WILLIAM MAXWELL

William Maxwell

EARLY NOVELS AND STORIES

Bright Center of Heaven
They Came Like Swallows
Stories 1938–1945
The Folded Leaf
Time Will Darken It
Stories 1952–1956
The Writer as Illusionist

THE LIBRARY OF AMERICA

The paper used in this publication meets the
minimum requirements of the American National Standard for
Information Sciences—Permanence of Paper for Printed
Library Materials, ANSI Z39.48—1984.

Distributed to the trade
in the United States by Penguin Putnam Inc.
and in Canada by Penguin Books Canada Ltd.

Library of Congress Control Number: 2007934857
ISBN 978-1-59853-016-2

First Printing
The Library of America—179

Manufactured in the United States of America

Christopher Carduff
selected the contents and wrote the notes
for this volume

Contents

BRIGHT CENTER OF HEAVEN

For Baba

Who is the most generous, the most beautiful,
the most astonishing of women.

Bright Center of Heaven

BREAKFAST at Meadowland—as Mrs. West invariably explained to people who came there for the first time—was a movable feast. It began at six, when Gust, the hired man, and Johanna, the cook, sat down to sausage and potato cakes in the kitchen. Their faces shone back at them from the bottoms of pots and pans and from the sides of the water-cooler, but they did not see. Nor were they consciously aware of the order in the cupboards and the heavy propriety of the cook-stove. The absence of order and propriety they would have noticed at once. In this brief period between six and seven, while the West family were turning in their beds and sleeping and waking and turning and sleeping again, Gust and Johanna divided the morning between them, and were secretly glad for the still seclusion of the kitchen.

At the first creaking of the floor boards overhead Johanna rose and made many trips between the kitchen and the dining-room, between the dining-room and the cupboard where the bright-blue china was kept. With the swift certainty of habit she set the gate-leg breakfast table by the north window, bringing knives and forks and spoons, bringing china, napkins, glasses, a pitcher of orange juice, a pitcher of cream, a bowl of buckwheat honey. Blindfolded, she could have set the table the same way, and put the coffee on the stove, and cut the bread for toast.

Johanna's coming and going did not trouble the deep serenity which lay upon the dining-room. During that portion of the night when the room had been dark and unoccupied, it had reestablished its identity. The curtains had fallen into their essential folds. The sideboard and the chairs had formed a more permanent relationship with the wall behind them. Bright indestructible sunlight fell upon the ledge of the east window, upon the polished floor, upon the broad oak table in the center of the room, giving clarity to the surface of these things. Upon the ledge of the west window garden poppies burned with yellow and green flames above a blue bowl. Through everything flowed the quick, immeasurable energy of the morning, yet nothing was disturbed by it. The room was utterly quiet, utterly self-possessed. Then Johanna, coming from the kitchen, heard a high clear voice. The voice was singing:

Today is the day
They give babies away
With a half a pound of Tay. . . .

All order was driven from the place by this extraordinary blitheness, and even the solidity of the sideboard and the huge oak table was imperiled. Johanna let out a small Bavarian grunt. Another day was beginning.

Even before Mrs. West appeared—and there was no way on earth Johanna could keep her from appearing, once she set her mind to it—Johanna could see the dark-blue band which invariably encompassed her grey hair, and her smile which had the brightness of confusion itself.

The door swung open.

"Good morning, Johanna." Mrs. West stopped before the mirror in the sideboard to straighten the dark-blue band, lingered at the window to poke the yellow poppies, and then sat down at the breakfast table. Johanna who had seen the doily rumpled on the sideboard and three yellow petals fall on the white window sill, retired to the kitchen.

As Mrs. West sipped her orange juice, her eyes wandered to the patches of yellow sunlight between the trees and along the fringe of the wood which began just outside the window. The wood was cool and deep and much too quiet. She listened a moment until she heard the reassuring strife of the red-winged blackbirds down in the marsh, and knew that the world was no better and no worse than it had been the day before; that it was, indeed, very much the same.

She heard the creaking of the floor boards overhead, and called to the kitchen, "I hear the children stirring, Johanna. You can start the toast." Back and forth over the ceiling the creaking went, while Mrs. West lingered over the dregs of her orange juice, and wondered if she were losing her mind. She had discovered three days ago the impropriety of calling her fifteen- and eighteen-year-old sons "the children." Now after bending the full force of her mind upon the matter for three whole days, she still said "the children" first, and when it was too late, remembered not to. What greater proof of insanity, she said to herself as she flooded a mountain of oatmeal in a sea of cream, what greater proof of insanity could anyone want?

All about her the low-ceilinged room seemed restive and uncertain of itself, as if the sideboard, the table, and chairs had spent the night in prowling and had only just now returned. Light, flecked and barred from the east windows, flowed down the wall and splashed upon the floor. The silver candelabrum on the sideboard glittered and gave off white sparks of sunlight. She could feel the day girding up its loins. She could hear it stomping down the stairs.

"Good morning, Muv."

Oh, the darlings! All elbows and shoulder-blades and legs like colts. She looked at Whitey with his wrists sticking out of his sweater sleeves, at Thorn's hair plastered down with water.

"Merry sunshine!" Her greeting was a ritual, having nothing at all to do with actual weather conditions. "Did you sleep well?"

"Can't remember," said Whitey, smiling sleepily into his glass.

Thorn only nodded, his attention apparently on orange juice. Mrs. West, for the ten-thousandth time, made an active effort to plumb the clouded pool of her oldest son's mind. She thought of orange juice.

"Muv, will you want me for anything this morning? I saw some burdock weeds growing in the ten-acre field yesterday."

He had eluded her again. It was always that way. When she was in orange juice, he was in the ten-acre field.

Johanna brought oatmeal and toast and a pot of coffee.

Mrs. West put one finger on the lid of the coffee-pot and leaned forward. "What about the pump? Did Gust bring the washers from Menaqua?"

Thorn buttered a piece of toast with quiet thoroughness before he answered. "They were the wrong kind."

Mrs. West held her hands to her head and moaned. To think of there being all kinds of washers. It was one more complication in a world already complex enough. "Never mind," she said, recovering quite suddenly from her agony. "Whitey can get the kind you want in Thisbe this afternoon."

"But, Muv,"—Whitey's voice rose in troubled flight—"you promised me the afternoon off to paint my canoe! You promised me three whole days ago."

"I know, Whitey, but I've got to have the washing. Besides, you can paint it when you get back. Thorn dear, pass me the honey."

"There won't be time enough." Whitey's clear, blue eyes grew dangerously bright. He focused his attention upon the bowl of yellow poppies.

At the breakfast table Mrs. West's maternal instincts were usually Spartan. "Nothing doing. I have to get the wash and Paul wants to do some shopping. Heavenly days! I almost forgot! Wouldn't that have been too dreadful! Jefferson Carter is coming on the four-o'clock, and so you've got to take me in to meet him."

It was a matter of no great consequence to Whitey that a Mr. Jefferson Carter was coming on the four-o'clock. A great many people came to Meadowland at one season of the year or another, and sometimes pretty funny people. But at the first mention of the name Paul he had given up all hope. Paul was a boarder and it was recognized in the family that the desires of the boarders were to be accepted without question. They were self-sufficient, like the laws of plane geometry, to which Whitey had been but lately introduced. If you asked why, it never got you any place.

Mrs. West watched her youngest son withdraw into his oatmeal, blinking. Poor lamb! "Johanna"—her voice and mind both wandered lightly through two swinging doors and into the kitchen—"do you suppose that in a world so full of uncertainties Master Whitey might have another piece of toast?"

*

Johanna grunted noncommittally. In her world there were no uncertainties—and she had almost no feeling for rhetoric. A word was the name of a thing, and not a thing in itself, to be made a game of. Since she had come to Meadowland to cook for the Wests there had been such a flood of words raining down about her Bavarian ears that she felt it incumbent upon her to stem the tide—in so far as she was able—with silence.

Silently she appeared in the dining-room, bearing a plate of toast.

In another part of the house a door closed. The kitchen door swayed, passing along the information to Mrs. West, who was helping herself to the toast, that Aunt Amelia was coming; that she was crossing the living-room; that in a second she would stop on the threshold of the dining-room to fasten the breast-plate and make sure the helmet of her invulnerable gloom.

"Merry sunshine, Amelia!" Mrs. West's voice flew toward her husband's half-sister like a volley of silver arrows, intending to undo with their brightness the work of years of indigestion. The arrows struck harmlessly against the breastplate and the helmet. They fell with a clatter at Amelia's feet.

"Good morning, Susan. Good morning, Benjamin—" Amelia alone out of all the human race called Whitey by his baptismal name. "Good morning, Thorn."

Now the breakfast table was become like unto the earth itself, one half light and the other half darkness.

"Johanna . . . Miss Bascomb's cottage cheese. Did you sleep well, Amelia?"

"I can't really say that I did." Amelia's tone implied that she would have liked to report better news, but candor compelled her to speak the truth. "I've been awake ever since three with that whippoorwill again, and before that I had the most frightful nightmare. I dreamed I was looking at myself in the glass, and there was a great patch on my forehead the shape of a gall-bladder."

Remembering that there had also been thunder and lightning during the night, and very heavy rain, Mrs. West smiled discreetly into her coffee cup. As usual, Amelia had slept better than she realized. "How strange, Amelia," she said aloud, trying to visualize the shape of a gall-bladder. Then, with the air of one making a contribution she added, "I dreamed I was having trouble with my arches, and I went into Bunnell's to see about getting a foot pad for the instep, and the clerk said to me, *I beg your pardon, madam, but did you know that you haven't got a stitch on?* And mind you, Amelia, I hadn't!"

Whitey sputtered over his last swallow of milk, rose, and disappeared into the kitchen. The firm brown mask of Thorn's face remained unshaken by mirth; he, too, rose from the table and followed his brother.

"Susan, I think you might be more careful what you say in front of the children."

Far in the back of Mrs. West's mind a thought took shape. Her eyes deepened for a moment, as if they were a patch of sunlit ground over which the shadow of a bird had passed. "They aren't children any more. . . ." This was as near as she could come to forming the idea which was like the shadow of a bird.

"Well, if it's all the same to you, I wish you wouldn't talk that way in front of Bascomb." Amelia's bloodless lips grew set.

"Amelia, you trouble yourself unduly over your favorite nephew. I shouldn't be afraid to turn him loose in Sodom and Gomorrah."

As if to offer himself in support of her statement, Bascomb appeared noiselessly in the doorway—a pale, gangly, hawk-nosed youth with his hair brushed forward from the temples instead of back. The effect was infinitely grotesque.

"Bascomb!" exclaimed Amelia, faintly. "Your hair!"

Mrs. West brightened. "I think it's very becoming."

Bascomb beamed his gratitude upon her. "I woke up in a Victorian mood," he explained, sliding into the place left vacant by Whitey, and picking up crumbs of toast. "I lay there looking at the chamber pot, and the pitcher and bowl on the wash-stand. They all had pink roses on them." His voice was high and rather unpleasantly nasal. Mrs. West wondered vaguely why it was that Amelia should prefer this strange creature—whose madness was amiable, to be sure, but none the less mad—to her own angels. "Then I got to thinking of the dear Queen," Bascomb was saying—"and of all the chamber pots, water-pitchers, wash-bowls, and shaving-mugs in Windsor Palace, each with pink roses on it."

Amelia, too scandalized for speech, wrapped her disapproval round her and laid the folds of it at her feet.

Mrs. West considered the matter of Windsor Castle. "Don't you think there might be forget-me-nots on some of them? In the top of the barn there's a slop-jar that has forget-me-nots."

"No! no!" Bascomb's excitement grew. "Forget-me-nots are much too obvious. They were *all* pink roses." He was radiant. "Aunt Susan, while I'm still feeling Victorian, may I please come to your room after breakfast and commune with your marble-top washstand?"

"By all means, my dear." Mrs. West smiled at him and beyond him. He *was* something of a dear, if you didn't take him seriously, and Heaven knows he didn't mean to be taken seriously. The trouble was he had been too well educated. She frowned to think what a mess tutors and guardians can make, once they start educating a child. Cram them full of history and mathematics—Mrs. West herself found it quite beyond her power to do sums—and never tell them how to use their knife and fork. It was outrageous!

"Aunt Susan—" Bascomb was still unsatisfied. Having disposed of Windsor Castle, there was the matter of the Empress Eugénie. "How old were you in 1870?"

"I didn't really begin being old until 1880."

"I was afraid of that." Bascomb looked downcast. "Now if you had been born about twenty years earlier, you could have dressed according to the Court of St. Cloud. As it is, I expect you went in for the hour-glass, instead."

"Very likely. That's such a long time ago, I don't altogether remember, but I rather think I did."

"Well what I don't see is"— Bascomb stopped a second. You could talk about anything under the sun to Aunt Susan, but you had to choose your words carefully—"when women wore such tight corsets, how could they have children?"

"My dear, we always took our corsets off." Mrs. West smiled maliciously at him. The young were so inquisitive. "Amelia, I forgot to tell you I asked Jefferson Carter to stop off on his way to New York."

"Carter?" There was apprehension in Amelia's voice. One generally had reason to suspect the worst of Susan's friends.

"Haven't I told you about him? Well, my dear, he's simply marvelous!" This was the unvarying preamble to one of Mrs. West's biographies. It represented an adjustment of *Friends, Romans, Countrymen* to the needs of the family breakfast table.

Bascomb recognized the signs, and knowing that his aunt had launched herself upon the full tide of a narrative, he straightway surrounded himself with the toast, the sugar, and the pot of honey.

Amelia composed herself quietly and waited.

Mrs. West paused a moment, like an experienced Chautauqua lecturer. "The winter I was in New York, Jerry Carson dropped in one evening and said, *Susan, you've got to go with me to hear Jefferson Carter at the Civic Club. He's a young Negro and very brilliant.*"

Amelia's sallow face flared up with amazement and dismay. With an effort, she kept from speaking.

"Of course, I was all agog," continued Mrs. West, having observed neither the flare nor the wild gleam of joy in Bascomb's eyes, "for I've always been a little hypped on the subject of Negroes. I always feel I can pardon them things I wouldn't put up with in my own, don't you know, because of what we have done to them. Well, we went, Jerry and I. I can remember so well. It was on a Wednesday evening, and Jerry said to me while we were having dinner, *Susan*, he said, *I managed to meet this chap at a publisher's tea*—Jerry's with Macmillan's you know—*and if you like him, I'll take you back and introduce him to you after he's through lecturing.*

"Well, the place was packed clear to the doors, and a most intelligent audience. Irita Van Doren and the Spingarns and —oh, all those people. And when he appeared, I give you my word, I have never seen anyone so stunning! Tall, and very black, and huge—a typical Negro. Simply stunning! Well I want you to know, he crossed his arms like this"—she stopped to demonstrate, using the breakfast table for the speaker's stand—"rested them in front of him, and then he began to talk. He talked for an hour and a half without moving. Well! I have never been so fascinated in all my life. . . ."

Bascomb's mind fluttered ineffectually. His natural inclination was to break up whatever was flowing and continuous, and a dozen times he was on the point of interrupting her. He didn't want to know about the definitive Jefferson Carter. It was more fun to be surprised. He didn't want to listen, but all the time he was conscious of her will that he should hear what she was saying. He struggled faintly, but in the end he was held and fascinated by the strenuousness of her words, and the dramatic quality which she injected into certain incidents, certain details, by the twist of her head, or the tone of her voice, or what she did with her hands.

Jefferson Carter was only one of innumerable flies preserved in the amber of his Aunt Susan's conversation. Perhaps he himself was one. He could imagine telling strangers about him, describing him each time with the same adjectives, using them as a straitjacket to inclose and bind his particular madness. He sat back in his chair, grinning at the idea of a Negro at Meadowland, and speculating upon the difficult situation which his Aunt Amelia's prejudices would almost certainly construct for her.

"—And Mr. Carter came to lunch the following week," Mrs. West was saying, "and we talked all afternoon, just as hard as we could talk. My dear, I wish you could know the things that poor soul went through. So poor and so eager to learn. . . . When he was a child he had to spend most of his time working in the fields. A few weeks in the summer and a few more in the dead of winter was about all the schooling he managed to get, but I wish my pampered offspring got half so much out of Thisbe High School with all its improved methods of education. He said that conditions in the country were so frightful that his mother finally forced his father to move into town where by hook or crook she could educate her children. She must have been a very remarkable woman, from what he has told me; *very* remarkable.

"Well things went along pretty well for a time, until a plantation owner got Jefferson's father to move out to Oklahoma, where everything was going to be marvelous. *You* know. . . . Of course what happened was that they got ears over appetite into debt for their railroad fare, and then the plantation-owner fixed it so they couldn't get out, no matter what they did. They worked and skimped and saved, and it was simply dreadful, until finally they decided to run away. They packed up bag and baggage and set out for Arkansas in the middle of the night. . . ."

Bascomb swayed from side to side, ecstatic with excitement. "Did the Red Sea divide, Aunt Susan, and then drown the plantation-owner and all his charioteers?"

But Mrs. West did not even hear him. "From that time on," she continued, "things began to look better for them. The children had a chance to go to a decent school, and Jefferson began to lay aside money to put himself through high school and college. He worked on construction gangs, mind you, when he was fifteen. And later he worked in a lumber-yard, doing a man's job. He skimped and scraped and saved and hoarded until he got enough to go away to a college for Negroes. . . ."

"Which one, Aunt Susan?"

"How do I know? From that point on he has simply gone up and up and up. Now he's doing marvelous work as a lecturer and teacher and as a leader of the Negro race." She took a sip of her stone-cold coffee and came slowly down off her mental rostrum.

"But, Susan"—Amelia clasped and unclasped her hands—"he's coming here? a Negro?" Her face grew dark with feeling.

"Why not?" said Mrs. West, absently, her mind on the laundry at the top of the stairs.

Before Amelia could find an answer, a shadow fell across the glass in the outside door. Immediately Mrs. West sang out to the kitchen, "Put in the baked eggs, Johanna. The boarders are coming."

*

The door of the boathouse down at the very edge of the marsh was flung wide open. A long-limbed girl ran swiftly across the porch, down the narrow board walk that led to the pier, and flung herself into the clear, copper-colored water of the Little Neenah. In due time her head appeared and she shook the water from her hair, like a puppy. Then it vanished again. The color from the leaves dead and drowned at the bottom of the stream stained her body bright yellow. Like a slim amber fish she swam beneath the water. Now she would double up and suddenly hurl herself upon the sky, white and gleaming, like a sword. And all about her bright jewels of sunlight would fall from the air. Now she would float quietly upon her back, looking into the overhanging branches; and small, inquisitive fish would swim up to her flanks and peck at them. Then she would turn or duck under, and the small fish would dart away, stricken with remorse. At last she swam slowly over to the pier, and with a glance to the right for the woods, and another to the left, to see that no one was in the garden, she pulled herself up out of the water, and fled dripping to the boat house.

The glow from her swim was still upon her as Nigel strode back and forth across the floor of the upper story of the boat house, drying her hair with a yellow bath towel—her hair which was short and thrush-colored, and fell about her face like a cloud. In her face there was something of the remoteness of a cloud, and something of the uncertainty.

She felt strangely like two people instead of one. There was a girl who had just been swimming and whose heart sang so within her that she could not sit down. And standing off to one side, detached and unspeakably weary, was a girl who had not closed her eyes all night. The girl who had been swimming was a live thing, part of the brightness of the morning; and the second girl, watching her, grew a shell of fear which fit so exquisitely that every part of her mind was covered and tightly bound. The first girl opened a drawer of the walnut dresser and drew out a pair of shorts. Then, passing the heavy, old-fashioned mirror, she tilted it until she could see her legs. When I am a great actress, the first girl said to herself, I shall play the final act of "Camille" in a chemise, and next morning Brooks Atkinson will say, "Miss Foley's legs are in the great tradition. . . ." The second girl smiled wanly at her, knowing that in all probability she would never have a chance to play "Camille" with or without a chemise.

Then there was only one girl, and that one sighed and pressed her hands against her head, realizing that all day she must endure this terrible constriction, as she had endured it the day before and the day before that. But there would be no more days after this. The night would bring a marvelous release from her predicament, or it would confirm disaster.

It seemed to her that if she could only tell some one, she would no longer be incased in futile armor, as if she were a crab. If she could only say to Susan casually, *Susan, I think I'm going to have a child. . . .* The very thought of the relief it would bring made her light-headed, but she was afraid to do it. There were too many years between them, and Susan's babies had arrived properly, with the sanction of the Church and the state. Hers, if she had one, would have only the sanction of the rose under which it was begotten. She could not tell Susan; and until she was certain of it she could not tell Paul. He would grieve so. He would blame himself so terribly for ruining her career. Poor darling, there were so many things he blamed himself for! Needless things. Things which might happen to anybody, especially if he were absent-minded. Until it was necessary, she could not hang this heavier weight upon him.

She sat down on the edge of the bed, and then stretched out on it, she was suddenly so weary. The morning light reflected from the creek below fell upon the dark ceiling and danced there. Nigel, remembering how Paul had first come to her, felt a physical excitement, an atomic movement which exactly corresponded to the play of light and shadow above her.

He had come into her dressing-room after her last scene. Jerry Carson had brought him. And when she caught sight of him in the mirror she was startled. It had been so long since she had seen a gentle person. Jerry leaned elegantly across the dressing-table at her, but she forgot all about being nice to him. She entirely forgot how influential he was and how he knew all the right people. From habit, and without in the least knowing what she was doing, she obliterated her face with cold cream, staring, the while, into the mirror at this strange man. Space had never before existed in her tiny dressing-room, but it did now, and he sat there quietly looking into it.

When they left, she wondered if he had even seen her; but apparently he had, for he came again and then again. And one night they sat across a table from each other in a little Greek restaurant for two and a half hours while he talked to her with his eyes, until at last she could not stand it any longer and said the words for him, and they went off down the night together.

At the remembrance her heart began knocking at the thin wall of her ribs. Lest the pressure be too much for them, she sat up and began putting on her sandals. There was still this day to be lived, whether she had a child or whether she didn't. Somehow she must consume this most difficult day, bit by bit, as if she herself were a child, confronted by some monstrous and unpalatable pudding which she must down before the Higher Authorities permitted her to leave the table. She bent over to fasten her sandals, and then crossed to the dresser. *Milady*—she spoke in her best stage voice, so that the room echoed about her—*if you will kindly permit me to settle this matter without your assistance, I shall be infinitely obliged to you.* She reached into the drawer for a brassière, put her arms through, and hooked it together. *Lord Andrew*—here she began striding back and forth again, her hair flying—*you must listen to me! Oh, you must! I had hoped to spare you this, which can only fill your declining years with grief. And now, because of your insane jealousy, you bring this bitter thing upon yourself.* She took a yellow woolen dress from a chair, lifted it over her head, and slid into it like a snake. Then in thoughtful silence before the mirror, she brushed the tangles out of her hair. With something of a shock she realized that the face which stared back at her from the mirror was in no way different. It was the same face which she saw every morning. Only tired. She followed the curve of her lips with a line of scarlet fire, and ran down the steps.

*

Thorn and Whitey were sitting on the stoop outside the kitchen door. Lighting Thorn's morning cigarette was a ritual, and Whitey shared in it in a way he was not even aware of. Now he sat solemnly watching his older brother until his attention was distracted by an enthusiastic licking of his left ear.

"Rats, stop it! Grow up, can't you?" With a quick jerk Whitey sent a handsome silver-and-black pup spinning head over heels across the ground. Rats was part collie and part police-dog, and not easily to be discouraged. This was a new game. He came back for more. Whitey picked up a stick and threw it. The stick was returned to him forthwith, but he did not throw it again. Instead, he sat weighed down by the burden of his secret woe, and looked off toward the smoke-colored hills to the south. Rats waited a moment, pushed the stick closer, and waited again. Then with a look in his eyes such as would have brought water gushing from the hard heart of rock, he went and laid his head on Whitey's knee.

"Goddamn all boarders," said Whitey, scratching the dog's ear with one hand, and his own mosquito-bites with the other.

Thorn blew a cloud of smoke through his nostrils, considered the profane problem-child beside him, and said nothing.

"Stinker! That's what she is. People who go back on their promises are stinkers."

Thorn threw his cigarette into a bed of ferns that grew beside the kitchen door, and with his hand rubbed the hair on the back of Whitey's neck—rubbed it the wrong way. "Forget it! I'll help you with your canoe this afternoon when you get back from town. The two of us can get it all sandpapered before supper, and it won't take you long to do the rest yourself."

"Thanks, West!" Whitey's sky opened and his sun shone through. The morning had suddenly become so fine he could no longer contain himself. He began shying pieces of gravel at a squirrel on a limb high overhead. He carved R-A-T-S on a piece of bare ground with a stick, and cried sic'm! to the bewildered pup. He considered one by one the possibilities of the flower-garden spread out brightly in the morning sun, the great oak tree which stood over it, and below that, the tool-shed, the water-tank, the banks of the creek, the boat-house, the marsh beyond the boat-house. . . . "If I had a thousand bucks, I'd dam up the creek and make a lake where the marsh is. You could do it for a thousand, couldn't you?"

A girl, slim and straight-shouldered, came out of the boat-house and started up the hill toward them.

"Couldn't you?"

The girl was wearing a yellow dress.

"West, *couldn't* you?"

The texture of Thorn's face changed. It took on the stiff immobility of wood. Only the eyes were alive and moved slightly as the girl in a yellow dress came up the hill.

Feeling obscurely disconsolate, Whitey got up and went off to the tool-shed, with Rats at his heels.

*

Down deep within Thorn a current of powerful feeling began to rise. As a swollen stream bearing dead logs and brush and the remnants of a bridge overleaps its banks and floods the wide defenseless fields, higher and higher the feeling rose. Thorn's heart grew wild with fear. A little higher and it would cover his heart.

"Good morning, West." A pair of auburn eyes looked down into his. The brush and the timber met an unyielding obstruction and jammed against it. The waters rose, dark and swirling in violent congestion.

"I'd like a cigarette, if you don't mind." Nigel took one from his package, waited for him to light it, and sat down beside him.

That was enough; that alone touched off the fuse. With a great soundless explosion logs and brush and streams of water shot into the air. The current beneath them swept on to the flat meadows and subsided there.

Thorn was too excited to speak. She smoked in silence while he examined the tips of her sandals. "You smoke too much," he said at last.

"I know." Nigel tossed her hair sadly back from her face and then pressed her hands to her head. There was a skewer running through it from temple to temple, and sometimes, if she pressed hard enough, the pain stopped for a moment. "Three yesterday and now this makes four in two days."

"I'm going down the creek this afternoon," he said, abruptly changing the subject. "Do you want to come along?"

Nigel shook her skewered head. "Woman's place is in the home."

Thorn's face lengthened. He felt acutely the disadvantage under which sensible persons labor in a world where so often people do not say what they mean, or if they do, mean nothing by it.

"But I have Thursday afternoons off, you know. . . ." Thorn was a nice youngster. Always so clean and well-scrubbed-looking, even around the ears. And he had nicely chiseled wrists and ankles.

Thorn continued to struggle with the problem of Thursday afternoons off. Nigel had all the time in the world. It was another joke, of course. And how should he answer it?

"You could get off by two o'clock, couldn't you?"

"Today isn't Thursday." She smoothed out Whitey's lettering and began to print N-I-G-E-L in place of R-A-T-S. If I had been a man, she thought, instead of merely having a man's name, I should have slept the last three nights, instead of turning and tossing and waiting for the sky to get light over the hills. It was strange having a man's name. You got circulars addressed to Mr. Nigel Foley, or to Nigel Foley, Esq. Even if your father did have his heart set on a boy, there was still no reason why he should pick out such a strange name to name it. It was on account of some one in a book, Aunt Eliza had said, but she couldn't remember what book it was, and Nigel was nearly grown before she found out. Most people shared Aunt Eliza's ignorance and were forever calling her Niggel, with a short i and a hard g, instead of a long i and a soft g. Niggel, as names go, was pretty awful.

"It is, too, Thursday." Thorn took a deep breath and held it, like a spent swimmer whose arms and legs stiffen with weariness, and whose sight grows dim.

Nigel had entirely forgotten that he was sitting beside her. There was something she liked especially about Thorn. Perhaps it was the way he kept things to himself; or perhaps it was only that his ears were small and pointed and lay close to his head. She looked at him to make sure which it was. "Yesterday was Tuesday, and it won't be Thursday until tomorrow sometime."

"Well if it were Thursday. . . ." His voice cracked under the burden of his anxiety, which was a little more than he could bear. "If it *were* Thursday, would you go down the creek with me?"

For the first time Nigel perceived that this matter of the canoe trip was tremendously important. She had been too concerned by her private anguish to see that Thorn had been looking at her with all of his heart in his eyes. Now that she had discovered it, she wanted to reach over and close his eyelids, as one desiring privacy for another might pull down the window-blinds. "If you really want me to go down the creek with you . . ." Nigel rose and put her hand on the knob of the screen door.

The gratitude which came into his face was so swift, so eager, that she turned away. If such a trivial thing could make him unspeakably happy. . ." Before the idea was even formulated she put it out of her mind. One distraction at a time was all she could stand. "When shall I be ready?"

"Let's make it two o'clock. We . . ." The words stuck in his throat. His eyes were starred with delight. "We don't want to get caught when Muv's nig arrives on the scene and have to stick around with him."

"Would you mind saying that over again?" Nigel sat down

on the stone steps, drew her skirt over her knees, and stared at him in wonder.

Thorn went scarlet with embarrassment. "Muv's hypped on the subject of Negroes. . . ."

"Yes, I know."

"Well, she's got one coming this afternoon on the four-o'clock, and he's going to stay a couple of weeks."

Nigel put her hands to her head. In her amazement she had forgotten the skewer for a second. Now she had cause to remember it. She pressed with all her might and tried to think about something else. This Negro of Susan's. Very likely there would be race riots at Meadowland before nightfall, and Amelia coming down to dinner in a Confederate flag, with a picture of Robert E. Lee pinned on her bosom.

"This is the first one," Thorn was saying.

"I see." Nigel nodded brightly, with a mental image of the skewer also nodding and also bright. "Not an old family custom."

The pain in her head gave an edge to the words that she had not meant them to have. She put out her hand to draw them back, but it was too late. The damage had been done, and Thorn was rubbing the back of his hand on his overalls. It was a special and excruciating kind of agony for him that Nigel should find his family queer. With every particle of his being he wanted to be like other people and do the things they did. But there was always his mother doing outlandish things, like bringing a Negro to Meadowland, and he had to stick up for her, no matter what. "They're all right, if you don't mind Negroes."

"I've never thought much about them, one way or another. What kind of a person is he?"

"Oh, he's grand high-mucky-muck of something or other. Ask Muv. She'll tell you all about him till you're blue in the face."

"Well, if he's a nice person—" Nigel hesitated. Unfortunately, niceness wasn't one of Susan's invariable tests for people. Sometimes she took up with them because she was sorry for them because they weren't nice. "If he's a nice person, I don't think I'll mind." Just now she didn't care if Susan imported a tribe of howling Uganda Hottentots.

"I don't mind very much," Thorn confessed sadly, "only I can't help wondering what Dad would think about it."

Nigel looked at him curiously. This was so much more of his feelings than Thorn had ever before revealed to her. That rising inflection on the word *Dad*. She had wondered more than once about Susan's husband, who was never mentioned. Sometimes she ran across his name in books—*Gordon West*. There was no trace of him at Meadowland, though there were traces everywhere of Susan and Susan's father, and of people even more remote. It was unsafe, of course, to go rooting around in other people's family closets. Judging by her own, one wouldn't have to look very far in order to turn up thieves and cut-throats and adulterers. But somehow it seemed unlikely that the unmentioned Gordon West was any of these. Anyway, there was no harm in asking. "What happened to your father?"

Thorn looked up at her in astonishment. "He's dead. He was an aviator during the war, and afterwards when my Grandfather Smith died, we moved out here, because Dad didn't like to live in town. He was a grand guy. He used to take us duck-hunting in October. Muv used to kick because we were missing school, but he'd laugh at her and say that school would wait and the ducks wouldn't. One day about five years ago all three of us went up the creek duck-hunting——"

Nigel thought that she had never seen Thorn's eyes grow so bright. They were as bright as his mother's.

"—I was thirteen and Whitey was ten—and we got caught in a cloudburst and soaked to the skin. He never paid any attention to the weather, himself, but he sent Whitey and me home in one duck-boat. He stayed there in the other all the rest of the day, and he didn't come home till dark. Then he had a chill and had to go to bed. And in a couple of days he was dead. That was crazy, wasn't it?"

"That was very crazy," said Nigel, softly, and she bent over to fasten her sandal, which had come undone.

*

After breakfast Paul returned to his room on the second floor of the Tower, and wrote a letter:

Dear Jerry,

So many times these last three weeks I have wanted to bless you for sending us to this place. As you foresaw, Susan took Nigel to her bosom, and she is now a member of the family. She even helps with the dishes on Johanna's day of rest.

Nigel, poor dear, never had a family—only aunts—and is as happy as a child. She thrives upon eggs and lettuce and country air, and long nights of quiet sleeping. She grows more beautiful daily, or so it seems to me.

Remembering your caution, we are most circumspect.

Nigel insists that the place doesn't really exist—that we shall both wake up some morning in a flat in Brooklyn. Sometimes when I go down to the pier to smoke my pipe and watch the water go by, it seems unreal to me, too. That comes of being a school-teacher for fifteen years, probably. In a college you're safe—at least you used to be—and nothing that happens in the world outside seems very real. Floods in China, I mean, and Peace Conferences. You sit and smoke your pipe, and life goes by just as the water goes by the pier. Even so, this is a strange place.

I have grown tremendously fond of Susan. Sometimes I think it is her ungovernable extravagance which charms me most—all her superlatives, her higgledy-piggledy conversation, and her unique faculty for making two complications spring up where there was only one before. She is warm and generous-minded, and to me she seems very much alive—more so than any woman I've ever known. She is forever doing, cleaning, cooking, supervising, changing. Sometimes she makes me think of the Jehovah of the Book of Genesis.

The boys are fine youngsters.

From what I have observed, the family affairs must be in a bad way. Susan has been economizing rather extravagantly, and has run into debt. That explains the boarders, though it doesn't explain why they are such a strange lot. Some of them you may remember. There is Aunt Amelia Bascomb, whose disposition is inclined to be dour and whose diet is limited to cottage cheese and tea—"very weak tea." And there is young Bascomb West from Philadelphia, a strange young man, full of whimsical conversation. Rather bad table manners. Below me in the Tower (and practising like fury at this very moment) is Josefa Marchand, a young pianist. Very forceful and masculine and genuinely gifted, I believe, though the milk of human kindness is not in her. On the top floor is Cynthia Damon, a rather plain woman with beautiful eyes, who paints. There is something strange about her manner —as indeed there is about the manner of all of us. I think she is beginning to be afraid she won't be able to make a go of it, that she hasn't really got the stuff in her. She'll take it on the chin, however. She's that kind.

The seventh boarder is coming this afternoon—a negro chap that Susan picked up in New York. He writes, as I remember, and goes around lecturing, and he used to do a little teaching, poor devil! Come to think of it, Susan met him through you. I can't remember his name, but you'll probably know who he is. If things go badly, we shall hold you responsible. For myself, I am not without misgiving— There speaks the academic mind! What I mean to say is, I'm sure as hell it isn't going to work. It doesn't matter in the least how much you rationalize: he is brilliant, talented—granted all that—and granted that when we have been dead fifty years, if anyone should open his grave and mine, only an anthropologist could tell which of us had been a white man and which a black. These are things we know. But the feeling persists even among cultivated people, and I have observed that people in general act according to what they feel, not according to what they learn in college. Therefore I fear for Susan's sociological experiment, though I am rather looking forward to it. Curiosity, of course. Meanwhile my Kentucky grandmother rests uneasy in her grave.

I mailed your galley-sheets to you yesterday. The book is good. To me it seemed genuinely enlightened. I liked especially what you have to say about marriage after fifty. If people could but realize —I speak with a lifetime of thirty-eight years behind me . . .

Paul put down his pen and looked at the words with rueful amusement. It would have been more accurate if he had said with a lifetime of seven months, for it was only seven months ago that he had first come alive. All the years behind him were unreal, and all the things that had happened to him he remembered but dimly, as if he had read them somewhere in a book he could no longer recall even the name of.

He sat and stared a long time out of the window, trying to

remember the day which had changed everything for him; to save his life he could not be sure whether it had been gray and dismal or bright, with the winter sun shining on the snow. And yet it was the most important day of his life.

He had been down with the flu for a couple of weeks. That much he was sure of. And when he started holding classes again, he found that the youngsters had been taking a holiday. There was nothing remarkable in that; they were healthy and honest youngsters who saw no reason why they should learn anything they didn't have to. He read them an essay by Stuart Chase, to fill up the hour, and from the way their jaws dropped, one might have thought it was the *Bagavad Gita*. Now looking back, it seemed such a trivial thing to start a row over. He didn't really care two whoops in hell about Stuart Chase—especially when he was so wabbly from the flu. It must have been the habit of ding-donging that he had got into from teaching school so long. It affects some people that way. Anyway, he lit into them good and proper, until finally that young ster stood up—a chemical engineer—Paul closed his eyes, trying to recall the earnestness of that square, sullen face, so concerned with the unanswerable and unimportant argument that these things were well and good, but they didn't have anything to do with life the way it was. Then Paul saw himself leaning over the desk at the boy and asking him questions. Had he ever gone walking in a March wind. The boy looked uncomfortable, as if Paul had trodden on delicate ground. No, he hadn't. He had been raised in Chicago, on the West Side, near Halsted Street. Had he ever written a poem? For a moment the boy looked as if he were going to laugh. Had he ever been in love? Had he ever felt anything remotely like an emotion? As the boy continued to stand there, waiting for him to finish, his silence had a curious effect. All the time that Paul was haranguing the class he was thinking to himself: *It's been a long time since you walked all the way around Crystal Lake. It's been twelve years since you wrote a poem, or anything that wasn't academic hackwork. You haven't been in love for so long, you've forgotten what it feels like.*

When the bell rang, and the class filed out, leaving him there alone by the desk, the curious feeling persisted. From that moment things began to stand out sharply in his mind. All during the week that followed—at staff-meetings, classes, departmental teas, wherever he went—he kept thinking to himself: *These things don't matter in the slightest. The enforcement of the no-car ruling and the meeting of the committee on requirements for graduation are as nothing compared with the needs of my immortal soul.*

It was the first time he had ever been at all certain that he possessed an immortal soul, and the discovery was so tremendous there was nothing for him to do but drop everything and scoot. There was no real reason, of course, why he should have gone off to New York. Any place would have done just as well, and perhaps better, except that——

"Christ Jesus!" exclaimed a deep masculine voice from the floor below. "What a place for an A-flat!" A fist descended in anger upon the blameless keyboard, and broken splinters of sound shot up through the quiet shaft of Paul's reflection.

"Well, Josefa," he inquired mildly, leaning over the balcony, "are you in difficulty?"

In answer there came a single discord, sharp and anguished. The shadow of irritation passed over his face. Then he smiled, quietly closed the door, and went on with his letter to Jerry Carson: *I speak with a lifetime of thirty-eight years behind me——*

*

"Ready, Paul?"

Paul went to the window and drew back the curtain. It was Nigel, waiting to go for the mail. She was standing beside the oak tree which grew by the door, and she looked so slim in her yellow dress, so slim and young, it made the blood rush to his head just to look at her. He told himself that merely to see her as she was now, standing beside the tree and looking up at his window, was worth all the security and comfort he had given up to possess her. Strictly speaking, he had never set eyes on her, or even so much as heard her name, when he gave up security and comfort; nevertheless it was on account of her that he had given up these things; she represented for him all that was quick and eager and alive.

"Are you ready, Paul?"

"Coming . . ." He licked the envelope, reached for his stick, and went downstairs quietly, so as not to disturb Josefa.

Everywhere in the room below his eyes fell upon profound and uncalculated confusion. He noticed, without thinking, the litter on the chaise-longue, the curtains knotted and looped and hanging in folded distress from the rod, Grandfather and Grandmother West and the Japanese nude all in varying degrees askew on the wall.

Josefa sat stiffly glaring at the piano, but her eyes were not focused on the Chopin *étude*. Instead, her whole being was withdrawn and concentrated about an inner core of anger. "Listen!" she said as he went past. Shaking her head until her straight bobbed hair began to swing back and forth, pendulum-wise, she laid before him her difficulty. It was a scale descending in double sets of fours, which reminded him of a game he used to play as a child. It took several to play the game and they went down three steps and up two, trying to see who could get to the bottom of the stairs first. He waited while Josefa clattered furiously down the scale until she came to the offending A-flat. Then with an utterly blank face and apparently no awareness that he was in the room, she pounded the one note with dull persistence.

As he came out of the door, Nigel beside the oak tree wondered whether there had ever at any time been so vague a man. The way he stood there on the stoop, blinking at the bright sunlight, and smiling at her as if he had never seen her before—it was almost enough to make her weep.

Side by side they followed the drive until they came to the entrance of Meadowland, where the road turned downhill in the direction of the Little Neenah. Paul lengthened his stride, and Nigel quickened her pace to keep up with him. He was passionately fond of walking, for he had discovered long ago the trick of timing his step with the steady pulsating of his blood, so that there was a sustained rhythm throughout his whole body, like that of a smoothly-running machine. In this ebb and flow of motion he found a release from the burden of physical consciousness, and his mind, set free, went off by itself into a pure and articulate region of thought.

Usually Nigel sauntered along beside him with her hand in

his coat pocket, talkative or silent according to her mood. This morning, however, she was whipped by her own intolerable restlessness, which drove her now to one side of the road, now to the other, ahead of Paul, behind him, sometimes backwards, looking up at him. At first the irregularity of her progress made him uncomfortable. Then he was reminded of the scarlet-and-green dragonflies—snakefeeders, he used to call them when he was a child—that wove an intricate aerial pattern over the steady-flowing water of the Little Neenah.

There was never more than the distance of the road between them, and yet for the first five minutes of their walk each of them moved in the farthermost regions of space. When a cottontail hopped out of the weeds and across the road, they both stopped dead in their tracks.

"Gust has been shooting them again," said Nigel, sadly, as the cottontail whisked into the bushes, and they started on. Now she was withdrawn to the far side of the road by the exigencies of her inward torment. "Every time I hear his gun banging, I want to cover up my ears and wail."

"They were eating the melon vines." Paul rather liked rabbits, but he could see Gust's point of view: a pest, no matter how charming, was still a pest. There was no use in pointing this out to Nigel.

They walked on down the road in silence. On either side were fields of young corn, row on row, spouting from the ground like fountains of green water, and falling back again upon the dark earth. Beyond these were other fields—green fields of corn, paler fields of oats, yellow fields of wheat waving lightly in the wind. Beyond these were the smoky hills, and then the bright sky overarching all the wide morning.

When they came to the bridge over the Little Neenah, they stopped and leaned their elbows on the railing, watching the water flow under their feet. A stick floated down, a long green blade of marsh-grass, another stick. Three copper fish advanced a few inches upstream and fell back. Time halted.

When it began again, they went on down the road past a wall of grape vine and three oak trees, until they came upon a lonely cow, grieving in a pasture. Nigel tried to comfort her with pats and small talk. Paul fed her a fistful of grass. Neither accomplished much. When they left her, the cow was still standing there by the fence, mournfully chewing the tag-ends of Paul's offering.

Paul walked along in contented silence, asking nothing of the morning except that it be quiet and bright and in no way disturb the procession of his thoughts. But Nigel exacted tribute of the roadside as she went. Now it was a milkweed blossom, now a burdock or a clover blossom, now the small fringe-like leaves of the honey-thorn tree.

Paul disapproved, but said nothing. For his part, he liked rather to see things growing. Women were always picking things and jamming them into silly little pots and vases. The flowers only lasted a day or two, at most. Wildflowers keeled right over and died as soon as you picked them. But the women went ahead and picked them just the same. He remembered a monstrous fat female he had once seen roving through a wood in springtime, her hands full of wilted Dutchman's-breeches, her eyes aglitter with the lust of possession. Nigel at least took only one of a kind. He watched her bend over a stalk of flame-colored butterfly-weed. When she straightened up, his eyes grew soft with delight. Something in the way she squared her shoulders always reminded him of a sturdy honest little boy. It renewed his faith in forthrightness, in dignity, in man's effort to subdue within himself all that is soft and clinging and parasitic.

He stopped and knocked the ashes out of his pipe. Then he stowed it away in his coat pocket and fell once more into his essential rhythm—not for thought this time, but that he might the more easily absorb the brightness which lay everywhere about him.

They came to a farmhouse and stopped to examine the low unpainted house, the cow-barn, the milking-shed, the horse-barn, the lean-to—all clustered about the farmhouse for protection and for defense, like a mediæval town about the castle of the lord.

"How would you like to spend a winter here?"

"At Meadowland?" Nigel was startled by this apparent irrelevance. She looked up at him sharply to see if anything lay below the surface of his question, but his eyes were thoughtful and not inquisitive.

"No. Here." He waved his stick at the bleak farm buildings.

"Thank you just the same." She breathed more deeply, realizing that she had merely read her own anxiety into his question. It was strange he didn't see that something was wrong with her. Sometimes he had a way of seeing right through her, when he seemed most vague. It was like the parting of a cloud.

"You wouldn't really, Paul." And it was strange that her face didn't give her away. But then she had looked in the mirror this morning, and it was the same face, so of course there was no reason why he should suspect anything. "It's too remote, and you know how you hate to go to sleep at night for fear you'll miss something."

"I don't think I'd worry much about that, with the snow ten feet deep in front of the door. Susan says it gets that way sometimes, in the drifts." He tried to imagine the buildings huddled together and ready for the siege of wind and sleet and falling snow. God knows a farmer's life was not an easy life, even at Meadowland, where there was everything to make the time pass pleasantly. It did pass pleasantly for the boarders, of course, but the family worked like Chinese cheap labor. On an ordinary farm like this it would be ten times worse. But there must be compensations for so much labor. In the fall, for example, just before the frost, when the days are cool and clear and the ripe odor of grapes lies on the air, and there is little to do except to cut wood against the coming of winter. It seemed to Paul that of the seasons of the year autumn was the most beautiful and the most satisfying. Perhaps that was because he was nearing forty, he told himself. And he could not help but think how strange it would be if he had to live always in a big city where there were no trees to mark the year's age and decline, and no bright autumn leaves. . . .

Having no further comment to make, Nigel had withdrawn again to the far side of the road. Paul continued walking down the highway, following in his mind an intricate stream of reminiscence which took him back to his first days in New York. For no apparent reason, he had preserved a vivid recollection of certain people—a drunken sailor with a herring in his hand, careening along the waterfront; an equally drunken Irishman who played the mouth organ for him, on the shuttle; an old woman poking and grubbing over the unspeakable contents of a garbage-can on East Eighty-third Street; the two likable young fellows who had lived at the same boarding-house. . . . Paul stopped, trying to recall their names. One of them was called Hendricks, and the other— What the devil? Mitchell, Meyer. . . . It didn't matter. He'd never see them again. They both worked in an insurance office, and although they were quite a little younger, they made nearly twice as much money as he had earned at the university. Very ordinary chaps they were, too. Started out every other Saturday afternoon and spent most of their pay check trying to forget how they had made it. With a sick feeling he remembered their routine, which he had fallen into for a time—night clubs and bad gin, and Monday morning waking up with a perfectly strange stenographer being sick at her stomach on the other side of the bed. It was all a part of that first general confusion when he used to go to bed at night with his head bursting. *Let em out pleez going up going down let em out pleez.* Sometimes he had been afraid to close his eyes, knowing that as soon as he did, he would see everything he had seen during the day, all at once, in different horizontal and vertical planes, and it was too much like being crazy. After a time he had grown deadened to these things, just as he had grown deadened to the hungry men who inhabited the parks by night and the streets by day. But once in a while the vertigo would return, and at such times he couldn't sleep for thinking how cold the poor old buggers must be, with their feet wrapped in newspaper and their heads tucked in a packing-box. Even now he could remember all too clearly something he had seen from the top of the Fifth Avenue bus one morning. There had been a light fall of snow during the night, and he saw an oldish-looking man sitting on a bench in the park, with his head thrown back unnaturally; and there was powdered snow on his shoulders and there was snow on his face. . . .

Remembering this man, and others he had seen, Paul felt a strange kinship with lost people. It seemed to him that they were lost because they were essentially incapable, and he suspected that the same thing was true of him; only they were unfortunate besides in not having any money, whereas he had never in his life known what it was to go hungry. Not yet.

Always he had assured himself that he could stop teaching whenever he pleased, and find some other kind of work. Once he had smiled over Henry Adams's observation that ten years of teaching, preaching, or fighting unfits a man for any other occupation. Now he found nothing humorous in the statement. It only made him think of all the letters of introduction he had presented to important people who were never in, or who told him to come back tomorrow, and the next day, and the next, and then gave him letters of introduction to tremendously important people who were never in. But that was not as bad as the interviews with personnel directors, male and female, who had no jobs to give, but who went on mechanically applying their yardstick all day long to discouraged and incompetent people like himself.

Perhaps he was not really incompetent. It might be that he had merely acquired the scholastic habit of absent-mindedness; and because his body and his mind were often worlds apart, sometimes when he had urgent need of both it was hard to get them together again. And even when there was no great need, when he and Nigel had been out driving in the Buick, for example, it was always Nigel who closed and barred the garage door while he was pulling himself sufficiently together to get out of the car.

If he wanted to, he could blame the times and not himself, that there was no work for him to do. The personnel directors had no jobs to give. They were merely applying the yardstick because that was what they were hired to do. Even so, it didn't take them long to find him wanting. One or two had bothered to ask, suspiciously, why he had thrown up a good job; and he had been foolish enough to try and explain about the chemical engineer and the faculty meetings. He blushed to think that he could have so given himself away to professional ears. However, the interview usually didn't last long after they found out that he had been a school-teacher. Somehow within two minutes he found himself standing by the glass door, smiling stiffly, and apologizing for having taken up so much of their time.

Nigel, behind him, stepped on one of his heels and then the other, by turns.

Paul turned back to her. "I've been thinking about New York," he said.

"So have I." She felt unaccountably better. Her headache

was gone. The walk and the brightness of the morning had done away with it.

"Have you made up your mind what you want to do in September?"

"I've been thinking of buying a half-interest in a fruit store. I still have a little money left, you know. It wouldn't take a great deal."

"I can't say very much for that idea." Nigel looked at him in vexation and wonder. Men were such romantic idiots. They never knew their limitations, or their possibilities, either. Here was Paul, by nature contemplative and impractical, and what did he do but cry phooey on the intellectual life and buy a half-interest in a fruit store. "For one thing, you're too well educated."

"You mean you don't think I could run a good fruit store." He looked at her steadily, challenging her.

"My only love, I'm certain of it."

"Probably you're right," he admitted, with sweet reasonableness. "I may try, however. Besides, I'm not so wonderfully well educated. I know a number—quite a number—of facts. Some interesting, some not very. But I've never discovered any real use for them. What I want, Nigel"—it was so difficult to find words which were not already worn and threadbare, and so difficult to find words which would not make this idea of his, which was altogether original and new, sound like the most utter commonplace—"what I want is to be of honest use in the world."

"That's a good Christian impulse."

"Oh, I don't mean that. . . ." The outer extremities of his eyebrows curved upwards with disappointment because she had failed to understand what he was trying so desperately to say. "Welfare work or anything like that is all cut and dried and thoroughly organized. And no office jobs! It's got to be something I like doing. . . . I was watching the youngsters yesterday, from my window. Thorn was in his shorts, washing the Ford, and Bascomb was sitting on the fence, saying clever things that were pretty much wasted on Thorn. Finally I heard Bascomb say, quite seriously, 'Some day I'd like to help you wash the car, West.' It was the first unclever thing he'd said in hours. Thorn very obligingly let him turn the hydrant on and off whenever he wanted to use the hose. And Bascomb was in seventh heaven. There's a case in point." Paul swung at a weed with his stick and decapitated it.

Nigel felt her own head fly off empathetically. "I take it that if Bascomb's guardian will only set him up in the car-washing business, he'll be happy the rest of his life." She did not mean to speak that way, any more than she had intended to speak so sharply to Thorn, but fear put an unintended edge to her words.

"Darling, whatever did you have for breakfast besides baked eggs?" Paul came over to her and stood there smiling and looking down at her. Her eyes changed from auburn to deep brown. "You know I didn't mean anything of the kind. What made Bascomb happy, whether he knew it or not, was that he was helping to do something that needed to be done, and doing a damn fine job of it. . . ."

Nigel rubbed her cheek against his tweed coat, deriving from the contact with his shoulder the comfort which she could not find in his words.

"It's only the combination that works. I might find it in a fruit store, or perhaps even on a farm. That's why I said I'd like to spend a winter here."

"With you for company," Nigel said, slowly, "I don't think I'd mind it very much myself. As for the combination"—she looked up at him squarely, trying to see him as he appeared to other people, stripping off the leaves of her protecting love so that she could appraise him for what he was worth—"I think you'd be much more likely to find it if you went back to teaching again."

"Perhaps you're right," Paul answered, and for no apparent reason, he bent down and kissed her mouth.

*

There was something about bedmaking that always made Mrs. West feel giddy. Perhaps it was the bending over. At all events, she could never do it without bursting into song.

"*Do you know how doth the farmer?*"

She folded the top sheet in a "hospital corner."

"Do you know how doth the farmer?
Do you know how doth the farmer?
Sow his barley and wheat?"

She pulled the spread smooth and stood off, looking at it in dismay. In spite of all her care, there was a wrinkle in the pad; it was clearly visible through two sheets and the spread. Recognizing the handiwork of the demon of confusion which was within her and which gave her no peace, she tore the bed apart and began all over again.

"See, 'tis, sow, sow, doth the farmer
See, 'tis, sow, sow, doth the farmer"

This war with the forces of confusion was an old one, and had been going on ever since she could remember. Battles were won daily on either side, and neither gave quarter nor received it. When the bed was remade, she went off to empty the slop-jar over the back fence.

Her heart was lightened by victory as she stopped a moment on her way back to watch Gust down on his knees in the field of sorghum. She blew a kiss at him and filled her lungs with the rain-drenched air. The rain had been very heavy, with much lightning and occasionally a shattering crack of thunder. Wide awake and frightened a little by the bright confusion outside, she had sat up in bed, reading *The Tale of Genji*. The remoteness of the story, both in time and place, took her mind from the storm; and she had been fascinated by the gravity with which these thousand-year-old characters analyzed one another's handwriting and by their concern for the quality of letter paper. "*Give a thought to the country folk who wait for moonlight on this cloudy night*," The Lady with the Red Nose wrote to Prince Genji. And to Mrs. West's amused delight, Prince Genji put the poem aside without looking at it, because the paper was faded and shabby, and because the upward and downward strokes of the writing were of the same thickness. Charmed by these intricate inclosures of convention and etiquette, Mrs. West soon forgot the bewildering succession of lightning and thunder. When her mind returned to the more familiar world of her bedroom, the storm had passed on and the moon was barging through a sea of small clouds.

Now there was no trace of the storm left in the whole sky. She took a last look about her and went back into the house bearing the empty slop-jar. On the way upstairs she remembered again that she had forgotten all about Jefferson Carter's arrival. She sighed with well-modulated despair. And he so fascinating, she said to herself as she put her slippers in the shoe-tray behind the door. Such understanding! such tolerance! such devotion to the Cause! she said to herself as she bent over and picked up a hairpin. So fine! she said to herself. Oh, my dear! she said to herself.

Then she stood looking at the room with a mild cast of horror over her face. Where to begin? There was the day's casual dusting, of course. And the lamp chimney needed washing. There were last night's clothes on the chair. The washstand needed attending to. The laundry which had been left at the top of the stairs ought to be sorted and put away. Then there were invisible tasks, no less imperative because they had been imposed rather by the mind than by themselves: a letter of condolence to Cousin Agnes, and butter cookies.

She seized the oil-mop and began feverishly circumnavigating the islands which were rugs, and the *terra incognita* under the bed, under the dresser, under the washstand. How strange a thing was time, she told herself. The words "past," "present," and "future"—what did they mean? You might just as well say "fiddle," "diddle," and "dee," because there was only "now," any way you looked at it. And yet if there was any pattern at all to people's lives, it was a pattern of time. When one was fifty-three, the beginning one knew, and the end one guessed from the beginning. It was a little like starting off to Milwaukee: One got on the train, settled one's bags, peered at everybody in the car, and then waited for the train to start. And all of a sudden one saw oneself *coming back* from the trip, settling the bags in the rack overhead, peering at everybody—and the journey all over before it was ever begun.

The trouble with these middle years, she told herself, as she shook the mop over the stairs, and then followed the lint down, dusting each stair as she went—the trouble with the middle years was one never got caught up. There were not hours enough in the day, even though one got up at four—as she sometimes did—to straighten and mend and cook and dust until long after dark. The past was still present, locked up in some untidy bureau drawer.

When she had reduced the bedroom to some semblance of order, Mrs. West shut from her mind all thought of the unsorted laundry by the stairs, and betook herself to the kitchen to consult with Johanna.

Here in the kitchen was not the semblance of order, but order itself. Row on row there were dippers, dishpans, blue-handled egg-beaters, large cooking-spoons, hanging from the whitewashed wall—big dipper, middle-sized dipper, little dipper. Big dishpan, middle-sized dishpan, little dishpan. . . . There was no spot on the floor, no crumb on the long table, no evidence anywhere that a three-hours' breakfast had but recently come to an end. Pots and pans, skillets, baking-dishes, broilers, pie-tins—all were securely imprisoned within the calm cupboard, and above everything, large and black and certain of its own substantiality, towered the cookstove.

"I've been thinking about lunch," said Mrs. West.

"*Ja*," replied Johanna, who had been cleaning out the ice-box.

"What do you say to some macaroni and cheese?"

Johanna felt that there was nothing she might be expected to say to macaroni and cheese, and so she said nothing.

"And deviled eggs, and lettuce with sour-cream dressing. You haven't forgotten how to make sour-cream dressing?"

"*Nein!*" Johanna shook her head eloquently. "*Aber was gibb's zu trinke'?*"

"Iced tea; it's such an intriguing day. You'd better open a jar of pickled peaches and we'll have some of the remnants of the ham. Meanwhile I'm going to fall to and make butter cookies. I haven't made any for——"

"Here's the mail!" Whitey burst into the kitchen by way of the screen door, waving a handful of letters and a rolled magazine. He was still too young to get letters, and his interest, therefore, was purely academic. It was none the less intense. "Four letters for you, Muv——"

Johanna put her two hands against the edge of the table, gripped it tightly, and waited.

"—and *The New Yorker* with a picture of a lady running a filling station. Look, Muv. . . . Isn't it swell? And a letter for you, Johanna, from Germany."

With an effort Johanna raised her eyes and looked at the envelope which Whitey held out to her. It was square and white. Her hands slowly relaxed. She took the letter and put it in her pocket without reading it. If her mother were dead they would not have used a plain white envelope. Whatever news the letter contained, it was not that. Her mother was still alive. . . . Johanna got down on her hands and knees again, and continued exploring the bowels of the ice-box. It was enough to know that her mother was still alive. Her mother was still alive three weeks ago when the letter was mailed. . . .

"Whitey, the flies! You forgot to shut the screen door again. Hand me my glasses, will you, dear? They're on the second shelf of the cupboard. These two are bills. This is from the Trust Company. Why! Here's a letter from Edith Paisley. Bless her darling heart! I wonder if she wants to come up?"

"Gosh! I hope not," said Whitey, gloomily. "There are enough people here already."

"Whitey! . . ." Mrs. West started to admonish her youngest born, but she saw that a button was missing from his shirt, and for the moment all else was forgotten. "There's a button off, Whitey. I must have missed it when I went through your clothes. In my room in the second drawer of my bureau you'll find my work-box. Bring it here and I'll sew it on this minute."

Whitey vanished through the swinging door which led to the dining-room.

"*Dear friend, I have wondered so much lately how it is with you*——"

Mrs. West began reading the letter aloud in an expressionless monotone, apparently for the benefit of Johanna, who was not listening.

"*—we have had so much sickness in the family the last few months I have not had the heart to write mother was taken sick very suddenly one Sunday afternoon last April just after dinner we rushed her to the hospital and tried to get a hold of Dr. Somebody or other I can't read the name she writes so poorly but he had*——"

"Muv, it's not in the second drawer."

"Well, look in the top drawer."

Mrs. West's brave diligence vanished again through the swinging door as she sat down on the high kitchen stool and went on:

"*—they decided to operate without him that night and they took out seven gall-stones the largest the size of a hen's egg she has felt so much*——"

"I looked in the top drawer, Muv, and it's not there, either."

Mrs. West waved him aside with her letter. "Never mind, then. I'll sew it on this afternoon if I have time—*wonder if you could put up with me for a week or two am much in need of a rest after going through so much with mother Dr. Doddy says a change of atmosphere would be very good for me and I should so love to see you all again let me hear from you when you have a moment's time with love to you all Edith Paisley.* Bless her heart! Such a darling she is, and so thoughtful of others. I give you my word, Johanna——"

But Johanna was not impressed with Mrs. West's word: it had been given to her on too many occasions. She went on solemnly restoring order to the ice-box. If Mrs. West chose to run a boarding-house and fill it with non-paying boarders, that was her business. It was not the way boarding-houses were run in Bavaria. . . . She put her hand against the side of her apron to be sure that the letter was still there.

"I have never in all my born days seen anything like the consideration that girl shows for her mother. She is simply—" Mrs. West felt about blindly for her handkerchief. She could never find one when she needed it. Never. At all the major crises of her life she had to drop everything and go find a handkerchief; or else do without. It was most exasperating. . . . With her eyes she searched the table, the ledge of the cupboard. Then seeing the unopened letter from the Trust Company she straightway forgot all about her handkerchief and ripped open the long official envelope. She read only the check which was inclosed with the letter. She gasped.

It was more like a sigh than a gasp. Nothing like so dramatic a gasp as she would have made if a cake had fallen. But Whitey, who knew her moods as well as he knew Wisconsin weather, was at her side instantly. "What's the matter, Muv?" He put his small pointed chin on her shoulder. Circles of concern shadowed his face. "What's the matter?" he repeated.

"Nothing, angel." Mrs. West put her arm around him and drew him closer to her. He was such a darling. . . . Then she withdrew her arm, remembering that boys do not like demonstrations of affection. "It's nothing."

Whitey was not lightly to be put off. He looked down at the check which lay open in her hands. "But, Muv—" His voice grew childish and shrill with amazement. "It isn't half as big as it usually is!"

What Whitey said was so desperately true she could think of nothing to say in return. Gordon had left enough to provide for them, and what with her inheritance from Father, there was always more than they needed. Until lately, that is, when the checks had been shrinking and shrinking, for no reason at all. It was like that story of the man with the magic skin that got smaller every time he made a wish, and, finally, pff! there wasn't any skin and there wasn't any man. She was almost in that predicament herself. There was a hundred twenty-five dollars in the bank which Cousin Agnes had sent her. But she had intended to spend that on something bright and extravagant. Now it would have to go for flour and chicken feed and——

"There wasn't any mail for me?" Amelia's sad face appeared at the kitchen window.

"Nope," Whitey answered. "Muv's got two bills and bad news and a lame-duck letter, and Johanna got a letter from Germany. That's all there was except *The New Yorker*." Whitey leered at her. "I'll get that if you want to look at it."

"Whitey!" Impertinence was even worse than missing buttons, and Mrs. West's voice conveyed as much disapproval as she could muster on such short notice. Amelia's dislike for *The New Yorker* was a family joke. She herself adored *The New Yorker*, all except the little king, which she couldn't understand, even after Whitey had explained it to her. But Whitey had no business making fun of Amelia to her face. For the moment, Mrs. West forgot her own enormous difficulties in feeling sorry for Amelia, who never got any mail, and who couldn't enjoy *The New Yorker.* "Here, Amelia . . ." She went to the screen door and opened it. "Stanch your wounds with this." Rats came up to her with his tail at an apologetic angle. She put her hand down absently to pet him. "It's from poor Edith Paisley. Such a time as she's been having! I must write to her this afternoon and tell her to— Get down, Rats! Whatever have you been rolling in? . . . Whitey, he's found something dead again!"

Sharp and clear over the green wall of sorghum came the sound of bugles. Rank on rank the shapes of confusion beset her from all sides. She had washed Rats only yesterday, and now it was all to do over again. Remembering the laundry at the top of the stairs, and her untidy closet, remembering the lost work-basket, the button off Whitey's shirt, the letter from the Trust Company, the couch cover left to soak in the "woodus," the box of old letters half sorted over, and three weeks' darning, she was quite undone. For the moment she could think of nothing to do. She would sit her down by the waters of the Little Neenah and weep.

Then it occurred to her that there was still time before lunch to make butter cookies. The thought gave her strength. She put from her mind the shapes which haunted it, and girded up her loins for battle.

"Whitey, you'll have to take Rats off to the creek and give him a good scrubbing. There's mange-cure in the 'woodus' cupboard, and you'd better do it now. You've got to go to town this afternoon.

"Johanna, as soon as you get through with the ice-box, you can start getting lunch under way. Don't forget about the sour-cream dressing, will you?"

The air about her grew bright with the combat. The enemy wavered. She must strike now! She went to the cupboard and took down certain of the golden crocks. Two shelves were completely disarranged by her haste. Twice she ran to the flour-bin, leaving each time a trail of fine white dust on the immaculate kitchen floor. Then to the ice-box for butter and cream. . . .

Johanna surveyed the ruin, a limp dishcloth held limply in her hands. Her face was without expression save for the utterly dead look of one who sees her sons slain by the invader, her daughters violated, and her house pulled down about her head.

*

Nigel paused a moment before the entrance to Cynthia's studio, which was a small box-like room on the top floor of the Tower.

"How lovely they are!" Cynthia was saying, and she bent over the flowers Nigel had brought her—burdock and clover blossom, milkweed and butterfly-weed and the fringe-like leaves of the honey-thorn tree. Then she got up, found a glass for them, filled it with water, and sat down again on her three-legged stool. "You're a darling to bring them to me." She took up a brush and began stroking it back and forth on her smock. "I'll make a drawing of them this afternoon, before they wither."

Nigel put her hand against the screen door and pushed it open. There was no use to stick around any more. She had hoped so much that Cynthia would ask her to stay. It would have made all the difference in the world if she could have unburdened herself of her secret anxiety. But she could tell by the tone of Cynthia's voice, and the restless way Cynthia was stroking the brush back and forth, that she wanted her to go away so that she could resume her struggle with the devil of curved essential form. Nigel saw the flicker of impatience which charged her large quiet eyes, and she knew exactly the way Cynthia felt. She had felt that way too many times herself. If some one came to her in the midst of a rehearsal, and said, "Here, I've brought you the crown jewels," she would probably stop and thank him, out of habitual politeness. She might even say: "How lovely they are! I'll wear them this afternoon before they wither." But all the time she would be fidgeting and wondering why in God's name they didn't go away and let her work in peace.

"Be good," she said, looking wistfully around at the bare, unmitigated room. Then she closed the screen door behind her and went down the stair.

*

The field of plumed sorghum which bordered the whole length of the lawn from the front gate to the garden was like a bank of green solid earth, and Gust, burrowing on his hands and knees between the rows, pulling sand-burrs, might very easily have been mistaken for an exceptionally large mole in blue overalls. As he moved through the interminable tunnel of leaves and the shadows of leaves, he was uncomfortably aware of a sharp pain in his right knee—the one he most often knelt on. He tried to spare it as much as possible, but there was no other way of pulling sand-burrs except to get down on his hands and knees. As the morning wore on, it seemed to him that the pain was getting worse. Once or twice he felt so sharp a twinge that the lines of his weatherbeaten face grew even more deeply set. Maybe it was because the day was so still, he told himself; no wind to blow away the heat. And maybe it was because he was old and going to pieces. Sixty-five was not a great age. The old man had reached seventy-three, and when he died he was as stout as a good piece of hickory. Sixty-five was not a great age. Only now, little things—this knee of his—seemed to bother him more than they used to. And sometimes lately he was tired for days at a time, so that when he woke up in the morning he felt exactly as if he'd just crawled into bed. It wasn't his muscles that were tired. They were still tough and stringy and good for as much work as they had ever been. He couldn't exactly describe this tiredness to himself, except that it was deeper than the other kind. It was in his bones. He was a good horse that was too old to work any more. . . . The lines which pain had set in his jaw, and at the corners of his eyes deepened with bitterness. He was too old to work any more, and pretty soon they'd find out and turn him loose in the pasture.

From the wages of a lifetime Gust had saved enough to buy a small piece of property on the Little Neenah, several miles below Meadowland. There was a house which could be fixed up for little money—he still had more than enough in the bank. On one side of the clearing there was a tamarack swamp and on the other, several acres of woods, and in the woods were deer. Often he caught sight of one when he was walking through the woods, but the deer ran so swiftly between the trees he could only catch a glimpse of it. It disappeared so quickly sometimes he was not quite sure whether he had actually seen a deer. It was more as if the thought of one had crossed his mind.

Again and again Gust had promised himself that someday, when he got around to it, he was going to retire to this little place and do all the things there had never been time for him to do. He would hunt squirrels in the woods and fish on the slough, and when the weather was bad he could sit in the doorway and smoke and listen to the rain on the roof. This dream of leisure for his body Gust had fabricated out of the infinite leisure of his mind, during the brief summer days in the fields, and the long winter days bent over his work-bench in the carpenter shop.

Now, as he shifted his weight carefully to spare his game knee, it occurred to him for the first time that he might turn his dream into actuality. There was seldom enough heavy work at Meadowland to keep two men busy, even in the summertime. The Boy was nearly grown. There was no great need of him any more. Of course there was always plenty of puttering to be done—building lattices and painting sheds—but nothing worth the bother. And if he quit, they'd be that much money to the good and the way things were going now it wouldn't do them any harm to save a penny. So long as he could remember, Meadowland had never paid for itself, even in the days when the old man was alive and watching over things. There was never any fussing then, and yet the farm ran like a clock. There was a place for everything, and it was always there when you went to get it. Now there were three places for everything, and it was usually not in any of them or else Whitey had just broken it. In the old days you could go from one end of the carpenter shop to the other, and never find a loose shaving or a nail unsorted. Now you were lucky if you could find a saw or a hammer when you needed one. The old man had money sense. He made his living out of other things, and, instead of clearing the forty acres of timber and trying to farm it, kept it intact, just as it was when he married and came to live on the place. The old man had money sense, but nobody in the family afterwards had any at all—except the Boy, who was the old man all over again. *She* didn't have the money sense God gave a jack rabbit. She didn't know how to make it, and, what was worse, she couldn't hang on to what she already had. The first scarecrow that came along could get anything he wanted out of her, so long as he looked hungry and needed a new pair of breeches. All these damned writers and painters and fiddlers that came every summer like a swarm of locusts and ate up everything in sight. If she didn't stop pretty soon there'd be nothing left for the Boy. The thought made him so angry that he stopped, when he came to the end of the row, and stood up to ease his back and his temper.

Mrs. West came through the garden gate and started up the hill, her arms full of blue and white larkspur. There was something so blithe about her—the way she was walking up the hill with her head held high, singing a funny little song. Gust could not take his eyes from her. She was an exasperating, silly woman— Barbs of pain shot through his knee. She was an exasperating, silly woman, and if she didn't stop pretty soon . . . The sharp lines of his face gradually softened and he stood staring after her with adoration in his eyes.

*

Bascomb hesitated at the door of the lowest story of the Tower, uncertain whether to go in and plague Josefa, who was still working over her descending scale, or to go up the outside winding stair which led to Cynthia's studio on the top floor. He liked better to watch Cynthia paint. But on the other hand, Josefa was more dangerous when unduly provoked, and Bascomb loved danger—of a sort.

He sat himself down before the door, tailor fashion, to consider the matter, and began drawing pieces of grass through his teeth. Bascomb's teeth were one of the things his somewhat absent-minded guardian had neglected, or perhaps it was his adenoids. One could never be sure which was responsible for the shape of his mouth. But at all events, he looked very like an amiable and engaging rat.

Out of a near-by hole a gopher came, and gave Bascomb his undivided attention for some time. Bascomb bowed politely and inquired after the gopher's health. The gopher suddenly remembered something, and dived back into his hole. Probably the gas stove, said Bascomb to himself, as he swatted a deer-fly. Another was zooming around the back of his head. When others came, he decided to seek shelter in the Tower.

"Can I come in to the ark of the Lord?" he said, opening the screen door. Like Jesting Pilate, Bascomb never stayed for answer.

Josefa got up from the piano and stood before him. She was an almost absurdly substantial woman with a peasant's broad face and a peasant's broad square shoulders. Her hair was black, straight, parted in the middle, and cut off a little below the line of her chin. Each move that she made had the power and the conviction of her whole body behind it. Her face, as she stood glaring at Bascomb, was like a masque of anger.

"Get out!"

"But Josefa . . ."

"Don't Josefa me. I'm working."

"I shouldn't have known it, really. I've been watching you through the door for fifteen minutes, and you haven't struck a note. That just goes to show—" He nodded pleasantly as he pushed a litter of books, papers, music, and magazines off the chaise-longue, and reclined thereon in what he hoped was the manner of the David Madame Récamier. The resemblance was not very striking.

"Bascomb, this is no time to be paying calls. And I've got too much work to do. If you don't get out of here—" There was a bright glitter in her enormous gray eyes.

"You're not at all hospitable." Bascomb helped himself from the package of cigarettes on the table. "That scale you were playing just now—as Lorado Taft says of Amiens cathedral: 'Pretty little thing. *I* like it.' "

Josefa was Bascomb's favorite audience, especially as she was now—passionate and resentful. He could not keep from grinning when she sat down before the piano and began to rock from side to side, her mouth drawn hard and straight, her gray eyes burning.

"Josefa, your surroundings are so delightfully chaotic." He waved a long limp arm vaguely in the direction of the stuffed owl and the confusion which he himself had just made on the floor. "In spite of all I can do with her, Aunt Susan spends every minute of her time straightening things. It's perfectly outrageous. I always say to myself, when I wake up in the morning and see my shirt on the floor and my socks in the water-pitcher, 'Bascomb, my boy,' I say to myself, 'neatness is the sign of a second-rate mind.' It really is, you know. And the sense of responsibility is another sign. That's your shortcoming, Josefa. Just now you were saying—don't deny it! I heard you with my very own ears—you were saying that you had too much work. Now according to Carlyle, Josefa, that would be impossible. You must read Carlyle. All about sea-green-incorruptible-mammonism. You'd love it! Now what's all this about having so much work?" Bascomb's voice became soft and honeyed with mock-solicitude.

Josefa bowed her head and stared at the keyboard, trying to devise some means of getting rid of Bascomb. Day after day he yapped and bit at her heels, like a little yellow dog. Some day he'd yap once too often and get a kick in the teeth. . . . The thought gave her enormous satisfaction far more than the thought of her highly successful concert last season in Town Hall. *What* a concert that was! She had bought a white satin evening dress with scarlet-lining in the sleeves, to take people's minds off the music. Then she played like a louse, forgot and went back, and made forty thousand mistakes, and it was the most brilliant concert of the year. . . . The ends of her mouth curled as she remembered how they had all come piling into her dressing-room afterwards—reporters and people waving movie contracts and envious-eyed music students. Such a jam they could hardly breathe. And she in the midst of them, jabbering and screaming, until she looked over their shoulders and saw *him* pushing his way to her, shoving and pushing, and so angry with her that the tears were streaming down his face.

"The trouble with you, Josefa"—Bascomb shook his head disapprovingly at her—"is that you're all hot and bothered because you're going to play with the Boston Symphony. That's wrong. All wrong. All wrong. You let Serge look after the Boston Symphony. He does it very well, and besides that's what he's paid for. I'll tell you exactly what to do. From now until the twenty-fifth of November you mustn't touch the piano. Do anything else you like. Take up golf, Josefa. You'll like golf. All you have to do is keep your head down. Besides, it's no end of fun wading after balls. By the way, do you mind if I take off my shoes? My feet always get so hot, and the only shoes I can wear with any comfort are Deauville sandals, which they don't make any more. The last pair I owned I lost going through a bog—or is it bawg?—bogg, bahg, bag, beg—I never can remember which it is. Well, to get on with the concert. After the twenty-fifth of November it'll be too cold for golf, and you can play a little Bach. You'd like Bach, Josefa. All you have to do is keep your head down. . . ."

He stopped, not altogether sure whether Josefa was pretending not to listen, or not even pretending to listen. "After you've done that for a month, your fingers will be loosened up, and you'll go to the concert feeling perfectly fresh, see? What you have to guard against, though, is the sense of responsibility. Hindoo psychology is the thing—you know—Yogi. That's exactly what you need. Now begin saying after me, 'Je suis an entity. Mon mind est mon instrument of expression.' "

Josefa turned around and looked at him. It seemed to her that his mind was like a clock improperly wound; you could never tell what hour it would strike next.

"You just say that over and over again all the rest of the morning, and in no time at all you'll find yourself becoming enlightened concerning the nature of the real self, and the secret knowledge whereby you may develop the consciousness and realization of the real 'I' within you . . ." He stopped for breath. "Tomorrow you spend the entire matin saying 'Je suis a center of thought. Around moi revolves mon mond.' Friday you say to yourself, 'Je suis independent of la body.' Saturday you say to yourself, 'A half-inch I in quotation marks avec a circle around it.' Sunday is a day of rest. Monday you say——"

Josefa rose deliberately from the piano bench and towered over her tormenter. One cuff and she could demolish him, break every bone in his ugly body. His eyes dared her to. "I have to work," she said, and turned back to the piano.

With an expression of delicate malice she began once more the descending scale. Over and over she played it, until she could tell, without turning around, that Bascomb was unhappy. Warming to her task, she let slip an occasional false note.

His ear was nice in such matters, she knew, though his taste in music was irresponsible.

From his intrenchment on the chaise-longue Bascomb for the first time considered the possibility of flight. Josefa's back was toward him, but he knew exactly what expression was on her face. Flight was out of the question.

He picked up a copy of a music magazine and thumbed noisily through its pages. Josefa's back became eloquent. He found a full-page picture of a soprano with a name like a typewriter. From the subtitle he gathered that she was bringing her vast bosom back to America on the *Berengaria*, for a concert tour. His agile mind leaped back and forth hopefully from sopranos to bosoms, from sopranos to bosoms to the *Berengaria*. None of them seemed to produce a vein of fruitful thought in him, so he got up from the chaise-longue, went over to the fireplace, and stuck his head into the opening. With something like a clatter he changed the draft from shut to open—from open to shut—from shut to open.

Instantly Josefa stopped playing false notes. She had accomplished all she had hoped. Now she went on playing the scale over and over again, trying her best to make it sound unendurably dull. She succeeded rather well.

Bascomb stood before the portrait of his grandfather, who looked like vinegar. With a few casual exceptions, himself included among them, the family stock had improved enormously. Perhaps Grandmother West was responsible. He passed on to her; then to the Japanese nude, who was of course in no way responsible, which was a pity. He would have liked nothing better than to be descended from a Japanese nude. Would that woman never stop that goddamned scale?

Beyond the outer fringes of his consciousness the shadow of a cloud appeared and grew larger. There was but one thing in heaven or hell that Bascomb could not endure. Fortunately, he knew the symptoms of boredom before it was well upon him. Rather than let that awful fate descend, he would declare an armistice with Josefa. "I'll go away and leave you if you'll only stop that tick-tacking and play something for me."

Josefa looked at him over her shoulder. Her eyes curved with mockery. She did not care greatly for his bribe, knowing that it was nothing more than the white flag of surrender. If she were to play but three notes of that scale—her mind toyed with the idea—if she were to play no more than three notes of that scale, he would go away and plague her no further.

She looked out of the window at the pasture where the bright green of the ground was woven into the bluer green of the summer trees. It had all been a mistake, her coming here. It was just as *he* said; they gave her no peace. She had been here weeks and weeks, without accomplishing a thing. She had been trifling with the *Allegro con fuoco* of the Tschaikowsky B flat Minor Concerto that she was going to play with the Symphony. She could not even do that the way she wanted, and all the long, arduous *Andante* still to be conquered. . . . She watched the bright green of the ground darken with the shadow of a cloud, and the blue-green trees grow purple. *He* would like that if he were here. He liked all subtle things. For example, that involved Bach air—the one which spins round and round, gradually withdrawing into itself. Involuntarily the fingers of her right hand sought out the notes. When she was certain of them she tried with the left hand another motif—a more simple one—from the same suite. Then she played the two together, softly, tentatively, until they merged and took shape. As they grew and put forth one flowering variation after another, she forgot entirely that Bascomb was in the room. She was playing for *him*. More times than she could remember he had come bursting into the room where she was practicing, demanding that she stop whatever she was working on and improvise for him. It seemed to quiet his nerves when he was worn and exhausted from teaching the same thing over and over again to the same thick-headed, thick-fingered pupils. He would sink down into his chair and shut his eyes, and the fine blue veins over his temples would pound slower and slower. Then quite suddenly he would be on the bench beside her, carving out in the bass clef a masculine accompaniment to her improvisation. She would think of the things she had known as a child. She would think of trees and the bare mountain-side, and heavy peasants and light-footed goats and thunder and lightning over the ponderous mountains. She would play all these things for him, and for a time he would follow wherever she led, so that they spoke with their hands a language of exquisitely adjusted sympathy. But it was never for long. Sooner or later—she could always tell when he was about to do it—he would wantonly destroy the mood of her playing. He did it always by the same curious trick of slipping from a dominant ninth in the key of D flat into a nerve-wracking augmented eleventh in the key of A flat, which shattered instantly the processional quality and the power and the quiet glory of her invented music.

It was so strange a thing. . . . She rocked back and forth on the piano bench, looking now out of the window and now past the disorderly room to a remote place where he now might be. It was so strange a thing, this speaking even for a brief time through one's hands instead of one's mouth. One had to begin by placing one's whole life in one's hands, breaking them in, as one would a horse, to do work which was contrary to their nature, and dull, and beneath their dignity. Scales and *études*. Scales and *études*. Until they were thoroughly broken and subservient to the mind. All this in order that one might decipher the testimony, left by others, of something more than mind—of a moment of Grace which came upon them, during which they heard a great many things all at once. And what they remembered they wrote down in succession and rearranged and made orderly, so that for other people there was something almost like a moment of Grace, though not Grace itself. . . . She moved an octave lower and continued in a different key. The shadows in the room grew quiet. She closed her eyes the better to see *his* face, and went on playing notes which the blind eye of the mind found for her. She felt the bench stirring beneath her. The room turned. Presently the earth began to move upon its ancient axis.

Bascomb, stretched out once more upon the chaise-longue, saw the shadow of the cloud fall below his mind's horizon, and sighed contentedly. He watched Josefa's massive torso bending and straightening over the keyboard. He envied her her arms, which were tough as carved wood, and her fingers, which were long and firm and apparently motivated by a life of their own. Gradually the sounds which he heard emerged upon his consciousness as music, and then as something more than music.

He saw a field, broad and curving under the autumn stars. And two friends walked in the field, their hands touching. They had heard the stars singing, and they followed the sound across the field and through the meadow beyond the field. When they saw the ground turn pale beneath their feet, they clasped hands and waited. . . .

"As Aunt Susan would say, that was most intriguing," Bascomb remarked in a far-away voice when Josefa had stopped playing. "What is it?"

"I haven't any name for it." She looked calmly out of the window, her broad white face drained of all expression. "Does it matter?"

"Certainly. I always want to know the names of things. That which we call a rose, you know, if designated as a cucumber, would smell like combination salad." He blushed with shame while his remark hobbled off to the limbo of the uncalled for. Thank God all literary allusions, witty or otherwise, were wasted on Josefa.

"This one has no name." She sat with her hands folded in her lap.

"It ought to have a name, Josefa. Everything ought to have a name, otherwise it's not nice." He stopped, thinking of the two friends and the stars which sang. "We'll call this piece of yours 'A Constellation for the G String.'"

"It would make better sense if you called it 'A G-String for the Constellation.'"

"No, no!" Bascomb sat up and began to shout. "Dreadful! Dreadful! How unspeakably vulgar you are!"

Josefa expressed with the help of her hands that which was inexpressible. When Bascomb assured her that she made his blood run cold, she gave no sign of being moved by the chemical catastrophe which was going on within him and for which she was allegedly responsible.

"While you were playing," he explained, "I had a lovely vision. I saw a field——"

Josefa looked good-naturedly at her hands while he related his lovely vision. She was still pleased over her last remark. When he had finished she made no comment.

"What's the matter? Don't you like it?" He looked crestfallen. "I'm disappointed in you."

What he meant was that he was disappointed in himself. Frustrated and uncomfortable, he began putting on his socks and shoes. "So you really don't think that's what it sounded like?" There was no conviction in his voice. "The field, I mean, and the two friends and the autumn stars?"

Josefa ran her fingers up and down the keyboard with excruciating precision, making no sound. "You can have it like anything you please, so far as I'm concerned. Any musician will tell you that it was only a series of variations in two different keys on two different themes by Bach, or perhaps stolen by him from Vivaldi. To me it was like—no matter what. Make whatever you please out of it. I'm going to work."

Bascomb was infinitely discouraged with himself. "I think I'll go call on Paul."

"He'll be delighted."

Halfway up the stairs Bascomb turned back. "Did you know that Aunt Susan's got a Negro boarder coming this afternoon?" He waited hopefully for the effect.

For answer, Josefa struck the first three notes of her descending scale, with the right hand at first and then with both. Bascomb had crowned his own discomfiture.

He continued up the stairs and found Paul in his room, reading by the window.

"Why Bascomb, come in! Come in. Won't you sit down?" Paul waved a hand toward the bed. There was only one chair in the room, and he himself was sitting in it.

"Thank you, I will." Bascomb put the cover on the slop-jar and sat down on it. This was a more hopeful beginning. Perhaps he should have come here in the first place. "I've come to give you a lecture on the unfoldment of consciousness." He crossed his legs precariously.

"That's very kind of you, I'm sure." Paul drew his pipe out of his pocket, and looked regretfully at the volume of Yeats, open on his lap. He had no desire to be interrupted at the moment, and he would rather have been called upon by a deputation from hell than by this pestilential and garrulous youth. There was only one thing to do—humor him. Otherwise he would stay much longer. Paul began filling his pipe.

"Well, really, it's very simple," Bascomb teetered on the slop-jar. "You begin by saying over and over to yourself, 'Je suis an entity'— Say, do you mind if I take off my shoes?"

*

Up and down the ten-acre field Thorn drove his team between the waving plumes of young corn while the sun wheeled higher and the morning wore away toward noon. From his seat on the cultivator, he shouted to the horses what must originally have been English words. But now, having lost their edge and shape through infinite repetition, they were monosyllabic injunctions in a private language known only to the horses and himself.

He had changed his overalls for a pair of khaki trousers. His bare lean back swayed from side to side with the movement of the cultivator. Most of the time his eyes were on the horses, but he knew without looking when the red-winged blackbirds rose beating the air above the marsh, and when a hawk circled over his head, its wings stretched and motionless.

These things were observed and recorded by him without astonishment or thought. They were the common phenomena of his world, along with the white horse named Bill, who had a mean disposition, and the sorrel horse named Jack, who did not; along with the burdock weeds and the corn and the young spruce trees his father had set out by the road; along with dry spells and rainy spells; along with the sweet smell of cut hay and the sour smell of horse manure.

The ten-acre field was Thorn's world. Its topography he knew by heart, and though he was not aware of the fact, he knew also the number of branches on the oak tree which his grandfather's perversity had left standing in the middle of the field.

The ten-acre field was bounded on the east by the Little Neenah, on the west by the road, and on the north and south by a horse-and-rider fence. These boundaries were geographical. To Thorn's eye, this morning, it was a ten-acre room with three walls of oak and one of willow, and a blue ceiling high overhead.

When Thorn's father moved his family to the country, it had been for the boy Thorn like coming home, though he was only four at the time, and had never been at Meadowland before. There had been generations of farmers on both sides of his family, but for Thorn's father the land had a half-remembered meaning. It troubled his mind when he was away from it, and yet he did not know quite what to do when he returned. He did not have the feel, and so he went duck-hunting in Octobers, and spent the intervening months playing with his sons. Even at four Thorn knew what his father did not. He would trudge along behind Gust's plow, overcoming the most tremendous difficulties in the way of clods and soft wet dirt. This he did sometimes for hours, until at last his stocky little legs gave out under him. When he was five, he learned to sit on one of the horses, and thereafter his labors were lightened.

He would follow Gust no matter where he worked, but he liked best the mornings when they started out together for the ten-acre field.

On his sixth birthday he and his father stood leaning against the south horse-and-rider fence, discussing gravely such grown-up matters as the value of timothy as opposed to clover for the second crop.

"It will never do," he had said, shaking his six-year-old head earnestly; and his father, who was a strange man occasionally given to unreasonable merriment, threw back his head and roared.

Thorn tried not to notice this lapse from strict sobriety. In a moment it passed and his father stood looking down at him curiously. Then he said, "I nearly forgot to mention your birthday present, son. I stopped in at the courthouse yesterday and made out a deed of transfer—with your mother's approval—for the ten-acre field. It's in your name now. You can do whatever you like with it."

The child looked up at him with eyes suddenly gone blind, and for a moment so far disgraced his manhood as to throw his arms about his father's neck. Then he ran off into the woods.

That night his mother, making her rounds with a candle to see that no harm was abroad, came to his small bed and found it empty. From room to room she went, calling his name softly, until she had searched the old house over for him. Then she grew frightened and roused the family.

They looked everywhere near the house, and their three nearest neighbors came across the fields, bearing lanterns, to help search for the child. Stretched out in a long line, they combed the dark wood, with very little help from the night sky, until they came at last to the ten-acre field, and there, curled up in a furrow of the warm soil, they found Thorn sleeping.

After that his father had taken him aside and explained to him the intricate unreasonableness of the feminine mind (most of which Thorn did not understand and none of which he could remember, now when he had need of it) and that furthermore it was expected of him as a man of property to make allowances for this irrationality, and even to forgo certain of his natural and legitimate pleasures, such as sleeping in the fields at night.

Though the ten-acre field came to be Thorn's on his sixth birthday, it was never merely a ten-acre field to him. Never a day passed without his going there at least once to see that everything was well with his possession. In the fall of the year, when he had to be ready by eight o'clock for the ten-mile drive to Thisbe to school, he would get up and dress by candlelight, and set out before breakfast for the ten-acre field. In winter when the farm and the woods lay buried deep in snow this seemed doubly necessary, and he would trudge there faithfully on the light snowshoes his father fashioned for him out of the frames of two old tennis racquets. To his child's mind it seemed that, unless he did so, the ten-acre field would grow very lonely during the long winter.

This morning it was not primarily the burdock weeds which were responsible for his coming here. He had something on his mind which he must straighten out, and it was necessary that he get beyond the sphere of his mother's influence to this place which, because it was utterly familiar, freed his mind from all thought of her confusion. He had come here this morning to think about his love.

Like all children raised in the country, Thorn was not in ignorance concerning the origin of life. So long ago that he no longer remembered, he had come upon a pasture scene before which he stood, dumb and wondering, until the details of the awkward, inexplicable coupling had been impressed upon his mind. Then he ran off and hid, and meditated in secret upon what he had seen. This was his first step beyond the protected world of his childhood; his first glimpse of terror.

As if certain scales had been removed from his eyes, he saw

everywhere about him in certain seasons of the year the quick lust of animals. But in a little while the sharpness and clarity of his first discovery wore off. He forgot entirely what he had seen in the pasture, and only the commonplace fact of breeding remained, made antiseptic by familiarity.

Occasionally he had read in books about people who were in love. . . . They were introduced to each other by a mutual friend. They fell in love at first sight. They danced. They went out on a balcony. The moon was very bright. He said would she marry him and she said she would. It was generally like that. He had read books which might have told him what he wanted to know. There was *Anna Karenina* in the bookshelf in his mother's room. But he did not have the kind of mind which relates what it reads to its own existence, and so he did not acquire experience vicariously.

As he passed up and down the rows, he moved certain experiences about in his mind, trying to make the edges of one fit into the edges of the other. It was as if his love were a jig-saw puzzle, and there were several pieces missing.

First of all, how could he account for this altogether new series of sensations which he had begun to feel: the bleeding which seemed to occur within him whenever he saw Nigel, as if each time an internal wound broke open at the sight of her, and bright blood flowed out of it in torrents; and the sense of not being quite able to get his breath sometimes when he thought of her; and the profound restlessness which seemed to locate somewhere in the small of his back; and the flame which fed upon his loins.

What did these things have to do with his love, and what did his love have to do with the breeding of animals and with the wild and shameful things which he sometimes dreamed. And what did his love have to do with that which had been between his father and mother, from which he had been shut out?

He remembered how much older his mother had grown the first night after his father died, and how often during the first long winter he heard her walking back and forth in her room. Whenever he heard her he would get up and come into her room to walk with her. But she would always gather him up and put him into bed with her, and the two of them would keep each other warm until he fell asleep watching her wide-open eyes staring at the ceiling.

Beneath these things and running all through them he felt the presence of some common meaning. If he could only put his hands on that, he would know everything he needed to know. If he could only find that.

A Ford joggled carelessly along the road and came to a full stop even with his cultivator. Thorn stopped his horses and went over to the car. In it sat Homer Hansen, a small Swede who lived two farms beyond Meadowland. He had once tried to cheat Mrs. West out of her share of the hay. Thorn, aged twelve, had put a stop to it. They had been on excellent terms ever since.

"We could stand a little rain." Hansen shifted his corn-cob pipe slightly.

Thorn put one foot on the running-board and leaned against the side of the car. "It rained some during the night."

"A couple of drops!"

Thorn nodded.

"That's a good stand of corn you got there."

"Not bad," Thorn agreed, modestly. It was the best, he knew, for miles around.

There followed a heavy silence during which Hansen sat mournfully chewing the end of his pipe, which was quite out. These silences always troubled Whitey and Mrs. West. They felt they must rush into the breach with conversation, and so they ruined everything. To Thorn country talk came natural. It was part of his feel for the land. It was evidence that he belonged with these people.

"Any trouble with potato bugs?"

"Not yet. Gust sprays them all the time. The rabbits are bad, though. They've eaten up half the melon vines."

Another silence, longer than the first, fell upon them. Hansen's Adam's apple worked its way up and down his neck. He put his hand inside his shirt and scratched reflectively. He moved his feet. "We got company coming today. From Oconomowoc."

"Is that so?" Thorn waited for him to go on.

"Cousins." Hansen's eyes changed color slightly. "Many folks staying at your place now?"

Thorn stiffened. He knew that look, and he knew the lustful, prying curiosity behind Hansen's simple question. Always it was this way. His mother was the chief source of gossip for the whole countryside. They had never admitted her right to be different from them, and more generous. They didn't really accept him, either, because he belonged to her. Always between him and these people whom he wanted to be like stood his mother. He must guard her against their curiosity. He must protect her in his father's absence.

He turned away slightly, that he might conceal from the neighbors the Negro reformer who was coming that afternoon, and the crazy woman who practiced on the first floor of the Tower, the man without a job who lived on the second, and the woman who painted oranges and oil-cans on the third. He turned away that he might conceal from the neighbors his love. Then he looked blandly into Hansen's eyes. "Nothing special," he said.

*

Cynthia had chosen her small, box-like room on the top floor of the Tower because it was high enough so that she could look out into the tops of the surrounding trees, and because she counted on the long, arduous climb to protect her against too frequent visitation. In the beginning she had been forced to do battle with Mrs. West, whose domestic instincts were thoroughly aroused at the thought of a room which did not have bright cretonnes, a chaise-longue, a bookcase, a waste-basket, a gate-leg table, andirons for the fireplace, and a suitable rug. Cynthia stood her ground bravely. In the top of the "woodus" she found a kitchen table which didn't wabble. This she used for her paints. From the loft of the barn she recovered a high three-legged stool. Except for these and her easel, which she leaned against the fireplace, the room was absolutely bare, so that she had almost as much room as she needed when moments of æsthetic difficulty arose and she was obliged to walk the floor.

Such a moment had but now come upon her. She stared down in quiet despair at the blob of vermilion on her palette, the blob of duck green, the half-dozen smooth areas of orange, all ambiguous from too much mixing.

Dead.

She scraped her palette clean and began with all the reds with yellow in them. Then she added quantities of yellow ocher, burnt umber, burnt sienna, emerald green—she was too weary to consider her extravagance.

This time she painted directly, without mixing the color on her palette. For a single moment she was almost satisfied with one stroke, it came so very close to being what she wanted. She stood off several feet to look at it, squinting now with one eye and now with the other. If you squinted slightly it was perfect. But if you looked at it squarely there was something——

She pushed her hair back from her eyes and reached for a clean brush. It was so simple a thing. She sat down and twisted her legs through the rungs of the three-legged stool. It was so simple a thing. She shut her eyes and began projecting oranges upon a large screen somewhere at the back of her tired brain—one after another, and each carved perfectly in space, until the firmament of her mind was filled and whirling.

She looked again at the canvas. Anybody could see that the oranges were oranges. The oil-can was clearly an oil-can. She could paint well enough where the thing itself was concerned. It was something more she wanted—some revelation of the identity within forms, of the relationship between two spheroids and a hemispheroid out of which emanated a thin curved spire. Now, after three weeks of passionate concentration, she had achieved two oranges and an oil-can.

She wiped her hands absently on her smock and began swishing a handful of dirty brushes around and around in a jelly-glass filled with turpentine. Watching the turpentine grow foul, Cynthia foresaw the coming on of one of the fits of despondency which swept over her from time to time, like a great wave. She slipped off her smock and went outside to await its coming.

From where she sat on the top step of the curving stair she could look down through layer upon layer of oak-leaves. It was only three stories to the gray-green ground below, but it seemed to Cynthia—so tired she was—that she could not even conceive of a place as far away as the ground must be. The distance from her top step was too great for the mind to establish the necessary relationships of place and space. She must be careful not to look down.

From limb to limb of the nearest oak tree a blue jay was shepherding a brood of young jays, cautiously and with many admonitions. Like Americans in Paris, thought Cynthia as she watched them. Save for the timorous exclamations of the young jays, and the maternal reassurances, the wood was as still as a wood can be. Then the sparrows came, and began fighting in the eaves trough, until the air was thick with the beating of wings.

At the corner where the railing turned, Cynthia saw two drops of rain water caught and suspended in a white spider web. One was oval and the other was round—more perfectly spherical than any natural thing she had ever seen. She bent forward and examined it closely so that she could see the green shadows reflected from the painted wood behind it, and the two points of white light borrowed from the sun.

An ant, grievously burdened with several grains of sand, crept up the railing level with her head. She looked at it as if she had never in her whole life been confronted with an ant. In a sense she never had. She did not know until this moment of intense perception that an ant had six legs, two pointed forward and four pointed back; that its body was like a string of small black beads—a large bead for the head, with two bent, anxious antennæ extending forward—a series of smaller beads, three in all, and each smaller than the preceding one—a strangely diminishing bead, as if the waist of the insect were drawn in and corseted—and finally a large abdominal bead, by way of finishing off the string with an ornament.

But the marvelous thing was that the string was alive and bore a burden of sand. Moved by the most god-like, dispassionate cruelty, Cynthia blew her breath upon it and watched it tumble hideously into the green depths below. With infinite slowness the wave of despondency began to rise. She held her breath and lay her head quietly on her knees. Then the wave came, all at once, and washed over her, and buried her.

So, contemplating disaster, she sat a long time until she heard a voice calling her name. Arm over arm she fought her way up through the waters of despair until she could see the thin sky and fill her lungs with clear air. She was not sure that she had really heard anyone, and her heart was still pounding wildly from its exertion. The way it had pounded one night when her dead mother's voice awakened her from a deep sleep, and she sat up in bed and answered, "Yes!"—desperately, like that. "Yes!"

"Cynthia. . . ."

The voice was real. Now there was no need to be afraid, as she had been that night sitting up in bed and listening with all her might to the silence in the dark house, which was empty as a shell and gave back to her from the hall outside her bedroom, and from the steep stairway, only the violent poundings of her own heart.

"Yes?" she called down. "What is it?"

"May I come up? It is I—Miss Bascomb."

An hour earlier, or a few minutes later, Cynthia would have resented this intrusion, but now she was glad for any human interruption which would help her to forget how near she had come to drowning.

"Certainly." And out of kindness she added, "Come slowly. The stairs are very steep."

Step by step Amelia mounted the stairs of the Tower, with the deliberate and slow progression of time itself adding minute to minute, hour to hour, piling month upon month, season upon season, year upon year. When Amelia appeared at the last corner, her face was drawn and a little paler than usual. On the third from the top step she sighed and caught her breath. "You live a long way up, my dear."

Watching her, Cynthia ached with sympathy. Amelia was so tall and gaunt and flat-chested. She was not really a woman at all. She did not have a woman's body, with a woman's breasts and full shoulders, a woman's firm round arms and legs. The line of her mouth was tight, as a man's sometimes is. Except for this there was nothing masculine about her—nothing strong, nothing alive. This was neither a woman's body nor a man's, but something in between and less than either—something gray which women become when desire dies out in them, for lack of cherishing; when no child takes shape within them. "You live a long way up, my dear. . . ." Amelia's words struck against some insubstantial wall of Cynthia's mind and echoed back, startling her into consciousness. To her knowledge, she had never heard Amelia call anyone "my dear," though Susan "my-deared" with every breath she took. . . . Whatever had caused Amelia to say that? But then, whatever had caused her to come at all?

As if in answer to Cynthia's unspoken question, Amelia explained: "I've come to see what you're doing." She rested a moment on the top stair, clinging to the narrow green railing for support.

Cynthia held the door open for her.

"Come inside, won't you?"

Their eyes met, and because each woman saw in the eyes of the other only kindness and good intent, a treaty was drawn up in silence, approved, signed and stamped with invisible seals.

Amelia passed over the threshold cautiously, as one entering an unfamiliar land submits to an unknown guide, trusting in good faith that there will be provisions and a lodging for the night. Once inside, Amelia stood looking around her. Window on the north, windows on the east and west. Fireplace on the south. Walls painted white, and so was the ceiling. Then her eyes fell upon the canvas. "Oh! . . ." She made an effort to conceal the disapproval she felt instinctively on first sight of Cynthia's study. The line of her mouth grew tighter. She willed away her disapproval because Cynthia and she were allies, and it would be a violation of the treaty between them if she disapproved of Cynthia's oranges and her oil-can.

All this effort Amelia might well have spared herself, for Cynthia was absorbed, for the moment, in the fact that walls painted white and left plain are peculiarly susceptible to light and shadow. She turned to the easel and began explaining her difficulties. "It's a— Did you ever paint?"

Amelia's face shone, as if for the first time in years she recalled something out of the charming past. "When I was young," she said, "I used to go twice a week, Wednesdays and Saturdays, to take painting lessons of a Mrs. Biedler—china-painting that was."

Cynthia caught the timid look. Poor Amelia was afraid she would look down on china-painting. "My mother painted china," she said, to reassure her. "I used to stand at her elbow for hours at a time, watching her. She taught me the names of the colors, and how to hold the brushes, and she let me make those funny little cotton pads that you cover with white silk and tie with a thread."

Amelia nodded. "I had rather a flair for violets," she said, modestly—"violets and yellow roses." She turned back to Cynthia's canvas and examined it carefully, almost professionally.

Cynthia returned to her original explanation. "It's a study in form, really—" She stopped to watch Amelia, knowing how little of what she had learned from Mrs. Biedler would have any bearing upon what she saw on the canvas. Then because the subject was so very real to Cynthia herself, she forgot almost immediately the limitations of her audience. "I used oranges," she began slowly, "because they are almost spherical, but not exactly. If they were exactly round, it would be a problem in mathematics, not in painting—you see?—and you might just as well use a pair of compasses. I made the two slightly different in size because I had an idea that if I could show the relationship that exists throughout natural forms—perhaps I can show you better what I mean with these flowers. Nigel brought them to me this morning from her walk." Cynthia stopped, remembering how Nigel had stood wistfully in the doorway, and then turned back for a second when she started down the stairs—as if there was something that she wanted to say and couldn't quite find the words. "Here's milkweed blossom, only all you have to do is look at it to see that it isn't really one blossom, but dozens of them, sticking out in every direction——"

Amelia nodded understandingly. "Like a cork ball with black pins in it."

"Exactly!"

The two women looked at each other and glowed with the pleasure of communication.

"In a deep shadow," said Cynthia, "you could scarcely tell the difference. The sepals are curled back against the stem, flat"—her eyes grew bright with enthusiasm—"the way a horse lays his ears back when he is angry. You know?"

Amelia did know.

"And this is butterfly-weed. The two are almost exactly alike, except for the color and arrangement on the stem. They may be of the same family, as these are, I suppose. Or they may not be the same kind of plant at all. Here's a blue-and-gold weed——"

Amelia could scarcely believe the testimony of her ears. It had been so long a time since anyone had bothered to talk to her as if she were an intelligent human being. They asked about her liver, if she had slept well, if her back hurt, if she had been to this doctor or that. Susan's conversation was intelligent sometimes, because she read a lot. But she had a way of forgetting the main point of what she was telling you. She'd start to tell you all about the amazing article she had just read on why cats can see in the dark, and she'd work up to the main fact, and then she'd have forgotten entirely why it was that cats could see in the dark. And there you were left high and dry.

Even if her mind didn't go wandering off the subject, even if she did remember what she was trying to tell you, it never seemed to make any difference to her whom she was talking to. If the pump handle had been an ear she would have derived just as much satisfaction from talking to the pump as she did from talking to her own sister-in-law.

But what Cynthia was saying was for her alone. And if some one else had been listening it would not have been said—at least, not in the same way. The thought made her a little dizzy. It was as if certain chambers of her mind, long unused, were suddenly thrown open to spring house-cleaning. First the shutters unhooked and the windows opened to light and air; then the rugs taken out and beaten on the clothes-line; then the chair covers removed, the floors scrubbed and waxed, the furniture oiled and polished, until the room was made habitable once more.

"The leaf," Cynthia was saying, "is like the honey-thorn. When you look closely at flowers, the same patterns keep turning up over and over, as if—" She looked slyly at Amelia and smiled. "As if the Lord lacked inventive powers and had to repeat himself frequently."

Amelia was a trifle shocked at the suggestion that God's power was in any way limited. But from the orthodox point of view, Omnipotence was not obliged to do anything, and therefore It was certainly not obliged to repeat Itself unless, of course, It chose to. Apparently It did choose to, because what Cynthia said was obviously true. "It's the same way with people, isn't it? I mean, they repeat themselves just the way plants do."

"Indeed yes!" Cynthia was laughing. "When I was in art school, studying portraiture, I made a chart of all the various kinds of noses I saw on the streets of New York. There were only thirty-seven, so far as I could discover. No two people really look alike, of course, no matter how closely their individual features may conform to type. That is, no two white people. I'm not sure about Chinese. They look as much alike to me as elephants. But then elephants probably don't have a bit of trouble telling one another apart."

A gust of fresh wind swept through the newly opened chambers in Amelia's mind. She laughed.

"People are much too complex," Cynthia continued, more seriously. "Once you begin to look at them, you discover too much that is individual. That's why I used oranges. The form is not so complex, and you can see the relationship more easily. If I can only get that—" She stopped short, remembering the travails of the morning. "If I can only get that, I shall try elephants, and then work up through Negroes and Chinese to the infinite complexity of the white race."

Amelia shook her head. "There's just as much difference among Negroes, my dear, as there is among white people."

"You've lived in the South?"

"In Charleston, South Carolina."

God bless us every one! thought Cynthia, with horror. And Susan bringing a Negro into the bosom of the family on the four-o'clock train! Had she— But then she must have known. She was always doing things that no one in full possession of his faculties would think of doing. This was one more brainstorm. "You don't talk like a Southerner."

"I've lived most of my life in the North," Amelia said, and rather sadly she added, "Not from choice."

Cynthia shook her head. "Nobody ever lives anywhere from choice. I spent the first twenty-five years of my life in Mason City, Illinois. When did you live in Charleston?"

"When I was a little girl. My mother and I went to live with my Aunt Jessamine Beal. I was only eight, but I remember quite well the first day we came there."

From where Amelia stood she could look out of the east

window, but it was not the old farmhouse at Meadowland that she saw, or the checkered fields; it was a busy street submerged in hot yellow sunlight. Enormous Negro mammies went prancing by, incased from wrist to ankle in billowing mullberry or lemon or pale green, brilliantly flowered. Their heads were bound with scarves—yellow, cerise, grass green—and they rolled their white eyes from side to side. Their dignity was stupendous.

In the dust and heat of the roadway others sat, row on row, their knees spread apart, their chins resting in their cupped hands. And all about their knees swarmed naked, pot-bellied pickaninnies, small and active copies of their shapeless fathers, who were standing on one leg, with their backs curved to the wall, swatting at flies.

Through this street that was never even for a moment quiet, through this bombardment of voices, with rockets of laughter exploding now and again upon the heavy air, rode Amelia, a child of eight, in a carriage behind two bay horses. On one side sat her mother, and on the other her Aunt Jessamine. Amelia remembered it all quite clearly. Suddenly her mother cried, "Jessamine!" and covered the child's eyes with her gloved hand. When she took her hand away they were in a quiet street completely shaded by trees that seemed to wash over the carriage like green waves.

What had happened back in the other street? Was some one hurt? Or was it something horrible or indecent, which a child should not be allowed to see? Years afterwards, when she asked about it, no one remembered.

"You don't like Negroes?"

"Not if they don't know their place!" Amelia's face grew dark and set. In the renovated chambers of her mind shutters were drawn, windows were closed and bolted, chairs were shrouded again. "Susan broke the news to me at breakfast."

"Perhaps if he's a very nice Negro——"

Amelia looked astonished.

"Pleasant, I mean—and well-mannered——"

"That's very possible," Amelia looked scornfully down the end of her nose, "but it doesn't have much to do with the matter. My sister-in-law never does things by half-ways. I haven't a doubt she'll put him at the table with us."

"You wouldn't care to sit at the same table with a Negro?"

Amelia looked sharply at her, suspecting sarcasm. If there was any intended, Cynthia's face did not betray her.

"Indeed I should not! It isn't as if Susan knew anything about Negroes. Each one she meets she says is marvelous and brilliant and beautiful—beautiful! It's just because they're Negroes. She hasn't the faintest idea of what they're really like, or what goes on in their thick heads, or the way they like to live. Most of them are too shiftless to stoop over and pick up a nickel. They lose or break anything you give them. And if you teach them that two and two make four, they forget it by the next day and have to be taught it all over again. I know what I'm talking about. I lived under the same roof with Negroes for years and years. When I first went to Charleston, I had a Negro mammy to take care of me and dress me. I was very fond of her. I think I was probably much fonder of her than I was of my Aunt Jessamine——"

Amelia saw a black turbaned face with very old eyes, and suddenly it occurred to her for the first time how strange a thing it was that anyone who was so loving—who had apparently never been treated unkindly in her life—should smile so resignedly. Was there something even about kindness that you had to become resigned to?

Somewhere in Amelia's mind a door was closed. An immaterial key turned in an immaterial lock.

"Even so," she went on, "I wouldn't sit at the same table with her." There was something final in the set of Amelia's jaw.

Cynthia ached for her because she seemed, for incomprehensible reasons, more drawn, more thin; because her breasts were utterly barren. "What are you going to do?" Cynthia spoke evenly, trying to hold back her compassion so that her voice would not betray it.

"I wish I knew," said Amelia. "I wish I knew."

*

Freed from her tormenter, Josefa descended into her work as a miner descends into a mine. The morning sunlight pouring in through the east window did not exist for her. She worked in a dark hole. She moved through tunnels and timbered passageways with no air but the pure oxygen of her intent mind.

Deep in the heart of her work she achieved a complete separation from the dimensions of life—from time and place, from everything except the technical difficulties of the brilliant *Allegro con fuoco.* When she rose to the upper regions again, she discovered that it was almost time for lunch, that she was ravenously hungry.

She got up from the piano bench, and as she stretched away the stiffness in her back she saw for the first time the intense and centrifugal confusion of the room. It looked very much as if she had taken a pole—a long pole—and stirred it round and round, drawing everything after it in a maelstrom of disorder. Josefa decided that on the whole she liked a certain amount of imaginative confusion. It made a room look as if it was being used for something.

And having decided that she quite liked confusion, Josefa went outdoors so that she would not have to look at it. She sat down on the steps, lit a cigarette, and relaxed, with her broad back against the screen door. The wood was strangely silent and, in contrast with the almost shadowless lawn, dark and rather forbidding. It was a perfectly harmless wood, as she very well knew, but by some trick of the midday light it had become sinister. She turned away from it and contemplated the lawn stretched out before her, green and deserted. Even the house seemed uninhabited. Actually it was in a ferment of preparation for lunch, Josefa knew. But at this time of the day the shades were invariably drawn in the living room, to keep out the heat of the sun. Bees moved about in the grape arbor, and the sound they made only accentuated the drowsy stillness of the landscape.

But what, Josefa wondered, are bees doing in the grape arbor? As she started across the drive to find out, a car drove over the rickety bridge at the foot of the hill. The sound was unmistakable. She stopped dead still in the shadow of an oak.

He was in that car. The moment she heard the loose boards rattling, and the deeper reverberation of sound over water, she knew that it was he. She had no reason to think that he might suddenly turn up in this way, but it did not matter. A letter had come from him only the day before, a letter posted in New York, which said that he was starting off to Maine for the rest of the summer. And that did not matter, either. She was glad beyond words, beyond the need of words, that he was here. As the car slowly climbed the hill, the drowsiness which had settled upon the farm slipped away behind the far blue hills and out of sight. The lawn and the house became tense with expectancy. The wood which had been sinister and lonely was now a dark and friendly place where they might walk until they lost themselves. In the green vines the bees roared loudly. The car drew nearer. Josefa felt the muscles about her heart twisting and twisting. She stepped out into the sunlight.

He was not in the car which turned in at the drive—an antique Oldsmobile that had to all appearances been ravished season after season by moths. Instead it was filled to overflowing with tourists who looked at Josefa and at the old white farmhouse and then at Josefa again, as if she were some outlandish creature—a pelican or a gnu—that they had heard about but never until this moment seen. They leaned out of the side of the car to get a better look at her, as they drove past and down the hill. Apparently Josefa was just what they expected a pelican to look like, only less impressive.

She threw out her arms in wide disgust and sought the shelter of the Tower. In a minute they would come chugging up the hill again, past the house, past the Tower, and out on the highway once more. It was an almost daily occurrence, and she would not have minded them except that she was so certain it would be some one else. How foolish of her to think that! She had no reason to expect him, and besides, he'd never drive out in an automobile, hating them as he did. He'd either walk or rent a horse. He was so unreasonable about cars. That time, for instance, when they were crossing the Plaza after Josef Lhévinne's concert and neither of them looking where they were going because they were so excited over Lhévinne's playing. . . . Josefa could not help but smile, remembering their excitement. *No one else can play like that*, he kept saying over and over, like a man in a fever. Then a voice, LOOK WHERE YOU'RE GOING! and the next thing she knew he was beating his fists against the windows of a taxi in amazement and fury.

If he did come to the farm, he'd never drive out from town in an automobile. That much was certain. . . . She stopped just inside the door, realizing with a shock that she was still expecting him. It was ridiculous, of course, but she couldn't get it out of her mind. And now the disorder which had seemed rather comfortable and picturesque was merely slovenly and unendurable.

He had gone off to Maine, she told herself as she stooped and began sorting the litter. He always went to Maine in the summer, she said as she straightened the rug with the back of her heel. And, anyway, if he were coming he'd certainly telegraph first. But if he should come— She released the curtains and straightened one after another of the pictures. But now if he should come, the room was ready.

*

When Amelia had gone, Cynthia returned to her perch at the top of the stairs, and considered the implication of Amelia's refusal to break bread with a Negro. She tried to remember all she had ever heard concerning race prejudice, but in the heart of that darkness she could find nothing to enlighten Amelia's dry, unintelligible woe. She sighed, feeling that it was all very confusing and she might better return to her own world of the colors and shapes of things.

Far below she heard the sound of a screen door banging. Then a voice called up to her——

"*Rapunzel, Rapunzel,*
Let down your gold braids."

It was Bascomb, and she had had enough company for one morning. First Nigel, whom she loved. Then Amelia, whom she could not understand. Now Bascomb, who was a nice enough youth, but he talked so much and his voice cut into her like blue steel.

She leaned her head weakly against the railing. Perhaps if I make no sound, she thought, he may go away. There was nothing she could do to prevent him from coming up. If she said to him, "Go away, go away. I'm working. You can't come up here," he'd come just the same.

"*Very well, Rapunzel;*
Don't let down your old braids."

She shut her eyes against the sharp sunlight and waited for the sound of his foot on the stair. The first step. The second step. The third— With no warning at all the backwash of the wave of despair struck her and whirled about her, breaking into pools of gray foam at her feet. With each step upon the stair the muddy water mounted higher and higher. She waited a moment, without breathing, and then turned her head away so that she might not be forced to witness this rape of her privacy.

*

The boarders were summoned to meals by a cow-bell which was rung, as a rule, before the food was even ready to put on the table. It was actually no more than a warning for Gust and Thorn to come up from the fields, because Mrs. West and Johanna had been putting their heads together, and lunch might happen anytime in the next half hour.

All this Paul knew by bitter experience. Yet, whenever he heard the cow-bell, reflex action compelled him to drop whatever he was doing and go down to the house at once. If worst came to worst, as it frequently did, and lunch was nowhere near to being ready, he would pull up one of the green shades in the darkened living-room and thumb through old numbers of the *National Geographic.* In the course of much waiting he had learned which mushrooms were poisonous and which were not. And he had picked up a considerable amount of information, interesting though perhaps irrelevant, about our friend the frog, and the nest life of the osprey. As the summer wore on, his interest passed to river-encircled Paraguay and burning Hadhramaut. There were even times when he felt that he must rush off on a travel jag and let no grass grow under his feet until he had climbed the Matterhorn.

Now, hearing the cow-bell, he put down his pen without a moment's hesitation, and went to the washstand. He poured water into the bowl from the large pitcher and wondered if he should ever get used to washing in rain water. It was always yellow, and it smelled curiously sour and fusty. No one else seemed to mind, so doubtless in time he too would get used to it.

Halfway down the stairs he stopped and exclaimed, "*Du lieber Gott!*" As he looked about him at the lower story of the Tower, his astonishment passed all bounds. Josefa was nowhere to be seen, and, so far as he could tell, disorder had fled with her. The curtains hung straight, if a trifle exhausted. The pictures were once more square with the world. The chaise-longue was cleared and the music was on the rack of the piano, where in the nature of things it was originally intended to be. Josefa must have interpreted Bascomb's visit as a warning from heaven.

Musing upon this latter-day miracle, he opened the screen door in time to hear the cow-bell a second time. . . . Something was up. In all three weeks of his stay at Meadowland the cow-bell had never been rung more than once. What portentous significance this second ringing might have, he could not imagine. Calamity, without a doubt. Calamity tagged as faithfully at Susan's heels as Rats did after Whitey. It must have overtaken her at last. Johanna had fallen from the stepladder and broken both legs; or perhaps Whitey forgot to go for the cream.

The air was cooler than it had been when he returned from his walk. He sniffed inquiringly. He looked up at the sky. Sure enough, it was clouding up. Like soapsuds. A little rain, perhaps.

Dead leaves rattled under the nearest oak tree. Paul looked down in time to see a spotted adder disappear into the tall grass. From far over the shadowed hills came a slow peal of thunder.

When he walked round the corner of the house, a strange and wonderful sight met his eyes. There in a long line extending down to the first pasture gate were all the people of Meadowland.

At the head of the procession was Nigel, in a blue-checked tablecloth which fell straight from her shoulders to the ground. On her head was a miter fashioned out of paper napkins, and she was waving a handful of knives, forks, and spoons in a highly pontifical manner.

Then came Josefa with a dish of something or other—probably something hot, by the way it was wrapped in a cloth. She was taking great peasant strides, as she always did, and she held the dish aloft as if it were a gift of frankincense and myrrh.

Behind her came Cynthia with a bucket of ice. Johanna, who followed after Cynthia with a large platter of deviled eggs, was taking short, harassed steps, as if she were only too aware that things were not as they should be; not at all as they were in Bavaria.

Whitey carried nothing at all, after the irresponsible manner of young boys. And Rats trotted along behind him after the equally irresponsible manner of young dogs.

As if to compensate for so much nonchalance, there was something painful about the way Thorn carried the large bowl of lettuce which had been intrusted to him. The bend of his elbows said to Paul, "This isn't the way people eat, is it? We ought to be sitting down at the table in the dining-room. I hope nobody drives through the outer lane."

What Gust was thinking as he stumbled along with a basket under one arm and a camp stool under the other, his elbows did not betray. He was limping rather noticeably, but there was nothing in his limp to suggest that he did not enjoy or approve of picnics. It seemed rather to suggest that there was something the matter with his right leg.

Though Gust apparently did not disapprove, Amelia did. There was profound disapproval in the very angle of inclination of her head.

At the sight of Mrs. West hurrying along with a round flat loaf of bread tucked under her arm, Paul could not help but notice how lightly her fifty-three years sat upon her, especially at such times as this, when she had just contrived to bring about a more than ordinary state of confusion.

"Aunt Susan looks like Little Red Riding Hood starting off to visit her sick grandmother," said Bascomb through his nose, and Paul was forced to agree with him. Bascomb himself brought up the rear, very dramatically, by waving on high a striped Nantucket jersey, tied by the sleeves to a somewhat disreputable broom-handle. It was a scene that definitely called for music—"Pomp and Circumstance," or the Triumphal March from "Aïda."

Paul felt that he ought to offer his services. "Can I bring anything?" he shouted to Mrs. West.

"Lord bless us, no!" Bascomb answered for her. "We've got everything but after-dinner mints and the garbage-pail, and you needn't bring either, because this is only lunch, and we'll throw the scraps to the chickens as we come back through the pasture. I tell you what, though. If you really want to do something, we'll let you be the flowers that go in the center of the table."

"If I had a boy like that," Paul said to himself, and went no further, realizing that he wouldn't do anything, of course, because there was nothing anybody could do about Bascomb. And so he quickened his steps and fell into line behind Mrs. West, not wishing to present an anticlimax to Bascomb's heroic figure.

"Everything was on the table," she shrieked back at him, "when I suddenly remembered what a heavenly day it was, and so I told Johanna we'd move the festive board down to the picnic-ground. Poor Johanna!"

Poor Johanna indeed, thought Paul. But what and where was the picnic-ground, that they should suddenly and with no warning transfer the festive board to it. "Picnic-ground?"

"My dear! Haven't you ever been down there? Well, wait till you see it!"

There was apparently no more information forthcoming and since communication was rather difficult, Paul felt that the most sensible thing he could do was to follow docilely after Mrs. West.

Confusion set in when the procession reached the farthest pasture gate. The column broke and began milling around. By the time Paul arrived at the gate, and could determine for himself the cause of the delay, there were definite signs of a stampede.

The difficulty was over the gate itself, which was so seldom used that a delicate sheath of wild-grape vines had woven itself around both the gate and the gate-posts.

"It's so lovely," Cynthia was saying. "We can just as well go round through the other gate." Her eyes filled with tears as she spoke.

Paul marveled at the depth of her feeling. Only once before had he stumbled on just such anguish for a torn and broken growing thing. He remembered now a youngster he had tutored while he was working his way through college, a pale, dark-eyed, thin-blooded child who wanted to read all the time. One day a big branch of a white lilac had broken off in a spring windstorm, at the time when the bush was in bloom. It was a large lilac and very beautiful. The family were sorry when the branch snapped, but the child had been more than sorry. He ran out in the midst of all manner of rain and wind—Paul could see him even now, trying to make the branch stay on, and weeping as if his heart would break.

"But how distressing!" Mrs. West was saying as she looked from the grape vine to the first pasture gate, which was nearly fifty yards away, and then back to the grape vine again. There was the law of the boarders to be considered, of course; but even so, what with the macaroni getting colder and colder, fifty yards was too great a distance, no matter how pretty the vines were. The practical ghost of her practical father rose before her. "My dear, do you mind?" she said to Cynthia, and without waiting for an answer she walked over to the gate and cut the Gordian knot.

Paul preferred not to look at Cynthia as the procession fell into line, and without further impediment straggled through the gate and across the pasture. In time they arrived at a second gate, narrower than the first and with no vines growing over it. They passed through at once, and on to a thin neck of land flanked by the Little Neenah, going upstream on one side and downstream on the other. As the land spread out and became a fan-shaped peninsula, the path led them into dense underbrush and thick overhanging branches.

"Keep the branches out of your hair and your hair out of the food," Mrs. West called, gaily, as one by one they disappeared into the thicket. "Do you feel like the Children of Israel going into the wilderness?" she asked Paul as he caught up with her.

"Rather."

"So do I. So do I. Fortunately, we don't have to wait around forty years before we get to the picnic-ground. As soon as we get there, all we have to do is march seven times round the walls of Jericho, and then we can have lunch." A branch swung back, by way of punctuation to her remark, and she was no more to be seen.

Paul made his way carefully along the narrow path, attending to brambles and thorn trees, and with one eye out for snakes. He could hear Josefa complaining bitterly that she had scratched her leg and would doubtless die of it. And he could hear Bascomb's voice—shrill and high as the sound of an insect—reassuring her. Considering the ruggedness of her frame,

Bascomb said, it was most unlikely that she would die by scratching.

It seemed to Paul that a really high-class insane asylum must not be so very different from this. Not so out-of-the-way, perhaps, and without the pleasant landscape. But the inmates could not be much farther from sober sanity than most of the people here. Doubtless in a nuthouse there was less going on, and the inmates were probably allowed to retire from time to time and be free from interruption in their padded cells.

He brushed away one more branch and there was the picnic-ground—a small clearing in the very heart of the peninsula. The grass was soft and unclipped, and in the center of the clearing was a fine slender elm. From where he stood, Paul could see through a line of fir trees to the opposite bank of the Little Neenah, and beyond that a field of marsh hay which had been cut and stacked. Row on row the stacks knelt down on their knees, like Moslems praying—their foreheads pressed devoutly to the ground.

Paul turned back to the clearing and held his breath. There was no serenity here! He looked at Josefa, who had found a stump and was loudly nursing her wounds; at Bascomb, who was trying to plant his standard in the sandy ground; at the rest of the Children of Israel clustered around Mrs. West. It was a good thing the Moslems had chosen the meadow to pray in.

Here on the peninsula a battle raged. Mrs. West clutched her head and pointed and gave innumerable orders. "Now don't put anything down till I spread the tablecloth. . . . Who's got the tablecloth? Who's got the *tablecloth*? Thank you, my dear. Now the plates. . . . Haven't you got them, Whitey? I told you to bring them. . . . Well, look in the hamper. If they're not in that, we'll just have to eat off our laps. Oh, there they are. Praise God, from whom all blessings flow. I hope you don't mind paper plates, because it won't do you any good. We're going to have them, anyway. Did the eggs arrive safely and in good spirits, Johanna?"

If I survive this, Paul said to himself, I shall never be fool enough to come here again. Then he went slowly into the center of confusion where Mrs. West directed the fighting, as from a flagship. All about Paul bombs were bursting and ships running aground. Try though he might, he could not shut his ears against the cries and groans of the dying. With something like awe he watched Mrs. West maneuver her difficult and unwieldy fleet around the blue-checked tablecloth. Partly by superior management and partly by brute force she managed to make Josefa and Thorn and Gust and Johanna and Whitey and Nigel and Bascomb and even Paul himself sit cross-legged in a square about the cloth, and in the same way she managed to make them fall to eating. Only then did she relax and draw a normal breath.

But Paul noticed, in the midst of helping himself to an egg, that her victory was not complete. Cynthia, for one, was present in body only. Her mind had gone off by itself. Some people could be alone in Bedlam, Paul thought to himself, envying such people. And Amelia was present in mind but not in body, for she had refused to trust herself to the bare ground, fearing insects or a cold in the head. She now sat on the campstool in the shade of the nearest tree, eating cottage cheese.

"The trouble with Aunt Amelia," Bascomb whispered to Paul, "is that she's too much like Little Miss Muffet grown past the age of innocence and still afraid of spiders. And the trouble with me is that I sound like an author commenting on his characters."

"Right." Paul took another egg. It was not until Whitey announced, with his mouth full of macaroni, that there was an ant in the butter-dish—it was not until then that Paul realized, with something of a shock, that he was at a picnic.

"Let him stay," Mrs. West commanded, from the head of the tablecloth. "He'll drown in a minute, and be an object-lesson to other ants." Her face grew pink with amusement. Clearly the picnic was going to her head.

"Here comes another one." Whitey looked dispassionately down into the butter-dish, which had become a sea of ice-water with yellow icebergs floating in it. "I think he'll go in, anyway. There!" He fished out both ants with his spoon. "Muv, he didn't pay any attention to the first ant."

Mrs. West nodded gravely. "We'll have to put up a sign."

Paul saw signals of appreciation and delight pass between Whitey and his mother. It was another of their jokes. In the course of an ordinary day they had a thousand of them, more or less. Some were private and unintelligible to anyone else.

Some were not particularly funny, or so it seemed to him. The strange thing was that Whitey never aped his mother's absurd vocabulary. He didn't say "an elegant ant," as she would have done, or "a large and influential ant." To that extent his sense of humor was more chaste than hers. But he had God's plenty of extravagance and fantasy, which he must have sucked with his mother's milk.

"Lettuce, Paul?"

He bent forward and took the large wooden salad bowl that Mrs. West held out to him.

"It's beginning to look like wilted lettuce, and it wasn't intended to at all. I don't think there's anything quite so uninteresting as wilted lettuce. It always looks the way I feel when I'm having trouble with my feet. Have some more, anyway, or we'll have to feed it to the chickens, and it isn't good for them to have too much of it. Sidney Trelease says that people never say, 'My feet hurt.' They always say, 'My feet hurt *me*.' Do you know Sidney? Well, my dear, you must. You simply must. He's the most amusing man I know. Do have some bread. It was fresh day before yesterday."

Having found a haven for the salad bowl, Paul took the bread-plate and held it. "Aren't you having any?"

Mrs. West did not hear him, and he said once more, "Susan, aren't you having any?" before he discovered that she was lost in contemplation of her eldest son. Paul followed her glance. There was nothing remarkable in what he saw. Thorn was eating macaroni, as one might very well expect him to, seeing that this was lunch and there was macaroni. And yet a puzzled expression lingered at the outer corners of Mrs. West's eyes, as if she found something mysterious and unfathomable in the way Thorn was stuffing himself.

Thorn felt the pressure of their eyes upon him, and looked up suddenly. That was all. But his face grew secretive as a wall, and as blank. There was no use to consider him further. Mrs. West sighed one small sigh, took the bread-plate which Paul had been holding out to her, and with no explanation remarked to him, "My dear, I think I am losing my mind."

Considering how frequently her mind voiced itself, and how variously, Paul felt that her anxiety was scarcely justified. He knew only too well that if the need arose, he could jump to his feet and deliver a twenty-minute lecture on The States of Susan's Mind: Its Likes and Dislikes, with copious footnotes and exhaustive bibliographical references. He turned his head just in time to catch what Nigel was saying discreetly in Whitey's ear. What Nigel said was, "How about another slice of ham?"

"If we had some ham," Whitey quoted, "we could have some ham and eggs, if we had some eggs. Every time we have deviled eggs it makes me want to belch." By way of demonstrating his point, he did so, rather mournfully. "See? What did I tell you?"

"I think you're wonderful," Nigel whispered back.

Watching her, Paul felt certain familiar winds blow over him—now hot and now cold.

"That's the advantage of eggs over olives." From across the table Bascomb put his oar into their conversation. "They don't leave any seeds behind. Would you look at that blob down the front of me."

Paul did look, and was properly amazed. It was not that Bascomb buttered his fingers as well as his corn-on-the-cob, or straddled his knife and fork, or brought on a small tidal wave by blowing into his soup. It was not that he did all these things and more, although of course he did. What amazed Paul was Bascomb's bland amusement at the frightfulness of his own manners.

"In Italy the mountains are so tall," said Cynthia, down at the other end of the table, "I never feel that I can breathe."

There was nothing peculiar about the remark itself, but coming as it did after Johanna's simple request for butter, it seemed very strange. In Italy the mountains are so tall—Paul said the words to himself and wondered why anything so completely irrelevant should have such intensity. I never feel I can breathe. Something must be the matter with Cynthia. . . . Paul could not keep from watching her. She sat looking down at her plate, which was loaded with food she had not touched, and her eyes grew peculiarly round. Paul wondered if perhaps he ought to say something to her; ask her how the painting had gone this morning. Then he decided that it was kinder to let her alone.

"I think I felt a sprinkle."

Paul turned now to Amelia, who was prophesying disaster from her camp stool. There was something Cassandra-like about Amelia. She was never believed, although she seldom prophesied falsely.

Even now Mrs. West was saying, "Nonsense, Amelia! It can't rain. The barometer is way up."

Paul smiled. How like Susan to be cocksure about the weather.

"Besides"—thoroughly aroused, she drove home her point—"the wind's from the south, and that means we can't possibly have rain for at least three days. Maybe not then."

"Say what you like, Susan. The sky *is* growing cloudy." With that Amelia rested her case.

At the first mention of the weather, both Thorn and Gust looked up, their faces quickened with interest.

"We could stand some rain." Thorn nodded to Gust, and Gust's weather-beaten head nodded back at him.

"But, Thorn, it just rained last night, hard. I woke up and heard it." Nigel had not yet learned that in the country there is no such thing as satisfactory weather.

Thorn smiled at her shyly. "That was just a sprinkle."

"Did it ever occur to you," Bascomb whispered to Paul, "how much Gust looks like an abandoned farm?"

It wasn't true, of course. Gust looked like anything but an abandoned farm. He was a tough-skinned old man with eyes that were sharp and black, like a beetle's. Furthermore, the comparison was not original with Bascomb. Paul himself had heard it somewhere. Who the devil said it? Never mind. It was about Calvin Coolidge, anyway, no matter who said it. "No, Bascomb, it never did."

At the sound of his voice, Nigel looked up and said, "I have a cramp in my leg." The look which accompanied her words said, *Darling, is it really true that you love me?*

"Why don't you stand on it, then?" Paul replied, and the look which accompanied his words said, *My dearest love, if anything happened to you, I think I should not go on living.*

"Buzz!" said Josefa to no one at all, as she bent over the salad bowl. "Buzz! buzz!"

Paul watched her pile her plate high with a ragged green mountain of lettuce and then begin to devour it, giant-wise.

He was moved to admiration by the spectacle. More than any person he had ever known, Josefa possessed the gift of concentration. Whatever she was doing—playing Bach or eating lettuce—all other things fell away before it. She seemed utterly oblivious to all the cross-currents of amusement and irritation which charged the life of Meadowland. Nigel might drop a stitch in her knitting, Susan might be swallowed up by catastrophe after catastrophe, Gust might fall out of the barn, and Johanna might burn the peas three times over. It was all the same to Josefa. She kept on practicing and practicing. So far as he could tell she had nothing on her mind except her lined and barred sheets of music. All outside channels of communication were cut off by her passionate concentration. She was miraculously immune.

Watching her, Paul decided it might be a wise thing to take piano lessons if playing the piano granted one this immunity which Josefa had. For he was so constituted by nature that he could not keep his mind on any natural function, no matter how interesting it was. He ate automatically without ever knowing what he was eating. And when he got into bed, he frequently got so interested in what he was thinking that he quite forgot to go to sleep. It was the same way with everything he did. Whatever he was doing was always overshadowed and complicated by what he was thinking. There were certain compensations for absentmindedness, however. Now, because his mind was not obliged to minister to his stomach, serving its baser needs, he was free to take in all that went on about him. All the intricate strands of conversation he picked up and wound together, like loose threads. Later, if he chose, he could unwind them again, clear down to the spool. He would remember then what Thorn said to Whitey, and what Whitey said in reply; what Bascomb said to Nigel, and what Nigel said to Bascomb, and what Bascomb said in reply to that, what Amelia said to Mrs. West, what Mrs. West said to Gust, what Gust said to Josefa, and what Josefa said to the salad-bowl.

Now Paul not only heard these things, but he also noted, as if for future reference, the spot of cheese baked dark brown against the side of the macaroni-dish. He noted the thin place in the bottom of Thorn's left shoe, the leathery texture of Gust's hands, the blob of salad-dressing still on Bascomb's shirt-front, the shade of blue in Mrs. West's eyes—which he had never before noted—and likewise the arrow of sunlight twisted in Nigel's hair.

There his mind lingered a moment, lovingly, and would have stayed. But there was no way of shutting out other perceptions, no way to keep from seeing Amelia's anxious glances toward the sky. Soon she would rise and cry "Woe! Woe!", cover her face with her hands, and wait for the rain.

And there was no way he could avoid seeing the deeper anxiety implicit in the shadows of Cynthia's large distracted eyes. Strange that nobody else noticed her. She hadn't eaten a thing, and all she had said during lunch was, *In Italy the mountains are so tall, I never feel I can breathe.* What mountains? Paul wondered. And why can't she breathe now? He looked up, half expecting to see great purple rocks jutting up on either side of the picnic-ground, but there was only the Little Neenah going upstream on one side and downstream on the other.

A turtle clambered out on a log in midstream and remained there, sunning itself. Paul tried to make up his mind whether the dash of red was on the turtle's throat or on his head. Then he let his attention wander to the Moslems kneeling in the hay-field; to the buildings posted up and down the hillside at irregular intervals; to the broad band of yellow light extending along the whole southern horizon; to the white sun directly overhead, appearing and disappearing behind banks of gray luminous clouds which had swiftly covered the greater part of the sky.

He turned back to Cynthia and watched her thoughtfully out of the corner of his eye for several minutes. Now she seemed to be talking to herself. He could see her lips moving rapidly, as if words were pouring out of her mouth in a great torrent. But no sound came—no sound, that is, until she suddenly stood up, brushed the crumbs off her lap, and screamed.

It was the precise moment when the morning achieved its consummation. The bare brightness of noon spattered down the sides of the trees and dripped from the restless twitching leaves.

Startled beyond speech, beyond all need of speech, The Children of Israel sat with their mouths open, staring at Cynthia.

"I wish I were dead," she said to them, and went quietly down the path, out of sight.

Paul turned to Mrs. West, and saw that her eyes had momentarily gone dark green with anger. The anger faded from her face, evenly, as heat lightning fades from the sky, and she reached for the platter of eggs. "Cynthia is a bit strange sometimes."

It seemed to Paul that she said it as one would say of a child. She is very sensitive; sometimes she cries over nothing at all. He was moved to take arms in Cynthia's defense. He bent toward Mrs. West and said, in a low voice, "Haven't you ever felt the same way?"

Mrs. West considered a moment, while she divided an egg with her fork. Then, looking up at him sharply, she said, "Not while I was eating my lunch."

*

Perhaps, out of deference to Mrs. West's opinion, and perhaps out of respect for the barometer, it was a very small rain which broke up the picnic party. Nevertheless, it came very suddenly and all at once. Before they could get back up the hill to the house, before they could even run to the shelter of the near-by elm, the sky opened and a cloak of white rain fell about their heads and shoulders.

Mrs. West took command at once. As admiral of the fleet she saw to it that the women and children got into the lifeboats first; then the passengers; then the crew. And though she did not remain with the picnic-ground until the sea closed over it, as the custom is among captains of ships, still she was the very last of The Children of Israel to start up the hill toward safety and dryness.

She was lashed and driven by fine whips of rain as she went through the pasture, but she minded not at all. The nice thing about being drenched to the skin was, of course, that you needn't be afraid of getting wet. She would have liked to go dancing about in the pasture, with a child's abandon, but the restraints of convention bound her arms tight against her sides, and time had taken from her legs the power to dance. Since neither time nor convention could bind or undo her delight, she danced with her mind, with her mind feeling the grass cool beneath her feet, and the rain wild in her hair.

"*Keemo*
Ky-mo
Karmo
Dell—"

It was a child's song that she sang, an old song that had come down in the family.

"*Ma-high*
Ma-ho
Ma-ram-sam-toodle-witch
Soup-back-turtle-wench
Ram
Sam
Hadgy
Widgy
Ky-mee-o"

The raindrops ran off the end of her nose. She laughed and shook her head, and still more ran off.

Ahead of her the procession scurried up the hill. There was Whitey—the lamb!—bounding and leaping along as if the rain were the fire of eternal torment. He didn't really mind rain, of course. He was no son of hers if he did. But how strange to make a game of fear! Thorn didn't. But then Thorn didn't make a game of anything. He walked through the rain quietly, with his head up. Rain was to him a familiar element, like air and sunlight. So it was to Gust, who limped along beside him.

But there was Johanna, as unhappy as a hen, ruffling her wet clothes and protesting in small irritated clucks. Mrs. West wondered to herself if it never rained in the Bavarian Alps.

And there was Paul, walking absently, as if he had totally forgotten that it was raining; as if he had outgrown rain some time ago and had put it aside with other childish things.

And there was Nigel running swiftly, marvelously, like a deer.

The same rain fell on them all, yet to each one it was a different thing. Not one of them loved it the way she did. Not one of them was dancing with his mind—right foot here, left foot there. But then not one of them was so glad to be alive.

Mrs. West caught up with Amelia and noticed that the corners of her mouth were turned up. It was like Amelia to enjoy the fulfillment of her prophecies, no matter how unpleasant that fulfillment might be to her. She was smiling now much as an Old Testament prophet might on the Day of Doom. Never mind, Mrs. West said to herself. After the Lord gets through with everybody else, he probably rounds up the prophets and judges them. The thought gave her comfort.

"Cold, Amelia?"

"Very."

"Ummm!" She could feel her own blood tingling and coursing through her veins. At least it seemed as if she could. Oh, this heavenly rain! "Have you plenty of aspirin?"

"Probably. But aspirin isn't enough to stave off pneumonia when you've been soaked to the skin." There was rancor in Amelia's tone. She was not annoyed that Mrs. West had refused to listen to her warning about the weather. Nobody ever listened to her warnings. But after the calamity had occurred, it was extremely annoying to have its importance underestimated. Plenty of aspirin! "I shall go to bed at once, and hold off the chill as long as possible."

"Perhaps you won't have a chill, my dear. It's a very warm rain." Mrs. West tried to make her voice sympathetic, but she really had no comprehension of what it meant to be ailing, and she knew that her expressions of sympathy were never convincing. If only Amelia weren't so sure she was going to have a chill long before her teeth began to chatter! This business of anticipating illness; there was no end to it. She herself never thought she was going to get anything, and of course she never did. Amelia was always certain she was going to have everything, and of course she did have everything.

"When you have time, Susan, will you send up some mustard and a pan of hot water?" Amelia's face was already haggard and ill-looking.

"Of course. The very first thing!" Mrs. West held the pasture gate open for Amelia to pass through. As she followed her up the hill, she considered in her mind Amelia's twenty years of the most complicated ill-health. It had all begun with an attack of the hives. Then she bit her tongue and couldn't talk for six months. What an amazing time that was! Thousands of notes a day, all about her tongue, to anyone who came near and would read them. When sinus became fashionable, she had sinus. Then an infected finger, two attacks of pneumonia in succession (contrary to all rules), then change of life and a nervous breakdown. For every ailment a dozen cures and a dozen doctors—none of them any good—at least, not half as good for Amelia as a first-rate witch-doctor would have been.

As Mrs. West went through the house and up the stairs, she lined up on a shelf in her mind all the pills, powders, capsules, drops, and serums Amelia had put inside herself during the last twenty years. The result seemed to her quite impressive, and just a trifle shocking.

*

Johanna sat alone in the wildly disordered kitchen, reading for the tenth time the letter which had come that morning from her sister in Bavaria: *Manchmal geht's ihr a bissel besser. . . .* Sometimes her mother was a little better. There was hope, a very slender hope, and her mind fell upon it in hunger. She read the sentence over again, lest there be in it some crumb of comfort which she had overlooked before. *Manchmal geht's ihr a bissel besser, den nächsten Tag ist's wieder schlimmer.* There was no comfort here. Nothing but hunger unsatisfied and hope turned dry and bitter to the tongue. *Sie fragt immer warum du nicht heim kommst* (*She keeps asking why it is you do not come home*). The very shape of the words cut like glass. As if there were any way that she could get home! As if she would willingly stay in this alien land, and her mother dying! *Sie sagt wenn du wissen tätst sie wär krank, wärst du nicht so lang fortgebliebe. Sie meint meine Brief' wären verloren gegangen* (*She says if you knew she was sick . . .*). Johanna sighed. The letters had not gone astray. Day and night for seven months she had known that her mother was sick. Day and night for seven months, while her body was in domestic bondage to the Wests, her mind had been with her mother, in the mountains of another continent, with a wide sea between . . . *She says if you knew she was sick, you would not stay away any longer.* No, she would not stay away any longer. She could not. She would get her things together. She would go this afternoon, after she had cleaned up the kitchen and peeled the potatoes for supper. *Mir sagen ihr immer* (*We tell her over and over again*) *du musst in Amerika bleibe.* She was not going home this afternoon? She was not going, after all. She had to stay in America—*und viel Geld verdiene* (*and earn money*) *für den Doktor und die Medizin die so viel kost* (*for the Doctor and the expensive medicines*). *Aber sie ist so alt* (*but she is so old*) *und vergisst's immer wieder* (*and she forgets*). . . .

Johanna put her head upon the kitchen table, wanting to weep, but no tears came.

*

When Mrs. West arrived, a few minutes later, with her hair piled high on the top of her head and her body incased in a silk kimono, Johanna was hard at work swabbing up the kitchen floor.

"My dear!"

Mrs. West surveyed the platters, the sopping tablecloth, the knives and forks, the remnants of the picnic food—all heaped skitter-skatter on the kitchen table. "My dear!" she repeated, following with eyes the trail of water which led into the dining-room. Heaven only knew how much farther it led, or how many of the boarders had contributed to it, as, trailing puddles of water behind them, they had gone off to their rooms to change into dry clothing.

"Was there ever such a catastrophe!" Mrs. West inquired of Johanna, rather as one seeking confirmation than as one asking to be informed. For Johanna there had been several just as great in the course of that day; but what was the good of saying so. She went on mopping the kitchen floor. Mrs. West, therefore, felt she might reasonably take it for granted that never in the whole history of man had there been anything to compare with this sudden shower and its consequences.

Back and forth she moved between the kitchen table and the sink, until by her efforts at restoring order she had spread confusion to the sink as well. "Is there plenty of hot water?" she asked, remembering her promise to Amelia.

Johanna wrapped her hands around the mop and twisted it. "*Ja.*"

Mrs. West prepared the mustard bath, and a cup of tea besides. Perhaps with this additional offering the gods might be appeased and Amelia would escape pneumonia.

Whitey appeared providentially, on his way to the creek for a swim, and was dispatched with the preventives. Almost instantly he returned with the news that Amelia had taken to her bed and did not dare to stir from it even to put her feet in the mustard bath. She was very grateful for the tea, even though it was too strong, and could she please have the hot-water bottle.

Mrs. West sighed. "Poor dear! By all means let her have the hottle-bottle. It's in the medicine-cabinet, Whitey. You know, hanging on a nail on the inside of the door. That's an angel . . ."

Whitey started off on this new errand.

"—and wait a minute. Before you go swimming, bring me the laundry list. It's on my bureau. Not the dresser, the bureau. And then I want you to pin it— Whitey are you listening?"

Whitey nodded.

"Well stop fiddling with your toes, then. Pin it on the blanket under the spread. If you want your jersey washed, put that in the basket, too; only, don't forget to put it under the spread." She paused and clutched her head. "I guess that's all, darling. Now go get the hottle-bottle."

Whitey departed straightway upon the first of his mother's errands. He was the family Ariel. To answer her best pleasure, he flew, swam, dived into fire, rode on the curled clouds.

"Soap," Mrs. West said thoughtfully as she sat down at the kitchen table and began to make out a list for the day's marketing in Thisbe.

Soap

—she wrote it down this time.

doz. lemons
cantaloupe
shoe-clnr.
nujol
junket
pancake flr.

There was something else she had to get, but she couldn't think of it. She looked up to see whether Johanna had started to clear away the kitchen table's confusion. Johanna had started. As befits one about to undergo an ordeal by dish water, she was scraping and piling the platters, putting the baking-dish to soak.

codfish

Mrs. West wrote, wondering what had ever made her forget.

Post-office
chicken feed
washing

What else was there? Oh, of course! The four-o'clock. That was the third time in the course of the day that she had forgotten Jefferson Carter's very existence. Without a doubt, when the train pulled in there would be no one to meet him. She would be off buying fifty pounds of chicken feed or a box of salted codfish.

At the thought of codfish, her mind grew pale. It was not that there was anything peculiar about codfish. But codfish was a symbol of her infamous servitude to the kitchen. If only she didn't have to keep her mind on food all the time! If she had the most marvelous cook in the world—Johanna was a dear, of course, but rather unimaginative in her ideas about food. Rather limited, poor dear—if she had the most marvelous cook she would sit in her room, and the cook would appear once a week for instructions. Together they would plan the meals, and the cook would have all sorts of ideas for new and intriguing dishes. That was the way it should be, and not this perpetual stewing about what to have for lunch, what to have for dinner. And the next day the same thing, only what to have for lunch that she didn't have yesterday. There was no end. She knew only too well that she would have to go right on planning meals until she died. And even then she would probably pass out of this sinful life with salted codfish on her mind, instead of her soul's salvation.

She sat staring out of the window, her eyes hard with rebellion. From behind the last gray cloud the sun came, quite unexpectedly, and shadows sprang into immediate existence on the lawn. There was color.

Gust appeared at the screen and broke in upon Mrs. West's secret meditations. "Going to town this afternoon?"

When she saw his face, she broke into lamentations. "Gust! Whatever is the matter with you?"

The furrows in his leathery cheeks were deepened with pain. The flesh seemed drawn tight against his skull. His eyes were sharp and glittering. "My knee. I hurt it." He spoke quietly and patiently, making every effort not to communicate his misery. "Started to hurt while I was pulling sand-burrs this morning. Beginning to swell a little now."

"Oh, you poor darling! Go in and lie down on the chaise-longue in the living-room. It's nice and cool in there. We'll be starting a little after two."

As she watched him move painfully away toward the dining-room her eyes grew bright. It was impossible for her to sympathize with Amelia. But Gust was another matter. Gust and the oak trees were the only things left to her out of the world of her childhood. Since then everything else had changed and taken on new functions, new identities. The milking-shed became a sleeping-house, and the summer-house became a pool for goldfish. The whole place changed except Gust and the oak trees. They had merely grown older.

At a time almost before she could remember, Gust had come to work for her father. He was a spare lad, then, with brown frightened eyes. He could handle a team of horses, and he could plow a straight furrow. But he didn't know any games. If there was no work to be done he would sit still with his arms in his lap, crossed at the wrist, as if they were handcuffed.

He was nearly a grown man before the frightened look disappeared forever from his eyes. How it had come there in the first place, Mrs. West never had known. If her father knew, he probably thought she was too young to be told about it. The boy was with him on the wagon, one night, when he drove into the yard, and there were never any explanations.

Gust himself never talked about his childhood. But then he seldom talked at all. Though she had reason to suspect that he would walk out and die, if there was need, for her or for either of the boys, it was not by his words that she knew this. For purposes of intercourse he seemed to prefer speechless things. He always spoke of the corn intimately, as if there were something personal between himself and the young growing stalks.

Once she was almost sure she heard him talking in the cornfield, with no one else around, or even within shouting distance.

And horses. He could do anything with horses. Anything. She could still remember that time a double team got stuck in a snowdrift just outside Thisbe, with a sled loaded down with wood. She closed her eyes and saw the drivers, swearing and beating the horses until the poor beasts were in a lather. The sled didn't budge. Strange how clearly it all came back to her. Then Gust unhitched the light Meadowland team and fastened them to the other sled, and talked to them quietly and sweetly—standing out on the shaft, with an arm thrown over the neck of each one—talked to them and coaxed them—until they pulled the sled out of the drift.

There were few moments in her life when she had been so moved.

Now, in a world full of unreliable people, there was always Gust—uncritical, unquestioning—like a mountain-side.

She began to count on her fingers the number of people who were going to town. Perhaps it would be better if some one drove Gust to town in the Ford. Otherwise they would all be crowded, and with his knee——

"Here's the hot-water bottle, Muv. It wasn't in the medicine-closet. It was in your room."

"How dreadful of me!" She beamed. "Now while I fill it, run up to Josefa's room and ask her if she minds driving Gust in to see the doctor."

Whitey whisked out of sight, and Mrs. West returned to her list. "How many pounds of butter have we, Johanna?"

Johanna's dish-towel stopped whirling. "*Zwei.*" By way of conveying the certainty and exactitude of her information, she nodded violently several times. Two pounds in the ice-box and a little over, in the brown crock on the third shelf of the lower right-hand part. Plenty of butter; and the ice-box was all clean, the way things should be. The way things were in her country, neat and tidy and clean. "*Sie fragt immer warum du nicht heim kommst.*" . . . As in a dream, only more clearly, she saw the Bavarian mountain-side above her own village as she had seen it one afternoon in winter, seven years ago. Seven years was such a long time. . . . There was the balcony on her mother's house. And Frau Rautenburg's just beyond it. Both covered with snow, like the church tower. Five minutes of two, the clock said. . . . With her eyes she could follow the line of houses that straggled up the opposite mountain-side. Above them was the fringe of dark gray pines, and then the great mountain all wrapped in snow.

"*—den nächsten Tag ist's wieder schlimmer.*" God must understand that she could not stay on here any longer in this terrible confusion. . . .

"She wasn't in her room, Muv." Whitey's head appeared at the corner.

"Then go up to the Tower." Mrs. West sighed, wondering at what age children reached the stage of reason.

"I did."

"Was she there?"

"Yes."

"Whitey, for Heaven's sake stop putting me off. What did she say."

"I told her you wanted her to drive Gustie into town——"

"And then what?" Mrs. West began to go over her list again.

"She said she couldn't; she was expecting some one this afternoon."

Mrs. West looked up in astonishment. "But how strange! She didn't say anything about it at lunch. Well I'll ask Paul if he minds waiting till tomorrow to do his shopping. Now hark, child—" Mrs. West's transitions sometimes staggered people less quick of mood than Whitey. "I expect you'd better give up your swim today——"

"But Muv, it's so nice just after a rain, and it won't take a minute." There were times when even Whitey was unprepared.

Poor darling! she thought, watching his face cloud up. He had wanted to work on his canoe this afternoon, and she hadn't let him do that, either. She was the worst kind of a tyrant. But never mind. There would be some way of making it up to him.

There never was any way of making up to Whitey the loss of his freedom. In her heart she knew this, and there were times when she felt certain misgivings on account of his bondage. But the trouble was that she had need of more legs than the customary two which had been provided for her, and she pressed Whitey into service because he was a good child, with clear eyes and a luminous heart, and because he gave himself gladly.

"I want you to go down to the barn for me and bring up one of those unvarnished little chairs that are hanging on the ceiling of the harness loft. We'll put it in Paul's room. Poor man, he hasn't any chair for company, and Bascomb has to sit on the top of the slop-jar when he comes to call. I expect you'd better wash the mouse off, too, and rub it down with wax before you take it up to the Tower. Did you get the laundry list?"

"Not yet, Muv." While she was speaking, his face had changed. It had grown subtle. He never looked that way unless he was about to kick over the traces. He might set fire to the house, perhaps, or tie knots in all the curtains. There was no telling. With one eye cocked for catastrophes, she said: "Trot up to Aunt Amelia with the hottle-bottle. Then take off your swimming-suit and don't forget to go find the laundry list. And one thing more—put it *under* the spread."

When Whitey had gone, Mrs. West summoned a vision of the cellar in her capacity of domestic genii. She saw the whitewashed stone walls, the cupboards of painted wood, the heavy joists of rough-hewn timber. She conjured up the shelf with oranges and lemons on it, and the one with blueberries spread out on a huge platter, and the one with cucumbers. She saw baskets of beans and bottles of olives; canned vegetables row on row, cans of tuna and shrimp, cans of anchovies and caviar and tomato soup. She focused her mind upon the somber corner where the preserves were, dark with age and powdered spider webs.

"While I am gone, Johanna, I wish you'd see what you can scare up in the cellar that might pass for preserves. Some of those elegant cherries that Cousin Agnes sent us, or some watermelon pickle." She began going over the list aloud: "Soap, scrub-boy, dozen lemons, cantaloupe—" She scratched off cantaloupe. She could never get cantaloupe in Thisbe. It was always green, or over-ripe. They sent the best of everything to the city. And there were probably more melon patches between here and Milwaukee than you could shake a stick at. . . . She put cantaloupe back on the list and looked up again in time to see Whitey pass through the room with the laundry list in his hand; he was quite naked. "O my immortal soul!" she gasped, and clutched her head.

"*Ach!*" Johanna had thrown her apron over *her* head, lest she be further contaminated by this new outrage.

"Whitey, what under heaven—" But of course. She told him to take off his swimming-suit and go find the laundry list. That was what he had done, exactly. She must act with a heavy hand. "Whitey, I want—" More than anything in the world, Mrs. West wanted to laugh. He did look so like a faun, standing there, grinning with his hands on his hips. A darling faun! She felt deep inside her a bubble of laughter. It was no use. He was the child of her own extravagance. She broke into chuckles, and tiny shrieks, and quiet, swift tears. So like his father. . . . She fished around in the bosom of her kimono until she found a handkerchief, to wipe the tears away.

When she had recovered a little from the excesses of her mirth, Whitey was gone. By her side stood Johanna, twisting her large parboiled hands.

"Please," Johanna was saying. "I have something I wish——"

Mrs. West grew sober instantly. Johanna never used English except for matters of life and death.

"Is it important, Johanna?" She felt intuitively that she must keep Johanna from speaking. "I haven't much time at the moment. I must go dress."

Johanna twisted and untwisted her hands. "Week from tomorrow, I think I go."

"Oh, my dear!" Mrs. West's voice sharpened with fear. "You mustn't think anything of what has happened just now. Whitey's only a child!"

Johanna shook her head. It wasn't what had happened. It was the words of her sister's letter: *She says if you knew she was sick, you wouldn't stay away any longer.* "Week from tomorrow," Johanna said, swallowing hard, "I think I go."

As too great a poison will sometimes fail to do its work, and the body will pass through the valley of the shadow of death and suffer no evil, so this announcement of Johanna's, being too great a calamity, passed over Mrs. West and did not destroy her. It merely left her breathless for a minute. When she could speak she said gently: "Very well, Johanna. Whatever you think best. We'll talk about it when there is more time. You won't forget about the watermelon pickle, will you?"

*

At quarter of two by the kitchen clock, Thorn came out of the house in his swimming-trunks and started down the hill to the pier. He stopped at the pump for a drink of water. The remainder of his second cup he threw into the bed of ferns beside the house. Then he tied a piratical red bandanna around his head, for protection against a possible onslaught of deer-flies, and proceeded down the hill.

As he passed behind the screen tent he saw that Nigel had not yet gone down to the boathouse. She was sitting there, knitting and talking to Paul.

Because of some inarticulate delicacy, he trod lightly on the grass so that the soundless sound of his bare feet would not disturb her. He always knew when she passed behind him. The whole region of his mind changed slightly, the way a room darkens when the sun goes behind a cloud. But now she kept right on talking and knitting—what a funny clicking sound knitting-needles made! That was a nice green dress she had on, but she was nicer in yellow, the way she was this morning. When she had on a yellow dress, she was like— His inexperienced mind went groping after some object or creature known to it, which might be compared to his love in a yellow dress. She was like that flower that Muv was so nuts about. You had to set bulbs out in the fall and it bloomed early in the spring. It began with a J— He could not remember, but, anyway, his love was like a flower that began with a J.

He leapt over the low stone wall.

Perhaps she had forgotten all about the canoe trip. Perhaps she would go right on sitting there with Paul all afternoon. The thought hovered over his mind like a butterfly over a milkweed blossom. Then it wandered off. Thorn drew breath again.

He hurdled a small fir tree set out year before last. He crossed the road. He went into the barn. There a familiar and yet highly intricate smell assailed his nostrils. It was a smell compounded from damp stone, dry hay, corncobs, saddle soap, dust, old leather, manure, and horses. Thorn loved it.

Stepping carefully, he went around to the front of the stalls. He took hold of the sorrel's nose and petted him. The sorrel stamped on the floor of his stall and whinnied amiably. Thorn reached down into the feed-trough for the halter and drew it over the sorrel's ears. Then he went to the next stall.

The white horse was pawing the floor boards, his ears back flat against his head.

Old Bill was without a doubt enough to make anybody swear. Always looking for trouble. But you didn't swear out loud at a horse. Not if you had any sense. Milk-Belly swore all the time at his horses, no matter what they did. You could hear him shouting at them three fields over. And look at them. Skin and bones, that's all they were. And they used to be good horses.

"Come on boy. Keep your shirt on. Steady. Steady. That's it." Now that he had managed to slip the halter over the head of Old Bill, he propped the barn door open with a stone and led the horses out, one at a time. Then with the halters in his hand, he led them over to the pasture gate. They stood in quiet impatience while he opened and shut the gate. But the minute he removed their halters and slapped them on the rump, they kicked up their hind legs and rolled over and over on the ground.

Thorn watched them until they galloped off down the pasture. Then he hung their halters on the gatepost, and went on down the hill past the Indian mound which was shaped like an eagle, and around the corner of the boathouse. There on the bank he saw the two canoes and the duckboats, all stretched out on their bellies. Beyond the creek bank was the hay-meadow, and beyond that the next hill rose smooth and green into the sky. The sky itself was bright blue and shining, as if some heavenly housemaid had just gone over it with soap and water.

As Thorn walked along the narrow boards to the pier, he turned himself upside down and walked the rest of the way on his hands, like an acrobat. It was unbecoming to one of his age, of course, but he *had* to do something. The afternoon had turned off so fine, and the sun was so warm on his skin, and the cup of his happiness was already running over before even a drop had been poured into it.

He stopped and righted himself before the first canoe, which was Whitey's. He examined the cracks in the paint. One of them went rather deep. It would need some filler. Whitey must have paddled right over the barbed-wire fence just below the slough instead of getting out and letting the canoe go over empty. Lazy little beggar. Always did things the easiest way, and then somebody had to do them over again after him. That .22 that belonged to Dad . . . Whitey wouldn't take time to oil it properly after he had used it, and now look at it! There was so much rust in the barrel you couldn't hit a cow with it. And the same way with his tools. There were nicks in his ax-blade, rust in his lathe, and every last one of his chisels and screw-drivers was twisted out of shape. Now it was, "West, can I borrow your this?" and, "West, can I borrow your that?" He had reached the borrowing stage.

To Thorn his younger brother was always in a "stage." There was no other way to explain his irresponsible actions. When Whitey lost his temper and Thorn had to hold his hands to keep him from throwing hammers at people, it was because Whitey was at that stage. If he went up the creek and didn't come back by suppertime, so that Mrs. West walked the floor and made Gust take the other canoe and go up after him, it was because he was at that stage. If Whitey's workbench in the carpenter shop was always upset and covered with rags, shavings, and disorderly tools, whereas his own was always in order—well, it was because *he* himself had got through that stage.

He looked up at the sun. It was almost time for Nigel to be coming down the hill. She'd have to change into her swimming-suit, first, and then they'd go down as far as the slough, where the water-lilies were. They'd be mostly closed up this time of day, but she'd like it, anyway. And there was good swimming in the clear space beyond the lily pads.

He must not forget to be back by four-thirty, so he could help the kid sandpaper his canoe.

Thorn righted his own canoe and shoved it carefully into the water. Then he ran back to the boathouse for paddles. The lower story of the boathouse was a large bare room with spider webs across the windows, boat-chains hanging from the ceiling, and a convocation of broken-down Victorian sofas and chairs which presided over and commented upon the comings and goings of whoever inhabited the upper story. Thorn took two of the paddles from the stack behind the door and returned to the creek bank.

"*She'll be comin' round the corner when she comes.*" He settled himself in the stern of the canoe and shut his eyes against the terrible glare of the sun.

> "*She'll be comin' round the corner when she comes;*
> *She'll be comin' round the corner,*
> *She'll be comin' round the corner,*
> *She'll be comin' round the corner when she comes.*"

A turtle, frightened by the prospect of this second coming, slid off a log and into the water with a plop. Thorn knew the sound and did not turn his head.

> "*We will kill that old white rooster when she comes.*
> *We will kill that old white rooster when she comes.*"

The tufted marsh grass swayed softly to the north. The crickets sang and sang, like dry fiddles. In the shallows the water caught bright bits of sunlight, held them for a second, and gave them up again to the bright air. Solemnly, like a procession, the current swept by the pier, bearing on its surface pieces of water-weed, sticks, fragments of leaves, white specks, air bubbles. And these in turn clung to the knees of the willow that had waded out into the water and knelt down there, the way cattle do.

In time the shadow of the willow also waded out into the stream, very, very slowly, until it reached Thorn's canoe. Feeling suddenly cool, Thorn sat up and looked at the sun. It had moved considerably while he was sitting there. It must be after two-thirty. Well after.

With a shove of his paddle, he freed the canoe and floated downstream a few feet, where he could see up the hill, through the tiger-lilies. She had forgotten all about him. She was still sitting there in the screen tent. He could see the green of her dress.

As a child he had schooled himself against disappointment. It was a thing unmanly to give way to. But now when something mattered—mattered tremendously—and he had need of this armor, it failed him. His hurt was like the sharp, unreasonable pain which comes from running into the corner of a table in the dark.

He could go up and get Nigel, of course. . . . Pride rose in his throat and choked him. With a vicious dig of his paddle he started on downstream. How could she forget? How could she do such a thing! All morning he had been counting on it, all the while he was going up and down the rows of corn in the ten-acre field. She said she'd go. . . . How could she forget all about it? As a hurt animal licks its wounds, licks them until the bright blood flows, nor will endure any bandage over them, so Thorn restated again and again the fact of his love's cruel forgetfulness.

At the first turning of the stream there were low overhanging branches. He gave a long pull and lay back while the leaves brushed over him. Then he began paddling again. Dip and back. Dip and back. It wasn't as if she had anything important to do, or anything on her mind that made her forget about the trip with him. She was just sitting there, knitting and talking to Paul.

Now the peninsula again. Dip and back. Dip and back. Dip and back. It was all his mother's fault. Paul wanted to go to Thisbe with them to do some shopping. If his mother hadn't made Paul stay home on account of the washing, Nigel wouldn't have had anybody to talk to and she wouldn't have forgotten their trip down the creek. For the first time it occurred to him that there might be something between Nigel and Paul. His jealous heart grew heavy as a stone.

Dip and back. Dip and back. He paddled by the picnic-ground without seeing it at all. Gradually his head cleared a little. It was true that Paul had brought her with him to Meadowland, and she did spend a lot of time with him. They went for the mail together every morning. That sort of thing. But they just talked to each other. They never looked pie-eyed, like that fellow that brought his wife to see Muv, the day after he was married. . . . They never called each other darling—never that he had heard. Come to think about it, he had never heard them call each other *anything*, and that was funny. . . . Another flame of jealousy consumed his flesh and licked his bones dry.

Once past the second turning he used his paddle only to steer with. As the canoe followed the current around the peninsula and along the edge of the pasture, the seed of a small hope put forth roots into the dusty soil of his mind and pressed upward. It couldn't be that she loved Paul. He was a good-enough egg. Sensible. Not weak in the head like Bascomb. And he knew about lots of things, even though he couldn't do much with his hands. Paul was nice enough, but he was an old man. He must be almost forty. There was a bald spot on the back of his head already. Nigel couldn't love a man as old as all that! The small hope grew leaves and blossomed.

So noiselessly did the canoe drift along that the turtles waited until it was almost upon them before they dived. And sometimes they raised their small inquisitive heads above the water again afterwards, as if they were still uncertain whether it had been worth while to disturb their sun-bathing for so silent an intrusion.

As a mountain climber is sometimes startled at the sight of one small flower growing miraculously out of the bare rock, and stops to gaze at its petals, white veined with blue, and at its yellow-and-blue center; and then the mountain-climber goes on up the precipitous wall of rock with less of weariness in his knees and a lighter pack on his back, so did the flower of Thorn's small hope refresh him and make the weight of his hurt feelings less burdensome to him.

Twice between the third and fourth turnings the marsh grass parted and a muskrat burrowed his way into the water, leaving a trail of brown mud in his wake. Each time Thorn felt the hair rise on the back of his neck, and laughed. He was like Rats at the sight of a rabbit.

Looking down at the spot of roiled muddy water, he thought of times during the last winter when he had got up before daylight to go look at his trap-lines. Sometimes the water would be frozen in the pitcher, and the floor would be cold as stone. He would pull on a pair of trousers and a sweater over his pajamas, as fast as he could, so that the heat of his body would not get out. Then his heavy boots, his leather coat, his stocking-cap and gloves. It was funny how Whitey would always jabber in his sleep and turn over. And it was funny how just as soon as he struck the outside air he would become so wide awake it hurt.

Sky and snow and bare trees would stagger a minute, and then cling more firmly to their places in the landscape. And he would fasten on his snowshoes and go crunch-crunch-crunch down the hill on the hard crust of the snow. The creek would be frozen over, hard and shining, and the dead grasses, stiff with ice, would tinkle in the wind. Even now, in all the heat of the summer sun, he could feel the cold wind through his sweater, through his heavy leather coat. And no sound anywhere except the grass tinkling and his snowshoes crunching as he went from one to another of the muskrat runways where his traps were concealed. And all the time, the snow getting bluer, and the sky lighter, and his hands and feet more senseless with the cold.

Then the warm sun reminded him that it was summer, that he was in his canoe going down the creek, that Nigel had forgotten her promise to go with him.

At the fifth turning he saw an enormous carp dozing in the shallow water. He flicked a few drops of water off the end of his paddle. Straightway there was no carp at all, and the water as calm as if he had only dreamed this fish.

As he held his paddle in the water for the sixth turning, he noticed a vine growing down to the water's edge; a vine with purple flowers and bright red berries on it.

Then came the bridge, where the life of man ended and the life of the marsh began. From that point on, the creek pursued its devious and uncertain course between solid walls of marsh grass and wild rice. At intervals there were cat-tails growing, and butterfly-weed, and pale blue marsh-iris. These Thorn knew, but there were dozens of delicate marsh flowers and flowering grasses which had no names for him, and which he thought very little about, except that he liked them much better than the petunias and phlox in his mother's garden.

The sun grew hotter and hotter until it seemed to him that he could feel the blood-stream thicken in his veins. His sensations grew narrower gradually until all things were shut out, at certain times, except a frightful and dizzy sense of motion—the forward motion of the canoe, and the backward-rushing of the overhanging branches. For long stages of his journey there was only dead quiet, with swift clouds and noiseless rushing branches. But every so often a fresh outcry would ring through the marsh and send the red-winged blackbirds crying wildly overhead.

Once he sat up just in time to see a slim yellow snake in front of his canoe bisect the stream by an almost imaginary line. Watching the snake trickle up the bank and into the grass, he did not see the mud-bank ahead of him until the canoe had very nearly run aground. But after that his journey was uneventful until he came to the old footbridge of a long-abandoned path through the marsh, and there, on the dilapidated railing of the bridge, he saw eleven great blue herons. They were beautiful—as beautiful as anything he had ever seen in his whole life. Very soft gray, with a band of black on their wings, and long slender necks. His heart beat wildly with excitement.

He had never seen so many all at once. Sometimes he would see one or two flying overhead, but never so many as this. And never did he get so close to them. They were like beings from another world. They were so detached and unafraid. The canoe drifted nearer and nearer. He wondered why his heart did not frighten them with the sound of its knocking. Nearer and nearer. . . .

Then one of the herons gave a startled cry. Instantly all of them rose into the air, crying and beating their very long wings. The cry sounded through the marsh, and from the high grass all around him twenty more rose stiffly. The air over his head grew dark with their wings, and he could not contain his delight.

When they had passed over the tamaracks and out of sight, and for some time afterwards, he remained in a state of Grace, like one who has seen a vision. Meditating upon this event which was as unforeseen and as wonderful as his love, he floated on downstream, past the weathered sign which said "no trapping and froccing allowed," past the abandoned rowboat, almost to the opening of the slough, which was his destination.

As the canoe drifted along he saw a scarlet snakefeeder lying on its back in the water, helplessly working its legs in the air. Because the exaltation had not yet departed from him he was moved to put out his paddle and rescue the insect. At the first attempt, the snakefeeder was washed off the blade of his paddle and disappeared under the water. When it reappeared it was out of reach, behind him.

With a few sharp strokes Thorn turned the canoe around in midstream and went back. He took greater pains this time, and he was successful. With infinite care he deposited the insect on a blade of marsh grass. Then he held the canoe close against the bank while he examined the snakefeeder. Half of one wing was broken off. It could never fly again. It would only cling there on the blade of grass until it died, or until one of the marsh birds discovered it.

In all the years he had been exploring the marsh he had seen hundreds of snakefeeders in the same plight, and never put out the blade of his paddle to help them. Now he was moved by this poor insect with the broken wing as he had never been moved by any creature's fate. He felt a cool well of pity deep within him, and certain words came to him, as if they had been spoken by a voice out of the marsh. It was because of the blue herons that he had tried to save the snakefeeder. It was out of the kindness of his love for the blue herons.

He lay back in the bottom of the canoe a long while listening and trembling, and the canoe drifted on down past the opening, into the slough.

*

Nigel and Paul sat in the screen tent consuming the afternoon between them, as if it were a cake that could be cut and parceled out, quarter by quarter hour, on a silver knife. Nigel's mind was hopelessly divided between her knitting and the view, between Paul's head, bent over his volume of Yeats, and her own private distraction.

The sweater was half finished—the front half—and there was still the skirt to be done before the summer ended. In September there would be no time for knitting, no time for anything at all. In September there would be rehearsals and learning lines, in the bathtub, on the subway. . . . All this summer day her brain, wearied to death by perpetual restatement of the same anguish, had fallen back into old and familiar grooves. As a person searching for a thing lost will look again and again in the same place, forgetting that he has looked there before and that it is not there, so Nigel continued to make plans for the fall, forgetting each time that in September she might not be going to New York at all; that she might have all time's delight in which to finish her sweater and skirt.

There was a secret involved in all this knitting. One afternoon the winter before, she had sat on the stairs backstage talking with Marski and eating pickles. It had been a wearing and unsatisfactory rehearsal which had left her greatly discouraged. Time and again Marski had shown her what he wanted her to do, only when she did it it wasn't the same. It wasn't, he complained, concrete. Then he would tell her to feel the thing, to do it instinctively, without thinking. She tried, and that wasn't right, either. In desperation Marski sent out for pickles, which they ate sitting on the stairs and watching the next scene. Then he turned to her impatiently and said *Darling*—Marski always darlinged everybody, even the janitors —*you will be as good as any of them. What you need*—Nigel was too weary to grasp the meaning of his words, and she followed instead the wide arc of his half-eaten concrete pickle—*what you need is to live a little.*

Not until hours later, when she was puttering around in the kitchen at home, did the words descend upon her inclosed in meaning. It was a new idea, and once she accepted it, she could no longer go on as she had before. No one had ever told her that if she worked hard and cultivated her natural talent for the projection of feeling, that still wasn't enough to be a great actress. She had been faithful and conscientious, and the other directors had been satisfied. But with Marski it was different. He kept trying to get something out of her that simply wasn't there.

His words were still in her mind when she boarded the train with Paul and came to Wisconsin. For the first time she surrendered herself to living. She took Susan's catastrophes on their face value, and was sympathetically laid low by each in turn, as long as she could do so and still keep her sanity. She experimented daily, and sometimes with a certain amount of success, so that she was able to conceive objectively the life which went on about her, and to discern the secret vitality which made things more real than thought. It was the knowledge of this secret vitality which made a great artist. It was the knowledge of this secret vitality which she must catch, somehow, and hold fast in a sweater and skirt so subtly knitted that no one seeing them would suspect that they were anything more than a yellow sweater and skirt; so subtly knitted that they would record in yarn all the happenings at Meadowland. And in the fall she would put on the sweater and skirt, she would go to Marski and say: "You see? I have lived. . . ."

Then remembrance came back upon her, and for the thousandth time she stood on a high place looking down, sick with giddiness. *My dear, what you need is to live a little. . . .* She could see him now, standing there in front of her, his funny round face crisp with impatience. But when she thought of his words, they were curiously twisted in meaning. She wished that he were standing in front of her now, so that she could ask him how it was one managed to live *a little*. To be safe you had to stay in a place where you couldn't live at all, as Paul had done before he came to New York; or else you had to be burdened beneath a weight of iron armor. Paul had come to New York without any such armor, and in seven months he had more wounds than poor dead St. Sebastian. And now if she took off her armor here in the country, only for a little while, only for half of June, July, and August, would not her life become so inextricably bound with his that she could never again do with it as she pleased. She looked up suddenly, expecting to find an answer to her question in the stream of brightness which flowed around the screen tent, and the enduring quiet of the view fell upon her mind, and it grew less distracted.

The screen tent was open on four sides and placed a little way down the hillside from the house. From there one could see every part of the farm except the ten-acre field, which was beyond the wood.

Because wire-screening conventionally comes in rolls a yard wide, the sides of the screen tent were divided into sections, and the whole farm was of necessity divided into panels a yard wide and six and a half feet tall. The effect was of a room hung with Chinese wall-paintings. No effort of the will or the imagination could give continuity and a third dimension to the view.

By slightly turning her head she could see from where she sat two wall-paintings depicting fragments of the house. The scene directly in front of her was rather more felicitous, being a fragment of wall—over-run with grape vine, a goldfish pond, and a low-hanging branch of an oak tree. The fourth panel was less interesting—a broad band of sky and a broad band of grass, separated by a narrow band of sorghum. The only point of accent was Rats, dozing on the lawn with his head on his paws. The fifth panel was definitely inartistic, because of a red barn on the next hillside. The sixth was a trifle sentimental—an old-fashioned garden overshadowed by a hundred-year oak. Beyond that the scenes were flawless, being made up of pasture and marsh, sky and the branches of trees. Then the farm buildings began, and the illusion was destroyed by unpicturesque realities—the barn, the garages, the ice-house.

And Paul, inside the tent, was likewise real and in no wise resembled a Chinese wall-painting. God defend me—thought Nigel, fervently—God defend me from a two-dimensional man. Without laying aside her knitting she peered at him under eyebrows which were arched in wonder. So vague a man, so marvelous a man. And he belonged to her. She shut her eyes and continued to see him just as plainly as before. Of all things in the world, her mind was surest of his face—the contour of his forehead, the fine delicate inclination of his under jaw, the straightness of his nose, the small lines radiating from the corners of his eyes, the hesitant and uncertain curve of his lips—all this her mind was utterly familiar with, and could instantly create, sharp and clear. That was more than she could do with any other face, even her own, which, being a woman, she had examined many thousand times.

Her hands knew Paul's body more than her own, which they had ministered to all these years. They knew Paul's body so well that they could have fashioned it out of modeling clay, with no trouble at all. The shape of the back of the head—so. The two muscles at the side of the neck, running into the shoulders, which were broader than her own and much harder. The shoulder-blades and the slender intricately muscled back. The small triangle at the base of the spine. All this it would have been as easy for her to fashion out of clay as the lumpish elephants and ducks she had made as a child, to the bewilderment of her aunts and uncles, who felt sure that a sculptor had come among them. And in front the small cavity at the base of the neck. The two flat planes of his chest and the sharp declivity where they ended. The hard solar plexus. The soft sensitive skin on his stomach. The deep well of his navel, and the line of soft curly hair that went downward from it to his loins. That was the way it would be in modeling clay. But alive, stretched out beside her, with his heart beating against his ribs—she grew dizzy at the thought of it, and dropped two stitches.

"What's the matter, darling?" He was looking up at her over the top of his book.

"I love you," she explained.

"Praise God for that! But why do you scowl so?"

"Was I scowling? I dropped two stitches and had to go back and unravel."

Their eyes met. They said nothing, one having too much to say and the other nothing that could be said in words. Nigel stood it until she knew that in another minute she would burst into unreasonable tears. She lowered her eyes and returned to her knitting, which was a safer occupation than looking into his eyes. He was a devil. Given half a chance, he could see through her as if she were water and her mind the yellow grains of sand on the bottom. It was no use to lie to him. If she started to, he would only put his hand on her, and she would want to lick it, like a faithful hound. If he so much as put his hand on her, she was almost too happy to go on living. It was something she couldn't possibly explain, even to herself.

"Nigel this is nice—'*Once every few months I used to go to Rosses Point or Ballisodare to see another little boy, who had a piebald pony that had once been in a circus and sometimes forgot where it was and went round and round. . . .*' Do you like that?" He rested his book on his knees, waiting for her to be amused.

"Darling," she said, marveling at herself that she could speak so lightly, and all her world unsteady and shaken, "you must never go with a circus."

"No, of course not." He smiled at her with his eyes. "But I think I will go in to town tomorrow, if Susan says I may. Would you like to come with me?"

"I can think of nothing more wonderful," Nigel answered, wondering if there would ever be a tomorrow, if she would ever get on the other side of this day, which was a particular thing, separate and interminable.

"I'm running low on tobacco, and I have no shaving-soap at all. Only one last squeeze. I could give up shaving, I suppose, but I have to have pipe tobac— HEY!"

Nigel's face went white with fear. "Whatever is the matter, Paul? I wish you wouldn't shout that way, so suddenly. You frightened me."

"I'm sorry, dear. It's Rats I was yelling at, not you. He's after the frog again. Rats! Get away from there!"

"Oh, stop him! stop him!" Nigel jumped to her feet in alarm, and all the knitting tumbled softly out of her lap. "If anything happened to that lovely frog——"

Together they left the screen tent and ran toward the goldfish pond.

The frog in question was a particularly green one who had hopped all the way up the hill from the bank of the creek and established himself comfortably in the goldfish pool. By day he would sit, unblinking, on a lily pad, while one member or another of the family talked to him or tossed pebbles into the water to frighten him. Like a small porcelain stoic he would sit absorbed in unshackled speculation. When a pebble came very near to hitting him he would sometimes chug faintly, by way of protest, being as yet too young to chug-a-rum. By night, when there was no one abroad to throw pebbles at him, he would grow more and more lyrical, until the antechambers of the night rang with his high-pitched croaking.

Paul was the first to reach the edge of the pool. He bent over Rats and then straightened immediately. By the way that he straightened his shoulders, Nigel knew they had come too late. "O Paul . . . !"

Taking her by the arm, he led her back to the screen tent. "Never mind, my dear." With the sound of his voice he tried to quiet her, as if she were a child. "Never mind . . . ."

There was one night when Nigel had knitted the croaking of the frog into the front of her sweater. It was a very still night, and the moon three-quarters full, with a yellow haze around it. She couldn't sleep because she wanted to go to Paul's room, and she knew she mustn't. So she sat up in bed with pillows at her back and knitted by candlelight for an hour and a half. She knitted both the croaking of the frog and the haze around the moon into her sweater until she grew quiet again, and fell asleep with the candle burning, and the frog croaking, and the knitting needles still in her hands.

"There are millions of frogs in the world," Paul was saying. "Millions of frogs. In time, another will come hopping up the hill to the goldfish pond."

How could he say such a thing! There were millions of frogs in the world, of course, but what difference did that make if none of them were as amiable as this one had been—as amiable and self-contained and green. Paul didn't really care at all. Men never did. They were all heartless. The death of the frog or the death of her heart's desire were all one to Paul—all one and nothing!

She looked up at him in anger and saw that while he spoke his eyes were bright and sorrowing. Then for her instant of disloyalty she quailed, as if the point of a spear had been thrust into the soft flesh of her side.

"Once when I was a little boy—about nine, I guess—I asked my father why it was that animals killed other animals. Whatever he said, I can't remember. Rats is overfed. It wasn't hunger that made him kill the frog. Apparently they do it for sport, like men."

He does care, Nigel told herself. And what he said is all true and strangely comforting. In time another frog will hop up the hill to the goldfish pond. Time fixes most things, and it will fix that. The mole, for instance, that tore off its hind leg in the trap Gust set for it on the terrace—it would learn to tunnel with three legs instead of four, and its blind life would go on. Or would it? For all one could tell it may have dragged itself off down its dark thoroughfare to a secret place of its own, and bled to death there.

Arguing thus with herself, she picked up her knitting and sat down again. Time wouldn't help the mole if he was dead. Or the frog, either. Time ended when they died. But then, so did everything else. She closed her eyes, and when she opened them, followed a faun-colored butterfly in and out of the stalks of sorghum. Then she bent over her yellow knitting and tried to imagine for herself a domestic existence, with a house to keep, dishes to wash, beds to make. She tried to imagine herself in the capacity of a mother, wiping small noses, scrubbing dirty knees, and tying up the same cut fingers over and over again. With the full strength of her imagination she tried to picture these things, and without success. It was a kind of imagining she had never before indulged in, and she lacked practice. She was far better at picturing herself as the star in a great scene, bringing the house down with her acting. She had been playing it almost since she could remember. On summer evenings, when she was a child, the little girl who lived next door and the little boy who lived across the way would meet at the pear tree in her backyard, and when she had finished her supper, Nigel would slip away from the table and go join them.

They had all the long summer twilight in which to contrive and act out their plays—Nigel's plays, as a rule—and Nigel's two aunts were the audience. They sat down on the side porch, and looked down in quiet amusement or quiet wonder at the scenes of passion and bloody death which were enacted before them; and they fanned themselves with palm-leaf fans.

Sometimes the children gave three or four plays in one evening. Nigel could no longer remember what they were about. All she could remember was the sensation of a reeling sky, as she flung herself upon the hard ground, mortally wounded by the dagger of the proud Spanish princess. That, and looking up into Thomas's round smudgy face as he bent over her, his eyes filled with honest tears.

Thomas was not always so absorbed in the drama. Sometimes, in the middle of a play, he would become bored, hideously bored. At such times there was nothing they could do but give in to him, and all three would withdraw to the backyard to catch lightning bugs, which they put in a bottle. As for the aunts, they went on fanning themselves, waiting for the night to come down.

When Nigel returned from the far country of her childhood, she discovered that Paul was looking at her, and had been, apparently, for some time. She could think of nothing to say, and after a second or two he took up his book and went on reading.

How marvelous to love a man who knew enough not to talk to you when you did not feel like talking! All the days of her life there would never be another man who made her feel as Paul did. If her mind grew wild with anguish or delight, the sound of his voice quieted it. If she uttered blasphemies against herself, he touched her with his hand, and she could not speak a single word. If she put her mouth to his mouth it was as if she had been walking for days through a dry rocky place, and suddenly came upon a spring of cool water. If she opened all the doors of her being to him he always came in quietly and kindly, like a man going through a deep forest, singing.

If he should die—the thought made her eyelids sting and grow hard, like marble. If he should die— The passing of the amiable frog had deepened the shadow which was already around her, though the afternoon was warm and bright and there were only white separate clouds in the sky.

Paul, I think I'm going to have a child. She shaped the words with her lips and said silently, *I'm more afraid than I've ever been.* She half expected him to look up from his book in amazement at her unspoken words. When he did not, she continued to stare at him. Once she had been desperately afraid of losing Paul, but she knew now that if anything happened to him, she would live through it and beyond it, although she did not know how.

Once he had promised to call for her after the play, and at twelve-thirty he hadn't come. Everyone else went home except the scrubwoman who pursued her across the dressing-room on her hands and knees. Nigel was certain that he had been run down by a taxi. He was so vague. He never looked where he was going. And while she walked the floor, jumping over puddles of soapy water and wringing her hands, she tried insanely to conceive how it was people managed to die . . . whether they went blind first, or stopped breathing, or whether they just stopped thinking. If anything did happen to Paul, she knew now that she would live through it and beyond it. Her fear now was an entirely different thing. It would be tragic enough if she had to give up her career, just as things were beginning to break for her. But it was not this that she was so desperately afraid of. If her love was not strong enough, if she held this blunder always against him, if she reminded herself each day when she woke and each night when she fell asleep again that it was because of him she had been undone . . . Her eyelids closed of their own weight, and she wondered if she would ever again feel so old.

"It isn't that I'm afraid of losing you—" To her surprise she said the words out loud.

Paul looked up at her quickly and smiled. His smile was ambiguous, but without a trace of reproach. "That would be good worry gone to waste."

"I know. I'd live through it somehow," she went on, leaving him to pick up the thread of her thought as best he might. "I'd work like hell. I wouldn't let myself think about it. But if—" How could she make him understand without telling him what was on her mind? "If I were to wake up in the middle of the night some time, and look at you, if you were to touch me, and I didn't feel anything at all, any more than if I had a stone inside of me—" She bent forward and took his hand in hers. "Do you see? If I should suddenly stop loving you?"

"I've thought of that." She could feel the blood coursing through his hand, but his eyes were steady and quite unfathomable.

"That would be worse for me—" She sought around in her mind for words which would make her feeling articulate. "That would be worse for me than if something happened to you—if you died, or went away. Do you remember Alda Robertson?"

"Yes. A small woman with very gray eyes."

"Very gray. Well, the first week of 'For Narrow Bed' I had to share a dressing-room with her."

"That was the week I went to Ipswich to see Sammy."

"Yes. It was the first time you had been away from me for any length of time, and I was most miserable."

"That was very nice of you."

She brushed his remark aside with her knitting-needle. "At night I'd go home and lie there in the dark for hours before I could go to sleep. And one evening I caught Alda looking at me in the mirror of her dressing-table. She asked me what was the matter, and I told her it was nothing. I was lonesome for some one.

"Then she wanted to know what it was like to be lonely. I didn't believe her at first, but she really meant it. I couldn't explain, exactly, except that it was like having the flu. It made your chest hurt. And she laughed at me. But her eyes—you remember how they are—her eyes grew so old—she's only fifty-two—they grew a thousand years old, as if she had found out everything there is to know, and she had long ago stopped caring how terrible things are, or how beautiful, or how kind."

Paul waited for her to go on, but when she said nothing more he asked, after a time, "Didn't she ever have a lover?"

Nigel nodded. "There was some one she knew in the south of France, when she was a young girl. But that was thirty years ago, and besides, he's dead."

"That does make a difference, I suppose."

"What do you mean?"

"Why, if you loved only one person in all your life, and even that person was dead."

Nigel stared at the points of her knitting-needles; then she said, slowly, "I think it was because she didn't love him that she looked so sad."

"Darling, listen to me!"

She let him take her other hand, and sat looking into his eyes.

"There are certain inevitable things—life and death and growth and change. These things all love, even ours, must submit to, because all of them are a part of love. More than likely the time will come when you wake suddenly in the night, and look at me with unloving eyes. And when that time comes we shall know what to do. But now you love me as I love you, and we are here in the screen tent, and it is five minutes to three by my watch——"

Nigel jumped up and looked at him with horror-stricken eyes. "It can't be that late! Oh, the poor lamb!"

"It is every bit that late. What's the matter?"

"I promised Thorn I'd go down the creek with him at two o'clock, and I forgot all about it!"

"Never mind. You can go tomorrow with him. The creek won't run off during the night."

"But you don't understand. This was something special."

Paul rubbed his chin thoughtfully. "In that case, you'd better take the other canoe and go down after him."

But Nigel ran out the door of the screen tent and started down the hill to the pier, without hearing a word he said.

*

At precisely eleven minutes to four, on the station platform of the Chicago, Milwaukee, and St. Paul Railroad, Bascomb turned over a new leaf. Henceforth, he promised himself, he would be an entirely different person, scarcely to be recognized by even his oldest acquaintances. For one whole Wednesday out of each week, he would discipline his tongue, put it on the shelf, give it a rest.

The circumstances which had brought on Bascomb's reformation occurred within the last half-hour.

While Whitey was struggling to get the clothes-basket out of the car, Mrs. West had fallen into conversation with the washwoman—a small Polish Mrs. Pielschowski whose children outnumbered the sands of the sea. The two women were merely discussing how much the littlest Pielschowski was gaining each week and what a nice disposition he had—female talk, and harmless enough, but by such minute occurrences are the lives of men completely altered. Bascomb had looked about him at the innumerable little Pielschowskis all smiling as only angels and the children of washwomen can, and he had merely remarked, in the most casual way, that with all due respect for the creative urge, did Mrs. Pielschowski know there was a place in Philadelphia where you could get pamphlets on birth-control? If Mrs. Pielschowski was interested, he would be only too glad——

That was all Bascomb had said, but even now, nearly half an hour later, he still felt the heat of Mrs. West's wrath. Even now he could hear her saying, "Bascomb, there are some things we do not say here."

Bascomb was not altogether sure whether his aunt meant there were some things one didn't say in the Middle West, or that there were some things one didn't say at Mrs. Pielschowski's. But no matter which she meant, this remark of his aunt's struck him with the impact of an altogether new idea. Always, until the moment when his reformation took place, he had assumed that he had an indisputable right to say whatever popped into his head.

Since most of the things which popped into his head were, so it seemed to him, quite entertaining, he had early in life dedicated himself to the high purpose of providing amusement. It was a thankless job, of course, and he was an unsung hero, but nevertheless he liked it, and on the whole he considered himself reasonably successful—so much so that if occasionally he said something that, well, might just as well have been left unsaid, it ought to be overlooked. So long as he kept up a fairly good batting average he ought to be allowed an occasional error.

But it was only too obvious that his Aunt Susan was not going to make any such allowances. Therefore, if he were to last out the summer at Meadowland, it would require the exercise of the severest discipline. There must be no halfway measures, no compromise. If he thought one thing and said another, it would inevitably lead to a split personality, or worse. He must go the whole hog. Not a sound would he utter from the crack of Wednesday's dawn until the crack of Thursday's.

With this one day of silence he would atone for a week's indiscretions. He would do penance for all the times he had gone the rounds of the boarders, quarreling with them and insulting them and keeping them from their work. He would do penance for lighting kerosene lamps in the daytime, for singing "Traviata" duets with both parts off key, for playing the "Petrouchka" suite on the antiquated victrola, and dancing until the plates fell off the pantry shelf.

Now, looking about him at the significant movement up and down the station platform, he glowed with the esoteric pleasure of the recently reformed. Without a doubt the railway station was the most exciting place in Thisbe. It was the point where the circular life of the town touched the tangential life of the world, and Bascomb found the tangency immensely dramatic.

With bright, reformed eyes he observed the comings and goings, all mysterious and incalculably important, of a very small urchin in very large overalls. He watched the baggage clerk hauling out wagon after wagon, many more than there was likely to be need for. He wondered at the rust-colored old man who sat in a pool of sunlight directly under the large-lettered THISBE which alone distinguished this station from four dozen others along the same line.

Having attended to these, Bascomb let his eyes wander over

the long line of box cars standing on the second track. They had every appearance of remaining there until the end of time, when a heavenly traffic agent would no doubt see that they were disposed of. From the sides of the car Bascomb learned as much as he cared to know of their capacity, and a good deal more which was fit to print only on the sides of box cars. At the moment, however, he was more interested in the non-paying passengers who squatted on top. Most of them were young—even younger than he was—and their eyes stared at him out of faces black with cinders and soot. He tried to imagine what it was like, riding on top of a box car—the violent rocking and the terrible blast of hot wind and cinders. Apparently they did not mind it. They looked cheerful enough, as if they could not conceive of a cosier method of travel.

Bascomb wanted very much to talk to them, and when one of them grinned at him he started forward immediately with every intention of getting acquainted. Then he remembered that this was Wednesday, that his life was completely changed. His disappointment was very great, especially when the boy stood up and began walking along the tops of the cars, jumping lightly from the end of one to the beginning of the next, landing always on his toes. Out of the depths of a very sheltered life Bascomb envied him his loose, shapeless army suit, his insouciant swagger, his ability to jump from one box car to the next, lightly, like a cat. It seemed to Bascomb that life must be an endlessly diverting spectacle viewed from the top of a box car, and for the moment he entertained serious thought of counter-reformation. If only counter-reformation were not so much like backsliding——

From this first trial of his strength he was rescued by the station agent, who came out on the platform, saw Mrs. West and called to her. "I've a telegram for you. It came through a little before noon. I've been trying to get you ever since. There's something the matter with your phone. I'll bring you the telegram in just a minute."

"Good Lord, Muv!" Whitey looked at her in despair. "I'll bet anything you turned off the phone last night on account of the storm, and this morning you forgot to turn it on again. You're *always* doing that."

"O my dear!" Mrs. West exclaimed, by way of confessing

her guilt, and as she stepped out of the car Bascomb sighed with admiration. She was one of those marvelous women who get out of cars frontwards like a man, instead of backing. In women that was a sign of genius. It was also a sign of genius to be able to pick out such becoming hats. That navy-blue turban now, over light gray hair. Most intriguing!

"O my dear!" Mrs. West said again, when the station agent came out of the depot with a folded telegram in his hand.

"It isn't for you," he explained. "It's for Miss Josefa Marchand."

Mrs. West read the telegram, arched her eyebrows. "How distressing!" she said, as she folded it and jammed it into her purse. "Don't let me forget about it, Whitey, will you?"

A Ford, antiquated and wholly disreputable, turned the corner and drove up to the depot with sighs of mechanical thanksgiving. With a full heart Bascomb recognized the Homer Hansens. There was Homer, small and faded out to the consistency of an old blue shirt. There was his enormously fat wife, as noncommittal as a leg of mutton. There were the two gangly, pale-eyed children.

"Just as if I'd given them their cue," Bascomb explained, rapturously, to himself, and he began jumping up and down on one foot, to the great astonishment of the urchin in overalls. It was too wonderful! Much too wonderful. In half an hour's time the whole countryside for ten or fifteen miles around would know that they were entertaining a Negro at Meadowland. The women would probably ring the bells for the farmers to come in from the fields, the way they did when somebody fished a skeleton out of the drainage ditch. It was too wonderful.

Solemnly, each from a different door, the Hansens emerged from their Ford. Mrs. Hansen backed, as Bascomb knew very well she would.

"Cousins from Oconomowoc," they explained to Mrs. West, who had called to them.

Bascomb nodded with satisfaction. Good enough. Oconomowoc should have the news by late tomorrow sometime, figuring all possible train schedules and all possible mail deliveries. There was a train at nine-thirty-seven, but then they might not come back to town again tonight. It would be safer to figure on the ten-five tomorrow morning. Meanwhile he could trust the station agent to see that all Thisbe knew about it.

Far up the track a train whistled. Bascomb started back to the car with the intention of telling Mrs. West to put down *The Nation*; Armageddon was at hand—and narrowly missed being run over by the baggage truck. Dear God! That made five of them, and there was never anything more than one sack of mail and a couple of empty egg-crates.

At a point somewhere beyond where the two parallel lines of track converged—at a point somewhere beyond infinity, perhaps—he saw puffs of microscopic smoke, and the excitement implicit in trains took possession of him. Now it was all going to happen. The train would come. Jefferson Carter would get off. Aunt Susan would say, "My dear—" Dense crowds would spring up out of nowhere, and police on horseback would have to clear a lane for them as ticker tape and the contents of waste-baskets rained down on their heads from above. It would be wonderful! wonderful! wonderful!

What happened after that Bascomb wasn't quite sure. He was standing on the platform, wringing his hands, and suddenly in the midst of his excitement he was calm, entirely calm. He saw, as in a mirror, a wide stretch of sea, and a pearl-diver standing in a shallow boat. It was all so clear he could see the sunlight splashing on the diver's wet shoulders, and it was not like a vision. Somewhere in the world he knew that such a pearl-diver existed. At this very moment the sunlight was splashing over his wet shoulders. And whether he dived into the water or whether he remained poised on the edge of his shallow boat, the pearl-diver could have no knowledge that he, Bascomb, existed. The diver would eat and sleep and live his life and be eaten by sharks, without ever touching at any point the life of Bascomb West. For the first time it became clear to Bascomb that he was not the very center around which the cosmos revolved. The thought was overwhelming; more so even than the great black train that went by with clouds of white steam, wheels roaring within wheels, and the terrible anguished cry of air-brakes grinding.

Bascomb watched the motion of the train growing slower and slower until he could see windows and then people in the windows. Mrs. West and Whitey appeared, one at each of his elbows. And there were the Hansens all in a row: tea, coffee, sugar, and salt. There was the baggage clerk, leaning against the first of his five trucks. But the urchin—where was he? In the very hour of crisis, had he vanished into air, into thin urchin air? It was too late now to find out, for the Punch and Judy show was already beginning. There was Mr. Punch getting off the train now. And there was the dog Toby, and there was the Blind Man with the Big Stick.

After these three came a tall thin woman who reminded Bascomb vaguely of the Princess Nicolai-Zybiskarenoff. Only just a shade thinner, perhaps. Behind the Princess was a fat man whose feet hurt, and after him a farmer's wife with a baby in her arms and two small children hanging to her skirts. It was time now for King Solomon in all his glory, but instead came a small boy with freckles and an Italian woman with gold rings in her ears. That was all. No Solomon and no glory.

Bascomb made his mind empty of all thought so that he might stave off the inevitable disappointment.

Far off and rounded, as if she were shouting through a tunnel, Mrs. West's voice came to him: "Why, there he is! He must have come in the parlor car." The words lay folded on the front steps of Bascomb's mind, like the morning paper. He took them up and opened them out. Carefully he read the headlines and knew that he could breathe once more.

He saw his aunt bearing down the platform toward a tall, broad-shouldered, very black Negro. "My dear—" she was exclaiming, three coaches down the platform. "My dear, how marvelous to see you!"

In the confusion of introductions Bascomb failed to observe whether the urchin reappeared in the nick of time, or if the baggage clerk had need of his five trucks, or what became of the Hansenian cousins from Oconomowoc. Indeed, he failed even to notice what effect the arrival of Jefferson Carter was having upon the town of Thisbe, Wisconsin.

The reason for Bascomb's defection was that he had been so preoccupied with the material arrangements for his Punch and Judy show—the audience, the setting, the mechanical equipment of puppetry—that if he thought of the protagonist at all, it was certainly as a lay figure. Now, the discovery that he had to do with a live, unpredictable person, whose movements were not controlled by wires and whose words were not spoken by someone concealed behind the scene, disturbed Bascomb so profoundly that he could not achieve the detachment necessary to the proper appreciation of drama.

"Did you have a pleasant trip, Jefferson?" What a marvelous woman his aunt was. Apparently she had expected a real person all the time.

"Why, yes; not at all bad——"

Since Pullman porters were the extent of Bascomb's association with the Negro race, he had, of course, expected Jefferson Carter to talk like a Pullman porter. Indeed, he had counted on it, and on the effect of yahs'm and noh'm said across the dinner table at Aunt Amelia. But this was a clearer, nicer English than his own!

"A little warm, for a while, but about two o'clock it cooled off, and after that it was very pleasant."

Whitey had made off with Jefferson's heavy Gladstone bag, and was floundering along toward the Buick. Mrs. West and Jefferson followed more leisurely. And Bascomb, for the second time that day, brought up the rear of a procession. He was glad of the chance to reflect upon what he had just seen, and to recover at leisure from his astonishment. Walking along in behind, he found more than a little of the Negro in the man ahead: his walk, the curve of his back, the hang of the arms from the shoulder, the inclination of the head. His laugh was a darky laugh—contagious and musical. He probably could sing——

Swing low, sweet chariot
Comin' fo' to carry me home

—like one of the grandfather angels. But there was nothing angelic about that face. Black and shiny as a kitchen stove, and built upon the low structure of the African skull.

From what Bascomb had heard, Jefferson might very well be thirty-five or forty years old, but then one could never be sure about Negroes. Jefferson might very well be as old as Uncle Tom, though he *wasn't* Uncle Tom, of course, because Uncle Tom had died and gone to heaven along with Little Eva and several bushels of large pink roses. That Bascomb was sure of. Besides, Uncle Tom didn't wear gold-rimmed glasses. Neither did any of the Pullman porters Bascomb had ever seen, but then Pullman porters probably didn't have much time for reading, and so they hadn't ruined their eyes.

Although it was obvious, from the thickness of the lenses, that Jefferson's eyes were ruined, they were nevertheless extremely intelligent eyes. Rather more than intelligent. They made Bascomb feel like a young whippersnapper, and mere intelligence never had that effect upon him. These eyes were unusually dark and sensitive. They expressed unusual dignity.

"Did I tell you," Mrs. West was saying, earnestly—"did I tell you in my last letter that I was losing my mind?"

Bascomb felt no scruples about eavesdropping. This was Wednesday, and there ought to be some compensations for keeping one's tongue in one's head.

"Well, I am. I turn off the phone and I can't remember names any more. I went to visit my Cousin Agnes Herrick in Hammond, and she had a house guest, a Mrs. Frost. Well, my dear, I insisted on calling her Mrs. Snow twenty times a day, until at last Agnes took me aside and said, 'Susan' she said, 'I don't like to seem rude, but Mrs. Frost is leaving tomorrow. Don't you suppose you could call her by her right name just once before she goes?' Whom do you go to, Jefferson, when you're losing your mind?"

Bascomb, listening, caught a deep chuckle, so deep it was almost like the low notes of an organ.

"I'm sure I don't know. But if you like, I'll make inquiries when I get back to New York."

"I wish you would. Now I've got no end of shopping to do. Can you bear it? If you can't I don't know what you can do about it. We could stop eating for a day or two, but I doubt if you'd like that, agreeable though you are. I guess you'll have to poke around with me, no matter what you feel like doing. Are you good at carrying bundles?"

"If you'd rather I waited in the car while you go in——"

Here—said Bascomb to himself without waiting to hear Mrs. West's reply—here is the Negro Problem I've been reading about.

*

When Whitey turned the car in at Meadowland, there was no evidence anywhere that the farm and all the buildings on it, and all the people in the buildings were older by three hours. Everything looked exactly as it had before, except that the geraniums in the window box were a shade more red, with the afternoon sun on them, and the shutters a shade more green.

As he brought the car to a stop before the door, Whitey's heart gave a leap in anticipation of his freedom. He twisted impatiently in his seat, waiting for the passengers to get out of the car. They were so slow! They took so much time over bundles and suitcases. He could have got in and out two dozen times, and lifted the things out besides, in the time it took them to get out once. But then his mother was telling the colored man all about the trouble she'd had with the people who came to fix the pump, and of course that slowed everybody up.

When they were all out he breathed a sigh of relief and put his foot on the clutch. "Don't forget about Josefa's telegram," he called to his mother, and with her arms full of packages and her mind already in the kitchen, Mrs. West called back that she wouldn't. The car coasted in silence down the curving hill. There was not a shred of doubt in his joyous mind that his brother would be there before him, perhaps already at work on the canoe. Thorn was an awful stick sometimes. So solemn about everything. But you could depend on him. Thorn never went back on his promises the way his mother did. Thorn was no stinker.

Anticipation bubbled up from within and broke into tiny spray on the surface of Whitey's mind. The car came to a stop in the garage. Without even so much as slamming the door behind him he jumped out and raced down the hill, seven leagues at a time. He rounded the corner of the barn and stopped dead in his tracks, his eyes wide with disbelief. There was no one waiting for him. Both canoes were gone. Thorn had gone back on his promise. Somebody had gone off with his canoe. With *his* canoe. Thorn had gone back on his promise.

The reeded banks of the Little Neenah, the marsh, the blue hills beyond the marsh—the whole familiar landscape was bent and splintered by Whitey's tears.

*

With the best of intentions, Mrs. West started off to the Tower with Josefa's telegram, but on the way she met Paul, who was also going there, and intrusted him with her errand. With the best of intentions Paul put the telegram in his pocket and continued on his way. Before he got there he passed a mole-trap which was sprung, and he fell to thinking of Nigel and the green frog and the rabbits who ate up the melon vines. Without a word he entered the Tower, closed the screen door softly, and started for the stairs.

Josefa smiled to herself, thinking what a good neighbor he was, and struck one more phrase from the *Allegro*. She was grateful now as she had been time and again, for his very ingratiating habit of minding his own business. Halfway up the stairs he turned and waited a moment as if there was something he wanted to tell her.

She looked up from her music. "Well, what is it?"

"Have you seen the Negro boarder?"

Josefa shook her head. "No. Have you?"

"Yes. He's a great man." There was awe in the tone of Paul's voice.

"What makes you think so?"

"Bascomb. He's stopped talking. If you ask him anything, he just swallows hard and looks goggle-eyed at you. Not a word can anybody get out of him."

"Mother of God!" exclaimed Josefa, and her astonishment broke out in diminishing chords. "Perhaps it's voodoo."

"I think it must be." Paul passed on up to his room with the telegram forgotten in his pocket.

Josefa sat musing upon the miracle of Bascomb's silence. She had vanquished him in the morning, the Negro had bewitched him in the afternoon. Perhaps by night some one would come along and annihilate him completely. That was a pleasant thought. The *Allegro* was beginning to take on form and substance, and that, too, was a pleasant thought.

In the course of the afternoon the sunlight had moved around to the west window. She put out her hand and light, yellow with the day's age, streamed over it. It must be late. After five o'clock. And still he did not come.

She bent over the keyboard, thoughtfully seeking a design in music which would correspond to the summer airs and the afternoon sunlight as it used to lie upon the slope of the mountains when she was a child. She had read somewhere that it was all a matter of correspondences. She was trying to find now a combination of notes which was like the tall trees, and also a combination of notes which was like the purple dust the shepherds raised driving their flocks down from high pastures.

As the pattern of the music that she played grew more and more like the patterned landscape which was in her mind, she closed her eyes and sought a combination of notes which was like a cloud coming up over the mountains. She found it, and then *he* came and sat down on the bench beside her. The moment he entered the room she knew. The roots of her hair tingled, he came so softly.

At once he began carving out a delicate accompaniment in the bass clef, as he had done so many times before. First he made shadows beneath the tall trees, and between the branches of them. He made the bent shadow of the shepherd move between two rocks. He dragged the shadow of a cloud over the mountains and across the meadows and the bare ground. A little more and Josefa's landscape would have been perfect and complete. But with a dominant ninth and the nerve-wracking transition to an augmented eleventh, he wantonly destroyed all that she had built.

"Oh, but why— —"

In sheer exasperation she turned upon him and opened her eyes. It was nearly a minute before she could make herself believe that there was no one in the room.

*

Jefferson Carter walked back and forth, back and forth across his bedroom. Now he stopped before the fragile bouquet of grasses and pale yellow flowers which Mrs. West had left on his dresser. Now he halted a moment in front of the long shelf of books and looked inquiringly at the backs. Now he opened the door of the closet and peered into its spotless vacuity. He was preparing himself for a change of atmosphere, and there were certain mental readjustments which he must make.

As he lifted the top of the walnut chest and stood looking down into it, he told himself that he was a fool ever to have come here at all. There were plenty of colored folk who knew how to dance the social cake-walk to the white folk's music. They did it very well, too. But that wasn't in his line. He might get to talking about the salvation of mankind, and in the social world that wasn't done.

Besides, he had a job to do, and spending pleasant days of idleness in the country was no part of that job. If he sat in a hammock under a shade tree, day after day, who would demand—when it was not too late to demand—that the Southern Negro have something more than a court lynching? Who would hound tax boards that held back the state appropriations for Negro schools? That was his job, and he shouldn't have taken the time to come here.

He wouldn't have, of course, if it hadn't been that he found Mrs. West a kind of angel, and if it hadn't been that he was sick unto death of hotel rooms. He wouldn't stay long, though. Just long enough to write an article for *The Crisis*, perhaps, and get his lungs full of clean air.

Even now, after so many months, it seemed to him that there was still some of the stale air of that Decatur court-room in his lungs. Dead smoke and the smell of people, grown heavier day after day. It would be a long time before he got it all out of his system, and it would be longer before he forgot the things that happened during the third trial. There was one thing that he would probably never forget: That smile of Andy Wright's which wasn't a smile at all, but a healed scar which drew back the corner of his mouth. Through layers of exhausted air he saw the boy sitting on the witness-stand, giving his testimony, giving his smile which wasn't a smile: *Yessuh, I was in the fight. I didn't do much fightin' myself because I had mah lil brother to take keer of, but I was in the car whar the fight was goin' on.* How strange a thing that a wound from the bayonet of a guardsman who was supposed to be protecting him from the mob should turn into a smile. *Nossuh, I didn't see no white girls. I didn't see them ontil they took us off the train at Paint Rock. Nossuh, I didn't do nothin' to no white girls. I was just in a rock fight, that's all. . . .*

Jefferson screwed up his face, made a queer little noise with his lips, and by way of driving the Scottsboro case from his mind, he walked over to the bed, put out his hand to feel the clean bed-linen, the stiff white pillow-cases. It was so clean here! He took a sensuous delight in the sheer cleanness of the white towels hanging on the rack, the stiff yellow curtains caught back at the windows, the yellow rugs on the floor. In such a room one had to be clean.

He laid his glasses carefully on the dresser, slipped off his tie, and worked himself out of his shirt and undershirt. As he bent over the washstand he caught the familiar reflection of his head and shoulders in the oval mirror. The sight was reassuring. He was in a strange country. He didn't know who was friend and who was enemy, but he did know from past experience that there would very likely be both. Some would be exceedingly nice to him, and sooner or later some one would turn up who could not eat or sleep or say his prayers until he had "put that nigger in his place."

No word of all the words Jefferson knew carried the sting of that word *place*. *Nigger* fell off as harmlessly as if it were a child's blunted arrow. Nigger was a cloak of contempt, but it was dyed in honorable blood. He wore it proudly. But the word *place* was to him a constant reminder of the great bitter fact: His race was still in bondage.

Just where did they get this *place* talk—he asked himself moodily as he washed his ears. So far as he knew, the Bible said nothing about class distinction in heaven. Apparently the seraphim and cherubim ate at the same tables and rode in the same railway coaches. The Lord wouldn't stand for it any other way.

He fastened a bath towel around his hips, tucked it in under his belt, and began to wash the soap off his chest and shoulders. His wet back and arms were beset by the late afternoon sun which showered him with splinters of green and gold. His shoulder-blades glittered and flashed. He bent over the washstand all unconscious of his glory.

But in hell there must certainly be class distinction. Perhaps the devil was called colonel, by courtesy, and all the fires were niggers being lynched.

The fantasy amused him elaborately. From the point of view of a white man, a lynching was not funny. But if you were born a Negro, you had given to you certain compensations for the color of your skin, and one of them was the ability to make jokes about it. That dialogue, for example, that Pickens was so fond of. The dialogue between the high-yellow and the coal-black—it was such joking as that which kept the Negro from committing murder and arson in wholesale quantities. That was why the colored folk were much happier than the whites—there were so many things they *had* to make jokes about. They made jokes which weren't jokes. Like Andy's smile which wasn't a smile.

Feeling more certain of himself now that he was washed, he dived into his Gladstone and brought out a green shirt. With thoughtful masculine deliberation, starting at the bottom and working upward, he buttoned it. Then once more into the Gladstone. This time he brought out a yellow tie. As he finished tying it there was a small, diffident knock at the door of his room. With a marvelously swift motion of his hands he swept his shirt-tails into his trousers. "Who is it?"

"Me—Whitey."

Jefferson finished buttoning his trousers and opened the door. There on the threshold stood a small boy with a pitcher of ice-water in one hand, a piece of sandpaper in the other. It was Mrs. West's youngest son, Jefferson decided. There had been so many things to see, he had scarcely noticed him on the way out to the farm. This lad must be very near the same age as his Marshall, and he was so tanned that his skin was almost the same color. Only the hair and the eyes were different. The hair bleached out to a pale yellow, and the eyes very bright blue, very candid, very disarming. Something in the way the boy stood, something in the way he held his head, reminded Jefferson of Mrs. West. Yes, he was obviously her son.

"I brought you some water," Whitey explained, and then he added, "—to drink," in case Jefferson, being a Negro, might not know what to do with ice-water.

"That was very kind of you." Jefferson took a glass from his washstand and filled it from the pitcher Whitey had brought. "And what am I to do with the sandpaper." He looked humorously down at Whitey over the rims of his glasses.

"Oh, that's to use on my canoe! I was going to sandpaper my canoe when I got back from town. My brother Thorn promised to help me"—Whitey's eyes grew large and sad; twice in one day people had gone back on their promises to him—

"but when I got back from town there weren't any canoes. I guess he took his canoe and went down the creek. I guess maybe he forgot about me."

Jefferson nodded in sympathy.

"We couldn't have done it, anyway, because somebody took my canoe out, too. Whoever it was won't get very far"—Whitey's face brightened at the thought—"because it leaks something awful. Since I couldn't sandpaper my canoe, I thought I might as well bring you some ice-water."

Jefferson mistook this for a personal kindness and was needlessly touched.

"Muv says if you want to take a cat nap before dinner, to help yourself. But if you'd like to make the grand tour——"

"What is that precisely?"

"Oh, she means, if you'd like to have a look around the farm and maybe go see the ducks——"

Jefferson nodded. "That would be very pleasant."

"I'll be waiting downstairs in the living-room when you're ready."

*

Mrs. West went from window to window in the living-room, raising the green shades which had been drawn to keep out the harsh sunlight. Faintly protesting, the room awoke from its long afternoon sleep. The chairs stretched, the curtains stiffened.

Mrs. West went from window to window in the living-room with a small china pitcher, watering the ivy—a seemingly harmless procedure which immediately brought about one violent and terrible invasion after another. First Whitey descended the narrow boxed stairs three and four steps at a time, managing to land, by a trick known only to him, in the center of the room. The glass pendants which hung from the candlesticks had not yet stopped quivering when Josefa broke in upon them, pale and distrait, to inquire if Cynthia was in her room. Mrs. West had hardly watered the second pot of ivy and Josefa had no more than ascended the stairs when Jefferson came down, all black and shining. And before Mrs. West had finished watering the third pot of ivy, Josefa fell down stairs.

Jefferson put out his arms to catch her, but Josefa, frightened by her fall, saw only a room full of objects which rose and staggered, rose and staggered, around a center of blackness. She twisted herself out of his grasp, her eyes blazing with anger.

O my dear, Mrs. West asked herself as she put down the china pitcher, are we going to have *that*? Jefferson had stepped back, waiting to see what would happen next. It was high time she took command of the situation. "Josefa, did Paul give you the telegram?"

"Telegram?"

"Can you believe it!" Mrs. West put her hands to her head and moaned. "Never in all my life have I known anyone so absent-minded. He was not more than fifty feet from the Tower when I gave it to him, and I saw him go in, with my own eyes, not two minutes later. Sometimes I think——"

"What did the telegram say?" Josefa cut her short, knowing that if the room continued to sway back and forth, describing an increasingly wider curve, everything was bound to fall in a heap in the middle of the floor, and then she would never find out.

"My dear, it was from somebody named Herman and he wants you to send him some money."

"Oh!" Josefa said, and then she added, "thank you!" as the room swung around once more and came to a full stop.

*

On the front terrace Jefferson and Whitey were met by a small and very clean dog who fell upon Whitey with immoderate delight, wagging his tail, whining softly, and licking Whitey's hand.

"This is Rats," Whitey explained, his eyes shining with a pure delight. "His full name is Aw Rats, but I call him Rats for short."

Rats eyed the tall, black-faced stranger a little fearfully. With due caution he approached and sniffed at Jefferson's shoes, at his ankles, between his legs. This was not at all the smell he was used to smelling, and he was not quite sure what he ought to do about it—nothing, certainly, with more sniffing. After considerable deliberation, he extended his head sidewards so that Jefferson could scratch his right ear.

Whitey broke into delighted laughter.

When Jefferson, in return for this sign of favor, had scratched not only the right ear but also the left, and the top of Rats' head, all three started off down the hill.

First they came to the goldfish pond. Jefferson counted six yellow water-lilies and one pink one, all half-closed. Beneath the green oilcloth lily-pads he could catch a gleam now and then as a goldfish swam nearer the surface of the water. He noticed along one side the fragment of stone wall overgrown with wild grapevine, and on the opposite side yucca plants and a small willow tree.

"There's a frog lives in this pond," said Whitey, "but I don't see him just now. That willow tree I fished out of the creek. It was just a stick floating along, and it had begun to sprout on one side, so I fished it out and stuck it in the ground, and now look at it."

Jefferson did look at it, with what he hoped was a fitting amount of wonder.

"That wall," Whitey went on, "was part of the foundation for a summer house Muv was going to build several years ago. But when they got the summer house half built, Muv changed her mind and decided she'd much rather have a goldfish pond there, and so they tore down most of the wall and made a goldfish pond. It leaks.

"And see that tree out there by the edge of the sorghum——"

Like a guide pointing out to travelers the main points of interest in the Roman Forum, Whitey called Jefferson's attention, quite professionally, to the major buildings of the farm—the "woodus," the Bright Idea, the carpenter shop, Hen's Delight, the boathouse, the garages . . . "And that's a corn-crib in front of the barn, even though it doesn't look like one, and beyond that is the icehouse, and beyond that is the he-john—just in case you didn't know where it is. Sometimes people don't notice it, when they first come, and go to the she-john up there behind the 'woodus.' I just thought I'd tell you.

"There's a pewee nest in the top of the he-john. Come on down and I'll show you. The little birds are only two days old."

They went to see the pewees in the he-john, and then through the barn, down to the boathouse, and along the narrow path into the marsh where the duck-pond was. Here were great numbers of ducks sailing without noise and without effort, from time to time lacerating the air with their quacking.

Jefferson leaned against the fence, watching the ducks and brooding over what he had discovered of Meadowland. It was the most complex farm he had ever seen—so many houses and sheds and shops of every sort, and he had not yet seen all there was to see. There was still the chicken-yard, and the woods, and the "Norwegian Village"—whatever that might be.

He was pleased with the cleanness of the farm. Each building was spotlessly white, with green trellises—so neat and so orderly. Yet taken all together they seemed to present a special kind of chaos. Perhaps there was a genuine need for so many buildings, but what of the effort that must be exerted to establish order over so many domains? That in itself must be rather a nightmare, a confusion springing from order.

Now as Jefferson watched a waggish elderly duck attended by the pomp and circumstance of seven ducklings embark on a hazardous sea journey, he wondered what connection there was between this disorderly order and the mind of Mrs. West, who was so charming, so like an angel. Because she was sympathetic, and so eager to help anyone who called upon her for help, and so free from prejudice of any kind, he felt both affection and admiration for her. But she was occasionally very disconcerting. Her mind jumped about so. He would be telling her of certain difficulties in the way of Negro franchise, and she would suddenly ask him how James Weldon Johnson was. One would hesitate to call her scatterbrained, but everything at Meadowland bore the stamp of her personality, and scattered was the word which best described Meadowland. He was forced to admit that he could make nothing out of her, but that she was very charming, very like an angel.

Under Whitey's guidance, Jefferson moved away from the duck-pond and through the wood, which was now cool and dark with shadows. Shafts of late sunlight broke through the walls of the wood and fell, as if a marching army of giants had camped for the night and cast their spears into the ground.

Jefferson felt the moss and dry leaves give way softly under his feet. Out of the carpet of leaves grew oak saplings, scarlet mushrooms, and feathery ferns. It was as if a green haze hung over the gray floor of the wood.

Soon they came to a group of thatch-roofed buildings which were open on the sides and filled with the strangest assortment of superannuated farm machinery. Among other things, Jefferson discovered two ox-yokes, which he found difficult to associate in his mind with the present mistress of Meadowland. And there were three curious, hand-hewn boats hanging upside down from the ceiling. These also bore testimony to an earlier occupation. He turned to Whitey for enlightenment. "How long have those boats been hanging up there?"

"Ever since I can remember. They're Indian dugouts. I guess they've always been there." By always Whitey meant from the beginning of time, but for him time began with his Great-grandfather Harrington who settled at Meadowland when the waters receded after the Flood.

"I see. Are there many Indians around here now?"

"There are some. There's a family of them living in a little house just on the other side of the first hill beyond the creek. The squaw comes here for food sometimes. She's awfully dark. She's almost as dark as a nig——"

The word caught on the edges of his lips, and remained there, half-spoken. Wave upon wave of scarlet confusion swept upward over his face, until Jefferson felt that he must take compassion upon the youngster and relieve his embarrassment. "Indians vary a little in color," he said calmly, "just the way Negroes do, but of course not anywhere near so much. There's a funny story—perhaps you know it—about two Negroes who were making fun of each other. One was very light, and one was coal-black. The light-skinned one said to the other: '*Man, you must ha' been born at midnight on de dark er de moon!*' And the dark-skinned negro said: '*Well, perhaps you mought hu' probably been born in de daytime—but de sun must ha' been in 'clipse.*' Then the light-skinned one said——"

Jefferson looked down at Whitey to see if he was being amused, and discovered that instead of lightening his embarrassment he had only added to it. He abandoned his story and, putting his hand on the boy's shoulder, said, gently, "Come,

Whitey; you promised to show me the chicken-yard before we went back to the house."

*

The saints in heaven, Mrs. West assured herself, could not have produced a more elegant arrangement of blue and white larkspur. She stood on one side of the dining-room table and then the other, shifting a stalk of white and admiring the effect, then shifting a stalk of blue and admiring that effect, until perfection hovered over the silver bowl.

Feeling the need of supplementary admiration, Mrs. West summoned Johanna from the kitchen. She would have preferred a more discriminating and articulate appreciation, but there was no one else within shouting distance.

Johanna appeared in the doorway encumbered, as she always was at such times, with her hands. Her eyes fell upon the flowers, and to Mrs. West's infinite agitation she burst into tears.

"But, Johanna!" she exclaimed. What with dinner coming on and a roast in the oven, it would have been better if Johanna were a little less moved by the centerpiece.

"But my dear!" She put her hands on Johanna's shoulders and shook her gently. "You mustn't go on like this! You'll make yourself sick!"

Johanna buried her face in her apron and broke into long even sobs, like a child.

"But what on earth—?" Mrs. West began to suspect that this distress of Johanna's was not entirely provoked by the exquisiteness with which she had arranged blue larkspur and white in a silver bowl. "Johanna, I want you to stay here, but if you aren't happy . . ." She stopped and reached for her handkerchief. Tears were so catching, and she was an utter fool. The idea of saying if you aren't happy to a person who was flooding the place with her tears. She sniffed, to make sure that there was nothing burning in the kitchen. "Johanna . . . listen to me. . . . You don't have to stay here, you know . . . if you don't want to." Her words had no effect whatsoever, and so she relapsed into the phrases she had used to comfort Thorn and Whitey when they were little. "Now," she said, softly. "Now . . . now." As if Johanna had skinned her knee or hideously bumped her head.

"*Heut' Morge'*"—Johanna reached down into her pocket—"*hab' ich a Brief bekomme'*."

With the letter in her hand, Mrs. West went off to the kitchen in search of her glasses. She wanted tremendously to look in the oven and see if the roast needed basting, but the oven door clanged so. And with Johanna in the next room giving herself over to grief, it seemed dreadful and unfeeling that she should even consider the roast.

She returned to the dining-room, sat down at the table, and began to frown over the difficulties of colloquial German and German script. Suddenly she looked up from the letter, her eyes blinking with sympathy. "But my dear," she said, softly, "why didn't you tell me?"

*

All the long summer afternoon Amelia lay in bed in her darkened room, waiting for a pneumonia bacillus to come and claim her. From time to time she coughed experimentally, but the results were neither alarming nor bronchial. She tossed back and forth in the bed until she felt hot enough to take her temperature. It was normal.

When at last it became apparent that she was not going to be sick, she relaxed and lay still. Because of the drawn shades there was a greenish cast to the walls and ceiling. It was as if her bedroom were a coral grot deep under the sea, where indolent ideas swam in and out, whispering among themselves. Now, with her eyes on the submarine ceiling, Amelia went over, again and again, the matter of Jefferson Carter. First, Prejudice took the stand and inflamed her mind with his passionate oratory. Necessity succeeded him and tore down his opponent's argument with brilliant logic and terrible common sense. Then Prejudice jumped up out of his seat and the two of them went at it hammer and tongs until Amelia was quite exhausted by the long, bitter contention. For the first time that she could remember, her will was thoroughly tired, thoroughly unable to drive the starved skeleton of a body to do its bidding. It was as if the will, too, were suffering from slow starvation.

Day in and day out for three years now, she had grown thinner and thinner, with nothing to feed her flesh upon except cottage cheese and weak tea. Without the rigidity of her will cottage cheese and weak tea would probably not have kept her alive. They would certainly not have given her the strength to rise each morning from her bed and go downstairs to face Susan's unbearable blitheness over the breakfast table.

But now even her will was exhausted. If she tried to move her arms from where they lay at her side she could not make them move. And if they continued to lie there, lifeless, under the sheet, how could she get up and dress for dinner? How could she get down the difficult stairs. She might get one foot on one step and one on the next and not be able to move either foot. She might have to stand there until some one came and helped her, until she fell.

Tears of self-pity scalded her cheeks and rolled down upon her pillow. Unable to check the flow of tears, unable to move, Amelia lay still and went over in her mind again the various aspects of her dilemma. Before the bell rang for dinner it was necessary for her to choose between two equally undesirable alternatives: She could rise—if she were physically able to rise—dress, and go down to dine with a Negro. Or she could stay in her room until after dinner, and then go away. Thorn would drive her in to the nine-thirty-seven train if she asked him to. And she had plenty of money. She could go wherever she wanted to. Wherever she wanted to? She didn't want to go any place. She wanted to stay here at Meadowland. The very thought of leaving it and living in hotels made her grow sick with terror. She could not endure to be alone. Now, in the shaded greenness of the room, she felt she could not even endure to go on living.

After a time she heard people coming up the stairs and Mrs. West's voice ricocheted from wall to wall of the upper hallway. The footsteps went on toward the guest-room. Lighter steps returned and stopped before her door. Amelia held herself rigid with agony lest Mrs. West should decide to invade her coral grot. Then the steps descended the stairs.

During the next few minutes Amelia lay still, listening to the sounds which came from the guest-room. Back and forth. Back and forth. The Negro was walking the floor. Something must be on *his* mind, too. She heard the sound of water splashing. He was bathing. Again the house grew quiet and again there were footsteps on the stairs, very light footsteps. There was a knock down the hall. She could hear Whitey's voice, and then a much deeper one, and Whitey's again. The voices blurred and grew indistinct. There were footsteps, and someone fell heavily so that the walls caught the sound and echoed it. She turned on her side and covered her ears with her pillow.

When the hall and her room grew still, she felt much stronger. In the midst of her anguish she had summoned the strength to press her pillow about her ears. Now she could get up and dress. She could go on living. Her will had taken up its work again.

She rose from the bed and raised the shades; the submarine green was exchanged for the yellow of the upper air. Slowly, so as not to put too great a strain upon her renewed energy, she washed and dressed. Feeling still woeful and unsteady, she coiled her hair into a rope and made a knot on the top of her head. She wished that she had some one to help her dress. Some one who was quiet and skillful and sympathetic. Like Cynthia.

But where is Cynthia? she said to herself as she secured the knot with a final hairpin. Cynthia's room was next to hers. She could not help but hear if she came in. There had been no sound all afternoon.

Amelia opened the door and looked stealthily into the next bedroom; it was empty. She retraced her steps in silence, emptied her wash-bowl into the slop-jar, and stood holding the bowl until the weight of it on her thin arms recalled her to life. She must preserve her strength. She must lie down and wait for the dinner bell.

The room grew more and more yellow. The sunlight crept up the wall. After a time the dinner bell rang. There were steps once more upon the stairs—steps and a knock at her door.

"Amelia . . ." She recognized Mrs. West's clear voice, and realized in a panic that there was now no time to reopen the hearing and go through the argument all over again. She must make up her mind one way or the other. She felt a knot of firmness forming in her head. She was not going down to dinner. Not if they took her out and stoned her.

"Amelia, do you feel like coming down, or shall I send up some cottage cheese and tea?"

The knot of firmness began to dissolve before the clarity of this voice, and the kindness of it. Amelia thought of the years she had lived at Meadowland. No one ever had been so unfailingly kind to her as Susan had been. Courtesy toward a guest. It was not so great a thing to ask, and Susan did not even ask that. She was willing to bring her food up to her; she wanted to spare her this embarrassment. The knot of firmness dissolved completely. "I'm coming, Susan," Amelia called. "I'm coming right away."

*

Mrs. West leaned over the table to light the candles. There was no real need for candle-light; though the clock maintained that it was evening, by the sun it was only late afternoon. But dinner, to Mrs. West, was an honorable occasion. It was the funeral feast of the day. After dinner you folded things and put them away. It was only fitting that there should be candles at dinner.

"*A kitten once to his mother said*
I'll never more be good;
I'll go and be a robber bold
And live in a lonely wood,
Wood, wood, wood,
And live in a lonely wood."

Amelia stood in the doorway. How gaunt she was! thought Mrs. West. How joyless! How old! "Well my dear, how are you feeling?"

Amelia did not answer. Slowly, stiffly, like a tragic fury, she made her way to the table and sat down in her accustomed place. Watching her, Mrs. West had a premonition that something extraordinary was about to happen. She shut her eyes and waited, but the world did not at that moment come to an end, and so there was nothing for her to do but go on lighting the candles on the sideboard.

"*—Howls, howls, howls,*
With three tremendous——"

"Hello Paul! Did you have a nice afternoon to repay you for giving up your trip to town? Sit down, please. Everything is ready."

In all my life, Paul thought to himself as he unfolded his napkin, I have never met such an astonishing woman. Even now at the end of the day her eyes are shining. With that delicate and firm profile, as delicate and firm as cut stone, how charming she looks; what she must have been like thirty years ago!

While Paul was meditating upon the nostalgic beauty of middle-aged women seen by candle-light, Bascomb appeared in the doorway with the voodoo still upon him, waited a moment, and then sat down beside Amelia.

"Bascomb," said Mrs. West, "did you see Whitey and Mr. Carter anywhere?"

Amelia's face became darkly illuminated, as if she sat facing a great conflagration. Bascomb opened his mouth to speak as the kitchen door swung open. There in the passageway stood Jefferson and Whitey, and both of them were smiling. Their entrance was so timely it made Mrs. West think of pageants, which she adored because they always seemed so prearranged. If only her household moved like a pageant— For a split second Whitey and Jefferson became grand symbolical figures representing the continents of Europe and Africa.

Mrs. West came forward to meet them. "I was just asking about you."

Amelia looked straight ahead, as if she had not seen anyone come into the room.

"Have you met everyone, Jefferson?"

Amelia thought of all the hot-water bottles Mrs. West had brought her, and all the powders and pills. She thought of how Mrs. West had tended her in sickness and in health these many years, while she had one thing after another— more ailments than the good Lord Himself could bear. She must do this for her.

"This is Mr. McKenzie. . . ."

Paul rose and offered his hand. Between the two men passed swift signals of surprise, of respect, of instinctive suspicion. Amelia stared at the blue and white larkspur in the center of the table; at the four silver candlesticks, one to the north, one to the south, one to the east, one to the west; at the fruit-cup which Johanna had left at her place, by mistake.

"Mr. Carter . . ."

Amelia braced herself and summoned all that was left of her thin starving will. In another second, she told herself.

"And my sister Amelia . . ."

Far off Amelia heard the words she had been waiting for. Now it was time. She opened her mouth to speak and no sound came. She tried to turn her head and nothing happened to it. There was nothing she could do. It was too great a thing to ask. The iron band around her head . . . the iron band around her heart . . . She stared at the white and blue larkspur. She counted the cubes of cantaloupe. She cleared her throat.

"But, Amelia——"

Mrs. West felt herself sliding down the side of the room, sliding and sliding. Everything she put her foot against came loose and rolled along with her. Every piece of furniture she caught hold of with her hands broke off at the roots. Faster and faster——

"We've been to the Norwegian Village——"

Mrs. West felt solid floor under her feet. She was afraid to move, afraid to breathe, lest this, too, should begin sliding. The floor held. Now that she could look about her, she found the room exactly as it was before. She looked up and saw Jefferson's immensely dark eyes speaking to her. They said, *It's all right. There's no harm done. This is what I expected to happen. It always does. See, it doesn't hurt a bit.* "We've been to the Norwegian Village——"

As soon as she heard the sound of his voice, she stopped being afraid of Amelia. She stopped being afraid of anyone. "Sit here by me, Jefferson—" And with her eyes she added, *I'll love you for this as long as I live.* "No, on the right. That's Gust's place, and he can't eat if he doesn't sit there."

Poor Aunt Susan! Bascomb thought, wondering if he could keep his tongue in his head much longer without going mad. Poor woman! Poor silly woman! Why didn't she reach out with a table knife and slit Aunt Amelia's throat. Slit— It would be so simple. Then all they would have to do would be to change the tablecloth and go on with dinner. Even now it wasn't too late. He bent forward to tell her, but she turned away and asked Paul where Nigel was.

"It's a long story," Paul began, sadly, for he had watched her age twenty years in the last two minutes. "Nigel promised Thorn she'd go down the creek with him——"

"Nigel is the young actress I was telling you about," Mrs. West explained to Jefferson. "She's the apple of my— Well, what happened, Paul?"

"Nigel got involved in the sweater she's knitting, and forgot to watch the clock. She was supposed to go about two, but it was after three before she remembered about it. By that time Thorn had gone off without her. There's a gallant son for you, Susan!"

"That!" Mrs. West exclaimed, "That from a child of mine! Whatever is the younger generation coming to!" She clutched her head and moaned, just as she clutched and moaned innumerable times since breakfast, but no one noticed, except Whitey, who had gobbled down his cantaloupe cubes and was more concerned over the fact that he would have to wait at least an hour for the second course. It was very trying, sometimes, to have a mother who clutched her head and moaned and slowed up the progress of dinner.

"Nigel belongs to the younger generation, too. That's the second half of the story. She took Whitey's canoe, and the last I saw of her, she was paddling downstream after Thorn."

"So that's where my canoe went!" Whitey said, with bitter indignation. "Well, the third half of the story is——"

But Mrs. West did not give him a chance to explain what the third half of the story was, for Gust had come in from the kitchen and taken his usual place.

"Jefferson, this is Gust. He's the prop of my old age, only just now he's got housemaid's knee."

The prop of Mrs. West's old age acknowledged the introduction and without further comment dug into his fruit cup.

"How does it feel now?"

"Better."

It didn't feel any better, but what else was there to say. If he told her the truth she'd get all upset. Women always got upset. And then they upset everything else. Like her bringing this nigger here. It was her business if she wanted to bring a nigger to Meadowland, he supposed, but all the same the old man wouldn't like it if he were alive. The old man wouldn't like it at all.

Gust chewed the first mouthful of cantaloupe analytically. It was a store melon and it wasn't ripe. If those damned rabbits hadn't eaten up all the melon vines they might have had some decent ones. At least they wouldn't be eating green ones. Still, it was hard to tell exactly when they ought to be picked. This one should have had about one more day.

"You're so seldom sick, Gust, I can't get used to it."

"I had malaria once." Gust offered the fact for whatever it was worth. They very seldom talked about anything that interested him. They couldn't very well, because most of them didn't know rye from clover, and they didn't even care about the weather. If it rained they went in the house, and that's all it mattered to them. In the old days, when the old man was alive, the people who came to the farm talked about railroads and new kinds of farm machinery. That was something to listen to. All this talk about writers and painting— He looked down the table at the double row of faces, all bending and eating. They were not his kind of faces and he was tired of looking at them. In the fall, he decided. And thinking pleasantly upon his little house and the woods which grew beside it and the deer which ran in the woods, he withdrew far into himself.

The candle flames wavered and bent unsteadily. In the open doorway stood Josefa. Mrs. West waved her spoon by way of greeting, and Josefa took her place at the table. From time to time she glanced up at Jefferson and at Bascomb, who remained silent as a trout.

In spite of the incident in the living-room before dinner, Jefferson was scarcely aware of her presence. He had met so many people during the last few minutes, and all of them peculiar. Just now his mind was concerned entirely with the lean sallow-faced woman at the other end of the table. She alone out of the whole roomful of people had refused to acknowledge the introduction. If she hadn't been there, perhaps he would have nothing to worry about. Everything would go smoothly, pleasantly. But then it was always that way. If she hadn't snubbed him, there would have been somebody else who would. The law of averages made it come out so. Out of the corner of his eye he watched Amelia. She was still looking at her fruit-cup as she had done ever since he came into the room. She would probably go right on looking at it. Probably a Southerner and still grieving for a cause seventy years lost. What wonderful haters Southern whites were. If only they had a little intelligence.

"*Dum dee da dum*," hummed Mrs. West, "*dum da dee da dum, dum da dee da da dum*. How did the practicing go today, Josefa?"

"It was fine," Josefa said, without enthusiasm. "I got more done than I have all the time since I've been here."

She looked disdainfully at Bascomb and returned to her fruit-cup. The strain was beginning to tell on Bascomb. Such a lovely opening. Like a box car. A couple of clever insults to start things going properly, and there would be a tong war in no time at all. Right there at the table. On the other hand, he did derive a certain perverse pleasure from mortifying his flesh. Tomorrow would be Thursday, and he would go insult Josefa bright and early.

How slow we are tonight, thought Mrs. West. Compared with the pangs attendant upon the birth of a meal, coming down to it was a very simple matter. You washed your face and hands, changed your dress, powdered your nose, and came down; that was all there was to it. Yet it had been hours and hours since the dinner bell rang, and they were not all down yet. And poor Johanna beside herself—she *was* still beside herself or she would never have put a fruit-cup at Amelia's place. Poor darling, she must find some way of helping her. They never seemed to be able to come down on time. Except Paul, of course, who had the farthest to come and drove her wild by coming hours too soon. He was a perfect dear, of course, but all men were trying, and he certainly was. The way he never seemed to know what he was eating, for instance; as if his mind were completely above such material things as cantaloupe cubes. And the way he watched everything that went on, every mouthful that she put into her head. If only she could look up some time and not find him looking at her. It was too exasperating. Some day she would have to speak to him about it. "Does anybody know where Cynthia is?" She looked down the table, and all the faces looked back at her, as blank as eggs.

"Perhaps she didn't hear the bell. Run upstairs, Whitey, and see if she's in her room."

Whitey rose from the table, but Amelia stopped him. "I looked before dinner, Susan. She isn't there. She hasn't been in her room since lunch."

"But what on earth?" The narrow edge of alarm crept into her voice. It was enough that Cynthia should disrupt the picnic at noon and bring on a thunder-shower. Now if she had gone and drowned herself in the Little Neenah, it would be too much. She saw Cynthia floating on the surface of the water, her hair waving around her head like water weeds. Cynthia was a dear, of course, but at the moment she had absolutely no patience with people who went and drowned themselves.

"Who is Cynthia?" Jefferson asked.

> "*Who is Cynthia*
> *What is she*
> *That all our swains adore her*——"

Mrs. West misquoted to no discoverable purpose. "Cynthia is the most adorable painter, my dear, and she has a room in the top of the Tower where she paints oil-cans and things. You know, all this business of abstract design and what not. It's such a climb up there that no one ever goes near—" Mrs. West stopped, unable to go on with her sentence, for Amelia had dipped her spoon into the fruit-cup which Johanna put at her place. "My dear! You'll have gas pains!"

"I expect to," Amelia answered. Now that she had disgraced herself forever, she saw no reason why she should not have gas pains if she chose to. She popped a cube of cantaloupe into her mouth and felt inexpressibly giddy. The table lengthened. The people grew tall, and rather out of shape. The candles soared toward a heaven of blue and white larkspur, and in the bright center of heaven Amelia saw a great black face with gold-rimmed glasses.

When you have eaten nothing for three years, nothing but cottage cheese and weak tea, you can get quite drunk enough on cantaloupe cubes.

Mrs. West was too fascinated to breathe. She had been trying to get Amelia to eat for so long, and now suddenly she was eating cantaloupe. . . . She would probably die before morning, but it was an end to be proud of!

Not until the fruit-cup was quite empty did Mrs. West remember her obligations as a hostess. Poor Jefferson! He must think he had come to a madhouse. She turned apologetically toward him. "Did Whitey show you our frog?"

Jefferson did not hear the first time, and she had to repeat. He was thinking of his family. In New York it would be nine-thirty by now. The children would be in bed. "Oh, I beg your pardon. He did show me where the frog lived, but the frog himself was either out or in. We didn't see him."

Paul shook his head. "I dare say you didn't. That's another long story, and a very sad one."

"Not really," Mrs. West cried out, and pieces of anguish splintered and shot into the far corners of the room. "If it's depressing, don't tell me. I sat in the car and read *The Nation* until Jefferson's train pulled in. I got so upset about the condition of the country that I can't stand anything more. If something has happened to that darling frog, don't tell me. I'm counting on taking him down to the picnic grounds with me for company, when I turn the farm over to Thorn. Thorn is my other son, you know, Jefferson. Just now he seems to be extremely late for dinner, but when he marries I'm going down to the picnic-ground and spend the remainder of my days in a teepee. I've got my teepee all picked out, but it isn't paid for yet."

"But, Muv, what will you do in the winter?" Whitey asked, from the other end of the table.

"In winter," replied his mother, "I shall move into an igloo. You don't happen to know anyone with a good stout igloo for sale, do you, Jefferson? It would have to be rather cheap——"

From the kitchen came Nigel and Thorn; Thorn was still in his bathing-suit.

"Oh, hello, darlings! I was beginning to worry about you. Where have you been?"

Nigel burst into laughter as she sat down at an empty place at the table. "We've had the most dreadful time! I forgot to meet Thorn when I promised to, and so I went down the creek after him——"

"But didn't it leak?" said Whitey.

"Did it leak! More than any canoe I ever want to ride in. By the time I got to the bridge, it was like trying to paddle a bathtub full of water. I was afraid to get out and turn it over because the creek is full of turtles. A snapping turtle as big as a soup-plate got up and walked off the very sandbar I was stuck on. I was scared almost——"

Mrs. West heard no more of Nigel's peril, for she turned to look at Thorn and discovered that he was standing there in the doorway with his eyes wide open, utterly stiff with happiness. Whatever had happened to him? She hadn't seen that unspeakably happy look on his face for years and years. Not since he was a little tike and Gordon made her give him the ten-acre field. And in the middle of the night—but that was a long time ago.

"And poor Thorn had to stop five times on the way home, and turn it upside down to get the water out. I've never had so much fun in all my life."

Paul watched her narrowly. It seemed to him that there was something strained about her gaiety, something a little unnatural about her excitement over the mishaps of her canoe trip. As soon as she stopped talking and bent over the fruit-cup, her face was quite drawn and tired.

"Thorn dear"—by an effort of will, Mrs. West forced Thorn to hear her—"run along and dress. I'll tell Johanna to put your plate in the oven." When he had vanished through the doorway, she tinkled her little silver bell. "Yes, Johanna, you may clear. And put Master Thorn's plate in the oven."

A current of cooler air blew through the room. The candles wavered and grew firm and wavered again. Mrs. West drew the scarf of her dress closer around her throat. It seemed to her that there was a touch of spring in the air. But this was the wrong time of the year for that. Before it could be spring again, they'd have to get through the rest of the summer and fall and winter. Before it could be spring again, they'd have to get through the rest of dinner.

She looked down the interminable table just in time to see Amelia reach for the fruit-cup at the empty place next to her.

*

According to Japanese legend there was once a criminal who, before his execution, promised the judge that he would return after death and haunt him. The judge was a skeptical fellow and demanded proof. "If you can come back after death," he said, "let's see you bite that stone over there, after your head is cut off." And sure enough, after the ax descended, the head bounded along the ground and set its teeth into the stone. But the judge was not at all upset, for he knew that only the very last thing a man wills before death can he accomplish afterwards; the condemned criminal had exhausted his ghostly strength in biting the stone and could trouble him no further.

So it was with Jefferson when Johanna appeared at the door of the screen tent a second time, bearing the elegant silver coffee-pot. He put all his strength of purpose into refusing a second cup of coffee and was therefore entirely defenseless against the blandishments of Mrs. West, who now set herself to make up for past neglect.

"Did Whitey show you the Indian dug-outs in the Norwegian Village?"

Her voice flew toward him through the twilight. He fumbled for the accumulated anger of an hour, and could not find it. "Yes, indeed. But he couldn't tell me how they came to be there in the first place."

"Couldn't he? Neither can I. Isn't that curious? They've been up there ever since I can remember. There were sheds down in the woods before I was born. They rot away, you know, and the roofs fall in from time to time, so they have to be replaced. But it still remains the Norwegian Village. There was a colony of Norwegians once, a little north of here." She put her cup and saucer on the table beside her until she had poked savagely at the pillows under her head. "We really have so little idea," she went on, having taken up her coffee, "how people lived here in the early days." She tipped the chaise-longue to an angle of twenty-five degrees—it was on rockers—and managing by a series of minor miracles to keep from spilling her coffee, she embarked upon the story of the Creation.

"In the beginning Grandfather Harrington bought Meadowland from a fur-trapper, and when he came here with

Grandmother Harrington and my mother—Mother was just a girl then—there was only a small clearing around the house. The rest was woods. All through the first year Grandfather cut down trees and broke the land just south of the house. Then the war came along and he had to traipse off to that, leaving Grandmother Harrington and Mother all alone up here in this desolate place. For a while they heard from him, and then the letters stopped. Poor Grandmother! She was almost out of her mind with anxiety. The heavy snows came. They were snowed in for two and a half months, with barely enough food to keep them going through the winter. And people talk about troubled times!

"Grandmother thought that Grandfather Harrington was dead, but he was in a Confederate prison in Charleston, and when the war was over he came home and finished clearing off the farm. There were Indians around here in those days—there still are some, of course, but they're pretty domesticated now—and once when Grandfather was walking through the wood with his gun laid in the curve of his left arm, like this"—she stopped to demonstrate, sitting bolt-upright in the chaise-longue and teetering perilously—"he heard a twig snap. Well, he turned around quick as a flash, and there stood an Indian with his tomahawk raised in the air and Grandfather's gun pointed right in his face. My dear!"

Mrs. West paused to let her audience recover from the excitement.

"I don't believe it, Aunt Susan!"

Jefferson wondered if he had ever heard such a high, unpleasant voice in a youth.

"I don't believe a bit of it. It sounds exactly like the stories Gust was telling about Uncle Will Bacon. You know, the one about his going to a party in hip boots, and dancing so hard and so long that when he got home and took off his boots, they were full of blood clear up to the top. And the one about the time he caught a baby elk, and saw the mamma elk coming at him, so he quick as a flash sat down on the hind legs of the baby elk and——"

"Bascomb—" Mrs. West's voice was polished with irritation. "If you can't distinguish in your own mind between Grandfather Harrington and Paul Bunyan's blue ox, I shall have to leave you to your own confusion. What was I talking about? Oh yes! My mother was nearly a grown woman by this time, and one day a young man stopped at the door for a drink of water. He was on his way west to look for gold. By the time he got there there wasn't any left, and when he came back with empty pockets, he stopped once more at Meadowland for a drink of water. And this time it was my mother who came to the door. He stood there smiling down at her, with one foot resting on the door-sill——"

Jefferson did not find himself particularly interested by this romance. He much preferred the earlier part of Mrs. West's story. Those people were important in the national life, and therefore he could imagine them more easily. Although it was not yet dark and the moon had not yet risen, he saw the figures of Mrs. West's saga moving noiselessly across the lawn, up and down the hill: Figures of hunters and trappers and woodsmen with coonskin caps and fringed leather jerkins, their guns across the curve of their left arm, so. Figures of Indians, moccasined and naked, creeping up to the edge of the clearing. Figures of a lonely woman and a little girl; of a tall raw-boned man fighting the woods with an insubstantial ax.

Back and forth these people moved through the outer darkness around the limited world of the screen tent. For Jefferson they were more alive than the people who sat with him in the tent. The specters outside were doing timeless things. They would live outside of time. Their lives had purpose, and so long as that purpose lived, they would keep on moving through the darkness, up and down the hill.

Jefferson looked about him at the seven people who sat in the screen tent, sipping their after-dinner coffee and fading slowly into the blue obscurity. They might have been seven hills, he knew so little about them, or seven rivers come together under the same sky. But seven hills or seven rivers might have had some meaning. There might be iron or copper in the hills, and ships might sail on the rivers. But so far as he could tell, these seven people had no meaning beyond themselves, which was to say that they had no meaning at all. They did not express the life of the nation. They had no visible work. They were all drones and winter would find them dead.

Jefferson lifted his face thoughtfully to the night. Over the farthest hills the sky was bright blue—the blue found on certain kinds of Chinese pottery. Rising out of a rack of silver-white clouds was a towering moth-colored thunderhead. It was like a great citadel out of which the gods might issue with their huntsmen and their hounds. Jefferson felt that the blue sky and the air all about him were charged with electricity. He could feel it in his hair, on his skin. There would be a storm before morning, and the unnatural air would be cleared by thunder and lightning. Some inherited sense for divination told him this. And before morning the unnatural strangeness with which the air of Meadowland was charged would also be cleared away. There would be trouble here. There would be thunder and lightning.

Mrs. West's saga had degenerated into the domestic trivialities of family history: How her mother tore her best dress, and how Grandmother Harrington mended it with her own hair, for lack of yellow thread.

While he was waiting for the small dribble of her talk to subside, Jefferson meditated upon what had been the longest meal of his life. First of all that gaunt woman who would not look at him nor speak to him. That was scarcely pleasant, of course, but it was an insult inflicted upon his own person, and not on his race. That he could stand easily enough. There had been a great many before this one, and there would be a great many more to come.

Then all these strange people dropping into their places one by one, right through dinner, and strangest of all, the way Mrs. West sat there watching that frightful woman eat, course after course. Sometimes she would remember to talk to him, and she would say something to get him started on the condition of the Negro in South Africa, or the number of firemen that had been shot off the Illinois Central trains going through Mississippi. But each time her mind would wander back to that woman, and she would sit there fascinated, like a bird watching a snake. Every bite of roast, every spoonful of peas that woman put into her head, Mrs. West counted. And so did all the others. He saw them do it. Sometimes they'd say things to him. Sometimes they'd say things to one another. But mostly they kept their eyes on her. It was as if they expected her to do something miraculous at any moment—prophesy, or lay a golden egg. Thank God she rose from the table and disappeared, just before they adjourned to the screen tent for coffee!

As for the rest—the broad-shouldered woman who fell downstairs, the hired man, the very pretty young girl, the man Mrs. West had told him about—the one who had been a school-teacher, the youth with adenoids, and the two boys—he could make nothing out of them at all, except possibly that he had come to a madhouse. For a moment he entertained serious doubts of the sanity of the entire group. There was something definitely light-minded about the way Mrs. West's attention wandered, even under normal conditions, and he had more than once been staggered by the transitions in her chain of thought. And what about that boy whom nobody had bothered to introduce to him—the oldest one. There was something queer about him, too. That wild look, as if he had become unexpectedly so happy that he was afraid each moment would be his last. There was something blinding about his look, like staring up at the sun. Jefferson had been forced to turn his face away, after a second or two.

Apparently the boy wasn't altogether normal, because he seemed totally unaware that there was a stranger at the table, and he didn't speak once through dinner. But the other youth—the one with adenoids and a large nose—he made up for both of them, before the meal was over. The way he suddenly broke put into a torrent of speech just before the cook brought in the dessert! Something about the geographical experience, whatever that was, and a pearl-diver which made him "get geography." Jefferson remembered a man he had once seen in Porto Rico—a man possessed by devils, who behaved in much the same fashion, pouring out thousands of words which had neither form nor substance. If they weren't all mad, then their conduct was inexcusable.

He looked from one to another of them, trying to make up his mind which they were, sane or insane, and a violent chemical precipitation began to take place within him. He grew unreasonably and uncontrollably irritated. He wanted to drag these people one by one out of the half-darkness. He wanted to say to them, "You there, ex-school-teacher! Look out!

There's going to be trouble this night. You'd better run for cover. . . . And you, boy with the face as happy as an idiot. Don't you see that big white weather-breeder? Have you lived in the country all your life and don't know that means thunder and lightning and rain before morning. . . ? And you, woman with the lovely face. Why are you bringing on the night with talking. You talk and talk and talk, and the air gets darker and darker. You'll bring down something darker than night, some day, with your talking. . . ." All these things he wanted to shout at them, dragging them out of the half-darkness, seizing them by the scruff of the neck, shaking them till they listened to him. But why he did want to say this, he did not know. It must be because the blood was pounding so in his temples. He must find something to hang on to, and hang on tight.

Then an angel came and held a flaming sword before Mrs. West's mouth, and there was silence. "I've been thinking about that generation of Americans," Jefferson began. "In some ways they were very brutal. In the North they broke the land, as your grandfather did. They cut down the timber, pulled up the stumps, and plowed under the green oak saplings. They made farmland out of what the Lord intended to be forests."

The wicker chaise-longue creaked and creaked. Mrs. West was not altogether gratified to have the word brutal applied to a member of her own family. She was broad-minded and all, but——

"In the South it was different. They didn't break new land any more. They exhausted the old, because it was so much easier. But they did break my grandfather's back with a club, so that all the rest of his life he walked with the upper part of his body at right angles to the lower." Jefferson hesitated. "I think the Lord intended him to walk upright, like a man."

"Oh, how dreadful! Oh, the poor dear!" Out of the darkness Mrs. West offered her sympathy as if it were a cloak, as if it were a warm, comfortable cloak.

"It isn't my grandfather I'm interested in now. You see, he's dead, and when you're in your grave it doesn't much matter whether you lie straight or crooked. What interests me is that brutal generation of men"—again the chaise-longue creaked—"who broke the land and broke—or tried to break—the Negro.

That generation made and unmade this country all at once, because they built by destroying."

Paul had not taught school for fifteen years without being able to tell when he was being lectured at. He knew the symptoms and the state of mind behind the symptoms. More times than one he had taken an idea in his teeth and run with it, as the Negro chap was doing now. "I should like to have that made a little clearer," he said.

Jefferson recognized the voice of the ex-school-teacher, and something in the quality of the voice—a certain dryness—told him that if he wanted to retreat, it would be better to do so now. But he did not intend to retreat, not until he had said what was on his mind. "Destruction," he went on, "was implicit in the growth of the nation because the pioneers exacted from the land——"

"But that's unreasonable!" There was something about Jefferson's positive way of speaking that made Paul contentious. "They had to exact from the land whatever they needed. They had to cut down trees or there would have been no place to plant corn, and nothing to build houses and barns out of. They had to trap and hunt or they would have had nothing to eat and nothing to keep them warm in winter. There is always a certain amount of destruction where there is growth."

"All that is true"—the blood pounded faster in Jefferson's temples—"but the fact remains that the pioneer was guilty of the great sin against nature——"

"And what, pray tell, is that?" Paul's voice had become like yellowed powder. He had the mild person's instinctive dislike for rhetoric. It was all very impressive to say the great sin against nature, but behind the statement was an appalling confusion of economics and Hebraic morality.

"The great sin against nature is taking more than you need."

Paul started to carry the discussion into more intricate realms of argument, but he suddenly remembered that he was arguing with a black man and not a white. If the discussion became heated, there would be social complications. It was better to stop now before it was too late.

"And so it was inevitable," Jefferson went on, "that in our period of maturity we should have to begin at the beginning and rebuild the land, and plant new forests to replace the ones which the Grandfather Harringtons cut down. That is what we must do in the North. In the South, we must rebuild a race. . . ."

This was the subject dearest to Jefferson's heart. He took these words in his two hands and held them high overhead, so that he could see them burning, burning, in the darkness.

"It takes a long time to restore land. You have to plant trees, and you have to wait a long time for them to grow big, and you have to watch day and night to keep them from being burnt down again. So it is with men, no matter what color their skin is. If you cut down their minds and keep them cut down for generations, you can't expect anything wonderful to spring up overnight. You don't realize, you can't realize what it means to a grown man not to be able to read and write——"

A cigar glowed intensely in the darkness. There was one person in the tent for whom Jefferson's explanation was unnecessary. Gust's cigar was a light shining from a lighthouse on the loneliest coast. If Jefferson had seen it, perhaps he might not have gone down on the reefs of race prejudice. But he was too full of what he had to say.

"Here is a whole race whom we must teach to read and write before they'll want to do anything more than sit around in the sun swatting flies. But that's what takes longest of all. Once they want to learn, there isn't anything they can't master."

"What about mathematics?" Nigel knew by the tone of Paul's voice that he had said all he was going to, and she felt a reckless desire to support him, even though she did it unwisely.

"Well, what about it?" Jefferson's voice grew louder and was keyed not for one person's ears, but for the unlistening world. He was no longer in the screen tent; he was no longer talking to these seven people. The mind of his race was on trial, and he was defending it. "What about mathematics?" he shouted. "Would you like me to demonstrate to you that the sum of the squares of two sides of a right-angled triangle is equal to the square of the hypotenuse. I'll be glad to, if you want to go into the house where we can have a light and pencil and paper. Or perhaps you would rather have me derive the formula for the sine and cosine of a thirty-six triangle?"

"We'll take your word for it." Against his will Paul was

forced to take up the discussion again, to protect Nigel. But it was very hard to speak calmly, with the fellow shouting so. Shouting at Nigel. When Paul spoke, his voice was not dry and powdery. It was like a tight fiddle-string. The words were plucked, and the vibration of anger lingered upon the flat unseen screens.

Something told Jefferson that he had gone too far. He ought to back track. He ought to give in. But with the blood pounding in his temples, there was no giving in. He must go on now, even to his ultimate doom. "I myself am no more than ordinarily intelligent, as Negroes go, and I was elected to Phi Beta Kappa at Harvard. What I have done my race can do, with a little help. But it won't be your help. We don't want that any more. Now we have leaders of our own to fight our battles and to lead us out of the wilderness where you left us. Our leaders can teach us one thing which yours never could do: They can teach us to have hope!"

Mrs. West turned and twisted and poked at the pillows under her head. She was very tired. She was very wretched. She could think of no way under heaven to make Jefferson stop shouting.

Jefferson seized the arms of his chair. "We cannot teach our people what to do with their lives, any more than you can. But we can give them the same tools to fashion their lives out of that you have had, because you are white, and that I have not had, because I am black. And what they accomplish with these tools you will have to recognize. There will be great musicians and great architects and great poets. There will be great statesmen and great mechanics. And you won't be able to deny them their greatness!"

"We don't want to deny them their greatness," Nigel protested. Paul put out his arm to stop her.

With the very last of his self-control, Jefferson kept from laughing.

"But until they are great musicians—" Josefa knew that they were already, but she was thinking of her fall and how the room rose and sank around a black pivot of fright.

"There are great ones now, and there always have been great ones." The wicker arms of Jefferson's chair groaned under the pressure of his fingers. "There are more great ones to come.

But for a long time yet they may have to devote most of their talent to keeping body and soul together. Now no matter what the kind of work, an incompetent white man is given preference over a trained and educated Negro."

"What about the shoe-shining business?" Bascomb inquired.

Jefferson heard the cruel sound of a whip cracking over his head. "Yes. There they have an equal chance. They have a chance wherever work is menial and degrading——"

"But that's not necessarily——"

Jefferson drowned Nigel's words in his own shouting. He did not even know she was speaking. Paul's anger rose, frothing and breaking, until it filled his whole mind. If it had been anyone but Nigel! If it had been anyone but Nigel who was shouted down! He struck in blind anger with all his might. "Until they have learned to behave like gentlemen, perhaps it is better that they be kept in their place."

Infuriated beyond the power of reason, Jefferson rose to his feet and stumbled forward. There were seven people looking at him in the darkness, and their eyes pierced his side in seven places. He stretched out his hands for the door. They met the unyielding screen. He tried again, and once more found a wall. He had forgotten where the door was, and the darkness was too thick for him to find it. He was caught, here in this grave.

"Oh Christ!" he shouted, and with his fists he beat upon the screen until it gave way.

The far hills grew pale with lightning as he stepped into the open night.

*

"And that just goes to show," said Bascomb, "that the hand is thicker than the eye."

"My dear"—Mrs. West spoke with the sound of autumn in her voice—"if only you didn't always have something to say." She turned on her side and stared at the invisible hole in the invisible walls of the screen tent.

Bascomb sighed heavily. "It must be that I am not appreciated here."

Paul's voice, deep and sober, came out of the darkness. "I doubt if any of us is appreciated just now. Susan, I'm very sorry . . ."

"Sorry . . ." The word dropped into the deep well of Mrs. West's distress and was drowned there.

"I was afraid just such a thing would happen."

"Yes? Then why did you let it happen?"

Nigel flew to Paul's defense. "But really, Susan, he *did* go too far."

There was no reply. Mrs. West had left the screen tent and was wandering in another more uncertain realm of being. Over and over she said to herself, "I have lived a long time, but I didn't think such a thing could happen to me."

She must go find Jefferson. And what could she say to him? What could anyone say to him? She could not bear the thought of the hurt which would be in his eyes. Really, there were some things one would rather not have lived to see. One would rather be dead before they happened.

The words echoed in her tired head until she remembered that once before, that day, they had been said when Cynthia stood up and brushed the crumbs off her lap and screamed. Poor Cynthia! And that was only seven hours ago.

Paul, unable to escape to a world beyond the screen tent, pressed his thumbs against his temples and tried to consider the matter rationally, knowing only too well that this was not at all a rational matter.

Nigel stared at the glowing end of Gust's cigar. Things had been done which could not be undone.

The crickets took possession of the night—of the night and all that was in it.

*

Thorn lay on his back on the pier, watching the moon climb with difficulty above the lowest bank of clouds. Over his head were branches spreading out so far that the lower ones nearly touched the water. Between the branches there were crevasses of darkness. Everywhere the crickets chirped in a rhythm as monotonous as the beating of a man's pulse.

While Thorn waited for Nigel to come down to the boat-house, he reviewed the afternoon in every detail, from the time when the low branches at the first turn swept over him until he came back up the creek and found Nigel stranded on a log in midstream. He had tried then, in the midst of righting the canoe, to tell her about the blue herons—how much they meant to him. But it was no use. All she would talk about was the turtle that was as big as a soup-plate. When she came down to the boathouse, when there were no turtles around, he would try again. It was important that he make her understand about the herons.

Above the senseless monotony of the crickets he heard the sound of a car starting, and saw headlights shining momentarily against the side of the carpenter shop, against the trunks of trees. Then the car was swallowed up by the woods.

It must be Whitey. But where in hell was he starting out for this time of night? It was after nine o'clock and he was supposed to be in bed by nine-thirty.

Pondering over this mystery, Thorn withdrew once more into his cavern.

*

"There, Gustibus," said Mrs. West as she put the last hot application on his swollen knee. Barbs of heat and of pain shot inward and met at the center of his knee joint. Gust shut his eyes and thought about the house in the woods where he was going in the fall when the first leaves were dropping and the nights were clear with frost.

"There! That's the last one." Mrs. West took away the application, and Gust regretfully laid aside his imagined season. "In the morning," she said, "you must come up before breakfast and let me bake it again."

Gust unrolled the leg of his trousers and carefully straightened his knee. "Good night," he said as he started for the door.

"But you've forgotten the hot-water bottle."

When he turned back to get it, he discovered that she was smiling at him as if he were still a young boy and not a man turned sixty-five.

"Do you know"—she hunched her shoulders slightly—"sometimes I get very tired of people who act and paint pictures and play the piano."

The lines of Gust's face moved in unaccustomed directions and astonishment broke through.

"I think it was much nicer," she went on, "in the old days

when Father was alive and the people who came here farmed or built railroads or invented cream-separators. You know, Gust, you are all I have left of that time. I should feel"—she hesitated and laid her hand gently on his sleeve—"I should feel quite lost without you!"

Gust wanted very much to say something, but after a lifetime of silence he was unused to words, and those which came to him now did not convey at all what it was he wanted to tell her. It was better, he decided, not to say anything. He opened the screen and her words, "Sleep well, my dear," went with him out of the door and into the night, which had somehow become larger than it was before. The sky was farther away and so were the dark hills. The oak tree beside the house rose taller and straighter, and its branches spread farther over the kitchen roof. The grass underfoot, the young spruce trees, the low flat roof of the garage, and the curve of the lawn as it went down the hill to the marsh—all were strange and new and very much more familiar than they had ever been.

*

The night sky was opaque with invisible drifting clouds and gave back almost no planetary light, but only the reflected glow of the earth itself. What few gray and tentative stars there were vanished as soon as the moon came out, yellow and subdued, from behind the clouds, like a night lamp burning at some heavenly bedside.

Across the terrace Nigel and Paul moved gravely. Their figures were thin and scarcely material. They whispered as they moved, communicating by the shadows of words, not words themselves.

"But, Paul!" Nigel's voice pleaded with him impatiently. "I *must* go up to the Tower and see Cynthia. Her light has been burning up there a long time."

"Please, darling, let's not wait. You can see Cynthia in the morning."

"But I'll only be gone five minutes, I promise you." A bat flew down out of the darkened air, down and past her head all at once, with a whirring sound. Nigel covered her hair with her hands.

"Please . . ." He touched her hand, smiling at her, and

Nigel faintly smiled, perceiving how difficult it was for her to deny him anything if he so much as asked for it. Her love had not the wisdom to withhold. Her love had no will against his will. That was well enough when they were together, secure against the hostility of time. But now she was alone, with neither wisdom nor will. . . . Besides, they oughtn't to go down to the boathouse this early in the evening. Some one would be sure to see them. They oughtn't to go at all. It seemed so outrageously irrelevant. It made her think of the summer evenings long ago when three children had made up plays and acted them. It was like Thomas' stopping the play and making them go catch lightning bugs to put in a bottle.

She drew away from him and shut her ears against the sound of his voice. His words were wings which beat ineffectually against her mind. They were as nothing compared with the weight in the locked chamber of her ribs and the unspeakable fear which lay coiled around her heart. She did not even hear his sigh. She thought only of Cynthia, who would understand, and share her secret gently.

Paul spoke to the night air, which was inattentive and full of inhuman voices. "I wish I hadn't said what I did. I was so mad I could have killed him when he shouted at you like that!" He was trying not to justify, but to explain, his cruelty. "And then suddenly I wasn't angry at all. There was the poor fellow trying so desperately to get away from us. I didn't know. I didn't know I could feel so sorry for any man. I wish I could go to him and —but nothing that I could say would do any good. Only I have such a huge desire to be kind to him. Curious. It makes me think of something that happened in New York. I was crossing Park Avenue at Forty-seventh Street. It was about midnight and bitterly cold, and as I stepped up on the curb a panhandler washed up against me. Could he have a dime? He had fifteen cents already and if he had a dime he could get a place to sleep for the night. When I had gone about ten steps beyond him, I heard—*It would be most kind of you. . . .* And do you know, darling, I couldn't move." Paul stopped, remembering how his feet had become stone because of these words, flung not so much at him as against the cold implacable night.

"It's so seldom one has a chance to be kind," he said, wistfully, in a tone which betrayed his own need of kindness. When there was no answer, he looked down at Nigel and saw that her eyes were closed, that she had not been listening. Her face was white and still, and there was no life in it. Her face was like a withered thing. And now he realized how strange she had been all day, how like some one wandering continually back and forth between this world and a farther planet; and suddenly the terrible conviction came to him that he had bungled once more, that he had brought some harm to this being who was so much dearer to him than all others, so infinitely dearer than his own life. With his teeth chattering, he took hold of her shoulders and shook her and cried out, "Nigel! Nigel!" And then, in agony, "What in God's name are you thinking about?" And when she did not speak, he took her face in his hands and called her by her name, over and over, until at last, far off in infinite space, she heard him and felt the pressure of his hands. Across all that distance it came to her, with the blinding clarity of truth, that her career, and all the things she had ever desired for herself, were as nothing beside her need of him, his need of her. Beyond the shadow of all doubt she was certain that if he let go, if he took his hands from her face even for a second, she would fall headlong. She would be bruised and battered against ten thousand unnamed stars.

As if it were for the first time, her eyes found his eyes, her mouth found his mouth. And the night, which had been between them, was now all around them.

"I've been away for a little while," she said; "but it's all right. I've come back again."

As they walked down the hill, now cloaked in the faint shadows of trees, unfolded and spread out upon the ground, and now exposed to the cool moonlight, this day, which had been a particular thing, separate and interminable, was joined to yesterday and tomorrow, and became a part of time.

*

Poor Gust! Mrs. West said to herself, remembering how the kerosene lamp on the table made a shadow of half his face, how the other half seemed all the more lined and weathered.

She took up her flashlight, turned down the lamp, and set out for the Tower, wondering how she could ever have been unkind, even in her thoughts, to Cynthia, who was such a darling. As she stepped outside the moon took refuge behind a rack of clouds. Between the light in the top of the Tower and the circle her flashlight made upon the ground lay the world, and the world was all in darkness. One could not be sure of anything. Jefferson might be sound asleep now, or he might be lying awake, staring at the dark. Earlier in the evening she had gone to his room and stood before the closed door a long time, until her courage failed her and she fled. When she went back there was no crack of light under the door. He, poor man, must be in bed.

Now, through a mist of uncertainty, Mrs. West followed the narrow path to the Tower, picking her way around the place where she knew Gust had set a mole-trap.

In order for her to reach the outside stairway which led up to Cynthia's room on the top floor, it was necessary for her to go past the door of the lower stories. As she passed this door she heard the strangest sound. It was like a soft object hitting against a wall, and fluttering. She stopped and listened to make sure. Birds in the Tower! Some one must have opened the draft in the chimney.

Inside the Tower, she pursued the fluttering with her flashlight until she discovered two young thrushes beating desperately against the walls, against the windows. "Poor things!" she murmured as she struck a match and began the complicated business of lighting a lamp. The birds fluttered more wildly than before.

When the room grew yellow with lamplight Mrs. West clutched her head and moaned for the third and last time. There were white droppings everywhere, on the piano, on the carpet, on the arms of the chaise-longue, on the window-sills. "O my dear!" she said to herself as she reached for the broom which was kept in the closet under the stairs. At sundown she had declared a truce with all confusion, but instead of withdrawing to bury its dead, as she had done, her ancient enemy had struck in darkness and in violation of all the honorable codes of war.

The birds fluttered in silent despair, as Mrs. West pursued them. The first she cornered in the window, and when she closed her hand about it the thrush was too frightened even to struggle. She carried it to the door, marveling that it did not beat its wings nor jerk its legs, that it did not even turn its head. When she opened her hand the bird flew upward into the trees as if it had been an arrow shot from a bow. It made no more noise than an arrow might have made.

The second thrush she cornered behind the door, and it lay so still in her hand that she thought for a moment it had died of fright, only she could still feel the heart beating wildly beneath the rumpled feathers. It did not fly so swiftly as the other, when she released it, but the cry it made sounded far down the night.

Mrs. West was so strangely moved by the sound that she put the broom back in the closet, turned out the lamp, and made her way back to the house without ever thinking of why it was she had come to the Tower.

For this one night Cynthia was safe.

*

Long before Thorn saw Nigel and Paul he knew that some one was coming down the hill. The moon was not bright enough for him to distinguish the outlines of their figures when they first appeared beyond the barn, but he could tell who it was by the lightness and the heaviness of their steps. He sat up, wondering whether to go toward them or stay where he was. What he had to say to Nigel couldn't very well be said in front of anyone else. No one else would understand. He'd better wait where he was until Paul had gone. He sat still, listening to the sound of their feet on the grass, and the much louder sound they made walking across the porch, and the protest of the screen door as they were received like shadows into the silence of the boathouse.

In a minute, Thorn said to himself, there would be a light on the second floor. But a minute passed, and another, and another, and still the boathouse remained as dark and as private as death.

Thorn sat in his cavern and waited until a quarter of the years of his life passed over his head, and with their passing a sudden wind sprang up, which rattled all the windows and banged all the doors of his mind, until he thought his head would crack open with the sound.

And then he heard a voice—his voice—speaking out of some other mouth, and the voice cried, *Come away! Come away!*

With his knees so unsteady that he could scarcely walk, and with all that slamming and banging going on in his head, it required his mind's most subtle devising to get from the pier to the moonlit road in front of the carpenter shop. But even after this had been accomplished, and there was no more need for silence, he could not rest. If he sat down on the steps of the carpenter shop, the rattling and the banging would get louder and louder, and they could hear it clear down there in the boathouse.

He turned toward the woods and ran swiftly, blindly, possessed by the accumulated terror of running. When he had no breath left in his body he ran until new breath came to him. And still he ran until the woods grew lighter and there was sky behind the tree trunks; until the ten-acre field lay before him, gray and still in the moonlight. There was no noise in his head any more. He leaned against the fence, waiting for the violence of his breathing to subside. Within his mind thousand upon thousand of sensations were renewed. All that he had ever heard, all that he had ever seen, each word that had been spoken, each thing as he had seen it, all whirled so swiftly and so relentlessly that his mind staggered. Year upon year he went back into time, searching involuntarily for something he had long forgotten, for something he did not want to remember.

With the full force of his will he tried to check this renewal of past time, but it was as if a fallen leaf, swept along on the current of the Little Neenah, should try with the full force of its will to remain fixed and motionless on the surface of flowing water.

He had turned away from the actual moment in order that he might not have to know that which was taking place in the boathouse, but all his running had only brought him nearer to a thing no less appalling, to a thing which was in reality that from which he had been running. He stood once more in a pasture dry, yellowed by the summer sun, and saw once more the fallow heifer, and heard the roar caught and echoing round and round within the hollow bowl which was the sky. An old internal wound that time had healed broke open. With the blood rising higher and higher toward his throat, he bent his mind in terror upon each spasm in the prolonged pattern of lust. Cold sweat broke out upon his forehead. In agony he curved his hands, and retching and spewing, he fell unconscious against the fence.

*

In the intense privacy of her room, Mrs. West unhooked and unbuttoned each part of the day, slipping it over her head or letting it fall in a pool at her feet. The laundry was still unsorted and the letter of condolence still unwritten, but they were no longer a burden to her mind. There was only the problem of Johanna.

"But of course!" she exclaimed as she unbound her hair. Of course. There was the hundred twenty-five dollars that Cousin Agnes sent her. She had meant to spend it extravagantly upon herself, and what with the bills and all, that was obviously impractical. They were much too hard up. Instead she would blow Johanna to an ocean voyage as an economy measure. On a hundred twenty-five dollars Johanna could get to Bavaria and tip taxi-drivers all the way. And Cousin Agnes would have the infinite satisfaction of knowing that her present had not gone for chicken feed. How wonderful! she thought as she stood before the mirror, combing out her hair. How marvelous! How nice!

The laundry was still at the top of the stairs, unsorted. But now that she had disposed of Johanna's troubles, she felt certain that she still had a long time to live. Perhaps before she died there would be time enough for everything.

With her reading-glasses perched precariously on the bridge of her nose, with pillows at her back and a lamp on the table beside her bed, she took up the Japanese novel where she had left off the night before:

At the side of the road he noticed a little orange tree almost buried in snow. He ordered one of his attendants to uncover it. As though jealous of the attention that the man was paying to its neighbor, a pine tree near by shook its heavily laden branches, pouring great billows of snow over his sleeve. Delighted with the scene, Genji suddenly longed for some companion with whom he might share this pleasure; not necessarily some one who loved such things as he did, but one who at least responded to them in an ordinary way.

The gate through which his carriage had to pass in order to leave the grounds was still locked. When at last the man who kept the key had been discovered, he turned out to be immensely old and feeble. . . .

Hearing the sound of a car, Mrs. West put down her book and waited; the day was not yet over. Who it was she could not imagine. Johanna retired with the sparrows. Gust was in his room in the carpenter shop, and asleep, more than likely. Bascomb was in bed, reading. When she went in to say good night to Amelia, she had found her already deep in quiet undyspeptic sleep.

Josefa's snoring came through the walls, so it could not be Josefa. The children were still up, in spite of all the rules and regulations, but they would not either of them be going or coming at this time of night. Perhaps Nigel and Paul——

She lay there quietly listening for the sound of footsteps upon the gravel. After a time the front door opened and closed.

"Whitey?" called Mrs. West, as the footsteps reached the top of the stairs.

"Yes, Muv." Whitey's head, golden and sleepy, appeared at the door.

"Was that you who came in just now with the car?"

"Yes, Muv."

"Well, what on earth were you doing?"

"Taking Mr. Carter to the nine-thirty-seven."

"O my dear. . . !" The words caught in Mrs. West's throat and came out still-born, with neither tone nor feeling. It was a very great pity that such a thing had happened. But once done it could not very well be undone. "Did he send any message, Whitey?"

Thought descended about Whitey's head like a nimbus of gold.

"Yes. He said to tell you he would write in the morning."

Mrs. West relaxed against the pillows. Poor dear, perhaps it was just as well for him that he hadn't stayed.

"Well, run along to bed. Good night darling. I love you."

"And I love you, Muv." With this answer, shyly spoken, Whitey closed the door behind him.

Once more Mrs. West took up the narrative of Prince Genji and the gatekeeper who turned out to be immensely old and feeble, but before she reached the end of the chapter she had fallen asleep, with her glasses still perched on her nose and the lamp still burning on the table beside her.

After a long time the sky above the trees grew suddenly yellow and then dark again; there was thunder in the tree-tops.

When the rain came Mrs. West turned on her side and woke up. The pillow was cool beneath her cheek, and the sound of rain steady and monotonous. The windows in the children's room. They would never think to close them.

The air in the hallway was warm and stuffy, but in the children's room it was cool. The curtains were flapping wildly in the west window, and the sill was wet.

Gently she closed the window and then turned back to the two narrow beds where her sons lay sleeping. An intense thumping under Whitey's bed told her that Rats was there. Whitey was all doubled up in a ball and breathing quietly, with his mouth slightly open. She bent down and pulled the covers over his shoulders. The lamb! Tomorrow he should have the whole day to sandpaper his canoe!

Thorn, too, was half-uncovered, but he lay on his side and perfectly straight, like a young tree. As she bent over him he stirred lightly in his sleep and turned his face to the wall.

Mrs. West sighed and made her way back to her own room. It seemed to her that in a way Thorn was no different from all the people of Meadowland, each one so extraordinary, and each one living within himself, so alone. When she came and looked at them, they always turned their faces to the wall.

Lying there awake in the darkness, listening to the rain upon the roof, upon the branches outside her window, Mrs. West thought of Prince Genji and his longing for some companion who might share his delight in the little orange tree and the heavily laden pine. Long ago she used to put her hand out in the night to feel Gordon's body beside her. She did the same thing now. Drawing her hand gently across the cool sheet and weeping quietly, she gave herself up to the remembrance of her dead marriage. But it was only for a short while; she was too much alive to sleep with ghosts.

She turned on her side and in the dark bed made a habitable place for herself, where she would be warm and sheltered for the night. High up in the trees a light was burning. It was Cynthia's light. Because of the birds she had forgotten it.

Her mind grew darker and darker as all the things which had been that day withdrew from her, one by one. She could no longer think why it was that the light burned there in the trees. What had she meant to do about it? Something. Something. There were the birds. Poor darling birds!

One of the prisoned thrushes flew into the trees like an arrow. The other cried out for joy.

THEY CAME LIKE SWALLOWS

Contents

They came like swallows and like swallows went,
And yet a woman's powerful character
Could keep a swallow to its first intent;
And half a dozen in formation there,
That seemed to whirl upon a compass-point,
Found certainty upon the dreaming air . . .

W. B. YEATS

BOOK ONE

Whose Angel Child

I

BUNNY did not waken all at once. A sound (what, he did not know) struck the surface of his sleep and sank like a stone. His dream subsided, leaving him awake, stranded, on his bed. He turned helplessly and confronted the ceiling. A pipe had burst during the winter before, and now there was the outline of a yellow lake. The lake became a bird with a plumed head and straggling tail feathers, while Bunny was looking at it. When there were no further changes, his eyes wandered down by way of the blue-and-white wallpaper to the other bed, where Robert lay sleeping. They lingered for a moment upon Robert's parted lips, upon his face drained and empty with sleep.

It was raining.

Outside, branches of the linden rose and fell in the wind, rose and fell. And November leaves came down. Bunny turned over upon the small unyielding body of Araminta Culpepper. Because he was eight, and somewhat past the age when boys are supposed to play with dolls, Araminta hung from the bed-post by day—an Indian papoose with an unbreakable expression on her face. But at night she shared his bed with him. A dozen times he drew her to him lovingly in sleep. And if he woke too soon and it was still dark, she was there. He could put out his hand and touch her.

Before him—before Peter Morison who was called Bunny—was the whole of the second Sunday in November, 1918. He moved slightly in order that Araminta Culpepper might have room for her head on the pillow. If it had been a clear day, if the sky were blue and full of sunlight, he would have to go off to Sunday school and sing hymns and perhaps hear the same old story about Daniel who was put in the lions' den, or about Elisha, or about Elijah who went to Heaven in a chariot of fire.

And what would become of his morning? As soon as he got home and spread the funny-paper out on the floor where he could look at it comfortably, some one would be sure to come along and exclaim over him: *For Heaven's sake, it's too nice a day to be in the house. Why don't you go outdoors and get some exercise?* And if he pretended that he was going to but didn't, they would come again in a little while. He would have to put on his cap and his woolly coat and mittens, whether he wanted to or not. He would be driven out of the house to roll disconsolately in a bed of leaves or to wander through the garden where nothing bloomed; where there were only sticks and crisp grass and the stalks of summer flowers.

But not now, Bunny said to himself, hearing the sound of water dripping, dropping from the roof. Not this morning. And somewhere in the front part of the house a door opened so that his mother's voice came up the stairs. A spring inside him, a coiled spring, was set free. He sat up and threw his covers to the foot of the bed. When he was washed and dressed he went downstairs. His mother was sitting at the breakfast table before the fire in the library.

"How do you do?" He threw his arms about her and planted a kiss somewhat wildly on her mouth. "How do you do and how do you do again?"

"I do very well, thank you."

She held him off in front of her to see whether he had washed thoroughly, and Bunny noticed with relief the crumbs at his father's place, the carelessly folded napkin.

"Did you have a good night? Is Robert up?"

Bunny shook his head.

"Stirring?"

"No."

"I thought that would happen."

While Bunny settled himself at the table she buttered a piece of toast for him. When she had finished she lifted the platter of bacon from the hearth.

"Robert stayed up until ten o'clock, trying to finish *The Boy Allies in Bulgaria*. I told him they wouldn't assassinate anybody without him, but he wanted to finish it just the same." She helped herself to another cup of coffee. "You know how he is."

Robert was thirteen and very trying. More so, it seemed to

Bunny, than most people. He wouldn't go to bed and he wouldn't get up. He hated to bathe or be kissed or practice his music lesson. He left the light burning in the basement. He refused to eat oysters or squash. He wouldn't get up on cold mornings and close the window. He spread his soldiers all over the carpet in the living-room and when it came time to pick them up he was never there; he had gone off to help somebody dig a cave. And likely as not he would come home late for dinner, his clothes covered with mud, his knuckles skinned, his hair full of leaves and sticks, and a hole in his brand-new sweater.

There was no time (no time that Bunny could remember) when Robert had not made him cry at least once between morning and night. Robert hid Bunny's thrift stamps and his ball of lead foil. Or he danced through the house swinging Araminta Culpepper by the braids. Or he twisted Bunny's arm, or showed him a fine new trick, the point of which was that he got his thumbs bent out of shape. Or he might do no more than sit across the room saying *Creepy-creepy-creepy* . . . pointing his finger at Bunny and describing smaller and smaller circles until the tears would not stay back any longer.

Before this day was over, it too would be spoiled like all the others. But while Robert was still upstairs in bed there was nothing for Bunny to worry about, no reason on earth why he should not enjoy his breakfast.

"It's raining," he said, and helped himself to bacon.

"I see it is." His mother took the plate from him and put it back on the hearth to keep warm for Robert. "It's been raining since five o'clock."

Bunny looked out of the window hopefully.

"Hard?"

Sometimes when it rained heavily for a considerable time he was not expected to go outside even though it cleared up afterward. The ground was too wet, they said. He might catch his death.

"Hard, Mother?"

"Like this."

Bunny tried to persuade himself that it was a heavy rain, but there was too much wind and not enough water. All the whirling and criss-crossing, the beating against the window and sliding in sudden rivulets down the glass—there was very little to it. The wind rose higher and the rain turned itself about and about. Inside, the room became intensely still. There was no sound but the logs crackling and singing in the fireplace. And because the lights were on in the daytime, the walls seemed more substantial, the way they did at night with curtains drawn across the windows and the room closed in upon itself.

"Do you think——"

Bunny hesitated, fearing at the last moment to expose himself.

"Rain before seven——" His mother got up from the table, having read his thought and answered it severely:

Rain before seven
Clear by eleven.

The words she had left unspoken remained cruelly before his eyes even when he looked down at his plate. With great concentration he began to eat his cereal. It would have taken a very little thing at that moment to spill his sorrow. Let the clock catch its breath, let one log fall with a sudden shower of sparks up the chimney, and he would have wept.

His mother sat down in the window seat and hunted through her sewing-kit impatiently. Bunny could hear her saying to herself that he was a grown man, or nearly so. Eight last August and not yet able to depend on his own strength, but coming to her again and again to be reassured.

Another time, he promised; another time he would try and not give in to weakness. If only she would not be severe with him now. He could not bear to have her that way. Not this morning. . . . Feeling altogether sorry for himself, he began to imagine what it would be like if she were not there. If his mother were not there to protect him from whatever was unpleasant—from the weather and from Robert and from his father—what would he do? Whatever would become of him in a world where there was neither warmth nor comfort nor love?

Rain washed against the window.

When his mother found the needle she had been looking for, she threaded it. Then she took up a square of white cloth. Her hand flew this way and that, over her sewing. Quite suddenly she spoke to him: "Bunny, come here."

He got down from his chair at once. But while he stood waiting before her and while she considered him with eyes that were perplexed and brown, the weight grew. The weight grew and became like a stone. He had to lift it each time that he took a breath.

"Whose angel child are you?"

By these words and by the wholly unexpected kiss that accompanied them he was made sound and strong. His eyes met hers safely. With wings beating above him and a great masculine noise of trumpets and drums he returned to his breakfast.

2

"What are you making? tea towels?"

Bunny noticed that his mother had a very curious way of shaking her head. Rather as if she were shaking away an idea that buzzed.

"They *do* look like tea towels."

The interest he took in her affairs was practically contemporary. If she were invited to a card party he wanted to know afterward who won the prize, and what they had to eat, and what the place cards were like. When she went to Peoria to shop he liked to be taken along so that he could pass judgment on her clothes, though it meant waiting for long periods of time outside the fitting-room. Nor did they always agree. About the paper in the dining-room, for instance. Bunny thought it quite nice the way it was. Especially the border, which was a hill with the same castle on it every three feet. And the same three knights riding up to each of the castles. Nevertheless, his mother had it done over in plain paper that gave him nothing to think about, and might far better, in his opinion, have been used for the kitchen, where it wouldn't so much matter.

"If they aren't tea towels, what are they?"

He waited impatiently while she bit off the thread and measured a new length from her spool.

"Diapers."

The word started a faint spinning of excitement within him. He went thoughtfully and sat down beside his mother in the window seat. From there he could see the side yard and the fence, the Koenigs' yard, and the side of the Koenigs' white house. The Koenigs were German but they couldn't help that, and they had a little girl whose name was Anna. In January Anna would be a year old. Mr. Koenig got up very early to help with the washing before he went to work. The washing-machine galumpty-lumped, galumpty-lumped, at five o'clock in the morning. By breakfast time there would be a string of white flags blowing in the autumn wind. They weren't flags, of course; they were diapers. And that was just it. People never made diapers unless somebody was going to have a baby.

Bunny listened. For a moment he was outside in the rain. He was wet and shining. His mind bent from the wind. He detached a wet leaf. But one did not speak of these things.

Always when he and his mother were alone, the library seemed intimate and familiar. They did not speak or even raise their eyes, except occasionally. Yet around and through what they were doing each of them was aware of the other's presence. If his mother was not there, if she was upstairs in her room or out in the kitchen explaining to Sophie about lunch, nothing was real to Bunny—or alive. The vermilion leaves and yellow leaves folding and unfolding upon the curtains depended utterly upon his mother. Without her they had no movement and no color.

Now, sitting in the window seat beside her, Bunny was equally dependent. All the lines and surfaces of the room bent toward his mother, so that when he looked at the pattern of the rug he saw it necessarily in relation to the toe of her shoe. And in a way he was more dependent upon her presence than the leaves or flowers. For it was the nature of his possessions that they could be what they actually were and also at certain times they could turn into knights and crusaders, or airplanes, or elephants in a procession. If his mother went downtown to cut bandages for the Red Cross (so that when he came home from school he was obliged to play by himself) he could never be sure that the transformation would take place. He might push his marbles around the devious and abrupt pattern of an oriental rug for hours, and they would never be anything but marbles. He put his hand into the bag now and drew out a yellow agate which became King Albert of Belgium.

A familiar *thump* brought him somewhat painfully again into the world of the library. *Thump thump thump*—all the way across the ceiling. Robert was getting up.

"I've been thinking—"

Bunny looked down in time to see his mother's hand spread over his and enclose it.

"—about the back room. I told Robert he could have a bed in there, and some chairs, and fix it up the way he likes. He's getting old enough now so that he likes to be by himself."

Bunny nodded. Sometimes when he and his mother were alone they discussed Robert in this way, and what should be done about him.

"If we do that, of course, there won't be anybody to stay with you."

He liked to have her bend down and brush the top of his head lightly with her cheek. But he would have preferred another time. Now it confused him. He turned his eyes toward the window and the damp trees, toward the rain-drenched ground. As soon as the window was clear enough for him to see through, a fresh gust drove against it from the other side and everything blurred. It was that way when his mother kissed him. This talk about moving Robert into the back room, where his Belgian city was, where he kept his magic lantern. What had that to do with diapers?

"You see—" His mother spread the white cloth over her knees, folded it, laid it with the others in a pile. "What we need is another person in the family. At least one other person."

"I think we're getting along quite well the way things are."

"Perhaps. But the room you're in. It's ever so much too——"

Her hand opened and lay still.

Some one to fill up his room. Like the Mr. Crumb that stayed at Miss Brew's, three houses down on the same side of the street.

"We're not going to take in roomers, are we?"

"No, not roomers, exactly. I wouldn't like that."

"I wouldn't either."

Mr. Crumb had such a large nose. It would be upsetting to wake and find him in Robert's bed early in the morning.

"What I had in mind was a small brother or a small sister—it wouldn't matter which, would it? So you wouldn't rattle around in there the way you do when you are all alone."

"No, I suppose not. But does that mean—"

His mother was not satisfied with just him. She wanted a little girl.

When she got up and went out to the kitchen, he did not follow her. Instead he sat absolutely still, watching the yellow leaves contract; watching the spider swing itself out upon the ceiling.

3

Although the library had been familiar at breakfast time, Bunny knew that it was now subject to change, to uncertainty. His father had come home again and would be home, said the big clock in the hall, for the day. . . . The little brass clock with clear glass sides emerged out of a general silence, asserting that it was not so; that Mr. Morison would go out again after dinner. . . . They argued then. The grandfather's clock made slow involved statements which the other replied to briefly. "Quarter of ten," said the grandfather's clock, untroubled by the irrelevance. "Ten till," said the little brass clock on the mantel. So long as that went on, Bunny could not be sure of anything.

His father had settled himself in his chair, with the Sunday paper. From time to time he solemnly turned the pages. When he read aloud he expected everybody to listen.

"*What is Spanish influenza? . . . Is it something new? . . . Does it come from Spain? . . . The disease now occurring in this country and called 'Spanish influenza' resembles a very contagious kind of 'cold' accompanied by fever, pains in the head, eyes, back, or other parts of the body, and a feeling of severe sickness. In most of the cases the symptoms disappear after three or four days, the patient rapidly recovering. Some of the patients, however, develop pneumonia, or inflammation of the ear, or meningitis, and many of these complicated cases die. Whether this so-called 'Spanish influenza' is identical with the epidemic of earlier years is not known. . . .*"

The word epidemic was new to Bunny. In his mind he saw it, unpleasantly shaped and rather like a bed pan.

". . . *Although the present epidemic is called 'Spanish influenza,' there is no reason to believe that it originated in Spain. Some writers who have studied the question believe that the epidemic came from the Orient and they call attention to the fact that the Germans mention the disease as occurring along the eastern front in the summer and fall of 1917.*"

By the calm way that his father crossed one knee over the other it was clear that he was concerned with the epidemic for the same reason he was interested in floods in China, what happened in Congress, and family history—because he chose to be concerned with such things.

When Bunny was very small he used to wake in the night sometimes with a parched throat and call for a drink of water. Then he would hear stumbling and lurching, and the sound of water running in the bathroom. The side of a glass struck his teeth. He drank thirstily and fell back into sleep. . . . Until one night across the intervening darkness, from the room directly across the hall, a voice said, *Oh, get it yourself!* For the first time in his life Bunny was made aware of the fact that he had a father. And thoroughly shocked, he did as he was told.

Ever since that time he had been trying to make a place for his father within his own arranged existence—and always unsuccessfully. His father was not the kind of man who could be fit into anybody's arrangement except his own. He was too big, for one thing. His voice was too loud. He was too broad in the shoulder, and he smelled of cigars. In the family orchestra his father played the piano, Robert the snare drum, Bunny the bass drum and cymbals. His father started the music going with his arms, with his head. And in no time at all the sound was tremendous—filling the open center of the room, occupying the space in corners and behind chairs.

". . . *In contrast to the outbursts of ordinary coughs and colds, which usually occur in the cold months, epidemics of influenza may occur at any season of the year, thus the present epidemic raged most intensely in Europe in May, June, and July. Moreover, in the case of ordinary colds, the general symptoms (fever, pain, depression) are by no means so severe* . . ."

Bunny saw that his mother was threatened with a sneeze. She closed her eyes resignedly and waited.

". . . *or as sudden in their outset as they are in influenza. Finally, ordinary colds do not spread through the community so rapidly or so extensively as does influenza. . . .*"

Bunny turned to his father. How was it that his father did not know? that he could go on reading?

"*Ordinarily the fever lasts from three to four days and the patient recovers. . . . As in other catching diseases, a person who has only a mild attack of the disease may give a very severe attack to others. . . .*"

The sneeze came. His mother's composure was destroyed by it. She fumbled for her handkerchief.

". . . *When death occurs it is usually the result of a complication.*"

"James——"

"Yes?"

"Do you mind reading about something else?"

"If it will make you any happier."

The largest and the smallest of Bunny's agates raced along a red strip in the pattern of the library rug. Maybe his mother would come around to his way of thinking—that it was neither wise nor necessary to take on a baby at this time. Later perhaps. . . . Remembering the wallpaper in the dining-room he felt sure that she would go ahead with her plans. From what he had observed (he went to call on the Koenigs occasionally when there was nothing better to do) it would mean a great deal of confusion.

"Bunny, I've lost my handkerchief. Get me another, like a good child, will you?"

Bunny nodded. They would have to buy dresses, knitted hoods, and soft woolly sweaters. . . . The race would be over in two shakes. Then he would get the handkerchief. He could always finish what he was doing before he got up and went on an errand for his mother. It was understood between them. The smallest agate was dropping behind.

"Son. . . ."

The folded paper lay across his father's knees.

"Did you hear what your mother said?"

"Yes, Dad."

It was a very little way to that wide green opening in the pattern which was the goal, with a chance that the smallest agate might . . .

"Then what are you waiting for?"

His father spoke quietly, but his voice and his firmness were like two unreasonable hands laid upon Bunny's shoulders. Bunny knew even while he resisted them that it was of no use. They would propel him straight up the front stairs.

"Nothing," he said, and got to his feet.

From the doorway he looked back. The library had changed altogether. In the chimney the dark red bricks had become separate and rough. There were coarse perpendicular lines which he had not noticed before. And the relation between the pattern of the rug and the toe of his mother's shoe escaped him.

The little brass clock had struck ten already, and now the grandfather's clock in the hall was getting started. There was a great to-do. The grandfather's clock stammered and cleared its throat like an old person. Once it had begun, nothing could stop it. Though the house fell down, it would go right on, heavily:

Bonng . . . bonng . . . bonng . . .

And each sound as it descended through the air was wreathed and festooned with smoke from his father's cigar.

"*Charlie Chaplin married. . . . The bride, a motion-picture actress. . . .*"

Bunny saw black clothes, a mustache and cane, feet widely turned. About the baby, he decided—it was just as well that his father had not been told.

4

From somewhere out of sight, beyond the passageway, came a soft *tput-tput-tput*. . . . Sadness descended upon Bunny, sadness and a heavy sense of change. There was only one thing in the world that made such a sound: his steamboat. Robert had filled the bathtub with water and was playing with his steamboat.

Bunny stood and looked in the door of the back room, which was to be Robert's. It was now empty except for his village.

Before long, Robert would have it. Robert's clothes would hang from hooks in the closet. Robert's shoes would tumble over each other on the closet floor. *Possession's nine-tenths of the law*, Robert always said when Bunny wanted his steamboat and Robert did not care to give it up.

That was because Robert was five and a half years older than he was. If *he* said that, Robert paid no attention to him. He had to get things from Robert by bargaining, or by appealing to his mother. Only she had said, definitely, that Robert was to have this room. It was all decided, just as it was decided what Robert was going to be when he grew up—*a lawyer*, Robert said to people who asked him. Always that; never anything else. (Bunny was going to be an architect.) Nothing would do but that Robert must practice law, try cases before a jury, like Grandfather Blaney. And be presented with a gold-headed cane, inscribed *To Robert Morison from the grateful citizens of Logan, Illinois.*

Nothing on earth could prevent Robert from becoming a lawyer; and in the same way nothing could prevent him from taking possession of the back room. Bunny knew that when the time came he would have to find another place for his blackboard and his magic lantern. He would have to pick up his Belgian village piece by piece and rebuild it in some other part of the house where people would be stepping over it every little while and complaining. And his magic lantern? What would he ever do about that? There were no dark green shades anywhere but in this room. His clothes closet had no window and was pitch dark, but it was not big enough. And besides, where would he attach the cord?

The soft *tput-tput* came to an end and Robert began talking to himself arrogantly. Bunny listened for a moment and then went and looked around the corner into the bathroom. Robert was declaiming, and in order to see his face in the mirror over the washstand he had pulled down the toilet-cover and climbed up on it. There balancing, he continued:

> "*And if thou sayst I am not peer*
> *To any man in Scotland here* . . ."

His sleeves were wet to the elbow, both of them. There was a tear in his stocking, acquired since breakfast. And one leg hung down, stiffly. Robert's *affliction*, people said, when he was not there to hear them.

Years ago, when Bunny was no more than a baby, and such a thin baby that he had to be carried on a pillow—Robert was hurt. Bunny knew only what he had been told. How Robert hopped onto the back end of a buggy and was run over. And they had to take his leg off, five inches above the knee. That was why Irene went up to Chicago and came back with the beautiful soldiers, the cavalrymen, which Robert kept on top of the bookcase, out of reach.

Now Robert was rehearsing. When he was satisfied with certain gestures he bared his teeth at his reflection in the mirror and going back a little, began:

"*And if thou sayst I am not peer*
To any man in Scotland here,
Highland
or low-land,
Far
or
near
Lord Angus, thou hast
LIED!"

The effect was fearful, even from out in the hall. Bunny withdrew quietly and went into his mother's room to get the handkerchief. Then he took it down to her and came up again, this time by the back stairs.

5

Sunday morning was an excellent time for invading a city. It was almost noon before Bunny's imagination flagged. But very suddenly the scene changed. Walls, gates, roofs, broken parapets and towers were then laid bare in simple actuality—two collapsible drinking-cups, a ruler, a block of stone, cardboard, brown paper, three pencils, and a notched wooden spool. After that it was no longer possible to pretend that his lead soldiers were shouting to one another and defending a Belgian town.

In actual weariness Bunny got up and went out to the back hall, where the clothes-hamper stood, where his mother kept the ammonia-bottle and rags for cleaning. She would know some way for him to pass the interminable time between now and time for dinner. . . . He felt his way down the gloomy, boxed-in stairs.

She was in the kitchen when he found her, at the table, with spoons laid out in rows and the silver polish open at her elbow. Bunny sat down without a word, and twisted his legs through the rungs of the high kitchen stool. The kitchen always seemed older than the rest of the house, although it was not. Older and more seasoned. Bunny could remember being here before he could remember anything else. The walls were dark with scrubbing, and the surfaces shone wherever there was metal or porcelain. Turnip tops flourished in bowls along the window sill.

The spoons his mother was polishing were plain for the most part. Not very interesting to do. But she looked through them until she found one with her name written on it—*Elizabeth*—and with roses and pineapples, and the sun going down behind the Kentucky State Capitol. As soon as Bunny took up a piece of rag and began to polish his mother's name, the sadness slipped away. Now that he was in the kitchen beside her, it was impossible to care very much whether Robert got the back room or whether he didn't.

Outside, the sky was growing lighter. The rain came down unevenly, in spurts. The kitchen curtains were turning brighter, fading, and turning bright again. Bunny looked up in time to see the pantry door open. It was Irene, tall and straight-shouldered, in a blue raincoat.

"Surprise!" she said.

He threw himself upon her.

"Nobody told me you were coming."

"Surprise, I said!"

She took hold of him by his arms, above the elbow, and began to turn. Round they went in the middle of the floor with the room tilting this way and that. Round they went. Round his mother went, and the cookstove, and Sophie in a pink apron, and the sink . . . faster . . . faster . . . the table . . . the stove . . . the sink . . . table . . . stove . . . sink streaking longer . . . upward and longer. . . .

After they stopped whirling, the kitchen went round and round for a while, all by itself. Always when Irene came for Sunday dinner it was that way. His mother alone was calm and unshaken. She got up from the table and went to meet Irene. They kissed haphazardly, in front of the stove.

Irene was his mother's sister, but she did not resemble his mother in the least. Irene's hair was much lighter than his mother's, and her eyes were a different color. His mother was dark. Her hair was almost black, and so were her eyebrows, and she was much heavier. They both talked about dieting all the time. *An ounce of prevention*, they said, and then ate hard, awful-tasting biscuits with their tea. (With Irene it was just talk; she didn't need to be any thinner, but when his mother went to buy clothes, the saleswoman said, "Something for the stylish stout?") And their hands felt entirely different and looked entirely different. From Irene's hands he drew excitement, and from his mother's the fact that she loved him. Irene and his mother were as different as the two faces of a coin. And yet they never seemed conscious of the difference. They loved being together. And the things they said to each other had little meaning, often, for other people. For instance, if Irene remarked *Butter's what I'm after*—they both grew hysterical. When he inquired what was so funny about that, they didn't explain.

"Have you enough to eat, Bess?"

Bunny looked toward his mother and was relieved when she nodded. It would be a great pity if Irene went right away.

"I mean *plenty*," Irene insisted. "Because there's no use in my staying if it isn't going to be worth while."

Then without waiting for an answer she went to take off her coat.

Bunny followed discreetly at her heels. The dining-room as they passed through seemed braced and ready for excitement. Although it was only a quarter after twelve, the little brass clock in the library started to strike. Irene did that to things. Most people's rubbers came off easily, but one of hers now sailed halfway across the floor. The other had to be rescued from under the hall-tree. And the moment she began pulling at her gloves there was a great burst of singing from above:

"*O when I die*
Don't bury me at all,
Just pickle my bones
In alkyhol . . ."

Bunny felt called upon to explain.

"It's only Robert," he said. "Upstairs, playing with my steamboat." Then by way of an afterthought, "Where's Agnes?"

"At her Grandmother Hiller's. She's there for the day."

It was not an unreasonable place for her to be, though as a rule Irene and little Agnes came together. After dinner he and Agnes played house behind the sofa. Agnes was the mother. She made beds and dusted and swept and talked to the grocery man over the telephone (he was the grocery man) and had lunch ready for her fat sofa-pillow children when they got home from school. At the end of the day the father came home (he was the father) and spanked all the sofa-pillows that hadn't minded their mother and gave French harps to all that had.

Friday was the usual day for Agnes to go to her grandmother's. On Friday his mother and Irene went to their bridge club. After school he and Agnes walked home together—Agnes to her Grandmother Hiller's and he to his Grandmother Morison's, who lived with Aunt Clara and Uncle Wilfred Paisley in a square white house in the same block. At five-thirty his mother called for him in the car. Irene was with her and they were wearing their best clothes. And then they stopped and got Agnes. That was the way it usually was, and he wouldn't have thought anything about Agnes's being there today except for the fact that a moment ago Irene was bright and cheerful. Now she was staring moodily past the top of his head.

"Irene?"

Apparently she did not hear him. If he asked her what he wanted to ask her, she might not like it. She might call him a *curiosity cat.* To keep himself from asking, he watched her pocketbook swinging back and forth on the tip of her index finger.

"Irene, why is it that Agnes is at her Grandmother Hiller's?"

"She's there to see her father."

The pocketbook stopped swinging and slid to the floor.

Bunny was deeply startled. He bent over and picked it up for her, but she did not seem to want it particularly. Agnes's father was Uncle Boyd Hiller, but he was not mentioned in the family. Or if he was, it was always by his initials—*B.H.* Never by his name. Not since the time they had to go to court to get little Agnes away from him. After that he went away and they didn't know where he was, or anything about him. Not for a long while. If he had come back now, it might mean all sorts of things. It might mean that he had come to take Agnes away. Or that Irene would have to go and live with him, the way she did before. It might mean——

The singing broke out again, on the landing, directly above them.

> "*'Tis better by far*
> *Not to spit at all*
> *Than to spit too far*
> *And hit the wall.*"

Robert appeared, steamboat in hand, singing. He had made a half-hearted attempt at combing his hair, but blond wisps stuck out in all directions. Irene's face brightened as soon as she saw him. Robert, from the very beginning, had been her favorite. But Bunny did not mind. He had his mother. And besides, Irene never thought he ought to be outdoors when he wasn't.

"Don't tell everything you know, Bunny."

Irene got up now and went toward the stairs. Bunny shook his head. He did, sometimes. He did tell everything he knew. But he didn't mean to. And this time he was practically certain that Robert (who didn't like to be kissed) would dodge suddenly before Irene could catch him.

6

Irene had a way of making things memorable.

So it seemed to Bunny as his father held out his mother's chair for her and they all sat down to dinner.

Because Irene was here, it was an occasion. Like Thanksgiving or Christmas. They unfolded their napkins with a more than ordinary anticipation. What they said was of no importance; merely to pass the time until Sophie appeared with the roast chicken and the occasion was confirmed. Then there were exclamations. His mother leaned forward anxiously, lest the chicken fail to be as tender as it looked. Bunny eyed the drumsticks. One of them went to him, as a rule.

"Hopefully yours," his father said, pointing the carving fork at him. And they all laughed. Even Sophie.

Then his father considered the chicken carefully. There was a moment of tension, and the knife slid in. Bunny could not help feeling that they would remember this afterward as the best roast chicken that ever they had.

"Just give me a little, James," his mother said—for she was always served first. "And no potato."

"Well you have to eat *some*thing. You'll get sick!"

"Yes, I know. . . . At the Friday club Amelia Shepherd was telling about a woman in Peoria who. . . ."

"There's no sense to it," his father said, gloomily. Then his disapproval passed, for lack of opposition, and he went on carving. A small slice of breast went to his mother, a much larger slice to Irene. When Robert got his wing, Bunny felt that he could look no more. He turned his head quickly and focused his attention upon the Japanese pilgrims who were climbing in and out among the folds of the curtains. He heard Sophie pass behind him and go back to the other side of the table. When he opened his eyes the drumstick was there, right on his plate. And the wishbone beside it.

Happily, Bunny looked about him at the circle of faces. His mother's eyes were dark brown, like his own. Robert's were hazel. Aunt Eth lived in Rockford and she had hazel eyes also. But Irene's eyes were gray.

Looking at her, he was reminded of his own drooping shoulders (hers were so straight) and thrust them back. No one noticed or thought to comment on his posture, so he relaxed after a second and began to eat.

The conversation became serious. There was talk about the war, and how the rumor started that the war was over. And talk about the last election, which his father took into his own hands immediately. When Bunny grew up he was going to vote Republican because his father was a Republican, and his father before him. It was all settled that way. Arthur Cook's father was a Democrat and they had a picture of President Wilson framed over the fireplace in their library. But his father said that was all Tomfoolishness. When Hughes was running against Wilson, Arthur Cook wore a little brass mule on the lapel of his overcoat and Bunny wore an elephant. And there was a time when they didn't walk home from school together in the afternoon. But that was all over now.

"Smart, I grant you——"

His father poured out the last spoonful of gravy and gave the bowl to Sophie, to be refilled.

"Exceedingly smart. But he made the blunder of a lifetime when he asked in the name of the American flag that the people of this country re-elect a Democratic Congress. In the name of the flag he asked the people for party control. And when he said that, he stepped down from the high office of the Presidency and became nothing more nor less than the leader of the Democratic party. If there's any greater mistake that a President could make, I'd like to know it!"

Although his father looked straight at him Bunny knew that he was not supposed to answer.

The statement hung on the air unanswered, burning with force, with enormous conviction, while his father helped himself to mashed potatoes.

"And what does it get him? Just tell me that. He loses control of the House and the Senate, both. He's still President, of course. They can't take that away from him. And so long as this country is at war, people should support him along patriotic lines. But there's nothing in the Constitution which gives the President right to undivided control of the legislative bodies, in wartime or any other time. And when it comes to furthering his own personal ambitions and the ambitions of a group of Southern Democrats who completely upset the machinery of national expenditure and taxation—when you come right down to it—*risk* the economic welfare of this country in the interests of . . ."

Bunny twisted in his chair uncomfortably. He remembered something that he had meant to tell his mother. About Arthur Cook. When his father held forth in this way, the quiet which belonged to the dining-room seemed to have escaped to other parts of the house. He thought of the upstairs bedrooms and how still they must be. His mother was eating her salad quite calmly, in spite of President Wilson. When she put her fork down, he might lean toward her and—but it was not easy to describe things. Especially things that had happened. For him, to think of things was to see them—schoolyard, bare trees, gravel and walks, furnace-rooms, the eaves along the south end of the building. Where among so many things should he begin?

Robert would not have had any trouble. *We were playing three-deep*, Robert would have said. *And Arthur Cook got sick.* That would have been the end of it, so far as Robert was concerned. He would not have felt obliged to explain how Arthur ran twice around the circle without tagging anybody. And how he stopped playing and said *I feel funny.* How he went over by the bicycle racks then, and sat down.

"At school last Friday——"

But he had spoken too loud.

"How would it be, son——"

His father let President Wilson alone for a minute and turned his entire attention on Bunny, so that he felt naked and ashamed, as if he were under a glaring light.

"—if you kept quiet until I finish what I'm saying?"

That was all. His father had not spoken unkindly. He was not sent from the table. No punishment was threatened. Nevertheless, Bunny withdrew sadly into his plate. And not even a second helping all the way round could restore his pleasure in this day.

His father commenced eating, and the conversation broke apart. Robert began to explain about the tie-rack he was making at school.

"You take and take a piece of wood about so long——" He indicated how long, with his hands.

Bunny could tell at a glance that Irene was not interested in Robert's tie-rack. He was not interested in Robert's tie-rack, either. He was not interested in anything of Robert's except the soldiers Robert would not let him play with, which were Robert's dearest possession.

"And when you get it planed down nice and even, you take a piece of sandpaper . . ."

Through the dining-room window Bunny could see Old

John stretched out on the back porch with his head resting on his black paws. John was very old and decrepit. In winter he got rheumatism in his legs and he had to be carried in and out of the house. Half his days were spent in looking for bones that he had long since dug up. And often he thumped his tail fondly when there was nobody there.

Robert finished with the tie-rack eventually. And then his mother and Irene exchanged recipes.

"I stir it," his mother said, "without ever changing the direction of the spoon. . . ."

"In cold water," Irene said, "and then I let it come to a boil, slowly. . . ."

Once when they were in the bathroom and Irene was in her thin nightgown, she said, *Bunny Morison, stop looking at my legs!* And he could not stop blushing. But why did she . . . And another time they went for a walk out past the edge of the town. They carried a book to read, and sandwiches in a pasteboard box. At the first shady lane (it was in June) they turned off and settled themselves under a tree. Irene read to him out of the book, which was about boy heroes of Belgium. And a cow came on the other side of the fence and looked at them. When they got hungry they opened the box and ate all the sandwiches. That was over a year ago, and there was dust on the road. The air was heavy. Irene's voice sounded like swords clashing, slashing at the leaves overhead.

He tried now to get her attention, to ask her if she remembered that day when they went out beyond the edge of town, but her face was shadowed by inattention. By the same vacant look that she had a little while ago in the front hall. His mother was talking about Karl: Would his father arrange to have Karl come some day next week—Monday or Tuesday—and take down the screens?

Meanwhile, Robert, unhindered, had eaten a third helping of everything. He was buttering a slice of bread whole, which he shouldn't; he should break the bread into pieces and then butter it. And there would be very little left for Old John.

When Sophie came to clear the plates away, Bunny noticed that everyone at the table fell into a silence which lasted, usually, while she brushed away the crumbs and until she brought the cream for coffee. Over the dessert his mother and Irene fell to discussing clothes. Something was gathered, his mother said, with a pleat in the back.

Bunny could not see what they found in such matters to interest them. He could have left the table when Robert did, or when his father rose and went into the library to take his Sunday-afternoon nap, but there was still something that Bunny had to say to his mother. He waited until there was a break in the conversation; until Irene began thumbing the pages of *Elite*, which she had brought with her to the table.

"At school, we were playing three-deep——"

"Broad bands of sealskin——"

Irene held up the magazine for his mother to see.

"—with a hobble skirt."

"It's too tight-waisted," his mother said. "I'm not in the market for anything that isn't cut along the lines of a circus tent."

Bunny peered across the table, hoping to see the picture of an elephant, but there wasn't any. Nothing but women's clothes: coats that were *gathered*, he supposed bitterly, and blouses.

"Mother——"

"You could wear that, Irene."

His mother had taken the magazine and was thumbing the pages wistfully.

"But so could you!"

"Don't be silly."

"Don't *you* be." Irene was excited. The very smallest spark was enough to set her off. "You could copy it easy as anything, Bess. And with the fullness where it is . . ."

Bunny thought of the schoolyard: gravel and dirt, with hardly a shred of grass; bare trees; the bicycle racks; and Arthur Cook's sick eyes.

"Mother, listen to me!"

He spoke louder than before, and plucked at her sleeve.

By the way her hand closed over his, he knew that she had heard him. All the time. And that sooner or later she would pay attention to nobody but him. Only just now he must keep still. He must not interrupt until they had finished what they were saying.

7

Bunny's nap was nearing its conclusion. Without making a sound, without moving, his body detached itself from the sofa. He moved freely among certain of the planets—Mars, the pink one, and Saturn with its rings. His dream, worn thin, began to give way around him. There was a moment of intense buzzing while he drifted back to earth. . . . Then, abruptly, he was awake.

Irene and his mother were having an important conversation at the other end of the living-room. Their voices were low and even, and he could just distinguish one word from another.

"You sure it isn't the war?" his mother said.

"Why should it be that?"

Bunny wanted to look at them, but he did not dare. Irene might notice him and stop talking. As a rule, people did, if they saw he was listening. They said *Little pitchers have big ears.* On the other hand, there were ways of keeping from being noticed. Playing under tables and behind chairs, very quietly. Or if it was night and he was away from home, getting extremely sleepy, so that they had to put him on a couch somewhere and cover him up. After a while if he kept his eyes closed and breathed regularly, they thought he was asleep. That way he found out all sorts of things.

"Well, because"—his mother spoke more distinctly now—"because his company is ordered to France and you may not ever see him again. It could be that, Irene, and nothing more than that."

"It could be, but I don't think it is . . . I wish you'd seen him, Bess. He looks much older."

"So do we all. I found three gray hairs yesterday."

Bunny's mind stirred lightly within his shell. Around one of innumerable corners he came upon a staircase that he remembered—not the one here, not this staircase at home. He looked down, cautiously, and saw Agnes kicking and squirming in her father's arms. Agnes was frightened. She kept saying, *I want my mamma . . . I want my mamma . . .* over and over. Whose house it was Bunny did not know. The remembrance was cloudy and uncertain, like a dream remembered in the midst of breakfast: Uncle Boyd carrying Agnes in his arms and the door closing upon them. There was meaning to it, and possibility of explanation; only he never dared to ask. And then Irene walked past him, talking to herself. He spoke to her, but she didn't even know that he was there. At the head of the stairs she waited, as if there was something she had just that minute thought of. Then she fell down, one step at a time, bumping.

"He looks older in a different way, and sad. It's very hard to explain, exactly."

"No doubt."

"But if you'd seen him! It's as if he were thinking all the time—even while he is making polite conversation—that he'd missed something people can't afford to miss."

"Whose fault could that be?"

Bunny had never heard his mother's voice sound quite so dry and unbelieving.

"His own, I suppose—but everything's that, in a way, for everybody."

"In a way. But I remember the last two months that you lived with him. I remember that you were like a crazy woman."

"I know I was. Though much of it was on account of Agnes. He was so jealous. But when I try to remember his fits of temper, and how unreasonable he was, I think of all sorts of things *I* started."

Through eyes that were nearly closed Bunny caught a glimpse of the living-room: moss-green wallpaper, and the green carpet, and a well of green shadow in the far corner of the room where Irene and his mother sat talking. He was not entirely awake, so that he saw things peculiarly. The white woodwork was unattached to the walls. The shape of the chairs was ambiguous. At a word from him (a magic word) the sofa would curve its back differently and the chair-arms protrude bunches of carved wooden grapes. The golden bowl which was suspended upside-down from the ceiling by three chains was now the size of a buckeye cup and now as large as the wading-pool at the Chautauqua grounds. Time and again, while he squinted his eyes, the walls relaxed and became shapeless.

He lost track of the conversation and when he started listening again, Irene was saying, ". . . and she had her son with her, a youngster about eleven years old. And every time they came on deck she'd light into him because he was sending all his post-cards to the same boy, instead of spreading them around.

"Boyd couldn't see anything funny in that, and after I explained, he still wasn't amused. It was completely unimportant . . ."

Bunny's eyelashes brushed and became momentarily entangled. Against the light from the bay window they seemed as large and long as spears. His mother got up and went over to the mantel. Then she came back and sat down again, with a box on her knee.

"Will you have some candy?"

"So soon after dinner. How can you, Bess?"

"You've forgotten what it's like to be—"

"Oh, of course. I did forget, as a matter of fact. I mean I forgot you were— But it is important that people laugh at the same things. Or at least enjoy them in something like the same way."

"If you went back to him, Irene, you'd find——"

"He was there when I took Agnes, this noon. I went in, anyway. I shouldn't have, I suppose. But I thought what's the use of going out of my way to make trouble when there's been enough already."

The last time Uncle Boyd came to the house, before he went away, Bunny saw him. Bunny was playing in the front hall with a china wolf-hound that used to be at Grandmother Blaney's before she died. And he looked out of the front window and saw Uncle Boyd coming up the walk. The doorbell rang. His father came to the door and opened it. And there he was—tall and thin, with a gray streak across his hair. And he said, *Is Irene here?* And his father said, *I haven't the least idea!*

"Boyd was very pleasant. He asked after you, Bess, and said how much he thought of you——"

"Yes?"

"And when I got up to go, he went with me as far as the front walk. We stood by the hitching-post and I said good-by, and he said good-by and he was very glad to have seen me, and then he shook hands very formally as if I were a visiting lady from Scotland. And then he went all to pieces. . . . The things he said—you wouldn't believe me if I told you. Standing there on the sidewalk with the tears running down his cheeks. . . . It was a mistake. For two whole years he had known it was all a mistake. And the way he found out was that he caught himself looking for me wherever he went. He'd notice some woman at the theater or walking in a park, and the back of her head would be like me. And he'd follow her, thinking possibly . . ."

Bunny narrowed his eyes as his mother got up, with the box of candy in her hand, and put it on the mantelpiece, where it wouldn't be so continual a temptation. Then she said, "Speaking of the backs of women's heads—I took Robert aside the other day and made him promise that if anything happened to me he'd break all my cut-glass. I don't want some other woman using it when I'm gone."

Bunny's eyes flew open. In the nick of time he remembered that he was pretending to be asleep, closed them, and opened them again—more deliberately. The spears waved. He was in a field of green corn.

8

The intense part of the afternoon was over when Irene got up to go home. Bunny and his mother were alone after she left. And it was clear that his mother was despondent over something, for she stopped hemming diapers and gazed thoughtfully into the fire for a long while. Once she sighed.

At the right moment Bunny told her about Arthur Cook, and how Arthur got sick at school. Bunny heard the nurse telling his teacher, outside in the hall, that it was a clear case of flu. This time there was no doubt about his mother's interest. She sat looking at him anxiously, the whole time. And certain portions of his narrative had to be repeated.

"Bunny, why didn't you tell me? Why didn't you tell me last Friday, instead of waiting until now?"

He started to explain fully, but she had already picked up the receiver of the telephone.

"I'm going to call Arthur's mother, and find out how he is. And while I think of it, there's something you can do for me: We're out of cream. Sophie forgot to order any. And if I make cornbread for supper, we'll need butter as well. Half a pound. . . . *Nine-nine-two.* . . . *Yes, that's right.* . . . I could send Robert for it when he gets home from Scout meeting, but he may be late."

It was the unexpected that happened, always. The empty gun, his Grandmother Morison said, that killed people. He would have to put on his rubbers and his coat and cap and gloves and go outdoors.

Weekdays he came straight home from school so that he could have his mother all to himself. At quarter after four Sophie wheeled in the teacart and there was a party: little cakes with white icing on them, a glass of milk for him and tea for his mother. Then he sat on her lap while she read to him from *Toinette's Philip* or from *The Hollow Tree and Deep Woods Book.* About Mr. Crow and the C-X pie. Or about Mr. Possum's Uncle Silas who went to visit Cousin Glenwood in the city and came home with a "man" and a lot of new clothes and a bag of shinny sticks.

When his mother read to him, her voice fell softly from above. It turned with the flames. Like the flames, it was full of shadows. While she was reading he would look up sometimes and discover that she had yawned; or she would stop and look into the fireplace absently, so that he would have to remind her to go on reading.

But today there was no pleasant hour with her before his father came home. When he threw open the back door, the sky overhead was clear, the air thin and without warmth. Old John rose and extended his paws unsteadily. Bunny recognized it as a gesture toward following him. But having made the gesture, Old John could do no more. He collapsed feebly upon his square of carpet.

If it had been Robert, Bunny thought sadly—if it had been Robert that called him, Old John would have come along.

Hoping to catch something off guard, he crossed the garden walk. But the sunlight was spread too evenly upon the ground and woven too firmly into the silence under the grape-arbor. Bunny did not disturb it in the least by his coming.

Only the Lombardy poplars were a trifle unprepared, so that when he picked up a stick and broke it, their few remaining leaves were seized with a musical agitation.

For a second Bunny wanted to climb up on the kitchen roof, which started behind the flue and from there sloped down almost to the ground, over the cellar stairs. Then he turned and went directly toward the front walk. An iron picket was missing from the fence. Once upon a time he could slip through by ducking his head. Now he had to bend double and squeeze. He was growing. Size nine or nine and a half. And yet the sidewalk seemed no farther away than it had ever been. With his head down, his eyes fastened upon the cement, he started toward the store.

Step on a crack
You'll break your mother's back

At the corner he looked up, for no reason. The outer branches of the elm trees met high overhead, shielding the street, which was empty and strewn with dead leaves. Mrs. Lolly's store was in the next block. Her porch was old and rickety and sagged in places, but it was high enough to stand up under. On the hard ground underneath Mrs. Lolly's porch three boys were kneeling, their arms outstretched, playing marbles. Johnny Dean, Ferris (who smoked cigarettes), and Mike Holtz. The afternoon became complicated—though it was clear, after the rain, and transparent to the farthest edges.

At the intersection Bunny crossed over. His knees were becoming drowsy with fear. He could go back, of course. He could go home and come again a little later. But what would his mother think? Opposite the store he crossed back again. Mike Holtz didn't see him, but he saw Mike Holtz. Saw his white face, jeering, his cap pulled down over one ear, his dirty fat knuckles. . . . If he could get as far as the steps, Bunny told himself carefully. He came to the steps, mounted over the very center of his fright, and closed the door safely behind him.

Mrs. Lolly was middle-aged and sagging, like her porch. She kept a yellow pencil in the knot at the back of her hair. Bunny was grateful to her, as he was grateful now to all things—things standing about in boxes and cases, on shelves all the way up to the ceiling. Everything was so substantial. The crates of apples and oranges, the pears in tissue-paper, the enormous cabbages. And most substantial of all—a very old woman who was worrying with her shawl.

Mrs. Lolly added up figures on a paper bag. When she stopped and looked at him blindly, Bunny saw that her eyes were full of arithmetic.

"Are you in a hurry?"

He shook his head. Not at all in a hurry. Not in the least. What he most wanted was for time to stand emphatically still, the way the sun and the moon did for Joshua.

The old woman, waiting, sucked at her teeth one after another until the pin came out of her shawl.

"Seven"—Mrs. Lolly went on counting—"and two to carry."

Bunny pressed his nose against the glass case. Looking intently, he tasted gumdrops, licorice, caramels, candy-corn.

"In Chicago," the old woman said, as she fastened her shawl closely about her shoulders, "I hear there's people dying of influenza. And in St. Louis."

A pleasant imaginary voice said: *Help yourself, Bunny. Take as much of anything there is in the case as you want.*

Mrs. Lolly jabbed the pencil straight into her head. "There's lots of sickness about," she said. "Come in again." And with what was left of the same breath, "Young man?"

"Cream," Bunny told her. "And half a pound of butter."

Then hoping by one means or another to delay matters he went in pursuit of Mrs. Lolly's tortoiseshell cat.

The cat dived under a cracker-barrel.

"Anything else?"

Mrs. Lolly held the cream out to him, and butter from her ancient ice-box. With no reason to stay, and nothing left to ask for, Bunny turned away. He and the old woman went out together. The steps were wet and so they both went slowly. When the old woman reached the sidewalk she stopped to catch her breath and went *phifft*—with her finger against her nose. Disgust encircled Bunny's throat.

Crossing the street in the old woman's wake, he remembered the first time he had ever seen anyone do that. A farmer. Some one they drove out in the country to see about some insurance premiums. His father left the car at the farmhouse. They climbed under a fence and walked side by side through a meadow where daisies were growing. And they came to a field and the man was in the field with his horses. His father talked about the price of wheat—whether it was better to sell now or hold on to it awhile. And everywhere about them the green corn was making a sound like——

"*There* he goes!"

A voice sang out, with no warning. The voice of Fat Holtz. The trees stumbled and the sidewalk turned sickeningly under Bunny's feet. He ran, ran as hard as he could, until legs tripped him from behind and hands sent him sprawling in the bitter dirt.

How Robert came to be there, who summoned him in this hour of need, Bunny did not know. Robert was there. That was enough. Robert pulled his tormentors off, one by one, and drove them away. Bunny sat up, then, and saw that there was a large hole in his stocking. And his knee was bleeding.

"Before all my friends," Robert said.

Matthews and Scully and Berryhill and Northway were crossing over to the other side of the street. They did not look back.

"In front of everybody," Robert said; "and you didn't even try to hit them."

Robert, too, was against him. Bunny looked at the broken glass and the white stain spreading along the walk, and burst into tears.

9

The little brass clock on the mantel struck seven sharply, to make clear that this second Sunday in November, 1918, which had begun serene and immeasurable, was very nearly gone.

From his place in the window seat Bunny observed that the rug was a river flowing between the stable and the long white bookshelves; turning at the chair where his mother sat, with light slanting down about her head and the blue cloth of her dress deepening into folds, into pockets.

When the little brass clock finished, the grandfather's clock cleared its throat, began to stammer. In the midst of this mechanical excitement Robert took a firmer hold on the lamp cord and with his free hand turned a page of *Tarzan and the Jewels of Opar*.

When the grandfather's clock had finished, it was seven (officially) and Bunny exchanged glances with his mother. His father got up to put a fresh log on the fire. Then he took a pack of cards and laid them face down in rows on the library table. His father grew restless if they remained overlong at the dinner table; fidgeted; contrived ways of transferring the conversation bodily to the library, where he could begin his shuffling and turning, his interminable dealing of cards. Bunny turned back to his mother.

"For this time of year," she said, "for November, it seems to be getting dark too soon."

She meant what she said, of course. And she meant also whatever she wanted to mean. Bunny was not surprised when his father stopped turning the cards and looked at her.

"I hadn't noticed it."

In this fashion they communicated with each other, out of knowledge and experience inaccessible to Bunny. By nods and silences. By a tired curve of his mother's mouth. By his father's measuring glance over the top of his spectacles. Bunny drew his knees under him and looked out. The room was reflected in the windowpane. He could see nothing until he pulled the curtain behind his head. Outside it was quite dark, as his mother said. Light from the Koenigs' window fell across their walk, across the corner of their cistern. If he were in the garden now, with a flashlight, he could see insects crawling through the cold grass. If he waited out there, waited long enough, he would hear blackbirds, and wild geese flying in migratory procession across the sky. . . . The curtain slipped back into place. Once more he could see nothing but reflections of the room. The night outside (and all that was in it) was shut away from him like those marvelous circus animals in wagons from which the sides had not been removed.

"I stopped in to see Tom Macgregor this afternoon," his father said.

"Seven of diamonds, sweetheart."

"I *see* it."

"Now, maybe, but you didn't."

Although she never paid any attention, his mother seemed to know by instinct when his father turned up the five of spades or the seven of diamonds that he was looking for. And she could tell clear across the room when his father began cheating.

"I did, too."

"Jack of clubs, then. . . . How was he?"

"How was who?" his father asked.

"Tom Macgregor."

Bunny listened with quickening interest. It was Dr. Macgregor who took his tonsils out; who sewed up a long gash over Robert's eye the time he fell off his bicycle, so there was scarcely the sign of a scar.

"He has a new hunting-dog."

"How many does that make?" His mother sat up suddenly and poked through her sewing-kit until she found the package of needles.

"Three, as I recall. But one of them has worms. I couldn't get him to talk about anything else."

"Did you see it, Dad?"

His father drew all the cards together and sorted those which were lying face up from those which were face down. Bunny could not bear, sometimes, having to wait so long for an answer.

"Dad, did you *see* the dog that had worms?"

"Yes, son."

"What did it look like?"

His father shuffled the deck loudly before he spoke.

"It was an English setter."

Bunny got up from the window seat in despair; he would go out to the kitchen and pay a visit to Sophie, whose conversation did not leave off where it ought to begin.

To get to the kitchen he must go through the dining-room, which was almost dark. And then the butler's pantry, which was entirely so. It was safe and bright in the kitchen, but overhead were dark caverns that Bunny did not like to think about—that end of the upstairs hall, where there was usually no light on, and the terrible back stairs.

"I think I'll go see what Sophie is doing."

His mother's nod reassured him. It said *Very well, my darling, but go quickly and don't look behind you.*

Under the pantry door there was a line of yellow light. And Bunny heard voices—Sophie, Karl, Sophie again. They were talking to each other in German, but they stopped when he pushed the door open. "Hello!" he said. The warm air of the kitchen enveloped him, instantly.

"And how is Bubi this evening?"

Karl was sitting very straight in the kitchen chair with his raincoat on. Tiny rivers of sweat ran down the sides of his face.

"My name isn't Booby, it's Bunny!"

"*Hein?*"

No matter how many times he corrected Karl, it was always the same. Karl never could remember. He always put his great hands together over his stomach and bobbed his head.

"That is good. And I all along was thinking—what you say it is? . . . *Bubi?*"

Sophie laughed then, and rattled the dishes in the kitchen sink—although there was no particular reason, so far as Bunny could make out, why she should do either. Every Sunday night this same conversation took place. Karl appeared after supper, scraped his feet on the mat, rain or shine, knocked once very gently, and came in. While Sophie washed and dried the dishes, Karl sat waiting with his coat on. And if Bunny came into the kitchen, Karl lit his pipe, gathered Bunny onto his lap, and told him a story.

After this unsteadying and unreasonable day when he had had so much to think about (the baby coming and Robert taking possession of the back room), after his encounter with Fat Holtz, Bunny gave himself up to the smell of leather and pipe tobacco; to the comfort of Karl's shoulder.

The story was always the same. Following the certain channel of Karl's sentences (*Already the ditch so deep was . . .*) he saw Karl's great-grandfather digging in mud and water up to his ankles. He saw trees falling, heard the great wind that blew and blew out of the ditch until at last it blew Karl's great-grandfather's pipe out—as Bunny was sure it would. And no sooner did Karl's great-grandfather's pipe go out than the real pipe which Karl held between his teeth, a deep-bowled one, went out also. And Karl had to stop and fill the real one before the story could go on.

First he couldn't remember what he had done with his tobacco-pouch. He looked earnestly on the kitchen table, under the chair, in all his pockets. He felt the sides of his trousers. He made Bunny get down so that he could search through his raincoat half a dozen times. After the pouch was located (in Karl's inside coat pocket, where he always kept it) Karl had to fill his pipe with great care. He had to tamp it down so that it was not too loose and so that it was not too tight. Then one match after another, before the pipe was lit properly. And just as Bunny was climbing back on Karl's lap, Sophie gave a final twist to her dishrag and hung it over the kitchen sink.

"*Aber* next time . . ." Karl said, smiling at him from the doorway.

But I wanted to hear the ending of the story now, not next time, Bunny thought sadly, as he turned out the light and made his way with one hand along the wall until he reached the dining-room.

"I told you, Bess. . . . There isn't any place else for her to go."

His father and mother were in the library still. By the tone of his father's voice Bunny was sure they were discussing Grandmother Morison. He waited for a moment among the dining-room chairs until he could decide whether the conversation was worth overhearing, and learned that Uncle Wilfred and Aunt Clara were going to spend Thanksgiving in Vandalia, with Uncle Wilfred's family.

"Why does your mother have to go any place? Why can't she stay right there while they are away? They could get some one to come in nights so that she wouldn't be alone."

"They're going to close the house up. The gas and electricity will be turned off."

"For *five* days?"

"Yes."

Bunny thought of Aunt Clara's house, standing there on the other side of town. And how Grandmother Morison and he went up the narrow stairs that lay behind a door in the Spare Room. Up to the attic which was Unknown Land, full of boxes he was not encouraged to look into, pictures, vases, trunks, broken pieces of furniture, magazines, books, old clothes—so much of everything and so many things that he could never get more than a confused geographical impression of the whole. By the double flue were toys that had belonged to Cousin Morison when he was a little boy. These he was not allowed to touch. . . . By the second dormer window was another collection, which belonged to Robert. Not so many, of course. Few of Robert's toys survived the treatment he gave them. Bunny was not allowed to touch these, either. . . . In the far corner of the attic beside the watertank were his own toys, all carefully put away in an egg-basket. These he could take down with him to Grandmother Morison's room, which smelled of camphor.

While she made quilting patterns out of brown tissue-paper, he played with the lovely Russian sleigh that worked on spools. With the paperweight Lion of Lucerne. With tables and chairs for the house where the three bears lived. And there were pictures in the basket, as well as toys. Pictures of Daniel, of Ezekiel in the valley, of Joshua with his sword drawn, bidding the sun and the moon stand still.

Bunny could not help regretting those other toys at Aunt Clara's which he was never allowed to play with. Especially the little gold piano with angels painted on it. Once, as he was going by, he put out his hand and touched one of the keys. And Aunt Clara called up to him through the floor that the little piano was Cousin Morison's (who died of typhoid fever) and he was not to touch it.

"I'm telling you what Clara said."

Bunny moved closer to the doorway. If he went any farther they'd stop talking, but at his back was the dark pantry, and the door into the kitchen was wide open.

"If it were at any other time. But we'll both be gone, and you know there's no telling what she may take into her head to do. I don't really mind her straightening my dresser drawers—I do mind, as a matter of fact—but she feeds Bunny gumdrops and horehound candy until his stomach is upset, and tells Sophie she won't go to Heaven because she was baptized in the Lutheran Church. . . . And what about Irene? Shall I tell her that we've changed our minds and don't want her to stay with the boys while we're away?"

"No, I'd rather she were here."

"So would I. Much rather. But the house isn't big enough to hold Irene and your—"

Bunny's question was decided for him by a disturbance on the back stairs—so sudden that his terrified heart nearly stopped beating. With arms outstretched he threw himself bodily upon the lighted room.

10

While Bunny waited, the cymbal in his left hand and the large padded drumstick in his right, Robert beside him tapped delicately on the edge of his chair. Light shone on the varnished surface of the piano, on the ivory keys. His father's hands proceeded up the keyboard in a series of chords twice repeated. Across the living-room his mother was looking at them. She was waiting for them to begin.

"Well, gentlemen?"

Bunny met his mother's eyes at the precise moment when his father started forth upon the opening measures of *Stars and Stripes Forever.* The flood of sound was so sudden and so immense that Bunny came near drowning in it. He caught at the regular six-eight rhythm as if it were a spar, and striking out with the cymbal in his left hand, the drumstick in his right, he tried frantically to save himself.

Ching . . .
Boom . . .
Ching . . .
Boom . . .
Boom . . .
Boom . . .
Boomdiddy-boom-boom . . .

Once started, the music swept along of its own momentum, carrying Bunny with it. He was helpless. So was Robert and so was his mother. The only opposition came from the room itself. What the green walls threw back, the fire caught at and sent up the chimney. What the fire could not reach, the ringed candelabrum turned nervously into light, ring upon ring.

After *Stars and Stripes Forever* came *Washington Post* and *El Capitan* and *The Fairest of the Fair.* Bunny's eyelids began to grow heavy. They were weighed down with music. He told himself anxiously that he must keep them open. He must not drop off to sleep. But in a very short while there was Karl's great-grandfather digging and digging with a pipe in his mouth . . .

digging . . .

and the water seeping into his ditch . . .

and the air grown darker . . .

and the high wind . . .

"Now what's wrong?"

The music had stopped and Bunny saw to his amazement that he was at home, in the living-room. And his father was frowning at him.

"He was falling asleep," Robert said.

"You can't expect to play with us, son, if you're going to fall asleep every five minutes. See if you can't do a little better."

Bunny stared self-consciously in front of him, past Robert's grave smirk.

His father turned back to the piano and with his left hand struck a chord, then another. "We'll quit in a few minutes and then you can go to bed." They took up *The U.S. Field Artillery* where they had left off. Bunny forced his eyelids so wide apart that they ached. If his mother would only look at him! Through the fading light he saw that she was reading. She had picked up a magazine. His eyelids closed for a second and when he opened them the room had darkened permanently. There was nothing, he found, that he could do about it. He heard the rhythm of the piano. Cymbal chinked blindly on cymbal and drumstick beat drum. But he was wrapped comfortably around in music so deep and so firm that he could lie back upon it. He was upheld for a long time and then moved forward into a darkened air where thunder burst concentrically out of red rings . . . green rings . . . lavender rings . . .

"For the love of God!"

"I wasn't falling asleep!" Bunny said, so wide awake now that he thought he was telling the truth.

"Oh balls!"

What this word meant when it didn't mean a ball that you throw or bounce, Bunny had no idea, but he knew it wasn't nice, whatever it was. And imprisoned inside him was another little boy who was nobody's angel child and who didn't like to be shouted at. That little boy said, "Balls your ownself!"

By the loud silence that had come over the room, Bunny realized that he'd gone too far. He looked at his mother, and then at Robert, who avoided meeting his eyes.

His father said sternly, "Go to bed, son. Go right now."

Bunny went over to the sofa, and as he bent down to kiss his mother good-night, his eyes searched her face for the indignation he was sure she felt, and he got a terrible shock: *She was trying to keep from smiling.*

She was not indignant with his father, she was on his father's side.

It was all that he could do to get up the stairs.

II

Bunny woke early to the sound of church bells, though it was Monday morning. Could it be Sunday all over again? Or was there something tremendously the matter?

While he lay in bed, wondering, the sky was split wide open by the whistle from the shoe-factory; by a second whistle from the waterworks. Then the fire alarm began, absorbing whistles and bells into its own dreadful moaning. Until sound became general and the morning throbbed with it.

When Bunny drew his head out from under his pillow Robert was gone, his bed disturbed and empty. One last turn and Bunny got up likewise. Washed himself, dressed, and went downstairs. At the door of the library he waited, uncertain how he might be received. Robert and his mother were eating breakfast before the fire. His father was sitting in the window seat, reading the *Chicago Tribune.* His father's coffee was there neglected on the window sill beside him. They looked so nice, sitting there. So like themselves. Was it possible, Bunny considered, that what he remembered about last night had never really happened?

"Good morning, everybody," he said, politely.

All three of them spoke at once:

"The War's over."

"Oh."

In his sleep he dreamed things that were quite real afterward. Could it have been that? Could he have dreamed that he talked back to his father and got sent up to bed? . . . He sat down in his place at the breakfast table and tied the napkin around his neck. Last night the music went on for a while without him, and then it stopped abruptly and Robert came upstairs. That much was true, not something he dreamed. And through the fringe of his eyelashes he had watched Robert undressing, taking down the straps of his wooden leg. Then darkness closed in around the sides of his bed and he was free to grieve. If *she* had been the one, he thought—if *she* had been in trouble, nothing in the world could have kept him from going to her. She did not really love him . . . Tears came, hot and effortless. Ran down his cheeks into the pillow, until he was exhausted and lay quiet, looking at the wedge of light under the bedroom door. After a time it grew wider. He heard them talking downstairs, and then the legs of the card table creak as they slid into place . . .

PEACE AT LAST

Bunny deciphered the headlines of the morning paper, upside down.

Germany Surrenders
Signs Armistice Terms

"Is that what all the noise is about?"

"Of course. What did you think?" Robert was almost unbearably superior.

"I didn't know. I thought maybe it was a fire."

"A fire! Listen to him. He didn't even know the Armistice is signed!"

Bunny looked to his mother for enlightenment. The word 'Armistice' was new to him, and he felt reasonably certain that Robert didn't know what it meant, any more than he did.

"It means *King's X*," she said.

"It means we beat the Germans," Robert said. He got up from the table and a moment later they heard the front door slam. Robert had gone to join the excitement.

His mother drew him to her. "Haven't you forgotten something?"

Hair? Teeth? Face and hands? He forgot to kiss her . . . In the night someone bent over him where he lay sleeping. Someone put Araminta Culpepper in his arms. She must have . . . Bunny saw that his father was waiting for their attention.

"You might listen to this, son. You might like to remember it when you're grown."

But instead of listening to the military terms of the armistice with Germany, Bunny went and put his head in his mother's lap, for he felt very odd inside of him. He heard her say, "James, this child is burning up with fever!" and he thought dreamily that it must be so. I'm going to be sick, he thought, grateful for the cool hand on his forehead and her nearness. And after that, life was no longer uncertain or incomplete.

BOOK TWO

Robert

I

THE grass under their feet was trampled and flattened down unevenly. They were hoarse from shouting. They knelt with their hands braced, with their toes balancing. Between their legs they saw the unstable sky

Nine . . .

Sixteen . . .

Thirty-seven . . .

and the roofs of houses.

Offside

Offside

Sixty-four . . .

Offside

Hunderd-and-eighteen shift

Watch it now

All right

WATCH it

All right

WATCH IT

They ran with knees high and trees spinning. The grey light of evening touched their foreheads, their thin dirt-drawn cheeks, their hands. Crying words, crying names, they fell together—impact of back and shoulder, down, on unknown thighs and the hard ground.

It's your turn to kick off

All right

It's your turn

Three . . .

Seventeen . . .

Thirty-eight . . .

McCarty's offside

Forty-seven . . .

Hang on to it
Hang on to it
Oh . . .
Do you stink, Northway

Into the clear circle of their voices Robert went, limping—McCarty's voice. Northway's voice, taut and protesting. The sky enclosed his shoulders.

Ah
Don't kick it
No
Knock a guy out doing that
What
Fooling like that
Come on
Come on, Morison, pass it
PASS it

Robert was thrown to the ground, alive and breathing.

Touchdown
Listen, after this . . .
Touchdown
It's not, either
For our side
Cryin' out loud
Touchdown
When
Time out I said
When did you
When

Robert picked himself up off the ground and adjusted the knees of his knickerbockers. Not gradually but all at once it was getting dark. He drew his sweater on over his head, weaving argument into it, and denial. They were going home now. Matthews and Scully and Northway and Berryhill (with the ball between his knees) and Engle and McCarty.

So long, McCarty
See you tomorrow
So long
Whose cap is this
So long

Somebody lost his cap
See you tomorrow I said
And don't forget
See you tomorrow

The sky hung down, dark and heavy upon the trees. Robert straddled his bicycle and with Irish between the handlebars left the field, riding now on the sidewalk and now in the street, which was old and full of unexpected hollows. The front wheel of his bicycle turned this way and that, jolting them.

"We should have had that touchdown," Irish said.

"By rights we should have had it, but what can you expect?"

Though it was Robert's bicycle, Matthews or McCarty or Berryhill would have offered to do the pedaling. They took it for granted that Robert wanted them to do the pedaling, on account of his leg. Irish never did. When it was time to go home he came and settled himself between the handlebars.

After the third long block the car tracks ended and there was level pavement. Street-lights went on at all the intersections. And houses withdrew beyond the rim of the fierce swinging light. Robert, turning, saw the shadow of his head and shoulders lag behind, saw leaves scattering. . . .

After the one-story house of old Miss Talmadge came the Bakers' and the McIntyres' and the Lloyds', then the driveway at the side of Irish's house, and the front walk. Irish got down.

"See you tomorrow."

"Sure, and thank your mother for lunch."

"Sure," Irish said.

There was a light in the kitchen window, but the rest of Irish's house was dark and uninhabitable.

"So long," Robert said.

Irish waited for some leaves to blow past.

"So long."

Through one last street lamp Robert rode alone—the shadow of his wheels elongated, preceding him. Beyond Miss Brew's and the Mitchells' and the Koenigs' (beyond the unseen, undreamed-of darkness) was home: the porch light and the front door, the white pillars along the front of the porch, and Old John waiting in the shadows to greet him.

"How are you, huh? How's the boy?"

Old John wagged in a slow difficult circle, his head and hind quarters and the tip of his tail.

"How's the boy, huh?"

Robert slanted his bicycle against the steps and then, opening the front door, passed into the circumscribed region of the front hall. Irene saw him at once, and started toward him.

"Look out, now." Robert gave her fair warning. "You'll get in trouble!"

If he pretended to go right and went instead to the left, he could always get by his mother. But with Irene it was not so easy.

"Look out, your own self!"

He charged straight at her and was caught, before he could get away. She bent her face down, smothering him.

Standing in the door to the library, his father said, "It is vitally important to keep her out of that boy's room. 'Tie her down,' Dr. Macgregor said, 'if you can't keep her out any other way.' "

Robert found suddenly that he was free.

He pulled off his cap and his outermost sweater. He would go now and stand beside his father, who did not subject him to these humiliating displays of affection. Irene knew he didn't like to be kissed. She only did it for meanness. . . . Robert was confused. The noise of the playing-field was still in his ears, ringing. When he hitched up his knickerbockers, Irene did likewise with her skirt.

"Where's Bunny?" he said, and made a face at her.

"He's sick." It was his father who answered him.

"What's the matter?"

"Spanish influenza," his mother said, coming toward them from the dining-room. Robert turned his eyes away. She was getting big around the waist, on account of the baby coming. He didn't mean to look, but sometimes he did, anyway, and it embarrassed her.

"If I'd only had sense enough," she exclaimed—not to them but to herself, apparently. "If I'd only taken Bunny out of school when the epidemic first started!"

The room seemed very bright to Robert, after being out-of-doors. He could feel the heat from the fireplace through his clothes.

"You can't be taking the boy out of school every time somebody in town gets sick."

"Robert, your hands—" By the way that his mother spoke to him, it was plain that she had not been listening. She roused herself. "You can wash out in the kitchen. Run along now . . . I want to slip upstairs for a minute."

Irene was in the doorway before her.

"I'll go, Bess."

"Thank you just the same, but——"

"I think you'd better let Irene go." His father spoke hurriedly and as if he were not altogether sure that he would be obeyed. Through heat and brightness Robert turned to look at his mother, who would not mind now whether he looked at her or not.

"Why?" she asked.

"Doctor's orders. You're to keep out of Bunny's room."

"But, James, how ridiculous!"

"That's what he said."

While his mother was still hesitating between anger and her original intention, Sophie appeared in the doorway. Sophie had a white apron on. And it seemed to Robert that she and the little brass clock on the mantel struck in unison.

"Dinner," they announced, "is ready."

2

Robert was awakened by a blow at the side of the house. With sleep still hanging to him, he raised himself tentatively on one elbow. It was daylight, and Karl's head and shoulders appeared at the window.

"*Wie geht's?*"

Karl had not spoken to any of them in German since America went into the war, and at first Robert could not answer him. He knew what the words meant, but he didn't know where he was until he saw the sewing-machine and the wire form his mother used for dressmaking.

"Good, I guess . . . only I don't like sleeping in this room."

Karl shifted his ladder slightly and peered in through the screen. It was not safe, they said, for Robert to be in the same room with Bunny. And so they moved him in here, in the sewing-room, where he had never slept before. The stairs creaked long after everybody had gone to bed. And the shade snapping kept him awake.

"I have to, on Bunny's account. He's sick. Did Sophie tell you?"

Karl nodded, thoughtfully. "That is bad." And then he smiled—a fine smile that ran off into the grain of his face.

"Soon I go back!" he said, shifting the ladder.

"Back where?"

"To the old country."

"To Germany? Why are you going to do that?"

Balancing himself, Karl began to take down the screen.

"If you have not seen your father," he said, "if you have not seen your mother, if you have not seen your brothers for seven year . . . ."

For Karl to be a German was one thing, it seemed to Robert. That couldn't be helped. But to want to go back there and be with a lot of other Germans was something else again. He yawned.

"How much will you take to close the window?"

With a great display of muscular effort, Karl managed to get the window down half an inch. Then he tucked the screen under his arm and withdrew out of sight. And there was consequently nothing that Robert could do about it, except to kick the covers off and close the window himself. While he dressed, he entertained himself by thinking of the time Aunt Eth came for a visit from Rockford. Irene was there, too. And it was her idea that they put a dress and a hat and a fur neckpiece on the wire dressmaking form and stand it at the head of the stairs to fool his father. Then they waited, snickering, behind the bedroom doors. . . . After the stump sock was on, Robert lifted his artificial leg from the chair, fitted his stump into it, and drew the straps in place over his shoulders. Then, partly standing, partly sitting down, he pulled his knickerbockers on.

Robert's *affliction*, people said, when they thought he wasn't listening.

The breakfast table was set before the fire in the library, as usual. Robert said good-morning to his mother, and to Irene, who was wearing a green silk kimono with yellow flowers on it. They were talking about Bunny.

"Hundred and two," Irene said; "and he complains of pain in his eyes."

Before he had time to unfold his napkin, she turned upon him.

"Stick out your tongue, Robert. I wouldn't be at all surprised— Just as I thought: it's red. It's very red. You must be careful. Just see, Bess——"

But his mother was in no mood for joking. "Here's the cereal," she said, "and sugar and cream. Now shift for yourself."

When Robert was halfway through breakfast there was a blow against the side of the house. He was not startled this time. With his mouth full of toast, he waited until Karl's head and shoulders appeared at the library windows. Then he reflected by turns upon Karl, who was going to Germany; and upon Aunt Eth, who was not like his mother and not like Irene, but in a way rather like both of them. Only she had gray hair, and she was quieter than his mother even, and she taught school in Rockford. When she came to visit, she brought wonderful presents—marbles or a peachy ball-glove for him, and building blocks or a book or paints for Bunny.

Bunny was always either painting or making something out of blocks. That was all he wanted apparently. He didn't play baseball or marbles or anything that other kids liked to do. At recess time while they were playing games he stood off by himself, waiting for the bell to ring. And if anybody went up to him and started pestering him, instead of hitting back at them, he cried.

Bunny isn't well, his father said. *You have to be careful how you play with him. He isn't as strong as you were when you were his age*. . . . He was careful, all right. But if he took Bunny out to the garage and they had a duel with longswords and daggers, the first crack over the knuckles would send Bunny on his way to the house, bawling. And if they played catch, it was the same thing. (Again the ladder struck, farther on. And Karl's head appeared at the third window. When he was gone Robert reached for the last piece of bacon.) He would have preferred a more satisfactory kind of brother, but since Bunny was the only brother he had, he tried his best to be decent to him. For instance, when Bunny got over the flu he was going to take down his good soldiers from the top of the bookcase and let Bunny look at them.

From this intention he was distracted by his mother, who laid her hand on his sleeve.

"While I think of it, Robert——"

He got up from the table, wiped his mouth with the back of his hand, and on second thought with his napkin. Whenever his mother just remembered something at this time on a Tuesday morning, it was the clean clothes. They came on Saturday, but she never got around to sorting them until it was time to send the soiled ones. If he stopped for Irish and got to school by eight-thirty, as he had promised Scully and Berryhill, he would have to hurry.

The clothes-basket was in the kitchen, on the other side of the stove, where he knew it would be. As he staggered through the library with it, he looked at his mother hopefully. But she was absorbed by what Irene was saying. Robert went on. He made it a practice never to listen to their conversation. It was generally about cooking or clothes, and it made him low in his mind. He set the basket down at the head of the stairs and while he was waiting amused himself by pulling horsehairs out of the sofa. Irish would be expecting him. They had promised to be at school by eight-thirty, both of them. If he had only known that his mother was going to talk so long. . . . When his patience gave way, he went to the railing and called down.

"Please, will you hurry? I have to go."

His mother called back to him from the library: "All right, Robert. I'm coming." But it was several minutes before she appeared in the downstairs hall. Irene was with her and they were still talking.

"That's the trouble. I never can think of anything for lunch that we haven't already had."

By leaning dangerously far out over the banister, Robert could look down on the tops of their heads. Irene came first. His mother followed, but more slowly.

"Why this unseemly haste?" she asked when she had reached the landing.

"I promised Irish I'd come by for him."

"If that's all it is, then I'm afraid Irish will have to wait."

"Oh, for cryin' out loud!"

"That's enough, Robert."

But it wasn't. It was nowhere near enough, so far as Robert was concerned. "The trouble with you, Mother"—he swallowed hard—"is you don't appreciate what a fine upstanding son you have. I wish you had Harold Engle around the house for about a week. You'd be hop-footing it over to the Engles' so fast, and saying, 'We have to have Robert back again, Mrs. Engle. I guess we can't get along without him.' "

"I expect I would, Robert."

Mollified, he put the stepladder in place beside the linen-closet.

"Try not to make any more noise than you have to. You'll disturb Bunny."

She bent over the clothes-basket, sorting underwear from pajamas; sorting shirts, napkins, tablecloths, towels. First she handed the sheets up to him, then the pillowcases. And then she began to sing, under her breath, so that he could scarcely hear what she was singing.

> "*There's a long long*
> *trail a-*
> *winding*
> *Into the land of*
> *my dreams . . .*"

Robert choked on his own haste.

> "*Where the night-*
> *in-gale is*
> *sing-*
> *ing*
> *And*
> *the*
> *pale——*"

The song ended so abruptly that Robert drew his head out from among the sheets and pillowcases to see what was the matter.

"There's a bird in here," Irene exclaimed and went back into the sick-room again, closing the door behind her.

His mother turned to him, her arms filled with winter underwear. "You'll have to do something, Robert."

This was more like it. . . . Robert slid down the stepladder, recklessly, having made up his mind to try the broom first. Then if that didn't work, they'd have to let him use his beebee gun.

When he came back upstairs, Irene and his mother were both in Bunny's room—Irene by the dresser and his mother on the edge of Bunny's bed, holding him. With feverish sick eyes, Bunny was watching the sparrow that flew round and round the room in great wide frightened swings. The windows were open as far as they would go.

"It's all on account of Karl taking down the screens," his mother said. And so far as Robert was concerned, her remark was neither helpful nor necessary. He took hold of the broom.

"You better get out of here, both of you. Because in a minute I'm going to start wielding this!"

Irene retreated at once, laughing and covering her hair with her hands as the bird brushed by her. His mother was not so easily hurried. "Lie still, lover," she said, with the bird flying from one side of the room to the other, swooping, turning, diving intently past her face. The door closed and right away Bunny was sitting up again, his eyes glittering with fever.

"Please don't hurt it, Robert!"

"Why not?"

Robert swung vigorously.

"Because I don't want you to."

"One sparrow more or less—"

"I don't care, I don't want you to hurt it!"

Robert swung and missed again. Nevertheless, the bird dropped and lay like a stone on the counterpane of Bunny's bed. As Robert's hand closed over it, he remembered: *It is vitally important to keep her out of that boy's room. . . .*

"I'll tell Mother on you!"

Tears ran down Bunny's cheeks.

Tie her down, the doctor said. . . . The sparrow escaped from Robert's fingers and with a sudden twist shot through the open window.

Tie her down . . .

And already she had managed to get in when they were all

excited. Already she had been sitting on the edge of Bunny's bed.

"Oh, shut up!" Robert said, and swung his broom upon the empty air.

3

All Thursday morning Robert raked leaves—raked them toward him until there was a crisp pile at his feet, and then another and another. With no more leaves to fall, the trees stood out in bare essential form, forgotten during the summer and now remembered. By noon the yard was swept clean on both sides of the house, and he had carried the trash up from the basement. There was nothing left but to burn the dead leaves and trash together, in the alley. And he could do that whenever he liked.

As soon as lunch was over, Robert went upstairs to get his football helmet and jersey. He was almost at the front door when his mother saw him.

"Where are you going?"

"To play football." He had done all that his father told him to do. The afternoon belonged to him. It was as good as in his pocket. "The whole gang——"

"I want to talk to you a minute."

His mother went on into the living-room and adjusted one of the shades which was not on a line with the others.

"Come here," she said.

"What's the matter?" he demanded suspiciously.

"I want to see what makes you bulge so."

"That's handkerchieves."

"One, two, three, four . . . So I begin to perceive. Your back pocket must be a place where they meet and congregate. Suppose you take them up to the hamper in the back hall, where they belong."

"Do I have to do it now? Can't I do it later?"

"If you like. But I'm afraid you can't play football this afternoon."

"Why not?"

"Various reasons. I want you to stay in your own yard, do you hear? Because if you run all over town, you'll be playing with all kinds of boys who probably haven't a thing the matter with them."

Robert looked at his mother unguardedly. She was smiling, but what she said wasn't funny and in fact didn't make a bit of sense. They had been up with Bunny for two nights—first Irene and then his father. And today was the third day, so that his fever would break, Dr. Macgregor said, or else it would go higher.

"I'm not going all over town. I'm only going to the vacant lot across from Dowlings' to play football."

"Please don't argue with me, Robert."

Don't argue with her! And already they were choosing up sides. As plainly as if he were there, Robert could hear them: Scully and Matthews and Northway and Berryhill.

"Crimenently——"

"There's no point in discussing it any further, Robert. Just do as I say."

His mother was tired. That was the whole trouble. She was tired and she didn't realize. . . . Robert went into the library and sat down. His father was there with stacks of papers around him—work that he had brought home from the office. He was vaguely aware of Robert's presence but no more, and for that Robert was grateful, because there was a lump in his throat that he couldn't seem to dispose of. He twirled his football helmet this way and that on the end of his finger, and tried not to think about things.

Partly it was all his own fault, because he let his mother into the room where Bunny was, so maybe it was right for him to be punished. Two days had passed and she didn't look any different, but maybe it was right anyway. Only what good, he asked himself as he got up and went over to the rocking-chair—what good was it having school closed? What good was all the time in the world? So long as he had to stay in his own yard, what good was anything?

No answer occurred to him, and therefore he rocked—gently at first, then with conviction.

"*She was goin' downgrade*
Makin' ninety miles an hour
When the whis-sul broke out

In a scream (Beep-Beep!).
He was found in the wreck
With his hand on the throttle
All scalded to death
With steam . . ."

Rocking and singing cheerfully, Robert was well into the second verse when his father took a pencil from behind his ear and said, "If you're going to stay in the house, you'll have to be quiet, son. I can't concentrate."

Robert jammed the football helmet on his head and went to the kitchen, where Sophie was washing the sheets for Bunny's bed. Sophie was always disagreeable lately. She flew around with her nose in the air, bossing everybody. And if he so much as asked for a piece of bread and butter, she would threaten to tell his mother on him.

"Now what do you want?"

"Last night's paper."

"Right there under the table. And don't get the rest of them in a mess, do you hear?"

People were always saying, *Do you hear, Robert? Do you hear me?* As if there was something wrong with his ears. But there wasn't. He heard everything that he wanted to hear and a lot more besides. The newspaper was on top. He folded it carefully and tucked it under his belt.

"What do you want last night's paper for?"

"None of your beeswax," he said, and slammed the door on his way out.

Old John followed him around to the back of the house, where the roof sloped down over the cellar stairs. There, by bracing his arms against two box elders which grew side by side, Robert could get up on the roof. As soon as he put his knee up, Old John whined.

"You better go somewhere else and play," Robert said, bitterly, and drew his other leg up after him.

Once he got as far as the kitchen roof, the rest was easy. Up there he was no longer at the mercy of anybody who chose to take a pencil from behind his ear, or raise or lower a window shade. He could look down on everything—on the back yard and the garage and the fence and the alley behind the fence, on Burnhams' trash pile and the row of young maples along the other side of the alley. To the right he could see the garden, the grape arbor, and the yard. To the left was the drive, and Bunny's sandpile under a big tree. Robert surveyed the whole scene carefully, before he sat down with his back against the chimney and opened the *Courier*. Page two. . . . There it was: "*SCHOOLS . . . The school board and the health officer have posted notices on the school houses and at places about town to the effect that the schools will be closed until further notice . . .*" Robert felt very small prickles in the region of his spine. He read the first sentence twice, to make sure that there had not been a mistake. . . . His mother couldn't keep him at home indefinitely. Things as awful as that didn't happen. She was just tired and cross this afternoon. And so there would be time for playing football and marbles, for making shinny sticks, for taking muskrat traps down from the top of the garage and cleaning them, for hunting rabbits and squirrels. . . . But there was more in the notice than that. It meant that something was happening in town, all around him. Not an open excitement like the day the Armistice was signed, with fire engines and whistles and noise and people riding around in the hearse. But a quiet thing that he couldn't see or hear; that was in Bunny's room, and on Tenth Street where Arthur Cook lived, and more places than that. Far down inside him, and for no reason that he could understand, Robert was pleased. . . . *The notice reads as follows: To the Parents . . . While the epidemic has not reached Logan to any extent, and while it may seem unnecessary to many, yet after consulting with the health officer and the medical authorities your school board decided to close the schools for this week at least, in the hope that no new cases will develop and that this community will be spared any serious epidemic. The Illinois committee on public safety strongly advises this course and cautions people against gathering in large numbers for any purpose, also traveling on railroad trains except when absolutely necessary.* . . . Robert closed his eyes. It seemed once more as if he could hear shouting. *First down and . . . four . . . to go* . . . Matthews and Berryhill shouting. And for that reason he wished (just for this afternoon) that Bunny, who was sick, anyway, had been the one to get run over and have his leg cut off above the knee.

But it was Crazy Jake that Robert heard, coming down the alley with his wagon and his old white horse. A long time ago, before Robert was born, Crazy Jake was held up by robbers who took his money from him and his watch, and hit him over the head. And because he was never able to think very well after that, he drove through alleys collecting tin cans for people. And he came at all hours. Robert had heard his mother say that lying awake sometimes in the middle of the night, she heard him.

"Hi, Jake!"

That was the thing about being on the roof. Robert could see Crazy Jake, who couldn't see him. It was like being invisible. Searching steadily, Crazy Jake emptied the Morisons' ash-can into his wagon. Then with his lips blowing, with his vacant face pressed to the sky, he drove on.

There was still part of the roof for Robert to climb—the upper level which extended out in the shape of a ledge. To reach it he made use of the rain-spout, the window frame, and the iron hook where the screen had been fastened. When he reached the top he was out of breath and a little dizzy with his accomplishment. The distance to the ground was considerable; enough to affect the pit of his stomach. He could reach out if he wanted to. He could almost touch the branches of the box elder. But also he might fall headlong and break every bone in his body. And they would all come running out of the house. His mother . . . . she would cry and take on about *him*, for a change. But she couldn't do anything. It would be too late. . . . Sometimes Robert fell from the roof of the garage, sometimes from the top of the flag-pole at the Chautauqua grounds. But in any case, people came running and took on over him.

At two o'clock Dr. Macgregor's car drove up before the Morisons' house. Until he could slip out of the grooves of his day-dream, Robert thought that Dr. Macgregor must be coming up the walk to see him. Then he remembered. It was Bunny who was sick, and this was the second time that Dr. Macgregor had come since morning.

Robert would have called out to him if he had dared. But he was not supposed to climb on this part of the roof, and they might hear him, inside. That was the trouble, he said to himself.

Whenever they got into a state, it was always on Bunny's account. They never had doctors for him. Not since he was run over.

It would be nice if his father read in the paper about a specialist who had discovered a way to make bones grow. Not really, of course. Because there wasn't any way to make bones grow, after they were once cut off. But just supposing. . . . They would take him to Chicago to see the specialist. And after looking him over pretty carefully the specialist would tell his father and mother to take him home again and put him to bed in a dark room with the shades pulled down. Only, before they did that they'd better go out to Lincoln Park and see the animals.

After he had been home a week his leg would be put in a special cast, made of elastic plaster. They would have a nurse for him, of course. And nobody else could come into the room unless he asked for them. And maybe for days and days he wouldn't ask for them. Just lie there and take dark green—no, dark *purplish* medicine through a glass tube, every hour and a half.

And the nurse's name would be Miss Walker.

At the end of a week the specialist would come and measure the outside of the cast, which would have expanded maybe the fraction of an inch. His mother would cry, and they'd have to take her out of the room. Or maybe it had better be Irene. Because his mother wasn't very easily upset. And the specialist would tell them he had to lie flat, that was the main thing. Lie flat on his back and not talk to anybody but Miss Walker (who was starched but not skinny, like the nurse that looked after him when he had his accident). Miss Walker was interested in football, so they talked about that, mostly. . . . Absorbed in these imaginary matters, Robert sat so still that the sparrows returned to fight with one another above the kitchen chimney. . . . When his stump began to hurt, they called the specialist by long-distance. He came and measured the cast and said it was all right: the stump was supposed to hurt. It was supposed to hurt now because the knee was forming. Within a month's time, he said, Robert would have a new knee.

The new medicine was red and thick like cod-liver oil, and the first spoonful made Robert sick. For a while they had to give it to him with orange juice. But then he learned to hold his nose and swallow it right down while Miss Walker said *That's the stuff.*

The cast began to get wider as flesh formed about the new bone. And the bone was growing, though it took time. He had to be patient and not think about it, because after a while the stump would begin to hurt again. And when it got to the foot, the specialist said it would hurt most of all.

Everything worked out just that way.

When it came time for them to remove the cast, they took him to the hospital. Dr. Macgregor was there—no, that was not right. There would be several doctors with masks on. Dr. Macgregor would give the anesthetic and the last thing he would remember would be Dr. Macgregor telling him to take deep breaths so they could hurry up and get it over with. . . . Sections here and there needed polishing, Robert decided. The end, especially, where he woke up and felt with his hand, through the covers. But on the whole it would do. At least until there was time to go over it.

For it was late in the afternoon. The sky all around him had lost its brightness and some of its color. And the heat had gone out of the tin roof, when he put his hands against it. Like an explorer long out of touch with the world, he advanced to the edge and looked down. Irene was there in the garden, alone.

There were signs, he told himself. If Irene had come outside now, it must mean something. Bunny's fever had broken. Or perhaps, as Dr. Macgregor said, it had gone higher. Slipping and sliding much of the way, Robert went down to find out. When he reached the box elders, Irene turned and started toward the kitchen door. She did not see him, apparently. She was going inside. He opened his mouth to call to her, but some one else did. Some one called her by her name, in a voice that Robert had not heard for years.

"Irene . . ."

The gate swung open, at the back of the garden, and Boyd Hiller came inside. He passed so close by the box elders that Robert saw grey hair at his temples, and his grey unhappy eyes.

"Irene, I've been waiting out there for hours. I couldn't go away—not without seeing you!"

Robert saw and understood everything, even the queer

tightness in his side, which was jealousy. And the tears that sprang into his eyes. Irene had come out into the garden to meet Boyd Hiller, and Boyd Hiller would ask her to go back to him. And if she did that, Robert wouldn't want to see her again. Not ever, he said to himself as he escaped between the trees and around the corner of the house. Not as long as he lived.

4

After dinner Robert had the library all to himself. His father and mother went upstairs immediately, but he did not join them, for fear of meeting Irene. With no homework to do, he ran his fingers along the top shelf of the bookcase and drew out *The Scottish Chiefs.* It was an old edition that had belonged to his Grandfather Blaney. The paper had turned yellow around the edges, and the print was small. But it began the way Robert liked books to begin, and by the second page he was submerged. The lamp cord was his only means of contact with the upper air. He clung to that, and shaped the words in silence as he read.

At eight o'clock his mother came downstairs and stood in the doorway a moment, looking at him. He did not know that she was there. Nor did he know when Dr. Macgregor came for the third time since morning. Robert was crossing the bridge at Lanark and saw the rising moon. Committed to him, as the worthiest of Scots, was the iron box which the false Baliol had given to Lord Douglas, and Douglas to Monteith. And he had five long miles to go before he could reach the glen of Ellerslie.

At ten o'clock Irene came and took the book away from him. He was too dazed; he had been too long in another world to remember that he had been avoiding her.

"It's time for you to go to bed."

"Who said so?"

"Your ancient and honorable father."

Robert pulled himself up out of the chair. If it had been his mother, he could have finished the part he was reading and maybe gone on into the next chapter to see what was happening there. But his father was different.

With men and horses moving beside him, Robert made his

way up the stairs to the sewing-room, undressed, and got into bed. For the first time he perceived how still the house was, how full of waiting. When he was little, he used to be afraid of the dark. He used to think that unnamable things were about to spring out at him from behind doors. Sometimes it was merely the house itself, tense and expectant, that frightened him. He was not afraid any longer.

He could hear voices—Irene and Dr. Macgregor and the sound of Irene's heels striking the stair. While he was waiting for her to come up again, he fell asleep.

It was still dark outside when he awoke. And no way that he could tell how late it was, or how early. Poised between sleep and waking, he got up to go to the bathroom. What he saw then when he hopped out into the hall was like a picture, and remained that way in his mind long afterward. There were lights burning everywhere, in all the rooms. At the head of the stairs Irene and his mother were standing with their backs to him. Because neither of them moved, Robert could not move; until Bunny raised up in bed quite calmly and said, "What time is it?"

Dr. Macgregor appeared from the bedroom across the hall and went into Bunny's room at once. When he came out again, his face was relaxed and smiling.

"Elizabeth," he said, "your angel child is going to get well."

5

The next few days were like a party, it seemed to Robert. There were cut flowers from the greenhouse and callers every afternoon. And Sophie had to spend most of her time running back and forth with the teapot.

All his mother's friends came to see her—"Aunt" Amelia, "Aunt" Maud, "Aunt" Belle—and stayed often until the stroke of six. Robert could not remember when the library had been so full of women drinking tea and talking about necklines. Or when his mother had been more happy, more like herself.

"Having a baby," she said to him privately, "is no worse than spring house-cleaning. It isn't even as bad. You don't have to take the curtains down."

He was not allowed to go out of the yard, and Irish couldn't come there and play. But one way and another (letting him stay up later, having his favorite desserts, listening to what he had to say about the high school football team) his mother made it up to him, so that after a while he didn't really mind.

What she wanted, apparently, was to make things up to everybody. She paid the paper boy six weeks in advance. And nothing would do but that old Miss Atkins, who came every Saturday with Boston brown bread and potholders (there were stacks of them in the linen closet), must stay to lunch. And the best blue china must be brought out for her.

Sophie alone was red-eyed and disagreeable. Robert and his mother agreed that it was on account of Karl. It was because Karl was going back to Germany.

"What I don't see," Robert explained, "is why she doesn't go to Germany with him."

"Perhaps she would," his mother said, "if Karl asked her to."

"Why does he have to *ask* her to?"

"For the looks of things."

"Couldn't she ask *him*?"

"She could but she won't."

"Then why doesn't she just go by herself?"

"That's what I'm afraid of. Whatever you do, don't put that idea in her head. It might be years before I could get some one to make as decent pie-crust as Sophie does."

"No," Robert said, gloomily, "I won't."

"As for *our* going away, that's arranged now—everything but the railroad tickets. And I do believe that with the least encouragement your father would go right down and get them. You know how he likes to have everything ready beforehand. . . . The only thing I have to do is to make sure that the baby is a girl. I don't care, particularly. I *like* scissors and snails and puppy-dogs' tails. But your father has his heart set on a girl. And if it turns out to be another boy, we may have to send it back. There's no telling. . . . Irene is going to stay with you and Bunny at night, so that you won't be alone. . . . If anything comes up, you're to call Dr. Macgregor. Only you're not to bother him unless it's something important—unless, for example, the house is on fire, or you catch Sophie upstairs trying on my hats. Do you understand? . . . You're old enough,

Robert, to take on responsibility, the way your father is always saying. And by that I mean it would be a good thing if you'd change your underwear from time to time, and not leave the light burning in the basement. . . . Also I want you to look after Bunny while we're gone. See that he goes to bed early even if you have to go when he does. He's been through such a siege, you know. . . . And that he eats the things he's supposed to eat, not just meat and potatoes. . . . And you're to write once a week, and brush your teeth night and morning, and not make any more trouble for Irene than you have to. . . . And while I think of it, how do you like the name *Jeanette—Jeanette Morison*—for a little girl?"

With his mother Robert was almost never constrained or ill at ease. It seemed easy and natural for her to be talking about whatever it was that was on her mind. She didn't stop what she was doing. Hardly ever. And that way he felt free to tell her all sorts of things. Because he always knew that she would go right on sorting the sheets and pillowcases.

But with his father it was different. He liked his father and he liked pretty much the same things his father liked. Old clothes, baseball talk, fishing, guns, automobiles, tinkering. When they were out in the country, his father and he turned to look at the same things. His mother liked trees and sunsets, but *they* liked horses plowing, orchards, and fine barns. They even liked the same kind of food, and put salt on everything, regardless. But if he came up behind his father and started to tell him something, he was always sorry afterward. It was never the way he had hoped it would be.

His father's comments embarrassed him. *I'm glad you told me, son. But now the best thing is to forget that as quick as you can. If you want to grow up to be decent and self-respecting, you haven't time for any foul-minded talk like that.* . . . Or, out of a clear sky his father would say *Remember now, it doesn't make any difference what kind of trouble you run into; your father will always be right here.* . . . Something that Robert knew perfectly well. And that somehow there was no need for saying.

Or else it was something that he didn't want to know. Like the time they were alone in the living-room and his father said, "I expect you've been wondering, Robert, why your mother has to go all the way to Decatur to have the baby—why she can't have it here at home. There's a reason, of course. A very good one."

Robert had taken it for granted that his father would not talk about *that.* . . . And he had not been wondering why they were going to Decatur, because mostly his father and mother didn't tell him why they did things and so he had long ago stopped wondering.

"When you were born, your mother had a pretty difficult time of it. There were several days when it didn't look as though she would pull through. And then Bunny came along, and it was the same thing. But there's a doctor in Decatur, a very fine specialist, who's developed a new treatment in dealing with childbirth. I could explain it to you, but the upshot is that Dr. Macgregor thinks we ought to take her over there, even at considerable expense."

"I see."

When Robert stood up to go his father laid the evening paper aside and stood up also.

"Because it's a pretty serious thing," his father said, and put his arm rather awkwardly around Robert's shoulder.

Together they paced, slowly, and without reason, from one end of the living-room to the other. After a time Robert began to feel the weight of his leg. He had only to say something about it and his father would stop, of course. But that would have meant giving in—admitting that there was something the matter with him.

So far as his mother was concerned, there wasn't anything the matter with him. If they were out fishing and had to crawl through a barbed-wire fence, his father looked back sometimes. Or called over his shoulder, *Can you make it, sport?* . . . But his mother went right on. She was like Irish in that respect.

And the same way with games. His mother took it for granted that he would learn to swim and dive, so he did. And everything that other boys did. And the only time she praised him was when he won the tennis singles at the Scout camp. The Scoutmaster was surprised and said how fine it was—meaning that Robert was handicapped with only one leg. And the news got into the paper, eventually, and his mother wrote:

Very nice. Mailed your clean underwear this a.m. Are you getting enough to eat?

Robert had the post card still. He kept it in a box, with his second-class Scout badge and his arrowheads.

"Things are going to be different now," his father was saying. "You'll have to do more for yourself. With a baby in the house you can't expect people to be picking up your things after you and keeping your clothes in order."

Once they went out into the hall solemnly. And once into the library. And so long as neither of them spoke, Robert could imagine that he knew what was going on in his father's mind; that they understood each other. But to have his father turn on him and say, "These things happen to everybody, sooner or later. We have to expect them," was altogether shocking. Robert looked around wildly as they bore down on the walnut sofa. They turned aside, of course, at the very last minute, but it was a narrow escape.

"Your mother is a fine woman," his father said.

6

Bunny was very pale after his illness, and he tired easily. The first time that he was allowed to come downstairs was an event. Robert got out his soldiers and laid the box on Bunny's knees.

The box was so large that it was all Bunny could do to hold it. And Robert stood by, in case Bunny should want to take the soldiers out of their places. When Bunny had looked at them a short while (at the lancers with silver breastplates and silver plumes, the cowboys, the Cossacks on white horses with bearskin caps and rifles slung across their backs) he indicated that Robert could put the lid on. His hands shook slightly, and there was satisfaction in his tired eyes.

"They're nice," he said. "Thank you, Robert. Thank you a lot." And then "Maybe sometime we could play with them together?"

Robert didn't answer.

"You take half and I take half, and then we could have a battle—how would that be?"

Robert returned the soldiers to the top of the bookcase

where they belonged. He wanted to be nice to Bunny because Bunny had been sick. But on the other hand, it wouldn't do to commit himself.

He said, "Maybe we could sometime," and went on to the living-room to practice his music lesson. Because there was an epidemic, his mother said, was no reason why he should get off practicing.

For a while—for fifteen minutes, perhaps—he practiced conscientiously. Then he made a series of trips out to the front hall to look at the clock. Each time that he came back he devoted considerable attention to the piano stool, which was either too high to suit him; or else too low. With half an hour still before him, he switched from *The Shepherd Boy's Prayer* to

Go tell

That was wrong——

Go tell

Aunt Rho

die her——

"Flat, Robert . . . B Flat!" his mother called from somewhere, from the butler's pantry. She was eating again. . . . That was the trouble. If they'd just leave him alone, he'd get along fine and maybe learn to play the piano so well that he could give recitals and people would have to pay money to come and hear him. Instead of that, they jumped on him—his mother jumped on him every time he struck a wrong note, so that he was always having to go back to the beginning, hour after hour, week after week, year in (he said to himself) and year out.

When he went again to see what time it was, Irene was standing in front of the pier-glass. She was poking long hatpins into her hat, and he tried to slip away while her back was turned. Nevertheless, she saw him in the mirror and stopped him. And this time it was not a matter of being kissed.

"What," she said, "did you think of my caller?"

Robert could think of nothing in reply, so he sat down on the bottom step of the stairs. When Irene was convinced that her hat was straight, she came and sat down beside him.

"I guess I didn't think anything," he said.

"That's a likely story."

Irene took his hand and covered the skinned knuckles with

her own. Robert considered a place in his trousers knee—a place which was about worn through. The trouble was that he couldn't tell Irene what he thought about her caller—not really. Besides, it wouldn't make any difference. If she was going to live with Boyd Hiller again, she'd do it regardless of anything he said.

Long ago, before he was hurt and almost before he could remember, there was a wedding in the Episcopal church, with lots of people. It was after dark and they went there in a taxicab—Irene and Grandfather Blaney. And Irene was afraid that he'd drop the ring if he carried it on a pillow, so she put it in his hand and closed his fingers over it. That much he remembered. And going down the aisle past all the people.

But there was more afterward. It was one of the family stories that he had heard over and over, until it seemed to him that he could almost remember it. When the time came for the ring, he wouldn't give it up. Boyd tried to take it from him and he said *No, it's Eenie's ring!* So loud that people heard him all over the church.

"The honest truth, Robert . . ."

Irene had to turn, they said, and take the ring away from him. But that part he didn't remember.

". . . the honest truth is that I didn't know Boyd was coming. I knew he was in town, of course. And when I took little Agnes to her Grandmother Hiller's, I saw him and talked to him for a few minutes. That was all."

Robert was not used to having grown-up people confide in him. First his father, and now Irene. . . . His mouth stiffened with embarrassment.

"I had been in the house all afternoon, you know, with Bunny. And your father came up to relieve me, so I threw a shawl around my shoulders and went outside to get a breath of air. . . . When I discovered who it was, Robert, I did the same thing you did—I ran away."

A week's suspense, a week of secret misery escaped in one breath, so that Robert felt very light and unstable. It wasn't that Boyd Hiller was to blame for his accident—because he wasn't, really. He didn't know that Robert was climbing on the back end of his carriage. He didn't even know that Robert was there until Robert got his foot in the wheel. And then it was too late. . . . He thought of that every time that he saw Boyd. He couldn't help thinking of that. But what troubled him now was something else. It was about Irene.

"The older you get, Robert, the less courage you have."

Robert stood up and put his hands in his pockets. He was glad of one thing, anyway. He would not have to avoid Irene any longer.

"You wouldn't like to see some muskrat traps, would you?"

"Not now. The taxi will be here any minute."

Robert glanced at the clock. They had already talked away six whole minutes of practicing.

"Next time, then?"

Irene buttoned her right glove and drew the left one on—all but the thumb. "Next time," she said, and kissed him soundly on the mouth.

7

Robert awoke into a bright cold room. There was snow on the window sill, and on the floor beneath. He looked out and saw that the walks were gone, the roofs buried under an inch of snow. And in the level morning light, which came neither from the sky nor the white earth but from somewhere between sky and earth, the maples stood out with stereoscopic clarity.

While Robert was trying to accustom himself to the change, his mother came in.

"I never knew it to fail," she announced as she closed the window.

"Never knew what to fail?"

"Sophie——"

Although it was a thing he had seen happen a thousand times, Robert sat up in bed and watched his mother turn on the radiator.

"She's gone and had all her teeth out. Every tooth in her head. Wouldn't you know! She came to work this morning feeling so miserable and she was such a sight, that I told her to go home. . . ."

The radiator began to kick and stomp, and only occasionally could Robert make out a word or two of what his mother was saying. When she left, he washed and dressed slowly. For long periods at a time his mind remained stationary and entranced, while he played with the buttons on his shirt. But there were moments in between, when he thought about teeth, and how he swallowed one at the age of seven; and about his Grandmother Morison, who had false teeth and kept them in a glass of water at night; and about Sophie, and what she would look like without any.

Eventually the smell of bacon frying aroused him. He went downstairs by the back way, and found his mother in the kitchen.

"Was it that," he said, "that was making Sophie so disagreeable?"

"I don't know."

His mother turned the gas down under the coffeepot.

"I didn't ask her. She was in no fit condition. If she had been, I'd have found out where she keeps the grapefruit knife. Because I've looked high and low. . . ."

After breakfast Robert wandered upstairs and stood looking at the back room that was some day to be his.

No change had been made since the day he came here with his mother and they planned together what they were going to do to fix it up. His mother suggested matting for the floors, in place of rugs. And pictures of birds. Also if they could pick up an old sea-chest somewhere—a chest that opened from the top. He thought it would be a good idea if the bed were built against the wall like a seaman's bunk, high and narrow, with long drawers under it where he could keep his things. There was to be a bulletin board where he could tack up notices and post-cards that he wanted to look at. And they both agreed that the door was to have a padlock on it.

Now that everything was so upset, with the baby coming and all, he couldn't expect them to do much about his room. Not for a while, anyway. Turning to go, he noticed the arrangement of rectangular walls and buildings: the ruler, the block of stone, brown paper, pencils, wooden spools. Bunny must have built it—whatever it was. He was the only one who ever came here. But Robert saw that with that piece of cardboard braced against the sides of the two largest buildings and curving upward he could construct a first-rate airplane hangar.

He carried out his idea immediately, and in a way that satisfied him beyond words. But he could not resist making one or two more serious changes, and he became so intent on what he was doing that he was startled when he heard Bunny's voice, close behind him: "What's that?"

"A flying field."

Bunny regarded him with suspicion.

"What did you think it was?"

Robert leaned back proudly, so that Bunny could see his handiwork. It was all neatly arranged—the hangar and three sheds, the road leading up to it, the corners of the field. He saw that Bunny, too, was pleased, or at least hovering on the edge of pleasure.

"Those are searchlights," he said, fearing that Bunny would miss them.

Bunny was looking at something else—at a cylindrical box which had once contained a typewriter ribbon.

"My village . . . you've torn up my Belgian village!"

Robert sighed. All he ever wanted to do was to play with Bunny. And whatever he did, the result was always the same.

"It can be fixed, Bunny. All you have to do is build it over again."

"It can't, either. And I wasn't through with it. I was going to play with it a lot more and now you've spoiled it!" Bunny looked so queer when he lost his temper: white as a sheet and like a little old man. "You've spoiled the whole thing."

"I know, Bunny, but I didn't mean to. . . . And I built you a new flying-field, didn't I? That's a lot better than any old Belgian village."

"If you'd only play with your own things," Bunny shouted, "and keep out of here where you don't belong . . ." Blocks, kindling-wood, pencils, wooden spools scattered noisily across the floor and out into the hall where his father stood, looking at them.

"What's all this?"

"My village. Robert went and——"

"I didn't, either. I didn't spoil anything. I was just——"

"Be quiet, both of you. And listen to what I have to say. Irene *was* going to stay with you but she's out of town."

"Where did she go?"

"Chicago."

"What for?"

"I don't know. You'll have to ask her. Sophie is in no fit shape to come to work, and so I've been talking to your Aunt Clara. You and Bunny are to go there and stay while we're gone."

As suddenly as that, everything was changed. Everything was different.

Robert was too uneasy to remain upstairs even while his clothes were being packed, and so he wandered disconsolately from room to room, with Bunny at his heels. Bunny was looking for his yellow agate which had got lost somehow, or mislaid. And he seemed to be more perturbed about that than he was over the change of plans.

For some time Robert stood before the bookcase in the library, uncertain whether or not to take his soldiers. He didn't want to go and stay at Aunt Clara's. He didn't like it there. But on the other hand, what if the house should burn down while they were gone. . . . At the last minute he decided to take both his soldiers and *The Scottish Chiefs*, which he had finished once, and read partly a second time.

"Hurry up, son," his father said from the doorway. "Dr. Macgregor is outside with his car, waiting. Say good-by to your mother and then we'll. . . ."

When Robert came into the hall his mother was standing before the pier-glass with her hat and coat on. He started toward her, but Bunny was there first, tugging at her and sobbing wildly into her neck.

"Why," she exclaimed through her veil. "Crying . . . at your age. What a thing to have happen!" And when Bunny cried the harder, "There, there, angel, don't take on so!"

Robert hesitated. He saw his father pull out his watch.

"Well, good-by," he said, though she probably didn't hear him. "Good by, Mother. Take care of yourself." And went on out to the car.

8

Aunt Clara was waiting for them behind the storm door.

"Well, how are my boys? And how are you, Doctor?"

Robert held his breath while she embraced him. Aunt Clara was a large woman—almost as tall as his father. And on weekdays she didn't wear any corset.

"Won't you take your coat off, Doctor? I say won't you take your coat off?"

Dr. Macgregor set their suitcases down in the front hall.

"Not today, thank you."

"When James called, I told him to bring the children right over. Mr. Paisley and I were going to Vandalia for Thanksgiving, but with the epidemic and so many people sick and all, we decided to stay home."

Blindfolded and set down like the suitcases in Aunt Clara's front hall, Robert would have known where he was. He would have known mostly by the smell, which was not like the smell of any house that he had ever been in, and not easy to describe, except that it was something like the smell of clothes shut up in boxes for too long a time.

The walls and the woodwork were dark, and the shades always at half-mast, except in the parlor, where they were all the way down, to keep the rug from fading.

While Robert stood with his cap and his overcoat still on, it occurred to him that he might slip out the back door and around the house to the car again, before anybody noticed what he was doing. He could stay with Dr. Macgregor until his father and mother came home, and then everything would be all right. He moved toward the dining-room, but just then Dr. Macgregor put his hand out to say good-by.

"If there is anything you want," Dr. Macgregor said; "if anything comes up, Robert—"

Aunt Clara answered for him: "If there's any occasion to, Doctor, we'll call you. I say we'll call you."

It was clear from the tone of her voice that there would be no occasion. In the doorway, with cold air rushing in between his legs, Dr. Macgregor turned and smiled at Robert approvingly. "Be good boys," he said, and closed the door behind him.

"Well," Aunt Clara said, "I wasn't looking for you quite so soon. Half after nine, your father said. Go stand your overshoes on the register, Robert. There's snow on them and it'll stain the carpet."

Robert had intended to watch until Dr. Macgregor drove away, but he did not dare go to the window when Aunt Clara had told him to do something else. He stood bravely still, however. For they were rubbers, not overshoes. And in the second place, Aunt Clara was not his mother. He didn't have to mind her. Unless he wanted to, he didn't have to do anything she said.

"Come upstairs with me, Bunny. I'll take the spread off, and the bolster, in Grandma's room. And then you can have some place to lie down. You must be careful for a while. You've been a sick boy."

Although his face was streaked with tears, Bunny was pleased with himself. Robert recognized the symptoms. And he saw that Bunny was making up to Aunt Clara—starting up the stairs in front of her as if she were the one person that he liked and depended on. Just as he did to Irene, or to Sophie, or to anybody who happened to be around and could get him what he wanted. When Bunny and Aunt Clara reached the landing, Robert went over to the register and stood on it, rubbers and all, preserving his independence by a kind of technicality while the hot air came up in waves, around his legs.

As soon as the rubbers were dry he took them off and his overcoat and cap, and went into the darkened parlor. He was looking for a place to put his soldiers. Though it was safe, or fairly so, the parlor would not do because it was never used except for company. Then Aunt Clara raised the shades halfway and people sat about in the big mahogany rocking-chairs, making conversation. On the piano there was a seashell that roared and a big starfish that came apart, once, in Robert's hands. He could still remember how he felt, holding it and trying to make the broken point stay on. Eventually, in fright, he put the starfish back the way it was, on top of the piano, and hoped that no one would notice. Aunt Clara discovered it the very next day, when she came to dust, and said would he please not touch things without asking.

All Robert wanted was to see what it looked like underneath. But if he had known what was going to happen, he would have let the starfish be.

In the sitting-room over the two doorways were plaster heads—a Negress in a red turban, and another (darker, and larger by several sizes) in a blue. Robert could never make up his mind whether he liked them or whether he didn't. And so he sat experimentally in various parts of the room, on the leather couch, in the big chair, holding his box of soldiers. Wherever he went, the Negresses followed him with their white eyes. He asked his mother once where Aunt Clara got them, and she said in darkest Africa. But that was only his mother's way of saying things. Aunt Clara had been to New York with Uncle Wilfred, and come home by way of Niagara Falls. And she had been to Omaha, to a funeral. But she had never crossed the ocean. Robert was quite sure of that. Just as he was sure that the heads were not real heads but plaster, and the fireplace not a real fireplace, though it had a fancy metal screen that looked as if it were screwed on over a grate.

One time when Aunt Clara was away at a meeting of the Ladies Aid, he took the screws out and discovered that there was nothing behind it but the wall. Only the metal screen wouldn't go back on again. He tried all afternoon until his mother came to get him, and still he couldn't make the screws stay in. But it was all right, because his mother told Aunt Clara to have a man come out and fix it, and she'd pay for it. And on the way home she wasn't even angry with him. For years, she said, she'd been wanting to do the very same thing.

For his part, Robert liked things to be whatever they were. And he liked them to work. Having reached that conclusion, he went and stood before the bookcase, helplessly interested by all the curious objects that he saw there, and that he was never allowed to touch—the coral, the starfish, the shells, the peacock feather, the parrot eggs, the ocarina, the colored stones. When he could not bear to look at them any longer, he turned away to the dining-room and the front hall. It was nearly ten. He waited in front of the cuckoo clock until the little wooden door flew open and the wooden bird fell out, gasping the hour. Then he went on, still searching for a place to put his soldiers.

At the top of the stairs, in the narrow hall, Robert was confronted by the framed high school and college diplomas of Aunt Clara and Uncle Wilfred, and the Morison coat of arms, and a picture of Grandfather Morison in his casket with all the funeral flowers. To the left were the Spare Room and Aunt

Clara's and Uncle Wilfred's bedroom, which looked as if it were never slept in, though it was, every night. To the right was Grandmother Morison's room. He stopped at the door and looked in. Grandmother Morison was in her rocking-chair by the window, and Bunny on the big mahogany bed with a blanket thrown over him. Neither one of them knew that Robert was there. The room was littered with dress-patterns, quilting-pieces, chalk, ribbon, old letters, spools, boxes and baskets and bags. *Come in if you're going to come in*, she always said. *Or stay out if you're going to stay out.* . . . He sniffed (there was a faint odor of camphor) and passed on down the hall to Uncle Wilfred's study—a narrow dark little room with a cot and a wardrobe and two chairs, a roll-top desk, a type-writer table, and a place in the middle to walk among them. The state agents of the Eureka Fire Insurance Company looked down at Robert from their oval frame, and stared him out of countenance. The wallpaper was brown and like a sickly sweet taste on his tongue. But the wardrobe was exactly what he had been looking for.

He put the soldiers on top of it, back and hidden from sight. As he turned to go out of the room he was stopped by the sound of a train whistle: two long, two short, and then a mournful very long . . . Robert listened until he heard it again. Two long . . . two short . . . And knew all in one miserable second that his father and mother were on that train; that they had gone away and left him in this house which was not a comfortable kind of house, with people who were not the kind of people he liked; and that he would not see them again for a long time, if ever.

9

Grandmother Morison could not remember the names of people, or where she put things. "James," she would say to Robert—"Morison—*Robert*," she would say; "have you seen my glasses?" And they would be on her forehead all the time.

When she had pulled them down, she would talk to Robert in a comfortable way about the *Lusitania*, or the assassination of President Garfield, or the Bombardment of Fort Sumter. And about his Great-uncle Martin, who owned a cotton plantation in Mississippi. And how if the Southern people had only been nice to the darkies and called them *mister* and *missus* there would never have been any war. And about St. Paul. And about Christ, who was immersed in spite of what anybody said to the contrary, because he went down *under* the water and he came up *out* of the water.

So long as Robert did not get up on the bed with his shoes on, or ask questions when she was involved in her crocheting, he could play with anything that he liked. And by trial and error he discovered that Grandmother Morison's room was the one place in the house where he was safe. Everywhere else a voice said *Robert* the minute he touched anything. If he grew restless (as he invariably did) and wandered into the Spare Room, or downstairs, it was only a matter of time before he was impaled by Aunt Clara's voice saying *Robert, I thought I told you not to play with Uncle Wilfred's scrap-book. . . . That darning egg, Robert, belonged to your Great-grandmother Burnett. I don't believe I'd play catch with it, if I were you. . . . Robert, do you think that's a nice kind of a song for singing? . . .* Until he was afraid to do or say anything, so he sat in the front hall folding and unfolding his hands. Or stood with his nose to the front window, watching the children pass—running, sliding, pushing each other on the icy walks.

He knew all of them by name. The boys who dragged sleds after them, and the little girls who made angels in the snow. He knew what marbles some of the older boys had in their pockets. But if they looked up and saw him, there was no flash of recognition. Nothing but wonder, as though they were looking at a Chinaman. He was cut off from them, estranged. Their mothers had not gone to Decatur to have a baby.

When there was nothing out-of-doors to interest him, Robert would turn and wait for the cuckoo clock to strike. The wooden door flew open, and the noisy little bird fell out, and that restored his interest in living. Also it reminded him of how he let his mother into the room where Bunny was—a thing he would rather not have remembered. When he had managed to forget it again, he was still aware vaguely that there was something he *had* been worrying about.

One day became for him hopelessly like another. Even Thanksgiving, because Aunt Clara had roast chicken instead of turkey, which was sixty cents a pound. But on the Saturday after Thanksgiving he made a discovery; something that he had overlooked. Under the table in the living-room was an unabridged dictionary, and on top of it seven or eight other big books arranged according to size. He took them all off at once, in such a way that he could put them back again the instant he heard Aunt Clara coming.

Finding the wrong kinds of words in the dictionary was not a crime. They couldn't put him in jail for it. But it was a thing he would not want to be caught doing, especially by Aunt Clara. It was like telling lies or listening to people who didn't know he was there.

The best way was to pick a letter (like *C*), close his eyes, and turn to whatever page he came to: *chilblain . . . child . . . childbearing . . . childbed . . . childbirth . . .* He had gone past what he was looking for. "With child," people said. A woman was with *child (chīld) n.; pl. children (chĭl'drĕn) . . .* 1. *An unborn or recently born human being; fetus; infant; baby . . . A young person of either sex, esp. one between infancy and youth; hence, one who exhibits the characteristics of a very young person, as innocence. . . .*

Robert flushed. He looked around at the empty chairs in the sitting-room and was on the verge of closing the dictionary. Then he thought better of it.

obedience, trustfulness, limited understanding, etc. . . . "When I was a child, I spake as a child, I understood as a child. . . ." His skin felt warm, under his clothing. He had gone too far again: fetus was the word *. . . fetter . . . fettle, fettle . . . fettling . . . fetus, foetus (fē'tŭs), n. a bringing forth, brood, offspring, young ones; akin to L.* fetus *fruitful, fructified, that which is or was filled with young . . . the young or embryo of an animal in the womb. . . .* Bunny came up behind him, so quietly that Robert did not even know he was in the room. Bunny waited a moment, and then made a slight noise. Robert slammed the book together, in panic.

"If she catches you," Bunny said, "if she finds out you've been using her dictionary, you'll get Hail Columbia!"

"She won't find out."

"What'll you do if she does?"

"Nothing."

"Why are you so red in the face, then?"

"I'm not."

"You are, too."

"I'm not, either. For cryin' out loud, Bunny, go play somewhere!"

"I will," Bunny said, hopefully, "if you'll let me have your good soldiers?"

"Nothing doing."

The page was creased where Robert had been reading. He put it back carefully. It might be some time before Aunt Clara used the dictionary, and then she might not be looking for a word that began with C . . . *The young*, he read, *or embryo of an animal in the womb. . . .*

Bunny went out of the room, leaving Robert free to thumb through the *W*'s . . . *wolves . . . wolvish . . . woman . . . woman's rights . . . womb . . . The belly . . . The abdomen . . . "Transgressors from the womb"—Cowper . . . Any cavity like a womb in containing and enveloping. . . .* Robert read and reread, skipping the brackets and the abbreviations but with never a glimpse of the meaning. The meaning was there, but he could not get at it. It was inside the words.

What Robert wanted, suddenly, was to be outdoors in a vacant field, running. He wanted to be running hard, and with a football against his ribs; to be tackled and thrown on something hard like the ground. With a sigh, he closed the dictionary and put the other books on top of it. Then he went to the front door to see if the mail had come. It had, and there was a letter for Aunt Clara, in his father's handwriting. Robert took it to her and waited, with his heart pounding inside his shirt.

"It's from your father," she said, as she wiped her hands on the roller towel in the kitchen. "I say it's a letter from your father." She opened the letter and read it from beginning to end, slowly. When she had finished, she put it back in the envelope and the envelope in the pocket of her kitchen apron.

"Has the baby come?" Robert asked.

"No."

"Does he say how my mother is?"

"Your mother is fine—getting along as well as can be expected, he says."

Robert looked at her. "Is that all he says?"

"Yes, that's all. . . ."

But it wasn't, Robert assured himself on his way upstairs. He could tell by her eyes. There was something in that letter which Aunt Clara hadn't told him. He might go to the phone and call Dr. Macgregor, perhaps, and find out how things were. But his mother said not to bother him unless it was something important and this might not be.

But then again, Robert said to himself as he reached the head of the stairs, it might. He turned down the hall and saw at once that Bunny was trying to get at his soldiers. Bunny had pulled Uncle Wilfred's swivel-chair across the study and was teetering on it, in front of the wardrobe.

"Hey!"

Bunny turned a frightened face upon him and lost his balance. The soldiers fell with him, all the way to the floor.

"I didn't go to . . . really I didn't!"

Robert brushed past him without a word. There were his Cossacks with arms broken off, and heads, and rifles, and the legs of their white horses. His mouth twisted in pity. There were his lancers.

"Damn you," he said. "Damn you, Bunny . . . *Damn* you!"

10

With glue and matches, wire, toothpicks, and pieces of thread Robert worked over his broken soldiers all Sunday morning. Fortunately the legs of certain horses were all in one piece. He could make those legs stay on. And if the horses wouldn't stand up afterward, he could always pretend that they were lame. Arms could be fastened on with wire, and heads with matches. So that anyone standing off at a distance from them could hardly tell that the soldiers were mended. The trouble was that Robert didn't play with them standing off at a distance.

Bunny wanted to help, but Aunt Clara said no, Robert didn't deserve any help after speaking to his brother like that—which was all right with Robert. When Bunny got big enough so that they were both grown up and the same size, he was going to take Bunny out in the back yard and clean up on him. That might not put any soldiers back together again, he told himself (and Bunny), but it would certainly make him feel a lot better. Because every so often, with the soldiers spread around him on the sitting-room floor—an arm here and part of a sword or a helmet there—he would suddenly decide it was too long a time to wait until Bunny grew up, and that something could be done right then and there. Uncle Wilfred was sitting in the big chair, with the Sunday paper, and so nothing was.

At five minutes to one, Aunt Clara called Robert and Bunny to come wash their hands for dinner. Bunny got to the kitchen sink first and took so long that it was time to sit down before Robert had his turn at the soap. He did not feel obliged, therefore, to wash with any great thoroughness or be too particular about not leaving any dirt on the roller towel. Besides, he said to himself as he sat down and unfolded his napkin, he was hungry.

At home it wasn't considered cheating if he started in on his salad before everyone else had been served. But no sooner did he commence than Aunt Clara spoke to him in a hushed voice.

"Robert, you've forgotten something."

He glanced up in surprise and saw that they were all looking at him—Aunt Clara, Uncle Wilfred, Grandmother Morison, and Bunny. He put down his salad fork and bowed his head. Uncle Wilfred in a disapproving voice said, "Bless us, O Lord, and these thy gifts. . . ."

Even after the blessing had been asked and they were free to receive it, Uncle Wilfred was not restored to a good humor. So far as Robert could make out, *he* was not responsible. It was the health officer, who had requested that for the duration of the epidemic the Christian Church (together with all the other churches) close its doors. To Uncle Wilfred's mind, there was no need for such action.

"It's one thing," he said, passing over the wing, which was Robert's favorite piece of chicken and giving him the drumstick, which he never ate if he could help it; "it is one thing to close the bowling-alley and the pool-halls. But to close the church of Jesus Christ is something else again. Anybody would think that church gatherings are unhealthy—that they're particularly conducive to the spread of disease."

Aunt Clara said, "It's true that there's lots of sickness about. I say that much is true."

"Church," Uncle Wilfred said, "is of so little importance that they can afford to suspend it at the slightest pretext. . . . There's no reason that I can see why people who come together for an hour on Sunday should be any more exposed to disease than they are all day long in stores and offices."

Robert was not hungry now. While Uncle Wilfred was talking, all desire for food left him.

"It's cold in here," he said, not expecting that Aunt Clara would get up and go look at the thermometer.

"I declare . . . seventy-six. Don't you feel well, Robert?"

He was all right. Perfectly. There was no reason why they should all be staring at him that way.

"Your eyes look bloodshot."

Robert pushed his chair back from the table. "No," he said, "I just thought it was cold in here." And before he could get upstairs to the bathroom, he was vomiting.

Aunt Clara undressed him, as much as he would let her; and pulled the covers back so that he could get into bed. In a little while, Dr. Macgregor came and took his temperature and asked him questions—all from too great a distance to be of any help. Robert was glad that Dr. Macgregor had come, and sorry when he went away. But there was nothing that he could do about it. He was cut loose. He was adrift utterly in his own sickness.

For three days and three nights it was like that.

Aunt Clara appeared every two hours—now fully dressed, and now in a long white nightgown with her hair in braids down her back. Sometimes her coming was so slight an interruption that he could not be sure afterwards whether she had been there at all. Again she stood beside his bed for an indefinite time, with two white tablets in one hand and a glass of water in the other.

On the morning of the fourth day, Robert awoke from a sound sleep and knew that he was better. He knew also that there was something that he had to find out, as soon as he could remember what it was. Aunt Clara appeared with his breakfast tray.

"Good-morning," she said. "How do you feel? I say how are you feeling, Robert?"

"Better."

His voice sounded weak and like the voice of somebody else.

"I think I'll get up, Aunt Clara."

"You'll do no such thing. You've been a sick boy, Robert. A mighty sick . . ."

The letter . . . Quite suddenly it came to him. Aunt Clara got a letter and she wouldn't tell him what was in it. He was going to call Dr. Macgregor and find out how things were. And when Dr. Macgregor came, he was too sick to remember it.

"Aunt Clara, can you tell me how my mother is?"

"She's getting along about as well as can be expected, the doctor says. And she's in the hospital, where she'll get very good care."

Robert was not at all satisfied. As soon as she went out of the room, he turned his back to the wall, so that he would not have to look at the insurance agents, and slept. At noon Aunt Clara awakened him to give him his medicine. He asked her the same question and got a similar answer. He closed his eyes and slept and woke up again and slept again until he had disposed of the greater part of a winter afternoon. The street lamp shone in squares upon the ceiling. Turning then, Robert saw, distantly, as through the wrong end of opera glasses, things that had taken place a month before. The last Sunday in October they wedged themselves into the car, among fishing-poles, baskets of food, skillets, automobile robes, water-bottles, and the can of worms. Then they drove out into the country until they came to a special gate. After that they had to crawl through a barbed-wire fence and lug all they had brought with them to a clearing on the banks of a creek.

With the automobile robes spread out on the ground and the food put away, his father went far downstream to cast for pickerel and bass. His mother sat on a high bank where all the sunfish in the creek would come, sooner or later, to be caught by her. Bunny sat near her among the roots of an old tree, and let the fish nibble the bait off his hook while he was dreaming. And Robert went up the creek and over a bridge to a place where he could cast without getting his line caught in the overhanging branches.

His mother smiled at him foolishly from the opposite bank. And it seemed to him that she was smiling at the sky also, and at the creek, and at the yellow leaves which came down, sometimes by the dozen, and sailed in under the bank and out again.

II

When Robert awoke it was quite dark outside, and what Aunt Clara was saying downstairs came up to him distinctly through the register.

"Yes. . . . Yes, Amanda. . . ."

Her voice was pitched for the telephone.

"I'm pretty well. How are you? . . . I say I'm pretty well. . . . Yes . . . he's better, I think . . . I say Robert's better. Been asleep off and on most of the day. . . . Yes . . . in Decatur. . . . Yes . . . in spite of every precaution . . . both of them . . . James, too. . . ."

Robert sank back on the pillow. It was his mother and father that they were talking about. Something had happened to his mother and father while he was sick. Or before, maybe. And Aunt Clara wouldn't tell him. When she came up with his dinner he would say *How is my mother? You have to tell me. . . .* But that was not the way that things worked out. Before it was time for his tray, Robert heard the front-door bell ring, and Irene's voice in the downstairs hall. He sat up in bed feeling very dizzy and not altogether sure that what he heard was not imagined.

"I don't know, Irene . . ."

Aunt Clara was arguing with her.

"I say I don't know whether Robert ought to see anybody or not. He's still running a temperature and the doctor's orders are that——"

Robert could not bear it another second.

"Irene," he called, "I'm up here!"

He heard the sound of high heels upon the stair, and knew beyond all doubt that there was one person in the world who was not afraid of Aunt Clara.

Irene switched the light on. She was very beautiful as she stood in the doorway. Her eyes were shining and she was all in black, with a black fur around her neck. She came and sat down on the bed, beside him, and Robert could smell her perfume.

That was a joke. Everything, suddenly, had become a joke. His hands (which she was holding) and the dun-colored wallpaper, the insurance agents. But most of all, the joke was on Robert himself—for being foolish enough to get sick at Aunt Clara's house.

"I've been to Chicago," Irene said, as if that too were foolishness.

So much had happened since she sat on the stairs with him. He did not ask why she had gone to Chicago. He did not care. When he was little and did something that he shouldn't—like turning the hose on Aunt Eth, who was starting out to the Friday Bridge Club—he set out for Irene's as fast as he could go. If he got there, he was safe. Irene would not let anybody come near him. Her eyes blazed and she put him behind her and said, *James Morison, don't you touch a hair of this child's head!*

Robert looked at Irene carefully, trying to memorize her face and the buckle on her hat so that he would have something when she was gone. In her handkerchief there was a sponge soaked in face powder, like the one his mother carried. He listened with only a part of his mind to the story that she was telling—how she got lost on the street in Chicago.

". . . When I was sure that I didn't have the vaguest idea where I was, I went up to a policeman and said *Can you please tell me how to get back to the Palmer House?* And he said *Lady, follow your nose.*"

Robert smiled and spoke her name slowly.

"Irene . . ."

"What is it?"

"There's a girl who called here a little while ago. Her name is Amanda Matthews."

"Yes, Robert."

"They talked about my mother. . . . When I ask Aunt Clara how she is, Aunt Clara always says *getting along as well as can be expected.*"

He could not frame the question that was troubling him, but Irene seemed to know anyway. She nodded to him just as if he had spoken it aloud.

"Turn over," she said. Then she pulled the covers down and

rubbed his back the way she used to do when he was little—rubbed it until he felt drowsy and quiet, far inside of him.

"Your mother and father both have the flu, and they're very sick."

When he turned around to look at her, she was staring out of the window.

"Your mother has double pneumonia."

Robert turned his back to the wall and closed his eyes. He had found out now what it was that he wanted to know.

"The baby was born yesterday . . . is still alive. I talked to the doctor this noon. He said that your mother was slightly improved. . . . She has an even chance, he said."

12

After Irene had gone, Robert sought in his mind and in his fever for a way to describe the situation. He did not want to use certain words that frightened him. *Double pneumonia*, Irene had said. And both his father and his mother were in the hospital.

And there was Aunt Amelia's husband, for instance. Mr. Shepherd had pneumonia (the plain kind) winter before last and there was something called *the crisis*. When that was over, he got well. But people didn't always.

Miss Harris at school didn't get well. She had "*T.B.*" and that was why she was so pale. She taught geography and all the kids used to bring her apples and oranges, and lilacs when they were in bloom. And for her birthday the whole class gave her sweet peas from the greenhouse.

When she had to stop teaching, Robert and Irish rode out to see her one afternoon on his bicycle. She was in a downstairs room, in bed, and she had changed so much during that short time that they hardly knew her. She coughed when she tried to talk to them. And there was a clock in the room that ticked loudly, and they were not allowed to stay but a minute or two.

That was several years ago. Before that Robert could remember about his Grandfather Blaney. Out in the country at a place called Gracelands they kept a ferret to drive the rats away. The ferret bit Grandfather Blaney in the ear while he was sleeping. Then he came home and was sick a long time, so that they had to have the Christmas tree upstairs in his bedroom. When the door was opened, Bunny and Agnes rushed in together—Agnes crying *See my rocking-horse*, and Bunny *Oh, see my doll!*

Then Grandfather Blaney died and the door of his room was kept tightly closed. Robert opened it once when there was nobody around, and went inside. They had taken everything out of the room except the furniture. There weren't even any clothes in the clothes-closet.

When he went home, he talked to his mother about it. She told him how they thought Grandfather Blaney was dead, and how he opened his eyes and looked at them and said, *Heaven is a providing-place.* . . . That was very much like something Mr. Stark read in Sunday school: *In my Father's house are many mansions.* The same thing, practically. If people were good, Mr. Stark said, and didn't break the Ten Commandments, they went straight to Heaven when they died. Cats and dogs, too. Only that wasn't right. Robert knew that for certain, because Irish's cat had kittens that had to be killed. And he and Irish buried one of them in a Mason jar with a little water in it. And two weeks later they dug the jar up again.

There were some things it was better not to think about. Without thinking at all, therefore, Robert lay quietly while moment after moment rose over him and set. Some one came upstairs. He heard the toilet being flushed and the sound of water running in the bathroom. Then there was no sound at all, until Uncle Wilfred brought his dinner up to him.

He would have liked to talk about his mother, but he didn't feel that he knew Uncle Wilfred well enough. Uncle Wilfred was kind and all that. He didn't force medicine down Robert's throat before he was half awake. And when he turned the light on, he always put a piece of paper around it. But on the other hand, Uncle Wilfred wasn't like other men. He didn't smoke or drink whisky or tell stories about how there were two Irishmen named Pat and Mike. He didn't have his hair cut often enough and he didn't believe in dancing. He wore shoes that turned up at the toe and he went to church three times on Sunday and there wasn't much of anything that Robert could talk to him about.

Each of them remained in a separate silence while Robert ate. But the moment Uncle Wilfred went out of the room, Robert was sorry that he had let Uncle Wilfred go, for he remembered, as soon as the light was turned out, that if anything happened to his mother, it would be *his* fault. He was frightened, then—more so than he had ever been. A terrible kind of fright, as if he were going to cry and be sick at his stomach, both at once. He doubled up his fists and buried his face in the hot pillow. The darkness was suffocating, but he stayed that way until he fell asleep, into a dream canopied with light.

He had come home.

He was in the little sewing-room at the head of the stairs.

It was night.

Waiting to go to sleep, he heard the stairs creaking.

And voices on the stairs.

The voices of his aunts, saying *Robert can't . . . Robert can't say . . . can't say fevver* . . . Aunt Clara, Aunt Eth, Irene. Their voices elongated in the dark and yet recognizable, saying the same thing one after another.

It made him uneasy. He turned, clutching the hem of his blanket.

Feather . . . Feather . . .

He could say it now without any trouble. Light as a . . . but not when he was little.

Feather . . .

The word snapped conclusively.

Feather . . .

It scraped against the dark side of the house and there was laughter on the stairs.

Feather . . .

The night wind bound him, dark, divided, on his hollow bed. Unwillingly, having premonitions of anguish, he settled farther into sleep.

In his dream he heard ringing, hoofs clopping, clopping on hard pavement. . . . He saw Dreyfus with his brown flanks shining. He heard Dreyfus with his harness jigging. . . . With faces white and intent Boyd and Irene drove past him in a high black carraige. He ran after them, crying *Irene! Irene!* but they did not hear him. And so he tried to climb on the back end of the carriage, crying

Irene!
(wildly)
As the wheels, turning
Do you hear me, Irene?
dragged him . . .
Torn bodily, torn by the roots out of his dream, he sat up in the dark. Some one was shaking him.
Robert darling, wake up!
It was his mother.
I am awake.
You're not.
I am, too.
Then tell me what's the matter?
Sighing, he lay back upon the pillow. The bedsprings creaked under his dead weight. He was very tired.
I don't know . . . I was having a bad dream.
I heard you, clear in my room.
She bent over him in the dark and brushed the hair back from his forehead.
It must have been a very bad dream.
Yes, it was.
Sleep was still under him, like a pit.
He could look down. . . .
If his mother would only stay with him, he would not drop into it immediately and dream that same dream. But he could not ask her to do that. He was too old. Much too old.
It's this room, Robert.
She seemed to have guessed, anyway.
Without his having to tell her, she went to the window and adjusted the shade so that it wouldn't snap.
You're not used to sleeping in this room.
She came back then, and sat down beside him on the edge of the bed.
His head cleared.
His lungs were no longer expanding and contracting with excitement.
When he was quite calm inside, he started down. . . . He was not afraid now. His mother was there, and she was not going away just yet. There was no need to hurry.

Once he looked back, trying to say good-night to her, but no words came.

He had gone too far.

There was a great distance between them.

At the very bottom, he turned and saw that she was still sitting on the edge of the bed where he had left her.

13

Robert was not supposed to get up. Tomorrow, Dr. Macgregor said, if he didn't have any fever. But it was not hard. So long as Robert braced his arms against the side of the bed, he felt all right. It was only when he stood. Or when he bent over to pull on his stocking. He had to rest a little. And again before he could finish tying his shoe. Then he stood, one-legged and shivering, while he measured the distance across the room to the wardrobe where Aunt Clara had hung his suit. The floor tilted slightly—not any more than he had expected and not enough to make him fall. He drew on his underwear and his shirt. While he was adjusting the straps of his leg, a sparrow came to peck at a grain of paint on the window sill and Robert waved his arms weakly to frighten it away.

Before he had finished dressing, the telephone rang and Aunt Clara's voice came up through the register. Robert drew his belt on and buckled it, listening.

"Hello. . . . Hello, James, I can't hear you . . . I say I can't hear you very well. Can you hear me? . . . Yes. . . ."

At the thought of his father, Robert had to sit down and with both hands cling to the edge of the chair.

"You don't mean it, James. . . ." And then a long silence and, "No, but I will . . . if you want me to."

Straining, Robert heard the click of the receiver. The stairs creaked softly.

"Bunny . . . *Oh*, Bunny. . . ."

Aunt Clara was already at the head of the stairs when Robert pulled his door open. She was neither surprised to see him nor angry.

"Come in here, Robert," she said. "I have something to tell you."

He followed her into Grandmother Morison's room. Bunny was there alone. And he was in his pajamas. Aunt Clara sat down in the rocking-chair and gathered Bunny onto her lap.

"It's about your mother," she said.

Her voice sounded hoarse, as if she had a cold. She began to rock back and forth, back and forth, until her eyes covered over with tears. Robert turned then and went out of the room.

He did not have to be told what had happened. He knew already. During the night while he was sleeping, she got worse. Then she did not have an even chance, like the doctor said. And she died. His mother was dead.

BOOK THREE

Upon a Compass-point

I

IF James Morison had come upon himself on the street, he would have thought *That poor fellow is done for.* . . . But he walked past the mirror in the front hall without seeing it and did not know how grey his face was, and how, all in a few days, sickness and suffering and grief and despair had aged him.

It was a shock to step across the threshold of the library and find everything unchanged. The chairs, the white bookcases, the rugs and curtains—even his pipe cleaners on the mantel behind the clock. He had left them there before he went away. He crossed the room and heard his own footsteps echoing. And knew that, now that he was alone, he would go on hearing them as long as he lived.

Sophie followed him when she had hung his coat and hat in the hall closet. "There's some letters for you," she said.

"Some what?"

"There's some letters for you and some bills. They come while you were gone."

"Oh," James said.

"I put them on the table."

He looked at Sophie for the first time and saw that her eyes were red from weeping.

"I thought I'd tell you," she said.

"Yes."

"In case there might be something important."

"Yes, I'll look at them"—he realized suddenly why she looked so different. It was because she had no teeth. And with her mouth sunken in, Sophie had become an old woman—"after a while."

"I turned the spread back in your room so you can lay down if you want to, Mr. Morison."

She saw that he didn't hear her and tried again. "Mrs. Hiller telegraphed from Decatur yesterday. She said to come and open the house this morning. And have the guest-room ready for Miss Blaney."

"For Miss Blaney? . . . Oh yes, I forgot about that. Or maybe they didn't tell me. It's all right, though. When is she coming?"

"The telegram didn't say. It just said to have the guest-room ready for her when she come. And Karl is going away."

"Where?"

"Why, didn't he tell you, Mr. Morison? He's going to Germany."

"Maybe he did. Yes, I guess so. When?"

"Right away. In a couple of days."

James put his hands over his eyes and felt the relief of darkness. His eyelids were cracked and hard. He had not slept for three nights. It did not seem likely that he would ever sleep again.

"You must tell Karl to be sure and see me before he goes."

Sophie nodded. "He was here early this morning. I had him build a fire in the grate. All you have to do is light a match to it."

"That's fine."

"When he comes I'll tell him you want to see him, Mr. Morison."

James took the stack of letters and sat down. *Mr. James B. Morison . . . Mr. James Morison, 553 W. Elm Street, Logan, Illinois . . . Mr. and Mrs. James B. Morison . . .* He read the envelopes again and again, without having the strength or the will to open them. *Mr. and Mrs. James B. Morison. . . .* When he closed his eyes for a moment and sank back, it was more than he could do to raise his head from the cushions.

"It's like being drunk," he said.

To his surprise, Sophie was still there and answered him.

"Once when I was a girl in the old country——"

James did not hear the end of her sentence. If he listened to Sophie, he would have to look at her. He would have to open his eyes.

When he relaxed, when he sat too long in one place, he invariably found himself on the railway platform downtown, with her. The train was coming in—the one they were going to take to Decatur. And there were people walking up and down the platform, waiting to get on. He shoved forward, knowing each time that if he'd only waited—but he didn't wait. That was the whole trouble. He was trying to get seats for the two of them before all the others got on. If he'd stepped back, he'd have seen the interurban draw up alongside the train. On the other tracks . . . The interurban had a parlor car that was almost empty. It would have been ever so much better to take that, don't you see? And turn their train tickets in later. That way they wouldn't have been exposed. But they had suitcases and all the people were pushing them forward and the train was crowded already. There was nothing to do but go up the steps and onto the train.

"You must take care of yourself, Mr. Morison," Sophie said. "You've got those three young children to think about. If anything happened to you now——"

"Yes," James said, "you're quite right." And sprang up suddenly and began tearing the envelopes open, one after another. He read the letters while he walked back and forth between the fireplace and the windows—read them over and over without retaining what he read. Then he threw envelopes and letters upon the library table and stood perfectly still, pressing his shoulder against the mantel.

For two days now (ever since they came into his room at daybreak to tell him) he had been getting on that train. And there was no way, apparently, that he could stop.

2

The coffin was set in the bay window of the living-room, and James wanted to be alone, but almost as soon as the undertaker's men were out of the house, Wilfred appeared, bringing James's mother and Bunny.

Bunny was weeping.

James bent down and drew Bunny to him, between his knees, and felt the soft wet cold cheek against his own rough skin.

"There, there," he said, gently. "You mustn't, son. You mustn't take on so. You'll be sick." He struggled with the large buttons on the child's coat.

"I put his rubbers on," Wilfred said.

James looked at him earnestly.

"I say I put Bunny's rubbers on."

"Oh . . . much obliged to you."

"That's all right," Wilfred said. "Glad to do it, only I think I got them wrong foot to."

James nodded. If they'd only wait, let him be by himself for a while.

"Clara said to tell you she'd be over this evening right after supper."

"You must take your coats off," James said. "You mustn't stand here in the front hall." And wondered if his words sounded as desperate to them—and as foolish.

His mother unwound a heavy woolen scarf and looked at him with faded eyes.

"James," she said solemnly, "she is gone to a better place, where she'll always be happy. Fourteen years ago your father died—in March. And it doesn't seem like any time at all. . . ."

Neither does what happened night before last, James wanted to say to her. He was only two rooms down the hall at the hospital, and Thursday night, when she was worse, he lay awake all night, listening. The gas-light came through the transom and cut a rectangular hole in the ceiling. It was through that hole that the sound of her desperate suffocated breathing came to him.

"You don't know, I said to Clara, how many times I get down on my knees and thank God for taking him, for not letting him suffer." She allowed Wilfred to help with her coat. "Every few days he'd have a spell of very bad pain. Then we'd have to give him morphine. . . ."

When Bunny stopped weeping and turned to look at her, James separated him from his coat and mittens.

"Sophie is out in the kitchen," he said. "Why don't you go out and say hello to her."

There was no point in a child's knowing these things.

"I'd been waiting for him to go," his mother said as they went into the library. "I'd been expecting it ever since he stopped eating. That's what carried him along, the doctor said—a good appetite. And he'd lost so much flesh. . . ."

With his eyes James begged Wilfred to take her away, but

Wilfred was unable or unwilling. He sat down in the largest chair and crossed one knee over the other permanently.

"I don't think your father weighed much over a hundred and twenty or maybe a hundred and twenty-five, because there was nothing to him but skin and bones. Even so"—she turned and looked into Wilfred's face to make sure that he was listening—"even so, I didn't get much rest. It was hard lifting him, you know, and I stayed right in the same room with him for months. He'd rather lie there and suffer than call anybody. And I knew if I was near I'd hear him move. He'd have pain, you know, James. And then he'd take medicine and sleep."

There was a silence. James said, "Did you have a nice time in Vandalia, Wilfred?"

"In Vandalia? Why, we didn't go."

"I thought you and Clara were going down there for Thanksgiving."

"We did intend to. But we'd have had to go on the train, and with so much sickness about, we were afraid to risk it. But I thought Clara told you all that when you called up about the boys?"

"Yes, I guess she did. Have they been all right? And behaved themselves?"

"Robert's been sick."

"Oh . . . is that so?"

"Yes, Robert's been a sick boy," his mother said. "A mighty sick boy!"

"The flu?"

She nodded.

"Yesterday morning," Wilfred said, "after you called, Robert got up out of bed before he was supposed to. Today, the doctor said. But Clara got in touch with him during the forenoon and he said it was all right if Robert didn't have any temperature. And he didn't—this was yesterday—so I guess it *will* be. He has to keep quiet, of course."

James caught a glimpse of a pocket knife: Wilfred was going to pare his finger nails.

"He didn't seem to take it as hard as Bunny did. But then I always thought Bunny showed his mother more affection." Wilfred closed the knife blade with a sigh. "Clara was going to tell you but in case she forgets—if you want to bring the baby home after the funeral, we'd be only too glad to take it and look after it for you."

James sat up. "I don't know." He steadied himself carefully with his hands. "They're going to keep the baby at the hospital for a week or so. The baby's all right, I guess, but they want to keep it there. And after that I don't know exactly what I want to do. I haven't had time to think about it."

The front door opened while James was speaking.

"We want to be of help," Wilfred said, "in any way that we possibly can."

"That's very kind of you."

"Until you get straightened around," Wilfred said.

Irene appeared in a draft of cold air. Her coat was half unbuttoned. She spoke to each of them. Then gravely, without any expression on her face, she made her way around Wilfred's feet and drew the curtains together across the library windows. With grateful eyes James followed her. She turned on the table lamp, and in the blue bowl on the mantel found matches to light the fire. When Bunny came in, the room was bright and habitable.

She smiled at him. "You know your agate?" she said, and took the blue bowl down from the mantel. "The yellow agate that you told me was lost? Well I've found it."

Bunny went on looking at her face.

"Here it is."

"Irene," Bunny said, "it's so terrible here!" And buried his face in the lining of her coat.

Irene's smile went all to pieces. She knelt down and put her arms about him. "Everything's going to be all right," she said. "Only you mustn't cry, do you hear? You mustn't cry."

Bunny dried his face with the back of his hand, and took the bowl and the yellow agate.

"I know," he said, and sat down on the floor to play.

Irene stood looking at him thoughtfully, until her eyes were no longer blurred. Then she turned to James and said, "When's Robert coming home?"

"He isn't, I guess."

"Why not?"

"He's been sick."

"I know he has. I just came from there."

"Clara doesn't think Robert ought to come home," Wilfred began. "He wasn't even supposed to——"

Irene interrupted him. "I called Dr. Macgregor and he said he'd seen Robert early this morning, and that it was all right if we wanted to bring him home. . . . Clara wouldn't listen, James. I told her . . . I told her everything Dr. Macgregor said. But she said Robert was going to stay there just the same. . . . I left him sitting in a chair by the front window with his rubbers on."

"If Clara doesn't think he ought to come home," James said, "perhaps it would be just as well to——"

"Don't you *want* him here?"

"Certainly I want him."

"Well do you mind if I call and tell her that?"

James shut his eyes. "Tell her anything you like."

He would have shut his mind, too, if it had been possible. He was very tired. And weak. And there was no reason why they could not make these arrangements among themselves.

From what Wilfred was saying—a word now and then, or a phrase—James gathered that the churches had been closed on account of the epidemic, but they were soon to be opened again. As for the epidemic, Wilfred said, that was on the wane. No new cases had been reported yesterday or the day before.

Against his will James listened and heard Irene's voice locked in argument.

"I know, Clara, but the doctor says it's all right . . . yes . . . Yes, James wants him here. . . ."

They had traced the epidemic, Wilfred said, to the original source and found that it was brought to this country in German submarines.

"Yes. . . . Yes, Clara. . . . Yes, I know!"

James turned and looked at Irene uneasily. There was no color in her face.

"Yes," she said, very slowly. "Yes . . . yes . . ."

The brilliant unreasonable laughter shocked them all and furthermore it didn't stop when it should have, but went on and on into the mouthpiece of the telephone.

3

It was Wilfred who took the receiver out of Irene's hand and told Clara to have the boy ready in fifteen minutes. For that James would be grateful always. Ethel came in from the late afternoon train and went upstairs right away to look after Irene. When his mother and Wilfred had gone, James stood with his back to the fire until the little brass clock on the mantel tick-tick-tick-ticked itself out of existence and the room grew quiet around him.

At five-thirty Robert came in. He had a book under one arm and the box of soldiers under the other, and he limped more noticeably than usual. When Robert was tired, he did not care how he walked, but led with his good leg, in spite of all that James had told him, and dragged his artificial leg behind.

Robert shook hands with his father solemnly and put the soldiers and the book on the library table. Then he went over to the windows and sat down.

"How are you feeling, son?"

"All right," Robert said.

"Weak?"

"Yes."

"So am I. We'll have to be careful for a while. Both of us."

Their eyes met and they agreed that there was something in the house which was not to be talked about. The best and possibly the only solution, so far as James could see, was for Clara to take the baby. And the boys, too. For he couldn't keep the house going—that was certain. He'd have to store what furniture he wanted. That wasn't much. He had never cared for antiques the way Elizabeth did. And sell all the rest. Sell the house, too, for what he could get.

Wilfred had not offered to take the boys, but it would be all right, probably. James would give Clara so much a month for boarding them and for their clothes—because he would not have Wilfred or anybody else paying for the support of his children. And he'd get a room near by. Clara's wasn't the kind of home they were used to, perhaps. But it would do until such time as he was able to make a better arrangement.

In the long run it was a mistake to have children. James did not understand them. He never knew what was going on in their minds. But that was Elizabeth's doing, after all. It was she who had wanted them.

There were some men who had a natural way with children. Tom Macgregor, for instance. They came to him in a room full of people, and pestered the life out of him. When Bunny and Robert were little, they would come to their father sometimes to have cigar smoke blown into their ears—Bunny did still—when they had the earache. But not very often. If they had been girls it might have been different. James felt more at ease with little girls. They came and sat on his lap and played with his watch-fob. And they seemed to like very much the riddles he told them. Robert and Bunny were forever arguing, contending with each other like Cain and Abel. So that it was mostly a matter of keeping them separated and making each one play with his own toys. And without her . . . James went into the front hall and stared for a long time at the umbrella-stand. Without Elizabeth it was more than he could manage.

On the second trip into the front hall he went through the white columns and into the living room. Then into the library by the door at the farther end. If he could only go back, if he could remember everything during the last ten days, why then he might—it was foolish of course, but the same idea occurred to him over and over—he might be able to change what had already happened.

In his whole life he had never been sick before—not seriously. And being sick, he could not make people do the things he wanted them to. They would not even let him get up and go into her room at the hospital and see her—except that once, late Wednesday afternoon.

The nurse brought a chair for him and made him sit some distance away from the bed. Elizabeth was better, she said. But he could not help seeing how difficult it was for her to breathe. It seemed to take all her strength for that.

He looked at her hair spread out over the pillow, and remembered the first time he had ever seen her. She was driving a pony cart on Tremont Street and she had two little girls in the cart with her and the little girls wore big blue hair-ribbons.

He leaned forward to ask her if she remembered meeting him

that day on Tremont Street, but just then the nurse came in. The nurse had the baby with her, wrapped in a white blanket. And Elizabeth smiled her slow smile and said, *Look, James, another peeing boy. . . .*

4

Each time that James passed through the living-room he was careful to look at the sofa or the French windows which led into the back part of the house. Nevertheless, he was drawn, pulled toward the bay window, until at last he could get no farther. The coffin was grey with silver handles. And if it was really Elizabeth, James thought—if he should see *her* when he stepped up to it (her dark hair and her forehead and the slope of her throat)—he did not know what he would do.

He stood there a few feet away, with his heart racing wildly like a machine, and Sophie had to call him twice to dinner before he understood.

Ethel and the boys were waiting for him in the dining-room.

"Would you like me to serve, James?" she said.

James looked at her in bewilderment. She pronounced her words precisely the way a school-teacher would.

"I always do the serving," he said.

"Yes, but I thought that perhaps if you weren't feeling well——"

"I'm all right," James said. "I'm quite all right."

They sat down together—Ethel in Elizabeth's place at the end of the table. When James was with her he found himself on guard for fear that he would make some mistake in his English. He spoke as well as the average person, he supposed. As well as anyone ought to speak. But Ethel had gone East to school. She had gone to Bryn Mawr and she never seemed to want to marry. When she was younger and before her hair turned grey, she was attractive enough. James knew of several men that she could have had. But she was too well educated for a woman and she didn't want any of them.

"For Miss Blaney," he said. And when Sophie took the plate that he handed her, James noticed that she was self-conscious on account of her mouth.

"How much are they going to cost, Sophie?" he said when she returned to his end of the table.

"What, Mr. Morison?"

"Your teeth."

"I don't know, exactly," she said, with the color mounting upward into her face. "About fifty dollars." She set Bunny's plate in front of him. "But if I'd known how much it would take, I don't guess I'd of had them out. But they were hurting me so, night and day——"

"You did the right thing, I'm sure," Ethel said. "And Robert needs more water."

James wondered if he had said something that he shouldn't have, if he had said something unkind. "When the time comes to get your new teeth, let me know, Sophie. I might be able to help you with them." He took up the carving-knife and began sharpening it. And Sophie beside him pulled the hem out of her apron in an access of gratitude.

When Robert had been served, she returned once more to the head of the table.

"That Karl is here . . ."

James unfolded his napkin.

"Tell him I'll be out as soon as we're through dinner," he said.

Sophie disappeared through the swinging doors, and James took up his knife and fork. When he tried to eat, the food turned solid in his throat and would not go down. There was nothing to do but sit with his plate untouched before him, and watch his sons, who were still too young to confuse grief with a good appetite.

When Robert passed things it was always without speaking and without looking up—as if the interruption were barely tolerable. With Bunny it seemed to be largely a matter of making him hear, for he ate with his eyes on some object (the corner of a dish now) and there was no telling where his mind was.

"How is Irene?" James said.

"Resting. I put cold cloths on her head. That's about all anybody can do, you know, after she's had one of those spells."

When Ethel was a little girl, Elizabeth had said, she could not bear to get dirt on her clean white stockings.

Bunny was recalled from wherever it was that he had been.

"Is it true, Aunt Eth— Is it true that Irene married Uncle Boyd Hiller for his money?"

In the silence that followed this question they could all hear the big clock ticking sullenly in the front hall, two rooms away.

"No, son, it isn't true," James said. "And you mustn't say things like that, do you hear?"

Bunny nodded, and would have gone on eating if Ethel had not leaned forward in her chair with hard bright eyes.

"Who told you that, Bunny?"

"It's something he's made up," James said.

"I didn't either make it up—it's what Grandmother Morison told Amanda Matthews."

Robert put his fork down with a clatter.

"Who is Amanda Matthews?" Ethel asked.

"She's a girl in Aunt Clara's Sunday-school class that was at Aunt Clara's house night before last."

James saw that Ethel was smiling at him queerly.

"Well, however it was," she said, "you misunderstood. Your grandmother wouldn't say such a thing."

"But she did, Aunt Eth. She said there was somebody else that Irene wanted to marry but Grandmother Blaney kept after her night and day, saying what a fine young man Uncle Boyd was, because he had been to Princeton and——"

"Bunny, that's enough."

The interurban was drawing alongside the train, on the other tracks. And James had to wait for a minute before he could go on speaking.

"Suppose you tell us, son, what you were doing all this time?"

"He was on the couch," Robert volunteered, "in the sitting-room, pretending like he was asleep."

"When I want information from you, Robert, I'll ask for it. . . . Go up to your room now, both of you."

They had made trouble enough for one evening—trouble that would last for months and months, and when Irene found out about it, breed more and more trouble.

"Well," he said, "what are you waiting for?"

As soon as they had gone—Robert looking injured and Bunny in tears again—James set about to deal with the image that obsessed him. With so much sickness, with the epidemic everywhere, it stood to reason that someone with influenza might have been on that interurban, too. They might have been exposed to the flu there, just as they were on the crowded train. And what point was there in torturing himself like this? What good did it do?

"You might have let them stay and have their dessert," Ethel said, from the other end of the table.

"They're my children, Ethel," James said, "and I'll do with them as I think best."

5

Wilfred returned with Clara almost immediately after dinner.

"It doesn't seem possible," Clara said. "I say it just doesn't seem possible! She was so young, and with so much to live for!"

James had no idea what to say, or what was expected of him. But as the evening progressed, more and more people came—Lyman and Amelia Shepherd, Maud Ahrens, the Hinkleys, the McIntyres, the Lloyds—until the library was filled with them. And by that time James had adjusted his mind to the rhetoric of the occasion. What bewildered him was not the set phrases, and not the repetition, but the fact that they were sincerely spoken. *Such a loss*, people said to him with tears in their eyes. *So tragic that she should have to be taken. . . .* Then because there were so many that they could not all talk to him, they fell back upon one another politely, as if that were why they had come. They discussed the peace terms and the price of meat. They talked about the weather, which was severe for December—only the beginning of the cold months.

James tried to take a suitable interest in the conversation, but he could not keep from glancing up when each new person came into the room, and strange ideas ran through his head. It seemed to him that except for an unwillingness to interrupt one another, people acted very much as if they had come here to a party. The house had taken possession of them—Elizabeth's house—and they were having a good time.

Clara and Wilfred went home, and then the Shepherds, and then the McIntyres, almost without James's noticing it. The air grew heavy with smoke. And after a while he discovered that it was not necessary for him even to seem to be listening. He was glad when eleven o'clock came and one by one they stood up to leave—all except young Johnston, who had brought his mail out to him from the office and did not know apparently how to go home.

While Johnston talked about the office and about the adjustment of a certain loss, James sat with his hand over his left side. It was something that he had never thought about until now, and there was no reason why it should occur to him particularly, except that he felt very wide awake after not having slept for days and days. But the strange thing was that he could hear his own heart ticking under his vest—keeping time there like a clock.

"I've come down from Chicago," a voice said—an unmistakable voice. James sprang up and went to the front hall, but he was too late. Boyd Hiller was there. He was inside the door, talking to Ethel, and there was that same tired handsomeness about him. He had not changed, except that it seemed to be an effort for him to carry himself so well. As Ethel started up the stairs, he turned and saw James in the doorway.

"Good evening," he said.

Once upon a time James met Boyd Hiller with Robert unconscious in his arms. And later (years later) James had shut the front door in his face. The extreme courtesy of Boyd's manner implied that he remembered both incidents.

In any family, James thought, it was like that. Nothing was ever forgotten.

There were no chairs in the front hall—only a sofa beside the window. Both men remained standing. When the tension became uncomfortable, James said, "Are you living in Chicago now?"

"For a short while."

Boyd cleared his throat.

"New York is my headquarters, though, and has been the last two years. I'm on the stock exchange."

"That must be interesting," James said, and thought grimly of the time Boyd put soap in the minnow-bucket for a joke.

"You get used to it."

"Yes, I suppose."

Irene was coming down the stairs in a green flowered kimono.

"You get used to anything," James said.

When Irene reached the bottom step, she waited, and Boyd waited at the edge of the dark red rug. "I can't tell you how shocked and how sorry I am!"

Irene stepped down and shook hands with him gravely.

"You've been sick," she said.

Boyd nodded.

"Flu?"

"It was a light case. When I was able to go back to the hotel I found your note, and here I am."

James understood now what had happened—why Irene had gone off to Chicago when they were counting on her to stay and look after the boys. Actually, there had never been much doubt in his mind. He knew her almost as well as he knew Elizabeth. She was very impulsive by nature, and excitable, and decided everything on the spur of the moment, and then had all the rest of her life to regret it in. It didn't take any great intelligence to see by the look on her face that she was about to run through that whole unhappy business with Boyd Hiller all over again. If they wanted to do that, James thought, it was all right with him. He turned and went back into the library.

6

The flowers in Irene's kimono were almost but not quite the color of her hair. And James decided that no matter what people said, it was not money. Irene had not married Boyd for that, nor would she go back to him for any such reason. There was no telling how she felt about Boyd now, but at one time, before they began quarreling so, she had been fond of him. On her wedding day she broke a mirror and perhaps it was that which ruined their marriage—bad luck as much as anything.

Somehow it was impossible to think of her leading a calm, ordinary life. Wherever Irene was, there was excitement. Now when she gathered the folds of her kimono and leaned toward the fire, her eyes glittered. Her hair gave off light.

"I think we know sometimes what is going to happen to us," she said. "I remember things that didn't seem to have any meaning till now, and they fit. . . . We were upstairs, James, in your bedroom, and Elizabeth was doing her hair. I was sitting on the bed, watching her, and I said, 'It's so complicated, the way you are doing your hair now,' and she stopped and looked at me in the mirror, and said, 'I know. I was just thinking that nobody will be able to do it for me when I am dead.' I said for her not to talk like that, because it was wrong and silly and there was no telling how long anybody would live. But she took the hairpins out of her mouth and said, 'Within three years.' "

James got up out of his chair and began to walk. He could not and would not believe what Irene was saying. He could not believe that Elizabeth had lain awake at his side, planning and arranging things for a time when she would not be there. With other people she sometimes covered up her true feelings, though not with him. Nobody had any idea, for instance, how deeply she still felt about Robert's accident; how at night she turned into his arms and wept. But if her life had been overshadowed by the anticipation of dying, he would have known it. She could not have kept it from him.

"It's the kind of thing that people remember," he said, "after some one is dead. You might never have thought anything more about it except for that. It's like any common superstition —thirteen at the table or a dog howling or a bird in the house."

"You know there was one," Irene said. "There was a bird in Bunny's room while he was sick. I didn't tell you afterward because I knew it would worry you— Not the bird, but something that it was too late to do anything about. It was my fault, really. Elizabeth sent Robert for a broom. Then in our excitement we both forgot and went into the room where Bunny was. When Robert came back he saw her sitting on the edge of Bunny's bed. . . . And ever since, he's been thinking that if anything happened to his mother, he'd be responsible. You didn't know that, did you, James? . . . Tonight when they were both in bed I went to see them. I talked to them for a while about their mother, and to my surprise Robert broke down and told me what was on his mind. You have to watch him, James, and talk to him more than you do, and find out what is back of what he's saying. Because he's at the age to get notions. . . . I explained to him that people caught the flu within three days after they were exposed to it. What he was worrying about happened weeks before his mother took sick. I don't know whether he believed me or not. I guess he did. It's things like that—don't you see? Now that his mother isn't here to keep an eye on him . . . And each of us has his private nightmare. Robert isn't the only one."

James looked at her oddly to see whether by some mischance she knew about the interurban.

"I keep remembering," she said, "how selfish I was those last weeks—always thinking about Boyd and whether I could bring myself to go back to him. And I sort of took what was happening to her for granted. That was the way it always was. As a person, James, I could never hold a candle to her. Nobody could. . . . I remember once we went, the two of us, to see a woman who had cooked for my mother, and who was very sick. She lived in an old house on Tenth Street, and it was filthy dirty. And after we left, Bess was furious with me. She said, 'Irene, I *saw* you gather up your skirts so they wouldn't touch anything! How *can* you be like that?' . . . She went over to the bed where the woman lay, and sat down, and took her hand."

James sighed. He had been along with them that day. It was just after Elizabeth and he were married. He had gone into the dirty ramshackle house on Tenth Street when they did. But Irene didn't remember. She was talking about Elizabeth for the pain it caused her, and possibly to keep from saying something she couldn't bring herself to say. They had always been friends, and with friends you oughtn't to have to say what both of you understand without its being said. Probably this was as near as she could come to speaking about that abrupt change of plans that had thrown them all into such an uproar. If it hadn't been for Clara, who, with all her faults, and she had plenty of them, nevertheless . . .

"And there's something else, James . . . something I have to tell you. At the last when she was so terribly sick she motioned with her hand. As if she wanted to write. I said 'Tell me what it is you want done, Bess, and I'll do it . . .'"

James got up and went to the window and threw it wide open, and small white papers that he had stuffed into the cracks to keep the drafts out were scattered across the room.

"'It's about my baby,' she said. 'I don't want the Morisons to have my baby.'"

The air was not as cold as James had expected, but dark and full of snow.

7

When he opened the door from the butler's pantry into the kitchen, he found only darkness. It was no more than reasonable, he told himself, that Karl should have got tired waiting and gone home. For it was after eleven, and he had promised to come out as soon as dinner was over.

The scene at the table had driven everything else out of his mind. And people began coming. . . . There was no need to say that to Ethel. She was a fine woman and he was fond of her. But if there was one thing that he could not stand, it was having somebody step in and tell him how to run his affairs. . . . He groped his way past the table to the light cord. Sophie had left the kitchen just as she always did, in perfect order. He was about to turn and go back to the front part of the house when he heard a scratching sound outside, and as he opened the door, there were two eyes shining at him out of the darkness. Old John hobbled across the sill.

"Did they forget you, old fellow?" James said.

The dog looked at him reproachfully.

It was beginning, James thought to himself—the final and complete disintegration of his house. Wherever he turned he would find it. Elizabeth was gone, and things would not be done which should be done. . . . He put his face down and buried it (for there was no one here to see him) in the cold fur of the dog's side. Old John whined softly.

Why, James thought, why am I doing this? And straightened up immediately and stood there waiting until the dog had made himself comfortable beside the stove. Then he turned the light out and went back the way he had come—through the butler's pantry and the dining-room and around the library to the front hall. Mr. Koenig had come over from next door, and he was in the library alone. And on the fifth step of the stairs James paused, remembering why people sat up all night with the dead.

Then he went on up the stairs and across the upstairs hall to the bedroom which Elizabeth and he had shared, and saw her dresses hanging in the closet, and was struck blind and almost senseless. When he could, he shut the closet door quickly, and pressed his forehead into the long cool mirror which was on the other side.

Satin
and lace
and brown velvet
and the faint odor of violets.

—That was all which was left to him of his love. In anger then (for she could have sent some word to him and she had not—only that message about the baby, which he didn't entirely believe) he went about the room picking up her brush or her ivory mirror or the tiny bottle of smelling-salts, and putting them down again. One after another he opened drawers, gathering small intimate things—hairpins, sachet-bags, a sponge soaked in powder, a score-card, a tassel, a string of amber beads—and made a pile of them on the dresser. For she had put him aside, he said to himself, casually with her life.

He stood in the center of the room, rocking forward and back; and in his ears heard that terrible last hour of her breathing. . . . He would sell the house, he thought over and over like a lesson to be memorized. A lesson that he would recite tomorrow when the time came. And Clara could take the children since she wanted them. And everything else—Elizabeth's clothes, her amethysts and pearls (he dumped them out on the dresser), her engagement ring, her enameled watch—he would give to Ethel, to Irene, to Sophie, to anybody with the kindness and mercy to have them. Because she was gone now. And when he had finished, there would be no trace of her anywhere. No one would know there had ever been such a person, he said to himself. And turned to the doorway, and saw Bunny staring at him with Elizabeth's frightened eyes.

8

When he had given Bunny a drink of water and tucked him in bed, James went downstairs and out of the house. The wind had fallen. There was an inch of snow on the front walk and more of it coming down steadily on James's coat sleeve and on his gloved hands and whirling in a silent frenzy about the street lamp. The crotches of trees were white with it, and each separate branch outlined. When James looked up he could see the night sky all dark, and the moist snow dropping into his face, into his open mouth.

He had come down the stairs and out of the house as he had done every day of his life, but with this difference—he was not going back. He would not enter that empty house again. Here on the sidewalk (with snow falling so thick that a man ten feet away would hardly know him) he was alone.

He turned to the left, as the snow turned, and walked past the first house, which was the Koenigs', and past the second, which was the Mitchells', and the third. . . . They were all asleep in their beds, with no knowledge of him, or that he was here on the sidewalk looking at their darkened houses.

The house of Elizabeth's father was on the other side of the street and occupied by strangers. He had nothing to fear from it. . . . He and Elizabeth lived there when they were first married, with her father and mother and with Irene. Elizabeth's father read Ingersoll and questioned every accepted idea on religion and morality, so that it was an education for a young man to be with him. But during his last illness he changed his mind about things, and he stopped questioning. *It's like this, James,* he would say. *There's the earth—the continents and the seas, and the moon revolving around the earth, and the sun beyond that, and all the constellations. And beyond the constellations are stars without number or name, millions of them, whirling in space. You know that, James, without my telling you. . . .* But for time or the passage of time they might be there now, talking—James himself, only younger, and an old man dying of a horrible blood infection in his head.

James leaned against a tree. The snow was all about him like a curtain. And he could almost believe that they were still in that house across the street. *Somebody made it—some power—according to laws that can't be changed or added to. . . . The same now as they were thousands of years ago. . . . It's got to be like that. Otherwise it wouldn't work. . . .*

When James put both hands behind him, he felt the rough bark of the tree through his leather gloves. His fingers were getting cold and stiff.

"But to what purpose?" he said aloud, and hearing the words, he lost their meaning and all connection with what had gone before.

He knew only that there was frozen ground under his feet, and that the trees he saw were real and he could by moving out of his path touch them. The snow dropping out of the sky did not turn when he turned or make any concession to his needs, but only to his existence. The snow fell on his shoulders and on the brim of his hat and it stayed there and melted. He was real. That was all he knew.

He was here in this night, walking across the corner of a yard, over a sidewalk, down a vacant street. When he stopped to get his bearings, he saw that without knowing it he had turned up the alley. There were deep frozen ruts along each side of the road, and telephone poles one after another leaning against the sky. Ahead of him he heard wheels creaking and the placing (muffled and delicate) of hoofs. The placing of hoofs on snow. And knew suddenly that it was all a mistake . . . everything that he had thought and done this day.

He was alive, that was the trouble. He was caught up in his own living and breathing and there was no way possible for him to get out. Elizabeth knew that, and she had come after him in the pony cart. She had come to take him home.

He was glad. He was immensely excited. His hands shook and his knees. He began to run along the alley, stumbling and falling and picking himself up again. He ran until he was stopped by the lean shape of a horse, and a wagon with a lantern on it. The lantern shone upward into a man's face that was thin and patient and crazy.

With the last of his strength gone out of him, James leaned against the firm lattice-work of his own back fence.

9

James awoke late into a room that was bright with the morning sun. On the dresser were Elizabeth's things lying in a heap as he had left them. When he looked outside the snow blinded him. He stretched his legs under the covers until they touched the foot of the bed, and wondered how many mornings of his life he had lain here—awake and watching the curtains blow in from the open window. And whether the lightness he felt inside him was grief. Or if he would ever be capable of any emotion again.

Slowly and with care he bathed and shaved and dressed himself in clean clothes. He staggered slightly when he went from the closet to the dresser to comb his hair. But his head was clear, and when he put his hands to his eyelids, they no longer felt cracked and hard. . . . There were formalities and customs, there was the funeral to be got through with somehow this day.

Ethel was in the guest-room, making her bed. He lingered at the door until she noticed him.

"You look rested, James," she said. "Did you sleep?"

He looked into her eyes and saw nothing but kindness there—kindness and a veiled sympathy. It had never been easy for her to express her feelings.

"Yes, I think I did."

"That's what you needed more than anything else."

For the first time it occurred to him that Ethel might keep from Irene what Bunny said last night at the table—that she had, in fact, no intention of telling her.

"Thank you," he said, and hoped that she would understand what for.

"Irene is off on some errand. With Boyd, I think. But your mother is here and Clara, too. You'll find them in the sewing-room."

At the head of the stairs James listened and heard their voices. They were arguing over which card had come with which flowers.

"I don't care what you say, Clara, the yellow roses were from the men in James's office. The carnations were from Bunny's class at school."

"If you'd only waited, Mother, and let me open them. I'm trying to write them down in this little book as they come. Otherwise we'll never know who sent what."

Though it was nearly ten o'clock, there was no one in the front hall or the living-room or the library. And James's place was still set at the dining-room table. He went on to the kitchen, which was warm and bright. Karl sat with his overcoat on and the sweat running down his face. Bunny was beside him at the kitchen table. And Sophie, rattling the breakfast dishes, created such a cheerful noise that none of them heard James, or knew that he was there.

Bunny was making a wreath of ferns. And it was hardly the thing, James thought. Bunny ought not to be making a game of flowers that had been sent to his mother's funeral. As James started forward he could have sworn, almost, that he felt a slight restraining pressure on his arm. And he turned, in spite of himself—in spite of the fact that he knew positively no one was there.

10

With his coffee James smoked a cigarette—the first since he had been sick. Irene came in before he had finished.

"I've been out driving," she said, and sat down beside him at the dining-room table.

"With Boyd?"

"Yes. Did Ethel tell you?" Irene unbuttoned her left glove and then buttoned it again. "I've made up my mind, James—or rather I've had it made up for me. Boyd has to live in New York and I'd have to live there, too, it seems, if I went back to him."

"What are you going to do, then?"

"Stay here and help you look after the children."

From her expression it was impossible to tell whether the choice had been easy.

"Boyd is fonder of little Agnes than he is of me. I don't think he knows that, but he is. After he carried her off that time, I knew it. And I was afraid to have him see her. But I don't feel like that any more. He's so frightfully lonely. And there's no reason why he shouldn't have her part of the year. If I could be sure that I might be a different person, or that he could—but what has happened once can happen again. No matter what it is or how hard you try to avoid it. And where the going hasn't been too good it seems better not to double back on my own trail."

"No," James said, "I suppose not." But sooner or later she must do something. As it is, she has no life at all.

He put out his right hand and produced a chord—G, D flat,

and F—on the dining-room table. Then he took a final drag at his cigarette.

"About the children, Irene—"

"It won't be easy, of course."

"I know that," he said.

"At first I wasn't at all sure that it could be done. Bunny was so close to his mother, you know. She seemed almost to be aware of every breath he took. And when they were in the same room together, he was always turning his face toward her. Last night when he came in and looked at me that way, I felt that there was nothing that you or I or anyone else could do for him. But this morning it's entirely different. The house is so bright, James, and so full of sunlight."

James leaned forward in his chair.

"I came in through the kitchen just now," Irene said, "and when I saw Bunny making wreaths, I knew somehow——"

Don't say it, James implored silently. *Don't say it!*

"I knew that there was a chance that things might work out all right. That we might be able to bring them up in the way she would have wanted."

II

While the man from the undertaker's went back for another load of chairs, there was time for James to walk—to make the circuit from the library out into the front hall, then through the living-room, which was filled with flowers, and into the library again.

He would have preferred to walk alone, but Robert stood waiting at the foot of the stairs and James did not have the heart to refuse him. Robert was freed from his mistake. It was evident from the way he walked. Neither Robert nor anyone else was responsible for Elizabeth's death. And anyway, it was what people intended to do that counted—not what came about because of anything they did. James saw that, clearly. And he saw that his life was like all other lives. It had the same function. And it differed from them only in shape—as one salt-cellar is different from another. Or one knife-blade. What happened to him had happened before. And it would happen again, more than once. Probably some one would lie awake all night in that very same hospital feeling his lungs contract and expand, contract, expand—until the whole of him was limited to the one effort of breathing for somebody else . . . But it would not be Elizabeth who was dying of pneumonia two rooms down the hall.

He would have liked to explain all this to Robert. And about the rectangle of light on the ceiling above his hospital bed. And also about the interurban, which no longer bothered him. It would be years probably before he could make Robert understand what happened when he met Crazy Jake collecting tin cans at midnight. But there was comfort at least in Robert's company, and in resting his arm on Robert's shoulders. Robert belonged to him. James could feel that in the way they walked together. They were of the same blood.

When he was Robert's age his father and mother went South and took him with them, for the winter. They rented a farmhouse on the side of a hill overlooking a Confederate cemetery. And he had no one to play with, being a Northerner, and he wanted to go home.

James remembered that winter, though of all the rest of his boyhood there was almost nothing left to him. The remembrance of a cellar door that sloped and could be used for hiding. A mulberry tree and the smell of harness, and brown stain of walnuts on his hands. . . . Even these things could not be shared with Robert, who was growing up in a different world.

Without their noticing it, they had changed the direction of their walking, and it now brought them straight toward the coffin. They stepped up to it, together, and it was not as James had expected. He did not break down, with Robert beside him. He stood looking at Elizabeth's hands, which were folded irrevocably about a bunch of purple violets. He had not known that anything could be so white as they were—and so intensely quiet now with the life, with the identifying soul, gone out of them.

They would not have been that way, he felt, if he had not been doing what she wanted him to do. For it was Elizabeth who had determined the shape that his life should take, from the very first moment he saw her. And she had altered that shape daily by the sound of her voice, and by her hair, and by her eyes which were so large and dark. And by her wisdom and by her love.

"You won't forget your mother, will you, Robert?" he said. And with wonder clinging to him (for it had been a revelation: neither he nor anyone else had known that his life was going to be like this) he moved away from the coffin.

STORIES 1938–1945

Contents

Homecoming

IT WAS nearly dark, and Jordan Smith, walking along with his eyes on the ground, came to a stretch of sidewalk where the snow had not been scraped off but was packed hard and icy. He looked up and, a trifle surprised, saw that he had come to the Farrels'. There were lights in the downstairs windows and the house was just as he had remembered it. Yet there was something wrong, something that made him stand doubtfully at the edge of the walk that had not been tended to.

He had come back to Watertown to spend Christmas with his family—with his father and mother, and his two brothers, who were both younger than he was and not quite grown. But they were not entirely the reason for his wanting to come home. Before he went away, he used to be with Tom and Ann Farrel a great deal of the time. So much, in fact, that it used to annoy his mother, and she would ask him occasionally why he didn't pack his things and go move in with the Farrels. And there was nothing that he could say; no way that he could explain to his mother that Farrel and Ann had somehow filled out his life for him and balanced it. They were the first friends that he had ever had. And the best, really. For that reason it would not do for him to go back to New York without seeing Farrel. He had never even meant to do that. But he had hoped to run into Farrel somewhere about town, coming or going. He had hoped that he wouldn't have to face Farrel in his own house now that Ann was not here. Now that Ann was dead, Jordan said to himself as he turned in and made his way up to the porch. He rang the bell twice. After a time the door opened slowly and a rather small boy looked out at him.

"Hello," Jordan said. "I've come to see your father, Timothy. Is he home?"

The boy shook his head. With a feeling which he was ashamed to recognize as relief, Jordan stepped across the sill into the front hall and the door closed behind him.

"How soon do you expect your father?" he said.

"Pretty soon."

"How soon is that?"

"I don't know." The boy seemed to be waiting stolidly until Jordan had proved himself friend or enemy.

"I expect you don't remember me. It's been three years since I left Watertown. You weren't so very old then."

Jordan had not meant to stay, but he found himself taking off his overcoat and his muffler and laying them across the newel post. The last time he had come here, Ann had met him at the door and her face had lighted up with pleasure. "It's Jordan," she had said. Even now, after three years, he could hear her voice and her pleasure at the sight of him. "Here's Jordan, Tom. He's come to say goodbye."

The front hall and the living room were both strangely still. Forgetting that he was not alone, Jordan listened a moment until the oil furnace rumbling away to itself in the basement reassured him.

"I can't stay," he said aloud to Timothy. On the hall tree was an old battered gray hat of Farrel's. Jordan started to hang his new brown one beside it, and then he changed his mind. With the hat still in his hand, he followed Timothy into the living room. There was a Christmas tree in the front window, with red balls and silver balls and tinsel and tin foil in strips hanging from it, and strand upon strand of colored lights that were not lighted. Under the tree Timothy's presents were still laid out, two days after Christmas, in the boxes they had come in: a cowboy hat, a toy revolver, a necktie and handkerchiefs, a giant flashlight, a book on scouting.

"Santa Claus must have been here," Jordan said.

Timothy did not consider, apparently, that this remark called for any answer. He waited a moment and then announced, "You're Jordan."

"That's right—Jordan Smith. But I didn't think you'd remember me."

He looked at the boy hopefully, but Timothy's face remained grave and a little pale, just as before. Jordan went over to the square, heavy, comfortable chair which was Farrel's favorite and sat down in it, and Timothy settled himself on the sofa opposite. For lack of anything better to do, Jordan took his hat and began to spin it, so that the hat went around wildly on his finger.

"You've grown, Timothy. You must have grown at least five or six inches since I saw you last."

Timothy crossed one foot over the other in embarrassment, and dug at the sofa with his heels.

"If this keeps up, we'll have to put weights in your pockets," Jordan said, and his eyes wandered past Timothy to the china greyhounds, one on either side of the mantel. "They're Staffordshire," Ann used to tell him proudly. "And if anything happened to them, I wouldn't want to go on living." Well, Jordan thought to himself—well, there they are. Nothing has happened to them. And the hat spun off the end of his finger and landed on the rug at his feet.

"Now look what I've done!" he exclaimed as he picked the hat up and placed it on Timothy's head. The hat came down well over Timothy's ears, and under the brim of it Timothy's eyes looked out at him without any eyebrows. This time Timothy was amused.

"It's too big for me," he said, smiling, and placed the hat on the sofa beside him.

"Now that it's dark outside," Jordan suggested, "why don't we light the tree?"

"Can't," Timothy said.

"Won't it light?"

Timothy shook his head.

"Get me the screwdriver, then."

A change came over Timothy. For the first time his face took on life and interest. "What do you want the screwdriver for?" he asked.

"Get me one," Jordan said confidently, "and I'll show you."

As soon as Timothy was out of the room, Jordan got up and went over to the fireplace. The greyhounds needed dusting, but there was nothing the matter with them. Not a crack or a chip anywhere. Jordan put them down again carefully and turned, hearing a slight disturbance outside. The *Evening Herald* struck the side of the house. It was a sound that he had never heard anywhere but in Watertown. He remembered it so perfectly that he couldn't believe that he had been away. Except for Ann, he said to himself as he made his way around the Christmas tree to the front window—except for her, everything was exactly the same. He had come home. He was here in this house that he had thought so much about. And, strangely, it was no satisfaction to him whatever.

Outside, the snow had begun again. Watching the paper boy wheel his bicycle down the icy walk, Jordan wondered why he had not stayed in New York over the holidays; why it was that he had wanted so much to come home. For weeks he had been restless, uneasy, and unable to keep from thinking of home. At night he could not sleep for walking up and down these streets, meeting people that he had known, and talking to them earnestly in his mind. Now that he was here, he didn't feel the way he had expected to feel. People were awfully nice, of course, and they were pleased to see him, but it was no kind of a homecoming. Not without Farrel and Ann. Wherever he went he found himself mentioning her, without meaning to especially. And it shocked him to see that people did not care about her any more. They had grown used to her not being here. Some of them—one or two, at least—complained to him about Farrel. They liked Farrel, they said. You couldn't help liking Tom Farrel. They still enjoyed having a drink with him every now and then. And there was no question but that Ann's death was a terrible loss to him. But if she had lived, the doctor said, she would never have been well, probably. And it was a year and a half since she had been rushed to the hospital in the middle of the night, to be operated on. Tom ought to begin now to get over it. He was nursing his grief, people said.

Jordan broke off a strip of tinsel from the Christmas tree, for no particular reason, and started with it for the kitchen. At the door of the dining room he met Timothy with the screwdriver. There was a woman with him also—a tired, tall woman with gray hair that was parted in the middle, and an uncompromising look about the corners of her mouth. Jordan nodded to her.

"I'm Mrs. Ives," the woman said. "What do you want with the screwdriver?"

"I want to fix the tree," Jordan explained, realizing suddenly why it was that Farrel had taken her for a housekeeper. If Farrel had got a younger woman and a more sympathetic one, there would have been talk. "Timothy says the lights don't work, and if we have a screwdriver we can tell which one is burnt out."

"Oh," the woman said. "In that case, I guess it's all right. You come to see Mr. Farrel, didn't you?"

"Yes." Jordan could see that she was trying to make up her mind whether or not she ought to ask who he was; whether it would be polite.

"Will Mr. Farrel be home soon?" he asked.

"Sometimes he comes right home from the office, and sometimes he doesn't." She answered Jordan's question patiently, as if it had already been asked a great many times. As if it were a foolish question, and one that nobody knew the answer to. "Mostly he doesn't come home till later."

"I see." Jordan turned to Timothy, who was tugging at his sleeve. Together they dragged a straight chair across the room from the desk to the Christmas tree. Jordan balanced himself on the chair and unscrewed the first bulb. Then he looked around for the housekeeper. She was not there any longer. She had gone back to the kitchen. "I may not be able to wait," he said, and handed the little red bulb to Timothy, who was standing below him. When Jordan applied the screwdriver to the socket, nothing happened. The lights did not go on. "It wasn't that one," he said.

Timothy handed the light back to him.

"No, sir," Jordan said, looking down at him thoughtfully. "It certainly wasn't."

Nor was it the second bulb, or the third, or the fourth. All of the lights on the first strand were good, apparently. As Jordan started on the second strand, he asked in what he hoped was a casual way, "Do you like Mrs. Ives?"

"She's all right," Timothy said. And he looked down then, as if Jordan had made a mistake and would after a second realize it. They did not speak for a time, but Jordan went on handing the bulbs to Timothy and testing the sockets with his screwdriver. When Timothy had no bulb to hold, he untwisted the wires with his hands. Quite suddenly, when Jordan came to the third bulb from the end, the whole tree blazed into light.

"It was that one!" he exclaimed, and took the new yellow bulb which Timothy held up to him. There was a moment when the lights went off again, but Jordan screwed the yellow bulb into the socket; then the lights came on and stayed on.

"How's that?" he asked.

"Fine," Timothy said, with the lights shining red and blue on his face.

Jordan stepped down from the chair and surveyed the tree from top to bottom. He could go now. There was no reason for him to stay any longer.

"When you grow up, Timothy," he said, "we'll go into the business." Then he picked his hat up from the arm of the sofa where Timothy had been sitting. "O.K.?"

"O.K.," Timothy said.

"Don't forget, then."

Jordan went out into the front hall and took his scarf from the newel post. He listened for the whir and rumble of the furnace, but this time it was not enough. Now that the Christmas tree was lighted, the house was even more unnaturally quiet. Up and down the street, in other houses, people would be sitting down to dinner, but Mrs. Ives had not yet turned the dining-room light on, and the dining-room table was not even set. It seemed wrong to go away and leave a child alone here, in this soundless house. Timothy was standing in the living room, watching him, and did not appear to be upset. But when he left, Jordan thought—what would happen to Timothy *then*?

He wound the scarf round his throat and held it in place with his chin until he had worked himself into his overcoat. When he had finished and was drawing on his gloves, he said brightly, "Smith and Farrel, Fixers of Plain and Fancy Christmas Trees."

Timothy was looking right at him, but there was no telling whether the boy had heard what he said. It seemed rather as if he hadn't. "Do you have to go?" Timothy said.

"I'm afraid I do." Jordan was about to make up a long, elaborate, and convincing excuse, but there were footsteps outside on the porch, and both of them turned in time to see the door thrown open. A man stood in the doorway, with snow on his shoulders and the evening paper clasped tightly under one arm.

"Jordan," he said, "for Christ's sake!"

"Sure," Jordan said, nodding.

"But I've been looking for you all over town!"

Jordan braced himself as the man caught at him slowly with his eyes, and with his voice, and with his two hands.

"And I've been right here," Jordan said helplessly, "all the time."

The Actual Thing

THE odor, if it was an odor, came from the other end of the attic, Mr. Tupper decided. He was looking about for a long wooden croquet box which had certain of his possessions in it—his Knights Templar sword, the works of Ingersoll, and an album of pressed flowers from the Holy Land. The attic was dreadfully hot and it might only be that, he thought—the dust and the heat. All at once he gave up pushing boxes and trunks around and went to the other end and stood sniffing in front of the bookcase. Then he began taking books down by twos and threes—"The Clansman" and "Truxton King," and dreary-looking textbooks that his nieces, Marjorie and Anne, and his nephew Joe had brought up to the country with them one summer or another and never opened. On the third shelf, behind the "Æneid," there was a dead blue jay. It had been dead a long time. A month, probably. The feathers were a dusty blue and the face was as dry and fragile and almost the same color as ashes. When Mr. Tupper bent forward to look at it over the tops of his glasses, the odor was quite sharp.

How did it ever manage to get in behind the books, he said to himself, and went to the window and threw it open. The air outside was saturated with August. There were voices calling, down by the tennis court. Young Joe's voice, high and uncertain. Then the voice of his friend, whose name Mr. Tupper couldn't for the moment remember. Stillwell or Stimson—some such name. "Thirty-forty," they said. "Deuce. . . . Deuce it is." And then, "My ad." Mr. Tupper, listening, felt as old as the hills. It was not probable, he said to himself—it was not even reasonable to *suppose* that he would live much longer. When he was gone, Henrietta, being his only sister, might keep his picture about somewhere, inconspicuously. And she would wait a year before doing his bedroom over into a guest room. But eventually she *would* do it over, and they would ask people out for the weekend—business acquaintances of Frank's who would undoubtedly stand at the window, as Mr. Tupper was doing now, and hear young voices coming up from the tennis court at the bottom of the hill.

The thought of such an end to his identity was sufficient to make Mr. Tupper lose whatever interest he had had earlier in the afternoon in the croquet box. He left the window open and turned and made his way down the attic steps.

In the living room it was pleasantly cool and dark, and Henrietta was there before him in a faded pink kimono and her gray hair pinned up on top of her head.

"Hello," he said.

She merely glanced at him from the sofa where she was sitting. She had a large pair of shears in her hand and a heap of flowered cretonne spread about her. Mr. Tupper stood and watched her. All Henrietta needed to do, apparently, was to lay an old curtain on the new material across her lap and in a careless way begin cutting. The cretonne was yellow and pale-green and mustard-color.

"Aren't you afraid you'll cut something you oughtn't to?" he asked.

But she was not afraid. "Perfectly simple," she explained without looking up. Mr. Tupper sat down near her and took out a cigarette. When it appeared that there weren't going to be matches in any of his trousers pockets, Henrietta gathered her shears and her curtain and the folds of her material into one hand and found him a packet of matches with the other, so that he didn't have to get up and go out to the kitchen, after all.

"There," she said, pushing an ashtray toward him. And when Mr. Tupper started to put the matches in his pocket, she said, "If you'll put them back in that little blue box," indicating the end table, "they'll be there when you want them the next time."

Mr. Tupper nodded. His sister was not really silly. It was just that she and Frank had been very poor when they were first married, and she had had to look after the children herself. From being alone with children so much, she had developed the habit of talking as if to a large audience of them.

"Etta," he said thoughtfully, "have you made your will?" She didn't answer him, but then she didn't always answer him, and so he went right on, "Because if you haven't, I think you ought to. Now that the girls are both married and have left home, it's important. It's really quite important."

"I suppose it is," she said as the shears cut through the centre of a large yellow poppy. "I suppose it is," she repeated. Then she stopped and looked at him oddly. It was the look she used to have sometimes when they were children, when she saw him coming toward her and knew that in a minute she would have to defend her dolls. Then the look changed. "Edward," she exclaimed. "Your hands!"

He glanced at them. They were, as a matter of fact, quite black.

"Where on earth have you been?"

"In the attic," he said. And for a moment he was on the verge of explaining to her about the blue jay. But then he realized that it was only a trick—Henrietta's way of taking his mind off what he was saying, and getting him to talk about something unimportant. "I haven't made one," he continued. "I haven't made my own will. I keep putting it off. But tomorrow I'm going in to town and do something about it. I think it's high time. I'm fifty-seven, Etta—be fifty-eight in January—and I might have kicked off any time during the last ten years." He glanced at her out of the corner of his eye to see whether or not she was shocked. Apparently the idea held no terror for her. "I'm convinced," he said, "that it was a mistake. I should have thought more about it."

"I really don't see why," she said.

Mr. Tupper looked at his hands. Then he got up suddenly and began to walk back and forth in the shadows of the living room. "Before Joe was born you thought about him, didn't you? You wondered whether Joe was going to be a boy or a girl and what you'd name him? And whether it would be hard on you when the time came?"

"That's different, Edward."

"What's different about it?"

"Well, for one thing, all this brooding about death is so . . ." She folded the material impatiently and cut at right angles to the two strips now hanging from her lap. "It's so morbid."

There! Mr. Tupper thought with satisfaction. That was what people invariably said. Death was morbid. Anything that people said about death was morbid. He came and stood beside his sister.

"How do you know, Etta—how do you know it's morbid to

think about death? You've never let yourself consider even the possibility of dying."

"Oh yes I have. Everybody does. Only I try not to let myself do it, Edward. I think about Joe or the girls, or I think of something around the house that needs fixing. And after a while it goes away." She bent her head over the flowered material so that he wouldn't be able to tell that she was upset. Mr. Tupper wheeled away from her and began walking again.

"From now on," he said, "I'm going to think about death a great deal. All the time, in fact."

"Very well. You may," she said, and her hand shook slightly as she began to cut again.

"What's more, I'm going to talk about it. I think everybody should talk about it. Everybody over forty. And there should be clinics in various parts of the country where people can go and learn about death. Because it isn't painful. The doctors say that death itself, the actual thing, is not at all painful. And people ought to know it. They ought to know how to get ready for it. How to put their affairs in order and how to compose their minds, so that when the time comes——"

"Oh dear!" Henrietta interrupted him. "Now I've gone and cut it all wrong."

Mr. Tupper stopped walking.

"Have you really?" he asked, without a great deal of sympathy.

"Yes, I have! And it's your fault, Edward. You came in here deliberately to bother and torment me!"

Mr. Tupper shook his head. It would have been easy enough to defend himself, but there were tears in her eyes, and he decided not to vex her any further. She was very good to him. She had made a home for him, of sorts, when it became apparent that he was never going to have one of his own. He bent over the coffee table and put his cigarette out.

"I told you," he said kindly, "I told you you were going to cut something you shouldn't."

In the attic the heat and the odor were quietly persisting. Mr. Tupper unfolded a month-old drama section of the Sunday *Times* and slipped it around the dead bird. All that remained was to carry it out to the rubbish pile and burn it there. A simple matter, he said to himself, that needn't involve anyone. But when he got outside he saw young Joe and his friend Stimson coming up the hill from the tennis court. It would be a long time, Mr. Tupper reflected, before they were interested in a clinic where people could go and learn about death. You could discuss such things with Henrietta, who was middle-aged, who was of an age for dying. But with boys it was different. Joe probably intended to go right on living forever.

Mr. Tupper stood and waited. The boys had their tennis racquets with them and they were hot and very red in the face from playing. When Joe saw Mr. Tupper he grinned cheerfully.

"Where are you going, Uncle?" he said. "Can I go with you?"

Mr. Tupper shook his head. "No," he said, "I should say not." And drew the folds of newspaper together in his hand. For the first time he seemed to realize what it was that he was carrying, and he wanted suddenly to throw the dry, horrible thing as far away from him as he could.

Young Francis Whitehead

THE Whiteheads lived on the sheltered side of a New Hampshire hill, less than half a mile from town. Their house was set back from the road, and there were so many low-skirted pine trees on both sides of the drive that Miss Avery, who had a parcel under her arm and was coming to see Mrs. Whitehead, was almost up to the house before she could see the green shutters and the high New England roofline. The driveway went past the garage and up to the front door, then around and down again to the road. Both garage doors were open and the afternoon sun shone upon Mrs. Whitehead's Buick sedan and, beside it, a new and shiny blue convertible. While Miss Avery was admiring it, an Irish setter came bounding out of the shrubbery. The dog barked and whined and stepped on Miss Avery's feet and blocked her way no matter where she turned, so that in desperation she gave him a shove with the flat of her hand.

As soon as she did that, a window flew open upstairs and young Francis Whitehead put his head out. "Go on, beat it!" he said. Apparently he had no clothes on. His hair and his face and shoulders were dripping wet, and for a moment Miss Avery wasn't sure whether Francis was talking to her or to the dog. "You silly creature!" he said, and whistled and gave orders and made threats until finally the dog disappeared around the side of the house. Then for the first time Francis looked at Miss Avery. "Oh," he said. "It's you. Come on in, why don't you?"

"All right," she said. "I was going to."

"I'm in the shower," Francis explained, "but Mother's around somewhere. She'll be glad to see you." He drew his head in and closed the window.

Miss Avery had stood by, in one capacity or another, while Francis learned to walk and to talk, to cut out strings of paper dolls, and ride a bicycle but they had seen very little of each other the last two or three years. Francis had been away at school much of the time. He was at Cornell. And Miss Avery decided, as she raised the knocker on the big front door, that he probably wouldn't care to be reminded of the fact that she had once sewed buttons on his pantywaists. The knocker made a noise, but no one came. Miss Avery waited and waited, and finally she opened the door and walked in.

The house was dark after the spring sunlight outside. Miss Avery felt blind as a mole. The first thing she saw was herself—her coat with the worn fur at the collar and her thin, unromantic, middle-aged face—reflected in a mirror that ran from floor to ceiling. She turned her eyes away and walked on into the library. Bookcases went nearly around the room. A wood fire was burning in the fireplace and the clock on the mantel was ticking loudly. Over by the French windows a card table had been set up. There was a pile of little baskets on it, and a number of chocolate rabbits and little chickens made out of cotton, and quantities of green and yellow wax-paper straw.

Miss Avery put down her parcel, which contained some mending that Mrs. Whitehead had asked her to do, and stood looking at the confusion on the card table until a voice exclaimed, "Happy Easter!" She turned and found Mrs. Whitehead smiling at her. Mrs. Whitehead had a china dish in one hand and a paper bag in the other. She advanced upon Miss Avery, put both arms about her, and kissed her.

"Easter is still two days off," Miss Avery said. "This is only Good Friday."

"I know it is. I was just indulging myself," Mrs. Whitehead said, and she carried the dish over to the card table and poured out the sackful of Easter eggs. "I was just thinking about you and here you are." She drew Miss Avery down beside her on the sofa and took both of her hands. "How's your mother? I've been meaning to stop in and see how she was but we've had so much company lately—Mrs. Howard from Portsmouth and Cousin Ada Sheffield right after that, and I really haven't had a moment. And tell me how *you* are. That's what I really want to know."

"Well," Miss Avery began without enthusiasm, but Mrs. Whitehead had already got up and was searching everywhere for little dishes and jars, lifting the tops and peering into them hopefully.

"I had some ginger, but it looks as if I'd eaten every scrap of it," she said. "There isn't a thing to offer you but Easter eggs."

Miss Avery tried to explain that it was all right; she didn't like ginger any better than she liked Easter eggs, but Mrs. Whitehead paid no attention to her. "I was just going to fix some baskets. My only child is home for his spring vacation, and I'm having eight of his cronies to dinner tomorrow night. And they all have to have Easter baskets." She gave up looking among the dishes and jars and sat down again, at the card table this time. "Francis brought a dog home with him, too," she said as she took one of the baskets and began lining it with green straw. "A perfectly mammoth setter. You know how huge they are. And so beautiful and so dumb!"

Miss Avery nodded, out of politeness. One dog was much like another so far as she was concerned.

"The boy it belonged to got a job somewhere," Mrs. Whitehead said, choosing first a yellow chicken from the pile in front of her, then a rabbit, and then a white chicken small enough to fasten on the rim of the basket. "Boston, I think it was."

"Providence," Francis said from the doorway. He came in and sat down quietly and stretched his long legs out in front of him. His hair was still wet, but it was combed neatly back from his ears. He had flannel trousers on, and a white shirt, and an old tweed coat. He was also wearing heavy leather boots that were laced as far as his ankles and came halfway up his shins. Miss Avery let her eyes wander from boots to coat, to the right-hand pocket of the coat, which had been ripped open by accident last fall when Francis was home for Thanksgiving. The cloth had been torn a little, too, but it was all right now, Miss Avery decided. She had made it as good as new.

"Providence, then," Mrs. Whitehead was saying. "Anyway, they had the dog in their dormitory all year and this boy couldn't take it to work with him, so Francis brought it home, without saying a word to anybody. Red, his name is. And I give you my word, he's as big as a pony. All morning long he's been going around knocking things over, tracking dirt in and out, stealing meat off the kitchen table—all the things boys do in college, I'm sure." She looked at Francis slyly. "And then every time he does something wrong, he comes and apologizes with those great brown eyes of his until I really don't think I can stand it much longer."

Francis drew himself up into his chair. "You exaggerate something awful," he said.

Mrs. Whitehead looked at Miss Avery. "It isn't so," she said meekly. "Is it, Miss Avery? Francis is always saying that I exaggerate." She turned to Francis. "Miss Avery's mother exaggerates, too, Francis, even with her hardening of the arteries." Then back to Miss Avery: "Though I never heard her do it, you understand. I daresay all mothers exaggerate." She looked from one to the other of them and then burst into laughter. "Miss Avery takes me so seriously," she said. "She always did. She never changes a bit. We're the ones who have changed, Francis. There's not one piece of ginger in the house."

She held the Easter basket off, admiring it from this angle and that. Then she put it aside and began on another one, which she lined with yellow straw. Before she had finished the second basket, the maid appeared in the doorway, carrying a wide silver tea tray. The dog followed after her, sniffing. "Annie, how nice of you to think of tea," said Mrs. Whitehead. When Annie tried to put the tray down, the dog came forward, blocking her way completely. Mrs. Whitehead was plunged into despair. "You see, Francis?" she said.

Francis rose and took hold of the dog's collar. "Red," he exclaimed fondly, "did anyone ever tell you you were a nuisance?" and dragged the dog out of the room.

"Don't put him in the pantry," Mrs. Whitehead called. Then she turned to Miss Avery again. "He can open the swinging door with his paw. Besides, he'll just be there for Annie to fall over."

From where Miss Avery sat, she could see into the front hall. Francis was whirling the dog round and round by his front legs and saying "Swing, you crazy dog, swing, swing!"

"Francis is going to leave school," Mrs. Whitehead said. "Last summer nothing would do but he must learn to walk the tightrope. Now he wants to leave school." She began arranging the teacups absentmindedly in their saucers. "He intends to go back and take his examinations in June. Then he's going to stop. I've talked until I'm blue in the face and it makes no difference to him. Not the slightest. . . . What kind of sandwiches are there, Annie?"

"Cream cheese," Annie said, "and guava jelly, and hot cross buns."

"Hot cross buns!" Francis said, coming back into the room. "Do you hear that, Mother?"

Mrs. Whitehead looked at him disapprovingly as he sat down. "The way you twist Annie around your little finger! I don't know what I'll do when you come home to stay."

Francis bent over, and having folded the cuffs of his trousers inside his boots, continued lacing them. "I'm not coming home to stay," he said, with his chin between his knees.

For a moment the room was absolutely still. Without looking at her son, Mrs. Whitehead put the tea strainer on the tray where the plate of lemon had been, reflected, and changed them back again. "Sugar?" she said to Miss Avery.

"If you please," Miss Avery said.

Annie brought her tea and the plate of sandwiches, the plate of hot cross buns. When Francis also had been taken care of, Annie waited to see whether Mrs. Whitehead wanted anything else of her and then withdrew from the room. Francis went on lacing his boots. After he had finished, he adjusted his trousers so that they hung over like ski pants. Then, quite by accident, he discovered his cup of tea. Nobody spoke. The dog returned, making soft, padded noises on the hardwood floor. Miss Avery thought that Mrs. Whitehead would probably object and that Francis would have to take hold of Red and drag him out again, but it was not that way at all. The dog came and put his head on Mrs. Whitehead's lap and she began to stroke his long, red ears.

"If you're not coming here, Francis," she said suddenly, "where *do* you intend to go?"

"New York."

"Why New York?" Mrs. Whitehead asked.

"I want to get a job," Francis said, and pulled a hot cross bun to pieces and ate it.

Mrs. Whitehead watched him as if it were an altogether new sight. When he had finished, she said, "You can get a job right here. There are plenty of jobs. Your Uncle Frank will probably make a place for you."

"I don't want a job in the mill," Francis said.

In a spasm of exasperation, Mrs. Whitehead turned away from him and poured herself a second cup of tea. "Really, Francis," she said, "I don't know what's come over you."

Miss Avery was ready to get up as soon as she caught Mrs. Whitehead's eye, and go home. But when Mrs. Whitehead did glance in her direction, Miss Avery saw that she was more than exasperated—that she was frightened also. Her look said that, for a few minutes at least, Miss Avery was not to go; that she was to relax and sit back in her chair.

"You do what *you* want, Mother," Francis said reasonably. "You like to have breakfast in bed, so Annie brings it up to you. I want to do the things *I* like. I've had enough school. I want to begin living, like other people."

Mrs. Whitehead pushed the dog's head out of her lap. "Being grown up isn't as interesting as you think. Your father and I always hoped that you would study medicine. He talked so much about it during his last illness. But you don't seem to care for that sort of thing and I suppose there's no reason why you should be made to go on with your studies if you don't want to. There are other things to think of, however. I can't rent this house overnight. People don't want so large a place, you know. It may take all summer. And you may not like it in New York after you get there. You'll miss the country and you'll miss your home and your friends. You may not even be able to keep your car. Had you thought of that?" She waited for him to say something, but he went on intently balancing the heel of one boot on the toe of the other. "We'll have to take a little apartment somewhere," she said, "and it'll be cramped and uncomfortable—"

"I'm sorry, Moth!" He stood up suddenly, and his voice was strained and uncertain. "When I go to New York I'm going alone," he said. "I want to lead my own life." Then he turned and went out of the room, with the dog racing after him.

When Mrs. Whitehead started talking again, it was not about Francis but something else entirely—a book she had read once long ago. The book was about New Orleans after the Civil War. She had forgotten the title of it, and she didn't suppose Miss Avery would remember it either, but it was about a little girl named Dea, who used to carry wax figurines around on a tray in the marketplace and sell them to people from the North.

Annie came in and carried the tea tray out to the kitchen. When they were alone again, Mrs. Whitehead seemed to have forgotten the book, or else she had said all there was to say about it. The moment had come for Miss Avery to bring forth her handiwork. She went and got the brown-paper parcel and sat down with it on her lap. Her fingers trembled slightly as she pulled the knot apart, and when the wrapping fell open she expected exclamations of approval. There were none. Mrs. Whitehead did not even see the mending. She was sitting straight up in her chair, and her eyes were quite blind and overflowing with tears.

"Francis is so young," she said. "Just twenty, you know. Just a boy. And there's really no reason why he should be in such a rush. Most people live a long time. Longer than they need to."

Miss Avery nodded. There was nothing that she could think of to say. She wanted to go home, but she waited until Mrs. Whitehead had found her handkerchief and wiped her eyes and given her nose a little blow and glanced surreptitiously at the clock.

Haller's Second Home

THE doorman, the two elevator men in the lobby all said "Good evening, Mr. Haller" to him and when he stepped off at the fourth floor he didn't ring the bell of the apartment directly in front of the elevator shaft but merely transferred the package he was carrying from his right arm to his left, opened the door, and walked in. A large grey cat was waiting just inside. "Well?" Haller said to it and the cat turned away in disappointment. There was only one human being the cat cared about and it was not Haller. He saw that the lights were on in the living room, but it was always empty at this time of evening. He put his hat and gloves on the front-hall table and, still wearing his raincoat, went in search of whoever he could find.

He had come here for the first time on a winter afternoon, when he was twenty-two years old. With a girl. Somebody else's girl, whom Mrs. Mendelsohn embraced and welcomed into the family. The girl was marrying Mrs. Mendelsohn's nephew, Dick Shields, who was Haller's best friend in high school in Chicago and on into college. And she and Haller were friends also. And she had asked him to come with her because he happened to be in New York—he had come down from Cambridge to go to the opera—and she was nervous about meeting these people who were about to become her relatives. The whole future course of her marriage and of her life might be affected favorably or unfavorably. And then what did she do but explain to them, before she had her coat off, that if she hadn't been marrying Dick she would have been marrying Haller. No one took this remark seriously, not even Haller. All in the world he wanted, behind those big horn-rimmed glasses, was to be loved, but he had his hands full with the Harvard Graduate School, and a wife would have been more than he could manage.

That first time, he rang the bell politely and, when the girl looked at herself in the round mirror of her compact, said, "Stop fussing. You look fine. You look like the Queen of the May." "I don't feel like the Queen of the May," she said, and they heard footsteps approaching and a woman's high, clear, beautiful voice finishing a remark that was addressed to someone in the apartment. Haller thought he was a spectator sitting on the sidelines, but in fact he was about to acquire a second home. This was eleven years ago: the winter of 1930–31. He was now thirty-three years old and still unmarried.

East Eighty-fourth Street was not noisy then, any more than it is now, and as always in New York a great deal depends on what floor you are on. The Mendelsohns' apartment was three stories above the street. Taxi horns, Department of Sanitation trucks, the air brakes of the Lexington Avenue buses—all such shattering sounds seemed to avoid the fourth floor and to choose a higher or lower level of the air to explode in. Even with the windows open, the Mendelsohns' living room was quiet. It was also rather dark in the daytime. Long folds of heavy red draperies shut out a good deal of the light that came from two big windows, and the glass curtains filtered out some more. These were never pulled back, and you had to part them if you wanted to see the brownstones across the way or the street below. It was hard to say whether the room was furnished with very bad taste or no taste at all. With time Haller had grown accustomed to the too bright reds and blues in the big Saruk rug, the queer statuary, the not quite comfortable and in some cases too ornate and in other cases downright rickety furniture. Though he was an aesthetic snob, there was nothing he would have changed. Not even a bronze nymph and satyr that would have been perfectly at home in the window of a Third Avenue thrift shop. What is a feeling for interior decoration compared to a front door that is never locked, day or night?

Through curtained French doors he saw a large female figure moving about the dining-room table and, being nearsighted, thought it was the Mendelsohns' cook. It turned out to be Mrs. Mendelsohn herself. "Hello, Haller darling," she said, and kissed him.

She was a stately woman, with blue eyes and black hair and a fine complexion. She was half Irish and half English—that is, her grandparents were. She favored the Irish side. The small, oval, tinted photograph of her on the living-room table, taken when she was nineteen, suggested that she had always been beautiful and that the beauty had been improved rather than blurred by the years. The blue eyes were still clear, the black hair had becoming lines of grey in it. She flirted with her husband. Her children admired her appearance, made fun of her conversation, and were careful not to bring down on themselves the full force of her explosive character. Haller had the feeling that her kindness toward him was largely because of his connection with her sister's son. There were flowers on the table—sweet peas—and dubonnet candles in yellow holders, and little arsenic-green crepe-paper baskets filled with nuts. "Looks like a birthday," he said.

"I don't know whether it is or not," Mrs. Mendelsohn said. "I got home late and there were no preparations of any kind. Ab has forbidden Renée to bake a cake, and so I'm just trying to rustle something together before Father comes up and is angry because dinner isn't ready."

"Where'll I put the present?" Haller asked.

"Present?" Mrs. Mendelsohn said. "You dare to give her a present?"

"Certainly. What are birthdays for if not to get presents?"

"Put it on her chair, then," Mrs. Mendelsohn said with a sigh, "and take the consequences."

He did as she suggested and then left the dining room and walked along the hall, looking in one door after another. Renée was in the kitchen. She was a West Indian, from Barbados, and she had only been with the Mendelsohns a few months, but in this short time she had become the family clearinghouse for all secrets and private messages. Nathan was her favorite; he told her things he told no one else, and made her feel very special indeed, and so was slowly pushing her toward the precipice where the rights of the employer and the obligations of the employed give way, in a moment of too great clarity, to the obligations of the employer and the rights of the employed. But while she lasted, and especially in the beginning, she was a delight to everyone but Mrs. Mendelsohn, who did not like her all that much. The Doctor joked with Renée and praised her cooking. "Enjoy yourselves!" she called when Nathan and Leo and Abbie and their friends went out the front door together, on a Saturday afternoon. "We will, we will," they promised.

Haller was tempted to go in and tell her what he had up his sleeve, but her back was turned and she looked busy, so he went on to the boys' room. The light was on in there but it was empty, like the living room. He took his raincoat off and laid it on one of the beds. Then he walked out again, and down the hall to the next door on the right. It was closed. The door of Abbie Mendelsohn's room was always closed—against what went on in the rest of the apartment and what went on in the world. Her brothers came and went without knocking, and Haller was permitted in there, and one or two other friends. He knocked lightly, and a voice said, "Come in."

The light went on as he pushed the door open and he saw that Nathan was lying on one of the twin beds and Abbie on the other. She sat up and looked at him. Then her blond head drooped. "Oh God," she said. "There's no use trying to sleep. How are you, Haller, dear?"

"I'm fine. Happy birthday."

"Happy what?" she said, sinking back on the bed.

"Would you like me to go someplace else?"

"Don't pay any attention to her," Nathan said. "She's just being difficult."

"I'm so tired my teeth water," Abbie said.

"Are you sure?" Haller asked. "I don't see how that's possible."

"It's what it feels like. I haven't slept for a week, on account of the kittens. They crawl on my face all night long. Be careful you don't step on them."

Haller made his way cautiously to the nearest chair and sat down. The Victorian sofa and chairs had belonged to the great-aunt for whom Abbie was named, and they gave this room an entirely different quality from the family living room. There were flower prints on the walls, the window looked out on a court, and the room was quiet as a tomb. "When are you going to start giving them away?" he asked.

"We gave one of them away this afternoon," Nathan said. "To a patient of Father's."

Officially the Mendelsohns had two cats—the altered male that was waiting at the door and a recently acquired alley cat whose standing in the family was doubtful. Dr. Mendelsohn did not like cats of any description and was convinced that they contributed to his asthma. "Two cats are one more than there is room for in a city apartment," he announced alarmingly from behind the *Evening Sun*, but so far he had done nothing about it.

The cat yowled up at Nathan from the courtyard one snowy night, and he went down in his bathrobe and slippers and rescued her. A month later she had a litter of four, behind the closed door of Abbie's room, and she was raising them without Dr. Mendelsohn's permission; without, in fact, his knowing anything about it. She nursed her kittens in a grocery carton on the floor between the twin beds, and now that they were able to stagger around on their own feet an opening had been cut in the side of the box for them to go in and out by. When they were not pushing at the mother cat's belly they clawed their way up the bedspreads, or collected in all but invisible groups on the mulberry-colored carpet, or went exploring. Except one, which Nathan now brought forth from the carton. This kitten could move, and it was apparently not in pain, but when he put his hand under it and tried to make it stand, the kitten collapsed and lay limp and miserable on the bedspread.

"The girl we gave the other kitten to is an orphan," he said. "First her mother died, and then she went to live with her grandfather and grandmother and *they* died."

"What a sad story," said Haller. "Do you believe it?"

Nathan was dark—dark hair, dark eyes, dark skin—and very handsome. Originally he had his mother's beautiful nose, but when he was a small child a dog bit him. He was playing with the dog, and teasing it, and it bit him on the nose. He had to have several stitches in it, and his nose was not the same shape afterward. His brother and sister mourned over this accident, as if it had been some tragic flaw in his destiny. He himself was resigned to his loss but did not minimize it.

"She's only eighteen," he said. "And her guardian was with her. A very nice woman. When I told her about the kittens she looked at the girl and said, 'Very well, we'll take the sick one.' But they took the one with the black mustache, instead. The one that looked like Hitler." He yawned.

"What you need is a change," Haller said, hanging over the arm of his chair to watch the kittens on the rug. "Why don't we all drive south into the spring. We could be as far south as Richmond, Virginia, the first night. We could see the tulips on the White House lawn."

"How do you know," Nathan asked, "how do you know there will be tulips on the White House lawn?"

"There will be something. If not tulips then there will be dandelions. When Moris Burge and I drove to Santa Fe last year we spent the first night in a wonderful tourist home in Richmond—"

"That Moris Burge," Nathan said.

"—and when we woke up the next morning we heard a cardinal singing in the backyard, and the lilacs were all in bloom. I'm not exaggerating. Why don't we drive south, the three of us, and go straight through the spring? We'll see iris in Alexandria, and in the southern part of New Jersey there will be pine forests with dogwood—white dogwood—all through them. Or we could go down the Shenandoah Valley and pick violets at Harpers Ferry, like I did when I was seventeen."

"You're such a traveler," Nathan said, but not unkindly.

"The West Indies when I was twenty-three. And Santa Fe, last summer. Where else have I been?"

"Boston."

"But you've all been to Europe."

"With Father."

"What were you doing in Harpers Ferry when you were seventeen?" Abbie asked, from her pillow.

"I went to Washington with a special train, from high school. We saw Mount Vernon, and Annapolis, and Fredericksburg, and Gettysburg. We saw George Washington's false teeth. And we had our picture taken in front of the Capitol Building. It was one of those moving cameras, on a track, and I was standing at one end of the group, and the boy who was standing next to me said, 'Come on!' and ran around in back, so I did too. We got in the picture twice. I had on an ice-cream suit. Twins is what it looked like. And perfectly plausible, except that I had one leg in the air because I'd just arrived. The next picture, everybody tried it and they had to give the whole thing up."

"Do you still have that picture?" Nathan asked. "I'd like to see it. I'd like to see what you'd be like if you were twins."

"It's somewhere. There isn't anything to look at in Gettysburg but wheat fields, but Harpers Ferry is remarkable. Three states meet there."

"Which three?" Nathan asked skeptically.

"West Virginia, Virginia, and I forget what the other is. But anyway, there are three states right in front of you—three mountains, green all the way to the top, with rivers between them, and the town is on a hill, and it's very old, and the streets are winding, and when I was seventeen I got off the train and ran all through the town and came back and picked violets by the tracks before the train started again. All this was in April."

"Haller, there's no such place, but I love you just the same." Abbie threw the quilt aside and sat up stretching.

"You haven't heard anything?" Nathan said. "No letter, I mean?"

"No," Haller said.

For three weeks, one of the people who was often in this unnaturally quiet room had been missing from it. A rubber stamp descending on a printed form separated Francis Whitehead from his civilian status. It was a grey day, and there was some snow mixed with rain. Governors Island offered a foretaste of things to come. Though now and then someone was sent back, the lines mostly moved one way. He was set down in a muddy Army camp, with a rifle and bayonet to take the place of his Leica and light meter, a footlocker for his earthly possessions—which, as it happened, he was indifferent to—and a serial number. He didn't really need a number to distinguish him from other soldiers, because he was the only one who could tell, in the dark, that the crease in the middle of the sheet he was lying on was not in the exact center of the bed.

There had been two letters from him since he went in the Army and they didn't say anything. He was not a letter writer, it seemed. He wrote notes, instead—on the backs of envelopes or other people's letters to him or laundry lists or old bank deposit slips. Not because of anything the messages were in themselves but because of something elusive in his character that made any clue seem interesting, Haller could never bear to throw these scraps of paper away. They drifted through his socks and handkerchiefs, in the top dresser drawer: *Why are you never home? If you want to lead a double life it's all right with me but I think you ought to live on the second floor. I'm tired of climbing these stairs. F.* . . . Or, *That new sport jacket is a mistake, you should have asked me to come with you. I can't make it tonight. What about Thursday? F.* . . . Or, *You are so pompous. F.*

When Francis Whitehead laughed his eyes filmed over with tears, but he kept his mouth closed, to cover his receding gums. This condition was apparent to his dentist and to him and to no one else. Like everything about him, his tight-lipped smile was charming. Before he went into the Army he was on the fringe of the world of fashion photography. Before that, he had been in the theater. His looks, the way he wore his clothes, his jokes, his talent for choosing just the present that would please above all other presents, his tormented smile enslaved people, but he himself did not quite know what he wanted, and so there was little prospect of his getting it.

Haller had written to remind him that today was Abbie's birthday. He didn't say—he didn't need to say—that if Francis could manage to call up from a pay station somewhere it would give her more pleasure than any present possibly could.

"Dinner's ready, children," Mrs. Mendelsohn said through the closed door. Abbie and Nathan scattered to wash. When Haller walked into the dining room, Dr. Mendelsohn was sitting down at the head of the table.

"Good evening, Haller," he said kindly and whisked his napkin into his lap. Mrs. Mendelsohn lit the candles, while Haller stood behind her chair. The others appeared one by one during the soup course. First Nathan. Then Leo, who had stayed at school for a meeting of the Geographical Society. He came into the dining room quietly, a tall thin youngster with the grey cat balancing serenely on his shoulders. Abbie was the last to turn up. She looked at the dining table and then said, "Mother, how could you?" but she was not really angry. The moroseness was overdone, and deliberately comic. It was true that she hadn't wanted any birthday celebration, but equally true that she was trying hard to grow up. And part of growing up was learning to accept the way her mother and father were, and not to hold it against them that they weren't the things she used to think they ought to be. If her mother wanted to decorate the table and bring home a birthday cake, it surely was possible to treat this as natural and not a crime, though silly.

She saw the package on her chair and said, "What's this?"

"It looks rather like a birthday present," Haller said.

"Do you mind if I don't open it until after dinner?" she said, and put the package on a chair at the far end of the room. And so indicated—rather too subtly for the people present to understand, but the guppies in the fish tank got it and so did the still life over the sideboard—that Haller had done something to her that, even if it was a long time ago, she had no intention ever of forgiving, though from time to time she forgot about it and from time to time she remembered and reminded him of it, and still he didn't understand. There was very little, as she observed to Nathan, that Haller did understand.

Haller didn't mind that his present had ended up in the far corner of the room. That is, he pretended that this, too, was funny and partially succeeded in believing that it was.

When Dr. Mendelsohn talked at the dinner table it was usually to one person only. Tonight it was Haller. He was telling Haller about one of his patients. "She's neurotic and self-pitying, you know what I mean? I gave the same treatment to somebody else that same afternoon and the whole thing was over in half an hour and the woman went home. But this patient was screaming before I ever got her on the table. Finally I had to say to her, 'Mrs. Weinstock,' I said, 'if you don't stop thrashing around, the instrument will pierce your bladder and you'll get peritonitis and die!' "

"Did she quiet down after that?" Haller asked politely.

"Yes, but she wouldn't go home. It was one-thirty and I was supposed to be at the hospital, so I . . ."

Haller didn't feel it was respectful to eat while Dr. Mendelsohn was addressing him, and his plate sat untouched in front of him. He compromised, however, by snitching cashew nuts out of the little crepe-paper basket. When he had eaten all there were, the two boys passed their paper cups around the table and Abbie slyly emptied them and finally her own into Haller's basket. He ate them all absentmindedly, and when Dr. Mendelsohn finished his story and took up his knife and fork,

Haller saw that the crepe-paper basket at his place was empty and said indignantly, "Somebody's been stealing my cashew nuts!"

The boys leaned against each other with laughter.

"Mr. Napier called today, Father," Mrs. Mendelsohn said, and the Doctor quickly and furtively raised his napkin and wiped away the particle of food that was clinging to his mouth.

He had his office on the ground floor of the apartment building, and the waiting room, with dark-green walls and uncomfortable, turn-of-the-century oak furniture and dog-eared back numbers of *Time* and *Field and Stream* and the *Saturday Evening Post*, was always full. His working day began at seven and he had every excuse to be tired and cross by six-thirty at night. Actually, the practice of medicine was pure pleasure to him; it was his family, not his patients, that made him irritable. He had grown up on the Lower East Side, in extreme poverty—the oldest son of an immigrant couple who did not speak English. When there was nothing to eat he went through the neighborhood searching for food in the refuse cans. Certain storekeepers knew this and took to leaving something for him. Working at odd jobs before and after school, he earned what money a boy could. He got conspicuously high marks in school, and he cured himself of a speech impediment by imitating Demosthenes—that is to say, he took the Coney Island Express to the end of the line and walked up and down the deserted beach reciting the Gettysburg Address with pebbles in his mouth. The rabbi had no fault to find with him, and neither did his father and mother. But he had no childhood whatever. When his favorite sister died of tuberculosis, the direction of his future was fixed. By a long unbroken chain of miracles he put himself through medical school. And how, lacking the hardships that had shaped his character, his children's characters were to be shaped and made firm was a riddle he could not find the answer to. Abbie had an excellent mind, and she was an affectionate daughter, but she did not know how to cook and keep house and sew, the way his sisters had at her age. When she was just out of college she and a dancer in a Broadway musical stepped into a taxi and got out at the Municipal Building and went inside, to the chapel on the first floor. The marriage lasted ten days. All she ever said, in explanation, was that they couldn't talk to each other. She was now working in a public-relations firm. Nathan didn't finish school. He had a job but could not have lived on his salary. His father considered him immature for his age, and lazy. And Leo had a preference for low company. Loudmouthed roughnecks, and their vulgar girls. When Dr. Mendelsohn looked around the dinner table a spasm of irritation would come over him—at the thought of what his children might be making of themselves and all too obviously weren't—and he would put his napkin beside his plate and push his chair back and go off and eat by himself at Longchamps.

His children understood how he felt, but at the same time there was very little they could do about it. They couldn't very well go and live on the Lower East Side, in conditions of extreme poverty. No one would have taken them in. Their Hungarian grandparents were dead and their father's brothers and sisters had, through their own efforts and his, all risen in the world. And if Abbie and Nathan and Leo had tried to sleep in an areaway their father would have come and stood over them, impatient and scolding, and made them come home where they belonged.

Dr. Mendelsohn's irritability was, so far as Haller could see, a matter of pride to his family. It gave him an authority that his physical presence alone—he was smaller than his wife—would not have provided, and it made all their lives more interesting. They never hesitated to provoke him, while pretending to go to considerable lengths to avoid this. His explosions were brief and harmless. But Nathan said that his father didn't like Gentiles, and Haller didn't know whether he came under this proscription or not. On the other hand, Dr. Mendelsohn didn't like most Jews either. This much Haller knew: He was a wonderful doctor.

After dinner, Abbie tore the wrapping off her present, which proved to be an album of Sibelius: "Night Ride and Sunrise" and "The Oceanides."

"I bought them on account of the titles," he said.

"The titles are beautiful," Abbie said. "And I'm sure they are too."

"I haven't the faintest idea what they're like," Haller said.

Unfortunately there was no way of finding out. When they went into the living room to play the records, they discovered that the machine wasn't working. It was connected to the amplifier and speaker of the radio, and where there should have been an empty space on the dial, free from broadcasting, three kinds of music were fighting for first place, none of them Sibelius.

Leo explained that it was a tube, and he and Nathan went out to buy a new one. Haller and Abbie sat down together on one of the beds in her room. He was expecting the telephone to ring, and his hand was ready to reach out for it as he watched her worrying over the sick kitten.

"You poor thing," she said, holding the kitten's head against her cheek. "Probably it's nothing but imagination—because he's only been this way since last night—but he seems thinner than the others, and his fur is dry and sickly looking."

"He doesn't look very happy," Haller agreed.

First she tried to make the kitten stand up, and then she took the others away and left the sick kitten with the mother cat. He soon lost interest, and Abbie tried to make him suck and found that it couldn't be done. She felt the kitten's vertebrae thoughtfully, and announced that its back was broken; there was a ridge that was definitely out of place. She made Haller feel it. When he said that if the kitten's back was broken oughtn't they to chloroform it, she decided that its back wasn't broken after all—though it was just possible that somebody had stepped on it. And moved by a sudden inspiration she gave the kitten cod-liver oil out of an eyedropper.

The boys came back with a new tube. When that didn't help, Leo sat down on the floor and began taking the radio apart with a screwdriver. Haller, with an unlit cigarette in his mouth, discovered that he had no matches.

"Leo, do you remember the time you soldered my glasses when they broke?" he asked fondly, going from table to table and not finding what he was looking for.

"Yes, I remember," Leo said.

"And do you remember how much it cost me afterward to have them fixed?" Haller said as he left the room and went down the hall. If he hadn't gone to the kitchen for matches he wouldn't have known about the plate that Renée was keeping warm in the oven. It was eight-thirty by the kitchen clock. Renée was sitting at the kitchen table. Her normally kinky hair was shining with pomade and hanging in straight bangs about her face. He saw the plate in the oven and said, "Who's *that* for?" She giggled mysteriously, and he opened his eyes wide in astonishment. "Tonight?" he exclaimed, and at that moment the doorbell rang.

By the time Haller got to the front hall, Francis Whitehead was inside, and Abbie and Nathan and Leo each had a piece of him, and were trying to go off somewhere with it. He put his little zipper bag down and then grinned at them. "A soldier," he said. And what a soldier. "Everything I've got on is several sizes too large for me," he said. "And I've lost ten pounds." With his hair clipped close to his skull he looked mistreated and ill. Haller was shocked.

"I've got till Tuesday," Francis said, rocking happily on his heels. "I've got thirty-six and a half more hours to do with exactly as I like. What do you think of my World War One pants?"

"They're lovely," Abbie said.

"Did you know he was coming?" Nathan and Leo were asking each other. "Did *you* know, Haller?"

"No," Haller said. "Renée is the only one who knew about it. All I was hoping for was that he'd call up."

"I called yesterday morning," Francis explained. "I picked a time when I was sure you'd all be out."

"That Renée," Abbie said, and began pulling him away from the others. "Have you eaten?"

Francis shook his head.

"Renée's got the whole dinner saved for you," Haller said.

Pushing and bumping into each other, they followed Francis Whitehead through the hall and the serving pantry into the kitchen. At the sight of them, the black woman turned her head away and laughed.

"Renée, you're wonderful!" Francis said, and threw his arms around her and hugged her. Then he sat down at the place she had just now set for him at the kitchen table. Abbie and Nathan drew up a stool and both of them perched on it, unsteadily. Leo sat on the kitchen stepladder. Haller paced back and forth, unable to settle anywhere, and asked questions that nobody paid any attention to. Francis looked at his plate heaped with chicken and creamed potatoes and asparagus and said, "I haven't seen food like this in so long. In the Army you never get a whole anything—just pieces of something. I dream about having a whole lamb chop." They were waiting to see him raise his fork to his mouth and he did, but then he put it down, with the food still on it. "I must go speak to your mother," he said, and got up and left the kitchen.

"How like him," Haller said, "to leave us all sitting here admiring his empty chair!"

When they couldn't get Francis to eat any more they tried to put him to bed but he curled up on the sofa in Abbie's room, with the other boys sitting on the floor as close to him as they could get, and he talked till one o'clock in the morning. He began with the group that had left Grand Central Station together. He described their clothes, and what they said, and how they acted. How the boy from Brooklyn who sat opposite him on the train nearly drove him crazy by reading a furniture ad in the *Daily News* over and over. He told them about the induction center: about the psychological examination, which consisted of hitting you on the kneecap and asking, "Any nervous disorders in your family, buddy?"; about the medical examination, which was perfunctory but nevertheless took hours, in a place so jammed with naked inductees that there was nowhere to stand without touching somebody. And how, one by one and still naked, they were started down the length of a long room while voices called out the sizes of shoes, socks, shorts, shirts, trousers, and they found themselves at the other end, fully clothed and outfitted in four minutes.

He didn't really mind being continually pushed and shoved, herded from place to place, and sworn at. After all, it was the Army. It was not a school picnic. What he couldn't stand, as the day wore on, was the misery that he saw everywhere he looked. A great many of the men were younger than he was, and they became so worn out finally that they lost all hope and leaned against the wall in twos and threes, with the tears streaming down their faces. Eventually, he worked himself into such a fury that he began to shake all over, and a tough Irish sergeant came up to him and put both arms around him and said, "Wait a minute, buddy. You're all right. Take it easy, why don't you?" in the kindest voice Francis had ever heard in his life.

But the strangest thing was the continual pairing off, all day long—on the train, at the induction center, at the camp, where, long after midnight, you found yourself still instinctively looking around for somebody to cling to, and look after. Somebody you'd never laid eyes on before that day became, for two hours, closer than any friend you'd ever had. When you were separated, your whole concern was for him—for what might be happening to him. While you had one person to look after, among the crowd, you were not totally lost yourself. When the two of you were separated for good, you looked around and there was someone in obvious desperation, and so the whole thing happened all over again.

When they arrived in camp, somebody talked back to a sergeant who was not Irish, and he said, "All right, you sons of bitches, you can just wait." And they did, from midnight until one-thirty, when they were marched two miles in what proved to be the wrong direction and three miles back, before they sat down, at 2:15 a.m., in a mess hall, before a plate of food they couldn't look at, let alone eat. All through the next day it continued—the feeling that each thing was a little more than you could stand. And the pairing off. But the next day was better. And the third day they began to relax and settle into their ordinary selves. . . .

Of the three boys sitting on the floor in front of Francis Whitehead, listening to him gravely, Leo was still too young for military service, Nathan had drawn a high number and didn't expect to be called before September or October, and Haller was 4-F because of his bad eyes. Most of the things Francis told them they knew already, from what they had read in newspapers and magazines. It was his voice that made the experience real to them. The voice of the survivor. And here and there a detail that they couldn't have imagined. And because it happened to Francis, whom all three of them loved.

When Haller went home, Nathan and Leo put up the overflow cot in their room, and Abbie brought sheets from the linen closet, and a blanket and pillow from the other bed in her room. The boys knocked on the wall when they were in bed, and she came back to say good night. Nathan was sleeping on the cot, Francis was in Nathan's bed, and Leo in his own. After she had turned out the light and gone back to her own room she could hear them talking together, through the wall. The talking stopped while she was brushing her hair, and then there was no sound but Francis's coughing.

She was almost asleep when the kitten commenced complaining from the box on the floor. She had entirely forgotten about it in the excitement of Francis's homecoming. "A little chloroform for you, my pet," she said, "first thing in the morning," and rolled over on her back. I'm twenty-five, she thought. Finally. Thanks to one thing and another, including Haller and his "Oceanides."

Then she thought about Haller—about her grievance against him, which was that he went on courting her year after year, as if faithfulness, the *idea* of love, was the answer to everything, and had no instinct that told him when she was willing and when she couldn't bear to have him touch her. Why, when he was so intelligent, was he also so stupid—for she did like him, and sometimes even felt that she could love him.

As for Francis, it was as Haller had said. Nothing that happens over and over is pure accident; and what they (and God knows how many other people) were faced with, at the critical moment, was his empty chair.

Out of habit, her mother referred to them as "the children," and it was only too true. She and Nathan and Leo. And Haller. *And* Francis. They were all five aiming the croquet ball anywhere but at the wicket, and playing the darling game of being not quite old enough to button their overcoats and find their mittens. But for how long? *For ever*, the curtain said, blowing in from the open window. But what did the curtain know about it?

The kitten was quiet, but the coughing continued on the other side of the wall. Listening in the dark, she decided that Francis didn't have enough covers on. If he had another blanket, he'd stop coughing and go to sleep. She could not get to the extra covers without disturbing her mother and father, and so she took the blanket from her own bed, slipped a wrapper on, and went into the boys' room. All three of them were asleep, but Francis woke up when she put the blanket over him. He didn't seem to know where he was at first, and then she gathered from his sleepy mumbling that he didn't want her to go away. When she sat down, he wormed around in the bed until his thighs were against her back and his forehead touched her knee. There he stayed, without moving, without any pressure coming from his body at all. This time it was not the empty chair but a drowned man washed up against a rock in the sea.

The Patterns of Love

KATE TALBOT'S bantam rooster, awakened by the sudden appearance of the moon from behind a cloud on a white June night, began to crow. There were three bantams—a cock and two hens—and their roost was in a tree just outside the guest-room windows. The guest room was on the first floor and the Talbots' guest that weekend was a young man by the name of Arnold, a rather light sleeper. He got up and closed the windows and went back to bed. In the sealed room he slept, but was awakened at frequent intervals until daylight Saturday morning.

Arnold had been coming to the Talbots' place in Wilton sometime during the spring or early summer for a number of years. His visits were, for the children, one of a thousand seasonal events that could be counted on, less exciting than the appearance of the first robin or the arrival of violets in the marsh at the foot of the Talbots' hill but akin to them. Sometimes Duncan, the Talbots' older boy, who for a long time was under the impression that Arnold came to see *him*, slept in the guest room when Arnold was there. Last year, George, Duncan's younger brother, had been given that privilege. This time, Mrs. Talbot, knowing how talkative the boys were when they awoke in the morning, had left Arnold to himself.

When he came out of his room, Mrs. Talbot and George, the apple of her eye, were still at breakfast. George was six, small and delicate and very blond, not really interested in food at any time, and certainly not now, when there was a guest in the house. He was in his pajamas and a pink quilted bathrobe. He smiled at Arnold with his large and very gentle eyes and said, "Did you miss me?"

"Yes, of course," Arnold said. "I woke up and there was the other bed, flat and empty. Nobody to talk to while I looked at the ceiling. Nobody to watch me shave."

George was very pleased that his absence had been felt. "What is your favorite color?" he asked.

"Red," Arnold said, without having to consider.

"Mine too," George said, and his face became so illuminated

with pleasure at this coincidence that for a moment he looked angelic.

"No matter how much we disagree about other things," Arnold said, "we'll always have that in common, won't we?"

"Yes," George said.

"You'd both better eat your cereal," Mrs. Talbot said.

Arnold looked at her while she was pouring his coffee and wondered if there wasn't something back of her remark—jealousy, perhaps. Mrs. Talbot was a very soft-hearted woman, but for some reason she seemed to be ashamed—or perhaps afraid—to let other people know it. She took refuge continually behind a dry humor. There was probably very little likelihood that George would be as fond of anyone else as he was of his mother for many years to come. There was no real reason for her to be jealous.

"Did the bantams keep you awake?" she asked.

Arnold shook his head.

"Something tells me you're lying," Mrs. Talbot said. "John didn't wake up, but he felt his responsibilities as a host even so. He cried 'Oh!' in his sleep every time a bantam crowed. You'll have to put up with them on Kate's account. She loves them more than her life."

Excluded from the conversation of the grown-ups, George finished his cereal and ate part of a soft-boiled egg. Then he asked to be excused and, with pillows and pads which had been brought in from the garden furniture the night before, he made a train right across the dining-room floor. The cook had to step over it when she brought a fresh pot of coffee, and Mrs. Talbot and Arnold had to do likewise when they went out through the dining-room door to look at the bantams. There were only two—the cock and one hen—walking around under the Japanese cherry tree on the terrace. Kate was leaning out of an upstairs window, watching them fondly.

"Have you made your bed?" Mrs. Talbot asked.

The head withdrew.

"Kate is going to a house party," Mrs. Talbot said, looking at the bantams. "A sort of house party. She's going to stay all night at Mary Sherman's house and there are going to be some boys and they're going to dance to the Victrola."

"How old is she, for heaven's sake?" Arnold asked.

"Thirteen," Mrs. Talbot said. "She had her hair cut yesterday and it's too short. It doesn't look right, so I have to do something about it."

"White of egg?" Arnold asked.

"How did you know that?" Mrs. Talbot asked in surprise.

"I remembered it from the last time," Arnold said. "I remembered it because it sounded so drastic."

"It only works with blonds," Mrs. Talbot said. "Will you be able to entertain yourself for a while?"

"Easily," Arnold said. "I saw *Anna Karenina* in the library and I think I'll take that and go up to the little house."

"Maybe I'd better come with you," Mrs. Talbot said.

The little house was a one-room studio halfway up the hill, about a hundred feet from the big house, with casement windows on two sides and a Franklin stove. It had been built several years before, after Mrs. Talbot had read *A Room of One's Own*, and by now it had a slightly musty odor which included lingering traces of wood smoke.

"Hear the wood thrush?" Arnold asked, as Mrs. Talbot threw open the windows for him. They both listened.

"No," she said. "All birds sound alike to me."

"Listen," he said.

This time there was no mistaking it—the liquid notes up and then down the same scale.

"Oh, that," she said. "Yes, I love that," and went off to wash Kate's hair.

From time to time Arnold raised his head from the book he was reading and heard not only the wood thrush but also Duncan and George, quarreling in the meadow. George's voice was shrill and unhappy and sounded as if he were on the verge of tears. Both boys appeared at the window eventually and asked for permission to come in. The little house was out of bounds to them. Arnold nodded. Duncan, who was nine, crawled in without much difficulty, but George had to be hoisted. No sooner were they inside than they began to fight over a wooden gun which had been broken and mended and was rightly George's, it seemed, though Duncan had it and refused to give it up. He refused to give it up one moment, and the next moment, after a sudden change of heart, pressed it upon George—*forced* George to take it, actually, for by that time George was more concerned about the Talbots' dog, who also wanted to come in.

The dog was a Great Dane, very mild but also very enormous. He answered to the name of Satan. Once Satan was admitted to the little house, it became quite full and rather noisy, but John Talbot appeared and sent the dog out and made the children leave Arnold in peace. They left as they had come, by the window. Arnold watched them and was touched by the way Duncan turned and helped George, who was too small to jump. Also by the way George accepted this help. It was as if their hostility had two faces and one of them was the face of love. Cain and Abel, Arnold thought, and the wood thrush. All immortal.

John Talbot lingered outside the little house. Something had been burrowing in the lily-of-the-valley bed, he said, and had also uprooted several lady's slippers. Arnold suggested that it might be moles.

"More likely a rat," John Talbot said, and his eyes wandered to a two-foot espaliered pear tree. "That pear tree," he said, "we put in over a year ago."

Mrs. Talbot joined them. She had shampooed not only Kate's hair but her own as well.

"It's still alive," John Talbot said, staring at the pear tree, "but it doesn't put out any leaves."

"I should think it would be a shock to a pear tree to be espaliered," Mrs. Talbot said. "Kate's ready to go."

They all piled into the station wagon and took Kate to her party. Her too short blond hair looked quite satisfactory after the egg shampoo, and Mrs. Talbot had made a boutonniere out of a pink geranium and some little blue and white flowers for Kate to wear on her coat. She got out of the car with her suitcase and waved at them from the front steps of the house.

"I hope she has a good time," John Talbot said uneasily as he shifted gears. "It's her first dance with boys. It would be terrible if she didn't have any partners." In his eyes there was a vague threat toward the boys who, in their young callowness, might not appreciate his daughter.

"Kate always has a good time," Mrs. Talbot said. "By the way, have you seen both of the bantam hens today?"

"No," John Talbot said.

"One of them is missing," Mrs. Talbot said.

One of the things that impressed Arnold whenever he stayed with the Talbots was the number and variety of animals they had. Their place was not a farm, after all, but merely a big white brick house in the country, and yet they usually had a dog and a cat, kittens, rabbits, and chickens, all actively involved in the family life. This summer the Talbots weren't able to go in and out by the front door, because a phoebe had built a nest in the porch light. They used the dining-room door instead, and were careful not to leave the porch light on more than a minute or two, lest the eggs be cooked. Arnold came upon some turtle food in his room, and when he asked about it, Mrs. Talbot informed him that there were turtles in the guest room, too. He never came upon the turtles.

The bantams were new this year, and so were the two very small ducklings that at night were put in a paper carton in the sewing room, with an electric-light bulb to keep them warm. In the daytime they hopped in and out of a saucer of milk on the terrace. One of them was called Mr. Rochester because of his distinguished air. The other had no name.

All the while that Mrs. Talbot was making conversation with Arnold, after lunch, she kept her eyes on the dog, who, she explained, was jealous of the ducklings. Once his great head swooped down and he pretended to take a nip at them. A nip would have been enough. Mrs. Talbot spoke to him sharply and he turned his head away in shame.

"They probably smell the way George did when he first came home from the hospital," she said.

"What did George smell like?" Arnold asked.

"Sweetish, actually. Actually awful."

"Was Satan jealous of George when he was a baby?"

"Frightfully," Mrs. Talbot said. "Call Satan!" she shouted to her husband, who was up by the little house. He had found a rat hole near the ravaged lady's slippers and was setting a trap. He called the dog, and the dog went bounding off, devotion in every leap.

While Mrs. Talbot was telling Arnold how they found Satan at the baby's crib one night, Duncan, who was playing only a few yards away with George, suddenly, and for no apparent reason, made his younger brother cry. Mrs. Talbot got up and separated them.

"I wouldn't be surprised if it wasn't time for your nap, George," she said, but he was not willing to let go of even a small part of the day. He wiped his tears away with his fist and ran from her. She ran after him, laughing, and caught him at the foot of the terrace.

Duncan wandered off into a solitary world of his own, and Arnold, after yawning twice, got up and went into the house. Stretched out on the bed in his room, with the Venetian blinds closed, he began to compare the life of the Talbots with his own well-ordered but childless and animalless life in town. Everywhere they go, he thought, they leave tracks behind them, like people walking in the snow. Paths crisscrossing, lines that are perpetually meeting: the mother's loving pursuit of her youngest, the man's love for his daughter, the dog's love for the man, and two boys' preoccupation with each other. Wheels and diagrams, Arnold said to himself. The patterns of love.

That night Arnold was much less bothered by the crowing, which came to him dimly, through dreams. When he awoke finally and was fully awake, he was conscious of the silence and the sun shining in his eyes. His watch had stopped and it was later than he thought. The Talbots had finished breakfast and the Sunday *Times* was waiting beside his place at the table. While he was eating, John Talbot came in and sat down for a minute, across the table. He had been out early that morning, he said, and had found a chipmunk in the rat trap and also a nest with three bantam eggs in it. The eggs were cold.

He was usually a very quiet, self-contained man. This was the first time Arnold had ever seen him disturbed about anything. "I don't know how we're going to tell Kate," he said. "She'll be very upset."

Kate came home sooner than they expected her, on the bus. She came up the driveway, lugging her suitcase.

"Did you have a good time?" Mrs. Talbot called to her from the terrace.

"Yes," she said, "I had a beautiful time."

Arnold looked at the two boys, expecting them to blurt out

the tragedy as soon as Kate put down her suitcase, but they didn't. It was her father who told her, in such a roundabout way that she didn't seem to understand at all what he was saying. Mrs. Talbot interrupted him with the flat facts; the bantam hen was not on her nest and therefore, in all probability, had been killed, maybe by the rat.

Kate went into the house. The others remained on the terrace. The dog didn't snap at the ducklings, though his mind was on them still, and the two boys didn't quarrel. In spite of the patterns on which they seem so intent, Arnold thought, what happens to one of them happens to all. They are helplessly involved in Kate's loss.

At noon other guests arrived, two families with children. There was a picnic, with hot dogs and bowls of salad, cake, and wine, out under the grape arbor. When the guests departed, toward the end of the afternoon, the family came together again on the terrace. Kate was lying on the ground, on her stomach, with her face resting on her arms, her head practically in the ducklings' saucer of milk. Mrs. Talbot, who had stretched out on the garden chaise longue, discovered suddenly that Mr. Rochester was missing. She sat up in alarm and cried, "Where is he?"

"Down my neck," Kate said.

The duck emerged from her crossed arms. He crawled around them and climbed up on the back of her neck. Kate smiled. The sight of the duck's tiny downy head among her pale ash-blond curls made them all burst out laughing. The cloud that had been hanging over the household evaporated into bright sunshine, and Arnold seized that moment to glance at his watch.

They all went to the train with him, including the dog. At the last moment Mrs. Talbot, out of a sudden perception of his lonely life, tried to give him some radishes, but he refused them. When he stepped out of the car at the station, the boys were arguing and were with difficulty persuaded to say goodbye to him. He watched the station wagon drive away and then stood listening for the sound of the wood thrush. But, of course, in the center of South Norwalk there was no such sound.

THE FOLDED LEAF

For Louise Bogan

Contents

Lo! in the middle of the wood,
The folded leaf is woo'd from out the bud
With winds upon the branch, and there
Grows green and broad, and takes no care,
Sun-steep'd at noon, and in the moon
Nightly dew-fed; and turning yellow
Falls, and floats adown the air.
Lo! sweeten'd with the summer light,
The full-juiced apple, waxing over-mellow,
Drops in a silent autumn night.

ALFRED TENNYSON
1833 (*aet.* 24)

BOOK ONE

The Swimming Pool

I

THE blue lines down the floor of the swimming pool wavered and shivered incessantly, and something about the shape of the place—the fact that it was long and narrow, perhaps, and lined with tile to the ceiling—made their voices ring. The same voices that sounded sad in the open air, on the high school playground. "Lights! Lights!" it seemed as if they were shouting at each other across the water and from the balcony stairs.

All of them were naked, and until Mr. Pritzker appeared they could only look at the water; they couldn't go in. They collected on the diving board, pushed and tripped each other, and wrestled halfheartedly. Those along the edge of the pool took short harmless jabs and made threats which they had no intention ever of carrying out but which helped pass the time.

The swimming class was nearly always the same. First the roll call, then a fifteen-minute period of instruction in the backstroke or the flutter kick or breathing, and finally a relay race. Mr. Pritzker picked out two boys and let them choose their own teams. They did it seriously, going down through the class and pointing to the best swimmers, to the next best, and in diminishing order after that. But actually it was the last one chosen that mattered. Whichever side had to take Lymie Peters lost. Lymie couldn't swim the Australian crawl. Week after week the relay began in the greatest excitement and continued back and forth from one end of the pool to the other until it was Lymie's turn. When he dived in and started his slow frantic side stroke, the race died, the place grew still.

Since he was not any good at sports, the best Lymie could do was to efface himself. In gym class, on the days when they played outdoor baseball, he legged it out to right field and from that comparatively safe place watched the game. Few balls ever went out there and the center fielder knew that Lymie couldn't catch them if they did. But in swimming class there was no place to retire to. He stood apart from the others, a thin, flat-chested boy with dark hair that grew down in a widow's peak on his forehead, and large hesitant brown eyes. He was determined when the time came to do his best, and no one held it against him that he always decided the race. On the other hand, they never bothered to cover up that fact.

This day two things happened which were out of the ordinary. Mr. Pritzker brought something with him which looked like a basketball only larger, and there was a new boy in the class. The new boy had light hair and gray eyes set a trifle too close together. He was not quite handsome but his body, for a boy's body, was very well made, with a natural masculine grace. Occasionally people turn up—like the new boy—who serve as a kind of reminder of those ideal, almost abstract rules of proportion from which the human being, however faulty, is copied. There were boys in the class who were larger and more muscular, but when the new boy stepped into the line which formed at the edge of the pool, the others seemed clumsy, their arms and legs too long or their knees too large. They glanced at him furtively, appraising him. He looked down at the tile floor or past them all into space.

Mr. Pritzker opened his little book. "Adams," he began. "Anderson . . . Borgstedt . . . Catanzano . . . deFresne . . ."

The new boy's name was Latham.

Mr. Pritzker, separated from the rest by his size and by his age, by the fact that he alone wore a swimming suit and carried a whistle on a string around his neck, outlined the rules of water polo. Lymie Peters was bright enough when it came to his studies but in games he was overanxious. The fear that he might find himself suddenly in the center of things, the game depending on his action, numbed his mind. He saw the words *five men on a side*; saw them open out like the blue lines along the floor of the swimming pool and come together again.

Eventually it was his turn to slip into the water, but instead of taking part in the shouting and splashing, instead of fighting over the ball with the others, he stayed close to the side of the pool. He went through intense but meaningless motions as the struggle drew near and relaxed only slightly when it withdrew (the water flying outward in spray and the whistle interrupting continually) to the far end of the pool. Once every sixty seconds the minute hand on the wall clock moved forward with a perceptible jerk, which was registered on Lymie's brain. Time, the slow passage of time, was all that he understood, his only hope until that moment when, without warning, the ball came straight toward him. He looked around wildly but there was no one in his end of the pool. From the far end a voice yelled, "Catch it, Lymie!" and he caught it.

What happened after that was entirely out of his control. The splashing surrounded him and sucked him down. With arms grabbing at him, with thighs around his waist, he went down, down where there was no air. His lungs expanding filled his chest and he clung in blind panic to the ball. After the longest time the arms let go, for no reason. The thighs released him and he found himself on the surface again, where there was light and life. The ball was flipped out of his hands.

"What'd you hang onto it for?" a boy named Carson asked. "Why didn't you let go?"

Lymie saw Carson's face, enormous in the water in front of him.

"If that new guy hadn't pulled them off of you, you'd of drowned," Carson said.

In sudden overwhelming gratitude, Lymie looked around for his deliverer, but the new boy was gone. He was somewhere in that fighting and splashing at the far end of the pool.

2

Miss Frank, pacing the outside aisle between the last row of seats and the windows, could, by turning her eyes, see the schoolyard and the wall of three-story apartment houses that surrounded it. The rest of them, denied her freedom of movement, fidgeted. Without realizing it they slid farther and farther down in their seats. Their heads grew heavy. They wound their legs around the metal column that supported the seat in front of them. This satisfied their restlessness but only for a minute or two; then they had to find some new position. In the margins of their textbooks, property of the Chicago Public School System, they drew impossible faces or played ticktacktoe. And all the while Miss Frank was making clear the distinction between participles and gerunds, their eyes went round and round the room, like sheep in a worn-out pasture.

The door was on the right, opposite the windows. In front on a raised platform was Miss Frank's desk, which was so much larger than theirs and also movable. If she stepped out of the room, the desk alone restrained them, held them in their seats, and kept their shrill voices down to a whisper. Behind the desk and covering a part of the blackboard was a calendar for the month of October, 1923, with the four Sundays in red. Above the calendar was a large framed picture. It had been presented to the school by one of the graduating classes and there was a small metal disc on the frame to record this fact; also the subject and the artist, but the metal had tarnished; you could no longer tell what class it served as a memorial to. At certain times of the day, in the afternoon especially, the picture ("Andromache in Exile," by Sir Edward Leighton) was partly obscured by the glass in front of it, which reflected squares of light and the shapes of clouds and buildings.

Miss Frank abandoned her pacing and stepped up to the blackboard in the front of the room. A sentence appeared, one word at a time, like a string of colored scarves being drawn from a silk hat. It was beautiful and exciting but they hardly altered the expression on their faces. They had seen the trick too often to be surprised by it, or care how it was done. Miss Frank turned and faced the class.

"Mr. Ford, you may begin."

"*At* is a preposition."

"That's right."

"*First* is an adjective."

"Adjective, Mr. Ford?"

"Adverb. *First* is an adverb, object of *at.*"

Ford had remembered to take his book home after football practice but he had studied the wrong lesson. He had done the last four pages of the chapter on relative pronouns.

"Prepositions do not take adverbs as their object, Mr. Ford . . . Miss Elsa Martin?"

"*First* is a noun, object of *at. Men* is a noun, subject of the verb *were*—"

"Of what else?"

"Subject of the sentence. *Were* is a verb, intransitive. *Delighted* is an adjective modifying *men*. *When* is a conjunction—"

"What kind?"

By reversing each number and reading from right to left, the *203* on the glass of the classroom door, which was meant to be read in the corridor, could be deciphered from the inside. Carson—third row, second seat—did this over and over without being able to stop.

"Not you, Miss Martin. I can see you've prepared your lesson. . . . Mr. Wilkinson, what kind of a conjunction is *when?*"

"*When* is . . ."

Janet Martin, Elsa's twin sister, but different, everyone said, as two sisters could possibly be, opened her blue enameled compact slyly and peered into it.

"Mr. Harris?"

"*When* is . . ."

"Mr. Carson?"

"I know but I can't say it."

Miss Frank made a mark in her grade book abstractedly, with an indelible pencil.

"Very well, Mr. Carson, I'll say it for you. But of course that means I get an 'S' for today's recitation and you get an 'F'. . . . *When* is a conjunction introducing the subordinate clause: *when they heard what brave Oliver had done* . . . Miss Kromalny, suppose you tell us as simply and briefly as possible what *they* is."

In spite of every precaution the compact closed with a snap. All over the room, heads were raised. Wide-eyed and startled, Janet Martin raised her head at exactly the same moment as the rest. She made no effort to hide the compact. There it was, in plain sight on top of her desk. But so were a dozen like it, on a dozen other desks. Miss Frank glanced from one girl to another and her frown, finding no place to alight, was dissipated among the class generally. She walked around to the front of her desk.

"That's right, Miss Kromalny. *What* is a relative pronoun used as object of the verb *had done*. *Brave Oliver had done what*. Go on, please."

"*Brave* is . . ."

But who knows what *brave* is? Not Miss Frank. Her voice and her piercing colorless eye, her sharp knuckles all indicate fear, nothing but fear. As for the others, and especially the boys —Ford, Wilkinson, Carson, Lynch, Parkhurst, and the rest of them—it would appear that bravery is something totally outside their knowledge or experience. They look to Miss Kromalny for enlightenment.

"*Brave* is an adjective modifying the proper noun *Oliver*. *Had* is . . ."

In the second row on the aisle there is a boy who could tell the class what none of them, not even Miss Kromalny, knows. But it is not his turn to be called on, and besides, he isn't listening. His face is turned to the windows and his jaw is set. Two hunkies from the West Side are waiting for him where Foster Avenue runs under the elevated. At three o'clock he will go to his locker and get the books he needs for his homework—a Latin reader, a textbook on plane geometry—and find his way out into the open air. There will be time as he stands on the school steps, dwarfed by the huge doors and the columns that are massive and stone, to change his mind. Wilson Avenue is broad and has traffic policemen at several of the intersections. It is perfectly safe. Nothing will happen to him if he goes that way. But instead he turns up the collar of his corduroy coat and starts walking toward the elevated. . . .

"What is *done*, Mr.—ah—Mr. Charles Latham?"

Caught between two dangers, the one he had walked into deliberately and this new, this unexpected peril, Spud clenched and unclenched his hands. He had all of a sudden too many enemies. If he turned his attention to one, another would get him from behind. His mouth opened but no sound came out of it.

"I could have sworn that Mr. Latham was with us at the beginning of the hour. Excuse me while I mark him absent."

The class was given time to titter.

"Miss Janet Martin, what is *done?*"

The blood drained slowly from Spud's face. His sight and then his hearing returned. With an effort he pulled himself up into his seat. Now that he was sitting straight, no one bothered to look at him. He had had his moment and was free until the end of the hour. He could think about anything he pleased.

He couldn't go back and attend to the hunkies under the elevated because they weren't there now. They never had been, actually. He had invented them, because he was homesick and bored and there was no one to take it out on. But it was all right for him to think about Wisconsin—about the tall, roomy, old-fashioned, white frame house the Lathams had lived in, with thirteen-foot ceilings and unreliable plumbing and a smell that was different from the smell of other houses and an attic and swallows' nests under the eaves and a porch, a wide open porch looking out over the lake. Or he could think about the other lake, on the other side of town. Or about the sailboats, in summer, passing the church point. Or about the railway station, with the morning train coming in from Milwaukee and the evening train from Watertown. Or about the post office and the movie theater and the jail. Or—it was all the same, really—he could think about Pete Draper and Spike Wilson and Walter Putnam; about old Miss Blair and the Rimmerman girls; about Arline Mayer and Miss Nell E. Perth, who taught him in first grade, and Abie Ordway, who was colored; about Mr. Dietz in the freight office, whose wife ran off with a traveling man, and his son Harold; about the Presbyterian minister and Father Muldoon and Fred Jarvis, the town cop, and Monkey Friedenberg and the Drapers' old white bulldog that rolled in dead fish whenever he found some and had rheumatism and was crazy. . . .

After a minute or two Spud's eyes came to rest on the mournful figure of Andromache. The class went on without him. When they had finished the sentence about brave Oliver, they opened their books to page 32 and the paragraph dealing with the subjunctive.

3

The ringing, brief but terrible, reverberated throughout all the corridors at five minutes before the hour. After the first bell no one, not even Miss Frank, could prevent them from talking out loud or from yawning openly. They were permitted to stand in the aisles and stretch. The girls could pry open their compacts and, without fear of being reprimanded, apply spit to their bangs and rouge to their thin young cheeks. The boys could poke each other. Hurrying from the school library—second floor at the front of the building—to an algebra class or a civics class or gymnasium or hygiene or Spanish 2B or commercial geography, Adams could step on Catanzano's heels, and if deFresne saw a friend climbing the stairs ahead of him, he could quietly insert a ruler between the familiar legs and so make them trip and sprawl. The relief this afforded was only partial and temporary. By the ringing of the second bell, they were once more in their seats. The door was again on the right, the windows on the left—unless, as occasionally happened, they were reversed—and the calendar hanging behind the teacher's desk at the front of the room. The picture, of course, had been changed. It was sometimes King Lear's daughter Cordelia, in white, taking leave of her two evil sisters; sometimes the chariot race from *Ben-Hur*. Or it might be some old monotonous ruin like the Parthenon, the temple at Paestum, the Roman Forum—they hardly noticed which, once they had settled down and become resigned to another hour of inactivity.

The ringing at five minutes to three in the afternoon was different. Although it was no louder than the others, it produced a nervous explosion, a discharge of every ounce of boredom, restlessness, and fidgeting stored up during the long school day. Classrooms were emptied and this time they did not fill up again. The doors of lockers were opened, revealing pictures of movie stars, football players, cartoons, and covers of *College Humor*. Books were tossed in blindly. Caps, plaid woolen scarves, and autographed yellow slickers were taken out.

They all had something to do, some place to go.

The Martin twins met at their lockers—second floor near the head of the center stairs—and parted again almost immediately. Elsa and her friend Hope Davison put on smocks and went down to the assembly hall where, with large brushes and buckets of paint, the stagecraft class was creating the seacoast of Illyria. Janet Martin went down the corridor to another stairway and out a side door of the building. When she appeared, Harry Hall left the cement pillar he was leaning against and came to meet her.

Carson and Lynch went to a movie on Western Avenue. It was called "The Downward Path" and a large sign outside the movie theater said no one under eighteen would be admitted. Carson and Lynch were only sixteen but they were large for their age. They stood and looked at the stills outside. Necking parties and girls half dressed, confronting their parents or the police. The blonde woman in the ticket booth accepted their two dimes without interest.

Rose Kromalny, whose family did not understand about art and music, waited for Miss Frank, to walk home with her.

The three boys who were trying out for assistant football manager met in Mr. Pritzker's office at one end of the gymnasium and tried not to look at one another.

The crack R.O.T.C. squad, consisting of Cadet Corporal Cline and Cadets Helman, Pierce, Krasner, Beckert, Millard, Richardson, and Levy, appeared in the schoolyard, in uniform, and commenced drilling. As always, there were those who stayed to watch.

There was a Junior Council meeting in Room 302 and a meeting of the business staff of *The Quorum* in 109. The Senior Sponsors held a brief meeting in the back of the assembly hall. The orchestra, as usual, practiced in 211. They had two new pieces: Mozart's "Minuet in E Flat" and the "Norwegian Rustic March" by Grieg.

Spud Latham, who had nothing to do and was in no hurry to go home since it wasn't home that he'd find when he got there, stood in front of his wooden locker and twiddled the dial. He was in the throes of another daydream. The school principal, on looking back over Spud's grades, had discovered that there had been some mistake; that they should all have been S's, not C's and D's. So he had the pleasure of coming home and announcing to his incredulous family that he was valedictorian of his class and the brightest student in the history of the school.

The pointer slipped by the last number of the combination and he had to work it over again. The second time he was successful. The locker flew open. His English grammar landed on the floor beside his gym shoes. He reached for his corduroy coat and, forgetting both the Latin reader and the textbook on plane geometry, closed the door of the locker. While he was moving the dial he glanced over his shoulder and saw a boy in a leather jerkin. The boy was waiting for him, apparently. For a moment Spud thought it was somebody he'd never seen before, but then he remembered. In the swimming pool when they were playing water polo. The kid who didn't have sense enough to let go of the ball. . . .

Spud turned quickly and walked away.

4

The way home from school led Lymie Peters past LeClerc's pastry shop. Without turning his head he looked in and saw Mark Wheeler in a coonskin coat, although the weather was mild, and Bea Crowley and Sylvia Farrell, who were trying to make a brown-and-white fox terrier sit up and beg for peanut brittle. And Bob Edwards, and Peggy Johnston, standing next to him in a dark red dress with a wide black patent leather belt. And Janet Martin and Harry Hall, sitting side by side, their hands almost touching, on a dead radiator.

There were a lot of others at LeClerc's that afternoon. Lester Adams, Barbara Blaisdell or a girl who looked like Barbara Blaisdell, Bud Griesenauer, and Elwyn Glazer were standing in one little group. Beyond their group was another one. A third group was over by the counter. In the eleven or twelve steps that it took Lymie to pass the shop window, he saw them all, including Mrs. LeClerc with her dark skin and her polished black hair. Other parts of his long walk home were accomplished miraculously, without his hearing or perceiving a single detail of all that was going on around him. He made his way blindly across busy intersections. Streetcars, taxicabs, and double-decker busses passed unseen before his eyes. Signboards, filling stations, real estate offices he ignored. He went under the elevated and came out again without knowing it. But LeClerc's was something else again. The girls in LeClerc's were like wonderful tropical birds, like parrots and flamingos, like the green jungle fowl of Java, the ibis, the cockatoo, and the crested crane. They may possibly have realized this themselves. At all events, their voices were harsh and their laughter unkind. They parted their hair in the middle sometimes, sometimes on the side, and encouraged it to fall in a single point on their cheeks. Their dresses were simple and right for school, but came nevertheless from Marshall Field's or Mandel

Brothers, never the Boston Store or The Fair. And their eyes, framed in mascara, knew everything.

The boys who hung out at LeClerc's had broad shoulders, or if they didn't, the padding in their coats took care of it. They wore plus fours as a rule, but some of them wore plus eights. Their legs were well shaped. Their bow ties were real and not attached to a piece of black elastic, like Lymie's. The little caps that clung to the backs of their heads matched the herringbone or the basket weave of their very light, their almost white suits. They had at their disposal a set of remarks which they could use over and over again, and the fact that there were a great many things in the world about which they had no knowledge and no experience did not trouble them.

The year before, they went to a Greek confectionery half a block up the street. Although the food in the school lunchroom was cheaper and more nourishing, so many of them insisted on eating at Nick's at noon that getting in and out of the door could only be achieved through force of character. You had to brace yourself and then shove and squirm and have friends make a place for you so that, together, you could elbow your way up to the counter. Once there, if you were lucky or if you had the kind of voice that outshouts other voices, you might come away with a bottle of milk and a ham sandwich or a cinnamon bun. But in the spring something (the same instinct, could it have been, that governs the migrations of starlings?) caused them to abandon the Greek confectionery and settle in LeClerc's, which was even smaller. Here every afternoon were to be found all the girls who never made the honor society or served as Senior Sponsors or took part in dramatics or played the viola; and yet who were, Lymie couldn't help noticing, so much better looking than the ones who did.

In the late afternoon LeClerc's was seldom overcrowded. If Lymie had pushed the door open and walked in, nobody would have indicated any surprise at seeing him. Mark Wheeler would have said "Hi there," over the heads of several people, and Peggy Johnston, who was in his division room, would probably have smiled at him. Her smile seemed to mean more than it did actually, but there were others. There were undoubtedly three or four groups he could have stood on the outside of, without anybody's minding it. After all, that was how it was done. Ray Snyder and Irma Hartnell and Lester Adams had all had to stand around on the outside before they were taken in. But Lymie didn't try.

He was too proud perhaps and at the same time too uncertain of himself. The fact that his legs were too thin for him to wear knickers may have had something to do with it; or that he had no set of remarks. Also, the one time that he had screwed up his courage to ask a girl for a date, she had refused him. Considering how popular Peggy Johnston was, he should have asked her at least two days before he did. She said she was awfully sorry but she was going to the Edgewater Beach Hotel that night with Bob Edwards, and Lymie believed her. It wasn't that he doubted her word. But deep down inside of him he knew as he hung up the phone what would have happened if he'd called earlier. And because he still carried that heavy knowledge around with him, when he got abreast of LeClerc's big plate glass window he looked in and saw everything there was to see but kept right on walking.

Perhaps it was just as well; Lymie was only fifteen.

But why, since he was so proud and in many ways older than his years, did he let himself be drawn into the Venetian Candy Shop farther up the street and come out half a minute later with a large red taffy apple and proceed to smear his whole face up with it, in public, walking along the street?

5

Mrs. Latham reached up and turned on the bridge lamp at her elbow, though it was still daylight outside, and the lamplight fell upon her lap, which was overflowing with curtain material. There were piles of it on the sofa and on the floor around her, and it was hard to believe all this white net could hang from the four living room windows that now were bare and looked out on a park.

She sat with her back not quite touching the back of the big upholstered chair and her head bent over her sewing. In shadow her face was expressive and full of character but when the light shone directly on it, although the features remained the same, it seemed wan. It was the face of a woman who might be unwell. Her soft brown hair had very little gray in it and was done on top of her head in a way that had been fashionable when she was a girl. Anyone coming into the room and seeing her there in the pale yellow light would have found her very sympathetic, very appealing. Without having the least idea what was in her mind as she raised the spool to her lips and bit through the white cotton thread, he would have felt sure that she had been through a great deal; that she had given herself heart and soul to undertakings which ought to have turned out well but hadn't always; and that she was still, in all probability, an innocent person.

Near the center of the park—it was no more than an open field with young elm trees set at regular intervals around the edge—boys were playing touchball. Their voices penetrated to the living room, through the closed windows. Mrs. Latham may or may not have heard them; she did not commit herself. A bakery truck passed in the street, and several cars, one of them choking and sputtering. The sound of footsteps on the cement walk caused Mrs. Latham to raise her head and listen. Whoever it was that she was expecting, this couldn't have been the one, for she went back to her sewing immediately and did not even bother to look out.

In spite of the solid row of front windows, the living room was dark. It was the fault of the wallpaper and of the furniture, which had obviously been acquired over many years, at no great expense, and perhaps even accidentally. There was barely enough of it here and there in the room to make it livable. A plain grayish-blue rug covered most of the floor. The sofa and the chair Mrs. Latham sat in were upholstered in a subdued green. There was a phonograph and three wooden chairs, none of them wholly comfortable. The table was mission, with a piece of Chinese embroidery for a runner, and a pottery lamp with a brown shade. Also a round ashtray with cigar bands glued in a garish wheel to the underside of the glass, and a small brass bowl. The bowl was for calling cards. It had nothing in it now but a key (to a trunk possibly, or to the storeroom in the basement) and thumbtacks. On the shelf under the table were two books, an album partly filled with snapshots and a somewhat larger one containing views in color of the Wisconsin Dells.

The opposite wall of the living room was broken by a

fireplace of smooth green tile made to look like bricks. The gas log had at one time or other been used. It was not lit now. At either end of the mantelpiece were two thin brass candlesticks, each holding a battered blue candle. Between them hung a framed sepia engraving of an English cottage at twilight. The cottage had a high thatched roof and was surrounded by ancient willow trees. The only other picture in the room hung at eye level above the sofa. It was a color print of a young girl, her head wound round with a turban, a sweet simpering expression on her face, and (surprisingly) one breast exposed.

Beyond the living room was the hall, with the front door bolted and chained, and then a rickety telephone stand. On the right was a door with a full-length mirror set into it, and another door that opened into Mr. and Mrs. Latham's bedroom. The hall opened into the dining room, which had two large windows looking out on a blank wall (this was not the apartment Mrs. Latham would have chosen if they'd had all the money in the world) and was a trifle too narrow for anyone to pass easily between the table and the sideboard at mealtime. In the center of the dining room table, on a crocheted doily, was a small house plant, a Brazilian violet which showed no sign of blooming.

After the dining room came the kitchen, and right beside it a bedroom—a girl's room by the look of the dressing table and the white painted bed. On the dressing table there was a letter. The room had a single window and French doors at the far end. The curtains must have been intended originally for some other room than this, since they did not quite reach the window sill. They were organdy and had ruffles. The glass in the French doors was covered with white net.

It was easy to guess that the door in the hall, the one with the mirror set into it, would, if opened, have revealed a closet. But these two French doors were tightly shut and without the help of Mrs. Latham there would have been no telling what lay beyond them. When the street lamps were turned on outside, something prompted her to stand up, brush the threads from her lap, and walk back here. She put her hand on a glass knob and turned it slowly. The door opened, revealing a boy's body lying fully clothed except for shoes, on a cot that was too small for it. The position—knees bent awkwardly, right arm dangling in space—seemed too inert for sleep. It looked rather as if he had a short time before been blindfolded and led out here to meet a firing squad. But such things seldom happen on a sleeping porch, which this clearly was, and besides, there was no wound.

6

When Mrs. Latham spread a blanket over Spud he turned and lay on his back. His face, freed for the time being of both suspicion and misery, was turned toward the ceiling.

It was too bad, Mrs. Latham thought as she bent over him, it was a great pity that they had to leave Wisconsin where they knew everybody and the children had so many friends. But at least Evans had been able to find another job. That wasn't always easy for a man his age. And in time he'd probably get a raise, like they promised him, and be making the same salary he had been making before. The children were still young. They'd have to learn to make new friends, and be adaptable.

She raised one of the windows a few inches and then closed the door behind her softly.

It was nearly six when Spud awoke. He drew the blanket around his shoulders without wondering where it had come from. For a moment he was quite happy. Then the room identified itself by its shape in the dark, and with a heavy sigh he turned on his side and lay with his hands pressed palm to palm, between his knees.

The light went on in the next room and he saw his sister Helen through the curtained doors. She seemed to be at a great distance. Remote and dreamlike, she was reading a letter.

The letter was probably from Pete Draper's brother Andy, Spud thought. "Gump" they called him. For three years now he had had a case on Helen, but his family didn't want him to marry her because she wasn't a Catholic. Every Friday night along about seven-thirty Andy used to appear at the front door with his dark blue suit on, and his hair slicked down with water. Sometimes he'd take Helen to a movie and sometimes they went to a basketball game. Once when Spud was coming home from a Boy Scout meeting on his bicycle, he saw them walking along the edge of the lake, and Andy had his arm around Helen. He was an awfully serious guy. Not like Pete. The night before they left Wisconsin, Helen sat out on the front porch talking to Andy for a long time. Spud was in bed but he wasn't asleep yet. Nobody was asleep in the whole house. His father and mother were in their room, and his mother was packing. He could hear her taking things out of the closet and opening and closing dresser drawers, and he kept tossing and turning in bed, and wondering what it was going to be like when they got to Chicago. His window was right over the porch and he could hear Andy and Helen talking. Several minutes would pass with no sound except the creak of the porch swing. Then they'd begin again, their voices low and serious. Spud thought once that Andy was crying but he couldn't be sure. And at a quarter to twelve his father came down, in his bathrobe, and sent Andy home.

By the way Helen tossed the letter on the bed, without bothering to fold it and put it back in the envelope, Spud could tell that his sister was not satisfied. Something she wanted to be in the letter wasn't in it, probably, but whatever it was, he'd never find out. She didn't trust him any more than he trusted her.

There was six years' difference between Spud's age and his sister's, and in order to feel even kindness toward her, he had to remember what she had been like when he was very small—how she looked after him all day long, defending him from ants and spiders and from strange dogs, how she stood between him and all noises in the night. Now, without either kindness or concern, he watched her dispose of her hat and coat in the closet, and brush her hair back from her forehead. His mother would have brushed her hair in the dark, so as not to waken him. Or if she needed a light to see by, she would have turned on the little lamp beside the bed, not the harsh overhead light. Helen never spared him. She didn't believe in sparing people.

The glare of the light raised Spud to a sitting position. He threw the blanket to one side, put his stockinged feet over the edge of the bed, and stretched until both shoulder blades cracked. The air that came in through the open window was damp and heavy and smelled of rain. He rubbed his eyes with the heel of his hand, yawned once or twice, and bending down, found his shoes. Having got that far he hesitated. All remembrance of what he was about to do with them seemed to desert him. He picked one of them up and stared at it as if by some peculiar mischance his life (and death) were inseparably bound up with this right shoe. When the light went off in the next room, the shoe dropped through his fingers. He yawned, shook his head feebly, and fell back on the bed. There he lay with his eyes open, unmoving, until Mrs. Latham came to the door and called him.

After she was gone he managed to sit up all over again, to put both shoes on, and to stand. Like a sailor wakened at midnight and obliged to make his way in a sleepy stupor up lurching ladders to the deck of the ship (or like the ship itself, pursuing blindly its charted course) Spud passed from room to room of the apartment until he found himself in the bathroom in front of the washstand. He splashed cold water on his face and reached out with his eyes shut until his hand came in contact with a towel. It was hanging on the rack marked SISTER but before he discovered that fact the damage had been done. He folded the towel, now damp and streaked with dirt, and put it back in what he imagined was the same way it had been before. Then he combed his hair earnestly, made a wild tormented face at himself in the bathroom mirror, and said, "Oh fuss!" so loudly that his mother and Helen heard him in the kitchen and stopped talking.

Their astonishment did not last. When he appeared in the doorway they hardly noticed him. He drew the kitchen stool out from under the enamel table and sat down and began to tie his shoes. When he finished, he straightened up suddenly. There was something that bothered him—something that he had done, or not done. Before he could remember what it was, Helen made him move so that she could get the bread knife out of the table drawer, and the whole thing passed out of his mind.

The kitchen smells, the way his mother took a long fork and tested the green beans that were cooking in a kettle on the top of the stove, the happy familiarity of all her movements, reassured him. It seemed almost like the kitchen of the house in Wisconsin. But then there was the rattle of a key in the front door, and Mr. Latham came in, looking tired and discouraged.

Before Mr. Latham had even hung up his coat in the hall closet, the atmosphere of security and habit had vanished. Nothing was left but a bare uncomfortable apartment that would never be like the house they were used to. And when they sat down, the food seemed hardly worth coming to the table for.

7

Evans Latham was an honest and capable man. He had worked hard all his life, and with no other thought than to provide for his family, but somehow things never turned out for him the way they should have. There was always some accident, some freak of circumstance that couldn't possibly have been anticipated or avoided. Bad luck dogged his heels wherever he went. It was not the work of his enemies (he had none) and must therefore have been caused by a disembodied malignancy.

If bright and early some morning the Lathams had left their apartment, which was not what Mrs. Latham would have chosen anyway, and had set up some kind of temporary quarters in the park across the street, among the nursemaids and the babies in their carriages; if Mr. Latham, with advice and assistance from the old men and the boys who gathered in the late afternoon to play touchball, had offered sacrifices—the phonograph, perhaps, or the garish ashtray; if he had then called upon all their friends, or since they had no friends, their neighbors, to join them by moonlight with faces blackened or with masks, and wearing swords or armed with shotguns and revolvers or shinny sticks or golf clubs or canes; and if, at a signal from Reverend Henry Roth of St. Mary's Evangelical Lutheran Church, they had rushed into the deserted apartment firing guns, overturning everything under which a malignant spirit might lurk, tossing the furniture out of doors, beating against walls and windows; and if the old men and the young boys had marched nine times around the outside of the apartment building throwing torches about, shouting, screaming, beating sticks together, rattling old pans, while the nursemaids ran up and down, up and down the cellar stairs; if all this had been done properly, by people with believing hearts, it is possible that the spirit would have been driven off and that, for a time anyway, prosperity would have attended the efforts of Mr. Latham. Unfortunately this remedy, tried for centuries on one continent or another and always found helpful, never occurred to him. He went on day after day, doing the best he knew how. And it wasn't seeing other men get rich off his ideas (oil had been found on the ranch in Montana two years after he had sold it) or any single stroke of bad luck, but the terrible succession of them, large and small, which had changed him finally, so that now he was seldom hopeful or confident the way he used to be.

When, like tonight, he was not inclined to be talkative, the others felt it and did not attempt to be cheerful in spite of him. Helen addressed an occasional remark to her mother but Mrs. Latham's replies were not encouraging and led nowhere.

Except when he was obliged to ask for the butter or the bread or the jelly, Spud ate in silence. Much of the time he was not even there. Mr. Latham had to ask him twice if he wanted a second helping. Spud managed to pass his plate without meeting his father's eyes and said, "What are we going to have for dessert?"

"Baked apple," Mrs. Latham said.

"I wish you'd make a chocolate cake sometime. You know the kind—with white icing?"

Mrs. Latham felt the earth around the Brazilian violet and then poured the water that was in her glass over it.

"When we get straightened around," she said.

"I don't think I want any baked apple," Spud said. "I don't feel hungry."

"First time I ever knew you to make a remark like that," Mr. Latham said. "Are your bowels clogged up?"

"No," Spud said, "they're not. I just don't seem to be hungry any more. Not like I used to. I haven't felt really hungry since we moved to Chicago."

Mrs. Latham signaled to him to be quiet but he paid no attention to her. "It's the atmosphere," he said. "All this smoke and dirt."

Mr. Latham stabbed at a couple of string beans with his fork. "Perhaps you'd better move back to Wisconsin," he said sharply. "I seem to remember that you ate well enough when we lived there."

"I would if I could," Spud said.

"There's nobody stopping you," Mr. Latham said.

Mrs. Latham frowned. "Please, Evans," she said. "Eat your supper."

"Well," he said, turning to her, "it's very annoying to come home at the end of a hard day and find all of you glum and dissatisfied."

"If you call this home," Spud said.

"It's the best I can provide for you," Mr. Latham said to him. "And until you learn to accept it gracefully, maybe you better not come to the table."

Spud put his napkin beside his plate, kicked his chair back, and left the room. A moment later they heard the front door slam. Helen and her mother looked at each other. Mr. Latham, carefully avoiding their glances, picked up the carving knife and fork and cut himself a small slice of lamb, near the bone.

8

Two pictures stood side by side on Lymie Peters' dresser. The slightly faded one was of a handsome young man with a derby hat on the back of his head and a large chrysanthemum in his buttonhole. The other was of a woman with dark hair and large expressive dark eyes. The picture of the young man was taken in 1897, shortly after Mr. Peters' nineteenth birthday. The high stiff collar and the peculiarly tied, very full four-in-hand were bound to have their humorous aspect twenty-six years later. The photograph of Mrs. Peters was not a good likeness. It had been made from another picture, an old one. She had a black velvet ribbon around her throat, and her dress, of some heavy material that could have been either satin or velvet, was cut low on the shoulders. The photographer had retouched the face, which was too slender in any case, and too young. Instead of helping Lymie to remember what his mother had looked like, the picture only confused him.

He had come into the bedroom not to look at these pictures but to see what time it was by the alarm clock on the table beside his bed. The room was small, dark, and in considerable disorder. The bed was unmade. A pair of long trousers hung upside down by the cuffs from the top drawer of the dresser, and the one chair in the room was buried under layers of soiled clothes. On the floor beside the window was a fleece-lined bedroom slipper. There was fluff under the bed and a fine gritty dust on everything. The framed reproduction of Watts' "Hope" which hung over the dresser was not of Lymie's choosing. During the last five years Mr. Peters and Lymie had lived first in cheap hotels and then in a series of furnished kitchenette apartments, all of them gloomy like this one.

The grandfather's clock in the hall and the oriental rug on the floor in Lymie's room had survived from an earlier period. The rug was worn thin and curled at the corners, but when Lymie turned the light on, the childlike design of dancing animals—dogs, possibly, or deer, worked in with alternating abstract patterns—was immediately apparent, and the colors shone. The grandfather's clock remained at twenty-five minutes past five no matter what time it was, but the alarm clock was running and it was seven-twenty.

Lymie went into the bathroom and moved the pieces of his father's safety razor, the rusted blade, the shaving brush, and the tube of shaving soap, from the washstand to the window sill. He let the hot water run a moment, full force, to clean out the bowl, and then he washed his face and hands and ran a wet comb through his unruly hair. The arrangement was that if his father didn't come home by seven-thirty, Lymie was to go to the Alcazar Restaurant on Sheridan Road and eat by himself.

At exactly seven-thirty-one he let himself out of the front door of the apartment building. The other boys in the block had had their dinner and were outside. Milton Kirshman was bouncing a rubber ball against the side wall of the building. The others were in a cluster about Gene Halloway's new bicycle. They nodded at Lymie, as he went by. The bicycle was painted red and silver and had an electric headlight on it which wouldn't light. A slight wind blew the leaves westward along the sidewalk, and there were clouds coming up over the lake.

The Alcazar Restaurant was on Sheridan Road near Devon Avenue. It was long and narrow, with tables for two along the walls and tables for four down the middle. The decoration was *art moderne*, except for the series of murals depicting the four seasons, and the sick ferns in the front window. Lymie sat down at the second table from the cash register, and ordered his dinner. The history book, which he propped against the catsup and the glass sugar bowl, had been used by others before him. Blank pages front and back were filled in with maps, drawings, dates, comic cartoons, and organs of the body; also with names and messages no longer clear and never absolutely legible. On nearly every page there was some marginal notation, either in ink or in very hard pencil. And unless someone had upset a glass of water, the marks on page 177 were from tears.

While Lymie read about the Peace of Paris, signed on the thirtieth of May, 1814, between France and the Allied powers, his right hand managed again and again to bring food up to his mouth. Sometimes he chewed, sometimes he swallowed whole the food that he had no idea he was eating. The Congress of Vienna met, with some allowance for delays, early in November of the same year, and all the powers engaged in the war on either side sent plenipotentiaries. It was by far the most splendid and important assembly ever convoked to discuss and determine the affairs of Europe. The Emperor of Russia, the King of Prussia, the kings of Bavaria, Denmark, and Württemberg, all were present in person at the court of the Emperor Francis I in the Austrian capital. When Lymie put down his fork and began to count them off, one by one, on the fingers of his left hand, the waitress, whose name was Irma, thought he was through eating and tried to take his plate away. He stopped her. Prince Metternich (his right thumb) presided over the Congress, and Prince Talleyrand (the index finger) represented France.

A party of four, two men and two women, came into the restaurant, all talking at once, and took possession of the center table nearest Lymie. The women had shingled hair and short tight skirts which exposed the underside of their knees when they sat down. One of the women was fat. The other had the face of a young boy but disguised by one trick or another (rouge, lipstick, powder, wet bangs plastered against the high forehead, and a pair of long pendent earrings) to look like a woman of thirty-five, which as a matter of fact she was. The men were older. They laughed more than there seemed any occasion for, while they were deciding between soup and shrimp cocktail, and their laughter was too loud. But it was the women's voices, the terrible not quite sober pitch of the women's voices which caused Lymie to skim over two whole pages without knowing what was on them. Fortunately he realized this and went back. Otherwise he might never have known about the secret treaty concluded between England, France, and Austria, when the pretensions of Prussia and Russia, acting in concert, seemed to threaten a renewal of the attack. The results of the Congress were stated clearly at the bottom of page 67 and at the top of page 68, but before Lymie got halfway through them, a coat that he recognized as his father's was hung on the hook next to his chair. Lymie closed the book and said, "I didn't think you were coming."

"I got held up," Mr. Peters said. He put his leather brief case on a chair and then sat down across the table from Lymie. The odor on his breath indicated that he had just left a prospective client somewhere (on North Dearborn Street, perhaps, in the back room of what appeared to be an Italian *pizzeria* but was actually a speakeasy); his bloodshot eyes and the slight trembling of his hands were evidence that Mr. Peters drank more than was good for him.

Time is probably no more unkind to sporting characters than it is to other people, but physical decay unsustained by respectability is somehow more noticeable. Mr. Peters' hair was turning gray and his scalp showed through on top. He had lost weight also; he no longer filled out his clothes the way he used to. His color was poor, and the flower had disappeared from his buttonhole. In its place was an American Legion button.

Apparently he himself was not aware that there had been any change. He straightened his tie self-consciously and when Irma handed him a menu, he gestured with it so that the two women at the next table would notice the diamond ring on the fourth finger of his right hand. Both of these things, and also the fact that his hands showed signs of the manicurist, one can blame on the young man who had his picture taken with a derby hat on the back of his head, and also sitting with a girl in the curve of the moon. The young man had never for one second deserted Mr. Peters. He was always there, tugging at Mr. Peters' elbow, making him do things that were not becoming in a man of forty-five.

"I won't have any soup, Irma," Mr. Peters said. "I'm not

very hungry. Just bring me some liver and onions." He turned to Lymie. "Mrs. Botsford come?"

Lymie shook his head. "Maybe she's sick."

"She always calls the office when she's sick," Mr. Peters said. "More than likely she's quit. It's a long way to come and she may have found somebody on the South Side to work for. If she *has* quit, she'll get in touch with me. She's got four weeks' wages coming to her."

"But I thought you paid her last week," Lymie said.

"I was going to," Mr. Peters said, "but I didn't get around to it." He glanced at the next table. "What kind of a day did you have at school?"

"All right," Lymie said.

"Anything happen, specially?"

A whistle blew faintly, Mr. Pritzker's whistle, and for a moment the splashing surrounded Lymie and sucked him down. He decided that it wasn't anything that would interest his father. School was one world, home was another. Lymie could and did pass back and forth between them nearly every day of his life, but it was beyond his power to bring the two together. If he tried now, his father would make an attempt at listening but his eyes would grow vague, or he would glance away for a second and hardly notice when Lymie stopped talking.

"No," Lymie said, "nothing happened."

Mr. Peters frowned. He would have liked the people at the next table to know how smart Lymie was and what good grades he got on his monthly report card.

There was a long silence during which Lymie might as well have been studying, but he didn't feel that he should when his father was sitting across from him, with nothing to read and nobody to talk to. When Irma reappeared with the liver and onions, it was a great relief to both of them. Mr. Peters cut a small piece of meat, stuck his fork into it, and raised it to his mouth. Just as he was about to take the meat from the fork, Irma leaned across the table and set a glass of ice water at his place. He put the fork down, broke off a piece of bread, buttered the bread carefully, and then put it on the tablecloth beside his plate. After that he raised the piece of liver to his mouth again, but instead of taking it he said thoughtfully, "Irma is a very fine girl. Too capable to be doing this kind of work. She ought to be in an office somewhere making twenty-five dollars a week."

Lymie, who had observed his father bending forward slightly so that he could see inside the neckline of Irma's uniform, said nothing. The fork remained poised. After a moment Mr. Peters lowered it with the piece of liver still on it, took a drink of water, and then after a moment picked the fork up as if this time he had every intention of eating. The front door opened and a man and woman came in. Mr. Peters turned to look at the woman's legs as she walked back through the restaurant. The liver fell off the fork, so he took a piece of fried onion and raised that halfway to his mouth.

This comedy went on for nearly twenty minutes and then Mr. Peters signaled to Irma to take his plate away.

"You haven't eaten anything," Lymie said.

"I wasn't hungry," Mr. Peters said. "All I want is some coffee," and once more there was a long silence, during which each of them searched vainly through his whole mind for something to say to the other.

9

Continuing the argument at the supper table, finding answers that made a monkey out of his father, Spud left the park, where he had been sitting all alone on a bench for the last hour and a half, and came to a neighborhood where the apartment houses no longer presented a continuous brick front to the street. Instead there were open spaces where the light from the street lamp shone on a cluster of shabby FOR SALE signs and signs beginning THIS CHOICE BUILDING SITE, with the rest of the lettering submerged in weeds. Sometimes there was only one three-story building to a square block, and no trees, no barberry bushes or bridal wreath to soften the hard outlines of the masonry. Here the air, although tainted with coal smoke, was freer, more like the air of open country.

Occasionally a car drove past, changing the aspect of the street by its headlights, making everything look thin and theatrical. The people Spud overtook on foot might have been young and beautiful and willing to hand over their lives to him, or they might have been older than death. So far as he was concerned they were shadows. He walked past them without even a sidelong glance. When he came to an iron bridge he loitered for several minutes, watching the water flow underneath, and no one caught up with him, which was odd. Possibly the others—the girl with the cloth rose on her hat, the Christian Science practitioner, the young boy with a canvas bag stuffed full of handbills, the piano tuner, and the woman whose blood pressure was higher than it should have been at her age—perhaps all these people had some destination or were expected somewhere. Spud was sailing before his own anger.

He walked on past a paint and varnish factory where, at the gate, an electric bulb shone down on the night watchman's empty chair. Across the street stood a row of ramshackle two-story frame houses, each with the same peaked roof, the same high sagging front porch. The houses extended for two blocks. Then the future asserted itself over the past and there were more apartment buildings with vacant lots between them, more signs, more weeds growing up through unfinished foundations.

A big Irishwoman in a black coat came toward Spud on the wrong side of the walk. She was feeling the effects of liquor and self-pity, and the least people could do, it seemed to her, was to get out of her way. Spud came straight on. At the very last moment her truculence turned to panic and she stepped off the sidewalk. But he was not, as she had thought, a blind man, so she shouted after him: "Damn kids! Think they own the earth . . ."

Spud turned and looked back, seeing the drunken woman for the first time. He shook his head and walked on. The members of his own family—his father, his mother, and his sister—all were against him; it was not surprising that, without knowing how or why, he should bring on himself the ill will of strangers.

At Christiana Avenue the sidewalk gave out abruptly and rather than continue through mud and have to clean his shoes when he got home, Spud turned south. After one long block, Christiana Avenue also gave out, and he turned back east again, zigzagging until he found another bridge and a street that brought him to the western edge of the park. In the park at the drinking fountain Spud found what all day long he had been searching for.

The other boy was astride a bicycle and apparently deep in conversation with two girls. He looked up as Spud walked past. Neither gave any sign of recognition. The other boy balanced himself on his bicycle with the front wheel turning this way and that, and his right foot resting against the cement base of the drinking fountain. His straight blond hair was parted in the middle and trained back like an Arrow collar ad, but it kept falling forward, and he had a nervous habit of tossing his head back.

Spud sat down on a bench near a young maple tree and crossed his legs so that his right ankle rested on his left knee. The girls giggled, which was to be expected, and when they bent over the drinking fountain, the blond boy made the water spurt up in their faces. After having this ancient trick played on them, they decided to turn the water on for each other, but the blond boy promised, and crossed his heart to die, and said honestly, until at last they gave him one more chance. Spud could have told them what would happen. He knew also that the argument by the drinking fountain was for his benefit. If the blond boy had been sure of himself, he wouldn't have wasted valuable time spurting water on girls and pretending to run over their feet with the front wheel of his bicycle.

Tilting his head back until he could look up at a street lamp that was directly behind him, Spud ignored the whole performance. His throat was dry and he could feel his heart pounding inside his shirt. He watched the moth millers beating against the glass globe, which was large and round and made the yellow leaves of the maple glow with light.

After a while the two girls (whether in real or mock anger there was no telling) walked away. Left to himself, the blond boy circled once around the drinking fountain and then rode past Spud so slowly that the bicycle wavered and nearly fell. Spud waited until he tossed his hair back, and then said quietly, "Why don't you get a violin?"

The blond boy didn't answer. He rode on about fifteen feet, made a sudden swift turn, came back, and stopped directly in front of Spud. One foot was on a pedal, the other resting on the sidewalk. "I don't like your attitude," he said.

Spud cleared his throat and spat carefully, so that it just missed the front wheel of the blond boy's bicycle. The wheel was withdrawn a few inches.

"You looking for trouble?"

"If I saw some," Spud said, "I don't know as I'd get up and walk away from it."

They were in position now, their moves as fixed and formal as the sexual dancing of savages.

"Because if you're really looking for trouble," the blond boy said, "I'd be only too happy to beat the shit out of you."

"You and how many other Swedes?"

That did it apparently, for the blond boy let go of his bicycle, which fell with a clatter, and Spud rose from the bench to meet him. They stood sizing each other up. The blond boy was taller than Spud, thicker through the waist, and larger boned. They each waited for the sudden twitch, the false movement which would release their arms and set them slugging at one another. They could not fight until the willingness to fight, rising inside them like mercury in a glass, reached a certain point; and that, rather than what they said or did or any ability to discriminate between a disparaging remark which could with dignity be allowed to pass and an insult which must be challenged if one is to maintain honor, cast the decision.

"There's a better place over there," the blond boy said, pointing to a dark clump of shrubbery.

"Okay," Spud said.

They walked into an open space among the bushes, took off their coats, their ties, unbuttoned their shirt collars, and rolled up their sleeves as if they were about to inspect each other's vaccination marks. There was a moment when they stood helplessly. Then the mercury began to rise again. The blond boy tossed the hair out of his eyes and shifted his balance, and Spud knew as definitely as if it had been announced over the radio what was coming. He ducked just in time.

No longer was it necessary to imagine two bohunks waiting under the elevated. He had an enemy now, a flesh and blood Swede with a cruel mouth and murder in his pale blue eyes. The Swede got through Spud's guard and landed one on the end of his chin. It only made Spud feel stronger, more sure of himself. All the rancor against his father for uprooting him, all his homesickness, his fear of Miss Frank's sarcasm, his contempt for the dressy boys who sat around him in the classrooms at school, his dislike for girls who painted their faces and for the other kind who knew their lessons and were superior, his resentment at being almost but not quite poor, at having to go through his sister's bedroom to get to his own—everything flowed out through his fists. At each impact he was delivered of some part of his accumulated misery and he began to feel larger than life size.

10

Janet Martin with her hair in curlers and her face scrubbed clean of rouge and powder and lipstick was not so different from her sister Elsa, after all. In the dark they talked across the narrow space that separated their two beds, and yawned, and broke the sudden silences with more talk. Their voices grew drowsy and the things they had to say to each other more intimate.

Carson and Lynch, in spite of what they had seen in the movie house on Western Avenue, fell into a dreamless sleep the moment their heads touched the pillow.

At quarter after eleven Lymie Peters was still awake.

On the way home from the Alcazar Restaurant Mr. Peters had stopped in at a cigar store and made a telephone call, the results of which were obviously satisfactory. As soon as they got back to the apartment he went out to the tiny kitchen and from one of the cupboards he produced two green demijohns, one containing alcohol, the other a little less than half full of distilled water. Then he made a trip to the linen closet, where he kept the glycerin and also a very small bottle containing oil of juniper. When alcohol, juniper drops, and glycerin had been added to the distilled water, in proper proportion, Mr. Peters took the bottle in his hands and shook it vigorously up and down, from side to side in wide sweeping arcs. After a time his arms grew tired and he called Lymie, who came and took turns swinging the demijohn.

To Lymie the word *party* had once meant birthday presents

wrapped in white tissue paper, ice cream in the shape of a dove or an Easter lily, and games like London Bridge and pin-the-tail-on-the-donkey. Now it meant a telephone call from the corner cigar store and the shades drawn to the window sills. The women who came to see his father had bobbed hair that more often than not was hennaed, they smoked cigarettes, their voices were raucous and hard, and their dresses kept coming up over their knees.

If he walked into the living room they usually made a fuss over him, and asked him to come and sit beside them on the sofa. Sometimes they straightened his necktie and slicked his hair down and asked him how many girls he had and if he knew why the chicken crossed the road. He did, actually, but he pretended that he didn't. No matter what he said, they always burst out laughing, and apparently it was about something which wasn't exactly the thing they were talking about, some joke that Lymie wasn't old enough to understand. He didn't stay long. He didn't want to, particularly, and he waited for his father to give him that look which meant it would be a good idea if Lymie said good night and went back to his own room.

Tonight, when the doorbell rang, Lymie raised his head and listened. He was prepared for what was coming. It had happened many times before. But nevertheless the expression on his thin pointed face was of anxiety. He heard his father's footsteps in the front hall. Mr. Peters was pressing the buzzer that released the vestibule door. A moment after he turned the double lock, a voice broke out on the stairs, a woman's voice, and when she reached the landing, Mr. Peters joined in, both of them talking loudly.

"*Whee I'm out of breath. Lymon, the next apartment you move into better be on the second floor before I develop heart trouble from climbing the stairs.*"

"*You're getting fat, that's all that's the matter with you.*"

"*I'm not either getting fat . . . Why do you say things like that?*"

"*What's this right here . . . feel it?*"

"*Don't be silly, that's just my . . .*"

Lymie got up noiselessly and closed the door of his room. It made very little difference. The woman's voice would have penetrated through stone. For a while after he had undressed and got into bed, he lay curled on his right side, listening. Then he began to think about the house where he was born. It was a two-story Victorian house with a mansard roof and trellises with vines growing up them—a wistaria and a trumpet vine. The house was set back from the street and there was an iron fence around the front yard, and in one place a picket was missing. As a child he seldom went through the front gate, unless he was with some grown person. Bending down to go through the hole in the fence gave him a sense of coming to a safe and secret place.

The odd thing was that now, when he went back to the house in his mind, and tried to walk through it, he made mistakes. It was sometimes necessary for him to rearrange rooms and place furniture exactly before he could remember the house the way it used to be.

The house had a porch running along two sides of it, and the roof sloped down so that it included the second story. The front door opened into a hall, with the stairs going up, and then the door to the library, the door to the living room. Beyond the living room was the dining room, and beyond the dining room was the kitchen. The stairs turned at the landing, and upstairs there was another hall. The door to his room, the door to the guest room, the door to his mother and father's room, and the door to the sewing room all opened off this upstairs hall. And there was a horsehair sofa where he sat sometimes in his nightgown, when there was company and he wanted to listen to what was going on downstairs. The sofa scratched his legs. There was also a bookcase in the upstairs hall, with his books in it, and a desk, and over the desk was a picture of a boy with a bow and arrow and a gas jet that was left burning all night. The bathroom was at the end of a long corridor and up one step. When you got to the end of the corridor you turned right if you wanted to go into the bathroom, and left if you wanted to go into the back hall, where the clothes hamper was, and the door to the maid's room, and the back stairs. The back stairs used to frighten him even in the daytime, and at night he never dared look to the left, as he reached the end of the corridor.

About the bathroom he was confused. Sometimes the

washbowl was in one place and sometimes it was in another. The tub was large and had claws for feet, he was sure. But was it at the far end of the room, under the window? Or was that where the toilet was?

He gave up trying to establish the arrangement of the bathroom and thought instead of the butler's pantry, which he had completely forgotten before. It was between the dining room and the kitchen. The butler's pantry was where the door to the cellar stairs was. You opened this door and the stairs went down to the furnace room, which was dark and full of cobwebs. And there was no railing.

There was also a door that opened off the kitchen, and another stairs which led to the cellar where his mother kept all kinds of fruit in jars on open shelves.

The discovery of these two sets of stairs, both of which he had totally forgotten, pleased Lymie. He thought about them for a minute or two and then suddenly the house went out of his mind, leaving no trace. He was back in his own bed, and it was the utter absolute silence that kept him from sleeping.

II

Mrs. Latham was still awake when Spud came in. She called to him softly from her bedroom. "Is that you, son?" It couldn't have been anyone else and it was really another question altogether that she was asking him. When he answered, the sound of his voice satisfied her apparently. "Turn out the light in the hall," she said. "And sleep well."

"Same to you," Spud said.

With his tongue he touched the cut on the inside of his cheek. There was a slight taste in his mouth which was blood. His shirt was torn all the way down his back. His hair was full of dirt and leaves. He was glad his mother hadn't waited up for him. It would upset her if she knew he had been fighting.

He tried not to make a sound going through Helen's room but he miscalculated the position of a small rocking chair and fell over it. Picking himself up he was as conscious of his sister's irritation as if she had spoken out loud, but there was no sound from the bed, not even the creaking of springs.

When Spud got his clothes off he was too tired to do anything but crawl in between the covers. Too tired and too happy. For the first time the room seemed his. It was a nice room, better than he had thought. It had all these windows. *The blond boy began to give way, to defend himself. Foot by foot they fought their way across the open space in the shrubbery, their breathing and the impact of their fists the only sound, their bodies the whole field of vision. When the blond boy, stepping backward, tripped and lost his balance, Spud fell on top of him.* Carlson, his name was: Verne Carlson. So he must have been a Swede. He was not especially different from a lot of guys in Wisconsin. Guys like Logan Anderson or Bob Trask, who think they are a lot tougher than they really are. But on the other hand (Spud yawned) not bad when you get to know them.

The night sky was split wide open by a flash of lightning and then another paler one. If it rained it would probably get the window sill and the floor wet but it didn't matter. Nothing mattered now. *The blond boy was tired. He got his legs around Spud's waist and then didn't have the strength to cut off Spud's wind. They lay that way, locked and not moving, until a sudden jerk pried the heavy legs apart and Spud rolled free.* He twisted around in the bed until he found the place he was looking for. *The blond boy made a grab for him and missed and grabbed again, but Spud knew what he was doing. He waited and saw his chance and pinned the blond boy's shoulders to the ground. Give up? he asked. Do you give up? The blond boy lay there panting, his eyes closed, his face streaked with sweat and dirt, and didn't answer.* Spud wanted to stay awake until he heard the sound of rain but his eyelids closed of their own accord and it didn't seem worth while opening them. Somewhere down the block a car started up and there were voices, people saying good night. And then his mother's voice saying . . . and the voice of the woman who passed him on the sidewalk. . . . No, that was what his mother said. Sleep well, she said. He flexed his fingers, sighed, and was almost gone when he remembered something. The splashing and the shouting in the pool. But that wasn't it. It wasn't while they were playing water polo, it was afterward. It was that skinny kid who. . . .

BOOK TWO

Partly Pride and Partly Envy

12

OF the many ways of knowing people, the eye's appraisal is surely the most complete; but Spud Latham's eyes, which saw only enemies, would never have perceived that the boy ahead of him was not like the others. Spud's eyes were bandaged now and for guidance he had to depend on his right hand, which was resting on a naked shoulder. The shoulder was very thin. The boy ahead of Spud (whoever it was) would have been no great help in a fight, but then this wasn't a fight exactly. The shoulder stiffened when there was danger, and when the danger was safely past, the shoulder relaxed. With a kind of wonder Spud felt the fragile collarbone moving, and the tendons, and made up his mind to follow trustingly.

The initiation should have been held in a long hut under the darkest trees in a forest, but that couldn't be managed; there are no forests, strictly speaking, anywhere near Chicago. The fraternity had engaged a suite of rooms on the fourth floor of a North Side residential hotel. The committee in charge had come early, bringing with them the paraphernalia for the initiation. They had unfortunately no masks, no slit gongs, no bull roarer. No one had told them about these things. But they had bananas, limburger cheese, a ball of kitchen string, French dressing, soured milk, tartar sauce, oysters, and a quart milk bottle full of stale tea. Because they were obliged to perform in one evening a ritual that, done properly, requires from two to three months, they yanked the shades down and hurriedly pushed the furniture out of the way. It would have saved them embarrassment later and also some expense if they had rolled up the rugs, which were a bloody shade of red, but they didn't think about it. Dede Sandstrom tore an old sheet of his mother's into strips that could be used for blindfolds. The other boys cut several lengths of string and on the end of each one they fastened an oyster.

Shortly after seven o'clock the pledges appeared, one at a time, in the hotel lobby. Their pockets were stuffed with chocolate bars, Life Savers, candy, and chewing gum. Their faces were scrubbed and shining, and they were dressed as for a Friday night date at the Edgewater Beach Hotel. This was a Wednesday—Wednesday, the twenty-fifth of January. The elevator boy delivered them, one at a time, at the fourth floor, where they parted from him reluctantly as though from a friend and made their way along the corridor, reading the room numbers. Lynch's hand sought his striped bow tie, lest it be at an angle, and two minutes later, at almost the same spot, Carson felt his wavy hair, plastered to his skull with water. Catanzano, caught off guard by a Florentine mirror, reassured himself by stretching his bull neck and squaring his heavy shoulders. In spite of the red arrows painted on the wall opposite the elevator shaft, Lymie Peters went the wrong way and had to retrace his steps. His face was flushed and he had a stitch in his side, from running. He had left home in what he thought was plenty of time, but then he had lingered in front of a butcher shop on Sheridan Road between Albion and Northshore Avenues. The shop was closed for the night and the floor was strewn with fresh sawdust, and in a row facing the plate-glass door stood a plaster sow and four little pigs. Caught in a timeless pink light they looked out at Lymie and he looked in at them until the big round clock on the wall of the butcher shop released him from this trap for children and sent him running down the street.

Spud Latham was the last to come, and he was several minutes late. This tardiness was intentional. His clothes had changed since last October. He wore plus eights, like Mark Wheeler and Ray Snyder, whom he counted among his innumerable enemies. He knew that they hated him (or at least that they didn't like his attitude) and he stood and faced the door of Room 418 with his jaw set, waiting for somebody to make a false move. When there was only silence he grew impatient, raised his fist, and rapped on the door with his bare knuckles.

"Who's there?"

The voice that spoke through the closed door was hollow and sinister.

Spud answered according to previous instructions: "Neophyte wishing admission to the Isle of Thura."

"Shut your eyes, neophyte, and face the other way on pain of deadly punishment."

The door was opened behind his back. Hands blindfolded him, and other hands pulled him roughly into the room, where they stripped him and disfigured his body with Carter's drawing ink and tincture of iodine. He submitted to this without protest, but then his coming here at all was an act of submission. Along with Spud's need for enemies was also the need to have friends, to be accepted by the right people.

He was pushed into the straggling line of naked, blindfolded neophytes, between Lymie Peters and Carson. After Carson came Lynch, with his bow tie retied around his bare neck. Then Ford, Catanzano, and deFresne—each with his right hand on the shoulder of the boy ahead of him. They were driven round and round the room, walking, running, hopping on one leg, and squatting duck-fashion until their knees went soft. They were driven over and under chairs, into the next room and out again, to the sound of paddles slapping, feet stomping, voices shouting, the whoosh of a broom descending (on whose buttocks?) and other often inexplicable noises.

The members of the initiation committee were enjoying themselves thoroughly. They had once undergone this same abuse and so it satisfied their sense of justice. But the real reason for their pleasure was probably more obscure. They were re-enacting, without knowing it, a play from the most primitive time of man. In this play the men of the village had a grudge against the nearly grown boys, or were afraid of them perhaps. In retaliation for some crime which the boys had committed or were about to commit (possibly some crime which the men themselves had once committed against men who were older than they) the boys of the village were torn from the arms of their mothers, rounded up, and made to undergo a period of intense torture. This torture may even have been a symbolic substitution for punishment by death. At all events it kept the committee busy from twenty minutes after seven until a quarter of eleven.

The neophytes were only kept in line half an hour. The more refined torment had to be administered singly. Carson wrestled for a long time with temptation. Lynch had to scramble like an egg, and Ford ate a square meal. DeFresne wore the skin off the end of his nose pushing a penny along the red carpet. And Catanzano, who was the biggest of the pledges and played guard on the football team, had to do as many push-ups as he could and then ten more. With the third he felt a hand on the small of his back. The hand pushed down cruelly whenever be pushed up. After a time he collapsed and lay still, not minding the catcalls and the obscene noises. He was a wop. His natural place was with the excluded. He was surprised to be here at all.

The fact that Lymie Peters was no good at games and that he never was seen in LeClerc's should have been enough to keep him from being pledged also, but Mark Wheeler had decided it would be a good thing for the fraternity to have somebody whose grades they could point to, if they ever got called up before the principal, and Mark Wheeler had persuaded the others. Having done that much for Lymie, he now knocked him off his feet with a frying pan. Bob Edwards made Lymie read a section of the classified telephone directory with the hot end of a cigarette directly under his nose. The others were fairly considerate. Lymie without his clothes on looked more delicate than he actually was, and they were afraid of injuring him. Also they were waiting for Frenchie deFresne. They wanted to see if they could make Frenchie cry.

When it was his turn they began by beating him with a broom to teach him that no one was kidding. They made him shadowbox blindfolded, hitting him occasionally and shoving him so that he scraped his knuckles on the rough plaster wall. They rubbed hard on the short hair at the back of his neck and also pounded incessantly on his collarbone (this produced an immediate and subtle pain) and made him do alternate knee-bends while they counted: 1, 3, 4, 7, 8, 2, 10, 6, 14, 19, 9 . . . When he had reached what they hoped was a state of physical exhaustion, Ray Snyder shouted: "Think of a nine-letter word beginning with S and ending with N or you'll be in a hell of a SituatioN. We'll throw you in the SheboygaN River, neophyte. It's damn cold there and no good SamaritaN can save you from pneumonia. The SuspicioN will be thrown elsewhere, neophyte, so don't try for revenge"—all the while pounding Frenchie's biceps and slapping his chest. Frenchie couldn't think of any nine-letter word beginning with S and ending with N, so they slapped him across the face several times. When he flinched, they slapped him harder until he quit flinching. After they had slapped him as hard as they could, fifteen or twenty times on both sides of his face, Frenchie cried and they were free to go on with the next part of the initiation.

The neophytes were lined up once more and subjected to divination to determine whether or not they had been experimenting with sex. All seven of them were found guilty and made to swallow a pill. To test their courage they were pushed one at a time up a tall stepladder from which, at a given signal, they were to throw themselves into space. Their blindfolds were raised for a second only, so that they could look down at the board full of rusty nails that they would land on. Carson's blindfold was not as tight as it should have been. He saw the rubber mat being substituted at the last moment for the board, but Lymie flung himself believing in the rusty nails and trusting that Mark Wheeler would be there to catch him. Nobody caught him. He landed on his hands and feet, unhurt, and the voice that cried out in pain was not his voice.

Spud Latham, who was next in line, jerked his blindfold off and saw that he had been fooled. The committee was astonished by this action, and somewhat at a loss to deal with it. They decided that there was no point in making Spud jump off the ladder after he knew what the trick was, so they tied his blindfold on tighter than before, and shoved him out of the way. Catanzano came next, then Ford, who hesitated when the signal was given and tried to back down the ladder. He had stepped on a rusty nail the summer before, at Lake Geneva, and he kept trying to explain about this; in the end they had to push him off.

The earth is wonderfully large and capable of infinite repetition. At no time is it necessary to restrict the eye in search of truth to one particular scene. Torture is to be found in many places besides the Hotel Balmoral, and if it is the rites of puberty that you are interested in, you can watch the same thing (or better) in New Guinea or New South Wales. All you have to do is locate a large rectangular hut in the forest with two enormous eyes painted over the entrance. You will need a certain amount of foolhardy courage to pass through this doorway and you may never come out again, but in any case once you are inside you will learn what it feels like to be in the belly of Thuremlin (or Daramulun, or Twanyirika, or Katajalina—the name varies in different tribes), that Being who swallows young boys and after the period of digestion is completed restores them to life, sometimes with a tooth missing, and always minus their foreskin.

When you have found your place in the circle on the dirt floor, it will not matter to you that Pokenau, the boy on your right, and Talikai, the boy on your left, are darker skinned than Ford and Lynch, and have black kinky hair. In that continual darkness, the texture of your own hair and the color of your skin and eyes will not be noticeable. The odor that you detect will be that which you were aware of in the Hotel Balmoral. The odor of fear is everywhere the same.

In the belly of Thuremlin a comradeship is established which will last Pokenau and Talikai and Dobomugan, and Mudjulamon and Baimal and Ombomb and Yabinigi and Wabe and Nyelahai the rest of their lives. They can never meet one another on any mountain path or in a flotilla of outriggers and not remember how month after month they sat in a crouching position, cross-legged, without moving; how they heard, not with their ears but through their hands, the strange tones which are the voices of spirits; how they learned to make the loud humming noise which so terrifies women; how one by one the mysteries were revealed to them—the sacred masks, the slit gongs, the manikin with the huge head and the gleaming mother-of-pearl eyes.

Along with the singing and eating, the boys are reminded again and again of how, as children, they were never far from their father's arms, and how their elder brothers hunted for them. Flutes play in the morning and evening, and when the boys are led to the bathing pool, the ghosts of their ancestors bend back the brambles from the path.

In a primitive society the impulses that run contrary to the patterns of civilization, the dark impulses of envy, jealousy, and hate, are tolerated and understood and eventually released through public ritual, through cutting with crocodiles' teeth, burning, beating, incisions in the boy's penis. This primitive ritual of torture is more painful, perhaps, but no more cruel than the humor of high school boys. Each stage of the torture is related to a sacred object, and the novices are convinced that, as a result of running the gantlet and being switched with nettles, they will have muscle and bone, they will grow tall and broad in the shoulders, their spirit will be warlike, and they will have the strength between their legs to beget many children.

Occasionally in New Guinea a boy will get into the wrong stomach of the Being, the stomach that is intended for pigs; and that boy cannot be restored to life with the others. But as a rule when the period of seclusion is over, all of the boys appear once more in the village, splendidly dressed in feathers and shell ornaments. Their eyes are closed. They still have to be led by their guardians and though they feel their mother's arms around them, they cannot respond. Even after they have been commanded to open their eyes, the most ordinary acts of life remain for a time beyond their understanding. If the support of their guardian is withdrawn, they totter. They do not remember how to sit down, or how to talk, or which door you enter a house by. When a plate of food is given them, they hold it upside down. Gradually they learn all over again what to do and how to take care of themselves, and the use of their new freedom. They can carry iron weapons after the initiation, and they are free to marry. And they neither fear death nor long for it, because death is behind them.

All this requires the presence and active participation of grown men. Boys like Mark Wheeler, Ray Snyder, and Dede Sandstrom aren't equal to it. In their hands, the rites of puberty are reduced to a hazing; and what survives afterwards is merely the idea of exclusion, or of revenge. The novices are in no way prepared to pass over into the world of maturity and be a companion to their fathers.

The night that Lynch was born, his father, then a young man of twenty-four, stood and stared at his son through the window in the hospital corridor with the tears streaming down his cheeks. Where was he now? Catanzano's father was dead, but why wasn't Mr. Ford at the Hotel Balmoral that evening?

He could have talked to his son quietly and perhaps coaxed him until Ford jumped from the stepladder of his own free will. Where was Carson's father? And Frenchie deFresne's? And what about Mr. Latham? That stupid pursuit of enemies that were sometimes imaginary and sometimes flesh and blood, to which Spud devoted so much of his time—Mr. Latham must have known, even though Spud didn't, who Spud's real enemy was, whose death he desired. The rites of puberty allow the father to punish the son, the son to murder his father, without actual harm to either. If Mr. Latham had been present and had taken part in the initiation, he might have been able to release Spud forever from the basis of all his hostilities. And Mr. Peters should have been there certainly. The call he made from the corner cigar store was not important even to him. It could have been made the next night, just as well. Now instead of being freed of his childhood, Lymie will have to go on smearing his face up with taffy-apples of one kind or another and being stopped by every plaster pig that he encounters, for years to come.

13

Mrs. Latham never stayed in bed after six o'clock. The light wakened her. In winter when it was dark until seven, habit made her get up anyway and dress and go out to the kitchen and start breakfast. At six-thirty she called Mr. Latham, and when he had finished shaving, he went into Spud's room and shook him.

The morning after the initiation, while he was still drugged with sleep, Spud discovered that there was something wrong with him. For a second he didn't believe it. I could be dreaming that I'm awake and standing here in the bathroom, he told himself. But he actually was awake; there was no doubt about it. And when he looked at himself in the mirror over the washstand, those two enemies sickness and fright had him just where they wanted him.

He pulled the lid of the toilet down and sat with his forehead against the washbasin, which was cool, though there was no comfort in it. "Oh . . ." he said very quietly, over and over, wanting to die. The minutes passed, and finally there was a sharp rap on the door. This was neither the time nor the place for despair.

He sighed and stood up and took his toothbrush out of the rack. Because there was, after all, nothing else to do, he scrubbed his teeth vigorously, avoiding his reflection in the mirror. Then he untied the strings of his pajama drawers, pulled the coat over his head, and reached for the cold water faucet that was connected with the shower. The cold shock on his face and on his spine kept him from thinking, but afterward, when he stepped out of the tub and began to dry himself, his mind took up exactly where it had left off. The last traces of ink and iodine came off on the towel.

Looking at them, Spud remembered, as though it were something that had happened long ago, how the neophytes, when the initiation was over and the blindfolds were jerked off, looked at one another with surprise and then at their own ink-stained, iodine-smeared, sweating, dirty bodies. Ray Snyder gave them the password (Anubis) and showed them the sacred grip, which turned out to be the same as the Boy Scouts'. After what had happened this morning, none of that mattered in the least.

At breakfast Spud sat with his head bent over his oatmeal and his mind off on a desperate search for some time or circumstance when he could have exposed himself. So far as girls were concerned, there weren't any. In Wisconsin they used to play postoffice at parties, and spin-the-bottle, but he hadn't even kissed a girl since he moved to Chicago. The trouble was, you didn't always need to get it from contact with a girl. The man who lectured in the assembly room of the high school (to the boys only; there was a woman who lectured to the girls) said you could get it in dozens of different ways; from drinking cups even, and from towels. Probably there was no use trying to figure out where he got it, since there were thousands of ways it could have happened. The only odd thing, the part Spud couldn't understand, was how people could wake up happy in the morning and dress and eat breakfast and go about their business all day without ever taking any precautions, without even *realizing* the danger that existed everywhere about them.

When Mrs. Latham said, "Do you feel all right?" he opened his mouth to tell her that his oatmeal dish would have to be washed separately, also the spoon he was eating with, and his eggcup; they'd all have to be sterilized, everything except his glass, which he hadn't touched yet. But he couldn't talk about such things to his mother. It was a part of life she didn't know about, and if he told her now what was the matter with him, it would be just the same as if he had spattered her with filth.

She put her hand on his forehead, and though it felt to him as if it were burning up, she didn't seem alarmed. "I guess you just aren't awake yet," she said, and got up and went out to the kitchen.

The sunlight, shining on the brick wall outside the dining room windows, cast Mr. Latham's face in shadow and also cast a shadow on the *Herald and Examiner*. He complained about this to Mrs. Latham when she returned with the coffee-pot, and Mrs. Latham suggested that he change places with her but he merely frowned and went on reading. Spud watched him, in the hope that his father would look up suddenly and realize that he ought to put the morning paper down and get up and go into some other room, where they could talk in private.

Helen got up from the table first. "What were you doing so long in the bathroom this morning?" she asked Spud, and without waiting for him to answer, went off to finish dressing. After she left, Mrs. Latham sat with a dreamy expression in her eyes as if, during the night, she had gone and done something quite unbeknownst to all of them. She took a sip of coffee occasionally, and the bottom of her cup grated when she returned it to the saucer. That and the rattle of the newspaper were the only sounds at the breakfast table. At last Mr. Latham stood up and, with the paper clutched in his hand, walked past Spud's pleading eyes.

Anyone at all familiar with Mr. Latham's habits could have told, by the sounds which came from the next room, that he had chosen a tie from the rack on the closet door; that he was tying it now, standing in front of the dresser; that now he was using the whisk broom on his coat collar. In a moment he would come out into the hall and open the hall closet and then it would be too late to stop him. With his hat in one hand and in the other his brief case containing samples of insulating material, Mr. Latham would be quite beyond the reach of his family. Spud pushed his chair back and went and stood in the bedroom door.

His father and mother's bedroom was a place that he seldom wandered into, and never at this time in the morning. Mr. Latham was in front of the window with one foot on the low sill, polishing his right shoe with a flannel rag. He switched to the other shoe and Spud went in and sat down on the edge of the unmade bed. It occurred to him, as his father passed between him and the light, that in all probability, since the disease took some time to show itself (ten days or two weeks, the man said) his mother and Helen were already contaminated by him.

Mr. Latham stuffed the flannel rag in a little brown bag which hung on the inside of the closet door. Then he turned to Spud and said, "Do you need some money?"

In a despair so complete that it blurred his vision, Spud shook his head and saw his father go out into the hall. A moment later the front door closed with a click. After a while Spud got up, went back to his own room, and gathered up the books he had brought home the afternoon before. I'll have to get through this day somehow, he decided. I'll have to go to school so they won't suspect anything, and come home, and eat supper the same as usual. When the lights are out and they're in bed and asleep, I can figure out some way to kill myself.

It was ten minutes of eight when Spud reached the schoolyard. The snow had melted in places, leaving patches of gravel exposed. Spud saw Lymie Peters coming up the walk behind him. He walked faster but Lymie hurried too and caught up with him as he started up the wide cement steps. They went into the building together. Neither of them mentioned the initiation but as they passed the door of the boys' lavatory on the first floor, Lymie said, "Did you pee green this morning?" and deprived Spud of the last hope, the one comfort left to him.

The disease showed.

If it had been any of the others, Spud would have swung on him. He couldn't hit Lymie. Lymie wasn't big enough. Besides, he remembered what he saw the night before when he ripped his blindfold off: Lymie, his thin naked body marked with circles and crosses and the letters I EAT SHIT, trying to get to his feet, without help from anyone. The scene had stayed in his mind intact. Also the curious feel of Lymie's shoulder under his hand. Instead of lying, which he would have done if it had been any of the others, he still had enough trust in Lymie to be able to say "Yeah," in a weak voice. "Yeah, I did."

"So did I," Lymie said. "I thought it might be—you know. So I asked my father. He said it must be that pill they gave us."

The sickness receded, leaving Spud without any strength in his knees.

"That was probably it. They figured they'd scare us," he said, with no outward sign that he had, in that instant, gone completely crazy. He wanted to laugh out loud and prance and dance and kick something (there was nothing to kick in the corridor) and hit somebody (but not Lymie) and throw his head back and screech like a hoot owl. He managed to walk along beside Lymie and to climb the stairs in the center of the building, one step at a time.

The door of Room 211 stood open, and high-pitched voices were swarming out of it. Spud and Lymie walked in together and down separate aisles. In spite of the babel and the steady tramping outside in the corridor, each of them heard the other's footsteps; heard them as distinctly as if the sound were made by a man walking late at night in an empty street.

14

The fraternity house which was referred to with such a carefully casual air in LeClerc's was a one-room basement apartment that Bud Griesenauer got for five dollars a month through an uncle in the real estate business.

They took possession on Ground-Hog Day and spent Saturday and Sunday calcimining the walls a sickly green. The woodwork, the floor, and the brick fireplace were scrubbed with soap and water, but there was nothing much that they could do about the pipes on the ceiling, and they decided not to bother with curtains even though small boys peered in the windows occasionally and had to be chased away.

The apartment was furnished with a worn grass rug, a couch, a bookcase, and three uncomfortable chairs from the

Edwards' attic. Carson brought an old victrola which had to be wound before and then again during every record, and sometimes it made terrible grinding noises. Mark Wheeler contributed a large framed picture of a handsome young collegian with his hair parted in the middle, enjoying his own fireside, his pennants, and the smoke that curled upward from the bowl of his long-stemmed clay pipe. The title of the picture was "Pipe-Dreams" and they gave it the place of honor over the mantel. The only other picture they were willing to hang in the apartment was of an ugly English bulldog looking out through a fence. This had been given to Mr. and Mrs. Snyder twenty-two years before, as a wedding present. The glass was underneath the slats in the fence and they were real wood, varnished and joined at the top and bottom to the picture frame.

To get to the fraternity from school the boys had to take a southbound Clark Street car and get off and wait on a windy street corner, by a cemetery, until a westbound Montrose Street car came along. It was usually dark when they reached the apartment and a grown person would have found the place dreary and uninviting, but they had a special love for it, from the very beginning. This was partly because it had to be kept secret. They could talk about it safely in LeClerc's but not at school, in their division rooms, where the teacher might overhear them and report it to the principal. And partly because they knew instinctively that sooner or later the apartment would be taken away from them. They were too young to be allowed to have a place of their own, and so they lived in it as intensely and with as much pleasure as small children live in the houses which they make for themselves on rainy days, out of chairs and rugs, a fire screen, a footstool, a broomstick, and the library table.

Sometimes the boys came in a body, after school; sometimes by two and threes. Carson and Lynch were almost always there, and when Ray Snyder came it was usually with Bud Griesenauer or Harry Hall. Catanzano and deFresne came together, as a rule, and Bob Edwards and Mark Wheeler. Lymie Peters attached himself to any group or any pair of friends he could find, and once Spud Latham turned up with a blond boy from Lake View High School, who kept tossing his hair out of his eyes. He didn't think much of the apartment and made

Spud go off with him somewhere on his bicycle. Later, without being exactly unpleasant to Spud, they managed to convey to him that he had made a mistake in bringing an outsider to the fraternity house, and after that, when Spud came, which was not very often, he came alone. Ford also came alone. As a result of his refusing to jump off a stepladder blindfolded he was now known as "Steve Brodie" and sometimes "Diver" and he had stopped going to LeClerc's.

The fraternity house was a place to try things. Catanzano and deFresne smoked their first cigars there and were sick afterwards, out in the areaway. Ray Snyder fought his way through "I Dreamt I Dwelt in Marble Halls" on the ukulele, and Harry Hall appeared one day with a copy of Balzac's *Droll Stories* which he had swiped from the bookcase at his grandfather's. It was referred to as the dirty book, and somebody was always off in a corner or stretched out on the couch reading it.

One afternoon when Carson and Lynch walked in they found Dede Sandstrom and a fat-cheeked girl named Edith Netedu side by side on the couch, with an ashtray and a box of Pall Malls between them. The girl sat up and began to fuss with her hair, and Dede said, "Haven't you two guys got any home to go to?"

Carson and Lynch had a feeling that maybe they weren't wanted but they took off their caps and coats and stayed. Dede wound the victrola and put a record on, and after the girl had danced with him a couple of times she asked Carson and then Lynch to dance with her. Both of them were conscious of her perfume and of her arm resting lightly on their shoulders, and they felt that the place was different. Something that had been lacking before (the very thing, could it have been, that made them want the apartment in the first place?) had been found. They went off to the drugstore and came back with four malted milks, in cardboard containers, and it was like a party, like a housewarming.

The other girls who ate lunch at LeClerc's knew about the apartment and were curious about it but they wouldn't go there. Edith Netedu was the only one. She was there quite often. She came with Dede Sandstrom but she belonged to all of them. They dressed up in her hat and coat and teased her about her big hips, and snatched her high-heeled pumps off and hid or played catch with them, and fought among each other for the privilege of dancing with her. She was a very good dancer and the boys liked particularly to waltz with her. She never seemed to get dizzy, no matter how much they whirled. They took turns, trying to make her fall down, and when one of the boys began to stagger, another would step in and take his place. Finally, when they were all sprawling on the couch or the floor, Dede Sandstrom would take over and dance with her quietly, cheek to cheek.

When she was there, the place was at its best. They sang and did card tricks. Ray Snyder's ukulele was passed around, and sometimes they just talked, in a relaxed way, about school and what colleges were the best and how much money they were going to make when they finished studying and got out into the world. Edith Netedu said she was going to marry a millionaire and have three children, all boys; and she was going to name them Tom, Dick, and Harry. When she and Dede Sandstrom put on their coonskin coats and tied their woolen mufflers under their chins and went out, they left sadness behind them.

15

When Spud Latham suggested that Lymie Peters come home with him to supper, Lymie hesitated and then shook his head.

"Why not?" Spud asked.

"Well," Lymie said, "I just don't think I'd better."

They were waiting for a northbound car with the brick wall of the cemetery at their backs, and it was snowing.

"Don't you want to come?" Spud asked.

"Yes, I'd like to very much."

"All right then," Spud said, "that settles it."

Actually it didn't settle anything for Lymie. He liked Spud, or at least he would have liked to be like him, and have broad shoulders and narrow hips and go around with his chin out looking for a fight. But nobody at school had ever asked him to come home like this, especially for a meal, and Lymie had a feeling that it wasn't right. Spud's father and mother would probably be nice to him and all that, but afterwards, when he had gone . . .

A streetcar came along and the two boys got on it, paid their fares, and went inside. The Clark Street car was always slow and this one kept stopping at every block to let people on or off. Lymie had plenty of time to wish that he had said no. He tried to suggest to Spud that maybe he oughtn't to be bringing somebody home like this without asking permission first, but Spud seemed to have no such anxiety. He raised his cap politely to a woman across the aisle who had been staring at them, and this sent Lymie off into a fit of the giggles. The woman was offended.

When the car stopped at Foster Avenue, Spud took Lymie by the arm and, partly dragging, partly tickling him, got him off. They stood and argued then on the corner, while the snow dropping out of the darkness settled in their hair and on the sleeves of their overcoats.

"I'll come some other time," Lymie said. "If I go home with you now, your mother won't be expecting me and she'll —"

"My mother won't mind," Spud said patiently. "Why should she?"

"Well," Lymie said, "it means a lot of extra trouble."

"If you think she's going to send me out for ice cream on your account——"

"That's not what I meant," Lymie said. "She may not be counting on anybody extra and she'll be upset."

"You don't know my mother," Spud said. "Honestly, Lymie, she likes to have me bring kids home. When we lived in Wisconsin I did it all the time. Pete Draper used to eat more meals at our house than he did at his own. When anybody asked his mother how Pete was, she'd say, 'I don't know. You'll have to ask Mrs. Latham.' Jack Wilson and Wally Putnam used to be there too on account of the ring I fixed up in the back yard, to shoot baskets. And Roger Mitchell and a lot of my sister's friends."

Under Spud's persuasion, Lymie gave in once more and then wished he hadn't. A block from the apartment building where the Lathams lived, he and Spud went through the whole argument all over again, stamping their feet and swinging their arms to keep warm. Still certain that it was wrong, that no good would come of it, Lymie watched Spud fit his key into the inside vestibule door and kick it open.

The Lathams lived on the second floor. When they got inside, Spud tossed his coat and muffler in the general direction of the chair in the hall and disappeared. The muffler fell where it was intended to, but the coat landed in a heap on the floor, between the chair and the hall table. Lymie picked it up and put it on the chair, with his own on top of it. When he turned and walked into the living room he knew instantly why it was that he hadn't wanted to come here, and that he ought to get out as soon as he possibly could. There, staring him in the face, was everything he'd been deprived of for the last five years.

He had thought he remembered what it used to be like but he hadn't at all. He didn't even have the house straight in his mind. It had taken on the monotonous qualities, the ugliness of the cheap hotels and furnished apartments he and his father had lived in ever since—all so similar that when he woke in the night he couldn't remember for a second whether he was in the one on Lawrence Avenue or the one on Howard Street or the one on Lakeside Place. He had totally forgotten how different furniture was that people owned themselves from the kind that came with a furnished apartment; and that tables and chairs could tell you, when you walked into a place, what kind of people lived there.

His eyes went on a slow voyage around the room, taking in every detail, fixing it (he hoped) forever in his mind: the curtains, the blue rug, the sofa, the lighted lamps, the phonograph, the Chinese embroidery, the sewing basket with the lid left open, the ashtrays, the brass bowl, the package of pipe cleaners, the fireplace, the brass candlesticks, the English cottage at twilight. This was how people lived, boys his own age, who didn't have to get their own breakfast in the morning, or wash their face in a dirty washbowl, or go to sleep at night in a bed that hadn't been made; boys whose fathers didn't drink too much and talk too loud and like waitresses.

When Spud came back, bringing Mrs. Latham, Lymie turned, ready to apologize and pick up his things and leave.

He saw that Mrs. Latham's hair was not bobbed, that she had no makeup on, and that her skirt was well below her knees.

"Mother, this is Lymie Peters," Spud said.

"How do you do, Lymie," Mrs. Latham said, and shook hands with him. Before Lymie could explain that he had changed his mind and wasn't staying for supper after all, she turned to Spud and said, "Show him where the bathroom is, and see that he gets a clean towel. We're all ready to sit down as soon as your father comes." Then she was gone.

"You see?" Spud said, straddling the bowl of the toilet while Lymie washed his hands. "All that fuss for nothing."

16

To know the world's injustice requires only a small amount of experience. To accept it without bitterness or envy you need almost the sum total of human wisdom, which Lymie Peters at fifteen did not have. He couldn't help noticing that the scales of fortune were tipped considerably in Spud's favor, and resenting it. But what gnawed at him most was that Spud should be, besides, a natural athlete, the personification of the daydream which he himself most frequently indulged in.

In this fantasy Lymie was in another place. His father had had to move, for business reasons, and he went along, of course, and they settled down in a nice big house in some place like New York or Philadelphia, where nobody knew them or anything about them. His father stopped drinking and was home every night for dinner, and they had a housekeeper who kept the place spick-and-span and saw to it that they had his favorite dessert (made of pineapple, marshmallows, oranges, maraschino cherries, and whipped cream) at least once a week.

One day, one Saturday morning, he was walking past a vacant lot where some guys were playing baseball, and he stopped to watch. In the last of the ninth inning the pitcher sprained his ankle and had to quit. They asked Lymie if he wanted to play. He didn't want to particularly but he didn't have anything else to do so he said all right and took his coat off and threw it on the ground. Then he tossed his cap beside it, loosened his necktie, and rolled up his shirt sleeves. They asked him if he wanted to pitch and he said "Sure." His side had a slight lead. The score was five to four, but there were three men on bases and no outs. Lymie (who had never pitched before) stepped into the dirt-drawn square which was the pitcher's box and with the heavy end of the batting order coming up, struck out three men, one right after the other, and won the game.

That was the way it was with everything he did in that place he moved to. He didn't care whether people liked him or not, so he didn't try to keep on the good side of everybody, and sometimes he got in a fight because this person or that didn't like his attitude, but he always came out on top, and the other guy apologized afterward and they became good friends.

After the guys found out he was so good at games, they always took him first when they were choosing up sides, and whichever side he was on won. He was never by himself any more because somebody always seemed to be waiting for him by his locker after school, and when the phone rang at night it was invariably for him. The guys were always after him to go to a movie or do something with them but he stayed home night after night with his father, reading or listening to the radio, and went to bed early and got plenty of rest. Because he'd been playing games a lot and exercising, his arm and leg muscles developed. He looked like all the rest of the guys in plus fours, only better. The girls smiled at him when he walked past with his chin in the air but he only nodded; he didn't smile back. He didn't have any time for girls. He hardly had time for his homework but he managed somehow so that he got all S's and was elected president of the senior class and captain of the football, basketball, baseball, and fencing teams, before he grew tired of daydreaming and let himself slip back into the actual world.

With gentle jabbing Spud propelled Lymie through the dining room, and Lymie's head swam for a second with the wonderful conglomeration of long-forgotten cooking smells that met him as soon as he set foot in the kitchen. The predominating one was of roast pork, which he could hear sizzling in the oven. A girl with light hair like Spud's was standing on a stool. In her hands was a large blue platter which she had just taken from the top shelf of the china cupboard.

"Hello, Lymie," she said, when Spud introduced her. "I hope you realize you've come to a bad end." Her voice was cheerful and contradicted her words. Lymie saw that she took his being there as a matter of course. Except for the color of her hair, she had almost no resemblance to Spud. Their dispositions seemed entirely different.

"Don't pay any attention to my sister," Spud said. "I don't listen to her, even. If she bothers you, tell her to go fan herself."

"I'm sure that Lymie doesn't talk to his sister that way," Mrs. Latham said. She had tied a kitchen apron around her waist and was holding a large aluminum basting spoon under the hot water faucet.

"Lymie hasn't got a sister, have you, Lymie?" Spud asked.

Lymie shook his head.

"You don't know how much you have to be thankful for," Spud said. "When do we eat?"

"As soon as your father gets home," Mrs. Latham said. "He may be a little late tonight."

"*O grim-look'd night*," Spud said. "*O night with hue so black! O night which ever art when day is not! O night! O night! alack, alack, alack! I fear my Thisbe's promise is forgot.*"

Helen got down off the stool carefully and pushed it under the kitchen table. "It's bad enough to have you out here in the first place," she said, "without your showing off."

"I wasn't showing off," Spud said. "That's poetry. Shakespeare."

"It's all the Shakespeare you know or ever will know," she said, and then, turning to Lymie: "When he was in seventh grade they did a scene from *A Midsummer Night's Dream*. You should have seen it. Spud was Pyramus and he had to make love to a freckle-faced boy named Bill McCann. They were both done up in old sheets and I've never seen anything so funny in all my life."

Lymie had a feeling that she was trying to use him as a weapon against Spud. He backed against the china closet, where he could hardly be considered more than a spectator.

"They kept forgetting their lines," she continued. "And the teacher had to prompt them."

"Is that so?" Spud exclaimed hotly. "You think you're so smart! What about the time you got up in assembly to make a speech and gulped so loud they heard you clear in the back row?"

"Go in the other room, all of you," Mrs. Latham said, "and stop arguing."

Lymie leaned forward, ready to follow Spud and his sister out of the kitchen; to his surprise neither of them showed any signs of leaving. There was a look about Mrs. Latham, a certain firmness in her mouth, which indicated that she could mean what she said. But apparently this wasn't one of the times.

Spud pulled the kitchen stool out and began to teeter on it. "If you won't let us talk about Shakespeare," he said, "what *do* you want us to talk about?"

"You don't have to talk at all," Mrs. Latham said severely. "You can get the bread knife and cut the bread and put it on the table."

This time Spud did as he was told.

Lymie would have liked to take part in the confusion and bickering but he didn't quite know how. He stayed close to the china closet until Helen came over and said, "One side. Have to get in there." Then he moved away cautiously and stood with his elbows resting on the kitchen window sill.

A door opened somewhere in the front of the apartment. After a second Lymie heard it close.

"Was that your father?" Mrs. Latham asked, when Spud came back from the dining room.

"It was," Spud said.

"*Der Papa kommt*," Helen said.

"German," Spud shouted contemptuously at her. "Who wants to talk German? If I were a Frenchman now, waiting in a shell hole, and you were a big fat Dutchman crawling toward me on your hands and knees——"

"Germans and Dutchmen are two different nationalities," Helen said. "Dutchmen are Hollanders. They didn't take part in the war. They were neutral."

"Yeah, the dirty cowards," Spud said.

Mrs. Latham opened the oven door and took the roast out. It was a large one, brown and crisp. She made no effort to prevent Spud from reaching out and snitching a small piece of fat that was hanging loose at the side.

"Just for that," Helen said, "you don't get any second helping."

"I pity the guy that gets you for a wife," Spud said.

A voice interrupted them, a deep masculine voice saying, "Anybody home?"

"We're all home," Mrs. Latham called out.

Everybody had something to do but Lymie. Helen began to mash the potatoes furiously. Spud let the water run in the sink and filled the cut-glass pitcher. Mrs. Latham transferred the roast to the blue platter and made gravy in the roasting pan on top of the stove. Feeling very much an outsider, Lymie picked up the gravy boat and held it for her, so that all she had to do was tip the pan. She thanked him, and then, as if she knew everything that was going on in his mind, said, "Now you're a member of the family, Lymie. You've been broken in."

She didn't smile, and Lymie realized that he could take what she said quite seriously. With a feeling of sudden and immense happiness he carried the gravy boat into the dining room and set it down in the center of the table.

17

All through dinner Spud addressed his mother formally. "Mrs. Latham," he said, pointing to the roast on the platter, "would you be so kind and condescending as to give me a piece of the outside." "Mrs. Latham, you're losing a very valuable hairpin." "Watch out, Mrs. Latham, you're dipping your elbow in the gravy."

He also announced that somebody was kicking him under the table and kept complaining about it until finally they all leaned over, raised the tablecloth, peered under it, and proved conclusively that nobody's foot was anywhere near him.

Lymie was so amused that his eyes filled with tears. It was the kind of thing that never happened at the Alcazar.

Helen and her mother cleared the table for dessert, and then it was Mr. Latham's turn. He rose and placed the knife blade between the prongs of his fork, transferring the musical sound to Lymie's glass, then to Spud's, and so on around the table. Mr. Latham could also (which was really astonishing) hold the sound back and release it whenever he wanted to. This was something he learned in the Masonic Lodge, he explained solemnly, and Mrs. Latham for the first time burst out laughing. Her face colored and she looked almost as young as Helen.

If Lymie had been told that all meals at the Lathams were not like this one, he would have refused to believe it. The others knew better, of course, but Mrs. Latham attributed the gaiety of the occasion to the roast, which was exceptionally tender and done to a turn. Mr. Latham felt that at last the apartment, which had seemed so dark and unlivable, was beginning to be like home. Spud was not given to analyzing. Helen alone knew the real cause—that Lymie's shyness and his delight at being there had affected all of them, arousing their feeling for one another and drawing them temporarily into the compact family that he thought they were. She felt sorry for him, but she was also suspicious of him. She was suspicious of everybody. The letters from Wisconsin had stopped coming. The last was in December, two days after Christmas. Now, so far as Helen was concerned, there was nothing good or kind anywhere, people lost their youth and grew middle-aged without finding anybody to love them, and happiness was a delusion.

The boys ate two helpings of peach cobbler, pushed their chairs back from the table, and went off to Spud's room. Mr. Latham retired to the living room and the solace of his cigar. Mrs. Latham and Helen cleared the table and got ready to do the dishes.

As Mrs. Latham was stirring the dishwater into a froth she turned and said suddenly, "Where on earth do you suppose Spud found that child?"

"The same place he gets all the others," Helen said. "There's a place he goes to that's like a dog pound and that's where he finds them."

Mrs. Latham shook her head. "I've seen him bring home some mighty strange creatures——"

"Strange!" Helen said.

"—just so he could have somebody to play football with. I suppose that's what he's meaning to do with this one."

"It's the wrong time of the year," Helen said. "You don't

play football when there's snow on the ground. Besides, did you notice his hands?"

"No," Mrs. Latham said, "what's the matter with them?"

"Nothing, except that they wouldn't go very far around a football."

"Ummm," Mrs. Latham said, and began to put the glasses one by one into the scalding hot dishwater. "Thinnest youngster I about ever saw. I'd like to keep him here for a month or six weeks."

"Where?" Helen asked, reaching for a dish towel.

"Oh, we could put him somewhere."

"I don't know where. He's too long for the couch in the living room and I won't have him sleeping with me."

"Don't be vulgar."

"I'm not being vulgar," Helen exclaimed. "Just practical. Let him stay at his own house."

"I suppose we'll have to, in any case," Mrs. Latham said. "But he doesn't look to me as if he got the right kind of food. Or maybe he's growing too fast and hasn't any appetite."

"It seemed to me he ate very well," Helen said. "He kept right up with Spud, helping for helping."

Neither of them said anything more for a while. Helen dried the glasses and stood them upside down on an aluminum tray on the kitchen table. Mrs. Latham filled the rack with plates and saucers. While she was pouring hot water over them out of the teakettle she saw a shadow in the doorway and looked up. The shadow was Spud. He had been showing Lymie his favorite neckties and the plaid golf socks with tassels on them that he wore whenever he wanted to pick a fight with somebody. Lymie had admired the Navajo rug on the floor and the picture of a four-masted schooner cutting its way through an indigo ocean. Now, while Lymie sat on the bed looking at the illustrations in *Mr. Midshipman Easy*, Spud was free to come back to the kitchen. He knelt down and began to root around in the bottom shelf of the cupboard. Six bars of Ivory soap came tumbling out on the kitchen floor. The kitchen cleanser, several wire brushes, a Mason jar filled with tacks, a tack hammer, a putty knife, a can of silver polish, and a ball of twine followed.

"What are you after?" Helen asked. "Do you know exactly?"

"Saddle soap," Spud explained.

"Why do you have to have it right now?" Mrs. Latham asked. "Couldn't you wait and use it some other time?"

Spud shook his head. "What have you done with it?" he asked. "It used to be right in here somewhere."

Mrs. Latham opened both doors of the cupboard and took out a cigar box with a heavy rubber band around it. "Did you look in here?" she asked.

The saddle soap was inside the cigar box.

"What about straightening up the cupboard?" Helen said, as Spud started for the dining room door. He glanced back at the confusion he had made.

"I haven't got time," he said. "We're going to saddle-soap my riding boots now. I'll clean it up later."

"That's a very nice boy you brought home," Mrs. Latham said. "Where does he live?"

"Over by the lake," Spud said.

"He has very nice manners. You can see that his mother has tried to bring him up properly," Mrs. Latham said.

"He hasn't got any mother," Spud said. "His mother is dead."

"What a pity!" Mrs. Latham exclaimed.

"Maybe it's a blessing in disguise," Helen said, but Mrs. Latham was not amused.

"Who looks after him?" she asked.

"I don't know," Spud said. "Nobody, I guess. He and his father eat out."

"No wonder he's so thin. Nothing but restaurant food," Mrs. Latham said.

"I ate at the Palmer House once," Helen said, as she finished the last of the dinner plates. "It was quite good."

"You wouldn't think so if you ate there all the time," Mrs. Latham said. And then to Spud. "You must bring him home with you again, do you hear?"

Spud stopped in the doorway to the dining room. "Who?" he asked.

"This boy," Mrs. Latham said. "Bring him as often as he's willing to come——"

But Spud was already on the way to his own room.

Mrs. Latham poured the dishwater out and it made a loud gurgling noise which prevented conversation for a minute. Then she said thoughtfully, "I'm really very glad. Spud needs somebody. He gets bored when he's alone and doesn't know what to do with himself. Lymie isn't the kind of boy I'd expect him to pick out for a friend, but he's a very well-behaved, nice youngster and maybe he'll be a good influence on Spud." There was a silence, while Helen spread her dish towel on the rack to dry; then Mrs. Latham said, "That explains everything, doesn't it?"

"What explains everything?" Helen asked. She had begun to clean up the mess in front of the cupboard.

"I mean the fact that his mother is dead. I knew there was something wrong the minute I saw him," Mrs. Latham said. She finished rinsing out the dishpan and hung it on a nail under the sink. Then she stood in the center of the floor and listened. The only sounds came from Spud's room, where the two boys were saddle-soaping his boots. Their voices sounded pleased and excited.

18

On the tenth of March, which was the anniversary of Mrs. Peters' death, Mr. Peters and Lymie got up early and went down to the Union Station. From Chicago to the small town they had once lived in was a trip of a little less than two hours, on the Chicago, Burlington, and Quincy Railroad. They made this journey every year. The scenery was not interesting—the cornfields of Illinois in March are dreary and monotonous—and there was no pleasure attached to the trip in the mind of either of them. But to live in the world at all is to be committed to some kind of a journey.

If you are ready to go and cannot, either because you are not free or because you have no one to travel with—or if you have arbitrarily set a date for your departure and dare not go until that day arrives, you still have no cause for concern. Without knowing it, you have actually started. On a turning earth, in a mechanically revolving universe, there is no place to stand still.

Neither the destination nor the point of departure are

important. People often find themselves midway on a journey they had no intention of taking and that began they are not exactly sure where. What matters, the only sphere where you have any real choice, is the person who elects to sit in the empty seat beside you from Asheville, North Carolina to Knoxville, Tennessee.

Or from Knoxville to Memphis.

Or from Memphis to Denver, Colorado.

Sometimes it is a woman with a navy-blue turban on her head and pearl earrings, pictures in her purse that you will have to look at, and a wide experience with the contagious diseases of children.

Sometimes it is a man who says *Is this seat taken?* Or he may not say anything at all as he makes room on the rack over your head for his suitcase, his battered gray felt hat, his muffler, and overcoat, and the small square package wrapped in blue paper and tied with red string. Before he gets off the train (at Detroit, perhaps, or at Kansas City) you will know what's in the package. Whether you want him to or not, he will spread his life out before you, on his knees. And afterward, so curiously relaxed is the state of mind engendered by going on a journey, he will ask to see your life and you will show it to him. Occasionally, though not often, the girl or the young man who sits beside you will be someone whose clothes, ankles, hands, gray-blue eyes all are so full of charm and character that, even though they are only there for a short time and never once turn and look at you, never offer a remark, you have no choice but to fall hopelessly in love with them, with everything about them, with their luggage even. And when they get up and leave, it is as if you had lost an arm or a leg.

Accidents, misdirections, overexcitement, heat, crowds, and heartbreaking delays you must expect when you go on a journey, just as you expect to have dreams at night. Whether or not you enjoy yourself at all depends on your state of mind. The man who travels with everything he owns, books, clothes for every season, shoe trees, a dinner jacket, medicines, binoculars, magazines, and telephone numbers—the unwilling traveler—and the man who leaves each place in turn without reluctance, with no desire ever to come back, obviously cannot be making the same journey, even though their tickets are identical. The same thing holds good for the woman who was once beautiful and who now has to resort to movement, change, continuous packing and unpacking, in order to avoid the reality that awaits her in the smallest mirror. And for the ambitious young man who by a too constant shifting around has lost all of his possessions, including his native accent and the ability to identify himself with a particular kind of sky or the sound, let us say, of windmills creaking; so that in New Mexico his talk reflects Bermuda, and in Bermuda it is again and again of Barbados that he is reminded, but never of Iowa or Wisconsin or Indiana, never of home.

Though people usually have long complicated tickets which they expect the conductor to take from them in due time, the fact is that you don't need to bother with a ticket at all. If you are willing to travel lightly, you can also dispense with the train. Cars and trucks are continually stopping at filling stations and at corners where there is an overhead stop light. By jerking your thumb you will almost certainly get a ride to the next town of more than two thousand inhabitants where (chances are) you will manage to get something to eat and a place to sleep for a night or so, even if it's only the county jail.

The appointment you have made to meet somebody at such and such a day at noon on the steps of the courthouse at Amarillo, Texas, you may have to forget. Especially if you go too long without food or with nothing but stolen ripe tomatoes, so that suddenly you are not sure of what you are saying. Or if the heat gets you, and when you wake up you are in a hospital ward. But after you start to get well again and are able to sit up a short while each day, there will be time to begin thinking about where you will go next. And if you like, you can always make new appointments.

The great, the universal problem is how to be always on a journey and yet see what you would see if it were only possible for you to stay home: a black cat in a garden, moving through iris blades behind a lilac bush. How to keep sufficiently detached and quiet inside so that when the cat in one spring reaches the top of the garden wall, turns down again, and disappears, you will see and remember it, and not be absorbed at that moment in the dryness of your hands.

If you missed that particular cat jumping over one out of so many garden walls, it ought not to matter, but it does apparently. The cat seems to be everything. Seeing clearly is everything. Being certain as to smells, being able to remember sounds and to distinguish by touch one object, one body, from another. And it is not enough to see the fishermen drawing in their wide circular net, the tropical villages lying against a shelf of palm trees, or the double rainbow over Fort-de-France. You must somehow contrive, if only for a week or only overnight, to live in the houses of people, so that at least you know the elementary things—which doors sometimes bang when a sudden wind springs up; where the telephone book is kept; and how their lungs feel when they waken in the night and reach blindly toward the foot of the bed for the extra cover.

You are in duty bound to go through all of their possessions, to feel their curtains and look for the tradename on the bottom of their best dinner plates and stand before their pictures (especially the one they have been compelled to paint themselves, which is not a good painting but seems better if you stay long enough to know the country in more than one kind of light) and lift the lids off their cigarette boxes and sniff their pipe tobacco and open, one by one, their closet doors. You should test the sharpness and shape of their scissors. You may play their radio and try, with your fingernail, to open the locked door of the liquor cabinet. You may even read any letters that they have been so careless as to leave around. Through all of these things, through the attic and the cellar and the tool shed you must go searching until you find the people who live here or who used to live here but now are in London or Acapulco or Galesburg, Illinois. Or who now are dead.

19

"When you grow up," Mr. Peters said, "there won't be anybody to make things easier for you."

Lymie, who had brought this lecture on himself by losing his return ticket, was walking ahead of his father down the white cemetery path. In his right hand he held a long narrow cardboard box done up in green florist's paper. In the other hand he carried a Mason jar filled with water, which slopped over occasionally. His shoes, which had been shined in the railway station at the same time as his father's, were now scuffed and muddy. He had no hat. The sun was out and it was windy but not cold.

"You'll want to provide yourself with a nice home and pleasant surroundings and all the comforts and conveniences you've been used to," Mr. Peters said. "You'll want to marry and have a family, which you can't do if you spend all your time reading and going to art museums."

So far as Mr. Peters was concerned, there was a definite connection between Lymie's absent-mindedness and the fact that he seemed to gravitate toward whatever was artistic and impractical. Mr. Peters wanted to be proud of his son and he was glad that Lymie had a good mind, but he was not a millionaire (how much Mr. Peters made exactly was nobody's business) and he had tried therefore to make Lymie realize that before you have a right to indulge in any kind of activity which is not practical, you must learn the value of money. If earning a living takes all your time and energy, it is something that you must resign yourself to. There is no use pretending that life is one long Sunday school picnic. Nothing is ever gained without hard work and plenty of it. But if a person is ambitious and really wants to make something of himself; if he can keep his chin up no matter what happens to him, and never complains, never offers excuses or alibis; and if, once he has achieved success, he can keep from resting on his laurels (also his equilibrium through it all and his feet on the ground) he will have all the more success to come and he need feel no fear of the future.

This philosophy was too materialistic to be very congenial to Lymie, and as a matter of fact Mr. Peters didn't take much stock in it himself. It was not something that he had learned from experience (his own business methods were quite different) but mostly catch phrases from the lips of businessmen he envied and admired. Where they got it, there is no telling.

Mr. Peters' career in business had never been very successful, never wholly unsuccessful. He was a salesman by accident rather than by disposition. His first job was with a bill-posting concern and had involved free passes to circuses, street carnivals, and moving picture houses. He still remembered it with pleasure. After that he tried real estate and life insurance, both of which had their drawbacks. When his wife died he decided that he wanted to move, to get away from anything and everything that reminded him of her, so he took a job with a wholesale stationery house, operating in the Chicago area. For the past five years he had remained in that business, though the concerns he worked for changed rather frequently. Each one, for a short while, was a fine company headed by men it was a privilege to work for. This opinion was eventually and inevitably revised, until a point was reached where Mr. Peters, for his own good, could no longer afford to work for such bastards. As a rule he quit before he was fired.

When Mr. Peters stopped on the cemetery path to light a cigarette, Lymie stopped also, his eyes busy with the mounded graves, the faded American flags in their star-shaped holders, and the tombstones, row after row of them, all saying the same thing: *Henry Burdine died . . . Mary his wife died . . . Samuel Potter died . . . Jesse Davis died . . . Temperance his wife died . . .*

"You get out of life," Mr. Peters said as they walked on, "just what you put into it."

Mrs. Peters' grave was at the far end of the cemetery, in a square lot with a plain granite tombstone on it about six feet high. On the stone was the single name *Harris.* Two small headstones marked the graves of Lymie's maternal grandfather and grandmother. A little apart from them were two other graves, one full-sized and one small, as if for a child. The inscription on the headstone of the larger grave said *Alma Harris Peters 1881–1919*.

Lymie set the Mason jar down and tore both string and paper off the box, which contained a dozen short-stemmed red roses. He tried to arrange them nicely in the Mason jar but the wind blew them all the same way and he caught the jar with his hand, just before it toppled. By bracing it against the headstone, in a little hollow, he could keep the jar from falling, but there was nothing he could do about the roses.

"Quit worrying with them," Mr. Peters said. "They look all right."

He stood with his hat in his hand, staring in a troubled way at the grave.

Lymie was embarrassed because he had no particular feeling,

and he thought he ought to have. He looked down at the low mound with dead grass on it and tried to visualize his mother beneath it, in a horizontal position; tried to feel toward that spot the emotion he used to have for her. He waited, knowing that in a moment his father would ask the question he always asked when they came here.

Though Lymie could remember his mother's voice easily enough, and how she did her hair, and what it was like to be in the same room with her, he couldn't remember her face. He had tried too many times to remember it and now it was gone. It wouldn't come back any more.

On the other side of the lot the ground dropped away abruptly. The cemetery ran along the end of a high bluff from which you could look off over the tops of trees to the cornfields and the flat prairie beyond. In the whole winter landscape the roses were the only color.

"Your mother has been gone five years," Mr. Peters said, "and I still can't believe it. It just doesn't seem possible."

Lymie remembered how his mother used to say his father's name: *Lymon*, she said, *my Lymon* proudly, and always with love.

He remembered the excitement of meeting his mother suddenly on the stairs. And the sound of her voice. And the soft side of her neck. And the imprint of her lips on the top of his head after she had kissed him. And being rocked by her sometimes, on her lap, when he had been crying. And being allowed to look at her beautiful long white kid gloves.

He remembered waking at night and realizing that she had been in his room without his knowing it—that room he remembered so clearly and that fitted his heart and mind like a glove. The bed he woke up in, and the dresser with all his clothes in it, and the blue and white wallpaper, and the light switch by the door, and the light, and next to it the framed letter which began *Dear Madam I have been shown in the files of the War Department a statement of* and which ended *Yours very sincerely and respectfully Abraham Lincoln*. And the picture over his head of a fat-faced little boy and a little girl with yellow curls, both of them riding hobbyhorses. And the bear that he slept with . . .

"Before she died," Mr. Peters said, "I was sitting on top of the world. I used to look around sometimes and see somebody I knew who was in a mess or having trouble of one sort or another and I'd think It's his own damn fault."

What became of the bear? Lymie thought. Whatever could have happened to it? Did somebody take it away?

"It didn't occur to me that I had anything especially to be thankful for," Mr. Peters said. "Probably if I had—" And then instead of finishing that sentence he asked the question Lymie had been waiting for: "Do you remember your mother, son?"

"Yes, Dad," Lymie said, nodding.

He remembered the time his mother saw a mouse and screamed and jumped up on one of the dining room chairs and from the chair to the table. She was deathly afraid of mice. And when they went to the circus at night they never could stay for the Wild West show because his mother grew nervous as soon as they started loosening the ropes. But she loved lightning and thunder.

He himself used to be afraid of noises in the night, and of the shadows which the gaslight made in the hall. The gaslight flickered, and that made the shadows move. But it also guided him on that long trip down the hall from the door of his room to the door of the bathroom, which he entered quickly, being careful not to glance to the left, where there was danger, darkness, and the back stairs. He was also afraid, horribly afraid deep down inside of him, when the man leaned over and put his face in the lion's mouth. But these were things that he had never told anybody.

"Your mother was a wonderful woman," Mr. Peters said. "I didn't know what I was getting when I married her. She was just young and pretty and always laughing and tying ribbons in her hair and I knew I had to have her. But that wasn't what she was really like at all, and it was quite a while before I found out."

Lymie remembered the tray of the high chair coming over his head and being lifted out of it when he choked. And later, when he was old enough to sit at the table in a chair with two big books on it. And taking iron through a glass straw. And sometimes having to take cod-liver oil. And the square glass shade that hung down over the round dining room table, with the red-and-green beaded fringe. And the fireplace with the tapestry screen in front of it during the summertime. And the Japanese garden with putty for the shores of the little lake, grass seed growing, and carrot tops sprouting with little green leaves, and a peculiar, unpleasant smell. And the real garden outside, beyond the grape arbor. And around in front the two palms in their wooden tubs on either side of the front walk. . . .

"Whatever she did and whatever she thought," Mr. Peters said, "turned out to be right."

When he talked like this it was largely to make himself suffer (he too had trouble remembering his wife's face, and the last years of his marriage had not been as happy as the first; there had been quarrels and misunderstandings, also that girl in the barber shop) and he did not expect Lymie to offer consolation. He took out his watch, glanced at it, and then put it back in his pocket.

The marble headstone of the small grave read:

Infant daughter of Lymon and Alma Peters
died March 14, 1919
aged 4 days

Looking at the inscription Lymie realized that he was not yet ready to go. He was suddenly filled with the remembrance of the sound of his mother's name: *Alma*, everyone called her. The richness and warmth of the sound. *Alma* . . . *Alma* . . . Like the comfort he got from leaning against her thigh.

When she was away there was the terrible slowness of time. Even when she was downtown shopping or at a card party. Though he knew she would be back at five o'clock, how could he be sure that five o'clock would ever come? And when his mother and father were away once on a visit to Cincinnati, that was really a long time. And they got home and she told him that she had a paint book for him in her trunk, and then that the trunks were lost.

But what he remembered most vividly of all as he turned away from the grave was the question that used to fill his mind whenever he opened the front door: *Where is she?* he used to cry. *Is she here? Has she come back yet?* And the rooms, the front hall where she had left her gloves, the living room where her pocketbook was (on the mahogany table), and the library beyond, where she had left a small round package wrapped in white paper, all answered him. *She's here*, they said. *Everything is all right. She's home.*

20

In April there was trouble over the fraternity house. It began on a rainy Monday afternoon. Six of them were there. Catanzano had a sprained ankle and was enthroned on the couch. The others were trying out his crutches. Lynch was about to play a medley of songs from "No, No, Nanette" on the victrola when the janitor, who was a Belgian, walked in. He had a couple with him—a very tall man whose wrists hung down out of the sleeves of his black overcoat and a woman in a purple suit with a cheap fur neckpiece, blondined hair, blue eyes, and very red skin. She looked around critically and then said, "Fourteen dollars?"

The janitor nodded.

"Well," the woman said, "I don't know." She crossed the room and would have tripped over Catanzano's bandaged foot if he hadn't drawn it hastily out of the way. The other boys stood still, like figures in some elaborate musical parlor game.

The man couldn't have been more than five years older than Mark Wheeler but life had already proved too much for him. There was no color in his long thin face. The skin was drawn tight over his cheekbones. His hair was receding from his temples, and something about him—the look in his eyes, mostly—suggested a conscious determination to shed his flesh at the earliest possible moment and take refuge in his dry skeleton.

The woman was almost old enough to be his mother but there was nothing maternal or gentle about her. She went into the bathroom and came out again, inspected the only closet, discovered that there were no wall plugs, and sniffed the air, which smelled strongly of wet wool. Still undecided, she wandered back to the door.

"I've never lived in a basement apartment before," she said, turning to the man, "and I'm kind of afraid of the dampness. On account of my asthma."

"Is not damp," the janitor said.

"Maybe not now with the heat on, but in summer I bet it's good and damp. . . . What about it, Fred?"

The young man was looking at the picture of the English bulldog. "It's up to you," he said. "I'll be away all day."

"Well I guess I'll have to think about it," the woman said, shifting her fur. The expression on her face was like a pout, but she wasn't pouting, actually; she was thinking. "I don't want to move in and unpack everything and then find out that I can't breathe," she said. And then, turning to the janitor, "We'll let you know."

She looked once more at the boys without seeing them and walked out. The janitor followed, and after him the young man, who had a sudden coughing fit in the areaway and left the door wide open behind him.

Lymie Peters was the first to recover. He was standing in a draft and he sneezed. Dede Sandstrom walked over to the door and slammed it. As if a spell had been lifted, the victrola needle came to rest on the opening bars of "I Want to Be Happy," and they all started talking at once. Their excitement, the pitch of their immature voices, the gestures which they made with their hands, and their uneasy profanity were all because of one thing which none of them dared say: Their house, their fraternity (which stood in the minds of all of them like a beautiful woman that they were too young to have) was as good as gone. If these people didn't take it, the next ones would.

The record came to an end and the turntable of the victrola went round and round slower and slower until at last it stopped. Mark Wheeler and Dede Sandstrom went out and called Bud Griesenauer, who wasn't home. His mother didn't know where they could reach him. On their way back to the apartment they met the janitor in the areaway. Mark Wheeler walked up to him and said, "What's the big idea?"

The janitor shrugged his shoulders. "I show the apartment, that's all."

"But it's our apartment," Dede Sandstrom said. "We pay rent on it."

"Maybe somebody else pay more rent on it," the janitor said, and disappeared into the boiler room.

The second indignation meeting lasted until almost dinner-time. On the way home Lymie Peters stopped in a drugstore and called Bud Griesenauer. This time he was at home. They'd all been calling him, he said. Wheeler and Hall and Carson and Lynch and everybody. And he'd called his uncle. It was probably a misunderstanding of some kind, his uncle said, and maybe the people wouldn't rent the apartment after all. But if they did decide to take it, there was nothing anybody could do. The boys didn't have a lease and the owner of the building naturally had a right to try to get as much money out of it as possible.

They held a special meeting the next afternoon, and it was decided that somebody should come down to the fraternity house every afternoon after school, in case the janitor showed the place to any more people; and that they should take turns staying there at night. The rest of the time they would lock the door with a padlock. They wrote days of the week on slips of paper and put them in Mark Wheeler's hat and passed the hat around. Lymie drew the following Friday, and Spud Latham offered to stay with him.

When they arrived Friday night, Lymie had three army blankets under one arm and a coffeepot under the other. Spud carried a knapsack containing all the equipment and food necessary for a large camp breakfast.

The apartment was very warm when they got there but they built a fire in the fireplace anyway. Lymie sat on the floor in front of the fire and took off his shoes, which were wet, and loosened his tie and unbuttoned his shirt collar. Spud took all his clothes off except his shorts. Then he emptied the knapsack out on the hearth, arranging the skillet, the coffeepot, the iron grill, the plates, knives, forks, salt, and pepper so that they would all be ready and convenient the next morning. The food he put in the bathroom, on the window sill, and the blankets he spread one by one, on the couch. Every movement of his body was graceful, easy, and controlled. Lymie, who was continually being surprised by what his own hands and feet were up to, enjoyed watching him. With the firelight shining on his skin and no other light in the room, Spud looked very much like the savage that he was playing at being.

When he had finished with the couch, he stretched out on top of the blankets and there was so much harmony in the room that he said, "This is the life. No school tomorrow. Nobody to tell you when to go to bed. Plenty to eat and a good fire. Why didn't we think of this before?"

"I don't know," Lymie said. "Why didn't we?"

"There's always something," Spud said. The full implications of this remark, in spite of its vagueness, were deeply felt by both of them. Spud picked up the volume of Balzac's stories and read for a while, lying on his back with his knees raised. Lymie continued to sit in front of the fire, facing him. The expression in his eyes was partly pride (he had never had a friend before) and partly envy, though he didn't recognize it as that. He was comparing his own wrists, which were so thin that he could put his thumb and forefinger around one of them and still see daylight, to Spud's, which were strong and square. The wish closest to Lymie's heart, if he could have had it for the asking, would have been to have a well-built body, a body as strong and as beautifully proportioned as Spud's. Then all his troubles would have been over.

When Spud turned and lay on his stomach, Lymie got up and sat down beside him on the edge of the couch, and began to read over Spud's shoulder: . . . *woman will heal thy wound, stop the waste hole in thy bag of tricks. Woman is thy wealth; have but one woman, dress, undress, and fondle that woman, make use of the woman—woman is everything—woman has an inkstand of her own; dip thy pen into that bottomless inkpot* . . . Without looking up, Spud rolled over on his back, so that Lymie could stretch out and read in comfort. But Lymie didn't move. His face was troubled. He started to say something and then, after a second's hesitation, he went on reading. *Woman makes love; make love to her with the pen only, tickle her fantasies, and sketch merrily for her a thousand pictures of love in a thousand pretty ways. Woman is generous and all for one, or one for all, must pay the painter, and furnish the hairs of the brush* . . . At the bottom of the page Spud looked up to see if Lymie was still reading. Lymie had been finished for some time. He was staring at Spud's chest.

"Let's do something else," he said.

"Why?" Spud asked. "This is interesting." He rolled over on his stomach again and was about to go on reading when Lymie surprised him by grabbing the book out of his hands. It sailed across the room into the blazing fire. Spud sat up and saw with a certain amount of regret that the flames were already licking at the open pages.

"What did you do that for?" he asked.

Instead of explaining, Lymie prodded at the book with the poker, so that the leaves burned faster. Pieces of charred paper detached themselves and were drawn, still glowing, up the chimney.

"You're going to have a hell of a time explaining to Hall about his book," Spud said.

"I'm not going to explain about it," Lymie said. His jaw was set and Spud, realizing that Lymie was very close to tears, sank back on the couch as if nothing had happened.

After a week in which no one, so far as the boys knew, was shown through the apartment, they gave up staying there at night, and with the warm weather they stopped going to the fraternity house altogether. It took too long, and besides, they were suffering from spring fever. When they emerged from the school building at three o'clock with their ties loosened and their collars undone, they had no energy and no will. They stood around in the schoolyard watching baseball practice and leaning against each other for support. Any suggestion that anybody made always turned out to be too much trouble.

There is no telling how long it would have taken them to find out about the fraternity if Carson hadn't wanted suddenly to play his record of "I'll See You in My Dreams." The record was at the fraternity and he asked Lynch to ride down there with him. Lynch's last report card was unsatisfactory and he wasn't allowed out after supper on week nights, so Carson went alone. When he came around the corner of the apartment building and saw the furniture clogging the areaway, he stopped short, unable to believe his eyes.

The couch was soggy and stained from being rained on. The chairs were coming unglued. There were wrinkles in the picture of the collegian, where the water had got in behind the glass, and the grass rug gave off a musty odor. The English bulldog was missing, but Carson was too upset to notice this. It was his victrola, the condition of his victrola, that upset him most. The felt pad on the turntable had spots of mildew, the oak veneer of the case peeled off in strips, and both the needle and the arm were rusted. When he tried to wind it, the victrola made such a horrible grinding sound that he gave up and went in search of the janitor. There was no one in the boiler room or in any of the various storerooms in the basement. He came back and tried the door of the apartment. The padlock that they had used was gone and in its place was a new Yale lock. No one came to the door.

The victrola records were warped and probably ruined, but he took them anyway and walked around to the front of the building, intending to peer in at the basement windows. They had net curtains across them and he could see nothing. He went off down the street with the records under his arm and his spirits held up by anger and the melancholy pleasure of spreading the news.

21

With school almost over for the year and summer vacation looming ahead, the loss of a meeting place made very little difference to any of them. Spud Latham and Lymie Peters met in the corridor by Spud's locker, after school, and went off together. Lymie had a malted milk and Spud had a milk shake and then they came out of the stale air of LeClerc's and separated. Or else Lymie went home with Spud. He never asked Spud to come home with him and Spud never suggested it. So far as he was concerned, Lymie belonged at his house, and had no other home.

No matter how often Lymie went there, Mrs. Latham always seemed glad to see him. She treated him casually and yet managed to watch over him. When she caught him helping himself out of the icebox as if he lived there, all she said was "Lymie, there's some fudge cake in the cakebox. Wouldn't you rather have a piece of that?"

At mealtime there was a place for him at the dining room table, next to Spud. From the other side of the table Helen teased him because he didn't like parsnips or because he needed a haircut, and Mr. Latham used him as an excuse to tell long stories about the heating business.

After supper Lymie and Spud studied together in Spud's room until their minds wandered from the page and they started yawning. Then they got up and went across the street to the park and lay on the grass and stared into the evening sky and thought out loud about what the future had in store for them. Spud's heart was fixed on a cabin in the North Woods where they (it was understood that Lymie was to be with him) could fish in the summertime and in winter set trap lines and then sit around and be warm and comfortable indoors, with the wind howling and the snow banked up higher than the windows of the cabin. Lymie chewed on a blade of grass and didn't commit himself. It all seemed possible. Something that would require arranging, perhaps (pleasant though such a life might be, there was obviously not going to be much money in it) but perfectly possible.

At nine-thirty or a quarter of ten he pulled Spud up off the grass and they went back across the street. Lymie gathered up his books and papers. As he passed by the living room door he said "Good night, everybody," and Helen and Mr. and Mrs. Latham looked up and nodded affectionately, as if he had told them that he was going down to the drugstore on the corner and would be right back.

One day Mrs. Latham discovered that there was a button missing from his shirt after he and Spud had been doing push-ups on the living room rug. They looked under all the furniture without being able to find it and then she made Lymie come into her bedroom with her while she hunted through her sewing box for another white button to sew on in place of the one he had lost. Something in the tone of her voice caught Spud's attention. He stood still in the center of the living room and listened, with a troubled expression on his face. His mother was talking to Lymie in a scolding way that was not really scolding at all and that he had never heard her use with anybody but him. He felt a sharp stab of jealousy. It was one thing to have a friend, but another to. . . . He raised the sleeve of his coat and looked at it thoughtfully. A piece of brown thread dangled from the cuff where a button should have been.

"Speaking of buttons," he said quietly.

"Oh, all right," Mrs. Latham answered him from the bedroom. "I've been meaning to fix it but I just didn't get around to it, with all there is to do in this house. Leave it on your bed when you go to school tomorrow. . . . Stand still, Lymie. I don't want to stick you. . . . And next time remember to save the button, do you hear? It isn't always easy to——"

She didn't bother to finish the sentence, but Spud's face cleared. He was reassured. His mother still loved him the most. She had heard him two rooms away, even though he hadn't raised his voice; and she knew exactly what button he was talking about.

Another afternoon when they got home from school, Spud was restless and wanted to go walking in the rain. They walked a long way west until they came to the Northwestern Railway tracks, where further progress was blocked by an interminable freight train. They stood and counted boxcars and coal cars and oil tankers, and the train shuddered violently once or twice and came to a dead stop. By that time they were tired of waiting for it to pass and so they turned back. The soles of their shoes were soaked through and the bottoms of their trousers were wet and kept flapping about their ankles. When they got home they hung their yellow slickers on the back porch to dry, and retired to Spud's room with a quart of milk and a box of fig newtons. Noticing the hollows under Lymie's eyes, Spud decided that he ought to take a nap. There was plenty of time before dinner, and he began to undo Lymie's tie. Lymie refused, for no reason; or perhaps because Spud hadn't given him a chance to consider whether he was tired or not. Spud got the tie off but when he tried to unbutton Lymie's shirt, Lymie began to fight him off. He had never really fought anybody before and he fought with strength that he had no idea he possessed.

At first Spud was amused, and then suddenly it became a life-and-death matter. He wasn't quite sure how to come at Lymie because Lymie didn't know the rules. He fought with his hands and his feet and his knees. He gouged at and he grabbed anything that he could lay hands on. Each time that Spud managed to get his arms around Lymie he twisted and fought his way free. The noise they made, banging against the furniture, climbing up on the bed and down again, drew Mrs. Latham, who stood in the doorway for a while, trying to make them stop. Neither of them paid any attention to her. The expression on Lymie's tormented face was almost but not quite hate. Spud was calm and possessed, and merely bent on making Lymie lie still under the covers and take a nap before dinner. He pried one of Lymie's shoes off and then the other. His trousers took much longer and were harder to manage, but in the end they came off too, and one of Lymie's striped socks. With each loss, like a country defending itself against an invader, Lymie fought harder. He fought against being made to do something against his will, and he fought also against the unreasonable strength in Spud's arms. He butted. He kicked. All of a sudden, with no warning, the last defense gave way. Lymie quit struggling and lay still. As in a dream he let Spud cover him with a blanket. Something had burst inside of him, something more important than any organ, and there was a flowing which was like blood. Though he kept on breathing and his heart after a while pounded less violently, there it was all the same, an underground river which went on and on and was bound to keep on like that for years probably, never stopping, never once running dry.

He watched Spud pull the shades down and leave the room without having any idea of what he had done.

BOOK THREE

A Cold Country

22

"ALASTOR is not antisocial," Professor Severance said, with a puckered expression about his mouth. Apparently there was something else he would have liked to add, something which was perhaps too flippant and would have destroyed (or come dangerously close to it) his hold on the class. "Alastor understands people rather better by getting away from them than by being buffeted by them." Heads bent over notebooks, fountain pens began to scratch. "In solitude only can we attune ourselves to the meaning of nature and the deep heart of man," Professor Severance said, teetering slightly, and with all traces of the flippant remark, whatever it was, gone from his rather tired, his definitely middle-aged, scholar's face. "So the poet turns from love to understand love."

This struck Mrs. Lieberman—the small, quiet-faced, prematurely white-haired woman sitting in the third row next to the window—as just nonsense. Her fountain pen remained idle in her hand. She was enrolled as a listener and so it didn't matter whether she took notes during the lecture or not. She wouldn't be called upon at some later date to fill two pages of an examination book with the house of cards that Professor Severance was now erecting, sentence by sentence.

"Alastor loves beyond the Arab maid," he continued, "and understands human nature beyond human intercourse." He spoke directly to Mrs. Lieberman, since she was the only person in the class who was looking at him. That he was well taken care of, there could be no doubt, she thought. But by whom? He was never without a fresh white handkerchief in his breast pocket, he never forgot his glasses. But on the other hand, Professor Severance didn't look like a married man. There was never a flicker of complacency, and also his lectures—always beautifully phrased, models of organization, style, and diction—from time to time showed a shocking (or so it seemed to her) lack of experience.

He picked up *The Complete Poetical Works of Shelley* in order to read from it, or perhaps in order to pretend to read from it, for his eyes only occasionally skimmed the page.

Earth, ocean, air, beloved brotherhood . . .

The voice in which Professor Severance read poetry was high and reedlike. The young man who sat on Mrs. Lieberman's right, the blond athlete with the block letter sewed on the front of his white pullover, thrust one long, muscular, football player's leg into the aisle and looked pained. In the row ahead of him, his exact human opposite—flat-chested with a long pointed face and straight dark hair that grew down on his forehead in a widow's peak—didn't seem to be listening either. His eyes were vacant. But when Professor Severance cleared his throat and said, "Mr. Peters, in what other English Romantic poet do we find these same 'incommunicable dreams,' these 'twilight phantasms' that invoke a greater responsiveness to 'the woven hymns of night and day'?" Lymie separated his legs, which were twisted together under the seat, and said, "Wordsworth?"

"Precisely!" Professor Severance exclaimed and Mrs. Lieberman decided that he must live with his mother.

It is always disturbing to pick up an acquaintance after several years. The person is bound to have changed, so that (in one way or another) you will have to deal with a stranger. Yet the change seldom turns out to be as great as one expects, or even hopes for. The summer that Lymie was seventeen, Mr. Peters found a place for him in a certified public accountant's office, downtown in the Loop. He wanted Lymie to learn the value of money by earning some. When Lymie went back to high school in September he saw that most of the boys his own age had put on weight. Some of them had put on as much as twenty-five or thirty pounds. That summer it seemed to happen to all of them. Their faces hadn't changed much, but they seemed to move differently. From being thin and gangly, they had spread out in the shoulders, their legs and arms had become solid, and they were beginning to be broad through the chest. Ford, who had never been heavy enough for anything but track, played football. So did Carson and Lynch.

Lymie had grown slightly more round-shouldered from sitting all day on a high stool in front of a comptometer, but that was the only physical change in him. He tried doing setting-up exercises morning and night in front of the open window, but they didn't help. And he had an uneasy feeling that he had somehow missed his chance.

Perhaps he attached too much importance to physical development. It is, after all, a minor barrier in the Grand Obstacle Race. The ordinary person manages it successfully (or doesn't) and goes on to leap (or fall into) the twenty-foot pit of shyness, to clear (or go around) the eight-foot wall of money, to climb (or fall headlong from) the swaying rope net of love, and so on and so on. Some fail at one obstacle, some at another. The sensible ones go on, if they fail, and try the next. Those with too much imagination keep throwing themselves at the first one they fail at, as if everything depended on that, and so forgot the others which they might have managed easily. When Lymie was in high school, not being able to hold his own in games had serious consequences. Now that he was a sophomore in college, it no longer mattered, or at least nothing like so much. But he still clung loyally to that one insurmountable barrier.

At nineteen he was almost painfully thin. The look of adolescence was gone from his face, his hair was less unruly, and his hands had taken the shape they would have for the rest of his life. His eyes still had a hesitant look, even when Professor Severance called on him and he produced the right answer out of the air. Which may have been the result of one failure after another on the high school baseball field and in the swimming pool. Or this hesitancy, this habitual lack of self-confidence, might well have been the cause of those failures.

When Professor Severance went on with his lecture, Lymie wrote something in his loose-leaf notebook which couldn't have had anything to do with Wordsworth or Shelley, because the two girls who sat on either side of him read it surreptitiously and smiled. They were friends, the three of them. They arrived at the classroom together, and small folded pieces of paper often passed between them, sometimes to the annoyance of Professor Severance, who, as a gentleman, could only combat rudeness by ignoring it.

Sally Forbes, the girl who sat on Lymie's left, had on a red leather coat and a close-fitting gray felt hat with a clump of cock feathers over each ear. Her father was a full professor in the department of philosophy. The cock feathers were light green and bright blue, and the ends curled over the brim of the hat and lay flat against her tanned cheeks. Her hair was straight and almost black. Bangs covered her forehead, and her mouth was large and a little too prominent, but nothing could destroy or in any way diminish the effect of her very beautiful, eager, dark brown eyes. She had entered college when she was sixteen, and was now seventeen, and looked older than that. Her shoulders were square, her back as straight as a child's, and she hadn't yet outgrown the childish habit of biting her fingernails. Her hips were narrow, her legs were slender but strong. Her breasts were small and there was no suggestion of softness about her anywhere.

Lymie and Hope Davison had known each other in high school, but not very well. They didn't actually get to be friends until they came down to the university. Hope's tan coat and skirt, white sweater, and brown and white saddleback shoes all said *There is a right and a wrong way to dress.* Hope disliked bright colors, loud-voiced people, and any display of egotism. Her face was small, delicate, and sober. Her mouth was nicely shaped but obstinate, and her light blue eyes had an unnerving effect on young instructors who were not used to lecturing from a platform. They left no room anywhere for the mysterious or the irrational. If voices had spoken to her out of a burning bush, in all probability she would have stood waiting for some natural explanation to occur to her.

Professor Severance did not mind being stared at. He had been teaching for twenty-two years, and knew that the faces that looked up at him would shortly be replaced by other faces not unlike them. His own face, at that moment, was turned toward the windows. Seeing handfuls of leaves coming down in a sudden stirring of the air outside, he spoke with such intensity of the despair that dogs every hope, and the resurrection through scourging, that his words at last reached the minds of his students. They realized uneasily that he had stopped talking about Shelley and was referring in a veiled way to himself. The fountain pens stopped scratching.

"Through crucifixion," Professor Severance said, "one arises to a new life. Death is a mere incident, for Alastor dies daily, entering more and more into eternity, so that when death comes to him it is somewhat overdue."

There was a solemn pause when he finished speaking.

"On Wednesday," Professor Severance said, "I shall take up the relation between Shelley's ethical philosophy and the idiom of his art. Will you please be prepared to recite on—" The bell rang before he could complete his sentence, and with the ringing of the bell, his power went out of him. He was Samson without his hair. Voices broke out all over the classroom. His students, a moment before so docile and so determined to get into their loose-leaf notebooks all that he had to say about the life of solitude, rose up in their seats and filled the aisles to overflowing. Professor Severance put the works of Shelley away in his battered brief case and gathered up his hat, his gray gloves, and his cane. The aisles were emptied almost immediately. He bowed Mrs. Lieberman out of the door ahead of him, and then marched briskly down the corridor.

Outside it was the very peak of fall. The sky was clear and very blue. The air was warm, the leaves were coming down in showers. Mrs. Lieberman was right behind Lymie and the two girls as they descended the iron stairs at the back of the building, and then were forced off the sidewalk by the two streams of traffic—one leaving University Hall, the other coming toward it. They stood a moment, talking, until dust and leaves, caught up in a miniature cyclone, made them turn their backs.

Hope said, "Hang on, Lymie—we don't want to lose you."

"Okay," he said, and took hold of her arm lightly.

"In case you think that remark was funny, Davison," Sally said, "you're sadly mistaken."

"I suppose I am," Hope said, "but on the other hand, I didn't mean to—"

"You never do," Sally said. "Why don't you hit her, Lymie?"

"I can't," Lymie said. "I wasn't brought up that way."

"Well, I wasn't *either*," Sally said, "but I knocked a boy out cold when I was nine years old, and nobody taught me how to do it. I just picked up a brickbat and hit him with it. Johnny Mayberry, his name was. He was a very nice boy. I don't remember what he did to me that made me so irritated with him, but anyway they had to take five stitches in his head, and his mother wouldn't let me come over and play in their yard for a long time afterward."

While she was talking, she opened a book and took out a gray envelope, pressed between the pages. Then with a strange asking look on her face she said, "Lymie, will you do something for me? Will you give this to your stuck-up friend?"

Lymie took the envelope and thrust it in his coat pocket. "He's not really stuck-up," he said slowly. "It was just a misunderstanding."

"I know it was." Sally nodded. "I just said that. But the thing is, a note probably won't be enough. And if it isn't, will you?——"

Mrs. Lieberman realized suddenly that neither of these girls was for Mr. Peters. Over a period of weeks she had built up an elaborate speculation about the intimacy in the row ahead of her and now in half a minute it was demolished. This was always happening to her, and it didn't really matter, except she was sorry for him. He needed someone. He needed fussing over and caring for. He needed lots of love. (She had two sons of her own, both in college, but when they came klop-klopping down the stairs in the morning, it sounded like horses, and they slipped past her and out of the house and into a world of their own making, where nothing she said ever penetrated.) And what grieved her as she started on down the walk, under the high nave made by overarching elm trees, was that she herself had no daughter to push at him—for she would have liked very much to take him home, fatten him, and keep him in the family.

23

The front corridor of the men's gymnasium was empty except for a set of scales facing the door and a glass case containing trophies. The prevailing odor was of chlorine, from the swimming pool. At either end of the corridor, a short flight of stairs went up and another flight went down, the result being in either case the same: row on row of metal lockers, long wooden benches, and shower rooms. In this part of the building, which was always overheated, the stale odor of male bodies met and grappled with the dank odor of drains.

The third floor of the gymnasium was a single vast room, light and sunny, with a narrow balcony running all the way around it and a high steel-ribbed roof. In the absence of partitions the floor space was divided by the equipment. Rings, parallel bars, ladders, tumbling mats, and a leather horse took up half the gymnasium. Most of the remaining area was required by the flying trapeze apparatus, but there was room under the balcony for several wrestling mats, and in the opposite corner a punching bag. Two sets of stairs led up to the balcony, which was an indoor running track steeply sloped at the curves and almost level on the straightaway. Three more sets of stairs went down to the locker rooms.

After four o'clock in the afternoon the gymnasium was like a men's club. The same undergraduates, the same faculty members came there day after day to work out and most of them knew each other, if not by name at least to speak to. Lymie came up from the locker rooms, in his street clothes, with his logic book under his arm, and his leather notebook, his anthology of nineteenth-century poetry. He stood for a moment at the head of the stairs. His eyes took in the little group around the high parallel bars, the tumblers doing double backflips, the mathematics instructor pulling at chest weights, and the two boys who were slowly swinging, head downward, from the iron rings. In a far corner he located the person he was looking for—a boxer who appeared at ten minutes after four every afternoon, in trunks and soft, leather boxing shoes, with his wrists taped, and on his hands a pair of pigskin gloves with the fingers cut out of them. The boxer was Spud Latham. There was no mistaking him, although in four years' time his face had grown much harder and leaner and his jaw more pronounced.

Spud was skipping rope when Lymie came up to him, and he acknowledged Lymie's presence with a curt nod. On the count of thirty-nine the rope caught on his heel. His face relaxed and he said, "This is one hell of a place. Nobody will put the gloves on with me."

"Did you try Armstrong?" Lymie asked.

"He's still sore on account of what happened last time," Spud said.

"You shouldn't have hit him so hard, probably."

"I didn't mean to," Spud said. "I just got excited, I guess, and the first thing I knew he was sitting on his can."

"Well," Lymie said, "you can't blame him for not wanting to do it again."

"I didn't hurt him," Spud said. "It just shook him up. You'd think with a whole gymnasium to choose from, somebody would be interested in something besides walking on their hands."

"What about Maguire?" Lymie asked.

"Same thing." Spud tossed the skipping rope aside and jabbed at the punching bag, making it *ka-slap, ka-slap* in whatever direction he wanted it to. His movements were quick, controlled, and certain, and there was a cruel look in his eye.

Lymie took off his shoes in order to practice skipping rope. His performance was not expert like Spud's. He was too tense. He missed on the count of thirteen and had to start over.

Spud was a year older than Lymie and his body showed it. His body was finished. It was the body of a man, slender, well-proportioned, compact, and beautiful. He had been a life guard all summer long at one of the street-end beaches in Chicago and his hair and eyebrows were still bleached from the sun. His skin was so tanned from the constant exposure that it looked permanent. He could have been a Polynesian. Though Lymie had seen him dress and undress hundreds of times, there is a kind of amazement that does not wear off. Very often, looking at Spud, he felt the desire which he sometimes had looking at statues—to put out his hand and touch some part of Spud, the intricate interlaced muscles of his side, or his shoulder blades, or his back, or his flat stomach, or the veins at his wrists, or his small pointed ears.

Spud turned away from the punching bag and went up on the balcony where the rowing machines were. While he was gone, a thickset boy with red hair picked up the boxing gloves which Spud had tossed aside, and started punching the bag. Spud came downstairs immediately and stood close by, watching him. When the redheaded boy turned aside to rest, Spud said,

"You wouldn't like to show me something about boxing, would you?"

The redheaded boy looked at him suspiciously and said, "Get somebody that knows something about it."

"There isn't anybody," Spud said. "They're all acrobats and like that. I can tell from watching you that you know a lot more than I do. And if you don't mind showing me a few things——"

The other boy pulled his sweat shirt off, over his head. "Okay," he said. "If you're that crazy to box, I'd just as soon."

Lymie tied Spud's boxing gloves on for him and then went over to the redheaded boy, who had finished tying one glove and was trying to manage the knot in the other. When Lymie took over, the redheaded boy said, "Much obliged," and looked past him at Spud.

"Three minute rounds," Spud said, "and no slugging."

"Better make it two," the redheaded boy said.

With Spud's pocket Ingersoll in his right hand, Lymie backed away and called "Time!" The two boxers closed in cautiously. The redheaded boy had at least twenty pounds advantage in weight, but he moved slowly. Spud walked round and round him, jabbing at him, blocking with his shoulder or his elbows, and breathing in through his mouth and out through his nose. Lymie looked down at the watch and then his eyes flew back to Spud. Once as Spud ducked, Lymie's head also moved sidewise. The movement was very slight, almost as if Lymie were asleep and dreaming that he was fighting.

At first the boxing was scientific and careful, but toward the end of the second round, Spud let go of one. He apologized and they went on fighting. In the third round the same thing happened again and this time he didn't apologize. Neither did the redheaded boy when he broke through Spud's guard a minute later and sent him sprawling.

Lymie called "Time!" sharply but nobody paid any attention to him. Spud got to his feet and resumed his shuffling and dancing, but he didn't box as well as he had before. The redheaded boy got through to him again and again—on the chin, on the side of the head, above his eye. Spud began to lose ground and eventually the two of them, still flailing at each other, ended up between the high parallel bars, to the annoyance of the boy named Armstrong, who jumped down and separated them.

"Why don't you stay over there where you belong, Latham?" he asked.

"Oh, don't be a sorehead," Spud said and turned his back on him. Lymie, who had followed the fighting anxiously all the way across the gymnasium, now untied the strings of their boxing gloves. Spud and the redheaded boy pulled their gloves off, shook hands, and went off to the showers together.

Left to himself, Lymie put his shoes on and picked up his coat, his books, the boxing gloves, and Spud's skipping rope. As he started down the stairs he saw by the big clock on the wall that it was now five-twenty-five. The trapeze performers had also decided to call it a day. They were dropping one after another into the net, like ripe pears.

24

When Sally left Lymie and Hope, she hurried home. It was her mother's "day" and she was expected to help. The Forbeses lived in a two-story bungalow a little over a mile from the university campus, in a quiet neighborhood. The outside of their house was white stucco covered with a thick, three-pointed ivy. Mrs. Forbes had grown it from a slip that she had carried away from Kenilworth Castle in her purse. Between the Forbeses' house and the Albrechts' house on the right, there was barely room for a narrow cement driveway. The apple tree in the Forbeses' back yard also shaded the flower garden of the economics professor and his wife whose house was on the left. The economics professor claimed the fruit that he could reach from his property, and a coolness had developed between the two families, partly as a result of this and partly because Professor Forbes, on summer evenings when the lawn needed sprinkling, very often placed the sprinkler so that most of the water went on the sidewalk, and passersby had to make a detour through the wet grass or walk in the street.

Mrs. Forbes was "at home" the second Thursday of every month. On these occasions Professor Forbes was on duty at the front door, where he shook hands with the arriving guests, and took their hats and coats from them, and if it was raining, their umbrellas and rubbers. During the fall and winter months there was always a wood fire burning in the living room fireplace. The curtains were drawn, the lamps were lit. In the dining room there were tall lighted candles in silver candlesticks, and the table was covered with a lace tablecloth and that in turn by stacks of hand-painted plates, rows of shining teaspoons, and platters of fancy sandwiches. Sometimes the woman pouring tea at the copper samovar was Mrs. Somers, the wife of the dean of the Graduate School. Sometimes it was Mrs. Severance, Professor Severance's mother. Or Mrs. Clark, whose husband was head of the English department. This afternoon it was Mrs. Philosophy Mathews, so-called to distinguish her from the Mrs. Mathews whose husband taught animal husbandry.

Mrs. Forbes herself, always serene, always handsome, stood in the living room receiving. Her guests presented a grand panoramic picture of the Liberal Arts faculty and the Graduate School. As with all such pictures (the "Coronation of Napoleon," for example, and "Men and Women of Letters of the Nineteenth Century") you have to have a key. A stranger would have seen a room full of middle aged and elderly people in groups of twos, threes, and fours, with teacups in their hands, talking a little too loudly in each other's faces. Mrs. Wentworth, whose husband was in the psychology department, and Mary Mountjoy, who taught Italian, were arguing about the best time to transplant dahlias. The head of the classics department and a young biology instructor were listening to a businessman who had married into the faculty. The world and his office, he was saying, could develop no trouble that two Manhattans wouldn't cure. After advancing this contention cheerfully and without opposition, he went on to assert that most people are enormously improved by liquor. The Althoffs and Helen Glover were twitting the head of the English department on his 8 A.M. broadcasts. Mrs. Baker, who taught the modern novel (with special emphasis on Henry James) and Alice Rawlings were standing in a corner trying to get away from the fireplace. They were discussing Mrs. Baker's Minnie, who was colored and who, after seven years of faithful service had had a major operation in August and then had declared that her boy friend was going to finance a whole year's vacation for her. Alice Rawlings said that she had given up and was going it alone with a superb houseman-yardman Fred, on Fridays. It was his one slum day, she said. He came straight from the Wilsons and the McAvoys, and was doing his best to make her back yard resemble their estates. Kathryn Shortall was saying what a blessing it was that her husband enjoyed eating out sometimes, and Sally's father, out in the hall, was talking to an exchange professor from the Sorbonne about Montaigne. Everyone knew everyone else and it was a good deal like progressive whist, or some game like that, since it involved a frequent change of partners. You went up to any group you felt like talking to. They opened automatically and amiably, and there you were, allowed to pick up the threads of the old conversation or start a new one.

There were several young girls, Sally among them, who came and went, bearing cups of tea and platters of sandwiches. Though Sally had known some of her mother's guests since childhood and was privileged to call many full professors by their nicknames, today she looked on everybody with the eyes of a stranger. There was no place for her in this world. She liked dogs, horses, sailboats, airplanes, climbing apple trees, staying up late at night, walking in the rain, driving round and round in an open car on a summer afternoon, sitting by a beach fire at night, lying on the ground and looking up at the undersides of leaves and at lightning bugs and falling stars, dividing her attention between a book that she had read many times and an apple, watching the sun go down and the moon come up, wondering what the boy she was going to marry would look like and where he was at that moment, and how long it would take him to find her. . . . The list was endless and made up entirely of normal human pleasures. If it had only included an appreciation of respectability, she would have been happier. Or at least she would have been spared a great many bitter arguments with her mother. The words "nice" and "proper" seemed to inflame Sally, and an attempt to consider her conduct in the light of conventional standards made her start talking furiously in a loud voice without much logic.

She loved her mother and father but she didn't love the things they lived by—professorial dignity, scholarship, old books, old furniture, old china, and brand new amusing gossip. She liked storms, lightning and thunder, excitement; and the climate of her home was unfortunately a temperate one.

When there were too many arguments in too short a time, she took a few clothes and moved into the sorority house, where she ran into similar difficulties. She was expected to be careful of her appearance and of her friends, and to remember at all times that she belonged to the best sorority on the campus. She didn't try to do any of these things and so there were more arguments, especially in chapter meetings. She moved around the house in a cloud of disapproval, which had the curious effect of making her clumsy. She tripped over rugs, her feet slid out from under her on the stairs. The girls that she wanted to have like her did, actually, but they also laughed at her, because she was so enthusiastic and so like an overgrown puppy; and this hurt her pride.

The girls who were not amused by her behavior were appalled by it. No room that she walked into was ever quite large enough, nothing was safe in her apologetic hands. She didn't mean to drop Emily Noyes' bottle of Chanel No. 5 or split open the seams of Joyce Brenner's white evening dress which she had asked to try on, but the result in each case was disastrous. The girls snatched fragile things from her if she showed any sign of picking them up, and the girl she bumped into hurrying around a corner of the upstairs hall took to her bed, with cold compresses on her head. It seemed to her that all girls were made of glass and she alone was of flesh and blood and constantly cutting herself on them. She gave up trying to please them.

Though she was undeniably a tomboy, there was nothing masculine about her appearance. She was a recognizable feminine type which the Greeks represented as a huntress with a crescent moon in the center of her forehead, a silver bow in her left hand, a quiver of arrows slung over one shoulder, and her skirts caught up so that her long thighs would be free and unhampered. During the annual festival which the Romans held in her honor, hunting dogs were crowned with garlands and wild beasts were not molested. Wine was brought forth and there was a feast consisting of roasted kid, cakes served piping hot on plates of leaves, and apples still hanging in clusters on the bough. It was not a type generally admired or often found in the university in the year 1927.

The one girl whom she made friends with, Hope Davison, was also a nonconformist, though of a different kind. She did nothing to call attention to herself, she had no sneak dates, and she never broke house rules. But she had a way of looking at people as if she saw through them, and didn't think too much of what was there. Her stare was, more often than not, unconscious, but the other girls in the sorority suffered from it, and from her remarks, which were more candid sometimes than there was any need for. After a year they had devised no adequate way of dealing with her or with Sally.

When Sally's nose was shiny, well it was shiny. Anybody who didn't like shiny noses could look the other way. The belt of Sally's red coat was sometimes missing for days. The left pocket had been ripped and not very expertly sewed up again. The lining was moth-eaten, and the coat itself had, on at least one occasion, been fished out of the waste basket where Mrs. Forbes had put it. Sally went on wearing it, partly because she loved it and partly because it was an offense to every self-respecting member of her sorority. Some of the girls threatened to burn the coat if she didn't stop wearing it, but this threat was never carried out. It would have been dangerous, and they knew it.

Sally and Hope had appeared together in Lymie Peters' freshman rhetoric class, the beginning day of the spring semester. The girls took the two empty seats beside him, and when the instructor didn't bother to alphabetize the class, they stayed there. By the end of the first week they were borrowing theme paper from Lymie. After the second week Sally and Lymie changed seats so that he was in the middle. Often when the class was over, all three of them would retire to a confectionery called the Ship's Lantern, which was long and narrow and pitch dark when they walked into it out of the sunlight. Sometimes they studied, but more often they sat and exposed their minds to each other while they made a mess out of melted ice cream and paper straws, cigarette ashes, and the dregs of Coca-Cola.

One afternoon soon after the semester had started, Spud

and Lymie met Sally coming out of the campus bookstore. She spoke to Lymie and he would have said "Hi" in return and walked on, but a sharp poke in the small of his back stopped him. After the introduction had been managed there was an awkward silence and Spud suggested that they go somewhere and have a Coke. This seemed to Lymie a very silly idea, since it was almost twenty minutes of six. Sally accepted the invitation, to his surprise, and all three of them went to the Ship's Lantern. Spud found an empty booth in the back and maneuvered Sally into the seat beside him. Lymie sat across from them. Lymie had never seen Spud in such a state of foolish excitement. He gave his imitation of an overstimulated horse, and of the flew-flew bird that swims backward to keep the water out of its eyes. He also found an occasion to exclaim: "*O grim-look'd night! O night with hue so black!*" and to demonstrate that it is possible to swallow a lighted cigarette without pain or even discomfort.

Sally was amused and delighted by everything he said. She was also very quiet, for her. Occasionally her eyes met Spud's for a second, but then she looked away immediately at his tie, or at the handkerchief folded and tucked so carefully in his coat pocket, or at his broad-knuckled hands. Her own, with their chewed-off fingernails, she kept out of sight under the table.

At six o'clock when Sally got up to go, Spud told her that if she cared to come down to the gym with him some afternoon he'd show her how to box.

"Oh, I'd love to," she said. Her eyes flew wide with pleasure at the prospect, and then she looked crestfallen. "You're just making fun of me," she said sadly.

"I'm not either," Spud exclaimed. Although he had been kidding, now that she spoke about it in this way, the whole idea seemed to take on a different aspect. "I mean it," he said.

"I'd love to," Sally repeated. "More than anything in the whole world."

"All right," Spud said. "I'll show you all I know about boxing. Here, put your hands up. Might as well give you the first lesson right now." He took hold of both her arms, by the wrists, and moved them into position. "There," he said. "The rest is easy."

Whether it was or not, she didn't have a chance to find out, for there were no more lessons. The next day Spud met her on the steps of University Hall and she looked right at him without speaking. He came home to the rooming house where he and Lymie were living, slammed his books around in a fury, and said the hell with her, the hell with all women.

Lymie asked Sally about it, the next time he saw her, and she had no idea what he was talking about. She hadn't seen Spud, she said. Really she hadn't! It was just that she was so nearsighted. She couldn't recognize her own grandmother six feet away, without glasses on. And that was why she hadn't spoken to him.

Spud wouldn't believe this at first, and after he did believe it he couldn't seem to get over his feeling that somehow (even though Sally hadn't recognized him) he had been snubbed. He refused to see or have anything more to do with her.

25

Lymie went down two flights of stairs, turned left, and went on until he came to Spud's locker. He put down the things he was carrying and turned the dial padlock until it fell open. Then he reached inside and brought out a clean towel. Farther down the row of lockers two boys were dressing. Lymie laid the towel across the bench and walked over to a door that opened into the swimming pool. There were half a dozen swimmers still in the pool. One of them was swimming back and forth, churning the water with his feet and ankles. The others were waiting their turn at the diving board. A boy with close-cropped curly blond hair did a high jackknife and then a tall freckle-faced boy tried a half gainer, which was not a success. He came up slowly and shook the water out of his eyes. The next boy placed both hands on the board, out at the very end, and then up went his naked legs, slowly and easily. He balanced himself for fifteen seconds, wavered, regained his balance, and dropped head first into the water. The tall diver returned to the board and Lymie could tell by the way he braced himself that he was going to try the half gainer again.

The two boys farther down the row of lockers finished dressing and slammed their locker doors shut. They saw the clean towel on the bench and their eyes turned from it to Lymie, standing with his nose pressed to the glass pane in the door. Once the towel was in their possession, no one could prove that it wasn't theirs. As they walked toward it, Lymie glanced at them, over his shoulder. They left the towel where it was.

The diver took a running jump from the end of the springboard. A moment later, Lymie turned away from the swimming pool and went back and sat down in front of the open locker. From his coat pocket he produced the gray envelope. *For Spud Latham* it said in Sally's round legible handwriting. The flap was unsealed. For a second Lymie was tempted to read it; he put both the temptation and the envelope aside.

Spud came up shining from his shower, found the towel Lymie had laid out for him, and dried himself. His eyes were clear and bright and full of happiness. "That was a good scrap," he said. "I enjoyed it. The guy was really mean, once he got started."

Lymie reached into the locker, found Spud's shorts, and handed them to him. "Didn't you hear me calling time?" he asked.

Spud shook his head. "I didn't hear anything," he said. "I was busy keeping from getting killed."

He sat down on the bench to dry his feet. When he had finished, his shoes and socks were waiting on the floor beside him, and the boxing trunks and jock strap that he had brought up from the shower room in his hand were hanging on a hook in the locker. It was not callousness that let him accept these attentions simply and without thinking about them. He wouldn't have allowed anyone else to do for him the things that Lymie did. And besides, he recognized that it gave Lymie pleasure to bend over and pick up the towel where he had dropped it, and to go off to the towel room and exchange it for a clean one.

When Lymie came back, Spud was dressed and tying his tie in front of a small mirror which hung at the end of the row of lockers. "I feel wonderful," Spud said. "What do you think we'll have for supper?"

"Wednesday, veal birds."

"I could eat a steer," Spud said, "without half trying."

Lymie buried his head in the locker, searching for Spud's big black notebook, and heard him say, "What's this, a communication from the dean's office?" and realized that he had discovered the gray envelope.

"It's for you," Lymie said.

Spud tore the envelope open and glanced at the note inside. "Here," he said, and tossed the note at Lymie. *Dear Spud*, it said, *We're having an informal house dance on the Saturday after Homecoming. Would you care to come? Sincerely yours, Sally Forbes.* Lymie folded the note, slipped it back in the torn envelope, and laid it on the bench. Homecoming was the twenty-fifth. The dance would be the second of November.

"What do you think?" Spud asked. "Do you figure I ought to go?"

"If it were me," Lymie said slowly (for he would have liked to be asked to the dance himself), "I'd go. You'll probably have a good time."

"Has Hope asked you yet?"

Lymie shook his head.

"Why hasn't she?" Spud asked.

"Maybe she's got somebody else in mind that she wants to ask," Lymie said. "Or she may be waiting to see whether you decide to come or not."

"We'll go together," Spud said suddenly. "And we'll tear the place down, shall we?"

"All right," Lymie said. "Anything you say."

He tossed the towel into the locker and closed it. On their way out of the gymnasium they stopped at the drinking fountain. Lymie held the lever down for Spud, who drank and drank. "Aah," he said as he straightened up. "That's better. I was dry as a bone."

"You're always dry as a bone," Lymie said. He bent down to the stream of water for a second only, and then wiped his mouth with the back of his hand.

In the front corridor they swerved from their path and went over to the scales. Lymie put his own books on the tile floor and took Spud's leather notebook from him. Spud planted himself firmly on the scales. The needle flew up to a hundred and fifty-seven pounds. He stepped down and Lymie took his place. This time the needle rose more slowly and wavered at a hundred and nine.

"Would you look at that!" Lymie exclaimed. "I've gained a pound and a quarter. It must be from skipping rope. It must be the exercise."

"Give me my notebook," Spud said. "You're cheating."

Without the notebook the scales declined to a hundred and seven and three-quarters. Lymie stepped down, his face shadowed by disappointment.

He and Spud were outside, almost at the front walk, when he remembered his own books. He ran back into the building for them, though he knew that Spud would wait. And when he had picked up the books, he hurried out again.

There were very few moments in the day when Lymie had Spud all to himself, and the last two summers they had been separated six days out of the week by their summer jobs in Chicago. Even on Sundays, when Lymie went to the beach to be with Spud, he had to share him with other people and pretend that he didn't mind when Spud rowed off in a boat with six other life guards, or lorded it over everybody on the beach from a high wooden perch where Lymie (although occasional marks of favor were bestowed on him) couldn't sit. There were so many things Spud liked to do that Lymie couldn't do with him, such as boxing, or playing football, or learning to fly an airplane, and Lymie spent a good deal of time watching from the sidelines, and waiting for Spud to come back to him. Oddly enough, Spud always did.

Before they went off to college, Lymie assumed that they would both belong to a fraternity, as a matter of course, but Mr. Latham put his foot down. It would take all the money he could scrape together, he said, if Spud was going to have four more years of schooling. For him to live in a fraternity and pay dues and have a lot of extra expenses, unless he could find some way to make the money himself, was out of the question. Lymie didn't want to belong to a fraternity if Spud couldn't and so when Bob Edwards, who had graduated the year before and was a Sigma Chi at the university, invited them both to stay at his fraternity house during Rushing Week, they wrote and declined the invitation.

The following September Lymie and Spud, Frenchie deFresne, and Ford all sat together on the train going down to the university, which was located in a small town something over a hundred miles from Chicago. Frenchie had been captain of the football team in his senior year, and he was staying at the Sigma Chi house. Ford had invitations from the Sigma Chi's, the Delts, and the Phi Gams, and he was staying at the Psi U house. Mr. Ford had been a Psi U, and so his son was prepared to be one too.

One of the Psi U's met him on the station platform and took his bag. Frenchie was surrounded by five upperclassmen, three of them letter men in football. Lymie and Spud saw him a few minutes later riding off in a rattletrap open car without fenders or top, and with signs painted all over it.

They checked their suitcases in the station and took a tiny streetcar which bounced and jounced and eventually went right through the heart of the campus. Lymie and Spud got off there and looked around. The buildings seemed very large, the stretch of green lawn interminable. Before they found a place to live that they liked, they walked up and down several of the streets bordering on the campus. Even without the sign ROOMS FOR BOYS in the front window, it was easy to tell which houses had rooms for students and which were private homes. The rooming houses invariably needed a coat of paint. There were no shrubs or flower beds around them, and the grass, when there was any, was sickly from too much overhanging shade.

Spud would have turned in at the first one they came to, but Lymie stopped him. They kept on walking until they found themselves in a slightly better neighborhood. At the first sight of the house with the mansard roof, Lymie said, "There's the place we're going to live!" It was painted white, and set well back from the street; and it had fretwork porches which ran around the front and sides of the house, on two stories, like the decks of a river steamboat.

They went up on the porch and twisted the Victorian doorbell, which gave out a hollow peal. Inside the house a dog started barking. Through the frosted glass landscape in the front door they could make out the shapes of furniture crowded into the front hall, as if the people who lived here were just moving in. They heard the dog quite plainly then, and a man's voice saying, "Pooh-Bah, for pity's sake, it's only the doorbell!"

The door swung open and they were confronted by a middle-aged man with gray hair and horn-rimmed glasses which hung on a black ribbon.

"Yes?" he said.

"We're looking for a room," Lymie explained.

The words were drowned out by the barking of the dog, a black and white spaniel trying frantically to work his way between the man's legs.

"Excuse me, just a moment," he said, and grabbed the dog by the collar. "Pooh-Bah, *will* you be quiet? I'll have to get a switch and whip you, do you hear? I'll whip you good!" Then with an expression of extreme agitation on his face, the man turned back to Lymie and Spud. "He must have thought you were the postman. Two separate rooms, did you say? Or do you want a room together?"

"We want to room together," Lymie said.

"Well," the man said, backing away from the door, "come in and let me show you what I. . . . Stop it, Pooh-Bah. I won't have this continual yiping and carrying on. These are two young gentlemen who are interested in a room, do you understand? Now one more bark out of you and I'll shut you up in the kitchen."

Single file they threaded their way through the spinning wheels and drop-leaf tables, the marble-topped washstands, the Boston rockers, andirons, horsehair sofas, chairs, and whatnots that cluttered the front hall.

"I hope you don't mind all this," the man said, waving at a collection of glass hats, hens, and hands. "My sign is being re painted just now so there's no way, probably, that you'd know it from the outside, but I'm in the antique business. The first floor is my shop, as you can see. I try to keep it tidy but people bring me things and suddenly there isn't room to breathe."

By the time they reached the foot of the stairs, the dog had stopped sniffing at Spud's trousers and was making overtures of friendship. Spud bent down and scratched his ear.

The rooms on the second floor opened one out of another, and no two of them seemed to be on the same level. The windows were large and the ceilings high, but the rooms themselves were cut up into odd unnatural shapes, apparently after the house was built.

"I have only two vacancies at the moment," the man said, "and one of them is too small for you, I feel sure. It's hardly more than a cubbyhole. But this one—" He threw open a door "—if you don't object to a north exposure and that Chinese gas station across the street, is quite respectable."

The room had two large windows and was furnished with two study tables, two unsightly wooden chairs, two cheap dressers, a Morris chair with a cigarette burn in the upholstery, and a small empty bookcase. The curtains were limp, and the rag rug was much too small for the floor; it was also coming unsewed in several places. Lymie looked from the pink and blue flowered wallpaper to the shades, which were green and had cracks in them. It was not the room they had imagined for themselves. It was not at all like the college room in the picture of the young collegian smoking a long-stemmed clay pipe. Spud looked inquiringly at Lymie, and then walked over to the closet with the dog following at his heels. The closet was a fair-sized one.

"Suits me," he said.

"How much is it?" Lymie asked.

"Well, I tell you," the man said thoughtfully, "I've been getting fifteen for it, for one person, a charming young man who graduated last spring. But it's really worth more than that: It's a good-sized room, as you can see, and I don't know that I can afford to rent it for any less than—my coal bills are really outlandish, you know, and so is the electric light. And of course you get hot water and all. Suppose I say eighteen dollars for the two of you?"

"A week?" Lymie asked anxiously.

"Oh dear no. I wouldn't dream of asking eighteen dollars a week. Not for a room like this. Not with all this dreadful furniture in it anyway. Eighteen dollars a month. Nine dollars apiece for each of you. I think you'll find, if you look around, that that's as good as you'll do any place. A room this size, and with a decent light and all. There's nothing the matter with it really. The only thing you may not like is living with so many people. There are eleven people living on this floor now—all of them students, of course—and somehow, I don't know what it is exactly, but whenever you get too many people under one roof, it always seems to lead to violence."

They decided to take the room.

That night after they had finished unpacking, they went out for a walk. There was a full moon, the biggest they could ever remember seeing. They were both aware that the world had grown larger, and that they had money to spend (though not a great deal) and that no one would inquire how they spent it. They had escaped from their families, from the tyranny of home. Feeling a need to celebrate all this they turned into a drugstore and ordered vanilla ice cream with hot fudge sauce. It was so wonderful when it came that they made up their minds to have ice cream with fudge sauce every night of the school year.

26

The antique dealer's name was Alfred Dehner. He occupied a large bedroom on the first floor, next to the kitchen, and slept in a four-poster bed with a soiled white canopy. There was no bathroom downstairs, so he used the one on the second floor and kept his toothbrush and tooth powder, his Victorian shaving mug, brush, and straight-edged razor, a cake of castile soap, iodine, and bicarbonate of soda in the medicine chest over the washstand. Although the boys stole from each other continually, they never touched his toilet articles.

Within a week after Lymie and Spud had moved in, they discovered that Mr. Dehner had jacked up the price of their room —two boys had occupied it the year before, not one, and they had only paid fifteen dollars a month. What Mr. Dehner had said about violence, however, proved to be true. The genteel atmosphere created by the antique furniture ended at the foot of the stairs. On the second floor the boys came and went from the shower naked or with a towel around their hips, and anybody who felt like singing did, at the top of his lungs. The boys seldom stayed in their own rooms but wandered aimlessly all evening long, looking for somebody who would let them copy his rhetoric theme, somebody who would loan them four bits till Friday, somebody to practice jujitsu, somebody to pester. Six or seven of them would crowd into a single room and sit around on the floor, talking about football or baseball or girls. Occasionally when the racket was louder than usual, one of the boys would look up from the serial in *Collier's* that he was reading and yell "Study hours!" but it never had the slightest effect. It was not intended to. It was just a remark, or perhaps even an excuse to start a fight.

Fights developed all the time, out of nothing at all—over a fountain pen that had been borrowed and then returned without any ink in it, over how many yards had been gained by a certain end run against the University of Illinois two years before, over who broke a string in the house tennis racquet. It was nothing to come home and find two figures in the upstairs hall, rolling over and over, grunting, gouging at each other, and kicking the floor with their heels. Mostly the fighting was good-natured but sometimes it was in earnest. If you wanted to stay and watch, you could. If you didn't, you stepped over the bodies and went on to your own room.

In the wintertime there was no heat in the radiators after ten o'clock. As the study rooms got colder the boys put on more clothes—sweaters, bathrobes, overcoats, and mufflers, until finally they had to go to bed to get warm. The dormitory was on the top floor, under the mansard roof. There was no heat in it, and the windows were left wide open from September until late in June.

At night, in the deepest quiet, bare feet would pad across the floor and a conversation started downstairs would go on gathering momentum until everyone in the dorm was awake and taking part in it. Sometimes two or three people in a row would stop when they came to Lymie's bed and shake him gently and say, "Want to pee, Lymie? . . . Do you have to pee?" Sometimes the door would fly open and a voice would cry "Fire! Fire! Steve Rush is on fire!" and ten or eleven boys would leap from their beds and rush to the second floor bathroom for water. If the fire spread, Freeman or Pownell also had to be put out. Usually Rush's bed was the only one that got soaked. He was a sound sleeper and also he had a mean streak in him and could be counted on to emerge from the dorm screaming and cursing and ready to kill anybody he could lay his hands on.

The noise and the confusion bothered Spud, who was used to quiet when he studied, but Lymie felt at home in the rooming house as soon as he sat down at his desk and wrote "Lymon Peters Jr., 302 South Street," in all his books. His desk faced one window, Spud's faced the other. When Lymie was studying, he seldom saw the boys who walked through continually on their way to some other room. When they tripped over the sill and started swearing, he looked up sometimes and smiled.

If there was no other sound, if peace descended on the second floor for five minutes, somebody was sure to start making faces at the dog and the dog would whine and bark and race around wildly until Mr. Dehner came running to the foot of the stairs.

"Are you teasing that poor animal again?" he would shriek up at them with his hand on the banister. "Really, such cruelty, such lack of any decent human feeling! If you don't stop it I'm going to call the dean's office! I give you my word! I'm going to call the dean's office and I'm going to ask to speak to the dean!"

Mr. Dehner's voice was shrill and penetrating, and his accent was not Middle Western. The *r*'s were slurred. The *a*'s were broad and for some reason they seemed to carry better than the flat kind. Whenever Mr. Dehner started talking loudly, Lymie put down his book and listened. Mr. Dehner was nearly always agitated about something—or, as it turned out nine times out of ten, about nothing. His voice would rise higher and higher, as if he were at last in real trouble, and Lymie would tiptoe to the head of the stairs, lean over, and discover that Mr. Dehner was talking to a couple of faculty wives about Paul Revere silver, or telling them how to take alcohol rings off the tops of tables with spirits of camphor.

The boys called him "Maggie" behind his back, but they liked him. They liked anything that was odd or extreme. They thought it was fine that Colter knew how to call pigs; that Fred Howard was a Christer and spent all his spare time at the Wesley Foundation; that Amsler's mother drove over from Evansville once a week just to see that he was getting enough to eat; and that Freeman every now and then at dinner took out six of his upper front teeth and tossed them into the water pitcher.

Far from holding it against Lymie that he was so thin, they bragged about him to strangers. Geraghty, who was a pre-medic, used to come into Lymie's room at night and make him take off his shirt. It was as good as having a skeleton, he said; he could find and name every bone in Lymie's body.

The boys took a brief dislike for Spud until he persuaded Reinhart and Pownell to go to the gym with him one afternoon and box. They nicknamed him "The Killer" and from that time on, he had his place in the gallery of freaks; he belonged.

Most of the boys ate at a mixed boarding club which was three blocks from the rooming house. The weekly meal tickets were five dollars and if you wanted a date of a certain kind, the boarding club was an easy place to get it. The boys from "302" ate at the same two tables breakfast, lunch, and dinner. Sometimes Lymie and Spud were separated when there was only one chair vacant at each table but usually they ate together.

In a fraternity house this would have been spotted almost instantly. One of the brothers would have said, "It's time to break that up." Spud and Lymie would not have been allowed even to walk to the campus together without someone stepping between them. At "302" nobody cared.

Sometimes, while Lymie sat at his desk with a book open in front of him, Spud got himself into trouble (the crime was unspecified) and Lymie took the blame for it and gladly and willingly spent the rest of his life in prison so that Spud could go free. Then they were in a lifeboat, with only enough food and water for one person, and Lymie, waiting until Spud was asleep, slipped noiselessly over the side into the cold sea. Then they were fighting, back to back, with swords, forcing the ring of their enemies slowly toward the little door through which one of them could escape if the other went on fighting. . . .

Spud spent at least an hour every evening tidying up the room. He lined up his shoes and Lymie's in a straight row on the floor of the closet. Then he rehung several pairs of trousers so that the creases were straight, and made sure that Lymie hadn't concealed the vest of one suit inside the coat of another. The objects on top of his desk—his pencils, his blotter, his fountain pen, ruler, and bottle of ink—had to be in an exact arrangement, and the desk and bureau drawers in order.

Otherwise there was no use in his trying to concentrate on calculus or German grammar.

Not all of this tidying was love of order. Spud's conscience wouldn't let him go to a movie on a week night or read detective story magazines; that wasn't what he had come down to college for. But he managed to put off studying until he had done everything else he could think of, and what with visitors and playing with the dog and other unforeseen interruptions, very often he would read two or three pages, yawn, and discover that it was ten o'clock, time to put the book down and get ready for bed.

He and Lymie were always the first ones to go up to the dorm. In the big icy-cold bed they clung to each other, shivering like puppies, until the heat of their bodies began to penetrate through the outing flannel of their pajamas and their heavy woolen bathrobes. Lymie slept on his right side and Spud curled against him, with his fists in the hollow of Lymie's back. In five minutes the whole bed was warmed and Spud was sound asleep. It took Lymie longer, as a rule. He lay there, relaxed and drowsy, aware of the cold outside the covers, and of the warmth coming to him from Spud, and Spud's odor, which was not stale or sweaty or like the odor of any other person. Then he moved his right foot until the outer part of the instep came in contact with Spud's bare toes, and from this one point of reality he swung out safely into darkness, into no sharing whatever.

27

The first afternoon that Sally brought Lymie home with her, she led him upstairs to Professor Forbes's study, where her father and mother were sitting with Professor Severance. Mrs. Forbes was darning socks. A pair of tortoise-shell glasses rested insecurely on the bridge of her nose. She had Sally's eyes, hair, and coloring but she was more self-contained. Her hair was parted in the middle and came down over her temples in two raven's wings. Her smile was charming but also rather ambiguous.

"I'm glad you decided to put in an appearance, Lymie," she said. "I was beginning to wonder about you. Some of the people Sally talks about don't exist, I'm sure. They couldn't. . . . This is Mr. Severance."

"Mr. Peters and I are already acquainted," Professor Severance said, nodding. "We see each other every Monday, Wednesday, and Friday at two."

"And that's my Pop," Sally said.

Professor Forbes rose and held out his hand. He was a tall, black-haired, black-eyed man with thick lips showing through his beard. He offered a box containing cigarettes and Lymie shook his head.

"Did you notice the tree as you came in?" Mrs. Forbes asked.

"Which tree?" Sally asked.

"The one between the curbing and the walk."

"No," Sally said, "what about it?"

"Your father ran into it today."

"No!" Sally exclaimed. "How could he? It's at least four feet from the driveway."

"He did it," Mrs. Forbes said triumphantly. "Don't ask me how. . . . My husband is learning to drive," she explained for Lymie's benefit. "He's had several lessons and today he took the car out alone, after lunch, and as he was coming back he turned into the driveway and knocked almost all the bark off one side of that huge tree!"

"You're exaggerating," Professor Forbes said, without removing his cigarette from between his lips. "The whole story is a gross exaggeration." The cigarette ashes drifted down on the front of his smoking jacket.

"I'm not exaggerating," Mrs. Forbes said. "I went out and looked at it."

"What about the Albrechts' bay window?" Sally asked.

"The Albrechts' bay window is still intact," Mrs. Forbes said.

Professor Severance shook with laughter.

"Couldn't we change the subject?" Professor Forbes asked irritably.

Mrs. Forbes looked at him over her glasses. "Maybe we'd better," she said, raising her eyebrows.

"How's Mrs. Sevvy?" Sally asked.

"Better, thank you." Professor Severance abruptly regained

his composure. "She's still in bed though. The doctor said another day or two wouldn't hurt her."

"Mr. Severance's mother is a most remarkable woman," Mrs. Forbes said, turning to Lymie. "She's seventy-three and serves the best food and gives the gayest parties of any woman in town. I hope you meet her sometime."

"When my mother's feeling better you must come and have dinner with us," Professor Severance said. "I've been wanting to tell you, Mr. Peters, how much I enjoyed reading your examination paper."

Lymie blushed.

"It's so discouraging to get your own words thrown back at you twenty or thirty times," Professor Severance went on. "I feel as if I were lecturing to a class of parrots. It's all on account of those miserable notebooks, of course. Some day I'm going to collect them all and throw them out of the window."

"You might as well throw the students with them," Professor Forbes said.

"Some of them are too large," Professor Severance said, "and too athletic."

"What about *my* examination paper?" Sally said, leering at him. "Wasn't it original, Sevvy?"

Professor Severance cleared his throat and then beamed at her affectionately. "Yes, my dear," he said, "almost wholly original. My one—ah—hesitation about it was that there seemed to be an insufficient acquaintance with the subject matter of the course."

"There," Sally said, turning to her mother, "you see?"

"Only too plainly, I'm afraid," Mrs. Forbes said. She excused herself and left the room.

A heavy silence descended. Sally was embarrassed by her mother's remark, and Professor Forbes had come to depend so on his wife's small talk that he had none of his own to offer. Politeness prevented Professor Severance from continuing the subject they had been discussing when Sally and Lymie appeared—Spenser's indebtedness to the *Orlando Furioso*—since it would probably have no interest for them.

Lymie's eyes wandered around the room. The ceiling was low and sloped down to the long bookcases on two sides.

There were Holbein prints on the walls and a colored map of Paris. Professor Forbes's desk was placed near two small front windows. Next to it was a large table with a lamp on it, and more books piled helter-skelter, some of them in danger of sliding off onto the floor. Lymie's glance came to rest on a large Chinese lacquer screen.

"That's a beautiful thing, isn't it?" Professor Severance said. "It's all very well about not coveting your neighbor's wife and his she-asses and his camels but when it comes to *objets d'art*, I find myself wavering sometimes." He got up and crossed the room so that he could examine the screen more closely. "Modern?" he inquired, over his shoulder.

"My brother-in-law sent it to us," Professor Forbes said noncommittally.

"The one who travels so much?" Professor Severance asked.

Professor Forbes nodded. "He got it in a hock shop in Manila."

"It's very beautiful," Professor Severance said.

The lacquer screen had three panels. On one side, the side facing the room, were white flowers which were like roses but larger and stiffer. Peonies, Lymie decided. The flowers were in square blue vases and the vases rested on carved teakwood stands, against a yellow background. Professor Severance folded the screen, turned it around, and opened it. On the reverse was a company of Chinese horsemen charging at an angle across all three panels.

The fat-rumped horsemen rode over pink flames and blue curlicues representing smoke. Their long, loose sleeves whipped from their elbows. Their tunics divided, revealing mail leggings and bare feet. The air was thick with arrows. Some of the horsemen rode with their lances set, their shoulders braced for the shock; others with daggers upraised, knees digging into their horses' sides. Here and there a rider twisted or rose in the saddle, and one of them hung from the stirrups with a spear coming out through the center of his back. Their faces were brick-red or deathly pale. All had identical thinly drawn mustaches and chin tufts, and expressions denoting fierceness or cruelty or cunning. The only calm face belonged to a severed head that had rolled under the feet of the horses and was gazing upward serenely toward heaven. The galloping horses shared in the frenzy of the riders. There were fat white horses, dappled horses, gold horses with the heads of dragons, ivory horses with gold manes and hoofs and tails, blue horses, pink horses, horses with scales and frantic, fishlike faces.

"I'd like to have known the man who made this," Professor Severance said. "The one who had the idea of putting still life on one side—those wonderfully placid white flowers—and warriors on the other."

"I assume it is a traditional juxtaposition," Professor Forbes said.

"No doubt, but somebody must have thought of it for the first time. The mutual attraction of gentleness and violence, don't you see, Mr. Peters? The brutal body and the calm philosophic mind."

"Don't talk to me about philosophic minds," Mrs. Forbes said. She came in carrying a tray with a silver teapot on it, teacups, a silver sugar and creamer, slices of lemon, and bread and butter cut paper-thin. "If I ever marry again it's going to be to a plumber. I've been trying for two days to get a man to come look at the hot water heater in the basement."

"Plumbing," Professor Severance said reproachfully, "is pure deductive reasoning."

"With a leak in it," Mrs. Forbes said.

He turned the screen around so that the flowers were showing as before. Then he sat down and with a curious intentness watched Mrs. Forbes arranging the cups and saucers on the tray.

"Sugar?" she asked, turning to Lymie. "Lemon?"

"No thank you," he said, both times.

"A purist," Mrs. Forbes said. She poured Professor Severance's tea without asking him how he liked it.

28

The night of the sorority dance it took Spud over an hour to dress. He and Lymie stood under the shower by turns, soaping themselves all over and washing the soap off again time after time, as if by this symbolical means they were getting rid of certain adolescent fears which had to do with women. Spud handed Lymie the soap and the nailbrush, and bent over with his hands braced against his knees. Lymie understood what was expected of him. He scrubbed until the skin from the base of Spud's neck to the end of his spine was red and glowing, and then turned around and submitted his own back to the same rough treatment.

When they were partly dressed, Spud got out the shoe polish and a rag and made Lymie stand with one foot on a chair, and then the other. Spud's shoes, already polished, were waiting with wooden shoe trees in them on the closet floor. He put them on, after he had finished with Lymie's, and tied the laces in a double knot. Then he attempted to cut his fingernails, which were thick and very tough. He could manage the fingers of his left hand without much difficulty but when he switched over, the nail scissors felt awkward and wrong. He made an impatient face, and Lymie took the scissors from him and finished the job.

Five whole minutes were consumed in picking out a tie for Spud, who had any number of them that he was especially fond of. The choice narrowed down finally to a blue bow tie with white polka dots and a knitted four-in-hand. Spud forced Lymie to pick out the one he thought Spud ought to wear, and Lymie chose the four-in-hand. Spud wore the bow tie, after explaining to Lymie all the reasons why it was better for this occasion, for a dance, than Lymie's choice. The bow tie had to be tied three times before the result was acceptable, and between the second and third attempt Spud decided that his collar was wrinkled, and changed to another white shirt. At nine o'clock he finished arranging the handkerchief in his breast pocket and was satisfied, or nearly satisfied, with what he saw in the mildewed mirror over his dresser. Lymie, who had been waiting for twenty minutes, said "Come on, let's go." A sudden wave of excitement carried both of them down the stairs, through the clutter in the front hall, and outside. The night air was crisp and cool, the November sky was blossoming with stars.

The sorority house was on the other side of the campus. From "302" the shortest way was through the university forestry, a narrow strip of woods which had sidewalks running through it and which at night was lighted at frequent intervals by street lamps. When the two boys emerged from the wood they were on the campus. The walk led them toward a series of new red brick Georgian buildings, each with dozens of false chimneys outlined against the starry sky. On the other side of the campus they passed a large unfinished building that was still under scaffolding—the new dormitory for men. As they came near the sorority house, they heard music.

"In Wisconsin," Spud said, "my sister used to go to dances at the lake club. She was fifteen and I was only nine or ten. They had dances every Saturday night. Sometimes my mother and father drove over in the car and watched, but I had to be in bed, because the dances didn't start until after nine o'clock. And I used to lie there on the screen porch and listen to the dance music. I used to wish I was older so I could be over there across the lake, like my sister. I used to wonder sometimes if I was ever going to be old enough to go to the lake club dances. Time seemed too slow then. One day lasted a lot longer than a week seems to now." Lymie put his right hand inside the pocket of Spud's coat, a thing he often did when they were walking together. Spud's fingers interlaced with his.

"Just when I was almost old enough to start going to the lake club dances," Spud continued, "we moved to Chicago. I don't know whether they still have them any more or not. I guess they probably do. They were nice. You could see the clubhouse through the trees, all lighted up with Japanese lanterns. And the music came over the water, the dance music. It was very plain. I used to lie awake listening to it."

Curtains were drawn across every window of the sorority house, upstairs and down. The two small lights on either side of the front door seemed brighter than usual. As Lymie and Spud turned in at the front walk, they could hear the orchestra playing "Oh, Katarina" rapturously. While they stood by the front door trying to make up their minds whether, since this was not like any ordinary evening, they ought to ring the bell, a boy came up the walk whistling, opened the door, and walked in. They went in after him.

There were a dozen boys standing in the front hall. Armstrong was among them. Lymie had never seen him anywhere except at the gymnasium and he wondered what would happen now if Armstrong, in his double-breasted dark blue suit, were to brace himself and do a handstand on the polished floor. He showed no signs of wanting to. He looked detached, very much at ease, very sure of himself. He recognized Spud with a slight flicker of surprise and spoke to him. Spud nodded coldly and went on to the coatroom, with Lymie in his wake.

All the hooks in the coatroom were taken and there were piles of coats on the floor. Spud took two of the coats off their hooks, dropped them on the floor, and hung his coat and Lymie's where they had been hanging. Then he combed his hair in front of the mirror in the lavatory, straightened his butterfly bow tie, and squared his shoulders until his coat collar came to rest against his neck. With his hand in the small of Lymie's back, pushing him, he came out into the hall once more.

On the opposite side of the stairs from the coatroom was another closet, the same size, where the house telephone was, and a set of electric bells which rang in the study rooms upstairs. Lymie pressed the ones marked *Davison: two long, one short* and *Forbes: one short, one long.* Then he came out into the hall again and stood next to Spud at the foot of the stairs. He had managed, during the walk across the campus, to mar the polish on his shoes. His long thin wrists hung down out of his sleeves, and his cowlick, that he had spent so much time plastering down with water, was sticking straight up. He stood stiffly with his back to the wide gilt mirror and didn't discover any of these flaws in his appearance.

Armstrong had gone now. His girl had come down the stairs in a white dress and he was dancing with her in the long living room, which was swept bare of rugs and furniture. The light everywhere downstairs was softened. There were yellow chrysanthemums on the white mantelpiece, and lighted candles. Oak leaves concealed the chandeliers. The dancers swung past each other performing intricate steps, their eyes half closed, their heads sometimes touching.

To pass the time while they were waiting, the boys in the front hall drew handkerchiefs out of their hip pockets and mopped their foreheads, or produced silver cigarette cases with an air of boredom, of disdain.

Lymie was expecting Hope and Sally to come down the stairs together, but Hope came first and alone. She was wearing a brown flowered chiffon dress that Lymie, who knew nothing about women's clothes, realized instantly was not right for her. It was not at all like the dresses the other girls were wearing.

Spud pulled Lymie's pants leg up a couple of inches in order to embarrass him, and although the effort succeeded, Hope didn't notice. She handed Lymie a small enamel compact, a lipstick, a tiny lace handkerchief, and said gravely, "Put these in your pocket." As they moved toward the entrance to the living room, the music ended. The couples stopped dancing and waited, in the subdued light. The girls were smiling with their eyes, or chattering. The boys reached inside their coats and drew their shirt sleeves up. Then, remembering where they were, they looked bored. The chaperons were in an alcove off the living room, playing bridge. The orchestra—a piano player, a drummer, saxophone, clarinet, trumpet, and slide trombone —was in another alcove partially concealed by potted palms. They made tentative noises with their instruments and then were silent. The dancers moved across the floor toward the dining room, toward the punch bowl, which was under the eye of Mrs. Sisson, the housemother. So far it had not been spiked. Lymie and Hope moved into a corner where they would not be noticed.

"People ought to dress up oftener," Hope said. "I've just decided that. It makes them nicer to live with. I stood in the upstairs hall and watched the girls go down." The girls whose fathers had not retired from business, she meant; the girls who could have new clothes whenever they wanted them. Aloud she said, "They looked so lovely, so unlike themselves," and raised her chin slightly, for she knew how she looked. She had seen herself in a full-length mirror in Bernice Crawford's room. Bernice had said, "You can't wear that, Davison. It doesn't look right on you!" and had offered to loan her a black dress with gold clips and a narrow gold belt, but the black dress was too tight. As Hope drew it off over her head she prayed that Lymie, who was always absent-minded anyway, would forget to come; that she herself would have an attack of appendicitis and be rushed to the hospital; that something, some merciful intervention would save her from having to go down the stairs. She decided to leave a note for Lymie and sneak out the back way, down the fire escape, and spend the rest of the evening in the Ship's Lantern, but it was already too late. Her bell rang, two longs and one short, as she was reaching into her closet for a coat.

"*You* look very nice tonight," she said to Lymie and before he had to answer her, the orchestra swung into the beginning of "Blue Skies." He put his arm around her and they started dancing. They were soon surrounded by other couples and in a moment Spud and Sally danced by. Spud danced very well and he looked smooth on the floor, Lymie thought. Spud didn't see them. His face when he danced was an unseeing mask. But Sally turned her head and called "Hello, Lymie, old socks!" She was wearing a peach-colored satin dress and her dark hair was piled on top of her head in a way that changed the shape of her face, made her look older, and emphasized her cheekbones and her wonderful dark brown velvet eyes. Lymie stepped on Hope's foot and apologized.

"Isn't Forbes *something!*" Hope exclaimed.

Lymie nodded without hearing what she had said. Here in this long dimly lighted room, where everyone had a price mark attached to him, he recognized Sally's value for the first time.

29

Lymie got home before Spud and passed through Dick Reinhart's room on the way to his own. Reinhart was in a sagging overstuffed chair and his feet, braced against his study table, were higher than his head. He looked up from Steve Rush's copy of *Psychopathia Sexualis* and said, "Well, Don Juan, did you have yourself a time?"

"I guess so," Lymie said. His mind was churning with images and excitement, and he wanted to talk to someone but not to Reinhart. "How late is it?" he asked.

"Quarter to one," Reinhart said. "Time all Phi Betes were in bed." His eyes were already searching for the place where he had stopped reading: *CASE 138. Z., age thirty-six, wholesale merchant; parents were said to have been healthy; physical and mental development normal; irrelevant children's diseases; at fourteen onanism of his own accord; began to. . . .*

Reinhart looked up from the page and saw that Lymie was still standing there. "You ought to read this book sometime," he said. "It's very interesting. I used to think I was a regular heller but compared to some of these guys I'm not so bad I guess. I could teach Sunday school if I wanted to."

Lymie went on to his own room and undressed. Then with his bathrobe pulled around him and his winter overcoat over his knees, he sat down in Spud's Morris chair and tried to read *The Eve of St. Agnes*, which Professor Severance had assigned for Monday. He got as far as the owl that for all his feathers was a-cold and then the page blurred, the words ran together like water. When his eyes focused again, he was looking at the row of suits, his and Spud's, hanging from the pole in the closet.

Lymie got up and went over to the closet and reached for the two victrola records which he kept on the shelf, under Spud's R.O.T.C. hat and spurs. He turned out the light and went into Pownell's room, which was also dark, and put one of the records on Pownell's victrola. The record was "Tales from the Vienna Woods" played by the Philadelphia Orchestra. As a rule he only played his records on Sunday morning early, when there was nobody around who might object to classical music. Now he drew a chair up and sat with his head between the doors of the machine. The room filled with waltzers, with girls turning and turning to the music, and he was in love with all of them, with their soft white arms, their small breasts, their dark eyes and their shadowy hair, which became Sally's hair, her coal-black bangs. She turned and smiled at him deliriously, and the peach-colored skirt flared out like the petals of a flower.

Lymie played the record twice and then turned the victrola off and sat with his forehead resting on the hard arm of the chair. There was a strange ache in his chest which he seemed to remember from a long time before, from when he was a child maybe. He sighed and then a few minutes later he sighed again.

Colter and Howard came in and passed through the room without turning the light on and without discovering him. Spud came home. Lymie recognized his step on the stairs and raised his head to listen. Spud stopped in Reinhart's room and Lymie heard them talking in low voices. A shoe dropped. Lymie was about to get up and go join them when he heard

Spud say quite distinctly, almost as if he were complaining: "I've seen it happen to a lot of guys but I somehow never thought it would happen to me."

"Yeah, I know," Reinhart said.

"The funny thing is," Spud said, "I don't know what to do about it."

"You don't have to do anything," Reinhart said. "You're hooked."

Lymie, listening, felt a double twinge of jealousy. The words could only mean one thing, no matter how you twisted them. And since it had to be that way, the least Spud could have done was to tell him about it first, not Dick Reinhart.

While Spud was in the bathroom brushing his teeth, Lymie crept up the stairs. He was, to all appearances, sound asleep when Spud crawled in beside him.

30

Dick Reinhart was from South Chicago. He had been raised a Catholic and wore around his neck a small silver scapular medal in the shape of a cross. It had been blessed by Father Ahrens of Hammond, Indiana, and was the equivalent of five holy and miraculous medals. At the top of the cross, in relief, were the head and shoulders of Our Lord, with the right hand raised in benediction and the left hand pointing to the Sacred Heart. This same symbol appeared again, larger, in the center of the cross. On the left arm were St. Joseph and the Infant Jesus. On the right was St. Christopher with his staff and the Infant Jesus on his shoulder. At the bottom of the cross was a full-length figure of the Blessed Virgin Mary, who was also on the reverse of the medal, supported by clouds, with the Infant Jesus in her arms and around her head a ring of seven stars.

When Dick was two years old his father died and about a year later his mother married again. Dick's stepfather didn't like children and so he was sent to live with his grandmother, a devout German woman, who used to sit beside him at the kitchen table and feed him from a big spoon, long after he was old enough to manage for himself. Although she had been dead for years now, whenever he wanted to he could still hear her voice saying, *Mund auf . . . Mund zu . . . kauen. . . .*

The year he was seventeen he fell in with a gang of hoodlums who were caught breaking into a freight car one winter night. The other boys took to their heels and got away, but Dick didn't run fast enough, and the judge sentenced him to six months in the state reformatory at St. Charles, Illinois. He made no effort to cover up the fact that he had been there, but when the boys at "302" tried to find out what it was like in the reformatory, he wouldn't tell them. He didn't seem to want to talk about it.

After he finished high school he got a job with a construction company in Cicero, Illinois, and was made foreman of a sewer gang. The men worked in continual danger of being buried under a cave-in. They were sullen and hard to handle. He never dared turn his back on them, for fear he would be hit over the head with a shovel, but he liked his job, even so, and he made friends with an Italian family who lived in the neighborhood. After the day was over he would sit in their kitchen drinking homemade wine with them.

When he had been working about six months, a man named Warner, who was in the office of the construction company, took a liking to him and taught him how to do elementary surveying. Warner was in his late forties and had been divorced twice. His second wife had been a parachute jumper and Warner was in love with her, he told Reinhart, but she tried two-timing him, so he walked out on her. When Warner found out that Reinhart liked to drink, he started taking Reinhart around with him at night. Warner could hold any amount of liquor without showing it, and he knew all the speakeasies in and around Chicago, and the women were crazy about him. No matter where they went, there were always three of them—Reinhart on one side of Warner and a woman on the other. He used to introduce Reinhart as his son, and he even talked about adopting him, but Reinhart never thought he would actually do it.

All this part of his life Reinhart told Spud one night when they were both staying up late in order to study for exams. Spud didn't get much studying done, but he didn't mind; he was finding out about life.

One day, Reinhart said, Warner called him into his office and asked him if he wouldn't like to go back to school. Unless he did, Warner said, there was no real future ahead of him in the construction business. He needed mathematics and a general background in engineering. Warner offered to give him the money for his books, tuition and room rent. The rest Reinhart would have to do for himself. The money was to be in the form of a loan, without interest. Reinhart could pay it back after he was out of college.

That fall he came down to the university and got a job in a drugstore, behind the soda fountain. There was no money in it; he worked five hours a day in exchange for his meals. Within a week he was pledged to a fraternity. It had a name like Beta Theta Pi, only one of the letters was wrong. The house was new and built of red brick with two-story white columns along the front of it, the architect having arrived at a compromise between the new Georgian architecture of the south campus and a Mississippi mansion. The house was out near the stadium, where land was cheaper. That meant a ten-minute walk to and from the buildings on the campus. The older fraternity houses were all within three or four blocks of the university. They had been built twenty years before, and they were not very impressive from the outside, but then they didn't have to be.

Reinhart had had no intention of joining a fraternity. What happened was that a kid who worked with him behind the soda fountain asked him to his fraternity house for a meal. The food was good and it was a beautiful warm night and that week there happened to be a full moon. After dinner a boy from Terre Haute played the banjo, somebody else played the piano, and the brothers stood around on the terrace outside the fraternity house, singing. It was exactly what Reinhart had always thought college would be like, and after three days of working behind a soda fountain, it made his eyes fill with tears.

A group of the boys took him indoors later and led him to a leather sofa in front of the big fireplace, where he could get a good look at the trophies on the mantel. When they produced a pledge button and asked him if he'd like to be one of them, he said he would, right away. He was afraid that if he hesitated, they'd change their minds about wanting him. Afterwards he realized that he ought to have asked Warner about it first. The trouble was, Warner had been a Phi Gam when he was in school and without seeing this beautiful new house or having a chance to get acquainted with the brothers, he was almost certain to think that Reinhart had made a mistake.

As soon as Rushing Week was over, the boy with the banjo cleared out. So did several others. They had graduated the year before, it seemed, but that fact wasn't made clear until now. The brothers who were left were not the ones Reinhart had liked especially. They were athletes, most of them, who had done well enough in high school to get their names and sometimes their pictures in the papers, but after they came to college they pulled a tendon or got water on the knee or became ineligible because of their grades. They stayed ineligible year after year and the greater part of the time they slept. Whenever Reinhart passed through the living room he found at least one of them stretched out on a leather couch, sound asleep with the radio going full blast in his ear.

Reinhart roomed with a senior who needed two and a half hours to graduate and was out tomcatting every night. Reinhart never saw anything of him; only his clothes strewn from one end of the study room to the other when Reinhart came down in the morning. The clothes, of course, had to be picked up, and there were pledge duties. Even though Reinhart was working and didn't have as much free time as the other freshmen, he had to sweep the front walk one week and the next week he had to see that the grate fire in the living room didn't go out, or to take the mail down to the railroad station at eleven-thirty at night, or to get up at six and go through the dorm waking the others at fifteen-minute intervals until seven-thirty. On Saturdays he had to wash windows and wax floors and clean study rooms with the other freshmen. The owner of the drugstore made him work longer hours than they had originally agreed upon, and he got so little sleep that the moment he opened a book his eyelids grew heavy. He began to fall behind in his engineering subjects.

Also, there was one sophomore who made trouble for all the pledges. They'd be in their study rooms after dinner and the sophomore would stick his head in, hoping that they'd gone out of the room and left the light on; or he'd want them to go on errands for him. He thought up more errands and gave more black marks than any other upperclassman in the fraternity. He seemed to have a particular dislike for Reinhart.

One night he came into Reinhart's room, backed him up against the wall, and gave him a lecture on his attitude: "Reinhart, you're one hell of a good guy, or could be if you weren't so goddam lazy. You're the laziest human being—I guess you're a human—that I've ever seen or heard of. You're so lazy. . . ." There was a great deal more of this, and Reinhart stood it all patiently. When the sophomore got through talking he pulled Reinhart across the hall into his own room and said to get busy and clean it up. Reinhart saw, in a bloody rage, that it was at least a two hours' job. The sophomore's room had been cleaned on Saturday and now you could hardly wade through it. He told the sophomore that he couldn't clean the room up; that he had to study. The sophomore gave him five more black marks for disobedience. When Reinhart said, "You dirty son of a bitch, clean it up yourself!" the sophomore took a poke at him and Reinhart laid him flat.

At this point in the story, Spud rolled his eyes and rocked with pleasure.

Half an hour later, Reinhart said, the upperclassmen held a special meeting in the chapter room, which was in the basement. When it was over, two of them came into his room and told him to be downstairs in front of the fireplace at quarter of eleven, for a paddling party. He took the pledge button out of his lapel and handed it to them, and the next day he moved into Mr. Dehner's rooming house, where there were no pledge duties, and where a sophomore was no better than anybody else.

Warner continued to send him money regularly all through his freshman year, and when summer vacation came around, Reinhart went back to his old job. Warner got married, very suddenly, on the Fourth of July, and his wife, a thin, rather nervous blonde, didn't like Reinhart. She thought he was a bad influence on Warner. In a moment of confidence he told Reinhart, but it would have been better if he hadn't, because Reinhart didn't like Warner's new wife very much either, and the more he saw of her the less he liked her. When Warner wanted him to go out drinking with them, on a Saturday night, Reinhart made excuses and finally Warner stopped asking him.

Toward the end of the summer Reinhart noticed, or thought he noticed, a change in the way Warner acted toward him. He made a very slight mistake on the job, something that was easily corrected and that ordinarily Warner wouldn't have paid any attention to. They had an argument about it, and Reinhart lost his temper. He apologized the next day, and Warner told him to forget it, but there was a speculative gleam in his eye which Reinhart saw several times after that. Apparently he thought Reinhart was trying to put something over on him.

Before Reinhart went back to school, Warner told him that his wife was going to have a baby. The baby was born early in April. It was a boy and Reinhart was very happy about it. He sent Warner a telegram, which Warner didn't answer for about ten days. The letter was typewritten and had been dictated to one of the stenographers in the office. At the bottom of the page, Warner had added a postscript in ink: he was very sorry but he had had a good many extra expenses lately and he wouldn't be able to send any more money.

It was very hot that April and the third floor was like an oven. The boys dragged their mattresses down to the second-story porch and slept there, until one night Reinhart, full of liquor, rolled off the porch and broke his arm. He had his scapular on when he fell, but then he could so easily have broken his neck. The next day the news of the accident was all over the campus and cars kept driving by with people hanging out to look. The other boys were proud, naturally. It gave their rooming house prestige. The first time Reinhart left for the campus with his arm in a sling, five of the boys just happened to be leaving at that moment and they surrounded him like a military escort of honor. For a long time afterward, people walking by "302" would say, "That's the place where the boy fell off the roof."

Without help from Warner, and unable to work in the drugstore with his arm in a cast, Reinhart was ready to drop out of school, but Mr. Dehner made an arrangement with him, apparently out of the kindness of his heart. Reinhart didn't in quire too closely into it. When his arm was well he washed windows and polished furniture for Mr. Dehner, made the beds in the dorm, and was general handy man for the place. In return for this, he was given his room free and enough money to eat on.

The work didn't take much time, but he was obliged to listen politely to Mr. Dehner, who lay in wait for him, in the front hall among the spinning wheels and the glass hens.

"Dick," he would begin, in a piercing whisper, "could I have a word with you? Steve Rush is—I know I've spoken to you about this before but he's two whole months behind now in his rent and something's got to be done. You know how fond I am of him and I don't want him to get thrown out of school or anything like that, but on the other hand there are certain fixed charges—light, heat, food for me, dog biscuit for Pooh-Bah, and the money I have to pay the bank every month—because they own this house, you know; I don't. I wouldn't take it if you gave it to me. It's too big and it's altogether too much of a responsibility. When I was younger perhaps but not now. Not at my age. I don't suppose the bank could sell it either, but then they don't want to, I'm sure. It's more profitable to rent it to some gullible person like me. You know the bank I mean? Not the bank across from the Co-op. The other one, the bank downtown. All they do there is sit around and clip coupons and give people two per cent interest on money they loan out for four and a half and five. It's shocking, I must say, and not like the antique business, but what can I do? I have to have a roof over my head, no matter what happens, and I have to eat. . . . What was I talking about? Dear me, I don't remember. Well, anyway, I don't want to keep you. You're sure you're dressed warmly enough? Because it's quite cold out. Much colder than it looks. You ought to have a sweater on, under your coat, in weather like this. It's strong healthy young creatures like you who die of pleurisy and pneumonia. . . ."

For two and a half years Reinhart had been listening to Mr. Dehner, who liked to talk to him because he was older than the other boys, and more patient. Dick was twenty-three now, and his hair was already getting thin. When he combed it, leaning over the washbowl, he would look down sometimes and count the hairs in the basin and shake his head sadly, but he never put oil on his scalp or did anything about it.

He went to Mass every Sunday but he also, from time to time, visited a house on South Maple Street. The eye of God must relax occasionally, and Dick seemed to know when this was about to happen. Once when he was waiting for a streetcar downtown a woman came along in a maroon-colored roadster and picked him up. They drove to a town thirty miles away, and spent the night there in the hotel. The woman was married and Dick knew that he had committed a sin with her, but after he had been to confession his sins no longer weighed on him.

Every so often he came home roaring drunk and sat up in bed and held an inquisition on himself and all the others. "You, Geraghty," he would say, "who do you think you're fooling? I saw you come in last night with that sly, satisfied look on your face. I know what you were up to. The first thing you know you'll get that poor girl in trouble, and then what'll you do? Where'll you get the money to have her taken care of? . . . And you, Howard, you Christer, isn't it about time you began sleeping with your hands outside the covers? . . . You needn't laugh, Colter. Don't think I don't know how you got through that physics course . . . Peters, what you need is a secret vice . . . And you, Latham, you're going to kill somebody some day, do you hear? You're going to kill somebody with your bare hands and you'll burn in hell for it . . . And you, Amsler, why don't you tell your mother to stay home? Because you don't dare, that's why. Because you're afraid of her, you damn, damn, double-damn fucking little coward. . . . I'm sorry, boys. I'm very sorry. I guess I've had a little too much to drink. Drink . . . Reinhart, you're drunk, you're pissyass drunk. You're so drunk the bed's going around. And whether you realize it or not . . . but it's so nice sometimes, it's such a wonderful, wonderful relief. . . ."

The boys didn't hold anything that he said against him afterwards, possibly because he sat around all the next day with his head in his hands and looked so gray and his misery was so acute that they could only feel sorry for him. But also because when Reinhart came home drunk, nobody escaped damnation and it cleared the air for a while.

31

It didn't seem to bother Spud or Sally that Lymie was with them a great deal of the time. They felt that in a way he was responsible for their happiness, and out of gratitude they included him in it. He accepted the role of the faithful friend, the devoted, unselfish intermediary. As such he was useful in many ways. When Sally met him on the Broad Walk between classes, she took all his books from him and shook them. If nothing fell out, it was Lymie's fault; he had lost the note somewhere, or left it in the wrong book, or was hiding it. When Spud had to ease his congested feelings by talking to somebody about Sally, there was Lymie, always at hand, always willing to listen, to encourage, and even (to a certain extent) sharing his delight, his wonder at what had happened to him and at the extraordinary change which had come over the world.

Sometimes all three of them sat in a booth in the back of the Ship's Lantern, and Spud and Sally talked about the house they were going to build as soon as they got married. Spud wanted a two-story sunken living room with a balcony. Sally agreed to the balcony but she was more concerned with the fireplace. It was to be stone, and very big. In addition to the dining room, kitchen, and usual number of upstairs bedrooms, there was also to be a library, a gun room, a billiard room, and a five-car garage. And the house was to be near the water, so that they could keep a sailboat. They drew plans and elevations on paper napkins or in Spud's loose-leaf notebook. So far as Lymie could make out, looking at these plans upside down, the house was of no recognizable style but merely enormous.

When they grew tired of arranging the future, Spud measured his hand against Sally's (she had stopped biting her nails) and was amazed each time at how much bigger a boy's hand is than a girl's. Or they sat and looked at each other and smiled and were sometimes pleased with the silence, or drove it away by talking a silly, meaningless language that they had invented between them. Because they felt free to say anything they wanted to in front of Lymie, they didn't realize that he was there, much of the time. But if he got up to go, they would get up too and go with him.

When the weather was bright they sometimes went walking along the Styx, a small creek that ran through the campus and across the town and out past the country club and then, a thin strip of woods along either side of it, into open farm land, the corn and wheat fields. Eventually they settled in some sunny spot and Spud would put his head in Sally's lap. Lymie lay on the ground near them, with his hands or his forearm cushioning his head, and looked up into the sky. If Sally wanted to kiss Spud, she went ahead and did it. And once when she was feeling particularly happy she leaned over and kissed Lymie. He took his handkerchief out and wiped his mouth with mock fastidiousness.

Sally made a face at him. "Lymie's an old woman-hater," she said. "He's the world's worst. But how could we ever get along without him?"

"Dandy," Spud said, rolling over. "We wouldn't have a bit of trouble. We need Lymie the way a cat needs two tails." He sat up then and picked a burr from his trousers and poked at Lymie and said, "Old friend, tell us a story."

"I don't know any stories," Lymie said.

"Yes, you do," Spud said. "Tell us that story you told me last summer on the beach. The one about the kid that fastened his sled on behind a big sleigh and couldn't get it loose."

"You mean 'The Snow Queen'," Lymie said. "That's too long. And anyway I don't remember all of it any more." He shielded his eyes from the sun with one hand. "I found a story in the library the other day. It was in a book of German legends but it's not a fairy story. It's about a man who had a coat that he liked very much. It made me think of you, Sally. But it wasn't the same kind of a coat, of course."

"Never mind what kind of a coat it was," Spud said. "Let's hear the story."

Lymie waited a moment before he began: "There was a man who had a coat which was woven in the design of a snakeskin but softer than velvet. He lived in a cold country but when he wore the coat he did not know whether it was winter or summer out, and at night when he fell asleep, it was with the coat spread over his blanket, so that he was as warm in his unheated balcony as his neighbors were who had tiled stoves to sleep on. And he still was not happy. He was perpetually examining his elbows to see whether they were beginning to wear out. He was haunted night and day by the thought that not this year perhaps or the next but certainly some day his beautiful snakeskin coat would wear out, and then he would be cold again."

Lymie turned his head slightly without taking his hand away, and saw that Spud had picked up a stick and was writing something with it on the bare ground. Sally was watching him. When they realized that he had stopped talking, Spud tossed the stick away and took Sally's hand instead. "Go on," he said. "We're listening."

"One night in a dream," Lymie continued, "the man saw himself giving the coat away to a beggar, and the light and the happiness from the dream lasted just long enough, after he had awakened, for him to see that that was what he must do with the coat—give it away. He sat all day with the coat across his knees, just inside the front door of his house, waiting. And although it was a part of town where many beggars lived and although seldom a day passed that one of them didn't come to his door asking for something, this day there wasn't a one.

"Toward nightfall, as he was about to give up his search, there were steps outside and he rushed out and found that a very rich man, with his horse and his two servants, was about to enter his house. He knew that the man was rich because he had fur on his collar and silver on his bridle and silver spurs on his heels. Without waiting to find out what had brought the rich man there, he pressed the coat on him and ran back into the house and locked the door. Almost immediately he realized that something was wrong, that he had acted in confusion, but by that time the rich man and his two servants were almost out of sight and he was ashamed to run through the streets after them.

"Instead of a coat to keep him warm that night, a coat which was woven in the design of a snakeskin but softer than velvet, he had only a slight hope that the rich man, in spite of the fur on his collar and the silver on his bridle and spurs, would understand the value of what had been given to him and find some use for it. And even so, he slept better than he had slept in a long time."

When Lymie finished, he took his hand away from his eyes. There was a silence and then Sally said, "I don't think I like that story very much. It's too sad. And besides, I don't know what it means exactly."

"It was just a story I read in that book I was telling you about. I read several of them. Do you want to hear any more?"

"No," Spud said. "One's plenty. I'm going to turn my attention, my undivided attention, to Miss Forbes. Are you happy, Miss Forbes?"

"About as happy as I ever expect to be," Sally said. "And you, Mr. Latham?"

"Tolerably happy," Spud said. "Just tolerably." He made a clucking noise with his tongue, and heaved a sigh as Sally pulled his head back into her lap.

After a time, Lymie grew restless and wandered off, but they soon came and found him. There is a species of cat that needs two tails.

32

One afternoon when Sally and Spud were sitting in a booth in the Ship's Lantern, Armstrong and his girl walked in. The girl's name was Eunice. She had fluffy light-brown hair and hazel eyes and at nineteen she was pretty in a sly, selfish way. She saw Sally and Spud, and without waiting to be asked, sat down with them. Armstrong moved in beside her. There was no room for Lymie when he appeared. Spud wanted to move over, so that he could squeeze in next to them, but Lymie insisted that he had a conference with his German instructor and fled.

Armstrong's girl was wearing his jeweled fraternity pin on her coral-pink cashmere sweater. She unpinned it for Sally to admire and Sally, turning it over to examine the safety clasp, dropped it.

"Oh, that's just like you, Forbes!" the other girl exclaimed.

"Well I didn't *go* to drop it," Sally said, trying to peer under the table. "It just slipped through my—"

"Don't step on it, anybody," Armstrong said. "Don't move your feet for a second while we look for it."

He and Spud slid out of their seats and got down on their knees in front of the booth and began searching.

"If that pin meant as much to you, Sally Forbes, as it does to me—" the girl said bitterly. Spud's head rose above the table. "Did you find it?" she asked anxiously.

He had the fraternity pin in his hand and put it on the edge of the table. As if the pin exercised a kind of foolish fascination for her, Sally started to pick it up again. The other girl snatched it from her and pinned it on the front of her sweater, above her heart. In her gratification at getting the pin back, she forgot to thank Spud.

Both boys got up, dusted the knees of their trousers, and then sat down again. The palms of Spud's hands were black from the dirt that he had been fingering, under the table. He tried to clean them off with his handkerchief. Armstrong's hands were still immaculate. He offered a package of Camels around. Spud shook his head but the girls each took one. Armstrong lit a match with his thumbnail and cupped his large hand around it as he held the match toward Eunice first and then for Sally. It was the gesture of a full-grown man, not a boy, and must have required practice.

Armstrong was a senior and a good campus politician. He had just missed out on being class president, in one of the off semesters. He looked well in his clothes and under all ordinary circumstances (that brief unpleasantness in the gymnasium hardly counted) he was easy and sure of himself. When people are too obviously and too variously blessed there is always a natural desire to find some flaw in them. The only thing that one could object to in Armstrong was that his full, heavy face, although handsome, had no character. Any number of boys in the university at that time could, from a distance, have been mistaken for him. And those qualities which made him outstanding in college probably meant that he would be a mediocrity later in life; though that didn't necessarily follow. He knew hundreds of people and had no trouble in keeping them straight. Boys kept nodding to him, on their way in or out of the Ship's Lantern with their dates, and he spoke to them by name. He spoke to the girls as well.

A tall thin boy with a crew haircut let his girl walk on ahead while he stopped and asked, "How are you, fella?"

"Not bad," Armstrong said.

"What did you get in that psychology exam Friday?"

"B minus," Armstrong said. "What did you get?"

"You're lying. You didn't get a B minus out of Lovat. He never gives higher than a C. No kidding, Army, what did you get?"

"I got a B minus, no kidding."

The tall boy put out his hand. "Let me feel you. I just want to touch a guy that got a B minus from Lovat."

"I got an A," Armstrong's girl said.

"That doesn't mean a thing," the tall boy said. "If you're a girl all you have to do is sit in the front row and cross your legs once in a while."

"You know Spud Latham?" Armstrong asked. "This is Bill Shearer."

"Glad to know you, Latham," the tall boy said and held out his hand. "I've seen you around."

There was no way that Spud could shake hands without revealing the dirt on the palm of his right hand. He nodded stiffly, and kept both hands under the table, making an easy enemy for the rest of his college life. The tall boy, flushing slightly, turned back to Armstrong.

"What about that accountancy problem for tomorrow?" he asked. "Have you done it yet? We could do it together."

"Okay," Armstrong said.

"Come over right after dinner."

"I can't," Armstrong said. "We've got a volley ball game with the A.T.O.'s."

"Who've they got?"

"Short and Harrigan and—"

"Harrigan's good."

"You're telling me. They've also got Safford, Rains—"

"Is Rains an A.T.O.? I thought he was a Delt?"

"That's his brother you're thinking of. His brother is a Delt. This guy's an A.T.O."

"I wonder why he didn't pledge Delta Tau Delta?"

"He could have, I guess," Armstrong said. "But you know how brothers are with each other. He probably wanted to show his independence so he came down to school and pledged A.T.O. But anyway, he's good."

"He's damn good," the tall boy said. "Herb Porter was talking about him. You know Porter, don't you?"

"Delta Chi?"

"Chi Psi."

"I meant Chi Psi. Yeah, I know him."

"Well, good luck anyway."

"Oh, we'll beat 'em," Armstrong said.

The tall boy shook his head admiringly. "You boys aren't overmodest, I'll say that for you."

Armstrong smiled. "Why don't you go bag your head, Shearer," he said.

"My girl's making motions. She'll give me hell if I don't. . . . Okay, fella. Be seeing you."

"Okay, fella," Armstrong said.

There were three of these conversations, all within fifteen minutes. Spud took no part in them. The girls talked to each other, but he sat back with a stiff expression on his face—the expression his mother put on sometimes when she found herself among women whose husbands were more successful than Mr. Latham, and whose diamond rings were more showy than hers. At four o'clock when Spud got up to go, Armstrong took the check and left with him. As soon as they had gone, Armstrong's girl leaned forward, as if she had something to say which must not be overheard. "Army noticed Spud at our house dance."

"Is that so?" Sally said.

"He likes Spud. He told me so. He thinks Spud is a very good guy. I do too, Sally. Only I think it's too bad that he doesn't belong to a fraternity. For your sake, I mean."

"I'll manage," Sally said.

"I don't mean that. Of course you'll manage. All I'm trying to say is that Spud *ought* to belong to a fraternity. I think it would be very good for him."

With her lips curling slightly, Sally said, "And very good for the fraternity."

When Lymie appeared on the top floor of the gymnasium later that afternoon, Spud and Armstrong were boxing. They went at it easy, and after a few minutes Army said that he had had enough, and pulled the gloves off and went back to the iron rings. Spud turned to the punching bag for a while and then he walked up to Lymie, took the rope away from him, and held out the pair of gloves that Armstrong had been using. "Here," he said, "put these on."

"Are you out of your mind?" Lymie asked.

"Go on." Spud unlaced one of the gloves. "Put your hand in here and shut up."

"I don't want to box with you."

"Why not?"

"Because I don't."

When the glove was on Lymie's hand, Spud wrapped the strings twice around Lymie's thin wrist and then tied them. "Hold out your other hand," he said.

"You'll forget," Lymie said, "and the first thing you know they'll be sending for the pulmotor."

"No, I won't, Lymie. Honestly. I'll take it easy. I promise. I just need somebody to practice with."

"Well, keep off my feet, whatever you do," Lymie said, and looked down at the gloves with distaste. Spud put on another pair and walked across the floor to the low parallel bars and held out his gloves for a sophomore named Hughes to tie.

"Now," he said, when he came back. "You want to fight with one foot flat, see? And your weight on the ball of the other foot. Or you can shuffle—the idea being that you always stand so that you can move somewhere else in a hurry."

"I see," Lymie said earnestly, and stood with one stockinged foot flat and his weight on the ball of the other.

"Watch me," Spud said. "Hold your arms like this and remember you've got to cover yourself no matter what happens." He stepped out of position and shifted Lymie's tense arms so that the elbows were in close to his sides and the gloves one in front of the other.

"Something tells me I'm going to get killed," Lymie said.

"Nothing's going to happen to you. Stop worrying."

"Okay," Lymie said, and led with his right and followed with his left and caught Spud almost but not quite unprepared.

"That's fine. Always get the first punch, if you can, for the psychological effect. . . . No, cover yourself. . . . That's it . . . there. . . . No . . . you're wide open, Lymie. . . . See, I could have taken your head off if I'd really wanted to. I could have knocked you cold. Keep covered . . . that's it . . . that's it. . . ."

Stepping backward, and then backward again, trying vainly to defend himself from the incessant rain of blows, Lymie tripped over his own feet and sat down.

"Did you hurt yourself?" Spud asked.

Lymie shook his head and got up again.

"You forgot what I told you about keeping on the balls of your feet. Keep moving, as if you were dancing almost."

When they stopped to rest, Lymie leaned against the wall, panting, his face red from the exertion. Spud turned away to the punching bag, and let fly all the energy he had been so carefully restraining. For a moment it seemed likely that the bag would break from its moorings and go flying across the gymnasium.

"Time," Spud said.

Lymie advanced from the wall to meet him. In the second round Spud tapped him on the nose harder than he had meant to. He dropped his arms immediately and said, "Oh God, Lymie, did I hurt you?"

Instead of stopping to feel the injury, Lymie lost his head and sailed into Spud with such a sudden and unexpected fury that he backed Spud against the brick wall. In Lymie's eyes was the clear light of murder. Spud made no effort to defend himself and after a few seconds Lymie stopped, confused by the lack of opposition. "What's the matter?" he asked.

Spud turned and leaned against the wall and laughed until he was weak. When he had gathered himself together again he saw that it was not Lymie's nose but his feelings that had been hurt. Spud put his arms around him and said, "There, Lymie, old socks, I didn't mean to laugh at you, honestly. I just couldn't help myself. The look on your face was so funny. You were doing right well, though. Fine, in fact. If you keep on like that, you'll be the next featherweight champion of the world. All you need is a few lessons."

But Lymie wouldn't box any more. He pulled the gloves off without bothering to untie them, and returned to the skipping rope. Later, after Spud was dressed and as they were leaving the gymnasium, Armstrong, whose locker was on the other side of the swimming pool, caught up with them and began talking about Christmas vacation, which was three weeks off. His remarks were addressed exclusively to Spud, although he had seen Lymie just as often upstairs and knew that they roomed together. Spud answered in monosyllables, and Lymie walked along with his hands in his pockets and his eyes off to the side—the nearest he could come to deafness, dumbness, blindness, and utter nonexistence.

He had to wait two days for Spud's reaction to these rather pointed attentions. The reference, when it came, was oblique, but Lymie was used to that. They were in their room studying, after supper, and although Spud's head was bent over his German reader, he had not turned a page for some time. When he was actually studying, you could always tell it. His eyes went back and forth continually between the day's assignment and the vocabulary at the back of the book.

"Do you think," he began, in a faraway voice, "—do you think Sally would like me better if I belonged to a fraternity?"

33

During Christmas vacation Mr. Peters' cousin, Miss Georgiana Binkerd, who was a very wealthy woman, came through Chicago. She had agreed to pay half the expense of Lymie's college education (Mr. Peters paid the other half) and now felt a proprietary interest in him. The three and a half hours that she allowed for having lunch with Mr. Peters and Lymie was ample, but it did not allow her to find out very much about them. From the fact that she had her hat on and was waiting when the taxi driver rang the bell in the vestibule of the apartment building, one might gather that Miss Binkerd had arrived in Chicago with her conclusions already formed (Mr. Peters was the black sheep of the family) and wished to leave with them intact.

Miss Binkerd was in her late forties and there was nothing about her to suggest that she had ever been any younger, but Mr. Peters could remember her when she was nine and had a brace on her right leg. Georgiana Binkerd's mother and his mother were half sisters, and as a boy he had been taken to visit the Ohio relatives every summer. His two little cousins used to tease him because he stuttered, and since they were both older than he was and both girls (so he couldn't hit them when he felt like it), they always got the best of every argument. At that time they lived outside of Cincinnati in a big square yellow brick farmhouse with a cupola on it and a double row of

Scotch pine trees leading from the road to the front porch. What Mr. Peters remembered best about this place was the long room which took up half of the downstairs and had parquet floors. It was intended as a formal drawing room but his uncle used it as a place to store feed. At night the rats ran all over the house, inside the walls. As a boy Mr. Peters used to lie awake listening to them and imagining that he had a shotgun in his hands.

He liked his aunt but he was afraid of his uncle, who had a beard and wore a gold collar button in his shirt on Sundays and didn't like children. During those years his uncle was a farmer. Later he made a fortune in railroad stock, lost it, and made another fortune in a patent medicine which was still on sale in drugstores, with his uncle's name and picture on it. They lived now—his aunt and Georgiana and her sister Carrie—in a big ugly house in the best residential section of Cincinnati. Mr. Peters had visited them there also, after he was grown. By that time the old man was stripped of his authority. No matter what he said, his wife and daughters corrected him. Under the guise of caring for his health, they had taken complete charge of his mind, his habits, the way he dressed, what he ate, his very life. When it finally dawned on the old man that he was never going to get any of these things back, he died. The women were still flourishing.

Georgiana Binkerd looked like her father except that he had been a large rawboned man and she was a small thin woman with pale selfish blue eyes that bulged slightly behind her rimless glasses. She had had infantile paralysis as a child and one leg was several inches shorter than the other and had no flesh on it. She was thrown off balance at every step and she walked with a nervous lurching which both Mr. Peters and Lymie, as they held the vestibule doors open for her, ignored. When they reached the cab, she turned to Lymie and put her claw-like hands on his shoulders and kissed him.

"Good-by, my dear! I wish you were my own child," she said, and with some awkwardness got her crippled body into the taxi.

Mr. Peters stepped in after her and closed the door from the inside. "The Union Station," he said, leaning forward and addressing the driver. From the tone of his voice one would have thought that it was he who had a train to make, not Miss Binkerd. She let it pass.

"Good-by, God bless you!" she called to Lymie, and he called back "Good-by, Cousin Georgiana," from the curbing. Though he continued to wave until the cab turned the corner, his mind was not on her but on her baum marten neckpiece, which was very lifelike. The cab turned south on Sheridan Road, then east for two blocks at Devon Avenue, then south again. Mr. Peters' mind was on the thick roll of American Express traveler's checks which he knew to be in Miss Binkerd's black leather purse.

"I can't tell you how much I've enjoyed this visit with you, Lymon," she said, swaying with the movement of the cab.

"It's been mighty nice having you," Mr. Peters said. His hand went toward the pocket where he kept his cigarettes, but he checked himself in time. "I've enjoyed every minute of it," he said. "And Lymie has too."

"He looks like his mother," Miss Binkerd said.

Mr. Peters nodded.

"I never saw Alma but the once, when I came for your mother's funeral," Miss Binkerd said. "But I remember her. She was a fine woman."

"She was indeed," Mr. Peters said. "Do you mind if I smoke?"

"It makes me cough," Miss Binkerd said.

Mr. Peters' hand withdrew from his pocket.

"There's one thing I'd like to say to you," Miss Binkerd announced impressively. "And that is, you deserve a great deal of credit for the way you've brought up your son all alone without any help."

"Thank you," Mr. Peters said.

"I watched him all through luncheon. He has very good manners. He could go among people anywhere and know what to do. The only thing that isn't as all right as it might be is his posture."

"I know," Mr. Peters said gloomily. "I nag him about it but it doesn't seem to do any good. He just won't stand up straight. Also, he's not strong, as you can see. He needs to be outdoors more. I've thought some lately of joining a country club if I can lay my hands on the money to do it. Golf is very good exercise and I could probably manage to play with him every week end during the summer months. It would do him a world of good, if I could only arrange it."

The sudden hard light that came into Miss Binkerd's eyes was not a reflection from her glasses. She had had a great deal of experience with remarks which could, if followed up, lead to a direct request for financial assistance.

"Lymie's a very nice boy the way he is," she said. "I wouldn't try to change him if I were you."

"Oh I don't," Mr. Peters said hastily. "I just meant that—"

"I've never been sold on country clubs. Cousin Will Binkerd belongs to one and I hear that the men drink in the locker rooms."

"Lymie wouldn't be likely to do that," Mr. Peters said. "He's not the type."

"No, I can see he isn't," Miss Binkerd said. "But even so. With boys you can't ever be sure. The quiet, well-behaved ones often cause their parents the most misery and heartache before they're through."

Mr. Peters suspected that this remark was directed obliquely at him, although as a boy he had not been conspicuously quiet or well-behaved.

"When Lymie was little," he said, "he used to have a terrible temper, and also he was very jealous. Especially of his mother. If he thought she was paying too much attention to some other child, he'd fly into a rage and she couldn't do a thing with him. Now that he's grown he never gives me the slightest trouble, except that I can't teach him the value of money. Slips right through his fingers."

"He comes by it honestly," Miss Binkerd said. This time there was no doubt whom the remark was directed toward. She peered out of the window of the taxi and said, "Is that the Edgewater Beach Hotel?"

Mr. Peters said that it was.

There was a silence which lasted for perhaps a minute and a half, and didn't seem to bother Miss Binkerd in the least. Mr. Peters, casting around uneasily in his mind for some way of ending it, said, "I wish we could have seen more of you—not just between trains."

"I know," she said. "Next time I'll pay you a real visit,

Lymon. But it's a long trip and I'm not as young as I once was, and it's hard for me to get around. I could have taken the sleeper from Kansas City to St. Louis, and not had to change stations. But I haven't seen Lymie since he was a year old, and Mother was curious to know how you were getting along."

"Well, you tell her we're getting along just fine," Mr. Peters said.

"I will," Miss Binkerd said, nodding. "I'll tell her. And she'll probably ask if you're still as handsome as you used to be. In that case I can fib a little."

She laughed and leaned back, happy that she had at last repaid him for calling her a spider when they were children, thirty-five years before.

34

The faces Spud saw around him were healthy, handsome, and intelligent but not too intelligent. There were no freaks in Armstrong's fraternity, nobody that you would ever need to be ashamed of.

The dining room walls were of solid oak paneling. The drapes were a plain dark red. There were six tables, and Armstrong sat at the head of one of them, with Spud on his right. Two boys from Chicago, a boy from Bloomington, another from Gallup, New Mexico, and a boy from Marietta, Ohio, filled out the table. The Chicago boys were talking about the new dance band at the Drake Hotel, where they had celebrated New Year's Eve. They may have been bragging when they talked about how drunk they had got, but in any case they weren't ashamed of it. They spoke with the natural, easy assurance of people who know that they are, socially speaking, the best; and that everywhere they go the best of everything will be reserved as a matter of course for them. Their attitude toward Spud could be gauged by the fact that they remembered to use his name each time that they spoke to him, by their polite interest in his description of the winter carnival at his home town in Wisconsin, and even by the way they offered him the rolls before they helped themselves. It was clear that he also belonged among the best people, otherwise Armstrong would never have asked him to dinner.

While the four student waiters cleared the tables after the main course, there was singing. First the university anthem, then a football song, then the fraternity sweetheart song, which was full of romantic feeling and required humming in places. Spud would have liked to join in but he didn't know the words and he also felt that, being a guest, he ought not to. He sat stiffly with his hands in his lap.

Between the salad and the dessert they sang again. They sang a long drawn-out dirty ballad which began:

Oh the old black bull came down from the mountain . . .
Houston . . . John Houston . . .

and ended with the old black bull, all tired out, going slowly back up the mountain. And then a song that somebody had put to the tune of "The Battle Hymn of the Republic:"

Mary Ann McCarthy she . . . went out to gather clams
Mary Ann McCarthy she . . . went out to gather clams
Mary Ann McCarthy SHE . . . went out to gather clams
But she didn't get a . . .

Forty-one spoons struck forty-one glass tumblers in unison, twice.

. . . clam
GLO-ry, glo-ry, hal-le-lu-jah

The voices soared out the refrain.

Glo-ry, glo-ry, hal-le-lu-jah
Glo-ry, glo-ry, hal-le-lu-jah
For she didn't get a . . .
(clink, clink)
. . . clam

The dessert was peach ice cream with chocolate cake on the side. It looked to Spud like the cake his mother made, and he bit into it hopefully. He was disappointed, but he ate it anyway.

A signal from Armstrong produced the simultaneous scraping of forty-two chairs. The boys hung back, hugging the wall until he and Spud were out of the dining room, and then closed in behind. Instead of going back into the living room, Armstrong took Spud on a tour of the two upper floors of the house. Spud was favorably impressed by the two bathrooms, each with a long row of washbowls, which made it unlikely that anybody would have to wait in line to shave; and by the study rooms. They opened off the long upstairs hallway, instead of one out of the other; there wouldn't be a steady traffic through them, the way there was through the rooms at "302." Each study room door had a padlock on it. At the rooming house Spud's favorite ties had a way of disappearing. They were not always in good condition when he found them, and two or three he had never been able to locate, though he suspected Howard. Padlocks were the only solution to the problem, obviously, and they were not, in Spud's mind, incompatible with brotherly love.

He was also struck by the fact that the dormitory, which was on the third floor, was the same temperature, or nearly so, as the rest of the house. In the daytime, Armstrong explained, the windows were kept closed, and there was heat from a couple of long radiators. At night when the windows were open, it was cold but not freezing. Spud nodded approvingly at the double-decker single beds, each with its cocoon of covers. He preferred sleeping by himself.

Study hours began at seven-thirty. The freshmen left the living room and many upperclassmen followed them. The dart game in the basement and the ping-pong table on the sun porch were deserted. There was no more shouting in the upstairs hall. In five minutes the house quieted down in a way that "302" seldom did before midnight.

Spud and Armstrong and two upperclassmen sat in front of the grate fire in the living room and talked. It was the time of year for arguing about basketball. Spud pretended that he was interested, but actually he was busy installing himself on the second floor, in a large corner room, with Lymie's desk next to his. He was wondering if it wouldn't work out better to put Lymie somewhere near by—down the hall, say, with another roommate for a change (better for Lymie, that is)—when the clock on the mantel struck eight. He got up to go, slipped his overcoat on in the front hall, tied his scarf correctly, shook hands all around, and left, very pleased with the house and the fraternal atmosphere, and rather pleased with himself.

A week later he was asked to dinner again and this time the

conversation in the living room was not about basketball but moved in a straight line. At the end of five minutes Armstrong produced a triangular pledge pin. Although Spud had been expecting it, he colored with embarrassment. It was not easy to explain, with four people looking at him, that he didn't have the money to join a fraternity.

"We can get around that difficulty," Armstrong said, "if you're willing to take a dishwasher's job or wait table." Then, correctly reading the look on Spud's face, he added, "It won't make any difference so far as your standing in the house is concerned. Also, it won't take much time from your studies. You'd naturally spend a certain amount of time sitting around after dinner, chewing the fat. The only thing you have to worry about is the hundred dollar initiation fee."

Spud nodded.

"Do you think you can manage that?" Armstrong asked.

"I'll have to think about it," Spud said.

Armstrong tried to press him, but he refused to commit himself, and his refusal was so firm that Armstrong gave way before it. "We're not in the habit of making open bids," he said. "And although in your case we're willing to make an exception, I think you ought to realize that there are plenty of guys—big men on campus—who would jump at the chance."

Spud did realize this, but he wasn't jumping, even so. He left, without a pledge button in his lapel, and went to the Ship's Lantern, where Sally and Lymie were waiting for him. They sat smiling while he described his evening, and once or twice a look passed between them which Spud intercepted. It meant nothing but that they were pleased with him for being so much like himself and so unlike anybody else, probably, who had ever lived. He began to suspect that there was some kind of a secret understanding between them, from which he was excluded.

"If you want to join it," Sally said, "go ahead. It's a good enough fraternity. The best there is, I guess. But of course they change. What's good one year isn't necessarily good the next. And I'm not sure I know what they mean by 'good' anyway."

"Wouldn't you be proud of me?" Spud asked.

"I am already," Sally said. "I won't love you any more because you've got a piece of fancy jewelry on your vest."

"You could wear it," Spud suggested.

"I don't need to," Sally said. "Everybody knows I've got you just where I want you."

"Humph," Spud said. What he wanted was for Lymie, who had everything to lose by the arrangement, or Sally, who had nothing to gain, to decide that it was to his best interest to join a fraternity. Then he would have been sure that he didn't want to. When Lymie said, "It's entirely up to you," Spud was thoroughly exasperated with both of them.

"It isn't entirely up to me," he exclaimed. "I don't know why you keep saying that. I can't walk off and leave you with that double room on your hands. If I go, you have to go too."

"So far," Lymie said, "nobody has asked me to join a fraternity."

"They will ask you," Spud said.

Sally said nothing. She had not said anything for a minute or so, but now Lymie was aware of her silence. It had changed its quality somehow. He smiled at her, by way of conveying that she didn't have to be tactful. He had known all along they were not going to ask him to join the fraternity. To Spud he said, "It doesn't really matter to me where I live, and it does to you, so you'd better decide."

"In the first place—" Spud began.

Lymie interrupted him. "I move this meeting be adjourned. All in favor say 'Aye.' "

"Aye," Sally said, peering into her compact.

"Motion carried," Lymie said, and picked up the check. "Forbes, it appears that you owe me a nickel. . . . Latham, twenty cents, please."

"Fifteen," Spud said. "Chocolate sundae is only fifteen."

"Twenty with nuts on it," Lymie said.

Spud put his right hand over his pants' pocket and then said, "How'd you like to treat me?"

"What would be the use of doing that?" Lymie asked.

"Well, I don't know," Spud said. "I thought you might enjoy it."

"Fork over," Lymie said.

"You're the tightest guy I ever knew," Spud said indignantly. "Barring none." He began systematically emptying all his pockets. There was no money in any of them.

35

When Reinhart offered to loan Spud a hundred dollars, he was so surprised that it didn't occur to him to ask questions. Even so, Reinhart felt that some explanation was necessary. "My aunt sent it to me," he said. "She does that once in a while. I don't happen to need it just now and I thought maybe you could use it." Reinhart who hadn't had a new suit in three years, who had no aunt, whose debts were as numerous as the sands of the sea.

"As a matter of fact I *could* use it," Spud said, and thought how wonderful it was that, just when you needed something very much (like a hundred dollars) along it came. For no reason. The exact amount. He was on the point of explaining to Reinhart about the fraternity, but then he remembered that Reinhart had had a bad experience with fraternities and would probably judge them all by the one he had been pledged to. "It's really damn nice of you," he said, letting gratitude take the place of explanations.

Reinhart shrugged. "I'm not giving it to you. It's a loan," he said, twisting a lock of hair between his thumb and forefinger.

"Even so," Spud said. He saw the rooming house, which he had for so long been ashamed of, and Reinhart slouched down in his overstuffed chair, with new eyes. It is foolish to contend that money doesn't make any difference. With a hundred dollars, the means of escape, in crisp clean bills in his right hand, Spud was no longer anxious to leave. After all, he had lived here for a year and a half, and these guys were his friends. When he needed help, they came across, without his even asking. Guys who did that were worth hanging on to.

Out of a sense of obligation Spud stayed and talked to Reinhart a few minutes longer and then walked across the campus to Sally's sorority house. She had told him that she was going home that afternoon, to get some clothes that she needed; but the hundred dollars had driven everything else out of Spud's mind. He had no intention of telling Sally about the loan, for that would have involved matters he didn't care to go into, such as how and when he was going to pay the money back. But he wanted to pin her down about the fraternity. He felt sure, although she had refused to influence his decision one way or the other, that she would be pleased if he were a fraternity man. After she had admitted this, he would tell her why he was going to turn the offer down.

He walked into the sorority house and pressed her bell, in the telephone closet. There was no answer. He pressed it a second time: *one short, one long.*

"Not in," a voice called down from upstairs.

Spud came out of the closet and stood at the foot of the stairs. "Know where she went?" he asked.

Hope Davison, with her hair in brown kid curlers, leaned over the banister. "Oh, hello, Spud. Don't I look a sight? Forbes has gone out. I think I heard her bell ring a little while ago, and then I guess she went out. Anyway she isn't here now."

"Was she with Lymie?" Spud asked up the stair well.

"I don't know," Hope said. "If she wasn't with you, she must have been with him. She's always with one or the other of you."

"Thanks," Spud said, and a second later she heard the front door slam.

During the first block, while he was calmly walking along, he beat Lymie to a pulp three times. With his bare hands he smashed Lymie's nose and closed his eyes and knocked his teeth in and made him spit blood. In the second block he hit Lymie in the stomach and knocked the wind out of him. Lymie crumpled, gasping, and Spud hit him again, on the way down. Lymie cried for mercy, begged for it, but Spud lifted him to his feet again and stood there a minute looking at him, at the guy that he had trusted, the guy that he had always thought was, of all the people he knew, his friend. He hit Lymie square on the chin with his bare knuckles, but he didn't feel a thing. All that he was conscious of was the change in Lymie's face. Lymie's eyes seemed to become glazed and then he seemed to wilt. In the following block Lymie came to, groaning. Spud knocked him down four more times and after that he made Lymie train with him every day. He made him drink lots of milk and fruit juices and eat fresh vegetables and get plenty of sleep and take exercise, and pretty soon Lymie began to put on weight. His chest filled out and his arms began to have some muscle and the first thing anybody knew, Lymie was a good boxer, quick and intelligent. He got to be a little better still, and soon he was the same size Spud was.

Then Spud took him on one day and beat the piss out of him. . . .

When Spud appeared on the top floor of the gymnasium Lymie was there, waiting for him. At the first sight of Lymie, Spud realized that it was no use. No matter how long Lymie trained, he would never be big enough for anybody to haul off and hit.

36

Professor Severance lived with his mother in a large white clapboard house which had been built in the 'eighties and was not far from the Forbeses' house. When Lymie rang the bell at six-thirty that same evening, a colored woman in a maid's uniform opened the door to him and took his coat and muffler. Then Professor Severance appeared and shook hands with him warmly. For the first few seconds Lymie missed the wooden desk and the low lecture platform. Being able to look straight into Professor Severance's eyes made him feel shy, and in the presence of a stranger. Through the double doorway he could see into a long brightly lighted living room, where an old woman sat waiting on a high-backed horsehair sofa.

It was a beautiful room, furnished with taste and with the help of money. The antique sofas and chairs, the little rosewood tables had been polished to a satiny texture. Against one wall was a square concert grand piano with the lid down, and on it were dozens of tiny painted clay figures—a Chinese wedding procession with men carrying banners, men bearing lanterns and spears, and horsemen riding behind the two palanquins of the bride and groom. Japanese prints hung at intervals around the room: a Hiroshige snow scene, the Hokusai great blue-and-white frothy wave on the point of breaking, two portraits of eighteenth century Japanese actors, a girl wading in blue water with her skirts tucked up to her knees; a group of women seated in a fragile black boat. In the bay window a card table had been set up with a bridge lamp shining on it, and cards laid out in rows, for solitaire.

For all its calm and elegance, the room was a battlefield. The card table, where Professor Severance had been sitting when Lymie arrived, and the copy of *Mansfield Park*, lying now on the table next to the sofa with a carved wooden paper knife in it, were sometimes the weapons with which Professor Severance and his mother attacked each other, sometimes the fortifications behind which they retired, when one or the other was momentarily victorious. The smoke of stale quarrels hung on the air. Professor Severance led Lymie over to the horsehair sofa and said, "Mother, this is Mr. Peters."

"How do you do?" the old woman said, in a voice that was clearer and stronger than Lymie had expected. Looking down at her, at the massive head and yellowish white hair and the colorless lips, Lymie thought how much like a St. Bernard she looked, except that the eyes were not only sad but sick as well. Even so, they managed a sudden yellow gleam that charmed him. Mrs. Severance sat, large and shapeless, in a gray silk dress with her long-fringed silk shawl slipping from her shoulders. A carved cane leaned against the corner of the sofa.

"Sit here beside me," the old woman said, patting the horsehair seat. "I want to talk to you. My son tells me you're a friend of Sally Forbes. You're in love with her, aren't you? It's all right. You don't have to blush like that. She's a darling girl. I've known her ever since she was born. She'll make you a good wife, I'm sure, though she's not as pretty as her mother was. Her mother was a real beauty. I always wanted her to marry William. I've never forgiven her for marrying Professor Forbes instead."

"My mother is of the opinion that everybody should get married," Professor Severance explained with a crisp smile. "The sooner the better."

"The sooner the better," Mrs. Severance said, nodding. "Look at William. He'll be forty-three next June and he gets more trying to live with every day of his life."

"I don't believe that's true," Professor Severance said mildly. "I should have said that I'm probably quite considerate, even-tempered, and in fact very little trouble to anybody."

Instead of answering him, Mrs. Severance asked Lymie how old he was, and he told her.

"Nineteen . . . Think of it!" she exclaimed. "I would have said he was fifteen at the most, wouldn't you, William?"

"No, I think he looks somewhere between eighteen and nineteen."

"At the most, fifteen," Mrs. Severance repeated. Then to her son, as if Lymie had suddenly vanished from the room, "Your students get younger and younger. When we first moved here, there weren't any that were fifteen years old. Or if there were, I don't remember them."

"But Mr. Peters isn't that young, Mother," Professor Severance said patiently. "He's just told you that he was nineteen."

"You're too young to be away from home," Mrs. Severance said, shaking her head at Lymie. "I feel quite certain of it. I dare say your mother feels the same way."

"My mother is dead," Lymie said.

The old woman's face took on a look of almost total blankness, as if she were listening to footsteps in the upstairs hall, or in some empty corridor of her mind. Then she looked at Lymie and smiled. "What a pity!" she exclaimed, reaching out toward him. "I'm so sorry!" Her clasp was warm and friendly. "What thin hands he has," she said, turning to her son. "They're as small and thin as a girl's."

Professor Severance rested his head on the back of his chair and half closing his eyes, said, "I've been trying most of my life to convince my mother, or to suggest, rather—for the suggestion by itself, adequately conveyed, would probably be enough—that it isn't polite to make personal remarks."

"Oh, pshaw!" Mrs. Severance exclaimed. "Mr. Peters is not offended, are you, Mr. Peters?"

Lymie shook his head.

"Besides," the old woman said, "I only say what I think, which is a compliment."

Professor Severance cleared his throat. The sound was noncommittal.

"William also tells me that you like poetry," she said. "Why don't you become a professor? It's a very pleasant life. So safe. Nothing to worry about as long as you live. You don't make any money, of course, but I can tell just by looking at you that you'll never make much money anyway. You're not the type. If I were you I wouldn't try. Settle down here and teach. William will tell you just how to go about it."

"Yes," Professor Severance said, nodding. "It's very simple. And I'm sure Mr. Peters would make an excellent, perhaps even an inspired, teacher, but he may prefer to be a poet instead."

"What nonsense," Mrs. Severance said. Twisting in irritation, she gathered the fringes of her shawl into a rope which she laid across her knees. "You can't starve in a garret these days. There aren't any. They've all been converted into apartments that cost thirty-five or forty dollars a month. Besides, you mustn't pay any attention to what William says. His students probably have a certain amount of respect for him, because he's read so much, but he's only a child, I assure you, in spite of all those books in his study. I'm sure that in many ways you are older than he is, Mr. Peters. Far older." She looked down at the large pink cameo which was pinned on the front of her dress and straightened it. "If this attachment between you and Sally Forbes doesn't work out," she said suddenly, "I wish you'd let me know. Because I have a granddaughter coming along, a dear sweet girl, and you might like her even better. She's fifteen now—just your age."

Professor Severance's eyebrows flew upwards and then settled again, into their usual repose.

"My niece lives in Virginia," he said. "I think you're safe enough, Mr. Peters. For the time being."

"Let me show you her picture," Mrs. Severance said. She reached across *Mansfield Park* and took a small framed photograph and handed it to Lymie. The photograph was tinted slightly, and he saw by the head and shoulders that Mrs. Severance's granddaughter had been even younger, probably about thirteen when the picture was taken. Compared to Sally she was not very interesting.

"It's very nice," he said, rather as if he had been asked to admire an antique gold bracelet or an amethyst ring.

"She lives just outside of Charlottesville in a beautiful old house that William's brother has bought there, with box hedges and holly trees and I don't know—I can't remember how many rooms with fireplaces in them. But anyway, she's coming for a visit in the spring. I'll see that you meet her."

The colored woman appeared in the doorway to the dining room and said, "Dinner is served."

"All right, Hattie," Professor Severance said, nodding.

Mrs. Severance placed the picture on the table and reached for her cane. With some difficulty she lifted her heavy bulk from the sofa. Then, leaning on the cane and with one hand through Lymie's arm, she stalked slowly toward the dining room.

The dining room table was large enough for eight people. Only three places were set, far apart, on a white damask cloth, the corners of which almost touched the floor. Between the two silver candlesticks in the center of the table was a crystal bowl filled with yellow and lavender stock. The air was heavy from the odor of the flowers, and Lymie had an uneasy feeling as he held Mrs. Severance's chair out for her and helped her dispose of the cane, that there were more people in the room than just the three of them. Even after he sat down, the feeling persisted (The fear of death, could it have been, standing patiently behind Mrs. Severance's chair? And behind her son's, the fear of being left alone with his decks of cards, his never-finished game of solitaire?) until the swinging door to the pantry flew open and the colored woman reappeared with a fourteen-pound turkey on an enormous blue china platter.

"I hope you're hungry," Mrs. Severance said. "It always exasperates me so when people don't eat."

No one saw or was conscious of the figure behind Lymie's chair.

37

When Spud appeared at "302" that night there was a pledge button in his lapel. Freeman and Amsler noticed it and withdrew from him as if he had contracted some fatal disease. They told Reinhart, who came into Spud's room with a puzzled expression on his face and stood watching Spud pack. He had emptied out his dresser drawers and his clothes covered the tops of both desks. Reinhart handed him a pile of shirts, when he saw that Spud was ready for them, and then a handful of socks, rolled up tight in the shape of an egg. There was absolutely no reason for Spud to avoid Reinhart's eyes. Unless he was drunk, Reinhart never made any comment, never offered advice. Nevertheless Spud took the things without looking at him.

A big suitcase and a canvas duffelbag held all of Spud's

earthly possessions. When he had finished packing, the room was tidy but it had a disturbed air and seemed larger than usual. Reinhart took the suitcase, Spud the duffelbag, which was full of books and soiled clothes, and very heavy. They passed by several open doors but no one spoke to them, no head was raised. At the front porch of the fraternity house Reinhart stopped and put the suitcase down. When Spud asked him to come in, he shook his head. "I'll be seeing you," he said, and went off down the walk.

The brothers were expecting Spud and gathered around him in a cluster at the front door and said, "Congratulations, boy. We're glad to have you with us!" One after another gave him (their little fingers interlocking) the pledge grip.

Armstrong wasn't there. He had taken his girl to a movie, and one of the other boys led Spud upstairs to his room. It was not the corner one, as he had hoped, but it was a large square room, with three windows, a comfortable chair for reading, two study tables, two dressers, green curtains, and plain cream-colored walls. His roommate turned out to be a boy named Shorty Stevenson, who was majoring in economics and wore glasses.

By ten o'clock Spud had finished putting his clothes away and he sat down at his new desk. His pencils, blotter, fountain pen, ruler, and ink were in their usual exact arrangement. His chemistry book was open before him, at the next day's assignment. The only thing that disturbed his sense of order was the boy who sat studying quietly, four feet away. Shorty Stevenson had on a maroon-colored bathrobe over green and orange striped pajamas. Lymie's bathrobe was blue and he always wore white pajamas.

In a sudden reversal of feeling Spud wanted to empty all the bureau drawers and start packing again. This isn't right, any of it, he said to himself.

He began to think about Lymie coming home to the bare ugly room on the other side of town. He saw the boys meeting him—Reinhart or Colter or Howard, maybe, or Freeman—at the head of the stairs, and telling him what had happened. Spud saw Lymie trying to pretend that it didn't matter, that he wasn't upset by it; and then a few minutes later, undressing and getting ready for bed and going up the stairs alone.

For the first time it crossed Spud's mind that he could have waited. He should have stayed there until Lymie got home from Professor Severance's. Or at least left a note for Lymie. It was that, he decided, that was causing him all this uneasiness. And in the next second he recognized that it had nothing to do with Lymie but only with himself; that he was frightened. He didn't like strangers and never had liked them.

All he had to do was to repack his things. But what would Shorty Stevenson think if he got up now and started taking shirts and socks and underwear out of the dresser and putting them back in an empty suitcase?

In a kind of slow panic Spud took his watch off, wound it, and placed it on the desk next to his chemistry book. Then he switched the goosenecked student lamp on and began to read. Sometimes his lips moved, shaping words and formulae. And sometimes his mind veered off toward things that had nothing to do with chemistry: *Why was he here where he didn't want to be? Who made him do it?*

They were both reasonable questions.

38

When Lymie managed through Reinhart to loan Spud a hundred dollars, so that he could join the fraternity if he wanted to, Lymie believed that he was acting under a wholly unselfish impulse. But if that was true, why wasn't Spud happy afterward? Why didn't the unselfish act (it had taken Lymie two long dreary summers to save that hundred dollars) lead to some good? From that which is genuinely good, good only ought to flow; not misery and misunderstanding.

The next morning when Spud awoke he was still lost, still unsure what he wanted to do. He was afraid to tell Armstrong that he had changed his mind. Armstrong would think he was crazy. They had given him all the time in the world to decide, and there was no way for them to know that he had done it all in a rush. The best thing to do, he decided finally, was to get Lymie into the fraternity as soon as possible.

He asked Lymie to dinner on guest night and Lymie came. He was all dressed up but with his shoes scuffed as usual, and the shirt he was wearing was not entirely clean. Lymie would never understand, Spud thought sadly looking across the table at him, how things like that counted against you. Lymie's feelings were deeply hurt, from the look in his eyes, and from the care that he took to make everything seem natural between them. But that, Spud decided, they could straighten out later, after Lymie had moved into the fraternity house. Spud didn't know quite how to suggest this to Armstrong but he figured that as soon as Armstrong and the rest of the brothers saw how bright Lymie was, they'd take him into the living room and pledge him.

After dinner Spud showed Lymie over the house. Lymie admired Spud's room and asked to be shown where he slept in the dorm. When Spud pressed him for his approval he said reluctantly that the house was very nice and that he liked the fellows very much. Spud revealed his plans, and Lymie shook his head. It was a fine idea, he said, but he was sure that they wouldn't ask him to join the fraternity.

He was invited for two guest nights in a row, and then he came and went casually. Sometimes he was at the fraternity house for a meal when the boys were on their ordinary behavior. They came down to the dining room helter-skelter, some of them without ties and their shirt collars open, and fought over second helpings and sang off key deliberately. Sometimes he and Spud studied together in Spud's room, of an evening. The boys in the fraternity were friendly toward Lymie, and accepted him, but as an outsider, a foreigner with all the proper credentials. Their attitude was a good enough indication of what he could expect, socially, the rest of his life. If he had been the kind of person who mixes easily and makes a good first impression, he wouldn't have walked past the plate glass window of LeClerc's pastry shop, years before, when he was in high school. Nor would he have felt the need of a special entrance to the iron fence that surrounded the yard outside his own house, when he was a child. He would have used the front gate, like other people.

39

As soon as Spud moved out of "302" the closet in his and Lymie's room, which had always seemed ample, contracted. It was too small even for Lymie's clothes. It was also very disorderly. Lymie made an effort to straighten it occasionally, though his idea of order was not Spud's. He didn't really mind confusion, but he was afraid that Spud might come over to see him and be upset because the closet wasn't the way he had always kept it. Day after day passed and Spud didn't show up. The closet became a catchall. Shoes, bedroom slippers, rubbers, a battered felt hat that belonged to nobody, wire coat hangers, a box of stale Nabiscos, shirts, underwear, socks, handkerchiefs, a suitcase, a crinkled necktie . . . all this and more was in the pile on the closet floor. The closet became indistinguishable from all the others on the second floor of the rooming house. When Lymie undressed at night, he hung his trousers upside down, by the cuffs in a dresser drawer. In the morning he left his pajamas where he stepped out of them.

He saw Spud every afternoon at the gymnasium. One day when Spud found somebody to box with, he brought his gloves over for Lymie to tie, as usual, but he stood looking past Lymie at the trapeze net. Lymie observed that his eyes had a cold glitter in them. When he finished tying the gloves, Spud walked away. At first Lymie thought that Spud must be sore at somebody else, since he himself had done nothing. But from that moment, Spud avoided looking at Lymie or speaking to him. Although Lymie was bewildered, he kept on coming to the gymnasium, day after day. The fact that he still had access to Spud's hands was a comfort to him. It was at least something. Afterward, while Spud was below in the shower room, he waited by the open locker. When Spud had finished dressing he managed, without either looking at Lymie or speaking to him, to indicate that he was ready to go. It would have been easy for him to hunt up Armstrong and walk home with him, instead of with Lymie, but he didn't. They weighed themselves in the front hall, and then, as they walked away from the gymnasium, Lymie usually made some careful, almost natural remark, to which Spud didn't reply.

Lymie went to bed every night at ten o'clock, as usual, but he had trouble getting to sleep. He was conscious of the cold all around the edges of the bed. Wherever he put out a hand or a bare foot, it was icy cold and it remained that way.

If you take a puppy away from the litter you can keep it from whimpering at night by bedding it down with an alarm clock and a hot water bottle. Deceived by the warmth, it will accept the ticking of the clock for the beating of its mother's heart. Lymie learned to make similar sad substitutions. The other pillow, the one Spud had slept on, at Lymie's back warmed him almost as quickly as a living body. By an effort of the imagination, his own arm, thrown lightly across his chest, became Spud's arm, and then he could sleep.

But it was sleep of a different kind, restless and uneasy. The dreams that came to him were troubled, even the ones that began in happiness and security. Usually when he awoke he could remember only certain threads—fragments of what had frightened him. But there was one dream that remained intact in his mind. He was standing on a street corner with Mrs. Latham. They were looking at a circus parade and they just had time, after the calliope had passed, to run to the next corner and see the parade all over again, coming back. Only this time the circus animals swerved and marched up onto the sidewalk, so that he was crowded back against a high wire netting which stretched between the sidewalk and the street. He left Mrs. Latham standing there and went into a large hotel, and downstairs to the men's room, where he urinated. When he came back the parade was over and Mrs. Latham was gone. He asked several people about her and one man pointed to a railway trestle, which was enclosed, with five stories built on top of the level where the trains ran. She was up there. Somebody, a man, a man with an evil face, had grabbed hold of her, while he was in the hotel, and had taken her away and now she was in trouble and it was his fault. He should never have left her alone on the street corner while the parade was passing by.

He thought he saw her at one of the windows high up on the trestle but it might not have been Mrs. Latham. There were many windows and people kept appearing at them, sinister people. The woman he saw, the one who appeared to be in such distress, might have been somebody else. The woman he saw in the street, later, *was* Mrs. Latham. She had disguised herself with a red wig, so that she looked much younger and like the women who used to come to see his father, the women whose voices were too loud and whose dresses kept coming up over their knees. He knew her, even so, but he couldn't go to her. She went up to an elderly man who was walking with his wife and put her arms around him and begged him to save her, but the man didn't understand, and his wife interfered, and people gathered around them in the street, so that there was no hope, even before the man with the evil face came down once more from the high trestle.

Whether the man took her away or what happened to her, Lymie didn't know because he found himself in a stony field. The field stretched as far as the eye could see, and he was still there, walking and walking, when the morning light awakened him.

40

During the last days of February, after a heavy snow, the thermometer went down to zero at night and rose only a few degrees in the daytime. The wind was from the north and nothing, not even a coonskin coat, was adequate protection against it.

The boys at "302" slept with their overcoats spread over the foot of their beds, and woke in the night and complained bitterly of the cold. Amsler, who had been sleeping alone, moved into Lymie's bed. Though Lymie had every reason to be grateful for human warmth, he waited until Amsler was asleep and then withdrew shivering to the farthest edge of the bed. For an hour and a half he lay there, not daring to move. Then he slipped out of bed and crept downstairs and spent the rest of the night in Reinhart's big chair, with two coats spread over him. At six o'clock, stiff with cold, and lightheaded from lack of sleep, he went into his own room and sat down at the desk. *Whatever it is that keeps you away,* he wrote, *so that we aren't able to talk to each other like we used to, I think it's time we did something about it. If I've done anything to offend you, I'm sorry. You haven't done anything to me. And even if you had it wouldn't make any difference. Since my mother died you're the only person who has meant very much to me . . .*

That afternoon, when Professor Severance started writing questions on the blackboard, the two seats on either side of Lymie were still vacant. Twenty minutes after the examination had begun, the classroom door opened and Sally tiptoed in and took her seat in the second row, next to Lymie. Her cheeks were red with cold. She looked at the questions on the board and then, in a slightly dazed way, at the blank examination book on the arm of her seat.

She barely nodded to Lymie. "The old English madrigal," she wrote, "was an amatory poem to be sung by three or more voices." The musical implications, Professor Severance had once said, were not to be lost sight of. Fortunately, she hadn't lost sight of them.

It was some time before Sally discovered the large question mark on Lymie's blotter. She shook her silver fountain pen, which had become clogged, and wrote "Hope" on the edge of her own blotter. Lymie had to wait until they emerged from the room where the examination was being held, for further enlightenment.

"The weirdest thing," Sally exclaimed as she closed the door behind her. "Hope had an exam in botany this morning, and she wasn't prepared for it—I was over at the house for supper last night, but I've been living at home. She told me she was going to tell Mrs. Sisson that she had appendicitis, and spend the morning in bed. And this noon I met Bernice Crawford and she said that Mrs. Sisson had called Dr. Rogers—you know that baldheaded little man with the goatee, the one that's always pinching people. Girls, I mean. I don't think he pinches boys. But anyway, he rushed Hope off to the hospital and took her appendix out before lunch. That's why I was late. I went to see her. She was still under the anesthetic, but they said she was coming along all right. Only there was nothing wrong with her, and she can't afford an operation. My God, Lymie, the things people get themselves into!"

"Maybe she really did have appendicitis," Lymie said.

"In a pig's ear!"

The door opened and Lymie moved to one side, so that two girls could get past.

"What are you looking so bedraggled about?" Sally asked.

"Who, me?" Lymie asked. "I feel fine."

"You don't look it. Maybe you'd better have your appendix out too."

"I can't," Lymie said. "I forgot to join the Hospital Association."

"Well then, you'd better not," Sally said.

He brought out the note and said, "Would you mind giving this to Spud?"

"Won't you be seeing him at the gym?"

Lymie hesitated and then shook his head. "Not this afternoon," he said. "I've got some work to do. I have to study for an hour exam."

"You aren't sore at each other?"

"No," Lymie said.

She sighed and put the envelope in her pocket. "I won't be seeing him until after supper probably. Do you know, Lymie, when I first knew you, you were different from the way you are now."

"In what way?"

"Well," she said slowly, "for one thing, you didn't tell lies."

41

Lymie went up to the dorm early that night, knowing that if Spud were coming it would have been before this, because pledges were not allowed out of the fraternity house on a week night after seven-thirty. He was hoping that he could fall asleep immediately and not know when Amsler came, but he turned and turned in the cold bed, without making a place for himself, and after awhile, he heard steps on the stairs. The door swung open and Howard and Geraghty came in.

"It's the whining," Geraghty said, as the door swung shut behind him. "If it wasn't for the whining I wouldn't care so much one way or the other. But this always wanting to know where you've been and who you were with and why you didn't call her up. It's enough to drive a guy nuts."

A bed creaked and Howard said, "Jesus, it's cold!"

"Somebody must have told her about Louise," Geraghty said mournfully. "She didn't say so but I'm pretty sure that's what must have happened."

Howard yawned. "Go to sleep," he said.

So Geraghty had a new girl, Lymie thought. And he hadn't got the old one in trouble after all, in spite of Reinhart's prophecies. Or maybe because of them. But why should Geraghty get tired of a girl who was so pretty and loving? Did he just want a change? And what would happen when Geraghty got tired of his new girl?

Lymie was not really interested in Geraghty or Geraghty's girls; he pulled the other pillow around to his back and waited. In a few minutes the door swung open again. It was Steve Rush this time. Freeman came shortly afterward. Then Pownell marched in, and Reinhart after him. Their beds creaked, and there was a soft rustling of covers as they settled down under the weight of coats and comforters. The wind tore at the corners of the house as if it had some personal spite against it and against all the people lying awake and asleep under the mansard roof. A floor board contracted. Lymie thought of Hope over in the university hospital. He heard the chimes in the Law Building strike midnight and wondered where Amsler was.

Lymie was hanging on the edge of sleep when he heard a step on the stairs, and it was something that he had imagined so many times the last few weeks that he didn't believe in it; not until the door swung wide open and the step (which couldn't be anyone else's) came nearer and nearer. Lymie waited. He felt the covers being raised, and then the bed sinking down on the other side, exactly as he had imagined it. Then, lifted on a great wave of unbelieving happiness, he turned suddenly and found Spud there beside him.

Spud was in his underwear and he was shivering. "My God, it's cold," he said. He pushed the pillow aside, and dug his chin in Lymie's shoulder.

Anybody else in the world, Lymie thought, anybody but Spud would have said something, would at least have explained that he was sorry. But Spud hated explanations and besides there was no need for them. It was enough that Spud was here, whether for good or just for this once; that it was Spud's arm he felt now across his chest.

Lymie lay back on the wave of happiness and was supported by it. The bed had grown warm all around him. Spud's breathing deepened and became slower. His chest rose and fell more quietly, rose and fell in the breathing of sleep. Lymie, stretched out beside him, wished that it were possible to die, with this fullness in his heart for which there were no words and couldn't ever be. All that he had ever wanted, he had now. All that was lost had come back to him, just because he had been patient.

He heard Amsler come in and go to his own bed. Then, managing to keep Spud's warm foot against his, Lymie turned and lay on his back, so that Spud's arm would go farther around him. He made no effort to go to sleep, and sleep when it came to him was sudden. One minute he was wide awake thinking, and the next he was lying unconscious, on his back, as if he had been felled by a heavy blow.

BOOK FOUR

A Reflection from the Sky

42

THOUGH it came from human throats the roar was animal. Certain voices rose above it screaming

Come on, colored boy

but the two fighters exchanging blow for blow didn't hear. Except when the referee came between them saying

Break it up, break it up

they were alone, under the smoky white light from the reflectors. They were in a world of silence and one of them was tired.

Uppercut, Francis . . . Old Man Uppercut . . . the head . . . up . . . up

He's tired too, Rudy

The head, not down there . . . up . . . up . . . throw it in his face

Oooh, that dirty nigger

The ice cream man moved in a world of noise, looking for upraised hands, for the quick turn of a head. At that moment all heads were turned away from him, all eyes were on the ring. The crowd moaned and moaned again as the white boy sank from the ropes to the canvas. In the back of the balcony a baby started crying. The referee waved the Negro to a neutral corner. On the count of seven the white boy rose to his knees. At the count of nine he was on his feet again but groggy.

Finish him off, Francis

Not there . . . up . . . up . . . atsa baby . . . a little higher and he's through

Come on, Francis . . . bring it up . . . up . . . that's it . . . cute . . . more

Good-by, Rudy

What hit him

Fall down, Rudy, you're through

Stop the fight
Come on, Francis . . . finish up fast
In the belly
That's it . . . downstairs, Rudy
He don't know where it came from . . . he still don't know
In the belly, Francis
It's all yours, Francis

The fight was not, as it turned out, all Francis's. At the end of the third round, the fighters broke apart. The Negro went on dancing until the decision was announced. Then the handlers stepped through the ropes, bringing robes and towels. Rudy's handlers congratulated him. There were several voices from the balcony assuring Francis that he had been robbed, but nothing was done about it. He and the white boy faded into the darkness, into the thick fog of cigar smoke, and two other fighters took their places.

The announcer moved up to the microphone.

Ladies and . . . gentlemen . . . this contest three rounds

One of the fighters was towheaded, with very white skin. His weight was distributed in chunks over his body, giving a look of boxlike squareness to his back and shoulders, his thighs, and the calves of his rather short legs.

From Chicago's West Side . . . wearing black trunks . . . weighing one-forty-seven . . . Larry Brannigan Junior

At the first sound of applause the towheaded fighter doubled up, as if from a stomach cramp, and with one arm held out stiffly he wheeled around backward in a complete circle—the favorite accepting homage from his admirers.

From the University of . . . wearing purple trunks . . . weighing a hundred forty-six and three quarters pounds . . . Spud Latham

Again applause. Spud raised his glove to his father, who was watching from the door to the dressing rooms. Mr. Latham saw the gesture, but didn't realize that it was for him. The past four nights, taking on all comers, Spud had wiped out his father's failures, one after another. Mr. Latham was no longer the same man.

The two fighters, their seconds, and the referee stood in the center of the ring under the glaring white light. The referee was heavy-set and had bushy black eyebrows. He was wearing gray trousers, a white shirt, a black bow tie, a black leather belt, and boxing shoes. His face suggested no particular nationality. Neither Brannigan nor Spud heard his instructions. They were sizing each other up. There was a cut over Spud's left eye which had three clamps in it. This caught Brannigan's fancy and he smiled. Hit properly, the clamps could be driven straight into Spud's head. The referee looked at the cut before he checked their hands and wrappings.

In his corner, waiting for the fight to begin, Spud suddenly felt limp. His handlers were hovering over him, telling him to feel Brannigan out in the first round. Spud nodded, wondering what they would say if he leaned forward now and confessed to them that he didn't have any stomach. His knees were moving all by themselves, and his hands, inside all of that tape, felt soft as putty. The whistle blew. He got up and scraped the soles of his shoes in the resin box. Then he stood with his gloves on the ropes, waiting. The rubber mouthpiece was forced between his lips. It was wet and it tasted wonderful. At the sound of the bell he swung around and saw Brannigan coming toward him fast. Spud crouched and let Brannigan have one—a left hook that caught him under the heart. The crowd moaned. Brannigan missed a wild left swing and took a left and right to the jaw. They went into a clinch and the referee separated them.

Atta boy, Brannigan, give it to him . . . open up that eye
Left, Latham
Keep punching that eye
There . . . that hit him
That's all right . . . Junior's taking it easy . . . he's not getting excited

Jab it . . . keep your left hand up, Latham, lead with your left hand, not the right . . . the left hand . . . keep the left hand in his face

Look out for your chin, dear friend
Go way from that
Keep your head, Junior . . . take it easy . . . three rounds
Ooh
That hit him . . . that's the only one that hit him
What a headache
What happened . . . what happened

Come on, Latham . . . let's go

Keep that left hand out there . . . left in his face will knock him out

He needs more than a left . . . he needs a left and a right for that boy

What happened . . . nothing happened . . . don't worry, Brannigan

He's a murderer

Hit him with a wet glove . . . a good one . . . a wet one

Spud backed Brannigan against the ropes and slugged him twice before the referee, for what reason it was not clear, came between them. There were boos and hisses from the crowd.

Go on . . . get out

Go way from there

He had no right to stop him . . . they were both on their feet

Right . . . right . . . so what

So he should leave him alone . . . the fellow was on the ropes

Maybe the referee has got bets on him

Use the left hand

Off the ropes, Junior

All of a sudden the referee they got him from Halsted Street

Keep away from those ropes, you fool

Shut up

Why should I shut up? I paid my admission . . . didn't I? . . . The guy had the fight in the first round and the referee steps between them

Keep it in his face, Latham . . . the left

Eh, Brannigan . . . what happened?

Between the first and second rounds Spud leaned back with his legs sprawled out in front of him and tried to relax. He felt the cold water being poured over his head and spilling down his chest. His gloved hands were taken from the ropes and placed on his knees. One of the handlers held the elastic away from his belly and massaged his chest and solar plexus. The other bent over him, talking earnestly. Spud was too keyed up to pay any attention. All he wanted was to get back in the center of the ring. This fight and one more and he'd have the Golden Gloves. The whistle blew. Spud pushed the mouthpiece back in, with his glove, and got to his feet. The stool was removed. The handlers crawled out through the ropes and went on talking to him, from outside the ring. Then the bell. Then he was fighting.

Apparently it made no difference to the referee that he was unpopular with the crowd. He continued to move quickly in wide circles around the fighters, coming between them frequently and forcing them apart with his hands. His face was extraordinarily serene, as if he knew the outcome of each fight before it began. He saw Brannigan graze Spud's chin with the lacing of his glove, and warned him about it, but most of the time he was looking at Spud and the expression in his eyes was sad.

Spud was certain that the first two rounds were his. He went into the third determined to win by a knockout. He could see that Brannigan's arms were so tired that it was all he could do to lift them. He himself felt fresh as a daisy. When Brannigan finally left himself wide open, Spud had the knockout blow all aimed and ready. Brannigan fell on his knees and Spud, in his excitement and haste, before he could stop himself, hit him again.

Standing there alone in the center of the ring, after the referee had stopped the fight, Spud heard the crowd for the first time. It took him several seconds to realize that they were booing at him.

43

Two figures rose up from where they had been sitting, their view of the ring partly cut off by a large pillar, and made their way through the aisles. One of them was a girl. Her coat was thrown open and she was wearing a bunch of purple violets pinned to the collar. The young man with her was about nineteen. He carried his overcoat and a Scotch plaid muffler over one arm, and the same distress that was in the girl's face was also in his, like a reflection from the sky.

To get from the arena to the dressing rooms it was necessary to go through a lounge which had orange wicker furniture in it. Around the green walls were framed autographed pictures of boxers and wrestlers. From the door of this room Mr.

Latham had watched Spud making his way to the ring. He was there waiting when Spud came back, his blue bathrobe tied around him and the sleeves hanging empty at his sides.

Disaster was something that Mr. Latham had had to contend with all his life. It didn't astonish him any more. But he was sorry, standing there in the doorway with a dead cigar in his mouth—that the run of bad luck was beginning now for Spud. When Spud's eyes met his father's for a second, Mr. Latham shook his head in sympathy and understanding.

Spud sat down on a wicker settee. His hair was soaking wet. The sweat was running down his forehead, down his chest, down the insides of his arms and legs. He had a headache and his mouth felt as if it were filled with cotton. He sat with his shoulders hunched, his wrists crossed under the folds of his bathrobe, handcuffed together by what had happened to him. The clumsy boxing gloves were resting on his bare knees. Another fight had already started in the arena, but Spud was involved in the last one. He couldn't get out of that moment when Brannigan had left himself wide open. From there things could have gone quite differently. *He slugged Brannigan and then he waited.* That was how it should have been, and how he kept making it be, over and over.

Although Mr. Latham seemed to be watching the fight, his look was inward. Lymie and Sally were almost close enough to speak to him before he saw them and stepped back from the doorway, so they could pass through it. When Spud saw them coming toward him across the room, he rose to his feet, ready to defend himself against both of them with his life's blood. *They were there. They had seen it.* But then he felt Sally's arms around him, hugging him, and he looked into her eyes and after that it was all right. That he had lost the fight with Brannigan didn't matter in the least.

It mattered to Lymie, though. "That dirty, double-crossing referee," he said. "You had the fight won in the first round."

Spud turned to him and smiled. "Pulled a fast one, didn't you?"

"We didn't know we were coming," Sally said. "I just couldn't stand it any more. You don't know what it was like having to wait for the next day's paper, and not being able to concentrate on anything for more than two minutes. I thought I was going crazy. So this morning Lymie and I looked up the train schedule and cut all our classes and came."

"What did your mother say?"

"She didn't say anything. She didn't know we were coming. I told Hope to call her after the train left."

Spud glanced uneasily at his father, while she was talking. When she finished he said, "Dad, this is Sally Forbes."

Sally took her hand away from Spud and put it in his. They smiled at each other and were, from that moment, friends.

"What happened to your eye?" Lymie asked.

"I got a bad cut," Spud said.

"When?"

"Last night. It bled all through the last round. After it was over they put some clamps in it."

"I'm glad I wasn't here," Sally said.

"I would just as soon have been somewhere else myself," Spud said. "That guy Brannigan, he kept trying to open it up but he didn't touch it once." His face lengthened. He was back in that moment when Brannigan left himself wide open. There was no hurry now.

"Don't worry," Sally said, with her cheek against his. "Don't even think about it."

Spud brought his arms out from under the bathrobe, and folded them around her.

"It seems as if you'd been away for years," she said sadly.

"Five days," Spud said. "It seemed like a long time to me too." He felt something soft and drew away from her. It was the violets. They had touched his bare chest. "Where'd you get the flowers?"

"Lymie bought them for me," Sally said. "He thought I ought to have some violets. I said this wasn't any symphony concert we were going to but he bought them anyway. And then we had dinner at a place called the Tip-Top Inn, where they have pictures of nursery rhymes on the walls, and an orchestra—all for eighty cents."

"It's across from the Art Institute," Lymie explained.

Spud took his arms away from Sally and appeared to be concerned with the lacing of his gloves. "I have to go back in there," he said, jerking his head toward the arena. "As soon as this fight is over."

Sally looked at him in bewilderment but he avoided her eyes.

"I'll get something out of it anyway," he said, "even if it's only third place. You better go back to your seats." His tone was harsh. He might have been speaking to strangers.

"We'll stay here," Sally said quietly.

Lymie, who from long habit should have been sensitive to the changes in Spud's mood, had no idea that anything was wrong. The person who is both intelligent and observing cannot at the same time be innocent. He can only pretend to be; to others sometimes, sometimes to himself. Since Lymie didn't notice that anything was wrong with Spud, one is forced to conclude that he didn't wish to notice it. Some impulse that he was not willing to admit even to himself must have prompted him to buy violets for Sally. They reopened an old wound that was far more serious than the cut over Spud's eye, and one that it wasn't possible to put clamps in.

At the sound of the bell Spud left them and disappeared into the crowd. A moment or two later he and another fighter emerged under the white light of the reflectors. All that had happened before happened again, like a movie film being run through a second time, but it didn't last as long. In the first round Spud did something so stupid that Lymie, watching him from the doorway, contracted his shoulders and turned away in despair.

Spud's opponent was an Italian boy with black hair and eyes and soft muscles. Spud was having everything his own way. The referee had just pried them apart and when the Italian boy came toward Spud again, Spud doubled up, caught the Italian boy in the pit of the stomach with his shoulder and then straightened up with a quick jerk. As if the rules had been changed suddenly and this was now a wrestling match, the Italian boy flew clear over Spud and landed flat on his back.

The silence lasted several seconds, during which a single voice could be heard saying:

Ice cream . . .

The referee blew his whistle. Then the catcalls began, and the screaming. Pop bottles flew through the air, and the booing was like the waves of the sea.

44

After the radio had been turned off there was an unnatural quiet in the Lathams' living room. Mrs. Latham was sitting on the sofa in the full glare of the overhead light. Her face was gray and blotched with suffering, and her eyes, wide open, saw only what was in her mind—terrible fantasies in which her son, her beautiful son, was brought home to her, bruised and bleeding.

Helen crossed the room and knelt beside her. "Mother darling," she said, "listen to me. He's all right. It's over now, and you mustn't think about it, you mustn't grieve about it any more. The cut over his eye isn't serious. It will heal in a week's time and nobody will ever know it was there." She took her mother's hands between her own and chafed them, as if they were cold.

"He's got a taste of it," Mrs. Latham said quietly. "And there's nothing anybody can do to stop him. He'll ruin his life."

"Well, let him," Helen said bitterly.

Mrs. Latham made a slight gesture which her daughter saw and understood. The gesture meant that she was not to say anything against Spud. Jealousy welled up in her. There was no way that she could keep herself from knowing that her mother loved Spud more than she did her, and always had, and always would. But that didn't make any difference. She would go right on looking after her mother, and making her life easier for her, and maybe some day. . . .

"Let him go ahead and ruin his life," she said aloud. "Let him go on boxing until he gets his nose broken and ends up with cauliflower ears, and looking like a thug. That's what he is anyway, so he might as well look like one."

Mrs. Latham shook her head.

"If he can come home the way he did Monday night and see you in the condition you were in then," Helen said, "and go right back and fight the next night, and the night after that, and again tonight, regardless of what it is doing to you, then I don't care what happens to him. Almost any stranger that walked in off the street I could have more feeling for than I have for him right now. It's a terrible thing to say but it's true."

Mrs. Latham was searching for her handkerchief in the folds of her dress. Before she found it, the tears had begun to slide down her cheeks.

"Oh, I'm sorry," Helen exclaimed. "Really I am. You know I don't mean it." She took her own handkerchief and dried her mother's cheeks, but there was no stopping the flow of tears, now that they had started. "Why do you wait up?" she said. "You're exhausted and you ought to be in bed this minute. Come on. Come take your clothes off. I'll turn the covers down for you and you can slip into bed. I'll wait up for them."

Mrs. Latham took the handkerchief and put it to her face and then, turning her head slightly, shook with sobbing. Helen put her arms around her and clung to her, weeping too. She thought of her mother always as a tower of strength, and to see her this way now, so stricken, so helpless, was more than she could bear. It also frightened her.

"I'm going to make you some coffee," she said. "You stay here and be quiet."

She went into the bathroom and held a washcloth under the cold water faucet, wrung it out, and then came back into the living room and laid it on her mother's face, on her eyes and her hot forehead. She did this several times before she finally went out to the kitchen and took the coffee down from the shelf of the cupboard, and began measuring it into the percolator with a big spoon.

All *they* ever saw in her mother was somebody who administered to their comfort, kept their clothes picked up and in order, fed them, and made a home for them to come to, when it suited their convenience.

When Spud was a child she had loved him, but now that he was grown, it was impossible. Nobody could love him. He was an entirely different person, ungrateful, unmanageable, ill-tempered and surly. There was no use trying to get her mother to stop caring for Spud, because she always would, but sooner or later her mother would have to realize that nothing could be done for him, and then she would give up trying.

If anything happened to her father, they'd have to give up the apartment, probably, and she and her mother could take a smaller place. It needn't be very luxurious. Just a couple of rooms, large enough so that they wouldn't get under each other's feet, and she'd work and make enough money to support them, and they could live together quietly and in peace.

This idea had been in the back of Helen's mind ever since the letters had stopped coming from Wisconsin. Mrs. Latham saw Helen always as a little girl, a very good, obedient child, and so, if she had known what her daughter was thinking, she would have been surprised, as one is now and then by what children do and say. The plan itself would not have appealed to her. She had every intention of keeping her family together and intact forever. But she couldn't drink the coffee after Helen made it and brought it to her, and Helen put the cup and saucer on the table next to the sofa. There the coffee gradually grew cold.

It was after midnight when the car drove up in front of the apartment. The windows on the second floor were still lighted but no face peered out from behind the living room curtains, and the street lamps strung at intervals through the park served only to show how deserted it was at this time of night.

Mr. Latham turned the motor off and said, "Well, here we are, home again."

Reluctantly, as if they had expected to spend the night in the back seat of the car with the robe over their knees, first Lymie, then Sally, and then Spud piled out. Sally pulled at her skirt and pushed her hair back under her hat. "Do I look all right?" she asked.

"You look fine," Spud said. The yawn that he was trying to suppress came out in his voice. She saw that he hadn't even been looking at her, that he was too tired to care how she looked. The elm trees at the edge of the park were rocking in the damp March wind. The sky was clouded over.

"I don't feel the least bit sleepy," she remarked, as she followed the two boys up the walk.

Spud had forgotten his key and they waited in the vestibule for Mr. Latham, who had stayed behind to lock the car doors. On the second landing they waited again. Lymie glanced surreptitiously at the violets on Sally's coat. They were beginning to curl. He had never bought flowers for a girl before. Looking at them, and then at Spud, who was leaning against the wall, Lymie thought: *If anything should happen to him, if he should be killed in an accident or something, Sally would probably marry me, because I'm Spud's best friend and I would cherish his memory.* . . . That this thought might involve a wish, he didn't perceive. It was merely one of those mixed-up ideas that occurred to him sometimes when he was very sleepy. He put it out of his mind immediately, and didn't remember afterward that he had ever thought it.

When Mr. Latham put his key in the door and pushed it open, Lymie saw that nothing was changed since he had been here last at Christmas time. It was one of the reasons he liked to come here. Nothing ever changed. He slipped his coat off, and his scarf, and dropped them on the chair in the hall, and then he walked into the living room. There his eyes opened wide and he stopped right where he was. The others had to move around him in order to get into the room.

Mrs. Latham was still sitting on the sofa, and in her violently altered condition Lymie recognized one of those changes which happened, so far as he could make out, only to women. His own mother, usually so loving and tender with him, at certain times used to withdraw, leaving him stranded, the center of his life a void. When she had one of her headaches, which came fairly often during the last years of her life, after his father started drinking, she retired into a darkened room and there lay motionless on her bed, with a damp cloth over her eyes, without knowing or caring what happened to Lymie. When he got home from school he used to walk round and round the house before he went in. If the shades were drawn in her bedroom, he knew.

Helen was bending over her mother anxiously, and as the others filed in she turned and faced them with a hatred which made no distinctions; they were all included in it. Spud went up to his mother and said, "It's all over now," which was as near as he could come to telling her that he was sorry. When she didn't answer, he turned away and went out into the hall. Helen bent over her mother again, as if the others (including the girl they had brought home with them, whoever *she* was) were not in the room, or were there with no right and would soon perceive this and go away.

Sally glanced over her shoulder at Spud, for help, but he seemed wholly concerned with hanging his coat in the hall closet. And Lymie, whom she was able to count on under ordinary circumstances, looked frightened and uncertain of what to do. Something was wrong, obviously. It was a scene that belonged to a house with a crepe hanging on the front door and a coffin somewhere and the odors of too many flowers. At that moment, when the only thing she could think of was flight, she felt a strong hand close over her arm. The hand propelled her, unwilling, toward the sofa. She heard a voice that she recognized as Mr. Latham's saying firmly, insistently, "Mother, we've brought one of Spud's friends home with us. This is Sally Forbes."

Mrs. Latham's eyes, so lost in the recesses of her own grief, focused slowly upon Sally. She raised her head with an effort and extended a frail hand. Sally took it and smiled. The eyes that looked into hers were red from weeping, and there was no reassurance in them. But something—politeness, a sense of obligation, of responsibility toward a guest—gave Mrs. Latham the strength to take hold and manage her family again.

"You'd better take your coat off, my dear," she said, and then, turning to Helen, "She can sleep in your room tonight, and you sleep in here."

The atmosphere in the living room changed immediately. Mr. Latham's face cleared. He felt in the breast pocket of his coat and brought out a cigar. Lymie went up to Mrs. Latham and kissed her on the cheek. There was no answering pat, but tonight he didn't expect it, and wasn't alarmed when she merely said, "Good evening, Lymie."

Spud came back from the hall and tugged at his sleeve. "You can sleep with me," he said.

They had already turned toward the hall when the ax fell.

"I think Lymie had better go to his own home tonight," Mrs. Latham said.

"The bed's big enough," Spud said. "We've slept together in it lots of times."

"You need your rest," Mrs. Latham said.

Lymie wasted no time picking up his scarf and overcoat. He saw that Spud was looking at him apologetically, and so he said, "I'll call you in the morning. . . . Good night, everybody!" and closed the door behind him.

On the way down the stairs he remembered the feeling he had had the first afternoon that he came home with Spud. It was a kind of premonition, he realized. Everything that he had thought would happen then was happening now. He had been wrong only about the time.

45

During the early part of April there was a week of undeniable spring. It was in the air first, before the ground or the bare trees gave any sign of it; and its effect generally was to make people miss appointments and forget what it was that they had been about to say. Along with the marriage of the earth and the sun, other strange influences were at work—the renewal of grass, the northward migration of birds, the swelling of buds on the trees.

Classroom windows were flung open, and instructors in economics and bacteriology and political science raised their voices above the sound of power lawn mowers. They spoke to empty seats, to a collection of figures that looked alive but were actually made of pieces of colored paper pasted over a framework of sticks, to ears that had no hearing, to minds that, masquerading in leaves and flowers, were even now on their way to the forest, up the mountainside, down to the seashore, where, according to ancient custom, certain rites were about to be performed which would make the earth fertile and green.

The university tennis courts were weeded and rolled and marked with new tape. All morning and all afternoon tennis balls bounced and were struck back. The scoring (*thirty-forty . . . love-five . . . deuce it is*) was added to the other spring sounds.

With all the windows open and the sunlight streaming in, the men's gymnasium was like a pavilion. The trapeze performers set up their apparatus outside on the grass, and there was a constant clatter of spiked shoes as baseball players came in and went out of the building. The empty football stadium (capacity seventy thousand) was taken over by thin, tense-faced runners, hurdlers, and high jumpers. Botany classes filed out of science buildings two by two. They were on their way out to the edge of town where, in the cold running water of the drainage ditch, spirogyra and chlodophora were to be found. The girls had charge of the green laboratory jars. The boys took off their shoes and their bright-colored socks, rolled their trousers above the knee, and waded in slowly, their bare feet searching for soft places in the gravel bottom. They came out of the water bearing slimy specimens in their hands and in their eyes the sorrowful realization of all that they had lost by starting to school at the age of six.

On the south campus two gardeners swept the cement bottom of the lily pond and then stood and watched it fill with clean water. The apple trees in the university orchards were sprayed, according to the latest methods. Lambs that had been born in March in the big university barns were now let out to pasture. Dogs were seen in pairs on the Broad Walk, and one of them made an obstinate attempt to attend Professor Forbes's lecture on St. Anselm and his logical proof of the existence of God.

The nights were languid and soft with a tropical odor that had its origin in the thawing corn fields outside of town. Nobody could study. The brick terraces of Tudor and southern colonial fraternity houses were crowded long after supper with boys looking at the moon. Under lunary influence many of them went off and drank spiked beer. Although the university authorities had forbidden serenading, between ten-thirty and eleven o'clock shadows collected in the shrubbery outside sorority houses. There was a campus policeman but he couldn't be everywhere at once. Young male voices, not always on pitch, rose to darkened second-story windows. The serenaders sang the university anthem, "When Day Is Done" and various plagiarisms on "The Sweetheart of Sigma Chi." Then with applause following them, they moved off down the street, unmolested. Around midnight, mattresses and blankets and pillows were hauled out onto flat roofs. Boys who were so fortunate as to belong to a fraternity fell asleep with the moon shining on their faces. And boys who had had to be content with living in rooming houses awoke, morning after morning, with the sun in their eyes.

There were only five people in the English seminar the night of the annual spring celebration. The air that came in through the open windows was too soft to blow papers about, but minds were not, of course, immune to it. Of the five people, four were graduate students with a Ph.D. oral examination to face, and no time to admire the moon or make love on the damp ground. The fifth was Lymie Peters. The scowling bitter face of Dr. Johnson looked down at them from the wall and approved of their industry, but the bust of Shakespeare was noncommittal.

A faint faraway sound was heard a little after nine o'clock. It might or might not have been cheering. One of the graduate students looked up from his barricade of books, took his glasses off, and announced the true cause of the disturbance. The others listened a moment and then all five went on reading. From time to time they also made crabbed, half-legible notes concerning the date of *Tottel's Miscellany* or the lavish use of similes in *Euphues and His England*. The cheering grew louder and more distinct.

Lymie, having finished the section of Dorothy Wordsworth's *Journals* recommended by Professor Severance, closed the book and restored it to the shelf where he had found it. He was ready to go home now and review separable and inseparable German prefixes. When he got outside the building, he saw that the sky to the south was pink from the glare of an enormous bonfire. The rooming house lay in one direction, excitement was in the other. Lymie started home, but he turned suddenly, hesitated, and then began to retrace his steps. Within half a block he was running.

The bonfire was in a muddy open field north of the stadium, and the field itself was swarming with dark figures. The boys nearest the fire stood out clearly. The firelight kept passing over their faces and hands. Others came out of the surrounding darkness, bringing fuel, and then went back again. Behind their movements there seemed to be some as yet unannounced purpose, some act of violence which would flare up all of a sudden and make the flames turn pale by comparison with it.

Lymie stood on the outer edge of the crowd, where he was not likely to get involved. The year before, in this same field, he'd lost a good coat and had the shirt torn off his back, in a mud fight between freshmen and sophomores.

After climbing forty or fifty feet into the sky, the flames, for lack of fuel, began to subside, and darkness gradually closed in on the field. A voice near the bonfire yelled, "To the campus!"

and there was an answering roar which produced a stampede. Lymie was caught up in it before he could retire across the street. He was swept along willingly enough, his feet mingling with all the other feet set so abruptly in motion. The running stopped after two blocks and those who had no desire to be part of the mob escaped from it. The rest proceeded through the fraternity district in a shambling, almost orderly fashion, filling the street and the sidewalks, and trampling on new grass.

When they got to the Union Building, the editor of the student daily newspaper, a tall, thin, hollow-cheeked blond boy, appeared on the steps above them and made a speech. "This is kid stuff!" he shouted. "What's the use of it? What's the use of destroying a lot of valuable property and getting into trouble and maybe thrown out of school?"

The mob, which had so far not destroyed anything, answered, "Drown him!" "Throw the son of a bitch in the Styx!"

"For what?" the thin-faced boy asked rhetorically. "For a little fun, maybe, that will reflect on the university and do serious harm. If you want to do something, then do something constructive."

There was a surging forward and the boy ducked hastily into the printing office and locked the door.

"Don't let him get away with that!" a voice cried, and another voice screamed, "Smash the door down!" but nobody wanted to be the one to do it. The mob had no leader. Voices were heard frequently but they didn't seem to be attached to a particular person, or at least not to anybody who was willing to appear boldly in front of the others and take charge. The mob waited, milling around outside the Union Building until some of them grew bored and went home. The rest eventually started toward the center of town, which was two miles from the campus. Their destination was the Orpheum Theater, where they would undoubtedly have interfered with the performance of some Japanese acrobats if they hadn't been stopped.

On the way, as they were passing through a little park, they met a student with his date, coming home from the movies. They surrounded this couple and separated them. When the boy struck out frantically, dozens of hands grabbed hold of him, tore his shirt off, gave him a black eye and a bloody mouth. They took the girl's skirts and pulled them over her head and tied them there. Somebody tripped the boy, who was still fighting, and as he fell, they pushed the girl, unharmed, on top of him. This little unpleasantness, this token rape, seemed to give the mob confidence.

When a streetcar appeared around a corner, twenty boys ran to meet it, and one of them managed to pull the trolley off the overhead wire. The streetcar was plunged into abrupt darkness. Before it even came to a stop, it was being rocked from side to side by a hundred hands. The motorman got out, swearing, and put the trolley back on. The boys stood off, and watched him with apparently no thought of interfering. The wooden streetcar lighted up, the motorman climbed on and clanging his bell furiously, moved forward about twenty feet before the lights went out again.

This happened three more times and the last time they pushed a small bonfire under the car, which made a good deal of smoke and frightened the passengers. But the mob had already had enough when that happened, so they let the motorman continue and would have continued themselves except that the Dean of Men appeared miraculously in their midst. He was a slight, almost boyish man of sixty-two. His hair and his mustache were snow white. He looked kind, humorous, and fatherly, but the effect on the boys was as if a rattlesnake had materialized right in front of them on the streetcar tracks. As they backed away from him he began picking certain figures out of the crowd and addressing them by name. "Hello, Johnston . . . Feldcamp, are you here too? . . . Morrison, if I had as much trouble with physics as you seem to have, I'd be studying tonight. . . . Peters, I think you had better beat it for home. . . ."

Lymie thought so too.

On the way he had to pass Spud's fraternity. He went up on the porch, opened the door, and walked in. By that time it was nearly eleven o'clock, and Spud had finished studying and was straightening his desk before he went to bed. After the Golden Gloves tournament he had set to work with two cans of paint, one turkey red, the other black. Everything in the room that could possibly be painted—the door, the window frames, the woodwork, the two study chairs, the tables, the two goose-necked student lamps, the closet curtain rod, the ceiling light fixture, and even the glass ashtray—was either one color or the other. Spud glanced at Lymie's flushed and excited face and then at his muddy shoes. "Where the hell have you been?"

"Spring celebration," Lymie said. He pushed his hat on the back of his head and sank down in a chair.

"I should think you'd have had enough of that, after what happened to you at cap-burning," Spud said.

"This was different," Lymie said.

"What happened? Where'd you go?"

While Lymie was telling him about the riot, Spud got undressed and put his bathrobe on.

"I don't understand it," he said, when Lymie had finished. "If they'd started breaking into sorority houses and throwing furniture out of the windows, the way they did once before, you'd have got yourself into a lot of trouble."

"I thought of that," Lymie said.

"Well," Spud asked irritably, "what did you get mixed up in it for?"

"I don't know," Lymie said. "I honestly don't. Why are you staring at me like that?"

"Because you need to have your head examined."

"I saw the bonfire," Lymie said, "and I guess I just wanted to see what they were going to do."

"You're crazy, that's all that's the matter with you," Spud said. "Or else you've got spring fever."

"I've got something," Lymie said, and stood up and sneezed violently three times while he was buttoning his coat.

46

What Lymie had was a bad cold which lasted ten days, and by the end of that period the ground was once more covered with dirty snow. He took to his bed and started dosing himself. This, instead of forestalling the cold, seemed to make it worse. The boys brought food in to him but he was alone all day in the dormitory. With no one to talk to, he slept a good deal, and one day woke up with a feeling that he was in some unnamable danger. Something, a person, a presence (he couldn't quite imagine it but it nevertheless knew *him*) was waiting outside the door. In a growing uneasiness he got up and went downstairs and dressed. It took longer than usual because he was weak from staying in bed, but his cold, from that moment, began to get better.

In April nothing stays. No purpose in the heavens and certainly no need on earth can keep the wind in any one direction. It blew from the east, from the west, and finally from the south. There were rain clouds and when it rained, thunder and lightning as well. With so much uncertainty in the atmosphere it was not really surprising that again Spud was not himself. Lymie first noticed it when Spud walked past him and asked Armstrong to tie his gloves for him.

Lymie didn't know what the trouble was, but he was not dismayed. He had worn Spud down once before and he was sure that he could do it again. Every day between four-fifteen and four-thirty he appeared at the gymnasium and stood a few feet away from the punching bag where Spud, if he wanted his gloves tied on or any small service like that, wouldn't have to go far to find him. When Spud came up from the showers, Lymie was there waiting by the locker, like a faithful hound. He made no move to open the lock, or to touch anything inside the locker that belonged to Spud. Occasionally while Spud was dressing and afterward on the way home, Lymie would say something to him, but Lymie was always careful not to put the remark in the form of a question, so there was no actual need for Spud to reply.

One day it occurred to Lymie that if he also kept quiet, if he just gave Spud a chance, the situation might change. It did, but not in the way he had expected. Once having joined Spud in that harsh silence, he couldn't escape from it; he had to keep still himself. He walked along, hearing the unfriendly sound of Spud's heelplates as they struck the sidewalk, and watching the swing of Spud's knees. Once or twice his glance went as high as Spud's mouth, drawn in a tight line. It was all that Lymie needed to see. When they came to the corner where Spud turned off to go to the fraternity house, Lymie's hand would rise in a half salute which did not break the silence and yet spoke eloquently. And Spud would nod and walk away.

In German class he and Lymie sat side by side, four days a week, without speaking. When Spud had no paper, Lymie took a sheet out of his notebook and handed it to him, ready to take it back if Spud decided to refuse the offer and write on the bare desk top instead. At such times, Spud longed to lean over and whisper, "How'd we ever get started this way, when you're the best friend I've got. The only one, when you get right down to it. Sally is something different . . ." But he had never been able to say things like that, and besides, Miss Blaiser was at the blackboard writing: (*1*) *When do strong verbs change their stem vowel?* (*2*) *Give the meanings and principal parts of beginnen, beissen, binden, bleiben, finden, gefallen, laufen, lesen, nehmen, rufen, schlafen, schliessen, schreiben, sehen. . . .*

There were also times when Spud would have been willing to leave the fraternity house and move back with Lymie, if the brothers had given him the slightest excuse. Instead of treating him as they did the freshmen, they acted as if he were already initiated. He had no pledge duties, he was never called down in front of the fireplace and paddled on Monday nights, nothing was ever said to him about his attitude or about the right fraternity spirit. Without a grievance he couldn't act, and the brothers wouldn't give him one. He looked everywhere and the nearest to an enemy that he could find was Lymie, who was also his only friend.

One afternoon Spud cut his chemistry class and walked across the campus to the rooming house. He wanted to talk to somebody and he decided to spill everything to Reinhart. When he arrived at "302," Reinhart's room was empty. Spud looked at the schedule of classes tacked to the wall above the desk and saw that Reinhart had no classes the rest of the afternoon. He sat down in the sagging, overstuffed chair to wait.

He had only been there a few minutes when Mr. Dehner's spaniel caught his scent in the front hall and raced to the stairs. He threw himself on Spud, who picked him up, tossed him almost to the ceiling, and caught him on the way down. The dog squirmed in Spud's hands, rolled his bloodshot eyes ecstatically, and wagged his stump of a tail. When Spud put him down, he backed off and with his head turned slightly made a queer sound that was half whimper and half bark.

"Well," a familiar penetrating voice said, "if it isn't Mr. Latham! How that poor dog has missed you."

Spud turned and saw Mr. Dehner standing in the doorway with a dust mop in his hand.

"Have you come back to us? I was saying just the other day to Colter I think it was, or maybe it was Geraghty. I said, 'Some day Mr. Latham will be back. You wait and see. He's not the fraternity type. And if he saw the way Mr. Peters keeps that room—' My dear boy, you ought to go and look at it. Just like the town dump. I'm terribly fond of Mr. Peters. He's so sensitive and all, but I declare I don't know how he finds his books when he wants to study. He must have some sixth sense. . . . Be quiet, Pooh-Bah! . . . I had a cousin—she was my mother's cousin, actually, who always used to pray to St. Anthony when she lost anything. She lived right around the corner from a church so it was very convenient. She found ever so many things that way. A garnet brooch, and the key to her safety deposit box, and my mother's seed pearls. We used to go running to her the minute anything turned up missing, and I must say she got results, even though it was pure superstition. Mr. Peters is not religious, is he? Nobody is religious any more. It doesn't seem to be fashionable. But it probably will come back, just like Victorian walnut. And then the churches won't hold them all. The intellectual types will drop Spengler and Einstein and take up St. Thomas Aquinas. For all I know they may be at him already. I must ask Mr. Peters. He's the student of the house. He looks like a student, doesn't he? So flat-chested. I wouldn't be at all surprised if he were tubercular. You don't think there is anything seriously the matter with him do you, Mr. Latham? I'd hate to have somebody in the house who was—you know. But probably he has lungs like a jack rabbit and will outlive all of us. I used to watch the two of you coming up the walk together. So comic, the combination. One all brains and no brawn, the other all brawn and—but grades aren't everything, are they, Mr. Latham? And people with brains so often seem to end up teaching school. That's undoubtedly what will happen to Mr. Peters—he's been very absent-minded lately—unless some kind fate intervenes. You never had any courses under old Professor Larkin, did you? No, of course you didn't. He died when you were in rompers, poor man. He was an authority on Chaucer or Milton, I don't remember which it was, and terribly absent-minded. He was famous for it. He once took a letter that he wanted to mail and left it on the hall table and went with the lamp, plug and all, out to the mailbox. They say that really happened. I don't know why absent-mindedness should go with teaching, but apparently there's some connection. Probably teachers don't want to be teaching any more than I want to keep roomers. They just wake up some morning and find themselves on a platform holding forth about Amenhotep III or heredity and environment. I do hope you're not planning to devote yourself to that sort of thing. You're not cut out for it, you know. You've taught Pooh-Bah to sit up and speak nicely for his biscuit, and he rolls over when you tell him to, which is certainly more than he does for me. But I don't feel that you belong on the faculty somehow, and I don't know that I would want you to if you could. It's a very questionable life. Safe, up to a point. But there's too much emphasis on expediency. And except for a few professors who have relatives that die and leave them a little something, everybody is so poor. Mr. Peters I don't worry about. He looks like the kind of person who would some day inherit a small legacy. But you, my boy, you belong in the wicked world. Don't worry if there are people who are brighter than you are. They'll never get to the top. There'll always be some well-connected person above them. Over the last five thousand years the human mind has had every possible chance to make something of itself and so far—" Mr. Dehner crossed the room and threw open the window and shook the mop violently several times. "So far," he repeated, turning his head to avoid the lint that blew back in the open window, "it has failed." He closed the window with a bang. "Now my dear boy, don't look at me like that. I can see by your eyes just what you're thinking: 'What does that old fool know about it anyway?' And you're quite right. The answer is nothing. Nothing but what I see going on around me every day."

He went off mopping carelessly under desks and around chairs and humming:

Old Heidelberg, dear Heidelberg
Thy sons will ne'er forget . . .

47

When Professor Severance did not appear, his class in Romantic poetry waited the customary five minutes for a full professor and then walked out. Lymie, Sally, and Hope did not separate until they were outside, and then only after considerable discussion. Lymie had a freakish black felt hat on—they were a sudden campus fad—and he pulled the hat, which was too small for him, down over one eyebrow, cocked the brim up in front, and said, "Now where are we going?"

"I've got a three o'clock gym class," Hope said. "I'm going back to the house and put my bloomers on. If you'd care to see me in a pair of bloomers, Lymie, you can hang around downstairs. It won't take me a minute to change."

"I think I'd rather go to the English seminar," Lymie said.

"Suit yourself."

"Well," he said, hesitating. "I don't have to see you in your bloomers to know what you would look like. I can imagine them."

"You may think you can," Hope said. "But I was never so surprised in my life as I was the first time I put them on. Forbes, are you coming?"

"I've got to go home," Sally said. "Mother's making me a new dress and I promised her I'd—"

"Do you have to do that today?" Hope asked. "I was thinking, if you and Lymie went to the Ship's Lantern I could meet you there before gym and we could do our French lesson together."

"Well," Sally said, "I'd rather, actually, but the thing is, Mother is expecting me. Also I want to wear the dress."

"Such selfish, disagreeable people," Hope said cheerfully, as she walked away. She had not had to drop out of school after the appendicitis operation because the sorority made her house manager, at a modest salary. As soon as she had something that set her apart from the others, she became pleasant to live with. Now her disparaging remarks were nearly always addressed to herself, and her opinions were no longer arrogant. When she stared at someone, it was obvious that she was worrying about unpaid house bills and didn't know that the person she was staring at was even there.

At the Broad Walk, Sally turned to Lymie and said, "Why don't you—oh, I forgot. You're going to the seminar."

"I don't *have* to," Lymie said.

"Well come on and walk me home then."

"All right."

They walked on in silence for almost a block before she lifted her head suddenly and said, "Spud's having one of his spells again."

Lymie nodded.

"I don't know when it began or what started him off," Sally said, "but every once in a while I catch him looking at me as if I were a perfect stranger to him. As if he were trying to size me up. We had a terrible fight last night, and then suddenly, when he was saying good night to me out on the front porch, he said, 'Hold me, Sally, just hold me!' It was terrible the way he said it. We sat on the front steps and leaned against each other and I held him as hard as I could for about half an hour, and when he went home he seemed a little better. He was all right, as a matter of fact, but I still don't know what was bothering him."

Lymie let her talk on and on until they reached the Forbeses' front walk. She put her hand on his sleeve then and said, "Somehow I can talk to you about Spud because I know that you feel about him almost the way I do."

She waved to him from the porch and then disappeared into the house. Lymie went on to "302." He had to go through Reinhart's room to get to his own.

When Lymie appeared in the door, Spud was there, and so was Reinhart. Spud stopped talking abruptly. The sight of Lymie's face, of his eyes blazing with happiness, was a too-exact, too-humiliating refutation of all that he had just been saying. There could be no question now of whose fault it was. Reinhart, sitting deep in his chair and twisting a lock of hair with his finger, would know everything.

The silence expanded like a soap bubble; expanded and expanded until it pressed against the four walls, the floor, and the ceiling. It seemed to Spud that it took a year for the light to go out of Lymie's eyes, for the expression on his face to change, for him to smile stiffly and walk on to the next room.

48

Spud took longer than usual with the wrapping of his wrists that afternoon, as if he were seeking for some kind of perfection which would automatically dispose of all his problems. The three o'clock gym classes had just been dismissed, and the aisle around him was clogged with boys opening lockers, pulling sweatshirts over their heads, stepping out of jock straps, arguing, singing, and snapping towels at each other's buttocks. He was so accustomed to this that he hardly saw them. He closed his own locker, picked up the skipping rope and the boxing gloves, and threaded his way through the crowded aisle without touching or pushing anyone.

As he started up the stairs he was conscious of a heavy feeling in his legs, though he had had plenty of sleep the night before. When he reached the floor above, he fought back an impulse to turn and go back down the stairs. Up till now Spud had done all his fighting with his fists and he didn't know how to cope with a stubborn, unyielding resistance that wasn't physical. He tried to pretend that this afternoon was like any other afternoon, to keep his eyes under control, and above all not to look for Lymie.

In spite of his lean, quick, well-trained body, in spite of the muscles in his arms and legs, there was a limit to Spud's strength and he had almost found it the night he got the cut over his eye. The cut had healed long since, but it had left a scar running through his left eyebrow. Spud drew a ringer that night—a Lithuanian who had no right to compete in that amateur tournament, since he was twenty-five years old and had been boxing professionally for years. He was tall and skinny with long arms. Spud took one look at him and was scared silly. He had reason to be. The Lithuanian hit him with everything but the ring post and Spud couldn't do anything about it. He couldn't get past those arms. The first three minutes seemed like three hours. It was the worst fighting Spud had ever come up against. In the second round he was knocked down and had sense enough to wait until the count of nine.

Then he got up and the bell saved him. At the beginning of the third round he got the cut over his left eye. The blood ran down the side of his face and some of it went into his eye, so everything he saw was filmed with red. The floor kept slipping out from under him, and it took all his strength to lift his arms. During that fight Spud discovered that you can hit a man and hit a man and hit a man and finally if he is still there and you hit him with everything you've got, he has to fall down or you're licked. Fortunately the Lithuanian fell down. Spud hit him with his Sunday punch and knocked him out. If he hadn't, Spud would have sat down right where he was. He was too tired to go on.

Lymie was there. He was standing against the wall near (but not too near) the punching bag.

I don't want to hurt him any more, Spud said to himself. I just don't want to go on hurting him. . . . Apparently he had no choice. He couldn't blow up at the referee for not stopping the fight because there was no referee. He could walk up to Lymie now and say, *For Christ's sake, go away, will you?* and Lymie would go away. But the next afternoon he'd be back again. And if he told Lymie to go away and not come back any more, Lymie would do that too. But he would stand outside the building waiting to walk home. Or if he wasn't allowed to do that, then he would follow at a distance. And even if he stayed away from the gymnasium entirely he would still be waiting, no matter where he was.

It must be something I did a long time ago, Spud thought suddenly—and don't remember. Maybe I didn't even know it at the time, but I must have done something to him or he wouldn't do this to me.

Ten minutes later while Spud was slapping half-heartedly at the punching bag, he felt a sharp, shooting pain all through his right wrist and up into his knuckles. He stopped and felt of his hand through the fingerless glove. It was okay as long as his hand was open and relaxed but it hurt when he moved his fingers. In disbelief that such a thing could happen to him, he drew his hand back, closed his fist, and hit the punching bag as hard as he could. Then he doubled up, holding his arms across his stomach.

Of the dozen boys working out in the gymnasium that

afternoon only one realized that something was wrong and came up to him. Spud recognized Lymie's face, through a blur of pain. Lymie was staring at him, with his mouth open and his eyes filled with concern; and it was that, Spud decided suddenly, that he wanted. Somebody to be concerned about him. Somebody to understand what it would mean if he could never box again.

His eyes met Lymie's for the first time in weeks and he said quietly, "I hurt my hand."

49

The shiny new Chrysler sedan that was parked in front of Professor Severance's house belonged to Dr. Rogers, who had taken Hope Davison's appendix out (unnecessarily perhaps) and who was always pinching young girls. He was inside, in the upstairs front bedroom. He had been called to attend Mrs. Severance, who had had a stroke and was lying in her huge walnut bed. He could have pinched Mrs. Severance until she was black and blue and she would not have felt it. Her face was ashen gray and her breathing was terrible to listen to. It had a kind of rising-falling rhythm, like someone putting his foot on the second rung of a ladder, then stepping down one rung, then two rungs higher, then one rung down. When she got to the top of the ladder she started down. At the bottom there was an interval of perhaps twenty seconds before she started up again.

Dr. Rogers bent over the bed and forced one of the sick woman's eyelids open with his thumb. The eyeball was rigid. He let his hand move down to her wrist, which was lying outside the cover. His serene, pale blue eyes went round the room, resting by turns on various objects: sewing basket, sachet bag, brush and comb and oval hand mirror, small silver-framed picture of William Severance at the age of eight in a white sailor suit by the seashore. Next to this picture was a larger one of a middle-aged man, handsome and distinguished-looking, but severe. The face bore a family resemblance to Professor Severance—the shape and length of the nose especially. It was his father. From the two pictures Dr. Rogers' eyes moved on to the large green checkbook which Mrs. Severance had been trying to balance, sitting at her desk, when the seizure occurred. Through daily use, all of Mrs. Severance's personal things seemed to have taken on her warmth of heart, her indomitability, foolishness, and charm.

The nurse that Dr. Rogers had brought with him waited in her starched uniform and cap on the other side of the bed. Professor Severance stood timidly in the doorway. When he was five years old his mother had taken him to New York for a visit. They saw the Central Park zoo and the aquarium. They observed the Statue of Liberty from a little boat that went all around the harbor. They rode on the elevated railway. He learned to take his hat off in the elevators of the tall buildings, and his mother, for the crowning treat of all, took him to the toy department of a big department store where he saw all the toys that he had ever dreamed of. She had an errand to do on the floor above and she thought he saw her go, but his mind was on a little piano with real keys, and suddenly he discovered that he was alone, that his mother had abandoned him. She was only gone five minutes, and the saleswomen gathered around and tried to comfort him, but a child lost goes on crying, right down to the end of time.

The late afternoon sun came streaming in through the open window and lay in squares on the white woodwork, on the polished floor, and on a section of wallpaper. The small yellow roses climbing up the wall seemed almost real.

"Well," Dr. Rogers said finally, "there's nothing to do but wait."

When he picked up his black bag and left the room, the nurse remained behind. Professor Severance followed him down the stairs and the two men stood talking on the front porch for perhaps five minutes. They kept their voices down, not because there was any danger that the patient upstairs might hear them, but out of respect for the seriousness of her condition.

The doctor got into his car and drove away, and Professor Severance went back into the house. He picked up one of the little clay figures that were on the piano in the living room—the figure of the bridegroom in a red robe, with a gold sash and green lining to his sleeves. After a moment or two Professor Severance restored the figure to the wedding procession and went out into the hall to telephone. The colored maid, coming into the dining room to set the table for dinner, heard him say, "Apparently there's nothing . . . Yes . . . Yes . . . Yes, I will . . . Of course I will, but there's nothing anybody can do now. We just have to wait . . . Yes, I will, Alice . . . Yes, of course . . ." and knew that he was talking to Mrs. Forbes.

When he came back into the living room he sat down at the card table, in his accustomed place, and his eyes went searching, out of habit, until they found a jack of spades to go on a queen of diamonds, a nine of hearts that he could place on the ten of spades.

In the middle of the night, some time between two o'clock and three, the lights went on at Professor Severance's, first in one room and then in another, upstairs and then down. The houses on either side of it, all up and down the block, were dark, and so were the houses across the street, but Professor Severance's house looked as if it were all lit up for a party, one of the parties for which his mother was famous, with fiddlers for the Virginia reel and a staggering buffet supper afterward and none of the guests as gay as or having a better time than the old lady herself.

50

Those who are brave enough go straight into the center of any dangerous situation and often come out alive on the other side. Most people aren't very brave, of course, and to try and skirt around a danger looks safer than to go right into the center of it. Unfortunately it isn't safer, because if you don't go through the center you meet with an ambush later on, and there the chances are totally against you. But the odd thing is that if you keep walking around a danger, if you choose the indirect, cautious method, avoiding an open conflict, it will seem for a time to work.

Spud broke a bone in his hand, that afternoon at the gymnasium, and afterward a strange happiness set in for him, and also for Lymie and Sally; the kind of happiness that people sometimes describe as "like old times come back again." Included in this description is the knowledge that the happiness seemed, the first time, as if it would last forever, and that they now know better than to think that.

Spud was still jealous. All that was necessary to unbalance his feelings was for him to meet Sally and Lymie coming toward him on the Broad Walk and see with his own eyes how interested they were in what they were saying to each other, before they looked up and saw him. But since he now made no effort to fight it, Spud's jealousy didn't last as long. Sometimes it only lasted a few minutes. If Spud was silent, Lymie stopped talking. When Spud's face cleared, all that Lymie had been thinking burst out of him in a flood of conversation.

With his right hand and wrist held immobile between two splints, there was no point in Spud's going to the gymnasium. He and Lymie and Sally sat in the Ship's Lantern until suppertime, or if Sally was busy, Spud went home with Lymie to the rooming house. He even stayed all night there once. In the morning a hand shaking Lymie's shoulder wakened him, and for a moment he didn't know whose hand it was. But then he opened his eyes and saw Spud sitting up in bed, and happiness flowed back into him like sunlight entering a room.

Spud wanted to be at the fraternity house for breakfast. They got up quietly without waking anybody and went downstairs. Lymie sat in his bathrobe and slippers, with his legs drawn up under him, and watched Spud dress. Every move that he made delighted Lymie. The way Spud rubbed the sleep out of his eyes with his uninjured hand, the majestic way that he put one foot on a chair and then the other, for Lymie to tie his shoelaces were pleasures so familiar and so long denied. When Spud went off to the bathroom, Lymie followed and pulled the lid of the toilet down and sat on it. He was amused at the violence with which Spud soused his face with soap and water, and he enjoyed knowing that in a moment Spud, with his head bent over the washbowl, would reach out blindly for the towel that he knew Lymie would have ready for him.

Washing and dressing required only a few minutes, and no amount of observation and delight could in any way prolong them. Back in Lymie's room, Spud turned to the closet and shook his head.

"It's a mess, isn't it?" Lymie agreed.

"I don't see how you stand it," Spud said.

"I don't know either," Lymie said. "I guess I just didn't see it. I haven't any eight o'clock class today. I'll come back right after breakfast and clean it up."

Spud looked at the closet regretfully—he would have enjoyed straightening it himself—and then at his watch. "I have to be going," he said.

Lymie went to the head of the stairs with him, leaned over the railing, and watched Spud make his way like a hero between two drop-leaf tables. Lymie waited until he heard the front door close, and then he went back to his room. He was too happy and grateful to go back to bed, and it was too early to get dressed. He walked up and down with his hands clasped together, thinking. He was not grateful to Spud so much as he was grateful to life itself. Because you are born, he thought, and you learn to eat and walk and talk, and you go to school, thinking that that's all there is, and then suddenly everything is full of meaning and you know that you were not born merely to grow up and earn a living. You were born to . . .

On the back of a chair he saw a sweater. He picked it up, held it out in front of him, and smiled. The shape and size identified it beyond question, among all the navy blue sweaters in the world. In a sudden access of feeling he buried his face in it. He didn't do anything about the closet.

That night, after supper, the three of them met in front of the Forbeses' house and played football by the light of a street lamp.

Neither Sally nor Lymie could hold Spud alone but they tackled him together. Sally grabbed the upper part of his body and Lymie dived for his legs. Even so, and handicapped as he was by an injured hand, Spud often got away from them.

When they had worn themselves out, they went up on the porch and sat in the swing and talked about places they'd like to go to, if they had plenty of money and nothing to worry about, like school or earning a living. Sally thought it would be nice to take a long ocean voyage to India or China. The nearest she had ever come to it, she said, was the trip from Boston to New York, on the night boat, which left Boston at five o'clock on a summer afternoon. Her mother and father were with her, but she had a stateroom all to herself. Around one o'clock she woke up, after being asleep for hours, and decided that the boat was pitching and tossing. When people were seasick (and at that moment she felt very queer) they got up and walked on deck. When she got outside, she found that they weren't out in the ocean at all; they were going through the Cape Cod Canal, and the boat was moving along steadily and quietly as if it were on a millpond. That was when she was twelve years old, and she could still remember the sound the bottom of the boat made, scraping, and the little shacks along the sides of the canal. The shacks were so close that you could almost reach down and pick the geraniums that were blooming in window boxes. Men with lanterns called up to her from the towpath, the captain shouted from the bridge, and there was a little dog that barked and also a girl with a baby in her arms—a wonderful baby that was wide awake at one o'clock in the morning.

The trip through the Cape Cod Canal was the first genuinely romantic thing that had ever happened to Sally. Until that time, her soul had been slowly perishing of a world where everybody was too well-bred and everything made too much sense. She wanted Spud and Lymie, her two closest friends, to understand about that inland voyage now, and share it with her, but unfortunately such an experience, the essence of it, cannot be communicated. And although Spud would have been glad of a chance to give blood transfusions or walk miles through deep snowdrifts for her sake, and Lymie would have sat for days at her bedside reading to her—on this occasion neither of them was willing to remain quiet and listen. Spud yawned openly, and Lymie kept fingering the chains which held the porch swing or pushing at a wicker chair to make the swing go sidewise. His eyes had a feverish luster that was not apparent in the dark, but when he spoke his voice was pitched to his own inner excitement, which made it impossible for him to listen to anyone very long without interrupting. This restlessness, this desire for something to be continually happening, had been with him since the afternoon Spud hurt his hand. It was with Lymie when he woke in the morning and it flung him into bed exhausted at the end of each day. His cheeks grew thinner and lines which would some day be permanent appeared between his nostrils and the corners of his mouth.

It was he, actually, who was responsible for the sudden, very violent wrestling match which made Mrs. Forbes turn on the porch light and gaze in astonishment at the tangled mass of arms and legs on the porch floor.

"Lymie," she exclaimed, "is that *you*?"

Nothing that Spud or Sally did ever seemed to startle her.

51

The university outdoor band concerts began late in April. Folding chairs were distributed over the steps of the auditorium, and on the stroke of seven the bronze doors opened and the sixty-odd members of the band filed out in their blue uniforms and found places. After an interval the band leader appeared and there was polite applause. Then a hush as his baton was raised and brought forth the first very faint sounds. The repertoire at these concerts was standard: "Pomp and Circumstance," Bizet's "Arlesienne Suite #2," the overture to "William Tell," the ballet music from "Rosamunde," and music equally familiar. The audience sat on the grass or walked about or stood in clusters. People listened to the music or not, as they pleased, and what the wind blew away didn't matter particularly.

The evening of the first spring concert Lymie walked over from the boarding club with Reinhart. Here and there in the crowd he saw someone he knew—a boy who had sat next to him in botany the year before, two girls who were in his German class, his physical education instructor. Ford and Frenchie deFresne were there, each with a girl. No one looking at Frenchie now, with his hair parted in the middle instead of on the side, and wearing fawn-colored flannel trousers, a brown tweed coat, a snow-white shirt, and a yellow tie, would ever have guessed that he had once been through hell because he couldn't think of a nine letter word beginning with S and ending with N. And though the girl who stood with her arm drawn through Ford's called him "Diver," it was something she had picked up from the boys in his fraternity, and even they had no idea where the name originally came from.

Bob Edwards was at the concert with his public speaking instructor, a woman who was clearly too old for him; and Geraghty was there, but alone. His new girl had stood him up for an Alpha Delt with a Packard roadster.

Mrs. Forbes was standing under the low branch of an elm tree, near the Broad Walk. Professor Forbes was with her, and so was Professor Severance. She waved to Lymie, but the two men were deep in conversation and didn't see him. Professor Severance had not worn a band of black cloth on his left sleeve or made any public show of mourning, and many of his students didn't even know that his mother had died suddenly during the night. But Mrs. Lieberman saw it in his face the first day that he taught his classes again. Professor Severance looked not only older but smaller, and it was all she could do to keep from speaking to him after the hour. *Now you can lecture*, was what she wanted to tell him. *You've passed over. And I'd like very much to hear what you have to say about Matthew Arnold or Swinburne or yourself* . . .

She was at the concert with her two sons. She smiled at Lymie and he smiled back, recognizing her vaguely. The redheaded boy with her was the boy Spud got to give him a boxing lesson, that day last fall. Hope was at the concert also, with Bernice Crawford. Lymie stopped to talk to them a moment, and then he and Reinhart walked on.

Sally wasn't with her mother and father, and Lymie assumed that she must be with Spud. He kept searching for them in the crowd and finding people who looked almost but not quite like them. The back of a girl's head or the slope of a boy's shoulders would be almost right but the carriage would be wrong or the girl would turn and he would see what he had known all along—that the girl was not Sally, not even like Sally.

He caught a glimpse of his logic instructor, a Welshman with wavy hair, and, later on, of his last year's rhetoric instructor with a woman who looked as if she might be his wife. Though dogs were not allowed on the campus, there were several of varying sizes and breeds, who pursued each other earnestly through the legs of the crowd.

The music out of doors was like a part of the weather. At one moment it sounded strong and clear and touched the hearts of those who were listening to it. The next moment it was scattered, lost on the largeness of the evening. Lymie had almost forgotten that Reinhart was with him when a remark, heard above the brasses and the clarinets, made him turn and ask, "*What* can't you stand any longer?"

"I don't know whether I ought to tell you," Reinhart said.

"Why not?" Lymie asked, with his eyes on a chain of migratory birds that were flying very high.

Reinhart shook his head. "It might make trouble."

"If it's something I ought to know—" Lymie said.

"Sometimes it's all I can do to keep from taking a poke at him. I'd probably get the shit beat out of me but it would be worth it. I'd feel better afterward. But anyway, I can't stand to see you following him around and getting kicked in the teeth whenever he feels like it."

Lymie looked at Reinhart oddly but said nothing.

"What the hell do you see in a guy like that?"

"A lot," Lymie said.

"I suppose you must," Reinhart said. "But if you feel that way about him, somebody ought to tell you something."

"What?" Lymie asked.

"You want to know?"

Lymie nodded.

"He's jealous of you. He's so jealous of you he can't stand the sight of you. He comes over to the house sometimes when you're at the library and he sits in my room and talks for an hour at a time about how much he hates you."

As a rule, Lymie's face gave him away. When he was embarrassed, he blushed to the roots of his hair. When he was frightened, he showed it. Now nothing showed.

"I guess I should have realized it," he said, and changed the subject.

The concert ended at eight o'clock with the playing of the university anthem. As the crowd began to drift toward the streets that led away from the campus, Reinhart tried to persuade Lymie to go to a movie with him, but Lymie said that he had to study, so they walked back to "302." Lymie went straight to his own room. He was loosening his necktie when Reinhart came in, sat down in the Morris chair, and lit a cigarette. He was in the habit of going from room to room during the evening, and Lymie was not compelled by politeness—since there was no pretense of it in the rooming house—to make conversation. He sat down at his littered desk and cleared a place in front of him. He knew that Reinhart was waiting for him to turn around, but instead he opened a book and pretended to read. Reinhart finished his cigarette and then got up and went on to Pownell's room. Five minutes later he was back.

"You're not sore at me, are you?" he asked hesitantly.

"Why should I be?" Lymie said.

"For telling you about Spud."

"No," Lymie said. "You did me a favor. Besides, I would have found it out sooner or later."

"That's what I thought," Reinhart said, and wandered back to Pownell's room.

A few minutes later he was back again. This time he didn't come in but lingered in the doorway. "Look, bud," he said, "I feel sorry about what I did. I shouldn't have told you. I know damn well I shouldn't. Now that I've made trouble between you two guys, I'm going out in a few minutes and get drunk." He turned away from the doorway and then came back one last time. "Why don't you come with me?" he asked. "You don't have to drink if you don't want to. Stay sober and keep an eye on me, because I'm going to need it." He saw by the expression on Lymie's face that he was getting ready to frame an excuse, and before Lymie could open his mouth, Reinhart said, "Never mind," and disappeared.

Between nine and nine-thirty, Colter and then Howard passed through Lymie's room without stopping. At twenty minutes of ten, Freeman came in and ransacked Lymie's closet for a sport coat which he had wanted to wear to the concert. He had gone through every other closet on the second floor without any luck, and so he thought he might as well try Lymie's. Lymie turned around and watched him. The sport coat wasn't there.

At ten o'clock Lymie undressed and went upstairs to bed. He was going to see Spud later. Beyond that he had no plan and yet he acted as if he had one, and as if it were essential to this plan that the other boys who lived at the rooming house should be in bed and asleep before he carried it out. The door swung open and closed, time after time. He thought he kept track of the boys who came in and got into their beds, but he miscounted. Reinhart and Pownell went out together, shortly after ten, and neither of them had come in when Lymie got up at midnight and slipped downstairs again.

Instead of getting dressed he put on a clean pair of pajamas and took his winter overcoat out of the closet. When he had combed his hair in front of the mirror he put the coat on, buttoned it, and left the house. It was a soft spring night and the moon, no longer full, was on its way down the sky. The houses Lymie passed were nearly all dark. Now and then a single harsh light burned in an upstairs room. In any other town a light in an upstairs window at that hour would have meant that someone was sleepless or sick. Here it was because a head was still bent over a book, a hand writing slowly. The campus was deserted. The massive familiar buildings were enjoying the peace and the silence in the corridors never allowed them in the daytime. The front door of Spud's fraternity house was unlocked; the brothers had no fear of being robbed by outsiders. There was a light in the front hall. Both the living room and the dining room were dark. The brothers had either gone out or up to bed, leaving the odor of stale cigarette smoke behind them.

Lymie went up four flights of stairs, with his right hand moving against the plaster wall, guiding him. The door which led to the dormitory had a pane of frosted glass in it, and groaned when Lymie pushed it open. He stood still, with his heart pounding, but no voice challenged him from the dark, no springs creaked suspiciously. Spud had shown him months before where he slept, and as soon as his eyes grew accustomed to the darkness Lymie made his way through the forest of double-deckers and found Spud asleep in his single lower, near the open window.

Lymie, who was always watching the others, who slipped into the water when it was his turn but never took part in the shouting and splashing, now for the first time watched himself. He was in the center of the stage at last, with an important part to play: he was the devoted friend, to whom a grave injury has been done.

52

Spud raised himself on one elbow and looked at Lymie without speaking. There was a second when Lymie was sure that he was about to fall back on the bed without ever knowing that anybody had awakened him. Instead he got up noiselessly and followed Lymie downstairs. At the door of Spud's room Lymie stepped aside. The door was padlocked and he didn't know the combination.

When they got inside Spud closed the door and went to his closet for a bathrobe; he had been sleeping naked. As Lymie took his coat off it occurred to him for the first time that Reinhart might have been mistaken. The whole thing could have been something that Reinhart had imagined, and the expression in Spud's eyes, the clouded look, might be due to the fact that his sleep had been broken. Lymie stared at the gray iris, the dark pupil, and then at the curve of the eyelids. There was no doubt about it, the expression was hate.

"There is something I have to tell you," he said.

Spud nodded.

"I went to the band concert with Dick Reinhart. He said you were jealous of me on account of Sally."

Spud's expression did not change.

"What I came over to tell you, you have to believe," Lymie said. "I'm not in love with Sally and she isn't in love with me. She doesn't love anyone but you and never has."

Spud nodded again, but it was not the kind of nod that means agreement.

"You believe me, don't you?" Lymie asked. "You have to believe me because what I'm saying is the truth."

To his horror he saw that Spud was smiling.

In the scene that Lymie had imagined, lying awake in bed on the other side of town, Spud had said to him, *I don't hate you, Lymie old socks. I couldn't hate you.* But there is so often a discrepancy between real life and the life of the imagination, and people tend not to allow for it, or at least not sufficiently. It hadn't occurred to Lymie that Spud would turn away, instead of speaking, and find a chair, and sit down with one leg crossed over the other and one fleece-lined slipper dangling in space. Spud was thoroughly awake now and his eyes were thoughtful, but the thought, whatever it was, remained locked inside of him.

Lymie saw that words were not enough. It would take some action, as yet unplanned but rising like a shadow behind him. On a sudden impulse he went toward Spud and knelt down and clasped Spud's knees. The movement came naturally to Lymie but it was also one of the oldest human gestures.

"Please listen to me," Lymie said. "Because if you don't, you'll be very sorry."

Spud had never read the *Iliad* and he was not moved by the pressure of Lymie's hands or the bright tears in his eyes. He had seen tears before and he himself never shed them.

When Spud lowered his eyes to his hands, Lymie looked at them too—at the tight bandage and the two splints on Spud's right hand, and the five fingers coming out of the gauze. When he is able to box again, Lymie thought, someone else will tie his gloves on for him. I no longer have access to any part of him.

There was a strange but not very long silence between them, and then Lymie got up from the floor, put his coat on, and turned the collar up around his throat. As he started for the door, Spud stood up too and followed him out into the hall. They went down the hall side by side, as if they were still on good terms with each other.

A door opened and Armstrong came out in his pajamas and bathrobe. His hair was rumpled. He had been studying late and he looked tired and sleepy. He glanced at Spud and then at Lymie, with interest. There had been a time when, if Armstrong had shown any knowledge of his existence, Lymie would have been pleased. Now when Armstrong said, "What are you doing up at this hour of the night?" Lymie didn't even bother to answer.

Spud followed him down the stairs and out onto the porch. The moon was going down behind the brick fraternity house across the street. Spud's face had relaxed and he looked almost kind. With this almost kindness Lymie would have no part. It seemed so unnatural, and so sad, to be separating for the last time. At the foot of the steps he turned and said, "I forgive you everything!" and then felt foolish, and wished he hadn't said it. It wasn't right. It wasn't even true. The sound of his voice had made it quite clear that he didn't forgive Spud anything.

53

Mr. Peters sat waiting in the outer office of the Dean of Men. His topcoat, neatly folded, lay on the chair beside him, and his gray fedora was on top of the coat. His eyes were bloodshot and he looked as if he hadn't slept well. Though he made no effort to attract attention to himself, the secretary to whom he had given his name managed to whisper it to the girl who was standing by the filing cabinet, and she in turn told the assistant dean, when he came out of his office to use the files. All three of them looked at Mr. Peters out of the corners of their eyes. They might as well have stared at him openly. He knew what they were whispering about.

He glanced at the clock on the wall, which said quarter after three, and compared it with his own gold watch. The clock was a minute fast. At twenty minutes of ten that morning he walked into his cubbyhole of an office, sat down with his hat on, reached into the top drawer of his desk, where he kept some aspirin, and took two, without any water. He lit a cigarette to take the taste out of his mouth, and as he put it down on the edge of the desk, the phone rang. He picked it up without having the slightest premonition of what was in store for him. "Mr. Lymon Peters?" the operator asked, and he said, "Yes, this is Lymon Peters speaking." "One moment please," the operator said, and then he heard a different voice. "Mr. Peters? Calkins speaking. George S. Calkins, Dean of Men at the University of . . . Can you hear me?"

"Yes," Mr. Peters said into the mouthpiece, and felt a cold sweat breaking out on his forehead. Lymie must have got into some kind of a scrape. . . . Mr. Peters hoped fervently that it wasn't a girl. If Lymie had got some nice girl in a family way. . . .

"Hardly hear you," the voice said. "Must be a bad connection . . . Operator?" The phone went dead for about thirty seconds and when Mr. Peters heard the voice again it was much louder. "Mr. Peters, I have something pretty upsetting to tell you. It's about your son."

"Lymon?" Mr. Peters asked, as if he had several. "What's he done?"

"Tried to commit suicide," the voice said. "Can you hear me now?"

Mr. Peters tried to answer but his throat seemed frozen and no sound came out of it.

"He's in the hospital," the voice said. "They took him there shortly after daylight this morning. And I've taken the liberty of hiring both a day and a night nurse. I hope that meets with your approval. Not that the floor nurse wouldn't do everything that's necessary, probably. But with cases of this kind, there is always a chance that they'll try again. So it's not safe to—"

"No," Mr. Peters said thickly. "I'm sure that's right, what you've done."

"I've looked up the train schedules for you," the voice said, "and I find there's one that leaves at . . ."

From the train Mr. Peters went to the hotel, registered, fortified himself with a shot of whisky, and then took a cab out to the university hospital. The dean had neglected to prepare him for the bandages around Lymie's throat and wrists, and at the sight of them the young man in Mr. Peters took his derby hat and departed.

Lymie was asleep. The doctor had given him a hypo and he had not even moved for nearly eight hours. Mr. Peters went over and stood beside the bed and looked down at Lymie's face. It was a dreadful waxy white, the thin skin drawn tight over the bones by exhaustion and revealing the secret shape of the skull. All the strength went out of Mr. Peters' legs, and he put his hand against the foot of the bed. There's only one thing to be thankful for, he thought, swaying slightly. And that is that the boy's mother isn't alive. It would have been too much for her. She couldn't have stood it. . . . He took out a handkerchief and blew his nose quietly. Then he turned to the nurse and said, "I don't suppose there is any use of my staying here. I have a room at the hotel, in case you need to get in touch with me. And I'll be back in the morning."

He had never been on the university campus before and what he saw, going from the hospital to the dean's office, wasn't very real to him. The sunshine and the big trees hanging far out over the street, and the sidewalks crowded with boys and girls Lymie's age, walking along with books under their arms, and all of them unconcerned, acting as if nothing were wrong anywhere in the world. But then the whole day was unreal to him.

The dean kept Mr. Peters waiting a full ten minutes before he was shown into the inner office, where the dean sat, at a heavy walnut desk, under a portrait of himself by a distinguished American painter. The money for this portrait had been raised partly by undergraduate subscription, partly by well-to-do alumni. The dean rose, walked around the desk, and offered his hand. His handshake, like that of most public men, was limp and impersonal, but the expression on his face seemed to Mr. Peters to be genuine sympathy.

"I'm very happy to meet you," the dean said, "though I regret the—er—circumstances under which we— Won't you sit down?" He regretted even more the alcohol which he detected on Mr. Peters' breath. . . . The dean was a teetotaler.

Mr. Peters settled himself in a chair beside the desk and waited for the dean to produce a letter addressed to him in Lymie's handwriting.

"It's not the first case of this kind we've had to contend with," the dean said. "At nineteen, you know, life often seems unbearable. I could show you statistics that prove—but you're not interested in statistics, I feel sure. Your son is in excellent hands, Mr. Peters. We have reason to be proud of our medical men. Dr. Hart is not my own doctor but I know him well and wouldn't hesitate to use him, if I were taken sick. He's both conscientious and thorough. I'm sure when you talk to him—"

"What did he do it with?" Mr. Peters interrupted.

"With a straight-edged razor," the dean said. There was a slight pause and then he added, "This must be very hard on you. I know how I'd feel in your place."

Mr. Peters looked at him and saw that the dean hadn't the faintest idea how he felt; that if anything, the dean was enjoying it, like the people in the outer office.

"I've talked to several of the boys in the rooming house where your son has been living, and to several of his teachers, and his two best friends—a boy named Charles Latham and a boy named Geraghty. You know both of them, probably?"

Mr. Peters nodded. He knew that Lymie had spent a good deal of time with a boy named Latham, when he was in high school, and that they had roomed together for a while when Lymie first came down here. "I've met Latham but not the other boy," he said.

"There is also a girl in the case," the dean said. "Her father is one of the prominent men here in the university. I couldn't get much out of the Latham boy. I found him sullen and distrustful. But Geraghty told me a good deal and so did the girl, without knowing it. She's a very open honest youngster. I've known her all her life. She says she didn't realize the situation, but it's obvious that your son was in love with her and tried to kill himself when he found out that she was in love with this Latham boy. I've been dealing with young people for thirty-five years now, and I've gradually come around to the belief that although they seem like children to us—to their parents especially—their problems, their emotional disturbances are not essentially different from the emotional disturbances of older people. The girl was rather distressed by our conversation this morning. She was crying when she left here, and she went to the hospital and tried to force her way in. We have a rule against mixed visiting at the university hospital, for reasons that I'm sure I don't have to explain to you. And in any case, the doctor doesn't want Lymie to have visitors for a day or so—that doesn't mean you, naturally. There are a couple of people that I have to talk to still—the president of Charles Latham's fraternity, a boy named Armstrong; and also the man who keeps the rooming house where your son has been living. I don't expect to find out anything from them that we don't know already."

Mr. Peters glanced uneasily at the pile of papers on the desk. "Did Lymie leave any word for me?" he asked.

The dean shook his head. "No word for anybody."

54

The statistics that the dean refrained from quoting show that there are more suicides in spring than in any other season of the year, that more single persons take their lives than married ones, that suicide is more frequent in peacetime than during a war, more common among Protestants than among Catholics.

Considering the whole of human misery, it is not unreasonable that now and then some unhappy person should want to take his own life. But certain customs and practices now fallen into disuse—the confiscation of the suicide's property, the brutal punishment inflicted on his corpse, the refusal of a Christian burial, and that strange practice of burying a suicide at a crossroads with a stake driven through his heart—testify to the horror aroused by this act. The horror may be due to the fact that all people share, in some degree, the impulse toward self-destruction; and when some one person actually gives way to it, all are exposed to the common danger. Or perhaps the horror stems from something else, something much less complicated: The suicide doesn't go alone, he takes everybody with him.

During the middle of the last century a French soldier hanged himself from the lintel of a doorway in the Hôtel des Invalides in Paris. For two years there had been no suicides there, and during the next fourteen days, five men were found hanging from the same beam. The passageway was closed off and there were no more suicides for a time at that institution, though men and women continued to jump from the Waterloo Bridge (also Highgate Archway and the Clifton Suspension Bridge), to swallow arsenic, to hold revolvers to their foreheads, and to throw themselves in front of trains.

The morning that Lymie was taken to the hospital, quiet descended on the second floor of the rooming house, and for nearly a week there were no fights, no wrestling matches at the head of the stairs. In one way or another each of the boys was affected. No one crossed the threshold of Lymie's room. The terrible expression that Colter and Fred Howard remembered seeing in Lymie's face that night when they passed through this room was, of course, the work of their own excited imaginations. Freeman remembered how Lymie had turned around sadly and watched him ransack the closet—and was ashamed. Pownell had come home about one-thirty that same night and heard someone being sick in the bathroom. He decided that it must be Reinhart, who had left him an hour before, good and drunk. He started to go in and hold Reinhart's head for him. But then he remembered that Reinhart owed him three dollars and had been asked for it repeatedly, so he went up the stairs to bed. For two days he kept from telling anyone about this, but finally he broke down and confessed that he was entirely responsible for Lymie's doing what he did, and there was no arguing Pownell out of it.

Amsler, who hadn't been home or allowed his mother to come and see him for over a month, sat down and wrote her a post card; she could expect him, he said, sometime late Friday. Mr. Dehner's reactions were perhaps the most peculiar, and made the least sense. When the telephone rang and he found himself talking to the dean at last, he was so confused he couldn't decide which boys, out of the dozen who lived in his house, were Lymie's friends. He saw Geraghty coming down the stairs at that moment and gave the dean his name. Mr. Dehner had been through a good deal. He had stood by while the plumber and his assistant had made the bathtub and the washbowl usable again, an experience that could easily have shattered a less nervous man. When he turned away from the telephone he went into his bedroom, locked the door, and lay face down on his four-poster bed, and wept; not for Lymie but for himself, because everything went wrong for him. No matter what he did or tried to do, the result was always the same.

After Geraghty left the dean's office he shut himself in a phone booth and called his old girl and they met in the Ship's Lantern and patched things up. Geraghty discovered that he was much fonder of her than he had realized. And he had not lied to the dean about his friendship with Lymie. He had always liked Lymie very much and had meant to be friends with Lymie, only he hadn't got around to it. What he told the dean was merely a statement of his intentions for the future—if Lymie survived. On the way home from the Ship's Lantern he stopped in to see his new girl, intending to tell her that it was all off between them. But for the first time in nearly a month she seemed really glad to see him and when she was like that, he didn't have the heart to tell her that he wasn't going to see her any more.

The only person in the rooming house who remained himself, calm and unexcited, was Reinhart, although it was he who had found Lymie at five o'clock in the morning, when he came home from a visit to the house on South Maple Street. He made Lymie lie down on the floor of his room, covered him with an overcoat, and then ran downstairs and called a doctor who lived in the next block. The ambulance came, twenty minutes later. Two interns brought a stretcher up the stairs. It was just getting light when they carried Lymie out of the house. The interns rode in the front of the ambulance and Reinhart rode in back with Lymie, who was conscious of everything that was going on but made no effort to talk. He didn't seem worried about himself or embarrassed about what he had done. Ordinary anxieties, the fear of what people might think, seemed to have dropped away from him. Reinhart took Lymie's hand and held it all the way to the hospital. At the door of the operating room the interns motioned Reinhart away but Lymie asked them to let him stay and so they put a sterile gown on him and a mask, and he stood near the door while the doctors questioned Lymie about the iodine he had swallowed and tried to find out whether he had cut his windpipe. Apparently he hadn't. The doctor took a long time cleaning and sewing up and dressing the wounds, and then he gave Lymie an injection for tetanus. The needles were inserted into his abdomen and they were an inch and a half long. Reinhart had to turn his eyes away when the needles went in. His body felt alternately hot and cold, and he thought he was going to faint.

When Lymie was wheeled off, Reinhart left the hospital and went to find Spud. It was six-thirty by that time and Spud was in his room getting dressed.

"Lymie?" Spud said. "Are you sure?"

"Yes, I'm sure," Reinhart said.

"But why?" Spud said. "What made him do a thing like that?"

"I didn't ask him," Reinhart said, "and he didn't tell me."

They both avoided each other's eyes.

Spud said, "I didn't think people—I mean, I thought he—"

Shorty Stevenson came into the room, in his pajamas, rubbing his eyes and yawning. They waited in silence while he put on his glasses, looked at them cheerfully, and stood scratching himself. "Did I interrupt something?" he asked, and when they still did not answer, he pulled his pajama coat off over his head, picked up a towel, and went off down the hall to the bathroom.

"Where's he now?" Spud asked.

"In the hospital. I just came from there."

"I guess I don't understand anything," Spud said, "but I thought— Tell me what happened."

He listened carefully with his eyes on the floor the whole time that Reinhart was talking. It was almost as if he suspected some trick, an April Fool's joke of some kind, and was on guard against it. But when Reinhart was finished, Spud said, "Wait a minute." While Reinhart stood there watching him, he finished dressing, picked up a couple of books and put them down again, looked around the room as if he were seeing it for the last time, then said, "Let's go."

On the way over to "302" they stopped at a dog-wagon and had breakfast. Reinhart lit a cigarette with his coffee and Spud asked him for one. Reinhart had never seen Spud smoke before, and as he lit a match and held it toward the end of Spud's cigarette, he thought: *this is the strangest part of all.*

Reinhart had an eight o'clock class, but his head seemed twice its natural size, from all the spiked beer that he had drunk the night before, and he knew there was no use trying to concentrate on anything. It would be better to get some sleep, if he could. He gave up that idea also when they started up the stairs at the rooming house and Spud looked at him suddenly with the face of a drowning man.

Reinhart stayed with Spud all morning, went to the dean's office with him, and was waiting when Spud came out from his interview with the dean. It was after twelve o'clock then, so they started for the boarding club. Reinhart turned off suddenly, not wanting to expose Spud to the curiosity of the boys from "302," and they ate in a drugstore. Spud seemed all right by that time. When they got to the rooming house, Reinhart went up to the dormitory and stretched out on his bed and fell asleep with all his clothes on.

It was late afternoon when he woke and came downstairs. His room was empty and he thought for a moment that Spud had gone back to the fraternity house. But then he heard someone moving about in the next room. He went to the door and looked in. Lymie's desk and the one that had been Spud's and the closet were in absolute order for the first time since Spud had moved out of "302." It must have taken hours, Reinhart thought. He looked at Spud, who didn't know that he was there. Spud was standing in front of Lymie's dresser. Reinhart turned away without making a sound.

A few minutes later Spud appeared in the door of Reinhart's room. Reinhart was at his desk studying, with his head supported by his hands. He didn't look up immediately. When he turned around, Spud was sitting in the big overstuffed chair. His eyes were closed and he was shivering and shaking as if he had caught a chill, as if he were chilled to the bone.

55

At two-thirty the next morning, Lymie opened his eyes in a bare hospital room. The light was on, shaded by a piece of yellow paper. Miss Vogel, the night nurse, saw that he was awake, came over to the bed, and took his temperature. She was a plump, middle-aged woman with dyed black hair and a black fuzz on her upper lip. She took the thermometer out from under Lymie's tongue and read it. Then she wiped his forehead with a damp washcloth, and straightened the covers. These first threads of dependency having been established between them, she bent over the bed, so that her face was close to his, and said, "Why did you do it?"

Lymie's eyelids closed of their own accord.

I didn't want to go on living in a world where the truth has no power to make itself be believed, he said, without moving his lips, without making a sound. *There was a small bottle of iodine in the medicine cabinet in the bathroom on the second floor of Mr. Dehner's rooming house. I took the cap off and drank all of it. The iodine burned the lining of my throat on the way down and formed a solid knot of burning in my stomach. The burning got worse and worse until suddenly I flung myself on my knees in front of the toilet and vomited the horrible yellow stuff into the bowl.*

Someone came upstairs about this time and I was afraid they would come into the bathroom and find me but they didn't.

Whoever it was went on up to the dorm. The burning lasted for a while and then it went away. I got up then and opened the medicine cabinet again and took out Mr. Dehner's straight-edged razor. With the warm water running slowly into the washbasin I began to cut my left wrist. The flesh parted with a stinging sensation and began to bleed. The blood turned pink in the lukewarm water and went down the drainpipe. I remember raising my eyes then, calmly, but with a wonderful kind of giddiness inside my head, and I looked at my face in the mirror. After a time the blood stopped flowing. The flow became single drops and the drops came slower and slower. I cut my wrist again, deeper. I made three separate incisions in my left wrist and each time the blood congealed, after a few minutes. So I transferred the razor to my other hand and cut wherever the veins showed through the skin.

There were moments when my strength failed and the light bulb dangling from the ceiling on a long cord seemed to grow much too bright. But these moments passed and I went on cutting. Finally (all this took a long time and I was very tired) I left the washbasin, knelt down beside the tub, and applied the edge of the razor to my throat. The blood flowed in a stream. The bottom of the tub was red with it almost immediately. The light dimmed and went out, and I remembered thinking then with surprise that this familiar thing, this comforting complete darkness that I had known every night of my life, was death.

When the blackness lifted, I was still there on my knees beside the tub. The razor was still in my right hand. I raised it and more blood flowed into the tub.

There is, for every person to discover, a limit, an end to his will, a wall before which he stands and has to say "This wall I can't climb over." At five o'clock, with the light showing gray in the bathroom window, I got up and acknowledged the fact that I was through. It had seemed so easy before I started, and it had proved to be so hard. I was too tired to cut any more. Some acts, particularly acts of violence, are not possible to certain people. Even when you try with all your strength, they just don't come off.

My white pajamas were soaked with blood. I picked up a bathtowel and wound it around my neck and then I started for my own room. Before I got there the front door opened and I heard singing. It was somebody coming home drunk, singing "Mary Ann McCarthy she went out to gather clams . . ." I went to the head of the stairs and waited there until Reinhart, lurching and stumbling and grabbing at the banister for support, looked up and saw me. "Want to pee, Lymie?" he said. "Do you have to pee?" Then his mouth fell open and he said, "Oh, my Christ, what have you done to yourself?"

56

"I expect Lymie has told you about me," Mr. Dehner said pleasantly. "My name is Alfred Dehner. I have the antique shop downstairs, and I'm his landlord, so to speak."

Lymie had never mentioned Mr. Dehner to his father, and Mr. Peters didn't like effeminate men. Instead of shaking hands he merely nodded.

"I just wanted to say how sorry I am. So shocking, wasn't it? Such an awful way to choose. Gas would have been much simpler, but probably he didn't think about it. And if he'd come downstairs and put his head in the oven I certainly would have heard him. I'm a very light sleeper. Have been for years. I fall asleep all right but then I wake up along about two o'clock and stay awake until daylight. And just before it's time to get up I fall asleep again. I said to Dick Reinhart this morning, 'Just when you think you're safe,' I said, 'and that everything has happened to you that can happen, that's the time to look out.' Lymie's always seemed like such a nice quiet boy. Not at all the sort that you'd expect to—although I must say, the first time I saw him, when I opened the front door and he was standing there, I had a feeling. Something told me that he—but that's the way life is. Always the unexpected. I've been horribly upset by all this. My nerves aren't strong, you know. I'm full of Luminal right this minute. It isn't habit-forming, the doctor says, but probably if you took a lot of it, over a long period of time, it might be. I'm expecting some ladies who are interested in a piecrust table that I found in the top of an old barn. It had to be refinished, of course, and when I first got it, it smelled of sheep manure, but it's a very fine piece. I don't expect you're interested in antique furniture. So few men are. If you want anything, you'll let me know, won't you. I'll be downstairs. . . . Come, Pooh-Bah."

The spaniel sniffed suspiciously at Mr. Peters' pants leg,

growled once, and then padded off after his master. Left to himself, Mr. Peters stood in the center of the room. He observed with satisfaction how neat it was. All the nagging he had done was evidently not in vain; Lymie had learned to pick up his things.

In a straight row at the back of the closet were a pair of rubbers and several pairs of scuffed shoes which couldn't belong to anybody but Lymie. I could have been a better father to him, Mr. Peters thought, looking at the shoes. *I could have stayed home oftener, and I could have been more patient. I could have spent more time with him, taken him to the movies occasionally, and gone to concerts and museums with him.*

While Mr. Peters was accusing himself, he heard a slight noise and turned around.

"There's something I want to tell you," Spud said. "I didn't know the money Lymie loaned me was from him."

Though Mr. Peters had only met Spud once, he recognized him immediately.

"I should have known it was from Lymie, but I didn't," Spud said.

"How much was it?" Mr. Peters asked.

"A hundred dollars."

Mr. Peters was shocked. A hundred dollars was a lot of money. Lymie couldn't have managed that on his allowance. He must have dipped into his savings. . . . The boy seemed to be waiting for reassurance, and so Mr. Peters said, "That's something Lymie hasn't told me about. But I'm sure that if he gave you the money, he wanted you to have it. You pay him back when you can."

"I will," Spud said, nodding. There was something about Mr. Peters—not his appearance so much as his choice of words—which reminded Spud of his own father. The silence between them was a comfortable one.

"Will you have a cigar?" Mr. Peters asked, reaching for his vest pocket.

Spud shook his head, but he was pleased. No grown man had ever offered him a cigar before. He watched Mr. Peters bite the end off of his and spit it in the wastebasket, and felt that he was on solid ground at last. Mr. Peters would never do some strange awful thing without letting you know beforehand.

"Have you seen him?" Spud asked suddenly.

"I saw him yesterday and again this morning," Mr. Peters said, searching for matches. Spud whipped out a package that he was obliged to carry as a pledge in a fraternity house. "Much obliged," Mr. Peters said. "He was sleeping both times. The doctor gave him morphine. He's in pretty bad shape, and of course he isn't a very strong boy to begin with, but they seem to think he'll pull through all right. I'm more worried about his mental condition than anything else. When he was younger, if I could have afforded it, I would have sent him to a military school. I wish I had anyway. It would have been good for him in lots of ways. The drilling, I mean, and the discipline. When Lymie was a child he used to have a terrible temper. You wouldn't think that now, would you? But if anybody teased him he'd fly into a rage. It was funny to see him sometimes—how anything so small could get so angry. Sometimes he looked almost as if he were ready to commit murder. After his mother died, I never had any more trouble with him, except that I can't teach him the value of— You wouldn't know by any chance whether he joined the Hospital Association this year? I'm sure he did because I told him to, and sent him the money, but at the dean's office they say they haven't any record of it."

"No," Spud said, "I'm very sorry but I don't know," and with no warning, he turned on his heel and left the room.

Mr. Peters stared after him and shook his head. First that business about the money, which the dean didn't know about. And the look of suffering in the boy's face. And what happened to his hand, that it was all bandaged up? Something was wrong somewhere. Nice boy, too. And probably not used to being mixed up in a thing like this. Probably very upset by it, like everyone else. . . .

Mr. Peters had always felt that he knew all there was to know about his son, and now suddenly it seemed as if he didn't know anything. Not even as much as the dean or this Latham boy, although there were probably things that they didn't know either. . . . He took a last look around, through layers of cigar smoke. What the room knew, it was not saying.

Mr. Dehner was waiting at the foot of the stairs with a folded sheet of paper in his hand. "I hate to bother you," he said, "when you have so much on your mind. But there's a small matter I'd like to discuss with you. I've been put to considerable trouble and expense by what happened the night before last. And I know that you'll want to do the right thing."

Mr. Peters glanced at the paper and saw that it was an itemized bill. "I'll attend to it," he said, and put the bill in his inside coat pocket. He started for the door, and Mr. Dehner followed him.

"There's one thing more. When Lymie is out of the hospital perhaps it would be better for everyone concerned if he found somewhere else to live. I can't have things like that going on in my house. I'm sorry but I just can't. The other boys would move out and it would give the place a bad name."

Mr. Peters waited until the front door had closed behind him, and then he drew the bill out of his pocket and looked at it.

To plumber on acc't stopped-up tub and washbowl . . *$25.00*
New razor *$10.00*
Bathroom rug *$4.00*
Bathtowel *$2.00*
Total *$41.00*

There was no charge for the iodine.

57

When Lymie awoke it was late afternoon and he saw his father sitting in the chair by the window.

"Well, sport—" Mr. Peters said quietly and Lymie smiled at him. Neither of them said anything more for a moment. Mr. Peters drew the chair over by the bed. His hands trembled more noticeably than usual.

"The next time you do a thing like that—" he began.

"There isn't going to be any next time," Lymie said, his voice low and rather indistinct. Mr. Peters leaned forward so that he wouldn't miss anything, but Lymie had finished. He lay perfectly still with his arms outside the covers.

"Well, anyway," Mr. Peters said. Sitting by the open window he had prepared this speech, and he felt obliged to deliver it, even though there seemed now to be no need. "I want you to remember that there are other people in the world, people who are very fond of you, and you have no right to hurt them, do you hear? You can't go on acting as if you had nobody to live for but yourself."

Lymie, who had not so far as he knew been living for himself, said nothing. His eyes moved toward the window. Just outside it there was a pear tree which was coming into bloom.

"There's something I wish you'd do for me," he said slowly.

"What is it?"

"There's a night nurse . . . I don't need her and I wish you'd tell them not to let her in here."

"Anything else?" Mr. Peters asked.

"No," Lymie said.

The day nurse came in with a box of flowers. She took the cover off and Lymie saw that they were long-stemmed red roses. There was a card tucked in among the waxed green leaves. The roses were from Mrs. Forbes.

When the nurse carried them off to put them in water, Mr. Peters stood by the bed, ready to go and yet not able to. He had decided not to say anything to Lymie about the Hospital Association. They could straighten that out later. Or about the itemized bill, which was outrageous. At least four times what any of those things could have cost. When he got home he'd cut the total in half and send the man a check.

"It wouldn't have hurt you to leave some word for me, son," Mr. Peters said suddenly. "You could have written me a line or two and I wouldn't have felt nearly as bad."

Lymie looked up at his father. To lie, to make up a kind excuse, required effort and he wasn't up to it yet.

"Why didn't you?" Mr. Peters asked.

"I didn't think about it," Lymie said.

He simply spoke the truth, but for a long time afterward, for nearly a year, Mr. Peters held it against him. With that one remark the distance which had always been between them stretched out and became a vast tract, a desert country.

58

In desert country the air is never still. You raise your eyes and see a windmill a hundred yards away, revolving in the sunlight, without any apparent beginning and for years to come without any end. It may seem to slow up and stop but that is only because it is getting ready to go round and round again, faster and faster, night and day, week in, week out. The end that is followed immediately by a beginning is neither end nor beginning. Whatever is alive must be continuous. There is no life that doesn't go on and on, even the life that is in water and in stones. Listen and you hear children's voices, a dog's soft padded steps, a man hammering, a man sharpening a scythe. Each of them is repeated, the same sound, starting and stopping like a windmill.

From where you are, the windmill makes no sound, and if you were blind would not be there. A man mowing grass must be accompanied by the sound of a lawn mower to be believed. If you have discovered him with the aid of a pair of binoculars then you have also discovered that reality is almost never perceived through one of the senses alone. Withdraw the binoculars and where is the man mowing grass? You have to look to the mind for confirmation of his actuality, which may account for the inward look on the faces of the blind, the strained faces of the deaf who are forever recovering from impressions which have come upon them too suddenly with no warning sound.

But who is not, in one way or another, for large sections of time, blind or deaf or both? Mr. Peters passed the Forbeses' house on his way to the hospital and Mrs. Forbes saw him, without knowing who he was, when she glanced out of her living room windows. She saw him returning an hour later and, even so, failed to perceive that for the first time in many years he had tried to speak from his heart and had failed. A person really blind might have heard it in his step, a deaf person could have seen it in the way he turned his face to the sun. All that Mrs. Forbes saw was a man getting old and heavy before his time.

The desert is the natural dwelling place not only of Arabs and Indians but also of people who can't speak when they want to and of those others who, like Lymie Peters, have nothing more to say, people who have stopped justifying and explaining, stopped trying to account for themselves or their actions, stopped hoping that someone will come along and love them and so make sense out of their lives.

There are things in the desert which aren't to be found anywhere else. You can see a hundred miles in every direction, when you step out of your front door, and at night the stars are even brighter than they are at sea. If you cannot find indoors what you should find, then go to the window and look at the mountains, revealed after two days of uncertainty, of no future beyond the foothills which lie in a circle around the town. If it is not actually cold, if you aren't obliged to hug the fire, then go outside, by all means, even though the air is nervous, and you hear wind in the poplars, a train, a school bell, a fly—all sounds building toward something which may not be good. For reassurance there is also a car horn, a spade striking hard ground, a dog barking, and an unidentifiable bird in the Chinese elm. For further comfort there is the gardener, an old Spaniard, squatting on his haunches near the house next door. He is cleaning out the winter's rubbish and rotting leaves from the fishpond. While you sit on your haunches watching him, he will catch, in a white enamel pan, the big goldfish and the five little ones that have as yet no color. Day after day he tends this garden for a woman who is always coming back but who never arrives. Patience is to be learned from him. His iris blooms, his roses fade, his potted pink geraniums stare out of the windows of the shut-up house. It is possible that he no longer believes in the woman's coming, but nevertheless, from time to time, he empties the goldfish pool and puts fresh water in it.

If the sound of somebody chopping wood draws you out of the front gate and into the empty lot across the road, you will find blue lupines growing and see blankets airing on a clothesline, and you can talk to the man who is adding a room onto his adobe house. A great deal is to be learned from him. Also from the man chopping wood, who knows even now that there is a thunderstorm coming over the mountains, brought on by the uneasy wind in the poplars.

If you go and live for a while in desert country it is possible that you may encounter some Spanish boys, barefoot, wearing blue denim overalls. It is important that you who have moral standards but no word for addressing a stranger and conveying instantaneous approval and liking, no word to indicate a general warmth of heart; who sleep alone if you can and have lost all memory of a common table and go to tremendous lengths to keep your bones from mingling with the bones of other people—it is vitally important that you meet the little Spanish boys.

If you speak to them too abruptly they may run away, or they may even turn into statues; and how to give them back their freedom and release them from their fright is something that you alone can solve. One of them will have patches on the seat of his overalls, which have come down to him from many older brothers with some of their animal magic still left. When he is sent for water, his brothers are there to protect him. All through the day he wears their magic, until night, when his brothers are with him actually, crosswise in the bed, or curled against him on a hard pallet on the floor.

One of the little Spanish boys will use expressions which were current in the time of Cervantes. Another will have a gray cotton sweat shirt with Popeye the Sailor on the back—the mark of the world and its cheapness upon him, innocent though he is of any world beyond this desert valley. And there will be another who is not innocent but born knowing the worst, though perhaps not where to find it. And two others will have Indians for ancestors and, for reasons that are hidden from them but urgent, will do things in a way that is different from the way that the others, the pure Spanish, the Mexicans, chose. Even the sleep of the little boys with Indian blood is different, being (in all probability) full of dancing and dreams which turn out to be prophecies.

The little Spanish boys have a word—*primo*, meaning cousin—which they use to convey their liking for strangers, their willingness to share the clothes on their back, the food on their table, their fire if they have one. This same uncritical love is offered frequently to goats, burros, dogs, and chickens, and it will be extended to you.

59

There was a screen between Lymie's bed and the door, and for a second he didn't know who it was that had come. He saw Reinhart first, and then coming behind him into the room someone else. Lymie was too weak to sit up but he made a slight movement with his hands which Reinhart saw. He moved to one side so that Spud could get past him and backed out of the room. Spud came and sat on the edge of the bed. His eyes were filled with tears. The tears ran down his cheeks and he made no effort to wipe them away. Neither he nor Lymie spoke. They looked at each other with complete knowledge at last, with full awareness of what they meant to each other and of all that had ever passed between them. After a moment Spud leaned forward slowly and kissed Lymie on the mouth. He had never done this before and he was never moved to do it again.

60

In the middle of the night, Reinhart cried out in his sleep, and the sound was so sudden and so terrible that it woke every boy in the dormitory at "302." They lay in their beds shivering and waiting for it to happen again.

On the other side of town, Lymie was also awake. It was the eighth night that he had spent in the hospital, and something (the anti-tetanus serum?) had made him break out in a rash. His whole body itched. He couldn't sleep. He couldn't even lie still but kept moving his arms and legs against the sheets for relief. After a while he turned on the light and read, and while he was reading he noticed a slight rigidness in his lower jaw. He put his book down and waited for it to go away and it didn't. Instead it grew worse. He tried not to get excited; like the rash, it could be a reaction from the serum. But the doctor hadn't said that his jaw would stiffen, and it was possible that the serum hadn't worked. They might not have given him enough of it, or they might have given it to him after it was too late. . . . He didn't want to die of lockjaw; he didn't want to die at all. He lay absolutely still, with the light on, wanting to cry out for help and not knowing where help would come from.

The truth is that Lymie had never wanted to die, never at any time. The truth is nothing like as simple or as straightforward a thing as Lymie believed it to be. It masquerades in inversions and paradoxes, is easier to get at in a lie than in an honest statement. If pursued, the truth withdraws, puts on one false face after another, and finally goes underground, where it can only be got at in the complex, agonizing absurdity of dreams.

When Lymie awoke at daybreak the rigidness in his jaw had begun to go away. He realized that, just before he woke, he had been dreaming. He was in a place by the sea, and there were houses, and he made his way along the street, searching for a particular house, which he couldn't find. He was looking for No. 28. He stopped people and they gave him directions which turned out to be incorrect, and the street numbers changed in front of his eyes, but finally he found the house he was looking for—No. 28—and then those numbers changed too, while he was looking at them.

61

The stiffness was entirely gone when the nurse came in at six-thirty to wash Lymie's face and hands. Though he had hardly slept all night long, he felt like singing. He was alive and he knew that he was going to live for a long time. He knew there were things he had not cared enough about, that he had taken for granted, that he would have missed if he had died. He wanted to get well and go back to school and study and walk under the big trees on the campus. He wanted to look into the faces of people that he didn't know and might never see again, hear rain in the night, and sleep, and turn in his sleep and have dreams. Good or bad, it didn't matter. The worst dream imaginable was better than nothing at all, no active mind, no waking up ever.

In the middle of the morning the nurse came in with a bowl of wildflowers—purple wood violets, Dutchman's breeches, jack-in-the-pulpit, trilium, and hepaticas. They had been dug up, dirt, roots, and all, and planted in a shallow blue bowl. They looked as if they had never been disturbed, as if they had grown that way, all in a cluster on the forest's floor.

"Who brought them to me?" Lymie asked.

The nurse didn't know. They had been left at the desk downstairs and there wasn't any card.

Lymie asked her to put the bowl of wildflowers on the night table beside his bed. While he was looking at them, his eyelids closed and he fell asleep. When he woke he went on looking at the wildflowers with all the strength of his eyes, and the narrow world he had lived in so long began to grow larger and wider. The world began to take on its own true size.

He slept on and off all day. That evening as it was beginning to get dark, he heard running footsteps in the corridor outside his room and then Sally put her head around the screen. She was out of breath.

"Well," she said, panting, "I finally made it. They wouldn't let me past the desk, so I sneaked in the ambulance entrance. How are you feeling?"

"I'm fine," Lymie said.

"You look a little peaked," Sally said. "And you've certainly got no business to be lying in bed on a day like today."

She came and sat on the edge of the bed and took his hand in hers. Then she turned her head and listened. There was no sound in the corridor. "Oh, Lymie!" she said, smiling down at him. Neither of them spoke for a minute or two. He was thinking how much she looked like a South Sea Islander, and she was trying not to look at the gauze dressings on his wrists and throat, and thinking that there are people for whom life just isn't going to be too easy, and that probably he was one of them and maybe she herself was another.

Putting her hand in the pocket of her red coat, she said, "Here's a letter for you."

Lymie took the envelope that she tossed to him. On it was written *For Lymon Peters Jr. Courtesy of bearer.* He pulled the letter out and read it.

Dear Lymie: I feel so important—I have just hired a janitor and fired a waiter. I suppose you would say the waiter was being abused, but really, Lymie, he was impossible—came when he pleased and was late then, sassed the cook and snooted me. So it is "check" for Mr. D. Evarts. I also have just completed 31 lines of blank verse for Professor Severance. It is very putrid blank verse but it is blank verse and I love it with a mother's love. I started out to ask you, Lymon, if you would care to come to our spring house dance? May twenty-eight. Reply by courier.

Faithfully,
Hope

When he had finished reading, he turned, frowning slightly, and looked out of the window. He'd have to wear a turtleneck sweater instead of a white shirt, and everybody there would know why he was wearing it . . . If Hope had the courage to ask him, if she wanted him, knowing that he. . . .

The pear tree was in full bloom.

"I have another message for you," Sally said. "Mother wants to know if you'd like to come and stay at our house for a week or so after you leave this dump."

"I'd like to very much," Lymie said.

"Then that's settled."

"What's settled?" a stern voice asked, and Sally glanced at the screen in alarm, but it was only Spud. He came in and sat down on the other side of the bed. He had moved back to the fraternity house, but every morning before he went to his first class, he came to the hospital. Today was the first day that he had come twice. The bandage and the splints had been removed from his right hand, and he held it out for Lymie to see, flexing the fingers slowly and then doubling up his fist.

"Do you want to know why my mother is so fond of you, Lymie?" Sally asked. "It's because she's sure that you are going to be a professor. She says she knew it the very first time you came to our house. You walked in, she says, and all you saw was the books."

"Doesn't your mother think I'm going to be a professor?" Spud asked.

"No," Sally said. "And you'd better not be, if you know what's good for you."

There were footsteps in the hall but they went on past.

Sally also knew who had sent the bowl of wildflowers. Mrs. Lieberman had stopped her after class and asked about Lymie.

"They're beautiful, aren't they?" Sally said. "Do you know her? Do you know who she is?"

He shook his head.

"She asked me to bring you to see her, and I said I would."

"That was very nice of her," Lymie said, turning to look at the flowers. The violets had closed for the night.

"She seemed like a nice woman," Sally said.

Spud walked over and examined the flowers closely. "They're just like the kind that grow in Wisconsin," he said.

When he came back he sat on the bed again, beside Sally this time. She took his hand in hers and Lymie's hand in her other hand, and with her eyes shining with mischief she said, "Well, here we all are!"

"You guys," Spud said disparagingly, and made Lymie raise his knees, so that he and Sally could go on a camping trip up and down the cover.

It was some time before the nurse came in and put an end to this childish game.

TIME WILL DARKEN IT

For my wife

Contents

The order observed in painting a landscape—once the canvas has been prepared—is as follows: First, one draws it, dividing it into three or four distances or planes. In the foremost, where one places the figure or saint, one draws the largest trees and rocks, proportionate to the scale of the figure. In the second, smaller trees and houses are drawn; in the third yet smaller, and in the fourth, where the mountain ridges meet the sky, one ends with the greatest diminution of all.

The drawing is followed by the blocking out or laying in of colors, which some painters are in the habit of doing in black and white, although I deem it better to execute it directly in color in order that the smalt may result brighter. If you temper the necessary quantity of pigment—or even more—with linseed or walnut oil and add enough white, you shall produce a bright tint. It must not be dark; on the contrary, it must be rather on the light side because time will darken it. . . .

Once the sky, which is the upper half of the canvas, is done, you proceed to paint the ground, beginning with the mountains bordering on the sky. They will be painted with the lightest smalt-and-white tints, which will be somewhat darker than the horizon, because the ground is always darker than the sky, especially if the sun is on that side. These mountains will have their lights and darks, because it is the custom to put in the lower part—after finishing—some towns and small trees. . . .

As you get nearer the foreground, the trees and houses shall be painted larger, and if desired they may rise above the horizon. . . . In this part it is customary to use a practical method in putting in the details, mingling a few dry leaves among the green ones. . . . And it is very praiseworthy to make the grass on the ground look natural, for this section is nearest the observer.

FRANCISCO PACHECO

1564–1654

PART ONE

An Evening Party (1912)

I

IN ORDER to pay off an old debt that someone else had contracted, Austin King had said yes when he knew that he ought to have said no, and now at five o'clock of a July afternoon he saw the grinning face of trouble everywhere he turned. The house was full of strangers from Mississippi; within an hour, friends and neighbors invited to an evening party would begin ringing the doorbell; and his wife (whom he loved) was not speaking to him.

As yet this quarrel was confined to the bedroom and he wanted if possible to keep it from spreading through the house. On his way upstairs he fixed the picture of Maxine Elliott so that it was straight with the world. As he closed the bedroom door from the inside, his eyes turned to the mahogany four-poster bed where his wife lay, face down, in a Japanese kimono. Her brown hair was spread out on the pillow like a sea plant, and one arm, with a heavy gold bracelet hanging from the delicate inert wrist, extended past the edge of the bed into space.

Austin loosened his tie and took off his coat and trousers and hung them on a hanger in the closet. When he had put on his bathrobe he stood waiting for some slight movement, some indication that the hand which had so often searched blindly for his hand was ready to make peace. There was no price that he was not willing to pay, no bargain too hard if only for the rest of this day all differences could be put aside, all wounds (old and new) disregarded and left to heal themselves. After a moment he sat down on the edge of the bed. Receiving no encouragement, he waited and then put out his hand. His fingers closed around his wife's elbow. The elbow was jerked away and drawn under her body where he couldn't get at it.

The childishness of this gesture made him smile, but it also meant that one avenue of reconciliation was closed.

"I'm sorry I did what I did," he said. "I should have talked to you first, before I wrote and told them to come. And if I had it to do over again—" There was no answer and he knew from past experience that there would be none. "I thought you'd understand and they wouldn't," he said.

His eyes rested uneasily on the design of the appliquéd quilt, the round lavender morning glories and the heart-shaped green leaves. The quilt was a present from his mother, who would have been shocked to see anyone lying on it.

Annoyed at himself for thinking about the quilt at a time like this, he crossed the room to the dressing table, picked up his wife's hairbrush, and, closing the bedroom door behind him, went into the room across the hall to look after his little daughter, who was too young to dress without help. Between them they decided which shoes and stockings, which dress she was to wear, and put them on her. Then, sitting in a rocker that was too low for him, Austin held her chin with one hand and managed the hairbrush inexpertly with the other.

The excitement of guests staying in the house made Abbey King talkative. "Is it true," she asked, "is it true that gypsies steal little children?"

Though more delicate and with a difference in spacing, her features were a reproduction of her father's—the high forehead particularly, and the eyebrows and grey-blue eyes. Her hair was light brown, like her mother's, and straight. When it was being brushed, it fluffed out and made crackling sounds, but Ab knew, at four years old, that her hair was too fine and too thin to be admired. Both of these drawbacks had been pointed out, not to the little girl but unfortunately in her presence. Mixed in with this sadness about her hair was the pleasure she had from standing between her father's knees.

"Do they, Daddy?"

"Sometimes," Austin King said, frowning intently.

"Do they steal tricycles?"

"I don't think so. They wouldn't have any use for tricycles."

"What happens to the children they steal?"

"Their fathers and mothers go to the police and the police find the gypsies and put them in jail," Austin said.

"What happens if they can't find the gypsies? What if they go so far away that nobody can find them and put them in jail?"

"Then their mothers grieve over them."

"Would Mama grieve over me?"

"Certainly. Stand still, Abbey. Stop jerking your head away. I'm not hurting you."

"You are too," Ab said, because it did hurt a little and because she liked to argue with people—with her father, with Rachel the cook, and most of all with her mother. She liked to wear her mother's temper thin. There was a limit that both of them recognized, a danger line past which Ab couldn't go and safely retreat from a spanking. Occasionally she stepped over it and then, after her mother's anger and her own tears, peace descended on the household. But with her father there was no such line. She could not drive him to the limit of his patience.

"What happens to the children?" she asked again.

"The children? Oh they grow up and become gypsies."

"Then what happens?"

"They go from place to place in their wagons."

Ab's next remark—a question really, though it took the form of a statement—was prepared for by an extended silence, during which Austin turned her around so he could tie her blue sash.

"Rachel says sometimes—*she* says if children are bad and if nobody can do anything with them or make them mind, then their mothers and fathers sell them to the gypsies."

"Surely not," Austin said.

"That's what Rachel says."

"Well nobody's going to sell you to the gypsies so stop worrying about it," Austin said, and got up from the rocker. His hands, as they gave a final twist to Ab's hair-ribbon, seemed meant for some work of exactness, like mending watches or making trout flies. Actually, Austin King was a lawyer.

"Now then," he said approvingly, "you're all ready for company even if your father and mother are not. See if you can stay that way for the next half-hour, till people begin to arrive."

He stood still and listened. Overhead, footsteps crossed and recrossed the ceiling. In the big, bare, third-floor bedroom (where the heat must be stifling, Austin thought) young

Randolph Potter was also making himself presentable for the party. He had come North with his father and mother and sister, hoping to escape the heat, and like a faithful hound running after a carriage with its tongue hanging out, the heat had followed them.

Until today Austin King had never set eyes on these foster relatives. When the name Potter crossed his mind at all, it was associated with two faded tintypes in the family album, on the page facing the stiff wedding-day portrait of his Grandfather and Grandmother King. Judge King, Austin's father, often used to speak of the man who took him in after his own father died, gave him a home as long as he needed one, and treated him exactly as he treated his own five sons. Both parties to this act of kindness—the homeless frightened boy and the gaunt Mennonite preacher—were now six feet underground, and the obligation could just as well have ended there, except that on the tenth of June the postman had delivered to the law office of Holby and King a letter addressed to Judge King, and therefore all the more binding on the person who broke open the sealed envelope. The letter was signed *Yrs. affy. Reuben S. Potter*, and it was full of allusions to boyhood matters that Austin didn't understand or know about, but he knew what his father would have written in reply to the final paragraph in which Mr. Potter, anxious to pick up the threads that had broken under the weight of time and distance, suggested bringing his family to Illinois for a visit.

Austin's whole long boyhood had been full of visiting aunts and uncles and cousins, who came and stayed sometimes for a month or more. Lawyers, judges, politicians, railroad men, business acquaintances, anybody that Judge King liked or was interested in or felt sorry for, he brought home from his office for a meal, for overnight, and never thought of letting his wife know beforehand. The dining-room table could be stretched out until it accommodated any number, and there was always plenty of food. Austin's mother was active and capable, and while Judge King was alive, able to manage any burden that he placed upon her. Having company meant putting clean sheets on the bed in this or that spare room and making up the couch in the billiard room so that some young cousin, or sometimes

Austin, could sleep on it, and then settling down to a nice long visit.

Such continuous open hospitality was dying out; it was a thing of the past. Martha King didn't entertain easily and casually the way Austin's mother had, and also, two days before the letter came, Dr. Seymour had told her that she was pregnant again. Faced with a choice between an inherited obligation and the consideration he owed his wife, Austin had sat down at his desk and tried to frame a letter that would explain, politely and regretfully and without giving offense, why it was not convenient to have the Potters at this time. He began and crumpled up one draft after another, until finally, trusting that Martha out of love for him would understand and approve, he dipped his pen in the ink bottle and with a heavy sigh committed them both.

Martha King not only didn't understand, she put an altogether different coloring upon his intentions; but instead of telling him how she felt, she waited, and when the Potters had arrived and it was too late for him to do anything about it, she made a scene behind the closed bedroom door, showered him with accusations (some just, some unjust), said that he didn't love her or he couldn't possibly have done such a thing when she was in no condition to have a house full of company, and then withdrew her support, leaving him to manage as best he could. To add to Austin's difficulties, she was ill in a way that she hadn't been before Ab was born; she was subject to morning sickness, making him feel that he had been unfair not only toward her but also toward the Potters, who should have been told, he now realized. They should at least have been given a chance not to come.

The footsteps stopped.

"Will there be any children for me to play with?" Ab asked.

Austin said, "No, this is a grown-up party and you mustn't interrupt people when they are talking, do you hear? Just be quiet and watch, and afterwards everybody will say, 'What a nice little girl.' "

He gave his daughter a pat on the behind and then, stepping over a doll's bed and a house of alphabet blocks, left her and went back into the bedroom across the hall.

2

Elm Street, the street the Kings lived on, had been finished for almost a generation when the Potters arrived for their visit. The shade had encroached gradually upon the areas of sunlight, and the outermost branches of the trees—maples and elms, cottonwoods, lindens and box elders—had managed to meet in places over the brick pavement. The houses reflected no set style or period of architecture but only a pleasure in circular bay windows, wide porches, carpenter's lace, and fresh white paint. Elm Street led nowhere in particular and there was never much traffic on it. The most exciting vehicle that passed on a summer day was the ice-cream wagon, painted white, its slow progress announced by a silvery *ka-ling, ka-ling, ka-ling* that brought children running to the curb. The ice-cream wagon was the high point of the monumental July or August afternoon, and much of its importance came from the fact that it was undependable. The children often waited for it in vain, their only consolation the chips that fell from the ice-man's pick. There were also gypsy wagons, but they were infrequent, not to be expected more than once or twice a summer. When they did come, the smaller children, clutching their playthings, withdrew to their own front porches where, in safety, they stood and stared until the caravan had passed by.

For a street only three unbroken blocks long—Elm Street below the intersection was another world entirely—there were an unusual number of children and it was they who gave the street its active character and its air of Roman imperishability. In feature and voice and attitude they were small copies of the women who shook dustcloths out of upstairs windows and banged mops on porch railings, of the men who came home from work in the late afternoon and stood in their shirt-sleeves dampening the lawns and flower beds with a garden hose. But for a time, for as long as they were children, they were almost as free as the sparrows.

With two alleys and any number of barns, pigeon houses, chicken coops, woodsheds, and sloping cellar doors (all offering excellent hiding and sliding places to choose from, all in the public domain), the children seldom left the street to play.

In the daytime boys and girls played apart, but evening brought them all together in a common dislike of the dark and of their mother's voice calling them home. They played games, some of which were older than Columbus's voyages. They caught lightning bugs and put them in a bottle. They frightened themselves with ghost stories. They hid from and hunted one another, in and out of the shrubbery. For the grown people relaxing on their porches after the heat of the day, the cry of *Ready or not, you shall be caught* was no more alarming than the fireflies or the creak of the porch swing.

Elm Street is now in its old age and nothing of all this is left. There are cars instead of carriages, no gypsy wagon has been seen in this part of the country for many years. The ice-cream wagon stopped being undependable and simply failed to come. Iceboxes make their own ice.

If you happen to be curious about the Indians of Venezuela, you can supply yourself with credentials from the Ministry of Education and letters from various oil companies to their representatives in field camps. With your personal belongings and scientific instruments, including excavating tools for, say, a crew of twelve men—with several hundred sugar bags for specimens, emergency food rations, mosquito netting, and other items essential for carrying on such archeological work—you can start digging and with luck unearth pottery and skeletons that have lain in the ground since somewhere around 1000 A.D. The very poverty of evidence will lead you to brilliant and far-reaching hypotheses. To arrive at some idea of the culture of a certain street in a Middle Western small town shortly before the First World War is a much more delicate undertaking. For one thing, there are no ruins to guide you. Though the houses are not kept up as well as they once were, they are still standing. Of certain barns and outbuildings that are gone (and with them trellises and trumpet vines) you will find no trace whatever. In every yard a dozen landmarks (here a lilac bush, there a sweet syringa) are missing. There is no telling what became of the hanging fern baskets with American flags in them or of all those red geraniums. The people who live on Elm Street now belong to a different civilization. They can tell you nothing. You will not need mosquito netting or emergency rations, and the only specimens you will find, possibly the only thing that will prove helpful to you, will be a glass marble or a locust shell split up the back and empty.

3

"If you want me to ask them to leave, I will," Austin said, turning to the four-poster bed. "I'll go right now and explain to them that it was all a mistake, and that we just aren't in a position to have company at this time."

To do this meant that he and the Potters would have to face each other in an embarrassment so hideous that he didn't dare think about it. Nevertheless, if that was what she wanted, if he had put a greater burden on her than she could manage, then he was ready, at whatever cost to himself, to set her free.

"Seriously," he said.

The offer was not accepted.

He turned away and opened the bottom drawer of the highboy, searching for summer underwear. "I'm going to take a bath and shave," he said. "It's almost five-thirty. Somebody has to be downstairs to let people in." He went off down the hall.

Now is the time to be quiet, to stand patiently in this upstairs bedroom and wait for some change in the position of the woman on the bed. So far as a marriage is concerned, nothing that happens downstairs in the living room or the dining room or the kitchen is ever as important as what goes on behind the closed bedroom door. It is the point at which curious friends and anxious or interfering relatives have to turn away.

The big double bed, like the quilt, is an heirloom and possibly a hundred years old. At the top of each heavy square post there is a dangerous spike, intended to hold the huge canopy that is now in the Kings' barn, gathering dust. The highboy, also of antique mahogany, contains a secret drawer in which (since Martha King had no secrets and Austin hid his elsewhere) are kept a velvet pincushion in the shape of a strawberry and odds and ends of ribbon. Originally dark, the woodwork in this room has been painted white. The windows extend to the floor and are open to the slight stirring of air that blesses this side of the house, carrying with it the scent of petunias from the window box. The ceiling of the bedroom is eleven feet high, indicating the house's age and some previous history—quarrels between husband and wife, perhaps, in this very room. If Martha King raises her head and listens, if she sits up suddenly and moves to the center of the bed, where she can see herself in the oval mirror over the dressing table—but that woman Austin King would not, in all probability, have married.

After twenty minutes he came back and went over to the dressing table. With his head bent forward so that the mirror would accommodate his reflection, he parted his damp hair solemnly on the left side and combed it flat against his skull. In sleep, in repose, in all unguarded moments, his face had a suggestion of sadness about it.

"Was it something that happened this afternoon?" he asked, standing beside the bed. "Did I do something or say something in front of them that hurt your feelings?"

With her voice half-smothered in the pillow Martha King said, "You didn't do anything or say anything and my feelings are not hurt. Now will you please go away?"

He leaned across her, trying to see her face.

"And please don't touch me!"

Austin had a sudden angry impulse to turn her over and slap her, but it was so faint and so immediately disowned that he himself was hardly aware of it. "Listen to me," he said. "You've got to get up now and come downstairs. I don't know what they'll think if you—"

"I don't care what they think. I'm not going downstairs."

"You've got to. We have company in the house and you've asked all those people."

"You go down if you want to. It's your company."

"But what'll I tell them?"

"Whatever you feel like telling them. Tell them you're married to an impossible woman who doesn't care what she does or how much humiliation she brings upon you."

"That isn't true," he said, in a tone of voice that carried only partial conviction—the intention to believe what he had just said, rather than belief itself.

"Yes it is, it's all true and you know it! Tell them I'm lazy and extravagant and a bad housekeeper and that I don't take proper care of my child!"

Austin's eyes wandered to the clock on the dressing table.

"Couldn't we postpone this—this discussion until later? I know I said something that hurt your feelings but I didn't mean to. Really I didn't. I don't know what it was, even." Again the voice was not wholly convinced of what it said. "Tonight after the party, we'll have it all out, everything. And in the meantime—"

"In the meantime I wish I were dead," Martha King said, and rolled over on her back. Her face was flushed and creased from the pillow, and so given over to feeling that one part of him looked at it with curiosity and detachment. Beautiful (and dear to him) though her ordinary face was, in coloring and feature, in the extreme whiteness and softness of the skin and in the bone structure that lay under this whiteness and softness, and the bluish tint of the part of her eyes surrounding the brown iris, it was a beauty that was all known to him. He saw something now that he might not ever see again, an effort on the part of flesh to make a new face, stranger and more vulnerable than the other. And more beautiful. Tears formed in the right eye and spilled over, and then both eyes were blinded by them. The detachment gave way and he gathered her in his arms.

"I don't see why you aren't happy with me," she said mournfully. "I try so hard to do everything the way you want me to do it."

He wiped the tears away with his hand gently, but there were more. "I *am* happy," he said. "I'm very happy."

"You can't be. Not as long as you're married to a woman who gives you no peace."

"But I am, I tell you. Why do I have to keep saying that I'm happy? If you'd only stop worrying about it and take things for granted, we'd never have these— Was it Nora Potter? Was it something about Nora?"

Martha shook her head.

"Sweetheart, Nora is like a cousin. She doesn't mean anything more to me than that. You don't have any cousins or you'd understand."

"I saw you when you helped her out of the carriage. You were smiling at her, and I knew you liked her better than you do me. I knew it would happen, before ever they came, and I don't know why I let it upset me. I just couldn't bear it." Now that she had at last accused him, she took his handkerchief and sat up and blew her nose.

"I don't know what you're talking about," he said with a guilty smile, though he had never in his life been more innocent. "Nothing happened. I don't remember smiling at her, or if I did—look, they invited themselves. I didn't ask them to come, and if I'd known they would give you a moment's unhappiness I'd never have allowed them to set foot in this house. You know that, don't you? Now that they're here, we might as well make the best of it. They won't stay long, probably, and we'll never have to have them again. We'll just go on living the way we have been, the three of us, and be happy."

So deeply did he mean and believe in this promise that the barricade of suspicion, the whole elaborate structure of jealousy and doubt that his wife had erected to keep him from reaching her, gave way before his eyes. The flesh gave up trying to make a new face and was content with the old one. Lightly, with the tips of her fingers, she stroked the fabric of his shirt. He took her in his arms again and rocked her.

Neither of them heard the steps on the front porch or the doorbell ringing in the pantry. With no sense of the passing of time, no anxiety because the guests had begun to arrive and there was no one downstairs to introduce the people from Mississippi, they held each other and lost themselves in the opening, unmasking tenderness that always comes after a satisfactory quarrel. At last, feeling utterly secure and able to cope with anything, Austin got up from the bed and finished dressing.

"I'll go right down," he said, "and tell them you were having trouble in the kitchen. Nobody will think anything about it."

"Do I look as if I had been crying?" she asked.

"Hardly at all. Put a cold cloth on your eyes."

At the door he took her in his arms once more and felt her cling to him. If he had held her a moment longer he would have given her all the reassurance she needed for some time to come, but he remembered the people downstairs, and let go. It was not his failure entirely. Women are never ready to let go of love at the point where men are satisfied and able to turn to something else. It is a fault of timing that affects the whole human race. There is no telling how much harm it has caused.

4

Rachel, the Kings' colored cook, heard the doorbell but Martha King had told her that she would be downstairs to let people in, and so, instead of hurrying through the front part of the house to answer it, she stood still and listened. Rachel never hurried, in any case, but set her course and let wind, wave, and tide take her where she had to go. Her daughter Thelma, who was twelve years old and had been got in to help, said, "They're beginning to come."

"All of them with big appetites," Rachel said, and opened the oven door and basted the ham.

On the front porch, old Mrs. Beach and her two daughters waited. At this hour of the day Elm Street was deserted, its inhabitants drawn to the supper table like nails to a magnet.

"Do you think we should call out?" Alice Beach asked, after what began to seem rather a long time.

"If they're downstairs they'll come," Mrs. Beach said. "And if they're upstairs they wouldn't hear us. Are we early?"

Lucy Beach glanced at the little gold watch that was attached to her shirtwaist by a fleur-de-lis pin and said, "It's five minutes after."

"Perhaps we ought to go home," Alice Beach said, "and come back later." Though she was in her early forties, she looked to her mother to settle the matter.

"When I was a young married woman," Mrs. Beach said, "and asked people for a certain hour, I was always ready to receive them. I hope when you girls marry that you'll remember to do the same. Not to receive your guests when they arrive is a mark of rudeness." She turned majestically and started for the steps.

Reluctantly her daughters followed. They had looked forward to this evening and there was reason to fear that, once they got home, even though it was only next door, their mother would refuse to stir out of the house.

"Are you coming to the party?" a small voice asked, and the

three women, startled, turned around and saw Ab peering at them through the screen door.

"We are if there's going to *be* a party," Mrs. Beach said.

"Oh, yes," Ab said.

"Well then, you'd better ask us in."

They trailed into the house, left their crocheted bags and their white kid gloves on the hall table, and seated themselves in an alcove of the long living room which, by its extreme order and high polish and glittering candlesticks and bouquets of white phlox, seemed to support Ab's statement. The little girl sat in a big wing chair facing Mrs. Beach.

"How are your dolls?" Alice Beach asked.

"They're fine, all but Gwendolyn," Ab said, after considering whether or not this interest was genuine, and deciding that it was.

"What's the matter with Gwendolyn? She looked remarkably well the last time I saw her."

"Oh, she broke," Ab said vaguely.

"You must have played too roughly with her," Mrs. Beach said. "I still have every doll that was ever given to me."

"Could I see them some time?" Ab asked.

"They're in the attic," Mrs. Beach said with discouraging finality.

A considerable stretch of silence followed. The guests looked around expectantly and then at each other. Ab, with no basis of social comparison, found nothing strange either in the silence or in the expectancy. All the windows were open and also the French doors leading out onto the side porch, but even so, it was very warm in the living room. Above the upright piano, in a heavy gilt frame, was an oil painting of the castle of St. Angelo. The clock in the clock tower was real, and its thin tick gradually dominated the silence and filled the room with tension.

Lucy cleared her throat and said, "How do you like your new relatives, Ab?"

"Fine," Ab said, "but I don't think my mother does."

Glances were exchanged again.

"And where *is* your mother?" Mrs. Beach asked.

"Upstairs," Ab said. "My father dressed me. He told me to stay clean till people arrived."

"Well you didn't quite make it," Mrs. Beach said. "You've got a smudge on your nose, from the screen door."

"Come here and let me give you a spit bath," Alice said. Ab got down from the chair obediently and came and stood before her, while she moistened one corner of a small lace-bordered handkerchief with her tongue and removed the smudge. "There," she said. "Now you're as good as new."

"Fix her sash while you're at it," Mrs. Beach said. "Anybody can see that it was tied by a man. . . . I'm sure there's some mistake."

"Perhaps it's the wrong day," Lucy said.

"Oh no," Ab said. "It's the right day."

No longer confident of her appearance, she withdrew to the front window as soon as Alice released her, and began to finger the curtains.

The clock in the castle of St. Angelo said twenty minutes past six as Mrs. Beach rose and motioned to her daughters to do likewise. Fortunately there was a step on the stairs. It was not the quick step of Martha King, but careful and deliberate —the step of a person farther along in years and well aware of the danger of falling. The woman who entered the room a moment later was so small, so slight, her dress so elaborately embroidered and beaded, her hair so intricately held in place by pins and rhinestone-studded combs, that she seemed, though alive, to be hardly flesh and blood but more like a middle-aged fairy.

"Well isn't this nice!" she exclaimed.

"I'm Mrs. Beach," the old woman said. "This is my daughter Lucy—"

"Happy to make your acquaintance."

"—and my daughter Alice."

"I'm Mrs. Potter. Do sit down, all of you. This reminds me of home." Mrs. Potter saw that the wing chair was vacant and settled herself in it. "Nobody is ever on time in Mississippi, but I thought Northerners were more prompt. Austin and Martha will be down directly. Won't you try this chair, Mrs. Beach? I'm sure you'd find it more— What about you, Miss Lucy?"

Though the old lady and her daughters sat stiffly on the edge of their chairs as if they might get up at any moment, they assured Mrs. Potter that they were comfortable.

"I expect you think this is hot," she said, fanning herself with a painted sandalwood fan, "but I give you my word it's nothing to the weather we've been having down home. People are always saying that Southerners are lazy and they are, but there's a reason. I don't know whether you've ever been laid up with heat prostration but— Do you live close by?"

"Right next door," Alice Beach said.

"Then it must have been your house I heard that delightful music coming from, while I was getting dressed. Just delightful. Do you play and sing, Mrs. Beach?"

"No," the old lady said solemnly, "but both my daughters are accomplished musicians. My daughter Lucy took lessons of Geraldine Farrar's singing teacher for a short while. Alice didn't have that privilege but we've been told there is a blood blend in their voices which is quite unusual."

"My husband is very fond of music," Mrs. Potter said. "His older brother was a drummer boy in the War Between the States, and we've always hoped that our children would turn out to be musical but neither one of them can sing a note. I hope you'll favor us with a concert while we're here," she added, turning from Mrs. Beach to her daughters. "Both of you."

"We're rather out of practice," Alice Beach said.

"They'll be glad to sing for you," Mrs. Beach said. "They both have very fine voices. My daughter Lucy could have had a career on the concert stage in Europe but I wouldn't allow her to. I didn't want her to be subjected to unpleasant experiences."

"I've never been able to keep either of my children from doing anything they set their minds on," Mrs. Potter said amiably. "I wish you'd tell me how you manage it."

Mrs. Beach did not feel that this remark called for an answer. Her daughters sat with their hands clasped nervously in their laps, and the clock threatened once more to take possession of the room. Before Mrs. Potter could start off on a new track there was a mixed trampling on the stairs and she called out, "Come in and meet these charming folks." And then, "This is my husband, Mrs. Beach . . . and my son Randolph . . . my daughter Nora. . . . Was that the doorbell? . . . Randolph, go see who's at the door."

Secure in the knowledge that this was going to be a party after all, that they had come on the right day and at the right time, even if there was nobody to receive them, Mrs. Beach and her daughters sat back in their chairs.

Ab slipped unnoticed out of the room and wandered out to the kitchen, where there was a bustle that she was familiar with and could understand, and wonderful smells. Though Rachel cried out at the sight of her, "Now you scat! We got no time for young ones," Ab was not in the least intimidated. She went straight for the kitchen stool, placed it in front of the cupboard, climbed on it and, balancing carefully, helped herself to a cracker.

5

The fear that always haunted Martha King before a party, that people would sit racking their brains for something to say, once more proved groundless. She came downstairs and found the living room full of her guests, all talking easily to one another. As she slipped into the empty place on the sofa, Mrs. Potter turned and smiled at her. The smile said *Here is your party, my dear. I've started it off right for you. Now I'll sit back and be a guest.* After that it was possible for Martha to look around quite calmly and see who was there. Austin was watching her and ready to come to her rescue, but she didn't need rescuing. She moved the pillow to one side, and then, deciding that Nora Potter was dressed in an unbecoming shade of old rose, Martha King sat back, as passive as the room itself.

"It's a feeling like . . . well, it's not possible for me to put it into words," Nora Potter said to Lucy Beach. "It's something you have to see in someone's face or hear in their voice." Her hair was a curious cinnamon color, parted in the middle and with bangs covering a forehead that went up and up. Her eyes were a blue-violet and seemed even larger and more vivid than they were because the rest of her face had no color in it. Her wide smile revealed two upper front teeth separated by a little gap that gave her a childlike appearance, as if she were seven or eight years old and just committing herself to the gangly stage. Though not at all beautiful, the Southern girl's face had a charming, touching quality that the women in the room failed to notice (or if they did, to care about); the men all saw it immediately. The blue-violet eyes were searching gravely for something that was not to be found in this living room or this town or perhaps anywhere, but that nevertheless might exist somewhere, if you had the courage and the patience and the time to go on looking for it. In a middle-aged or even a young married woman the same sincerity, the same impossibly high-minded principles, the refusal to compromise would not have appealed to them. These qualities had to be combined with the sweetness of inexperience. Glancing at Nora the men were reminded of certain idealistic plans they had once had for themselves, plans that for practical reasons had had to be put aside. *You must be careful*, they longed to say to her. *You are young and inexperienced. You may think you know how to take care of yourself but life is hard and there are pitfalls. However, you don't have to be afraid with me. I can be trusted. . . .*

The little colored girl broke up the conversation in the living room by opening the French doors and saying "Dinner is served." Every face was turned toward her. The idea that had been, off and on for the last half hour, in all their minds—food—was now a shining fact. Martha King rose and led the way into the dining room. The other women followed, according to age: Mrs. Beach, Mrs. Danforth, Mrs. Potter, Lucy and Alice Beach, young Mrs. Ellis, who had recently come to town as a bride, Nora Potter, and Mary Caroline Link. Mary Caroline had been asked so that young Randolph Potter would have someone of his own age to talk to.

At the head of the dining-room table was Rachel's ham on a big blue platter. At the foot of the table was a platter of fried chicken. Between these two major centers of interest were any number of minor ones—the baked macaroni, the stuffed potatoes, the tomato aspic, the deviled eggs, the watercress, the hot rolls covered with a napkin, the jellies and the preserves, the stack of dinner plates, the rows of gleaming silver, the napkins that matched the big damask cloth. Like a tropical flower, the dinner party had opened its petals and revealed the purpose and prodigality of nature.

"Well, Martha," Mrs. Beach said, without bothering to hide her astonishment, "I must say this looks very nice . . . I won't have any of the ham. I can see it's delicious by the way it cuts, but ham always gives me heartburn." She glanced at the plate Martha King was fixing for her and was reassured; the chicken was white meat. "And a stuffed potato and a roll, thank you . . . no, that's plenty. I'm an old woman and I don't need as much to keep me going as you young people. Pshaw! you've given me too much of everything, my dear . . . Alice . . . Lucy . . . come help yourselves. This is a buffet supper and you're not supposed to hang back in the doorway."

"Aunt Ione, let me give you a better piece of chicken," Martha said to Mrs. Potter. "You've got the part that goes over the fence last."

"It's the piece I like," Mrs. Potter protested. "I never get it at home because it's Mr. Potter's favorite. I wouldn't dare take it if we weren't visiting."

"Well, here's the wishbone to go with it."

"If this keeps up I'll go home stuffed out like a toad," Mrs. Potter said, helping herself to celery and then a ripe olive and crabapple jelly. "You must give me your receipt for pocket-book rolls. Mine never turn out like this."

"I don't suppose there's any way to get the men to continue their conversation in here," Martha said. "Alice, you haven't anything on your plate at all. Here, let me help you. . . . Now then, don't forget the roll. . . . There's no onion in the salad, Mrs. Danforth. I remembered that you don't eat it. . . . Mrs. Ellis, what will you have? A wishbone? The wing?"

"When I was a girl," Mrs. Beach said, "young women of good family were taught to cook as a matter of course, even though there often wasn't any need for them to, after they were married. Unless you know how food should be prepared, you can't tell someone else how to do it." (And even if you tell your daughters how to act at a party, there is nothing you can do about the look of sadness that returns after every effort at animation.) "I used to entertain a great deal when we lived in St. Paul. Mr. Beach was in the wholesale grocery business there, and he loved to invite people to our home. I often spent days getting ready beforehand. Now the young women just slap something together and call it a dinner party."

"Cousin Martha," Mrs. Potter said slyly, "if you just slapped this together—"

"Martha is an exception," Mrs. Beach said, and passed on down the table.

The men appeared to be in no hurry to get into the dining room. While they stood in a little group outside discussing the price of hogs, Austin King went to the closet under the stairs and got out the card tables for Thelma. When these were set up, one in the study and three in the living room, he stood with his back to the fireplace enjoying a moment of pride in the house and in his wife. He had watched her come down the stairs in a white dress with a large cloth rose at her waist, looking as lovely (the dress was his favorite and she had worn it to please him) as any woman ever looked. The roomful of people had stopped talking for a few seconds, and then unable to remember what they had been about to say, they went on talking about something else.

In the dining room Nora Potter said, "I don't know what will happen to me if I ever get married. I can't cook and I hate sewing. Brother says if I never learn to keep house, somebody will always have to do it for me. But just the same, I do envy and admire you, Cousin Martha."

"You haven't any salad," Martha King said. "Here . . . let me help you to it."

Immediately afterward Nora plunged back into the conversation with Lucy Beach, a conversation that had nothing to do with housekeeping. "Do you think people are happiest," Martha heard her say as they moved out of the dining room, "when they don't even know that they're happy?"

At that moment the men, who had merely been biding their time, closed around the table and with no pretense of a poor or finicky appetite, helped themselves to everything within reach.

Old Mr. Ellis, returning to the living room with his plate in his hand, provided a moment of suspense for everybody. He was frail and uncertain in his movements but no one dared to take the plate from him, and the catastrophe they were all expecting did not occur. Avoiding the table where Mrs. Beach had established herself, he sat down between Nora Potter and Alice Beach.

"I've been meaning to call on you," the old man said as he tucked one corner of his napkin into his shirt collar. "And I will, one of these days." He turned to Nora. "You'd never think it, but this young lady I used to dandle on my knee."

"You used to give me peppermint candy," Alice told him.

"I was always partial to you," the old man said.

"How do you like it up North?" Alice asked. Nora had already been asked this question four times, but she answered with enthusiasm.

"You could've come at a better time of year," Mr. Ellis said. "It's too hot in July and August. Spring or fall is best."

"I'd like to come some time in winter," Nora said. "I've only seen snow once in my whole life."

"We get plenty of it," old Mr. Ellis said, "but nothing like what we used to get when I was a boy. I don't know what's happened, but the weather isn't the same."

"Mr. Ellis is full of wonderful stories about the old times," Alice said, turning to Nora. And then turning back, "Tell Miss Potter about The Sudden Change."

"Oh you don't want to hear me tell that story again," the old man said, smiling at her. "You've heard me tell it a hundred times."

"Miss Potter hasn't heard it. And besides, I always enjoy your stories."

"I've forgotten most of them," Mr. Ellis said. Ten years before, he had been an imposing representative of the world sensitive little boys are afraid of—the loud, ample, baldheaded, cigar-smoking, cigar-smelling men. And then suddenly, before anyone realized what was happening, Mr. Ellis' hair had turned white and with it his bushy eyebrows and the long black hairs growing out of his nose and ears. He was now a little old man with a tired mind and the violent emotions of second childhood. He discovered the plate in front of him and made a futile effort to cut his fried chicken.

"Can't I do that for you?" Alice asked.

"I can manage it," the old man said. "I'm still able to feed myself." Then he put down his knife and fork and began: "The Sudden Change occurred on the afternoon of December 20, 1836. It was one of the most remarkable phenomena ever recorded. There were several inches of snow on the ground that day and it had been raining long enough to turn the snow to slush. In the middle of the afternoon it suddenly stopped raining and a dark cloud appeared out of the northwest, traveling very rapidly and accompanied by a roaring sound that . . ."

With her plate in her hand, Martha King stood looking around the living room. The only vacant place was next to Nora Potter, who glanced up as Martha approached and said, "Mr. Ellis is telling us the most wonderful story. It's a privilege to hear him."

"You're very sweet, my dear," the old man said, taking advantage of his great age to pat her hand.

"Please go on," Martha said. "I came to this table especially to hear you."

"There were two brothers in Douglas County overtaken by this same cold wave I was speaking about," Mr. Ellis continued. "They were out cutting down a bee-tree and they froze to death before they could reach their cabin. Their bodies were found about ten days afterward. But the most remarkable case of suffering happened to a man named Hildreth. My father knew him well and heard the story from his own lips. He left home in the company of a young man named Frame, both intending to go to Chicago on horseback. They had entered a large prairie and were out of sight of human habitation when the cold came over them in all its fury. Fifteen minutes from that time, their overcoats were like sheet iron. The water and slush was turned to solid ice. Their horses drifted with the wind or across it until night closed in. Finally they dismounted, and Hildreth killed Frame's horse, and then they took out the entrails and crawled into the cavity and lay there, as near as Mr. Hildreth could judge, until about midnight. By this time the animal heat was out of the carcass, so they crawled out, and somehow the one that had the knife dropped it. . . ."

A few minutes before, while Martha King was serving her guests, she had been ravenously hungry. Now that she could eat and had a plate piled high with food in front of her, she discovered that she had no appetite. She raised her fork halfway to her mouth and then put it down.

"I wish Pa could hear this," Nora said, turning around in her chair. "He'd be very interested."

But Mr. Potter had discovered that the woman who sat next

to him was interested in singing. He was now telling her about all the great singers—Nordica and Melba and Alma Gluck and John McCormack—who had sung at the French Opera in New Orleans, and about the time he happened to be standing on the platform of the railway station in Birmingham when Paderewski's private car passed through. Mr. Potter had heard none of these artists and his own taste in music did not rise above Sousa's marches, but he managed nevertheless, out of scraps and hearsay, to make Lucy Beach's face bloom suddenly, and to place her beyond all doubt in the company from which Geraldine Farrar's teacher, after a few lessons, had dismissed her.

". . . Hildreth returned to the river bank," Mr. Ellis said. "And when he found that the ice was strong enough to bear his weight, he crawled across. The man came out and watched him trying to get over the fence and didn't lift a finger to help him. Finally he tumbled over the fence anyway, and crawled into the house and lay down before the fire. He begged for assistance and when the man relented and would have done something for him, his wife prevented it." Mr. Ellis began searching for his napkin, which had fallen to the floor. Alice restored it to him. He tucked it into his collar again and then said impressively, "The man's name was Benjamin Russ. His wife's name is not known, and nobody cares to remember it. They both had to leave the country afterward, there was so much indignation among the neighbors. Mr. Hildreth always expressed the opinion that they imagined he had a large sum of money on him, and that they could secure it in case of his death. Such hardheartedness was very rare among the early settlers, who were noted, like you Southerners"—the old man made a little bow to Nora—"for their hospitality."

"Grampaw, you've told that story at every gathering you've been to in the last twenty years," Bud Ellis said loudly, from the table in the alcove. "Why don't you keep still for a while and let somebody else talk?"

"All right, all right," the old man said. "I know I'm a tiresome old fool, but just remember that people can't help it if they live too long. You may live too long yourself."

The embarrassment that followed this remark was general. The visitors from Mississippi began talking hurriedly. The

Illinois guests were silent and looked down at their plates. No amount of coaxing could make Mr. Ellis finish his story. He sat sulking and feeling sorry for himself until Thelma came to take the plates away and bring the ice cream.

6

After the card tables had been cleared and put away, Randolph Potter sat down beside Mary Caroline Link and began to tell her about his favorite riding horse, a jumper named Daisy, that had recently gone lame. The young Southerner was so strikingly handsome that he drew the attention of the others in the room to the couple on the sofa. Mary Caroline's pink linen dress was charming, but she herself was plain, with a receding chin and heavy black eyebrows. She had no easy compliments like the girls Randolph was used to, and her shyness forced him to keep thinking up new subjects for conversation.

Across the room, Nora Potter let her eyes come to rest on her brother.

"A penny for your thoughts," Bud Ellis said.

"I was thinking," Nora said, "of the words 'homely' and 'beautiful'—of the terrible importance people attach to whether somebody's nose is too long or their eyes too close together. How it must puzzle the angels!"

"You're way over my head," Bud Ellis said, and got up and joined his grandfather and Mr. Potter at the far end of the living room.

The sun had gone down but the heat remained on into the long July twilight. The curtains hung limp and still. In the dining room Thelma moved about, putting away silver and china. The word "nigger," which was so often on the lips of the Southerners, she did not appear to notice, and the Potters were unaware of any lack of tact on their part, even when Austin King got up quietly and closed the dining-room doors.

Martha King had settled down for the evening beside Dr. Danforth, who was old enough to be her father and whose fondness for her was uncritical and of long standing. Though his infirmity—he was hard of hearing—sometimes made him difficult to talk to, she was utterly at ease and herself with him, knowing as she did that if she were to lean forward and say to him: *I think I've killed somebody*, the expression on his face might change from pleasure to concern but the concern would be for her, and he would probably say: *You did? Well, my dear, I'm sure you had some very good reason for doing it. Can you manage by yourself or do you need my help?*

After a while, Mrs. Potter called across the room to her. "Martha, change places with me. You've had that delightful man to yourself long enough!"

This move having been accomplished, Mrs. Potter sat fanning herself and smiling around at the company for a moment or two. Then, turning to Dr. Danforth, she said, "Warm, isn't it?"

"I didn't catch that?" Dr. Danforth said, and cupped his hand behind his ear.

"I say it's very *warm!*"

"Ninety-six in the shade on the east side of the courthouse at two o'clock this afternoon," Dr. Danforth said.

"If I'd known it was going to be like this up North," Mrs. Potter said, fanning him as well as herself, "I'd never have had the courage to pack up and come. And in that case, I'd have missed knowing you, Mr. Danverse."

"Danforth . . . Dr. Danforth. I'm a veterinary."

"Well you must just excuse me. I've met so many charming people here this evening, and as I get older I have trouble remembering names. My girlhood friend Clara Huber, from Greenville, Mississippi, has a daughter who married a man named Danforth. I wonder if you could be any kin?"

"My people come from Vermont," Dr. Danforth said.

"Now isn't that unusual," Mrs. Potter said. "You hardly ever meet anyone who comes from Vermont. Not down home, anyway. But I was going to say, if you're a horse-doctor you must like horses, so why don't you come down and visit us? We've got a whole stable full of horses you could ride. I tell Mr. Potter he's fonder of horseflesh than he is of his wife. Just joking, you know . . . I say *just joking* . . . Yes. But seriously, Mr. Danforth, you ought to come down to Mississippi. You've never seen cotton growing, have you? Well, you'll find it interesting. A field of cotton is a beautiful sight if you can just look at it and not have to worry about the practical side. The menfolks will show you around the plantation. The old slave quarters and the live oaks with moss hanging from them. You don't have anything like that up North, do you? And the family burial ground. Just drop us a penny post card and let us know when you're arriving. We're simple country folks. We don't put on any dog. But Mr. Potter loves company and so do I, and we'll show you a good time, you and your very charming wife."

Mrs. Potter had already asked several other people to come and stay at the plantation and each invitation had started, in the person who received it, a chain of subdued excitement and planning that would take months to exhaust itself. She stopped fanning and called across the room to her son. "Randolph, what is the name of the man Clara Huber's eldest daughter married? Danforth? Danverse?"

"Tweed," Randolph said, barely turning his head. "Charlie Tweed." Mary Caroline was telling him about the high school debating contest that had as its subject: *Resolved that Napoleon was defeated, not by the Russians or the English or the Austrians, but by Destiny.* Her side had been given the affirmative.

"Charlie Tweed," Mrs. Potter said to Dr. Danforth. "So he's probably no relation to you. He's a cotton broker and lives outside of Columbus, Georgia."

The conversation of the Southerners was sprinkled with place names that in an Illinois living room in 1912 were still romantic—Memphis and Nashville and Natchez and Gulfport and New Orleans—and that conveyed to the people of Draperville a sense of strange vegetation and of an easier, more picturesque life than they themselves were accustomed to. Mr. and Mrs. Potter depended, for the most part, on half a dozen topics: the Delta country, the plantation, cotton, kinship, their own emphatic likes and dislikes, and the behavior of various eccentric persons back home. These topics formed a complicated series of tracks and switches, like a railroad yard. Sometimes their separate conversations merged, so that Mr. and Mrs. Potter would be telling the same story simultaneously in different parts of the room. But the next moment they would go steaming off in opposite directions, calling on their son or daughter for confirmation of details, for names and dates momentarily forgotten. They thought out loud, recklessly, and sometimes heard their own remarks with surprise and wonder.

They were in the North and among strangers, a situation that was unnatural to them, and that could only be corrected by making lifetime friends of every person they talked to. It didn't occur to them that they might bore anyone, and no one was bored by them or less than delighted with their soft Mississippi accent.

Mr. and Mrs. Potter talked about themselves and the people they knew because they had as yet nothing else to talk about, but as they began to feel better acquainted, the direction of their concern sometimes veered, sometimes reversed itself, and the full heat of their charm and interest was applied flatteringly to the listener, while they extracted his likes and dislikes, his hopes, plans, and history. The person taken hold of in this way had the feeling that they would never let go, that he and everything about him would always engage the attention and sympathy of these Southerners. The fact that the Southerners did let go a moment later, and let go completely, was not important. The contact, though brief, had been satisfying.

Randolph Potter left Mary Caroline and went out to the kitchen on some errand which he did not explain, and Mrs. Danforth came and sat down beside her. It was all Mary Caroline could do not to put out her hand and prevent Randolph's place from being taken. Mrs. Danforth was a very homely woman with a disconcerting habit of twisting her head like a parrot and looking at the person she was talking to with an expression that seemed half-inquiring and half-mocking. Mary Caroline answered Mrs. Danforth's questions about her mother, who had not been well lately, but her eyes kept straying. Mrs. Danforth saw the direction they took, and then, in her survey of the room, that her husband had said something to Mrs. Potter which made her tap his arm coquettishly with her fan. Pleased that he was enjoying himself, Mrs. Danforth turned back to Mary Caroline and said, "What a pretty dress, my dear. Did you make it yourself?"

In a kind of dream, Abbey King had been passed from one lap to another. Worn out by the excitement, the perfume and cigar smoke, and the effort of trying to follow so many conversations, none of which made the least concession to inexperience, she fingered the silk rose at her mother's waist.

"When I was nine," young Mrs. Ellis said to Martha King,

"we moved from the part of town where we knew everybody, and I thought I wouldn't ever again have any friends. I used to sit in my swing in the back yard of the new house and watch the two little girls who lived next door. I envied their curls and their clothes and everything about them. And then one day I caught them using my swing. They were swinging each other and eating licorice, and they gave me some. . . . But it took a long time, it took years for me to realize that wherever I went there would always be someone who—"

"You'll find people very friendly here," Martha said, stroking Ab's hair.

In the evening air outside, the throbbing sound of the locusts rose and ebbed. Austin King left the circle of men and came across the room. What he had to say was for his wife's ear alone. She nodded twice, and he sat down at the piano and played a series of chords which produced a brief and respectful silence. "We're going to play a game called Mystic Music," he said. Mrs. Potter had never heard of this game and, instead of listening to the rules as Austin explained them, she kept going off into descriptions of parlor games that they played in Mississippi. The men were reluctant to leave their closed circle and the subject of Teddy Roosevelt, who out of egotism had split the Republican Party.

Though it was taken so seriously that night in the Kings' living room, the split in the Republican Party was as nothing compared to the split between the men and the women. Before dinner and again immediately afterward, the men gathered at one end of the room near the ebony pier glass and the women at the opposite end, around the empty fireplace. What originally brought the split about, it would be hard to say. Perhaps the women, with their tedious recipes and their preoccupation with the diseases of children, drove the men away. Or perhaps the men, knowing how nervous the women became when their husbands' voices were raised in political argument, withdrew of their own accord in order to carry on, unhampered, the defense of their favorite misconceptions. Both men and women may have decided sadly that after marriage there was no common ground for social intercourse. At all events, the separation had taken place a long time before. In Draperville only the young, ready (like Randolph and Mary Caroline) for courtship, or the old, bent (like Mrs. Potter and Dr. Danforth) on preserving the traditions of gallantry, were willing to talk to one another. They met as ambassadors and kept open the lines of communication between the sexes.

Austin King continued his efforts at the piano until eventually one person at a time relinquished his right to speak and the room was ready for the new game. Young Mrs. Ellis was chosen to be the first victim, and left the room. Austin began to improvise. He played the same mysterious little tune over and over, the end being woven each time into the beginning, until the company arrived at the stunt that Mrs. Ellis must do. She was called back from the study and the music became louder. She changed the direction of her steps and the music diminished. Now louder, now softer, it led her around the living room on invisible wires until at last, hesitantly, she transferred a vase of white phlox from the table to the mantelpiece and the music stopped altogether.

The next victim, Randolph Potter, had to stand before Mary Caroline Link, bow from the waist, and ask her to dance with him. Under the spell of the music, Alice Beach (whose sister had sung for Geraldine Farrar's teacher, though she herself, being the younger one, had had no such opportunity) took a book out of the bookcase in the study, returned to the living room, sat down in the wing chair, and commenced to read aloud.

Since Austin couldn't see into the study, this required assistance, and so did the next stunt, when Dr. Danforth went all the way upstairs. The piano was moved so that Austin could see into the front hall, and confederates were stationed on the landing and at the head of the stairs. By prearranged signals they conveyed to the pianist whether Dr. Danforth was getting warmer or colder. A false move on his part produced an abrupt fortissimo chord, which was sometimes succeeded by others even louder, because of Dr. Danforth's infirmity. At last he came down the stairs wearing a white coat of Martha King's and a black hat with ostrich feathers on it. This feat was regarded by the Mississippi relatives as a triumph of the human mind.

After Dr. Danforth, it was Ab's turn. She had not expected to have any. But little girls can be seen and not heard and still be the center of attention. Now, with all eyes upon her, she was obliged to leave the room. She sat with her legs tucked under her in a wicker chair in the study, and listened to the low murmur in the next room. It threatened to become intelligible but didn't quite, and finally they called to her.

As Ab came into the living room she saw and started toward her mother. The music stopped her in her tracks. She blushed. She would have liked to escape but the music held her fast. She moved tentatively toward the fireplace. The music grew softer. There were three people confronting her—Mrs. Potter, Dr. Danforth, and Miss Lucy Beach. Ab knew she was supposed to do something to one of them, but which one? And what was it that she was supposed to do? She advanced toward Dr. Danforth. Once when she had an earache, he blew cigar smoke in her ear and the pain went away. The music grew louder, obliterating him.

Through the music her father was saying something to her which she couldn't understand, but which was nevertheless insistent and left her no choice except the right one. She stepped back and would have walked in the opposite direction, but the *DEE dum dum dum* grew loud and frightening. Lucy Beach sat there smiling at her, but some instinct—what the music was saying seemed clearer to the child now, though it was not yet plain—made her move instead toward her great-aunt from Mississippi. The music grew soft and caressing. The music suggested love to the little girl. She saw an invitation in her great-aunt's eyes and, forgetting that it was a game, leaned toward her and kissed her on the cheek. To Ab's surprise, the music stopped and the room was full of the sound of clapping.

"You sweet child!" Mrs. Potter exclaimed, and drew Ab into her arms. While Ab was enjoying her moment of triumph, she heard her mother's voice announcing that it was way past time for little girls to be in bed. A moment later she was led off, having gone around the circle of the company and said good night to everyone.

The sense of triumph was still with her on the stairs, and it lasted even after she had been tucked in bed. She was pleased with her first excursion into society, and she realized drowsily that the grown people were, beyond all doubt or question, pleased with her. The sudden prompting which had seemed to arise from inside her, the impulse toward love, was, as it turned out, exactly what they had meant for her to feel all along.

7

The sounds of an evening party breaking up are nearly always the same and nearly always beautiful. For over an hour the only excitement on Elm Street had been provided by the insects striking at the arc light. Now it was suddenly replaced by human voices, by the voice of Mrs. Beach saying, "Feel that breeze . . . Good night, Martha . . . Austin, good night. Such a nice party . . . No, you mustn't come with us, Mr. Potter. We left a light burning and we're not afraid."

The light could not protect Mrs. Beach and her daughters from death by violence, or old age, or from the terrible hold they had on one another, but at least it would enable them to enter their own house without being afraid of the dark, and it is the dark most people fear, anyway—not being murdered or robbed.

"Good night . . . good night."

Mrs. Danforth had left no light on, but then her husband was with her.

"Good night, Martha . . . good night, my boy."

"Good night, Austin . . . good night, Martha . . . good night, Mrs. Potter . . . Here, Grampaw, take hold of my arm."

"I don't need any help. I can see perfectly . . . good night, Miss Potter . . . good night."

Old Mr. Ellis had been listened to, and at his time of life he asked for nothing more. All the Draperville people had been so complimented, so smiled at and enjoyed that they felt as if a weight had been lifted from their backs.

"Good night, Mrs. King. I don't know when I've had such a lovely time."

"You must come again, Mrs. Ellis."

"Good night, Mr. King."

Though Mary Caroline lived next door to the Ellises, everyone expected Randolph Potter to take her home and she found him now (so firmly and relentlessly does the world push young people at one another) by her side.

"No, you don't have to take me home, Randolph, really. It's only a step. . . . Well, all right then, if you insist."

If it had been twenty miles, the distance from the Kings' front porch to the Links' front walk would have been too short for Mary Caroline. The summer night was barely large enough to enclose a wandering sanity, a heart that must—somewhere on the way home—sigh or break. Such a pressure around her heart the girl had never felt before. Randolph did not touch her or even take hold of her elbow as they crossed the street, but his voice was music, the night insects were violins.

Faced with a sea of empty chairs, Austin and Martha and the Potters sat down to appreciate the quiet, recover their ordinary selves, and exchange impressions of the evening.

"Your friends are just charming," Mrs. Potter said. "I can't get over how nice they were to us."

"There was salt in the ice cream," Martha said.

"It tasted like nectar and ambrosia to me," Mrs. Potter said. "Austin, toward the end of the evening, I couldn't help thinking of your father. You look like him, you know. And he would have been so proud of you."

The expression on Austin King's face did not change, but he was pleased, nevertheless. Mrs. Potter had found the only compliment that could touch him, that he would allow himself to accept.

"I always like a mixed party," Mr. Potter said. "You get all kinds of people together, young and old, and they're bound to have a good time."

Nora smothered a yawn. It had been a long evening, and now she wanted to go to sleep and never wake up again. She kept her head from falling forward.

"Rich and poor," Mr. Potter said.

"There was nobody here who was very rich *or* very poor," Austin said.

"Well, people like the Danforths and the old lady with the two daughters—Mrs. Beach. They're people of culture and refinement. They've traveled all over Europe, she told me. You can see they've always lived well. And poor old Mr. Ellis. We had a little conversation after dinner. I always feel sorry when a man gets that old and has to worry about money."

"The Ellises don't have to worry about money," Martha said, tucking a loose hairpin into place.

"Old Mr. Ellis likes to give the impression that he's hard up," Austin said, "but actually he owns four hundred acres of the best farmland around here."

"You don't say!"

"It's Mrs. Beach who has a difficult time," Martha said. "They used to be well off—not rich exactly but comfortable—and then Mr. Beach died and left them barely enough to get along. But of course you'd never know from talking to her. She's terribly proud."

"Always has been," Austin said, nodding.

"Nora, go to bed," Mrs. Potter said. "You're so sleepy you can hardly keep your eyes open. Cousin Martha will excuse you."

"I'll wait up till Randolph comes."

"What time do you have breakfast?" Mrs. Potter asked, turning to Martha.

"Don't worry about breakfast," Austin said. "Sleep till noon if you feel like it."

The two men withdrew to the study for a nightcap, leaving the women to straighten the rugs and put back the chairs, to discover that Mrs. Danforth had forgotten her palm-leaf fan and Alice Beach a small, lace-bordered handkerchief with a smudge in one corner. Randolph's step on the front porch broke up the exchange of confidences in the living room and the matter-of-fact conversation about farming in the study. Amid a second round of good nights, the Potters went upstairs to bed.

"You go on up," Martha said to Austin. "I want to see if Rachel has put everything away."

"I'll wait," he said, yawning.

The kitchen was all in order, the remains of the ham in the covered roasting pan on the table in the larder, the sink white and gleaming, the icebox crammed with leftovers. Martha started back, turning out lights as she went. Finding no one in the study or the living room, she called to him.

"Out here," he answered.

He was on the porch, looking up at the sky. She came and leaned her head against his shoulder. Without speaking, they went down the steps and out into the yard where the grass, wet with dew, ruined Martha King's bronze evening slippers. The moon was high in the sky, so bright that they could see the shapes of the flower beds and here and there, dimly, the color of a flower. When they came to the sundial, they stopped. The mingled odor of stock and flowering tobacco Austin had smelled before, but he had never realized until now how like the natural perfume of a woman's hair it was. A foot away from him, Martha stood as still as a statue.

Tonight after the party we'll have it all out, he had told her, hours before. Everything, he had said. But if it was that she was waiting for, she wouldn't be standing there with her face raised to the sky. She'd be looking either at or away from him. The small flicker of resentment that had persisted all through the evening—she needn't have put him through so much when there were guests in the house and people coming—he laid aside.

"You must be dead tired," he said.

There was no answer from the moonlit statue. Every rustle, every movement in nature had withdrawn, leaving them in the secret center of the summer night. *There will be other summer nights*, the sundial said, *nights almost like this, but this night won't ever come again. Take it while you have it.*

"We better go in," he said after a moment or two. "Tomorrow we both have to be up early."

Taking her arm, he led her gently back through the garden to the lighted house.

PART TWO

A Long Hot Day

I

THE far end of Elm Street dipped downhill in a way that was dangerous to children trying out new bicycles, and at the intersection with Dewey Avenue the pavement ended. From here on, Elm Street made no pretense of living up to the dignified architectural standards of the period. Instead, it was lined on both sides with small one-story houses that under the steady pressure of a first and second mortgage were beginning to settle, to soften, to crack open.

If there had ever been any graceful trees below the intersection, they were gone by 1912. The cottonwoods and box elders had been planted by the wind—the same wind that later broke off limbs and lopped the tops out of them. There were no flower beds, no fern baskets, no potted palms, no brick driveways. The grass fought a losing battle with dandelions, ragweed, thistles. Chimney fires and evictions were not uncommon.

In this down-at-the-heel neighborhood a few white families and most of the Negroes of Draperville lived on terms of social intimacy, to which there were limits; but no taboo prevented the women from calling to each other (*How's your husband's back, Mrs. Woolman? Is it still giving him trouble? . . . I saw your Rudolf heading for the gravel pits with some older boys and told him to come home, but I don't think he heard me. . . .*) or the children from playing together in swarms.

In winter the residents of lower Elm Street kept themselves warm with stoves or took to their beds when the woodpile gave out. Their windows were nailed shut the year round, and the stale air they breathed they were accustomed and resigned to, just as they were accustomed and resigned to roofs that leaked, ceilings that cracked and fell, floors that were uneven, and the scratching of rats at night inside the walls. In their lifetime few of them had known anything better, though as a matter of fact there was one—there was a colored boy who finished high school and went off to St. Louis to study medicine, much to the amusement of the white families who brought their washing to his mother once a week in big wicker baskets.

Something like a great pane of glass, opaque from one side, transparent from the other, divided the two halves of Elm Street. Beulah Osborn, the Ellises' hired girl, Snowball McHenry, who worked in Dr. Danforth's livery stable, and the Reverend Mr. Porterfield, who looked after Mrs. Beach's furnace from October until April and her flower garden from April until October, knew a great deal about what went on in the comfortable houses on the hill. But when they or any of their friends and neighbors passed under the arc light at the intersection, the comfortable part of Elm Street lost all contact with them.

In one of these shabby houses, in what was actually a railroad caboose covered with black roofing paper and divided into two rooms by a flimsy partition, Rachel, the Kings' cook, lived sometimes with one man and sometimes with another, and raised her five children. The two small windows on either side of the front door had once looked out on a moving landscape, on Iowa and Texas and Louisiana and West Virginia. Because every house in Draperville had to have a porch, Rachel's also had one—a platform four by four, with an ornamental balustrade that unknown hands had deposited in a tree near by, one Halloween. In the front yard under a box elder was a rain-rotted carriage seat with the horsehair stuffing coming out of it, and a funeral basket set on two round stones. There were a number of other things in Rachel's yard that were not easily explained—a bassinet, a rusty coach lantern, a coffeepot, a slab of marble that might have been a table-top or a tombstone. The effect of all this was strangely formal, a fancy-dress nightmare made out of odds and ends, suggesting (if you didn't look too closely) an eighteenth-century garden house.

The morning after Martha King's party, Rachel opened her eyes and saw the commode with a pitcher and bowl, and a full slop jar standing on the floor beside it. A magazine cover was tacked on the wall above the washstand. The child in this picture had rolled off the printing press a little white girl, but someone had since painted the hands and face a chocolate brown, and now it was a little colored girl who hugged the grey kitten to her breast.

Rachel hung for a moment between sleep and waking, and then realizing that the other half of the bed was empty said, "You, Thelma—what you doing?"

Thelma appeared in the doorway to the kitchen. She was in her underwear and in her left hand was the piece of wrapping paper Rachel had used to bring home some leftovers from the party—a little chicken and ham that would never be missed. As a piece of sculpture Thelma was astonishingly beautiful. The receding slope of her forehead, the relation of the cheekbones to the slanting, dreamy eyes, the carving of the thin arms and legs, the rounded shoulders, the hollow chest were the work of a tormented artist who had said, in this one fully accomplished effort, all that there is to say about childhood; said (unfortunately, from the point of view of a work of art) a little more, spoiling the generality of his design by something personal.

"You want to see what I been drawing?" Thelma asked.

Rachel brushed the picture aside. "What time that clock say?"

"Twenty minutes to seven."

"Whoo-ee, I got to get up out of this bed right now. Go wake up your brothers."

As Rachel bent over the china washbowl, she heard the couch in the kitchen being shaken, and then groans and protests.

"Time to get up, Alfred," Thelma said.

"Time to knock your head off if you don't leave me alone," Alfred said.

"Hush up, all of you!" Rachel commanded.

Thelma came back in the front room and sat on the bed. Rachel glanced at her daughter suspiciously and, as she was drying her face and hands, said, "There seems to be something weighing on your mind."

Thelma pulled a feather through the ticking of the pillow and said, "I don't want to go to Mrs. King's no more."

"So that what's bothering you."

"I don't so much like it there. The Southern people they—"

"I guess I'm mistaken," Rachel said. "It don't look as if you was my child, after all. Mrs. King give you them nice crayons and when she needs a helping hand, you aren't a bit willing."

"Yes I am," Thelma said quickly. "I'm your child."

"Get away from me," Rachel said, and found herself, at ten minutes of seven, when the coffee ought to be in the pot and on the stove, with a broken heart to mend. She took Thelma on her lap and said, "I don't know what to do with you. I just don't. Let me see that picture you drawed." She felt around in the bedclothes and uncovered the piece of brown wrapping paper. "Alfred . . . Eugene . . . Get up out of that bed before I come pull you out. Your pappy come home one of these days and I tell him a few things."

The two little boys asleep on the narrow cot at the foot of Rachel's bed stirred and untwined their bare legs without waking.

Rachel held the picture out at arm's length and considered it critically. The artist had taken certain liberties with perspective and altered a few facts, but there nevertheless, for all time, was the Kings' living room, the ebony pier glass, the upright piano, and the bouquets of white phlox, just as they had appeared to the innocent eye, the eye that sees things as they are and not the use they are put to. The café-au-lait ladies distributed about the room on sofas and chairs wore long lace dresses, diamond necklaces, too many rings on their fingers, too many jeweled pendants and rhinestone ornaments in their hair. The men were more aristocratic. They might have been dark-skinned dukes and earls. No one was fat or ugly, no one was old.

"Yes," Rachel said nodding. "You're too tender for this world. I got to harden you up some way or you won't survive."

2

The breakfast table was set for seven, and four of the places had not been disturbed. No sound came from the upper regions of the house. When Austin and Martha spoke to each other or to Ab, their voices sounded subdued, as if they were either listening or afraid of being overheard. Except for this and the empty places, there was no indication of company in the house. One might almost have thought that the Mississippi people had packed their bags and stolen away in the night.

Austin passed his cup down the table to be refilled. With the fumes from the coffeepot Martha felt a wave of returning nausea, and bent her face away. "Be careful and don't spill it," she said, handing the cup to Ab.

"That's very good coffee," Austin said.

The telephone rang a minute or two later. He looked at his wife questioningly. She nodded, and he got up and went into the study to answer it. Young Mrs. Ellis wanted to say what a nice time they had had and how much they had enjoyed the Potters. Austin barely had time to return and sit down before the telephone rang again. The second call was from Mrs. Danforth, to say the same thing. "Well I'll tell Martha," she heard him say. "Oh no, she's fine."

At eight-thirty he folded his napkin and slipped it through a silver ring that had his first name engraved on it and was a relic of his childhood. "I'll be home a little after twelve," he said as he pushed his chair back from the table. Although he said nothing about the Potters, it was clear from the look in his eyes and from his doubtful expression as he bent down to kiss his wife that he wanted to ask her to be gracious, to be friendly whether she felt like it or not, to do nothing that would make the Potters feel unwanted.

As he was starting out the front door, Martha heard him say, "Hello, where have *you* been?"

A moment later, Nora Potter came through the study and into the dining room. She was wearing a green dress with black velvet bows and two black velvet ribbons braided into her cinnamon-colored hair. The dress was becoming, but strange for this time of the day. It made Nora look like a tintype in a family album—some fourth or fifth cousin, who is shown a few pages later with her rather vain-looking husband, and then again as an old lady, formidable and all in black, with her elbow resting on an Ionic pillar.

"I woke up around six o'clock," Nora said as she began to eat her cantaloupe, "and couldn't get back to sleep, so I got up and put on my clothes and went out walking. Wasn't that enterprising of me?"

"Very," Martha said.

"Did I waken you?"

Martha shook her head. "We thought you were still asleep," she said, reaching for the china serving bell.

"I tried to slip out of the house as quietly as I could. What a nice sound that bell makes. Our bell at home makes such a racket. It came down through the Detrava side of the family so Mama insists on using it."

"This one came down through Mr. Gossett's gift shop," Martha said. "Did you enjoy your walk?"

"There was dew on the grass and after the heat yesterday everything seemed so fresh and clear cut. Maybe because I'm in a strange place, seeing everything for the first time. Or maybe it's because I'm happy. All my life I've wanted to come North." She put down her spoon and with her raised eyebrows conveyed the seriousness and the intensity of this desire. "Ever since I was a little girl."

The horrible odor of frying eggs penetrated through two swinging doors and filled the dining room.

"Well now that you're here, you must make the most of it," Martha said.

"I mean to," Nora said earnestly. "At home it doesn't cool off at night and you wake up exhausted. Here everybody and his dog were out sweeping and watering their window boxes and I don't know what all. You'd think they were getting ready for a celebration."

Martha leaned over and wiped a dribble of egg from Ab's chin. "You make me wish I'd been out with you," she said. "There was nothing so interesting going on here."

"And red geraniums. Everybody has red geraniums and I'm so tired of magnolias. What would they have done if I'd walked right past them into their houses and had a look around?"

"It all depends on whose house you walked into. The Murphys would have let you go upstairs and downstairs and anywhere you wanted to. Old Mrs. Tannehill would probably have called the police."

"Would she really?"

"Yes, I think she would," Martha said. "But Austin would have come and bailed you out."

"It's a game I'm always playing with myself," Nora said. "That I'm invisible and can go wherever I want to go and watch people when they don't know anybody is watching them." She finished her cantaloupe and pushed it aside. "There was so much going on this morning I almost came back here to get Brother. You know how—not always but sometimes—you feel If I only had someone with me?"

"I know," Martha said.

"And then," Nora said, "sometimes when you do have someone with you and you think they're going to enjoy things the way you do, it turns out not to be the right person." Her eyes came to rest on the silver napkin ring. "You and Cousin Austin seem so suited to each other. I woke up thinking about you."

"And I woke up thinking about you," Martha said.

"Did you really?" Nora's eyes opened wide. "Wasn't that a coincidence! And yet if we were to try and tell somebody, they probably wouldn't believe that such a thing could happen. I'm always having strange things happen to me. I don't know what it is."

The pantry door swung open and Rachel appeared with a platter of bacon and eggs. "Morning, Miss Nora," she said glumly.

"Good morning, Rachel. How are you this morning—at least *I* think they're strange. But what I was about to say is I'm so glad you and Cousin Austin found each other."

"Do you take cream and sugar in your coffee?" Martha asked.

"Neither," Nora said. "I just take it black." Her expression changed and became uncertain. In Mississippi a genuine liking conveyed with candor usually brought a similar protestation in return. Also, there was something about Martha King's manner—so encouraging one minute and the next so blank, as if she had no idea what Nora was talking about—that made some of Nora's pleasure in the summer morning dwindle away. At the risk of seeming foolish she added, "And so glad I've found you both," and was partly reassured by the wan smile from across the breakfast table. "I often wonder why people marry the people they do marry, and what they find to say to each other, day in and day out. There's so much that must be difficult—"

"You're excused, pet," Martha said to Ab.

"I haven't finished my milk," Ab said.

"Never mind. You don't have to finish your milk this morning. Go in the study and play with your dolls."

"Do you mind my talking in such a steady stream?" Nora asked, as Ab left the room. "We all talk more than we should, except Randolph. It's a family failing. The thing is, you don't have to listen. Not if you don't feel like it."

"Oh but I *am* listening," Martha said. "And with great interest."

"If people don't talk," Nora said, "it's so hard to know what's on their minds. Tell me, Cousin Martha, do you ever hear voices?"

The telephone began ringing, and Martha went into the study to answer it.

"Yes," Nora heard her say. "Well I'm glad. I hoped everybody was having a good time . . . Yes, I'll tell them. They aren't up yet. Only Nora . . ."

At the sound of her own name, Nora felt the cold damp wind of dislike blowing through the dining room, and wondered what she had said or done to deserve it.

"Oh no!" Martha exclaimed, over the telephone, "What a pity! Perhaps it was the fried chicken . . . yes . . . yes, of course. . . . Well, you tell her I'm terribly sorry. . . . I can look it up, but I think I remember it . . . a teaspoonful of baking powder and then you beat it thoroughly until it's stiff. . . . That's right . . . yes . . . yes, Alice . . . yes, I will. And thank you for calling."

"I'm so sorry about all these interruptions," she said, when she came back into the dining room. "That was Alice Beach calling to say what a nice time they had last night and how much they liked you all."

"I hope you told her how much we liked them," Nora said.

"What was it you were saying?" Martha asked. "Here, let me fill your cup."

Oh, it's no use, Nora thought. I ought never have tried to make friends with her. She doesn't want to be friends with anybody.

"I hear these voices," she began, as she passed her cup across the table, "saying 'Nora, where are you?' and I say, sometimes right out loud: 'On the side porch' or 'Upstairs'—depending on where I am at the time. They aren't real voices—"

Martha tilted the coffeepot and it gave out a last thin trickle.

"*Now* where are you going?" Nora asked anxiously.

"To make a fresh pot of coffee."

"Can't I do it?"

"I'd better go do it myself," Martha said. "Rachel's in a bad mood this morning. She might bite your head off. . . . They're not real?" she asked, with her hand on the swinging door.

"Cousin Martha, that bed!" a voice said. Mrs. Potter swept into the dining room, wearing a lace cap to hide her curl papers and an old brocade dressing gown that Nora had begged her to leave at home. "Good morning, daughter."

"Nora and I have been having such an interesting conversation," Martha King said.

"I hope she hasn't been talking about Life, at the breakfast table."

"Oh no," Martha said. "Nora and I have been talking about voices."

"I can't always follow her, before my eyes are open. Nothing but toast and coffee for me," Mrs. Potter added as she sat down. "Mr. Potter likes his two eggs and a little fried ham, if you have any, but I just have toast and coffee. My dear, it was like sleeping on a cloud."

3

The law office of Holby and King, on the north side of the courthouse square, was reached by a flight of rickety stairs in which deep grooves had been worn by the feet of people coming to inquire into their rights under the Law, or to be treated by Dr. Hieronymous, the osteopath whose office was across the hall.

In the outer room of the law firm, surrounded by tier upon tier of fat calf-bound books on jurisprudence and equity, Miss Ewing guarded the gate through which people were usually but not always allowed to pass. She was a thin, energetic, nervous woman with a raw complexion, pale blue eyes, and pince-nez that reflected the glitter of overhead lights but no mercy on mankind. Around her cuffs she wore sheets of legal foolscap held in place by paper clips, and her hair was a grey bird's nest full of little combs, bone hairpins, puffs, and rats. The age of anyone born and raised in Draperville was either common knowledge or easily arrived at by mental calculation—Miss Ewing was fifty-one. But how she did her hair up the same way every morning of her life was a secret known to no other living person.

Miss Ewing was friendly with clients, rude to insurance salesmen and peddlers, and self-important generally; but she did the work of two secretaries and an errand boy, was never ill, and gave up all claim to a life of her own in the sincere and fairly accurate belief that without her the firm of Holby and King would not have been able to function. She alone understood the filing and bookkeeping systems, and she had hundreds of telephone numbers and addresses in her head, including some that belonged to people who were now retired from business and in certain cases dead.

This morning she was sitting at her L. C. Smith double-keyboard typewriter thrashing out five copies of an abstract that Austin King had left on her desk, and waiting for a farmer named John Scroggins to come out of Mr. Holby's office so she could go in and take his dictation. There were a number of matters that Mr. Holby ought to have been attending to, but instead he was addressing the farmer as if they were both in a crowded courtroom. "We had more enjoyment in the days of bare rough floors and mud chimneys than the people of today, who tread upon velvet and recline upon cushioned seats, clothed in purple and fine linen . . ."

The farmer was clothed in an old dark blue suit, and he had come to consult Mr. Holby about the mortgage on his farm. It was coming due shortly and the bank was threatening to foreclose.

"Life then," Mr. Holby said, "was more real. Humankind possessed more goodness. Virtue had a higher level, and manhood was set at a higher key . . ."

Miss Ewing went on typing.

Austin King's door was closed. Although he was the junior partner in the firm, his office was the larger of the two, and looked out over the square and the stately courthouse elms. It had been Judge King's office. Partly out of respect for his father's memory and partly so that his father's friends could come here and smoke a cigar and perhaps feel his loss less keenly, Austin had kept the office the way it was during Judge King's lifetime. But the big slant-topped desk, the green and red carpet, the stuffed prairie dog, and the framed photograph of the old Buttercup Hunting and Fishing Club were not enough. Something was gone from the room and these memorials only made the old men sad. When they came at all, it was generally on business.

Judge King was the nearest the town of Draperville had come to producing a great man. During the last years of his life, honors had been heaped upon him. He was twice judge of the circuit court and several times a director of the county fair association. In 1880 he was a delegate to the Republican National Convention at Chicago, and four years later he was one of the presidential electors for the state of Illinois. In 1896 he was asked to run for governor and declined. (The offer had strings attached to it.) And shortly after the conclusion of his most celebrated case, *The Citizens of Dunthorpe County v. James Long*, he was publicly presented with the gold watch which Austin now carried.

Judge King's largeness of mind, his legal talent, and his wisdom in political affairs were balanced and made human by his fund of stories, his love of good living, and the pleasure he took in people of all kinds, especially women. He preferred them to be young and pretty, but whatever they were like, he rose to meet them as if they were, entirely in themselves, an object of pleasure and an occasion for ceremony. He made them little complimentary speeches and with his own eyes dancing looked deeply into theirs, to see what was there. They were always charming to him. Refusing to recognize what everyone knew to be a melancholy fact, he went on notes for friends and made a number of loans of which his executors could find no written record. But in a place where gossip and scandal flourished, Judge King left a good name.

It was never his intention that Austin should become a lawyer. He died in 1901, before Austin knew what profession he wanted to follow. His father's memory, tenaciously preserved in the minds of the people who loved him, the sense of personal loss, and perhaps most of all the realization that he had never really known his father made Austin choose law as a career.

After seven years of practicing in his father's office, he still did not feel that it was his own. But when he arrived in the morning there was usually someone waiting to see him. He was not consulted about political appointments or asked to serve on honorary committees, but men who wanted to be sure that in the event of their death their families would not be taken advantage of had Austin King draw up their wills and appointed him sole executor. He could spot a trick clause in a contract far more quickly than his father ever could. He had read more widely and was better at preparing briefs. On the other hand, there were things that Judge King had learned as a lean and hungry young man in the offices of Whitman, James, and Whitlaw in Cincinnati that no law school has ever learned how to teach. Judge King had been a brilliant trial lawyer of the old school. Austin settled cases, whenever he could, out of court; settled them ably and without fanfare. This was not wholly the difference between father and son. The times were changing.

During the period between 1850 and 1900, when Draperville was still a pioneering community, the ownership of land was continually and expensively disputed. The government extinguished the Indian title to the prairie, and the land was subject to settlement either before or after it was surveyed. The settler had no paper title—merely the right to possession, which he got by moving onto the land and raising a crop. The amount of the crop was not legally specified. A rail fence of four lengths was often seen on the prairie, with the enclosed ground spaded over and sown with wheat. This gave the settler the right to hold his land against all others until he had purchased it from the government (or until, through some unfortunate clerical mistake, someone else had) and it also left a chaos of overlapping claims. Laws were passed but they were full of loopholes, and consequently, for the next two generations, able lawyers were held in the highest respect. In the eyes of simple and uneducated men, the Law assumed the status, dignity, and mystical content of a religion. The local lawyers, even though they were the heirs of Moses, sometimes charged very high fees. A farmer accused of having improper relations with his daughter would have to hand over his farm to the Honorable Stephen A. Finch before that eminent swayer of juries would take his case. But the older lawyers also took on a great many cases where there was no possibility of remuneration, merely so they could argue in court. They were dramatic figures and people attended their trials as they would a play, for the emotional excitement, the spectacle, the glimpses of truth behind the barnburning, the murderous assault, the boundary dispute, or the question of right of way.

By 1912 the older generation, the great legal actors with their overblown rhetoric, their long white hair and leonine heads, their tricks in cross-examination, their departures from good taste, had one after another died or lapsed into the frailty of old men. There was also, throughout the country, an abrupt change in the legal profession. The older Illinois lawyers were trained on and continued to read assiduously certain books. Their bible was Chitty's *Pleadings*, which Abraham Lincoln carried in his saddlebags when he went on circuit in the forties and fifties; they also read Blackstone's *Commentaries*, Kent's *Commentaries*, and Starkie on *Evidence*. The broad abstract principles set forth in these books were applied to any single stolen will or perjured testimony, and on these principles the issue was decided. With the establishment of the Harvard Law School case system, the attention of lawyers generally was directed away from statements of principle and toward the facts in the particular case. They preferred more and more to argue before a judge, to let the court decide on the basis of legal precedent, to keep the case away from a jury, and to close the doors of the theater on the audience who hoped to hear about the murder of Agamemnon and see Medea's chariot drawn by dragons. The result was that the Law lost much of its moral and philosophic dignity, and required a different talent of those who practiced it. The younger men regarded themselves as businessmen, and Miss Ewing (never quite respectful, never openly disrespectful) considered them one and all as schoolboys slip-slopping around in the shoes of giants.

Through the old-fashioned oratory in Mr. Holby's office she heard the measured tread which meant that Austin King was walking the floor. So far as Miss Ewing could see, it was the only trait that he had inherited from his father. More times than she could remember, she had heard Judge King pacing the length and breadth of his inner office. At such times he did not suffer himself to be interrupted. The governor of the state had been kept waiting for forty-five minutes until the pacing stopped.

When she had finished typing the abstract, she arranged all five copies neatly in a pile, got up from her desk, and took them into Austin's office. He stopped pacing and looked at her, but the expression in his eyes was remote, and she was not at all sure that he knew she was in the room.

"Mrs. Jouette called," she said. "I made an appointment for her to see you at ten o'clock on Tuesday."

The thread of his thought broken, he nodded and (judging by the shade of annoyance in his voice) sufficiently aware of her presence, said, "Thank you, Miss Ewing."

If he doesn't want to be interrupted, she said to herself as she sat down at her desk in the outer office, all he has to do is say so.

She knew perfectly well that he would never tell her not to come in when the door was closed, and so long as he didn't tell her, some perverse impulse drove her to break in upon him with details that could just as well wait. At times, when Miss Ewing was overtired, she considered the possibility of getting a position elsewhere, though she knew that there was no office in Drapervile where she would receive as much consideration or be paid anything like her present salary.

The outer door opened and Herb Rogers came in. Miss Ewing did not waste on him the smile that was reserved for clients.

"I'm selling tickets for a benefit at the opera house," he said hesitantly.

"Mr. Holby has someone in his office," Miss Ewing said, "but if you'd like to see Mr. King—"

"I don't want to bother him if he's busy. I can come back later."

"It's all right," Miss Ewing said cheerfully. "You can go in."

4

Sit down, won't you? the rubber cousin said. *You're rocking the boat.*

I never try to make my children mind, the elephant cousin said.

I wish you'd tell me how you manage, the rubber cousin said.

Oh I don't know, the elephant cousin said. *I give them presents from the ten cent store. They manage the rest.*

I give Humphrey lots of presents, said the mother.

That's news to me, said Humphrey.

Well I don't know whether it is or not, said the mother.

Sit down, Edward, before I slap you, said the rubber cousin.

My name isn't Edward, Humphrey said.

"From now on, it is," Ab said.

Well my advice, said the father, *would be to go out in the kitchen and see what there is to eat. Wash your hands, everybody.*

The telephone began to ring and Ab made no move to answer it. She didn't even seem aware of the ringing on the other side of the room, but the doll party on the window seat was suspended when Martha King came into the study and took the receiver off the hook.

"Yes? . . . Oh yes, Bud . . . no, we haven't. . . ."

Ab always enjoyed listening to her mother on the telephone. Where grown-up conversations were concerned, the half was usually more interesting than the whole.

"Yes . . ." her mother said several times into the telephone. "Well I'm afraid it's going to be very warm, but just let me ask them. . . ." Martha King put the receiver on the telephone stand and left the study. Ab turned back to her dolls.

Hot cocoa, said Humphrey, whose name was now Edward.

And crackers with white icing on them, the father said.

That's a good idea, the elephant cousin said. *Whose idea was it?*

That was my idea, said the mother.

Martha King came back and said, "Bud? . . . We'd like to very much . . . yes . . . All right, I will . . . good-by."

With a brief, absent-minded glance at the dolls lined up in a row on the window sill, she went through the living room and out onto the porch. The doll party came to a sudden end.

". . . and the terrible part of it was," Mrs. Potter was saying as Ab opened the screen door, "they seemed so happy!"

She had taken possession, for the rest of the visit, of a wicker armchair that just suited her. The chair commanded a view of the sidewalk and the street, and the right armrest was designed to hold magazines or a knitting bag. Mrs. Potter kept her silk bag with the round raffia base in her lap. The bag contained crocheting and it went everywhere Mrs. Potter went. Mr. Potter kept the swing in motion with his foot. Nora was out in the side yard reading a book, with her head bowed to the white page.

"So Rebecca came home with a six-months-old baby," Mrs. Potter said, "and she's been home ever since. . . . Daughter, you oughtn't to be out there on the damp ground. Cousin Martha will give you a blanket to sit on."

"It isn't damp," Nora called back, "and I don't want a blanket to sit on."

"Nora is a great reader," Mrs. Potter observed. "She takes after her Great-Aunt Selina, who used to cook with a book in her hand. When Nora was fourteen she started in and read right straight through the historical novels of Harrison Ainsworth. I tried one of them once. It was about the Tower of London and very interesting. I always meant to go on and read the rest of it. Aunt Selina married a man named . . ." The crochet needle jabbed in and out, emphasizing this point or that in Mrs. Potter's family history. When Mr. Potter showed increasing signs of restlessness, she glanced up and said, "You haven't seen the barn."

"You don't have to worry about me," Mr. Potter said. "I can always look after myself."

But he didn't. He sat in the swing, with one leg crossed over the other and his arms folded expectantly, and did nothing whatever to amuse himself. He was waiting for the telephone to ring, for people to arrive, for last night's party to begin all over again.

"Aren't there any dogs in this town?" he asked suddenly.

"At home Mr. Potter always has at least three hunting dogs trailing after him," Mrs. Potter said. "Every chair in the house has dog hairs on it, and we have to barricade the beds to keep Blackie off of them. She comes and goes like a princess."

"Blackie's a good dog but she's getting old," Mr. Potter said mournfully. "She can't see any more. Five years ago I wouldn't have taken a hundred dollars for her."

He got up from the swing and announced that he was going to have a look around. He meant the barn; enough time had elapsed so that the idea was his now and not his wife's. As he disappeared around the corner of the house, she said, "Mr. Potter is not himself this morning. You'll just have to excuse him. He misses the horses. His whole life revolves around horses and dogs. Raising cotton is just a sideline. But it's good for him to get away some place where he has to fall back on people for companionship. . . . Now, my dear, I want to hear all about you. Are your mother and father living? I thought maybe we'd have the pleasure of meeting them last night."

"My mother died before I was old enough to remember her," Martha said. "She died of consumption, and my father died shortly afterward. I was raised by an uncle and aunt."

Mrs. Potter had reached a crucial turn in her crocheting and didn't answer for a minute or two. Then she drew a length of thread through her fingers and said, "Was she your mother's sister?"

"My father's," Martha said. "My mother didn't have any sisters or brothers. She was an actress. I have a picture of her upstairs, in *The Taming of the Shrew*. I can just barely remember my father. From what I've heard of him, I don't think he was much like the rest of the family. They're all very religious."

In her voice there was a note of tension, of fright, as if she were a schoolgirl undergoing an examination for which she was not at all prepared. Mrs. Potter heard it, and without seeming to change the subject, began to talk about the house on Elm Street. Apparently it is not easy for women to make friends. Except for certain critical periods of their lives, they seem almost not to need them. But for Mrs. Potter, too, the visit stretched out interminably. It had not been her idea to come North this summer and she didn't know, actually, why they were here. She only knew that part of the month of July and part of the month of August had to be crossed somehow, and so she set out to cross them. With her crocheting to support her, as it had in every other crisis of married life, she commented on rooms, rugs, curtains, wallpaper, the arrangement of tables and chairs—all this interspersed with descriptions of the plantation house in Mississippi, and how various pieces of furniture had come down through the family. Under the praise of her house (which was praise of her) Martha King began to feel easier, to feel safe. She explained about the alcove in the living room and the open bookshelves in the study and, after a time, about the people who had raised her and who were now in China working as Christian missionaries.

"My religion has been a great comfort to me," Mrs. Potter began. Ab closed the screen door softly so as not to attract attention to herself, and went back to the library. The dolls were worn out from the party. The elephant and Humphrey Edward lay face down on a cushion and for the time being, they all refused to come to life.

Ab went upstairs to her room and got her celluloid animals—a duck, a green frog, and a goldfish—and started down the hall to the bathroom. When she pushed the door open, Randolph Potter was lying in the tub in water up to his chin. Ab stood holding her celluloid toys, and made no move toward the washstand.

"I've lost the soap," Randolph said. He moved his legs gently so that the black hairs stirred with the current.

"Can't you find it?" Ab asked.

"Not without an extensive search. What have you got there?"

Ab held the toys out to him.

"I have a duck at home," he said, and sat up slowly. "A live duck." The water parted, revealing the bald slope of his knee. "I wish I had him here right now."

"In the bath with you?" Ab cried.

"He swims round and round," Randolph said, nodding. "And when I lose the soap he dives for it."

"Why does he do that?"

"Because he knows I need it."

"Why do you need the soap?"

"For the same reason little girls need to ask questions they already know the answer to." When he drew his hand out of the water, his fingers were closed around a cake of castile soap.

"What is the duck's name?"

"I call him Sam," Randolph said, and glanced at the open door.

Now that they had something to talk about, Ab pulled the toilet cover down and set the celluloid animals on it. Randolph began to soap his arms and chest. Where the soap went, Ab's eyes went also.

"He follows me wherever I go," Randolph said. "And he likes raisins and crackerjack."

"What does he do with the prize?" Ab asked.

"He wears it on a string around his neck. When he gets in the bath with me, I take if off so he won't lose it. And when he swims, he goes like this." Randolph made a movement with his hands which churned the water around the tub clockwise.

"I take a bath with my mother sometimes," Ab said, drawing nearer.

"When Sam gets tired of swimming one way, he turns around and goes the other."

There was a sudden upheaval in the tub and Randolph stood up, dripping, and began to soap his back, his belly, and his thighs. He saw where Ab's stare was directed. Having got what he wanted, he said, "I don't think you ought to be in here with me . . . You better go now before somebody comes," and watched the child's curiosity turn to fear.

In her desperate hurry to get away from the bathroom, Ab slipped and fell thump-thump-thump, all the way down the treacherous back stairs. Her screaming brought Rachel, who picked her up and moaned over her and rocked her in her arms.

The world (including Draperville) is not a nice place, and the innocent and the young have to take their chances. They cannot be watched over, twenty-four hours a day. At what moment, from what hiding place, the idea of evil will strike, there is no telling. And when it does, the result is not always disastrous. Children have their own incalculable strength and weakness, and this, for all their seeming helplessness, will determine the pattern of their lives. Even when you suspect why they fall downstairs, you cannot be sure. You have no way of knowing whether their fright is permanent or can be healed by putting butter on the large lump that comes out on their forehead after a fall.

5

The July sun mounting higher and higher in the sky brought both heat and glare with it. By the middle of the morning, animals moved with a noticeable slowness, and the leaves of the trees hung limp and dusty. Women with errands to do downtown kept as much as possible in the shade of awnings. Men meeting on the steps of the courthouse or in front of the bank stopped to compare thermometer readings, to observe how the new asphalt paving blocks buckled with the heat, and to prophesy a thunderstorm out of the brassy sky before night. Farmers driving into Draperville for their Saturday marketing left their teams on shady side streets or in Dr. Danforth's livery stable. Everybody bore the heat patiently and without complaining; no heat, no corn. In stores, the overhead fans whirred to little if any purpose. The windows in the two upper floors of office buildings were flung wide open, as if the masonry were gasping with the heat. At eleven o'clock, the big round sprinkling wagon drove twice around the square. The spraying cooled the streets and the air temporarily but by noon, when Austin King left his office, the pavement was dry and dusty again.

He waited under the awning of Giovanni's ice-cream parlor and moviedrome until a streetcar came along. It was the open car that went out past the cemeteries to the Chautauqua grounds, and would let him off two blocks further from Elm Street than the other car, but it was cooler and so he took it. As he turned in at his own front walk, Mr. Potter got up from the porch swing. "It's a scorcher, isn't it?" Austin said.

"We're all waiting for you," Mr. Potter said.

"Am I late?"

"The womenfolks decided to have an early lunch," Mr. Potter said. "Bud Ellis called and invited us to drive out to their farm this afternoon."

"In this heat?"

"Well, he seemed to think today would be a good time. And we're used to heat. Down home—" Mr. Potter hesitated, searching for justification for the ride and apparently expecting Austin to provide it.

For a minute Austin said nothing. Then pleasantly, in his usual tone of voice: "If that's what you all want to do, fine."

He held the screen door open for Mr. Potter, and followed him into the house. Randolph was in the study. He had Austin's fishing box open on his knees and was examining the trout flies. Mrs. Potter was in the living room, playing the piano loudly and firmly. Ab was sitting on the living-room floor, with her collection of Singer Sewing Machine birds spread out around her.

"Where's Martha?" Austin asked.

"In the kitchen," Mrs. Potter said, still playing.

The whole atmosphere of the house had changed since breakfast. The Potters seemed to have taken hold (after all, he might have been consulted about the drive this afternoon), to have asserted their rights and privileges as guests, and he could feel *his* rights and privileges withdrawing timidly into the cellar, into closets, and beyond the trap door to the attic.

"If you'll excuse me," he said, "I'd better wash up before lunch."

He came down by way of the back stairs, and found Martha in the pantry putting sprigs of mint in a row of tall iced-tea glasses. "You look as pale as a ghost," she said. "Was it hot downtown?"

"No worse than it was here, probably."

"We're just having sandwiches and leftover salad."

"Did everything go all right this morning?" he asked.

"Randolph came down to breakfast at ten-thirty. Ab fell on the stairs. And they want to go driving."

"So I hear."

"I tried to put it off, but Mr. Potter gets restless just sitting around the house. And Nora has been reading."

"That shouldn't upset anybody," Austin said.

"Maybe it shouldn't but it did. You know that set of books from your father's library—tall green books?"

"*The Works of Robert Ingersoll?*"

"Well, Nora found them, and Aunt Ione discovered what she was reading and made her stop. He's an atheist, isn't he? Aunt Ione has been playing hymns to purify the atmosphere. Nora got mad and went over to the Beaches' house, and the girls asked her to stay and eat with them. I wanted to get out of the house for a while myself, to give the Potters more room, but it was time to start lunch."

"I don't think Nora had a very good time at the party last night," Austin said.

"Did she say anything to you?"

"No," Austin said, "it's just a feeling I had. We ought to have invited somebody for her—somebody her own age." He touched a damp curl on the nape of her neck. Martha moved away from him.

"You don't seem too happy yourself at this moment," he said.

"Does everybody have to be happy? Go on in and tell them to sit down. We're all ready."

He looked at her in astonishment. Though he knew he had already said too much, he said one thing more: "I'm sorry you had such a difficult morning." But it was no use. She was already far, far out of his reach. He waited a moment with his hand on the swinging door and then went on into the dining room.

During lunch Martha King behaved toward her guests exactly as she had before, but she looked past her husband instead of at him—a thing that all three of the Mississippi people were instantly aware of. Out of politeness and not because they had any fear of scenes, they talked—talked constantly, often including Rachel in their conversation as she moved around the table. The gleam and roll of her very white eyeballs conveyed extreme acuteness of perception and sometimes open mockery, both of which the Potters were used to in their own servants.

As soon as Austin had finished his dessert, he put down his napkin and escaped to the barn. The horse, a handsome sorrel, had been harnessed and fed. Austin backed Prince Edward into the shafts of the high English cart that was his special pride and drove around to the front of the house, where the Ellises' surrey was waiting. He tied the reins to the other hitching post and then went back inside. Bud Ellis was standing in the front hall with his straw hat in his plump hand. Mrs. Potter had put on a long linen duster and was adjusting her veils in front of the ebony mirror in the living room. Mr. Potter and Randolph, also in dusters, were waiting impatiently.

"Where is Miss Nora?" Bud Ellis asked, shifting his weight from one foot to the other. "Isn't she coming?"

"Nobody knows," Randolph said gloomily.

There was a step on the front porch and Mrs. Potter, turning away from the pier glass, said, "There she is now."

"I'm not going," Nora announced as she walked in. "I'm going to stay home with Cousin Martha."

"There's no need for you to do that," Mrs. Potter said.

"But I don't *want* to go!" Nora exclaimed.

"You don't want to miss the ride," Mrs. Potter said firmly. "And Cousin Martha probably has things that she wants to do this afternoon."

Seeing Nora's face fall, Mrs. Potter thought how selfish her children were, how seldom they did anything for anyone else if it required the least effort or sacrifice. She herself would have liked very much to stay home out of the heat, but here she was, ready to do what everybody else did, and to give every appearance of enjoying it. "We're all waiting for you," she said.

Reduced to the status of a child, Nora put on the linen duster her mother held out to her, and then a series of green veils. The whole company trooped out of the cool house into the blinding hot glare. The English cart, though it was very handsome and painted red, did not have a top to protect them from the sun. Mrs. Potter gathered her long skirts with one hand, put her right foot on the little iron step, and with Mr. Potter's help mounted to the back seat of the cart. After a brief pause, to give Austin a chance to offer him the reins, Mr. Potter got up after her. Screened by the purple clematis on the Links' front porch, Mary Caroline saw Bud Ellis help Nora into the front seat of the surrey, saw Randolph leap into the front seat of the cart, beside Austin King.

Actuality, no matter how beautiful or how charming, can never even approximate the heartbreaking vision of the beggar looking in at the feast. To Mary Caroline, Mrs. Potter was not a middle-aged woman from Mississippi but a queen—some legendary queen of France or Denmark; and Randolph was not a person at all but everything that is kind or fair. For this glimpse of him, as the carriages drove off, she had been waiting since breakfast and would have gone on waiting, patiently, for years.

6

The road to the Ellis farm led out past the fair grounds, the baseball park, and the coal mine into flat open country, where the whole of the horizon was visible, very much as it is in the Delta country. Occasionally, the sweep of land is interrupted there by a line of willows and cypresses, indicating water. Here the interruption was likely to be a hedge fence or a windbreak of pines on the north side of a farmhouse. The clouds that pass over the Delta are larger and in the evening create the gold and rosy color that they later pass on to the sky. But the Mississippi people, looking around them, saw the shimmer that they were accustomed to.

Nora Potter, riding beside Bud Ellis in the front seat of the surrey, found she had misjudged him; he was much nicer than he had seemed the night before, and she could talk to him about the things that were worth talking about. "It's just that sometimes I feel so full of longing," she explained, "all kinds of longing—for happiness, for sympathy, for someone who won't be startled by what I say."

"I've been thinking," he said, "about what you said about faces. It's true what you said, every word of it. People do make too much of a fuss about—men especially—about whether a girl is good looking or not. They ought to look for something deeper. It's a funny thing, but that's what made me call this morning. I wanted to hear what else you had to say."

In the fields on either side of the road the grain had been cut and was now standing in yellow shocks flattened by their own weight and by the weather. The corn was a dark, dusty, summer green.

"We crossed the Ohio River just as it was getting light yesterday morning," Nora said. "I was awake and I kept looking out of the train window. It was like coming into a foreign country. Here the past doesn't hang over you all, the way it does over us. You're just yourselves, leading your own lives and not grieving over the War Between the States and Sherman's army. You wake up in the morning and it's that morning you wake up to. At home I wake up in a world that's always remembering something—the way things used to be. And trying to get back. And there isn't any getting back, so of course there isn't really any waking up. Except for the niggers. They're happy and irresponsible. I hear them outside my bedroom window, laughing and quarreling as if they owned the place and we were just there to take care of them. Sometimes I wish I were a nigger or an Indian or anything that would keep me from having to be myself, Nora Potter, who goes to parties and pays calls, and sits by quietly, with nothing to say, while Mama does all the talking."

"I know what you mean," Bud Ellis said, nodding. "But there are a lot of people who wouldn't."

"I have a great deal to say, but it isn't receipts, and that's all the women at home ever talk about. Cooking and sewing and their children and family matters."

"It's practically all they talk about here."

"If you say something that's an *idea*," Nora said, "they look at you as if you'd just gone out of your mind. They actually get embarrassed and after a minute or two start talking about something else. I haven't anybody at home I can talk to—except Brother, of course. He understands me, in a way, but it isn't a very good way. There's no comfort in it. You can't ever depend on him for anything, and he's so vain. He spends hours looking at himself in the mirror. I can go to him when I've been having trouble with Mama, because he knows how exasperating she is, and how hard I try to get along with her. But when I tell him what I've been thinking, what I really believe, he doesn't listen. Sometimes he looks at me as if he wished I'd quit talking and quit worrying and quit trying so hard. But I have to keep trying. If you don't do that down home, you're done for."

"You're not telling me a thing I don't know about," Bud Ellis said gloomily. "Not a thing, Nora."

"There's so much food, and you eat and eat until you can't breathe, and take longer and longer naps, and plan new clothes and talk about who is related to who, and it's like a dream. All you need to do is use that easy charm all Mississippi people have—Randolph, Mama, and Papa, everybody but me."

"Offhand I'd say you have the most charm of any of them," Bud Ellis said, very seriously.

"You don't mean that. You're only being polite, and you don't need to be with me."

"I wasn't being polite. Cross my heart."

Nora shook her head. "Don't you see—" she began.

Although Austin King knew the road, he kept his eyes on the surrey, maintaining just enough distance between the two carriages so that the dust would have a chance to settle ahead of him. When Bud Ellis stopped so that Nora, who had never seen a threshing combine, could watch the farmers pitching the bound sheaves into the maw of the red machine and the straw spraying out of the big metal snout, Austin stopped. The surrey started up, after a minute or two, and he touched Prince Edward lightly with his whip and drove on between more stubbled fields, more fields of tall Illinois corn. He was beginning to get used to the Mississippi voices, and to hear more in them than a soft Southern accent. When Randolph had anything to say it was generally addressed to the back seat. Austin's mind was free to return to town, to the house on Elm Street and the figure of his wife, closing the door of the bedroom where Ab lay in the deep restoring sleep of childhood, taking clean towels out of the linen closet, talking to Rachel, and searching, in all probability, for some new grievance against him. This mirrored image was inaccurate; for a long while that afternoon Martha King sat in the window seat in the library, doing nothing at all. And in one point, Austin's image of his wife reflected more truth about him than about her. But at least it made him forget the heat and the tiresome drive until suddenly the rich Southern voices, raised in argument, brought him back to reality.

"For heaven's sake, stop admiring your hands!"

"What else is there to admire?" Randolph asked.

"You can admire the view," Mrs. Potter said. "Cousin Austin, what are those green warty things?"

"Hedge apples," Austin said.

"Are they good to eat?"

"I've never heard of anybody eating them."

"How interesting," Mrs. Potter said.

"For God's sake, Mother!" Randolph exclaimed. "You've seen hedgerows all your life!"

"Maybe I have," Mrs. Potter said. "I don't always notice every little detail, like you and Nora. I certainly don't remember any such warty things growing on the plantation. . . . Cousin Austin, would it be too much trouble for you to stop the carriage a moment so Randolph can hop down and pick one?"

"I'll do no such thing," Randolph said. "If you'd never seen a hedge apple before, I'd get you one gladly, but the grass is dusty and they don't grow within reach, and the trees have thorns on them. If you want one, you can climb up and get it yourself."

Austin brought the carriage to a stop, handed the reins to Randolph, and jumped out. In the ditch by the side of the road he found a stick and started throwing it.

"Don't anyone ever talk to me again about the manners of a Southern gentleman," Mrs. Potter said.

"You're the one who's always talking about Southern gentlemen," Randolph said. "I don't know that I've ever seen one."

"You've seen your father," Mrs. Potter said.

After several attempts Austin knocked down one of the hedge apples and brought it over to the cart.

"Thank you, Cousin Austin," Mrs. Potter said. And then, as they drove on: "Yes, I do believe I've seen them before. It seems to me that old Mrs. Maltby has a receipt for making jam out of them. Or perhaps it's quince I'm thinking of. In any case, I'm going to take it home and ask her. There ought to be something you can do with them, since there are so many."

In the surrey the conversation had right-about faced, and it was now Bud Ellis who was doing most of the talking. "When anybody tries that hard, you can't help feeling sorry for them."

"I know," Nora said.

"But feeling sorry isn't enough. It ought to be, but it isn't. Not if you're a person who—well, never mind. I don't know how I got started talking like this, except that you're kind enough to listen to me." He gave a slap with the reins and made the horse go faster. "She's very sweet and affectionate and all that, but I know everything she's going to say before she says it. And the things I say to her half the time she doesn't hear. Or if she does hear, she doesn't understand. She gets it all wrong, just the way when she tries to tell the simplest story every single fact comes out changed. Last night I heard her telling your mother about an old stone quarry that we drove out to, a week or so ago. It's full of water and the kids go swimming in it. I used to swim there a lot when I was growing up, and I heard her saying that the walls were a hundred feet high. Actually, they're only twenty-five or thirty feet high. I know it's a small thing and I ought to be able to overlook it, but I sat there chewing my fingernails and thinking if she'd only get something right, just once!"

Nora glanced around, to see if the English cart was still following. Once before, in Mississippi, a conversation with a married man had taken just such a turn, and she didn't want this conversation to end up where that one had.

"Even though our paths have led along such distant trails—which I very much regret—I can talk to you and you understand what I'm saying. Mary and I don't speak the same language or see eye to eye about anything. Our pleasures are never the same. When I come home at night I wonder sometimes why I come to that particular house—why not just any house, since there isn't going to be anything for me when I get there."

Nora knew that she ought not to be listening to him. Most of what he said probably wasn't true, and she ought to be heading him off, now while there was still time. But instead she sat and looked at her gloves. She couldn't help feeling sorry for him. He was so idealistic, just the way she was, and it seemed as if everybody in the world, whether they were married or not, was looking for the same thing and never finding it.

Staring straight ahead at the dusty road, Bud Ellis said, "I'm going to tell you something I've never told any living person. I wasn't in love with her when I married her. I thought I was, at first, and then I woke up one morning and knew it was all a mistake."

Now is the time, Nora said to herself, but the flippant remark, the observation that would set them back on the right track again, refused to come.

"By that time the wedding announcements had been sent out and all the arrangements made, and you know how it is. I just couldn't do it. A thing like that, women don't get over very easily. Especially some women. I thought maybe after a month or two I'd fall in love with her, that it would come about of its own accord, but it hasn't, and now I know it never will. We just aren't right for each other, and it's a great shame, because she could have made some man very happy. Sometimes I've thought I ought to tell her I don't love her, but when she looks at me in that way—so sort of anxious and waiting to see whether I'm going to like her new dress or something she's bought for the house, I just can't say it. It's all the same to me whatever she wears. But I tell her she looks fine and she believes what I tell her. That's the funny part about it. She's perfectly happy and satisfied. Maybe some day I'll find a woman I really care about, someone I can share my inmost thoughts with and know that they're understood—a woman that just being with means everything in the world. If I do, I'll screw up my courage and make a clean breast of it to Mary. It'll be hard on her to accept, but not as hard as it would be if there is nobody I care about more than I care about her. Meanwhile, we'll just have to go on living together and yet utter strangers. I don't blame her, you understand; it's my fault, the whole business. I shouldn't have been so softhearted in the beginning. But there are things I know now that I didn't then. And if a man is going to make his mark in the world and accomplish his ambitions, he has to have a woman behind him who understands those ambitions and is driving him on. . . . This may be taking a liberty, but there's something I want to ask you, Nora. Do you think you could find room in your heart for one more friend?"

Why, Nora wondered wildly, *why* should it always be a married man who maneuvers his way around the room until he ends up sitting beside me? Is it something I do that I shouldn't, and that makes a serious conversation, a conversation about life, suddenly turn into something else?

People often ask themselves the right questions. Where they fail is in answering the questions they ask themselves, and even there they do not fail by much. A single avenue of reasoning followed to its logical conclusion would bring them straight home to the truth. But they stop just short of it, over and over again. When they have only to reach out and grasp the idea that would explain everything, they decide that the search is hopeless. The search is never hopeless. There is no haystack so large that the needle in it cannot be found. But it takes time, it takes humility and a serious reason for searching.

7

The surrey and then the English cart turned from the road into a narrow lane with deep ruts in it. The lane led through empty wheatfields to a gate, and beyond it the farmyard, where a buggy stood with the shafts resting on the ground. Bud Ellis drove around to the side of the house and Austin followed him. While they were helping the ladies to alight, Mr. Ellis and his tenant farmer came out of the barn and walked toward the carriages.

"So you came, after all," the old man called to them. "I wasn't sure whether you would or not."

"You ought to know we wouldn't let an opportunity like this slip by," Mr. Potter said, mopping his face with his handkerchief.

"I wouldn't have blamed you any if you'd changed your mind. It's a long drive in this heat . . . Meet Mr. Gelbach."

The tenant acknowledged the introduction with a nod and then said, "Be quiet, Shep!" to the dog that was barking at them from ten feet away.

The barking dog and the odor from the pigpen mingled with the other summer smells were like medicine to the restlessness that had afflicted Mr. Potter's legs all morning. "A fine place you have," he said, glancing around.

"The house needs paint and one thing and another," Mr. Ellis said. "Just now it's not much to look at, but I'll get it all fixed up one of these days. With corn selling at thirty-three cents at the grain elevator, I may end up living here." No one took him seriously and he did not mean that they should. He was knocking on wood in case the ancient gods of agriculture should have noticed his prosperity and consider that it had passed all reasonable bounds.

The tenant farmer unhitched the two horses and led them off to the barn.

"I've got something you ladies would enjoy seeing," Mr. Ellis said. "My new colt, born two days ago."

The colt and the mare were in a pasture behind the big

barn. "Pretty as a picture," Mr. Potter said, leaning on the pasture fence. "Yes, that's worth coming all the way from Mississippi to see." He called a long string of coaxing invitations to the colt but it wouldn't come to him.

They went on to take a look inside the big white barn, smelling of manure, hay, dust, and harness; at the corn cribs empty until fall; at the new windmill; at the sheds filled with rusty farm machinery; at the pigs; at the vegetable garden; and finally at an Indian mound down by the creek. A head, ears, nose, legs, and tail were all easily discernible to the people from Mississippi, and Mr. Potter knew about an Indian mound in Tennessee which was said to resemble the extinct Megatherium.

After the Indian mound Mr. Ellis turned toward the cornfield, and at this point the women were left behind. They were not expected to take an interest in farming, and besides, their shoes were not suitable for walking over plowed fields. Austin King and the tenant farmer walked along side by side with nothing to say. Each imagined that the other was mildly contemptuous—the farmer of the city man, the man who worked with his head of the man who worked much longer hours and harder because he had nothing to work with but his calloused hands.

Austin King was in many ways the spiritual son of Mr. Potter's tall, gaunt, bearded father, and would certainly have been a preacher if he had been born fifty years earlier. Mr. Potter had had all the justice and impartiality he could stand in his boyhood. He had more than once been tied to the stake and burned alive in his father's righteous wrath. And so he went on ahead with old Mr. Ellis and his grandson.

No one was ever made to feel morally inferior in Bud Ellis's presence. Money was what Bud Ellis was after, and this cold pursuit has a tendency to elbow its way into the category of the amiable weaknesses, where it does not belong. For the sake of their warmth and protective coloration, the man whose real pursuit is money will also pursue women or drink too much, or make a point of sitting around with his coat off, his tie untied, his feet on a desk, killing or seeming to kill time. And in that way he can safely say that anyone who appears not to be governed by materialistic or animal appetites is a blue-nosed hypocrite.

As they stripped off ears and compared the size of the kernels, Mr. Potter made the opening move in a game that must be played according to certain fixed rules, like chess—a game in which (as no one had more reason to know than Mr. Potter) hurry is often fatal. He admired whatever old Mr. Ellis admired, and listened to his long, rambling, sometimes pointless stories. Mr. Potter also told stories himself, stories in which he himself was invariably the shrewd hero, sly, tactful, humorous, always coming out on top at the end. These stories, taken together, tended to establish Reuben S. Potter as a sound man of business.

Mr. Ellis was himself a sound man of business. His four hundred acres had been acquired at a tax sale. The old man was quick to scent out a game and usually ready to play—on his own terms, of course, which would not in the final showdown be wholly to the advantage of Mr. Potter.

Without his family to restrain him, Mr. Potter's voice grew louder and his bragging more open. "I knew what I was up against. I'd had dealings with Henry Fuqua before. So when he come to me and said he'd heard I had a pair of mules I was fixing to dispose of and how much did I want for them, I said, 'Henry, you got a good mule now. What do you want with two more?' 'Well I do,' he said, 'and furthermore I got my eye on them two white mules.' 'Well,' I said, 'tell you the honest truth, I don't know as I want to sell that pair of mules. They're nicely broken in now and used to each other and I might have trouble finding another pair that would satisfy me. Why don't you go talk to Fred Obermeier? I was out by his place the other day and he's got some nice mules, two or three of them.' 'If I wanted to talk to Fred Obermeier,' he said, 'I'd be talking to him now. I wouldn't be here dickering with you. I'll give you eighty dollars for the two of them.' Well, eighty dollars is a good price down home for a pair of mules, but I figured if they were worth that to Henry, they were worth more to somebody else, because he can't bear to part with a nickel he don't have to, so I said, 'Tell you what I'll do. You can have Jake, if you want him, but Olly belongs to the children. They raised him and he's kind of a pet. You know how it is, Henry,' I said, 'if I was to sell Jake and Olly both, they'd probably feel bad.' 'Make it eighty-five,' he said. 'No, Henry,' I said. 'That's a decent enough offer, but these mules—I don't know as I can see my way clear to selling them. Not at this time, anyway.' So we argued back and forth, and the sum and substance of it was . . ."

Mr. Ellis dropped back beside Austin King and the tenant, a short stocky man of about forty, with light hair, blue eyes, and a dark sunburned neck. "My oats aren't as good this year as last," Mr. Ellis said. "We had a lot of rain in the late spring and planted late. But the corn will even things up—isn't that right, John?"

"It ought to, if this weather holds," the tenant said, his voice low and unemphatic.

"John had his own farm until a few years ago," Mr. Ellis said, turning to Austin. "He's a very good man, a hard worker. They both are. When we're short of help she comes right out in the field and works alongside of him. They've got three nice children and she puts up enough vegetables to last through the winter and keeps the house neat as a pin. I want to get her some linoleum for the kitchen floor when I sell my corn. It always pays to keep the womenfolks happy, you know. Some people are eternally changing tenants but I've had this couple on the place for the last seven years and we get along fine."

When the corn was delivered to the grain elevator, the tenant would claim his share of the profits. Meanwhile, he allowed old Mr. Ellis to take full credit for plowing this forty-acre field, for sowing the seed, for disking and harrowing in dry weather. As they walked along under the enormous sky and in the midst of heat so luxuriant and growth so swift that they could almost be seen and heard, the tenant farmer's arms remained always at his side as if he had no power of gesture, and his eyes, not even angry, reflected no pride, no pleasure, no possession of anything that they saw.

8

When the men disappeared into the cornfield Mrs. Potter didn't have Dr. Danforth to fall back upon. There was Nora, of course, but to fall back upon Nora in time of need was to take up all manner of unsolved problems that Mrs. Potter, who loved peace and harmony, had agreed to let alone. She couldn't make friends with the dog because Randolph had bewitched it, and Randolph himself was never to be counted on. He was only there when she didn't need him. He was kneeling in the dust now, his face hidden by his crossed arms, and the dog was walking round and round, nosing Randolph, trying to get in past his hand, past his elbow. Mrs. Potter retired to the porch, opened her silk bag, and found her spectacles.

When the men came back from the fields, she could stuff her crocheting into the bag again and with the extreme adaptability which marks the lady, be ready to please, to console and comfort, to mother old Mr. Ellis, who was twenty-five years her senior but who would nevertheless need mothering after he had been so long in the hot sun.

"It's cooler out here," Nora called from the shade of a cottonwood tree.

"My knees," Mrs. Potter called back.

Nora offered to drag the rocker out onto the grass but Mrs. Potter would not allow it. She was happier where she was. Occasionally she raised her eyes from her crocheting and let them wander over as much of the farm as she could see from the porch. It distressed her that there were no old trees around the farmhouse, no lawn, no flower garden. Neatness and order were wasted upon her and so was the fertility of black soil. She wanted something that gratified her sense of family tradition, of home as the center of the universe. What Mrs. Potter saw was a flayed landscape that a hundred years earlier had been one of the natural wonders of the world—the great western prairie with timber here and there in the distance, following a stream, and the tall prairie grass whipped into waves by the wind, by the cloud shadows passing over it, mile after mile, as if the landscape, once an inland sea, remembered and was trying to reproduce its ancient aspect.

The farmer's three children huddled in a group by the windmill and watched Randolph and the dog for some time before they overcame their shyness and allowed him to charm them with tricks. The laughter and the squealing of the children reached the porch and caused Mrs. Potter to peer down at them over the railing. With a sigh she began another round on her centerpiece. No matter where Randolph was, he had to be loved; he couldn't rest until he had made someone, even if it was only a long-nosed collie, a victim to his charm.

The crocheting grew under Mrs. Potter's fingers until it was the size of a small saucer, and then the farmer's wife came out of the house with a jelly glass in her hand, worked the rusty pump-handle, and brought Mrs. Potter a drink of cold water.

"Now aren't you kind!"

Mrs. Potter could not invite the farmer's wife to visit her in Mississippi but she was ready, even so, to make a friend. She pressed her crocheting flat on her knee and explained the pattern, so like a snowflake under the magnifying glass, and the farmer's wife invited her to come inside out of the heat.

Under the cottonwood tree Nora amused herself by picking blades of sunburnt grass and measuring them, one against another, discarding in each case the shorter one. Drowsy with the heat, her mind drifted helplessly, now coming to rest against the children's voices, now returning to the house in town. What I don't see, she said to herself, is why life should be so simple for some people; why everything that Cousin Martha could possibly want or need should be granted to her, with no strings attached, happiness within reach, where she has only to bend down and gather it, day after day. And other people . . . Cousin Martha doesn't hear voices that aren't real, or want to watch people when they don't know they're being watched. Motives don't interest her the way they do me. She has things to do, and if I had been allowed to stay home with her this afternoon, I might have found out her secret—what it is that makes it possible for her to be so sure of herself. But since I'm here instead, something ought to happen to me. Things that start ought to be finished, even if it takes twenty or thirty years. We were asked out to his farm and therefore something ought to come of it, for all of us, and for Cousin Austin. Most of all for Cousin Austin, because he didn't want to come. He was tired and he didn't want to drive us out into the country. Nothing but politeness made him do it. He's seen the farm before and he doesn't care about farming or expect anything to come of this drive. It's one thing for me to expect something and not get it, but if people who expect nothing come away empty-handed, then there is really no hope.

No hope, said the heat, the only actor on this wide empty stage, drawing the last moisture out of the ground. *The whole business of expecting and receiving (or not receiving) is an illusion.*

Frightened by this communication from the landscape, Nora stood up suddenly, brushed her skirt off, and walked toward the porch. Every window in the house had been closed since early morning and the blinds pulled to the window sills to keep out the sun. The downstairs room had an air of scrubbed, solemn poverty. When Nora came into the parlor, Mrs. Potter and the farmer's wife paused and then (since she seemed to have nothing to tell them, no message from the men) turned back to each other and went on talking about their canning, their church work, and their children.

9

Between quarter of two and quarter after three, an age of quiet passed over the house on Elm Street—over the richness contained in cupboards, the serenity of objects in empty rooms. The front stairs creaked, but not from any human footstep. The sunlight relinquished its hold on the corner of an oriental rug in the study in order to warm the leg of a chair. A fly settled on the kitchen ceiling. In the living room a single white wheel-shaped phlox blossom hung for a long time and then dropped to the table without making a sound. On a dusty beam in the basement a spider finished its web and waited. Just when the arrangement of the furniture, the disposition of light and shadow, the polish and sweet odor of summer seemed final and the house itself a preserved invaluable memory, Ab awoke and called out to her mother.

Between three-thirty and quarter of four, the leaves on the trees began to stir. There were dust eddies, dry whirlpools in Elm Street. The locusts grew shriller. One of the little Ritchie girls, walking and skipping on her way to the store for a loaf of bread and two pounds of small yellow onions, passed the Kings' house and saw Martha King in the garden, cutting

Shasta daisies. Mrs. Danforth looked out of her kitchen window and saw her at about the same time—saw Ab pulling flowers off the trumpet vine while Martha arranged the daisies in a cut-glass vase on the back steps. So did Rachel's son, Eugene, who came to the back door that afternoon, talked to his mother for a few minutes, and went out the driveway eating a slice of bread with butter and sugar on it.

When Martha King had finished arranging the flowers, there was nothing more for her to do. She went upstairs to her room and stood looking around and frowning, as though something had brought her here and she could not remember what it was. The closet door, slightly ajar, drew her attention. Half the closet was dedicated to Austin King—his suits, his shoes, his ties, his sober presence. The empty coat-sleeves, the trousers hanging upside down, reminded her of how she had been irritable with him before lunch when he was only trying to do his best by the company from Mississippi and by her. Resolving to do better by him and by them, she let her eyes rove through her own wardrobe, feeling the pleasure of deep blue against flamingo red, stopping at a row of white blouses then going on to folds of velvet or silk. She lifted the white dress she had worn the night before from its hanger and, holding it in front of her, consulted the dressing-table mirror. Then she sat down in the chair by the window and with a pair of sewing scissors she snipped the threads that held the cloth rose in place.

When Austin King went away to law school, Martha Hastings was a girl who had only just lengthened her skirts and been permitted to leave off wearing hair-ribbons. Three years later, when he began to practice law in his father's office overlooking the courthouse square, she was a grown woman, quite different from the girl he remembered, with mysterious shadows in her face and beautiful brown eyes that were sometimes sad, sometimes willful and arrogant. For a long time he merely watched for her in any group of people where she was likely to be, and wondered about her when he was falling asleep at night, finding now this explanation and now that for the mysterious shadows, investing her with the sweetness and gentleness and pliability of a story-book heroine, walking with her, in his imagination, over moon-dappled grass, their hands sometimes touching, their faces reflecting one another's need. Accident at last brought them together; the Women's

Club decided to produce Erminie *with local talent. After a rehearsal at the Draperville Academy, Austin King asked if he could escort Martha Hastings home. He was, and always had been, shy with girls. If she had rewarded him with the slightest encouragement, it is more than likely that he would have seen no more of her. But from the very beginning she fought against him. The never-ending effort to do what is right, upon which Austin King spent so much of his energy, she had already had more than enough of at home. She had been boxed in by Christian unselfishness, by church and Sunday school, by the Epworth League, from the time that she was old enough to be at all aware of her surroundings.*

In an atmosphere laden with Methodism, people smiled at her, the same complacent, oversweet smile that they smiled at everyone else. They had no idea who she was or what she was like. They weren't taking any chances. They were singing their way to Eternal Salvation and she didn't want to be saved. She wanted to run risks and there weren't any offered to her. What she missed was excitement, weakness in her knees, the sense of falling and falling and nothing under you to break the fall, nothing but empty space, and who knows what, when you land or if you ever land at all. Wasn't there anyone, she asked herself, standing on the church steps in the brilliant sunshine, or holding a plate of strawberry ice cream at a church social—wasn't there someone who would give her the sense of danger, a man who would look at her and make everything go dim around her? A man that she would see only once and know that she would marry him if he raised his little finger to ask her to; even though she didn't know anything about him, maybe not even his name, or whether he was kind or false, loved her or was making a game of love?

The first time that Austin kissed Martha Hastings good night on the front steps of her uncle's house, her arm rose in an involuntary gesture and then, feeling his uncertainty, she let her arm drop to her side and said, "You didn't have to do that." Martha King slipped the white dress on over her head. Standing in front of the mirror, turning slowly, she considered the effect without the cloth rose. The face in the mirror became doubtful. Without the flower, the pleated silk sash didn't look right. It might be the way the sash was draped, but on the other hand, sashes were not being worn so much any more. If the dress was plainer . . . She took it off and very carefully cut the threads that held the sash in place, and then went on cutting and removed the lace inset at the throat. It made the dress look too sweet, she decided, too much like a young girl's first party dress.

The next day she received a letter asking her to marry him. Her first reaction was pleasure, wholly unexpected, like coming outdoors on a May morning and finding that the Baltimore orioles had arrived. He's so gentle, she thought, and so trusting. Some girls would take advantage of him, and so I'd better marry him and protect him from them. Then, in a spasm of irritation at her own foolishness, she tore the letter into small pieces and dropped it in the wastebasket.

Sitting in the porch swing that night she told him that it was no use, that she didn't love him and never would love him, and that sooner or later she would have to ask him to stop seeing her. "When that time comes," he said solemnly, "all you have to do is tell me and I won't bother you any more."

The time didn't come, though she often threatened him with it, always with such pain in her voice—as if it were he who had threatened to send her away and never let her see him any more. This contradiction between what she said and the voice that said it confused and encouraged him. Part of him was ready to agree with her. It was impossible that he would ever possess a beautiful woman. Nevertheless, he kept coming, night after night, drawn by the desire to see her face and hear the sound of her voice, to be near her. Her voice was sometimes young and confiding, sometimes harsh, and occasionally altogether hopeless. Martha Hastings had many different voices, each one so full of shading and meaning that even to think about them was to cause shivers of delight to pass over his body.

Though Austin King was, by Mrs. Beach's standards, an eligible young man, attractive, of good family, well-mannered, ambitious, and kind, his own opinion of himself was not very high; not as high as—taking human nature by and large, all the grossness, selfishness, and loutish cruelty—it might have been. He knew that Martha Hastings did not want to marry him, but he also remembered how her arm had come to rest for a second on his shoulder, and from his physical memory, this sensation which the shoulder could produce at will, he derived hope. He even tried a little experiment. Instead of asking her, as he had been doing each night when he left, if he could see her the next night, he deliberately omitted this question, and when he arrived the following evening—tall, thin, hollow-cheeked, with a bunch of white roses in his hand—she was expecting him. But she did not like the roses. "I don't mind them when they're just buds like this," she said, with a troubled expression on her face. "But I don't like them when they open." After that he brought her other flowers—violets, carnations, lilies of the valley, whatever the florists had that reminded him of her. Instead of kissing her good night against her will, he watched her carefully, studied her moods, listened for anything in her glance or her voice that would give her away to him.

Since it is the nature of women to want to be loved, too great encouragement ought not to be derived from the fact that if you kiss one of them on a summer night, her arm rises and involuntarily comes to rest on your shoulder. Although so much time and effort have gone into denying it, the truth of the matter is that women are human, susceptible to physical excitement and the moon. This susceptibility is only skin-deep.

Something would have to be done about the ugly seam that held the skirt and waist together, Martha King decided. She tried draping the sash in various ways and then, with a reckless gleam in her eyes, burned her bridges behind her. No dress with one long sleeve and one short has ever yet looked right. If the dress was short sleeved, wouldn't the waist have to be higher? Or was it the embroidered panel that was causing all the difficulty?

Every woman is a walled town, with ring after ring of armed reservations and hesitations. They can hold off an army for years, and they are not always to be trusted even when they open the gates of their own accord. The citadel has cells, secret places where resistance can survive long after the enemy is, to all appearances, in possession. The conqueror has to take all, the defeated lose everything before the natural balance and pride of either can be regained.

What distinguished Austin King from the God-fearing, church-going people who attended Wednesday-night prayer meetings was that he allowed her to be angry and unreasonable and unfair. He also revealed something of himself—not the effort to do right but a simple falling into it at times, as if there was no other choice open to him—which touched her heart. Even so she would not marry him.

Nothing is accomplished in the way of courtship that does not first take place in the pursuer's imagination. One evening, as he was crossing the street in front of her house, the words "I, Austin, do take thee, Martha" came unbidden into his mind. His life was quite changed and his chances were greatly improved when he reached the other side of the street and stepped up on the grass between the curbing and the sidewalk. He carried himself more confidently. There was a different look in his eyes. Martha Hastings, watching him cut across the lawn instead of coming up the walk, took fright. The enemy had got through the outer wall.

The gentlest person has depths of cunning, resources of patience and persistence and strategy. Knowing that Martha Hastings was frightened, and wanting in so far as possible to be kind, Austin never again asked her to marry him. Instead he began to talk about the future as though it were now settled. He appeared to be happy and serene when he was with her. She was not taken in by this subterfuge, but on the other hand there seemed to be no way to combat it. Austin brought to life, one by one, four imaginary children, each with a name and nature of its own. The oldest was a boy, a blond, white-faced dreamer, late to meals, moody, and frequently irritable. Then a girl, a passionate, unpredictable child, never saddened or elated by the same things that affected other children, now needing to be petted and loved, now fearlessly scaling roofs, climbing apple trees. Then a thoroughly conventional boy whose only concern was to be like other people and who disapproved of his family. The third boy was short and stocky and brave, a hero in the small size, all heart and no subtlety, always running to catch up with the others.

The idea of marriage with Austin King, Martha Hastings could reject, but there was no denying that he was the father of these children who were so real to her. For a while, in self-defense, she spoke of them as his children, and when that failed her, she had to accept not only them but also the house that he conjured up one night in the porch swing—the house surrounded by very old apple trees, with the snow lying a foot deep outside, and the children asleep upstairs, and the two of them talking in low voices by their own fireside.

Realizing, finally, that it was too late to send him away, that his will and his imagination were stronger and more persistent than hers, she did the one thing left for her to do. She packed a suitcase and ran away, leaving no word for him or even an address where he could write to her. Her uncle and aunt, sworn to secrecy, put her on the train one damp November morning, and in a mood of wild and laughing elation she looked out of the train window and saw the town of Draperville slipping away from her.

Between four and four-thirty, the locusts grew still. Martha King finished cutting the threads that held the waist and skirt together and then glanced at the clock. It was later than she thought. They ought to be coming home any time now. She folded the pieces of what had been Austin's favorite dress and put them away in a chest where she kept sewing materials. When she went downstairs she opened the screen door and called "You'd better come in now," to Ab, who was riding her tricycle up and down the walk.

"Just one more time," Ab said.

The sky was clouded over with running clouds. Martha turned and went out to the kitchen. "There's going to be a thunderstorm," she said to Rachel. "It'll cool the air, but I do wish they'd come."

10

The clock face in the courthouse dome said five o'clock when Austin King drove around the square and down Lafayette Street with Nora on the front seat beside him and Randolph in back, between his mother and father, holding a bloody handkerchief to his forehead. The horse was in a lather. Austin had driven him harder than he would have under ordinary circumstances on such a hot day, but it had not been fast enough for the Potters, who by their anxious silence had urged him to drive faster.

He stayed in the cart in front of Dr. Seymour's office while the Potters went inside. When they came out, ten minutes later, Randolph had a neat bandage over his left eye and looked handsomer than ever, but the gravity had not left their faces.

The tops of the trees were swaying wildly in the wind and

the first drops of rain splashed on the pavement as the cart turned into Elm Street and drove up before the Kings' house. The Potters got out and Austin drove the horse and cart around to the barn.

"What on earth happened?" Martha King asked, as the people from Mississippi burst in upon her.

"The man warned Randolph about the dog," Mrs. Potter said, "but you can't keep that boy from making friends with an animal."

"Accidents will happen," Mr. Potter said.

"Randolph, go on upstairs and lie down," Mrs. Potter said. "I'll be up in a minute."

"We were about ready to leave," Mr. Potter said, "and I was trying to round everybody up so we wouldn't get caught in the storm when—"

"Randolph began running in circles," Mrs. Potter interrupted her husband, "with the dog after him. They disappeared around the corner of the house, and when Randolph came back there was a gash in his forehead—"

"About two inches long," Mr. Potter said, "down his forehead and through his eyebrow—"

"It was bleeding," Mrs. Potter said.

"The dog wasn't frothing at the mouth?" Martha asked.

Mr. Potter shook his head.

"Randolph isn't used to these Northern dogs," Mrs. Potter said. "He should have been more careful. Apparently the dog got excited and leapt at his face."

"The doctor took eight stitches in it," Mr. Potter said impressively.

"It hurt his feelings," Mrs. Potter said as she turned toward the stairs, "but he'll get over it. Cousin Martha, you should have been with us. We had a very nice drive, in spite of the way it turned out."

Austin unharnessed the horse, led him into the stall, threw a blanket over him, and gave him some oats. Then he stood in the doorway, looking out at the rain. The sky had turned from black to olive green and the garden was illuminated by a flash of white lightning which was followed by a clap of thunder that made him thrust his neck forward involuntarily and hunch his shoulders, as if the thunderbolt had been intended for him.

His face was relaxed and cheerful. The storm had released all the accumulated tension of the long hot day. He didn't mind being marooned in the barn or the fact that the house was full of visitors. Something inside him, he did not know what, had broken loose, had swung free, leaving him utterly calm and at peace with the world.

Mrs. Danforth, looking out of her kitchen window, thought how deceptive appearances are; Austin King, usually so restrained and dignified beyond his years, was running through the rain with long leaping strides like a boy of twelve.

II

The bedroom lights were on because of the unnatural darkness outside, and Austin, all dressed and ready to go downstairs for dinner, was sitting on the edge of the bed. His hair was neatly combed, and his starched collar and Sunday suit imparted a certain stiffness to his gesture of apology.

"I'm sorry," he said. "It never occurred to me."

"That's what I say," Martha said calmly. "It never occurred to you."

She was seated at her dressing table in her petticoat and camisole. Her waist was tightly corseted, and her full bust and shoulders had a curving elegance that was of a piece with the carved monogram on the silver brush and comb and hand mirror on her dressing table.

"I thought if you wanted to come, you'd say so," Austin said.

"I did say so."

"When?" he asked, in amazement.

"Before lunch," Martha said, still looking in the mirror.

"I don't remember your saying that you wanted to come driving with us. I must not have heard you."

"I said I'd like to get out of the house for a while."

"Is that what you meant?" Austin said. "I wasn't sure at the time. I thought you were just tired and irritable and wished they'd never come."

"If you weren't sure, you might have asked me."

"It was so hot and all, and I'd have given anything to have stayed home myself instead of taking a long drive, so naturally I—"

The rain had started coming in through the screens. Austin got up and closed both windows, and then went back and sat down on the bed. What does she see? he wondered. What on earth does she see when she holds her hand mirror and looks sidewise into it?

One sometimes notices in public places—in restaurants, especially—women dressed elaborately, wearing furs, with big diamonds in the rings on their fingers, and their faces so hideous that the observer turns away out of pity. Yet no pity is asked for; nothing but pride looks out of the ugly face.

If Austin King had suddenly said, "You have the most lovely eyes of any woman I have ever seen, and wherever I go I am always looking, always comparing other women with you. Of them all, my darling, you are the most beautiful, the most romantic. I love, beyond all reason or measure, the curve and width of your upper eyelids, and your hair, that always looks as if you had been out walking and the wind had swept it back from your forehead. I love your mouth, and the soft shadow right now at the side of your throat . . ." the chances are that Martha would have listened carefully and perhaps in some inner part of her nature been satisfied for a moment. But only for a moment.

She put the hand mirror face down on the dressing table and looked into the large mirror in front of her. She never looked into either a moment longer than necessary. If she had cared to look at her husband, all she needed to do was to shift her glance to meet his, also reflected in the dressing-table mirror, but she avoided his eyes, apparently without any effort on her part.

The beautiful blind passion of running away is permitted only to children, convicts, and slaves. If you are subject to the truant officer and the Law of Bedtime there will be doorways that will shelter you and freight cars that will take you a long way from home. If you are a safe-cracker and cannot walk in a straight line for more than a hundred yards without coming face to face with a high stone wall, there are ways of tunneling under the wall, under the five-year sentence, and confederates waiting outside. If you cannot own property but are owned yourself, you may, hiding in the daytime and traveling across country by back roads at night, eventually reach the border. But if any free person tries to run away he will discover sooner or later that he has been running all the while in a circle and that this circle is taking him inexorably back to the person or place he ran away from. The free person who runs away is no better off than a fish with a hook in his mouth, given plenty of line so that he can tire himself out and be reeled in calmly and easily by his own destiny.

"I wouldn't have gone if you had asked me," Martha King said. "There were too many things that had to be done here. It's just that I don't like to have it taken for granted that I never go anywhere."

In a happy panic Martha Hastings left town and went to Indianapolis to stay with Helen Burke, who was teaching school there. They had known each other since they were little girls, and Helen (whom no man had ever asked to marry) listened patiently night after night while Martha talked about Austin, twisting his words about to suit her own purposes, throwing a sinister light on innocent circumstances, and, on rather flimsy evidence, convicting the man she loved. Helen Burke believed everything that Martha told her, sympathized with and was caught up in the excitement of her friend's dramatic dilemma. "I don't know how you lived through it," she would say, and her eyes would fill with tears over the monstrous cunning and misbehavior of a boy she had known ever since the first grade and whose name always headed the honor roll. "And I had no one to turn to," Martha would say, "except you." When at the end of ten days, Martha Hastings packed her bag and said good-by, Helen Burke was too emotionally exhausted to do anything about it. Offering fresh counsel and foreseeing new difficulties, she went with Martha to the station, before school opened in the morning, and had trouble all that day enforcing discipline in the classroom.

The movements of Martha King's arms, her gestures as she pinned her hair in place on top of her head, were dreamy and thoughtful. "The whole thing is of no importance," she said. "I just mentioned it in passing. I don't want to spoil your pleasure in any way. And so long as you are—"

"But it *is* important," Austin protested. "If you think for one minute that I don't enjoy having you with me—"

"I'm useful to you as someone to run the house. I know you appreciate that."

There was an extra loud clap of thunder and Martha winced.

She was not afraid of electrical storms but they made her nervous.

Martha Hastings had written to her aunt and uncle that she was coming, but no one but Helen Burke knew that she was on the 11:15 train. She sat looking out of the dirty window at fields and farmhouses and roads leading in all directions and felt her own hold on life to be very slight, to be slipping away from her like the flat landscape. If she could have stayed on the train forever she would have, but it was leading her toward a decision that she was not yet prepared to make, and suddenly, as though a familiar voice had spoken, it came to her that she must let chance decide. If Austin was at the station to meet her, she would marry him. It would be the hand of fate, and she would have no choice but to follow where it pointed. If the station platform was deserted, if he didn't know just by his love for her that she was coming back to him, then they were not meant for each other. In a state of peace with the world and with herself, she sat and looked out at the red barns and the round silos, at a white horse in a pasture and at cows huddled around a tree for shade. "Draperville!" the conductor shouted. "Draperville!" and the train began to slow down. Through the plumed smoke outside the window she saw a church steeple, the monument works, and then the station. The train would go on to Peoria and for a second, standing in the aisle, she considered wildly the possibility of going on with it. There was no one she knew in Peoria, no friend waiting to give her shelter. As she stepped down from the train he was the first person she saw, his head above the other heads on the station platform. He had seen her and was coming toward her. The face that she presented to him was one he had never seen before—quiet, relaxed, without the slightest trace of indecision or of anxiety.

That night, sitting in the porch swing she told him that she would marry him. She also asked him not to tell anyone, but this request, in the midst of his happiness, he failed to attach any importance to. The next night, when he went to see her, her serenity was gone. She said that she didn't want to be engaged yet, that she needed time to think it over. And then, seeing the strange expression that passed over his face, she said, "You haven't told anyone, have you?"

"I've told my mother," he said. "She's going to give you a dia-

mond pin that belonged to Grandmother Curtis. She asked me to bring you to tea tomorrow afternoon."

"Oh Austin, how could you?"

"And I told Mr. Holby," he said.

"How can I face your mother when I don't know yet whether I want to marry you? I told you not to tell anyone!"

"I'm sorry," Austin said helplessly. "I forgot. If you want me to, I'll tell them we're not engaged. That it was a mistake."

This humiliation she could not bear for him to have.

Sad of heart, he had to go on accepting congratulations. Martha had not actually broken the engagement, she had suspended it, left it open and in doubt. She kept the diamond pin but did not wear it. He came back night after night, he was gentle with her, he was patient, he was unyielding. During all this time he did not reproach or blame her, even to himself. Martha Hastings was catapulted into a dreamlike series of showers, engagement presents, congratulations, and attentions from Austin's family, and in the natural course of events found herself with Austin's mother addressing a pile of wedding invitations.

"I don't know what else I can say except that I'm very sorry," Austin said. "And since you didn't really want to go anyway, I don't exactly see what harm is done."

"No," Martha said. "What does it matter? It's a small thing that I've married a man who doesn't care for me."

She was rewarded with a look which said quite plainly: "I am married to a stranger and there is no possibility of ever coming to terms with her." It only lasted for a second and was replaced by a look of such understanding, and such sadness as the result of understanding, that she had to turn her face away. Once more he had found her out, got through the barrier and seen her for what she was—a beautiful woman who could not believe in her own beauty or accept love without casting every conceivable doubt upon it. Now and every other time that they quarreled, she was merely seeing how far she could go, leading him to the edge of the pit and making him look down, threatening their common happiness in order to convince herself of its reality.

"I'm going downstairs," he said. "Ab's tricycle is out in the rain and it'll get all rusty."

PART THREE

A Serious Mistake

I

THE gash that ran down Randolph Potter's forehead and through his left eyebrow healed rapidly without becoming infected. Because of it he was, for a time, both a hero and a household pet. Nora changed bedrooms with her brother so that he wouldn't have to sleep in the oven-like heat engendered by the sun on the tin roof. During the daytime he lay stretched out on a sofa in the living room or on the porch swing and held court. Someone was always at his side, anxious to wait upon him, eager to run upstairs for a clean handkerchief or out to the kitchen for a glass of cold water. He saw the evening paper before anyone else did, and he had only to bite his lip or frown or sit up and arrange the pillows at his back and people stopped talking and inquired if he was in pain.

The Ellises, feeling responsible for the accident, dropped in to see Randolph every day. Sitting between his mother and sister, he took no part in the conversation. In his eyes there was a look of tired contentment. His family and all the people around him had abandoned their ordinary preoccupation with their own affairs and were now concerned about him for a change; not merely about him, about a very small part of him. He was quite satisfied.

Mrs. Beach advised that the collie's head be sent to a laboratory in Chicago for testing. When Martha King failed to convey this suggestion to the Ellises, Mrs. Beach conveyed it herself. The dog was kept under observation for a week, and when neither it nor Randolph developed symptoms of rabies, Dr. Danforth sent the dog back to the farm.

During the week of waiting, Mr. Potter got volume MUN–PAY of the encyclopedia in the study and made Nora read aloud the article on Pasteur. He was particularly moved by the closing words of Pasteur's oration at the founding of the Institute: "Two opposing laws seem to me now in contest. The one, a law of blood and death, opening out each day new modes of destruction, forces nations always to be ready for battle. The other, the law of peace, work, and health, whose only aim is to deliver mankind from the calamities which beset him . . ." When Nora had finished reading, Mr. Potter with tears in his eyes said, "Those are the words of a great man. If it weren't for Pasteur and General Robert E. Lee, the world would be far worse off than it is today. They're the leaders and the rest of us follow along after them and owe what we have to their wisdom and self-sacrifice."

"But that isn't what it means," Nora said.

"That's what I got out of it," Mr. Potter said. "You can interpret it any way you please. I know that if your father were here, Austin, he would agree with me. All this talk about education—what good does it do to teach a nigger to read and write? They're put here on earth for a definite purpose, just like the rest of us, and when you try to change that, you're going against the Lord's intention."

"What Nora is trying to say—" Austin began.

"It's all in the Bible," Mr. Potter interrupted, "right down in black and white: 'A little knowledge is a dangerous thing.' Women and men are different and anybody who says that a woman can do the same things a man can do is talking through his hat. Woman's place is in the home, and if only a lot of crackpots, busybodies, and old maids would stop agitating for equal rights, the vote, and all the rest of it—"

"Nora has just as much right to her opinion," Mrs. Potter said, drawing out her crochet thread, "wrong though it may be—"

"But it isn't a matter of opinion," Nora cried. "It's a matter of words, and they only mean one thing. Scientists, it says, are trying to—"

"They'll ruin the country," Mr. Potter said. "Mark my words. Every radical and every reformer will join hands with the suffragettes, and the first thing you know—"

Nora got up from her chair and left the room. A moment later they heard the screen door slam.

"*Now* what did I say?" Mr. Potter asked, turning helplessly to his wife.

The cigar-smoking, cigar-smelling men, simple, forthright, and forever dangerous—to themselves as well as to other people—swing from prejudice to hanging prejudice in the happy delusion that their feet are on solid ground, and any small table or delicate vase or new idea they come near stands a good chance of being knocked over. Even so (or perhaps because of the very great number of tables and vases and ideas that he had at one time or another upset) Mr. Potter waited for some reassurance from his wife, some gesture of approval.

"I expect she's gone over to the Beaches'," Mrs. Potter said; and then, pursuing the one comparison that never lost its charm for her, "At home Nora always goes to see Miss Washburn when she wants to let off steam. Miss Washburn was one of her teachers at the seminary. She doesn't think I've been all that I should have been to Nora. She told someone that, and I haven't spoken to her since. It's easy for people who— This fall, she's leaving Mississippi for good. She's going East to teach at some girls' college and she wanted to take Nora with her."

"If I had my way she'd ride out of town on a rail," Mr. Potter said bitterly. "Anyone who tries to come between children and their parents, and especially a dried-up old maid that no man ever looked twice at—"

"Mr. Potter doesn't believe in education for women," Mrs. Potter interrupted him. "And I must say, I don't either. At least, not very much. There are other things they can do, I always say. Some day the right man will come along and Nora will marry and have a home and children of her own and then she'll come to her father and thank him for knowing what was best. But it was a terrible disappointment to her. She's a great reader, you know. Just now, she doesn't know what she wants to make of her life. She's all mixed up, and try as I may, I can't seem to help her."

Randolph touched the edge of his bandage lightly with his finger.

"She just has to work it out for herself," Mrs. Potter said. "Does your wound bother you?"

"I think it's draining," Randolph said.

"Well, stop touching it," Mrs. Potter said. "You've been very brave, but if you don't stop worrying it—"

Having brought the conversation around to where he and not Nora was the center of attention, Randolph let his bandage alone.

When he grew tired of lying still, he usually got up and went out to the kitchen, and Martha King, coming into the pantry on some errand, would hear derisive laughter that stopped abruptly as she pushed open the swinging door. Rachel had washed and ironed the blood-stained shirt so to Randolph's satisfaction that he wouldn't let Martha King send his shirts to Mrs. Coffey with the family washing. Rachel took them home and did them late at night. He wouldn't allow his mother to heat the water for the hot applications Dr. Seymour had ordered; only Rachel, his favorite, could do this. No matter how late Randolph came down to breakfast, there was a place set for him, at the dining-room table, and usually some mark of favor—fried chicken livers, a lamb kidney or a chop—that hadn't been served to the others. Under his patronage, Rachel's position in the household rose considerably. The Mississippi people plied her with compliments on her cooking and when they got into an argument among themselves, asked her to corroborate their opinions. "Isn't that so, Rachel?" they would ask, and Rachel would answer, "That's right, Mr. Potter. You tell them!" And then, "Miss Nora, that's a true fact what you just said," and retire to the kitchen leaving them both convinced that she was on their side.

The conversations between Randolph and Rachel in the kitchen were not all a matter of sly joking. There were sometimes intimate revelations, things Randolph told her about himself, about the members of his family, that he would not have told any white person. Rachel got so she listened continually for his step, coming through the pantry toward the kitchen, and her manner toward Mrs. Potter was not always wholly respectful. Randolph had become her child, as he had been long ago in the past the child of some other black woman who watched over him in the daytime, put him to bed at night, sang to him, told him stories, and was there always, the eternal audience for anything he had to say.

"The trouble with you," Rachel said to him one day, "is you want everything. And you don't want to do no work for it."

"That's right," Randolph said nodding. "There's a crippled

boy at home—Griswold, his name is—had infantile paralysis when he was small and the other boys used to pick on him a lot. I don't think he ever had a friend till I came along and was nice to him. Griswold's very smart. He notices everything, especially people's weak points, and that way, when the time comes, he gets what he wants. The other day . . ."

Most people, when they are describing a friend or telling a story, make the mistake of editing, of leaving things out. Fearing that their audience will grow restless, they rush ahead to the point, get there too soon, have to go back and explain, and in the end, the quality of experience is not conveyed. Randolph was never in a hurry, never in doubt about whether what he had to say would interest Rachel. By the time he had finished, she had a very clear idea in her mind of the crippled boy who knew how to wait for what he wanted, and she also knew one more thing about Randolph Potter.

Turning from the sink, she asked out loud a question that had been in the back of her mind for days: "What you want to go and hurt that dog for?"

"I didn't hurt it," Randolph said, and then when Rachel rolled her eyes skeptically, "I tell you I didn't!"

"You was just petting it and it bit you?"

"Ummm," he said. Their eyes met and he smiled slowly. "I don't really know what happened. I was tired of playing with her, and she kept jumping on me and asking for more so I kicked her."

He looked at Rachel to see if she was shocked, but her face revealed nothing whatever. If she had been shocked, it would have been all right. Or if she had been sufficiently under his spell that she had laughed, but all she did was look at him thoughtfully.

"I kicked her in the head," he said. "And if she'd been my dog and bit me like that, I'd have taken a gun and shot her. You don't believe me, do you?"

"I believe you," Rachel said. "I reckon that's what you'd of done, all right."

"That's where you're wrong," Randolph said, and got up from the stool and left her. From that day on, he never came into the kitchen, never looked at Rachel when she was passing platters of food around the table, never spoke to her when they met on the back stairs.

2

Nora Potter tried again and again to make friends with Martha King, and each time the effort spent itself without accomplishing any more than waves accomplish when they wash over rock. Sympathy is almost never to be had by asking. It comes of itself or not at all. And those who are engaged in work of great moment, such as fomenting conspiracy or carrying a child inside them, do not really have it to offer.

Martha would sit and listen to Mrs. Potter (who wanted nothing except to be a decent, pleasant, untroublesome guest) by the hour. But when she found herself alone with Nora, she usually got up after a minute or two and went to look at the loaf of nutbread baking in the oven or to count the sheets that had come back from the wash. Defeated time after time by these tactics and with no idea why they were being used against her, Nora would go across the side yard to the Beaches, who were always delighted when she came. Mrs. Beach put down her volume of aristocratic memoirs, the girls left the piano, and they all settled down on the porch or in the shade of a full-grown mulberry tree in the back yard.

The Beach girls said very little, and the few remarks they made were generally corrected or cut short by their mother. "The sky this morning reminds me of Florence," she would remark, while with one hand she made sure that her cameo breastpin had not come undone. "The same deep blue. You'd love Florence, Nora. I wish we could all go there together. Perhaps we will, some day. Such a beautiful city . . ." Or, "I'll never forget my first glimpse of Venice. We arrived on a Saturday night and left the railway station in a gondola and found ourselves on the Grand Canal . . ."

No one coming into the Beaches' house could have remained unaware of the fact that Mrs. Beach had traveled. In every room and on every wall there was some testimony to this wonderful advantage which she had had over nearly everyone else in Draperville. A huge photograph of the Colosseum hung in the front hall. The Bridge of Sighs and St. Mark's Square were represented, one in color, one in black and white, in the living room. In the dining room the Beaches ate with the Cumaean Sybil and Raphael's Holy Family looking on.

The greatest concentration of *objets d'art* was in the parlor, where there was a Louis XV glass-and-gilt cabinet full of curios —ornamental scissors from Germany, imitation Tanagra figurines, Bohemian glass, Dresden china, miniature silver souvenir albums of Mont-Saint-Michel and the châteaux country, woodcarvings from the Black Forest, a tiny spy-glass that offered a microscopic view of the façade of Cologne cathedral, and enough other treasures to occupy the eyes and mind of a child for hours. Over the piano a row of familiar heads—Beethoven, Mendelssohn, Schubert, and Schumann—testified to the importance and value of great music, and did what they could to make up for the fact that the piano was not a Steinway.

Nora Potter soon felt so at home at the Beaches' that to knock or pull the front-door chime when she came to see them would have seemed an act of impoliteness. She walked in one morning and wandered through the house until she found Lucy in the kitchen, fixing a tray.

"Mother had a bad night," Lucy said. "We were up with her until past daylight." Nora started to say that she would come back some other time, but Lucy said, "No, don't go. She's awake now and it'll do her good to see you."

Mrs. Beach's room was high-ceilinged and gloomy, with massive golden oak furniture, and on the walls and dressing table, on the bureau and the nightstand, a hundred mementos and votive offerings to Mrs. Beach's marriage and motherhood. The old lady herself was lying propped up in bed and, for someone who had been keeping people up all night, looked quite well indeed. "Pshaw," she said when she saw Nora. "Just see what they've gone and done to me!"

"If you *will* eat things you know you're not supposed to," Lucy said.

"It wasn't the baked beans. They never hurt anybody, and you can tell Dr. Seymour I said so. There was an onion in the stewed tomatoes. I tasted it."

"I've told you twenty times—" Lucy began.

"Onion never agrees with me," Mrs. Beach said. And then

to Nora, "You were a dear to come and entertain an old woman like this. I wish you were staying with us instead of at the Kings'. I could be dying up here and Martha King wouldn't come near me."

"Mother, you know that isn't true," Lucy said indignantly.

"True enough." Mrs. Beach lifted the napkin that covered her tray and peered under it. "I don't think I'd better eat any toast, especially since you put butter on it. Just a cup of tea is all I want. Did you remember to scald the pot?"

Her daughter nodded impatiently, and Mrs. Beach, still skeptical, put her hand against the side of the Limoges teapot. "All right, dear," she said. "I'll call you if I want anything."

All the things that in her own mother annoyed Nora—her mother's unreasonableness, her arbitrary opinions, her interminable stories about the past—she could be patient with in Mrs. Beach. She dragged a white rattan chair over to the bed and showed such interest in Mrs. Beach's symptoms that the invalid developed an appetite, drank two cups of strong tea, and ate all the buttered toast. Nora took the tray away when Mrs. Beach had finished with it. Then she adjusted the pillows successfully—a thing that neither Lucy nor Alice ever managed to do.

"I can see a change in the girls just since you've been here, Nora," Mrs. Beach said. "You're very good for them, you know. They spend so much time with me when they ought to be going to parties or at least seeing someone nearer their own age. I've tried my best to encourage them to bring their friends here, but they don't seem to want any outside companionship. Or else there isn't anybody that interests them. They've had more than most girls, though I dare say they don't appreciate it. I didn't appreciate the things my father and mother tried to do for me until I was older and had children of my own. But the girls are not like me. They're not like any of my people, so far as I can see. Mr. Beach had a sister; possibly Lucy and Alice take after her, though she was a cripple all her life, and could hardly have been expected to . . ."

Nora's friendship with the Beaches was happy because it was with the whole household. This morning, for the first time, she felt herself being plucked at, being forced, whether she wanted to or not, to take sides. Her eyes fell on the faded picture of

Mr. Beach—a dapper, middle-aged man who in effigy was no more help than he had been in real life.

"If they would only talk to me," Mrs. Beach said. "I have to worm information out of them. There was a young man who liked Alice for a time. His father owned some land, I believe, out near Kaiserville, and he was a nice enough boy, Mr. Beach thought, but no polish or refinement, of course, and that dreadful red neck all farm boys have. I had a little talk with him one evening and he didn't come back any more. Alice isn't strong, you know. She could never have done the work a woman is expected to do in the country. And besides, the girls had their music. . . . Tomorrow or the next day, when I'm feeling better, remind me to show you the album of pressed flowers that we brought back with us from the Holy Land. . . ."

Nora said nothing while the old lady criticized her daughters, but her silence struck her as disloyal, and if it had been possible she would have sneaked out of the house without stopping to talk to Lucy and Alice. It wasn't possible. There was only one staircase and they were waiting for her at the bottom of it. As she stood up, Mrs. Beach said, "Remember me to your dear mother and father, and if Austin should ask about me—I know Martha won't—tell him I spent a bad night but that, thanks to you, I'm feeling much better."

The house next door is never the sanctuary it at first appears to be. If you reach the stage where you are permitted to enter without knocking, you are also expected to come oftener and to penetrate farther and in the end share, along with the permanent inhabitants, the weight of the roof tree.

3

What was missing from Austin King's office overlooking the courthouse square was sociability. With a good cigar in his fist and his feet on Judge King's slant-topped desk, Mr. Potter set about correcting this condition. It was not too difficult, and the only real opposition was supplied by Miss Ewing, who thought all Southerners were lazy and shiftless and should be kept waiting.

Mr. Potter waited once. He waited more than half an hour,

and when Miss Ewing finally said, "Mr. King will see you now," he went inside and discovered to his astonishment that Austin was alone and hadn't even been told that Mr. Potter was waiting.

"Now don't you bother, Miss Ewing," he said as he walked into the outer office the next day. "Stay right where you are. I don't want you jumping up and down for me."

"Mr. King has someone in his office," Miss Ewing said.

"Yes?" Mr. Potter said. "I wonder who it could be."

"Alfred Ogilvee," Miss Ewing said indicating with a slight turn of her head the chair Mr. Potter was to take advantage of. "Mr. King will be free in just a few minutes."

"Well, if he's busy, I don't want to interfere," Mr. Potter said. "But I'd better tell him I'm here. Otherwise he'll be wondering about me. I'll go in and get my business over and leave right away. . . . Now you go right ahead, my boy, and don't mind me!" Mr. Potter closed the door of the inner office behind him. "I know you two have something you want to talk over, and I'll just sit here by the window and watch the crowd. . . . I don't know anything about these legal matters, Mr. Ogilvee. I'm just a plain farmer. I run a cotton plantation down in Howard's Landing, Mississippi, and when they start using all those big words, I have to take a back seat. The party of the first part and the party of the second part. It's enough to drive an ordinary man crazy. But Austin here understands it. He can tell you what it all means, in simple language that anybody can follow. I wish I had his education. I wouldn't be a farmer if I did. I'd get me a nice office somewhere and a girl to keep the books and answer the phone, and I'd sit back and watch the money roll in. If we could all write our own wills any time we felt like it and get up in court and address the judge in high-flown language, the lawyers would go hungry. I dare say that time'll never come . . . You put your money in land and you may have a thousand and one worries, but there's one thing you don't have to worry about. The land won't run off. It's there to stay. I've known men—very smart men they were, too—worked hard all their life and everybody looked up to them, bankers and lawyers and men that had factories working day and night, and every reason, you might say, to feel high and dry—who went to bed worth forty or fifty thousand dollars and woke up without a cent to their name. May I ask what line of work you're in, Mr. Ogilvee? . . ."

Alfred Ogilvee had come to have Austin draw up a deed of sale for a corner lot, but he stayed to visit, to discuss farming and politics and the old days when a horsemill was looked upon as a very important enterprise, and everything movable wasn't placed under lock and key. What happened with Alfred Ogilvee happened with other clients. Recognizing that a change had set in, they not only stayed but came again, a day or two later, and on finding out from Miss Ewing that Mr. Potter and Mr. Holby were in Austin's office, they went on in.

Mr. Potter had no sense of the relentless pressure of time. In keeping Austin from working he was, Mr. Potter assumed, doing him a favor. Once Austin realized that there was no way to dam the flow of Mr. Potter's sociability or cut short his visits, he began to enjoy them. So long as he was kept from working, it didn't matter how many men were sitting around in his office with their hats tipped back, their thumbs hooked to their vests, interrupting their own remarks to aim at the cuspidor, and wondering if there was any reason to suppose that the improvement of the next fifty years would be less than the improvement of the last fifty. Religion, politics, farming and medicine, the school tax, the war between capital and labor, feminism—all had their innings. One way or another, everything was settled, including how to ascertain the age of sheep. For the most part, Austin sat and listened. While the air grew thick with cigar smoke, he had the satisfaction of feeling himself taken in and accepted in a way that he had never been accepted before.

Anxious to be liked, to be looked up to, like the men who had gone to sleep worth forty or fifty thousand dollars, Mr. Potter found ways of ingratiating himself with the merchants of Draperville. Instead of fighting the Civil War over again, he said solemnly, "The South has come to see the error of its ways. What we need down there now are modern farm machinery and modern business methods, factories run the way they are up here. . . ." Any true Southerner, in 1912, would have rejected Mr. Potter's ideas along with the accent that it had taken him many years to acquire. The merchants, with no basis of comparison, saw no reason to find fault with anything Mr. Potter did or said.

As a young man he had left the North to seek his fortune in Mississippi at a time when Northerners were not at all welcome there. In order to set foot inside certain doors, to hold down the job of credit manager to a mill, Mr. Potter had had to be something of an actor. Where he shone was not in the role of Hamlet but as a vaudeville actor, an entertainer. His humorous stories, though they had often been told before, were still wonderful in the way they conveyed (as if Mr. Potter's life depended on it) every nuance of character, every detail of setting, and above all the final rich flower of point. The stories always ended in a burst of laughter, and it was for this that they had been so painstakingly told.

Sometimes, when there was no one else in Austin's office, Mr. Potter actually did sit by the window and watch the crowd, but there were so many activities going on down below in the courthouse square, so many matters of interest that crossed Mr. Potter's mind. Both required comment and the comment usually required an answer. In the end, Austin found himself turning, without too great reluctance, from his littered desk.

4

Though the drive out to Mr. Ellis' farm ended in a disaster, it was nevertheless followed by so many other afternoon and evening drives that it often seemed as if the visit were taking place on wheels. After supper Austin drove the cart around to the front of the house and waited for the screen door to open. There was no use trying to hurry the Potters. They came in their own good time, when Mr. Potter had finished reading the article on the seasons of the antipodes, in the evening paper; when Randolph facing some mirror had considered long enough how he looked with a bandage across the left side of his forehead; when Mrs. Potter had finished telling Martha King about a certain dress that she had not brought with her, high-waisted, of orange velvet and Irish crochet, covered with black marquisette; when Nora had found her gloves. If Austin attempted to hurry the Potters, it only injected a note of crisis into the proceedings. Eventually the screen door burst open and the rich Southern voices, arguing happily, saying "What do you need gloves for anyway on a night like this?" or "Cousin Austin, why didn't you tell us you were waiting?", took possession of the stage.

Sitting beside Austin King on the front seat of the cart, Mr. Potter talked on and on, his voice pitched to carry above the unhurried clop-clopping of the horse's hoofs and the chorale of the locusts. Sometimes Mr. Potter tried Austin's patience by telling him things he already knew.

"You've got a very fine wife," he said. "I don't know how you persuaded her to marry you, but you must have done something, because I can see she just worships you. She's a fine girl, pretty as they come, and full of spirit, which I always like in a woman, provided it doesn't go with strong-mindedness. . . ." Or Mr. Potter said, "Now my boy, I'm going to give you some advice, and I want you to take it in the same spirit that it is offered. When I was your age, nobody could tell me anything because I wouldn't listen to them, but I got all that knocked out of me, and I don't know as I would want you or Randolph here to go through what I went through before I got my feet on the ground . . ."

Don't be misled by the advice of old people, the locusts said. *Or the clop-clopping of horses' hoofs. There is no ground under your feet, or any solid place. If you start down, looking for it, you will just keep on going down and down. Nothing is safe any more, but if you must trust yourself to something, try resting on the air. Make a spinning sound like us and maybe that will support you.* The mindless, kindless voice of nature, audible enough to poets and other crackpots, Mr. Potter did not hear or want to hear.

"If you want to get ahead in the world," he said, "and I'm sure you do—you're ambitious, the same as any other young man—learn to be more like other people. Your father was a very able, clever man, but he was no saint. I could tell you a thing or two about him that isn't generally known, but I don't think any the less of him for being human. If you want people to come to you, you've got to meet them halfway. Somebody asks you to drop into a corner saloon with them, do it. Don't always be making excuses that you have work to do, or that you have to get home to your wife. The work will keep and so will your wife. I've lived a long time and I know what I'm talking about. . . ."

Try scraping your wings together, said the locusts. *Maybe that will put off the coming of the first hard frost. That's the theory we operate on, and so do the katydids, but if you don't like that theory, find one of your own that you do like and operate on that, and don't trust people who know what they're talking about.*

"We all make mistakes," Mr. Potter said. "It's the only way we learn. But if you can profit by someone else's experience, it saves a lot of time and heartache, believe me."

Except for a nod and an occasional "That's the fair grounds we're passing now," or "That's the jail," Austin sat and held the reins.

If offering advice made Mr. Potter happy, there was no reason why he shouldn't listen to it, even though he often didn't agree with what Mr. Potter said. There were certain matters that Austin would have liked to have someone's advice about: Whether it wouldn't be better if he dissolved the partnership with Mr. Holby and started out on his own. And what to do about his mother, who, now that she was older, leaned on him in a way she had never leaned on his father, and let the money he sent her from time to time slip through her fingers. What to do when Martha (whose happiness was far more important to him than his own) let herself strike out at him, wildly and carelessly, as if it were a matter of complete indifference to her whether the next bitter thing she said would be the remark that neither of them would ever forget. And why what he did for one person took away from what he tried to do for another, so that no matter what he did or whom he tried to please, he still felt somehow in the wrong. These things he couldn't discuss with Mr. Potter.

The evening drives ended before dark. The afternoon drives were longer and required preparation in the way of veils and dusters. Sometimes they went in the cart, sometimes with Bud Ellis in his surrey. The men sat in front, and wisps of their conversation—the words "alfalfa" and "timothy," the words "first and second sweepings"—drifted back with the cigar smoke. Ab sat on her mother's lap or, if Martha King stayed home, on Mrs. Potter's, which she found quite comfortable after she got used to the projecting corset stays. With its big red wheels, the English cart was enough higher than the general run of rigs and surreys so that, on dirt country roads, they almost never had to eat other people's dust but rode along smiling and superior. The conversation in the back seat came steadily and placidly. There were never any exchanges of private information when the men were present, never that carefully subdued, serious tone, just above a whisper, which was calculated to escape Ab but which invariably acted instead as a warning signal to her wandering attention. When the household secrets, the recipes, the ways of keeping silver from tarnishing, rose loud enough to be overheard in the front seat, Bud Ellis would sometimes wink at Mr. Potter and say, "Blah-blah-blah. . . ." Ab knew (and Bud Ellis didn't) about the unfettered talk of the women on those occasions when no men were present.

In one corner of the porch of the house on Elm Street, there was a clay flowerpot filled with sand which she emptied out on the floor and then put back, a handful at a time, very quietly. Most of the talk that flowed over her head was cheerful and reassuring, but she waited patiently for those moments when the conversation took a darker tone. For example, the conversation between her mother and Aunt Ione, interrupted by the return of Mr. Potter from the barn.

"Nora and I used to be much closer," were the words that caught Ab's attention, "but because of an unfortunate thing that happened—I don't know exactly how to tell you about it or whether I ought to, even, but there was a time when Mr. Potter and I—there were certain things about him that I didn't understand or make allowance for, as I should have. So many doors were closed to us—neither of us were born and raised in the South, you know. And we had a darky nurse who took care of the children, and I sat around all day, ready to receive callers who never came. I couldn't see that Mr. Potter needed me, and it didn't seem that my life was leading anywhere. And then I met someone who cared very deeply for me. . . . It's strange how just talking about it brings all the old feelings back. He kept begging me to run away with him, and I tried not to listen, even though I felt I belonged to him and not to the man I had married, and that it was my one chance for happiness. I know now that we none of us have that right. But anyway, I did finally. I left Mr. Potter and the children and went off with him. We lived in Charleston for a while, and then in Savannah. I thought he was happy. He seemed *quite* happy, but it turned out he wasn't. It was just blindness on my part. He had a very fine mind and I knew I was no match for him in that, but I thought I could make it up to him in other ways. He had to tell me, and even then it was hard for me to realize that he . . . Mr. Potter never reproached me. If he had, it might have been easier. I had no one but Nora to talk to. By that time she was older and there was no way of keeping from her what had happened. I dare say I told her more than I should have. She was always a very serious child. For a while, as I say, we were very close, and then after a year or two she withdrew into herself. She never talks to me any more about what's in her heart, and I try not to burden her with my feelings. . . ."

During this recital, Ab sat as still as a stone. In those moments when life is a play and not merely a backstage rehearsal, children are the true audience. With no lines to speak, they remain politely on their side of the proscenium unless (after the hero has blinded himself with his own hands) the playwright chooses to have one or two of them led onto the stage to be wept over and then frightened with some such blessing as *May heaven be kinder to you than it has been to me.* Although children are not always equipped to understand all that they see and overhear, they know as a rule which character is supposed to represent Good and which Evil, and they appreciate genuine repentance. By all rights, when the play is finished, the actors should turn and bow to them, and ask for their applause.

5

If Ab, tired of eavesdropping, tried to break in upon the conversation of her mother and Mrs. Potter, Martha King would turn her head and convey in a glance that this was not the time to test the invisible line past which Ab could not go without a spanking. Along with a great many other things, spankings had been postponed until the visit of the Mississippi people was over. There was no telling when that would be. They had come a long way (a whole day and a whole night on the train) and Ab had been told that she must not ask them how long they were going to stay.

There were compensations. Mr. Potter brought home thin twisted peppermint sticks in a glass jar, and if coaxed he would walk the length of the living room with Ab sitting on his foot. And Cousin Randolph was always at her disposal. He allowed her to crawl all over him, to twist his necktie, to whisper inaudible secrets in his ear, and one rainy day he even played dolls with her. But every one of these delights was paid for, sooner or later, with confusion. If she told Randolph that gypsies came and set fire to the barn during the night, he not only believed her but made the gypsies set fire to the house as well, and also to the Danforths' house. The fire department arrived and the conflagration became too real, so that Ab was driven back upon the truth, which was that she herself had lighted a match—a thing she was never supposed to do; and the truth Randolph would not believe, in spite of her anxious efforts to convince him of it.

Sometimes when they were alone, he would sit and stare at her with what seemed like intense dislike, though she knew that, since he was her cousin, it couldn't be. Everywhere he went, Ab followed or walked ahead of him like an animal on a leash, and when Martha King tried to put a stop to this on the grounds that Ab was being a nuisance, Randolph insisted that he liked to have Ab with him, that he needed her to protect him from Mary Caroline.

The Links lived four houses down, on the opposite side of the street from the Kings'. Mr. Link owned a small factory where he manufactured inexpensive paper-soled shoes to be worn on one occasion only—by dead people. He believed in frugality and would not let his wife pay out good money for a hired girl when she had two grown daughters to help with the housework. There was a dining room and kitchen on the ground floor of the house, but the family cooked and ate in the basement.

When Mary Caroline was seven years old she stopped playing with dolls and instead haunted any house on Elm Street where there was a baby. In dozens of ways she conveyed her dependability, with the result that when other girls were playing jackstraws or skipping rope she was wheeling a baby carriage up and down the shady sidewalks, tipping the carriage to produce a toothless smile and a crinkling of tiny eyelids, jiggling the carriage when the baby fretted, or sitting still while a hand so small as to seem miraculous clasped her forefinger. Any baby would do so long as Mary Caroline could guard it from other children who might want to pick it up, and who in their carelessness might forget about the soft spot on the crown of the head; any baby that was helpless, cried, smiled at her, wet its diapers, was sweet-sour smelling and soft as silk.

All that Mary Caroline would have asked for, if asking would have done any good, was to belong to a large family where babies recur frequently, and not be forced to roam the neighborhood in search of them. The year between her eleventh and twelfth birthdays moved so slowly that at times it seemed to her she would never get through it. But once it became a physical possibility for her to have a baby of her own, her whole concern was disparagingly for her mirror. She cut out dresses from tissue paper patterns and pieced them together on the floor of her bedroom—an undertaking that often ended in tears. She tried twenty ways of pinning up her hair and in the mirror she was twenty different women—young, old, animated, bored, modest as a nun, evil beyond shame or boldness. She bathed constantly and took great care of her nails.

All this went on in her bedroom, at the end of the upstairs hall. She presented to the world—to her mother and father and sister, her schoolmates, her teachers—the image of a fourteen-year-old girl with sturdy legs, a thick waist, thick eyebrows, a receding chin, an awkward manner, and a tendency to blush. Where there should have been mysterious shadows in her face, to correspond with the mysteries that absorbed all her waking mind, there was only a painful shyness.

In the town of Draperville the fourteen-year-old girls were the natural prey of older boys. At their moment of budding, the girls left the boys of their own age (still in kneebritches, in love with bicycles) behind. The older boys were waiting in Giovanni's ice-cream parlor, with the dark and the whole outdoors (and sometimes the girl as well) on their side.

The five boys, all of decent respectable families, who lured a Polish miner's daughter out to the cemetery one May night would not have dared to do what they did if it had been, say, one of the Atchison girls instead. But they managed, now and then, singly, to seduce some girl whose father was cashier of the bank, or county superintendent of highways, or a hardware merchant or a lawyer or a doctor. The Lathrop boy, so well brought up, so polite always with older people, persuaded Jessie McCormack to go with him out into a cornfield at the edge of town. And afterward, when he urinated on the moonlit weeds, he felt a sensation of burning pain that frightened him and robbed him of all pride in his wonderful new accomplishment. Since there seemed to be no other way to renew this pride except by telling on the girl, he did that—only to one boy, but that was enough. That boy told the others. And in the end, the word *cornfield* was a signal for Jessie McCormack to turn away and find other company.

What was done to the Polish miner's daughter was an act of horror, but at least her body was old for her age. The McCormack girl was prematurely pretty, with blue eyes and straight blond hair and bangs, and her mother dressed her like the doll in *Tales of Hoffmann* and she had not meant to do anything that the other girls didn't do. A single word can age people, wash away any youth, any attractiveness they were intended to have. At seventeen, no longer a doll and disappointing as a woman, she sat alone in the porch swing on Saturday evenings and watched the couples go by.

The high school boys compared experiences in the locker rooms and washrooms at school (*I don't ever want to have anything to do with her again. I hate a girl that* . . .), but in all their tattling, their wondering and recounting and imagining, they left Mary Caroline untouched. The boy who asked Mary Caroline to the senior play, her last year in high school, wore glasses and went out for the track team (unsuccessfully) and in his social inexperience let her walk on the outside until somebody shouted "Girl for sale!"

And all the while her eyes saw, on every side, the strong arms and straight backs and widening shoulders. Her ears caught the husky music in voices that had only recently deepened. There was, she discovered, a hollow center in her body which drained all the strength out of her legs whenever she met James Morrissey in the corridor—James Morrissey who had curly blond hair and a cracked laugh and white teeth and cheeks like apple blossoms, and who wrote notes to Frances Longworth and to Virginia Burris but never to Mary Caroline. And then suddenly it was no longer James Morrissey but now Boyd Mangus who affected that highly sensitive nervous center. Then it was Frankie Cooper. Then Joe Diehl. Like a cloud shadow, love passed over the field, having nothing to do with actual boys but only with something which for a brief time was given to them.

Mary Caroline had always been studious, but when the Potters arrived and she suddenly started acting like her older sister, gossip lumped both girls together permanently. The gossip of Draperville was often irresponsible and unjust. Mary Caroline was not boy crazy; she had received a sign. She who had looked in the mirror so many times with sickness and dislike for herself had seen mirrored in a human eye her need for love. She had seen it only once, at the Kings' evening party for the people from Mississippi, but it had been unmistakable.

Although the world firmly and relentlessly pushes young people together, it does so with an object in view and has very little patience with them once it becomes apparent that the object is not going to be served. *If this one won't love you, then for heaven's sake go find another who will*—so says the world, and the young, unless they are unusually obstinate, obey. Mary Caroline came back, day after day, in the hope of seeing again what she had seen the night of the Kings' party, and always with an excuse in her hands—a dish of homemade fudge, a book of poems for Mrs. Potter (who never read poetry), one of her mother's coffee cakes, or a bouquet of the same flowers that bloomed so abundantly in Martha King's garden. When these offerings had been received and disposed of, Mary Caroline sat in a shy silence, never taking her eyes off Randolph, and sometimes it was necessary for Martha King to ask her to meals.

6

"You'll stay for lunch?" Alice Beach asked at the foot of the stairs.

"I'd love to," Nora said, "but Cousin Martha is expecting me. I told her I'd be right back."

"It's all right," Lucy Beach called from the dining room. "I just telephoned Martha. It was perfectly all right. She's having a light lunch the same as we are. And this way we can have you all to ourselves for once. Everything is ready. Come and sit down."

From their strange manner, which conveyed a subdued excitement, it was clear that the Beach girls had something on their minds and were debating whether to tell Nora. The secret, like all secrets, came out eventually. Lucy and Alice were thinking of starting a kindergarten. There was a place downtown, it seemed—two rooms over Bailey's Drug Store that were for rent very reasonably.

"I've spoken to Mr. Bailey about them," Lucy said, "and he's waiting to hear from us before he lets anyone else have them. There has to be some equipment—the more the better, naturally, but it all takes money and we haven't got very much. We're going to have some long low tables, and some chairs that are the right size for children, and colored yarns for them to weave, and scissors and blocks and colored paper for them to cut out—"

"Tell her about the book," Alice said. "We sent off for—"

"We have a book written by an Italian woman," Lucy said. "Sometime while you're here—"

"It's very difficult reading," Alice said. "There's a lot I can't make head or tail of."

"You haven't tried," Lucy said. "I don't suppose, Nora, with all you have to do, that you'd have time or even be interested—"

"Oh, but I would," Nora said. "I'd be very interested. I am already."

The rest of the lunch party was given over to the kindergarten plans. When Lucy came back from the kitchen with a large dish of sliced peaches and the teapot, she said, "What we want to ask you, Nora, is this: Would you, as a kindness to us, speak to Mother about it? Maybe if you said it was a good idea, she might let us go ahead with it."

"I don't know that I have that much influence over her," Nora said, "or any, as a matter of fact. But of course I'll try. Just tell me what it is that you want me to say to her and I'll—"

Before she could finish, the telephone began to ring. Lucy

jumped up from the table to answer it. "Yes," they heard her say. "All right, I will."

"Who was it?" Alice asked when Lucy put the receiver back on the hook.

"That was your mother," Lucy said. "She said to tell you that they're waiting for you to go driving with them."

"Oh, it's so stupid," Nora said, rising from her place. "I don't in the least want to go driving. Couldn't I stay and talk with you?"

From the upstairs part of the house came the tinkle of a little bedside bell, bought in the open market in Fiesole long ago.

"Couldn't we—" Nora began.

"That's Mama," Lucy said. "I better go see what she wants. It was so nice of you to stay and have lunch with us, Nora, and Alice will give you the book."

7

All her stubbornness aroused, Nora sat under the mulberry tree in the Beaches' yard, with the dark blue book that had been ordered from Chicago open on her lap, and in a short while her family (quite as if she didn't exist) came out of the Kings' house with Bud Ellis and got into the Ellises' surrey. When Martha and Ab joined them, the surrey started up briskly and without even a backward glance they drove away. That's what they're like, she thought. And if anything happened to me, they'd just go on being themselves, so why do I worry so about them?

She waited a little longer, until Rachel came out of the kitchen door with a bundle under her arm and called, "They was looking for you, Miss Nora. They wanted you to go driving with them."

"I know," Nora called back. "I didn't want to go driving."

"Well you're safe now. You outsmarted them. You got the whole house to yourself," Rachel said and went off down the driveway.

The book failed to hold Nora's attention, under the mulberry tree or in the window seat of Austin King's study. She rejected for a while the temptation to explore the house, entirely empty and for the first time at her disposal, but in the end she put the book aside and wandered from room to room. There was very little that she hadn't seen before, but observing the house the way it was now, unsoftened and unclaimed by the people who lived in it, she saw more clearly. Rejecting, approving, she tried to imagine what it was like to be Martha King.

The house was so still that it gave her the feeling that she was being watched, that the sofas and chairs were keeping an eye on her to see that she didn't touch anything that she shouldn't; that she put back the alabaster model of the Taj Mahal and the little bearded grinning man (made out of ivory, with a pack on his back, a folded fan, and his toes turned inward) exactly the way she found them. The locusts warned her, but from too far away. The clocks all seemed preoccupied with their various and contradictory versions of the correct time. The glimpse that Nora caught of herself in the ebony pier glass was of a person slightly wary, involved in an action that carried with it an element of danger.

A glance into the guestroom, when Nora went upstairs, was enough. This room, which might have held some clue on the day they arrived, now offered only an untidiness no different from the untidiness, year in and year out, of a familiar bedroom in the plantation house in Mississippi. Nora hesitated, standing in the upstairs hall, between Ab's room and the room that belonged to Austin and Martha King. The door of this room (the one she wanted most to see when it was unoccupied) was closed. She went into Ab's room, looked around, and came out again, no wiser in the ways of children than she had been before. She listened and heard no sound but the beating of her own heart, which grew louder when she put her hand on the knob of the closed door and turned it.

The bedroom was empty and in perfect order.

Nora stared at the mirror. It was drained of life and purposeless. She went over to the dressing table and, careful not to upset the bottles of toilet water and perfume, she pulled out drawer after drawer: face powder and hairpins, enameled earrings, a little blue leather box containing Martha King's jewels, tortoise-shell combs, scented handkerchiefs, folded white kid gloves, stockings, ribboned sachets. Here, too, Martha King, whom she liked and envied and couldn't even seem to know, eluded her. The paraphernalia of femininity, softness, sweetness, and illusion might have belonged to any beautiful woman.

Nora passed on to the bureau, pulled open the big drawers, and discovered the little secret one containing a velvet pincushion, odds and ends of ribbon, and a letter addressed to Austin King. Observing how it lay among the ribbons so that she could restore it to the exact same position, Nora lifted the letter out of the drawer, examined the handwriting (feminine) and the postmark (Providence, R.I.). With the letter in her hand she went out into the upstairs hall, bent over the banister and listened, ready, if there was the slightest sound, to slip the letter back in the drawer and be in her own third-floor bedroom by the time anyone reached the landing. There was no sound. With her hands trembling, she drew the letter from the envelope and began to read slowly, for the writing offered certain difficulties.

Austin, my dearest, my precious, my most neglected:

You have sent me all the money there is in the world! I know there cannot be more. And I cannot say anything or even thank you at all. I wonder why we are so inadequately equipped with words that will express? Words are the tools of man and could not express what the spirit can feel.

But if you only knew what a load is taken from me, right off my back, as it were, all because you love me. I'm just going to try with might and main (whatever that does mean!) not to feel obligated. That is the worst of me. I am such a poor receptacle. I want to do all the pouring, or so it seems, and do not get the joy out of great or small gifts because I so want to give those that are greater. That is not right, so I intend to enjoy my relief and forget what you gave me. Perhaps I can even go so far as believing that I gave it to you?

The carpenters are here. It has simply poured all day and to see them sitting about unable to shingle was just too much for all of us. But tonight the wind has shifted to the west and we believe we shall have a fine day tomorrow.

And new shingles are on the south side of the house and the west side of the barn. Tomorrow if the day is fair the barn will be all right and in order and that makes me glad. I have worried over the roof for so long that I shall miss it, the worry. There are new planks under the floor of the barn, in front, you know, where it was rotting, and the eaves are to be fixed too, and the barn is to have some paint, much needed. I think I shall freshen up the walls downstairs, in the dining room. Did I tell you that Jessie gave me Aunt Evelyn's dining table and buffet? I have the most annoying time of it trying to remember what I have written you three children. I cannot for my life tell whether I told you, or Charles, or Maud, or each one of you several times. Well, anyhow, told or untold, she did—Jessie gave me that table. It came yesterday, is sixty inches across and solid mahogany. Enormous. It weighs a ton.

That you weigh one hundred and sixty pounds is a great solace. Do you walk to work each day? Above all, you must get exercise and in fresh air. Last evening your Aunt Dorothy held forth about you and certainly she paid you the highest compliment one human can pay another. I'll not tell you now. But sometime. She is so fine and level. And kind—and generous. But I'll not start on her.

About myself. You see I have been acting sort of uppish ever since last summer's adventures in high finance and I have not responded to all the tests and various treatments according to my usual docility. Now don't get the idea that I am seriously ill. I'm not, but I am also opposed to being ill if it can be avoided. Yesterday I went to see Dr. Stanton again, and that after a week away, and was told to return in two weeks. Meanwhile, I am loaded with pills and potions, and my leg is still lame and blue.

I have not told all this to Maud because I felt certain she would get ideas, think I was worse off than I am and worry about it. Of course I shall say nary a word to her or to anybody about your generosities, but I cannot understand why your sister should feel as she does.

Last Sunday I heard a wonderful sermon by my pet, Dr. Malcolm LeRoy Jones, which ended with a story about Voltaire and Benjamin Franklin. It seems that Franklin took his son, a lad of seventeen, to see Voltaire who was very old. When they entered Voltaire's room Franklin said, "I have brought my son to you and I want you to tell him something he will remember all his life." Voltaire arose and said, "My son, remember two words, GOD & LIBERTY."

Dearest and beloved Austin, take care of yourself. Remember that without health there is no happiness in success. I am very proud of you and no one loves you as I do.

Mother

8

"Anybody home?" Austin King called, standing in the front hall at five o'clock that afternoon.

The answer came from the study, and it was not his wife's voice but Nora's that he heard. When she appeared, he thought for a moment she was ill, she looked so listless, dejected, and unlike herself.

"There's something I have to tell you," she said.

"Is that so?"

"Something I have to confess."

"Very well." Austin put his hat away and, as he started for the study, said, "Let's go in here." He sat down, crossed one knee over the other, and waited. He had been particularly careful about Nora all during the visit. He never maneuvered her into the front seat of the cart when they went driving—in fact, he occasionally maneuvered her out of it. And when he came home from the office and found her sitting alone on the porch, instead of following his natural inclination to be friendly, he stood with one hand on the screen door, asked her what kind of a day she had had, and went on into the house. When Nora was set upon by her family for expressing some idea that seemed to him reasonable and just, he sometimes raised his voice in her defense, but what he said ("I agree with Nora. . . ." or "I think this is what Nora is trying to say. . . .") was usually drowned out in the same clamor that did away with Nora's opinions. If this cautious show of friendliness had been enough and she was able to come to him when she had something on her mind, he was pleased. "Now tell me all about it," he said encouragingly.

In the window seat, facing him, Nora was silent.

"Don't worry," he said. "Whatever it is, I promise I won't be angry with you."

"You ought to be angry," Nora said. With her head bent, she examined her hands—the palms and then the backs—with a detachment that reminded him of Martha in front of her mirror.

"I've been through the house," she said at last, and then waited, as if for him to understand from this vague preliminary what it was that she really had to confess, and so spare her the difficulty and pain and humiliation of telling it.

"Well," Austin said, "why not, if it interests you?"

"But that's not all," Nora said. "I did something I've never done before, and I don't know what made me do it this time. They went off driving without me, and I found the letter and read it."

"What letter, Nora?" He couldn't think of any correspondence that was in the slightest degree incriminating, but even so, a chill passed through him.

"Upstairs. I don't know what made me do such a thing. All I know is I feel dreadful because of it."

"Upstairs?"

"In the little secret drawer in your bureau. I found the letter from your mother and read it."

"Oh that!"

"It was a very nice letter but I had no right to read it. I felt terrible afterwards. I felt so ashamed."

"You mustn't take it so to heart. There was no reason why you shouldn't have read it if you wanted to." Though it was odd, of course, that she had been going through his bureau.

"But I didn't want to. Something made me. I didn't even want to be alone in the house. I didn't feel right about it. I kept thinking maybe someone would come. And it was so still—the way it is sometimes when there's going to be a storm. And afterward I wanted to hide so I wouldn't have to face you and Cousin Martha ever again. Because you've been so kind to us all and that's the way we repay kindness."

"There was nothing in the letter that I didn't want you to know. But for your own sake, I'm glad you told me. Because now you won't ever have to think about it again."

"I can't help thinking about it. If you only knew how I—"

"I don't remember ever reading someone else's mail," Austin said, "but I know I wanted to, lots of times, and I did other things—when I was a boy—that I was ashamed of afterwards."

"I've learned my lesson," Nora said. "I won't ever do such a thing again as long as I live."

When people say *I have learned my lesson*, what they usually mean is that the lesson was expensive. This one had cost Nora the conversation she had been looking forward to, the conversation that was to have revealed what Austin King felt about life. Instead of talking to him as one grown person to another, she had to come to him now in a storm of childish repentance and like a child have her transgression forgiven.

"I don't see how you really can forgive me!"

"There's nothing to forgive." Austin was hot and tired and he wanted to escape upstairs and put his face in a basin of cold water. He could not escape because Nora did not allow him to. She sat with her mouth slightly open and her eyes had a sick look in them, as if in a moment of absentmindedness she had allowed some beautiful and valuable object to slip through her fingers and was now staring at the jagged pieces on the floor.

Outside, a carriage stopped in front of the King's house. Mr. Potter got down and handed Ab from her mother's lap to the sidewalk. While the others were telling Bud Ellis how much they had enjoyed the afternoon, Ab wandered up the sidewalk and into the house.

"Forget about it," Austin said. "So far as I'm concerned, it never happened."

The one person he didn't care to have read this letter was Martha, whose name was nowhere mentioned in it and for whom the letter contained no affectionate messages. His mother never criticized Martha, but he had waited in vain for some indication that his mother loved his wife; and Martha did love his mother. His brother Charles lived in Detroit and was in the real estate business—a simple, amiable man who loved his wife and children, and threw himself into whatever he happened to be doing with an enthusiasm and pleasure that were never complicated by introspection. "This is wonderful!" he was always saying, no matter whether he was swimming or riding or playing tennis or merely out for a Sunday-afternoon walk. "Gosh, I feel fine!" he would tell people, or "I wouldn't have missed this for anything on earth!"—and mean it. Maud lived in Galesburg, was married to a professor at Knox College, and was a very different story. She had the measuring eye that waits to see how cakes and affection are going to be divided, and was not only jealous but also moody and implacable. If the letter had been from either his brother or his sister, he could have told Nora that he seldom saw or heard from Charles and that, although they liked each other, they had nothing to say when they met; and that his sister had certain terrible difficulties to contend with, inside herself, and he had learned to get along with her by remaining always in a state of armed readiness to avoid trouble. In this way he would have aroused Nora's interest and turned her mind away from the fact that she had had no reason (except curiosity) to read the letter in the first place. Since the letter was from his mother this was impossible. He knew far less about his mother than he knew about Nora. If he had tried to tell Nora about his mother, he would only have ended up telling her about himself, and he did not want any of the Mississippi people, so long as they were guests in his house, to know what he was really like. Otherwise, nowhere, neither in the attic nor in the basement nor behind closet doors, would he have been safe from them. And so he said, "If I'd thought, Nora, I'd have told you that any letter you find in this house you can read. I give you my complete permission and approval, do you understand!"

"Do you really mean that?" Nora asked.

He nodded.

"I'm so glad," she said. "Not that I'd dream of ever doing such a thing again. But just the idea that you wouldn't mind if I—" She stopped, aware of Ab standing in the doorway watching them.

"If this and that," Austin said, "and a half of this and that, and four make eleven—"

Ab's face lit up at this old joke between them.

"—how much is this and that, and a half of this and that?" Smiling he picked her up and carried her into the front hall, where the tired travelers were divesting themselves of gloves, linen dusters, and veils.

To remain free of people you need some disguise, and what better, more impenetrable false face can any man put on than the letters (so various, so contradictory in their assumptions and their appeals) of his family and his friends? It was an inspiration, and like any inspiration it worked—far more powerfully than Austin had intended. It put an image between Nora Potter and the sun. From that time on, she was conscious of no other presence in the house but his. And when his gentle grey eyes came to rest on her for a moment, they left her so drained and weak that it was all she could do to stand.

9

"The way I've got it figured out," Mr. Potter said painstakingly (though this story was not going to end in a burst of laughter), "is that now is the time. Land in Mississippi is cheaper than it has any right to be. I'm going to buy the plantation next to mine and cotton-farm the two at a big saving. I reckon on taking three or four people into it with me, to swing the deal, but there'll be money for all."

By "all" Mr. Potter did not mean Miss Ewing, who was listening outside with her head just far enough away from the pane of glass that it would not cast a shadow; or Dr. Hieronymous, the osteopath. He meant Bud Ellis and Judge Fairchild and Alfred Ogilvee and Orin McNab, the undertaker, and Mr. Holby and Dr. Seymour and Louis Orthwein, who owned and published the *Draperville Evening Star.* While Mr. Potter walked the floor and talked and gestured, they sat still and listened and asked questions that had to be answered. In their eyes there was the light of—not ambition, precisely, but rather the awareness that life had quickened for them, that they were in the presence of their Big Chance.

When the door opened and the men filed out, Miss Ewing was seated at her desk and the typewriter was thrashing out so many legal words a minute that no one realized how quiet the outer office had been for the last hour and three-quarters. They said nothing to Miss Ewing about the offer that had just been laid before them, but the sound of their feet on the worn stairs was a dead giveaway. It was not beautiful like the sound of an evening party breaking up, but it had its own excitement and fear of the dark.

Faced with a circle of empty chairs, Austin and Mr. Potter sat down to appreciate the drop in tension.

"When you're dealing with Northern businessmen," Mr. Potter said, "everything has to be worked out so they know where they stand. That's where you come into it, my boy. I want it all down on paper, so it's legal and proper and there can't be any trouble later on. Of course if you want to put some money into the venture, that's another thing. I'm not urging you to. I'd rather not do business with relatives. It sometimes makes for hard feelings. But when a golden opportunity is knocking at your door—"

"What about old Mr. Ellis?" Austin asked.

"Bud wants to put up three thousand dollars," Mr. Potter said. "I don't know whether we can let him have that much stock in the company or not. We'll have to see when the time comes. I haven't spoken to the old gentleman yet. Old people are just naturally conservative, as you may have discovered. Mr. Ellis doesn't know much about any but Illinois land, which is very good, there's no getting around that; but land prices in the North are high. The South has possibilities for development that have never been realized. There has been poor management, poor equipment, poor everything. Mr. Ellis may hold off for a while, until he sees how the others react, but then he'll be glad to be included. I thought I'd let Dr. Danforth in on it, and you, naturally, if you are interested. When your mind is made up, there'll be plenty of time to discuss the details." Mr. Potter dropped his cigar in the cuspidor with a gesture of finality.

"In any case," Austin said, "I'll be very glad to draw up the papers for you."

Mr. Potter reached for his soiled Panama hat. "I'd better be getting along now," he said. "I told the ladies I'd be home by four. Mrs. Potter will be wondering what's become of me. Of course, we expect to pay you for any legal work that you do."

"There won't be any charge," Austin said.

10

In spite of failing mental powers, which made old Mr. Ellis forget sometimes what he had started to say, he knew a surprising amount about the boll weevil. He also behaved very childishly, lost his temper the second time that Mr. Potter's plan was explained to him, shouted at his grandson, and stalked out of the parlor of the farmhouse. During the party Mary Ellis gave for the Potters that evening, Mr. Ellis remained upstairs in his room, sulking.

A list of guests, an account of the refreshments, and a description of the Japanese lanterns which made the Ellises' yard look like fairyland appeared in the *Star* the following evening but actually it rained during the late afternoon, and the lawn party was held indoors. The children of Elm Street, for reasons of their own which had nothing to do with the Ellises' lawn party, appeared pulling streetcars—shoe boxes with a lighted candle in them. In Bremen and Hamburg the same custom prevailed at this period and it may have been brought to Illinois from one or the other of those German cities. The star-shaped and moon-shaped and plain rectangular windows were covered with colored tissue paper, and there was a round hole directly over the candle. Drawn by a string, one after another, the cardboard boxes made a soft shuffling sound and threw shafts of colored light on the cement sidewalk.

Mrs. Potter, watching the procession from the Ellises' porch, said, "You know, I miss the darkies. They're the chief thing I miss up North. Rachel's little girl that Cousin Martha has in every now and then to help serve—I've grown so attached to her. If it were only possible, I'd take her home with me in my purse. . . . When you were a child, Mrs. Danforth, did you wake up expecting that overnight the house you went to sleep in had become a palace with marble floors and footmen to wait on you, and you had to put on a pink satin ball dress to eat breakfast in? I go into the kitchen sometimes to boil the water for a cup of tea and I see Thelma has a piece of asparagras fern and two half-dead daisies in a jelly glass by the kitchen window, and I want to say to her, 'Strange as it may seem, I was a little girl once. I remember what it was like.' And I do remember, Mrs. Danforth, and I'm sure you do too. I had tasks set for me, and all that, but what I liked to do best was to sit with my hands in my lap, thinking about all the wonderful things that were some day going to happen to me. My hair was in two braids down my back and there was a dreadful time when I thought I was going to have big feet, but it was only that they were growing and the rest of me hadn't started yet. . . ."

Involuntarily, Mrs. Danforth tucked her own feet farther under the swing. In the dark the parrot-like turn of the head was not visible and people forgot that she was homely and were aware instead of the warmth and gentleness of her voice. There was a good deal of laughing and loud talking in the parlor, which came out to them through the open window. Mrs. Danforth saw that Bud Ellis and Mr. Potter had her husband in a corner and were talking to him earnestly.

"My feet are quite small," Mrs. Potter said, "now that I've caught up to them, but when I started to grow taller, something happened to me. I forgot about being a princess and I stopped being surprised that I was not eating off golden plates. . . ."

To approach Dr. Danforth with a business proposition during a social evening was an error in tactics. Mr. Potter had to raise his voice to carry above the other conversations in the room, and a sure thing shouted has either a dubious or a desperate sound.

"It wasn't as if that little girl died or anything," Mrs. Potter said. "She just stepped aside, and she's still there, waiting. I look at Thelma and I know that so far as she's concerned the practicing that comes from the house next door isn't the Beach girls, it's the court musicians. The garden is full of fountains splashing and rose trees, and the rats that run in the walls at night—you've seen the place where Rachel lives—are kings' sons coming and going. 'Well, dear child,' I want to say to her, 'that's right. They *are* kings' sons."

The children with their lighted shoeboxes were coming back now, on the other side of the street.

"It's all I've arrived at," Mrs. Potter said, "after a long and in some ways difficult life. The rats really are kings' sons, and anyone who says they are rats wouldn't know a king's son if he saw one."

II

During the second and third week in August, the center of Draperville shifted from the courthouse square to a section of wooded land and shallow ravines two miles south of town. Rocking and swaying, the open streetcar that all the rest of the year went only as far as the cemeteries now went on to the end of the line. The passengers got off, passed over a narrow footbridge, and presented their season tickets at the gates of the Draperville Chautauqua.

A cinder drive led past the ice-cream tent, the women's building, the administration and post-office building, the dining hall, and the big cone-roofed auditorium, built on the brow of a hill and open on the sides to all kinds of weather. Every year the sloping floor of the auditorium was sprinkled with fresh tanbark and the bare stage decorated with American flags and potted palms. The acoustics were excellent.

Spreading out from the auditorium in a series of circles were the cottages, rustic, creosote-stained, painted white or green, or with crazy Victorian Gothic embellishments for children to climb on, and with the names that small, cramped cottages always have—Bide Awee, Hillcrest, and The House That Jack Built. Between the cottages there were brown canvas tents with mosquito netting across the entrance flaps and ropes and stakes for the unwary to trip over after dark.

The cottages were occupied by the same families year after year. They did not come for the simple life—life being, if anything, too simple in town; they came for self-improvement, and because it was a change, with new neighbors and unfamiliar china and kerosene stoves to worry over and a partial escape from the heat. Mornings at the encampment of pleasure were for breakfast, for cot-making, for leisure and social calls. For the women there was the cooking school, for the children the slides and swings of the playground. At two o'clock a bell high up in the rafters backstage summoned everybody to the auditorium for a half-hour of music, followed by a lecture. The audience kept the air stirring with palm-leaf fans and silk Japanese fans and folding fans and sections of newspaper. The finer shades of meaning were sometimes wafted away but at all events there was rhetoric, there was eloquence, there was the tariff question, diagrammed by the swallows flying through the iron girders of the cone-shaped roof. When the afternoon program was over, the baseball game drew some of the audience, the ice-cream tent others. Dinner, and then the bell once more, its harsh sound turned musical as it passed through layer upon layer of lacquered oak leaves.

After the evening concert, the part of the audience that had come out from town for the day crowded the streetcars that were waiting for them outside the entrance gates or got into buggies and drove back to town, choking all the way in a continuous cloud of dust that they themselves helped to create. Because of the dust, the route was marked at intervals by gasoline lamps that spluttered and flared up occasionally, frightening the horses. The campers followed this or that winding cinder road until they came to their own tents and cottages. By eleven, when the curfew rang, all lights were out and the Chautauqua was as dark and quiet as it was on those nights when the chain hung across the entrance and the north wind and snow had their season.

Austin King came home from his office at noon and hitched the horse and, as soon as lunch was over, drove his guests out to the Chautauqua grounds. Mr. Potter liked best the military band, Randolph the light opera company that gave a performance of *Olivette* (with interpolations from *Robin Hood*, *The Bohemian Girl*, and *The Chimes of Normandy*), but to Mrs. Potter it was all one and the wonderful same. She did not wait for the bell to ring but left the others in the dining hall or on the porch of the Ellises' rustic cottage and went on ahead with her pillow, her fan, and her bottle of citronella. No string trio was ever too long for her, no lecturer ever dull. She was equally delighted with William Jennings Bryan, the explorer who had been in Patagonia, and the man with a potter's wheel who turned out clay vases and made a larger than life-size head of Marie Antoinette grow old and fretful.

Sunday cast its shadow over the Chautauqua grounds as it did in town, but the religious services were shorter. After Sunday school and church at the auditorium, the atmosphere brightened, and by evening there might be glee singers or the "Anvil Chorus" performed with real anvils. Martha King, feeling unwell, missed the second Sunday in the 1912 season. The picture on the bulletin board outside the administration building showed a group of twenty handsome young men in white uniforms heavy with gold braid. Traveling from Chautauqua to Chautauqua, the White Huzzars may have lost track of the days of the week. Or perhaps they were the instruments of Change, pointing toward the fast automobiles, the golf courses, and the Sunday-night movies of the future. Anyway, their musical selections and their behavior were lighthearted and without a precedent in the history of the Draperville Chautauqua. Halfway through the evening they grabbed up their clarinets and trumpets, shoved their folding chairs in a double line, and went for a sleigh ride. This was not culture—they were enjoying themselves! The grey-haired members of the audience, guardians of an uncomplicated Calvinistic era and with fixed ideas of what entertainment was appropriate to a day of worship, sat shocked and disapproving. The rest applauded wildly, reminded of something they had almost forgotten or known only in snatches—of how wonderful it is to be young.

When the last encore was over, Austin took Ab from Mrs. Potter's lap and lifted her like a limp sack to his shoulder. Her head collapsed of its own weight and her eyelids remained closed but she knew they were moving slowly up the aisle of the big auditorium, with people all around them.

Austin started to hand the sleeping child up to Mrs. Potter in the back seat of the carriage, but Nora said, "Oh, let me hold her!" so earnestly that, over Mrs. Potter's protests, Austin handed the child up to the front seat instead. When the carriage wheels started to turn, Ab stirred and seemed on the point of waking, but then a woman's hand cushioned her head in the hollow between two breasts and held it there, and she fell fast asleep.

Austin drove back to town the long way round to avoid the dust. The night was cool, and the people in the English cart spoke in murmurs and then not at all. As they passed the cemeteries Nora said, "I've never held a sleeping child before."

"She's not too heavy for you?" Austin asked.

With the reins lying loose in his hands, he was free to turn and look at his daughter and at the girl beside him. With wisps of soft hair blowing against her cheek, Nora's face looked very young and open and vulnerable. "Will you promise me something," he said suddenly. "Before you marry, bring the man to see me. I want to look him over."

"What if I never find such a person?"

"You don't have to find him. He'll find you. But it has to be the right kind of a man or you won't be happy."

"Will you be able to tell, just by looking at him?"

"I think so," Austin said.

"All right," Nora said quietly, "I promise."

As they entered the outskirts of town, Ab felt the change from country dirt road to brick pavement, and wakened sufficiently to hear a voice say, "Cousin Austin, do you believe in immortality?" Shortly afterward a great many hands lifted her and carried her up a great many steps, brought her through long hallways, and undressed her. When she woke up, it was morning and she was in her own bed, with no knowledge of how she got there.

12

The Potters' visit lasted four weeks and three days. During the final week Mr. Potter held a series of business meetings in Austin King's office, and the plan was put down on paper so that there couldn't be any trouble later on. After sober consideration Austin King decided that his other obligations (especially the money that he had to send his mother from time to time) made it inadvisable for him to invest in the Mississippi corporation. Dr. Danforth also stayed out of the venture. But in a town the size of Draperville it was not difficult to find six men who were ready and willing to make a fortune.

Mrs. Potter wanted very much to stay on till the end of the Chautauqua season, but Mr. Potter had received a letter from the bank in Howard's Landing and business came before pleasure. The banging sound that Ab heard when she was supposed to be taking her nap turned out to be Mr. Potter and Randolph hauling the two trunks up from the basement.

They went one last time to the Chautauqua grounds and when the afternoon lecture was over wandered into the museum, a log cabin not unlike the one old Mr. Ellis was born in, except that in the old days log cabins didn't have a water cooler just inside the door and visitors were not handed small printed cards urging them, in the name of the First National Bank, to save for a rainy day.

There were barely enough relics in the museum to go around—a gourd that had been used as a powder flask during the battle of Fort Meigs, a pair of antlers, a baby's dress, a tomahawk, a bed with rope springs, a few letters and deeds. By all rights, the first hoe that shaved the prairie grass and so brought an end to one of the wonders of the world should have been here, but historically important objects that are useful in their own right seldom can be spared for museums.

It is hard to say why Nora Potter chose this place to announce to her father and mother that she was not going back to Mississippi with them. Perhaps the regimental flags and the rifle that had originally come from Virginia encouraged her to take a defiant stand. Or possibly it was her mother's annoying interest in a stuffed alligator that was swung on wires from the ceiling. At all events, with no warning or preparation, she turned and said, "I'm not going home." Mr. Potter bent down and signed the register in the full expectation that it would guarantee his immortality. Mrs. Potter gazed up at the alligator. "So lifelike," she murmured, and then "What do you mean you're not going home?"

"The Beach girls are starting a kindergarten and they want me to work with them. I told them I would."

Mrs. Potter's face took on a sudden angry flush. "It's preposterous!" she exclaimed. "I never heard of such a thing."

The present with its unsolved personal relationships and complex problems seldom intrudes upon the past, but when it does, the objects under glass, the framed handwriting of dead men, the rotting silk and corroded metal all are quickened, for a tiny fraction of time and to an almost imperceptible degree, by life.

Martha whispered something to Austin and, pushing Ab ahead of them, they went past the water-cooler and out into the sunlight. While the Potters converged (*God and Liberty*, Voltaire said) upon Nora, their hosts waited uneasily in the cinder drive. The sound of angry Southern voices came through the open door of the museum but nobody stopped to listen, and Ab was prevented from following this very dramatic scene by her mother and father's resolute and uninteresting conversation about Prince Edward, who was showing signs of lameness from being driven so much. After a time the Potters appeared, with blank faces. Mr. Potter drew Austin aside and said gravely, "Mrs. Potter thinks we'd better not stay for the evening performance."

Late that night, after the others had retired to their rooms, Mrs. Potter in her brocade dressing gown knocked on Nora's door, opened it, and went in. Nora was sitting up in bed reading. Mrs. Potter sat down on the edge of the bed, and picked up Nora's book. "What's this, if I may ask?"

"Certainly you can ask," Nora said. "It's a book the Beach girls loaned me."

Mrs. Potter read the title of the book aloud, dubiously: "*The Montessori Method* . . . I don't understand. I really don't. How you can talk about leaving your family and your home and everyone dear to you! Why do you want to stay up North among strangers?"

"They're not strangers. They're my friends."

"You have friends at home, if that's all there is to it. Plenty of them. What is it you want, Nora?"

"I want to make my own life," Nora said, raising her knees under the cover and resting her chin on them. "I want to be among people who do things instead of merely existing. I want to see snow. I don't know what I want."

"No, you don't know what you want. Ever since you were a little girl you've been that way. Do you know the first word you ever said? Most babies begin with 'Mama' but the first word you ever uttered was 'No' and you've been saying it—not to other people, just to me—ever since. I've tried to be a good mother to you. As good as I knew how, anyway. I nursed you through scarlet fever and whooping cough, I've fed and clothed you, I've protected you against your father when he was impatient or wanted to make you do things you didn't feel like doing, and all the same you're against me, and have been, since the beginning. Do I get on your nerves—the way I talk, the things I do? What is it?"

Nora shook her head. For a minute neither of them spoke, and then she said slowly. "Mother, listen to me. Now's your chance, do you hear? I know that when I start to talk about what I really think and want and believe, something comes over you, some terrible fit of impatience, so that your knees twitch and you can't even sit still long enough to hear what I have to say. You listen to other people. Anybody but your own daughter you have all the patience in the world with. I've watched you. You know just what to say and what not to say.

With everybody but me you're wonderful. I wish I had a mirror. I wish I could show you what you look like right now, your face flushed and set, and that expression of grim endurance. Why do you have to endure your own daughter? I get furious at you but I don't endure you. What is it you want me to be? Do you want me to be domestic like Cousin Martha, and worry about meals and whether the cook is in a bad temper and whether my husband is looking at some other woman? I haven't any husband to be jealous of, and I haven't any house, either. So I can't very well be domestic, can I? Or worry about the temper of the cook who doesn't exist? Do you want me to be afraid of you the way the Beach girls are afraid of their mother, so that when you're around all the life and hope goes out of me, and everybody thinks what a pity it is that such a charming delightful woman should have a dull daughter? Well, I won't be dull for anybody, not even you. I'm not dull, so why should I pretend to be? Or easygoing, or self-controlled, or anything else . . . What you are thinking now I know. I can read it in your face. We've been over this a thousand times, you're saying, so why do we have to go over it again? But we haven't been over it a thousand times. I've never really talked to you the way I'm talking now, never in my whole life. Always before I've spared you, spared your feelings, and this time I'm not going to. I don't see any reason to spare your feelings. You're a grown woman and you had enough courage to leave my father and to come back to him, which I wouldn't have been able to do. I'd have died first. Don't look so horrified. You know what he's up to with Bud Ellis and those other men. You know why he brought us all up North when we were perfectly comfortable at home. You don't live with someone for thirty years without knowing what they're like. Somewhere inside of you, you have accepted him, for better or worse. And you've accepted Randolph. You know why that dog bit him. You know how he gets people and animals to love him and then turns on them suddenly when they're least expecting it. If I were a collie, I'd have bit him a hundred times. I did try to kill him once when we were little. Do you remember? I chased him round and round the summer-house with a butcher knife and everybody but Black Hattie was afraid to come near me. You were afraid too, Mother, I saw it in your eyes, but I wouldn't have stabbed you. If you'd only walked right up to me when I was wild with anger and trusted me enough to put your arms around me and hold me —that's all I ever wanted. Somebody to hold me until I could get over being angry with Brother. Then we wouldn't be sitting here like this, like two strangers who don't know each other very well, or like each other. . . . Why haven't you ever accepted me, Mother? Didn't you want to have a daughter? Or was it that you suddenly started to dislike me, after I— Oh, it's no use. I don't know why I go on trying. It's like talking to a tree or an iron doorstop. . . . Look, I want to stay up North because I feel, deep down in my heart, that there's something here for me. There's nothing at home and I'm young, Mother. I can't bear to wake up in the morning and know what's going to happen all day long, what we're going to have for lunch, what you and Father and Randolph are going to say before the words are out of your mouth. If a wagon goes by with two niggers in it and a yellow dog, that's enough for you. You run to the window at the first sound of the wheels and say 'There's Old Jeb and Sally and their yellow dog,' and you're as pleased as if you'd seen a circus parade. But I don't care if it *is* Old Jeb, or if my new dress doesn't fit right across the shoulders, or if Miss Failing's sciatica is worse, or the minister is going to leave. There'll be another minister to take his place. There always has been, and the new one will go right on trying to raise the money to fix the church roof, so what difference does it make? I don't care about the big blue willow salad bowl and platter that should have come to you after Great-Aunt Adeline died, only Cousin Laura Drummond snitched it while the rest of the china was being packed. Let Cousin Laura have her salad bowl and platter. I want excitement. I want to live in the real world, not in Mississippi with my head in a brown paper bag just because you married Father instead of Jim Ferris, who would have given you a big house in Baltimore and a fine carriage and plenty of servants to wait on you. I'm your daughter and you ought to help me. You ought to want to help me get away and lead the kind of life you would have had if things had turned out differently. Who knows? You help me now and maybe I can help you later. Maybe I can make a lot of money teaching kindergarten, and you won't have to be worrying always for fear the whole plantation will collapse on your head some day and the Detrava sofas be sold at auction. Maybe I'll marry a millionaire. Maybe I'll—"

Like an alarm clock that had finally run down, Nora stopped talking. Her eyes filled with tears. If her mother had argued with her she could have found new arguments to answer the old ones, but her mother didn't argue with her. The angry flush was gone, and instead of the resisting, restless gestures of incomprehension there was a quietness so intense that the room rang with it.

"Nora, I need you," she said slowly. "If you leave me now, I don't know how I'll manage. You're more help to me than you know. I can't live in a house where nobody is honest or brave or in any way dependable. I did before you were old enough to understand things, but I can't any more."

13

"I know old man Seligsberg isn't your client," Miss Ewing said, "but since Mr. Holby is out of town and it's rather important, I thought maybe you might want to handle it for him."

"All right," Austin said, without glancing up. "Just put it on my desk and I'll look at it later."

Mr. Holby's procrastination was a problem that had to be handled delicately. If he had been as successful and as universally respected as Judge King, he might have found it easier to make decisions. Office work bored him. What he needed to marshal his energies was the smell of the courtroom, the sound of the judge's gavel, whispered consultations at a moment of crisis, a shaky witness to cross-examine, and an audience that he could sway by reason or emotion, depending on the cards he had up his sleeve.

The mantle of the older lawyers should have fallen on his shoulders, but when the time came for him to receive it the mantle was threadbare and he found himself cheated out of the honor that they had had. His little overnight trips to Springfield and Chicago and St. Louis extended themselves to three days or sometimes to a week and longer. When he was in the office he spent more time talking to old cronies than he gave to legal work. "Just put it there in that pile I have to look over," he would say, indicating a wire basket full of dusty manila folders. "I'll take care of it first thing tomorrow morning." Or "Let's wait another month or six weeks and then see where we stand. If we hurry it through—"

Austin King was not entirely free from procrastination himself, and for that reason found it twice as irritating in his partner. Forty minutes passed before he got around to looking at the large document that Miss Ewing had placed on his desk. During that time a fashionably dressed young woman entered the outer office and asked to see Mr. King. "If you'll just take a chair," Miss Ewing said. "Mr. King will see you as soon as he is free." There was nothing she liked better than to keep people waiting, and it often annoyed her that Austin did not use this simple means of building up his prestige. When he called to her finally, she got up from her desk, smiling, and went into his office.

"Where did you find this deed? It should have been recorded months ago."

"It was in the files," Miss Ewing said.

"Did you know it was there?"

Miss Ewing nodded. "I've spoken to Mr. Holby several times about it, but—"

She and Austin exchanged a brief, understanding look, and then he said, "I'd better get right over to the county clerk's office with it."

"Miss Potter is waiting to see you."

With difficulty Austin turned his mind away from the things he would have to say not only to the county clerk but also to Mr. Seligsberg, and to Mr. Holby when he returned from his trip to Chicago.

"Miss Potter?" he repeated. "Tell her to come in."

When Miss Ewing ushered Nora in, Austin got up from his chair. "Well, this is very nice!"

"The county clerk's office closes at noon today," Miss Ewing said, and withdrew, shutting the door after her.

"I won't stay but a minute," Nora said. "I know you're terribly busy."

Unable to deny it in the face of Miss Ewing's instructions about the county clerk's office, Austin with a wave of his hand offered Nora the chair beside his desk. She remained standing.

"What's keeping that girl?" Mrs. Potter asked. "I declare, whenever we want to make a train, she's always late. It's enough to drive you to drink. . . . *Nora?*"

"Coming," a voice called down from upstairs.

"We may as well start on out to the carriage," Mrs. Potter said.

Outside in the bright sunlight all sense of hurry seemed to leave her. At the foot of the steps she put her arm through Martha King's and as the two women went slowly down the walk, Mrs. Potter said, "I don't know what to say or how to thank you. The truth of the matter is that I couldn't feel any closer to you, not even if you were my own child. . . . Write to me, won't you? I want to know everything that you're doing, all about Ab and Rachel and that darling black child of hers who is always drawing when she should be doing the dishes. She gave me one of her pictures to take home. And about the Danforths and Mrs. Beach and the Ellises and all the people we've met. But mostly about you, because you're the one who really matters to me. All those years when I might have had you, instead of those people who didn't understand you. If only I'd had you then, after your mother died . . . but she *knows*. She's watching us."

Mrs. Potter searched the bosom of her dress for a handkerchief, wiped the tears away, and pulled her veil down over her troubled face. Randolph helped his mother into the back seat of the cart and then got in after her. The screen door opened and Nora came out, dressed exactly as she was when she went upstairs; no hat, no gloves, no pocketbook, no light summer coat.

"*Now* what?" Mrs. Potter cried.

"She's not going," Mr. Potter said.

"Nora, go back into the house and—" Mrs. Potter attempted to rise, but Randolph put a restraining hand on her shoulder.

"Her mind is made up," he said.

"But she can't stay here," Mrs. Potter said, looking around wildly. "Cousin Austin and Cousin Martha have their own life to lead, and I won't have her imposing on them in this way!"

"Mrs. Beach has offered me a room in their house," Nora said.

"Oh, I don't know what will become of her!" Mrs. Potter exclaimed. "Mr. Potter, do something! Don't just sit there!"

Mr. Potter went halfway up the walk and stood talking to Nora so quietly that the others couldn't hear what he said or what Nora said in reply. He bent down and kissed her, and then came back and climbed into the front seat of the cart. Austin looked at his watch.

"We'd better be starting," Mr. Potter said.

As the carriage drove away, Nora and Martha King both waved, but there was no response from the back seat.

Hiding behind the purple clematis, Mary Caroline had one last glimpse of Randolph. He was saying something to his mother, and suddenly he turned. It could have been an accident; he needn't have been thinking of Mary Caroline as they drove past her house, but with such small signs and tokens all of us keep the breath of life in our chimeras.

15

For most people, having company for more than three or four days is a serious mistake, the equivalent to sawing a large hole in the roof and leaving all the doors and windows open in the middle of winter. Out of a desire to be helpful or the need to be kind, they let themselves in for prolonged spells of entertaining, forfeit their privacy and their easy understanding, knowing that the result will be an estrangement—however temporary—between husband and wife, and that nothing proportionate to this is to be gained by the giving up of beds, the endless succession of heavy meals, the afternoon drives. Either the human race is incurably hospitable or else people forget from one time to the next, as women forget the pains of labor, how weeks and months are lost that can never be recovered.

The guest also loses—even the so-called easy guest who makes her own bed, helps with the dishes, and doesn't require entertaining. She sees things no outsider should see, overhears whispered conversations about herself from two rooms away, finds old letters in books, and is sooner or later the cause of and witness to scenes that because of her presence do not clear the air. When she has left, she expects to go on being a part of the family she has stayed with so happily; she expects to be remembered; instead of which, her letters, full of intimate references and family jokes, go unanswered. She sends beautiful buggy and drive as far as the iron watering trough on the east side of the square.

"It's more than likely that we will see each other again, sometime. And in any case, just because you are going back home doesn't mean that I will disappear from the face of the earth."

"Doesn't it?" Nora said anxiously. "You mean I can write to you?"

"If writing helps, you can write to me."

"But you won't answer my letters?"

"Perhaps not always. It's hard to know now what will be best later on. But whatever seems best for you, I will do, Nora."

They stood for several minutes more, looking out on the courthouse and the rectangle of asphalt streets. Then, without turning to him, she said, "No one has ever felt the way I do when I am with you. They couldn't. I feel as if I had just come through a terrible fever where everything was distorted and weird and frightening. We'll never be any nearer to each other, you and I, than we are this moment. Somehow I don't ever see myself being able to manage the love I have for you, or controlling it so that it isn't apparent to everyone. I can't ever be friends with you—really and truly friends—because no one who knows me could ever see me with you and not know I love you. It's so mixed up, isn't it?"

Very, said the typewriter in the outer office.

"I may write to you, or I may not," Nora said. "But even though I do not write, you will feel me thinking of you. I don't see how you could help it."

She moved away from the window and stood memorizing the contents of his desk—the litter of papers, the stains on the green blotter, the shape of the pen, the position of the old-fashioned inkwell.

"I'm going now," she said. "I'm sorry I stayed so long. You aren't angry with me for coming?"

"No."

"It's hard for me to leave, knowing that we probably won't ever have another chance to talk like this. Standing by the window I began to feel so calm inside. Everything was so wonderful. But I still can't look at you. I look in your eyes and the whole room falls apart. It's a quiet feeling, like being suspended in space, but the trouble is I want to go on looking and looking, and I know I must stop. And it's frightening when you consider that I'm supposed to be a grown woman, not a girl. I was so unkind to Mama last night, and I hate myself for it, and I can't bear being unkind to her. I wish I could die."

With her gloved hand on the doorknob, Nora turned back once more. "I will go on writing to you forever."

"Possibly," he said, "but I don't think so."

"You won't disappear, will you? You'll remember you promised not to be angry with me if I—"

"No matter what happens," Austin said, "I won't disappear and I won't be angry with you."

14

The Potters' visit, which had seemed so spacious in the beginning, came to a hurried end. At eight o'clock on the last morning, the railway express wagon came and took away the two trunks and five suitcases. The Potters had only themselves to worry about—only gloves, pocketbooks, spectacle cases, last-minute regrets.

At quarter after nine, Austin drove around to the front of the house.

Randolph took one last conscientious look in the pier glass, as if the mirrors here in the North were more to be trusted than the ones he would find when he got home. "Cousin Martha, don't forget," he said. "You're coming down to stay with us next winter."

"Is it time to say good-by?" Mrs. Potter asked. She picked Ab up, kissed her, said "God bless you!" and set her down. Then she turned to Austin. "I'm going to kiss you, too."

"I'm going to the train with you," Austin said, accepting her embrace.

"So you are!" Mrs. Potter exclaimed. "I completely forgot. Well, I'll kiss you again at the station. Where's Nora?"

"I gave you the address of the bank in Howard's Landing, didn't I?" Mr. Potter said to Austin, and then, turning to Martha, "Good-by, my dear. You've made us all happy with your wonderful hospitality."

"I came to ask you something."

"Something of a legal nature, perhaps?" Austin smiled at her.

"No," Nora said, pulling at her gloves.

The errand that had brought her downtown must be a serious one, Austin decided; otherwise she wouldn't be so uneasy with him. Again his hand made the same gesture without his being altogether aware of it, and Nora shook her head. "There's no need for me to sit down," she said, "and I don't want to take up any more of your time than I have to. It's simply this—I came here to ask why you—why you look at me the way you do."

"Look at you?"

"Yes. Whenever we're in the same room or anywhere together I see you watching me, and before I go home I want to know why. I want to know what it is that you are trying to convey to me."

Austin flushed. "If I have been making you uncomfortable, Nora," he said, "I'm very sorry. I wasn't aware of what I was doing. Now that you've told me, I—"

"Is that all?" Nora's lips trembled.

"What do you mean 'all'?"

"I mean—oh, why are you so cautious? You can say anything in the world to me, *anything*, do you understand?"

"But I really don't have anything to say to you."

The clacking of the typewriter in the outer office added to his sense of helplessness. *This is a place of business*, the typewriter said. *Personal matters should be taken care of after office hours, not here.*

Nora turned toward the door, and he said "Wait!"

"Please let me go," she said with her back to him.

"Not just yet. I want to talk to you. If I had had any idea that you—"

"You must have known that I was in love with you. Everything else about me you understood so perfectly without my having to tell you. I thought you wanted me to be in love with you."

"But I *didn't* know it," he said, "and I don't believe that you are in love with me. You don't know anything about me." He looked around for some material evidence in support of this statement. The stuffed prairie dog and the photograph of the old Buttercup Hunting and Fishing Club offered, unfortunately, too much evidence. They proved that nobody knew anything about Austin King; that he had taken very good care that people shouldn't know anything about him.

"I know that you are the kindest, most understanding person I have ever known," Nora said. "And that I love you and you don't love me."

"You're very young, Nora. Any feeling that you have for me now you will soon get over."

"How can I get over it when I can't talk to you? I want to talk to you but I can't say the things I need and want to say. You don't want to hear them."

"Possibly not," Austin said, "but I want to help you."

"Besides, I can't look at you."

She went to the window, and stood looking down. The firemen were sitting in their shirtsleeves in front of the fire station. A buggy went by, and then a farm wagon drawn by two heavy grey horses. A man came out of Gersen's clothing store and stood looking up and down the sidewalk, as undecided as a fly walking on a ceiling.

"I don't have to look at you," Nora said. "I know exactly how you look anyway. I know you are trying to help me. But when you say kind things, gentle things, it makes me want to die." Her voice rose in pitch and Austin was sure that Miss Ewing in the outer office could hear everything. The typewriter clacked one more legal sentence and then was still. Any girl who threw herself at a married man could expect no sympathy from Miss Ewing, and neither could the man.

"What I am feeling now," Nora said, "is, of course, being terribly in love, and I don't know quite what to do. Sometimes I feel this cannot be happening, must not be happening to me."

Austin went over to the window, hoping that if he stood near her, she would lower her voice. "You will be all right, Nora," he said. "Nothing bad will come of it."

"Tomorrow I am going home and I won't ever see you again. You'll forget that I exist, but I can't bear not knowing where you are every minute of the day or what's happening to you. I may begin to imagine all sorts of things."

Austin saw Dr. Seymour come out of his office, get into his

some upstairs bedroom, just as he himself was lost in a private hush; saw the inevitable change from adolescents to men and women who told lies about each other, about themselves, and about the true nature of the world they lived in, never for a moment admitting what he and everybody else knew to be a fact—that the apple had gone bad a long time ago and slugs had eaten the rose, that the hay had mildewed in the barn, and the last hope of fair dealing was lost in third-grade arithmetic.

An incomplete vision may last for generations but anything complete, like any act of will, is bound to crack in a much shorter time. With Dr. Danforth the change came when he began to look at people as if they were no different from dumb animals. The light in the human eye, the sudden coloring under surprise and emotion, the stiffness around the mouth, the movement of the hands were all, he discovered, essentially truthful; as if in those moments when people were most anxious to deceive they were also desperately eager to convey that they were lying. Lying very plausibly—the eye, the skin, the mouth, the hands said—but lying nevertheless, and with no real desire to be believed. *The motive is money*, said the eye. *Ambition*, confessed the nervous hands. *Fear*, said the mottled skin. *Envy*, said the hungry mouth.

As for his own lies, which had once filled him with horror and pride, he saw that he was not even in a class with Snowball, who lied like an artist, in several dimensions, for pleasure sometimes, sometimes out of boredom, now maliciously, now simply out of a confused sense of fact. Since Dr. Danforth loved Snowball, he had to believe everything that the Negro said—tentatively, provisionally, never trying to pin him down, because one lie exposed always gave rise to another, and Snowball himself was apparently incapable of grasping the idea, let alone the ideal, of truth.

Into this crack, bit by bit, enough of the apocalyptic vision disappeared so that when Ella Morris came into the stable one Decoration Day to hire a rig, he was ready for her. She was then past thirty—a very homely, very intelligent woman with a queer habit of twisting her head to one side when she talked to people and considering them with detachment, with an unsentimental curiosity. Dr. Danforth, as a young man, had known her father and used to call on Mr. Morris sometimes when he needed advice. Ella wanted a carriage to drive her mother out to the cemetery. She didn't shout at him as people so often did. She didn't even talk slowly but in a perfectly normal voice asked, "Why don't you ever come to see us?"

He thought at first that he must have misunderstood her, but she seemed to be waiting for an answer, so he said, "I don't go anywhere. People don't like to talk to a deaf person."

"You can understand me, can't you?" she asked, twisting her head and looking at him.

He nodded.

"Mother would be very pleased if you came to see her," Ella Morris said. "She often speaks of you."

For two days he tried to put this invitation out of his mind. Then he went out and bought a new suit, a new white shirt, and a new tie and hat, and that evening he went to call on the Morrises. The old lady talked to him about her dead husband. When Dr. Danforth said what a fine man he was, she said, "Isn't it strange, nobody misses him. All the people that knew him, and all the people he helped. It's just as if he had never lived. I don't know how people can forget so quickly."

"They don't forget," he said. "It's just that they have so much else on their minds—most of it not very important."

Ella sat quietly, following the conversation. But the questioning look, the look of reservation, or perhaps of unkind curiosity was not there. She seemed, in some way, to have made up her mind about him.

They talked about the old days for a while and when he got up to go, the old lady said, "I hope you'll come again," and took his hand and looked deeply into his eyes, trying to see, apparently, whether he really did remember her husband.

When Ella went to the door with him, he was afraid that she was going to comment sarcastically about his new suit, but all she said was, "I hope Mother didn't tire you. She lives a great deal in the past."

He went to see the Morrises again, and then again, and one night they asked him to go to a church supper with them. Because he was with the Morrises, people seemed to treat him differently. They went out of their way to draw him into conversation, and he wasn't shy. He talked to people, with his eyes turning occasionally toward Ella Morris, and on the way home presents to the children at a time when she really cannot afford any extravagance, and the presents also go unacknowledged. In the end her feelings are hurt, and she begins to doubt—quite unjustly—the genuineness of their attachment to her.

During their stay, the Potters had managed to invest the rooms they slept in with much of their personality. They had moved things, chipped things, left rings in mahogany, left medicine stains, left the impression of their bodies in horsehair mattresses. Living partly out of suitcases and partly out of untidy dresser drawers, with disorder lying on the floor of their closets and toilet articles spilling over their rooms, they had achieved a surface of confusion that Martha King had long since given up trying to do anything about.

With their heads tied up in dustcloths, Martha King and Rachel went to work. Turn a mattress and who can say what manner of person has been sleeping on it? A bed remade with clean sheets and a fresh counterpane will look as if it had never been slept in. By nightfall, the guestrooms had regained their idealized, expectant air, and there was a square package (containing a black velvet bow, a sandalwood fan, a toothbrush, a necktie . . .), all addressed and ready to mail, on the downstairs hall table.

Without the two extra leaves, the dining-room table was round instead of oval, and brought Austin and Martha and Ab much closer together under the red-and-green glass lampshade.

"Is the steak the way you like it?" Martha inquired from her end of the table.

"Yes," he said, from his.

"Not too done?"

"No, it's fine. Just the way I like it."

"I asked Mr. Connor for veal chops and he said he had veal but he wouldn't recommend it, so I got steak instead."

"Mr. Holby is going to Chicago next week," Austin said, after a considerable silence.

"Again?"

"He's going to be gone four or five days. There's a meeting of the State Bar Association."

There was another long silence and then he said, "Old Mrs. Jouette was in the office today. She asked after you."

"That was nice of her," Martha said.

PART FOUR

The Cruel Chances of Life Baffle Both the Sexes

I

If I live to be a thousand years old, Nora said to herself as she rearranged her ivory toilet articles on the dresser scarf, I'll never get used to these curtains.

Neither will we ever get used to you, the faded black and red and green curtains said. *We may learn to tolerate each other but no more. That bed you slept so badly in, last night, is Mr. Beach's bed. He died in it. This was his room. And even though your comb and brush are on the bureau and your dresses are hanging in the clothespress, it all belongs to him.*

The black walnut bed was enormous, a bed that was meant for husband and wife, for marriage and childbirth. No single person could possibly feel comfortable in it, or anything but lost to the world. Lying between the high, crenelated headboard and footboard, she had dreamed about Randolph; she was in trouble and he saved her. In real life, of course, he never did save her. He was only harsh and impatient with her for getting into trouble when he, for some reason or other, never did. She could be drowning and as she came up for the last time he would look down at her from the bank and say *I told you it wasn't safe to swim into a waterfall. . . .*

When Nora had made the bed Mr. Beach died in, she looked around timidly for something else to do, some household chore that would justify her being there, and discovered that neither Alice nor Lucy had straightened their rooms that morning. Though there were no cotillion programs tucked in the dressing-table mirror, no invitations to parties or football games, no letters beginning:

My dear Miss Beach,

So delightfully urged I succeeded in getting an invitation to the Draperville Academy dance next Friday. I write to ask per-

mission to take you and to have the supper dance with you. I will call tomorrow evening and then learn whether or not I may have the pleasure of . . . both rooms seemed to say that it is not kind to pry into the secrets of young people. Lucy's room was larger, with a window seat and a view of the mulberry tree in the back yard. The prevailing color was a pink so inappropriate to Lucy's age that Nora decided Mrs. Beach must have chosen it for her. Alice's room, directly across the hall, was in blue and white. The two brass beds were the same ones Alice and Lucy slept in when they were children. A stranger to the family, passing down the hall and glancing in at these two doors, would have thought to himself *The girls' rooms*, never suspecting that two mature women came here each night, undressed, took the combs and pins out of their greying hair, and lay down to sleep in the midst of so many frills and ruffles.

Feeling like an intruder, Nora put the two rooms in order and escaped to the downstairs part of the house, where she sat in the parlor and looked at a large souvenir book of photographs of the Columbian Exposition, and waited for Martha King to call.

If the Kings had asked Nora to stay on with them, she would have refused, even though their house was so much more cheerful and comfortable than the Beaches'. But they hadn't asked her. And furthermore, Martha had let two whole days go by without coming across the yard to see whether she was settled and happy in her new surroundings.

The telephone rang several times during the morning, and each time Nora hurried into the dining room, ready to be pleasant and natural, to keep her hurt feelings from betraying themselves, to make water run uphill. While one part of her said into the mouthpiece of the telephone, "This is Nora Potter, Miss Purinton. . . . Yes . . . for a while, anyway . . . Just a moment, I'll see if she can come to the phone. . . .", another part of her cried out: *How can she not call when she knows I'm waiting to hear from her?*

Answers to this question came and crowded around Nora. Cousin Martha had meant to call and then someone had dropped in and was gossiping and keeping her from the telephone; or perhaps she had tried to call and the line was busy. It might be that, out of nervousness (they had never been altogether easy with one another), she had put off calling as long as she could, without being rude; or that the telephone was out of order and she was waiting for a man from the telephone company to come out and fix it. In which case, she could have come over, unless she was sick. And if she was sick, wouldn't Austin have called and told them?

It was possible—just barely possible—that Cousin Martha (though she didn't seem that kind of a person) had taken this way of showing Nora that she didn't like her and didn't want her here. Down home, people would never act that way. Whether they liked you or not, they called and pretended that . . . Or it might be that she was annoyed because . . .

Like the early systems of astronomy, the answers were all based on the assumption that the sun goes around the earth. By lunchtime Nora had considered and exhausted every explanation except the right one—that she was not as important to Martha King as Martha King was to her.

It would be difficult, she decided, living right next door to them and never seeing or speaking to Cousin Martha, but if she didn't call, that must be what she intended Nora to do. She would walk past the Kings' house without looking at it, and if they were on the porch and didn't speak . . . This image, involving a third person, was too painful and had to be put aside in favor of another. . . . If Nora were, say, with Lucy and Alice and they called *Good evening, Martha*, then Nora would have to pretend that she didn't hear or wasn't aware that anyone was being spoken to. She would have to be ready, when Cousin Martha came over to see Mrs. Beach, to step aside into some room, to be always busy in some remote part of the house. She couldn't take the children to kindergarten, as Lucy wanted her to do, because that meant turning up the Kings' front walk, ringing the doorbell, and standing there in front of the door until Cousin Martha opened it. But everything else she could manage, and maybe even that. If she sent some child and she herself remained on the sidewalk, turned slightly away, looking after the other children . . . Whatever lay in her power to do, for Austin's sake, she would do. If she couldn't be friends with Cousin Martha, she would do the next best thing. She would keep out of her way. Though it would be difficult and not at all the way it was when her family was here, no one would ever know. People would think it was an accident that she and Cousin Martha were never seen together. And her mother, who was very fond of Cousin Martha, need never find out how badly Nora had been treated.

Having prepared herself again and again all morning for the call that didn't come, Nora had no strength left to fight the idea that recurred to her at quarter of two—that perhaps Martha King was waiting for *her* to call; that it was, in fact, her duty to call, after having been a guest in the Kings' house for over a month. Pride counseled her to wait in the parlor, but Fear said *What if Cousin Martha never calls?* By that time, Nora was too nervous to trust her own voice over the telephone.

"I'm going over to the Kings," she called out to the silent house. "I'll be back in a few minutes," and ran across the yard to get at the little white-throated, whisking animal of uncertainty.

2

After dinner, Martha King took her coffee cup and went into the living room. Austin followed her and built a fire. The living-room fireplace smoked a little until the flue was warm, and as he stood holding the evening paper across the upper part of the opening, he said, "Did you call Nora or go over to see her today?"

"I meant to," Martha said, "but before I got around to it, she came over here." She was silent for such a long time that he finally looked at her over his shoulder.

"I'm worried about her," Martha said.

"Why?"

"Well she's up here among strangers, and she's young and impulsive, and with nobody to keep any kind of check on her—"

"The Beaches aren't strangers," Austin objected.

"They aren't like her own family. They don't have any control over her. I wouldn't want anything to happen, for Aunt Ione's sake. I feel that she trusts us to look after Nora as much as we can, even though Nora isn't staying with us."

The flue was now drawing properly and the newspaper no

longer needed, but Austin continued to stand facing the brick fireplace, keeping the paper from being sucked up the chimney.

"I have a feeling that Nora is in trouble and that she needs—"

"What kind of trouble?"

"Oh, Austin, you make me so impatient sometimes. You know perfectly well that Nora is in love with you and that that's why she didn't go home when they did."

"Did she say so?"

"Of course not."

"Then how do you—"

"I saw it on her face when she walked in. She wanted to know if I thought she'd done right in staying, and we talked about that and about her family. And then we talked about you."

Austin crumpled the newspaper into a ball and threw it into the fire.

"I offered to introduce her to some young people," Martha said, as he sat down, "but it turned out that she likes being with older people. She finds them more stimulating. Besides, she doesn't think of us—of you and me—as being old."

"We're not as young as we once were. That's no reason to smile at her."

"Very well," Martha said. "I won't smile at her. You have a way—you've never done it with me but I've seen it happen with other people—"

The creaking of the front stairs made her turn her head for a second. The Kings' house, being old, was subject to unexplained noises, most of which came from the cellar and the pantry, and from the front stairs when there was no one on them. This creaking of the stairs, so like the sound of someone trying not to make a sound, often caused Abbey King's heart to stop beating for several seconds. The footsteps did not, like those in ghost stories, continue down the stairs and stop just outside the library door. There was only one, and then a long agonized waiting for the next step, which never came.

"You have a way," Martha went on, "of being very kind and gentle sometimes, and of seeming to offer more than you really do. If you act that way with Nora—"

"What am I supposed to do? Tell her that she's got no business to be in love with me?"

Martha shook her head. "I didn't say that. But if you tell her—or even allow her to guess that you know, it'll be all over with her. She's got as much as she can manage now to keep from telling you or me or anybody that she thinks will listen sympathetically. The only thing that makes it possible for her to pretend that she isn't in love with you is that she doesn't know how you might take it. You might laugh at her or think she was just being very young and she can't bear that. She has that much pride still. As long as she doesn't know how you feel, she'll go on trying to pull the wool over my eyes and waiting for a sign from you. At least I think she will. If she breaks down and starts to confide in you, you can refuse to listen."

He sighed.

"If you can't stop her any other way, you can always turn your back and walk off. I may be wrong but I don't think Nora has ever been in love before. And for that reason—"

"I don't see how she can be interested in a man of my age," he said. "But whatever feeling she has for me now, she'll get over, as I told her."

"Do you mean to say she came right out and told you she was in love with you?"

"More or less."

"When?"

"The day before they left." He recounted briefly what had happened between Nora and him in his office. When he finished, he sat staring at the cortege of nymphs that followed the car of Apollo, over the mantelpiece, and thinking how strange it was that Martha showed no signs of being jealous. So many times before when her jealousy had no grounds whatever, she had been very difficult and unreasonable. Apparently, even though she made scenes and accused him of things he wouldn't have dreamed of doing, she didn't really believe or mean what she said. Otherwise, how could she sit considering the design of the coffee cup so calmly and dispassionately.

"She seemed very upset because she had to go back to Mississippi with them, and so I told her that she could write to me—which there won't be any occasion for her to do now. And also that I'd do anything I could to help her."

Martha King picked up her coffee cup and started for the dining room. As she reached the doorway she turned and asked, "You're not in love with her, are you?"

He saw that she was looking at him, waiting for his answer with no fear and no anger because she felt it necessary to ask such a question, but in a way that was more serious for both of them, if his answer was yes, than either fear or anger.

"No," he said soberly, "I'm not in love with her."

3

When Nora had finished drying the supper dishes for Lucy, she went upstairs to the room that she shared with Mr. Beach and, standing in front of the dresser, she brushed and braided her hair. From the room at the end of the hall, she heard an old voice complaining.

In a way that was hardly noticeable to anyone but herself, Mrs. Beach was failing. She had difficulty remembering names. Her handwriting began to take on certain of the shaky characteristics of the handwriting on old envelopes in the attic. Her glasses had to be changed. She had to stop and rest on the stairs. All her life she had been busy pointing out the difference between black and white. Now, as a result of these new symptoms, she had to attend to the various shades of grey. This necessary task was instructive; it forced her to reconsider her marriage and rearrange her girlhood; but she was not grateful for it, any more than the woman who has occupied the prize room of a summer boarding-house until a declining income forces her to move into cramped quarters at the head of the back stairs is grateful for the opportunity to acquaint herself with the kitchen odors and the angry voice of the cook. The complaining was bewildered, as if Mrs. Beach had not yet discovered the proper authorities to complain to, and realized that there was no point in laying her grievance before Alice.

Nora daubed cologne on her neck and throat, and after one last quick look at herself in the mirror, she opened a dresser drawer, took out a soft bundle wrapped in a handtowel, turned out the light, and went down the hall to the head of the stairs.

Lucy was waiting for her in the parlor. Nora settled herself on the plush sofa and unpinned the towel, which contained a ball of grey wool and a pair of knitting needles. With Lucy's help, she was learning to cast on. Listening for the sound of footsteps on the front porch, Nora sometimes lost the thread of Lucy's conversation, but then she picked it up again and, nodding, said, "I know just what you mean." A mistake in her knitting was more serious. She had to unravel back to the point where her mind had wandered. There was no reason to think that he would come tonight, any more than any other night, and if he didn't come, she still had every reason to be happy that she was here. In Mississippi, she could wait a hundred years, for all the good it would do her.

"You're doing your hair a new way," Nora observed.

"I changed the part," Lucy said.

"It's very becoming the way you have it now. I've tried dozens of ways of doing my hair and this is the only way that doesn't make me look like somebody in a side show. Mama has such beautiful hair—or at least it was beautiful before it turned grey. But I don't know why we sit here talking about hair when there are so many more interesting things to talk about. What would you like to have, Lucy, if you could have anything in the world you asked for?"

"If I could have anything in the world? Why I'd like to—"

"Once you've declared your wish, you have to stand by it. You can't change your mind and have something else instead. So before you—" Nora turned her head to listen.

If the Dresden shepherd with his crook and saffron knee-britches and violets painted on his waistcoat and the shepherdess with her petrified ribbons, tiny waist, and sweet expression are sometimes separated by the whole width of the mantelpiece, it may be that the shepherdess is an ardent, trusting, young girl, inexperienced in the ways of the world, the shepherd a married man, years older than she, with a china wife and child to think about and scruples that have survived the firing and glazing. Or perhaps the hand that put them there was more interested in ideas of order and balance than in images of philandering.

At quarter of nine Lucy yawned and said, "I rather expected Austin King to drop in." She got up from her chair, picked up the souvenir book of the Columbian Exposition, which Nora had left out on the parlor table, and put it away on the bottom shelf of the glassed-in bookcase where it belonged. “Don’t feel you have to go to bed when we do, Nora. We’ve got into the habit of retiring with the chickens.”

“If you don’t mind,” Nora said, “I think I will wait up a little longer. I’m not a bit sleepy.”

Once or twice she got up and went into the dining room, where she could see the lights in the Kings’ house, and at one point she wandered out into the hall and stood looking at the door chime, which needed only a human hand to make it reverberate through the quiet house. At ten o’clock the lights went out downstairs in the house next door and the upstairs lights went on, shortly afterward.

When Nora went upstairs, no one said (as they would have if she had been at home): *Is that you, Nora?* From the room at the end of the hall came the sound of Mrs. Beach’s breathing, as regular and mournful as a buoy bell. Nora tiptoed past the two open doors that offered absolute silence and turned the light on in her room.

When she was ready for bed, she turned the light off and raised the shade so that, lying in bed, she could still see the thin slice of light upstairs in the house next door. After a time the window was raised a few inches, but the light stayed on. Turning and tossing, lying now on her right side, now on her heart, Nora invited and prevented sleep. The light went out, the clock in the downstairs hall struck twelve, and then one, and finally two. After Nora had given up all hope of ever dropping off, she realized that she had been somewhere, that something had happened to her, that she had been dreaming.

4

As a result of his having drawn up the necessary papers (so that Mr. Potter’s plan would all be down on paper, legal and proper, and there couldn’t be any trouble later on) Austin found himself involved in an active correspondence with the bank in Howard’s Landing, and from this correspondence he learned a number of facts that Mr. Potter had apparently not found time or thought it necessary to go into. The indebtedness on the plantation was larger than Bud Ellis and the other shareholders had been given to understand, and the mortgage (which would have to be satisfied before the Mississippi corporation began to coin money) covered not only the plantation house but the land and the farm implements as well. Mr. Potter's reassurances, by return mail, were convincing enough, if you took each explanation by itself, but they didn't quite dovetail. Austin began to wonder about the elk's tooth charm, the courtly manners, and the stories in which Mr. Potter invariably outsmarted the other fellow.

Mrs. Potter's bread-and-butter letter—full of misspelling and arbitrary punctuation, words written in and crossed out, the margins crammed with messages and affectionate afterthoughts, and bits of information about people that Austin and Martha had never heard of—quieted for a short while his uneasiness about the business transaction that had taken place in his office. They would never forget the wonderful time they had had, she wrote, or their dear friends up North. The pity of it was that they couldn't get on the train and come back whenever they felt like it, which was often. Since her return home, she had been as busy as a cat in a fish store. Cousin Alice Light, who lived in Glen Falls, had come with the children, twins. Little Alice very bright for her age, and the boy into everything the minute his mother's back was turned. And then old Mrs. Maltby died before Mrs. Potter had a chance to ask her for the receipt for making hedge apple jam, and Mrs. Potter, though no kin to the Maltbys, had taken charge, made all the arrangements for the funeral, buried the dead and entertained the living. After the funeral the relatives came back to the house and fought over the furniture, and the little dropleaf table that was supposed to go to Mrs. Potter went to one of the daughters-in-law instead.

Mrs. Potter missed the yellow bedroom of the house on Elm Street—as girls she and her sister always had that color. And Mr. Potter had bought an automobile, a Rambler, and was learning to drive. Randolph had been offered a job in the bank but couldn't decide whether to take it or not. His father wanted him to, but Randolph wasn't sure that he'd like working behind a cage and taking money from all kinds of people. Besides, he would have to live away from home, and naturally he'd rather be with his family. The weather was still warm, like the middle of summer. They had started picking cotton that week. . . .

The letter contained no mention of Nora, not even in the postscript. Reading the letter, one would almost have thought that Mrs. Potter had no daughter, or else that she was afraid. In places where witchcraft is still practiced, people are extremely careful about disposing of hairs that they find in combs, and of fingernail parings. Possibly some such instinctive or superstitious caution kept Mrs. Potter from writing Nora's name.

The postman also left in the mailbox of the house on Elm Street a souvenir of the Mardi Gras, addressed to Miss Abbey King. When opened out it proved to be a long narrow strip of colored pictures of horse-drawn floats—boats and thrones, gigantic spiderwebs, witches' caverns, cloud-capped palaces, and caves under the sea. Across the bottom Randolph had scrawled *Do you remember me?* which was foolish and unnecessary, since Ab in her nightly prayers remembered everybody.

With these samples of their highly characteristic handwriting, the Potters proved that they had gone home, that they were now safely disposed of in the shadowy untroublesome country of absent friends and relations, but Austin King found himself wondering why Mr. Potter, with his affairs in such an unsettled state, had bought an automobile; why Randolph hadn't jumped at the chance of a job in the bank; why Nora never came to see them. Occasionally he saw her, in the side yard or on the porch of the house next door, and waved to her and Nora waved back. Instead of stopping to talk to her, he went on into the house, carrying with him the image of a startled face, the eyes wide open, the expression doubtful, as if Nora were not certain that he was waving at her.

5

After a long summer of green, the prairie towns have their brief season of color. The leaves on the trees begin to turn—first a branch, then a tree, then a whole street of trees, like middle-aged people falling in love. The maples turn bright orange or scarlet, the elms a pale poetic yellow, and before the color has reached its height, the leaves begin to detach themselves, to drift down. Lawns have to be raked, and then raked again. Children play in leaf houses, and leaf fires smoldering in gutters change the odor of the air. The sun finds a way through bare branches to make new patterns of light and shade. The daytime, between nine o'clock in the morning and two in the afternoon, is like summer; but after the evening meal, women sitting in porch rockers send this or that child into the house for a shawl and are themselves driven indoors by the dark a few minutes later. The lawn mowers stand idle, frost stills the katydids and puts an end to the asters, and sadly, a little at a time, people get used to the idea of winter.

During the long September and October evenings, Austin King found time to collect the family snapshots and paste them in a big black scrapbook. This scrapbook was part of a set, of the great American encyclopedia of sentimental occasions, family gatherings, and stages in the growth of children. The volumes are not arranged alphabetically and it doesn't matter very much which one you open, since each of the million or so volumes is likely to contain, among other things,

a picture of a statue in a park
of children playing in the sand at the seashore
of the horses waiting at the paddock gate
of the float that won first prize
of the new house before the roof was finished
of a winding mountain road
of Sunset Hill, of Mirror Lake
of a nurse wheeling a baby carriage
of a tree leaning far out over the bank of a creek
of the tennis court when there was no one on it
of two families seated along the steps of a band pavilion
of the dead rattlesnake
of a sign reading Babylon 2 miles
of a row of rocking chairs on a hotel verandah
of the view from the ridge
of girls with young men they did not marry
of a picnic by the side of the road
of a camping wagon
of the cat that did not stay to have its picture taken

of a boy holding his bicycle
of summer cottages on a small inland lake
of the dog that was run over
of the little boy in a pony cart, with a formal flower bed and the stone gates of the asylum in the background
of a man with a string of fish
of the graduation class
of the oak tree in the garden
of the children wading with their clothes pulled up to their thighs
of a parade
of a path shoveled through deep snow
of a man aiming a rifle
of a boy walking on his hands
of a Christmas tree taken when the needles were beginning to fall off
of Starved Rock
of two children in a swing
of the party stepping into a gasoline launch
of the bride and groom with their arms around each other
of the son in uniform, standing beside the back steps, on a day when the light was not right for taking Kodak pictures
of the pergola
of a fancy-dress party
of the river bank at flood level

Here and there, among so much that is familiar and obvious, you suddenly come upon a scene that cries out for explanation —four women seated around a picnic cloth and gazing calmly at a young man who is also seated and holding what appears to be a revolver in his right hand; or a picture with the center torn out of it, leaving an oval-shaped hole surrounded by porch railing, lawn, trees, a fragment of a woman's skirt, and the sky. If there are clues in the form of writing (*Just after smashup on mountain*, or *The Hermitage 1910*), they are usually unsatisfactory. You never learn what smashup on what mountain or where the hermitage is. There is seldom any pretense that the subjects were doing anything but having their pictures taken. The scenes are necessarily static, and in the faces there is that strange absence of tension that exists in all casual photographs taken before the first World War. One's immediate impression, looking through old photograph albums, is likely to be *Why, there has been no change, no change since childhood.* And then *But how they give themselves away!* And who held the camera is a question that recurs again and again; what person voluntarily absented himself from the record in order to preserve for posterity the image he saw through the small glass square on the side of the camera?

Austin King worked over the scrapbook at his desk in the study, with his back to the fireplace. His careful hands moved from the pastepot to the cloth, from the cloth to the box of curling, unmounted snapshots. The logs that had been drying out all summer on the woodpile snapped and shuddered and were consumed quickly by the flames and fell apart. When he looked up, he saw the lighted room and himself reflected in the window panes against the darkness outside. Martha would have drawn the curtains, but she was not there; she had taken to going upstairs soon after dinner.

If you are of a certain temperament, patient and methodical, pasting snapshots into an album or any work that is simple and done mostly with the hands is pleasant, but it has one important drawback; it leaves the mind free and open to its own dubious devices. Sometimes, to escape from or clarify his own thoughts, Austin King screwed the lid on the pastepot, got up from his desk, and began to walk back and forth in front of the fireplace. He walked from the door that led to the hall (where he turned) to the door that led to the dining room (where he turned again). Occasionally, while the minute hand and the hour hand of the Dresden china clock on the mantelpiece moved slowly toward bedtime, the classic drama in the fireplace was interrupted by some irrelevant stage business—a door creaking somewhere in the back part of the house, a ghost on the stairs.

Before Austin King could go up to bed there were a number of things that, night after night, had to be done. He stood the logs on end in the study fireplace so they wouldn't burn away before morning. He tried the lock on the kitchen door. He opened the door in the pantry, went down the unsafe cellar stairs, and banked the furnace fire. Some of these precautions were necessary (Rachel sometimes forgot to lock herself out, and the kitchen door had once or twice blown open in the night); some had a strange ritualistic quality. No one had been in the living room all day, but he looked to make sure that the damper in the living-room fireplace was closed. He glanced out of the dining-room window at the thermometer, which had not changed perceptibly since he looked at it two hours before. He went around turning off certain radiators and turning others on, night after night. These acts had the look of precautions against something—the presence on the stairs, possibly; or the enemy who, when Austin opened the front door before locking it, was never there.

6

In the upstairs hall of the Beaches' house, under a combination gas and electric light fixture, there was a large steel engraving of an old woman selling apples. In a gilt frame that was ornately carved and cracked, it had outlived by many years the sentimental age that inspired such pictures. The old woman had snow-white hair, square steel-rimmed spectacles, and an expression that was a nice blending of natural kindness and the determination to be kind. There were three children in the picture. The well-dressed boy and girl on the old woman's left had a marked family resemblance. A china doll hung dangling from the little girl's right hand and she had already taken a bite out of her apple. The little boy was apparently saving his until a burning question had been decided. Facing the brother and sister a barefoot boy with ragged clothing searched deep in his trousers pocket for a penny. The barefoot boy was the center and whole point of the picture—his rapt eyes, his expression conveying a mixture of hope and fear. It was evident that he could expect no financial assistance from the well-dressed children. Either there was a penny in that or some other pocket, or else he would get no apple from the old woman with the square spectacles. When Mrs. Beach was a little girl, she had often had trouble getting past this picture, and a voice (now long dead) had to remind her that she had been sent in quest of a gold thimble or a spool of thread.

Nora was gazing at the picture one rainy afternoon when a voice called from the foot of the stairs. From her room at the end of the hall, Mrs. Beach called back, "Is that you, Martha? Come on up."

Unable to move, Nora heard the footsteps mounting and at the last moment, panic set her free and she vanished into her own room. Martha King, having seen the flash of skirts and the door closing, said to herself, Then she *is* trying to avoid me.

"In my room," Mrs. Beach called, and Martha went on down the hall.

Mrs. Beach was seated at her sewing table fitting together the complicated pieces of a pink and white and green quilt. The big double bed, which dominated the room, was made up and the pillows tucked into a round hollow bolster. The rest of the room was in such disorder as one might expect if the occupant were packing for a long sea voyage, but Mrs. Beach had merely been straightening her bureau drawers. The chairs were piled with odds and ends whose place in the grand scheme of things she had not yet decided upon.

"Just move that pile of shirtwaists," she said, with a wave of her stork-handled scissors. "I'd rather you didn't sit on the bed."

"I can't stay," Martha said.

"You always say that, and it's not polite. If you come intending to leave right away, you might as well not come at all. Have you heard from Mrs. Potter?"

Martha nodded.

"I think it's so strange that she doesn't write to me," Mrs. Beach said, "with Nora staying in our house. If Alice or Lucy were staying with the Potters I'd certainly feel that it was my duty to write and show my appreciation, but I gather that Nora and her mother are not very close. That may be why she doesn't bother to put herself out, where Nora is concerned. Now that I think of it, it seems to me that you might have done more for Nora than you have, these past weeks. Or would you have preferred that she went home with her family?"

In order to carry on an amicable conversation with Mrs. Beach, most people found it necessary to let a great many of her remarks pass unchallenged. Far from being grateful because they had come to see her, she usually found pleasure in pointing out to them how long it had been since their last visit. She also asked questions that were inoffensive in themselves but that steered the conversation inexorably around to matters that were sometimes delicate and sometimes none of Mrs. Beach's business.

"I've had only one letter from her," Martha said. "She asked to be remembered to you. Austin hears from Mr. Potter."

"I must say she seemed very fond of us all when she was here, but out of sight, out of mind, apparently. This is the wild rose pattern." Mrs. Beach held the quilt out for Martha to admire. "I've made one for Lucy and now I'm making one for Alice. I want them to have something to remember me by when I'm gone."

"It's lovely," Martha said. "But I wish you wouldn't talk of dying, on a gloomy day like this."

"After you reach sixty," Mrs. Beach said, "you don't expect to be around forever. I don't know that I even want to be. The world was a much nicer place when I was a girl. Good breeding and good manners counted for something. My mother began her married life with her own carriage and a large staff of servants. In the summer we went to . . ."

Mrs. Beach kept Martha for three-quarters of an hour, talking about the vanished world of her girlhood and about the kindergarten, and then she said, "Please don't think I'm driving you away, my dear, but if I don't have my afternoon rest—"

"If you wanted to lie down," Martha said, rising, "why have you been keeping me here? I tried to leave three times in the last fifteen minutes, and each time you—"

"Don't be so touchy," Mrs. Beach said, and smiled. Her smiles were rare, in any case, and seldom as amused or as genuinely friendly as this one was. "All old people have their failings," she said. "Stop and see the girls on your way out. They'll be hurt if you don't."

The Beach girls were on the glassed-in back porch, painting little wooden chairs. They had spread newspapers over the floor but there was no way they could avoid getting paint on themselves. Lucy had a streak of robin's-egg blue running through her hair where she had touched her head in a gesture of weariness. Their hands and aprons were covered with paint.

"Be careful and don't brush against anything!" she said when Martha appeared in the kitchen doorway.

"They're for the kindergarten? How beautiful!" Martha said. "And what a lot of work!"

"There's no end to it," Lucy said. "If I'd known what we were letting ourselves in for—"

"Mother's upstairs," Alice said.

"I've just been up to see her," Martha said, "but I really came over to talk to you. About Ab, I mean. I haven't decided definitely whether to send her to kindergarten or not. She's so young."

"You mustn't let our friendship influence you," Lucy said.

"Oh I wouldn't," Martha said. "If I don't send her, I know you'll understand. When are you going to start?"

"The first week in October, if everything is ready by that time," Lucy said. "We're having trouble with the tables. Mr. Moseby keeps promising them by a certain date, and then they're never ready. It's so discouraging."

They discussed at some length whether Ab would be happy in kindergarten.

"She doesn't want to be anywhere unless I'm there too," Martha said. "Also, I don't want to be separated from her. I really feel very queer about it, but I suppose it will pass. I can't go on like this, feeling anxious about everything. But if she cries—"

"She won't cry," Lucy said. "At the Montessori School in Rome—"

"Look out for your dress!" Alice cried, too late, as Martha backed against one of the freshly painted chairs.

The blue smudge came out with a little turpentine, and Alice went as far as the front door with Martha King, and then turned toward the stairs. Mrs. Beach was lying on her bed with her eyes closed, but as Alice started to tiptoe from the room, she said, "Well, *is* she or isn't she going to send Ab to kindergarten? I never saw Martha so undecided about anything before."

"She's going to think it over," Alice said.

"This shilly-shallying isn't like her," Mrs. Beach said, opening her eyes. "I think she's going to have another baby."

Mrs. Beach had a talent for divination. With the aid of a soiled pack of fortune-telling cards she sometimes correctly foretold the future, and she could often guess at a glance what was inside a wrapped package or in the back of someone's mind. If this was perhaps nothing but acute observation arriving at the truth by way of shortcuts and back alleys, it never ceased to confound and confuse her daughters, and Mrs. Beach had absolute faith in her own intuitive powers.

"If she were going to have a baby, wouldn't it show?" Alice asked, aware that, while they were talking, Nora had come into the room.

"Not necessarily," Mrs. Beach said. "For Austin's sake, I hope it's a boy. I don't know that everybody would agree with me and I don't care whether they agree with me or not—*I* think Austin is every bit as fine a man as his father was."

This was not her usual opinion of Austin King, and Alice recognized that her mother was in a special mood—the one where she didn't like to hear anybody criticized.

Out of contrariness, as she knelt down and began picking up scraps of material from the rug, Alice said, "Sometimes I wonder about him. I mean, if he is as nice as he seems. Because if he is that way, why does Martha get so furious with him?"

"I've never seen the slightest trace of irritability in Martha," Mrs. Beach said. "Vague, yes, and unable to make up her mind. But not irritable."

"I've seen her ready to pick up an axe and hit him over the head with it," Alice said.

"You're imagining things," Mrs. Beach said. "May, June, July, August, September—"

"No I'm not," Alice said, and realized how still Nora was. Throughout the conversation, she hadn't said a word. And yet Nora had lived in the house next door for a month and must have a pretty good idea of what they were like. Austin was her cousin, of course, and with some people that would be enough to prevent them from discussing him. But Nora talked about her own mother and father and brother without the least reticence, and if she didn't join in the conversation about Martha and Austin, it couldn't be because of any family scruples, but only because she didn't want to say what she thought.

As Alice Beach reached toward a pin, an idea came into her mind that startled and then frightened her. She glanced hurriedly around to see whether her mother or Nora had read her thoughts.

"—October, November, December, January," Mrs. Beach said. "I wouldn't be at all surprised if the baby came in January."

7

It wasn't that Ab didn't want to go to kindergarten. She woke that morning in a warm nest of bedclothes, and when her mother came into the room and said, "Today is the day," Ab felt both proud and singled out. But there was something she didn't understand, that might have been explained to her and wasn't, and disaster is often merely an event that you don't have a chance to get used to before it happens.

"Did you go to kindergarten?" she asked as she stepped into the underwear that her mother held out for her.

"No," Martha said. "There wasn't any kindergarten when I was a little girl."

"Did Daddy go to kindergarten?"

"No."

"Did Rachel?"

"No, Rachel didn't go to kindergarten either. Just you."

Ab submitted to the washrag and soap with less than the usual amount of complaints, and she didn't dally over her breakfast. As soon as she had finished her milk, she asked to be excused and slid down from her high chair. The house was full of clocks, but they were of no earthly use to her. She could go to her mother and say, "What time it is?" and her mother would glance at the china clock on the mantelpiece in the study and say, "Twenty minutes of two," or her father would put down his newspaper and extract his gold watch from his vest pocket, open the case, and announce that it was a quarter after seven; but such statements were never in the least enlightening. And there was no way of telling beforehand when anything was going to happen. So far as Ab could discover, it happened when the grown people decided that the time had come for it to happen.

She played, that morning, within sight and hearing of her mother, who lingered at the breakfast table, her hair piled in a loose knot on top of her head, and the sleeves of her negligee pinned above the elbows. At quarter of nine the doorbell rang.

When her mother opened the door, Ab saw Nora Potter with a little boy and two little girls.

"Oh, hello," Martha King said. "I didn't expect you quite so early."

Ab withdrew behind her mother's skirts. Since they had come too early, they would have to sit down in the living room and wait until her mother was dressed.

Martha went to the long closet under the stairs and a moment later emerged with Ab's blue coat and bonnet in her hand, and even then Ab was unprepared for the shock that followed —the shock of hearing her mother say, "Now be a good girl, won't you?" Her mother must know that she wouldn't think of going to kindergarten without her. It was out of the question.

"I'm not going," she announced firmly.

"But we talked about it, and you decided you wanted to go," her mother said.

"I don't want to any more," Ab said, successfully preventing her right arm from being forced into the right sleeve of the coat.

"Abbey, please don't make a scene. You know you're going to kindergarten. It's all decided. Now stand still and let me put your coat on."

"I don't want to put my coat on."

"You must. You can't go through life changing your mind every five minutes and keeping people waiting."

"What will all these little girls and boys think of you?" Nora said, smiling at her.

Ab saw Nora coming nearer and threw herself at her mother's knees, clutching them, clasping her hands around her mother's skirts.

After that, nothing was real or made the slightest sense; not her mother's tears, nor the shamed look on the faces of the other children, nor the detached sound of her own screaming.

The kindergarten rooms were three-quarters of a mile from the house on Elm Street, and Ab was carried, kicking and screaming and fighting for breath to scream again, the whole way. People who passed the strange procession turned and looked back and wondered if they ought to interfere. Nobody did. The frightened screaming ("I want my mother! I want my mother!") sounded like grief—heart-rending, impersonal; grief for the world and all who are obliged to live in it.

8

The porchlight went on, directly overhead, and Dr. Danforth opened the door. "Come in, come in, my boy. How are you? I was just saying to Ella—"

"You aren't busy?" Austin asked, as he stepped over the threshold.

"I didn't get that?"

Austin shouted his question.

"Busy?" Dr. Danforth repeated in the low even voice of the deaf. "What would I be busy about at this time of night? Let me take your hat."

The Danforths' house was built by Mrs. Danforth's father at the height of his material prosperity. Mr. Morris had been a banker and also something of a philanthropist. When his bank failed on "Black Friday," he turned everything he had over to his creditors and eventually got back this house and a fraction of his once very considerable means. After that, he could not go on putting promising boys through school or supporting the hospital and other worthy organizations, but at least his family were not in want. For lack of a better word, people who came to the house for the first time usually said "Oh, what a beautiful house!" by which they meant that it was dark, cave-like, and quiet; that it invited daydreaming; that it belonged to the past. The rooms were large and opened one out of another, and the cherry woodwork had the gleam of dark red marble. The dark green walls of the dining room were stenciled with white peacocks above the dado, and in the music room there were cupids and garlands of pink roses. These long-faded murals had been painted by an itinerant Italian artist whose sick wife, debts, and dirty children had touched old Mrs. Morris' always susceptible heart.

The parlor fireplace was of molasses-brown tile, with mirrors set into the complicated Victorian mantelpiece. On the mantelshelf there was a brass clock with the works visible through panes of thick beveled glass, and several family photographs. Over the sofa there was a huge oil painting of a storm at sea and a Byronic shipwreck. Mrs. Danforth's chair was beside the heavy carved table, where the lamplight would shine on her needlework. The lampshade was of hammered brass, four-sided, with pin-points of light shining through in the design of some long-tailed bird—the phoenix perhaps. Dr. Danforth's chair was beside the sofa. The lamp that shone on his newspaper came from a mahogany floor lamp with a red silk shade. In front of the other window was a large silvered gazing globe that belonged in a garden but had found its way, pedestal and all, into the Danforths' parlor. The gazing ball was not pleasant to look into, since it reflected all people as ugly and deformed.

The room offered no clue to what the Danforths had been doing when the doorbell rang. There was no open book, no workbasket, no card table laid out for solitaire. The big lump of cannel coal in the grate was unlit. Though Dr. and Mrs. Danforth were pleased to see Austin King, there was nothing in their manner to indicate that he had rescued them from an empty evening or from each other.

"How is Martha?"

"Tired out. She went upstairs after supper," he said and had to repeat this statement louder for Dr. Danforth's benefit.

"Nothing serious?" Dr. Danforth asked.

"Fall house-cleaning."

"She mustn't overdo," Mrs. Danforth said.

"I know," Austin said gravely. "But how to stop her?"

Dr. Danforth leaned forward eagerly as if he knew and were about to tell them, but what he said was "I have a horse downtown that I'm anxious to have you see. A sorrel, five-gaited and gentle. You might want to get him for Martha. Prince Edward is too big for a woman to handle. This horse would be just right for her."

"Except that he shies occasionally," Mrs. Danforth said.

"What's that?" Dr. Danforth asked.

"I say Martha doesn't want a horse that shies," Mrs. Danforth said placidly.

"I think I can cure him of that. He wasn't ridden properly in the beginning. You can have him for just what I paid for him."

"I don't know that I can afford to buy another horse just now," Austin said. "But I'd like to see him."

"You come around tomorrow sometime," Dr. Danforth said, nodding.

Austin moved forward until he was sitting on the edge of the sofa. "I brought these over to show you," he said, indicating the sheaf of papers in his lap. "Maybe it's nothing to be worried about, but I'd like your advice."

"Why don't you go in the library, where you won't be disturbed?" Mrs. Danforth said. Her husband was looking at Austin and didn't know that she had spoken. She waited until he turned to her again and then repeated the suggestion as if for the first time.

"Come along, my boy," Dr. Danforth said.

"If you don't mind?" Austin said to Mrs. Danforth.

"Not at all."

The two men went into the next room and Dr. Danforth found his spectacle case, spread Austin's letters and documents out in front of him on the big roll-topped desk, and began to read. After a while the swivel chair swung around so that Dr. Danforth's back was to the litter of papers—deeds, documents, the correspondence between Austin and the bank in Howard's Landing, between Austin and Mr. Potter. He rubbed his nose thoughtfully with one finger, started to speak, and then changed his mind. At last he said, "I can't advise you, my boy. You'd better talk to someone who knows something about cotton farming. Fred Meister was down there a few years ago. Why don't you go talk to him?"

"But does it seem all right to you, just on the face of it?" Austin asked.

"No, I can't say that it does. The indebtedness is larger than we were given to understand. I only had that one talk with him about it, and I don't hear all that people say, so maybe—"

"It's considerably larger," Austin interrupted.

"Did he say anything about a second mortgage?"

Austin shook his head. "That only came out after I began writing to the bank. Do you think he's dishonest? He didn't seem like that kind of a man when he was here. He seemed—you knew that Mr. Potter and my father were raised together? In some ways he reminds me—"

"I never saw the Judge go out of his way to make anybody like him, but I know what you mean," Dr. Danforth said. "I wouldn't say that Mr. Potter was dishonest. When I'm trading with a man I'm supposed to get the better of him, and he's supposed to get the better of me."

"But this isn't horse trading."

"I was just giving that as an example." Dr. Danforth turned back to the desk and began to read the letters again, moving his lips silently and occasionally shaking his head. "Has Judge Fairchild seen this letter?" he asked finally.

Austin got up and came over to the desk. "No," he said, looking over Dr. Danforth's shoulder. "That one just came today."

"Show it to him. It could be that there is something funny going on between Mr. Potter and the bank. I'd show him everything."

"Wouldn't it be better to wait?"

"Bring it all out into the open," Dr. Danforth said. "It's going to end up there sooner or later anyway, and you'll be doing yourself and everybody else a favor by hurrying the thing along."

Mrs. Danforth opened a drawer of the parlor table and took out her crocheting. In the carved furniture all around her there was a great variety of natural forms—flowers, grasses, ferns, leaves, acorns, occasionally a butterfly or a grasshopper or some small animal such as a lizard or a frog. Before he became a banker, Mrs. Danforth's father had taught wood-carving at Hampton Institute, and after his death, as a kind of legacy, he had left everywhere in the house carved tables, chairs, footstools, firescreens, and chests—his version of the fable of creation. Mrs. Danforth, being of a more abstract turn of mind, was content with a six-pointed star. Though she had crocheted hundreds of white table mats in the previous eighteen years, and scattered them through a dozen households, she never varied from this one design.

The sound of the men's voices, low and serious, came to her from the open door of the den. After a few minutes she got up and went through the house, turning on lights in the dining room, the pantry, and the kitchen. When she had unlocked and opened the back door there was a light pattering of animal footsteps and a stiff-legged, shaggy black dog came loping out of the darkness and up onto the porch.

"Well, Hamlet," she asked, "did you decide it was time to come home?"

The dog stretched in front of her, as if he were making an exaggerated bow, followed her into the house, and back through the kitchen, the pantry, and the dining room, to the parlor, where he turned around three times and subsided on the rug at her feet.

When he sighed deeply she peered down at him over her glasses and said, "Nobody knows what it means to be a very old dog, do they?"

He rolled his eyes up at her, thumped his tail, and sighed again, a shipwrecked creature that had, against all hope and expectation, found his way to shore.

9

Dr. Danforth had begun to lose his hearing when he was a very young man. First the minute sounds—the clock ticking, the click of a fingernail, the scrape of a cup in its saucer—and then all buzzing, droning, hammering, sawing, singing, all echoes and reverberations, and finally the whole auditory perspective vanished from his consciousness without his knowing that this had happened. He had to ask people more and more frequently to repeat what they said to him, and was annoyed with them for mumbling. At the same time his own voice was pitched lower and lower, and people had trouble catching what he himself said, though he was under the impression that he spoke distinctly. His naturally kind, calm face was screwed up in a permanent grimace by the effort to understand what was going on around him, until one day he saw a horse stomp and realized that the hush he lived in hadn't in any way been impaired. He went out into the street and stood there listening. The sounds that he knew must be there, as solid and undeniable as the courthouse itself, failed him. He saw movement, people passing on the sidewalks, carriages in the street, clouds in the sky, but they made no sound. And when old man Barnes came up to him and began to shout in his ear, he turned abruptly and went back into the darkness of the stable, a stranger to himself and, from that day on, a friend to no one.

His deafness had the effect of making the world seem a

larger place, the streets wider, the buildings farther apart, the sky vast again, the way it had seemed to be when he was a country boy. It also showed him that every man was a liar, and he himself—the eternal horse trader—was of course the greatest, the most complete liar of them all.

The truth is necessarily partial. Every vision of completeness is a distortion in one way or another, whether it springs from sickness or sanctity. But in the visions of saints there are voices that speak reassuringly of the cloud of Unknowing. Dr. Danforth did not even hear the occasional good that people spoke of him. When they came to the livery stable to hire a carriage, he directed them to Snowball McHenry, the Negro stableboy, and betrayed himself only in the way that his hands petted and stroked and captured the heart of every dumb animal that came near them. In time he learned to use his infirmity to advantage, reading lips when he wanted to understand, and when it served his purpose not to understand, making people repeat, until in the exasperation of continual shouting, they gave the game away.

That's Dr. Danforth, deaf as a post but nobody ever got the better of him in a horse trade. . . . Lives all alone, never goes anywhere or sees anybody. . . . Doc's a fine man. The trouble is, he won't let anybody do anything for him. His father was like that toward the end of his life.

So, charitably, Dr. Danforth was assigned a place; he became a town character, like the Orthwein boy who was born without a soft palate, and Joe Walsh, the blacksmith, who never cut his hair but wore it in a pigtail tucked inside his shirt collar—because of an illness, some people said, and others said he had made a bet with somebody and lost.

Dr. Danforth knew everything that went on in Draperville but from a distance, from the greatest distance of all, which is the outside. Ten years passed without its ever occurring to him that he needed a new suit of clothes. He was often seen with a stubble on his chin. He didn't know or care how he looked. On his way home to the boardinghouse on Hudson Street, he stepped over little girls who were too engrossed in their sidewalk games to realize that they were in anybody's way; saw them leave their colored chalk, their jacks and skipping ropes and rubber balls, and go off to lose themselves in the mirror of

that night a great wave came over him of happiness and hope. Sitting on the front porch, after the old lady had excused herself and gone indoors to escape the night air, Ella asked him to marry her. It was so strange, not being able to hear the words and yet knowing, by his own wildly beating heart, that they had been said. He was frightened at what she had done and he thought, for a second, that the only thing left for him to do was to pick up his new hat and run, but he couldn't even do that, because Ella was still talking, in that inaudible voice, her eyes focused on the porch railing, and her face so beautiful with trouble that he realized he couldn't go; that unless he took her in his arms, something terrible would happen.

"If you're sure," he said; but that was several days later, and it was all he ever said.

From that night everything was different for him. He wasn't on the outside any more, looking at lighted windows. He was sitting down at the table in the dining room or beside the parlor lamp. He didn't walk down the street and nod to people on their front porches, on summer evenings. He had a porch to sit on, a place where he was expected.

10

"I saw you coming out of the bank," Nora said, "but you didn't see me."

"Why didn't you stop me?" Austin asked. He had just come through the revolving door of the post office, and the sun was shining directly in his eyes.

"You were lost in thought," Nora said.

"Was I?" Austin said. Her manner with him was friendly and natural—or almost natural—but since her visit with Martha, Nora hadn't come either to the house or to the office. During the past week he had seen her only once, in the side yard of the house next door. Though he was glad to see her now, if he had had a chance to choose where they met, it would not have been in so public a place as the steps of the post office. He shaded his eyes from the glare and said, "What do you hear from your family?"

"They're fine," Nora said. "Pa had an accident with the new automobile, but it wasn't so very serious. He ran over a culvert and bent the front axle, I think it was, and had to be towed into Howard's Landing. But it's all right now. And Brother has a new hunting dog, and they've had lots of company." She moved up one step in order to be on a level with him. "Mrs. Beach is complaining because you and Cousin Martha never come to see us."

"We haven't gone anywhere," Austin said. "Martha hasn't felt up to it. You know we're—"

"Yes, I know," Nora said. "I'm very happy for you. I—" She hesitated as a man came up the steps toward them.

"I just sold my corn, Austin," the man said.

"Good time to sell," Austin said, nodding, and waited until Ray Murphy had disappeared into the post office. Then he said, "Are you getting along all right, Nora?"

"Yes," Nora said. "You don't have to worry about me any more. I don't know where I got the courage to speak to you as I did that day, but it must have been from you. Because even now, as I look back on it and realize what an unthinkable thing I have done, somehow I'm not ashamed or humiliated. So it must be because of you."

"There's no reason for you to feel ashamed."

"I hope you've forgotten all I said to you, because I have. I've put it out of my mind forever. It was just something that at the time seemed very real but wasn't actually, and I'm very grateful to you for talking to me the way you did, because some men—but you aren't like that, and so there's no use in my going into it. I wasn't in love with you—or if I was, I'm not any more. It's just like you said. I'll always know that I can come to you if I'm ever in trouble, and you'll do everything in your power to help me, and for that reason I'm not entirely sorry. But you mustn't worry any more about me because there's nothing to worry about."

The post-office door opened and Nora went right on talking. "The chief thing I want to say to you is how truly grateful to you I am, and how sorry I am that you should ever have become involved enough to feel that you . . ."

If Ray Murphy was surprised to see them still standing there, his face did not show it. He nodded at Austin and went on down the steps and crossed the street.

". . . Sometimes I feel like writing to Cousin Martha,"

Nora said, "and telling her how kind you were to me, and how you put me on the right track."

"I don't believe I'd do that, if I were you."

"Oh I wouldn't dream of writing to her!" Nora exclaimed. "She might not understand and I wouldn't want to cause you or her a moment's unhappiness. It's just that she has so much —she has you and little Abbey and that beautiful house and all—and I feel like telling her how much she has to be thankful for. But she knows, of course. There's no need to tell her things that she already knows."

"No," Austin agreed. He saw Al Sterns coming across the courthouse lawn and, turning to Nora, said, "Would you like to come up to the office and talk to me there?"

"Don't you see I can't come up to your office and talk to you?" Nora said. "Of course I want to, but what is the good? I'd just rattle on and on. If I could only be still or talk sensibly, but I can't do either. I know I'm an emotional person. I'm aware of all these things. But if you only knew how badly I want you to like me and approve of me!"

"I do like and approve of you," Austin said. Al Sterns waited for a wagon to pass and then started across the street toward the post office.

"I want desperately to be friends with you, but I don't know how. It's not your fault. You are doing everything possible to make things easy for me, but even thinking about going to your office with you makes me want to run miles away, because I know I'd only make a fool of myself. Sometimes when I haven't seen you for several days I think 'Maybe he isn't like that. Now think. How could you remember exactly what he looks like? Part of it is in your head.' But then I see you coming up the walk and you are just as I remember you, of course. This is my compensation for being all mixed up in general—that I have certain things—faces, mannerisms, and so forth, so impressed on my mind that I can never forget them."

"Austin, how's the world treating you?"

"Can't complain, Al. . . . This is my cousin, Miss Potter."

"Pleased to meet you, Miss Potter," Al Sterns said and put out his hand. "Austin, they tell me you—"

"Or even color them in imagination," Nora said. "They are just as they are."

"I'll drop in and see you later," Al Sterns said, and went on up the steps.

"*You* are just as you are," Nora said. "I think of you all the time, because I can't help doing that. But I don't think of you in any woebegone way. Just sometimes when I can't find anything to do to keep me busy or at night when I'm falling asleep, I suddenly wonder where you are and what you're doing. And if we do find ourselves face to face, by some accident, the way we are now, I know I'll always have something to say to you, because I think in terms of you. Whenever I see anything that moves me, makes me smile or feel sad, I always think of you. But no one need ever know. I never talk about you, about how wonderful you are, or drag compliments out of people so I can repeat them to you, or make over Ab, or do any of the things girls do when they're hopelessly in love. I won't run in and out of the house on some flimsy pretext, and on the other hand, if I don't come to see you very often, you mustn't think it's because I don't have any interest in you, because I do."

"I understand," Austin said. He had been expecting Al Sterns to come out again, but he saw now that Al had come out of the side entrance and crossed the street in front of the fire station.

"Last night I dreamed about you, and today I can't remember the dream. All I know is that we were at home and that you were going into town with us, and somehow in the dream we went off and left you. . . ."

It was a long involved dream that Nora recaptured, piece by piece, standing on the post-office steps. Though Austin kept his eyes rigidly on her face, he heard very little of it. In his mind he said *Nora, I have work to do. . . . There's somebody waiting in my office . . .* over and over, hoping that Nora would grasp what he was thinking, by mental telepathy. *I don't want to listen to your dream. . . .*

". . . we were driving through this section of the country," Nora went on. "I can't remember whether this was part of the same dream or another one. Anyway, there were two other people with us. Actually a couple who are not really friends of our family but the man is one of Pa's business associates, with their twelve-year-old son. I can remember distinctly being at your house, Cousin Austin. I don't remember arriving there, having you greet us and so forth, but suddenly in the dream I was leaning against the window sill with my chin in my hands—"

The Jouettes' shiny black surrey drove up before the post office. The colored boy jumped down from the front seat and took old Mrs. Jouette's letter from her.

"—staring at you," Nora said. "The window was closed, which was queer because it was in summer, and you were outdoors watering the lawn, paying absolutely no attention to us at all."

Old Mrs. Jouette, all in shiny black, like the carriage, turned to the sad-faced young girl beside her and said, "Who is that standing on the steps?"

"Austin King."

"It can't be," Mrs. Jouette exclaimed.

"It is, all the same," the girl said listlessly. "I don't know who she is, but they were standing there when we drove by before."

"I had the feeling in my dream," Nora said earnestly, "I had the distinct feeling that you had been cordial and polite to everyone but me. I kept staring at you, trying to make you look at me. . . ."

Seeing the old lady's lorgnette trained upon him, Austin lifted his hat and bowed. The bow was returned, but without any accompanying smile of pleasure, and old Mrs. Jouette turned her attention to the courthouse lawn. Lord Nelson, Austin thought, at Trafalgar, in his admiral's uniform, with all his medals showing. . . .

". . . And you would not," Nora said. "You absolutely refused to look at me. Yet you knew, of course, that I was staring at you for that express reason. . . ."

II

The voices in the study grew louder and Martha King, sitting in the living room with young Mrs. Ellis, heard Bud Ellis say, "Of course it's not your fault, Austin. All you did was draw up the papers. But naturally, since he was a relative of yours, we assumed—"

"Let's keep to the facts," Judge Fairchild said. Martha got up and dragged her chair nearer the sofa.

"I'm just stupid, I guess," Mary Ellis said. "But it seems harder than anything I've ever tried to do. I sit down with three cookbooks in front of me, and they all tell you to do something different, and never the thing you really want to know. If Bud weren't particular about his food, it wouldn't matter, but his mother was a very fine cook and he tells me things she used to make for him, like peach cobbler and upside-down-cake and salt-rising bread. And when I try the same thing, it never turns out right, for some reason. And I have to worry about things that Father Ellis can chew, and sometimes if he doesn't like what we have, he gets up from the table. Bud says he does it just to make a scene, but naturally it makes me feel bad, after I've tried to please him. Bud's mother never used a recipe, he says. I don't see how anybody can cook without a recipe. I don't see how you begin, even."

"Probably she learned from *her* mother," Martha said.

"I never had a chance to do that," Mary Ellis said. "My mother was an invalid and we had a series of housekeepers. I was never even allowed in the kitchen."

"It'll come, with practice," Martha said, trying to follow the conversation in the study. "You get so after a while it's second nature. You don't even have to think about it."

"I don't know," Mary Ellis said despairingly. "I don't think I'll ever get to that point. I like to keep house and I like sewing—I make all my own clothes—but I don't think I'll ever learn to cook. It just isn't in me."

"You mustn't feel that way," Martha said. She was struggling with herself to keep from getting up and going into the next room. They were solidly against him, and appealing to his sense of honor, which was so easy to do if you were Bud Ellis and didn't have any. But if she appeared in the doorway and said *Stop it. I know what you're doing, and I won't allow it!* Austin would never forgive her.

"It isn't that I don't have enough time," Mary Ellis was saying. "Although I'm busy, of course. But not like women who have children to think about. Did you have Ab right away?"

"She was born a little over a year after we were married," Martha said.

"I envy you so," Mary Ellis said. "Bud and I have been married nearly a year now and—"

"Just because you don't have a baby the first year doesn't mean anything," Martha said. "I know women who were married ten or twelve years before their first baby came."

"But I don't want to wait that long. I want to have my children when I'm young. Every time I see a child I want to touch it and hold it on my lap, and it's making Bud very unhappy."

"That goes without saying," Bud Ellis said in a loud voice. "But four thousand dollars is four thousand dollars. And if we'd known what we do now, we'd never have put money into the venture. I'm not accusing *you* of anything, Austin, but I'd like to know one thing: Why did you stay out of it?"

Martha King waited, hoping against hope for the sound of her husband's fist against Bud Ellis' jaw. There was no such sound.

"I try not to feel that way," Mary Ellis said. "I know it's foolish of me to . . ."

Surely he won't explain, Martha said to herself. Oh don't let him stoop to explain.

"I couldn't afford to take the risk," Austin said, in the next room.

"Then you knew it *was* a risk?" Judge Fairchild said, as if he were leaning down from the bench to question the witness on the stand.

Martha King looked across at the Danforths' house, saw that it was dark, and realized that she wouldn't have called Dr. Danforth even if they had been home. It was Austin's battle, and she would have to sit by quietly and let him lose it.

It is a common delusion of gentle people that the world is also gentle, considerate, and fair. Cruelty and suspicion find them eternally unprepared. The surprise, the sense of shock, paralyzes them for too long a time after the unprovoked insult has been given. When they finally react and are able to raise their fists in their own defense, it is already too late. *What did he mean by that?* they say, turning to the person nearest them, who witnessed the scene and who might also have been attacked, although he wasn't. There is never any help or enlightenment from the person standing next to them, and so they go on down some endless corridor, reliving the brutal moment, trying vainly to recall the precise words of what must—and yet needn't have been—a mortal insult. Should they go back and fight? Or would they only be making a fool of themselves? And then they remember: This is not the first time. Behind this unpleasant incident there is another equally unpleasant (and another and another), the scars of which have long since healed. The old infection breaks open, races through the blood, producing a weakness in the knees, and hands bound, hopeless and heavy at their sides.

"Have you been to a doctor?" Martha King asked.

"Yes. Dr. Spelman. He just told me to get lots of rest and not to get upset by things." Mary Ellis seemed completely unaware of what was going on in the study. When Bud Ellis said, "I think you might have had the decency to tell us, Austin," her face remained unchanged, hopeless, unhappy.

Martha waited and said, "There's something you can try, if you want to. Grace Armstrong told me about it. It's something her mother discovered. Grace says that she would probably never have come into the world otherwise, and neither would her children. If you want to try it—"

"I'll try anything," Mary Ellis said.

"Well, then," Martha said, "this is what you must do. . . ."

12

The people who lived on Elm Street seldom spoke or thought of the Beach girls as separate personalities. It is true that they had a marked family resemblance and that their remarks and timid mannerisms were often interchangeable, but more important, it was generally recognized that they would never marry, and if they were ever to enter the ark with the other animals, two by two, it would have to be in each other's company.

At the kindergarten the children never for a moment confused them. If a child fell down during a game of tag or drop-the-handkerchief and skinned his knee or struck his elbow, it was Alice Beach that he rushed to. She wiped the children's tears away, approved of their weaving, admired and sometimes correctly interpreted the drawings they brought to show her. When they grew tired of playing, she held them in her lap. If they started quarreling over an alphabet plate or a necklace of wooden beads, she found something else to distract them temporarily from the emotion of ownership. So long as she was in the room there was a center of love, of safety.

In a child's world, where there is a mother there must also be a father. There was nothing about Lucy Beach that could be considered masculine and yet she was able, when the children grew overexcited, to calm them. "Now that's enough," she would say. "No more." And it would be enough and there was no more of that particular frenzy. She never spoke harshly to the children or punished them with a quick spanking, but they seemed to have decided by common consent to be afraid of her.

Nora went from house to house in the mornings, collecting the children, who fought for the privilege of walking beside her. And because she was young, because she laughed easily and played London Bridge-is-falling-down and drop-the-handkerchief with as much pleasure and excitement as they did, they presented her with samples of their handiwork—crayon drawings and lopsided raffia baskets which she was expected to admire and keep always. When she sat down for a moment on one of the low kindergarten chairs, small arms encircled her neck. The children leaned upon her (all except Ab) and rubbed against her like cats and were in love with her without knowing it, and this in no way interrupted or inter fered with their relation to Miss Lucy, the agent of punishment, and Miss Alice, the agent of comfort.

Love and fear are so well taught at home that no educational system need be concerned with these two elementary subjects. The first stage of the Montessori Method is to develop the sense of touch, sight, and hearing. This is done through games, and by guiding the children's attention to the association of objects, names, and ideas. They are taught the difference between hot and cold objects, between objects that are rough and those that are smooth. And by teaching children the words "hot," "cold," "rough," "smooth," you extend their sense of language before any question of reading or writing arises. They get their ideas of form and color from playing with blocks and cylinders of varying sizes, which are fitted into frames that match them. There are no set lessons, no classes, no prizes or punishments of the usual kind. The only incentive is the pleasure, in a room where all kinds of interesting occupations are being pursued, of succeeding and getting things right.

Though Alice and Lucy Beach had read Mme. Montessori's famous book, their own education had been at the hands of their mother. Touch, sight, and hearing were developed not by games but by crises. They were taught the difference between a warm, kind mother and a cold mother and how, by a simple act of disobedience, a failure in sympathy, they could change "kind" to "cold," "smooth" to "rough." As they grew older they became extremely adept at fitting their hopes into a frame that did not match. There were set lessons which, once learned, could not be unlearned. There were prizes, in the shape usually of a trip to Europe. And there were punishments of an unusual kind, which sent them weeping to their rooms and then brought them back to be forgiven by the person who had done something unforgivable to them.

If Mrs. Beach had realized how easy it was to start a kindergarten, how simple to find a dozen mothers who were anxious to have their children out from under foot three hours every weekday morning, she would never have given her consent to the modest establishment over Bailey's Drug Store. It was only one of many ideas that the two girls had hatched up, and the other ideas had always been exhausted in talk. This one they had carried through, to her amazement, and for the time being she could think of no way to put a stop to it.

From nine until eleven-thirty, five mornings a week, the children accepted the kindergarten routine as they would have accepted an act of enchantment. When Lucy played the piano, they marched and sang. They wove hammocks and rugs out of colored yarns. With scissors and paste and sheets of colored paper they made houses and stores and churches with pointed steeples. At certain times, memory overtook them as it overtook Ulysses on the shore of Calypso's island, and then they would come to Nora and say, "When are we going home?" or "Will my mother be home when I get there?"

Every day when it came time to deliver the children to their homes, Nora had to stand and see one child after another leave her and run into outstretched, waiting arms. It was something she never got used to.

13

"Why are you responsible?" Dr. Danforth asked. "All you did was draw up the papers."

"I know," Austin said, "but I invited them here. They were guests in my house and don't you see, that makes it look as if I—"

Dr. Danforth didn't at first understand, and then he said, "No . . . no, you mustn't do that, my boy. They went into it with their eyes open. Or at least they should have gone into it that way. It was speculation pure and simple. And you have Martha and Ab to worry about, and another child coming. It wouldn't be right at all. The thing will work itself out some way. Just give it a chance."

"I found out one thing," Austin said, examining the tips of his shoes, "while they were here. It seems that there was a time when Mr. Potter was very hard up, and turned to Father for help."

"Is that so?" Dr. Danforth peered at Austin over his glasses. "I never heard about that."

"Father refused him."

"It wasn't Mr. Potter that the Judge was indebted to, if I remember correctly," Dr. Danforth said.

"I know," Austin said.

"It's true that they were raised under the same roof and you might expect, for old times' sake, that the Judge would want to do whatever lay in his power to help some member of his foster family. But you can't judge people's actions unless you know what went on in their minds at the time. Even if the Judge were alive today and you could go to him and ask why he refused to help Mr. Potter, he might not give you any satisfaction. He was a very proud man. It was his only fault, as far as I can see, and with him it wasn't exactly a fault; he had reason to be proud. He might rather let you think ill of him than defend himself against a charge that he figured you ought to know was false. That's the way he was."

"Perhaps you're right," Austin said, "but I remember hearing him say a number of times how deeply indebted he was to the people who raised him, and that he could never pay them back."

"You can't pay people back for the kindness they show to you when you're in trouble. There isn't any way of measuring, in terms of money, what you owe them. You can go on paying them back forever, and still be indebted to them. Sometimes they don't need any help. Or maybe the kind of help they need you can't give them. All you can do is look around for somebody that *is* in need of help and do what you can for them, figuring that it will all be canceled out some day. I'm sure that's the way the Judge looked at it. He was always helping somebody out of a tight spot, his whole life long. People that are near to you and that you have every reason for trusting—if they do something that doesn't look quite right to you, why you wait and give them time to explain themselves. And if they can't explain because they've passed on, you still oughtn't to . . . The chances are that the Judge paid off this debt as he paid off every other, but felt obligated, even so, to the end of his life, and that's why you heard him speak as he did. I don't doubt that the story Mr. Potter told you about turning to the Judge for help and being refused is true, every word of it. The Judge could say no. But in every one of these letters there is something held back, and I doubt if he told you the whole story. Maybe that wasn't the first time Mr. Potter turned to the Judge for money. Maybe it was the fourth or fifth time. Maybe the Judge went on his note and had to make it good afterward, the way he did for so many other people that pass as honest men. Or it could even be that he had some reason to distrust Mr. Potter. After all, they knew each other as boys. Maybe the Judge realized that any help he gave would just be frittered away on something foolish, like an automobile. Sometimes, with men like Mr. Potter, there is no real way of helping them, even if you try. The more help anybody gives them, the deeper in they get. But I'll tell you one thing—I wouldn't believe any man that spoke ill of Judge King."

"I wasn't speaking ill of him," Austin said soberly. "I just wondered, that's all."

Dr. Danforth looked startled. "I wasn't talking about you,"

he said. He took his spectacles off, restored them to their case, and put the case in his vest pocket. "I didn't really get to know my own father until just at the end of his life. And even then there were things I couldn't ask about, or tell him about myself, for fear of upsetting him. I know what he was like as my father, but the rest of him, all that part that had nothing to do with me . . ." With a smile that apologized for the tears in his eyes, Dr. Danforth took out his handkerchief and blew his nose vigorously.

Death, about which so much mystery is made, is perhaps no mystery at all compared to the history of one's parents, which has to be pieced together from fragments, their motives and character guessed at, and even then the truth about them remains deeply buried, like a boulder that projects one small surface above the level of smooth lawn and, when you dig around it, proves to be too large ever to move, though each year's frost forces it up a little higher.

14

"The house seems a little chilly," Mrs. Danforth said when her husband came back from the Kings'. She was sitting in her accustomed chair and her hands were engaged in the creation of the same white six-pointed star.

"I'll see what I can do about it," he said.

The rumble of furnace grates being shaken went through the silent house. A shovel scraped in the coal bin, an iron door clanged shut, and again there were heavy footsteps on the basement stairs. Mrs. Danforth looked up as her husband came into the room. He went over to his chair, sat down, rubbed his eyes with his hand, sighed, and said nothing. After a time he said, "Well, I've been over the whole business with him. He listened to everything I had to say, but he's still going ahead with his plans."

"I thought he probably would," Mrs. Danforth said.

"He feels responsible because he drew up the papers and because the arrangements were made in his house. If there's anything in the world that boy doesn't feel responsible for, I don't know what it is. He has to borrow four thousand dollars. On his house. The bank won't take the stock as collateral."

"Is that so," Mrs. Danforth said.

"I told him, 'You'll be lucky if you get out of this without having to go into bankruptcy.'"

"What did he say to that?"

"He didn't say anything."

"Austin will never go bankrupt," Mrs. Danforth said calmly.

"The others are willing to ride along, in the hope of getting their money back some day. It's Bud Ellis who's making the trouble. He threatened to bring suit against Austin."

"Why against Austin?"

"Because if they brought suit against Mr. Potter and won, the chances are they still couldn't collect anything. So far as Austin is concerned, they haven't got a leg to stand on. The case would be thrown out of court."

"Austin must know that."

"Certainly he knows it, and so does Bud Ellis. It isn't right. 'Let them stew in their own juice,' I told him. 'You've paid off your father's debts and provided for your mother. That's enough.' . . . He mustn't make a pauper of himself for people who aren't even related to him."

"No," Mrs. Danforth agreed.

"I told him all that and a lot more, but it was so much wasted breath."

"Well, you've had your say," Mrs. Danforth said, searching through the table drawer for a missing crochet hook. "Whatever happens now, it won't be your fault."

15

"How nice you look, Nora," Alice Beach said.

To her surprise, Nora went back into her room and took off her earrings. The look of expectancy on her face, as she went down the hall and said good night to Mrs. Beach, could not be taken off. Martha King's long-delayed invitation had included them all, but Mrs. Beach had eaten something that disagreed with her and was in bed, and one of the girls was obliged to stay home and take care of her. Which one should go and which one should miss this pleasant change from their ordinary routine had been decided long ago when Lucy took lessons from Geraldine Farrar's singing teacher and Alice stayed below in the little reception hall, listening to the sound of her sister's voice ascending and descending the scale that ended with a chord on the piano.

"Do you have your key?" Mrs. Beach asked.

"In my purse," Lucy said. "We'll be home early."

On her face also there was a look of expectancy, but what Lucy Beach expected from this evening was by no means clear. She could not have been hoping that the Kings, after knowing her for many years, would suddenly accept her as their most intimate friend, ask her for dinner again and again, and feel somehow incomplete unless she was with them. Nevertheless, the look was there, and it implied something of this kind or order.

"The cat came back," Nora said, as Austin opened the door to them. Having waited so long for an invitation to dinner, she now produced this poor joke in self-defense, to show that the waiting was unimportant, was nothing. The gloved hand that was about to reach out and touch his coat-sleeve, she checked in time. Nervously, knowing that her happiness could not last because he would not let it last, she looked around to see what changes had taken place in the house during the past three months.

"It's nice to see you," Austin said, as he put their coats away in the hall closet.

Though it was so important that Nora look at him right then, before his expression changed, she could not. Once before he had seemed to want something of her, and then it turned out that he . . . That was how it all began, the mistake above all other mistakes she must guard against making. But would he have said that he was glad to see her unless he meant to imply something more besides?

"Martha will be down in just a minute," he said, and led them into the living room.

"Mother and Alice were so sorry they couldn't come," Lucy said.

"I'm sorry, too," Austin said, and then, as Lucy chose an uninviting chair, "Wouldn't you be more comfortable by the fire?"

I know exactly how I feel when I'm with him, Nora said to herself, but I don't know how to stop feeling it.

They sat stiffly making conversation until Martha King came down the stairs. She was wearing a silk shawl, but she showed quite plainly that she was carrying a child. Austin talked to Lucy, and Nora was left with Martha King, whose one effort at making conversation with Nora that evening came to nothing. While Martha was talking to her, Nora's glance wavered toward the other couple in the room, and then traveled to the sheet music on the piano. She wondered what it would be like sitting here alone with him in the evening, listening to his playing (so much more expressive and musical than her mother's thumping) and watching his sensitive hands moving over the keyboard. She realized suddenly that Martha had asked a question.

"Mama? Oh, she's fine."

"And your father?"

"He's all right. They're all fine and sent their love to you and Cousin Austin," Nora said, and felt as if she had awakened abruptly in the midst of a dream. Though the dream remained in her memory, as sharp and clear as a winter day, she couldn't get back into it. "I notice that Cousin Austin comes home much later than he used to last summer. I'm afraid we interfered with his work."

"He's been very busy with the fall term of court," Martha said.

"Oh," Nora said, and nodded, and then after a pause she said, "I'd like very much to hear him speak in court. Would it embarrass him, having someone there that he knows?"

Martha picked at the fringe of her shawl and Nora thought for a moment that she had not understood. "If you think it would embarrass him, I won't say anything to him about it," she said.

"He won't let me go and hear him," Martha said, "but that's probably because I— Why don't you ask him and see what he says. He might enjoy having you there."

"You can come if you like," Austin said, turning away from Lucy. "The case I'm trying now is not very interesting, the way a criminal trial would be."

"I wouldn't care about that," Nora said, her face suffused with pleasure. "All I want is to see a case tried."

"Dinner is served," Rachel said.

After they were seated, Nora turned to Austin, prepared to be anything that he wanted her to be, because she loved him so much and because he was so wonderful and she was so happy just being with him. All she needed was some positive indication from him of the role he wanted her to play in his life, and until that came she would have to go on feeling shy with him (it was strange how someone could take up so much of your thoughts and still be as remote as a star) and painfully aware of the fact that she wanted him to love her, knowing that he couldn't and telling herself that it didn't matter, so long as she was here and could love him.

Austin's efforts at commonplace table conversation were not taken up by Nora and he had to fall back on the food. Martha tried to talk to Lucy but there were distractions. Rachel had forgotten to warm the plates, and she passed the mint sauce after they had finished eating their lamb.

Lucy Beach, dining out for the first time in years without her mother and sister, failed to notice the frequent silences. Her hand kept reaching for the cut-glass tumbler. She drank a great deal of water, and smoothed and folded the napkin lying across her lap. When, after an interruption, Martha King took up the conversation at some place other than the place where Lucy had left off, she was neither discouraged nor hurt. Her European table manners returned to her; she ate without transferring her fork from her left hand to her right.

When they were ready for dessert, Martha rang the little china serving bell beside her place and nothing happened. As if it were customary for people to ring and have no one answer, they sat and waited. Eventually, Rachel put her head in at the pantry door and said, "The frogleg man."

"At this time of night!" Austin exclaimed. He felt in his change pocket and drew out fifty cents for Rachel. Then turning to Nora, he explained, "Mr. Barrett. We never know when he's coming, and if we don't take them, he won't come back any more. They're bullfrogs, and I suspect that he catches them with a flashlight, which is against the law, but . . ." The frogleg man carried them safely through the rest of the meal, on his eccentric back. When they left the table and returned to the living room, they discovered the fireplace had been smoking in their absence. Austin opened the windows and they sat coughing and shivering with the cold. The acrid smell of wood smoke reminded Nora of the time they kept smelling a strange odor in the plantation house at Howard's Landing. "It wasn't like any smell I've ever smelled before. It was dry and dusty, and a little like the smell of vinegar, and nobody could make out where it was coming from, until one day—" Austin left the room and Nora waited until he had come back with a big log in his hands before she went on and finished her story.

The log made the fire burn properly. The smoke went up the chimney instead of out into the room, and in time they were able to close the windows. The Kings and their two guests sat in a circle around the fire, and Austin, finding an appreciative audience, talked shop. Martha sat braiding the fringe of her shawl. Austin's stories about the involved litigations, lawsuit after lawsuit, of the picturesque Jouette family she had heard before. From time to time she pressed a yawn back into her throat and, exerting all the will-power at her command, kept from glancing at the clock. Lucy Beach contributed nothing to the conversation but her animated interest. Looking at her, one would have thought that a great many things were now being made clear to her that had not been clear before. Actually, she was planning in her mind what she would say to Alice when she got home. *Austin got started talking about the Law, and he talked very well. I wish you could have heard him. . . .*

Lucy sat and listened as long as Austin included her in the conversation. When he forgot to do this, she turned to Martha King and began to talk about a problem that had arisen in connection with the kindergarten.

"We have an arrangement with Rachel's son Eugene to come and start the fire in the stove so the rooms will be warm when the children get there. A couple of weeks ago I noticed that the chairs had been rearranged and the alphabet plates were on a different shelf of the cupboard from where I'd put them the day before. I didn't know whether to speak to Eugene or not. He's a very nice boy, and I didn't want to hurt his feelings. But soon after that, a piece of green paper was missing, and some of the crayons were broken. Something had to be done, so I went downtown an hour earlier one morning, and guess who the culprit was?"

"I can't guess," Martha said. "Who was it?"

"Thelma."

"What did you say to her?"

"What could I say to her," Lucy said, "except that if she came any more, I'd be forced to tell her mother about it."

What Lucy actually said was "Have you been coming here every morning, Thelma?"

Instead of answering, Thelma looked down at her own small black hands that had at last got her into serious trouble.

"You know that you shouldn't have used the crayons and paper without asking?"

Again no answer.

"And that I'll have to tell your mother on you?"

Still no answer.

With a long pole Lucy opened one of the windows at the top and let out some of the hot dry air in the room. When she had put the pole in the corner, she turned and said, "What will your mother do when I tell her?"

"Whip me."

"And do you want her to do that?"

"No, Miss Lucy."

"Well, I don't want her to, either. Now suppose you put your coat on and go home and we neither of us say anything about it. But I don't want you to come back here any more, do you understand?"

So contagious is remorse that Lucy said, "You can take this with you if you like," and presented Thelma with her own half-finished drawing of a woman in a garden, with shears and a basket full of flowers—poppies or anemones or possibly some flower that existed only in Thelma's mind. Shortly afterward, the children arrived, as noisy and active as birds, and took possession of the kingdom that was reserved for them.

Some dissatisfaction with her part in this scene, or with the circumstances which had obliged her to act as she did, kept Lucy from going into the particular details, which could have no interest, she felt, for Martha King. She turned her head so as not to miss what Austin was saying.

". . . so Father called old Mr. Seacord into his office and said, 'George, I want you to go down to the bank in Kaiserville and tell Fred Bremmer to look around and see if he can find that will anywhere. If an offer of two hundred acres of land will help him find it, you can make the offer in my name, and I don't care how you split the land between you.' The will was in Father's office by nine o'clock the next morning."

"How amazing," Nora said, and felt the world moving off on an entirely new orbit, from which it would very likely never return to pursue its usual path. She had had a vision during the past half-hour, and the way was now open to her. She would read, she would study, she would pass the bar examination with flying colors. She saw herself defending the innocent (who would otherwise be convicted of crimes they had no knowledge of), astounding old and learned judges with her irrefutable logic, the foremost woman lawyer in the state of Illinois, a partner in the firm of King and Potter.

Lucy looked down at her gold watch and exclaimed, "Why, we must go home! We've stayed much later than we should have. . . . Nora, I hate to talk about going when everybody is having such a good time, but we really must."

In the front hall, while Austin was helping Nora on with her coat, she said, "It's all so fascinating. I won't be able to sleep for thinking of the things you've told me." And Lucy said to Martha King, "It's so nice of you to ask us. As soon as Mother is over her little upset, you must come and have dinner with us. Then Alice can be in on it, too."

She carried her expectant look with her out into the November night.

16

The night of Martha King's dinner party, a traveler returned—a Negro with no last name. He came on a slow freight from Indianapolis. Riding in the same boxcar with him since noon were an old man and a fifteen-year-old boy and neither of them ever wanted to see him again. His eyes were bloodshot, his face and hands were gritty, his hair was matted with cinders. His huge, pink-palmed hands hung down out of the sleeves of a Mackinaw coat that was too small for him and filthy and torn. He had thrown away his only pair of socks two days before. There was a hole in the sole of his right shoe, his belly was empty, and the police were on the lookout for him in St. Louis and Cincinnati.

The shadow that the Negro met under the arc light at every cross street did not surprise him. He had seen it in too many back alleys where it is better to have no shadow at all, and he was a man who lived by surprising other people. When he came to Rachel's shack he stopped and looked up and down the street. Then he moved quietly up to the window. He stood there motionless for some time before he turned toward the door.

"Where's your Ma?"

The five frightened faces might just as well have been one. There was no variation in the degree or quality of terror.

"I asked you a question."

"She ain't home, Andy," Everitt said.

"That's mighty strange. I thought she'd be here tonight," he said, and closed the door. "She ain't expecting me?"

There was no answer.

"I don't call that much of a welcome," he said. "Your pappy come three hundred miles to see you, and they ain't none of you get up off their ass to welcome me home."

"We didn't know you was coming," Eugene said in a whisper. "You didn't send no word."

"So I got to send a notice to my own family before they condescends to receive me. I got to write them a letter say I be home on such and such a day, after I been away three whole years. Well, next time maybe I do that. And maybe I don't. Who's your Ma working for, these days? That same old white woman?"

"No," Eugene said.

"Where she work?"

"She work for the Kings," Everitt said.

"Huh? You don't say. She getting up in the world. Fast. Mighty fine clothes you all got, for niggers. Looks to me like you're well fed too. Mighty sleek. Looks to me like I come to the right place."

"I'll go tell her you're here," Thelma said.

"Another country heard from. You stay here. . . . Eugene, git up off of that couch and let your Pappy lie down. He's come a long way and he's tired. Your Ma fix me a little supper and then I'm going to sleep. I'm going to get in the bed and sleep for a week. Get up, you hear? Before I make you. You think you're grown, maybe, but you ain't grown enough. I show you. I show you right now."

What happened inside the shack was of no concern to the funeral basket, the two round stones, the coach lantern, and the coffeepot. They were merely the setting for a fancy-dress nightmare, not the actors. Evil moves about on two legs and has lines to speak, gestures that frighten because they are never completed. He can be blond, well bred, to all appearances gentle and kind. Or the eyes can be almond-shaped, the eyebrows plucked, the lids drooping. The hair can be kinky or curly or straight. Features and coloring are a matter of make-up, to be left to the individual actor, who can, if he likes, with grease paint and eyebrow pencil create the face of a friend. If the actor wears a turban or a loincloth, the dramatic effect will be heightened, provided of course that the audience is not also wearing turbans or loincloths. What is important is that Evil be understood, otherwise the scene will not act. The audience will not be able to decide which character is evil and which is the innocent victim. It is quite simple, actually. The one comes to grief through no fault of his own, knows what is being done to him, and does not lift a hand to defend himself from the blow. If he defends himself, he is not innocent. The other has been offered a choice, and has chosen Evil. If the audience and the actors both remember this, they will have no trouble following or acting out the play, which should begin, in any case, quietly, in a low key, suggesting an atmosphere of peace and security and love. The funeral basket, the two round stones, the rain-rotted carriage seat, the coach lantern, and the coffeepot are very good. And for a backdrop let there be a quiet street on a November night in a small midwestern town. A woman comes down the street toward an arc light at the foot of a hill. Under her arm she has a brown paper parcel containing scraps of leftover food. A colored woman, with her head down, her shoulders hunched, indicating that it is cold. If there is a wind-machine in the wings, the effect will be more realistic. There should be lights in the houses. The trees have shed their leaves. The woman stops suddenly and conveys to the audience by a look, by the absence of all expression, that a chill has passed over her which has nothing to do with the wind from the wings. She looks back at the arc light. And then she begins to run.

17

There was no reason why the ringing of the doorbell the following night should have made the hairs rise on the back of Austin's neck—unless he expected, when he opened the front door, to see the disembodied spirit that lived in the cellar, in the butler's pantry, and on the stairs.

"Oh," he said. "I couldn't imagine who it was. Come in, Nora."

"I saw your light," Nora said. "I won't stay but a minute. I know you're very busy."

"I brought some work home from the office," Austin said, as he closed the door. "How is Mrs. Beach?"

"She's feeling better," Nora said as she followed him into the study. "Cousin Austin, there's something that I want very much to talk to you about."

"Yes?"

"Something of the utmost importance. To me, I mean," she added, as she sat down in the chair Martha King used when she was doing her mending, and tucked her legs up under her skirt.

Austin's eyebrows rose, conveying both a question and a slight apprehensiveness.

"I spent the afternoon in the public library," she said, "reading Blackstone's *Commentaries.*"

This piece of information was delivered in such a way as to suggest that Nora expected Austin to be amazed by it. If he was amazed, his face failed to show it. He said, "Is that so?"

"I read the first forty-two pages," Nora said.

"What did you make of it?"

"There were lots of things I didn't understand," Nora said. "The language was new to me, but I found it very interesting. . . . Cousin Austin, do you think I could be a lawyer?"

"That's a hard question to answer."

"I know it is," Nora said, "and I don't expect you to tell me right off. I didn't know whether you'd even listen to the idea. Really I didn't. I thought, I'll tell him and then see what he—"

"Why should you want to be a lawyer, Nora, when there are other fields that are just as rewarding and much more—"

"Because it's the one thing that appeals to me," Nora said. "I know there are other things I *could* do, but I want something where I can do some good. All day I've hardly allowed myself to hope. I was afraid that if I did and then it turned out that there was no chance for me, the disappointment would be too—tell me this much: Do you think, knowing me as you do, that it's impossible?"

"It's not impossible," Austin said, "but on the other hand, it's not easy."

"Oh I know that," Nora said quickly.

"There was a girl in my class at Northwestern—quite a nice girl, as I remember. It was generally assumed that a girl in law school wouldn't last more than one semester, and as a matter of fact this girl did drop out. I never knew why or what became of her, but I do know that there are several women practicing law in this state. They may not have an easy time of it at first, but then nobody does. It all depends on how serious you are about wanting to do it, and whether you're willing to apply yourself. You'd have to work very hard for a long time. Otherwise there's no use even considering it."

"I'm very serious," Nora said. "Terribly serious. Something inside of me says I can do it. I know I can if you'll only help me. I wouldn't want to embarrass or inconvenience you, but would it be possible for me to come to your office in the afternoons and read there? For a short while, I mean. Just long enough for you to decide whether or not there is any use in my trying."

The case against women in the practice of law has been nobly expressed in an opinion by Chief Justice Ryan (39 Wis. page 352):

The law of nature destines and qualifies the female sex for the bearing and nurture of the children of our race and for the custody of the homes of the world and their maintenance in love and honor. And all life-long callings of women, inconsistent with these radical and sacred duties of their sex, as is the profession of the law, are departures from the order of nature; and when vol-

untary, treason against it. The cruel chances of life sometimes baffle both sexes, and may leave women free from the peculiar duties of their sex. These may need employment, and should be welcome to any not derogatory of their sex and its proprieties, or inconsistent with the good order of society. But it is public policy to provide for the sex, not for its superfluous members; and not to tempt women from the proper duties of their sex by opening to them duties peculiar to ours. There are many employments in life not unfit for the female character. The profession of law is surely not one of these. . . . Discussions are habitually necessary in courts of justice, which are unfit for female ears. The habitual presence of women at these would tend to relax the public sense of decency and propriety. If, as counsel threatened, these things are to come, we will take no voluntary part in bringing them about.

The habitual presence of women in courts of law was to come, even though Chief Justice Ryan took a voluntary part in preventing Miss Lavinia Goodell from practicing before the Supreme Court of the state of Wisconsin.

Nora's interest in the law had taken Austin by surprise and appeared to be rather sudden, but it was also true that she had a very good mind, clear and logical, except where her emotions were involved. The fact that she had plowed through forty pages of Blackstone was in itself remarkable. Very few women would have got past the first page. With help, and if she applied herself . . .

"Let me think about it, a day or two," he said. "Mr. Holby will be back in town on Tuesday. I'll talk the matter over with him. He may object to your being in the office, in which case—"

"If you only knew what it means to me," Nora said.

As she said good night, her face, under the porchlight, was transformed.

18

"If you want Nora near you," Martha said as she dealt herself a hand of solitaire.

"But that's not the point," Austin said. "I don't want her near me. I'm merely trying to help her. It will be something of an inconvenience having her in the office, day in and day out.

It means giving her a certain amount of my time, if she is going to make any progress—"

"Well, if you have the time, why not?"

"I don't have. I've never been entirely caught up since they were here last summer. And Mr. Holby does less and less. From a purely selfish point of view, there's no use even considering the idea. It's bound to cause a certain amount of talk, and it may lead to friction with Mr. Holby. Since I'm doing three-quarters of his work and he is taking sixty per cent of the profits of the firm, I suppose I shouldn't worry about exerting pressure on him."

"The person I'd worry about is Miss Ewing."

"I'm going to have a talk with him about that, too," Austin said. "The time has come when the percentage should be reversed. I'm going to insist on at least a fifty-fifty basis. . . . Why Miss Ewing?"

"I don't know but I rather imagine she won't like having another woman in the office, especially under the arrangement you're considering."

"She'll have to like it," Austin said. "In the old days I used to be able to come to you with problems that were bothering me, and we could talk them over. Now when I try to talk something over with you, you seem to resent it. I always understand things better after I've talked to you, and I often follow your suggestions."

"Not recently," Martha said, glancing over the rows of cards for a black ten that the nine of diamonds could go on.

"Maybe not recently," Austin said, "but that's because you have a kind of blind spot where Nora is concerned, and always have had. There's more at stake here than Nora. Every time a woman manages to break through the barrier of prejudice that keeps them out of the professions—"

"This interest in feminism is fairly recent with you, isn't it?"

"Not as recent as you think."

"Well in any case, this much I do know," Martha said, scooping the cards into a pile. "If you were a doctor, Nora would be spending her time poring over a medical dictionary and persuading the nurses to let her into the operating room at the hospital. And if you were a school teacher, she'd care terribly about education."

"You're not being fair to her."

"I'm being quite fair to Nora, and you're wrong in thinking I dislike her," Martha said. "I not only like Nora, I admire and respect her courage. The last three months can't have been easy for her. The person I am unfair to is you, Austin, because I know you want to be helpful, you want to help everybody, and instead of encouraging you to do that—after all, it's a perfectly natural desire—"

She began shuffling and reshuffling the cards, as if shuffling were all that there was to the game.

19

"Well, my boy," Mr. Holby said, "I'm glad you brought the subject up. It's time we gave it some consideration. I have a tendency to let things ride, as long as they seem to be going well, and it didn't occur to me that you might not be satisfied with the present arrangement."

"I'm not dissatisfied," Austin said, feeling, from Mr. Holby's tone of voice, and also a certain sadness in his manner, that Mr. Holby was not going to put up a fight; that his case was won. "It's just that when I came into the firm, it was with the understanding that someday—"

"I know," Mr. Holby said, nodding. "I realize all that, and I've been aware for some time that you were carrying perhaps a little more than your share of the burden. But that's what happens, of course. As a young man I went through the same thing, and charged it off to valuable experience, figuring that it would eventually correct itself—as, of course, it did. Part of it has been beyond my control. As you know, Mrs. Holby's health hasn't been any too good this last year. I'm quite worried about her. I wouldn't want anybody but you to know this, but I talk to you as if you were my own son. I've had to think about her more than I would have if she'd been as strong and active as most women of her age. I've had to take her to Hot Springs and other places that we hoped would do her good, which means, of course, spending a good deal of money, but these things come up in family life, and there's really no choice. They have to take precedence, for a time, over everything else. I'm telling you all this so you'll understand that it hasn't been just my own pleasures and desires that I've had to consider."

"Oh, I know that," Austin said quickly.

"As we get older, we tend to lean more on the younger men around us, to depend on their energy and willingness to see that the details are carried out, without which, of course, the maturer wisdom and judgment that come with age and that are concerned with broader matters would be seriously hampered. I fancy that an outside viewpoint would consider that the two just about cancel each other out. At least they make a very good working team. You've done extremely well for so young a man, and I'm confident that some day your name will mean as much, will command the same respect that your father's did. But it takes time, and you mustn't be impatient. It will all come to you, everything that you hope for and deserve in the way of recognition. I've done what I could to guide you and keep you from making rash mistakes, and I intend to go on giving you the benefit of my experience and knowledge, so that when the time comes that I have to step down and you have to carry on alone or with the help of some younger man, the ideals that the firm of Holby and King has always stood for will be ably represented. I look forward to that day, as I'm sure you do, too. Meanwhile, of course, there are other, more pressing matters to consider. In your eagerness to get ahead, I think you underestimate one or two angles of the situation. I'm the last man in the world to countenance an injustice. Not even for five minutes. My life has been dedicated to the cause of truth and fair play. People who complain that lawyers are interested only in their fee fail to take into consideration that the Law is the only profession whose aim is to correct the evils of society, defend the innocent, and see to it that the guilty are meted out their due punishment. Without the legal profession the world we live in would be chaos. In Law you have order, you have responsibility, you have decency, you have the only arrangement whereby society can function. It isn't enough to pass laws. They must be interpreted. One cause, one legal claim must be balanced against another. You and I, sitting in this room, cannot—and still be worthy of the name we call ourselves by—see the question of partnership in any but the broadest light. When I've been away from the office, it may have seemed to you that I was frittering away my time in social pleasures, enjoying the company and cultivation of time-honored associates, reaping my just rewards, probably, but nevertheless—and for the moment—allowing my mind to be diverted from the work that lies waiting for me this very minute on my desk. I wouldn't blame you if you had thought that. It would be a very natural mistake for you to make under the circumstances. The truth of the matter is that my mind is never idle. I am continually deliberating and meditating upon some legal problem, so that when the time comes and the decision must be made, I have covered the whole question, every crack and cranny of it, and am ready to act. In a world where people are continually acting on some blind impulse, never stopping to consider what is the wise, what is the right course to pursue, the intellectual faculties are not always given their due, but without them where would we be? What hope would there be for mankind? On the one hand, you'd have barbarism and ruthless aggression, on the other, slavery. Someone must digest, must ponder and weigh the consequences, study the causes, give thought to the ultimate values that must never be lost sight of, and dismiss those considerations that are trivial or misleading, that are mere side issues. Now as things stand, I find myself in agreement with you about the division of profits of this firm—that an equal sharing, even though it tends to set a valuation on certain qualities that cannot in the very nature of things be evaluated, is reasonable and fair. Or if not precisely and mathematically so, then it will so soon become that way that we ought to feel ourselves free to anticipate the future, and even to do this with a certain amount of confidence that we are acting properly. I say 'as things stand.'

"A short time ago you mentioned to me the possibility of taking a young woman into the office—Miss Potter—with the understanding that she would read and prepare herself for the bar examination. It is perhaps a rather radical departure from what is customary, but even so, I have no objection. I believe, as I'm sure you know, that conditions change, that we must abide by the Law of Progress in so far as we can interpret it. I'm sure you have looked into Miss Potter's qualifications thoroughly and would not countenance such a step if she were lacking in the requisite mentality. And I appreciate also that, in view of your association with her family, you would want to offer her any assistance that lies in your power. But I hope you have also considered what it means to the firm. She will require desk space, it will put an added burden on Miss Ewing, who is already overworked. And if Miss Potter is to advance with any speed toward her goal, she will require a great deal of your time and guidance. So much of each, in fact, that it seems to me quite to upset the balancing of values, yours and mine, that we were just now speaking of. If you want to have her here, I am willing to withdraw any objections I might have to it, with the understanding that, for the time at least—I don't mean that the question of division of profits cannot be reopened in the future, you understand—until we see how this new arrangement works out, I feel that it is better to let things ride along the way they have been going. I leave it entirely up to you, my boy. Whatever you decide will be satisfactory with me."

PART FIVE

The Province of Jurisprudence

I

Of the literary arts, the one most practiced in Draperville was history. It was informal, and there was no reason to write it down since nothing was ever forgotten. The child born too soon after the wedding ceremony might learn to walk and to ride a bicycle; he might go to school and graduate into long pants, marry, move to Seattle, and do well for himself in the lumber business; but whenever his or his mother's name was mentioned, it was followed inexorably by some smiling reference to the circumstances of his birth. No one knew what had become of the energetic secretary of the Chamber of Commerce who organized the Love-Thy-Neighbor-As-Thyself parade, but they knew why he left town shortly afterward, and history doesn't have to be complete. It is merely a continuous methodical record of events. These events can be told in chronological order but that isn't necessary, any more than it is necessary for the historians to be concerned with cause and effect. Research in Draperville was carried on over the back fence, by telephone, in kitchens and parlors and upstairs bedrooms, in the back seat of carriages, in wicker porch swings, in the bell tower of the Unitarian Church, where the Willing Workers met on Wednesdays and patiently, with their needles and thread, paid off the mortgage on the parsonage.

The final work of shaping and selection was done by the Friendship Club. The eight regular members of this club were the high practitioners of history. They met in rotation at one another's houses for luncheon and bridge. The food that they served was competitive and unwise, since many of them were struggling to maintain their figures. After the canned lobster or crabmeat, the tunafish baked in shells, the chicken patties, the lavish salads, the New York ice cream (all of which they would regret later), the club members settled down to bridge, with their hats on and their shoes pushed off under the card table, their voices rising higher and higher, their short-range view of human events becoming crueler and more malicious as they doubled and redoubled one another's bids, made grand slams, and quarreled over the scoring. No reputation was safe with them, and only by being present every time could they hope to preserve their own. The innocent were thrown to the wolves, the kind made fun of, the old stripped of the dignity that belonged to their years. *They say* was the phrase invariably used when a good name was about to be auctioned off at the block. *They say that before Dr. Seymour married her she was running around with . . . They say the old lady made him promise before she died that he'd never . . . They say she has cancer of the breast. . . .*

If you come upon footprints and blood on the snow, all you have to do is turn and follow the pink trail back into the woods. You may have to walk miles, but eventually you will come to the clearing where hoofprints and footprints, moving in a circle, tell of the premeditated murder of a deer. You can follow a brook to the spring that is its source. But there is no tracing *They say* back to the person who said it originally.

They say Ed came home one afternoon when he was not expected and found her and Mr. Trimbull . . . They say old Mr. Green went to him and said either you marry Esther or . . . They say that Harvey had a brother who was in an institution in Fairfield and that he kept it from Irene until their second child was born. . . .

The flayed landscape of the western prairie does little to remind the people who live there of the covenant of works or the covenant of grace. The sky, visible right down to the horizon, has a diminishing effect upon everything in the foreground, and the distance is as featureless and remote as the possibility of punishment for slander. The roads run straight, with death and old age intersecting at right angles, and the harvest is stored in cemeteries.

They say Tom went right over and made her pack up her things and leave. They haven't any of them spoken to Lucile since. . . . They say he drinks like a fish. . . . They say it was all Mr. Tierney's brother's fault. While he was visiting them he came down with a mild case of diphtheria and their little girl—such a pretty child—caught it from him.

By December, the historians had gathered together all the relevant facts about Austin King's young cousin from Mississippi, knew that she was madly in love with him, and were not surprised when he took her into his office. The historians called on Mrs. Beach with gifts of wine jelly and beef broth, and when they met Nora on the street with the children, they stopped her and asked questions that appeared to be friendly but that were set and ready to spring, like a steel trap. The historians were kind to Miss Ewing, and they remembered that Martha King (whose side they were on) was very careless about repaying social obligations and when asked to join the Women's Club had declined on the grounds that she didn't have time. This ancient border skirmish, nearly forgotten in the light of more recent improprieties, was resurrected detail by detail with appropriate comments (*If I have time, with three children, and Sam's mother living with us . . .*), as fresh as if it had happened yesterday.

What is the chief end of Man? the historians might well have asked over the bridge tables, but they didn't. When they met as a group, they slipped all pity off under the table with their too-tight shoes and became destroyers, enemies of society and of their neighbors, bent on finding out what went on behind the blinds that were drawn to the window sill.

They say . . . they say . . . from quarter of one till five o'clock, when the scores were tallied; the prize brought out, unwrapped, and admired; and Jess Burton, Bertha Rupp, Alma Hinkley, Ruth Troxell, Elsie Hubbard, Genevieve Wilkinson, Irma Seifert, and Leona McLain tucked their hand-painted scorecards into their pocketbooks to give to their children, slipped on their torturesome pumps, and went home full of news to tell their husbands at the supper table.

2

"What?" Nora asked, looking up from *Province of Jurisprudence Determined.*

"I said I hope my typewriter doesn't disturb you," Miss Ewing said.

"Oh, no." Nora said. "I wasn't even aware of it. Please, you mustn't worry about me, or I'll feel I oughtn't to be here."

"Some people find it very disturbing until they get accustomed to the sound," Miss Ewing said. "Do you find jurisprudence interesting?"

"What?" Nora asked, looking up once more. "Oh yes. Very."

"I noticed you're wearing a sweater today. It's a good idea if you're going to sit so near the window. With an old building like this, there are always all kinds of drafts, and if there's one thing I can't stand, it's a draft down the back of my neck. The janitor said he'd do something about stuffing the cracks with paper, but of course he hasn't. I'll have to speak to him again about it."

"That's very kind of you," Nora said, "but please don't bother. I'm quite comfortable, really I am. All I need is a good light to read by."

"You find the light all right there?"

"Oh yes."

"These dark winter days, I usually turn the lights on at three-thirty or quarter of four, but if you'd prefer to have it earlier, just say so."

"I will," Nora said, without looking up this time.

"You don't want to strain your pretty eyes, reading that fine print," Miss Ewing said, as the typewriter commenced thrashing.

The telephone rang, clients came and went, with a curious glance for the desk at the window, where a red-haired girl sat reading with her chin resting in her hand. The mailman walked in, on his afternoon rounds, handed the bundle of mail to Miss Ewing, and said, "I see they've finally taken pity on you and given you an assistant."

"Not exactly," Miss Ewing said, as she paid him two cents postage due on a long thin letter. Though she usually took the mail from him and sent him on his way, this afternoon she kept him for five minutes with questions about his mother, who was ailing, of what disease neither the doctor nor the mailman could say. The ancient filing cabinet made a grinding noise every time Miss Ewing pulled out one of the drawers.

At three-thirty Miss Ewing said, "I'm going to take Mr. Holby's dictation. Do you think you can manage all right?"

"Yes, thank you," Nora said.

While Miss Ewing was in Mr. Holby's office, a man came in, looked around hesitantly, coughed, and said, "I beg your pardon, Miss—"

Nora looked up and said. "Oh, excuse me. Did you want to see Mr. King?"

"Well, as a matter of fact," the man said, "I came to see Mr. Holby. On business."

"Just a minute," Nora said. "I'll see if he—"

"You're new around here, aren't you? I'm Will Avery."

"I'll tell him you're here, Mr. Avery," Nora said. She knocked timidly on Mr. Holby's door and Miss Ewing opened it, with her notebook in her hand.

"There's someone who—" Nora began.

"Mr. Holby doesn't like to be interrupted when he's giving dictation," Miss Ewing said. "Oh, hello, Mr. Avery. Would you like to see Mr. Holby? Just go right in."

As she sat down at her desk Nora said, "He asked to see Mr. Holby, and I didn't know what to do, so I—"

"It's quite all right," Miss Ewing said. "There's bound to be some confusion at first. I just thought I'd better tell you so you'd know, after this, not to interrupt him."

Will Avery left the door open as he went in, and Nora was able to hear the entire discussion of whether Mr. Holby should slap a sheriff's notice on the family who lived over the billiard parlor and were three months in arrears with their rent. When Will Avery got up to go, Mr. Holby accompanied him as far as the stairs, and then came over to see what Nora was reading.

"An extremely important subject for you to grasp," Mr. Holby said. "It involves the larger concepts of the Law, which all of us must keep straight in our minds, even when we are dealing with the most petty concerns. The human race—suppose we conceive of it in this way—the human race is parceled out into a number of distinct groups or societies, differing greatly in—shall we say—circumstances, in physical and moral characteristics of all kinds. But you will find that they all resemble each other in that they reveal, on closer examination, certain rules of—if you like—*conduct*, in accordance with which the relations of the members *inter se* are governed. Each society naturally has its own laws, its own system of laws, its own *code*, as we say. And all the systems, so far as they are known, constitute the appropriate subject matter of jurisprudence.

"The jurist may deal with it in the following ways: He may first of all examine the main conceptions found in all the systems, or in other words"—Mr. Holby raised his voice so that it would carry above the sound of the typewriter—"define the leading terms common to them all. For example, the terms *law*, *right*, *duty*, *property*, *crime*, and so on and so forth, which, or their equivalents, may . . ." The filing cabinet slammed shut. ". . . may, notwithstanding certain delicate differences of connotation, be regarded as common terms in all systems. That kind of inquiry is known as analytical jurisprudence. It regards the conceptions we've been talking about as fixed or stationary, and aims at expressing them clearly and distinctly and showing their logical relations with each other. What do we really mean by a *right* and by a *duty*—" The harsh overhead light went on. Mr. Holby, startled, turned and looked at the light fixture, and then, turning back to Nora, he said, "Where was I?—oh, yes—what is really meant by a *right* and by a *duty*, and what is the underlying connection between a *right* and a *duty* are types of questions proper to this inquiry. Now suppose we shift our point of view. Regarding systems of law in the mass—do you follow me?" Nora nodded. "—we may consider them not as stationary but as changeable and changing. If we do that, we may ask what general features are exhibited by the record of the change. This, somewhat crudely put, may serve to indicate the field of historical or comparative jurisprudence. In its ideal condition it would require— Come into the office, my dear, where we won't disturb Miss Ewing."

3

Martha King, her movements heavy and slow, went back and forth between the dining room and the kitchen, stacking the breakfast dishes. This can't go on, she said to herself. I'm going to have it out with her when she comes. She can either turn up in the morning when she's supposed to or—

There were footsteps outside, and Rachel pushed the back door open. Her eyes were bloodshot and doleful. She looked around at the confusion in the kitchen without seeing it, and then took her coat and stocking cap off and hung them on a nail beside the door.

"Now don't you worry about me being late, Mrs. King. I'll just do these dishes and get to the upstairs."

Martha's anger had deserted her at the sight of Rachel's face. In a helpless silence she turned and lit the gas under the coffeepot and then said, "Are you sick, Rachel?"

"No'm," Rachel said, "I'm not."

"You'd better have a cup of coffee with me. It may make you feel better."

Sitting across the kitchen table from her, Martha said nothing and let Rachel drink her coffee in peace. Day after day when she looked around her and found nowhere the strength to begin, it was Rachel who gave her a push—by encouragement, by example, by insisting (just as she was being sucked down in a whirlpool of things undone) *Now you leave that to me*. In exchange for four dollars a week, Rachel took the mop out of her hand and sometimes the weight off her heart. When the house seemed large and lonely, all she had to do was to go to the kitchen. Rachel was never disapproving, never surprised by anything that Martha King said or did. Her occasional bad moods had nothing to do with the woman she worked for, any more than Martha King's moods had anything to do with Rachel. But in spite of the freedom which they allowed each other, Rachel could say, *Now don't you feel blue, Mrs. King*, or *You're making things out worse than they are*, and Martha King could not.

"I won't ask you if you're in trouble," she said aloud. "I don't need to ask. I've never pried into your affairs, but you know that you can come to me, don't you, if you need help?"

"I know," Rachel said, but she did not explain why she sat with her shoulders hanging limp and heavy and her feet twisted under the chair, or why she looked old and frightened.

"There's been many a time," Martha said, turning and looking out of the window, "when you've helped me."

"It's not that kind of trouble," Rachel said.

Martha King finished her coffee in silence. Rachel got up and carried the cups and saucers to the sink, and began to dispose of the orange peels and eggshells that Martha had left there in the hurry of getting Austin to his office and Ab ready for kindergarten. Martha pushed her chair back and started for the pantry door.

"Would it be all right," Rachel said, above the sound of the running water, "if I was to keep Thelma here when she's not in school?"

This request ought to have made the whole thing as clear as daylight, and perhaps would have, if it hadn't been for the great pane of glass, which kept one part of Elm Street from knowing what the other part was up to. Even so, the gulf that separated Rachel and Martha King was not a simple matter. It was more than the difference between the front and back door. Rachel's trouble was something that Martha King would never have to cope with. She was protected by the thousand and one provisions in the code of respectability, and had been, from the moment she was born. Her husband took out his anger against her by straightening pictures and turning off lights that had been left burning in empty rooms. He carried a pearl-handled pocketknife, not a razor, and he used it to sharpen pencils with.

And it was not fear of the razor that made Rachel look old. She had been born and raised in the knowledge of it. It was the way his eyes followed Thelma, the fact that his cuffs and kicks were for the boys, never for her; the thick softness in his voice when he spoke to her; the idea that had formed in that low black skull, as simple and easy as death.

"Why, yes," Martha King said. "Of course it'll be all right. Keep her here as much as you like." And pushing the door open, she went on into the front part of the house.

4

"Here, puss . . . Here, puss, puss, puss . . . Here puss. . . ."

Leaning over the railing of her second story porch, Miss Ewing looked up and then down the alley. Though she called and called, the big yellow tomcat did not come. "I can't wait any longer," she said to herself out loud. "I'm late enough as it is," and went back into the kitchen, locked and bolted the back door, and put the saucer of milk in the icebox. This was not the first time that the cat had failed to come when she called, and it could just look after itself until she got home.

Left to her own devices, Miss Ewing would never have taken on the care and responsibility of an animal. This one had adopted her. One autumn night when she got home from work, the cat, half-starved, was sitting on her front steps. She stopped to stroke it and the cat purred at her touch. It sat so quiet, so gentle, and so trustful that she toyed with the idea of keeping it, and then after a moment said, "Go home, pussy!" and went on up the stairs to her flat. Ten minutes later she hurried down and opened the street door. The cat was still there, and bounded up the steps after her as lightly and eagerly as a kitten.

She let the cat out every morning when she left for work and when she got home in the evening it was there waiting for her. She learned (or thought she learned) its habits and the cat learned hers. It was company, it was someone to talk to and worry over, and it was, in spite of its condition when she found it, a very superior creature. After she had fed it a few weeks it filled out and became quite handsome. But then it took to wandering, and she never knew whether it would be there or not when she was hurrying home. Sometimes it was gone for two or three days. And one morning when she opened the back door, she saw something that caused her to let out a low moan. What she took at first sight to be the pieces of a cat—*though not her cat*—proved to be something else; a section of bloody fur, a piece of raw red flesh, and the hideous dismembered tail of a rat. The cat, having eaten all the rest, had left these three pieces on Miss Ewing's porch in front of her back door, to chill her with horror (or perhaps as a mark of friendship and favor). And after that terrible and instructive sight Miss Ewing could not pet the cat or hold it on her lap or feel toward it as she had before. She continued to feed it, and the cat, accepting the change in her, came and went as it pleased.

Miss Ewing's flat was in a row of identical two-story buildings a block from the railroad. It was dark in the daytime and larger than she needed. It would have been too large for her except that she had crammed into it most of the furniture that had once been scattered through a house on Fourth Street, leaving herself barely enough room to move around in. As an only child, Miss Ewing had inherited everything, including, for about fifteen years, the problem of supporting her parents, both of whom were now dead. In the front room there were two large, oval, tinted photographs under convex glass of her mother as a young woman and of her father before he took to drink.

Ordinarily it was easy for her to get to the office of Holby and King, dust and arrange the two desks in the inner offices, and be at her typewriter when Austin King walked in. But for over a week now, she had found it harder and harder to get up in the morning. She heard the alarm clock go off and lay in bed unable to move, unable to lift her head from the pillow, exhausted by the effort of producing plays and parts of plays in which the characters changed roles with one another and spoke lines that were intended to make the audience laugh (although the play was a tragedy), and the dead came back to life, and everything took place in a half-real, half-mythical kingdom against a backdrop of pastel sorrow. The cat figured frequently in Miss Ewing's dreams. So did her mother. And so, in one disguise or another, did Nora Potter.

When Miss Ewing went to work for the firm of King and Holby she understood, without having to be told, that the big calf-bound books that lined the walls of the outer and inner offices were not to be taken down and read by her. She could copy deeds and abstracts to her heart's content. She had the run of the filing cabinet. She could take dictation, and she could put in long-distance telephone calls and say (sometimes to Springfield, sometimes to Chicago), "Just a minute please, Mr. Holby calling . . ."

Miss Ewing knew as much about mortgages, wills, transfers, property rights, bills of sale, clearance papers—all the actual everyday functioning of a law office—as the average attorney ever needs to know. With a little reading on the side, she might have been admitted to practice, along with Miss Lavinia Goodell; but instead she had chosen to dedicate her energies to the best interests of the firm of King and Holby, and later, the firm of Holby and King. She not only knew all their clients by name, but also where the income of these clients was derived from and among what relatives their property would be divided when the undertaker had made away with the mortal remains. She knew what Austin King thought of Mr. Holby and what Mr. Holby thought of Austin King. She knew who (in all probability) killed Elsie Schlesinger on the night of October 17th, 1894. The only thing Miss Ewing didn't know was how to drive Nora Potter out of the office, how to send her weeping down the stairs.

She interrupted Nora's reading whenever she had a free moment to do this in. She took delight in leaving the door into the hall open so that, although a cold draft blew around her own ankles, it also blew around Nora's. She found a black velvet bow and holding it between her thumb and forefinger as if it were unclean, deposited it in the wastebasket. She spoke one day with a Southern accent and instead of appreciating the true nature of this pleasantry, Nora smiled at her and said, "Why Miss Ewing, you're beginning to talk like a Southerner just from being around me." Nora offered to stamp and seal envelopes when Miss Ewing's desk was inundated with outgoing correspondence. Nora said, "Can't I do some typing for you, Miss Ewing? I can only use two fingers but that won't matter, will it?" Nora said, "Can't I help you with that old filing?" Nora said, "If you'd like me to, Miss Ewing, I'll . . ." Day after day Nora was kind and thoughtful and cheerful and pleasant and friendly in a way that no one (if you exclude the cat Miss Ewing could no longer bear to touch) had ever been. And perhaps it was this as much as anything that made Miss Ewing wake up so tired in the morning.

In her hurry to get as much work as possible done and out of the way before one-thirty, she made mistakes. She filed papers away in the wrong folders, she found sentences in her shorthand notebook that she could not decipher, she left a whole clause out of a contract that Austin King had given her to copy. When he pointed this out to her, she flushed, mumbled excuses, and retired to the outer office to copy the whole thing over. This time, she inserted the carbon paper the wrong way so one of the carbon copies had the same words on the back, inverted, and the other was a clean white page. As it drew nearer and nearer to one-thirty, Miss Ewing's eyes kept turning to the clock. Her hands were clammy and moist, and she had to wipe them continually. She was short with the wrong people and patient with people whose reasons for climbing the stairs were dubious. But when one-thirty came, and Nora walked in, there was an abrupt change. Composed, patronizing, ironical, Miss Ewing looked up from her typewriter and said, "Good afternoon, Miss Potter. What is it to be today—Blackstone or Sir James Maine?"

5

The bed creaked in the room across the hall and then a voice answered, "Yes, Alice, what is it?"

"Are you awake?"

"Well, I'm talking to you. I suppose I'm awake. What is it?"

"I thought I heard something."

"In Mother's room?"

"No, downstairs. It sounded like somebody walking around down there. Did you lock the back door?"

"Yes. Go to sleep."

In the summer night such marauders as are about—the night insects, the rabbit nibbling clover on the lawn, the slug sucking the iris blade—all go about their work of destruction in a single-minded silence. Sleep is disturbed not by noises but by the moonlight on the bedroom floor. But in the late fall and early winter, especially before the snow comes, there is a time of terror when field mice, rats, and squirrels, driven indoors by the cold, make ratching-scratching sounds inside the walls; the stairs creak; some part of the house settles a thousandth of an inch (the effect of a dead man's curse or a witch in the neighborhood); and people whose dreams are too active wake and hear sounds that (so the pounding in their left side tells them) have been made by a prowler.

"If it *is* somebody," Alice Beach said, "they probably won't come upstairs where we are. They'll probably just take the silver and leave. That's what I'd do if I were a burglar."

"Oh, Alice, you're so silly. There isn't anybody downstairs."

They both held their breath and listened, with their hearts constricted by fear, the pulse in their foreheads beating against the pillow.

"Sh—sh—"

"Very well," Lucy said. "I'm going downstairs and find out what it is. Otherwise you'll keep me awake all night."

"Oh, Lucy, please! *Please* don't! It isn't safe!"

"Fiddlesticks!"

The light went on in the room across the hall and Alice got up out of bed also, put her dressing gown on, and followed Lucy to the head of the stairs. The light at the foot of the stairs went on, then the light in the parlor, in the dining room, the kitchen, the laundry. With every light in every room of the whole downstairs turned on, Lucy Beach opened the door to the basement and stood at the head of the cobwebbed stair, waiting. The cause of their disturbance was not there.

It is never easy to live under the same roof with someone in love. Even when the secret is known to all and can be openly joked about, there is something in the atmosphere that promotes restlessness. If the family is divided into those who know and those who don't know and mustn't under any circumstances find out, then instead of restlessness there is a continual strain, the lamps do not give off their usual amount of light, the drinking water tastes queer, the cream turns sour with no provocation. The conspirators avoid each other's eyes, take unnecessary precautions, and read double meanings into remarks that under normal circumstances they would not even hear. The person they are doing their best to protect keeps giving the secret away. Now on one pretext, now on another the cat is continually let out of the bag and it is then up to those who know about this animal to rush immediately and corner it before the fatal damage is done.

"You see?" Lucy said, and closed and locked the cellar door. Turning out lights as they went, they found themselves at last in the front hall. Lucy opened the door of the coat closet, where a man could have been hiding among the raincoats and umbrellas. "Now if you're satisfied," she said, "we can go back to bed."

6

"I know you're busy, Mr. King," Miss Ewing said, "but Mr. Holby has someone in his office and I thought—if you could give me a minute, that is. I— If you don't mind, I'll close the door."

Austin had given her a great many minutes without her feeling any need to ask apologetically for them, and her manner now was so hesitant, so deeply troubled that he motioned her to a chair. Miss Ewing sat and twisted her handkerchief and at last said, "I haven't been feeling well lately. The doctor tells me I ought to take a rest."

"The office is very busy just now," Austin said, "but I guess we can manage somehow. We don't want you to get down sick. How much time do you plan to take off? A week? Two weeks?"

"I'm afraid it would have to be longer," Miss Ewing said. "I know this is a hard time for you, and I don't like to do it, Mr. King, but Dr. Seymour thinks I ought to give up my job entirely."

"I'm sorry to hear that," Austin said, neither his voice nor his expression conveying an adequate amount of regret. It takes time to accept a catastrophe, and in the face of the first intimation that the golden age of Miss Ewing had come to an end he was almost cheerful.

"I'm sorry to have to tell you," she said. "I thought maybe I could keep on a while longer anyway, but I haven't been sleeping at all well and—"

"It's not a question of money, is it? Because if it's a question of money, I'd be glad to speak to Mr. Holby about a raise for you. I'm sure it could be arranged."

"No," Miss Ewing said. "It isn't that. You and Mr. Holby have always been generous with me. More than generous. It's just that I'm getting along in years and I don't seem to be able to stand the work I used to. My mind is tired, and it makes me so nervous when things don't go just right—when I make mistakes."

Austin searched his conscience for some mild reprimand, some abrupt or impatient gesture that might have hurt Miss Ewing's feelings.

"I'll never forget how good your father was to me when I first came to work here. I was just a girl and I didn't know anything about law or office work. He used to get impatient and lose his temper and shout at other people, but with me he was always so considerate. He was more like a friend than an employer."

Austin nodded sympathetically. What she said was not strictly true and Miss Ewing must know that it was not true.

His father had often lost his temper at Miss Ewing. Her high-handed manner with people that she considered unimportant and her old-maid ways had annoyed Judge King so that he had, a number of times, been on the point of firing her. He couldn't fire her because she was indispensable to the firm, and what they had between them was more like marriage than like friendship. But there is always a kind of truth in those fictions which people create in order to describe something too complicated and too subtle to fit into any conventional pattern.

"He was a wonderful man," Miss Ewing said. "There'll never be anybody like him."

Austin's glance strayed to the papers on his desk and then returned to Miss Ewing. "When would you want to leave?" he asked.

"As soon as possible."

"I'm afraid there are a good many things that Mr. Holby and I don't know about. We've leaned so heavily upon your experience and knowledge of the firm. If you could stay on a few weeks, say until the new girl is broken in."

"Oh I expected to do that," she said eagerly. "The way things are now, I'm the only one who—"

She stopped talking and looked at him with such a strange pleading in her eyes that, half in fright, he started to get up out of his chair.

"Mr. King, I'm not the person you think I am. You shouldn't have trusted me. I've done something I never thought I'd do. Something so . . ."

What was left of her ordinary self-composure gave way entirely and she began to cry and to tell him that she had done terrible things, so terrible that he'd have to put her in jail for it. From her hysterical confession he could make out only one incredible fact—Miss Ewing had stolen money from the firm. How much he couldn't discover, but apparently it had been going on for over a year. First, small sums from the cash box. Then she had forged his and Mr. Holby's signatures and in that way withdrawn considerable sums from the bank, which her knowledge of bookkeeping had enabled her to conceal.

"If you had come to me and told me that you needed money," Austin said.

"I didn't need it. I don't know why I took it. At first I just wanted to see if I could, as a kind of game, I guess. And when I found out how easy it was to deceive you and Mr. Holby, I went on doing it. If Judge King had been alive I wouldn't have dared. He'd have guessed somehow. But you kept coming in, day after day, always the same, always trusting me, and I couldn't stand it any more. I just had to tell you and get it over with before I went crazy. You don't know what it's like to have something gnawing at your conscience day and night. No peace of mind, no rest, until finally you think everybody knows and is just waiting to catch you at it. Anything, even going to jail, is better than the worry you go through in your own mind. I hope you never know. But that's what you have to do with someone like me—call the police and have them take me away. . . ."

She broke into a fresh storm of weeping, and Austin got up from his chair and went around the desk and put his hands on her thin shoulders to comfort her.

"Please don't!" she exclaimed, shaking herself free. "I don't deserve kindness, and I can't stand it. I can't stand anything more."

Austin left her weeping in the chair that was reserved for people who came to inquire into their rights under the Law, and went out into the outer office and called a cab. When it came, Miss Ewing put her hat and coat on, and took one last wild hopeless look at her cluttered desk. Austin helped her down the stairs and told the Mathein boy who was driving his father's hack to take her home. Then he went back into his office, closed the door, and called Dr. Seymour.

In his excitement, while he was talking over the telephone, there was a certain hardness—the hardness of triumph. All these years Miss Ewing had rubbed his nose in the fact that he was not the man his father was. And how the mighty were fallen! But he said, "She's put in many years of faithful service, and if she's sick—she'd never have behaved this way otherwise—naturally we'll take care of her"; and so preserved that inner image, the icon that no one, kind or unkind, is ever willing to change.

7

"Why my darling!" Martha King exclaimed as she lifted Ab onto her lap. "My precious angel! Nobody can ever take your place, not even for one solitary second!"

Ab's tears were stopped by the quick comfort of softness and her mother's "There, there . . ." When she sat up she was smiling.

"Where will the baby sleep? Will the baby sleep in my room?"

"If you'd like it to," Martha said. With her hand she brushed Ab's bangs back from her high forehead and then, bending down, kissed the soft place where the bones had long since grown together.

When Ab left her to go and play, Martha got up from her chair and went over to the window seat and the pile of mending. Rachel had failed to show up, that morning, and Martha King was weighed down by a premonition. The tangle of socks, the shirt collar that needed turning, remained untouched. For over an hour she sat with her forehead against the window, looking out on the driveway and the house next door, on the kitchen pump and the mulberry tree now stripped of both leaves and fruit.

What she thought of, sitting there all that time, she could not have told later. She saw a leaf dropping, people passing on the sidewalk, the grey overcast Saturday. But all this was out of any time sequence and often part of a long chain of ideas and images that seemed to have no connection with each other and that led nowhere. There is a country where women go when they are pregnant, a country with no king and no parliament. The inhabitants do nothing but wait, and the present does not exist on any calendar; only the future, which may or may not come. Yet something is accomplished there, even so, and that inescapable tax which in the outside world is collected once every lunar cycle, in blood, is forgiven and remains in the hands of the taxpayer.

The castle in which all are confined is surrounded by a moat fed by underground springs. There are no incoming and outgoing heralds, no splendor falls on the castle walls. The windows are narrow slits looking out through stone upon a landscape of the palest colors. The view from the highest turret is always the same, except that sometimes there is no view at all.

The inhabitants of the castle are often seized with cramps and vomiting. They are extravagantly hungry one moment and without appetite the next. Consistency is not required of them. Eccentric woolgatherers, in summer they huddle each one beside an ornamental stove that is always lit and there for her alone. In winter they put their arms through the slits in the stone walls and feel the warm rain. Emotions are drowsy, remembered, and vague. Bitterness, hatred, and fear are watered and tended and turned so that they can grow evenly, and then are forgotten before they have a chance to flower. Intending becomes pretending. The children's voices that are heard occasionally are not the voices of children who will grow up and marry and beget more children but those of Cain and Abel quarreling over the possession of a tricycle or a rubber ball.

Now and then someone tries to escape from the country but this is difficult. There is bound to be trouble at the frontier. The roads, although policed, are not safe after dark. People are robbed of the calcium in their bones, and of their life's savings in dreams. The featureless landscape turns out to be littered with dirty things, maggots crawling, disgusting amoebae that move and have hairy appendages, or the bloated body of a dead animal.

A sound outside made Martha King turn in time to see Mr. Porterfield wheeling his bicycle up the brick driveway. As she opened the kitchen door, her eyes traveled to the note in his right hand.

The Reverend Mr. Porterfield was a slight, neatly dressed Negro of uncertain age. His hands and face were grave, his manner (neither obsequious nor race-proud nor quick to see insult where no insult is intended) a model for white people to follow in dealing with black. Every Sunday evening, from the platform of the African Methodist Episcopal Church, he justified the ways of God to his congregation, and when they were in trouble they came to him for help.

"I don't know what I'm going to do without her," Martha

said, after she had finished reading Rachel's note. "Is she all right?"

"Yes, ma'am."

"She didn't say where she was going or what her plans were?"

"Well, no," he said carefully. "She requested me to deliver the message to you and I said I would. But where she was going she didn't exactly say."

"I see," Martha said. "Won't you come inside? It's very cold out today."

"Thank you, ma'am, but I have to be getting on downtown."

As he righted his bicycle Martha said, "Did she take the children with her?"

"Oh, yes," Mr. Porterfield said. "Yes, she took the children."

"Well, if you hear anything from her . . ."

"Be glad to. If I hear anything, I'll certainly inform you of it. . . . Good day, ma'am, and remember me to Mr. King."

He knows and he won't tell me, Martha King thought as she watched him wheel his bicycle down the driveway. She started back into the house and then hesitated. Her eyes took in the icebox and the accumulation of things destined for the barn loft, as if somewhere—behind the mildewed print of the U.S.S. *Maine*, perhaps, or in the box of tarnished evening slippers—was hidden the disturbing reason for Rachel's conduct, why she trusted Mr. Porterfield and not Martha King.

8

"Wait till I get there, Nora," Alice Beach called out from her room, where she was getting dressed.

"We're waiting," Nora called back. "I haven't told them a thing."

Each evening when she came home from the office of Holby and King, she brought life and excitement not only into the Beaches' gloomy house but also into the even gloomier sickroom. The atmosphere of illness had had to give way before it. The invalid's eyes were bright with curiosity, and she had permitted Nora and Lucy, as a mark of special favor, to sit on her bed.

"Austin asked me if I'd come back this evening and help out. They've been searching all afternoon long for somebody's will. Apparently Miss Ewing had her own system of filing and—"

"You are too telling them!" Alice called out.

"No, I'm not," Nora said. "Nobody can figure out what it is. The whole place is turned upside down, Mr. Holby is leaving for Chicago in the morning, and poor Cousin Austin—"

"Now," Alice said coming into the room. From the color in her cheeks, the eager expression on her face, she might have been expecting a gentleman caller.

"Miss Ewing's mother used to sew for me," Mrs. Beach said, forgetting that she had told Nora this vital fact several times already. "I had her for a week in the spring and a week in the fall. She was honest as the day is long, but slow—terribly slow."

"Well," Nora said, sitting back and with her arms crossed, looking from one interested face to another, "guess what."

"Oh, don't keep us in suspense any longer!" Alice cried.

"I won't," Nora said. "It was all in her imagination. The auditors have gone over the books with a fine-tooth comb, backwards and forwards, and every penny has been accounted for."

"No!" Lucy exclaimed.

"Well, I'm glad, for her mother's sake," Mrs. Beach said.

"There isn't a word of truth in Miss Ewing's story," Nora continued, "and I don't know how many people she's told it to. For instance, she hasn't been near the doctor in two months."

"It's the strangest thing I ever heard of," Alice said.

"Austin can't convince her—he stopped in to see her this afternoon and asked me to go with him. She still insists that she's a thief and ought to be sent to the penitentiary. It's very hard to know what to do with someone in that upset state. When you try to reason with them—"

"Was she in bed?" Lucy asked.

"No," Nora said. "She was up and dressed. She has a cat, a big yellow tomcat, and she didn't want me to pick it up, but it came straight to me and sat in my lap as contented as you please, all the time we were there."

"Austin shouldn't have left everything in her hands," Mrs. Beach said. "I'm surprised at him. I thought he was a better businessman than that."

"But if you knew Miss Ewing—" Nora began.

"I had to watch her mother like a hawk," Mrs. Beach said. "If I didn't, every stitch had to be ripped out and done over again. Part of the trouble was that she was going blind and didn't know it. Miss Ewing must have *wanted* to steal the money. Otherwise, it wouldn't be so on her mind. . . . When Lucy was six years old, she took a dollar bill from my pocketbook to buy lemonade," Mrs. Beach went on. "I knew all about it. The neighbor boy who had the lemonade stand stopped me as I was coming home and gave me the change, but I wanted her to tell me and so I waited . . ."

Lucy flushed, and when the painful story came to an end, Nora tactfully led the conversation around to Miss Ewing again.

"They've arranged for her care in a nursing home in Peoria until she's better. The thing is to get her to go there."

"Who's footing the bill?" Mrs. Beach asked.

"Cousin Austin offered to. Mr. Holby refused to have any part of it. But something has to be done with her. She's threatened to kill herself. Tonight as we left each other, Cousin Austin asked if I'd mind going to see her again tomorrow, alone. He thinks maybe she might listen to me where she wouldn't listen to a man, and of course I told him I'd be glad to. I feel that anything I can do to help her, I ought to do, especially when they've all been so kind to me."

9

The chairs in Dr. Seymour's waiting room were straight-backed and hard, and time passed very slowly there. The dark varnished woodwork, the soiled lace doily on the center table, the ancient *Saturday Evening Posts*, the brass lamp, and the leering, pink plaster billikin, all went with the atmosphere of antiseptic and worry, which remained intact, in spite of the continual substitution of one worried person for another. The waiting room was full: Austin and Martha King, an old man with his left hand wrapped in a dirty bandage, a woman with a little girl, a red-cheeked man who was the picture of health but who could not have been what he appeared to be or he wouldn't have been here. They sat, sometimes looking at each other, sometimes staring at the pictures on the wall. One was of a doctor in a long frock coat walking down a moonlit road with his medicine bag in one hand and his umbrella in the other. The umbrella was held in such a way that the doctor cast ahead of him the shadow of the stork. In the other picture, the doctor was at the bedside of a sick child, whose anxious father and mother were standing in the shadows.

After a time, an elderly woman being treated for the cataract on her right eye was led out by a woman who might have been her daughter. While she was inside, the elderly woman had been told something that she had not expected to be told; something good or something bad that it would take her a while to get used to. In the meantime, she had to be guided. Someone had to manage her purse for her, and show her the way to the door.

The man with the dirty bandage went inside, and Austin looked at Martha. She surprised him now by a patience that he (who was always so patient) did not have. He fidgeted, he was restless, he turned nervously and looked out of the window. His usual sense that everything would be all right, that he was not threatened by the disasters that overtook other people, had deserted him. These consultations had taken place before and they were always the same, always reassuring. He ought to have been at his office at this moment, but Martha couldn't have managed the streetcar, and he didn't want her to come in one of Jim Mathein's dirty old hacks, so he had harnessed Prince Edward and driven her down here himself.

The little girl was suffering from some skin disease. She looked at Martha and then away, looked again, and finally buried her head in her mother's lap. The two women exchanged glances and smiled. Gradually the little girl overcame her shyness to the point where she could come and lean against Martha's knee.

"How old are you?" Martha asked.

"Five," the mother said. "She doesn't talk."

"Oh," Martha said. She leaned forward so that the child could finger her beads. It was all that Austin could do to keep from interfering, but Martha had no concern apparently about the skin disease and whether it might be contagious.

For a while nothing happened in the waiting room—nothing more interesting or dramatic than the sun's coming out from behind a cloud, outlining the window on the linoleum floor and transferring the lace curtains there also, as if they were the kind of decalcomania pictures that schoolboys apply to their hands and forearms with spit. Of the illness that for forty years had passed through the waiting room, there was no trace. People with tuberculosis, people walking around with typhoid fever germs inside them, women with a lump on their breast that turned out to be malignant, men with an enlarged prostate, children who failed to gain weight. People with heart trouble, with elephantiasis, dropsy, boils, carbuncles, broken arms, gangrenous infections, measles, mumps, a deficiency of red corpuscles, a dislocated spine, meningitis, facial paralysis, palsy. Women with wrinkled stockings who would shortly be led away to the asylum, women who could not nurse their children, babies born to linger a short while like a bud on a sickly plant. The little boy whose legs are in braces, the little girl who has breasts at three and begins to menstruate at four but is otherwise normal. The man whose breath is choked by asthma, whose heartbeat is irregular and tired. The woman with swollen joints. The woman whose husband has infected her with gonorrhea. All saving their worry and fright for the inner office, all capable of being cured or incurable. The illness of the soul inextricably bound up with the illness of the body. The ones who ought to recover and won't, the ones whose condition is hopeless and yet who live on. Like the pattern of the lace curtain on the linoleum, they came and went, leaving no trace.

The man who had gone into the inner office with a dirty bandage wrapped around his hand came out with a clean one. The office girl said, "The doctor will see you now, Mrs. King," and Martha got up out of her chair.

Austin waited until the door closed behind her, and then his eyes dropped to the floor, searching for the outline of the window frame, which was so pale now that it was hardly visible, and soon went out altogether. He sat, crossing and uncrossing his legs. After a time he took out his watch and looked at it. The examination in the inner office was lasting longer than usual.

10

"I don't know what you must think of me," Mary Caroline Link said. "I've been meaning to come ever since you got here, only there's so much to do. This is my last year in high school. I'm graduating in June. And what with the glee club and the triangular debate and outside reading—Did you ever have to read *The Heart of Midlothian*? It's a terribly sad book—I don't know where the days go. But it isn't right not to have time for your friends."

Her conversational manner suitable to a woman of forty, Mary Caroline sat on the sofa in the Beaches' parlor. She had come on a Sunday afternoon with an offering of Boston brown bread.

"I didn't think anything about it," Nora said.

"I hear you're reading law in Mr. King's office," Mary Caroline said. "I'm sure you must find it interesting."

"Yes," Nora said. Her smile was both vague and lavish with some shining inner pleasure.

"How is your brother?"

"He's fine," Nora said. "I guess he's fine. He never writes. Nothing in the world would make him write a letter."

Mary Caroline noticed that there was something about the shape of her eyes and the curve of her mouth that was like Randolph. Nora was nice looking, she looked like someone it would be exciting to know, but her face didn't, of course, make all other faces look flat and commonplace the way his did. There was only this fleeting similarity of expression. Mary Caroline was surprised that she had never seen it before, when it was quite noticeable.

"Do you like the girl he's engaged to?"

"Engaged?"

"Perhaps I shouldn't have asked about it. He told me in confidence, but I thought of course that you knew."

"No," Nora said kindly. "I'm afraid I don't even know what girl you're talking about."

"There must be some mistake," Mary Caroline said, coloring. "I must have misunderstood him. But he told me—at least I *thought* he said he was engaged. It seems to me—I *could* be mistaken—that he said she was a beautiful girl from New Orleans, whose father was a millionaire."

"Oh, that one," Nora said. "No, he's not engaged to her, and never has been, so far as I know. Did he really tell you that?"

"Yes."

"I don't know what makes him tell such terrible lies," Nora said. "Except that he can't bear things the way they really are. Do you have any brothers?"

Mary Caroline shook her head.

"I've often wished that I had another brother besides Randolph," Nora said. "Because as it is, there's no basis of comparison. I don't know whether the way Randolph acts is usual with boys or not."

Nora could have told Mary Caroline how to get even with Randolph, and have led her to the holly tree from which the arrow would have to be fashioned that slew the darling of the gods. What Randolph could not endure was indifference. All Mary Caroline would have had to do was not to be touched by his beauty, not to care in the least whether he lived or died, and he would have moved heaven and earth to make her care.

"I know lots of boys at school," Mary Caroline said, "and I assure you that Randolph isn't at all like them."

"Probably not," Nora said, patting a pillow into shape. "But sometimes I wish he weren't so vain."

"Is he vain?" Mary Caroline asked, sitting forward in her chair.

"Terribly."

"Well, I've never seen that side of him," Mary Caroline said. "But I suppose it's hard not to be vain if you look like Randolph. I'm glad you told me. I feel I understand him better. And it's nice, don't you think, when people who seem so perfect in every way turn out to have some small fault? It makes you like them all the more."

As a result, apparently, of this remark, the vague and yet shining smile was once more interposed between them.

From where Mary Caroline was sitting, she saw a rig drive up and stop in front of the Kings' house. She leaned closer to the parlor window and then said, "It's Dr. Seymour. Is somebody sick at the Kings'?"

"Mrs. King," Nora said gravely.

"Oh dear," Mary Caroline said. "Nobody told me."

"She has to stay in bed all the time, from now until the baby comes."

"What a *shame!*" Mary Caroline said. "I must go and see her."

Feeling that she had already said more than she should about Randolph to his sister, Mary Caroline began to talk about the glee club cantata. She stayed until it began to get dark outside, and Nora went with her to the door. She had heard very little of what Mary Caroline said during the last half hour, and she had no idea that part of an undying devotion had been transferred from Randolph to her.

"I'll call you in a day or so and perhaps we can do something together," Mary Caroline said.

Watching her go off into the twilight and the rain, Nora said *You must not think I don't appreciate all you have done for me. If I don't speak of it, it's because . . .*

Deeply committed to a conversation with Austin King that never ended, Nora did not forget that he had a wife, but she found no room in her heart for jealousy. Cousin Martha was married to him and that was all. She had no interest in his work, no curiosity about what went on in his mind. For that he turned to Nora, who gave him her complete and rapt attention, no matter where she was or what claims the outside world made on her. *I realize perfectly that there are things which I cannot possibly say to you, which you do not wish to hear*, she said as she shepherded the children past the dangerous interurban crossing. *I think I have discovered something important*, she said as she put the pots and pans away in the cupboard. *No, I didn't actually discover it. You directed my thinking and there it was. . . . You may have friends who are nearer and dearer to you*, she said to the image in the mirror while she brushed and braided her hair, *but I doubt if there is anyone who cares more deeply about your happiness than I do. . . . I hear everything you say, everything*, she said, and let the coffee boil over on the stove.

II

"I appreciate your thoughtfulness in coming to tell me," Martha King said. "But you and I know, Miss Ewing, that Mr. King isn't that kind of a man."

This statement, which didn't follow logically what Miss Ewing had just been saying, confused and dismayed her. She was not in the habit of paying social calls on Mrs. King, and the long wait downstairs had given her ample time to consider whether it wouldn't have been better not to come. If she had known that Mrs. King was not well, that she would be received in Mrs. King's bedroom, her courage would have failed her. It was sustained now by the belief that what she was doing was for the best interests of the firm of King and Holby. Leaning forward anxiously, she said, "Of course, there's no one like Mr. King. That's why I was so surprised when he called her into his office and—"

What other strange visions Miss Ewing's eyes had seen lately —the synagogue of Satan, the four beasts full of eyes before and behind and within, hail and fire mingled with blood and all green grass burnt up, the star that is called Wormwood falling from heaven, and the air darkened by reason of the smoke of the pit—their unnatural glitter attested to.

"Naturally I'm sorry to learn that people have been talking about him and Miss Potter," Martha said kindly. "But it's something he is in no way responsible for. People have to gossip and if they can't find something that's true to gossip about, they're likely to make something up. I'm sure you'll do everything in your power to stop it. What a lovely umbrella. Is it new?"

"It was my mother's," Miss Ewing said, her attention shifting helplessly to the carved umbrella handle, in the likeness of a monkey's head with the two paws covering the mouth. Though Martha King was lying in bed, she managed to convey that her guest had stayed as long as politeness would allow. Miss Ewing rose and, further dismayed by the glimpse of herself which she caught in the dressing-table mirror (she certainly had no intention of being a busybody and a meddler), took leave. Outside in the hall, she made a wrong turning and soon afterward found herself face to face with the backstairs. Rather than run the risk of having to stop and explain this social error if she retraced her steps, Miss Ewing went on, arrived in the pantry, and, trembling with agitation, eventually found her way out of the labyrinth.

"I don't think anybody would believe her stories," Martha said when she finished telling Austin about her visitor that evening, "except that she isn't the only person who has been talking. You said it would cause a certain amount of talk and it has. Mrs. Jouette felt obliged to warn me of what people—mostly Mrs. Jouette, I have no doubt—are saying. I also heard it from Mrs. Ellis."

"Why didn't you tell me?" Austin asked.

"Because I didn't want to worry you. I knew you'd take it seriously, even though it's so preposterous, and a week from now they'll be gossiping about somebody else. But Miss Ewing's stories were really quite vicious. She's let her imagination run away with her, and if she's told anyone else what she told me this afternoon—"

"Let them talk," Austin said.

"It can't do us any harm," Martha said slowly, "but what about Nora? If being in your office is going to give her a bad reputation—"

"But how *can* they talk that way about her?"

"They can and will as long as Nora behaves as she does," Martha said.

"What do you mean?"

"Apparently she tries very hard to pretend that she's simply a friend of the family. But she mentions your name a good deal oftener than there is any need for, and the way she looks at you as you walk through the outer office is enough under the circumstances to convict you both. If she shouted her love from the housetops, people wouldn't be any quicker to believe the worst."

"Oh," Austin said. And then, "I suppose if she gives up her plan of becoming a lawyer, and it's understood that she isn't to come to the office any more, or here, and if she manages to avoid speaking to me when we happen to meet somewhere, then they'd be satisfied?"

"It would help," Martha said.

"They can't hurt Nora," Austin said.

12

"Come in, come in," Austin called cheerfully, and to his surprise Dave Purdy said, "Hello, Austin, how are you?" and walked into Mr. Holby's office instead.

A few minutes later Miss Stiefel brought Austin some letters to sign. Unable to find a trained law secretary, he had taken a girl out of business college. Her typing was adequate but not to be compared, of course, with the perfection of Miss Ewing's. Miss Stiefel was pale, with light-blue eyes, and hair and eyebrows and eyelashes so blond that they seemed almost white.

"That *was* Dave Purdy, wasn't it?" Austin asked.

She nodded.

"Did you tell him I was busy?"

"No," the girl said. "He wanted to see Mr. Holby."

"But I handle all his legal business," Austin said. "Mr. Holby doesn't know anything about it."

"Shall I ask him to step in on his way out?"

"Never mind," Austin said. And then, as she was leaving the room, "Will you let me know when Mr. Holby is free?"

Although he had not asked her to, she closed the door into the outer office, absentmindedly, perhaps. But it could also be, Austin realized suddenly, that she was following instructions from Mr. Holby—instructions based on the fact that the junior partner was socially no longer an asset to the firm.

When Miss Stiefel opened the door half an hour later, Austin was sitting at his desk with his head in his hands, and she had to speak to him twice before he heard her.

"Mr. Holby is free now."

Mr. Holby didn't as a rule stand upon his dignity. If he knew that Austin wanted to see him, he came to Austin's office. In a dull flash of anger, with the words of his resignation all framed in his mind, ready to offer if the occasion required it of him, Austin got up and went through the outer office. Mr. Holby went right on reading for a few seconds and then, glancing up, said, "Did you want to see me, young fellow?" He had not called Austin "young fellow" since the early weeks of their partnership.

Austin sat down. Mr. Holby offered him a cigar but no explanation of Dave Purdy's visit. Austin was sure that Mr. Holby would have preferred to ignore the incident. Mr. Holby didn't like explanations when rhetoric would do just as well. When the occasion demanded—in cross-examination, for instance—he could get to the point with the speed and directness of aim of a rattlesnake.

"Dave Purdy came to see you instead of me," Austin said.

Mr. Holby nodded. "He wanted to change his will. Nothing very complicated. I made a note of the change. Would you like to see it?"

"No," Austin said, "if he came to see you about it, you'd better go ahead and handle it. What I want to know is if there have been any others?"

For almost half a minute Mr. Holby didn't reply, and Austin saw that he was trying to make up his mind whether to take refuge in pompous vagueness or to speak frankly. In the end he took the cigar out of the corner of his mouth and spoke frankly.

"It's the women. They're out to get you."

"Why? How do you know?"

"I don't know," Mr. Holby said. "I only guess it; what usually happens when a man begins having trouble with his wife. They band together and take her side, and if they want to, they can do a good deal of damage in a business way."

"But I'm not having trouble with my wife," Austin said, with a rising sharpness in his voice.

"I didn't say that you were," Mr. Holby said blandly. "These stories start circulating, sometimes with no basis in fact, or at best a very slight one, and the first thing you know—"

"You're sure that's why Dave Purdy came to see you instead of me?"

"Positive."

"Have there been others?"

Mr. Holby inhaled twice in succession on his cigar and then nodded slowly.

"Would you like to dissolve the partnership?" Austin asked.

"It may not be necessary," Mr. Holby said. "It all depends on what happens. I mean between you and Martha."

"But I tell you—"

"I know I can speak frankly to you," Mr. Holby interrupted, "as one man of the world to another. Miss Ewing, I'm sorry to say, has done a good deal of talking. I'm no saint and I don't know anybody who is, but you can't expect to have an affair with another woman right under your wife's nose and not get into trouble. I'm not blaming you for it. Miss Potter is a very attractive young woman and it was probably something that you couldn't either of you help. What's done is done, and there's no use crying over spilt milk. We'll—"

"If you'd just listen to me for a minute!" Austin exclaimed. "Miss Ewing is as mad as a March hare. She—"

"The time has come for *you* to listen to *me*," Mr. Holby said. "We'll weather the storm, and I don't mind telling you there has been a storm. It isn't only a matter of people coming to me instead of you. Bud Ellis has served notice on me that he is taking his business to Chappell and Warren from now on. Well, let him, I say. It's going to cost him a pretty penny before he's through. Meanwhile, anything you can do to patch things up between Martha and you, I advise you to do. Take some time off. Take a trip with her somewhere. It'll be all right with me."

"I'm afraid I can't afford a trip just now," Austin said. "And Martha is expecting a baby in January, so I doubt if she'd enjoy it."

"Suit yourself," Mr. Holby said, and got up from his desk and went toward the hatrack. Standing in the door, with his overcoat on and his silk muffler neatly arranged, he turned and said, "If Martha would care to talk to me, I'd be very happy to see her at any time," and went out, leaving Austin alone, his long legs stretched out in front of him, his eyes staring, and his anger with no outlet.

13

On the morning of the day before Christmas, Martha King did not come downstairs and the door of her bedroom remained closed. Austin stayed home from the office, and Ab followed him wherever he went, except that she was not allowed to use the basement stairs, which had no railing, and so, while he was searching for some boards to make a stand for the Christmas tree, she stood at the top and asked questions of the dark dusty rooms below. With the wreath of holly on the front door, the red candles on the mantelpiece in the living room and in the study, and the tree lying on its side beside the icebox on the back porch, her mind was crawling with questions, the answers to which bred new questions that occasionally had to be repeated because Austin's mind was taken up with matters that had nothing to do with Santa Claus. *Put her to bed and keep her in bed*, Dr. Seymour had said. The slight hemorrhaging had lasted only that one day, but the fear that it might begin again at any time kept Austin from sleeping, made him irritable and unlike himself. If she's only all right, he said to himself as he came up the stairs with the boards for the stand; if she just gets through this last month without any more trouble, that's all I ask.

With Ab after him, he went to the pantry and began searching through the drawer where the hammer should have been and wasn't. I should have realized, he said to himself, that something was the matter, that it was different this time from the way it was before Ab was born. I should have gone and talked to Dr. Seymour myself. Instead of which, I was so immersed in my own affairs that I— "Frieda, have you seen the hammer? It should be here in this drawer."

"No, Mr. King," Frieda said from the kitchen. "You were the last person that used it. If it isn't there, I don't know where it could be."

The Kings' new cook was a middle-aged widow who had raised a family of five sons and then, just as she was ready to sit back and be taken care of by them, they one after another married. She was very religious, with thin tight lips and a streak of grey running through her hair. They ate early on Wednesday evening so she could get to prayer meeting on time, but that wasn't of course the same thing as contributing to the support of foreign missionaries in far-off places like India and China, who would have been grateful (she managed to convey as she cleared the table) for the piece of gristle, the remainder of a slice of bread that Austin or Ab left on their plates.

The hammer turned out to be in the larder, a room that Austin King hadn't been in for over a month.

"How does Santa Claus bring presents to children who live in a house where there isn't any fireplace?" Ab asked at his elbow.

Austin answered this question to the best of his ability and then said, "Now if somebody hasn't made off with the nails."

"With his bag and all the presents?" Ab asked.

"Certainly."

With the boards, the hammer, and nails, Austin went out to the back porch and saw a grey sky and soft rain descending. The ground, which should have been covered with snow, was soggy after a week of rain.

"How does Santa Claus get here in his sleigh if there's no snow?"

"There's plenty of snow at the North Pole," Austin said, sawing at one of the boards he had brought up from the basement. When he had finished making the stand, he nailed it to the bottom of the tree and carried it through the kitchen, the pantry, and the dining room, leaving a trail of pine needles behind him, and discovered that the tree was too tall to stand upright in the bay window of the living room.

He decided that, for the sake of the shape of the tree, he would have to rip the stand apart and saw another foot off the trunk. He dragged the tree through the house once more, and out on the back porch.

If she takes good care of herself, he said to himself, as he pried the stand apart, and if she gets plenty of rest. And if I see to it that nothing happens that could in any way upset her . . .

But suppose she does take care of herself and something happens to her anyway? said the rain, the same slow steady rain that was falling on the graves in the cemetery. *Suppose you are left in this house? Suppose you have to go on living without her, the way other men have had to do who lost their wives?*

She's just got to be all right, he told himself.

The stand, which had been all right the first time, now gave him trouble. The tree leaned to one side, and so he tried more nails, explaining meanwhile to Ab about Mrs. Santa Claus and her remarkable geese.

"And whenever she plucks one of them it snows."

"Then why doesn't she pluck one of them now so Santa Claus's sleigh will have something to run on?" Ab asked.

"Because nothing is ever that simple."

"Why isn't it that simple?"

The tree, when he stepped away from it, teetered and in a spasm of exasperation he threw down the hammer and cried, "Oh, Abbey, I don't *know!*"

She backed away from him in surprise. He had never before spoken sharply to her and now, just when everything else was so confusing, it turned out that with him, too, there was a line that she must not cross. She looked at him as if, before her eyes, he had suddenly turned into a stranger. He picked her up in his arms and carried her into the house.

"You stay inside with Frieda," he said. "You're getting cold."

He was once more her kind, patient father, but that did not in any way alter what had just happened.

She sat watching him from a remote sofa while he set the tree up in the alcove of the living room. Her face was long and thin with reproach. When he sat down beside her and lifted her onto his lap, her expression changed gradually. He saw that she had forgiven him and that she had another question, which she was afraid to ask. He was tired to death of questions, hers and his own and everybody else's, and he sat holding her and looking at the bare Christmas tree. At last, feeling her so quiet against him, he said, "Well, Abbey, what is it?"

14

At quarter after eleven on Christmas morning, the Kings' living room was strewn with tissue paper from the ebony pier glass to the dining-room doors. The candles on the Christmas tree had burned low and been put out, for fear of fire. Their red and white and green and blue wax had dripped on the pine needles, the artificial snow, the gold tinsel, and the colored balls that managed to reflect in their curved sides the whole disorderly, uninhabited room.

The square flat package on the hall table was for Nora. It was wrapped in red tissue paper tied with white ribbon and contained a handkerchief. On the sofa in the living room, the presents Austin had received were arranged in a neat pile that contained nothing more interesting or exciting than a belt with a silver monogrammed buckle (he already had a pearl-handled pocketknife) and a game that required the throwing of dice. The person or persons who sent Ab the box of dominoes, the box of tiddlywinks, and the mechanical dancing Negro minstrel would never be properly thanked; Martha King was not in the living room when these presents were opened, and the cards that came with them were now somewhere in the mass of tissue paper.

The ringing of the doorbell produced footsteps in the upper hall, and Austin came down the stairs, with Ab following, one step at a time.

"Merry Christmas!" Nora cried, as he opened the front door.

"Merry Christmas," he said, and took the pile of Christmas packages that she held out to him so she could close her umbrella and take her coat off.

"When I went to bed last night," she said, "I was so sure it was going to snow by morning. How is Cousin Martha?"

"Just the same," Austin said.

Nora did not hear him. She had caught sight of the Christmas tree and was exclaiming over it.

"This room looks as if a cyclone had struck it," he said apologetically.

"We just have a small one," Nora said. "On the dining-room table. At home every year— Oh, Austin, I've left you standing there holding all those packages! I'm so sorry." She took them from him and put them on a table. "Cousin Abbey, this is for you." Nora handed Ab the largest and most impressive-looking of the presents she had brought over.

Ab, jaded by the continual opening of packages, ripped the big rosette of red ribbon and the tissue paper off and discovered a Noah's ark. It was large, it was painted in bright colors, and it was undoubtedly the most expensive toy that had found its way into Mr. Gossett's shop in time for Christmas.

Nora glanced around the room and said, "Oh isn't that a sweet doll's house! I had one when I was little—with real andirons in the fireplace that I just loved."

Ab found the catch that released the hinged roof, and dumped Noah and his wife and the wooden animals matter-of-factly on the floor.

"I'm afraid you've been much too generous," Austin said. "We'll put it away until she's older and can appreciate what a beautiful thing it is."

"No, let her play with it. . . . Cousin Abbey, show me what else Santa Claus brought you." In the midst of this tour of inspection Nora suddenly turned to the pile of packages once more. "This is for Cousin Martha—it's a quilted bed-jacket. And this is for Cousin Martha, too. I couldn't remember what kind of cologne she likes, so I got her violet. And this is for Cousin Martha from Mama. It's the crocheted centerpiece that she started when she was here. She said to tell Cousin Martha that it was her masterpiece. . . . And this is for you, Austin."

His present turned out to be a grey woolen scarf that Nora had knitted herself.

"That's very thoughtful of you, Nora."

"If you don't like the color I can make you another. All I have to do is get some wool and—"

"No," Austin said. "This is just right. Thank you very much."

"There's a present here for you," Ab said.

"Go and get it," Austin said. "It's on the hall table."

As Ab started out of the room, Nora said, "I didn't know what to get for Frieda."

"You didn't have to get her anything," Austin said.

"Well, I wanted to," Nora said happily. "I didn't know what she'd like so I got her a handkerchief. . . . Is this for me?"

"Yes," Ab said.

Austin turned his face away while Nora carefully and painstakingly untied the ribbon. Her exclamations of pleasure, her praise of Martha's taste, he only partly heard.

"Abbey, take these up to your mother," he said, handing her the three packages. "And be careful you don't slip on the stairs."

There was no use waiting until tomorrow to tell Nora what he had to tell her. He might as well get it over with, along with all the other unpleasantness.

With her head framed by the Christmas wreath in the

window, Nora sat and listened quietly while he explained to her how grateful he and Mr. Holby were for all the help she had given them after Miss Ewing's breakdown, but how with the added burden and confusion of breaking in a new girl they couldn't—they neither of them had the time to—

Nora looked at her hands, at the holly on the mantelpiece, at the wooden animals that had fallen out of the ark. She said, "I know. . . ." She said, "I understand, Cousin Austin, I know exactly. . . ." And by the time he had finished, she was apparently quite reconciled. She tried to pretend that it wasn't a great disappointment to her but only something natural and to be expected on Christmas Day. She smiled, she went on talking about other things for a short while, and as she was leaving she said, "Tell Cousin Martha I love the handkerchief. I always lose mine wherever I go and I never have enough."

15

"What I'd really like is to behave naturally toward you," Nora said. "And the knowledge you have that I do love you—and knowing *I* know that nothing can be done about that, but that you are willing to act as though this did not affect your attitude toward me as a person and so forth—I don't know whether I am expressing myself so badly that you may not be able to follow what I am trying to say. I hope you do understand, because it is terribly important to me—all these things help me to act toward you as I know I should. I may appear to be giving a very poor performance of trying to help myself, but I *am* trying."

For a while she sat silent, with her arms embracing her knees, lost in thought. The loudness of the clock testified to the lateness of the hour. Nora stared at the design of the carpet without realizing how the silence prolonged itself. At nine-thirty, when she came for the fourth night running, she said that she was only going to stay for five minutes. She had been discussing, analyzing, explaining herself for over three hours now.

"I can't accept the nice things you say to me," she said. "Accept them gracefully, I mean. And yet the very least little thing that you say to me pleases me so. It makes wonderful things happen inside of me. Do you know how good it makes me feel, how glad, sitting across from you in this room? I know that, being you, you know exactly what I am going through, and you are trying to help me. It seems like something without beginning or end, you and I in this room. Everything is so simple now, I say to myself. He knows how you feel. He knows you love him. He knows, in fact, everything. Go ahead and talk, if you must talk, only don't look at him. . . . Isn't it strange the trouble I have looking at you?"

If she had looked at him, she would have seen that his eyelids were drooping. The lines that gave his face character and distinction had melted. He was very tired. He had tried, like a man walking a tightrope blindfolded over Niagara Falls, to keep himself and the wheelbarrow in balance, but whereas Nora went away each night looking relieved, easier in her mind, and more hopeful, he himself was so exhausted by her that he could hardly get up the stairs.

"Sometimes I've thought about you and wondered. If you had known me first, would things have been any different? I don't mean necessarily that you would have wanted to marry me, but you'd have liked me, wouldn't you? Because I'm not like other girls, am I? Not just another girl who loves you and is afraid of becoming a nuisance?"

"No."

"In spite of my general muddleheadedness," Nora said, "certain aspects of this thing are clear, irrevocably clear. I know that nothing can ever again be as empty as the life I lived before I knew you. When I have moments of despair and think it would be so much easier for me just to give up, I can't. Everything in me fights it at every turn. . . . What do you do? What happens when you are caught between two things? When you can't get where you are headed but it is impossible to turn back? I know that you have been kind and gentle when you might have been angry and lost all patience with me, and I would not have done anything but accept it from you, because that's how it is. Besides, in letting me come and read in your office, you have opened an entirely new world to me. I'm sorry, naturally, that it had to stop, but that doesn't alter the fact that you have been good and wonderful. How can you help but love a person who has been the sort of person you have been? I have nothing but the most profound admiration for you. . . . Oh, don't you see, if I keep this up, this wild talking, it's because I'm saying over and over 'I love you and you don't love me and how can I go on? What am I going to do?' . . . Sooner or later you will become discouraged with me. You will feel I am not making any real effort to overcome an emotion which can only spoil everything for us. I mean make it impossible for us ever to talk to each other again the way we are doing now. . . . But if, in permitting me to say anything and everything to you, we have only succeeded in having me fall more in love with you, we must be on the wrong track. . . . Oh, it wasn't entirely wrong, because if, up to a point, I hadn't been able to talk to you as I did that day in your office and as I have been these last few nights, I think—"

There was the sound of a step on the stair, which Austin didn't pay any attention to, until it was followed by a second and a third.

"—and I am thinking of this very carefully," Nora said. "I think I should have . . ."

The third step was followed by a fourth and a fifth. Austin's eyelids lifted. His face came back into focus. He turned toward the doorway into the hall. Nora went on talking and broke off only when Martha King came into the room, wearing a long loose negligee over her nightgown, and with her light brown hair down her back. She walked between them, over to the window seat, sat down, and drew her skirt together over her knees. For a moment nobody said anything. Nora colored with embarrassment. "I'm so sorry," she said. "I didn't mean to disturb you."

"It's quite all right," Martha said. "Your voice carries." Then turning to Austin: "What do you want of her? Why do you go on making her suffer?"

Nora felt a flicker of elation, which gave way to sorrow—to a sorrow that was very deep, as if the woman sitting in the window were her first friend and final enemy, someone whose coming had been long expected and planned for. "He hasn't made me suffer," she said. "He hasn't done anything. It's all my fault. I'm so sorry. I'm so very sorry this happened. Please forgive me!"

"Nora, I think you'd better go now," Austin said. "It's late. It's after midnight."

From the hall doorway, Nora turned and looked back and saw that they were waiting in a silence from which she was excluded.

"I really didn't mean to do this," she said, fumbling with the latch on the front door. "I couldn't have meant to do this."

16

There are only two kinds of faces—those that show everything openly and tragically, and those that, no matter what happens, remain closed. From the one every old loss cries out each time you meet it. Every fresh doubt calls attention to itself. The beginning of cancer or of complacency are immediately apparent, and so is the approach of death. From the other kind you get nothing, no intimation of strain, of the inner war of the soul—unless, of course, you love the person who looks out at you from behind the blank face. In that case, some day, instead of saying *How well you are looking*, as the last acquaintance before you has done, you may be shocked and ask abruptly *What on earth has happened?*

The same thing is true of houses, for anyone who is interested enough to look at them, at what is there. Rachel's shack cried out that she was gone, taking her children with her. The funeral basket lying on its side ten feet away from the two stones said *Keep away unless you are looking for trouble.* The wicker bassinet, half full of leaves, said *Man is his own architect.* The coach lantern and the coffeepot had disappeared, the front door stood open.

On the unmade bed, on sheets that were twisted and sooty, Andy lay abandoned, flat on his back, barefoot, with trousers on and a woolen shirt unbuttoned over his chest. The breath that came from his open mouth, with each snore, was frosty. He turned onto his side and huddled there like a fetus.

A dry leaf had drifted in and was now resting on the edge of the rag carpet before it went even further. On the table were dirty dishes, dried food, cigarette butts, and a small pool of vomit. The patchwork covers were in a heap at the foot of the bed, but the hand that reached slowly out went in a different direction, over the side, down, fumbling until the fingers closed over the neck of a bottle and stayed there. The drawers of the old varnished dresser had at some time or other been pulled open and ransacked, and then left with garments dripping over onto the floor. In the kitchen Thelma's picture of the evening party at the Kings' had come loose and hung from one tack, flapping. All the food and cooking utensils had been knocked down from the shelves. There was a broken cup under a chair, and on top of the stove a mixture of coffee grounds and cornflakes.

The man on the bed sat up slowly, with the bottle in his hands. His eyes opened. Bloodshot and frightened, they looked around the room with no recognition in them, not even when they were focused on the open door. The man raised the bottle to his lips and drank until the bottle, upended, proved conclusively that it was empty. He flung it across the room and the bottle shattered. The figure on the bed sank back solemnly, the hands opened and closed twice, as if in surprise (*Pharaoh's army got drownded*), and then the only movement was the frosted breath rising thinner and thinner from the purple mouth.

The Kings' house showed nothing, that day. To Mary Caroline Link, on her way to high school, and to the Reverend Mr. Porterfield, riding by on his ancient bicycle, the house looked exactly the same as always. The iron fence was enough, in itself, to keep out every threat the world has to offer, but Mrs. Danforth was uneasy. From her parlor window she had seen the setting sun reflected from the windows across the way a thousand times. She could predict almost to the minute when the lights would go on—first in the kitchen, then in the front part of the house. She knew also how the house looked when it was completely dark. She had looked out on the flower garden in summer when it was a mass of bright color, in clumps and borders, and when the mounded beds, with snow on them, looked like a small family graveyard in a corner of a country field. The Kings' house—the east side of it—and her own house were like her left and right hand. And when there is something wrong with your hand you know it, whether other people are aware of it or not.

Mrs. Danforth opened the pantry door and listened, convinced that she had heard the telephone, that they were trying to communicate with her from the house next door. Then she went about her housework, made the big double bed in the front room, and with the dustmop in her hands, worked her way down, frowning at the lint that had collected on the stairs.

17

"*Now* where are you going?"

"Upstairs," Ab said.

Frieda moved between her and the doorway into the dining room. "No you don't, young lady," she said. "I have my orders and I'm to keep you with me, so just sit down on that stool over there and don't make any trouble, if you know what's good for you."

"I want my mother," Ab said.

"Well, you can't have her."

"I can too have her," Ab said. "And I don't have to mind you."

"Your mother doesn't want you up there. She's sick. You try anything funny and you'll get what Paddy gave the drum."

"I'll tell my father on you when he comes home," Ab said.

"Go ahead and tell him. See how much good it does you."

"I will tell him."

"You're not to bother your Daddy either. He has other things to worry about. You stay here in the kitchen with me and be a good girl and maybe I'll let you lick the dish."

"I don't want to lick the dish, and I don't like it here. You're a bad woman."

"Sticks and stones may break my bones but words will never hurt me," Frieda said.

"If you don't let me see my Mama, I'll call the police. They'll come and take you away and put you in jail."

The thin mouth stretched to a grim slit, and a dark red flush told Ab that she had once more stepped over the line.

"Very well, young lady, call the police. I've taken all I'm going to from you. March right into the library with me and call the police. You'll see soon enough who they'll take off to jail."

She took hold of Ab's arm roughly, pulled her from the high stool, and forced her, stumbling, through the swinging doors, through the dining room, and into the study.

"Sit right down there," Frieda said, giving Ab a final push toward the desk. "I'll wait here while you do it."

Ab looked at the black instrument. In spite of many imaginary conversations into a glass telephone that came filled with red candy, she had never thought of using the real one and she did not know what would happen, what voice would answer if she took the receiver off the hook. It might be Mrs. Ellis or Alice Beach or the man at the grocery store, or it might be the voice of her Sunday school teacher or of the man who came to the back door with froglegs.

"Go ahead," Frieda said. "I'm waiting."

Ab looked at the telephone and then wildly around for help.

18

"If only Alice hadn't come down with the grippe," Lucy said.

"Oh, it's so beautiful!" Nora said, standing at the parlor window with her fur hat on, and peering through the lace curtain at a world that was even more lacelike. The evening before, along about dusk, it had started snowing, and the snow had been coming down all night long. The walk and the front yard were buried there was no telling how deep. Beyond that, Nora could not see because of the snowflakes that filled the air with a massed downward movement. "I want to get out in it," she said. "Twice in the night I got up out of bed and went to the window and stood shivering in my nightgown, trying to see the snow. Now I want to be out in it. I want to feel it on my face."

"I don't think you ought to try it," Lucy said. "Let me call the mothers. It probably would be better to, anyway. If the children get their feet wet, they'll all come down with colds."

On a newspaper beside the front door there were three pairs of overshoes. Nora found hers and sat down to put them on.

"By tomorrow," Lucy said, "it will have stopped snowing and the walks will be cleaned and you won't have such a time getting there."

"Who knows what it will be like tomorrow," Nora said gaily. "Maybe the snow will be six feet deep. Maybe we won't be able to get out of the house. Do the drifts ever come up as high as the second-story window?"

"I think I'd better come with you," Lucy said. "I really think I'd better. It'll be hard enough for you, but you don't know what it's like for children. You'll have to carry them, and you can't all that distance."

"They can walk behind me," Nora said. "I'll make a path for them."

She put her arms into the man's winter coat that Lucy held for her. The coat had belonged to Mr. Beach. It was very heavy, it was much too large for Nora, and it was lined with rabbitskin.

"Now for the mittens. This is just like 'East Lynne,'" Nora said, and pushed the storm door open. The snow was banked against it, blown there during the night, and the storm door cut a deep quarter-circle into the new level of the porch. "Don't worry about me."

The front steps were rounded over so there was scarcely an inch drop from one to the next. Nora put her foot down cautiously where the walk ought to be, and discovered that the snow was six or seven inches deep. She took a big step and then another and another. At the place where the lawn curved down to meet the sidewalk there were three more steps, which she found under the snow. And then she stopped and looked around. The houses across the street had rounded white roofs with black chimneys sticking out of them. The trees were thickened, whitened, lightened with snow, and, placed in a perspective of much greater depth than the eye usually was aware of, reminded her of her grandmother's stereoscope, that must still be somewhere in the attic at home in Mississippi.

"Oh, no wonder!" she exclaimed.

Love falling on her face, love falling on her hair, love smooth and untracked, filling up every previous impression, space closing in, distance diminished, the shape and outline of every house, every tree, every hitching post transformed, made beautiful, made into the great lace curtain.

With the heavy coat weighing her down, Nora floundered through the snow until she got as far as the Kings' front walk. Someone had shoveled a path from the porch steps to the sidewalk, and the path was already filling in, more than half obliterated. She saw large footprints which must be Austin's, and as she walked where he had walked, put her foot down in the print of his, all sense of cold left her. She rang the doorbell and then, turning around, saw the world as he had seen it, a few minutes ago, from his own front steps. If I can have this and no more, Nora said to herself, it's enough. I'll be happy forever. I've had more than I ever expected to have on this earth.

But there was more. The arrangements (by whomever made) were generous. The snow kept on falling.

"She isn't going," a voice said in the intense stillness. "Her mother thinks it's snowing too hard for her to go to kindergarten."

"Thank you, Frieda."

"You're welcome, I'm sure."

It isn't snowing too hard, Nora thought as she turned and went back into the excitement of high freedom. It isn't snowing hard enough.

Of the eleven children that she was supposed to collect, only four were expecting her, and walking with them was as difficult as Lucy Beach had foreseen. They had to walk backwards part of the time so that they didn't face the wind. There were stretches of sidewalk where no one had walked. There were deep drifts. They were sometimes forced out into the street. The children walked behind Nora, in the path that she scuffed for them, and when they got as far as the high school, the little Lehman boy began to cry. His overshoes were full of snow and his feet were cold and wet and he had lost one of his mittens. Nora tried to coax him and succeeded for a little way. Then he sat down in the snow and refused to go any farther, so she picked him up and carried him, as heavy as lead, until they reached the beginning of the business district. Here the sidewalks had been cleaned, and walking was easier.

"When we get to the kindergarten it will be all right," Nora kept saying to them. "The kindergarten will be warm. We'll play games. We'll play that it's Christmas."

At nine-thirty, she unlocked the door of the kindergarten rooms and walked in with the children following after her. Though it was immediately apparent, by their visible breath, that there was no fire in the stove, she went over to it and touched it with her hand. The stove was cold. The man had not come.

There was a closet off the hallway, and in it Nora found

some kindling; not much but if she was careful it would be enough. There was a bucket of coal by the stove, with a folded newspaper lying on top. The fire smoked but there was no crackling sound, and very soon it went out.

"It probably has something to do with the draft," Nora explained to the children. She raked the coal and blackened kindling out onto the floor. There was no more newspaper, so she snatched a long colored-paper chain from the chandelier and stuffed it into the stove. The fire, rebuilt, burned feebly, without giving off any heat. The children stood around, all bundled up and shivering. In the hall closet, while she was rummaging for more paper, Nora found a can of kerosene.

19

Mary Ellis had been asked to the Friendship Club, at Alma Hinkley's house on Grove Street, as a substitute for Genevieve Wilkinson, who was out of town. There were the usual two tables and the scorecards were decorated irrelevantly with a hatchet and a spray of cherries. At five minutes after five, the four women in the living room had finished their final rubber and were replaying certain hands in retrospect while they added up their scores. The table in the parlor had fallen behind because of Bertha Rupp, whose hesitations were sometimes so prolonged and whose playing was so erratic that for years there had been talk of asking her to resign from the club.

Ruth Troxell opened the bidding with a heart and then said, "It must have been a shock to Martha King, in her condition."

"It was a shock to everybody," Mary Ellis said.

"I pass," Irma Seifert said.

Mary Ellis passed and the bidding reached a standstill while Bertha Rupp considered the thirteen cards that chance had dealt her. "Two clubs," she said impulsively and then tried to change her bid to two diamonds, which the other players refused to allow.

"But I meant two diamonds!" she exclaimed.

"It doesn't matter what you meant. Two clubs is what you bid," Ruth Troxell said, and then glancing at the score pad beside her, "Two hearts." She was high at the table.

Irma Seifert and Mary Ellis passed.

"Why did they have a can of kerosene in the kindergarten rooms in the first place?" Irma Seifert said.

"That's what I can't figure out," Mary Ellis said. "Alice says that both she and Lucy knew it was there but they never— Are you waiting for me? I passed."

"We're waiting for Bertha," Ruth Troxell said.

There was a long silence and then Bertha Rupp said, "Two hearts."

"Ruth has already bid two hearts," Irma Seifert said.

"Two spades then," Bertha Rupp said, clenching her cards.

"You're sure you don't want to go to three hearts?" Ruth Troxell asked.

"No, two spades."

"Three hearts," Ruth Troxell said.

"With only the word of four-year-old children to go on," Irma Seifert said, "I don't suppose we'll ever know. Three no-trump."

"I pass," Mary Ellis said. "Mrs. Potter is the one I feel sorry for."

"They say she has aged overnight," Ruth Troxell said.

"Austin met them at the train," Mary Ellis said, "and they drove straight to the hospital. Nora was conscious. She knew them."

"Who are they staying with?" Irma Seifert asked. "Your bid, Bertha."

"Oh, they're staying with the Kings, the way they did before," Mary Ellis said.

"I wouldn't have any of them in my house if I were Martha," Ruth Troxell said.

"At a time like that," Irma Seifert said, "you don't know what you'd do. Take these nuts away from me, somebody, before I make myself sick."

PART SIX

There Is a Remedy or There Is None

I

"I WOULDN'T care how disfigured her face and hands might be," Mrs. Potter said, "if she'd only get well; if I could take her home with me and keep her there, forever and ever."

She was lying fully dressed on the bed in the yellow guestroom. "From the moment they're able to walk, they start trying to get away from you," Mrs. Potter said. One arm was thrown across her face, to hide the effort it required for her to remain in possession of her feelings. "They want to escape from your arms, get down out of your lap and leave the house where they were born. I don't know what it is. Nora never had anything but kindness at home. Her father worships the ground she walks on. So do we all. Love her to pieces. But it isn't enough, apparently. I don't know why this had to happen or what we could have done to prevent it."

"Nothing," Martha said. "You couldn't have prevented it or you would have. And you mustn't blame yourself."

Mrs. Potter had experienced The Sudden Change. While she was still trying to close the useless umbrella of the Past, the cold wave of the Present had come over her and, miles and miles from home, she wandered, sometimes with the wind, sometimes across it.

"She keeps trying to talk to me through all those bandages and it's so terrible. Are you sure Dr. Seymour is a good doctor, Martha?"

"We've always had him," Martha said. In open disregard of Dr. Seymour's orders, she was up and dressed and sitting in a chair by the front window of the guestroom. She had her own reasons for what she was doing—reasons that Dr. Seymour probably wouldn't understand or approve of, but this wouldn't prevent her from putting herself in his hands when the time came to trust someone with absolute trust. "If you don't feel satisfied, and want to call some other doctor in for a consultation, I'm sure it would be all right with him."

"I keep wishing we'd brought Dr. LeMoyne with us," Mrs. Potter said. "He's just a country doctor but he knows a great deal. He brought both my children into the world, and he would have come except that he's so old now. He's eighty-three and he would never have stood the train journey."

There had been a fresh fall of snow during the night. The limbs of the trees were outlined in white against a tropical sky. The tree ferns and palm fronds that went with the blue sky were drawn in white, on the window pane.

"This doctor seems very fond of Nora and anxious to do anything he can to relieve her suffering. The thing I don't understand is that she doesn't want to live. She keeps saying there's no place for her anywhere. I haven't told Mr. Potter. It would only upset him. But there must be some reason, something that is troubling her."

Looking out through the patterns of frost, Martha saw that the Wakeman children were trying to make a snowman. The snow would not roll properly; it was too dry, and instead of becoming larger and larger, the snowball crumbled and fell apart.

"You mustn't think too much about what she says in her delirium."

"I can't help thinking about it," Mrs. Potter said. "And besides, she wasn't delirious when she said that. She was in her right mind. 'I don't have to go on living if I don't want to,' she said. . . . Part of the time she knows me, and then other times when I say something to her, she doesn't hear."

A chunk of snow, dislodged by the wind, left a branch of the big elm tree and was scattered on the brilliant sunshine.

"If I only knew what it is that's troubling her, I might be able to do something about it. But I've asked her and she won't tell me. Did she ever talk to you and Cousin Austin?"

"She talked to Austin," Martha said.

"It surely wasn't the kindergarten," Mrs. Potter said.

"No," Martha said. "She was very good with the children. They all loved her."

"It must be something else," Mrs. Potter said. "Sometimes

I think it was those law books. I told you, didn't I, that she never wrote us that she was reading law in Cousin Austin's office?"

"Yes."

"Was it Cousin Austin's idea?"

"No, it was Nora's," Martha said.

"Well, it was very thoughtful of him to allow her to do it. I should have thanked him before this. He's always so ready to help. Some day he'll get his reward. . . . I've been low in my mind, but I have never not wanted to live, and I can't seem to find the right thing to say to comfort her. There's something else she said last night: 'It looks different without the leaves.' Whatever could she have meant by that?"

"I don't know," Martha said. "You're sure she said 'leaves'?"

"Yes. And then she said, 'I ought never to have allowed myself to hope.' I asked her what it was that she hoped, but she didn't hear me. And right after that, the nurse said something about her condition and she flared up and we had difficulty quieting her. I oughtn't to tell you these things. Everything ought to be happy around you. I don't know why you didn't tell us last summer—why you let us come and impose on you that way when there was no need."

"Last summer was a long time ago," Martha said. "Your being here now doesn't change anything so far as Austin and I are concerned. I'm just sorry that there's so little we can do."

"Don't say that," Mrs. Potter said, withdrawing her arm. "You and Cousin Austin have meant more to us in these last few days than I can ever begin to tell you."

"I'm going to leave you alone for a little while," Martha said. "You must get some rest before you go back to the hospital."

The comforter who says *I know, I know* (and doesn't know) or *You must be brave* (when all people are brave and it doesn't help them when the blow comes) is nevertheless serving a purpose. Martha King made it possible for Mrs. Potter to talk about her grief, and when the words were out of the way and the bedroom door had closed and the comforter had gone off down the hall, she wept, but freely, easily, and with satisfaction. She wept for Nora and she wept for herself—for the death of all her hopes. She wiped the huge scalding tears away again and again, as if weeping were the one thing in the world she understood and had a natural talent for.

2

On the door of room 211 in the hospital was a sign that read NO VISITORS. This did not apply to Dr. Seymour and the nurses or to Mrs. Potter, who slept on a cot in Nora's room and went home some time during the day to change her clothes, be with her husband, and rest. The sign did apply to Austin King.

While he was at his office, he was safe; he could turn his mind to other things and forget for a while about Nora, though even here the trouble intruded. He would find himself staring at a legal paper he had read over and over, without knowing a single word he had read. When he was at home, his eyes kept turning toward his desk where, in the left-hand cubbyhole, there was a letter from Nora. Though Austin needed to talk to someone about this letter and all that had led up to the writing of it, there was no one willing to listen night after night with eyelids grown heavy, and no one came down the stairs and put an end to his investigation of blind alleys and his consideration of what might have happened in the light of what actually had. He was quite clear in his mind about what he had meant to do for Nora, but he had been patient, he had listened to Nora instead of turning his back on her the day she came to see him at his office, and if he hadn't treated her gently, would she have stayed up North? So much depended on the answer to this question and there was only one person who could tell him (through bandages) what he needed to know.

The Mississippi people returning brought three small suitcases with them and left behind all desire to please, to charm, to acquire new friends. Though there was a question of how long they would stay, their reason for coming was clear to everyone. Time did not pass the way it had before in a whirl of carriage rides, picnics, and trips to the Chautauqua grounds. Time had slowed down and was threatening to stop entirely.

The friends the Potters had made on their previous visit did not desert them. The callers filled the living room and overflowed into the study. What had happened was too tragic to be mentioned, and so the callers depended on their mere physical presence to convey how sorry they were, and talked about other things—about the weather, about the new oiled road from Draperville to Gleason, about the new fashions in women's dress, about their own sciatica or rheumatism or about the great number of people who were down with the grippe—in an effort to divert the Potters from their only purpose in coming to Draperville. Lucy Beach threw herself into Mrs. Potter's arms and wept, but then the Beach girls had always been queer, and if they hadn't taken it into their heads to start a kindergarten, the whole thing might have been avoided. When Lucy had been led from the room, the conversation was resumed where it had left off, the full social strength was mustered to cover this lapse from decorum.

Mr. Potter acted like a man who had been stunned. He was neither restless nor interested in anything that went on around him. He sat most of the time in the big chair in the study, unable to take part in any conversation or to check the involuntary tears that at certain moments filled his eyes and slid down his leathery cheeks. Rather than disturb him, Austin and Martha King found themselves turning to Randolph when there were messages of sympathy that had to be acknowledged, decisions to be made.

Of the many things that would not fall into any proper place during this second visit, one of the strangest was the change in Randolph Potter. He was able to pass the mirror in the hall and the ebony pier glass in the living room without so much as a glance at his reflection. His handsomeness forgotten, he had become overnight the prop of the family. Mrs. Potter leaned on him as if from years of habit. When Ab offered herself to him, Randolph lifted her onto his lap, but instead of playing games or teasing her, he went on talking quietly to the callers or to Austin and Martha, and after a few minutes she got down and went off to play. Mary Caroline Link called and Randolph talked to her in a way that was pleasant and friendly but that aroused no expectations. It was almost as if he were her older brother, home from college and trying to fit once more, or at least appear to fit, into the family circle he had now outgrown. He asked about Rachel the first night, when a strange white woman moved around the dining-room table with platters of food. Martha King explained that Rachel had disappeared shortly before Christmas, taking her children with her, and Randolph nodded absently as if he had known all along that was what Rachel would eventually do.

He was not grotesquely cheerful the way his mother sometimes was, nor openly grief stricken, like Mr. Potter. It was almost as if Randolph, who always walked by himself and never made common cause with his family, were now justifying the wisdom of his past selfishness by assuming full responsibility for his family and for the confusion and distress they brought about, sooner or later, wherever they went. Randolph was kind, he was thoughtful, he was anxious not to make trouble for Martha King and solicitous about her health, and he dealt sensibly with the problems which Austin and Martha brought to him. More wonderful than anything else, he carried for eight whole days, all alone, the burden of conversation in a house where nobody felt like talking. His mild jokes and stories said, or seemed to say, *You understand that it is not lack of feeling that makes me able to tell about the time Pa paid a call on the new minister. I know my sister is lying in the hospital badly burned and that there is nothing any of us can do about it. But if you listen carefully, you will perceive that the jokes I make, the stories I tell, are not the ones I would choose if we were all light-hearted and Mama were not waiting for us to leave the dining-room table so she can go back to the hospital. But somebody has to carry the load, otherwise you would sit and stare at your food, and Pa would begin to cry again, and it only makes things worse.*

One day when he and Austin were alone in the study, Austin brought up the subject that no one was willing to talk to him about. "For a while," he began, "we didn't see as much of Nora as we ought to have, living right next door."

"You and Cousin Martha weren't in any way responsible for what happened," Randolph said.

"I know, but I blame myself for—"

"You mustn't. Sister shouldn't have stayed up here on her own. Mama tried to prevent her. We all did. But she had this idea about being a kindergarten teacher, and wouldn't listen to reason. I know you both love her and that's enough, as I keep telling Mama. She thinks if she'd only allowed herself to realize that Nora was a grown woman, and not kept harping at her—but you know Mama is just as set in her ways as Nora is. After a little, when things are straightened out, I hope you'll come and stay with us. You'd like it very much down South, Cousin Austin. I'll take you around and show you the country. Take you coon hunting, if you like."

3

"I just don't know," Mrs. Potter said.

Austin's question had taken her by surprise. The hack was waiting in front of the house and Mrs. Potter, with her hat and coat on, was waiting at the foot of the stairs for Mr. Potter to come down and drive off to the hospital with her. She glanced around for a place to sit down. The only chair near her was a rickety antique that had been put in the front hall purposely because in the hall there was less likelihood of anyone's being tempted to sit on it. The chair creaked ominously but it sustained Mrs. Potter's weight, which was not much, in any case.

"The doctor said— You couldn't give me the message?"

He shook his head.

"You want to see her alone?"

"Yes," Austin said, coloring. "I wouldn't want to do anything contrary to Dr. Seymour's orders, but if it's all right with you, and you don't mind asking him—"

"Oh, it's perfectly all right with us," Mrs. Potter said doubtfully. "And I'm sure that if Nora weren't in pain, she'd be delighted to see you. She's always admired you so. But if it's something that would upset her—"

"I'd be very careful."

"I know you would," Mrs. Potter said.

From the troubled expression on her face, she might have been sitting in front of some closet door that she had walked past a hundred times in the last week without once noticing that it was there. The beating of her own heart told her now that the closet contained something of interest to her. But was it something that needed to be discovered? Wouldn't it be better and wiser to keep on walking past the closet door as she had been doing? She raised her eyes and met his questioningly.

Then it's here—Nora's secret—where I never thought to look for it? Is this why she doesn't want to go on living?

That's right.

Mrs. Potter parted the fur on her black sealskin muff with her fingers while she deliberated. At last she said, "I don't know why you shouldn't see her, if you want to. You're our own kin, practically. I know you won't stay too long or do anything to wear her out. I'll speak to the doctor about it. If he says it's all right for you to see her . . . Whatever can be keeping Mr. Potter? He knows we have to be at the hospital by four and it's now—"

"I'd be deeply grateful if you would," Austin said.

4

"I didn't mean to hurt your feelings, Miss Stiefel," Austin said, standing in the outer office. "But you do understand, don't you, that legal work has to be done right. Otherwise there's no point in—"

When it came time for Miss Ewing's successor to take dictation, she sat with her note book on her knee and a frightened look on her face that nothing could erase. Austin dictated much slower than usual, and spelled out words as he went along, but the letters she brought in to him to be signed were full of mistakes. Worried lest he himself let something slip by that would cause difficulties later on, he called the head of the business college. She had no one to send him who was any better than Miss Stiefel, or as good, and so he went on struggling with her, the struggling being interrupted occasionally by tears and apologies.

"I realize that the work is still new to you," he said, "and it takes a while to get used to the legal phraseology, but after this when you aren't sure about something—" Her eyes were on the doorway and she was not listening to what he said. Austin turned around and saw Randolph Potter. "Be with you in a minute," he said. "After this, come to me with it and don't try to guess what it should be, because nine chances out of ten it won't be right, and it only makes more work for both of us. Mr. Griffon is coming in at four. Do you think you can have that lease ready by then? . . . You better make two carbons, while you're at it. We'll keep one here in the files. . . . Did you walk down?" he said, turning to Randolph.

"I came on the streetcar," Randolph said.

"Any news from the hospital?"

"Mama asked me to tell you that she's spoken to Dr. Seymour and it's all right. You can see Sister tomorrow afternoon at four o'clock."

Austin said, "Come inside."

"I know you're busy," Randolph said. "I just dropped in for a minute. I've got a check here that I wanted to get cashed, and I thought maybe, since they don't know me at the bank—"

"How much money is there in the cash box?" Austin said, turning to Miss Stiefel.

"Not very much," Miss Stiefel said. "Mrs. Holby was in, and Mr. Holby took ten dollars out of it for her, so—"

"Never mind. I'll endorse it and you can take it over to the First National Bank. You know where that is?"

Randolph nodded, took out his leather billfold, and extracted a check, folded in two. Without bothering to look at the amount or the bank that the check was drawn on, Austin borrowed Miss Stiefel's pen and wrote his name.

"Take this to the third window," he said. "If there's nobody there, ask for Ed Mauer. I'll call him and tell him you're on the way over."

Before Austin could make this telephone call, the client he was expecting came in, and soon afterward the telephone rang. "Excuse me just a minute," he said, and picked up the receiver. A voice that he recognized as Ed Mauer's said, "There's a fellow here says he's a cousin of yours. He's got a check—"

"Oh yes," Austin said. "I was just about to call you."

"—for a hundred and seventy-five dollars. I wanted to make sure the endorsement was genuine."

Though Austin was in the habit of dealing with his suspicions so summarily that he was hardly aware that he had them, this one was not to be ignored. It leered at him and said *Well?* The receiver shook in his hand. He thought of the letter from Nora that was in a cubbyhole of his desk at home. He thought of Mrs. Potter's face the day he had met her at the station and she said *Don't keep anything from me, that's all I ask.* . . . He thought of the night in the study, when Bud Ellis said *Naturally, since he was a relative of yours, we thought* . . . Some day, somehow, there would be an end. And meanwhile . . .

"It's all right, Ed. I endorsed it. Much obliged for calling me."

5

That evening it appeared that for once there would be no callers. Randolph left for the hospital with Mr. Potter soon after dinner, and Austin and Martha King settled down in the living room.

"Do you feel all right? Is the house warm enough?"

"Yes," Martha said.

"I'll be glad when it's over with," Austin said.

"You're not worrying?"

"No, not exactly," he said. "It's just that—"

"There's nothing to worry about. I feel fine, and it's going to be a boy."

"You thought Ab was going to be a boy."

They were like two people meeting by accident at a large party after years of not seeing each other and uncertain whether to fall back into their former intimacy or be on their good manners.

"Do you remember, Austin, the beautiful fires you built for me when we were first married?"

"You don't care for this fire?"

"It's all right. I have no objection to it," Martha said. And then, "Ab can stay at the Danforths', but I don't know what to do about you."

At such meetings, silences have the weight of words chosen carefully, and words convey now single, now double meaning, and the conversation moves forward in strides that take miles and miles for granted.

I keep hearing the sound of my own footsteps, Austin tried to tell her, silently. *Everywhere I go* . . .

"Maybe if you went to the office, at least part of the time—"

"No," Austin said, "I want to be here."

In desperation at the clotted feeling inside him that cried out *Oh I do love you!* he raised his hand as far as his forehead and slowly took off his mask. No one is ever fooled by false faces except the people who wear them. The doorbell rings on Halloween, and you go to the door and what do you find? A policeman or a Chinaman, four feet high. The face might be convincing enough if you are nearsighted, but how can you fail to recognize and be touched by the thin arms and legs of the little Ludington boy who lives two houses down the street and who, for all his fierceness on this occasion, you know to be a delicate child and a worry to his mother?

The face under Austin King's mask was just the same as the mask, but the eyes betrayed anxiety.

"I know you do," Martha said.

They sat looking into the fire in a silence that was familiar and trusting. Austin wanted to tell her that he was going to see Nora, and he also wanted to explain his reasons for doing this, so that the trust and deepest level of contact between them wouldn't be destroyed. He let half a minute slip by and then said, "Aunt Ione has arranged for me to see Nora, tomorrow afternoon. I wanted to tell you about it first so you'd understand. I would have waited until she was out of the hospital, but—"

"You *asked* to see her?"

"Yes," Austin said. "I had a letter from Nora, written that night after she left here. You said you didn't care to discuss her or anything to do with her—"

"I still don't."

"—so I didn't show it to you. Martha, in the letter she—"

The doorbell chose this moment to ring. Austin looked around the room helplessly and then at his wife, who had turned away and was looking into the fire. He got up and went to the door.

Sitting on Martha King's carved walnut sofa, with his rubbers still on and one leg crossed over the other, old Mr. Ellis looked very small, like a shrunken boy. He had dressed himself up very carefully but there was a large spot on his mottled green tie and his shirt collar was badly frayed. Mary Ellis would never have let him out of the house with it on, but then she and Bud had gone out after dinner. They had gone to call on the Rupps, and as soon as the old man was sure that it was safe, he had shaved—nicking his face in several places—dressed himself, and with a fine satisfaction in disobeying orders had come calling.

"It's been a strange winter," he said. "I don't ever remember one like it. Everybody is on edge, it seems like. You go in the stores and the clerks act like they don't want to wait on you. People I've known for forty years pass me by on the street. I know I'm an old man and I forget sometimes what it was that I was going to say, but I used to feel that I was welcome when I went places and now I don't any more."

"You're always welcome here," Martha said quietly. "I oughtn't to have to tell you that."

"I know I am," Mr. Ellis said. "I saw your lights and so I thought I'd just drop in for a minute. Bud and Mary don't want me to go anywhere. They're afraid I can't take care of myself, but I'm just as able to take care of myself as I ever was. I was out sprinkling ashes on the walk this morning and you'd have thought— You folks weren't going any place?"

"No," Martha said. "I don't go out much in this weather."

"I don't want to keep you if you've got to go someplace," Mr. Ellis said. "And they're always keeping things from me. Things I have a right to know. Nelson Streuber died and they didn't tell me. I didn't get to the funeral."

"They probably didn't want to upset you," Martha said, avoiding Austin's eyes.

"He was five years younger than I am, and I never expected to outlive him. . . . That nice young girl—what's her name? —from Mississippi?"

"Nora Potter," Martha said.

"I saw her the other day," old Mr. Ellis said. "I saw her on the street with some children and stopped to talk to her. She's always nice to old people. 'You don't belong here,' I said to her. 'You ought to go home. You don't look happy like you did when you come out to the farm that day with your folks,' and she said, 'Mr. Ellis, I'm going soon. I've learned my lesson.'" Old Mr. Ellis nodded solemnly. "'I've learned my lesson,' she said. I always enjoy hearing Southerners talk. It's softer than the speech you hear ordinarily, and it seems to belong to them."

Austin examined his hands as if they contained the terribly important answer to some riddle like *As soft as silk, as white as milk, As bitter as gall, a thick wall, And a green coat cover me all.*

"Mr. and Mrs. Potter will be sorry that they missed you," Martha said.

"Are they still here?" Mr. Ellis asked in surprise. "Why, I thought they'd gone home long ago. . . . Austin . . . Martha . . . There's something I want to say to you. I'm an old man. You may not see me many times more. I've seen a great many things happen. I've had almost as much experience as it's possible to have in a lifetime, and people ought to value it. Because that's all there is to growing old. You just gradually accumulate a store of experience. But nobody wants it. Nobody cares what I've seen or what I think. Times have changed, they say, but that's where they're wrong. There's nothing new. Only more of the same. Gradually you accumulate a store of experience—but I said that, didn't I? Bud gets so annoyed with me when I repeat myself. In the summer it's all right. I can go out to the farm every day, and I'm not under foot. But now I have to stay pretty close to home, on account of the ice and snow, and I don't want to catch cold and have it turn into pneumonia. An old man like me, I could go off just like that. I wouldn't mind too much. I've outlived my usefulness, but dying isn't something you can do whenever you have a mind to. You have to wait out your time. My father lived to be almost ninety. The last two years he was bedridden, but his mind was clear. And when he died we were all there around the bed and saw him go. . . ."

Mr. Ellis stayed a long while—long enough for Austin to surrender his last hope of restoring the atmosphere of trust and affection that had been broken in upon. What he had to say he would say, but it would not sound the same now.

He helped Mr. Ellis on with his coat and handed him his muffler. In repayment for this courtesy, old Mr. Ellis said with a twinkle in his eyes, "The greatest hardship in the old days was courting the girls. There was only one room in the house and the old folks would sit and watch the proceedings. It was exceedingly hard on a bashful young man like me. But I managed. We all did, somehow or other."

He would have gone off without his hat if Austin hadn't forced it on him, and he refused to be helped down the icy steps. "I'm all right," he said. "I'll just hang onto the railing." Slowly, a step at a time, as if it were the grave he was descending to, he made it, and said one last good night, quite cheerfully for one so old and so tired out by waiting.

Austin shut the door upon the cold, and turned around in time to see Martha start up the stairs.

"Don't go up just yet," he said. "I haven't told you why it's so important that I see Nora right away."

"I understand that it *is* important and that's enough."

"You don't understand a damn thing," he said, furious at her. The sound of footsteps on the porch made him turn. Mr. Potter and Randolph had come home from the hospital.

6

The waiting room on the ground floor of the hospital had a tile floor, cream-colored walls, a mission table, three hard straight chairs, and a wooden bench. The one window looked out on the back wing of the hospital—a red brick wall with a double row of windows that were green-shaded, curtained, quiet, and noncommittal. The grey day had been warm. There were bare patches in the snow. The trees had here and there a trace of their white outline, and from the icicles hanging along the gutters drops of water fell at regular intervals as if from a leaky faucet. The light was failing, the afternoon all but over when Austin put his hat and coat and muffler on a chair and sat down to wait for Dr. Seymour.

Over the bench was a sepia print of Sir Galahad with his young head bent, brooding, and his arm thrown over his charger's neck. There was also a wall vase with artificial flowers in it. The flowers were made of crepe paper dipped in wax. They did not resemble any actual flowers and there had been no attempt to convey a general truth, such as what a flower is or why there are such things as flowers, but merely to make one more disconcerting object. There were no magazines on the mission table. It was not part of the hospital's intention to offer entertainment or to make the time pass more quickly for visitors who, more often than not, stayed too long and ran the patients' fever up and were a nuisance, all around.

Austin crossed and uncrossed his legs impatiently and

waited for Dr. Seymour to appear in the doorway. Nora's letter he had put off answering until it was too late for anything but remorse because he hadn't answered it. He wasn't, as she thought, indifferent to her feelings or to what happened to her, and never had been. He didn't despise her and there was no reason for her to feel that she had forfeited all claim to his approval and friendship. She had done nothing wrong. If anyone was to blame, he was, for not realizing sooner that there was no way he could guide her through an emotional crisis that he himself was the cause of. But to think of her lying there day after day, in pain, not wanting to live, because she thought the one person in the whole world that she loved had no use for her, that she was nothing, that there was no place for her anywhere . . . *You're young, Nora. This won't go on forever. And I do love you, in a way. . . . No, that isn't right. It's not love exactly but tenderness and concern. I want you to be happy and to have everything that life has to offer. I don't want you to lose hope or think that you have to compromise. I want you to go on fighting for the things you believe in. The feeling I have for you isn't like the feeling I have for Martha or for anybody else. It's somehow different and unlimited, and whether we see each other or not . . .*

When Dr. Seymour walked in, he brought with him the hurry of an orchestra conductor arriving late, with the audience already seated and impatient and the musicians waiting in the pit. He was a clean-shaven man in his sixties, small-boned, brusque, with mild blue eyes that had a certain vanity in them (his treatment of chronic nephrosis had been published recently in the monthly bulletin of the American Medical Association) and very little interest in or patience with people who were not sick.

"How's everything at home?" he asked.

"All right," Austin said.

"Nothing happening yet?"

Austin shook his head.

"It will shortly. If it doesn't we'll make it happen. Her pains should have started by now. . . . About this visit upstairs—I don't want you to tire her out, do you understand? If it had been anybody else, I wouldn't have let them come, but I know I can depend on you not to stay too long. Terrible thing that was. I don't know why people can't learn not to pour kerosene on a fire. Remember now—five minutes and no more."

7

If everything I do is wrong, Austin said to himself as he paced the length and breadth of his office overlooking the courthouse square, *then I will not do anything. I will not raise my hand . . .*

The meeting with Nora had not come off the way he had hoped it would. Instead of putting her mind at rest, he had had to go searching from room to room, all up and down the corridor, looking for a nurse to come and quiet Nora's hysterical weeping; and then he had to stand, shamefaced and humiliated, while the nurse gave him a piece of her mind.

He would not try to help anybody in trouble ever again. There was no help, and even if there were, he was in no position to offer it. He could only make things worse—unbearable trouble out of what was no greater and no less a calamity than being born. After this he would keep out of it, let them sink or swim.

It was a pity Martha wasn't at the hospital. She ought to have seen that performance. If he told her about it now, she wouldn't believe it. Nobody would, in their right mind, but it was the last show of that kind he would ever put on. He knew now what it was and why he did it. Other men were vain of their appearance or their clothes or because they were attractive to women or because they could drive a four-in-hand, but he had to be better than anybody else; he had to distinguish between right and wrong.

She came to his office that day all dressed up in a long white dress and a big hat with red roses on it, but that was all the good it did her. He was incapable of doing anything that wasn't upright and honest. He couldn't carry on behind his wife's back with some girl who threw herself at him because that wouldn't be Austin King. He didn't laugh at Nora or treat her like a child (which was what she was) or lose his temper or do anything that would have made it easier for her to forget him or him to forget her. He sent her away thinking of him as a sincere, high-minded man who wouldn't allow himself to fall in love with her because he was already married to somebody else. For that she admired him, naturally, because she was young and didn't know any better. But he knew better. And so did Martha. After they were married, he expected Martha to be to him what his mother was to his father—unquestioning, loyal, bound by a common purpose. He waited to hear her say to Ab *Your father says* . . . in the same tone of voice his mother used with him, and Martha never did and never would. He had made her marry him against her will, or if not against her will then before she was ready. He rushed her into it. Later he said *If she won't work with and beside me, then I will do it for both of us* . . . In his pride he said *I can do everything that is necessary. I can make a marriage all by myself.* . . . Well he hadn't, and the only thing that seemed at all strange was that he had tried so hard, that it was so difficult for him to stop trying, even now, when he no longer cared what happened . . . unless possibly something inside him didn't want to try, didn't want their marriage to work out.

And how did he know that his mother was unquestioning, loyal, and devoted? When the first of the year came around, his father, confronted with the annual bill from the dry-goods store and worrying about where he'd get the money to pay it, demanded *Why did you need these three spools of cotton thread?* and *What's this five yards of flowered calico?* and then his mother cried and in the end he couldn't think of any better way to deal with it and so she went right on charging things. But it was a source of great bitterness between them. They were in business together, the business of having a home and raising a family. And if he hadn't been trying so hard not to discover it, he would have seen, by the time he was ready for long pants, that habit and money and fear are what hold married people together, not love. Love has nothing to do with it.

Well, he was finished. Let the bills accumulate on the hall table. He was tired of paying bills. Mr. Holby could find a new partner and take over the front office for himself, as he had all along wanted to do. This wasn't really his office anyway but his father's, and he couldn't fill his father's place here and ought never to have tried. He ought never to have tried to do anything. What happened was bound to happen, from the beginning, and all you needed to do was to lie back and let it happen. . . .

The ringing of the telephone broke in upon his thoughts. He stopped and waited a moment, and then realized that it was nearly seven, Miss Stiefel had gone home, and the outer office was dark. The ringing was repeated and insistent and like a voice calling his name. With his hand on the receiver he hesitated.

I'm through, he said to himself. *Let accident decide. Let—*

The telephone stopped ringing.

8

"About six o'clock or a little after," Mrs. Potter said. "We were all at the supper table, and I heard her call Austin, so I put down my napkin and went up to see if she wanted anything and—"

"You say the pains have stopped coming?" Dr. Seymour said.

"They stopped soon after I talked to you."

"How long did she have them?"

"Oh, about an hour," Mrs. Potter said. "I had some trouble getting you at first. I called your office and they told me you were at the hospital, and when I called the hospital they said you had just gone, so I waited and called the office again, and that time—"

"I'll go on up and have a look at her," he said. He took off his coat, his scarf, and his fur-lined gloves and left them in a neat pile on the chair in the hall.

"She's resting quite comfortably," Mrs. Potter said. "I took her up some toast and tea, and she ate that, and she says she feels fine."

"I'd much rather she didn't feel fine at this point," Dr. Seymour said, and started up the stairs.

When he came down ten minutes later, Mrs. Potter said, "Is everything all right?"

"No," he said, "it isn't. The pains may start again in a little while, but if they don't— Where's Austin? Why didn't *he* call me?"

"Cousin Austin isn't here."

"Where is he?"

"I don't know," Mrs. Potter said. "When he didn't come home for supper, I supposed that he had made some other plans. But Martha doesn't know where he is either."

"Did you call his office?"

"I've called three times."

"Well, keep on trying," Dr. Seymour said. "I don't like what's going on upstairs. I'm going to move her to the hospital, and then if anything happens, we're at least prepared for it."

"She was expecting to have the baby here," Mrs. Potter said.

"I don't care where she was expecting to have it, and two hours from now she won't either, I hope. I want you to go up now and get her dressed and ready. Don't hurry her. I don't want her to be frightened. Just get her dressed and bring her downstairs. The telephone is in here, isn't it?"

9

"He *was* here," the waitress in the dining room of the Draperville Hotel said. "He came in and ordered the steak dinner."

"What time was that?" Randolph asked.

"About seven o'clock or a little after."

"You're sure it was Mr. King and not somebody else?"

"Oh, no," the waitress said. "It was Mr. King, all right."

She was tired and her feet hurt. From years of watching people eat, she had contracted a hatred of the human race (and of traveling salesmen in particular) that was like a continual low-grade fever. If arsenic had been easily obtainable and its effects impossible to trace, she would have sprinkled the trays with it and carried them into the dining room with a light heart. But the handsome young man with the Southern accent confused and troubled her. She wanted to say to him, with her hand on his coat-sleeve: *Why do you care?*

"He sat over at that table in the corner and he was alone. At least—no, I'm sure there wasn't anybody with him. I noticed that he didn't eat anything after it was brought to him, and I meant to ask if his steak was all right, but I was busy and pretty soon he got up and went out."

"How long ago?"

"Oh, maybe half an hour, maybe a little more. I couldn't say exactly. He left a dollar bill on the tablecloth, and the dinner only came to—"

"If he comes back," Randolph said, "tell him to call home immediately—no, tell him to go straight to the hospital."

"Is anything wrong?" the waitress asked, ready to take off her apron and put on her hat and coat and go out into the night with him. Her question went unanswered.

As Randolph opened the door of the hack that was waiting outside, he said, "Drive around to the south side of the square. He may have come back in the meantime."

There were no lights in the windows that were lettered *Holby and King, Attorneys at Law.*

"I'm going to try once more, even though the place is dark. Keep an eye out for him. He may be walking around the streets somewhere," Randolph said to the cabman. He jumped out of the hack, ran up the stairs, and rattled the doorknob. It was still locked.

"Austin?" he shouted.

No answer. Not a sound. He pounded on the locked door, waited, and then pounded again. A door opened at his back and, turning around, Randolph saw Dr. Hieronymous, the osteopath. He was a large man with grey hair and a grey face. His heavy shoulders could easily have broken the door down for Randolph. He said in a mild voice, "Were you looking for somebody?"

"I'm looking for Mr. King."

"He was just here. At least I heard somebody come up the stairs. I don't know whether it was Mr. King or not."

"About five minutes ago?"

"Why, yes," Dr. Hieronymous said. "I'd say it was about that. Not more than ten minutes anyway."

"And was there anybody just before or just after?"

"No, I don't think there was."

"Then it wasn't Mr. King you heard, it was me," Randolph said, and resumed pounding on the door.

10

The nurse rang the bell of the elevator repeatedly before the elevator ropes and then the elevator descended past their eyes. It was operated by a lame Negro who had difficulty opening and closing the doors.

"We're going to put you in the room at the end of the hall," the nurse said as she stepped out on the second floor. "It'll be quieter."

"I'm not sensitive to noise," Martha King said.

"I was thinking of the other patients," the nurse said cheerfully and then laughed.

The room at the end of the hall had two windows, one looking out on Washington Street and the other on the street in front of the hospital, where Dr. Seymour's horse and rig were waiting, with the reins tied to the hitching post.

This is not at all the way I wanted it to be, Martha said to herself. *I thought I'd be at home, in my own bed, with everything around me the way it always is. I thought Austin would* . . .

"Do you want a cup of tea?" the floor nurse asked.

"Yes, I do," Martha said. "I had some tea just a little while ago, but I'm terribly hungry."

"You'll have to work fast," the floor nurse said, "or you'll be hungry a long time. How long ago did you have your first baby?"

"Four and a half years."

"Dr. Seymour is going to deliver it?"

"Yes."

"The first thing to do is to get into bed. Do you have any pains now?"

"No," Martha said. She surrendered her pocketbook and gloves, and allowed the nurse to help her off with her coat.

Standing across the street from Mike Farrell's saloon, Austin heard mournful singing, and then an argument that ended abruptly with the sound of breaking glass and a man being thrust out through the swinging door.

In the alley that ran beside the pool hall, Austin stopped beside a window with the blind drawn, offering a view of several pairs of feet under a table. The window was open about an inch, and he heard the sound of cards being shuffled and very little difference between winning and losing.

He stood in the alley looking under the drawn blind for a very long while. On a street beyond the post office, where there was a row of shabby houses, Austin King leaned against a tree and saw the third house from the corner visited by a man on guard against watchers—a man who came in stealth and left twenty minutes later, less alive and (judging by his walk, his carriage) less hopeful than when he came. The man who crossed over to the other side of Lafayette Street to keep from being recognized Austin would not have known anyway, but neither did he know the man with the miner's cap who spoke to him by name.

Here and there he saw a light in some house, a night light left burning for a child or a sick person afraid of the dark. Austin was grateful for any illumination—for the dim light in the lobby of the Draperville Hotel, and for the light in the hack-stand next door, and for the light in Dr. Danforth's livery stable, where Snowball McHenry slept on a pile of horse blankets.

The jewelry store had an iron grating across the windows and a heavy padlock on the door, and a light was left burning so that Monk Collins, the policeman on night duty, could see into the back of the store. Shapiro's Clothing Store and Joe Becker's shoe store were dark, and so was the hardware store, the barber shop, the lumber yard, the two banks. The sign-boards outside of Giovanni's confectionery and moviedrome (where if you bought an ice-cream soda you could sit in the back room and watch a moving picture of a man hanging over the edge of a cliff by his fingers) had been taken in off the side-walk for the night, but there was a light on the first floor of the courthouse, for the night watchman, and on the second floor of the telephone building, and there were also the overhead arc lights where Austin King met and parted company with his shadow.

The sound of a violin coming through closed shutters kept him standing on the sidewalk in front of a shack on Williams Street for twenty minutes, during which time he experienced all the sensations of earthly happiness. The music stopped and Austin walked on.

Standing across the street from the jail he found himself talking to an old man named Hugh Finders, who was, many people believed, in some way connected with a brutal murder some twenty years before. Where he came from, Austin had no idea. The old man simply materialized out of the night.

"I seen you around, since you were in kneebritches," he said to Austin, "but this is the first time I ever talked to you, I guess. Everybody's so busy these days. I see them ride by in their fine carriages, but they don't have no time to talk to poor old Hugh."

There was a time when people talked to poor old Hugh. For three days, various lawyers kept him on the witness stand, trying to find out about the bloodstains that were discovered on the inside of his hack. The questions they asked he did not feel called upon to answer, and all that the street light revealed now was an old man with a cancerous skin condition and wisps of dry white hair sticking out from under a filthy cap. "You live on Elm Street, don't you?" he said. "I know. Big white house. The old Stevenson place. You're married and got a little girl, ain't you? Pretty little thing. I seen her with your wife. She don't know me, I expect. I was always interested in you on account of your father. He was a fine man. Nobody ever went to him in trouble that didn't get help. First he'd give you a lecture, take the hide right off you, and then he'd reach down in his pocket. He used to think I drank too much and I guess maybe he was right, but we can't all sit up there, high and mighty, and pass judgment on our fellow men. Some of us poor devils has to be judged. Otherwise your daddy would of been out of a job. I always meant to pay back the money he loaned me but I never managed to, and he never pressed me for it. . . ."

With a slight weave in his walk, he started toward the street light at the end of the block, but to the best of Austin's knowledge he never got there. Somewhere between the jail and the corner Hugh Finders disappeared and his secret vanished with him.

Austin walked through a park where there were band concerts in the summer-time, and then through the deserted courthouse square. The lighted clock face, so like his father's gold watch hanging in the sky, told him that it was late and that he would have to begin the next day without enough rest, but clocks have been known to be wrong. There might be no next day.

He passed the stairs that led up to the office of Holby and King without taking advantage of the refuge they offered him, without even knowing they were there. He was very tired. He didn't remember ever being as tired as this. And a little bit at a time, over a period of hours, he'd been letting himself down. He'd been watching what other people do, so he could learn to be more like them. And somehow, maybe because he didn't understand what he saw or it could have been that he was just too tired, it didn't seem worth the bother. Turning right at the corner, he walked one more block, crossed the interurban tracks, and ended up on the brick platform that ran in front of the railway station.

The through train from St. Louis, due in at 2:37 A.M., was late, and Austin waited on the station platform with his back turned against the icy wind. It was late January, and so the wind was due also, bringing another consignment of winter to the ice-locked lakes of Wisconsin, the snow-covered cornfields of Illinois. There was a potbellied stove in the station, and Austin went inside, thinking to warm his hands, but the heat and the stale odor made him lightheaded, and so he walked out again immediately. He was in a state of shivering excitement that required air.

Facing the station was a block of stores: the cigar store and Mike Farrell's saloon, Dalton's grocery, the shoe repair shop, the bicycle shop, and the monument works—all dark at this time of night. Across the tracks the bird house on a pole—with its porches and round windows, doors, gables, and cupola, a fairly accurate statement of the style of architecture most admired around the year Eighteen-eighty and still surviving along College Avenue—was untenanted. The flower bed that in summer spelled Draperville in marigolds and striped petunias had been erased by heavy frosts. This could have been almost any station anywhere along the line. As Austin passed and repassed the station master's lighted cage, in an effort to keep warm, he could hear the telegraph clicker and see the ticket agent with a green eyeshade on his forehead.

The signal lights switched far down the tracks, south of

town. The ticket agent came out of the station. His description afterward of what happened that night would in no way have agreed with Austin King's. *Number 317 was coming in a little late*, one of them would have said. The other would have said *Time was cool and flowed softly around me. I didn't like to put my head down in cold that might not be too clean, and it was hard to swim against the current without doing that, so I drifted downstream toward the monument works and then fought my way back. Twice I tried to crawl out onto the platform but it didn't work. Each time I lost my hold. The platform, the station, the empty birdhouse, the stars, and Mike Farrell's saloon fell away from under me and I was swept downstream. The third time I put my head under and swam straight toward the light. It was easier than I imagined. When I stopped swimming I was well within the wedge made by two parallel steel rails meeting at infinity, and the light was shining right on my face. I tried to stand up but there was no bottom. There was nothing to stand on, and when I came up for air a second time I was still inside the wedge. Although I had been swimming much harder than before, I hadn't got anywhere. I was out of breath and I knew I was somewhere I had no business to be.*

You don't have to have water to drown in. All it requires is that your normal vision be narrowed down to a single point and continue long enough on that point until you begin to remember and to achieve a state of being which is identical with the broadest vision of human life. You can drown in a desert, in mountain air, in an open car at night with the undersides of the leafy branches washing over you, mile after midnight mile. All you need is a single idea, a point of intense pain, a pin-prick of light growing larger and steadier and more persuasive until the mind and the desire to live are both shattered in starry sensation, leading inevitably toward no sensation whatever. . . .

The station master said something that Austin (with the light falling all around him from a great height) did not hear.

. . . *He's right, I guess. He must be right. I've known Fred Vercel for years and never knew him to say anything that wasn't so. If he did call to me, as he says—if he warned me, I probably stepped back, in plenty of time, and the rest is some kind of strange hallucination. But I never had any such feeling before. I know he spoke to me, but the way I remember it, I couldn't hear what he said. I couldn't hear anything but the sound of the approaching engine, and even that stopped when I went under. I had never been in a situation I couldn't get out of, and I held my breath and felt myself being rolled over and over, helpless, on the bottom. My mind, in an orderly fashion, reached one conclusion after another and I knew finally that there wasn't going to be any more for me. This was all. Here in this place. Now. And I felt the most terrible sadness because it was not the way I expected to die. It was just foolish. I shouldn't have looked into the light so long. I knew better. And I was not quite ready to die. There were certain things that I still wanted to do. I suppose everybody feels that way when their time comes.*

I don't know how I got home. I just found myself there, looking through the dining-room window at the thermometer to see how cold it was, turning off the lights, going up the stairs to bed. On my pillow there was a note from Mrs. Potter, and after I had read it I went back downstairs, turning on the lights I had just turned off. Until daylight I paced the floor of the hospital waiting room alone. Then Doc Seymour walked in and said, "We're in for a long wait. Austin, I think you'd better go home and get some rest."

II

"The waiting room is right down the hall," the nurse said, smiling. "Try not to take it too hard."

"I know where it is," Austin said.

He sat down and let his head back so that the wall would have the burden of supporting it. The artificial flowers and Sir Galahad reminded him that he had been here the day before, as well as earlier this morning. He tried not to look at them. He was conscious of a strange sensation in his mouth, as if his teeth were watering. The rims of his eyelids felt hard and dry.

In the confusion of dressing and breakfast and getting a suitcase packed for Ab and delivering her at the Danforths' front door, he had left his gold watch under his pillow. He got up and went out into the hall. What had seemed like half an hour had actually been two and a half minutes. This error in calculation was destined to repeat itself at varying intervals all through the day.

12

With her nose pressed to the window pane and her forlorn back reflected in Mrs. Danforth's silver gazing globe, Abbey King looked out on the same perspective that she was accustomed to seeing from the window in the front hall and the front living-room window at home. The only difference was that she could see one more house to the left and one less house to the right. No one came in or went out of or walked by the houses. The ground was bare, the trees and shubbery appeared to have given up forever the idea and intention of producing green leaves. With shreds of brown attached to it, a lateral shoot of the pink rambler trained to grow up the trellis on the east side of the Danforths' house was bowing and bending in the wind, a few inches from Ab's face. If it should turn out that there is no such place as Purgatory, there is at least Elm Street on a grey day in January.

"Would you like to put on your things and go outside and play?" Mrs. Danforth asked.

"I don't care," Ab said.

"We'll bundle up warmly, and if you get cold, tell me and we'll come in."

Entrusting her mittened hand to Mrs. Danforth's gloved one, Ab made a tour of the yard, and Mrs. Danforth lifted her up so that she could look in the window of the playhouse, made of two piano boxes. The key to the playhouse was lost and no one had been in it for many years. Ab saw a school desk, a blackboard, and some dusty paper dolls, and was satisfied that the playhouse, like the flower garden, was finished for a while. Occasionally, her eyes turned to the house next door. She knew that her mother was not there. Whether anyone else was, and what they were doing, the house did not say, and Ab, in exile, did not ask.

A dray went past the Danforths' house, past the Kings' and stopped in front of the Beaches'. A man got down from the driver's seat, and immediately, as if by some prearranged signal, a pack of children appeared around the corner of the house across the street, crossed over, and gathered on the sidewalk.

"You want to join them?" Mrs. Danforth asked.

Ab stood timidly pushing her hands further into her mittens. She was not allowed to go beyond the confines of her own yard, but then she wasn't at home now and the Danforths' yard had no fence but was open to the street.

"It's all right," Mrs. Danforth said. "I'll stay here and watch you."

The sight of the blue kindergarten chairs and the children's excited comments were enough to break the thread (slight in any case) that bound Ab's right mitten to Mrs. Danforth's left glove. She started slowly off down the sidewalk, broke into a run as she passed her own house, and then slowed down again to a walk. There was no Miss Lucy or Miss Alice to coax Ab into the group. She stood on the outskirts, ignored by the others, who left her standing there and went from the sidewalk down into the street. *Don't go in the street*, her mother's voice said. Ab looked back. Mrs. Danforth nodded. Taking her life in her hands, Ab pressed through the children until she was able to see into the back end of the dray.

"Look out!" a boy in a corduroy coat said to her. "You'll get conked on the head if you aren't careful."

This offhand admonition, neither friendly nor unfriendly, was very important. First of all, it recognized her existence, a fact that would otherwise have remained in doubt. Second, it conferred citizenship papers on her. From now on she was free to come and go in a commonwealth where the games were sometimes rough and where the older inhabitants sometimes picked on the younger ones but nobody ever had to deal with or try to understand emotions and ideas that were thirty years too old for them. Abbey King attached herself to the hero in the corduroy coat, followed him from the street to the sidewalk and back again, and with her eyes on his dirty, tough, young face, waited to see what remarkable words, what brave acts, he would spontaneously produce.

Satisfied that Ab no longer needed watching, Mrs. Danforth turned and went back into the house that invited daydreaming, that was dark, cavelike, and full of objects which had demonstrated conclusively how things survive and people all too often do not.

13

When the dray loaded with kindergarten furniture drew up before the Beaches' house, Alice propped the storm door open wide with a brick covered with carpet from the house in St. Paul, and then went back inside. As she peered out through the front window, the expression on her face was of relief, almost of happiness. The chairs were scattered over the frozen lawn, and the children sat down on them as if they had been invited to a party. The two movingmen started up the walk, carrying a table between them. Except that they held it by the ends instead of by silver handles at the side, the effect was that of pallbearers carrying a coffin. The box of colored yarn which they had set on top of the table might so easily have been flowers sent by some close friend of the family. When they reached the steps, Alice came outside again. The man in front put his end down for a moment, tipped his hat, and said, "Where do you want it, lady?"

He was short and stocky, his face so capable and kind that she was tempted to tell him everything, but the other man was still holding his end of the table, so she said timidly, "In the attic, please." She was prepared if the two men exchanged a glance not to notice it, but no such unpleasantness occurred. Tracking soot in after them, they headed for the stairs. "Easy," the man in front said. "Watch the newel post." The man in back was enormous, loose limbed, open mouthed, and entirely at the mercy of the mind that directed his strength. At the turn of the stairs, he managed to leave a cruel scratch that no amount of furniture polish would ever remove from the banister.

Halfway down the upstairs hall, the attic door stood open. On the wall beside it, a glass knob the size of a dollar shone red, an indication that the light was on in the attic. The hall was narrow and the table had to be turned on end before it would go through the door and up the steep attic stairs. Lucy stood waiting for them by the chimney, with a man's heavy sweater on over her cotton dress. She had cleared a space for the kindergarten equipment from the accumulation and welter of years—suitboxes, trunks, old furniture, lampshades, riding boots, books and magazines stacked in piles, boxes that were not always marked as to their contents and might contain

Christmas tree ornaments or Mr. Beach's clothes. The men made five trips in all, and Alice went with them each time in an effort to prevent further damage to the stairs.

Lucy remained in the attic, where the kindergarten equipment looked strangely bright and fresh; too bright and too fresh to be what it really was, the death of all her hopes. Why is it we never give anything away? she wondered. Other people discard and dispose of things and start afresh with only what they need and can use, but everything we ever had is here, ready to speak out against us on the Day of Judgment. . . . She pushed the chairs closer together so that the kindergarten equipment took up less room, and rearranged the colored paper, the yarns, and the boxes of scissors in a neat pile.

"Are you still up there?" Alice called from below, and, receiving an answer, came up the attic stairs.

"It doesn't look like very much, does it?" she said, staring at the tables and chairs.

"Well, it's paid for," Lucy said. "That's the main thing. Maybe we can sell it some time."

"Or maybe we can use it ourselves," Alice said, "after people have forgotten."

"No," Lucy said. "It's done for. I don't know why we keep it. We'll never have any use for it, and we'll never sell it. It's just going to stay up here, with the trunks and the Baedekers." Her eyes took in the corner where the suitcases were, splattered with labels—*Lago di Como*, *Cadenabbia*, *Grand Hotel Nice*, *Roma*, *Firenze* . . .

"Any time we want to start living our lives all over again, everything we need is here—except courage."

"Maybe some day we'll have houses of our own," Alice said, "and then whatever will we do with it all?"

"That's done for, too," Lucy said. "I'm forty-seven and you're forty-three. People may call us the Beach girls but we're no spring chickens, either of us. We've had our chance and missed it, and I'm so tired I don't care any more. All I want to do is rest. I don't know why people don't tell you when you're young that life is tiring. It probably wouldn't have done any good, but then again it might have."

"I don't feel that way," Alice said. She took a kindergarten chair and sat down, facing a bookcase crammed with glass and china. On a level with her eyes there was a milk pitcher which she remembered from her childhood. It was blue and white, and two young women (sisters, perhaps) walked in a garden, each with her hand through a young man's arm. A duenna with a dog at her feet sat watching them, approvingly. And in the background there was a ruined temple, undoubtedly to the shaggy god who, from his place under the handle, kept an eye on both couples. Under the spout there was a motto which Alice Beach knew without having to read it:

For every evil
under the sun
there is a remedy
or there is none,
if there be one
try and find it,
if there be none
never mind it.

She turned her face away from this familiar message and looked out of the attic window at the bare branches of a big maple tree. After a while she said, "Sometimes I have to stop and remember how old I am."

"You've got a few more years to go," Lucy said. "Then you'll be tired, too, like me. You won't care any more what happens to you or what might have happened. Don't look at me like that."

"I can't bear to have you say such things."

"You don't have to listen. And besides, I don't have to say them. I can just think them instead, if that will make it any easier for you."

"It won't."

"Well, then, you'd better go away. I'll even help you."

"Where would I go?"

"Anywhere. I can manage here without you, now. You can go anywhere in the world you please. There never was enough money for two but there's enough for one, and you might as well take it and go abroad. You always liked the Dalmatian Coast. Go back to Ragusa and try it there for a while."

"What about Mama?"

"Well, what about her?"

"It might kill her if I left home now."

"Nothing will kill her. She'll outlive both of us. She'll outlive everybody on Elm Street. She's not ever going to die. It's time you realized that. She's going to live forever. And she can't stop you from going because I won't let her. I could have stayed in Europe if I'd really wanted to. I can manage her now and I could have managed her then. Deep down in my heart I didn't want to. I wanted her to manage me. And she has, I'll say that for her. She's never been so sick or so tired and discouraged with Papa and us and herself that she didn't manage things the way we wanted her to manage them. So pack your bag and put on your hat and go, and it'll be all right. Go to Mississippi if you don't want to go abroad. Go stay with the Potters on their plantation. Mrs. Potter asked us to last summer. All you have to do is tell her you'd like to go with them when they go. Maybe you'll find someone down there. Sometimes a widower with children will—"

Lucy turned her head to listen. Both of them heard, faint and far away, the ting-a-ling of a bedside bell.

"I'd better go see what she wants," Alice said.

"Let her wait," Lucy said. "This is more important. And don't look so frightened. Try and think calmly and clearly. Try to see what it is that you really want to do. And whatever it is, I don't care if it's to be a bareback rider in a circus, I'll help you."

These offers which come too late or at the wrong time, in words that are somehow unacceptable, are the saddest, the most haunting part of family life.

"Lucy, please stop!" Alice exclaimed as she started for the stairs. "I don't pick at you. Why can't you let me alone?"

14

"Mama?"

"She isn't here," Mr. Potter said. "You've got a new nurse."

"Where is she?" Nora asked.

"She went back to the house to rest. She didn't get much sleep last night, so I said I'd take over. Is there anything you'd like me to do for you?"

"What's that awful shouting?"

"Some poor soul is having a hard time of it, I guess," Mr. Potter said.

"It seems like it's been going on for hours and hours. I don't see why they don't put her somewhere where nobody can hear her. It's awful to have to listen to. . . . When's Mama coming back?"

"Pretty soon. How do you feel?"

"All right. Only I'm so tired of lying here."

"It won't be much longer. The doctor says you're coming along fine."

"I want to go home," Nora said.

"We'll take you home," Mr. Potter said, "just as soon as you're able to be moved."

"I want to be in my own room. I don't ever want to see this place again."

"Just be patient a little while longer," Mr. Potter said. "It doesn't do to try and rush things."

"But I've been here so long and this bed's so uncomfortable."

"Rome wasn't built in a day."

The screaming was resumed.

"What time is it?" Nora asked.

"Half after two."

"Did Mama say what time she was coming back?"

"She'll be along directly. Now that you're getting better, you mustn't expect her to be at your beck and call. You've put her through considerable strain, and she's worn out. From now on, it's up to us to spare her anything we can. . . . It's a bad thing to grow old, Nora, and know that you've been a fool."

After this abrupt revelation, the first that he had ever made to his daughter, Mr. Potter sat quietly and watched her eyes close and saw her breathing change gradually to the breathing of sleep.

The knowledge that you have been a fool hurts just as much, is just as hard to admit to yourself if you are young as when you are old. And Mr. Potter was not going to change his ways. Every error that people make is repeated over and over again, ad infinitum, ad nauseam, if they know what they are doing and cannot help themselves. The curtain goes up night after night on the same play, and if the audience weeps, it is because the hero always arrives at the abandoned sawmill in the nick of time, the heroine never gives in to the dictates of her heart and marries the man with a black mustache. There is not only a second chance, there are a thousand second chances to speak up, to act bravely for once, to face the fact that must sooner or later be faced. If there is really no more time, it can be faced hurriedly. Otherwise, it can be examined at leisure. The result is in either case the same. Windows that have been nailed shut for years are suddenly pried open, letting air in, letting love in, and hope. Cause is revealed to be, after all, nothing but effect. And the long, slow, dreadful working out of the consequences of any given mistake is arrested the very moment you accept the idea that there is waiting for you (and for your most beautiful bride, who with garlands is crowned, whose lightness and brightness doth shine in such splendor) six feet of empty ground.

15

Part of the time Martha King was convinced that there was some dreadful mistake—that they were trying to bury her alive. At other times she was quite rational, knew why she was there, answered correctly when Dr. Seymour leaned over the bed and asked, "How many fingers have I?" and was able to distinguish between her own screaming and the chant that came from the next room: *Oh doctor, doctor . . . oh my doctor . . .* sometimes pleading, sometimes a shriek, sometimes a singsong, but in the next room. Not the same as *Oh this is strong! The pain comes in waves! It's all in my back!* (she said that); or, *It's gone, isn't it?* (the nurse); or *Are my eyes swollen? It feels as if I were peeking through them . . . Oh now it's starting, it's starting!*

At three-thirty the nurse stopped referring to her watch, and time was measured by the slow progress of a patch of sunlight on the hospital floor.

To experience the emotion of waiting, in its purest form, you must pass through that stage when pacing the floor, or drumming with your fingers, or counting, or any of the mechanical aids gives release, and enter into the stage when the arrival of the minute hand of the clock at twelve is separated from the sound of striking by so long an interval that the whole nervous system cries out in vain for an end of waiting. Pain is movement, the waves of the sea rising, receding; waiting is the shore they break upon, the shore that changes, in time, but never noticeably. The will that waits and endures is not the same will that makes it possible for people to get out of bed in the morning or to choose between this necktie, this silk scarf, and that. It is something you never asked for and that never asked for you. You have it and live. You lose it and give up the ghost.

When the wall would no longer support the weight of Austin King's head, he got up and walked, his nerves on edge, his mind coming up against a high blank fear every six or seven paces. He felt his ribs encased in a delicate pressure that might, if he took too deep a breath, be shattered, and with it the last chance that things would turn out all right. A single nervous gesture, a word addressed to himself out loud, and his life, like a round glass paperweight turned upside down, would be filled with revolving white particles of terror. Then his natural patience would gain the upper hand and he was able to sit down and wait. And then in a little while his forehead would contract in furrows and his eyes cloud over with the suspicion that everything that could be done upstairs was not being done, and he would get up and walk again, with his hands clasped behind his back.

The sunlight reached the foot of the hospital bed and began to climb. Martha King's pains recurred at the same unchanging interval. A scrubwoman, in slavery to a bucket of soapy water and a grey mop, reached the doorway and looked in.

"What's the matter? Won't the baby come out?"

It was not a question but merely comfort, freely given and gratefully received.

"Have you any children?" Martha King asked, turning her face to the door.

"Nine alive and one dead."

"Was your second as hard as the first?"

"That's right. And with the second one I suffered the same pain."

The scrubwoman went on mopping the corridor. She did not know or ask who the patient in labor was. There was no lace on the hospital gown, and pain had first disfigured and was now busy disposing of the beautiful woman. Pain did its work so well that the Reverend Mr. Porterfield would not have recognized Mrs. King. Neither would the Beach girls nor Mrs. Danforth nor anyone who ever saw her gathering flowers in her garden of a late summer afternoon. First the beauty went, then the smile, then the light in the brown eyes, then the perfume, then the softness, then the fiery temper, and finally the deeper patience of love. All that was left was a creature writhing on a bed, trying to come to acceptable terms with agony.

The fading outside light was replaced by the glare of electric bulbs, and a black velvet cloth was hung outside the hospital windows.

"The only thing that frightens me is hearing that woman scream," Martha King said.

It was her own screaming that she heard, this time. The next room was as quiet as doom.

Disfigure and dispose of Martha King as, say, Mrs. Beach or old Mr. Ellis knew her and you have a nameless animal creature, but the creature is not the end and certainly not the answer. There is finally the self, biting its hands and shouting *It's awful . . . Oh please . . . It's so awful . . . Oh God I don't like it. . . .*

Out in the corridor there was the sound of dishes rattling, of talking and occasionally laughter. People who work in hospitals have their own sanity to think about and preserve.

16

When Ab had said her prayers, Mrs. Danforth lifted her into the big bed in the guestroom and drew the covers around her. "I'll leave the light on in the hall," she said, "and if you want anything in the night, call me and I'll hear you."

Ab looked up at her without answering, her eyelids weighted with sleep. Nobody but her mother had ever tucked her in bed before, and though Mrs. Danforth was kind and gentle with her, it wasn't the same. She wanted her mother. The sound of Mrs. Danforth's heels descending the stairs was not the sound her mother made.

The gaslight in the hall threw moving shadows and filled the bedroom with an uneasy light. From where Ab lay she could see a picture on the wall: A man in a white nightshirt, his legs sprawled across the sheets, was dreaming of a steeplechase, and horsemen in pink coats were jumping their horses over a brook. Ab did not understand that it was a dream picture. What she saw, by the flickering gaslight, was that the horses were going to land on the man in bed and trample him to death.

17

The mop, swishing in wet wide circles, brought the scrubwoman face to face with a glass window which acted as a frame to a picture that never hangs on the walls of the waiting room of doctors' offices. The operating table was tipped, so that the patient's feet were higher than her head, and the upper half of the body was covered by a sheet. The hands strapped to the side of the operating table looked bluish. The sheet moved up, down, up, down, with hard breathing. Dr. Seymour was cutting into the abdominal area, blotting up blood with a towel as the incision grew larger and larger. The scrubwoman made several wide swipes with the mop and then looked again. This time the incision was completed and the skin, held back by clamps, revealed a lake of blood, which the nurses were struggling to dispose of. Dr. Seymour, looking like a butcher, fitted the forceps into the abdomen and pulled. The forceps slipped and he put them in again and pulled with all his strength. Then, dispensing with the forceps, he reached in with his hand, wrist deep in blood and water, and pulled out a baby, dripping, waxlike, and limp.

The scrubwoman who had had ten children (of which nine were still living) stayed long enough at the window to make sure that this child was alive, and then moved slowly down the corridor, swirling the mop in wider and wider circles that left cloud patterns and wave patterns on the hexagonal tiled floor.

18

In the middle of the night Abbey King was awakened by a commotion downstairs at the front door. All sounds, all sensations that in the daytime are weakened or explained away by the mind's comforting interpretation in the night are magnified. This sound, so loud and so frightening, Ab never doubted for a second was on account of her. They were coming for her. They were going to get her and punish her at last for having been so many times a bad girl. Her only hope—that Mrs. Danforth wouldn't hear the knocking, or if she did hear it, wouldn't answer it—lasted only until she heard footsteps in the hall. Mrs. Danforth in a long dressing gown, with her hair in two braids down her back, went past the bedroom door.

Just one more chance, Ab begged, to her mother far away and to God farther away still. The steps went on down the stairs and Ab heard the chain unfastened, the key turn in the door, and a voice that wasn't a policeman's or a gypsy's but her father's voice said, "It's a boy."

Though there was now no reason for terror, it drained away very slowly.

"How's Martha?"

"She's all right. . . . I saw your light and thought I'd stop in and tell you."

"Did she have a hard time?"

"Toward the end. But they gave her morphine and she came through the operation without any difficulty. The baby weighs five pounds." There was an excitement and a happiness in her father's voice that Ab had never heard there before. She lay perfectly still waiting for him to ask about her, to start up the stairs, to call out when he reached the landing.

"You must be done in."

"No, I'm fine."

"You may be fine but you look like a ghost. Let me make you some coffee," Mrs. Danforth said. "It won't take but a minute."

"No," her father said. "Thank you just the same. It's been a long ordeal and I'd better go on home."

The last thing Ab heard was the sound of Mrs. Danforth's soft slippers on the stairs. Sometime during the remainder of the night, the pink-coated horsemen rode over her on their terrible horses, and she died without dying, and cried *Daddy!* . . . and woke up with arms around her and heard a voice saying "There, there . . . There, there . . . You've been having a bad dream."

19

"But I've told her repeatedly," Mary Caroline said. "She knows it's my favorite blouse and that I don't want her to wear it. She has lots more clothes than I do, and I don't think it was a bit nice of her."

"You mustn't be selfish with your things," Mrs. Link said.

"I'm not," Mary Caroline said. "But when I showed her the spot that won't come out, she just said she was sorry and let it go at that."

"The next time I'm downtown," Mrs. Link said, "I'll get some material and—"

"I'd rather pick it out myself. If you don't mind," Mary Caroline said.

"No, I don't mind."

Tolerant and serene, loving both her daughters equally, Mrs. Link viewed the neighborhood as they walked along. There was a hack waiting in front of the Kings' and as Mary Caroline and Mrs. Link passed on the opposite side of the street, the Mathein boy came out with two suitcases, which he stowed away on the front seat of the hack.

"Did you remember to go and say good-by to the Potters?" Mrs. Link asked.

"Yes," Mary Caroline said. "Mrs. Potter asked me to come and visit them."

"Well, that was nice," Mrs. Link said.

The lace curtains in the Mercers' front window were new, and the Webbs' house looked all shut up as if they might be away. For a week now, Mrs. Link had been meaning to sit down with her needle and thread and change the yoke in her navy blue dress, so she could wear it to church on Sunday, and they really ought to stop and see Mrs. Macomber, who was all alone in that big house. . . . Dimly conscious of the fact that Mary Caroline had just asked her a question, she said, "What's that, dear?"

"I said are Mr. and Mrs. Mercer in love?"

"Why? What makes you ask?"

"I just wondered," Mary Caroline said.

If she'd only thought to bring Mrs. Macomber's blue cake plate, she could have killed two birds with one stone. On the other hand, it was hardly polite to return the plate with nothing on it. She would take over a loaf of orange bread after she baked on Tuesday. This time of year it always seemed as if there was nothing to look forward to but ice and snow, but it was February and so the winter was really half over. It didn't get dark till nearly five-thirty, and if Mr. Link was ever going to order the seeds for the vegetable garden, he'd better get ready and do it right away. The Sherman house, too bright a yellow when it was first painted, had faded to a pleasant color, but it would never look the way it had when it was white. And Doris shouldn't have taken Mary Caroline's blouse without asking.

"Are Mr. and Mrs. Sherman in love?" Mary Caroline asked as they turned in at their own front walk.

The hack was still standing in front of the Kings'. How poor Mr. King had managed all this time, with his wife in the hospital and a house full of company.

"I don't know, dear," Mrs. Link said. "I suppose they are. How can you tell?"

20

Half an hour before the hack arrived to drive them to the station, the Potters were all downstairs, ready and anxious to leave. Mr. Potter took his watch out and compared it with the clock in the hall. As he put the watch back in his vest pocket, he said, "Cousin Abbey, I think we're making a big mistake not to take you with us. You could have a pony to ride and lots of little pickaninnies to play with."

"Mr. Potter, stop teasing that child." With her hat and coat on, and her veil pinned over her face, Mrs. Potter sat down at the piano. She had just remembered a hymn that she hadn't thought of in years. With several false starts she made her way through the first half, and then time after time produced a wrong chord and had to go back and start over again. She was thinking about Nora—about the patches of drawn, purplish or whitish skin on her face and neck, which Dr. Seymour said would never go away, though they would lighten with time . . . *Oh that same wrong chord! So maddening.*

"Do you feel all right?" Randolph asked, bending over the sofa.

"Yes," Nora said, "but I wish Mama would remember the rest of that hymn. It's driving me crazy."

"If you want Mama, you'll have to take her hymns with her," Randolph said, and wandered out into the front hall, where a suitcase was waiting for somebody, some conscientious helpful person, to carry it out to the curbing.

"Cousin Austin said he'd be here by ten," Mr. Potter said, "and it's five after." And then, in response to the ringing of the front doorbell, "Now I wonder who that could be?"

"He'll be here. Don't go borrowing trouble," Randolph said.

"There's someone at the door," Mrs. Potter called from the piano.

"Do you think we ought to answer it?" Mr. Potter said. "We've said good-by to everybody I can think of."

"Maybe Cousin Austin forgot his key," Randolph said. He opened the door and a long conversation followed, while the cold swept in along the floor.

"For heaven's sake, shut the door!" Nora exclaimed.

"Is that right?" Randolph said. "Well, I'm sure they didn't mean to. How much is it? . . . I'll tell him. I certainly will . . . yes . . . Well, I don't think that's at all fair to you. . . . I'll tell you what you do. You come back next Saturday, there'll surely be somebody here then."

He closed the door and, turning to his father, said, "The paper boy. He hasn't been paid in weeks."

"How much was it?" Mr. Potter asked.

"Forty cents. They take it out of his earnings instead of waiting till he gets paid. He showed me a book with a lot of little coupons in it, so it must be right. Funny that Cousin Austin hasn't paid him. The boy's name is Dick Sisson, and he's saving his money to buy a new bicycle."

"It's twelve minutes after," Mr. Potter said, eyeing his watch.

Mrs. Potter, having remembered the rest of the hymn, left the piano triumphantly and said, "Randolph, come help me with your sister."

Together, they got Nora up off the sofa, put her hat and coat on her, and sat her, like a doll, on the chair in the front hall.

"The hack is here," Randolph said, "and no Cousin Austin. Now what do we do?"

"We can't leave without saying good-by," Mrs. Potter said. "Cousin Austin would be hurt."

"Well, why isn't he here then?" Randolph asked.

"Oh, I don't know!" Mrs. Potter exclaimed. "I wish you wouldn't ask questions that nobody knows the answer to. . . . It's all right, Nora. If we miss this train, we'll take the next one."

The Potters, accustomed to keeping other people waiting, now sat and waited themselves—waited and waited. At last Mrs. Potter said, "Cousin Abbey, will you tell your father that—"

"It's no use," Mr. Potter said. "The train leaves in seven and a half minutes. We'd just have a wild ride for nothing."

They sat looking at each other. A minute went by, and another, and then the front door burst open. "I'm terribly sorry," Austin said. "I was detained."

"It's all right," Mr. Potter said. "We'll take the evening train. Or the one tomorrow morning."

Nora's eyes filled with tears that were not, Austin saw, for him. She wanted to go home. The tears were merely from childish disappointment. A long time ago, he thought, I used to feel like that sometimes.

"If I can't take that train, I'll die," Nora said.

Mr. Potter shook his head. "It's no use," he repeated.

Without bothering to search through that part of his mind where old unhappy memories were stored (whatever the disappointment was that had been more than he could bear, he had lived through it) Austin picked up the remaining suitcase and opened the front door. "We can try," he said. "The train may be late."

21

When Martha King came back to the house on Elm Street it was as a traveler returning after a long adventurous life to the place where that life had begun. The lighted windows, the known dimensions of the yard, the half-seen shapes of trees and shrubbery all appeared to her in a perspective of time, from too great a distance for her to feel any direct happiness but only wonder at the place for being, after all this while, unchanged.

The nurse went ahead with the baby, while Martha with Austin supporting her made the trip slowly, pausing at the porch steps. She still hadn't got her strength back and there was a question in her mind whether she ever would. The lamps were lighted, the floors and the furniture shone. A hand that might have been hers had been at work, and nothing varied by a hair's breadth from its right place.

"It looks as if we were about to give a party," she said as Austin was hanging her coat in the hall closet.

"Hadn't you better go straight up to bed?"

"After dinner," she said.

When she was settled on the sofa in the living room with a wool afghan over her knees and pillows at her back, she said, "Austin, would you go upstairs and see if there's anything she needs? . . . And find Ab," she called after him.

She lay back on the sofa with her eyes closed until a sudden thunder of feet on the stairs made her sit up and turn toward the hall. Austin came into the living room with Ab riding on his back. They were both flushed and laughing.

Ab slid limply into her mother's arms and Martha said, "You oughtn't to come down the stairs like that with her."

"I wouldn't drop her," Austin said.

"You might stumble and fall." As she rocked Ab and smoothed her hair, Martha King felt as if some part of herself that she'd thought she had lost forever had now been restored to her.

"If you knew how much I missed my baby!" she said, and the room blurred with her tears.

"I missed you too," Ab said.

"Did you?"

"Mama?"

"What is it?"

"And . . ."

"Yes, Abbey?"

"Rachel's out in the kitchen."

"No!" Martha exclaimed. And then turning to Austin, "That's what you were so pleased with yourself about?"

"I wanted to surprise you," he said. "I found out where she was and wrote to her."

"Did you fire Frieda?"

"She gave notice the day the Potters went. She said she couldn't stay in the house alone with me. It wasn't proper."

"And you've had nobody to cook for you all this time?"

"I managed," Austin said.

They heard someone moving about in the dining room. Martha called, "Rachel, is that *you?*"

Rachel appeared in the dining-room door and smiled—a broad, bright, gleaming smile that made Martha feel taken up and held, as she herself was holding Ab.

"It was simply awful without you," she said.

"Is that right?" Rachel said. "I give the whole house a good going over."

"I see you did. It's beautiful. Have you been up to see our boy? He's not much to look at. He only weighs eight and a half pounds."

"I reckon he'll improve, now you've got him home," Rachel said.

Hours later, lying in bed and watching Austin undress, she said solemnly, "I can't tell you what it feels like to be here, after the hospital." What it was like was music, like wave upon wave of rising, ringing happy voices singing *Let us praise the Creator and all that He has made.*

With the light off and Austin in bed beside her, she found herself suddenly wide awake, restless, and wanting to talk. "There's something that worries me. When Ab was born I loved her right away, but I don't feel the same about this baby."

"You will."

"When I hold him he cries as if he doesn't want to come to me."

"Show me the baby that doesn't cry."

After a short while he withdrew his arm from under her head and turned over on his side. She was still not ready to go to sleep. She said, "Austin, does Nora write to you?"

"No."

"You're telling me the truth? You wouldn't lie to me about it?"

"Why should I lie to you? She hasn't written to me and she won't, and if she did write I wouldn't open the letter."

"There's no reason for you to say that. I wouldn't mind if you did. If you want to write to her, it's all right with me."

"But I don't want to write to her. And I don't want her to write to me. It's all past and done with."

"For you, maybe."

"Oh, sweetheart, forget about it. Go to sleep."

"All the time I was in the hospital I kept thinking about what it would be like to be home, and the very first night—"

He heaved himself over and sat up in bed, staring down at her in the dark. "This is something you started your own self. I didn't mention her."

"What difference does it make who mentioned her? She's still here," Martha said, and felt the bed give as he lay back once more.

"She's in Mississippi," he said, "so help me, God!"

They lay side by side, silent, in the dark.

After a while she said, "I guess it's just that I don't know you any more. You've changed . . . but I've changed, too. I don't mean this unkindly, Austin, but I think we ought to see things as they are, instead of trying to. . . . It's something I realized in the hospital—that you have only one life and if you spend all your time and energy trying to force something that, in the very nature of things, is impossible and hopeless, you might as well not have lived at all. People ought to follow their deeper instincts and be what they are meant to be, even if it causes unhappiness. They can't be themselves and still go on pretending that everything is all right when it isn't. By being honest with each other, we can at least—" She stopped, informed by his breathing that he was asleep.

How could he do that to her? How *could* he not care, when she was speaking to him for the first time, opening her heart in a way that she had not done all the years of their married life? She had been through the most terrible experience, and the minute it was over, he had no more interest in it or in what she had been through. All that mattered to him was his sleep.

In a cold rigid fury she lay beside him, trying not to hear the deep regular breathing of the man who had beaten her down with his persistence and his unbending will, and now no longer cared enough about her even to stay awake five minutes. She was weak and exhausted and trapped by the children she had borne him, but he was fine.

Unable to bear his nearness any longer, with her nerves stretched taut, she moved slowly and carefully out from under the covers, and could not find her dressing gown in the dark and so put his on, and sat in the rocking chair by the front window in the guest room. She wouldn't stay in the house with him a day longer than she had to. She would take the children and Rachel and find some place where they could live, even if it was only some little flat downtown, over a store. And in the summer-time she could rent a cottage at the Chautauqua grounds so that the children would have a place to play outdoors, and they'd manage somehow. And when the children got old enough to look after themselves, she could go to Chicago and find a job there. Rachel had managed, and what Rachel could do, she could.

How long Martha King sat in the rocking chair by the front window in the guestroom, with the robe drawn around her, planning, she had no idea. She looked out at the street and saw the street lamp as the life she had been meant to lead and the circle of light cast by it as the place she must get to. She was drunk with certainty, with finality, with decision. After a while she went into the next room. The nurse was lying on her back snoring and did not waken when Martha King bent over the crib and picked her baby up and carried him back to the guest room.

The baby did not waken either, though he stirred and she felt his tiny hands pushing against her side. She examined the baby's face by the light of the street lamp: so small and helpless, so much in need of protection against the cruelty of the world. The protection had better come from within. She would bring him up not to be nice, not to be polite, not to try and make the best of things, but in full knowledge of what life is, to make his own way, fight for what he wanted, and above all else to feel. To be angry when he was angry, and when he was happy, to bring the house down with his joy . . .

The clock in the downstairs hall struck one, and she got up and put the baby back in his crib, and then because the house was cold, and she was not well and there was, after all, no place else to go, she got back into bed and lay there, with her eyes wide open, looking at the reflection of the street light on the ceiling.

Austin stirred, and put his arm across her, and she took hold of it, by the wrist, and removed it, but when she moved away from him, toward the outer edge of the bed, he followed again in his sleep, and curled around her in a way that made her want to shout at him, and beat his face with her fists. She pushed the arm away, roughly this time, but he still did not waken. The arm had a life of its own. All the rest of him, his body and his soul, were asleep. But the arm was awake, and came across her, and the hand settled on her heart, and she let it stay there for a moment, thinking how hard and heavy it was compared to the child she had been holding, how importunate, how demanding; how it was no part of her and never would be, insisting on a satisfaction, even in sleep, that she could not give. She started to push it away once more but her own arms were bound to the bed. Only her mind was awake, able to act, to hate. And then suddenly the fine gold chain of awareness, no stronger than its weakest link, gave way. Circled by the body next to her, enclosed in warmth, held by the arm that knew (even though the man it belonged to did not), Martha King was asleep.

STORIES 1952–1956

Contents

The Trojan Women

THE business district of Draperville, Illinois (population 12,000), was built around a neo-Roman courthouse and the courthouse square. Adjoining the railroad station, in the center of a small plot of ground, a bronze tablet marked the site of the Old Alton Depot where the first Latham County Volunteers entrained for the Civil War, and where the funeral train of Abraham Lincoln halted briefly at sunrise on May 3rd, 1865. Other towns within a radius of a hundred miles continued to prosper, but Draperville stopped growing. It was finished by 1900. The last civic accomplishment was the laying of the tracks for the Draperville Street Railway. The population stayed the same and the wide residential streets were lined with trees that every year grew larger and more beautiful, as if to conceal by a dense green shade the failure of men of enterprise and sound judgment to beget these same qualities in their sons.

The streetcar line started at the New Latham Hotel and ran past the baseball park and the county jail, past the state insane asylum, and on out to the cemetery and the lake. The lake was actually an abandoned gravel pit, half a mile long and a quarter of a mile wide, fed by underground springs. Its water was very deep and very cold. The shoreline was dotted with summer cottages and between the cottages and an expanse of cornfields was a thin grove of oak trees. Every summer two or three dozen families moved out here in June, to escape the heat, and stayed until the end of August, when the reopening of school forced them to return to town. After Labor Day, with the cottages boarded up and the children's voices stilled, the lake was washed in equinoctial rains, polished by the October sun, and became once more a part of the wide empty landscape.

On a brilliant September day in 1912 the streetcar stopped in front of the high school, and a large, tranquil colored woman got on. She was burdened with a shopping bag and several parcels, which she deposited on the seat beside her. There were two empty seats between the colored woman and the nearest white passengers, who nodded to her but did not include her in their conversation. The streetcar was open on the sides, with rattan seats. It rocked and swayed, and the passengers, as though they were riding on the back of an elephant, rocked and swayed with it. The people who had flowers—asters or chrysanthemums wrapped in damp newspaper—rode as far as the cemetery where, among acres of monuments and gravestones (Protestant on the right, Catholic on the left), faded American flags marked the final resting place of those who had fallen in the Civil or Spanish-American wars. It was a mile farther to the end of the line. There the conductor switched the trolley for the return trip, and the colored woman started off across an open field.

A winding path through the oak trees led her eventually to a cottage resting on concrete blocks, with a peaked roof and a porch across the front, facing the lake. Wide wooden shutters hinged at the top and propped up on poles gave the cottage a curious effect, as of a creosote-colored bird about to clap its wings and fly away.

The colored woman entered by the back door, into a kitchen so tiny that there was barely room for her to move between the kerosene stove and the table. She put her packages down and dipped a jelly glass into a bucket of water and drank. Through the thin partition came the sound of a child crying and then a woman's voice, high and clear and excitable.

"Is that you, Adah Belle?"

"Yes'm."

"I thought you'd never come."

The colored woman went into the front part of the cottage, a single disorderly room with magazine covers pasted on the walls, odds and ends of wicker furniture, a grass rug, and two cots. Japanese lanterns hung from the rafters, as if the cottage were in the throes of some shoddy celebration, and the aromatic wood smell from the fireplace was complicated by other odors, kerosene, camphor, and pennyroyal. A little boy a year and a half old was standing in a crib, his face screwed up and red with the exertion of crying. On his neck and arms and legs were the marks of mosquito bites.

"What's he crying about now?" the colored woman asked.

"I wish I knew." The woman's voice came from the porch. "I'll be glad when he can talk. Then we'll at least know what he's crying about."

"He's crying because he miss his Adah Belle," the colored woman said and lifted the little boy out of the crib. The crying subsided and the child's face, streaked with dirt and tears, took on a look of seriousness, of forced maturity. "Don't nobody love you like Adah Belle," she said, crooning over him.

"Virginia saw a snake," the voice called from the porch.

"You don't mean that?"

"A water moccasin. At least I think it was a water moccasin. Anyway it was huge. I threw a stick at it and it went under the porch and now I'm afraid to set foot out of the house."

"You leave that snake alone and he leave you alone," the colored woman said.

"Anything could happen out here," the voice said, "and we haven't a soul to turn to. There isn't even a place to telephone. . . . Was it hot in town?"

"I didn't have no time to notice."

"It was hot out here. I think it's going to storm. The flies have been biting like crazy all afternoon."

A moment later the woman appeared in the doorway. She was thirty years old, small-boned and slender, with dark hair piled on top of her head, and extraordinarily vivid blue eyes. Her pallor and her seriousness were like the little boy's. "Adah Belle," she said, putting her white hand on the solid black arm, "if it weren't for you—if you didn't come just when I think the whole world's against me, I don't know what I'd do. I think I'd just give up."

"I knows you need me," the colored woman said.

"Sometimes I look at the lake, and then I think of my two children and what would happen to them if I weren't here, and then I think, Adah Belle would look after them. And you would, Adah Belle."

The little boy, seeing his mother's eyes fill with tears, puckered his face up and began to cry again. She took him from the colored woman's arms and said, "Never you mind, my angel darling! Never you mind!" her voice rich with maternal consolation and pity for the lot of all children in a world where harshness and discipline prevail. "This has been going on all day."

"Don't you worry, honey," Adah Belle said. "I look after them and you, too. I got you some pork chops."

"Then you'll have to cook them tonight. They won't keep without ice. The first of the week I'm going in and have things out with the ice company." The white woman's face and manner had changed. She was in the outer office of the Draperville Ice & Coal Co., demanding that they listen to her, insisting on her rights.

"That flying squirrel been into the spaghetti again," Adah Belle said.

"You should have been here last night. Such a time as I had! I lit the lamp and there he was, up on the rafter—" The woman put her hands to her head, and for the moment it was night. The squirrel was there, ready to swoop down on them, and Adah Belle saw and was caught up in the scene that had taken place in her absence.

"I was terrified he'd get in my hair or knock the lamp over and set fire to the cottage."

"And then what?"

"I didn't know what to do. The children were sitting up in bed watching it. They weren't as frightened as I was, and I knew they oughtn't to be awake at that time of night, so I made them put their heads under the covers, and turned out the light—"

"That squirrel getting mighty bold. Some one of these days he come out in the daytime and I get him with a broom. That be the end of the squirrel. What happen when you turn out the light?"

"After that nothing happened. . . . Adah Belle, did you see Mr. Gellert?"

The colored woman shook her head. "I went to the back door and knock, like I ain't never work there, and after a while *she* come."

"Then she's still there?"

"Yes'm, she's there. She say, 'Adah Belle, is that you?' and I say, 'That's right, it's me. I come to get some things for Miz Gellert.'"

"And she let you in?"

"I march in before she could stop me."

"Weren't you afraid?"

"I march through the kitchen and into the front part of the house with her after me every step of the way."

"Oh, Adah Belle, you're wonderful!"

"I come to get them things for you and ain't no old woman going to stop me."

"She didn't dare not let you in, I guess. She knows I've been to see a lawyer. If I decide to take the case into court—"

With the single dramatic gesture that the white woman made with her bare arm, there was the crowded courtroom, the sea of faces, now friendly, now hostile to the colored woman on the witness stand.

"You going to do that, Miz Gellert?" she asked anxiously.

"I don't know, Adah Belle. I may. Sometimes I think it's the only solution."

From her voice it was clear that she also had reason to be afraid of what would happen in the courtroom. *If anybody is to blame, Mildred is,* her friends were saying over the bridge tables in town, women grown stout on their own accomplished cooking, wearing flowered dresses and the ample unwieldy straw hats of the period. Their faces flushed with the excitement of duplicate bridge and the combinations and permutations of gossip, they said, *If she can't stand to live with Harrison, then why doesn't she get a divorce?* Behind this attack was the voice of fear (in a high-keyed Middle Western accent), the voice of doubt.

They were not, like Mildred Gellert, having trouble with their husbands. Their marriages were successful, their children took music lessons and won prizes at commencement, and they had every reason in the world to be satisfied (new curtains for the living room, a glassed-in sun porch), every reason to be happy. It was only that sometimes when they woke in the middle of the night and couldn't get to sleep for a while, and so reviewed their lives, something (what, exactly, they couldn't say) seemed missing. The opportunity that they had always assumed would come to them hadn't come after all. *You mark my words,* the women said to each other (the words of fear, the counsel of doubt), *when cold weather comes, she'll go back to him.*

But could Mildred go back to him? After all, with his mother staying there keeping house for him, he might not want her back.

Oh he'll take her back, the women said, on the wide verandah of the brick mansion on College Avenue. *All you have to do is look at him to tell that. . . .*

The hangdog expression, they meant; the pale abject look of apology that didn't prevent him from nagging her about the grocery bills or from being insanely jealous whenever they were in mixed company and she showed the slightest sign of enjoying herself.

But it really was not fair to the friends who had stood by her again and again. The first two times Mildred Gellert left her husband, the women one and all stopped speaking to him, out of loyalty to her, they said. And then when she went back to him, it was very embarrassing to go to the house on Eighth Street and have to act as if nothing had happened. This time when he tipped his hat to them, they spoke. *There's no use fighting other people's battles*, they said, slipping their pumps off surreptitiously under the bridge table. *They never thank you for it. Besides, I like Harrison. I always have. I know he's difficult, but then Mildred isn't the easiest person in the world to get along with, either, and I think he tries to do what is right and she ought to take that into consideration.*

The tragic heroine takes everything into consideration. That is her trouble, the thing that paralyzes her. While her lawyer is explaining to her the advantages of separate maintenance over an outright divorce, she considers the shape of his hands and how some people have nothing but happiness while they are young, and then, later, nothing but unhappiness.

Much as I like Mildred, the women said, driving back from the lake after listening to a three-hour monologue that had been every bit as good as a play, *I can't get worked up over it anymore. Besides, it's bad for the children. And if you ask me, I don't think she knows what she wants to do.*

This was quite right. Mildred Gellert left her husband and took a cottage out at the lake, in September, when all the other cottages were empty and boarded up, and this, of course, didn't solve anything but merely postponed the decision that could not be made until later in the fall, when some other postponement would have to be found, some new half measure.

Did you hear her ask me if I'd seen Harrison? the women said as the carriage reached the outskirts of town.

She wanted to know if he'd been at our house and I said right out that Ralph and I had been to call on his mother. She knows the old lady is there, and I thought I might as well be truthful with her because she might find it out some other way. I was all set to say, "Well, Mildred, if we all picked up our children and left our husbands every six months—" but she didn't say anything, so naturally I couldn't. But I know one thing. I'm not going all the way out there again in this heat just to hear the same old story about how Harrison wouldn't let her go to Peoria. And besides she did go, so what's there to get excited about? If she wants to see me, she can just get on the streetcar and come into town. After all, there's a limit.

The limit is boredom. Unless the tragic heroine can produce new stories, new black-and-blue marks, new threats and outrages that exceed in dramatic quality the old ones, it is better that she stay, no matter how unhappily, with her husband. So says the voice of doubt, the wisdom of fear.

In the front room of the cottage out at the lake Adah Belle said, "She's been changing things around some."

"What?"

"She's got the sofa in the bay window where the table belong, and the table is out in the center of the room."

"I tried them that way but it doesn't work," Mildred Gellert said.

"It don't look natural," the colored woman agreed. "It was better the way you had it. She asked me did I know where to look for what I wanted and I said I could put my hands right on everything, so she sat down and commenced to read, and I took myself off upstairs."

"When Virginia was a baby, Mother Gellert came and stayed with her so Mr. Gellert and I could go to Chicago. When I got back she'd straightened all the dresser drawers and I thought I'd go out of my mind trying to figure out where she could have put things. She'd even got into the cedar chest and wrapped everything up in newspaper. She smiles at you and looks as though butter wouldn't melt in her mouth, and then the minute your back is turned— Did she ask for me?"

"No'm, I can't say she did."

"Or about the children?"

The colored woman shook her head.

"You'd think she might at least ask about her own grandchildren," Mildred Gellert said. Her eagerness gave way to disappointment. There was something that she had been expecting from this visit of Adah Belle's to the house on Eighth Street, something besides the woolens that Adah Belle had been instructed to get. "Was there any mail?"

"Well, they was this postcard for little Virginia. It was upstairs on the table beside the bed in her room. I don't know how that child's going to get it if she's out here. But anyway, I stick it inside my dress without asking."

"It's from her Sunday school teacher," Mildred Gellert said, and put the postcard—a view of stalagmites and stalactites in Mammoth Cave, Kentucky—on the mantel.

"While I was at it, I took a look around," Adah Belle said.

"Yes?"

"Judging from the guest-room closet, she's move in to stay."

"That's all right with me," Mildred Gellert said, her voice suddenly harsh with bitterness. "From now on it's her house. She can do anything she likes with it." As she put the little boy in the crib, her mind was filled with possibilities. She would force Harrison to give her the house on Eighth Street; or, if that proved too expensive for her to manage on the money the court allowed her, she could always rent those four upstairs rooms over old Mrs. Marshall. Adah Belle would look after the children in the daytime, and she could get a job in Lembach's selling dresses or teach domestic science in the high school.

"She save brown-paper bags. And string."

"Don't get me started on that," Mildred Gellert said. "Did she say anything when you left?"

"I call out to her I was leaving," Adah Belle said, "and when she come out of the library she had these two boxes in her hand."

"What two boxes?"

"I got them with me in the kitchen. 'Will you give these to the children,' she says. 'They're from Mr. Gellert. I don't know whether Mrs. Gellert will want them to have presents from their father or not, but you can ask her.'"

"As a matter of fact, I don't," Mildred Gellert said.

Out in the kitchen she broke the string on the larger package and opened it. "Building blocks," she said. The other box was flat and square and contained a children's handkerchief with a lavender butterfly embroidered in one corner. "I wish he wouldn't do things like that. With Edward it doesn't matter, but the sooner Virginia forgets her father, the better. He ought to realize that."

"He don't mean no harm by it," the colored woman said.

Mildred Gellert looked at her. "Are you going to turn against me, too?"

"No'm," Adah Belle said. "I ain't turning against you, honey. All I say is he don't mean no harm."

"Well, what he means is one thing," Mildred Gellert said, her eyes fever-bright. "And what he does is just exactly the opposite!" The next time they drove out, her intimate friends, to see her, she would have something to tell them that would make them sit up and take notice. It wasn't enough that Harrison had driven her from the house, forcing her to take refuge out here, in a place with no heat, and fall coming on; that didn't satisfy him. Now he was going to win the children away from her with expensive gifts, so that in the end he'd have everything and she'd be left stranded, with no place to go and no one to turn to. He'd planned it all out, from the very beginning. That would be his revenge.

"What you aim to do with them? Send them back?" Adah Belle asked, looking at the two boxes she had carried all the way out from town.

"Put this on the trash pile and burn it," Mildred Gellert said and left the kitchen.

Outside, under a large oak tree, a little girl of five, her hair in two blond braids, was playing with a strawberry box. She had lined the box with a piece of calico and in it lay a small rubber doll, naked, with a whistle in its stomach. "Now you be quiet," the little girl said to the doll, "and take your nap or I'll slap you."

From her place under the oak tree she watched the colored woman go out to the trash pile with the flat square box, set a match to the accumulation of paper and garbage, and return to the kitchen. The little girl waited a moment and then got up and ran to the fire. She found a stick, pulled the burning box onto the grass, and blew out the flames that were licking at it. Then she ran back to the oak tree with her prize. Part of the linen handkerchief was charred and fell apart in her hands, but the flames hadn't reached the lavender butterfly. The little girl hid the handkerchief under the piece of calico and looked around for a place to put the strawberry box.

When she came into the house, five minutes later, her eyes were blank and innocent. She had learned that much in a year and a half. Her eyes could keep any secret they wanted to. And the box was safe under the porch, where her mother wouldn't dare look for it, because of the snake.

The Pilgrimage

IN a rented Renault, with exactly as much luggage as the backseat would hold, Ray and Ellen Ormsby were making a little tour of France. It had so far included Vézelay, the mountain villages of Auvergne, the roses and Roman ruins of Provence, and the gorges of the Tarn. They were now on their way back to Paris by a route that was neither the most direct nor particularly scenic, and that had been chosen with one thing in mind—dinner at the Hôtel du Domino in Périgueux. The Richardsons, who were close friends of the Ormsbys in America, had insisted that they go there. "The best dinner I ever had in my entire life," Jerry Richardson had said. "Every course was something with truffles." "And the dessert," Anne Richardson had said, "was little balls of various kinds of ice cream in a beautiful basket of spun sugar with a spun-sugar bow." Putting the two statements together, Ray Ormsby had persisted in thinking that the ice cream also had truffles in it, and Ellen had given up trying to correct this impression.

At seven o'clock, they were still sixty-five kilometers from Périgueux, on a winding back-country road, and beginning to get hungry. The landscape was gilded with the evening light. Ray was driving. Ellen read aloud to him from the *Guide Gastronomique de la France* the paragraph on the Hôtel du Domino: "*Bel et confortable établissement à la renommée bien assise et que Mme. Lasgrezas dirige avec beaucoup de bonheur. Grâce à un maître queux qualifié, vous y ferez un repas de grande classe qui vous sera servi dans une élégante salle à manger ou dans un délicieux jardin d'été. . . .*"

As they drove through village after village, they saw, in addition to the usual painted Cinzano and Rasurel signs, announcements of the *spécialité* of the restaurant of this or that Hôtel des Sports or de la Poste or du Lion d'Or—always with truffles. In Montignac, there were so many of these signs that Ellen said anxiously, "Do you think we ought to eat *here*?"

"No," Ray said. "Périgueux is the place. It's the capital of Périgord, and so it's bound to have the best food."

Outside Thenon, they had a flat tire—the seventh in eight

days of driving—and the casing of the spare tire was in such bad condition that Ray was afraid to drive on until the inner tube had been repaired and the regular tire put back on. It was five minutes of nine when they drove up before the Hôtel du Domino, and they were famished. Ray went inside and found that the hotel had accommodations for them. The car was driven into the hotel garage and emptied of its formidable luggage, and the Ormsbys were shown up to their third-floor room, which might have been in any plain hotel anywhere in France. "What I'd really like is the roast chicken stuffed with truffles," Ellen said from the washstand. "But probably it takes a long time."

"What if it does," Ray said. "We'll be eating other things first."

He threw open the shutters and discovered that their room looked out on a painting by Dufy—the large, bare, open square surrounded by stone buildings, with the tricolor for accent, and the sky a rich, stained-glass blue. From another window, at the turning of the stairs on their way down to dinner, they saw the delicious garden, but it was dark, and no one was eating there now. At the foot of the stairs, they paused.

"You wanted the restaurant?" the concierge asked, and when they nodded, she came out from behind her mahogany railing and led them importantly down a corridor. The maître d'hôtel, in a grey business suit, stood waiting at the door of the dining room, and put them at a table for two. Then he handed them the menu with a flourish. They saw at a glance how expensive the dinner was going to be. A waitress brought plates, glasses, napkins, knives, and forks.

While Ellen was reading the menu, Ray looked slowly around the room. The "*élégante salle à manger*" looked like a hotel coffee shop. There weren't even any tablecloths. The walls were painted a dismal shade of off-mustard. His eyes came to rest finally on the stippled brown dado a foot from his face. "It's a perfect room to commit suicide in," he said, and reached for the menu. A moment later he exclaimed, "I don't see the basket of ice cream!"

"It must be there," Ellen said. "Don't get so excited."

"Well, where? Just show me!"

Together they looked through the two columns of desserts,

without finding the marvel in question. "Jerry and Anne were here several days," Ellen said. "They may have had it in some other restaurant."

This explanation Ray would not accept. "It was the same dinner, I remember distinctly." The full horror of their driving all the way to Périgueux in order to eat a very expensive meal at the wrong restaurant broke over him. In a cold sweat he got up from the table.

"Where are you going?" Ellen asked.

"I'll be right back," he said, and left the dining room. Upstairs in their room, he dug the *Guide Michelin* out of a duffel bag. He had lost all faith in the *Guide Gastronomique*, because of its description of the dining room; the person who wrote that had never set eyes on the Hôtel du Domino or, probably, on Périgueux. In the *Michelin*, the restaurant of the Hôtel du Domino rated one star and so did the restaurant Le Montaigne, but Le Montaigne also had three crossed forks and spoons, and suddenly it came to him, with the awful clarity of a long-submerged memory at last brought to the surface through layer after layer of consciousness, that it was at Le Montaigne and not at the Hôtel du Domino that the Richardsons had meant them to eat. He picked up Ellen's coat and, still carrying the *Michelin*, went back downstairs to the dining room.

"I've brought you your coat," he said to Ellen as he sat down opposite her. "We're in the wrong restaurant."

"We aren't either," Ellen said. "And even if we were, I've *got* to have something to eat. I'm starving, and it's much too late now to go looking for—"

"It won't be far," Ray said. "Come on." He looked up into the face of the maître d'hôtel, waiting with his pencil and pad to take their order.

"You speak English?" Ray asked.

The maître d'hôtel nodded, and Ray described the basket of spun sugar filled with different kinds of ice cream.

"And a spun-sugar bow," Ellen said.

The maître d'hôtel looked blank, and so Ray tried again, speaking slowly and distinctly.

"*Omelette?*" the maître d'hôtel said.

"No—ice cream!"

"*Glace*," Ellen said.

"*Et du sucre*," Ray said. "*Une*—" He and Ellen looked at each other. Neither of them could think of the word for "basket."

The maître d'hôtel went over to a sideboard and returned with another menu. "*Le menu des glaces*," he said coldly.

"*Vanille*," they read, "*chocolat, pistache, framboise, fraise, tutti-frutti, praliné . . .*"

Even if the spun-sugar basket had been on the *menu des glaces* (which it wasn't), they were in too excited a state to have found it—Ray because of his fear that they were making an irremediable mistake in having dinner at this restaurant and Ellen because of the dreadful way he was acting.

"We came here on a pilgrimage," he said to the maître d'hôtel, in a tense, excited voice that carried all over the dining room. "We have these friends in America who ate in Périgueux, and it is absolutely necessary that we eat in the place they told us about."

"This is a very good restaurant," the maître d'hôtel said. "We have many *spécialités. Foie gras truffé, poulet du Périgord noir, truffes sous la cendre*—"

"I know," Ray said, "but apparently it isn't the right one." He got up from his chair, and Ellen, shaking her head—because there was no use arguing with him when he was like this—got up, too. The other diners had all turned around to watch.

"Come," the maître d'hôtel said, taking hold of Ray's elbow. "In the lobby is a lady who speaks English very well. She will understand what it is you want."

In the lobby, Ray told his story again—how they had come to Périgueux because their friends in America had told them about a certain restaurant here, and how it was this restaurant and no other that they must find. They had thought it was the restaurant in the Hôtel du Domino, but since the restaurant of the Hôtel du Domino did not have the dessert that their friends in America had particularly recommended, little balls of ice cream in—

The concierge, her eyes large with sudden comprehension, interrupted him. "You wanted truffles?"

*

Out on the sidewalk, trying to read the *Michelin* map of Périgueux by the feeble light of a tall street lamp, Ray said, "Le Montaigne has a star just like the Hôtel du Domino, but it also has three crossed forks and spoons, so it must be better than the hotel."

"All those crossed forks and spoons mean is that it is a very comfortable place to eat in," Ellen said. "It has nothing to do with the quality of the food. I don't care where we eat, so long as I don't have to go back there."

There were circles of fatigue under her eyes. She was both exasperated with him and proud of him for insisting on getting what they had come here for, when most people would have given in and taken what there was. They walked on a couple of blocks and came to a second open square. Ray stopped a man and woman.

"*Pardon, m'sieur*," he said, removing his hat. "*Le restaurant La Montagne, c'est par là*"—he pointed—"*ou par là?*"

"*La Montagne? Le restaurant La Montagne?*" the man said dubiously. "*Je regrette, mais je ne le connais pas.*"

Ray opened the *Michelin* and, by the light of the nearest neon sign, the man and woman read down the page.

"*Ooh,* LE *Mon*TAIGNE*!*" the woman exclaimed suddenly.

"LE *Mon*TAIGNE*!* the man echoed.

"*Oui, Le Montaigne*," Ray said, nodding.

The man pointed across the square.

Standing in front of Le Montaigne, Ray again had doubts. It was much larger than the restaurant of the Hôtel du Domino, but it looked much more like a bar than a first-class restaurant. And again there were no tablecloths. A waiter approached them as they stood undecided on the sidewalk. Ray asked to see the menu, and the waiter disappeared into the building. A moment later, a second waiter appeared. "*Le menu*," he said, pointing to a standard a few feet away. Le Montaigne offered many specialties, most of them *truffés*, but not the Richardsons' dessert.

"Couldn't we just go someplace and have an ordinary meal?" Ellen said. "I don't think I feel like eating anything elaborate any longer."

But Ray had made a discovery. "The restaurant is upstairs,"

he said. "What we've been looking at is the café, so naturally there aren't any tablecloths."

Taking Ellen by the hand, he started up what turned out to be a circular staircase. The second floor of the building was dark. Ellen, convinced that the restaurant had stopped serving dinner, objected to going any farther, but Ray went on, and protesting, she followed him. The third floor was brightly lighted—was, in fact, a restaurant, with white tablecloths, gleaming crystal, and the traditional dark-red plush upholstery, and two or three clients who were lingering over the end of dinner. The maître d'hôtel, in a black dinner jacket, led them to a table and handed them the same menu they had read downstairs.

"I don't see any roast chicken stuffed with truffles," Ellen said.

"Oh, I forgot that's what you wanted!" Ray said, conscience-stricken. "Did they have it at the Domino?"

"No, but they had *poulet noir*—and here they don't even have that."

"I'm so sorry," he said. "Are you sure they don't have it here?" He ran his eyes down the list of dishes with truffles and said suddenly, "There it is!"

"Where?" Ellen demanded. He pointed to "*Tournedos aux truffes du Périgord*." "That's not chicken," Ellen said.

"Well, it's no good, then," Ray said.

"No good?" the maître d'hôtel said indignantly. "It's *very* good! *Le tournedos aux truffes du Périgord* is a *spécialité* of the restaurant!"

They were only partly successful in conveying to him that that was not what Ray had meant.

No, there was no roast chicken stuffed with truffles.

No chicken of any kind.

"I'm very sorry," Ray said, and got up from his chair.

He was not at all sure that Ellen would go back to the restaurant in the Hôtel du Domino with him, but she did. Their table was just as they had left it. A waiter and a busboy, seeing them come in, exchanged startled whispers. The maître d'hôtel did not come near them for several minutes after they had sat down, and Ray carefully didn't look around for him.

"Do you think he is angry because we walked out?" Ellen asked.

Ray shook his head. "I think we hurt his feelings, though. I think he prides himself on speaking English, and now he will never again be sure that he does speak it, because of us."

Eventually, the maître d'hôtel appeared at their table. Sickly smiles were exchanged all around, and the menu was offered for the second time, without the flourish.

"What is *les truffes sous la cendre*?" Ellen asked.

"It takes forty-five minutes," the maître d'hôtel said.

"*Le foie gras truffé*," Ray said. "For two."

"*Le foie gras*, O.K.," the maître d'hôtel said. "*Et ensuite?*"

"*Œufs en gelée*," Ellen said.

"*Œufs en gelée*, O.K."

"*Le poulet noir*," Ray said.

"*Le poulet noir*, O.K."

"*Et deux Cinzano*," Ray said, on solid ground at last, "*avec un morceau de glace et un zeste de citron. S'il vous plaît.*"

The apéritif arrived, with ice and lemon peel, but the wine list was not presented, and Ray asked the waitress for it. She spoke to the maître d'hôtel, and that was the last the Ormsbys ever saw of her. The maître d'hôtel brought the wine list, they ordered the dry white *vin du pays* that he recommended, and their dinner was served to them by a waiter so young that Ray looked to see whether he was in knee pants.

The pâté was everything the Richardsons had said it would be, and Ray, to make up for all he had put his wife through in the course of the evening, gave her a small quantity of his, which, protesting, she accepted. The maître d'hôtel stopped at their table and said, "Is it good?"

"Very good," they said simultaneously.

The *œufs en gelée* arrived and were also very good, but were they any better than or even as good as the *œufs en gelée* the Ormsbys had had in the restaurant of a hotel on the outskirts of Aix-en-Provence was the question.

"Is it good?" the maître d'hôtel asked.

"Very good," they said. "So is the wine."

The boy waiter brought in the *poulet noir*—a chicken casserole with a dark-brown Madeira sauce full of chopped truffles.

"Is it good?" Ray asked when the waiter had finished serving them and Ellen had tasted the *pièce de résistance*.

"It's very good," she said. "But I'm not sure I can taste the truffles."

"I think I can," he said, a moment later.

"With the roast chicken, it probably would have been quite easy," Ellen said.

"Are you sure the Richardsons had roast chicken stuffed with truffles?" Ray asked.

"I think so," Ellen said. "Anyway, I know I've read about it."

"Is it good?" the maître d'hôtel, their waiter, and the waiter from a neighboring table asked in succession.

"Very good," the Ormsbys said.

Since they couldn't have the little balls of various kinds of ice cream in a basket of spun sugar with a spun-sugar bow for dessert, they decided not to have any dessert at all. The meal came to an abrupt end with *café filtre*.

Intending to take a short walk before going to bed, they heard dance music in the square in front of Le Montaigne, and found a large crowd there, celebrating the annual fair of Périgueux. There was a seven-piece orchestra on a raised platform under a canvas, and a few couples were dancing in the street. Soon there were more.

"Do you feel like dancing?" Ray asked.

The pavement was not as bad for dancing as he would have supposed, and something happened to them that had never happened to them anywhere in France before—something remarkable. In spite of their clothes and their faces and the *Michelin* he held in one hand, eyes constantly swept over them or past them without pausing. Dancing in the street, they aroused no curiosity and, in fact, no interest whatever.

At midnight, standing on the balcony outside their room, they could still hear the music, a quarter of a mile away.

"Hasn't it been a lovely evening!" Ellen said. "I'll always remember dancing in the street in Périgueux."

Two people emerged from the cinema, a few doors from the Hôtel du Domino. And then a few more—a pair of lovers, a woman, a boy, a woman and a man carrying a sleeping child.

"The pâté was the best I ever ate," Ellen said.

"The Richardsons probably ate in the garden," Ray said. "I don't know that the dinner as a whole was all *that* good," he added thoughtfully. And then, "I don't know that we need tell them."

"The poor people who run the cinema," Ellen said.

"Why?"

"No one came to see the movie."

"I suppose Périgueux really isn't the kind of town that would support a movie theater," Ray said.

"That's it," Ellen said. "Here, when people want to relax and enjoy themselves, they have an apéritif, they walk up and down in the evening air, they dance in the street, the way people used to do before there were any movies. It's another civilization entirely from anything we're accustomed to. Another world."

They went back into the bedroom and closed the shutters. A few minutes later, some more people emerged from the movie theater, and some more, and some more, and then a great crowd came streaming out and, walking gravely, like people taking part in a religious procession, fanned out across the open square.

What Every Boy Should Know

SHORTLY before his twelfth birthday, Edward Gellert's eyes were opened and he knew that he was naked. More subtle than any beast of the field, more rational than Adam, he did not hide himself from the presence of God or sew fig leaves together. The most he could hope for was to keep his father and mother, his teachers, people in general from knowing. He took elaborate precautions against being surprised, each time it was always the last time, and afterward he examined himself in the harsh light of the bathroom mirror. It did not show yet, but when the mark appeared it would be indelible and it would be his undoing.

People asked him, Who is your girl? And he said, I have no girl, and they laughed and his mother said, Edward doesn't care for girls, and they said, All that will change.

People said, Edward is a good boy, and that was because they didn't know.

He touched Darwin and got an electric shock: ". . . the hair is chiefly retained in the male sex on the chest and face, and in both sexes at the juncture of all four limbs with the trunk. . . ." There was more, but he heard someone coming and had to replace the book on the shelf.

He stopped asking questions, though his mind was teeming with them, lest someone question him. And because it was no use; the questions he wanted to ask were the questions grown people and even older boys did not want to answer. This did not interrupt the incessant kaleidoscopic patterns of ignorance and uncertainty: How did they know that people were really dead, that they wouldn't open their eyes suddenly and try to push their way out of the coffin? And how did the worms get to them if the casket was inside an outer casket that was metal? And when Mrs. Spelman died and Mr. Spelman married again, how was it arranged so that there was no embarrassment later on when he and the first Mrs. Spelman met in Heaven?

Harrison Gellert's boy, people said, seeing him go by on his way to school. To get to him, though, you had first to get past his one-tube radio, his experimental chemistry set, his growing ball of lead foil, his correspondence with the Scott Stamp & Coin Co., his automatically evasive answers.

Pure, self-centered, a moral outcast, he sat through church, in his blue serge Sunday suit, and heard the Reverend Harry Blair, who baptized him, say solemnly from the pulpit that he was conceived in sin. But afterward, at the church door, in the brilliant sunshine, he shook hands with Edward; he said he was happy to have Edward with them.

In the bookcase in the upstairs hall Edward found a book that seemed to have been put there by someone for his enlightenment. It was called *What Every Boy Should Know*, and it told him nothing that he didn't know already.

Arrived at the age of exploration, he charted his course by a map that showed India as an island. The Pacific Ocean was overlooked somehow. Greenland was attached to China, and rivers flowed into the wrong sea. The map enabled him to determine his latitude with a certain amount of accuracy, but for his longitude he was dependent on dead reckoning. In his search for an interior passage, he continually mistook inlets for estuaries. The Known World is not, of course, known. It probably never will be, because of those areas the mapmakers have very sensibly agreed to ignore, where the terrain is different for every traveler who crosses them. Or fails to cross them. The Unknown World, indicated by dotted lines or by no lines at all, was based on the reports of one or two boys in little better case than Edward and frightened like him by tales of sea monsters, of abysses at the world's end.

A savage ill at ease among the overcivilized, Edward remembered to wash his hands and face before he came to the table, and was sent away again because he forgot to put on a coat or a sweater. He slept with a stocking top on his head and left his roller skates where someone could fall over them. It was never wise to send him on any kind of involved errand.

He was sometimes a child, sometimes an adult in the uncomfortable small size. He had opinions but they were not listened to. He blushed easily and he had his feelings hurt. His jokes were not always successful, having a point that escaped most people, or that annoyed his father. His sister Virginia was real, but his father and mother he was aware of mostly as generalities, agents of authority or love or discipline, telling him to sit up straight in his chair, to stand with his shoulders back, to pick up his clothes, read in a better light, stop chewing his nails, stop sniffing and go upstairs and get a handkerchief. When his father asked some question at the dinner table and his mother didn't answer, or, looking down at her plate, answered inaudibly, and when his father then, in the face of these warnings, pursued the matter until she left the table and went upstairs, it didn't mean that his mother and father didn't love each other, or that Edward didn't have as happy a home as any other boy.

Meanwhile, his plans made, his blue eyes a facsimile of innocence, he waited for them all to go some place. Who then moved through the still house? No known Edward. A murderer with flowers in his hair. A male impersonator. A newt undergoing metamorphosis. Now this, now that mirror was his accomplice. The furniture was accessory to the fact. The house being old, he could count on the back stairs to cry out at the approach of discovery. When help came, it came from the outside as usual. Harrison Gellert, passing the door of his son's room one November night, seeing Edward with his hand at the knob of his radio and the headphones over his ears, reflected on Edward's thinness, his pallor, his poor posture, his moodiness of late, and concluded that he did not spend enough time out-of-doors. Edward was past the age when you could tell him to go outside and play, but if he had a job of some kind that would keep him out in the open air, like delivering papers . . . Too shocked to argue with his father (you don't ask someone to give you a job out of the kindness of their heart when they don't even know you and also when there may not even be any job or if there is they may have somebody else in mind who would be better at it and who deserves it more), Edward went downtown after school and stood beside the wooden railing in the front office of the Draperville *Evening Star*, waiting for someone to notice him. He expected to be sent away in disgrace, and instead he was given a canvas bag and a list of names and told to come around to the rear of the building.

From five o'clock on, all over town, all along College Avenue with its overarching elms, Eighth Street, Ninth Street, Fourth

Street, in the block of two-story flats backed up against the railroad tracks, and on those unpaved, nameless streets out where the sidewalk ended and the sky took over, old men sitting by the front window and children at a loss for something to do waited and listened for the sound of the paper striking the porch, and the cry—disembodied and forlorn—of "Pay-er!" Women left their lighted kitchens or put down their sewing in upstairs rooms and went to the front door and looked to see if the evening paper had come. Sometimes spring had come instead, and they smelled the sweet syringa in the next yard. Or the smell was of burning leaves. Sometimes they saw their breath in the icy air. A few minutes later they went to the door and looked again. Left too long, the paper blew out into the yard, got rained on, was covered with snow. Their persistence rewarded at last, they bent down and picked up the paper, opened it, and read the headline, while the paper boy rode on rapidly over lawns he had been told not to ride over, as if he were bent on overtaking lost time or some other paper boy who was not there.

In a place where everybody could easily be traced back to his origin, people did not always know who the paper boy was or care what time he got home to supper. They assumed from a general knowledge of boys that if the paper was late it was because the paper boy dawdled somewhere, shooting marbles, throwing snowballs, when he should have been delivering their paper.

Every afternoon after school the boys rode into the alley behind the *Star* Building, let their bicycles fall with a clatter, and gathered in the cage next to the pressroom. They were dirty-faced, argumentative, and as alike as sparrows. Their pockets sagged with pieces of chalk, balls of string, slingshots, marbles, jackknives, deified objects, trophies they traded. Boasting and being called on to produce evidence in support of what ought to have been true but wasn't, they bet large sums of unreal money or passed along items of misinformation that were gratefully received and stored away in a safe place. Easily deflated, they just as easily recovered their powers of pretending. With the press standing idle, the linotype machine clicking and lisping, the round clock on the wall a torment to them every time they glanced in that direction, they asked,

What time is the press going to start?—knowing that the printing press of the Draperville *Evening Star* was all but done for, and that it was a question not of how soon it would start printing but of whether it could be prevailed upon to print at all. When the linotype machines stopped, there was a quarter of an hour of acute uncertainty, during which late-news bulletins were read in reverse, corrections were made in the price of laying mash and ladies' ready-to-wear, and the columns of type were locked in place. The boys waited. The pressroom waited. The front office waited and listened. And suddenly the clean white paper began to move, to flow like a waterfall. Words appeared on one side and then on the other. The clittering clattering discourse gained momentum. The paper was cut, the paper was folded. Smelling of damp ink, copies of the Draperville *Evening Star* slid down a chute and were scooped up and counted by a young man named Homer West, who never broke down or gave trouble to anyone. Cheerful, even-tempered, he handed the papers through a wicket to the seventeen boys who waited in line with their canvas bags slung over one shoulder and their bicycles in a tangle outside. One of them was Homer's brother Harold, but Homer was a brother to all of them. He teased them, eased the pressure of their high-pitched impatience with joking, kept them from fighting each other during that ominous quarter of an hour after the linotype machines fell silent, and listened for the first symptoms of disorder in the press. When it began chewing paper instead of printing, he pulled the switch, and a silence of a deeply discouraging import succeeded the whir and the clitter-clit-clatter. The boys who were left said, I can't wait around here all night, I have homework to do. And Homer, waiting also, for the long day to end and for the time still far in the future when he could afford to get married, said, Do your homework now, why don't you? They said, Here? and he said, Why not? What's the matter with this place? It's warm. You've got electric light. They said, I can't concentrate. And Homer said, Neither can I with you talking to me. He said, It won't be long now. And when they insisted on knowing how long, he said, Pretty soon.

The key to age is patience; and the key to patience is unfortunately age, which cannot be hurried, which takes time (in which to be disappointed); and time is measured by what happens; and what happens is printed (some of it) in the evening paper.

Just when it seemed certain that there would be no more copies of that evening's *Star*, the waterfall resumed its flowing—slowly at first, and then with a kind of frantic confidence. One after another the boys received their papers through the wicket, counted them, and, with their canvas bags weighted, ran out of the building to mount their bicycles and ride off to the part of town that depended on them for its knowledge of what was going on in the outside world in the year 1922.

After their first mild surprise at finding Eddie Gellert in the cage with them, the other boys accepted his presence there, serene in the knowledge that they could lick him if he started getting wise, and that they had thirty-seven or forty-two or fifty-one customers in a good neighborhood to his thirteen in the poorest-paying section of town. His route had been broken off one of the larger ones, with no harm to the loser, who, that first evening, went with him to point out the houses that took the *Star*, and showed him how to fold the papers as he went along and how to toss them so they landed safely on the porch. After that, Edward was on his own.

The boys received their papers from Homer in rotation, and it was better to be second or third or fourth or even fifth than it was to be first, because if you were first it meant that the next night you would be last. "Pay-er . . ." Edward called, like the others. "Pay-er?"—with his mind on home. His last paper delivered, he turned toward the plate kept warm for him in the oven, the place it would have been so pleasant to come to straight from school. But he was twelve now, and out in the world. He had put the unlimited leisure of childhood behind him. As his father said, he was learning the value of money, his stomach empty, his nostrils burning with the cold, his chin deep in the collar of his mackinaw.

How much money his father had, Edward did not know. It was one of those interesting questions that grown people do not care to answer. Since his mother was also kept in the dark about this, there was no reason to assume he could find out by asking. But he knew he was expected to do as well some day, and own a nice home and provide decently for the wife and children it was as yet impossible for him to imagine. If all this were easy to manage, then his father would not be upset about lights that were left burning in empty rooms or mention the coal bill every time somebody complained that the house was chilly. Life is serious and without adequate guarantees, whether your mother takes in washing or belongs to the Friday Bridge Club. Poverty is no joke—but neither is the fear of poverty never experienced. Every evening Edward saw, like a lantern slide of failure, the part of town he must never live in, streets that weren't ever going to be paved, in all probability, houses that year after year the banks or the coal company or old Mr. Ivens saw no need for repainting or doing anything about, beyond seeing to it that the people who lived in them paid their rent promptly on the first day of the month.

On Saturday mornings he came with his metal collection book and knocked and the door was opened by a solemn, filthy child or a woman who had no corset on under her housedress and whose hair had not been combed since she got out of bed. The women gave him a dime and took the coupon he held out to them as if that were the commodity in question. If they asked him to step inside he held his breath, ignoring the bad air and an animal odor such as might have been left by foxes or raccoons or wolves in their lair. The women wadded the coupon into a ball or, if they were of a suspicious turn of mind, saved it for the day when he would try to cheat them, and they could triumphantly confront him with the proof of his dishonesty. If they didn't have a dime (often the case in that part of town) or were simply afraid, on principle, to part with money, they put him off with every appearance of not remembering that they had put him off the week before and the week before that. He turned away, disappointed but trying desperately to be polite, and the paper kept on coming.

Regardless of how many customers paid or put off paying the paper boy, the *Evening Star* claimed its percentage every Saturday morning. Any other arrangement would have complicated the bookkeeping, and the owners of the paper did not consider themselves responsible for the riot that broke out, one Friday afternoon, in the cage next to the pressroom. The boys refused to take the papers Homer held out to them through the wicket, and nothing that he said to them had any effect, because their grievances were suddenly intolerable and they themselves were secure in the knowledge (why had they never thought of this before?) that the *Star* was helpless without them. The word "strike" was heard above the sound of the press, which had started on time, for once, and which went right on printing editorial after editorial advising the President of the United States to take over the coal mines—with troops if necessary, since the public welfare was threatened.

At quarter of five, home was not as Edward had remembered it. There was nothing to do, nobody to talk to except Old Mary, and she said, Now don't go spoiling your supper! when all in the world he wanted was company. He went back through the empty uneasy rooms and settled in a big chair in the library with a volume of *Battles and Leaders of the Civil War* on his lap. He didn't read; he only looked at the pictures (a farmhouse near Shiloh, the arsenal at Harpers Ferry) and listened for the sound of a step on the front porch. It was dark outside, and people all over town were beginning to look for the evening paper. His mind was still filled with remembered excitement, triumph that blurred and threatened to turn into worry. But then he turned a page. This had the same effect as when a dreamer, waking, escapes from the nightmare by changing his position in bed.

Virginia came in, and Edward called out to her, but she rushed upstairs, too absorbed in her own world of spit curls and charm bracelets, of what Ossie Dempsey said to Elsie McNish, of TL's and ukuleles, to answer her own brother. And where was his mother?

Mildred Gellert, unable to get along with her husband, unable to bear his bad temper, his nagging, had tried leaving him. Sometimes she took the children with her and sometimes, with her suitcases in the front hall, she clung to them and told them they mustn't forget her, and that when they were older they would understand. The trouble was, they did understand already. For a time it was very exciting, full of subtle moves (she communicated with Harrison through her lawyer) and countermoves (his mother came and kept house for him) like a chess game. The Gellerts' house, no matter who ordered the meals and sat at the opposite end of the dining-room table from Harrison Gellert, had a quality of sadness. This was partly architectural, having to do with the wide overhanging eaves, and partly because the shrubbery—the bridal wreath and barberry—had been allowed to become spindly and the trees kept the sunlight from the lawn. Neither surprised by its own prosperity, like the Tudor and Dutch Colonial houses in the new addition to Draperville, nor frankly shabby, like other old houses of its period, the Gellerts' house and yard were at a standstill, having reached their final look, which owed so much, apparently, to accident, and so little to design or intention or thought.

When Edward walked into Virginia's room she was lying on the bed reading a movie magazine, and she implied that she would just as soon he went somewhere else. Not that he cared. He sat slumped in a chair until she said, "Do you have to breathe like that?"

"Like what?"

"With your mouth open like a fish."

Nothing made him so uncomfortable as being reminded of some part of himself that there was no need to be reminded of. It took all the joy out of life. "This is the way you breathe," he said indignantly. "Just let me give you an imitation."

She laughed scornfully at his attempt to fasten on her a failing she did not have, and so he reminded her—a thing he had meant not to do—that she owed him thirty cents. This led to more insinuations and denials, in the heat of which he forgot he was home early until his mother, standing in the doorway with her hat on, said, "If you children don't stop this eternal arguing, I don't know what I will do!" Neither of them had heard her come upstairs. They looked at each other, conspirators, on the same side. "We're not arguing."

Convicted without a hearing (their mother went on to her own room), they drew apart from each other again. Virginia said, "That was all your fault. I didn't ask you in here, and you're not supposed to come in my room unless I ask you in." Which was a rule she made up, along with a lot of others.

Before they even realized they were arguing again, a voice called, "Children, please! please!" Their mother's voice, so nervous, unhappy, and remote after the Friday Bridge Club. It embarrassed them, reminding them of scenes at the dinner table and conversations between their mother and father that floated up the stairs late at night after they were in bed.

Edward went into the bathroom and ran lukewarm water into the washbasin. It takes patience and some native skill to make a pumice stone float. Absorbed in this delicate task, Edward forgot about his grimy hands and also about the hands of the clock. A warning from his mother as she started down the stairs (how did she know he was in the bathroom?) woke him from a dream of argosies, and the stone boat sank. He arrived in the dining room out of breath, his blond hair slicked down and wet, his hands clean but not his wrists, and an excuse ready on his tongue. He had decided not to mention the strike but it came out just the same. Halfway through dinner it burst out of him, and he felt better immediately.

"How did it start?" Harrison Gellert asked. The lamp that used to hang low over the dining-room table, with its red and green stained glass, its beaded glass fringe, had been replaced, in the last year or two, by glaring wall brackets, a white light in which nothing could be concealed.

"I don't know," Edward said. He passed his plate for a second helping. The plate was filled and passed back to him, and then his father said, "You were there, weren't you?"

"Yes."

"Well, all I'm asking you to tell me is what happened. Something must have happened. How did the strike get started in the first place?"

"I don't remember," Edward said.

He glanced at his sister, across the table. She had stopped eating and with a lurking smile, as if to say *You're going to catch it*, waited for him to flounder in deeper and deeper. He did not hold this against her. The shoe was often enough on the other foot.

"It seemed like it just happened," Edward said, hoping that this explanation, which satisfied him, was truthful and accurate, would also satisfy his father. "I left my arithmetic book in my desk at school and had to go back and get it."

Pleased to have recalled this detail, he stopped and then saw that his father was waiting for him to go on.

"When did the boys decide they weren't going to deliver their papers, before you got there or after?"

"After."

"But the trouble had already started?"

"Not exactly."

"You mean it was like any other evening."

Edward shook his head. What he could not explain was that the boys were always threatening to strike, to quit, to make trouble of one kind or another.

"What are you striking about?"

"The collection. We're supposed to go around collecting on Saturday morning. And people are supposed to pay us, and we're supposed to pay the *Star*. We pay Mrs. Sinclair seven cents and keep three. Only lots of times when we ask for the money, they— You want to see my collection book?"

"No. Just tell me about it."

There were times when, if it hadn't been for the reassurance of Edward's monthly report card, Harrison Gellert would have been forced to wonder if his son were a mental defective. No doubt he was passing through a stage, but it was a very tiresome one.

"Sometimes we have to wait five or six weeks for the money," Edward said.

"But you get it eventually?"

Edward nodded. "But she takes her share right away, out of whatever we do collect, and it's not fair."

"What's unfair about it?"

"She has lots of money and we don't."

"What else are the boys striking for?"

"When the press breaks down, sometimes we don't get home until after seven o'clock. One night it was nearly eight."

"It isn't Mrs. Sinclair's fault that the press breaks down."

To this Edward made no answer.

"What else?"

"We want more money."

"How much more?"

"Oh, let the poor child alone!" Mildred Gellert exclaimed, raising her wan, unhappy face from her salad and looking at her husband.

"He's not a child," Harrison Gellert said. "And I'm not picking on him. How much did you make this week?"

"Thirty-three cents," Edward said. "But some of it was back pay. I only have thirteen customers. Barney Lefferts has the most. He has fifty-two. He makes about a dollar and a half a week when he gets paid."

"That's very good, for a boy."

"I guess so," Edward said.

"Did anybody take the trouble to explain to Mrs. Sinclair why you were refusing to deliver the paper?"

"Oh, yes, but she didn't listen to us. She was awful mad. And Homer was standing there, too."

"What did she say to you?"

"She was inside, where the press and the linotype machines are."

"But what did she say?"

"She tried to get us to deliver the papers. So we all went outside and left her."

"And then what happened?"

"The other guys jumped on their bicycles and rode off."

"And what did you do?"

"I came on home."

"Who's going to deliver our paper?" Virginia asked.

"Nobody, I guess. They can't, if we're all on strike." Edward turned back to his father. "Do you think I did wrong?"

"It's something you're old enough to decide for yourself," Harrison Gellert said. Edward was relieved. On the other hand, it wasn't the same thing as being told that he had his father's complete and wholehearted approval to take part in a strike any time there was one. If he hadn't gone on strike with the others, it would have been uncomfortable. He would have had enemies. The school yard would not have been a very safe place for him, and neither would the alley in the back of the *Star* Building, but actually he had wanted to go out on strike and he had enjoyed the excitement.

"They'll have to take us all back, won't they?" he asked. "Since we all did it together?"

"Finish your potato, dear," Mildred Gellert said. "You're keeping Mary waiting." She was not young any more; she had given up searching for her destiny and had come home, for the sake of the children. Acceptance has its inevitable meager rewards. The side porch was now enclosed, and it was generally agreed that the new green brocade curtains in the living room had cost Harrison plenty.

During dessert, Edward remembered suddenly that he was saving his money to buy a bicycle, and the rice pudding stuck in his throat and would not for the longest time go down. When the others left the dining room, he lingered until Old Mary finished clearing the table and with her hand on the light switch said, "You figure on sitting here in the dark?"

Edward got up and went into the library, where his mother and Virginia were. His mother was sewing. She was changing the hem on Virginia's plaid skirt. Edward sat down, like a visitor waiting to be entertained. He heard the front door open and close, and then his father came in and sat down in his favorite chair and (quite as if he hadn't understood a word of all that Edward had been telling him) opened the evening paper.

When the paper boys ran out of the building, Harold West got as far as the door when Homer called to him. Homer said, "You stay here, Harold," and Harold stayed. After he had delivered his own papers, he rode back downtown and with a list supplied by the front office, he and Homer had started out together. Ever so many houses had no street numbers beside the front steps or on the porch roof; or else the numbers, corroded, painted over five or six times, could not be seen in the dark. Not every subscriber to the Draperville *Evening Star* got a paper that night. The lists were incomplete, and there is no adequate substitution for habit. The office stayed open until ten, and there were a few telephone calls, but most people were not surprised that the evening paper, arriving at such different times every night, should finally have failed to arrive at all.

On Saturday morning, Edward went downtown. He saw a knot of boys standing on the sidewalk in front of the *Star* Building. The riot was over, the strike had collapsed, and though they had counted on him to act with them, they had not bothered to inform him of their surrender. If he hadn't been led there by curiosity, he would have been the only one not now apologizing and asking to have his route given back to him.

Riot, in the soul or in an alley, wears off. It is not self-sustaining. Reason waits, worry bides its time. The recording

when it was run over. It happened on a Saturday noon. Hungry, in a hurry to get home for lunch, he rode up in front of the *Star* Building. A voice in his head reminded him that the boys were not allowed to leave their bicycles in front of the building, and another voice said promptly, She won't see it, and even if she does, this once won't matter. . . . He leaned his bicycle carefully against the high curbing and went inside. There were two boys ahead of him. While he was counting the money in his change purse, a boy opened the street door and shouted, "You better come out here, Gellert! Somebody just ran over your new bicycle!"

Without any feeling whatever, as if he were dreaming, Edward went outside, and a man he'd never seen before said, "I didn't know it was there, and I backed over it."

Edward kept right on, without looking at the man, until he reached the edge of the sidewalk and could look down at what ought to have been somebody else's ruined bicycle, not (oh, please not) his.

His mouth began to quiver.

The man said, "I'm sorry," and Edward burst into tears. What had happened was so terrible, and he felt such pity for the mangled spokes, the tires torn from their rims.

Mrs. Sinclair, seeing that there was trouble of some kind in front of the building, left her desk and went to the door. She looked at the bicycle and then at Edward standing there blindly, with the tears streaming down his face. "You're not supposed to leave your wheels in front of the building," she said, and went inside. People gathered around Edward, trying to console him. The man who had run over Edward's bicycle got into his car and drove away. Someone told Edward his name, and where he lived.

That night Harrison Gellert backed the car out of the garage and, with Edward in the front seat beside him, drove out to the edge of town and stopped in front of a one-story frame house in a poor neighborhood. "You wait here," he said, and got out and went up the brick walk. A man came to the door, and Edward saw a lighted room. His father said something and the man said something. Then he held the screen door open, and his father stepped inside and the door closed. Edward waited in perfect confidence that his father would tell him that it was all settled and the man was going to buy him a new bicycle. Instead, his father came out, after about five minutes, and got in the car and started the engine without saying a word. They were halfway down the block before he turned to Edward and explained that the man didn't know anything about his bicycle.

"But they *said* it was him!"

"I know," Harrison Gellert said. "He may not have been telling the truth."

Conscious of how quiet it had become in the front seat, he added, "Would you like to drive downtown for an ice-cream soda?"

They parked in front of the ice-cream parlor, and his father honked and a high-school boy came out, with a white apron around his hips, and took their order. A few minutes later he reappeared with two tin trays and two tall chocolate sodas. The soda was as good a comfort as any, if Edward had been allowed to eat it in silence, but Harrison Gellert was genuinely distressed and sorry for his son, and his sympathy took the form (as it had in the past when he tried to comfort his wife) of feeling sorry for himself. "As you get older," he said, "you will find that a great many things happen that aren't easy to bear. Things you can't change, no matter how you try. You have to accept them and go right on, doing the best you can."

"But it isn't right!" Edward burst out. "He ran over it. It's his fault!"

"I know all that."

"Then why doesn't he have to pay for it?"

"If it was his fault, he *ought* to pay for having your bicycle repaired. But you can't make him do it if he doesn't want to."

A year earlier, Edward would have cried out, "But *you* can!" He thought it now, but he didn't say it.

"We'll find out from Mr. Kohler how much it will cost to have your bicycle fixed, and I'll go fifty-fifty with you, when it comes to paying for it."

Edward thanked his father politely, but there was no use talking about having his bicycle fixed. It would never be the same. The frame was sprung, and you could always tell a re-painted bike from one that was straight from the factory. His father could go to court if necessary, and the judge would make the man pay for ruining his bicycle, and maybe fine him besides.

"It may be cheaper in the end to get a secondhand bicycle," Mr. Gellert said.

With an effort Edward kept the tears from spilling over. He didn't want a secondhand bicycle. He wanted not to leave his new bicycle in front of the *Star* Building where it would be run over.

And Mr. Gellert wanted to say and didn't say, "I hope this will be a lesson to you."

It was a lesson, of course, in the sense that everything that happens, good or bad, is a lesson.

Edward Gellert was thirteen going on fourteen when the paper boys went on strike against the *Evening Star*, and he was fourteen going on fifteen when his bicycle was run over. One half the individual nature never seems any different, from the cradle to the grave; the other half is pathetically in step with the slightest physical change. Edward's voice had deepened, hairs had appeared on his body where Darwin said they should appear, his feet and hands were noticeably large for the rest of him, and something would not allow him to kneel in the dark beside his bed and ask God to give him back his new bicycle. People might be raised from the dead, as it said in the Bible, but a ruined bicycle could not by any power on earth or in heaven be made shining and whole again.

The French Scarecrow

I spied John Mouldy in his cellar
Deep down twenty steps of stone;
In the dusk he sat a-smiling,
Smiling there alone.
—*Walter de la Mare*

DRIVING past the Fishers' house on his way out to the public road, Gerald Martin said to himself absentmindedly, "There's Edmund working in his garden," before he realized that it was a scarecrow. And two nights later he woke up sweating from a dream, a nightmare, which he related next day, lying tense on the analyst's couch.

"I was in this house, where I knew I oughtn't to be, and I looked around and saw there was a door, and in order to get to it I had to pass a dummy—a dressmaker's dummy without any head."

After a considerable silence the disembodied voice with a German accent said, "Any day remnants?"

"I can't think of any," Gerald Martin said, shifting his position on the couch. "We used to have a dressmaker's dummy in the sewing room when I was a child, but I haven't thought of it for years. The Fishers have a scarecrow in their garden, but I don't think it could be that. The scarecrow looks like Edmund. The same thin shoulders, and his clothes, of course, and the way it stands looking sadly down at the ground. It's a caricature of Edmund. One of those freak accidents. I wonder if they realize it. Edmund is not sad, exactly, but there was a period in his life when he was neither as happy or as hopeful as he is now. Dorothy is a very nice woman. Not at all maternal, I would say. At least, she doesn't mother Edmund. And when you see her with some woman with a baby, she always seems totally indifferent. Edmund was married before, and his first wife left him. Helena was selfish but likable, the way selfish people sometimes are. And where Edmund was concerned, completely heartless. I don't know why. She used to turn the radio on full blast at two o'clock in the morning, when he had to get up at six-thirty to catch a commuting train. And once she sewed a ruffle all the way around the bed he was trying to sleep in. Edmund told me that her mother preferred her older sister, and that Helena's whole childhood had been made miserable because of it. He tried every way he could think of to please her and make her happy, and with most women that would have been enough, I suppose, but it only increased her dissatisfaction. Maybe if there had been any children . . . She used to walk up and down the road in a long red cloak, in the wintertime when there was snow on the ground. And she used to talk about New York. And it was as if she was under a spell and waiting to be delivered. Now she blames Edmund for the divorce. She tells everybody that he took advantage of her. Perhaps he did, unconsciously. Consciously, he wouldn't take advantage of a fly. I think he needs analysis, but he's very much opposed to it. Scared to death of it, in fact . . ."

Step by step, Gerald Martin had managed to put a safe distance between himself and the dream, and he was beginning to breathe easier in the complacent viewing of someone else's failure to meet his problems squarely when the voice said, "Well—see you again?"

"I wish to Christ you wouldn't say that! As if I had any choice in the matter."

His sudden fury was ignored. A familiar hypnotic routine obliged him to sit up and put his feet over the side of the couch. The voice became attached to an elderly man with thick glasses and a round face that Gerald would never get used to. He got up unsteadily and walked toward the door. Only when he was outside, standing in front of the elevator shaft, did he remember that the sewing room had a door opening into his mother and father's bedroom, and at one period of his life he had slept there, in a bed with sides that could be let down, a child's bed. This information was safe from the man inside—unless he happened to think of it while he was lying on the couch next time.

That evening he stopped when he came to the Fishers' vegetable garden and turned the engine off and took a good look at the scarecrow. Then, after a minute or two, afraid that he would be seen from the house, he started the car and drove on.

*

The Fishers' scarecrow was copied from a scarecrow in France. The summer before, they had spent two weeks as paying guests in a country house in the Touraine, in the hope that this would improve their French. The improvement was all but imperceptible to them afterward, but they did pick up a number of ideas about gardening. In the *potager*, fruit trees, tree roses, flowers, and vegetables were mingled in a way that aroused their admiration, and there was a more than ordinarily fanciful scarecrow, made out of a blue peasant's smock, striped morning trousers, and a straw hat. Under the hat the stuffed head had a face painted on it; and not simply two eyes, a nose, and a mouth but a face with a sly expression. The scarecrow stood with arms upraised, shaking its white-gloved fists at the sky. Indignant, self-centered, half crazy, it seemed to be saying: *This is what it means to be exposed to experience.* The crows were not taken in.

Effects that had needed generations of dedicated French gardeners to bring about were not, of course, to be imitated successfully by two amateur gardeners in Fairfield County in a single summer. The Fishers gave up the idea of marking off the paths of their vegetable garden with espaliered dwarf apple and pear trees, and they could see no way of having tree roses without also having to spray them, and afterward having to eat the spray. But they did plant zinnias, marigolds, and blue pansies in with the lettuce and the peas, and they made a very good scarecrow. Dorothy made it, actually. She was artistic by inclination, and threw herself into all such undertakings with a childish pleasure.

She made the head out of a dish towel stuffed with hay, and was delighted with the blue stripe running down the face. Then she got out her embroidery thread and embroidered a single eye, gathered the cloth in the middle of the face into a bulbous nose, made the mouth leering. For the body she used a torn pair of Edmund's blue jeans she was tired of mending, and a faded blue workshirt. When Edmund, who was attached to his old clothes, saw that she had also helped herself to an Army fatigue hat from the shelf in the hall closet, he exclaimed, "Hey, don't use that hat for the scarecrow! I wear it sometimes."

"*When* do you wear it?"

"I wear it to garden in."

"You can wear some other old hat to garden in. He's got to have something on his head," she said lightly, and made the hat brim dip down over the blank eye.

"When winter comes, I'll wear it again," Edmund said to himself, "if it doesn't shrink too much, or fall apart in the rain."

The scarecrow stood looking toward the house, with one arm limp and one arm extended stiffly, ending in a gloved hand holding a stick. After a few days the head sank and sank until it was resting on the straw breastbone, and the face was concealed by the brim of the hat. They tried to keep the head up with a collar of twisted grass, but the grass dried, and the head sank once more, and in that attitude it remained.

The scarecrow gave them an eerie feeling when they saw it from the bedroom window at twilight. A man standing in the vegetable garden would have looked like a scarecrow. If he didn't move. Dorothy had never lived in the country before she married Edmund, and at first she was afraid. The black windows at night made her nervous. She heard noises in the basement, caused by the steam circulating through the furnace pipes. And she would suddenly have the feeling—even though she knew it was only her imagination—that there was a man outside, looking through the windows at them. "Shouldn't we invite him in?" Edmund would say when her glance strayed for a second. "Offer him a drink and let him sit by the fire? It's not a very nice night out."

He assumed that The Man Outside represented for her all the childish fears—the fear of the dark, of the burglar on the stairs, of what else he had no way of knowing. Nor she either, probably. The Man Outside was simply there, night after night, for about six weeks, and then he lost his power to frighten, and finally went away entirely, leaving the dark outside as familiar and safe to her as the lighted living room. It was Edmund, strangely, who sometimes, as they were getting ready for bed, went to the front and back doors and locked them. For he was aware that the neighborhood was changing, and that things were happening—cars stolen, houses broken into in broad daylight—that never used to happen in this part of the world.

The Fishers' white clapboard house was big and rambling, much added onto at one time or another, but in its final form still plain and pleasant-looking. The original house dated from around 1840. Edmund's father, who was a New York banker until he retired at the age of sixty-five, had bought it before the First World War. At that time there were only five houses on this winding country road, and two of them were farmhouses. When the Fishers came out from town for the summer, they were met at the railroad station by a man with a horse and carriage. The surrounding country was hilly and offered many handsome views, and most of the local names were to be found on old tombstones in the tiny Presbyterian churchyard. Edmund's mother was a passionate and scholarly gardener, the founder of the local garden club and its president for twenty-seven years. Her regal manner was quite unconscious, and based less on the usual foundations of family, money, etc., than on the authority with which she could speak about the culture of delphinium and lilies, or the pruning of roses. The house was set back from the road about three hundred yards, and behind it were the tennis courts, the big three-story barn, a guest house overlooking the pond where all the children in the neighborhood skated in winter, and, eventually, a five-car garage. Back of the pond, a wagon road went off into the woods and up onto higher ground. In the late twenties, when Edmund used to bring his school friends home for spring and fall weekends and the Easter vacation, the house seemed barely large enough to hold them all. During the last war, when the taxes began to be burdensome, Edmund's father sold off the back land, with the guest house, the barn, and the pond, to a Downtown lawyer, who shortly afterward sold it to a manufacturer of children's underwear. The elder Mr. and Mrs. Fisher started to follow the wagon road back into the woods one pleasant Sunday afternoon, and he ordered them off his property. He was quite within his rights, of course, but nevertheless it rankled. "In the old days," they would say whenever the man's name was mentioned, "you could go anywhere, on anybody's land, and no one ever thought of stopping you."

Edmund's father, working from his own rough plans and supervising the carpenters and plumbers and masons himself, had converted the stone garage into a house, and he had sold it to Gerald Martin, who was a bachelor. The elder Fishers were now living in the Virgin Islands the year round, because of Mrs. Fisher's health. Edmund and Dorothy still had ten acres, but they shared the cinder drive with Gerald and the clothing manufacturer, and, of course, had less privacy than before. The neighborhood itself was no longer the remote place it used to be. The Merritt Parkway had made all the difference. Instead of five houses on the two-and-a-half-mile stretch of dirt road, there were twenty-five, and the road was macadamized. Cars and delivery trucks cruised up and down it all day long.

In spite of all these changes, and in spite of the considerable difference between Edmund's scale of living and his father's—Dorothy had managed with a part-time cleaning woman where in the old days there had been a cook, a waitress, an upstairs maid, a chauffeur, and two gardeners—the big house still seemed to express the financial stability and social confidence and belief in good breeding of the Age of Trellises. Because he had lived in the neighborhood longer than anyone else, Edmund sometimes felt the impulses of a host, but he had learned not to act on them. His mother always used to pay a call on new people within a month of their settling in, and if she liked them, the call was followed by an invitation to the Fishers' for tea or cocktails, at which time she managed to bring up the subject of the garden club. But in the last year or so that she had lived there, she had all but given this up. Twice her call was not returned, and one terribly nice young couple accepted an invitation to tea and blithely forgot to come. Edmund was friendly when he met his neighbors on the road or on the station platform, but he let them go their own way, except for Gerald Martin, who was rather amusing, and obviously lonely, and glad of an invitation to the big house.

"I am sewed to this couch," Gerald Martin said. "My sleeves are sewed to it, and my trousers. I could not move if I wanted to. Oedipus is on the wall over me, answering the spink-spank-sphinx, and those are pussy willows, and I do not like bookcases with glass sides that let down, and the scarecrow is gone. I don't know what they did with it, and I don't like to ask. And today *I* might as well be stuffed with straw. The dream I had last night did it. I broke two plates, and woke up unconfident and nervous and tired. I don't know what the dream means. I had three plates and I dropped two of them, and it was so vivid. It was a short dream but very vivid. I thought at first that the second plate—why *three* plates?—was all right, but while I was looking at it, the cracks appeared. When I picked it up, it gave; it came apart in my hands. It was painted with flowers, and it had openwork, and I was in a hurry, and in my hurry I dropped the plates. And I was upset. I hardly ever break anything. Last night while I was drying the glasses, I thought how I never break any of them. They're Swedish and very expensive. The plates I dreamed about were my mother's. Not actually; I *dreamed* that they were my mother's plates. I broke two things of hers when I was little. And both times it was something she had warned me about. I sat in the tea cart playing house, and forgot and raised my head suddenly, and it went right through the glass tray. And the other was an etched-glass hurricane lamp that she prized very highly. I climbed up on a chair to reach it. And after she died, I could have thought—I don't ever remember thinking this, but I could have thought that I did something I shouldn't have, and she died. . . . Thank you, I have matches. . . . I can raise my arm. I turned without thinking. I can't figure out that dream. My stepmother was there, washing dishes at the sink, and she turned into Helena Fisher, and I woke up thinking, Ah, that's it. They're *both* my stepmothers! My stepmother never broke anything that belonged to my mother, so she must have been fond of her. They knew each other as girls. And I never broke anything that belonged to my stepmother. I only broke something that belonged to my mother. . . . Did I tell you I saw her the other day?"

"You saw someone who reminded you of your mother?"

"No, I saw Helena Fisher. On Fifth Avenue. I crossed over to the other side of the street, even though I'm still fond of her, because she hasn't been very nice to Dorothy, and because it's all so complicated, and I really didn't have anything to say to her. She was very conspicuous in her country clothes." He lit another cigarette and then said, after a prolonged silence, "I don't seem to have anything to say now, either." The silence became unbearable, and he said, "I can't think of anything to talk about."

"Let's talk about you—about this dream you had," the voice said, kind and patient as always, the voice of his father (at $20 an hour).

The scarecrow had remained in the Fishers' vegetable garden, with one arm limp and one arm stiffly extended, all summer. The corn and the tomato vines grew up around it, half obscuring it during the summer months, and then, in the fall, there was nothing whatever around it but the bare ground. The blue workshirt faded still more in the sun and rain. The figure grew frail, the straw chest settled and became a middle-aged thickening of the waist. The resemblance to Edmund disappeared. And on a Friday afternoon in October, with snow flurries predicted, Edmund Fisher went about the yard carrying in the outdoor picnic table and benches, picking up stray flowerpots, and taking one last look around for the pruning shears, the trowel, and the nest of screwdrivers that had all disappeared during the summer's gardening. There were still three or four storm windows to put up on the south side of the house, and he was about to bring them out and hang them when Dorothy, on her hands and knees in the iris bed, called to him.

"What about the scarecrow?"

"Do you want to save it?" he asked.

"I don't really care."

"We might as well," he said, and was struck once more by the lifelike quality of the scarecrow, as he lifted it out of the soil. It was almost weightless. "Did the doctor say it was all right for you to do that sort of thing?"

"I didn't ask him," Dorothy said.

"Oughtn't you to ask him?"

"No," she said, smiling at him. She was nearly three months pregnant. Moonfaced, serenely happy, and slow of movement (when she had all her life been so quick about everything), she went about now doing everything she had always done but like somebody in a dream, a sleepwalker. The clock had been replaced by the calendar. Like the gardeners in France, she was dedicated to making something grow. As Edmund carried the scarecrow across the lawn and around the corner of the house, she followed him with her eyes. Why is it, she wondered, that he can never bear to part with anything, even though it has ceased to serve its purpose and he no longer has any interest in it?

It was as if sometime or other in his life he had lost something, of such infinite value that he could never think of it without grieving, and never bear to part with anything worthless because of the thing he had had to part with that meant so much to him. But what? She had no idea, and she had given some thought to the matter. She was sure it was not Helena; he said (and she believed him) that he had long since got over any feeling he once had for her. His parents were both still living, he was an only child, and death seemed never to have touched him. Was it some early love, that he had never felt he dared speak to her about? Some deprivation? Some terrible injustice done to him? She had no way of telling. The attic and the basement testified to his inability to throw things away, and she had given up trying to do anything about either one. The same with people. At the end of a perfectly pleasant evening he would say "Oh no, it's early still. You mustn't go home!" with such fervor that even though it actually was time to go home and the guests wanted to, they would sit down, confused by him, and stay a while longer. And though the Fishers knew more people than they could manage to see, he would suddenly remember somebody he hadn't thought of or written to in a long time, and feel impelled to do something about them. Was it something that happened to him in his childhood, Dorothy asked herself. Or was it something in his temperament, born in him, a flaw in his horoscope, Mercury in an unsympathetic relation to the moon?

She resumed her weeding, conscious in a way that she hadn't been before of the autumn day, of the end of the summer's gardening, of the leaf-smoke smell and the smell of rotting apples, the hickory tree that lost its leaves before all the other trees, the grass so deceptively green, and the chill that had descended now that the sun had gone down behind the western hill.

Standing in the basement, looking at the hopeless disorder ("A place for everything," his father used to say, "and nothing in its place"), Edmund decided that it was more important to get at the storm windows than to find a place for the scarecrow. He laid it on one of the picnic-table benches, with the head toward the oil burner, and there it sprawled, like a man asleep or dead-drunk, with the line of the hipbone showing through the trousers, and one arm extended, resting on a slightly higher workbench, and one shoulder raised slightly, as if the man had started to turn in his sleep. In the dim light it could have been alive. I must remember to tell Dorothy, he thought. If she sees it like that, she'll be frightened.

The storm windows were washed and ready to hang. As Edmund came around the corner of the house, with IX in one hand and XI in the other, the telephone started to ring, and Dorothy went in by the back door to answer it, so he didn't have a chance to tell her about the scarecrow. When he went indoors, ten minutes later, she was still standing by the telephone, and from the fact that she was merely contributing a monosyllable now and then to the conversation, he knew she was talking to Gerald Martin. Gerald was as dear as the day was long—everybody liked him—but he had such a ready access to his own memories, which were so rich in narrative detail and associations that dovetailed into further narratives, that if you were busy it was a pure and simple misfortune to pick up the telephone and hear his cultivated, affectionate voice.

Edmund gave up the idea of hanging the rest of the storm windows, and instead he got in the car and drove to the village; he had remembered that they were out of cat food and whiskey. When he walked into the house, Dorothy said, "I've just had such a scare. I started to go down in the cellar—"

"I knew that would happen," he said, putting his hat and coat in the hall closet. "I meant to tell you."

"The basement light was burnt out," she said, "and so I took the flashlight. And when I saw the scarecrow I thought it was a man."

"Our old friend," he said, shaking his head. "The Man Outside."

"And you weren't here. I knew I was alone in the house . . ."

Her fright was still traceable in her face as she described it.

On Saturday morning, Edmund dressed hurriedly, the alarm clock having failed to go off, and while Dorothy was getting breakfast, he went down to the basement, half asleep, to get the car out and drive to the village for the cleaning woman, and saw the scarecrow in the dim light, sprawling by the furnace, and a great clot of fear seized him and his heart almost stopped beating. It lay there like an awful idiot, the realistic effect accidentally encouraged by the pair of work shoes Edmund had taken off the night before and tossed carelessly down the cellar stairs. The scarecrow had no feet—only two stumps where the trouser legs were tied at the bottom—but the shoes were where, if it had been alive, they might have been dropped before the person lay down on the bench. I'll have to do something about it, Edmund thought. We can't go on frightening ourselves like this. . . . But the memory of the fright was so real that he felt unwilling to touch the scarecrow. Instead, he left it where it was, for the time being, and backed the car out of the garage.

On the way back from the village, Mrs. Ryan, riding beside him in the front seat of the car, had a story to tell. Among the various people she worked for was a family with three boys. The youngest was in the habit of following her from room to room, and ordinarily he was as good as gold, but yesterday he ran away, she told Edmund. His mother was in town, and the older boys, with some of the neighbors' children, were playing outside with a football, and Mrs. Ryan and the little boy were in the house. "Monroe asked if he could go outside, and I bundled him up and sent him out. I looked outside once, and saw that he was playing with the Bluestones' dog, and I said, 'Monroe, honey, don't pull that dog's tail. He might turn and bite you.'" While she was ironing, the oldest boy came inside for a drink of water, and she asked him where Monroe was, and he said, "Oh, he's outside." But when she went to the door, fifteen minutes later, the older boys were throwing the football again and Monroe was nowhere in sight. The boys didn't know what had happened to him. He disappeared. All around the house was woods, and Mrs. Ryan, in a panic, called and called.

"Usually when I call, he answers immediately, but this time there was no answer, and I went into the house and telephoned the Bluestones, and they hadn't seen him. And then I called the Hayeses and the Murphys, and they hadn't seen him either, and Mr. Hayes came down, and we all started looking for him. Mr. Hayes said only one car had passed in the last half hour—I was afraid he had been kidnapped, Mr. Fisher—and Monroe wasn't in it. And I thought, When his mother comes home and I have to tell her what I've done . . . And just about that time, he answered, from behind the hedge!"

"Was he there all the time?" Edmund asked, shifting into second as he turned in to his own driveway.

"I don't know where he was," Mrs. Ryan said. "But he did the same thing once before—he wandered off on me. Mr. Ryan thinks he followed the Bluestones' dog home. His mother called me up last night and said that he knew he'd done something wrong. He said, 'Mummy, I was bad today. I ran off on Sadie. . . .' But Mr. Fisher, I'm telling you, I was almost out of my mind."

"I don't wonder," Edmund said soberly.

"With woods all around the house, and as Mr. Hayes said, climbing over a stone wall a stone could fall on him and we wouldn't find him for days."

Ten minutes later, she went down to the basement for the scrub bucket, and left the door open at the head of the stairs. Edmund heard her exclaim, for their benefit, "God save us, I've just had the fright of my life!"

She had seen the scarecrow.

The tramp that ran off with the child, of course, Edmund thought. He went downstairs a few minutes later, and saw that Mrs. Ryan had picked the dummy up and stood it in a corner, with its degenerate face to the wall, where it no longer looked human or frightening.

Mrs. Ryan is frightened because of the nonexistent tramp. Dorothy is afraid of The Man Outside. What am I afraid of, he wondered. He stood there waiting for the oracle to answer, and it did, but not until five or six hours later. Poor Gerald Martin called, after lunch, to say that he had the German measles.

"I was sick as a dog all night," he said mournfully. "I thought I was dying. I wrote your telephone number on a slip of paper and put it beside the bed, in case I *did* die."

"Well, for God's sake, why didn't you call us?" Edmund exclaimed.

"What good would it have done?" Gerald said. "All you could have done was say you were sorry."

"Somebody could have come over and looked after you."

"No, somebody couldn't. It's very catching. I think I was exposed to it a week ago at a party in Westport."

"I had German measles when I was a kid," Edmund said. "We've both had it."

"You can get it again," Gerald said. "I still feel terrible. . . ."

When Edmund left the telephone, he made the mistake of mentioning Gerald's illness to Mrs. Ryan, forgetting that it was the kind of thing that was meat and drink to her.

"Has Mrs. Fisher been near him?" she asked, with quickened interest.

He shook his head.

"There's a great deal of it around," Mrs. Ryan said. "My daughter got German measles when she was carrying her first child, and she lost it."

He tried to ask if it was a miscarriage or if the child was born dead, and he couldn't speak; his throat was too dry.

"She was three months along when she had it," Mrs. Ryan went on, without noticing that he was getting paler and paler. "The baby was born alive, but it only lived three days. She's had two other children since. I feel it was a blessing the Lord took that one. If it had lived, it might have been an imbecile. You love them even so, because they belong to you, but it's better if they don't live, Mr. Fisher. We feel it was a blessing the child was taken."

Edmund decided that he wouldn't tell Dorothy, and then five minutes later he decided that he'd better tell her. He went upstairs and into the bedroom where she was resting, and sat down on the edge of the bed, and told her about Gerald's telephone call. "Mrs. Ryan says it's very bad if you catch it while you're pregnant. . . . And she said some more."

"I can see she did, by the look on your face. You shouldn't have mentioned it to her. What did she say?"

"She said—" He swallowed. "She said the child could be born an imbecile. She also said there was a lot of German measles around. You're not worried?"

"We all live in the hand of God."

"I tell myself that every time I'm really frightened. Unfortunately that's the only time I do think it."

"Yes, I know."

Five minutes later, he came back into the room and said, "Why don't you call the doctor? Maybe there's a shot you can take."

The doctor was out making calls, and when he telephoned back, Dorothy answered, on the upstairs extension. Edmund sat down on the bottom step of the stairs and listened to her half of the conversation. As soon as she had hung up, she came down to tell him what the doctor had said.

"The shot only lasts three weeks. He said he'd give it to me if I should be exposed to the measles anywhere."

"Did he say there was an epidemic of it?"

"I didn't ask him. He said that it was commonly supposed to be dangerous during the first three months, but that the statistics showed that it's only the first two months, while the child is being formed, that you have to worry." Moonfaced and serene again, she went to put the kettle on for tea.

Edmund got up and went down to the basement. He carried the dummy outside, removed the hat and then the head, unbuttoned the shirt, removed the straw that filled it and the trousers, and threw it on the compost pile. The hat, the head, the shirt and trousers, the gloves that were hands, he rolled into a bundle and put away on a basement shelf, in case Dorothy wanted to make the scarecrow next summer. The two crossed sticks reminded him of the comfort that Mrs. Ryan, who was a devout Catholic, had and that he did not have. The hum of the vacuum cleaner overhead in the living room, the sad song of a mechanical universe, was all the reassurance he could hope for, and it left so much (it left the scarecrow, for example) completely unexplained and unaccounted for.

THE WRITER AS ILLUSIONIST

The Writer as Illusionist

A Speech Delivered at Smith College
March 4, 1955

ONE of the standard themes of Chinese painting is the spring festival on the river. I'm sure many of you have seen some version of it. There is one in the Metropolitan Museum. It has three themes woven together: the river, which comes down from the upper right, and the road along the river, and the people on the riverbanks. As the scroll unwinds, there is, first, the early-morning mist on the rice fields and some boys who cannot go to the May Day festival because they have to watch their goats. Then there is a country house, and several people starting out for the city, and a farmer letting water into a field by means of a water wheel, and then more people and buildings—all kinds of people all going toward the city for the festival. And along the riverbank there are various entertainers—a magician, a female tightrope walker, several fortune-tellers, a phrenologist, a man selling spirit money, a man selling patent medicine, a storyteller. I prefer to think that it is with this group—the shoddy entertainers earning their living by the riverbank on May Day—that Mr. Bellow, Mr. Gill, Miss Chase, on the platform, Mr. Ralph Ellison and Mrs. Kazin, in the audience, and I, properly speaking, belong. Writers—narrative writers—are people who perform tricks.

Before I came up here, I took various books down from their shelf and picked out some examples of the kind of thing I mean. Here is one:

"I have just returned this morning from a visit to my landlord—the solitary neighbor that I shall be troubled with . . ."

One of two things—there will be more neighbors turning up than the narrator expects, or else he will very much wish that they had. And the reader is caught; he cannot go away until he finds out which of his two guesses is correct. This is, of course, a trick.

Here is another: *"None of them knew the color of the sky. . . ."*

Why not? Because they are at sea, pulling at the oars in an open boat; and so are you.

Here is another trick: "*Call me Ishmael. . . .*" A pair of eyes looking into your eyes. A face. A voice. You have entered into a personal relationship with a stranger, who will perhaps make demands on you, extraordinary personal demands; who will perhaps insist that you love him; who perhaps will love you in a way that is upsetting and uncomfortable.

Here is another trick: "*Thirty or forty years ago, in one of those gray towns along the Burlington railroad, which are so much grayer today than they were then, there was a house well known from Omaha to Denver for its hospitality and for a certain charm of atmosphere . . .*"

A door opens slowly in front of you, and you cannot see who is opening it but, like a sleepwalker, you have to go in.

Another trick: "*It was said that a new person had appeared on the seafront—a lady with a dog . . .*"

The narrator appears to be, in some way, underprivileged, socially. She perhaps has an invalid father that she has to take care of, and so she cannot walk along the promenade as often as she would like. Perhaps she is not asked many places. And so she has not actually set eyes on this interesting new person that everyone is talking about. She is therefore all the more interested. And meanwhile, surprisingly, the reader cannot forget the lady, or the dog, or the seafront.

Here is another trick: "*It is a truth universally acknowledged that a single man in possession of a good fortune must be in want of a wife . . .*"

An attitude of mind, this time. A way of looking at people that is ironical, shrewd, faintly derisive, and that suggests that every other kind of writing is a trick (this is a special trick, in itself) and that this book is going to be about life as it really is, not some fabrication of the author's.

So far as I can see, there is no legitimate sleight of hand involved in practicing the arts of painting, sculpture, and music. They appear to have had their origin in religion, and they are fundamentally serious. In writing—in all writing but especially in narrative writing—you are continually being taken in. The reader, skeptical, experienced, with many demands on his time and many ways of enjoying his leisure, is asked to believe in people he knows don't exist, to be present at scenes that never occurred, to be amused or moved or instructed just as he would be in real life, only the life exists in somebody else's imagination. If, as Mr. T. S. Eliot says, humankind cannot bear very much reality, then that would account for their turning to the charlatans operating along the riverbank—to the fortune-teller, the phrenologist, the man selling spirit money, the storyteller. Or there may be a different explanation; it may be that what humankind cannot bear directly it can bear indirectly, from a safe distance.

The writer has everything in common with the vaudeville magician except this: The writer must be taken in by his own tricks. Otherwise, the audience will begin to yawn and snicker. Having practiced more or less incessantly for five, ten, fifteen, or twenty years, knowing that the trunk has a false bottom and the opera hat a false top, with the white doves in a cage ready to be handed to him from the wings and his clothing full of unusual, deep pockets containing odd playing cards and colored scarves knotted together and not knotted together and the American flag, he must begin by pleasing himself. His mouth must be the first mouth that drops open in surprise, in wonder, as (presto chango!) this character's heartache is dragged squirming from his inside coat pocket, and that character's future has become his past while he was not looking.

With his cuffs turned back, to show that there is no possibility of deception being practiced on the reader, the writer invokes a time: He offers the reader a wheat field on a hot day in July, and a flying machine, and a little boy with his hand in his father's. He has been brought to the wheat field to see a flying machine go up. They stand, waiting, in a crowd of people. It is a time when you couldn't be sure, as you can now, that a flying machine would go up. Hot, tired, and uncomfortable, the little boy wishes they could go home. The wheat field is like an oven. The flying machine does not go up.

The writer will invoke a particular place: With a cardinal and a tourist home and a stretch of green grass and this and that, he will make Richmond, Virginia.

He uses words to invoke his version of the Forest of Arden. If he is a good novelist, you can lean against his trees; they will not give way. If he is a bad novelist, you probably shouldn't.

Ideally, you ought to be able to shake them until an apple falls on your head. (The apple of understanding.)

The novelist has tricks of detail. For example, there is Turgenev's hunting dog, in "A Sportsman's Notebook." The sportsman, tired after a day's shooting, has accepted a ride in a peasant's cart, and is grateful for it. His dog is not. Aware of how foolish he must look as he is being lifted into the cart, the unhappy dog smiles to cover his embarrassment. . . . There is the shop of the live fish, toward the beginning of Malraux's "Man's Fate." A conspirator goes late at night to a street of pet shops in Shanghai and knocks on the door of a dealer in live fish. They are both involved in a plot to assassinate someone. The only light in the shop is a candle; the fish are asleep in phosphorescent bowls. As the hour that the assassination will be attempted is mentioned, the water on the surface of the bowls begins to stir feebly. The carp, awakened by the sound of voices, begin to swim round and round, and my hair stands on end.

These tricks of detail are not important; they have nothing to do with the plot or the idea of either piece of writing. They are merely exercises in literary virtuosity, but nevertheless in themselves so wonderful that to overlook them is to miss half the pleasure of the performance.

There is also a more general sleight of hand—tricks that involve the whole work, tricks of construction. Nothing that happens in Elizabeth Bowen's "The House in Paris," none of the characters, is, for me, as interesting as the way in which the whole thing is put together. From that all the best effects, the real beauty of the book, derive.

And finally there are the tricks that involve the projection of human character. In the last book that I have read, Ann Birstein's novel, "The Troublemaker," there is a girl named Rhoda, who would in some places, at certain periods of the world's history, be considered beautiful, but who is too large to be regarded as beautiful right now. It is time for her to be courted, to be loved—high time, in fact. And she has a suitor, a young man who stops in to see her on his way to the movies alone. There is also a fatality about the timing of these visits; he always comes just when she has washed her hair. She is presented to the reader with a bath towel around her wet head, her hair in pins, in her kimono, sitting on the couch in the living room, silent, while her parents make conversation with the suitor. All her hopes of appearing to advantage lie shattered on the carpet at her feet. She is inconsolable but dignified, a figure of supportable pathos. In the midst of feeling sorry for her you burst out laughing. The laughter is not unkind.

These forms of prestidigitation, these surprises, may not any of them be what makes a novel great, but unless it has some of them, I do not care whether a novel is great or not; I cannot read it.

It would help if you would give what I am now about to read to you only half your attention. It doesn't require any more than that, and if you listen only now and then, you will see better what I am driving at.

Begin with breakfast and the tipping problem.

Begin with the stealing of the marmalade dish and the breakfast tray still there.

The marmalade dish, shaped like a shell, is put on the cabin-class breakfast tray by mistake, this once. It belongs in first class.

Begin with the gate between first and second class.

Begin with the obliging steward unlocking the gate for them.

The gate, and finding their friends who are traveling first class, on the glassed-in deck.

The gate leads to the stealing of the marmalade dish.

If you begin with the breakfast tray, then— no, begin with the gate and finding their friends.

And their friends' little boy, who had talked to Bernard Baruch and asked Robert Sherwood for his autograph.

The couple in cabin class have first-class accommodations for the return voyage, which the girl thinks they are going to exchange, and the man secretly hopes they will not be able to.

But they have no proper clothes. They cannot dress for dinner if they do return first class.

Their friend traveling first class on the way over has brought only one evening dress, which she has to wear night after night.

Her husband tried to get cabin-class accommodations and couldn't.

This is a lie, perhaps.
They can afford the luxury of traveling first class but disapprove of it.
They prefer to live more modestly than they need to.
They refuse to let themselves enjoy, let alone be swept off their feet by, the splendor and space.
But they are pleased that their little boy, aged nine, has struck up a friendship with Bernard Baruch and Robert Sherwood.
They were afraid he would be bored on the voyage.
Also, they themselves would never have dared approach either of these eminent figures, and are amazed that they have begotten a child with courage.
The girl is aware that her husband has a love of luxury and is enjoying the splendor and space they haven't paid for.
On their way back to the barrier, they encounter Bernard Baruch.
His smile comes to rest on them, like the beam from a lighthouse, and then after a few seconds passes on.
They discover that they are not the only ones who have been exploring.
Their table companions have all found the gate.
When the steward unlocked the gate for the man and the girl, he let loose a flood.
The entire cabin class has spread out in both directions, into tourist as well as first class.
Begin with the stealing of the marmalade dish.
The man is ashamed of his conscientiousness but worried about the stewardess.
Will she have to pay for the missing marmalade dish?
How many people? Three English, two Americans cabin class, three Americans first class.
Then the morning on deck.
The breakfast tray still there, accusing them, before they go up to lunch.
The Orkney Islands in the afternoon.
The movie, which is shown to cabin class in the afternoon, to first class in the evening.
The breakfast tray still in the corridor outside their cabin when they go to join their friends in first class in the bar before dinner.

With her tongue loosened by liquor, the girl confesses her crime.
They go down to the cabin after dinner, and the tray is gone.
In the evening the coast of France, lights, a lighthouse.
The boat as immorality.
The three sets of people.
Begin in the late afternoon with the sighting of the English islands.
Begin with the stealing of the marmalade dish.
No, begin with the gate.
Then the stealing of the marmalade dish.
Then the luncheon table with the discovery that other passengers have been exploring and found the gate between first and second class.
Then the tray accusing them.
What do they feel about stealing?
When has the man stolen something he wanted as badly as the girl wanted that marmalade dish for an ashtray?
From his mother's purse, when he was six years old.
The stewardess looks like his mother.
Ergo, he is uneasy.
They call on their friends in first class one more time, to say goodby, and as they go back to second class, the girl sees, as clearly as if she had been present, that some time during the day her husband has managed to slip away from her and meet the stewardess and pay for the marmalade dish she stole.
And that is why the breakfast tray disappeared.
He will not allow himself, even on shipboard, the splendor and space of an immoral act.
He had to go behind her back and do the proper thing.

A writer struggling—unsuccessfully, as it turned out; the story was never written—to change a pitcher of water into a pitcher of wine.

In *The Listener* for January 27th, 1955, there is a brief but wonderfully accurate description of a similar attempt carried off successfully:

"Yesterday morning I was in despair. You know that bloody book which Dadie and Leonard extort, drop by drop from my breast? Fiction, or some title to that effect. I couldn't screw a word from me; and at last dropped my head in my hands, dipped my pen in the ink, and wrote these words, as if automatically, on a clean sheet: Orlando, a Biography. No sooner had I done this than my body was flooded with rapture and my brain with ideas. I wrote rapidly till twelve . . ."

It is safe to assume that on that wonderful (for us as well as her) morning, the writer took out this word and put in that and paused only long enough to admire the effect; she took—on that morning or others like it—the very words out of this character's mouth in order to give them, unscrupulously, to that character; she annulled marriages and brought dead people back to life when she felt the inconvenience of having to do without them. She cut out the whole last part of the scene she had been working on so happily and feverishly for most of the morning because she saw suddenly that it went past the real effect into something that was just writing. Just writing is when the novelist's hand is not quicker than the reader's eye. She persuaded, she struggled with, she beguiled this or that character that she had made up out of whole cloth (or almost) to speak his mind, to open his heart. Day after day, she wrote till twelve, employing tricks no magician had ever achieved before, and using admirably many that they had, until, after some sixty pages, something quite serious happened. Orlando changed sex—that is, she exchanged the mind of a man for the mind of a woman; this trick was only partly successful—and what had started out as a novel became a brilliant, slaphappy essay. It would have been a great pity—it would have been a real loss if this particular book had never been written; even so, it is disappointing. I am in no position to say what happened, but it seems probable from the writer's diary—fortunately, she kept one—that there were too many interruptions; too many friends invited themselves and their husbands and dogs and children for the weekend.

Though the writer may from time to time entertain paranoiac suspicions about critics and book reviewers, about his publisher, and even about the reading public, the truth is that he has no enemy but interruption. The man from Porlock has put an end to more masterpieces than the Turks—was it the Turks?—did when they set fire to the library at Alexandria.

Also, odd as it may seem, every writer has a man from Porlock inside him who gladly and gratefully connives to bring about these interruptions.

If the writer's attention wanders for a second or two, his characters stand and wait politely for it to return to them. If it doesn't return fairly soon, their feelings are hurt and they refuse to say what is on their minds or in their hearts. They may even turn and go away, without explaining or leaving a farewell note or a forwarding address where they can be reached.

But let us suppose that owing to one happy circumstance and another, including the writer's wife, he has a good morning; he has been deeply attentive to the performers and the performance. Suppose that—because this is common practice, I believe—he begins by making a few changes here and there, because what is behind him, all the scenes that come before the scene he is now working on, must be *perfect*, before he can tackle what lies ahead. (This is the most dangerous of all the tricks in the repertoire, and probably it would be wiser if he omitted it from his performance: it is the illusion of illusions, and all a dream. And tomorrow morning, with a clearer head, making a fresh start, he will change back the changes, with one small insert that makes all the difference.) But to continue: Since this is very close work, watch mender's work, really, this attentiveness, requiring a magnifying glass screwed to his eye and resulting in poor posture, there will probably be, somewhere at the back of his mind, a useful corrective vision, something childlike and simple that represents the task as a whole. He will perhaps see the material of his short story as a pond, into which a stone is tossed, sending out a circular ripple; and then a second stone is tossed into the pond, sending out a second circular ripple that is inside the first and that ultimately overtakes it; and then a third stone; and a fourth; and so on. Or he will see himself crossing a long level plain, chapter after chapter, toward the mountains on the horizon. If there were no mountains, there would be no novel; but they are still a long way away—those scenes of excitement, of the utmost drama, so strange, so sad, that will write themselves; and meanwhile, all the knowledge, all the art, all the imagination at his command will be needed to cover this day's march on perfectly level ground.

As a result of too long and too intense concentration, the novelist sooner or later begins to act peculiarly. During the genesis of his book, particularly, he talks to himself in the street; he smiles knowingly at animals and birds; he offers Adam the apple, for Eve, and with a half involuntary movement of his right arm imitates the writhing of the snake that nobody knows about yet. He spends the greater part of the days of his creation in his bathrobe and slippers, unshaven, his hair uncombed, drinking water to clear his brain, and hardly distinguishable from an inmate in an asylum. Like many such unfortunate people, he has delusions of grandeur. With the cherubim sitting row on row among the constellations, the seraphim in the more expensive seats in the *primum mobile*, waiting, ready, willing to be astonished, to be taken in, the novelist, still in his bathrobe and slippers, with his cuffs rolled back, says *Let there be* (after who knows how much practice beforehand) . . . *Let there be* (and is just as delighted as the angels and the reader and everybody else when there actually is) *Light*.

Not always, of course. Sometimes it doesn't work. But say that it does work. Then there is light, the greater light to rule the daytime of the novel, and the lesser light to rule the night scenes, breakfast and dinner, one day, and the gathering together of now this and now that group of characters to make a lively scene, grass, trees, apple trees in bloom, adequate provision for sea monsters if they turn up in a figure of speech, birds, cattle, and creeping things, and finally and especially man—male and female, Anna and Count Vronsky, Emma and Mr. Knightley.

There is not only all this, there are certain aesthetic effects that haven't been arrived at accidentally; the universe of the novel is beautiful, if it *is* beautiful, by virtue of the novelist's intention that it should be.

Say that the performance is successful; say that he has reached the place where an old, old woman, who was once strong and active and handsome, grows frail and weak, grows smaller and smaller, grows partly senile, and toward the end cannot get up out of bed and even refuses to go on feeding herself, and finally, well cared for, still in her own house with her own things around her, dies, and on a cold day in January the funeral service is read over her casket, and she is buried. . . . Then what? Well, perhaps the relatives, returning to the old home after the funeral, or going to the lawyer's office, for the reading of the will.

In dying, the old woman took something with her, and therefore the performance has, temporarily at least, come to a standstill. Partly out of fatigue, perhaps, partly out of uncertainty about what happens next, the novelist suddenly finds it impossible to believe in the illusions that have so completely held his attention up till now. Suddenly it won't do. It might work out for some other novel but not this one.

Defeated for the moment, unarmed, restless, he goes outdoors in his bathrobe, discovers that the morning is more beautiful than he had any idea—full spring, with the real apple trees just coming into bloom, and the sky the color of the blue that you find in the sky of the West Indies, and the neighbors' dogs enjoying themselves, and the neighbor's little boy having to be fished out of the brook, and the grass needing cutting—he goes outside thinking that a brief turn in the shrubbery will clear his mind and set him off on a new track. But it doesn't. He comes in poorer than before, and ready to give not only this morning's work but the whole thing up as a bad job, ill advised, too slight. The book that was going to live, to be read after he is dead and gone, will not even be written, let alone published. It was an illusion.

So it was. So it is. But fortunately we don't need to go into all that because, just as he was about to give up and go put his trousers on, he has thought of something. He has had another idea. It might even be more accurate to say another idea has him. Something so simple and brief that you might hear it from the person sitting next to you on a train; something that would take a paragraph to tell in a letter . . . Where is her diamond ring? What has happened to her furs? Mistrust and suspicion are followed by brutal disclosures. The disclosure of who kept after her until she changed her will, and then who, finding out about this, got her to make a new will, eight months before she died.

The letters back and forth between the relatives hint at undisclosed revelations, at things that cannot be put in a letter. But if they cannot be put in a letter, how else can they be disclosed safely? Not at all, perhaps. Perhaps they can never be disclosed. There is no reason to suspect the old woman's housekeeper. On the other hand, if it was not a member of the family who walked off with certain unspecified things without waiting to find out which of the rightful heirs wanted what, surely it could have been put in a letter. Unless, of course, the novelist does not yet know the answer himself. Eventually, of course, he is going to have to let the cat—this cat and all sorts of other cats—out of the bag. If he does not know, at this point, it means that a blessing has descended on him, and the characters have taken things in their own hands. From now on, he is out of it, a recorder simply of what happens, whose business is with the innocent as well as with the guilty. There are other pressures than greed. Jealousy alone can turn one sister against the other, and both against the man who is universally loved and admired, and who used, when they were little girls, to walk up and down with one of them on each of his size-12 shoes. Things that everybody knows but nobody has ever come right out and said will be said now. Ancient grievances will be aired. Everybody's character, including that of the dead woman, is going to suffer damage from too much handling. The terrible damaging facts of that earlier will must all come out. The family, as a family, is done for, done to death by what turns out in the end to be a surprisingly little amount of money, considering how much love was sacrificed to it. And their loss, if the novelist really is a novelist, will be our gain. For it turns out that this old woman—eighty-three she was, with a bad heart, dreadful blood pressure, a caricature of herself, alone and lonely—knew what would happen and didn't care; didn't try to stop it; saw that it had begun under her nose while she was still conscious; saw that she was the victim of the doctor who kept her alive long after her will to live had gone; saw the threads of will, of consciousness, slip through her fingers; let them go; gathered them in again; left instructions that she knew would not be followed; tried to make provisions when it was all but too late; and then delayed some more, while she remembered, in snatches, old deprivations, an unwise early marriage, the absence of children; and slept; and woke to remember more—this old woman, who woke on her last day cheerful, fully conscious, ready for whatever came (it turned out to be her sponge bath)—who was somehow a symbol (though this is better left unsaid), an example, an instance, a proof of something, and whose last words were— But I mustn't spoil the story for you.

At twelve o'clock, the novelist, looking green from fatigue (also from not having shaved), emerges from his narrative dream at last with something in his hand he wants somebody to listen to. His wife will have to stop what she is doing and think of a card, any card; or be sawed in half again and again until the act is letter-perfect. She alone knows when he is, and when he is not, writing like himself. This is an illusion, sustained by love, and this she also knows but keeps to herself. It would only upset him if he were told. If he has no wife, he may even go to bed that night without ever having shaved, brushed his teeth, or put his trousers on. And if he is invited out, he will destroy the dinner party by getting up and putting on his hat and coat at quarter of ten, causing the other guests to signal to one another, and the hostess to make a mental note never to ask him again. In any case, literary prestidigitation is tiring and requires lots of sleep.

And when the writer is in bed with the light out, he tosses. Far from dropping off to sleep and trusting to the fact that he did get home and into bed by ten o'clock after all, he thinks of something, and the light beside his bed goes on long enough for him to write down five words that may or may not mean a great deal to him in the morning. The light may go on and off several times before his steady breathing indicates that he is asleep. And while he is asleep he may dream—he may dream that he had a dream in which the whole meaning of what he is trying to do in the novel is brilliantly revealed to him. Just so the dog asleep on the hearthrug dreams; you can see, by the faint jerking movement of his four legs, that he is after a rabbit. The novelist's rabbit is the truth—about life, about human character, about himself and therefore by extension, it is to be hoped, about other people. He is convinced that this is all knowable, can be described, can be recorded, by a person sufficiently dedicated to describing and recording, can be caught in a net of narration. He is encouraged by the example of other writers—Turgenev, say, with his particular trick of spreading out his arms like a great bird and taking off, leaving the earth and soaring high above the final scenes; or D. H. Lawrence, with his marvelous ability to make people who are only words on a page actually reach out with their hands and love one another; or Virginia Woolf, with her delight in fireworks, in a pig's skull with a scarf wrapped around it; or E. M. Forster, with his fastidious preference for what a good many very nice people wish were not so.

But what, seriously, was accomplished by these writers or can the abstract dummy novelist I have been describing hope to accomplish? Not life, of course; not the real thing; not children and roses; but only a facsimile that is called literature. To achieve this facsimile the writer has, more or less, to renounce his birthright to reality, and few people have a better idea of what it is—of its rewards and satisfactions, or of what to do with a whole long day. What's in it for him? The hope of immortality? The chances are not good enough to interest a sensible person. Money? Well, money is not money any more. Fame? For the young, who are in danger always of being ignored, of being overlooked at the party, perhaps, but no one over the age of forty who is in his right mind would want to be famous. It would interfere with his work, with his family life. Why then should the successful manipulation of illusions be everything to a writer? Why does he bother to make up stories and novels? If you ask him, you will probably get any number of answers, none of them straightforward. You might as well ask a sailor why it is that he has chosen to spend his life at sea.

APPENDIX

Contents

Introduction to "They Came Like Swallows"

AN English instructor at the University of Illinois, who was my mentor during all four years of college, had a sabbatical some time about the year 1930 and went around the world. I don't know in what country he picked up a copy of the Tauchnitz edition of *To the Lighthouse*. Shortly after he got home he offered it to me, saying, "I couldn't read this but you may like it." His idea of the perfect novel was Fielding's *Tom Jones*. I perhaps don't need to explain that the central figure of *To the Lighthouse*, Mrs. Ramsay, is a woman who, by her protecting nature and desire for harmony, is able to reconcile, briefly, and only to a certain extent, the clashing temperaments of her husband and children and of the guests who have been invited to stay with the Ramsays in their house on the coast of Cornwall. On the very first page I came upon my doppelgänger:

> Since he belonged, even at the age of six, to that great clan which cannot keep this feeling separate from that, but must let future prospects, with their joys and sorrows, cloud what is actually at hand, since to such people even in earliest childhood any turn in the wheel of sensation has the power to crystallise and transfix the moment upon which its gloom or radiance rests, James Ramsay, sitting on the floor cutting out pictures from the illustrated catalogue of the Army and Navy Stores, endowed the picture of a refrigerator, as his mother spoke, with heavenly bliss.

My mother's death, in the epidemic of Spanish influenza of 1918, so scarred my soul that I would, I am sure, have written about it sooner or later but in any case the way I did write about it was strongly affected by the style and narrative method of *To the Lighthouse*. Saul Bellow, speaking at a literary symposium at Smith College in the fifties, said, "A writer is a reader who is moved to emulation." I took it that he did not mean mere copying. Mrs. Woolf was strongly affected by reading Proust. ("Oh if I could write like that!" she said. And decided that she could. And discovered she couldn't.) In the paragraph I have quoted there is an echo of his syntax.

I saw in Mrs. Ramsay a woman rather like my mother, who was acutely responsive to other people's happiness or distress, whose voice I associate with velvet, who lived by the pure feelings of the heart. That this reflects a child's point of view is obvious. Because Virginia Woolf disposed of Mrs. Ramsay's death in a brief, terrible parenthesis, leaving the reader in ignorance of what led up to it, I felt my hands were not tied. I could go where she had chosen not to.

If you toss a small stone into a pond, it will create a ripple that expands outward, wider and wider. And if you then toss a second stone, it will again produce a widening circle inside the first one. And with the third stone there will be three expanding concentric circles before the pond recovers its stillness through the force of gravity. That is what I wanted my novel to be like. No directions came with this idea. I have tried to recall, across the intervening sixty years, how I went about writing *They Came Like Swallows* and what I remember instead is the places I wrote in.

When I was seventeen I had a summer job on a farm near Portage, Wisconsin, and it became a second home. Middle-western farms do not usually offer much pleasure to the eye but this one did. Besides a log house and a frame house that was much older, there was a horse barn and the usual outbuildings, a forty-acre stand of oak trees, hay meadows, and a marsh with a small swift-running stream meandering through it. The banks were lined with wild rice, which in the fall Indians harvested from their canoes. What was originally a water tower had been converted into a three-story frame building. On the first floor there was a single room with a grand piano. Josef Lhévinne, the great Russian pianist, was a friend of the family and came to the farm at least once during every summer. The piano was for him to use when he was preparing for a season of concertizing. On my hands and knees in the vegetable garden, pulling weeds, I would hear the beginning notes of the Chopin A Minor Étude, Opus 25, and straighten up to listen: In the upper half of the keyboard, musical fireworks. In the lower half, the imperturbable melodic line. The second floor of the tower was his bedroom. The third floor, reached by an outside stairway, was a little study with a brick fireplace, white wicker furniture covered with a cheerful cretonne, and a desk facing a window. I went there once at the end of winter and found, between the cushions of the chaise longue, the dry odorless body of a dead squirrel. It had come down the chimney, been unable to get up it again, and died there of hunger and cold. If I had understood and allowed myself to feel the full implications of this lonely death I would have become, in that instant, a mature novelist.

When I began to write seriously, this room among the treetops was turned over to me. I forget how many months I sat in that room, at that little desk, struggling. I needed to forget Virginia Woolf and establish contact with a figure out of antiquity —the old, often blind, professional storyteller who made his living by standing on the riverbank by the ferry landing or by some crossroads, telling tales that began "Once upon a time there was a . . ." As I searched for the form I believed was implicit in the material, I would hear the crows bad-mouthing one another. A goldfinch or a robin would settle on the branch outside my window and then fly off. Sometimes I stopped typing in order to enjoy a summer thunderstorm. I tried telling the story in the first person and in the third. Neither one worked. The omniscient author knew too much and at the same time too little. I did seven versions of Part One, each about a hundred pages long, and wasn't satisfied with any of them.

The summer of 1935 I had a fellowship to the MacDowell Colony. There I was given a fieldstone studio to write in, with a desk and a typewriter, a table and some chairs, a fireplace and plenty of logs to burn in it. I slept in the men's dormitory. At noon a picnic basket containing my lunch was left on the doorstep of my studio and usually I was sitting there waiting for it. In the afternoon I went walking. The air of southern New Hampshire is fresh and smells of pine needles. I would stand and watch huge cloud formations turn on some invisible axis and in an instant become deep blue sky. Sometimes I walked in the woods, sometimes I went downhill into the village of Peterborough, where I stepped into the bookstore or walked up one street and down the next admiring the old houses. In a grove of trees in the center of town I discovered a pond large enough to swim in and quite deserted. After that, when I went walking I usually took my swimming trunks with me. Many years later, I learned that the hours I kept were the subject of amused comment by the other colonists, who spent the whole day working in their studios, but my judgment failed along about twelve-thirty and after that there was no point in my sitting in front of a typewriter.

Among the colonists that summer there were only three with any conspicuous talent—the surrealist painter Louis Guglielmi, who died young; the composer David Diamond, who was only seventeen; and the poet and translator Robert Fitzgerald. About the others the most you could say was that they were pleasant company. Among them was a Brazilian composer who was writing a triple fugue, a woman who was doing her Ph.D. thesis on the last ten years of Wordsworth's life, during which he wrote nothing of any consequence, and a poet whose copy of Elinor Wylie's *Angels and Earthly Creatures* had been plagiarized from so often that the pages were coming unsewed. The Brazilian composer was carrying on an extensive correspondence with orchestra managers all over the world and enlisted my help, his English not being up to it. From time to time I rebelled and then he would sit down at the piano and play Busoni's transcription of the Bach chaconne, after which I would go on turning his pidgin English into something more businesslike. A painter named Charlotte Blass needed a model and I sat for her. Husbands, wives, friends, lovers came and went. The bachelors complained of sexual impotence and suspected Mrs. MacDowell of putting saltpeter in the coffee. Diamond saw Elinor Wylie's ghost. It struck me that living in an artists' colony was a little like sleeping six in a bed.

Fitzgerald grew up in Springfield, Illinois, thirty miles from where I was living most of that time. We became friends during the year I spent as a graduate student at Harvard. He was two years younger and much better educated. His mother died when he was three, his younger brother when he was seven. And while he was away at boarding school, a year or two before I met him, his father, whom he worshipped, died of tuberculosis of the bone. I learned far more about literature from him than I did from my encounters with the English faculty at Harvard. Except for a brief bad period in my sophomore year, my college days had been happy and I was cheerfully skittering around on the surface of things. Fitzgerald loathed the undemanding, the mindless, the merely charming, and he took me, almost literally, by the scruff of the neck and forced me to recognize the tragic nature of life. That summer at the MacDowell Colony he was collaborating with Dudley Fitts on a verse translation of the *Alcestis* of Euripides. In this play the heroine dies and is brought back to life through the intervention of Hercules. Without the help of Hercules I was trying to do much the same thing. Fitzgerald's room at the colony was directly above mine and I used to listen attentively to the sound of his footsteps climbing the outside stairway or pacing back and forth across the ceiling. His very presence was a help to me. I managed to break through, finally, into a kind of narrative that didn't deliquesce by the following morning.

On the first of September his stay expired and he left to spend a few weeks in the house of a relative in Annapolis. Mine, God knows why, had been extended to the end of the month. During that time I finished an eighth version of Part One, that I felt would stand, and began Part Two.

It had been agreed that on my way home to Illinois, at the beginning of October, I would stop off and see Fitzgerald in Annapolis, and that he would meet me in the train station in Baltimore, but when I stepped down from the train I didn't see him. It took me a minute or two to accept the fact that he wasn't anywhere, and I didn't have his telephone number. I waited around for an hour and then took the trolley to Annapolis. It was night by the time I got there. I gave a taxi driver the address, in Epping Forest, which I took to be a development but it turned out to be a real forest, full of cottages that were boarded up for the winter. We drove round and round in the dark peering at street signs and finally saw a house with a lighted window. While he waited with his motor running, I knocked on the door and a middle-aged woman opened it. "Oh, yes," she said. "I know where Miss Stuart's house is, and I could show it to you from where we are standing if it were daytime, but I don't think I can tell you how to get there. . . . Come in. . . . My niece has gone to the movies. When she gets home she'll take you there."

I paid the driver and sat down in a straight chair with my suitcase beside me. It had been a long day. I wondered if something had happened to Fitzgerald—like a car accident. I thought how trusting people were in the South. I glanced at my wristwatch. It was still early. The woman said, "I can see you are tired. Why don't you go to bed in my niece's room, and I'll wait up for her." So I did. And woke to bright sunlight, and dressed, and the woman, whose name I told myself I would remember all the days of my life but that I have nevertheless forgotten, gave me toast and coffee and pointed out the house, across a small ravine, where Fitzgerald would be staying.

He didn't appear to find it remarkable that I had managed to make my way to where he was.

"I meant to come and meet you," he said, holding the screen door open. We sat down at a table and I watched his face for signs of approval or disapproval as he read the chapter about Robert and his friends playing football.

I settled down in Urbana, Illinois, in the house of a retired banker, whose daughter, Garreta Busey, was a member of the English Department and also my friend. The arrangement we made was that in exchange for room and board and four dollars a month I would read her examination papers, which she said she could no longer bear the sight of. I suspect that she wanted to help me get on with my novel and chose this tactful way to go about it.

There was nearly always a student or two living in the house. In the past I had been one of them. It stood on half a block of ground and had the settled, softened look that old places tend to have. There was a violet bed by the front walk, and a cucumber tree had grown one very long limb protectively around the side porch. The downstairs woodwork was of cherry. The rooms were well lighted and of such generous proportions that it seemed a privilege to walk through them. I think it unlikely that anyone ever lived there who didn't appreciate its meditative stillness. Including the arsonist who, a dozen years ago, poured gasoline here and there and burned the place to the ground. I had a large bedroom and an adjoining room to write in, with only one window, which looked out on a section of tin roof so lacking in interest that after a brief glance I turned back to the typewriter. On a good day I managed to do a page that didn't end up in the wastebasket. Objects—Bunny's yellow agate, Robert's toy soldiers, the clocks that could not agree about what time it was—even though they didn't exist anymore were at my disposal. Turning an actual person into a character in a novel was more tricky. Facts alone did not supply them with the breath of life. I had to believe myself in their created existence.

I have dealt, in one partly autobiographical novel or another and in short stories, with the disaster that overtook our family in the year 1918. Because I was only ten at the time of my mother's death, there were things I didn't know or that were kept from me. I think that in the end I got all the circumstances right. But I am not sure that these later retellings are as affecting as the first one, where I made myself two years younger than I actually was, played ducks and drakes with chronology, gave one person's experience to another, introduced domestic habits from households I came to know later, and freely mixed fact with fiction. It may be simply that when I was writing *They Came Like Swallows* the heartbreaking actual events had not yet receded into the past.

It took all winter to finish Part Two. I wrote Part Three in ten days. Much of the time I walked the floor, framing sentences in my mind and then brushing the tears away with my hand so I could see the typewriter keys. I was weeping, I think, both for what happened—for I could not write about my mother's death without reliving it—and for events that took place only in my imagination. I don't suppose I was entirely sane.

1997

Preface to
"Time Will Darken It"

Time Will Darken It was begun in the summer of 1945, shortly after I was married, and I had had the feeling that, for someone as happy as I was, writing was not possible, but one day, habit reasserting itself, I sat down at the typewriter and began describing an evening party in the year 1912. It took place in the house I lived in as a child. I seemed to have no more choice about this than one has about the background of a dream. I also hadn't any idea about what was going to happen to the characters. The evening simply unfolded moment by moment until it was time for the guests to rise and say *Good-night . . . Good-night . . .*

The next day, when I returned to my typewriter, there they all were waiting for me. In a way that had never happened before and has never happened again, the story advanced by set conversations. A, who was late to work, had to stop and deal with the large wet tears of B, C tried unsuccessfully to reach out to D at the breakfast table, but E, who was older and wiser about people, managed to . . . as if I were writing a play. When I started a new chapter it was a matter of figuring out which of them hadn't talked to each other lately. When my judgment faltered—usually around lunchtime—I would take what I had written and read it to my wife, sitting outside on the grass.

Why the Mississippi relatives? They were simply *there*. I knew that the party was given for them when I sat down to write about it. When I was a little boy my mother and father had a visit of some duration from my Grandmother Maxwell's sister and her family, who came north from Greenville, Mississippi, to escape the heat. Their syntax, their soft Southern way of speaking, the intensely personal interest they brought to any social encounter made them seem very different from the Middle Westerners I was used to. They charmed everyone they came in contact with, but the resemblance of the Mississippi characters in the novel to my flesh-and-blood relatives went no farther than that. As a rule, unless real people have suffered a sea change and become creatures of the novelist's imagination, the breath of life is not in them.

Some novels don't require much in the way of a setting, if the interior or exterior dialogue is sufficiently compelling. This story, I felt, needed things for the eye to rest on. Houses all up and down a quiet street. Hitching posts. Elm trees arching over the brick pavement. Sounds, too: the ice cream wagon, the locust and the katydid. And smells from the kitchen or the pigpen. So I surrounded the characters with the summer and winter of a small town set in farmland so flat that, once you have left the outskirts behind you, you can see in every direction all the way to the horizon. Or, to put it differently, the book needed as much poetry as prose fiction can accommodate without becoming too fancy.

Though the characters were so talkative, there was one subject they were reticent about, and I had to decide for myself whether or not Austin King was unfaithful to his marriage vows. I tried it both ways, with the result that the novel went off simultaneously in two directions, and I followed each one for a considerable distance before I finally decided that he probably would not have allowed himself to sleep with his young cousin, much though he may have wanted to. He kept himself always on a very short rein.

Some readers have understood the last chapter to mean that the Kings' marriage was finished. This was not my intention. In the year 1912, in a town like Draperville, women did not leave their husbands except in fear for their life. Lying awake in the dark, Martha King threw the book at Austin in order to prepare herself to forgive him.

1992

CHRONOLOGY

NOTE ON THE TEXTS

NOTES

Chronology

1908 Born William Keepers Maxwell Jr., August 16, in Lincoln, Illinois, second child of William Keepers Maxwell (b. 1878) and (Eva) Blossom Blinn Maxwell (b. 1881). (Parents, both Lincoln natives, married June 2, 1903; first child, christened Edward but called "Hap" after funny papers' Happy Hooligan, born March 25, 1905.) Baby William ("Billie"), delivered at home, is fragile and sickly, weighing only 4½ pounds at birth, at six weeks even less: "Mother's milk did not agree with me, nor did anything else until the family doctor suggested goat's milk." Coaxed toward health by constant attentions of Blossom, whom he will remember as a stout, handsome, brown-eyed woman "acutely responsive to other people's happiness or distress." Father, chief Illinois agent for Hanover Fire Insurance Company, travels state every Tuesday through Friday for annual salary of $3,000. (Additional income will later come from renting out 360 acres of farmland east of town, purchased with small inheritance from his father, Robert Maxwell [1850–1904], a lawyer.) Brought up in the Christian Church, a fundamentalist American offshoot of Scottish Presbyterianism, William Sr. is thrifty, sober, practical, emotionally distant; Maxwell will remember him as a good father but a man of his period, who "felt responsibility for his children rather than pleasure in them." Family lives in small house at 455 Eighth Street; neighbors include many relatives, including boys' maternal grandparents (Edward Blinn, a judge of the court of claims, and Annette Youtsey ["Nettie"] Blinn), paternal grandmother (Margaret Turley Maxwell), four aunts and an uncle (Annette, Edith, and Ted Blinn; Maybel and Bertha Maxwell). In 1908 the town of Lincoln—seat of Logan County, 165 miles southwest of Chicago, at the very center of the state—has population of nearly 11,000. Neighborhood where Maxwell grows up is northwest of Lincoln's downtown but connected to it by electric streetcar line. Elms, silver maples, box elders, and cottonwood trees canopy brick and cobblestone streets, which in every direction trail off into dirt and gravel roads leading into cornfields. At age

50, Maxwell will recall hometown as being "small enough and sufficiently isolated for the people who lived there to have not only a marked individuality but also a stature that still seems to me larger than life-sized. They did not know how to be dull, and nothing that had ever happened was forgotten."

1909 In front of Eighth Street house, five-year-old Hap climbs onto wheel of Aunt Annette's buggy. When she, not seeing him, starts her horse, his leg becomes tangled in wheel and is later amputated above the knee. "By the time I was old enough to observe what was going on around me," Maxwell will write, "my brother had an artificial leg—of cork, I believe, painted an unconvincing pink." Despite his "affliction," Hap is an extroverted, irrepressible handful: throughout their shared boyhood, he plays with Billie "the way a cat plays with a chipmunk or a mole, hoping to produce signs of life," which usually come in the form of angry tears.

1910 Family moves into larger house at 184 Ninth Street, catercorner to Blinn residence. This comfortable late Victorian, with its 11-foot ceilings and, in winter, drafty windows, its cheerful white walls and woodwork, its many snug and semi-secret places to read, and its upstairs bedroom shared by the two brothers, will figure into much of Maxwell's fiction: it is, in his phrase, his imagination's home.

1911 In spring, parents build cottage on extreme outer edge of 120-acre Lincoln Chautauqua Grounds, two miles southwest of town. Family will spend this and many later summers here. During six-week Chautauqua season, from mid-July through August, they hear opera stars, jazz orchestras, and William Jennings Bryan, watch ballgames, swim in the Wading Pool, and make nightly visits to the ice-cream tent. Mainly they relax in the shade of the overarching oak trees.

1912–13 In July 1912, William Sr.'s Aunt Ina, wife of a plantation owner in Mississippi, visits Ninth Street with her large extended family. After their long, delightful visit, a series of misfortunes: Grandmother Nettie suffers massive stroke, Uncle Ted loses left arm in automobile accident, and Aunt Annette, impatient with kitchen fire that will not stay lit, pours kerosene on grate and severely burns her hands. In November 1912, Grandfather Blinn is bitten by a ferret and contracts blood poisoning; he dies in January 1913, at age 68. Nettie follows him almost one year later, at age 65.

1914 In fall, starts kindergarten at private preschool run by two progressive-minded middle-aged women in rooms above storefront near Lincoln's courthouse square. His daily escort to and from class is the pretty 25-year-old teachers' assistant, Grace McGrath. A parlor soprano with a taste for popular songs of the day, she will come to play a leading role in the Maxwells' musical evenings at home, hosted by William Sr., a talented pianist.

1915 One January afternoon, Blossom takes six-year-old Billie downtown to pick up a book that she loved as a child and has ordered for him. "When we got home," Maxwell will remember, "she sat down on the divan and I sat beside her and she began to read the book to me. It was *Toinette's Philip*, by Mrs. C. V. Jamison, a writer of children's books who was once well known. It was set in New Orleans, around the turn of the century, and it had an elaborate plot and fully developed characters. And it had scenes that moved me, just as they had my mother. How much influence this moment had on my future I cannot be sure, but I would think a great deal."

1916 Enters Lincoln Central School (grades 1–8) and from the start is avid but introverted pupil. Excels in art, and throughout school years is convinced he is meant to be a painter or a picture-book illustrator. Physically slight, gangly and uncoordinated, he is always last to be picked in playground games: "I was born to describe boys playing baseball, not to do it." He and Hap, with parents' blessing, attend not the Christian church but the less dogmatic Presbyterian Sunday school, where they dislike sermons but enjoy singing hymns and learning Bible stories.

1918 Beginning in late August, Spanish influenza sweeps North America, killing nearly 600,000 persons in U.S. by year's end. Pandemic reaches Lincoln in early October, infecting some 2,000 and killing nearly 100 in just three months. On December 24, William Sr. takes Blossom, pregnant with their third child, on 30-minute train ride to Bloomington, Illinois, to deliver in Brokaw Hospital. Boys are left in care of Aunt Maybel, who lives with her husband

and Grandmother Maxwell on Union Street, three blocks from Ninth Street house. On Christmas morning, boys suffer first symptoms of flu and are confined to separate bedrooms. In Bloomington, parents, too, come down with flu, and are hospitalized.

1919 On New Year's Day, Blossom gives birth to third son, (Robert) Blinn Maxwell; severely weakened by flu and labor, she dies of double pneumonia on morning of January 3, at age 37. Father phones Maybel, who tells the boys. ("My childhood came to an end at that moment," Maxwell will later say.) Next day, William Sr., still recovering from flu, returns to Lincoln with Blossom's remains: "His face had turned the color of ashes, and would stay that way a whole year." Funeral service performed at home, with the casket resting in the angles of the bay window of the front room. "The worst that could happen had happened," Maxwell will remember, "and the shine went out of everything. Disbelieving, we endured the wreath on the door, and the undertaker coming and going, the influx of food, the overpowering odor of white flowers, and all the rest of it, including the first of a series of housekeepers, who took care of the baby and sat in my mother's place at mealtime." In days, weeks, and months that followed, "my mother's sisters and my father's sisters and my grandmother all watched over us. If they hadn't, I don't know what would have become of us, in that sad house, where nothing ever changed, where life had come to a standstill."

1921 On October 5, not quite three years after Blossom's death, William Sr. marries Grace McGrath. Family begins new life together in place with no associations with the past: a rented, semi-furnished house on Eighth Street. William Sr. sells 184 Ninth Street and buys vacant lot on town's northern frontier; the two-story stucco house he builds there, 226 Park Place, will be ready for occupancy in spring 1922. Billie reads Waverley novels and popular works in Scottish history, delivers Lincoln *Evening Courier* on his blue and silver bicycle, and finds distraction from sorrow through working hard at school.

1922–23 In September 1922 begins freshman year at Lincoln Community High School, and following week is elected class president. When assigned *Treasure Island*, reads it five times before turning to something else: "I had read for pleasure all through my childhood, but this was my first encounter with literature." In spring 1923, first attempt at short fiction, the story of an aristocrat who hides inside a grandfather clock to survive the French Revolution, is published in school's annual literary magazine.

1923 Father accepts promotion to state office of insurance company; in spring he and Grace sell house and move to two-bedroom apartment in North Chicago neighborhood of Rogers Park. Billie and Hap remain in Lincoln, guests of Grace's mother, to complete school year; four-year-old Blinn is looked after by Aunt Maybel, her husband, and Grandmother Maxwell. In June older boys join father and stepmother in Chicago, but Blinn, at grandmother's desperate request, stays behind. In the end, William Sr. allows the Lincoln Maxwells to bring up Blinn, a decision he will always regret, as it results in a lifelong physical and emotional distance between him and Blinn, and decades of indifference between Blinn and Billie. (In contrast, Blinn and Hap will become close friends and, after World War II, share a successful legal practice in Oxnard, California.) In September, Hap leaves Chicago for Urbana and freshman year at University of Illinois, while Billie enrolls as sophomore at Nicholas Senn High School, one of Chicago's largest, with student body of 3,400, nearly six times that of Lincoln High. Billie soon becomes aware that he has "left a good enough school for a great one," remarkable for its dedicated teachers and strong *esprit de corps*. Draws and writes for school yearbook, whose sponsor, Miss Karssen, takes him to the Art Institute, the Chicago Symphony, and the theater (they see Mrs. Fiske in *The Rivals*). English instructor Miss Sedgewick directs his reading and chooses books for him from the Chicago Public Library: Shaw, Barrie, Galsworthy, H. G. Wells, Conrad. Meets Jack Scully, his class's top athlete, and Susan Deuel, the brightest girl in sophomore English, both of whom become close friends.

1924 Brings home from school library a copy of Mark Twain's *Mysterious Stranger* with intention of testing religious convictions: "They were not, it turned out, very strong." Calls himself an atheist, a label that, as years pass, will mellow into "unbeliever": "I would like to believe in God but not all that much, is, I sometimes think, the truth of the matter."

1925 In June accompanies Jack Scully to Portage, Wisconsin, where Jack has summer job as lifeguard on Mason Lake. When job Jack prearranged for him falls through, finds room and board in exchange for doing chores at Bonnie Oaks, a nearby farm and summer artists' colony. Maxwell sees that farm's owners, businessman Harrison Green and his charismatic, culture-loving wife, Mildred Ormsby Green, "were not ordinary people—that is, they were not farmers. Only when I came to read *The Cherry Orchard* years later did I find people who were anything like them." His first chore is to deliver a box of strawberries to the Greens' celebrated neighbor Zona Gale, a woman of letters whose *Miss Lulu Bett* had won the Pulitzer Prize for Drama in 1920. "She was wonderful to me," he will later write. "She talked about art, music, books, and the mystical aspects of daily existence. She also—and it is the one thing that always makes an adolescent's head swim—treated me as an intellectual equal." The visits to Zona Gale that summer are many, and by end of August she has appointed herself his mentor: "It was understood that I would make something of my life, but meanwhile it was life that she talked to me about. . . . I had been immeasurably enriched, in ways I didn't even try to understand."

1925–26 In senior year is associate art editor of high-school magazine, for which he writes series of essays on American paintings in the collection of the Art Institute of Chicago. Spends most Saturdays in galleries and museums, and decides that, after graduation, he will enter studio program at the school of the Art Institute. Friendship with Jack Scully deepens into passionate attachment.

1926–27 At end of summer, Jack returns from lifeguard job at Lake Geneva, Wisconsin, with acute pleurisy, almost too weak to enroll as planned at the University of Illinois. Maxwell accompanies him to Urbana to help him through orientation, and Hap arranges a few days' room and board in his fraternity house. Then, "what with one thing and another, including the full moon," both boys accept pledge pins from Hap's fraternity and Maxwell revises college plans: he will spend a year at the U. of I.

before going to art school. Takes several English classes, and is delighted that Susan Deuel is in most of them. Finds faculty friend in freshman composition instructor Paul Landis, who suggests courses and recommends him to fellow teachers. In spring, takes advanced course, English Romantic Poets, taught by Bruce Weirick, who requires students to write poetry—an ode, a ballad, a sonnet—"so that they might have a less distant feeling toward Coleridge and Wordsworth." In May, Weirick persuades Maxwell to abandon plans to transfer to Art Institute and instead continue at Urbana, develop as poet and scholar, and study to become professor of English.

1927–28 In sophomore year joins Illini Poetry Society, a dozen or so faculty and student poets who meet on Sunday evenings: "Every week, you had to read a poem you had just written, and mine betrayed a fondness for Elinor Wylie and Walter de la Mare." Other members include Landis, Weirick, and junior faculty member Garreta Busey, who for Maxwell represents "the outside world": she has lived in New York City, and until recently was on the staff of the *Herald Tribune*'s Sunday book review. Finds himself increasingly attracted to Margaret Guild, stepdaughter of English department chairman Jacob Zeitlin. After weeks of courting (mostly with opera records) introduces Margaret to Jack Scully. When she and Jack become lovers, Maxwell is devastated: "I thought I didn't want to live any more and cut my throat and wrists with a straight-edged razor." After release from hospital, wears heavy gray turtleneck sweater—"the only turtleneck sweater to be seen anywhere on campus"—to cover bandages. Receives note from Susan Deuel, inviting him to Kappa Alpha Theta spring dance; he goes, wearing turtleneck, and she and her sorority sisters see to it that he is never without a partner.

1928–30 Resumes friendship with Jack and Margaret, but in lower emotional key. (After graduation couple will marry, move to Wisconsin, and pay visits to Maxwell throughout their troubled marriage.) Continues studies in English, with minor in French. In May 1929, Poetry Society votes Maxwell's "Sleeping Beauty" their Prize Poem for 1929; publication in *Illini Poetry 1924–1929*, edited by Landis, marks his first book appearance. Writes two one-act comedies, one of which, "Polly Put the Kettle On: A

Mother Goose Phantasy," wins the English department's Play Prize for 1930. Graduates May 1930, with Highest Honors and as class salutatorian (second highest grade-point average among 1,200 students).

1930–31 At recommendation of Weirick, Harvard Club of Chicago grants Maxwell paid scholarship to Harvard Graduate School. In Cambridge makes friend of poet and translator Robert Fitzgerald, then only a sophomore but already being published in leading literary journals. Takes courses taught by critic Theodore Spencer and poet Robert Hillyer, and is visited by Zona Gale, who urges him to pursue his own work as well as his formal studies. Enjoys studying Old English epic and Old French romance, but encounters psychological block against learning required German: even most common words remain unrecognizable no matter how often he consults dictionary. Ends year with B in German, which disallows renewal of scholarship. Unable to afford tuition, leaves Harvard humbled but with master's degree.

1931–33 Returns to Urbana to teach freshman composition and take further graduate courses. Rooms at home of Garreta Busey, where he meets Charles Shattuck, a self-taught Shakespeare scholar who will become a lifelong friend. (Later Shattuck will marry Susan Deuel, and eventually will become professor of English at U. of I.) In February 1932, through arrangements made by Busey, begins reviewing popular novels for the New York *Herald Tribune*, which will publish some 20 items through October 1933. In May, Busey is approached by a friend, Yale historian Wallace Notestein, to do research for a collection of brief lives of English "characters"; she enlists aid of Maxwell, who reads two-volume biography of Thomas Coke of Holkham (1754–1842), an eccentric M.P. and agriculturalist, and rewrites book as 40-page essay. "Working with Garreta I discovered the pleasure of writing prose narrative," he will remember. "To keep the pleasure alive I began working on a long story, which I hoped would turn out to be a novel." On assignment for the *Herald Tribune*, reads *One More Spring*, by Robert Nathan, "a silly novel" about a group of dreamers who keep house in an abandoned tool shed in Central Park. "The gist of the book was that life is to be lived—and, well, it is, of course. Anyway, that book made me restless with my prospects. I saw myself being promoted from assistant to associate to full professor, and then to professor emeritus, and finally being carried out in a wooden box. This was 1933"—the height of the Depression—"and only an idiot would have thrown up a job at that point. But I did anyway."

1933 In early May, travels to New York with vain hope of securing job at the *Herald Tribune* book review. Returns to Bonnie Oaks at invitation of Mrs. Green, who provides free summer room and board and the leisure to undertake writing novel. Works and sleeps in a room on third floor of a frame building that was once the farm's water tower, leaving it only for meals with Mrs. Green and fellow guests. (Maxwell will later say that most characters in his first book "were largely, but not wholly, extensions of parts of myself; [others] were derived from people living on the farm at the time, so it was a handy place to be. I finished the book in four months, with the help of Virginia Woolf, W. B. Yeats, and Elinor Wylie . . .") In early September takes complete draft of novel to Zona Gale, who, despite reservations—she thinks it is missing a concluding chapter—offers warm congratulations and unsolicited letter of recommendation to prospective publishers: "It is modernity come of age, mellow, intelligent, casual, done with enormous delicacy." Returns to Urbana, where book is read by friends and faculty. In November Jacob Zeitlin, who has friends in New York publishing, sends copy to Eugene F. Saxton, editor-in-chief of Harper & Bros. Meanwhile, Maxwell, inspired by a travel book by Lafcadio Hearn, plans tour in the West Indies: "I was in search of the next thing to write about." In New York in mid-December, boards tramp steamer bound for Martinique: "I stayed in Fort-de-France. I spoke only rudimentary French and the natives spoke patois. I had nothing to do all day except wander around looking at what there was to see. That month seemed as long as a year. . . ."

1934 In late January, receives word that Saxton wants to publish novel, pending decision by his boss, Cass Canfield. Upon Maxwell's return to New York, Saxton offers fall publication and advance against royalties of $200, with which Maxwell finances 10-month stay in the city. Living at the Y.M.C.A. near Grand Central, quickly revises novel to meet April 15 delivery deadline. Proposes many titles—"Snakefeeders," "Thundercloud," "Today Is the Day"—before Canfield agrees to *Bright Center of Heaven*. First printing of one thousand copies, released in September, sells out quickly, but second thousand, printed in December, sells hardly at all. When money runs out, in mid-December, returns to Bonnie Oaks, where, through May 1935, he does small chores in exchange for room and board.

1935 In winter, finishes three short stories and hires New York agent to place them in magazines; V. S. Pritchett, a reader for the London quarterly *Life and Letters To-Day*, recommends one to the editor, who purchases it for issue of Winter 1936. Plans autobiographical novel about death of his mother; writes seven drafts of the opening section but is happy with none of them. At suggestion of Robert Fitzgerald, applies to MacDowell Colony, artists' retreat in Peterborough, New Hampshire, where Fitzgerald has summer residency; there, from early June through end of September, he completes successful draft of first third of book, using Fitzgerald as sounding board. ("In Fitzgerald's view, life was tragic," Maxwell will later recall. "Under his influence I gave up Galsworthy and Barrie and Wylie and accepted the idea that literature was serious business.") In October, returns to Urbana, where Garreta Busey strikes a deal: in exchange for grading her students' papers, she will give Maxwell $4 a month, room and board, and the privacy necessary to continue his work. "Without this arrangement," he will later say, "I doubt very much that the book would ever have been finished or that I would have continued to be a writer."

1936 In February, completes novel, *They Came Like Swallows*, which Saxton acquires for Harper's in early summer. Story "Remembrance of Martinique" appears in *Life and Letters To-Day* and is reprinted in July issue of *The Atlantic Monthly*. Through Saxton's influence, Katharine S. White, fiction editor of *The New Yorker*, purchases Maxwell's other completed stories, "Mrs. Farnham Puts Her Foot Down" and "A Christmas Story," both of which she schedules for December publication. In late August, Maxwell moves to New York and finds inexpensive lodging in rooming house on lower Lexington Avenue. Writes synopses of bestsellers for Paramount Pictures, and interviews for entry-level editorial jobs with Malcolm Cowley at *The New Republic*, Christopher Morley at *The Saturday Review of Literature*, and, in late October, Katharine White. During their meeting, Mrs. White asks what he is looking for in way of salary: "Some knowledgeable acquaintance had told me I must ask for $35 a week or I wouldn't be respected, so I swallowed hard and said, 'Thirty-five dollars.' Mrs. White smiled and said, 'I expect you could live on less.' I could have lived nicely on fifteen. A few days later I got a telegram from her asking me to report to work the following Tuesday"—November 3 —"at the salary agreed on: $35 a week."

1936–37 Initial duties at *The New Yorker* include informing cartoonists of acceptances and rejections; he especially enjoys conversations with cover artist Ilonka Karasz, a Hungarian-born designer and painter. By Christmas, Mrs. White and senior editor Wolcott Gibbs begin training Maxwell as editor of fiction, memoir, and humor. In January 1937, becomes occasional book critic for the *Saturday Review*, which will publish 17 items through February 1940. *They Came Like Swallows* published in March to positive reviews. Christopher Morley, member of selection committee of Book-of-the-Month Club, chooses novel as club's dual main selection for April; Maxwell's initial payment is the "overwhelming sum" of $8,000. Finds room-and-a-half on Patchin Place, in the West Village; at request of Mrs. White, installs a phone, which, when it rings, he refuses to answer. By year's end has published three more stories in *The New Yorker*, the last of which, "Never to Hear Silence," prompts admiring letter from a regular contributor, poet Louise Bogan.

1938 Stories "Homecoming" (January 1) and "The Actual Thing" (September 3) published in *The New Yorker*; edits work by Daniel Fuchs, Oliver La Farge, John O'Hara, Sylvia Townsend Warner, Joseph Wechsberg, and others. In spring, receives award of $1,000 from Friends of American Writers, a Chicago women's club, for *They Came Like Swallows*. In December, Mrs. White announces that she and her husband, staff writer E. B. White, are moving to a farm in mid-coastal Maine from where she will continue her editorial duties; she appoints Maxwell her office liaison. When Zona Gale dies suddenly on December 27, at age 64, Maxwell is bereft: "I am only beginning to understand how much, in the way of literary taste and craftsmanship, I received from her."

1939 Wolcott Gibbs appointed *New Yorker* theater critic, and Maxwell assumes most of his editorial duties; job becomes so burdensome that he writes almost nothing. Suffers insomnia and takes to walking city late at night; is happy only at country home of Ilonka Karasz or in company of new friend Louise Bogan. In July, meets Sylvia Townsend Warner during one of the English writer's rare visits to America: "Her conversation was so enchanting it made my head swim. I did not want to let her out of my sight. Ever." Trains Gus Lobrano, a friend of E. B. White, as assistant editor, and is deeply hurt when Mrs. White quickly promotes him to Maxwell's salary level. Hurt lingers, even after Mrs. White chooses "Homecoming" for inclusion in *Short Stories from The New Yorker* (1940), her selection of best fiction from magazine's first 15 years. On April 8 *The New Yorker* publishes "Good Friday" (later collected as "Young Francis Whitehead") and on December 18 the first of eight "lighter" stories—formula fiction written mainly for Christmas and other occasions—that will appear, under pseudonym "Jonathan Harrington," through August 1942. When, in November, Lobrano is given Mrs. White's old office, Maxwell is indignant: "I thought, If this is the way things are, I will leave and become a writer." Resignation accepted, with sadness and concern, by editor Harold Ross; Maxwell will quit office on March 15, 1940.

1940 On March 1, leaves city for rented saltbox in Yorktown Heights, New York, an hour from Grand Central and 15 minutes from country home of Ilonka Karasz. Writes short stories, not all of which are purchased by Mrs. White. In June, drives to Santa Fe with friend Moris Burge, an official with American Association on Indian Affairs, and works for five weeks in home of Burge's fiancée. Enjoys extended visit with *New Yorker* writer Oliver La Farge, who lives among the Navajo, and in mid-July returns to Yorktown Heights "with the whole state of New Mexico up my sleeve." Begins what he hopes will be third novel, a short book based on impressions of Desert Southwest. Plants rosebushes, paints shutters, and enjoys keeping house in rural Westchester County; reads widely, especially in Russian fiction: Chekhov, Tolstoy, Turgenev.

Lobrano phones to ask if he would do some freelance editing, and by October Maxwell, won over by Lobrano's sincerity, returns to fiction department three days a week. In fall, spends two months in Bermuda, which becomes subject of his only Reporter at Large piece (January 4, 1941). In December, Saxton attends party in honor of new fiction editor of *Harper's Bazaar*, Mary Louise Aswell, who knows Maxwell's work and asks to see his stories.

1941 In February, *Harper's Bazaar* purchases "Abbie's Birthday" (later collected as "Haller's Second Home"); will publish in August issue. In May, at party hosted by Mrs. Aswell, Maxwell meets Eudora Welty, a young writer visiting New York from Jackson, Mississippi; they become instant friends and lifelong correspondents. Shows Louise Bogan work-in-progress, an autobiographical story about two contrasting but complementary teenaged outsiders, frail, bookish Lymie Peters and athletic, inarticulate Spud Latham; she tells him it is not a story but the first chapter of his next novel. Maxwell immediately sees book in situation, but not how to dramatize painful, personal material. Over next four years, he will send Bogan everything he writes about Lymie and Spud; she in turn will read it with critical attention, providing the audience and encouragement he needs to sustain him in his work.

1942 Ilonka Karasz proposes collaboration: Maxwell will write a novella based on his experiences in Martinique, she will illustrate it with egg-tempera paintings. After 10,000 words and a few full-color studies, project is abandoned as too expensive to print in wartime economy. They try again with picture book for children, a tale in which the figures of the zodiac come down from the heavens and take up residence on a Wisconsin farm. Harper's agrees to do book only if art is designed to print in one color: Karasz chooses deep blue of nighttime sky and makes experiments on scratchboard. Meanwhile, Maxwell pushes on toward middle of novel, tentatively titled "No Word for Anybody."

1943 In winter called for military service, and obtains deferment due to "anxiety neurosis." In spring, uses savings to buy small, sturdy house—an early prefab, built in late 1930s—on Baptist Church Road, in Yorktown Heights: it will be his country place for the rest of his life. Eugene Saxton nominates Maxwell for membership in the Century, an exclusive social club for writers and artists whose clubhouse is a block away from the *New Yorker* offices. In June, Saxton dies of heart attack; his successor at Harper's is Edward C. Aswell, Mary Louise's husband. Mrs. White returns to the *New Yorker* office and Maxwell's daily workload lightens. By July, has been at work on novel for three years and is still struggling with material. Lobrano, seeing that Maxwell cannot complete first draft without a sabbatical, speaks to Harold Ross, who hands Maxwell an unsolicited five months' leave at full salary, beginning August 1. Works without interruption in Yorktown Heights, and completes second draft by New Year's Eve.

1944 Returns to magazine in January, again on part-time basis, and works on third draft of novel. Doubting quality of work and convinced that, "like a tree whose central stem had been cut," he is no longer maturing, begins analysis with Theodor Reik, a protégé of Sigmund Freud whose private practice includes many artists and writers. Reik reads all of Maxwell's work, including novel-in-progress, and by March is meeting with him an hour a day, five days a week. Completes third draft of novel and submits it to Edward Aswell, who acquires book for Harper's and sets delivery date of November 15. Maxwell rewrites and revises until day of deadline, incorporating many suggestions made by Aswell, Reik, and Louise Bogan. While novel is in production, Bogan finds better title—*The Folded Leaf*—and in gratitude for all she has done for him, Maxwell dedicates book to her.

1944–45 In October 1944, phones Emily Gilman Noyes, a young woman he had met earlier that year, when, just graduated from Smith College, she interviewed for job at *The New Yorker*: "She wore her hair piled on top of her head, and she had a hat trimmed in fur, and I thought I had never seen anyone so beautiful. . . . I couldn't get her out of my mind." He invites her to join him for a drink at the Algonquin Hotel, where they talk about poetry and painting, her childhood visit to France, and her current work with children at an Upper East Side nursery school. In November, he takes her to a friend's party, after which he surprises both her and himself by asking her to marry him. She says no, but invites him to call on her again after New Year's. In December, Maxwell sublets apartment at Park Avenue and 92nd Street, mainly to be near her. Throughout January he sees her almost every evening, and in February her parents fly to New York from Portland, Oregon, to meet him. On March 20, he again proposes, and this time is accepted. He and Emily marry, in private ceremony, in chapel of First Presbyterian Church, New York City, on evening of May 17. The bride is 23, the groom, 36; Gus Lobrano and Emily's mother are witnesses.

1945 In June, Maxwell ends therapy with Reik, upon whose couch, he says, "the whole first part of my life fell away, and I had a feeling of starting again." *The New Yorker* publishes story "The Patterns of Love" (July 7) and a signed book review—Maxwell's first for the magazine—of Reik's *Psychology of Sexual Relations* (September 15). In April, Harper's publishes *The Folded Leaf*, with jacket design by Ilonka Karasz, one of several she will do for him over the next 25 years. Reviews are many and enthusiastic: Edmund Wilson, in *The New Yorker*, calls it "a quite unconventional study of adolescent relationships—between two boys, with a girl in the offing—very much lived and very much seen. This drama of the immature . . . is both more moving and more absorbing than any of the romantic melodramas which have been stimulated by the war." By year's end 200,000 copies are in print, including Book Find Club edition and digest-sized paperback distributed to armed forces.

1946 The Maxwells keep house in Yorktown Heights, and, in Emily's words, lead "a Wordsworthian life: long walks, reading aloud, organic gardening." She paints, writes poetry, and quickly proves to be Maxwell's most trusted reader: he calls her "the critic on the hearth." Maxwell edits stories by Nancy Hale, Mary McCarthy, and J. D. Salinger. Revises proof of collaboration with Karasz, *The Heavenly Tenants*, published by Harper's in September, and writes long short story, "An Evening Party," set in 1912 in "Draperville," a semi-fictionalized Lincoln, Illinois. Because of provincial setting, story cannot be published in *The New Yorker*: "Harold Ross edited a cosmopolitan magazine," Maxwell once explained, "and had a map of acceptable settings for fiction" that included the East

Coast, Hollywood, Florida, Paris, "but not the Middle West, which rather tied my hands." Sends story to Cyril Connolly, editor of London literary monthly *Horizon*, who writes: "It is really the very exciting beginning to a novel . . . One wants another 30 chapters, and I hope you will do it that way." At Christmas writes fairy tale, "The Woodcutter," as gift for Emily; it is the beginning of a tradition he will observe for many Christmases, birthdays, and anniversaries to come.

1947 Continues work on Draperville novel, writing quickly but somewhat distractedly. Deciding that "the burden of living a double life, of working at a somewhat demanding job and trying to write a book, is difficult to sustain," again quits *The New Yorker*, effective May 1. Completes final draft of novel by Thanksgiving; Emily discovers title, *Time Will Darken It*, in pages of recently published anthology *Artists on Art*. Edward Aswell acquires novel and sets publication date of September 1, 1948.

1948 In January, Aswell resigns from Harper's, leaving Maxwell without a sponsor there. Revises *Time Will Darken It* in proof and approves final galleys by end of May. He and Emily plan long-deferred honeymoon in Europe, mainly in Emily's beloved France. On July 1 they depart New York aboard the *Queen Elizabeth*, burdened with typewriter, too many over-packed suitcases, and four months' supply of goods then unobtainable in France—cigarettes, coffee, nylons, writing paper. Land in Cherbourg, visit Mont-Saint-Michel, and sunbathe on the coast of Brittany; lodge for six weeks with family in Blois and explore the châteaux country; attend the Salzburg Music Festival, make tour of Northern Italy, and linger a week in Rome; sublet apartment in Paris and make side trips to Nice, Cannes, Chartres, and Versailles. On October 19 they board the *Mauritania* for voyage home. For Maxwell Europe, and especially France, is a revelation: "I remembered every town we passed through, every street we were ever on, everything that ever happened, including the weather." Upon returning to Yorktown Heights—"with my hat still on my head and our suitcases on the front porch"—types two-page outline for book about newlywed Americans' encounter with postwar Europe. Writing this book will be his chief literary project throughout the 1950s.

1948–49 In fall 1948, Maxwell, dismayed by poor sales of new novel and by lack of enthusiasm at Harper's, returns to *The New Yorker* on part-time basis. Is admitted to the Century; he will be a lifelong member of the club, having lunch there almost daily for the next three decades, attending events and sitting on committees for even longer. After Maxwell sends her a copy of *Time Will Darken It*, Sylvia Townsend Warner becomes constant correspondent: during her remaining three decades they will exchange more than 1300 increasingly affectionate personal letters. To ease commute from Westchester, rents floor-through walkup in building where Ilonka Karasz now lives, a three-story brownstone on East 36th Street at Lexington Avenue; the Maxwells will spend weekdays there, returning to country on weekends and during summer. Plans sequel to *Time Will Darken It*, which he intends to publish as a series of short stories and later rework into novel; is discouraged when *Harper's* and *The Atlantic* reject first installment, "The Trojan Women."

1950 Struggles to imagine opening scene of book about France, but is undecided whether material would be better treated in first or third person, as fiction or as straightforward travel memoir. In fall he and Emily, after five years' trying to conceive a child, attempt to adopt, but Maxwell's age, 42, presents bureaucratic difficulties.

1951 *Perspectives U.S.A.*, a new quarterly financed by the Ford Foundation and edited by Jacques Barzun, Lionel Trilling, and others, purchases two Draperville stories, "The Trojan Women" (published Fall 1952) and "What Every Boy Should Know" (Spring 1954). In summer Harold Ross, diagnosed with lung cancer, begins long hospitalization; dies after surgery on December 6. His handpicked successor, former managing editor William Shawn, immediately widens magazine's editorial compass and encourages Maxwell to solicit, acquire, and edit fiction outside Ross's definition of "a *New Yorker* story." Among Maxwell's earliest purchases for Shawn are "The Bride of the Innisfallen" by Eudora Welty, her first story in the magazine, and "Madeline's Birthday" by Mavis Gallant and "The State of Grace" by Harold Brodkey, their first stories anywhere.

1952 Maxwell's satisfaction with editorial work deepens as he helps shape fiction department's new direction. At office, friendships with colleagues grow stronger, especially with staff writers and local contributors including Brendan Gill, Philip Hamburger, Joseph Mitchell, Francis Steegmuller, Natacha Stewart Ullman, and the Irish-born short-story writer Maeve Brennan. Continues work on French novel, with limited success.

1953 In January, Eudora Welty visits the Maxwells in New York apartment and gives private reading of short novel *The Ponder Heart*; Maxwell will edit it for *The New Yorker*, and, when published as a book, Welty will dedicate it to him, Emily, and Mrs. Aswell. In April, the Maxwells visit England and Sylvia Townsend Warner. Story "The Pilgrimage," based on experiences in France, published in *The New Yorker* (August 22), while manuscript of French novel grows chaotically, its many and various drafts filling a large grocery carton in Maxwell's study.

1954 When Jack Huber, a psychologist and close friend of the Maxwells, learns that the couple is desperate to adopt, he pulls strings at a Chicago agency where friends are on the board. After much paperwork, the Maxwells interview at agency, fly home, and wait. Then, having shown "that we are longing for a child so deeply that we are willing to bring up somebody else's child—anybody's child whatever—[the gods decide] we may as well be allowed to have our own." Daughter, Katharine Farrington ("Kate") Maxwell, born December 19.

1955 When rent for brownstone becomes unaffordable under new owner, the Maxwells return to living year-round in Yorktown Heights. Maxwell—upset by loss of apartment and worried about financial future, his books out of print and his current novel stalled—decides to give up writing and become a full-time editor. Accepts invitation to speak at Smith College symposium "The American Novel at Mid-Century" but dreads writing speech, whose assigned topic is "the novelist's creative process." Does not begin draft until he boards train to Northampton, but then his words flow so freely, and he believes in them so passionately, that he knows he cannot give up writing fiction. On evening of March 4 delivers speech, "The Writer as Illusionist," to receptive audience including fellow-speakers

Saul Bellow, Brendan Gill, and Alfred Kazin. In fall, John Cheever and short-story writer Jean Stafford invite Maxwell and Daniel Fuchs to appear with them, not in an anthology, but in the literary equivalent of a group exhibition of recent work. The resulting volume, called *Stories*, will include three items by Maxwell: "The Trojan Women," "What Every Boy Should Know," and a new story, "The French Scarecrow."

1956 Gus Lobrano dies, March 1, at age 53, and Maxwell inherits several of his authors, including Cheever, V. S. Pritchett, and long-time acquaintance Frank O'Connor. Hires assistant, Elizabeth Cullinan, an aspiring writer whose stories of Irish-American life Maxwell will edit for the magazine from 1960 through 1975. "The French Scarecrow" published in *The New Yorker* (October 6). Second daughter, Emily Brooke ("Brookie") Maxwell, born October 15. *Stories* published in December by Farrar, Straus & Cudahy.

1957 In September, poet Robert Lax prints Maxwell's fairy tale "The Anxious Man" (later collected as "The Old Man Who Was Afraid of Falling") as a limited-edition broadside. Encouraged by friends' response, Maxwell revises nine other fairy tales for publication in *The New Yorker*; they will appear throughout 1958, in four installments of two or three tales each, under the heading "Old Tales about Men and Women."

1958 In March receives letter from publisher Alfred A. Knopf: "Brendan Gill tells me that all may not be well between you and Harper & Brothers. . . ." In June signs contract with Knopf for French novel, with delivery date of January 1, 1960; he also signs contract for reprints of three of his previous novels, to be published in paperback under Knopf's new Vintage Books imprint. (Declines Knopf's offer also to reprint *Bright Center of Heaven*: upon reading it for first time in 20 years, finds it "hopelessly imitative" and "stuck fast in its period.") In May is surprised and encouraged by $1500 grant in literature from the American Academy of Arts and Letters. In August is visited by Frank O'Connor, to whom he confesses that, although he has promised to deliver his French novel in 18 months, he has reached an artistic impasse. When O'Connor asks to read manuscript Maxwell is "appalled" but allows his friend to drive away with grocery carton full of typescript. Within weeks O'Connor writes that Maxwell seems to have written two novels—one about the American couple, the other about the French family they lodge with—and suggests they be combined and told from the Americans' limited point of view. "My relief was immense," Maxwell later recalls, "because it is a lot easier to make two novels into one than it is to make one out of nothing whatever. So I went ahead and finished the book." Meanwhile, learning that Vintage editions of early novels will be newly typeset, Maxwell takes opportunity to revise them, beginning with *The Folded Leaf.* "When I was writing [that novel]," Maxwell later tells *The Paris Review*, "I was in analysis with Theodor Reik, who thought the book should have a more positive ending. And Edward Aswell at Harper's thought the book would be strengthened if I combined two of the minor characters [Hope and Mrs. Lieberman]. I was so tired and so unconfident about the book that I took their word for it. Later I was sorry. And when the book came out in the Vintage edition . . . I put everything back pretty much the way it was in the first place."

1958–59 In September 1958, when Kate starts kindergarten at the Brearley School, family moves from Yorktown Heights to convenient address of One Gracie Square, a 15-story apartment building near 84th Street and the East River. Father dies, January 15, 1959, while Maxwell is revising *They Came Like Swallows*; rewrites certain passages mainly to soften portrait of stern and disapproving father character. Works himself to near exhaustion to finish his French book, provisionally titled "Leo and Virgo." Knopf extends delivery date to June 1960. Vintage edition of *The Folded Leaf* published in September.

1960 "Leo and Virgo" is read by biographer, translator, and friend Francis Steegmuller, whose many queries prompt Maxwell to write epilogue, "Some Explanations." When Maxwell delivers book to Knopf, editor-in-chief Harold Strauss proves so unenthusiastic—he dislikes epilogue, and urges Maxwell to cut it—that Mr. Knopf assigns novel to Judith Jones, who will edit this and all of Maxwell's later books for the firm. Vintage edition of *They Came Like Swallows* appears in April.

1961 In March, *The Château* published to mixed reviews but strong sales: in May and June it spends three weeks on the *New York Times* bestseller list, and by October more than 17,000 copies are in print. Despite strong interest from foreign publishers, Maxwell forbids U.K. and Continental editions in effort to protect privacy of originals of certain European characters. Katharine White retires from *The New Yorker* and Maxwell becomes senior editor in fiction department; inherits several of Mrs. White's authors including Vladimir Nabokov and John Updike. Mentors young writers Larry Woiwode, the gifted protégé of Charles Shattuck at Urbana, and Shirley Hazzard, whose first short story he discovers in the "slush pile." Begins light but thorough revision of *Time Will Darken It*.

1962 *The Château* short-listed for 1962 National Book Award in Fiction (won by Walker Percy's novel *The Moviegoer*). Vintage edition of *Time Will Darken It* published in September. Signs contract for collection of fairy tales, to be delivered to Knopf in 1965. Writes "A Final Report," first story set in historical Lincoln, not fictional Draperville, and narrated in his own voice: "I found I could use the first person without being long-winded or boring, and at the same time deal with experiences that were not improved by invention of any kind."

1963 "A Final Report" published in *The New Yorker* (March 9); Maxwell dismayed by interference from magazine's legal department, which demands substitution of fictional names for those of real-life persons and places. On May 22, inducted as member of the National Institute of Arts and Letters; citation reads, in part: "His grace and wit delight his readers, while his wisdom enlarges their understanding of the human heart."

1964 *The New Yorker* publishes "The Value of Money" (June 6), Maxwell's fictional tribute to his father. At request of widow of Oliver La Farge (1901–1963), edits and writes foreword to *The Door in the Wall* (1965), a collection of 12 La Farge short stories.

1965 On May 1, family moves to 544 East 86th Street, their final New York City address. Completes his book of tales, 16 of which are serialized in *The New Yorker*, in five installments of two to four tales each, under heading "Further Tales About Men and Women." *The New Yorker* publishes "A Game of Chess" (June 12), story dramatizing Maxwell's troubled adult relationship with brother Hap; to spare Hap's feelings, uses byline "Gifford Brown."

1966 In February *The Old Man at the Railroad Crossing*, collection of 29 tales, published by Knopf, with dedication to Emily. Frank O'Connor dies on March 10, at age 62. In summer, Maxwell takes family on car tour of Wales, England, and France and revisits many persons and places of 1948 trip. When Elizabeth Cullinan leaves the magazine, hires new assistant, Frances Kiernan; in 1972 will train her as an editor in fiction department.

1967 After reading family genealogy compiled by late first cousin William Maxwell Fuller, begins planning nonfiction work that is part personal memoir, part family history, part imaginative re-creation of folkways, religious life, and biographical particulars of four generations of Blinn and Maxwell ancestors. To collect facts and anecdotes, begins extensive correspondence with distant family members and with archivists and local historians in Ohio, Kentucky, and Illinois. To find narrative voice, rereads E. B. White and further refines first-person persona previously explored in "A Final Report."

1969 "The Gardens of Mont-Saint-Michel" published in *The New Yorker* (August 9). In May, Maxwell elected president of the American Academy of Arts and Letters; will serve through May 1972. During his term, secretary of Academy is poet William Meredith, who becomes a dear friend.

1970 Louise Bogan dies, February 4, at age 73; Maxwell writes obituary for *The New Yorker*. Finishes manuscript of *Ancestors*, his nonfiction narrative.

1971 *Ancestors* published in June by Knopf, to mixed reviews. In writing book, Maxwell will later say, "I came to feel that life is the most extraordinary storyteller of all, and the fewer changes you make [in facts and details] the better, provided you get to the heart of the matter."

1972 Stepmother Grace McGrath dies, October 15, at age 83; returns home for funeral and discovers friend in step-cousin Tom Perry, executor of Grace's estate and manager of Maxwell family farm. In Lincoln is reminded of schoolmate whose father, in winter 1920–21, killed his wife's lover and then himself. Upon return to New York attempts short story based on this tragedy; in need of concrete details, asks Tom Perry to research files of the Lincoln *Evening Courier* for contemporary accounts.

1973 Charles Shattuck nominates Maxwell for honorary degree of Doctor of Letters from the University of Illinois. Upon accepting diploma at commencement exercises on June 9, Maxwell says: "Though I have lived in New York City for nearly 40 years, when I sit down at the typewriter and begin to write, it is nearly always of Illinois. I have no choice, really. Other places do not have the same hold on my imagination. I am very moved by the high honor the university has bestowed on me—how could I not be, when what it amounts to, in the logic of emotions, is that the place where I belong has laid formal claim to me."

1974 "Over by the River," a long story ten years in the writing, published in *The New Yorker* (June 26).

1975 Company policy obliges Maxwell, 66, to retire from magazine on December 31; before doing so, hires and trains fiction editors Charles McGrath and Daniel Menaker.

1976 "I slid into retirement and hardly noticed the jar. . . . It is wonderful not having to break off writing after four days and pick it up again three days later. Also, I rejoice in the thought that I shall never again write a letter beginning 'I am very sorry, but your story isn't right for . . .' etc. The solitude is pleasant, but it is solitude, and I had got into the frame of mind of defining myself in terms of my relations with other people. . . . Shawn very kindly offered me an office to write in, but I like to go the typewriter in my bathrobe and slippers, straight from the breakfast table, and anyway I feel it somehow not right, and perhaps not dignified, to hang around after you are gone." At home begins, but soon abandons, novel drawing on memories of Bermuda in 1941. Prepares collection of 12 short stories published over previous 38 years, revising most from their magazine versions and arranging them, not chronologically but thematically, in the following order: "Over by the River," "The Trojan Women," "The Pilgrimage," "The Patterns of Love," "What Every Boy Should Know," "The French Scarecrow," "Young

Francis Whitehead," "A Final Report," "Haller's Second Home," "The Gardens of Mont-Saint-Michel," "The Value of Money," and a new story, "The Thistles in Sweden," published in *The New Yorker* for June 21. Dedicates book to Sylvia Townsend Warner, and commissions jacket illustration from daughter Brookie.

1977 Mentors Alec Wilkinson, 25-year-old son of a Yorktown Heights neighbor, coaching him through every draft of an account of his year with the Wellfleet (Massachusetts) Police Department, later published in *The New Yorker* and as the book *Midnights* (1982). Using research material compiled by Tom Perry, returns to subject of Lincoln murder-suicide but now treats material in first person, crafting a work part memoir, part fiction, part historical reconstruction of a "true crime." In September, *Over by the River and Other Stories* published by Knopf, to very good reviews.

1978 Aged and ailing, Sylvia Townsend Warner asks Maxwell to act as co-executor of her literary estate. She suggests that certain friends and readers "might like a volume of letters," and asks that he collect and edit them. In late April, flies to England for a leavetaking but is too late; she dies on May 1, at age 84. Maxwell feels poorly, and is diagnosed with lymphoma; responds dramatically to chemotherapy. Lincoln novel develops quickly; he plans to call it "The Palace at 4 A.M.," after sculpture by Giacometti in the Museum of Modern Art, but *New Yorker* poetry editor Howard Moss objects: he once wrote a play with that title.

1979 New novel, now called *So Long, See You Tomorrow*, published in two installments in *The New Yorker* (October 1 and 8). In fall, over lunch at the Century, an admirer, art critic Hilton Kramer, urges David R. Godine, a Boston-based publisher starting a paperback list, to reissue Maxwell's major works, beginning with *The Folded Leaf*. Between 1981 and 1989, Godine will reprint eight books, seven with new covers designed by Brookie.

1980 Dedicates *So Long, See You Tomorrow* to Robert Fitzgerald; book published by Knopf in April to uniformly positive reviews. On May 21, Eudora Welty presents Maxwell with the William Dean Howells Medal of the American Academy of Arts and Letters; the prize, for *So Long, See*

You Tomorrow, is awarded once every five years in recognition of the most distinguished work of American fiction published during that period.

1981 *So Long, See You Tomorrow* named finalist for Pulitzer Prize in Fiction (won by John Kennedy Toole's *A Confederacy of Dunces*). On May 26, Ilonka Karasz dies, at age 85, after a long illness.

1982 In spring, makes final visit to France: five weeks in Paris, with Emily and Brookie. Interviewed for *The Paris Review*'s "Art of Fiction" series (Fall 1982); is so pleased by results of painstaking collaboration with editors that he adopts practice of giving only written responses to questions from print interviewers and insisting on right to correct proofs.

1983 In January, *Sylvia Townsend Warner: Letters*, edited and with an introduction by Maxwell, published by Viking. *The New Yorker* publishes "Love" (November 14), inaugurating a decade-long series of first-person stories about figures from Maxwell's Lincoln boyhood.

1984 *The New Yorker* publishes "My Father's Friends" (January 30) and "The Man in the Moon" (November 12). To honor Eudora Welty on her 75th birthday (April 13), writes story "With Reference to an Incident at a Bridge" for tribute volume privately printed by friends. On April 26, in ceremony at the Guggenheim Museum, receives the Brandeis University Creative Arts Medal for Fiction; among the jury for this lifetime achievement award are John Updike and Irving Howe.

1985 Robert Fitzgerald dies, January 16, at age 74; Maxwell delivers tributes at the spring meeting of the National Institute of Arts and Letters, April 2, and again at a memorial reading at the Guggenheim Museum, November 5. Brother Hap dies, August 23, at age 80; as a memorial, writes story "The Holy Terror," published in *The New Yorker* (March 17, 1986).

1986 "The Lily-White Boys," a story of New York, published in special 100th issue of *The Paris Review* (Summer/Fall 1986).

1987 Writes memoir of Zona Gale for *The Yale Review* (Winter 1987), expanding on a private tribute delivered at the American Academy of Arts and Letters in 1972.

1988 *Five Tales*, a small book of previously uncollected fairy tales written for his family, is edited by Emily and privately printed as surprise gift to Maxwell and his admirers on his 80th birthday.

1989 In April, Knopf publishes *The Outermost Dream*, 19 essays on literary subjects, most of them revised or entirely rewritten versions of book reviews that first appeared in *The New Yorker* between 1956 and 1987. None of the essays considers fiction; instead they appreciate the diaries, letters, autobiographies, and lives of favorite writers (Virginia Woolf, E. M. Forster, Isak Dinesen, Samuel Butler, Byron, Colette) and friends (Louise Bogan, Frank O'Connor, V. S. Pritchett, Sylvia Townsend Warner, Eudora Welty, E. B. and Katharine White). Story "Billie Dyer" published in *The New Yorker* (May 15).

1990 Edits, with Charles McGrath, *A Final Antidote* (1991), 56-page selection from the journals of Louise Bogan, privately printed in edition of 220 copies.

1991 Writes "The Front and the Back Parts of the House," published in *The New Yorker* (September 23); submits it and six other recent Lincoln stories to Knopf under the title *Billie Dyer and Other Stories*. Barbara Burkhardt, a Ph.D. candidate at the University of Illinois writing her dissertation on Maxwell's work, helps plan "special Maxwell issue" of *Tamaqua* (Fall 1992), the literary biannual of Parkland College, Champaign, Illinois. Maxwell writes "What He Was Like" expressly for *Tamaqua* but story is published by *The New Yorker* (December 7, 1992), which enjoys right of first refusal. Instead he prepares a long excerpt from abandoned Martinique novella of 1942 ("At the Pension Gaullard"), writes a new tale ("The Old House"), and, from October 1991 through July 1992, fashions a long interview, mainly through the mail, with Burkhardt.

1992 In February, *Billie Dyer* published by Knopf. When asked by interviewer whether the book is memoir or fiction, Maxwell replies: "For me 'fiction' lies not in whether a thing, the thing I am writing about, actually happened, but in the form of the writing. The important distinction is between reminiscence, which is a formless accumulation of facts, and a story, which has a shape, a controlled effect, a satisfying conclusion—something that is, or attempts to be, a work of art. . . . I admire writers who don't have to depend on personal experience for their material and storytelling"—Tolstoy, for example—"but I am not one of them." Writes prefaces for Quality Paperback Book Club omnibus of *Time Will Darken It*, *The Château*, and *So Long, See You Tomorrow*. Asks Barbara Burkhardt to help him catalog papers for eventual donation to University of Illinois Library.

1993 Maeve Brennan dies, November 1, at age 76; Maxwell writes obituary for *The New Yorker*. Enjoys visits from, and correspondence with, brother Blinn and his family, and the attentions of young admirers including poets Michael Collier and Edward Hirsch, fiction writers Richard Bausch, Charles Baxter, Benjamin Cheever, and Donna Tartt, and literary scholar Michael Steinman. He calls these new, unexpected, and affectionate friendships "a gift from life."

1994 Arranges and revises texts for *All the Days and Nights: The Collected Stories of William Maxwell*, comprising 23 short stories (including complete contents of *Over by the River* and *Billie Dyer*) and 21 tales or "improvisations" (mostly from *The Old Man at the Railroad Crossing*). In spring, publishes three improvisations in *Story* magazine, and, in fall, four more in *The New England Review*. Become client of agent Andrew Wylie, who untangles Maxwell's rights history and negotiates deal with Vintage Books for uniform edition of paperback reprints.

1995 In January, *All the Days and Nights* published by Knopf, occasioning a year of awards and acceptances: Ivan Sandrof Award for Lifetime Achievement in Literature (National Book Critics Circle); Mark Twain Award (Society for Study of Midwestern Literature, Michigan State University); Gold Medal for Fiction (presented by Joseph Mitchell, American Academy of Arts and Letters); Heartland Award in Literature (Chicago Tribune Foundation); PEN/Malamud Award for the Short Story; Ambassador Book Award (English-Speaking Union of the United States), and American Book Award. In March, *Mrs. Donald's Dog Bun and His Home Away from Home*, a picture book for children with watercolors by *New Yorker* cartoonist James Stevenson, published by Knopf. In November, records *So Long, See You Tomorrow* in its entirety for the American Audio Prose Library, together with an interview by series' producer Kay Bonetti.

1996 In May, *The Happiness of Getting It Down Right*, Michael Steinman's edition of the Frank O'Connor–William Maxwell letters, published by Knopf. Writes memoir of Maeve Brennan for *The Springs of Affection*, posthumous collection of Brennan's Dublin stories (1997). On his 88th birthday, interviewed by Edward Hirsch for *DoubleTake* magazine (Summer 1997). Writes introductions to the Modern Library editions of Joseph Mitchell's *Joe Gould's Secret* (1996) and his own *They Came Like Swallows* (1997).

1997 Donates majority of personal and professional papers to University of Illinois Library. Writes memoir, "Nearing Ninety," for *The New York Times Magazine* (March 9); will revise it for inclusion in *Best American Essays 1998*, edited by Cynthia Ozick. Lymphoma returns, and again Maxwell responds well to chemotherapy.

1998 Christopher MacLehose, of Harvill Press, London, publishes paperback edition of *So Long, See You Tomorrow*; over next four years will make five other Maxwell books available to British and Commonwealth readers. An interviewer for *Illinois Alumni* magazine asks Maxwell to name the happiest and most significant moments in his long life and career: "Perhaps when meeting the Wisconsin novelist Zona Gale when I was 16. Perhaps when I looked through a porthole at age 40 and saw the coast of France. Certainly the day when my wife agreed to marry me. And the days when my two daughters were born. And when I first read Tolstoy's 'Master and Man.'" In summer, Emily discovers she has ovarian cancer, and undergoes first of three rounds of chemotherapy. In October, the Century presents gala dinner and literary evening in celebration of Maxwell's 90th birthday and his 50th year as member of the club. Story "The Room Outside" published in *The New Yorker* (December 28, 1998 & January 4, 1999).

1999 Writes introduction to *The Music at Long Verney*, Michael Steinman's choice from Sylvia Townsend Warner's uncollected stories, and afterword to *The Element of Lavishness*, Steinman's edition of the Maxwell–Warner letters (both published by Counterpoint in 2001). On June 7 *The New Yorker* publishes "Grape Bay (1941)," not a new story but the revised opening of abandoned Bermuda novel of the late 1970s. Two final improvisations published in *DoubleTake* (Fall).

2000 Health begins to fail: suffers pneumonia, near blindness, anemia, and return of lymphoma. Meets with family lawyers, and asks Michael Steinman to be his literary executor. In spring, Emily refuses to undergo fourth round of chemotherapy; she dies at home, on July 23, at age 78. Maxwell, surrounded by family and friends, follows her eight days later, on July 31, at age 91. A joint memorial service, organized by daughters, is held on September 8, at the Cathedral of St. John the Divine, New York City, and attended by hundreds.

Note on the Texts

This volume presents a selection from the fiction that William Maxwell published between 1934 and 1956. It contains the texts of four novels—*Bright Center of Heaven* (1934), *They Came Like Swallows* (1937, revised edition 1960), *The Folded Leaf* (1945, revised edition 1959), and *Time Will Darken It* (1948, revised edition 1962)—and nine short stories, as well as the text of a speech, "The Writer as Illusionist" (1955), and, in an appendix, two later prose pieces: the introduction to the Modern Library edition of *They Came Like Swallows* (1997) and the preface to the Quality Paperback Book Club reprint of *Time Will Darken It* (1992).

Maxwell made notes for *Bright Center of Heaven*, his first novel, in the spring of 1933, when he was teaching freshman composition at the University of Illinois at Urbana-Champaign. The first draft was written from June through September 1933 at Bonnie Oaks, a working farm and summer artists' retreat near Portage, Wisconsin. Jacob Zeitlin, a professor in the Illinois English department with friends in New York publishing circles, sent a copy of the novel to Eugene F. Saxton, editor-in-chief of Harper & Brothers, in December 1933. Saxton accepted the manuscript in February 1934, and Maxwell quickly revised the novel, delivering a final version on April 15. An examination of the setting copy, which is among the papers Maxwell donated in 1997 to the Rare Book and Manuscript Library at the University of Illinois at Urbana-Champaign, shows that the Harper's copyeditor retained many of Maxwell's inconsistencies in spelling, capitalization, and punctuation, while making changes in diction such as substituting "wabbly" for "wobbly," "overalls" for "Koveralls," and, at page 96.10 of the present volume, "a cow" for "the ass end of a cow." *Bright Center of Heaven* was published by Harper & Brothers in New York in September 1934. Although the first printing of 1,000 copies quickly sold out, a second printing of 1,000 in December 1934 sold poorly. There were no further printings of the novel in Maxwell's lifetime. This volume prints the text of the 1934 Harper & Brothers edition.

Maxwell wrote his second novel, *They Came Like Swallows*, between 1934 and 1936. (In his introduction to the Modern Library edition, printed on pages 927–33 of the present volume, Maxwell gives an account of the novel's composition.) It was published in the United States by Harper & Brothers, where his editor was again Eugene Saxton, in March 1937, and in England by Michael Joseph Ltd.

in September 1937. Maxwell provided both publishers with copies of the same setting text, which each copyedited in its own style. The Harper's copyeditor used a light hand, mainly inserting serial commas, while the copyeditor at Joseph preserved Maxwell's punctuation but made the text conform to English spelling conventions (e.g., "colour," "waggons"). A contradiction in the setting copy led to a significant variant in the two editions: in the Harper's edition, Book Two is titled "Robert," while in the English edition it is titled "Scissors and Snails." (The setting copy in the University of Illinois collection has one version on the part-title page, and the other on the opening page of the part.) Several errors in the English edition, especially in paragraphing and italicization, indicate that Maxwell, who carefully went over the proofs of the Harper's edition, was not closely involved in its production.

In June 1958 Maxwell signed a contract with Alfred A. Knopf providing for the hardcover publication of the novel-in-progress that would become *The Château* (1961) and for the publication of *They Came Like Swallows*, *The Folded Leaf*, and *Time Will Darken It* in Knopf's new Vintage paperback line. Maxwell revised *They Came Like Swallows* in the winter of 1958–59 by cutting pages from the Harper's edition and mounting them on typing paper, then penciling deletions and other marks directly over the original pages and typing or penciling insertions in the margins. He wrote in a letter to his friend Frank O'Connor that, upon rereading the novel, he was "moved helplessly by the material, which will only cease to move me when I am dead, I suppose," but was also dismayed by his work's shortcomings: "All the judgments are so harsh and, as I eventually discovered, in many cases quite wrong. But there was nothing I could do short of rewriting it out of existence, except here and there to do the small detail work that pulls a character back into recognizable human focus, and to restore a grand scene that I mistakenly deleted, in which I was impertinent to my father, who, of course, had a minute before been impertinent to me." (The restored passage Maxwell referred to appears at pages 210.1–17 in this volume.) Maxwell approved final proofs on December 2, 1959, and the Vintage Books edition of *They Came Like Swallows* was published in April 1960. This volume prints the text of the 1960 Vintage edition.

Shortly before Maxwell joined the staff of *The New Yorker* in November 1936, he began contributing short stories to the magazine, where his editor was Katharine S. White; in 1941 he also contributed two stories to *Harper's Bazaar*, where Mary Louise Aswell was his editor. The five stories collected in this volume as "Stories 1938–1945" were selected from the nearly two dozen that Maxwell published during the 1930s and 1940s. They were first published as follows: "Homecoming," *The New Yorker*, January 1, 1938; "The Actual Thing," *The New Yorker*, September 3, 1938; "Young Francis Whitehead" (under the title "Good Friday"), *The New Yorker*, April 8, 1939; "Haller's Second Home" (under the title "Abbie's Birthday"), *Harper's Bazaar*, August 1941, and "The Patterns of Love," *The New Yorker*, July 7, 1945. "Homecoming" and "The Actual Thing" were never collected by Maxwell, although "Homecoming" was reprinted without change in *Short Stories from The New Yorker* (1940), an anthology anonymously edited by Katharine S. White. Maxwell revised "Young Francis Whitehead," "Haller's Second Home," and "The Patterns of Love" while compiling his collection *Over by the River and Other Stories*, published by Alfred A. Knopf in 1977, and made further small revisions for their inclusion in *All the Days and Nights: The Collected Stories of William Maxwell*, published by Knopf in 1995. The present volume prints the texts of "Homecoming" and "The Actual Thing" published in *The New Yorker*, and the texts of "Young Francis Whitehead," "Haller's Second Home," and "The Patterns of Love" published in *All the Days and Nights.*

In early 1940 Maxwell wrote a vignette about two high school students who form an unspoken alliance at the school swimming pool. He showed the piece to his close friend Louise Bogan, the poetry critic for *The New Yorker*, who told him that he had written not a short story but the opening pages of a novel. Over the next four years Maxwell sent her his work-in-progress, chapter by chapter, and came to rely heavily on her critical response to the installments. By July 1943 he had been at work on the novel for more than three years and was still struggling with the material. At the suggestion of *New Yorker* fiction editor Gus Lobrano, Harold Ross, the editor of the magazine, offered Maxwell five months' leave at full pay. Working without interruption at his small house in Yorktown Heights, New York, Maxwell completed a second draft by the end of the year. He returned to *The New Yorker* on a part-time basis in January 1944, and finished a third draft in the spring. He submitted this version to Edward Aswell, who had succeeded Eugene Saxton as Harper's editor-in-chief. After Aswell asked for revisions, Maxwell delivered a final draft on November 15, 1944, under the title "No Word for Anybody." While the book was in production, Louise Bogan suggested changing the title to *The Folded Leaf*, an allusion to Tennyson's "Song of the Lotos-Eaters." *The Folded Leaf* was published by Harper & Brothers in April 1945. Maxwell made a number of small changes in the Harper's text for the English edition, published by Faber & Faber in September 1946. Faber also edited the text to make it conform to English spelling conventions and rephrased many of Maxwell's Midwestern colloquialisms (e.g., changing "you'd of drowned" to "you'd have drowned").

Maxwell began revising *The Folded Leaf* for publication by Vintage Books shortly after signing his contract with Knopf in the summer of 1958, probably following the same procedure he had used when preparing the paperback edition of *They Came Like Swallows.* (The whereabouts of the setting copy for the Vintage edition of *The Folded Leaf* are unknown.) He used the opportunity to undo several significant changes he had made in 1944 at the recommendation of Aswell and of Theodor Reik, his analyst at the time, but had later come to regret; as a result, the text of *The Folded Leaf* published by Vintage in September 1959 is very close to the version Maxwell originally submitted to Aswell. This volume prints the text of the 1959 Vintage edition.

Maxwell began writing *Time Will Darken It*, his fourth novel, in Yorktown Heights in the summer of 1945, and delivered it to Aswell in December 1947. The novel was published in the United States by Harper & Brothers in September 1948 and in England by Faber & Faber in 1949; Maxwell provided both publishers with copies of the same setting text, which each copyedited in its own style. In winter 1961–62 he revised the text of *Time Will Darken It* for the Vintage Books edition, published in September 1962. (Only a few pages of the setting copy of the Vintage edition are at the University of Illinois; the whereabouts of the remaining pages are unknown.) This volume prints the text of the 1962 Vintage edition.

The four short stories collected in this volume as "Stories 1952–1956" were selected from the six that Maxwell published during the 1950s. They first appeared in periodicals as follows: "The Trojan Women," *Perspectives U.S.A. 1*, Fall 1952; "The Pilgrimage," *The New Yorker*, August 22, 1953; "What Every Boy Should Know," *Perspectives U.S.A. 7*, Spring 1954, and "The French Scarecrow," *The New Yorker*, October 6, 1956. "The Trojan Women," "What Every Boy Should Know," and "The French Scarecrow" were included in *Stories*, a collection of short stories by Jean Stafford, John Cheever, Daniel Fuchs, and Maxwell published by Farrar, Straus & Cudahy in 1956. Maxwell revised these three stories, as well as "The Pilgrimage," for their inclusion in *Over by the River* (1977) and made further small changes for their publication in *All the Days and Nights: The Collected Stories of William Maxwell* (1995). The texts printed in this volume are taken from *All the Days and Nights.*

"The Writer as Illusionist" is based on a speech Maxwell delivered at a symposium, "The American Novel at Mid-Century," held at Smith College, in Northampton, Massachusetts, March 3 and 4, 1955.

Later that year Maxwell revised the text and had it privately printed as a 16-page, saddle-stapled pamphlet, bound in white paper wraps, and with the publisher identified on the inside front wrap as "Unitelum Press." (The name was chosen by Maxwell because his venture in self-publishing had the "one end" of bringing out the pamphlet.) He presented most of the copies of the pamphlet to friends and colleagues as a gift, but some were sold in New York City bookstores at fifty cents each to recover the printing costs. "The Writer as Illusionist" was not reprinted during Maxwell's lifetime; the text printed in this volume is taken from the pamphlet edition.

The appendix to this volume presents two essays written by Maxwell in the 1990s as prefaces to reprintings of his works: the introduction to *They Came Like Swallows* was published in the 1997 Modern Library edition of the novel, and the preface to *Time Will Darken It* was one of three prefaces published in the 1992 Quality Paperback Book Club omnibus edition of *Time Will Darken It*, *The Château*, and *So Long, See You Tomorrow*. The texts printed in this volume are taken from, respectively, the 1997 Modern Library edition and the 1992 Quality Paperback Book Club edition.

This volume presents the texts of the original printings chosen for inclusion here, but it does not attempt to reproduce nontextual features of their typographic design. The texts are printed without change, except for the correction of typographical errors. Spelling, punctuation, and capitalization are often expressive features, and they are not altered, even when inconsistent or irregular. Except for clear typographical errors, the spelling and usage of foreign words and phrases are left as they appear in the original texts. The following is a list of typographical errors corrected, cited by page and line number: 6.27, "Johanna."; 10.27, stand; 11.7, Gracelands; 12.5, negroes; 12.18, Boarders; 23.28, Halstead; 31.38–39, "Some . . . West." 37.8, *much*——; 38.9, Muv"; 38.24, and——"; 45.32, her,–; 46.4, it is; 48.11, *flat*; 50.19, nice.; 50.39, Frustrate; 51.38, yourself;; 54.9, forego; 54.23, so the; 56.26, breech; 60.14, She; 61.26, oilcan; 62.3, thread.; 62.35, enthusiasm.—; 65.38, nose; 68.30, 31, Lhevinne's; 69.8, come—She; 70.8, Boarders; 75.17, moslems; 77.17, hurt,; 78.16, Bascom; 81.7–8, Woe!" cover; 81.15, upon; 85.30, *verlorn gegange*; 86.22, Boarders; 87.28, "Soap."; 91.4 the the; 91.19, town——; 99.31, though; 101.4, imaginery; 103.7–8, discourged; 114,19, Boarders; 120.19, twenty-times; 123.15, base; 129.35, "woodus."; 142.16–18, *Who . . . her*——; 151.38, "That; 152.38, you rather; 153.11, negroes; 154.4, negro; 155.35, renewed; 156.16, Gustibus"; 164.13, undispeptic; 188.13–14, groceryman; 192.7, be; 205.33, He; 215.16, handle-bars; 221.9–10, "We . . . him."; 221.35, pillow-cases; 245.36, *Luisitania*; 254.16, *head!*"; 272.12, I; 307.39, wan't; 311.37, a half; 342.25, de Fresne; 408.10, wrist;

412.37, Lynch; 417.4, Profesor; 434.16, himself); 512.39, begun; 529.16, oclock; 547.29, luminal; 554.17, Pop-Eye; 573.25, 1,000; 581.33, heir; 584.8, yourselves This; 594.1, old bent; 603.14, Rachael's; 608.4, ask; 632.29, sewing; 654.7, tanagra; 674.7, Why; 681.6, postoffice; 708.5, postcript; 714.12, It's; 720.4, shinging; 720.27, eargerly; 726.6, said.; 727.32, glad see; 748.8, coffepot; 761.3, hesistantly; 761.40, it's; 767.2 know; 786.38, Mr; 803.7, said; 812.1, makes; 813.3, end,; 816.33, courtesty; 824.19, The; 865.26, *qualifé*; 870.22, suddenly.; 871.12, *foi*; 902.27, laying; 918.29, Knightly; 927.7, Tauschnitz; 927.23, rest.

Notes

In the notes below, the reference numbers denote page and line of this volume (the line count includes headings). No note is made for material included in standard desk-reference books. Biblical quotations are keyed to the King James Version. Quotations from Shakespeare are keyed to *The Riverside Shakespeare*, ed. G. Blakemore Evans (Boston: Houghton Mifflin, 1974). For references to other studies, and further biographical background than is contained in the Chronology, see *William Maxwell: A Literary Life*, by Barbara Burkhardt (Urbana and Chicago: University of Illinois Press, 2005), *A William Maxwell Portrait: Memories and Appreciations*, ed. Charles Baxter, Michael Collier, and Edward Hirsch (New York: W. W. Norton, 2005), *My Mentor: A Young Man's Friendship with William Maxwell*, by Alec Wilkinson (Boston: Houghton Mifflin, 2002), *The Element of Lavishness: Letters of Sylvia Townsend Warner and William Maxwell, 1938–1978*, ed. Michael Steinman (Washington, D.C.: Counterpoint, 2001), *What I Think I Did: A Season of Survival in Two Acts*, by Larry Woiwode (New York: Basic Books, 2000), *The Happiness of Getting It Down Right: Letters of Frank O'Connor and William Maxwell, 1945–1966*, ed. Michael Steinman (New York: Alfred A. Knopf, 1996), and *Ancestors*, by William Maxwell (New York: Alfred A. Knopf, 1971). Significant interviews with Maxwell, for which he provided written, not oral, responses, include those by Edward Hirsch (*DoubleTake*, Summer 1997), David Stanton (*Poets & Writers*, May/June 1994), Barbara Burkhardt et al. (*Tamaqua*, Fall 1992), and John Seabrook and George Plimpton (*The Paris Review*, Fall 1982).

The editor wishes to thank the Rare Book and Manuscript Library of the University of Illinois, Urbana-Champaign, whose award of a research grant through the John "Bud" Velde Visiting Scholars Program supported his work on this volume.

BRIGHT CENTER OF HEAVEN

2.1 BABA] Maxwell's pet name for Mildred Ormsby Green (1872–1964), at whose estate—Bonnie Oaks, a working farm and summer artists' retreat near Portage, Wisconsin—most of this novel was written.

4.5–7 *Today is the day /. . . half a pound of Tay. . . .*] From a soldier's ditty of the First World War era, which continues: "If you know any ladies / Who want any babies / Just send them round to me."

10.3 Jerry Carson] Gerald Hewes Carson (1899–1989), an Urbana native and a product of the University of Illinois English department, was, after 1922, a journalist, editor, book reviewer, and advertising copywriter in New York City.

10.21 Irita Van Doren and the Spingarns] Van Doren (1891–1966) was editor-in-chief of the book-review supplement of the Sunday New York *Herald Tribune* from 1926 to 1963. Joel Elias Spingarn (1875–1939), American educator and man of letters, was from 1913 one of the white leaders of the NAACP. He and his wealthy wife, Amy Einstein Spingarn (1883–1980), were patrons and critical champions of many writers of the Harlem Renaissance.

13.21 "Camille"] *Camille* is the English title for *La Dame aux camélias* (1852, tr. 1856), a play by Alexandre Dumas *fils* (1824–1895). Adapted by Dumas from his first novel (1848), it tells the story of a French youth's affair with a beautiful and doomed courtesan.

13.22 Brooks Atkinson] Atkinson (1894–1984) was chief drama critic of *The New York Times* from 1925 to 1960.

23.10–11 Stuart Chase,] American economist and essayist (1888–1985) whose criticism of advertising, technology, and the wastefulness of consumer society appeared in *The Nation* and other left-leaning publications.

23.12 *Bagavad Gita.*] The *Bhagavad-Gita* ("Song of the Divine One") is an ancient Sanskrit text of 700 verses, constituting chapters 25–42 of the *Mahabharata.* It takes the form of a dialogue, in which Krishna, an incarnation of Vishnu, instructs the warrior prince Arjuna in the Hindu philosophy of life.

23.34 *Crystal Lake.*] Two-hundred-thirty-acre lake in McHenry County, Illinois, about 50 miles northwest of Chicago.

30.1 Henry Adams's observation] Cf. Adams, in Chapter 7 of *The Education of Henry Adams* (1907): "No man, however strong, can serve ten years as school-master, priest or senator, and remain fit for anything else."

32.36 "*Do you know how doth the farmer?*"] Nursery song and circle game, akin to "Do You Know the Muffin Man?" and "The Farmer in the Dell."

33.23 *The Tale of Genji.*] Novel by the Lady Murasaki (Murasaki Shikibu, 978–1031) describing love and politics in the imperial court of Heian Japan. It was introduced to the West through a translation by the English Orientalist Arthur Waley, which, when published in six installments between 1925 and 1933, became a transatlantic literary phenomenon.

35.28–29 "*Nein! . . . Aber was gibb's zu trinke?*"] "No! . . . But what would you have to drink?"

38.17 story of the man with the magic skin] *Le Peau de chagrin* ("The Wild Ass's Skin," 1831) by Honoré de Balzac.

38.35 the little king,] Popular series of pantomime comic strips by Otto Soglow (1900–1975) featuring a benign, pleasure-loving, roly-poly monarch. "The Little King" originally appeared in *The New Yorker* from 1931 to 1934, then continued as a long-lived Sunday newspaper strip.

44.5 Jesting Pilate,] Cf. Francis Bacon, "On Truth," in *Essays* (1601): "What is truth? said jesting Pilate, and would not stay for answer."

44.22 the David Madame Récamier.] In a full-length portrait (1800) by the Neoclassicist painter Jacques-Louis David (1748–1835), the young Jeanne-Françoise ("Juliette") Récamier (1777–1849), hostess of an intellectual salon in Napoleon's Paris, lounges barefoot on an Empire sofa, her back turned toward the viewer, at whom she looks over her right shoulder.

44.29 Lorado Taft] Taft (1860–1936) was a monumental sculptor and a writer of popular works of art history. An Illinois native, he taught at the Art Institute of Chicago and later, during Maxwell's years as a student there, at the University of Illinois at Urbana-Champaign.

45.9–10 sea-green-incorruptible-mammonism.] Conflation of two phrases coined by the Scottish historian and social critic Thomas Carlyle (1795–1881). In *The French Revolution* (1837) Carlyle used "The Sea-Green Incorruptible" as an epithet for Robespierre; in *Past and Present* (1843) he called Victorian England's earnestness about making money the "Gospel of Mammonism."

45.34 Serge] Russian-born conductor Serge Koussevitsky (1874–1951) was music director of the Boston Symphony Orchestra from 1924 to 1949.

46.2 Deauville sandals,] Slip-on sandals with a single, wide, cloth band, in a style made popular on the resort beaches of Deauville, Normandy, in the 1920s.

47.11 *Berengaria*,] R.M.S. *Berengaria* sailed for Cunard from 1919 to 1938. With the *Aquitania* and the *Mauretania*, she was one of the company's trio of great passenger ships on the Southampton–Cherbourg–New York line.

48.10–11 Tschaikowsky B flat Minor Concerto] Piano Concerto No. 1, op. 23 (1874–75), by Pyotr Ilyich Tchaikovsky (1840–1893).

50.11–12 That which we call a rose,] Cf. *Romeo and Juliet*, II.ii.43–44.

53.15 horse-and-rider fence,] Rude, all-wood post-and-rail fence, with the rail-ends stacked in alternating fashion between double posts.

68.29–30 Josef Lhévinne's] Lhévinne (1874–1944), a Russian-born concert pianist and music teacher, was a close friend of Mildred Ormsby Green and a summer resident at Bonnie Oaks from 1922 through 1943. For Maxwell's personal impressions, see page 928.31–38.

70.36–37 "*Du lieber Gott!*"] "Dear God!"

72.30 Nantucket jersey,] Long-sleeved crew-necked sweatshirt.

72.32–33 "Pomp . . . "Aïda."] *Pomp and Circumstance*, or "The Land of Hope and Glory," op. 39, no. 1 (1901), march by Sir Edward Elgar; Triumphal March, from Act II, Scene 2, of *Aïda* (1871), opera by Giuseppe Verdi.

77.16 Sidney Trelease] Sidney Briggs Trelease (1896–1983) was a businessman in Champaign, Illinois, renowned locally for his wit. The husband of an English instructor at the University of Illinois, he was a fixture at the school's social functions, where, Maxwell once wrote, "he was as much an anomaly among the professors as Bottom the Weaver in Titania's bower."

78.7–8 "If we had some ham . . . if we had some eggs.] Depression-era one-liner of unknown authorship but wide currency.

85.23 *den nächsten Tag . . . schlimmer.*] But at nighttime she is worse again.

85.29–31 *Sie sagt . . . verloren gegangen*] She says if you knew she was sick, you would not stay away any longer. She wonders if my letters have gone astray.

87.27 Ariel. . . . clouds.] See Shakespeare, *The Tempest*, I.ii.190–92.

87.36–37 *nujol / junket*] Nujol for Constipation was a brand of mineral-oil laxative, Junket a brand of powdered custard mix.

95.26 Indian mound] Earthwork, usually at a burial site, by one of many of the pre-Columbian peoples of North America collectively known to modern anthropology as the Mound Builders. The mounds are most often found in the Ohio and Mississippi river valleys and take many forms, from cones to massive walls to truncated pyramids. Those in the shapes of animals are also called effigy mounds.

101.33 froccing] That is, "frogging."

101.36 snakefeeder] Dragonfly; see page 26.7.

106.26–29 '*Once every few months . . . round and round. . . .*'] From *Reveries over Childhood and Youth* (1916), the first of W. B. Yeats's six autobiographies.

111.27 'For Narrow Bed'] The title of this nonexistent play is an allusion to "The Song of the Mad Prince" by Walter de la Mare (1873–1956), in his collection *Peacock Pie* (1913): "Who said, 'All Time's delight / Hath she for narrow bed; / Life's troubled bubble broken'?— / That's what I said."

124.17 *The Crisis*,] Official organ of the NAACP, published continuously since November 1910.

124.20–37 that Decatur court-room . . . *that's all* . . . .] The third trial of the so-called Scottsboro Boys was held in Decatur, Alabama, July 14–24, 1933. The "Boys" were nine black youths who, on March 25, 1931, fought with two white men in the boxcar of a Southern Railroad freight train after two white women, passengers on the train, accused them of rape. The train was stopped near Paint Rock, Alabama, and the youths were arrested by posse and incarcerated in Scottsboro, seat of Jackson County. A swift trial (April 6–9, 1931) ended in eight death sentences and a hung jury. The U.S. Supreme Court reversed the convictions on procedural grounds, and a second rape trial (spring 1933) ended in confusion when one of the plaintiffs recanted her testimony. The U.S. Supreme Court demanded a third trial, which ended in five acquittals, three life sentences, and a death sentence. Andrew Wright was one of those sentenced to life; he was paroled in 1943. His little brother, Leroy "Roy" Wright, 13 at the time of the incident, was acquitted. In the end, all the convicted Scottsboro Boys were paroled or pardoned, the last in 1976.

124.29–37 *Yessuh . . . that's all . . . .*] Maxwell's source for quotations from Andrew Wright's testimony is journalist Hamilton Basso's account of the third trial of the Scottsboro Boys, published in *The New Republic* for December 20, 1933.

126.1 Pickens] William Pickens (1881–1954), Yale-educated orator and writer, was a founding member of the NAACP and later its longtime Southern field secretary. Maxwell met him at Bonnie Oaks in the summer of 1925, and memories of that experience, together with details selected from Pickens's *Bursting Bonds* (1923, an expanded edition of *Heir of Slaves: The Autobiography of a "New Negro,"* 1911), contributed to his characterization of Jefferson Carter. For "the dialogue between the high-yellow and the coal black," see page 131.29–35.

130.27 James Weldon Johnson] Diplomat, journalist, and man of letters, Johnson (1871–1938) was the author of the novel *The Autobiography of an Ex-Colored Man* (1912), the U.S. consul to Venezuela and Nicaragua, and the national secretary of the NAACP from 1915 to 1930.

131.29–35 "There's a funny story . . . the light-skinned one said——"] Cf. "Discriminating the Color Shadings," in William Pickens's *American Aesop: Negro and Other Humor* (1926).

133.3–4 "*Heut' Morge' . . . hab' ich a Brief bekomme'.*"] "This morning . . . I got a letter."

136.20–25 "*A kitten once . . . And live in a lonely wood.*"] Here and a few lines later, Mrs. West misquotes passages from "The Robber Kitten" (1858) by the Scottish writer R. M. Ballantyne (1825–1894), who wrote "robber *fierce*," "*dreary* wood," and "*two* tremendous howls."

142.16–18 "*Who is Cynthia / . . . swains adore her*——"] Cf. Shakespeare, *Two Gentlemen of Verona*, IV:ii:39–40: "Who is Silvia? What is she, / That all our swains commend her?"

145.1–12 According to Japanese legend . . . no further.] Maxwell's source is "Diplomacy," in *Kwaidan: Stories and Studies of Strange Things* (1904) by Lafcadio Hearn (1850–1904).

163.34–164.7 *At the side of the road . . . old and feeble. . . .*] From Chapter 6 of Arthur Waley's translation of *The Tale of Genji: Book I* (1925).

THEY CAME LIKE SWALLOWS

167.1 THEY CAME LIKE SWALLOWS] Maxwell wrote the following descriptive copy for the back cover of the 1960 Vintage paperback edition of the novel:

"This is a novel that dramatizes most touchingly one of the deepest fears of childhood—that the mother of the family will go away and never come back. The only remarkable thing about Elizabeth Morison was that she made it possible for the people around her to be happy. Her husband, her two young sons, her sister whose marriage had ended badly, all continually turned their faces toward her in the way that flowers turn toward the sunlight. When she was with them they were themselves. While she was there the Morisons' house was beautiful and warm and bright and safe against all the terrors of the dark. The force that was at work through her was what is meant by 'the power to love.' She should have lived to a ripe old age, with her grandchildren around her knee; instead she was cut down in full flower, like an armful of wheat, because no house is safe against death, no family immune from the events of its time. It is unbearable, and it happened. The writing of this book is such that not merely the characters in Mr. Maxwell's story but the reader himself struggles to find some point of balance in the void, to accept so serious a loss."

171.1–6 *They came . . . air . . .*] From "Coole Park, 1929," in *The Winding Stair and Other Poems* (1933) by W. B. Yeats (1865–1939). Copyright © by Anne Yeats. Reprinted from *William Butler Yeats: The Poems* (Revised Edition), edited by Richard J. Finneran (New York: Macmillan, 1997). Macmillan Library Reference U.S.A. is an imprint of Scribner, a division of Simon & Schuster, Inc., New York. All rights reserved.

174.21–23 "How do you do . . . again?"] Cf. the nursery rhyme "One Misty, Moisty Morning."

174.36–37 *The Boy Allies in Bulgaria.*] The syndicate-written "Boy Allies" books—23 volumes published by A. L. Burt, New York, from 1915 through 1919—followed the adventures of American and British youths caught up in the major land and sea campaigns of World War I. Titles included *The Boy Allies on the Firing Line* and *The Boy Allies at Jutland* but not *The Boy Allies in Bulgaria.*

175.14 thrift stamps] Stamps issued by the U.S. Treasury Department's War Savings Stamps program during World War I. The stamps, designed to encourage patriotism and thrift, were issued in small denominations and sold primarily to schoolchildren.

183.25 *Charlie Chaplin married. . . .*] On October 23, 1918, Chaplin, age 29, married 16-year-old Mildred Harris (1901–1944), the first of his four wives. The bride was an actress whom Chaplin mistakenly believed was pregnant with his child.

184.36–37 "*And if thou sayst . . . Scotland here . . .*"] Cf. Canto 6, Stanza 14 of *Marmion, a Tale of Flodden Field* (1808) by Sir Walter Scott.

187.22 *Butter's what I'm after*] In the first edition of *They Came Like Swallows* (1937), this paragraph concludes: "When he inquired what was so funny about that, they couldn't possibly explain. It was a family joke, that was all—a joke so old that neither of them could remember what the point of it was."

188.1–4 "*O when I die / . . . alkyhol . . .*"] From "Little Brown Jug," American folk song of the Civil War era.

188.18 French harps] Harmonicas.

191.3 Hughes] Charles Evans Hughes (1862–1948), Republican Party candidate for president in the election of 1916, which was won by Woodrow Wilson.

192.9 *three-deep*] Or Three Deep, a children's circle game for dozens of players, with a chase-and-tag element.

194.10 *Elite,*] *Elite Styles* (1897–1929), American women's magazine that, like its longer-lived competitor *Butterick's*, featured illustrated fashion news and dress patterns for the amateur seamstress.

199.17 *Toinette's Philip*] Novel for children (1894) by Mrs. C. V. Jamison (née Celia Viets Dakin, 1837–1909). Set in Old New Orleans, it concerns a white orphan raised by his black "mammy."

199.17 *The Hollow Tree and Deep Woods Book*] Volume of tales (1901) by Albert Bigelow Paine (1861–1937), with drawings by J. M. Conde. It collects the contents of Paine's *The Hollow Tree* (1898) and *In the Deep Woods* (1899) and additional related stories about Mr. Crow, Mr. Possum, Mr. Rabbit, and other animal characters.

205.12 "*Hein?*"] "Come again?"

208.18–19 *Stars and Stripes Forever*] March (1896) by John Philip Sousa (1854–1932), American bandmaster known as "The March King." He was also the composer of *The Washington Post* (1889), *El Capitan* (1896), *The Fairest of the Fair* (1908), and *The U.S. Field Artillery* (1917) among dozens of other marches.

211.3 "The War's over."] On Monday, November 11, 1918, at Compiègne, France, the Germans signed an armistice agreement prepared by the Allied powers, ending World War I.

211.37 *King's X,"*] Playground cry of the American Midwest, now obscure. A child who wanted to call a time-out in a game of tag, or to call off a fight he was losing, exclaimed "King's X!," "King's Cross!," or "King's Cruce!," usually while holding up crossed fingers.

217.28 "*Wie geht's?*"] "What's up?"

221.21–33 "*There's a long long / trail . . . pale*—"] From "There's a Long, Long Trail" (1915), American popular song of the World War I era by Alonzo "Zo" Elliott, words by Stoddard King.

224.36–225.5 "*She was goin' downgrade . . . With steam . . .*"] From "The Wreck of the Old 97," ballad by Henry Whitter, words by Charles Noell, commemorating the wreck, on September 27, 1903, of Southern Railroad mail train No. 97. The train was en route from Washington, D.C., to Atlanta when it jumped the tracks outside Danville, Virginia, killing nine, including the engineer, Steve Broady.

226.15 shinny sticks,] Homemade hockey sticks, used for playing street hockey with a can or a small ball.

230.13 *The Scottish Chiefs.*] Historical novel (1810) by Jane Porter (1776–1850) concerning William Wallace, Robert the Bruce, and the rebellion they led against England's Edward I.

236.13 *The Shepherd Boy's Prayer*] American parlor song (1879) by A. W. Holt.

236.16–18 *Go tell / Aunt Rho / die*] American folk song: "Go tell Aunt Rhodie / Go tell Aunt Rhodie / Go tell Aunt Rhodie / Her old gray goose is dead."

244.16 Ladies Aid,] Most congregations of the Presbyterian Church (U.S.A.) have a Ladies Aid Society, whose chief mission is to raise funds for maintaining and improving the church building and grounds.

247.26–27 "*When I was a child . . . as a child . . .*"] I Corinthians 13:11.

248.17 "*Transgressors from the womb*"] See Book 5, line 829, of "The Task" (1784) by William Cowper (1731–1800); also Isaiah 48:8.

252.24 automobile robes] Early automobiles were unheated, and so outfitted with lap robes or "buggy blankets" to help keep the driver and passengers warm. These robes hung on rails attached to the backs of the front seats.

256.13–14 *Heaven is a providing-place.*] The phrase is not from Scripture but from Maxwell family history, as recounted by Maxwell in *Ancestors* (1971), pages 248–49. Hours after his apparent death, Maxwell's Grandfather Blinn opened his eyes and, looking toward his daughters keeping vigil by his deathbed, said: "Heaven is a providing-place." They believed that he had come back for one brief moment, with a message just for them. "After that," Maxwell writes, "nothing could shake [their] belief that there is a life without end."

256.15–16 *In my Father's house are many mansions.*] John 14:2.

280.20 Ingersoll] Robert Green Ingersoll (1833–1899), "The Great Agnostic," American orator whose forceful and eloquent antireligious arguments, delivered on the Chautauqua circuit and later collected in books, provoked American audiences and scandalized the clergy.

STORIES 1938–1945

298.5 Knights Templar sword] The Order of Knights Templar, an elite division of the secret fraternal society known as the Masons (U.S.A.), issues ceremonial swords and other regalia to its members.

298.5 Ingersoll] See note 280.20.

298.11 "The Clansman"] Historical novel (1905) by Thomas Dixon Jr. (1864–1946) romanticizing the Old South's resistance to Reconstruction and the rise of the Ku Klux Klan. It served as the basis of D. W. Griffith's film *The Birth of a Nation* (1915).

298.11 "Truxton King,"] Bestselling romance (1909) by the American writer George Barr McCutcheon (1866–1928). It is the third of six intricately plotted novels about love and intrigue in the royal court of Graustark, a tiny Central European principality repeatedly threatened with extinction by its powerful northern neighbor, Axphain.

308.35–36 a book she had read once long ago.] *Lady Jane* (1891), a novel for children by Mrs. C. V. Jamison (see note 199.17).

311.23 Saruk rug,] A Persian carpet, usually with a large central medallion against a dark blue background.

319.24 Demosthenes] Athenian statesman and orator (384–322 BCE).

320.11 Longchamps.] Chain of moderately expensive white-tablecloth restaurants that flourished in Manhattan from the 1920s through the 1960s.

320.34 Sibelius:] Finnish composer Jean Sibelius (1865–1957); his "Night Ride and Sunrise," op. 55 (1909), and "Oceanides," op. 73 (1914), are symphonic tone poems.

329.16–17 *A Room of One's Own.*] Book-length essay (1929) in which Virginia Woolf argues that "a woman must have money and a room of her own if she is going to write."

THE FOLDED LEAF

335.1 THE FOLDED LEAF] Six months after the publication of *The Folded Leaf*, Maxwell attempted but never finished an essay about the composition and themes of the novel, presumably as an introduction for the London edition, published by Faber & Faber in 1946. Among the existing fragments, the following is the most polished and complete:

"The novelist who chooses to write about grown people sits down to his typewriter with the happy assumption that, if he does his work honestly and intelligently, the reader will be interested. If the novelist writes about children, he can depend on the reader's pleasure in reliving his own childhood. But if you write about adolescents, the question that immediately arises is how to make them seem important enough to read about. This is partly due to the literary tradition of Thomas Bailey Aldrich and Booth Tarkington, which presents growing up as something inescapably comic. It is also partly due to certain facts of our culture. Adolescents are allowed no part in the political life of the nation. If they find a job this does not, as with grown people, confer economic independence upon them. They are encouraged to study and to play football, but not to marry or to find any direct release from sexual tension. And for what is, anthropologically speaking, an unreasonably long time they are forced to take a passive part in the life around them, to wait, their talents unused and for the most part undiscovered, their true nature as much a matter of mystery to them as if they were shut up in a pitch dark room. No life is open to them except the life of feeling. That this is the richest life of all, nobody ever tells them, and they have no way of judging for themselves. Their conversation, if overheard, is nearly always trivial or foolish or dull, because they have not yet learned that it is possible to talk about things that really interest them and be understood. But actually, what they are engaged in, the process of growing up, is both serious and important, as serious and important as any experience except death, and something like it . . . ."

336.1 *Louise Bogan*] Poet, translator, and from 1931 to 1968 the chief poetry critic for *The New Yorker*, Bogan (1897–1970) encouraged Maxwell throughout the writing of *The Folded Leaf.* In his obituary of her, published in *The New Yorker*, Maxwell wrote: "She was a handsome, direct, impressive, vulnerable woman. In whatever she wrote the line of truth was exactly superimposed on the line of feeling. One look at her work—or sometimes one look at her—made any number of disheartened artists take heart and go on being the kind of dedicated creature they were intended to be."

339.1–10 *Lo! . . . night.*] From "Song of the Lotos-Eaters" (1833) by Alfred, Lord Tennyson (1809–1892).

344.16–17 ("Andromache in Exile," by Sir Edward Leighton)] Maxwell tweaks the name of academic painter Lord Frederick Leighton (1830–1896) and conflates the titles of two of his famous canvases, "Dante in Exile" (1864) and "Captive Andromache" (1888).

344.21 A sentence appeared,] The sentence being diagrammed, *At first men were delighted when they heard what 'brave Oliver' had done*, is from G. M. Trevelyan's *England Under the Stuarts* (1904). It refers to Oliver Cromwell's forcible dissolution of England's "Rump" Parliament on April 20, 1653.

348.26 *College Humor.*] Glossy monthly magazine (1920–1932) that featured light fiction, comic pieces, cartoons, and, on its covers, pin-up-style illustrations of flappers and co-eds.

348.34–35 the seacoast of Illyria.] See Shakespeare, *Twelfth Night*, II.i.

348.40 "The Downward Path"] Five-reel silent film (1900) directed by Arthur Marvin (1857–1911). It tells the story of a country girl who runs away from home, is forced by her scheming lover to dance for money in a big-city saloon, and at last drinks poison to end her degraded life.

349.21–22 "Norwegian Rustic March"] Part of the *Lyric Suite*, op. 54 (1891; orchestrated 1904), by the Norwegian composer Edvard Grieg (1843–1907).

351.5–6 plus fours . . . plus eights.] Knickerbockers that fastened four inches, or eight inches, below the knee.

355.30 "Gump"] Chinless, hapless Andy was the head of the comic-strip family the Gumps, created in 1917 by Sidney Smith (1877–1935) for the *Chicago Tribune.*

361.5 "Hope"] Allegorical painting (1886) by the English symbolist George Frederic Watts (1817–1904). Watts depicts Hope as a blindfolded young woman sitting atop the globe, plucking the one remaining string on a broken lyre.

374.22–23 slit gongs . . . bull roarer.] Musical instruments that, among the aborigines of Australasia, are used exclusively in male-initiation rituals. A slit gong is a tall wooden cylinder that stands upright like a man and is often topped with a carved male head. The gong is fashioned from a log that has been hollowed out through one narrow opening (the "slit") and whose walls have been carved to varying degrees of thickness. When struck with mallets, the walls can produce a wide variety of low, liquid notes, "the strange tones which are the voices of spirits" (see page 379.28–29). A bull roarer is a low-pitched, deeply resonant wooden whistle attached to a cord; when the cord is swung like a lasso, the whistle emits "the loud humming noise which so terrifies women" (see page 379.30).

376.4 Thura] Greek word meaning "gate" or "door."

376.29–30 a play from the most primitive time of man.] Maxwell's chief source of details about Australasian myth and ritual is *The Golden Bough: A Study in Magic and Religion* (3rd ed., 1922) by the English anthropologist Sir James George Frazer (1854–1941); see especially Chapter 67, Section 4: "The

Ritual of Death and Resurrection." He also consulted "The Puberty Rites of Savages," in *Ritual: Four Psychoanalytic Studies*, by Theodor Reik (1919; tr. 1931).

382.19 (Anubis)] In ancient Egyptian mythology, the jackal-headed god who conducts the soul into the afterlife.

387.7 "Steve Brodie"] Charismatic Bowery bookie (1863–1901) who allegedly jumped off the Brooklyn Bridge on a $200 bet. The jump (July 23, 1886) was probably a hoax; it was widely thought that an accomplice threw a weighted dummy off the bridge while Brodie waited in the water. Whatever the case, Brodie became an instant urban legend, and the saloon and "living museum" he opened at 114 Bowery became a thriving tourist attraction.

387.12 "I Dreamt I Dwelt in Marble Halls"] Aria ("The Gipsy Girl's Dream") from the light opera *The Bohemian Girl* (1843) by Michael W. Balfe, libretto by Alfred Bunn.

393.19–21 "*O grim-look'd night . . . forgot.*"] Shakespeare, *A Midsummer's Night Dream*, V.i:170–73.

397.33 *Mr. Midshipman Easy,*] Sea adventure (1836) set in the Napoleonic era, by the English naval hero turned novelist Captain Frederick Marryat (1792–1848).

408.8 "No, No, Nanette"] Broadway musical (1925) with book by Otto Harbach and Frank Mandel, music by Vincent Youmans, and lyrics by Harbach and Irving Caesar. Hit songs from the show include "I Want to Be Happy" and "Tea for Two."

411.20–33 *woman will heal . . . hairs of the brush*] From the "Author's Prologue to the Third Ten Tales," in *Droll Stories: Collected from the Abbeys of Touraine*, vol. 3 (1837; tr. 1874), by Honoré de Balzac.

412.26 "I'll See You in My Dreams"] Song (1924) by Chicago bandleader Isham Jones, words by Gus Kahn. The recording by the Ray Miller Orchestra, with vocalist Frank Bessinger, topped the charts in 1925.

417.4 "Alastor] See "Alastor; or, The Spirit of Solitude" (1816), long poem by Percy Bysshe Shelley (1792–1827).

419.2 comptometer,] Early-model business calculator; a shoebox-sized adding machine that was also capable of multiplication and division.

429.32–430.2 the Greeks represented . . . clusters on the bough.] Cf. Frazer, *The Golden Bough*, Chapter 1, Section 1 ("Diana and Virbius").

441.33 "Maggie"] In the comic strip "Bringing Up Father," created by George McManus (1884–1954) in 1913, Maggie was the personification of social propriety and social aspiration, forever censuring her husband, Jiggs, an Irishman of low tastes and behavior.

444.6 that's my Pop,"] Comic catchphrase of the 1920s, coined by cartoonist Milt Gross (1895–1953) in his illustrated newspaper column "Gross Exaggerations."

445.36 Spenser's indebtedness to the *Orlando Furioso*] *The Faerie Queene* (1590), romantic allegory by the Elizabethan poet Edmund Spenser (1522?–1599), owes much of its structure and many of its episodes to *Orlando Furioso* (1516) by the Italian poet Ludovico Ariosto (1474–1533).

449.31 "Oh, Katarina"] Novelty song (1924) by L. Wolf Gilbert and Richard Fell, in which the singer warns his overweight lover: "Oh, Katarina, / Oh, Katarina, / To keep my love you must be leana. . . ."

452.5 "Blue Skies."] Song (1926) by Irving Berlin (1888–1989). It was already a hit when Al Jolson performed it in *The Jazz Singer* (1927).

452.25 *Psychopathia Sexualis*] Collection of case studies in sexual deviancy (1886; tr. 1892) by the German psychiatrist Richard von Krafft-Ebing (1840–1902).

453.7 *The Eve of St. Agnes*,] Narrative poem (1884) by John Keats.

453.17–18 "Tales from the Vienna Woods"] *Geschichten aus dem Wienerwald*, op. 325 (1868), waltz for orchestra by Johann Strauss II (1825–1899).

454.38 *Mund auf . . . kauen.*] Mouth open . . . mouth shut . . . chew.

463.20 'The Snow Queen',"] Modern fairy tale ("Sneedronningen," 1884) by Hans Christian Andersen (1805–1875).

469.8 pulmotor."] Lightweight emergency pulmonary-resuscitation device once widely used by ambulance medics, firemen, midwives, and the like.

473.6 baum marten] Furrier's name for the European pine marten (*Martes martes*), a mink-like mammal prized for its thick, golden brown fur.

482.37 *Mansfield Park*,] Novel (1814) by Jane Austen.

509.3 crepe] Victorian-style black-crepe funeral wreath.

511.15 St. Anselm] French-born cleric (1033?–1109) who succeeded Lanfranc as Archbishop of Canterbury in 1093. His "logical proof of the existence of God" is put forth in *Monologium* (1070) and its sequel, *Proslogium* (1087).

511.28 "When Day Is Done"] Song (1926) by Robert Katscher, lyrics by Buddy De Sylva. The recording by Paul Whiteman and His Orchestra was a hit in 1927.

511.29 "The Sweetheart of Sigma Chi."] Fraternity song (1911) by F. Dudleigh "Dud" Vernor, words by Byron D. Stokes, popularized by a 1927 recording by Fred Waring and His Pennsylvanians.

512.13 *Tottel's Miscellany*] Anthology (1557), also known as *The Book of*

Songs and Sonnets, edited and published by Richard Tottel (1530?–1594?), a London bookseller. It collected for the first time the work of several esteemed English poets, including Sir Thomas Wyatt and Henry Howard, Earl of Surrey, and sparked the Elizabethan vogue for poetry miscellanies.

512.14 *Euphues and His England.*] Part Two (1580) of *Euphues*, early novel by John Lyly (1554?–1604). Part One, *The Anatomy of Wit*, was published 1578.

518.27 Spengler] Oswald Spengler (1880–1936), German historian and philosopher, author of the two-volume *Decline of the West* (1918, 1922; tr. 1926, 1928).

520.1–2 *Old Heidelberg, dear Heidelberg / Thy sons will ne'er forget . . .*] *That golden haze of student days / Is round about us yet.* From "Heidelberg," a drinking song from the comic operetta *The Prince of Pilsen* (1902) by Gustav Luders, book and lyrics by Frank Pixley.

530.15–18 "Pomp and Circumstance" . . . familiar.] *Pomp and Circumstance*, see note 72.32–33; *Arlésienne Suite* (1872) by Georges Bizet (incidental music for the play *D'Arlésienne* by Alphonse Daudet); *Willliam Tell* (1829) by Gioachino Rossini (overture to the opera *Guillame Tell*); *Rosamunde* (1823) by Franz Schubert (incidental music to the ballet *Rosamunde, Fürstin von Zypern* ["Princess of Cyprus"], based on the play by Helmina von Chézy).

540.35–541.26 The statistics . . . in front of trains.] Maxwell's chief sources of anecdotal detail about the social phenomenon of suicide are *Suicide* (1897; tr. 1951) by Émile Durkheim, and *Masochism in Modern Man* (1937, tr. 1941) by Theodor Reik

547.29 Luminal] Brand name for phenobarbital, a barbiturate prescribed as a short-term sleeping aid or calming agent.

TIME WILL DARKEN IT

565.1–30 *The order . . . observer.*] From *Arte de la pintura* ("The Art of Painting," 1649), by Francisco Pacheco del Rio, a portraitist and religious painter who worked mainly in Seville and was first the mentor, then the father-in-law, of Diego Velázquez. The passage was excerpted, and translated from the Spanish, by Marco Treves, in *Artists on Art: From the XIV to the XX Century*, compiled and edited by Treves and Robert Goldwater (New York: Pantheon Books, 1945).

567.14–15 Maxine Elliott] Elliott (1868–1940), an American actress, was a star of the London and Broadway stage (c. 1890–1920) and one of the most frequently photographed beauties of her time.

581.13 Geraldine Farrar's] American soprano Geraldine Farrar (1882–1967) was a star of the Metropolitan Opera from 1906 to 1922. Her most popular role was Cio-Cio-San, in Puccini's *Madama Butterfly*, which she sang in its U.S. première on February 11, 1907, and in nearly a hundred subsequent performances.

584.19 receipt] Recipe.

584.19–20 pocketbook rolls.] Crusty buns made from ovals of dough folded over into a pocketbook-shape; better known as Parker House rolls, after the Boston hotel that popularized them.

586.17 The Sudden Change."] Maxwell's source for Mr. Ellis's story is "Coldest Night Ever Recorded," an article published in the Lincoln (Illinois) *Daily Courier* on February 13, 1905, and reprinted many times thereafter.

588.2–3 Nordica . . . McCormack] Lillian Nordica (1857–1914), American soprano; Dame Nellie Melba (1861–1931), Australian soprano; Alma Gluck (1884–1938), Romanian-born American soprano; John McCormack (1884–1945), Irish-born American tenor. All had sung with the Metropolitan Opera before 1912 and made numerous early phonograph records.

588.6 Paderewski's] Ignacy Jan Paderewski (1860–1941), Polish composer and phenomenally popular concert pianist.

588.8 Sousa's marches,] See note 208.18–19.

609.19–20 L. C. Smith double-keyboard typewriter] The Smith Premier (Syracuse, New York, c. 1889) was a standard-model early typewriter. It had a separate key for each character, upper and lower case, and a keyboard seven rows deep. Its popularity waned after the introduction of the key-shifted type basket in 1904.

612.18–21 Chitty's *Pleadings* . . . Starkie on *Evidence.*] *Practical Treatise on Pleading, and on the Parties to Actions and the Forms of Action* (1809) by Joseph Chitty; *Commentaries on the Laws of England* (1765–69) by William Blackstone; *Commentaries on American Law* (1826–30) by James Kent; *A Practical Treatise on the Law of Evidence* (1826) by Thomas Starkie.

615.21–22 Harrison Ainsworth.] William Harrison Ainsworth (1805–1882), English novelist and playwright, published 39 historical romances in the manner of Sir Walter Scott, including *The Tower of London* (1840).

620.6 Singer Sewing Machine birds] Like many other businesses of the late 19th and early 20th centuries, Singer printed trade cards—small cardboard cards, usually with advertising copy on one side and a color-lithograph picture on the other—that were given away by retailers and salesmen to promote the company's products. Singer's most popular and various series of cards depicted the birds of America, and these, like today's baseball cards, were avidly collected and traded by both children and adults.

620.33 *Robert Ingersoll?"*] See note 280.20.

625.34 "Hedge apples,"] A hedge apple, or hedge ball, is the yellow-green, grapefruit-sized fruit of the Osage orange tree (*Maclura pomifera*).

630.11 Indian mound] See note 95.26.

630.12–13 Megatherium.] Giant ground sloth that flourished in the Americas during the Pleistocene era.

637.1 Erminie] English comic opera (1885) by Edward Jakobowski, libretto by Claxton Bellamy and Harry Paulton.

637.10 *Epworth League,*] Youth ministry of the former Methodist Episcopal Church (North), named after Epworth, Lincolnshire, the boyhood home of John Wesley. The league was active from 1889 until 1939, when it was absorbed into the Methodist Youth Fellowship of the United Methodist Church of America.

648.33 Pasteur] French bacteriologist Louis Pasteur (1822–1895) perfected the rabies vaccine in 1885. The Institut Pasteur, Paris, was founded by the French government in 1887 to help Pasteur and his fellow-researchers develop new techniques and medicines to improve public health.

654.4–5 Cumaean Sybil] Detail from Michelangelo's ceiling for the Sistine Chapel.

654.7 Tanagra figurines,] Painted terracotta figurines, mainly of women in informal poses, in a style that flourished throughout the Mediterranean in the fourth and third centuries BCE. In 1873–74, thousands of these figurines were uncovered by archeologists in the necropolis at Tanagra, Greece, and reproductions quickly made their way into homes around the world.

659.37 marquisette,] Diaphanous but sturdy woven fabric, usually of nylon or other synthetic fibers, used chiefly in curtains and mosquito netting.

666.19–20 the doll in *Tales of Hoffmann*] In one episode of the fantastic *Contes d'Hoffmann* (1881), posthumously produced opera by the French composer Jacques Offenbach (1819–1880), the hero falls in love with "Olympia," a life-size clockwork coquette usually costumed in a frilly baby-doll dress.

672.32–33 *Voltaire and Benjamin Franklin.*] The 84-year-old Voltaire received Franklin and his son in Paris on February 15, 1778. He recorded the visit in a letter to his confessor, the Jesuit Abbé Gaultier, dated February 21, 1778.

673.1 *without health there is no happiness in success.*] Cf. Thomas Jefferson, in a letter to his son-in-law, Thomas Mann Randolph Jr., dated July 6, 1787: "With your talents and industry . . . you may promise yourself anything—but health, without which there is no happiness."

682.18–19 *Olivette . . . The Chimes of Normandy*),] *Olivette* (*Les Noces d'Olivette*), French comic opera (1879) by Edmond Audran; *Robin Hood*, American comic opera (1890) by Reginald de Koven, libretto by Harry B. Smith; *The Bohemian Girl* (see note 387.12); *The Chimes of Normandy* (*Les Cloches de Corneville*), French comic opera (1877) by Robert Planquette.

682.33 "Anvil Chorus"] Gypsies' work song ("*Vedi! Le fosche notturne spoglie* . . .") from Act II, Scene 1, of *Il Trovatore* (1853), opera by Giuseppe Verdi.

682.38 White Huzzars] The White Hussars, a "military-march and swinging band" formed in 1911 by the cornet-player and composer Al Sweet (1876–1945), were one of the first jazz acts to tour the Chautauqua circuit.

684.38 battle of Fort Meigs,] In the spring and summer of 1813, General William Henry Harrison and his men held off British attacks on Fort Meigs, the U.S. fort they had established that February on the Maumee River near Perrysburg, Ohio.

686.9 "*The Montessori Method*] Book (*Il Metodo della Pedagogia Scientifica*, 1909; tr. 1912) by the Italian educator and physician Maria Montessori (1870–1952) outlining her innovative method of preschool education. In 1907, she opened a "little school" in Rome for children aged three to six. There, in a classroom equipped with custom-built child-sized furniture and rich in art supplies and easy-to-manipulate playthings, she refined a repertoire of "learning games" designed to encourage "learning through doing" rather than through following a teacher's explicit instructions. She and her staff did not "teach"; instead they permitted children to experiment, exercise, play, and ask questions, all toward the end of helping deepen their intellectual curiosity, sensory appreciation, manual dexterity, and autonomy. Even before her book was translated into English, her work was popularized in America by professors of education and psychology at Harvard and by articles in *McClure's* magazine. The first U.S. preschool founded on the Montessori method was opened in Tarrytown, New York, in February 1912.

699.19 Columbian Exposition,] The World's Columbian Exposition, popularly known as the Chicago World's Fair, was held at a 600-acre site on the shore of Lake Michigan from May to November 1893 in commemoration of the 400th anniversary of Columbus's landing in North America.

703.27–28 the cortege of nymphs . . . Apollo,] Reproduction of *Aurora* (1613–14), a fresco by Guido Reni (1572–1642) created for the Casino dell'Aurora, Rome.

709.27 *Sunset Hill . . . Mirror Lake*] Resort locations in the White Mountains of New Hampshire.

710.17 *Starved Rock*] Cliff overlooking the Illinois River between La Salle and Ottawa, Illinois.

722.26 Hampton Institute,] Historically black and Native American coeducational college founded in 1868 in Hampton, Virginia; it was renamed Hampton University in 1984.

725.35 Decoration Day] Annual holiday, first observed on May 30, 1868, to honor the Union dead of the American Civil War. After World War I, the name was changed to Memorial Day and the observance broadened to honor all those who have died in service to the country.

736.35 Ulysses . . . Calypso's island,] See *Odyssey*, Book 5.

750.32–751.18 The case against women . . . state of Wisconsin.] Lavinia Goodell (1839–1880) was the first woman to practice law in the state of Wisconsin. Admitted to the Rock County bar in June 1874, she soon found it necessary to argue a case before the Wisconsin Supreme Court, which required that she also be admitted to the Wisconsin State Bar. Her application was filed in December 1875 (39 Wis. 232), and the following February a panel of three justices, including Chief Justice Edward G. Ryan, unanimously denied it on grounds that women were unfit to practice law (39 Wis. 245). In protest, John Cassoday, speaker of the Wisconsin State Assembly, introduced a bill that would admit qualified women to the state bar. The bill was signed into law on March 22, 1877, and Goodell was admitted on June 18, 1879, nine months before her death by cancer at age 40.

753.33–34 Hot Springs] City in central Arkansas, site of Hot Springs National Park.

759.35–36 *Province of Jurisprudence Determined*] Three-volume work on the origins and development of Western law (1832) by the English jurist John Austin (1790–1859).

768.5 Sir James Maine?"] Sir Henry James Sumner Maine (1822–1888), author of *Ancient Law* (1860) and professor of historical and comparative jurisprudence at Oxford and Cambridge.

775.25 U.S.S. *Maine*,] Battleship whose unexplained explosion in Havana harbor, on February 15, 1898, killed 260 men and contributed to the outbreak of the Spanish-American War.

777.36 billikin,] Billiken—the small, seated figure of a smiling, squint eyed, pointy-headed imp, "the god of the way things ought to be"—was sculpted in 1908 by Florence Pretz, a commercial artist in Kansas City, Missouri. When mass-produced by the Billiken Company of Chicago, Billiken figurines became a national craze, which peaked in 1911.

780.12 *The Heart of Midlothian*?] Novel (1818) by Sir Walter Scott.

781.20–22 the holly tree . . . darling of the gods.] In Norse mythology, Odin's son Balder was the handsomest, kindest, and best loved of the gods. He was also virtually invincible because his mother, Frigg, had exacted a promise not to harm him from every thing in nature. When jealous Loki, the god of mischief, learned that Frigg had overlooked the holly tree (or the mistletoe), he fashioned a dart from a sprig of it, gave it to Balder's brother Hoder, and teased him into tossing it at Balder. The dart pierced Balder's neck, killing him instantly. See Frazer, *The Golden Bough*, Chapter 61 ("The Myth of Balder") and Chapter 66 ("Balder and the Mistletoe").

783.20–24 synagogue of Satan . . . smoke of the pit] These visions come from the Revelation of St. John: the synagogue of Satan (2:9), the four beasts full of eyes (4:6), hail and fire mingled with blood (8:7), Wormwood falling from heaven (8:10–11), the air darkened by reason of the smoke of the pit (9:2).

796.24 *Man is his own architect.*] Cf. Sallust (Gaius Sallustus Crispin, 86–34 BCE): "Faber est suae quisqu fortunae" ("Man is the architect of his own fortune"). This aphorism was a favorite of Theodor Reik (1888–1969), Maxwell's Freudian psychoanalyst in 1944–45.

797.17 (*Pharaoh's army got drownded*)] From the chorus of the spiritual "Mary, Don't You Weep."

800.11 'East Lynne,'"] Novel (1851) by Mrs. Henry (Ellen) Wood, which features, among other sensational elements, a snowstorm and an adulterous heroine disfigured in a fiery train wreck.

815.40–816.2 *As soft . . . cover me all.*] The answer to this Anglo-Saxon riddle is "A walnut."

817.26 sepia print of Sir Galahad] "Sir Galahad" (1864), painting by the English symbolist George Frederic Watts (1817–1904).

833.24 Baedekers."] Small-format travel guides published by the firm of Karl Baedeker Verlag, Leipzig, from the 1850s through 1943. Baedeker so dominated the international market for such books that, until World War II, the words "travel guide" and "Baedeker" were almost interchangeable.

834.10–17 *For every evil /. . . never mind it.*] Traditional English rhyme, first published in *English Proverbs and Proverbial Phrases* (1869), collected by William Carew Hazlitt (1834–1913).

837.13–15 (and for your most beautiful . . . such splendor)] Cf. "Coronemus nos Rosis antequam marcescant," poem by Thomas Jordan (1612?–1685). The Latin title is an allusion to the Wisdom of Solomon 2:8: "Let us crown ourselves with roses before they be withered."

847.24–25 *Let us praise the Creator and all that He has made.*] Cf. Psalm 148.

STORIES 1952–1956

855.1 *The Trojan Women*] The title alludes to the tragedy by Euripides (first performed 415 BCE), which dramatizes the fate of widows and fatherless children in the aftermath of the Trojan War.

865.24–28 “*Bel et confortable . . . jardin d’été . . . .*”] “Beautiful and comfortable establishment of well-deserved fame, happily managed by Mme Lasgrezas. Courtesy of a skilled chef, you will enjoy a first-class meal, served to you in an elegant dining room or a delightful summer garden. . . .”

865.30 Cinzano and Rasurel] Cinzano is an Italian vermouth aperitif; Rasurel, a French line of women’s swimwear.

866.16 Dufy] Raoul Dufy (1877–1953), French artist and illustrator whose signature paintings feature large flat areas of saturated color and a spontaneous graphic line.

868.7–8 “*Vanille . . . praliné . . .*”] “Vanilla . . . chocolate, pistachio, raspberry, strawberry, tutti-frutti, praline . . .”

871.13 *Œufs en gelée*] Poached eggs in aspic.

874.1 *What Every Boy Should Know*] In 1998, in response to an editor’s request that he provide a narrative “caption” to a found photograph (“Lincoln [Illinois] Rotary Club Meeting, c. 1950,” by Larry Shroyer), Maxwell wrote a 400-word autobiographical fantasy that can be seen as a footnote to this story. Published in *DoubleTake* (Winter 1999), under the title “Recognition,” it reads:

“The press that printed the Lincoln (pop. 11,000) *Evening Courier* was old and had a tendency to break down, in which case fourteen boys—I was one of them—milled around restlessly in a small space until it stopped chewing paper and started printing again. On Saturday mornings the subscribers often found excuses for not paying me and I had to pay the newspaper out of my earnings until they did. In January and February the icy wind from the Illinois prairie went through my corduroy coat and my hands were sometimes so stiff with cold I could barely manage to throw the paper in the direction of the subscriber’s front porch. Home seemed very far away. For National Boy Scout Day the town went through a kind of charade: On that day a Scout became the fire chief and another the police chief and still another the mayor. I think because I was the only delivery boy who was also a Boy Scout, I was picked to be the editor of the newspaper. Wearing my Scout uniform I sat in the office of the actual editor, Brainerd Snyder—a high-strung but kind man in his forties. At first he showed me what he was doing, until the phone began ringing and he got too busy. At twelve o’clock he took off his green eyeshade and reached for his jacket, saying ‘We’re going to Rotary.’ The Rotary Club luncheon took place once a week in the dining room of the New Lincoln Hotel, which in 1921 was no longer very new. This day there were thirty or forty men and a handful of Boy Scouts. Halfway through lunch, Brainerd Snyder clinked his water glass with his knife and, under his breath, told me to stand up. When the room grew quiet, he said ‘Gentlemen of the Rotary, I want to introduce the editor of this day’s *Courier*,’ and something like pandemonium broke out. Chanting ‘We’re for you, Billie Maxwell!’ the Rotarians pushed their chairs back and formed a snake dance and went weaving through the tables singing 'For he's a jolly good fellow, that nobody can deny . . .' I felt physically larger. And surprised (I didn't think that they even knew who I was). The Boy Scouts who were mayor, police chief, and fire chief must have received similar ovations, but I remember only my own apotheosis."

874.18–21 ". . . the hair . . . trunk. . . ."] From Chapter 2 of *The Descent of Man, and Selection in Relation to Sex* (1871) by Charles Darwin (1809–1882).

881.26 TL's] True Loves.

892.1 *The French Scarecrow*] In April 1970, a high school senior in Newport News, Virginia, wrote to Maxwell asking what, exactly, the scarecrow in this story represents. In answer, he wrote:

"Most people go about their daily lives carefully ignoring whatever keeps them from feeling safe and secure, or, at most, taking a glance at such things out of the corner of their eye and then looking away—for example, illness, financial insecurity, death, the fear that they are not really loved, and so on. All these carefully ignored fears are what the scarecrow represents. The story doesn't make a statement about anything, it is just a series of events related in one way or another to a single idea . . . Insofar as there is any conclusion, it is that in general people have no choice but to live with the fears that they themselves create."

892.2–5 *I spied John Mouldy . . . alone.*] From "John Mouldy," poem by Walter de la Mare, in his *Songs of Childhood* (1902).

894.6 *potager,*] A French-style kitchen garden, both practical and ornamental, planted with fruit trees, vegetables, herbs, and decorative flowers.

897.34–35 spink-spank-sphinx,] Cf. the refrain of "Robert of Lincoln," a poem for children by William Cullen Bryant (1794–1878): "Bob-o'-link, bob-o'-link, / Spink, spank, spink."

THE WRITER AS ILLUSIONIST

909.2 *A Speech*] Maxwell prepared this speech for "The American Novel at Mid-Century," a symposium at Smith College, Northampton, Massachusetts, March 3 and 4, 1955. The event was organized by Daniel Aaron, Newton Arvin, Charles Hill, and other members of the English department at Smith. The keynote speaker was Alfred Kazin, the William Allen Neilson Visiting Professor for 1954–55; the other speakers were Saul Bellow, Brendan Gill, and Maxwell. Mary Ellen Chase, a novelist and a professor at Smith from 1926 to 1955, was master of ceremonies, and Professor Aaron moderated a panel discussion among the speakers. After the panel discussion, the four speakers fielded questions from the audience, members of which included fellow-novelists Ralph Ellison and Ann Birstein (Mrs. Alfred Kazin).

909.6–7 There is one in the Metropolitan Museum.] Maxwell refers to the Metropolitan's 18th-century study copy of "Spring Festival on the River," a hand-scroll by the master Zhang Zeduan (or Chang Tse-tuan, 1085–1145), widely thought to have been a court painter of the Northern Song Dynasty.

909.18 spirit money,] Ceremonial paper, representing earthly money, burned as an offering to the dead during Chinese rituals of ancestor worship.

909.28–30 "*I have just returned . . . troubled with . . .*"] First line of *Wuthering Heights* (1847) by Emily Brontë.

909.36 "*None of them . . . sky. . . .*"] First line of "The Open Boat" (1898) by Stephen Crane.

910.3 "*Call me Ishmael. . . .*"] First line of *Moby-Dick* (1851) by Herman Melville.

910.9–13 "*Thirty or forty . . . atmosphere . . .*"] First line of *A Lost Lady* (1923) by Willa Cather.

910.16–17 "*It was said . . . dog . . .*"] First line of "The Lady with the Dog" (1899) by Anton Chekhov, in the translation by Constance Garnett (1917).

910.26–28 "*It is a truth . . . wife . . .*"] First line of *Pride and Prejudice* (1813) by Jane Austen.

911.4–5 humankind cannot bear . . . reality,] See "Burnt Norton" (1935), one of Eliot's *Four Quartets* (1943).

913.28–29 Bernard Baruch . . . Robert Sherwood] Baruch (1870–1965), "The Lone Wolf of Wall Street," was a self-made American financier and a wartime economic adviser to Woodrow Wilson and Franklin D. Roosevelt; Sherwood (1896–1955), an American playwright and screenwriter, perhaps best known for his Oscar-winning script for William Wyler's *The Best Years of Our Lives* (1946).

915.38–916.6 "Yesterday morning . . . till twelve . . ."] From a letter to Vita Sackville-West from Virginia Woolf, dated October 9, 1927, quoted by Sackville-West in her article "Virginia Woolf and *Orlando*," *The Listener*, Vol. 53 (January 25, 1955), pages 157–58.

916.38 The man from Porlock] In a note on his unfinished poem "Kubla Khan"—written in Linton, England, in 1798, and published 1816—Samuel Taylor Coleridge describes how his work on the poem was interrupted (and indeed destroyed) by an unannounced visit from "a person on business from Porlock," a neighboring town.

918.28–29 Anna . . . Mr. Knightley.] Hero and heroine of, respectively, *Anna Karenina* (1877) by Leo Tolstoy, and *Emma* (1816) by Jane Austen.

APPENDIX

927.3 An English instructor] Paul Landis (1893–1970), Maxwell's freshman composition instructor and self-appointed English-department adviser.

927.7 Tauchnitz edition] Inexpensive, pocket-sized, English-language volume, published by the firm of B. Tauchnitz, Leipzig, and for sale throughout continental Europe. Tauchnitz inaugurated its "Collection of British and American Authors" in 1841, and the firm published more than 5,400 titles in the series before going bankrupt during World War II.

927.31 a literary symposium] See note 909.2. Bellow's speech, "The Novelist and the Reader," was never published in the form that he delivered it at Smith. Certain of his comments were drawn from "The Writer and the Audience," an essay he had recently published in *Perspectives U.S.A. 9* (Fall 1954); others were later incorporated into "Distractions of a Fiction Writer," his contribution to *The Living Novel: A Symposium*, edited by Granville Hicks (1956). Neither piece, however, contains the remark quoted here, which for Maxwell became a touchstone.

928.32 Josef Lhévinne] See note 68.29–30.

929.26–27 MacDowell Colony.] First artists' colony in the United States, founded in 1907 by the composer Edward MacDowell (1860–1908) and his wife, Marian Nivens MacDowell (1857–1956), on the grounds of their 450-acre farm in Peterborough, New Hampshire. Today the colony, in operation year round, provides free room and board to up to 32 artists at any one time, each artist staying for up to eight weeks.

930.8–11 Louis Guglielmi . . . Robert Fitzgerald.] Osvoldo Louis Guglielmi (1906–1956) was raised in the Italian slums of Harlem. Heavily influenced by both Ben Shahn and Giorgio di Chirico, he was a surrealist with a social conscience, often depicting America's working poor moving through distorted, nightmarish cityscapes. David Diamond (1915–2005), a native New Yorker, was 20 years old in August 1935, not, as Maxwell has it, 17; he would write 11 symphonies and a great number of orchestral and chamber pieces. Robert Fitzgerald (1910–1985) was a lyric poet, a translator of the Greek and Latin classics, and, after 1965, the Boylston Professor of Rhetoric and Oratory at Harvard University. He and Maxwell were lifelong friends: Maxwell dedicated his novel *So Long, See You Tomorrow* (1980) to him, and Fitzgerald his posthumously published book of essays, *The Third Kind of Knowledge* (1993), to Maxwell.

930.12–18 Brazilian composer . . . unsewed.] The Brazilian composer was Burle Marx (1902–1991); the woman writing her dissertation, Frederika Beatty (1897–1965; Ph.D., Columbia, 1939); and the poet, Nancy Byrd Turner (1880–1971).

930.16–17 *Angels and Earthly Creatures*] Posthumously published sonnet sequence (1929), mostly on themes of death and sexual passion, by the American poet Elinor Wylie (1885–1928).

930.22 Busoni's . . . Bach chaconne,] In 1893, the Italian pianist Ferruccio Busoni (1866–1924) made a piano transcription of Johann Sebastian Bach's Chaconne in D minor (BWV 1004), part of Bach's Partita for Solo Violin No. 2 (c. 1723).

930.24 Charlotte Blass] Blass (1908–1981), a painter in watercolor and oils, was a student of George Luks at the Art Students League in New York. Her signature subject was the landscape and Native American people of Texas and the Desert Southwest. Her painting of Maxwell in the summer of 1935 was reproduced on the jacket of the Modern Library edition of *They Came Like Swallows* (1997).

931.6–7 Dudley Fitts] When Fitts (1903–1968) was a young instructor in the classics at the Choate School, in Wallingford, Connecticut, he mentored his gifted student Robert Fitzgerald, only seven years his junior. Together they translated several Greek tragedies, into which, Maxwell once commented, "they poured their own poetic talent, producing an excitement you won't find in Gilbert Murray." Their first collaboration, the *Alcestis*, was published in 1936.

932.20 Garreta Busey,] Busey (1893–1976) provided Maxwell a window onto the professional life of the writer; by the time he met her, in 1931, she had been a member of the staff of the New York *Herald Tribune* Sunday books section and had published scores of poems and reviews in national magazines. Maxwell once described her as "a wise, patient, supportive friend" who helped him, in "all the ways a person of courage can transmit this to a person who doesn't have very much," to quit academic life and become a novelist.

THE LIBRARY OF AMERICA SERIES

The Library of America fosters appreciation and pride in America's literary heritage by publishing, and keeping permanently in print, authoritative editions of America's best and most significant writing. An independent nonprofit organization, it was founded in 1979 with seed money from the National Endowment for the Humanities and the Ford Foundation.

1. Herman Melville, *Typee, Omoo, Mardi* (1982)
2. Nathaniel Hawthorne, *Tales and Sketches* (1982)
3. Walt Whitman, *Poetry and Prose* (1982)
4. Harriet Beecher Stowe, *Three Novels* (1982)
5. Mark Twain, *Mississippi Writings* (1982)
6. Jack London, *Novels and Stories* (1982)
7. Jack London, *Novels and Social Writings* (1982)
8. William Dean Howells, *Novels 1875–1886* (1982)
9. Herman Melville, *Redburn, White-Jacket, Moby-Dick* (1983)
10. Nathaniel Hawthorne, *Collected Novels* (1983)
11. Francis Parkman, *France and England in North America*, vol. I (1983)
12. Francis Parkman, *France and England in North America*, vol. II (1983)
13. Henry James, *Novels 1871–1880* (1983)
14. Henry Adams, *Novels, Mont Saint Michel, The Education* (1983)
15. Ralph Waldo Emerson, *Essays and Lectures* (1983)
16. Washington Irving, *History, Tales and Sketches* (1983)
17. Thomas Jefferson, *Writings* (1984)
18. Stephen Crane, *Prose and Poetry* (1984)
19. Edgar Allan Poe, *Poetry and Tales* (1984)
20. Edgar Allan Poe, *Essays and Reviews* (1984)
21. Mark Twain, *The Innocents Abroad, Roughing It* (1984)
22. Henry James, *Literary Criticism: Essays, American & English Writers* (1984)
23. Henry James, *Literary Criticism: European Writers & The Prefaces* (1984)
24. Herman Melville, *Pierre, Israel Potter, The Confidence-Man, Tales & Billy Budd* (1985)
25. William Faulkner, *Novels 1930–1935* (1985)
26. James Fenimore Cooper, *The Leatherstocking Tales*, vol. I (1985)
27. James Fenimore Cooper, *The Leatherstocking Tales*, vol. II (1985)
28. Henry David Thoreau, *A Week, Walden, The Maine Woods, Cape Cod* (1985)
29. Henry James, *Novels 1881–1886* (1985)
30. Edith Wharton, *Novels* (1986)
31. Henry Adams, *History of the U.S. during the Administrations of Jefferson* (1986)
32. Henry Adams, *History of the U.S. during the Administrations of Madison* (1986)
33. Frank Norris, *Novels and Essays* (1986)
34. W.E.B. Du Bois, *Writings* (1986)
35. Willa Cather, *Early Novels and Stories* (1987)
36. Theodore Dreiser, *Sister Carrie, Jennie Gerhardt, Twelve Men* (1987)

37A. Benjamin Franklin, *Silence Dogood, The Busy-Body, & Early Writings* (1987)

37B. Benjamin Franklin, *Autobiography, Poor Richard, & Later Writings* (1987)

38. William James, *Writings 1902–1910* (1987)
39. Flannery O'Connor, *Collected Works* (1988)
40. Eugene O'Neill, *Complete Plays 1913–1920* (1988)
41. Eugene O'Neill, *Complete Plays 1920–1931* (1988)
42. Eugene O'Neill, *Complete Plays 1932–1943* (1988)
43. Henry James, *Novels 1886–1890* (1989)
44. William Dean Howells, *Novels 1886–1888* (1989)
45. Abraham Lincoln, *Speeches and Writings 1832–1858* (1989)
46. Abraham Lincoln, *Speeches and Writings 1859–1865* (1989)
47. Edith Wharton, *Novellas and Other Writings* (1990)
48. William Faulkner, *Novels 1936–1940* (1990)
49. Willa Cather, *Later Novels* (1990)

50. Ulysses S. Grant, *Memoirs and Selected Letters* (1990)
51. William Tecumseh Sherman, *Memoirs* (1990)
52. Washington Irving, *Bracebridge Hall, Tales of a Traveller, The Alhambra* (1991)
53. Francis Parkman, *The Oregon Trail, The Conspiracy of Pontiac* (1991)
54. James Fenimore Cooper, *Sea Tales: The Pilot, The Red Rover* (1991)
55. Richard Wright, *Early Works* (1991)
56. Richard Wright, *Later Works* (1991)
57. Willa Cather, *Stories, Poems, and Other Writings* (1992)
58. William James, *Writings 1878–1899* (1992)
59. Sinclair Lewis, *Main Street & Babbitt* (1992)
60. Mark Twain, *Collected Tales, Sketches, Speeches, & Essays 1852–1890* (1992)
61. Mark Twain, *Collected Tales, Sketches, Speeches, & Essays 1891–1910* (1992)
62. *The Debate on the Constitution: Part One* (1993)
63. *The Debate on the Constitution: Part Two* (1993)
64. Henry James, *Collected Travel Writings: Great Britain & America* (1993)
65. Henry James, *Collected Travel Writings: The Continent* (1993)
66. *American Poetry: The Nineteenth Century,* Vol. 1 (1993)
67. *American Poetry: The Nineteenth Century,* Vol. 2 (1993)
68. Frederick Douglass, *Autobiographies* (1994)
69. Sarah Orne Jewett, *Novels and Stories* (1994)
70. Ralph Waldo Emerson, *Collected Poems and Translations* (1994)
71. Mark Twain, *Historical Romances* (1994)
72. John Steinbeck, *Novels and Stories 1932–1937* (1994)
73. William Faulkner, *Novels 1942–1954* (1994)
74. Zora Neale Hurston, *Novels and Stories* (1995)
75. Zora Neale Hurston, *Folklore, Memoirs, and Other Writings* (1995)
76. Thomas Paine, *Collected Writings* (1995)
77. *Reporting World War II: American Journalism 1938–1944* (1995)
78. *Reporting World War II: American Journalism 1944–1946* (1995)
79. Raymond Chandler, *Stories and Early Novels* (1995)
80. Raymond Chandler, *Later Novels and Other Writings* (1995)
81. Robert Frost, *Collected Poems, Prose, & Plays* (1995)
82. Henry James, *Complete Stories 1892–1898* (1996)
83. Henry James, *Complete Stories 1898–1910* (1996)
84. William Bartram, *Travels and Other Writings* (1996)
85. John Dos Passos, *U.S.A.* (1996)
86. John Steinbeck, *The Grapes of Wrath and Other Writings 1936–1941* (1996)
87. Vladimir Nabokov, *Novels and Memoirs 1941–1951* (1996)
88. Vladimir Nabokov, *Novels 1955–1962* (1996)
89. Vladimir Nabokov, *Novels 1969–1974* (1996)
90. James Thurber, *Writings and Drawings* (1996)
91. George Washington, *Writings* (1997)
92. John Muir, *Nature Writings* (1997)
93. Nathanael West, *Novels and Other Writings* (1997)
94. *Crime Novels: American Noir of the 1930s and 40s* (1997)
95. *Crime Novels: American Noir of the 1950s* (1997)
96. Wallace Stevens, *Collected Poetry and Prose* (1997)
97. James Baldwin, *Early Novels and Stories* (1998)
98. James Baldwin, *Collected Essays* (1998)
99. Gertrude Stein, *Writings 1903–1932* (1998)
100. Gertrude Stein, *Writings 1932–1946* (1998)
101. Eudora Welty, *Complete Novels* (1998)
102. Eudora Welty, *Stories, Essays, & Memoir* (1998)
103. Charles Brockden Brown, *Three Gothic Novels* (1998)
104. *Reporting Vietnam: American Journalism 1959–1969* (1998)
105. *Reporting Vietnam: American Journalism 1969–1975* (1998)
106. Henry James, *Complete Stories 1874–1884* (1999)

107. Henry James, *Complete Stories 1884–1891* (1999)
108. *American Sermons: The Pilgrims to Martin Luther King Jr.* (1999)
109. James Madison, *Writings* (1999)
110. Dashiell Hammett, *Complete Novels* (1999)
111. Henry James, *Complete Stories 1864–1874* (1999)
112. William Faulkner, *Novels 1957–1962* (1999)
113. John James Audubon, *Writings & Drawings* (1999)
114. *Slave Narratives* (2000)
115. *American Poetry: The Twentieth Century,* Vol. 1 (2000)
116. *American Poetry: The Twentieth Century,* Vol. 2 (2000)
117. F. Scott Fitzgerald, *Novels and Stories 1920–1922* (2000)
118. Henry Wadsworth Longfellow, *Poems and Other Writings* (2000)
119. Tennessee Williams, *Plays 1937–1955* (2000)
120. Tennessee Williams, *Plays 1957–1980* (2000)
121. Edith Wharton, *Collected Stories 1891–1910* (2001)
122. Edith Wharton, *Collected Stories 1911–1937* (2001)
123. *The American Revolution: Writings from the War of Independence* (2001)
124. Henry David Thoreau, *Collected Essays and Poems* (2001)
125. Dashiell Hammett, *Crime Stories and Other Writings* (2001)
126. Dawn Powell, *Novels 1930–1942* (2001)
127. Dawn Powell, *Novels 1944–1962* (2001)
128. Carson McCullers, *Complete Novels* (2001)
129. Alexander Hamilton, *Writings* (2001)
130. Mark Twain, *The Gilded Age and Later Novels* (2002)
131. Charles W. Chesnutt, *Stories, Novels, and Essays* (2002)
132. John Steinbeck, *Novels 1942–1952* (2002)
133. Sinclair Lewis, *Arrowsmith, Elmer Gantry, Dodsworth* (2002)
134. Paul Bowles, *The Sheltering Sky, Let It Come Down, The Spider's House* (2002)
135. Paul Bowles, *Collected Stories & Later Writings* (2002)
136. Kate Chopin, *Complete Novels & Stories* (2002)
137. *Reporting Civil Rights: American Journalism 1941–1963* (2003)
138. *Reporting Civil Rights: American Journalism 1963–1973* (2003)
139. Henry James, *Novels 1896–1899* (2003)
140. Theodore Dreiser, *An American Tragedy* (2003)
141. Saul Bellow, *Novels 1944–1953* (2003)
142. John Dos Passos, *Novels 1920–1925* (2003)
143. John Dos Passos, *Travel Books and Other Writings* (2003)
144. Ezra Pound, *Poems and Translations* (2003)
145. James Weldon Johnson, *Writings* (2004)
146. Washington Irving, *Three Western Narratives* (2004)
147. Alexis de Tocqueville, *Democracy in America* (2004)
148. James T. Farrell, *Studs Lonigan: A Trilogy* (2004)
149. Isaac Bashevis Singer, *Collected Stories I* (2004)
150. Isaac Bashevis Singer, *Collected Stories II* (2004)
151. Isaac Bashevis Singer, *Collected Stories III* (2004)
152. Kaufman & Co., *Broadway Comedies* (2004)
153. Theodore Roosevelt, *The Rough Riders, An Autobiography* (2004)
154. Theodore Roosevelt, *Letters and Speeches* (2004)
155. H. P. Lovecraft, *Tales* (2005)
156. Louisa May Alcott, *Little Women, Little Men, Jo's Boys* (2005)
157. Philip Roth, *Novels & Stories 1959–1962* (2005)
158. Philip Roth, *Novels 1967–1972* (2005)
159. James Agee, *Let Us Now Praise Famous Men, A Death in the Family* (2005)
160. James Agee, *Film Writing & Selected Journalism* (2005)
161. Richard Henry Dana, Jr., *Two Years Before the Mast & Other Voyages* (2005)
162. Henry James, *Novels 1901–1902* (2006)
163. Arthur Miller, *Collected Plays 1944–1961* (2006)

164. William Faulkner, *Novels 1926–1929* (2006)
165. Philip Roth, *Novels 1973–1977* (2006)
166. *American Speeches: Part One* (2006)
167. *American Speeches: Part Two* (2006)
168. Hart Crane, *Complete Poems & Selected Letters* (2006)
169. Saul Bellow, *Novels 1956–1964* (2007)
170. John Steinbeck, *Travels with Charley and Later Novels* (2007)
171. Capt. John Smith, *Writings with Other Narratives* (2007)
172. Thornton Wilder, *Collected Plays & Writings on Theater* (2007)
173. Philip K. Dick, *Four Novels of the 1960s* (2007)
174. Jack Kerouac, *Road Novels 1957–1960* (2007)
175. Philip Roth, *Zuckerman Bound* (2007)
176. Edmund Wilson, *Literary Essays & Reviews of the 1920s & 30s* (2007)
177. Edmund Wilson, *Literary Essays & Reviews of the 1930s & 40s* (2007)
178. *American Poetry: The 17th & 18th Centuries* (2007)
179. William Maxwell, *Early Novels & Stories* (2008)
180. Elizabeth Bishop, *Poems, Prose, & Letters* (2008)
181. A. J. Liebling, *World War II Writings* (2008)

This book is set in 10 point Linotron Galliard,
a face designed for photocomposition by Matthew Carter
and based on the sixteenth-century face Granjon. The paper
is acid-free lightweight opaque and meets the requirements
for permanence of the American National Standards Institute.
The binding material is Brillianta, a woven rayon cloth made
by Van Heek-Scholco Textielfabrieken, Holland. Compo-
sition by Dedicated Business Services. Printing by
Malloy Incorporated. Binding by Dekker Book-
binding. Designed by Bruce Campbell.

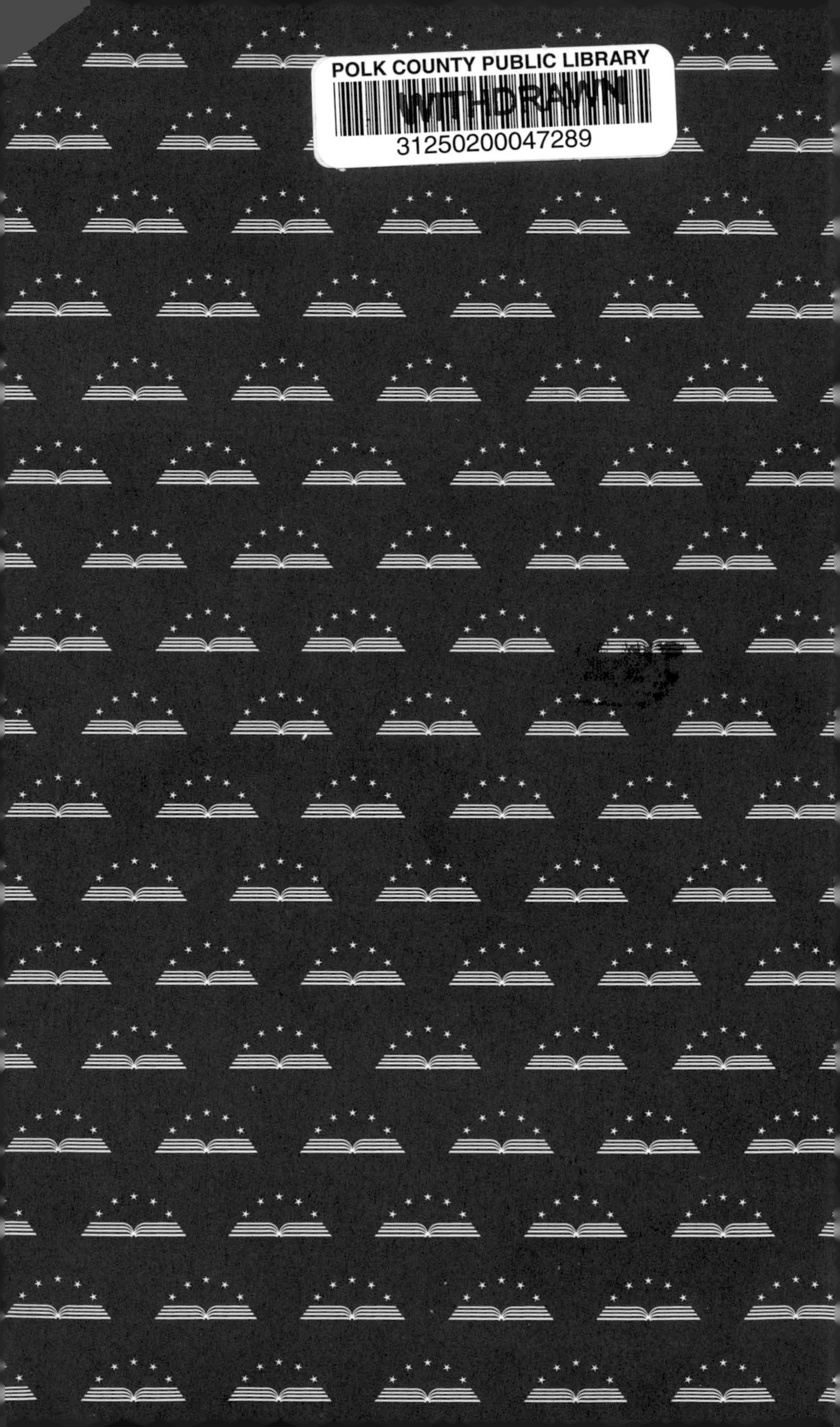
POLK COUNTY PUBLIC LIBRARY
WITHDRAWN
31250200047289